THE END OF ALL THINGS

The Complete Series

MIKE KRAUS

MUONIC
PRESS

THE END OF ALL THINGS
The Complete Series

By
Mike Kraus

© 2024 Muonic Press Inc
www.muonic.com

www.MikeKrausBooks.com
hello@mikeKrausBooks.com
www.facebook.com/MikeKrausBooks

CONTENTS

THE RUINATION

THE DARKNESS

THE DEVOURING

THE REDEMPTION

WANT MORE AWESOME BOOKS?

Find more fantastic tales right here at books.to/readmorepa.

***

If you're new to reading Mike Kraus, consider visiting his website at www.mikekrausbooks.com and signing up for his free newsletter. You'll receive several free books and a sample of his audiobooks, too, just for signing up, you can unsubscribe at any time and you will receive absolutely *no* spam.

SPECIAL THANKS

Special thanks to my awesome beta team, without whom this book wouldn't be nearly as great.

Thank you!

THE COLLAPSE

CHAPTER ONE

Alice Burton
West Palm Beach, Florida

Warm rays of sunlight beat on the dark waters of the mid-Atlantic, shimmering across its surface, highlighting the frothy waves as they tumbled in, pushing their way up the flattened sand to sip at the shoreline. Seagulls pecked at the water's edge, looking for fruits and seeds that had blown in or dead fish tangled in seaweed. It was late in the afternoon on Calico Beach, dog walkers and kite fliers in the distance and a couple of boats out on the wavy water, pulling skiers across the glistening surface. Alice, Jake, and Sarah had the place all to themselves, their beach house nestled behind a dune with the nearest bungalows a hundred yards in either direction.

Alice sat up from her white beach towel. "You guys ready to get in the water? It looks amazing."

"Looks *scary* to me," Sarah replied from beneath her tilted umbrella, the twelve-year-old leaning into the sun. "You know I hate when I can't see my feet."

Alice laughed. "Trust me, you'll love it."

"I'm ready!" Jake tossed his phone aside and stood.

"Let's refresh our sunscreen first, kiddo. Ten minutes out there and you'll be burned to a crisp. Here, I'll put it on Sarah's back. Sarah, you can do your brother."

Nodding, Sarah scooted closer to her mother, took the sunblock, and waited for Jake to sit. "Are you sure it's safe to swim out there?" Sarah asked.

Alice glanced at the water as she rubbed sunblock into her daughter's skin. "Do you think the water's dangerous?"

"I was reading about that big oil spill out in the Gulf, and I wonder if that could reach here? I don't want to swim in contaminated water."

"It shouldn't be contaminated out where we are, honey. That happened in the Gulf, and we're on the Atlantic side. While it's definitely a tragedy, the oil won't reach here. The water's perfect. Go ahead and get in. I'll be down in a second."

Laughing and jostling, Jake and Sarah kicked up sand as they sprinted down the beach and hit the surf running, feet splashing as they leaned into the first wave, crashing against it and coming up sputtering. Alice turned to her beach bag and took out her phone, checking for messages from James and finding one waiting for her.

Conference is over. Just got back to the hotel... flight out of Denver tonight at midnight! Can't wait to see you all!

. . .

Smile widening, Alice sent a reply.

Can't wait to see you, too. Get here soon!

She tapped on her usual news app but caught herself before it could open, closing it and putting the phone on silent and tossing it into her beach bag. It was supposed to be a vacation from the daily grind, a seven-day retreat from electronics, social media, and the twenty-four-hour news cycle. James had already missed the first two days, but he'd be there soon, and it would be "phones in suitcases" from that point forward.

Alice stood in front of the long mirror, checking her aqua green summer dress, pushing her hair back over her shoulders, touched by a light breeze blowing through the open windows as the air filled with fresh ocean and light perfume.

She hollered over her shoulder. "Kids, are you just about ready?"

"Yeah, Mom!" Jake called. "I'm starving, but Sarah's taking forever!"

"Am *not*!"

"We need to get going if we're going to make our reservations at Seafood Jack's!"

"How does a place with a name like that even *have* reservations?" Jake yelled back.

Alice chuckled as she closed and locked the windows, then she met the kids downstairs, locked the front door and guided them along a paved walkway that ran parallel to the beach. They moved north past vibrant beach houses as the surf roared nearby, the kids in their light summer clothes and tennis shoes trotting along beside her. The smells of seafood hit them as they approached a row of restaurants on the right with wide canopies above open dining areas, and they climbed wooden stairs to the boardwalk with its timber framework and bright white railings, tropical-themed restaurant signs and menus hanging in the windows.

Reaching Seafood Jack's, Alice guided the kids past an older couple, the woman pulling her husband by the hand on their way out. She and Alice exchanged polite smiles before a hostess seated the Burtons at a table overlooking the beach. A waitress took their orders and returned with their tropical drinks, promising their food would be right up. While they waited, Alice looked through the glass storefront and into the parking lot where vacationers walked to their cars in their bright shirts with bags full of sundries and souvenir cups.

"When Dad gets here, can we go out on a boat?" Jake asked excitedly.

"I'm sure we will."

"You guys go ahead." Sarah frowned. "I just want to sit on the beach and read my books. My e-reader is packed full. I have a new book about this girl who gets enrolled in this magic school, and…"

Sarah's explanation faded in Alice's ears as she spotted the older couple out on the side of the road, staring at their stalled car. The man was scratching his head, gesturing while the woman held her phone up, tapping on the screen before putting it up to her ear. Several other cars drifted by, losing power, their drivers angry and pounding on their steering wheels, and even more were stalling as they were pulling out, drivers getting out and cursing as some of the vehicles swerved around and into each other.

"Mom? Earth to Mom!" Sarah was waving her hand in front of Alice's face. "I was telling you about my book."

"Oh, I'm sorry, honey." A nervous twitch drove Alice to her feet. "Can you guys stay here a second? I'll be right back."

Alice left the table and wove through the crowd, letting the hostess know she'd be back in a moment, striding to a short set of stairs and down to the parking lot where she rushed over to where the older couple was standing by their car, looking confused.

"Hey, there." Alice waved as she crossed the street. "What's going on? Car trouble?"

"That's right," the man huffed. "It started fine, but as soon as we tried to hit the road, it died."

"That's a rental, right?"

"Yep. It ran great all week. Looks like other people are having the same issue. Weather, maybe?"

"What are you going to do?"

The man shrugged and circled to the driver's side. "I'll give it another try. Maybe it's flooded or something."

"Modern cars don't flood like they used to, hon," the woman said, sighing but getting in.

"Well, I'm going to try it anyway."

The woman flashed Alice a friendly smile through her open window. "We'll figure it out, thanks."

"Okay," Alice replied with a faint wave, making sure no cars were coming as she backed up across the road, watching the woman motion at her husband in agitation while he kept turning the key, foot slamming repeatedly on the gas pedal.

As Alice reached the opposite side of the road and glanced back, the couple's car was replaced by a hot flash of light and heat, blowing the back end several feet straight up, flipping over the entire vehicle and shedding pieces of plastic and metal as it landed with a smash onto its roof. Alice flew backward, landing hard on her backside with a cry as debris zipped past her head, ricocheting off other cars, pieces falling like hot hail to clank on hoods and roofs or land smoking on the pavement. Ears ringing, head spinning with horror, she blinked as the older couple burned inside the wreckage, the woman inside waving her arms as flames and smoke consumed her obscured form until she stopped moving a moment later.

Alice uttered a cry for help that died on her lips, as she was suddenly ducking and rolling as more explosions erupted near her, glass shattering in every direction as fierce roars filled the air. Vehicles flew skyward, riding springs of fire, flipping and landing with heavy crashes in a buckling of metal and death screams. A pickup rocketed sideways when its fuel tank blew with a sharp echo of sound, the tail spinning into the parking lot, sweeping over a family of six and wiping them across the pavement to leave only bloody streaks where they'd been standing.

The sudden stench of burning bodies and fuel filled the air, causing her to retch as she scrambled to her feet, sprinting through the parking lot past dumbfounded onlookers as more vehicles went up. She dashed up the stairs and into the restaurant, flying past the horrified hostess as a chunk of a fender plunged through the front glass and landed just inside. People leaped from their tables, knocking full drinks over to crash on the floor, slamming into each other as they clumped together near the back rail away from the explosions and noise. Reaching the kids, Alice hovered over them protectively as she retrieved her phone.

"What's happening, Mom?" Sarah's eyes were as wide as saucers.

"I don't know yet," she replied through tight lips, hand shaking as she scrolled down a string of text messages and missed calls from James. Opening the first one, she scanned the words with a blink.

Alice... Get to safety now. Something's going on. It's very big. Very bad. Pick up, please. This is really, really bad.

Taking the kids by their hands, she guided them outside, hustling past panicked people and out the front door, ducking and flinching as car parts whizzed by. Coming down the stairs, Alice threw glances over her shoulder as more explosions ripped through the cool early evening like volcanic dominoes, waves of heat covering everything. Curious tourists watching through the storefronts or coming up from the beach were suddenly turning to flee as flaming debris flew at them, sharp pieces shattering windows and puncturing flesh, big chunks knocking people down in a shrapnel storm, hundreds of them injured and dying right before her eyes.

Slowing to a frantic walk, Alice dialed James's number and handed the phone to Jake. "Read your father's texts to me." At the same time, she dug out an earbud and popped it in her ear, waiting for her husband to answer, but greeted by a series of clicks and silence.

Jake's voice shook, glancing back at the explosions behind them, flinching as each one went off. "Y...you want me to read, Mom?"

"All the messages he sent," Alice said. "One at a time."

"Okay, here's the first one." Jake swallowed and read. "Nobody knows what's going on... there's been massive explosions on TV right now all across the country... cars and trucks exploding, going up in smoke..." The boy looked up. "What's going on?"

"That's what we're trying to find out," Alice picked up her pace. "Keep reading, please, faster."

"Here's the next one..." Jake continued. "Seriously, where are you guys? Did you leave your phone on silent again? Will text soon... need to get out of here now. Please be safe!" Jake's voice trembled. "This last one came a few minutes later, and Dad says ...we've been directed to evacuate the airport, and I'm doing that right now... on foot. I'll send another text when I reach safety. Please contact me as soon as you can!" Jake's eyes watered with fear. "Should I... keep reading, Mom?"

"Yes!"

"Okay. Next one says... Alice, I hope everything's okay there. There are planes falling from the sky... balls of flame, I'm not kidding. Stay safe. Call me!"

With every message, Alice's frown grew grimmer, yet she hustled the kids along, glancing back to where even more explosions were ripping off deeper inside the resort town, coming not just from the vehicles but the buildings as well. Flame and black smoke curled upward into the afternoon sky, painting a swath of darkness across the fading blue that joined other billowing clouds in a nightmarish tapestry.

"Mom, what does Dad mean?" Jake asked, jogging to keep up with her.

"I don't know, but something bad *is* happening. Don't worry, we're getting out of here right now."

They gave the bungalows and driveways a wide berth as more cars and buildings caught fire, charred debris everywhere. One economy van with surfboards strapped to the top had been launched forward through a beach house door, left perched at an awkward angle with the front end buried in the living room. Flames curled up from the inside, licking out from the windows and catching in the bungalow's rafters. As they approached their own beach house, Alice spotted their rental car lying on its side, the entire thing roaring with flames, fingers of scalding heat baking their faces as they walked by.

"Are we going to be okay in there?" Sarah asked as tears streamed down her face.

"The flames haven't spread to the house," Alice responded. "We'll be safe for now." Letting them in, she said, "Go upstairs and get all your things packed. I want to be ready to leave at a moment's notice."

Wordlessly the kids tromped up the steps as Alice shut the door, took her phone out, dialed James's number, and huffed in frustration when nothing but static came back. With worry nagging at her stomach, she sent him a quick text reply.

We're safe at the beach house, but people are going crazy here. Cars are exploding everywhere, just like what you said. Call me ASAP. Please be safe.

Moving into the kitchen, she placed her phone on the breakfast bar, arms folded as she stared through the rear window at the setting sun. Mind racing, she paced into the front room and looked toward town as an orange glow engulfed the rooftops, dark trails of smoke mixing with the darkening sky, smaller explosions marked by a dozen bright flashes in the distance. Biting her lip, Alice closed her eyes against the chaos, praying James was okay, trying to wrap her mind around what was happening.

Far above the Burton's beach house, the fading sunlight cast a dark hue over the town as wrecked vehicles raged with flames. Cinders rose on a cool Florida breeze to whisk across the rooftops and twirl against businesses and shops, wedging into cracks, tiny sparks growing in the crevices, catching the frameworks on fire while screams and shouts echoed out in the distance, disbelief, anger and death spreading like a plague.

Ships off the Gulf Coast were not spared from the conflagration as they worked on the oil spill, and they too soon blazed in the night, the flames spreading across the water's surface, boiling the brine and sending thick folds of smoke twirling upward in the scorching winds. Travelers on the Florida highways got caught in a hellscape as they abandoned their burning cars, sprinting across the expressway, clothes aflame and trailing tendrils of smoke as the remnants of oncoming traffic struck them, sending their torched forms rolling across the highway.

In every city and town throughout the United States, the explosions tore open the night sky, the air filled with cinder storms that spun across the cityscapes, lighting everything in a nightmarish glow.

CHAPTER TWO

Ryan Cooper
Somewhere Outside East Lansing, Michigan

Ryan stood at the large bay window at the back of his daughter's house, looking out over the twenty-five plus acres that made up a large portion of their overall property. A soft dirt lane had a right-hand branch leading off to animal pens and barns, and in the distance stood a wide green pasture fenced in with a herd of sheep, a pair of goats, and a donkey, all being watched over by three Great Pyrenees lounging in the shade of a corkscrew willow.

The yard was a beautiful rolling landscape of green with rangy patches of wooded areas off to either side, sugar maples mixed with medium-sized pink and white flowering trees and a spattering of droopy-leafed black maples dotting the yard. Soft footsteps sounded behind him, and he turned to greet Helen, who came around to face him with a cup of coffee in each hand and a soft smile on her delicate lips.

"Here you go, dear."

"Thanks," Ryan said, taking the warm cup and wincing at the hot side before finally getting his finger through the handle and holding it up with a smile. "Got it."

As Helen laughed, he blew across the surface and had a sip, enjoying the rich aroma drifting to his nose, the dark bitterness sliding over his tongue to give his senses a kick.

"This is really good. Thanks."

Helen smiled and turned to face the backyard with him, drawn to the chicken coop where hens pecked at the ground near the feet of a large rooster who strutted around like he owned the place. Another coop stood off to the side, guinea fowls and peafowls free ranging nearby, and beyond those structures stretched a small pasture where a peacock sauntered by with its feathers folded and lying straight back.

"That peacock doesn't look too proud today," Helen said.

"Probably hasn't had his coffee yet."

Laughing, Helen play-slapped his arm as she admired the grounds. "Alice and James have done so much with the place, don't you think?"

"Well, it's not like our place was," he scoffed, "but I have to admit, they've done a great job." Slipping his arm around her waist, he looked off to the side where a bed of flat black panels sat turned up to the sky, soaking up the sunlight as the afternoon waned on. "We taught our little girl well, and James is no slouch. He did well with the solar panels."

"You should see the ones in the barn. It looks like they want to go totally off grid."

"Let me live in peace knowing I still got a few things up on the youngsters," Ryan chuckled, sipping deeply from his coffee cup, a pleasant warmth running through his body, following behind the first pinch of alertness. With a smile, he turned, limping slightly, holding his right leg to massage it as he headed back to the kitchen. "I'm getting seconds. You want anything?"

"I can get that for you, honey," Helen said, following him across the gray tile to the breakfast bar where he angled for the coffee maker and placed his cup next to it.

Pot in hand, he started pouring when a muffled thump caught his ear. It was a distant sound, almost like a bump from the dryer when an exceptionally heavy load rolled inside it, though they weren't running any laundry.

Placing the pot down, he turned to Helen. "Did you hear that?"

"I heard something," she replied, leaning her hip against the counter, holding her cup with both hands. "But it sounded like the HVAC unit or furnace or something. You know how it sometimes knocks and clicks?"

"Yeah, should be off, though...." Not completely convinced, Ryan reached for the creamer, starting to pour it into his mug when a pair of muffled thuds went off, louder than before, shaking the house and causing the glass and silverware to rattle gently in the cabinets. "That sounded like explosions... close, too."

"Explosions?" Helen stepped back to peer through the large bay window again. "I don't see anything out back."

"Because it was out front," he said, leaving his coffee. "I'm sure of it."

Walking past Helen, he crossed into the dining room to stand before a pair of windows with the curtains pulled to the side, sunlight bathing the yard in warm light. A spattering of flowering trees stood out near the edges, a pair of red oaks off to the right guarding the house, their brilliant red leaves glowing like fire in the sun's rays. A long lane flanked by ponds of blue water led down to a gate. Parts of the yard were filled with berry bushes and fruit trees, but it was the bright orange blooms of fire and smoke in the neighbor's driveway that held his gaze, two vehicles flipped over in heaps of twisted metal, flames licking from the windows.

"Are their *cars* on fire?" Helen asked.

"I think so." A thin hint of panic rose in his stomach, rising to a quick crescendo. "Oh, no. It could catch their house on fire. We've got to go help them."

Helen gasped and slapped her hand over her mouth, and Ryan spun and grabbed his jacket where it hung on a chair, heading for the garage as he called back, "Do the kids keep a fire extinguisher in the garage?"

"That's what Alice told me," Helen confirmed, placing her coffee cup on the dining room table, snatching her jacket and hustling after him along the hall to the garage. Ryan hit the garage door button as he entered, a light coming on to illuminate shelves of gardening supplies, weed killer, and other odds and ends. A big fire extinguisher sat next to James' workbench and Ryan hefted it, pointing to another smaller one clipped onto the wall above the workbench.

"You grab that one and follow me. Let's go."

They went fast down the gravel driveway and hustled along the lane to the front gate, ducks quacking and flapping their wings in the ponds, spooked by both the people disturbing them and by the billowing clouds rising high into the sky, coalescing into a mini mushroom cloud. By the time they reached the gate, Ryan's leg ached from ankle to knee, the muscles straining all the way up through his hip like they always did when he pushed himself too hard. He refused to slow down, unable to take his eyes off the flaming cars, the blinding heat, and the smoke gusting at them even though they were still a respectful distance away. One vehicle had flipped over, still basically where it had been parked, but it was teetering back and forth as flames and smoke rolled up from the bottom in continuous waves. The other car was at an odd angle off to the side, fire engulfing the entire rear end, tires melted, rubber burning in greasy black fumes that twirled together in a cyclone. Car parts lay scattered everywhere, acrid vapor stinging his nostrils as the pair ran up into the yard, Ryan with a sheen of sweat forming on his face.

Glancing over his shoulder, he watched Helen's golden-gray hair singe at the edges, feeling the heat burning his cheeks, and he grabbed her arm and pulled her back and around to the left. Since the nearest car had blown toward the street, they circled it using the path to the driveway. Arm thrown up to shield his face, he blinked at the detached garage where the first vehicle had popped straight up and flipped to leave flaming parts raining on everything. The garage was burning fast, the door blown off, the front right corner collapsed inward, crumbling as they watched the fire dance across the rooftop and crawl along the sides. A third vehicle had been parked inside when it caught fire, sitting askew in its spot, the shape outlined by raging flames.

Turning to Helen, he pointed. "See the third car inside? That's why the garage went up so fast. And the cinders are drifting over to the house."

"How are we supposed to do anything with these?" Helen lifted her extinguisher, gesturing at it helplessly.

The Jones family came flying into view on their left, Mike dragging a hose as Anita and their older kids were dowsing the grass with buckets of water before running back inside to refill them. Jaw set with grim determination, Mike pulled the hose toward the garage, a skinny, lone man against all the heat and flame, getting as close as he dared, pointing the nozzle up and letting fly with an arc of cool water that fizzled out into steam the moment it touched the flames.

"We're going to help them keep their house from burning down."

Ryan rushed up and grabbed Mike's attention, showing him the fire extinguisher and gesturing toward the flames that burned a ragged hole in the garage's side, threatening to leap to the nearby house. Stepping aside, Mike made room, still drenching the siding as Ryan cut in and placed the extinguisher on the ground. With the nozzle pointed at the charred spot, he pulled the pin and jerked the handle, white spray ejecting from the spout and billowing up the wall like a snowstorm.

Fire and retardant battled, producing a grayish smoke shocked through with orange flames that burst from the vents in the eaves. Helen stepped in beside Ryan, adding her extinguisher to the fight, but as much as they waved and sprayed the fire retardant, they only managed to put out a small section before they ran dry. Tossing his extinguisher aside, Ryan grabbed Helen's arm and drew her away from the heat, wiping the sweat out of his eyes. Mike turned his hose on the spot they'd been working on, the water drenching everything, hissing and dousing some of the flames.

"You're making progress!" Ryan shouted. "I've got another hose in the garage. Let me run over and grab it. I'll be right back."

Without waiting for a reply, he waved off Helen's protests while he raced back to the house. Pain lanced up his leg, but he ignored it as he ran back up the long drive to the front stoop where Alice had a hose wrapped up in a wheeled cart. Detaching it from the spigot, he dragged it along the long driveway, pulling it across their neighbor's yard and up to the house, the wheels rattling against gravel and grass. Attaching it to the Jones' front spigot, he cranked it on and hauled the hose to the side of the house, pointing the nozzle at the flaming eaves.

"We have to soak everything," Ryan shouted. "I've got a more powerful nozzle, so I'll hit the top section, and you work on the lower parts. Okay?"

Mike nodded, his expression calming with the arrival of a second hose in the fight, aiming his hose at the base of the garage and soaking it. As Helen joined Anita and the kids with buckets, cups, and anything to saturate the bushes and grass between the two structures, Ryan took aim and fired, shooting water up through the vents, hoping it flew into the rafters or dripped down the other side. Heat hissed and spat at him, sending rolling smoke over the walls to cover him, lungs filled with an acrid bite, forcing him to back off but not abandon his position. Between them they got control of the fire, keeping it off the house side of the garage, letting the other side burn as the wind changed direction, blowing cinders and smoke away from them.

When it became clear that they had gotten the inferno under control, Ryan took Mike by the arm and pulled him back. "What in tarnation happened here?"

"I have no idea," Mike replied, turning off his nozzle, right hand closed into a fist as his soaked T-shirt hung off him. He shook his head at the destruction, then shifted his attention toward the cars. "My Toyota just exploded, followed by Anita's Mitsubishi." With sudden realization, he slapped his thigh and winced as he stared into the garage. "But before those two exploded, my mustang must have gone up. I'd just restored it!"

"I hope you have insurance for it."

"I do, but what in the world am I going to tell the insurance company?"

"What are *any* of us going to tell them?" Ryan had caught sight of something down the road and dropped his hose, walking as close as he dared to the driveway where the vehicles were still burning. The area was rural, the houses spaced hundreds of yards apart, sometimes miles, though his daughter's family's part of the old country road had several houses in relatively close proximity. Distant balls of smoke and flame were ripping toward the sky, dots of bright orange glowing in a haze that seeped over the grassy plains and drifted through the surrounding woods.

"Geez," Mike said in a quivering tone. "That's the Willoughby's house down there. It's on fire."

"Almost all of them are," Ryan said. "Cars and more houses, both. There, way up on the right where the road curves. See them?"

"Yeah." Mike scratched his head as he turned his hose on his burning sedan out in the yard, his voice mystified as he half-heartedly tried to put it out. "What the heck's going on? I just don't get it."

"Me neither." Ryan scratched his head and rubbed his smudged cheeks, face drenched with sweat and water. "What about the fire department? Have you called them?"

"Anita called 911 as soon as it started, but the lines were busy. She'll keep trying, though." Mike groaned as he looked back at the vehicles. "Insurance is going to be a pain in my ass."

Ryan patted his shoulder with a tired sigh. "When we get back to the house, we'll give them a try, too, but I'm not sure if...." Ryan looked to the distant skyline, even more plumes of fire and smoke rising above the hills, and when he looked in the other direction past James and Alice's, more black marks raced toward the clouds, huge swaths of darkness churning upward. "I just hope they can get to the rest of these folks in time."

"Me, too. Oh, and Ryan? Thanks a lot, man. You guys helped save our house. Sure am glad ya'll are house-sitting for your daughter."

"Don't mention it. I'm just happy we were able to keep the damage to a minimum. You all need anything else, just holler."

Ryan turned to see Helen hugging Anita and the kids as he walked over with a smile. They gave a last wave and circled around the smoldering vehicles, heads turned away from the smoke, and made their way back to the gate at the end of the driveway. Slipping inside, Ryan closed it and let the latch fall, throwing the padlock through the loop and snapping it shut. With a tired smile at his wife, the pair slowly headed up the gravel lane back to the house, Ryan rubbing at his leg the whole way.

Sensing his discomfort, Helen locked her arm through his, offering support, and he leaned on her, letting her take some of his weight as they moved up the drive. The ducks had settled back down, and if he ignored the billowing smoke on the horizon, the farm looked beautiful, the red maples standing on either side like guardians heralding their return. When they reached the top of the driveway, Ryan stopped and stared at their car where it sat unblemished, still in one complete piece, the shiny maroon paint glinting in the sunlight.

"What is it, honey?" Helen asked, looking back.

"Oh... nothing. Just wondering, that's all."

Lost in his thoughts, Ryan let his arms fall around her waist and guided her up into the house.

CHAPTER THREE

James Burton
Denver, Colorado

Sitting at Gate 42, getting ready to board his plane, James Burton put his book aside and picked up his phone, looking for some mindless news to distract him from the exhausting engineering conference he'd attended. The panels had been demanding as the competition was growing exponentially more challenging, putting a lot of pressure on him and his associates to make airtight presentations with sales quotas constantly in the backs of their minds.

Sitting in the hard blue chair in the middle of the row, James watched people as they milled around or got a last-minute coffee. Kids were playing video games on their phones, staring into their laps despite the huge scenic window in front of them showing off the powerful jets as they flew in and took off, their bright lights blinking against the evening sky. With a dry smile, aware of the irony, he lifted his own phone and checked a few random news stories, scrolling idly. It was only when a swelling murmur filled the gate area, people mumbling, pointing, and walking up to the window to look outside that he, too, looked up. He put his phone aside, rising curiously in his seat, jaw dropping at the sight of several huge plumes of smoke climbing into the afternoon sky. James grabbed his book and tucked it under his arm, scooped up his duffel bag, and swept it onto his shoulder as he crossed to the window.

The black clouds were growing at the far end of the tarmac, spreading out, covering the star-filled sky, though he couldn't tell what exactly was burning. Off to the left, a fuel truck cruising toward a waiting plane suddenly ignited in a whoosh of fire and smoke, the tail end careening off to one side, the crowd leaping back with a startled gasp before stepping forward to watch a tire roll across the tarmac. Flaming debris arced toward them, peppering the window with clanks and thuds and causing everyone to titter nervously, though no one moved to step away.

"Stay back!" James shouted, gesturing, though no one was paying attention, too busy watching the events happening out on the airstrip.

Before he could continue, a massive *thump* rocked the floor a few gates down, another fuel truck spinning sideways across the pavement, screaming airport workers throwing their arms up as sharp pieces of the tank swept at them, slicing their bodies before they were knocked through the air like rag dolls. More trucks leaped upward on springs of flame, one bouncing ten feet high and landing in a fireball that bloomed outward around the edges, catching aircraft ground crew in its scalding embrace, blasting over them and sending them staggering across the tarmac with their clothes smoking.

He glanced up at the TV screens mounted throughout the room, watching as the images from different news channels showed similar incidents happening in Philadelphia, Sacramento, and Miami. On one TV, a ticker scrolled along the bottom. "Disaster in DC. Reports of multiple, high-yield explosions are occurring at Ronald Reagan Airport at the nation's capital... tens of thousands estimated dead..."

Swallowing a dry lump, he tried calling Alice twice, but both times he heard only endless ringing, and he shot her a text instead.

Alice... Get to safety now. Something's going on. It's very big. Very bad. Pick up, please. This is really, really bad.

The crowd surrounding James began breaking off, mumbles and groans beginning a slow climb into panic as more flowering explosions and scorched bodies reflected off the tinted glass. A fire truck on the way to assist went up like a firecracker, pieces of ladder and its bright red sides punching outward to scatter over the pavement in a wave of flying glass and metal. Around James, members of the airport staff pushed everyone back, but people were glued to the scene, frozen, one woman arguing with a staffer who tried to turn her away, shoving back, getting aggressive with a snarl on her face.

Shrapnel from the explosions continued peppering the glass, a sizeable chunk of metal striking high on the edge, the impact with a weak point sending a lightning bolt-shaped crack shooting to the bottom of the massive window. More smoking pieces struck hard and fast, like a heavy hailstorm, creating a sprinkle of tiny breaks and spiderweb marks in the glass, showing the passengers how vulnerable they were. Over James' right shoulder, another large window shattered under the stresses it was enduring and the crowd screamed en masse, people pushing and shoving, knocking James aside, causing him to accidentally strike a man with his duffel. The throng moved like it had a mind of its own, thousands of pounds of humanity flowing in one direction before shifting unpredictably in another random direction. Reeling, heart kicking up another notch, he plunged into the crowd, working his way along the gate lane and wincing as something heavy hit the roof of the building, followed by more pieces that sent dust trickling on their heads as the tiles above rattled and the metal groaned.

Most everyone was shoving their way in the same direction as him, yet a subsection were pushing toward the windows to see what was going on as they tried to get out, screaming when the debris finally broke through the glass and showered them with shards and heavy, smoking chunks. Turning sideways, James squeezed past them all, throwing himself into the clusters of carry-ons and backpacks people had on, tripping over a dropped handbag, causing him to stagger and almost fall. The shrieking crowd suddenly parted and he cut briskly through the throng, alarm bells ringing in his head, yet he kept himself calm and breathing as steadily as he could, ducking and weaving to avoid panicked travelers shrieking past him to find their loved ones. The far end of the gate was a long way off and he broke into a slow jog, hopping, twisting, and dodging as he tried to avoid knocking people down.

From the side, an electric transport cart barreled into view, the driver gripping the wheel in sheer panic, foot pressing the accelerator to the floor and glancing back as the throng broke toward him calling for him to stop. James was closer to him than most, though, and he lowered his head and sprinted after it, almost running a woman over, spinning and lunging, grabbing the vehicle's back rail as the cart fishtailed and swerved, nearly jerking his arm from its socket as he hauled himself aboard with a mighty grunt. Scrambling to hold on as he glanced at the red-faced runners too slow to copy his motions, James crawled to the front and climbed over the divider, landing in the passenger seat next to the driver.

"What's going on here?" he shouted as he grabbed the support bar on the dashboard and hung on.

The panicked driver looked over and locked eyes with him in surprise, shrugging and shaking his head. "No clue, man. I just know the whole damn place is going up in flames, and I need to get out of here."

"I agree with you there," he replied, glancing back at the crowd of hundreds chasing them.

One by one, people got their feet twisted or were stepped on, faces planting onto the carpeted gateway only to be trampled, hands reaching out and grasping for help just before they vanished beneath pounding shoes. The transport pulled into a wide square with restaurants surrounding them and a set of escalators in the middle. James jumped out and nearly slipped on a puddle of something pink with pieces of ice, but he got his feet under him, adjusting his duffel and lunged toward the escalators. Grabbing the rail, he skidded on and leaned against the side, panting, trying to catch his breath as the crowd drew closer. With a gasp, he stood and descended the slick metal steps, dodging between people just standing still with dumbfounded looks, flying past them two at a time as they gaped.

"What's happening?" a twenty-something man asked, staring at his phone, hardly noticing James as he went by.

"The news is saying everything is blowing up," his girlfriend replied with a rising question in her voice, oblivious to the swiftly approaching danger. "How can *everything* be blowing up?"

James reached the bottom and stepped off to the side, glancing at the televisions on the walls as they displayed destruction on every screen, anchors babbling in panicked voices and gesticulating wildly as lists of cities rolled across the bottom of the screens.

Pausing for a moment to catch his breath, he frantically sent another text to Alice.

Nobody knows what's going on... there's been massive explosions on TV right now all across the country... cars and trucks exploding, going up in smoke.

He dashed into the middle of an open area with signs everywhere, causeways and stairs, escalators and a set of elevators at the far end. He searched for the nearest exit as more explosions rattled the terminal and debris flew past the windows and clattered off, glass shattering, the panic spreading to all floors as people pushed and shoved, trying to get to their luggage or the exits. Sweaty faces gaped at him as they ran by, one line of people clinging to each other's shoulders, the lead man a massive brute who'd put his head down and was charging ahead and bowling people over indiscriminately. The air reeked with perfume, sweat, body odor and the unmistakable scent of fear, and from the loudspeakers came a woman's monotone voice ordering everyone in all terminals, gates, and restaurants to make their way to the nearest exit in an orderly fashion. Someone slammed into him, almost knocking his phone out of his hand, yet he held on to it and spun away as he shot Alice another message.

Seriously, where are you guys? Did you leave your phone on silent again? Will text soon... need to get out of here now. Please be safe!

Turning in a full circle, he glared at the sea of humanity that was growing more panicked by the second, their frantic energy fueling his own fear. James had been to the Denver airport many times and usually knew his way by heart, but in the confusion all the signs blurred together, arrows pointing to the different terminal pickup and drop-off zones, the obvious exits still packed with people. A mob of hundreds or more were heading for security, pushing past the airport police and airport staff who were backing up, holding their hands up and forming a paltry barrier against the furious, onrushing crowds. One uniformed man tripped, staggered backward, and collapsed, not a single person trying to help him, feet stomping over him as he curled up and held his hands up to defend himself, finally disappearing beneath the mindless throng.

As more people jostled him, James hunted for a way out until he caught sight of a hallway with *Restrooms* marked across the top. Putting his head down, he rammed forward, shouldering one man aside, dragging his duffel bag over a woman who was on her knees and trying to climb to her feet. With a glance at her terrified face, he turned to help her up when the crowd shifted, pushing everyone in the opposite direction and sweeping her out of his sight. James kept moving, reaching the hallway, looking back to see a few people following him and hoping he knew a different way out. While the restrooms themselves didn't have exits, there were sometimes employee doors in such side halls. When he got clear of the crowd he spotted the steel door with *Employees Only* emblazoned on its placard and grabbed the handle and flipped it open, entering a short landing with a storage room off to the left and a metal stairwell leading down.

"Bingo," he muttered, clutching the rail and swinging himself around, thumb flying over his phone screen to send another text to Alice.

We've been directed to evacuate the airport, and I'm doing that right now... on foot. I'll try you again when I reach safety. Please contact me as soon as you can!

Descending the stairs, he leaped the last four and landed hard at the bottom, pushing through another door with his phone gripped tight. The throng drove against him but he pushed back and knocked people off him, adrenaline pulsing through his veins. Head finally clear, he realized he'd come around to the terminal check-in where kiosks stood in a row with travelers running past them for the doors while dragging their luggage and families in tow. James leaped in behind a young couple and pushed his way outside, hit by an unexpected wave of blistering heat, the harsh scent of smoke wafting over the entire airport as clouds of black drifted by overhead. Taxis and Safe Drive cars were lined up letting people off for their flights, the new arrivals looking agape at the mass of humanity exiting in waves of palpable panic, many heading for the three-level parking garage across the street. He squeezed between a taxi and a transport van who were dropping people off from a nearby hotel, pausing while cars cruised by and glancing over the lot numbers, trying to remember where he'd parked.

"Was I in 2C, or was it 3C?" Scratching his head, he waited for the next car to pass before jogging to the other side of the road where a wide, grassy patch separated the pavement and the garage.

A new pair of explosions shook the air and a tremendous force shoved him from behind, sending him airborne, arms windmilling as the toe of one shoe clipped the curb and dropped him face-first in the grass. He slid a couple of feet, cheeks and nose stinging as he rolled to lie on his duffel bag, staring at a car door hurling past where he'd been standing to land in the parking lot with a heavy *clang*. Another boom shook him, the ground vibrating as a commuter van thirty yards to his left leaped off the pavement, twisting and spinning at the same time to clip a woman in the forehead, partially decapitating her in an instant, her body spinning into the flames from yet another vehicle. People screamed, scattered or hit the concrete, a burst of fire from one gas tank catching a man in mid-run, setting him ablaze, dropping him flat after five more steps to flail weakly as he burned. Many of those unfortunate enough to not be snuffed out by the immediate blasts were hit with blazing shrapnel and razor-sharp glass, eliciting screams of agony as they fell to the ground. A woman and her child ran from the mess of wreckage, clothes smoking, hair lit with bright orange tendrils as they shouted and patted their heads, backs peppered with pieces of glass and plastic.

Tears in his eyes, James scrambled to his feet, legs wobbly but holding as he ran toward the parking garage entrance, until a pack of people bulled past him and knocked him to his knees. Up on the third deck, a pair of cars leaped high in the air on waves of heat, slamming into each other and plunging straight down to split on the upper rail, spilling slowly over the edge before plummeting downward in a blazing torrent to crash on the heads of the people who'd knocked him down. Two of them dodged to the side, turning and screaming for their loved ones who'd just been crushed, backing away when a gust of flames beckoned.

With a desperate cry, James rolled to his feet, lowered his head and ran as more vehicles inside the parking lot burst into flames in the dark recesses, clouds of soot and smoke squeezing between the layers along with pieces of hot steel and glass to flick across his skin, cutting his upraised arm and face as he fled down the road. Hot winds blew at him from both sides, carrying with them noxious fumes and the reek of flash-bombed flesh, screams cut off as those trying to flee were pulverized with car parts, almost all of them dropping on the spot and leaving a few to crawl and groan with gut-wrenching injuries. The young couple he'd followed through the exit were running up ahead of him off to the right and as the man glanced back, a shard of something zipped in from the right side and nicked his neck, the piece whizzing past James and sending a light spray of blood across his cheeks. The woman turned back to catch the falling man, calling for help, but James raced by without slowing despite a sharp pang of guilt, unable to stop what was happening and unwilling to turn back for even a second lest it mean a quick and brutal death.

He got clear of the worst of the chaos, panting and sweating, legs aching as he jogged through the last smoke cloud and slowed to a fast walk. Behind him, the drop-off lane was covered in rubble and bodies. Most were dead, some were crawling, and others were lying face down on the pavement with their hands thrown over their heads as fiery debris continued to fall. Facing forward again, he spotted more trouble ahead as the vehicles continued to erupt in flames, burning in the middle of the road as they crashed and spun out, a few injured survivors managing to crawl away, though far fewer than had been in the vehicles to begin with.

A sedan hung precariously off the guardrail above the terminal's entrance road where it circled back on itself creating an overpass, front wheels tilting up and down slowly as smoke and flame licked out of the interior. James slowed to a halt, panting hard and bending over with his hands on his knees as he watched the vehicle for a long moment. Gravity won in the end as some unseen fuel source ignited behind it, pushing the vehicle over, sending it toppling down in a cascade of scorched metal. Before it had hit the ground, James took two steps, grabbed the guard rail and swung his legs over, dropping ten feet to hit the sloping grass, feet slipping out from under him as he landed hard on his backside and slid toward the bottom.

The raging debris cleared the guardrail and plummeted down in a clatter of jangling parts. With a cry, he rolled over, crawled, and lunged to get out of the way as a sizeable chunk of the sedan's engine block slammed the pavement where he'd been standing. The impact sent fire and cinders scattering everywhere, chasing him up the underpass's cement incline where he stayed crouched beneath it, putting a thick layer of concrete and steel rebar between himself and the death raining down.

After the worst of the debris fell past him, slamming into the hillside and rolling down in a tumble of clanking metal and flames, he crept toward the edge of the underpass and peered into the sky where a pair of winged fireballs arced beneath the clouds in streaks of wavering orange and black, leaving long trails as they hurtled toward the earth. James estimated the airplanes' trajectory as they plummeted toward the main terminal where thousands of people were still stuck in a congested throng of humanity. He ducked back beneath the underpass, finding a nook to squat in and keeping the reinforced concrete between himself and the flying shrapnel, wrapping one arm around his knees while sending another text to Alice, praying that he'd survive long enough to hit the send button.

CHAPTER FOUR

Agent Alan Harris
Washington, D.C

President Birk stood at the podium atop the steps of the Rose Garden drilling down through a list of bullet points, aggressively highlighting the features of his administration's new energy plan. Flanked by perfectly manicured bushes, the press corps occupied five rows of seats in the grassy courtyard, surrounded by swaths of vibrant green foliage, verdant brush bursting with white chrysanthemums and purple-headed flowers that nodded in the breeze. Public officials and representatives of carefully selected corporate entities were seated in three rows in front of the press, each man and woman in attendance watching the President with rapt attention.

"Bottom line? What this plan will do," Birk gestured to the crowd, smiling confidently, "is usher in the next age of renewables, making our country far less dependent on imports from other countries and increasing our self-sufficiency. And with the new combination of nuclear and geothermal sites we'll be developing, we believe the United States can be a nearly ninety percent net exporter of oil, bolstering our economy and delivering on our pollution promises decades ahead of schedule."

Cameras snapped as the President spoke, the attendees hanging on his every word, the live feeds rolling, swaths of cabling running back through the grass to television trucks assembled just past the hedgerows. His tall form gave the impression that he was looming over them and looking down from striking blue eyes beneath black hair and over a chiseled jawline, though he wasn't purposefully trying to be intimidating.

Dressed in a dark suit and tie, hands clasped in front of him as status reports filtered through his earpiece, Secret Serviceman Alan Harris stood to the President's left, tucked behind a porch pillar. He gazed across the audience as camera flashes rose to a swell each time Birk made a point.

"Looks like a quiet night." Security Chief Westbrook spoke in his ear. "Just a handful of protesters outside the public gate, but facial surveillance came back negative with no big troublemakers on the list. I want Harris and... wait. Standby security team."

A spattering of muffled booms echoed in the distance, sounding like backfiring vehicles only much deeper and denser, their tails ending in a series of longer whooshes. The noises caught Harris' attention enough to look out over the public grounds, gaze shifting to the West Wing, noting three other agents with their fingers pressed to their earpieces, at least one of them with a cocked eyebrow as he glanced upward. Several members of the press corps had turned to look as well, searching the sky curiously before shifting back to the man standing at the podium.

"Attention agents in the Rose Garden," Security Lead Westbrook came through Harris' earpiece, "you may have heard some muffled explosions coming from inside the city. We're checking on those now. Please stand by."

Harris glanced around one more time, his gaze widening as thick plumes of smoke began rising off the city streets outside the grounds, gathering in a slow-moving cloud picked up by the winds and carried to the northeast. President Birk briefly looked upward but didn't miss a beat as he continued with his speech, though two more explosions ripped off close by, followed by a distant scream. The agent instinctively moved toward the podium and searched the crowd, alarm bells hammering in his head. A threat could come from anywhere; the sky, the ground or even the gathered media and it was his job to figure out what that was, when it was going to happen, and become the wall between that harm and his charge. Protocols flashed through his mind as he waited on direction from his security lead, eyes and ears sharp, shoulders tense beneath his coat as he kept his hands at the ready position. The detonations grew louder, sounding like they were coming from the public parking lots where lingering visitors were heading back to their vehicles after the Rose Garden's recent closure. The sky glowed orange as a dozen explosions split the late evening before dissipating into the darkness, and a million scenarios ran through his head as Westbrook piped in.

"Attention agents in the Rose Garden. We're receiving reports of multiple explosions in the city, three dozen or more and growing."

"Sir, we've got explosions out here in the visitors' lots," Harris said, tearing his eyes away from the sky and searching the crowd as he slowly circled toward the President.

"Are you serious, Harris?"

"Yes. We're all looking at them, sir. Everyone's noticing, even the President... but he's not moving."

"That's it," Westbrook said. "*Skylark* to the bunker, now!"

Harris was already striding briskly toward the podium, glancing at another agent approaching from the other side as they descended on the President, pulling on his arms and drawing him away from cameras and confused murmurs as reporters stood and stared in awe at the blooming sky around the White House.

Birk gave him a questioning look as he was pulled away. "What is it, Agent Harris?"

"Come with us, sir. We'll explain on the way."

The President was primed to protest when the television trucks around the garden went up in a pulse of blinding light, their tops blossoming like volcanic flowers, their antennae and dishes collapsing as scalding fire cooked the nearby foliage and turned it all to charred ash as a wave of heat followed, hot gusting cinders washing over the press corps and sending them scattering with screams and alarmed cries.

Birk tried to speak, but his words fell flat as the pair of Secret Service agents dragged him away, surrounding him as debris landed in the grass behind them, a few pieces clanking against the windows and leaving soot marks on the glass.

"This way, sir!" Harris pointed to the Oval Office door as his partner opened it, all three rushing in, greeted by two more agents who joined the huddle around the President, a few reporters still snapping pictures as they fled.

"We've got Skylark, and we're heading to A-3." Harris breathlessly reported into his wrist mic.

"Good, Harris. Pro—"

Before the Rose Garden doors could close, a boom rocked the building, knick-knacks vibrating on the tables, a picture of Neil Armstrong on the moon rattling off the wall to crash on the floor. Harris snapped his head around to catch a huge fireball rolling upward into the night sky and lighting it up like a sun, bits of debris pattering against the windows to send cracks through the triple-reinforced glass.

"What was that?" Harris hissed, guiding the hunch-shouldered President across the room.

There was a pause before the security chief came back. "Marine One was parked on the tarmac."

"*Was?*"

"It's not there anymore. We lost it."

"What the hell is going on?" The President tried to turn to look behind him as his agents barreled him forward. "Are we under attack?!"

"Take a right when we get into the hall." Harris spoke through tight lips, stepping ahead of the President, scooting sideways with his arms out to keep scrambling White House staffers from bumping into them.

"What's happening, Harris? Answer me, dammit!"

"Explosions, sir."

"Terrorists?"

"Unknown. But we've lost Marine One."

"So it is an attack?"

"I don't make those calls, sir. It's important we get you to the bunker right away."

"Can I call my wife?"

"Not right now, sir."

"She won't be happy."

"Sorry to hear that, sir."

They entered a series of twists and turns, Marines and more Secret Service rushing from an inner corridor as they guided members of the Joint Chiefs of Staff and high-profile politicians into another section of bunkers on the east side of the building. When they reached the end of a hallway, another brutal eruption shook their feet, causing paintings on the wall to shiver and dust to trickle from the ceiling.

"Be advised Rose Garden agents," Westbrook said. "The President's motorcade have all gone up. The bunker is *the* secure location. I say again – all transportation is non-functional at this time."

"Sir, we've lost both your primary and secondary transports," Harris said as he and the other agents led the President down a short, plain hallway with a single thick slab of metal at the end with a keypad and massive latch built in.

"The motorcade?"

"Yes, sir."

"That's right under our feet. How could they have infiltrated so deeply?"

Cries broke over Harris' earpiece before he could reply, more agents with their channels open capturing screams and explosions across the grounds, scenes of terror filling his head as he imagined what they must be going through. Still, Harris kept a steady expression as he punched the correct code into the keypad and grabbed the heavy latch, heaving it open with a grunt and gesturing for the President and the other three agents to enter. As soon as they were all inside, Harris shut the door and squeezed past them, hitting a steel stairwell with thick railings and a slip-proof surface that wound downward several floors lit by dim lights set into the cold concrete walls.

As they descended, the President quipped, "You'd think they could have jammed an elevator in here."

"It's designed this way on purpose," Harris murmured, more to keep his own nerves in check than to answer the President's vague query. "Along this stairwell, the electric switches to its own bunker-supplied power. I was told they wanted to keep it simple to avoid anyone getting stuck—"

"Just kidding, agent," Birk replied, wearing a troubled grin. "I should be happy I'm getting my cardio in."

"Yes, sir."

Several floors down, solidly beneath the White House grounds, they entered a circular chamber with five short, branching passages with gray walls made of steel-reinforced concrete and designed to withstand earthquakes, bombs, and even a direct nuclear strike on the capital. Running on its own separate power and air filtration systems, each passage led to a different part of the facility, complete with a kitchen, recreation room, and sleeping quarters for three families, giving the residents an extended survival time should they be forced underground.

Harris nodded for two of the agents to stand guard at the bottom of the stairs, then he picked a passage, half turning as he swept his arm to indicate where Birk should go, their pace still quick, but the need to huddle around their ward somewhat lessened due to their location. "This way, sir."

With the signal to his earpiece buzzing with static, he tapped it once, saying, "Chief Westbrook, we've got Skylark into the bunker and are taking him to the command center now."

"Good. We'll remain in total lockdown until the emergency protocol is lifted. Is that clear?"

"Yes, sir."

Birk allowed his smile to grow slightly wider. "I'll bet you didn't expect to be doing this your first week on assignment with me, did you, Harris?"

"No, sir."

At the end of the hall, they ran into another thick metal door, and Harris punched in the right code and waited as the slab popped with a loud *clack* and opened inward. He shoved it wide enough for the President to enter, gesturing for the last secret serviceman to remain outside before he pulled the door shut behind him. The bunker was a fifty square-foot area with steel I-beams running across the ceiling and braces scattered throughout the room, riveted into the ceiling and the floor with big metal plates. In the far corner was a plain door leading to the restroom, and dead center stood the President's desk carved from a massive slab of steel with the Presidential seal emblazoned on the front and facing the door. Stomach turning, he remained calm despite the terrifying noises still filtering in through his earpiece, sirens wailing, alarms ringing through the White House corridors as a fire raged on the first floor near the West Wing.

Harris interrupted the line. "Be advised. Skylark is now fully secured in the command center."

Birk had already circled to a plush office chair on the other side, facing two computer screens, the metal desk with panels of buttons and phones with blinking lights flanking a coal-black keyboard.

"Secret Service and Marines have been deployed across the White House grounds," Westbrook said in Harris's earpiece. "They're being supported by our bomb squads and dogs. Stand by."

Face illuminated by the screens, the President glanced up as he worked. "What are they telling you, agent Harris?"

The agent moved to the President's side. "We've secured the building, sir. Agents and Marines are moving out across the grounds with bomb squads attached to their hips."

"Good." Birk kept looking through his screens. "I'm about to join a meeting, so you're going to hear a lot of confused and angry people. If you see me motion for help," the President chuckled, "get ready to shoot the computer, got it?"

"Yes, sir."

"That was a joke, Harris." Birk patted the young man on the shoulder. "You did good, son. We're safe now."

"Of course, sir." Harris moved to the front of the President's desk, standing stock still with his hands clasped at his waist, eyes narrowed and looking at the floor as he listened.

Voices filtered in through a speaker sitting between the monitors, some of them muffled like they were calling in from cell phones or had spotty connections. Harris recognized the voices of top commanders, members of the Joint Chiefs, and the Secretary of State, all expressing disbelief and incredulity as the banter grew raucous. Birk finally pressed a button on his keyboard and leaned closer to a goose-neck microphone on the side.

"Okay, everyone, settle down. Just FYI, I'm locked in the bunker." He glanced up at Harris. "And I'm well-protected and safe. We can get on to the business of figuring out what's going on. Robert, what are you hearing from Canada and Mexico?"

"Toronto's been hit. Mexico City, too."

Birk's shoulders sagged with morbid relief. "So, it's a bigger situation than a direct attack on the United States, or the White House?"

"It seems that way, sir. Moscow called thirty seconds after you were whisked away, demanding to know why we were attacking them."

"You straightened that out?"

"Yes, and our diplomats are working hard... it took a few minutes to assure China we hadn't just started World War III with them. I've personally got my counterparts from the UK and France on the horn. The casualty reports coming in are... staggering. Paris is burning. They're estimating tens of thousands are dead or missing, and those numbers are skyrocketing. Support services are overwhelmed. It's the same in London, and, well, everywhere, sir."

"Thanks Robert. What about *us*, General?"

A baritone voice punched through the line, so loud it vibrated the speaker. "Sir, this is General Pulaski. Whatever is happening, it's in every major US city and every active military base."

"*Every* base?" Birk asked, one eyebrow arched as he leaned forward with the beads of sweat on his brow glimmering in the monitor lights.

"That's right, sir. I've got hundreds of thousands of vehicles burning... tanks, troop transports... our *jets*. Fuel storage, too. It's all we can do to try to put the fires out."

The President leaned back in his seat, face blank and expressionless as a paleness washed over him. "I understand, General. Thank you." Momentarily shocked, he blinked at the activity pulsing on his screens with incoming messages or updates as he tried to follow them. Swallowing hard, jaw set, the color returning to his cheeks, he punched his finger on the desk surface. "Okay, people. We need to figure this out, and we need to figure it out *now!*"

On the east side of the Potomac River, Washington was awash in flame. Massive clusters of detonations rocked the pavement as civilian vehicles, city buses, delivery trucks and vans, and government vehicles alike erupted in flame. Shards of plastic, steel, and glass shot skyward, hanging for a moment before falling in a rain of shrapnel on the heads of innocent bystanders. They threw their arms up only to be cut to ribbons by the descending storm while others were caught in the flames directly as multiple explosions congealed in a cyclone of light and heat, scorching the sides of buildings, citizens scrambling to dive under stoops and into dumpsters, only to be cooked alive when the flames reached them. A Dodge

Charger zipped between screaming traffic and slammed into an ambulance, the entire thing going up in an orange blast, the car's shiny black finish crawling with fire as the driver was charbroiled alive.

A bus pulling away from the National Gallery of Art exploded, its windows blowing out and cutting into a group of college kids on a field trip, waiting for the next bus to come in. Their screams and wails rose in a furious chorus, many falling where they stood, hit by flying debris while others stood gaping with deep furrows in their cheeks and foreheads from a dozen cuts, blood seeping into their eyes before they could even fathom what was happening.

Blazes broke out on every street, devilish flames dancing up the walls, hot enough to shatter glass, smoke climbing higher into the atmosphere to join in a black cloud that hung over the city, a harbinger of the doom that was spreading as fast as the flames could find new fuel to burn. A gas station on a corner lifted from the pavement as the tanks buried beneath it erupted like pipe bombs, fissures forming in the concrete within a forty-yard radius, breaking open, splitting with molten light before lava-hot fire flashed upward. The concussion rippled through the city streets for blocks as a massive ball of flame rose in slow motion, connected to the earth by a tendril of gray smoke. At its apex, the fire curved outward in a mushroom shape that curled in on itself and continued on into the sky, leaving widespread destruction at its feet.

CHAPTER FIVE

Alice Burton
West Palm Beach, Florida

Ocean waves crashed against the beach, their simple motions in stark contrast to the fires raging along the shoreline and beach houses burning to the ground, while the wharf and all its restaurants still blazed bright in the deepening evening. The burning township cast fluttering shadows in the sky as the rising smoke blotted out the moon and stars, the whole scene something out of a nightmare.

It was well before midnight and Alice was finishing stuffing two changes of clothes, some toiletries, a flashlight, and her phone charger into a tote bag, pausing to rest her hands on her waist, trying to figure out how to pack everything they had brought plus what they had purchased since arriving. She kept shifting things around, trying to get the best fit, finally giving up and turning to the dresser to scoop up her phone and check her messages. There'd been nothing from James since his last text, and no connection bars on her phone, and whenever she resent a message, it failed almost immediately. The power had gone out an hour and a half ago, but she'd scrounged up an old radio from the kitchen closet with working batteries and brought it upstairs, placing it on the dresser to listen while she was getting her things together.

"... my name's Steve Jasper, and I'm broadcasting from WFLA out of Miami. I've sent the staff home except for myself and a few volunteers to keep the broadcast rolling, combining stories from the National Weather Service, National Headline News, and call-ins from local residents who are reporting from the ground. Stay tuned for more updates as they come in. If you're listening to this broadcast in South and Central Florida, your power is probably out and you know the explosions have something to do with vehicle malfunctions that are occurring across the broader United States. As of right now, the nation's military is on high alert, and almost every city has issued a state of emergency from New York to our own governor DiCarlos here in Miami, his press release coming just prior to Florida losing power. Our police scanners are jammed with emergency calls and communications, though city services have all but shut down across the board. Two hours ago, just outside the studio, I watched a Florida news helicopter explode in the sky right before my eyes. It was... terrible."

Though the station manager was trying to remain professional, his voice quivered as it piped through the old single speaker radio. "We've not heard an official explanation from Washington, yet, and there've been reports that the President of the United States has been taken into hiding for his own protection."

Alice stopped shifting things in her tote bag and shook her head, chin falling as her eyes watered with tears, the disaster so incomprehensible that she could barely wrap her mind around it. Her parents were back home house sitting, and James was trapped somewhere in Denver where his status was unknown.

"As far as we're aware, the government's emergency channel is urging citizens to stay indoors and avoid populated areas. They also advise everyone to stay away from motor vehicles of all types as the reports of spreading fires continue to roll in. The police lines are busy, and... well, to be frank, there's no way they can get to you, so stay safe out there and keep an eye out for looters. We have limited battery power here at the station, so I'm going to sign off to conserve energy. I'll open the channel once again in one hour, so don't forget to dial in for the latest news and information about the disaster. This is Steve Jasper, reporting from WFLA, Miami, Florida." The reporter's brutal honesty was both shocking and refreshing, given the situation.

Stuffing her phone in her pocket, Alice exited her bedroom and called down the hall to the kids. "All right, guys. I've got everything I can carry, and I'm heading down. You've got five minutes."

Sarah hollered from her room. "But mom! I can't fit everything I want into my backpack."

"What are you trying to fit?"

"All my clothes and my computer tablet and my e-reader. No matter how I fold everything and stuff it in, it just doesn't fit."

"And it's not going to," she replied, pausing with her hand on the stair rail. "Just bring a couple of changes of clothes and your shoes and socks. And all your sandals, too. We might be doing a lot of walking."

"But we just went shopping for all my new stuff before we came here."

"Forget all that." Alice gave the girl's bedroom doorway a pointed look. "Just bring shoes, socks, and a couple of sets of clothes. If you notice a flashlight up there in any of the drawers, grab that, too."

"Okay, mom. I'll see what I can do."

"Five minutes, Sarah!"

Jake stepped out of his room with his beach backpack on his shoulder and a smile on his face as he stopped in front of her. "I'm ready to go, Mom. I already figured since the cars were blowing up that we have to walk, so I've got both pairs of tennis shoes and ten pairs of socks."

"Good job." She ruffled his hair as she came down the steps.

Halfway, she paused, peering through the foyer window with her arm out to hold Jake back. "Wait a minute. Go back upstairs."

"What is it, Mom?" The boy climbed to the top and turned around, craning his neck to see.

"Just stay here a second... I see someone outside."

From her position on the stairs, she could see the top half of two people walking by on the sidewalk, a man and a woman, squinting at the flaming rental car as they gave it a wide berth, each carrying duffel bags and backpacks. The woman was staring down the lane at the burning beach houses and, forcing the man to pause by gripping his shirt, she turned him and pointed at the Burton's rental house, arguing until he allowed himself to be led back up the walkway toward their front stoop.

With a shushing gesture to Jake, Alice headed downstairs and stepped up to the door, peeking through the decorative sidelight glass which was frosted except for small patterns of clear spots the designs didn't cover. Two shadows approached, coming straight up to the porch and climbing up like they were going to knock before pausing as they seemed to whisper to each other while gesturing at the door.

With panic squeezing her chest, Alice crossed through the wide, open entryway into the recreation room and looked around for a weapon. The room was large and elaborately laid out with a pool table, two small arcade games, a dartboard, and a small liquor bar and refrigerator. The walls were decorated with nautical artifacts; a steering wheel, a painting of a sailboat, and a sign that read *Captain on Deck!* They'd barely had time to enjoy the house before the events of the evening, much less find something she could use as a weapon.

Alice pressed her hand into her thigh, murmuring, "*Think, think, think...*" There were some pool balls resting on the pool table, and she picked up the eight-ball and stuffed it in her pocket. Turning back, she spotted a rack of pool sticks in the corner, grabbing one in each hand and carrying them into the foyer. Spinning to the sidelight, Alice peered through the frosted glass again, catching whispers on the porch and watching as the pair shuffled closer while continuing to argue. Glancing upstairs, she gestured for Jake to come down, finger pressed to her lips as he descended quietly, gingerly stepping on the far edges of each step to keep them from squeaking.

Smart.

Eyes wide with questions, Jake glanced at the frosted glass and the shadows standing beyond it, then he turned back to his mother and swallowed hard.

She held out a pool stick, whispering, "Here, take this and stand behind the door. Don't say a word. Got it?"

Jake accepted the weapon, nodding when Alice took it out of his hand and flipped it over so that he was holding the skinny end, adding weight to the business end if he needed to hit someone.

"Okay, back up in the corner there."

The voices outside were whispering louder, caught in the middle of an argument, though she couldn't make out what they were saying. They continued edging toward the door, leaving her field of vision as they got ready to knock. Alice placed the second pool stick in the other corner and rested one hand on the doorknob, closing her eyes and taking a quick breath before she turned the handle and whipped the door open with a glare. They were a ragged pair, dressed in ratty jeans and soiled shirts, tennis shoes scuffed and barely hanging on their feet, their backpacks bulging where they hung on their shoulders. Their hair was lank and greasy, faces thin, pale arms riddled with scabs with clothes sagging off their frail bodies.

Alice snapped with gruff agitation, "Can I help you?"

The man stood frozen and the woman jumped back with shifty eyes above sallow cheeks, her gaunt expression surprised for a moment before a half smile appeared on her face. Stepping hesitantly forward, she glanced past Alice to peer into the house. "Sorry to bother you, but we were just down by the wharf earlier. Saw you and your kids come back here after all that stuff blew up down there."

"That's right," the guy added, his voice rough, his chest full of congestion. "We were down there, and we saw you..."

The woman shot him a dark glance before smiling wider at Alice. "Anyway, it seemed like one of you folks might've gotten hurt, since there was a lot of debris flying around and all. Thought it might be nice to come down and check on you. You know, since there're no police or ambulances around."

"You just wanted to make sure we were okay, right?" Alice spoke skeptically.

"That's it, ma'am."

"We're fine."

"Well, that's great," the man said, glancing past her into the house. "Good to know you folks are okay. Are the little ones okay, too?"

"They're fine," Alice replied flatly.

"That's what we like to hear." The man sniffed and scratched at the scabs on one of his arms. "With kids, this must be hard. You happen to know what's going on?"

"Nope," Alice snapped as she gripped the doorknob harder.

The man took another step toward the door, coming within three feet of her and ignoring her heated glare. "We've been all up and down the lane here, and we've helped quite a few people already. We really love being neighborly."

"I'll bet," Alice snapped gruffly. "I'll bet you *really* helped everyone lighten their load. Good citizens, that's what you are. But we don't need any help, so you can just go somewhere else."

The man glanced past her again, stepping forward a little more, the woman giving Alice a hungry glare as she pushed in next to him. "Why do you have to be like that?" she asked. "If you'd just give us a chance, we could show you." A slow grin spread across her face, revealing an upper row of missing teeth and a few yellowed ones lining the bottom.

Alice tightened her grip on the door knob and shouted. "No! Leave, *now!*"

With a quick jerk of her arm, she slammed the door shut, pressed her foot against it, and twisted the deadbolt home with a sharp clack. Backing away, she wiped sweat off her forehead and shot a glance at Jake as he stood with the pool stick in his hands, shoulders tense as the piece of wood quivered in his grasp. He glanced up the stairs, and Alice turned to see that Sarah had come halfway down, blinking with a frightened expression.

"Come on," Alice whispered, gesturing for her to join them. Taking both kids by the arms, she guided them into the hallway between the foyer and kitchen where they stood in the shadow of the steps.

"What's going on, Mom?" Sarah asked. "Who are those people?"

"I saw them in the sidelights," Jake said. "They look like druggies."

Alice shushed them both, whispering. "I don't know why they're here, but it's not for anything good. Now, here..." She grabbed the other pool cue out of the corner and handed it to Sarah, bringing the kids around to the stairs and gesturing for them to go up. "I want you guys to go about halfway up where they can't spot you through the sidelights."

Both children turned to go up, but Sarah paused and looked back. "Are we going to have to fight them, Mom?"

"I don't know, honey. Just go upstairs and stay out of sight, but be ready if I need you. Go on, do as I say."

The kids flew up the stairs, briefly illuminated in the firelight from outside, the bright orange glow casting shadows across the ceiling and chandelier. Close to the top, they turned and crouched behind the rail, partially hidden in the darkness as they peered at her through the spindles. Pivoting back to the door, Alice pressed her ear to the thick wood, squinting and listening to the junkies' shuffles and whispering voices.

"We can't just leave," the woman was saying. "They've got to have some good shit in there."

"Yeah, but that didn't go like we thought it would." The man snarled his reply. "She's not going to open the door for us." His voice went even lower. "What if we just go on in? What are they going to do to stop us?"

"It's just a woman and two brats," his partner agreed. "She doesn't look tough, and the kids looked like pushovers."

Alice glanced over her shoulder to see both her children scooting down the stairs, Jake holding the pool stick higher. She threw up her hand, shaking her head, making gentle pushing motions to show they should stay right where they were and stay *quiet*.

Alice watched the shadows flit around outside as the pair whispered and put their hands on the cloudy glass. The man tromped through the flowerbeds along the front of the beach house, tearing up the mulch and cursing as he tripped over the bushes. Alice peeked around the door frame at the window, glancing over her shoulder to keep both looters in view.

"There's got to be some good stuff in here," the man said, jerking on the window, trying to get it open even though Alice had shut and locked them before they'd left the house earlier. "Looks like some games and pinball machines."

"We can't carry that stuff," the woman shot back. "We need computers and phones. Money and jewelry, too, if we can find it." The woman's shadowy face moved down the decorative glass, shifting from one eye to the other and looking through the clean spots as Alice hugged the wall and kept out of sight.

"Wait, I think I found something," the man said, and Alice edged around the door frame to see him staring down at the bags the kids had left over by the pool table.

The woman's shadow straightened and turned toward him. "Well, what is it?"

"Looks like a couple of bags. Like they're all packed up and ready to leave."

"Maybe we should relieve them of their burdens," the woman replied with a chuckle, coming off the porch and staggering over the flowerbed to stand by his side. A moment later, both faces were staring at the bags through the glass. "Oh, man. Score!"

"Let's break the glass," he grunted excitedly.

The woman turned around. "Get the thing out of my backpack."

"Where'd you put it?" He rooted inside her bulging backpack, objects clanking as he moved them around.

"It should be right at the top. Hey! Quit pushing me around."

"Here it is." The man held up a bulky black flashlight, the kind with the heavy rubber coating that was supposed to be indestructible, with a glass breaker on one end. He smashed it through the glass, breaking a big section before sweeping up the sides and top to knock out the jagged shards. Alice fell back into the foyer with the pool stick clenched tight in her sweaty hands. Waves of fear ran up her arms, giving her goosebumps as adrenaline pulsed in her veins. The man boosted his partner up to climb inside as her ratty coat caught on the sharp glass still stuck in the pane. Bent over the windowsill, she squirmed and strained, finally landing hard on the floor with a grunt. The man jumped up behind her, grunting and wiggling until he fell through with a heavy thump that shook the walls.

"Shhh!" The woman hissed into his ear as she helped him up, Alice's cheeks turning hot as she watched them from around the door frame.

"What are you talking about?" the man snapped. "You were twice as loud as me. Come on... the bags are over there."

A stale reek wafted off them as they shuffled to the pool table, each taking a piece of luggage and placing it on the green felt. The woman glanced into the foyer just as Alice pulled back, gripping her weapon harder but waiting to attack. The man unzipped Jake's suitcase, flipped open the top, and exposed some clothes, his sandals, and a hand-held gaming system.

"Bingo! This is worth a couple of hundred bucks. Let's look around in the other rooms."

Glancing up the steps at the kids with a fearful shudder and sweat beading on her skin, Alice experienced a moment of indecision. If she tried to get the kids and run out the front door, the junkies might chase them. Worse, they'd lose all their supplies and be helpless in a world of danger. Jaw clenched, Alice looked up at the kids, then she turned and charged into the room with a few silent, broad steps, sweeping the pool stick in from the side and striking the man in the face with a sharp crack, rattling her hands and nearly knocking the cue out of them. The blow stiffened him straight, screaming in surprise as blood rushed from a wide cut across his forehead and ran into his eyes.

"GAH!" The man took one step back and crumpled to the floor, head cracking against the edge of the pool table on his way down. Alice danced away, waving the pool stick threateningly as the man moaned and rolled around while the woman stared at him for a moment, then she lifted her gaze slowly as she bared her teeth.

"You hit my baby!" she shrieked, stepping over him with her clawed hands up and ready to strike.

Alice backed up and waved the pool stick, pointing to the window they'd come through and screaming at the top of her lungs. "Get out of here, now! I already called the cops!"

The woman's glare was piercing, nostrils flaring as she crept forward. "Cops ain't going to help you now, lady! You hit my baby, an' you're going to pay for it!"

With another high-pitched shriek, she charged in, but Alice struck first, hitting the woman across her upper arm with the pool cue, failing to stop the crazed junkie but altering her course enough to save her face. One gnarled hand grabbed Alice's shirt, while the other snatched a fistful of hair. Screaming in surprise and pain, Alice dropped the stick, made a fist, and gave the woman a sideways blow to the head that sent her reeling backward but didn't break her grip.

"Gah! You bitch!" the woman roared, yanking Alice by the hair and swinging her around.

The pair spun into the rec room and banged against the table, clawing and jostling for position as they tore at each other. Alice kept her center of balance, unwilling to be pulled down, feet shuffling across the floor as the woman kicked at her shins. A shockingly strong hand clutched her throat, squeezing her windpipe and choking the life out of her, but Alice grabbed the wrist with a screech, thrusting it upward as she head-butted the junkie in the chin. The woman slumped from the shock as her teeth slammed together, giving Alice a chance to drive her forward and slam her into the pool table.

Grunting, snarling, the junkie roared to life, shoving Alice a couple of steps toward the foyer to get her off her feet, though Alice twisted sideways and absorbed the pressure to stay upright. Over the woman's shoulder, she saw the man starting to get up, head shaking as he got to his knees and spotted them fighting through blood dripping into his eyes. Alice arched her back and drove her legs, shoving and thrusting the woman hard enough into the pool table to draw a sharp and satisfying cry of pain from the junkie's dry, chapped lips. Fumbling with her pocket, Alice grabbed the eight-ball, raised it high, and smashed it against the woman's head with a sharp crack, dropping her straight to the floor. The man was still struggling to rise, gripping the table's edge with white knuckles, expression furious as he lunged for her throat. Gasping and coughing, Alice scrambled around the pool table as the man chased her, staggering and half-walking himself around the table's edge on his hands as blood dripped from his chin. In her haste, Alice slipped backwards and caught herself on the edge of the pool table, giving the man a chance to snatch her wrist and jerk her upright as he raised his fist to strike. A pool stick cracked the man across the back, the wood splintering with the force of the impact as the man released her and fell back to the floor with a heavy thud to reveal Jake standing behind him, eyes wide and frightened as he held the fractured stick.

"Get back, Jake!" Alice's hand was stinging as she scrambled backward, crawling, gripping the edge of the table and straining to rise.

Sarah had come the opposite way and grabbed her mother's arm, helping her to her feet and holding out a fresh pool stick. Alice took it and waved it threateningly as she guided the children past the bedraggled woman and into the foyer, arm thrown out to keep the kids behind her. Once in the hallway, she unlocked the deadbolt, grabbed the handle, and threw the door wide.

Body stiff with rage, she pointed outside, screaming, "Get out of here... *now!*" Her voice sounded like a stranger's, riding a wave of primal energy from somewhere she couldn't explain. Heart pounding, her breaths shallow and loud, Alice pointed at the open door and bellowed. "Come on! Let's go! *Out!*"

The dazed pair struggled to their feet, their nasty expressions wiped clean from their faces, the woman turning to wait for her man as she eyed the menacing pool stick. Holding each other up, they shuffled by with groans and mutters, bumping against the door frame and almost falling. When they were outside, Alice grabbed the doorknob, slammed the door shut, and locked the deadbolt with a clack. Snapping around, she put her face to the sidelight and watched as the pair staggered along the walkway to the street, holding each other for support as they turned left and moved along the sidewalk. With the immediate danger averted, Alice put her back to the door and slowly let herself sink down to the floor, breathing heavily while the kids fell to their knees next to her with horrified expressions on their faces.

Jake still held the broken pool cue, the piece quivering in his hand as he touched her shoulder. "Are you okay, Mom?"

Alice blinked at him dazedly, though when Sarah leaned in and rubbed her mother's forehead, she snapped awake. "Yes, I'm... fine... I think. Are you two okay?"

Both nodded, but Sarah barely held her panic in check. "What just happened, Mom?"

"Seems like people are getting crazier a little faster than I thought they would." Alice peered into the recreation room.

"Hey, it looks like they left some bags behind." The man's backpack had dropped to the floor and spilled its contents everywhere. "Guys, help me up."

Each child grabbed an arm and got her to her feet, then Jake walked over and fell to his knees next to the backpack, spreading the top open as he peered inside. "Sarah, bring me the flashlight, would you?"

"Yeah." The girl crossed to where it had fallen and scooped it up, taking it to Jake with Alice right behind her.

"Be careful, Jake. You don't know what's in there."

"Um... it looks like just some canned food, some bottled water, and a new pack of men's T-shirts, still in the bag..." Jake moved them aside, smartly placing the survival items next to him. "And... wow! Look at all this jewelry!" He pulled out strings of pearls, elegant golden necklaces with pendants that shined in the flashlight beam, and a pair of chokers all entwined in his fingers.

"I'm not a jeweler," Alice said, "but that looks like expensive stuff."

"I can't believe they'd steal so much." Sarah wore a disgusted expression. "We can't keep any of it."

"No, we're not taking any of the valuables. Let's put that stuff in a jar in a cabinet in the kitchen. Once this is over, I'll notify the beach house owner and let them know they have some stolen property inside. Can you do that for me, Sarah?"

"Absolutely!" Sarah took the jewelry from her brother with a smile and then carried a handful of it along the hall and into the kitchen.

"What about the rest of the stuff?" Jake asked, holding the bag open and shining the flashlight beam inside.

"Looks like this is a few houses' worth of goods." Alice chewed on the inside of her lip for a moment. "We'll take the food and bottled water, whatever we can carry." Patting the pool table, she said, "Go ahead and line up everything here."

Footsteps came down the hall, and Sarah popped back into the room. "Did I hear you say we're taking the food and water?"

"That's right. We're packing up and *leaving*."

"Going out *there*?" Jake nodded at the window.

"We can't stay in the beach house. More people like them will be by soon, looking to loot and hurt people, and these pool sticks won't be a very good defense against them."

"Seems like we did pretty well with them," Jake replied as he lined up several cans of spaghetti and meatballs, ravioli, and soups.

"We got *extremely* lucky, kids," Alice explained in a shaky voice. "If it had been anyone except a pair of drugged-out junkies, I'm not sure this would have gone so well for us. No, we can't defend ourselves here, and besides, I'm not interested in hanging out in a remote house on the beach of all places. We need to get moving and *keep* moving."

"Where will we go?" Sarah asked in a plaintive tone, her worried expression deepening as she put her arm around her mother's waist.

"We're going home. Somehow." Alice returned the hug. "Come on. Let's finish packing up a few things but keep it light. Then we'll head out and see just how bad the world's become."

CHAPTER SIX

James Burton
Denver, Colorado

The distant explosions from the terminal and nearby parking lots haunted James for hours as he alternately sat, knelt and laid on the concrete slope beneath the overpass. There were massive puddles on the road, and the bottom of the embankment was soggy and wet. Where the debris had landed in the water, pieces sizzled and popped, leaving an oily sheen on the surface with larger chunks smoldering and giving off trails of smoke that rolled up into the sky.

Several vehicles had exploded beneath the underpass before he'd gotten there, spreading wreckage across the pavement. Car parts, fenders, and seats were scattered everywhere, and a foul smelling smoke rolled off the smoldering leather and cloth coverings, wafting through the girders and I-beams above him, pouring around the edges of the overpass to billow away.

James raised the water bottle he'd been holding between his knees and took a couple of gulps, lifting it above his head to splash a bit on his forehead, cooling his chafed face. Using his shirt from his duffel bag to dry himself off, he stood and started preparing to leave. He'd been waiting for the worst of the disaster to be over, hoping there'd be less of a chance of having flaming debris rain down on his head before setting off. Still, every hour of inactivity that passed brought a gnawing anxiety and the desperate need to reach his family that fueled his anxiousness to get moving once again. His inability to reach anyone via phone or text didn't help, either, and sitting still for hours had pushed his fears and paranoia to new heights.

With a heavy sigh, he swung his bag on his shoulder and started down the concrete slope. At the bottom, he turned a full circle, looking away whenever an especially thick cloud of smoke drifted by. The road east swept up toward the airport terminal, a less than desirable direction, so he looked past the puddles and up the oil-slicked embankment. If he could make it up the embankment, he could take the road coming in from the city, which – while assuredly not a cakewalk – would undoubtedly be a less treacherous path than the alternative. Stepping carefully over the stagnant water, he jumped onto a piece of metal, almost slipping on its greasy surface before he threw his weight forward and landed on the slope. He fell to his hands and knees immediately, crawling up through the slick grass, getting twelve feet before his forward movement stalled and he started sliding straight down. Cursing softly, he waited until he reached the bottom, spun, and hopped across the piece of metal to land back on the pavement.

"That's not going to work." He sighed, adjusted his bag, and began walking west, focusing on the darkness, his path lit by hundreds of small fires still simmering beneath the overpass, exposing the tangled mess he'd have to go through to reach the city's edge.

James picked his way between the smoking rubble, stepping over a catalytic converter and kicking plastic pieces aside.

Tires lay on their sides with the scent of burning rubber clogging his nose. Foam cushions smoldered, soggy with fuel and oil and antifreeze, giving off a horrible, bitter stench that stung his nasal passages even more. Stopping for a moment, James tied a spare shirt from his bag around his face, folding it into a bandanna and dampening it with a bit of his bottled water to keep the worst of the smoke and smells out. He started off again, finding an overturned eighteen-wheeler at the far end of the overpass, the cab blown off by the twin fuel tanks attached to its sides. The entire cab had crashed in one piece but lay spun so that the truck's front grill faced sideways. The cab doors were blown open and the trucker's personal possessions had spilled out into the oily mess. Still in his seat, unable to escape the violence of his rig's explosion, the driver's charred arm hung over the door, his flannel shirt soaked with blood that dripped from his fingers.

Turning away, James walked to the trailer, its thin walls split wide open to leave barrels of chemicals spilled into the roadway. Between the bridges were solid walls of concrete he couldn't climb, so he was forced to pick a path through. Getting on his knees, he ducked under the trailer, entering a space filled with twisted metal and broken cables hanging loose. Falling onto his elbows, he crawled ahead, wincing every time the viscous fluid dripped on his head and neck between cracks in the flimsy trailer floor. Coming out the other side, he wiped his skin clean, dousing himself with water to make sure that whatever was on him didn't burn before he moved off again, striding along an open patch of pavement, the concrete walls giving way to steeply sloped grass embankments and fencing.

Moving to the next section, James navigated more wreckage, his path lit by raging truck beds that had been hauling flammable goods. When he stepped into an open spot devoid of wafting smoke, he caught sight of the distant city off to the left. Denver was burning, flames crawling up the sides of buildings, illuminating the bloated clouds in the sky with a tortured glow, though not much could be made out through the dim lighting and thick, acrid smoke.

Heading back into the rubble, James clambered and climbed over the blown-up sedans and pickups when he couldn't slide between their scorched husks. Once, he stopped to investigate some specially marked trailers that had spilled airplane parts and equipment everywhere, tens of millions of dollars lying broken on the pavement. He moved on, stepping over dead bodies lying in the roadway, giving each mangled and twisted form a brief nod of respect as he passed, trying to see them more as things than people lest his rising nausea overwhelm him.

As the road swung him farther to the north, the congestion grew thicker, mostly traffic that had been entering the terminal area and catching fire at the same time. Pieces of aluminum hung from the highway rails, forcing him to skirt an entire pickup truck balancing up there, half hanging on and looming above his head. A small part of him expected to hear cries for help from around the area, though the silence was nearly complete except for the crackling flames and ticking metal, nauseous vapors making him dizzy with their fumes as they penetrated his makeshift mask. Puddles of oil and other chemicals coated the pavement, dripping from the wrecks above as they seeped through the cracked concrete. Brick dust trickled on his head, and he was forced to dodge larger pieces that smashed around his feet.

After an hour of crawling and ducking through the dangerous debris, James stepped from beneath the last overpass, leaving the mess of crushed shapes behind, their twisted metal forms ghoulish in the firelight. Out from the smoke and noxious vapors, he took a deep breath of cleaner air, saying a silent goodbye to the hundreds of corpses still stuck in their vehicles or shredded into pieces by flyaway metal and parts. James turned back to the road, walking north over an open stretch of pavement with fewer pileups and less destruction, letting out a long, deep breath of relief for having made it through the gauntlet. The grassy fields on either side were dotted with pieces of aircraft, and a massive section of fuselage had crashed near the road, its tube shape crushed like a soda can. Behind the windows were the vague forms of passengers still locked in their seats where they slumped forward in death, blood dripping from their pale and soot-covered faces.

Wiping away stinging tears, James looked across at Denver burning ahead of him, the details becoming clearer the closer he got. The tops of the buildings were cast in shadow, fingers of flames licking from the windows of the lower and middle floors to leave scorch marks up the walls. The streets shimmered like the coals of a massive furnace, glowing even brighter when a gust of wind blew through the narrow channels, coaxing the furnace to a feverish intensity. On the north side of town, past the businesses that comprised the backbone of the city, the conflagration burned at a lower degree, though the fires were rising as more homes caught and turned the sky deeper shades of reddish orange. Distant sirens wailed, accompanied by flashes of blue and red lights that spun from the tops of the debilitated city vehicles. There was no movement to the emergency lights that still shone, just a torrid flood of blistering heat and waves of smoke engulfing the skyline. James imagined the screams of the dying as he walked a mile and a half toward the growing destruction, not relishing the idea of having to find a way through such a place.

The wide-open fields around him were cast in pitch blackness to add a surreal tone to the night, and the thought of Alice and the kids struck him again. He dug out his phone from his pocket and turned it on for what felt like the hundredth time, staring at the screen for several seconds before checking to see if there were any messages. Scoffing at the lack of signal, James shook his head at his empty inbox and fought back a wave of dread. Powering down the phone again to save the battery, James put the device away and gazed ahead of him, noticing a blazing parking lot off the opposite lane to his left. Angling across the median, he strode to the other side and turned into a short entrance lane. At its head was a guard booth, check-in kiosk, and a big sign that read *Long-term Parking, Lot B.*

Gazing out across the lot and its smoking vehicles, he wondered if there was something left that he could drive.

"Can't be that every single one has blown up." James murmured to himself as he ducked beneath the gate and stepped into the first row of glowing metal on his left, the heat singing his cheeks as he strode through the raging wreckage of cars twisted every which way.

SUVs, pickups, and sedans with their paint peeled off lay everywhere, glass shattered and twinkling on the pavement, clouds of sweet antifreeze and the flatter taste of oil hanging heavy in the air. There were areas in the center of the lot where the flames were simply too hot to approach, vast swaths of vehicles that had detonated at the same time to land in a pile of tangled steel. A blue sedan with its nose pointed at the ground was squeezed between a couple of trucks as the pungent scent of burning flesh rolled off the wreckage in waves. James pressed past a white town car and a sporty civic whose front ends were crushed together, left unburned as the rear parts spouted flames and smoke. Beyond those hulks, the west lot came into view, but as he strolled past the wrecks, he couldn't spot a single car or truck that wasn't damaged beyond repair, nothing that would get him on the road and out of danger.

Squinting and peering through a break in the flames, he noticed a darker section up near the north corner where the shapes of living, breathing people shifted and moved. Arm thrown up to protect his face, he leaped upon a hot hood and slid across to the other side, jogging away from the worst of the blaze toward the milling people. Approaching cautiously, he did a quick count of roughly three dozen standing in a section of the lot where there weren't too many cars, and the ones that had blown up had already burned out. An elderly Hispanic woman sat on the back of one car where just a faint trickle of smoke rose from the engine block, gusting in a fitful wind. She was sobbing, face in her hands, heels propped on the bumper as a younger man consoled her. More people were gathered close by, many sitting on the pavement or on pieces of luggage, weeping as friends, family and strangers consoled them. Still others stood off to the side, hugging themselves, being sick in the grass or sobbing uncontrollably.

Swallowing the growing lump in his throat, James approached the woman sitting on the hood and the man consoling her. "Excuse me. Are... you guys okay?"

The man whirled and held up his hand and James backed up a step, raising his hands in surrender.

"Oh, no, no I'm not here to hurt you or ask you for anything. I was supposed to get on a plane to Florida back there." Voice wavering with exhaustion, he pointed over his shoulder at the still flaming terminal. "Everything just blew up, including my plane and I've been walking for... I don't know how long."

The man lowered his arm and nodded slowly. "We'd just gotten off a flight from Florida," he said with haunted eyes. "We were disembarking when our plane exploded. It took out the entire gate..." He swallowed and shook his head, his face illuminated by the fires to show a bevy of smudge marks and tiny cuts on his forehead and chin.

"So many people around us were *dying*!" The woman behind him spoke with a thick Hispanic accent. "It was terrible. I have never seen anything like that in my whole life. A woman was screaming for us to help, but we could not."

The man shrugged. "It was bad. People were running everywhere, and—"

"No, I get it," James replied with a nod. "It was crazy back there, so don't feel too guilty. I hope you two get to wherever you need to go, and I'm glad you're okay."

James turned away from them and stepped deeper into the crowd of survivors, striding over to a family who were sharing water bottles and candy bars between kids who sat on small pieces of luggage.

"Hey, folks." He waved and nodded. "Is everyone here okay?"

The parents had been watching him approach, and he saw tears on the woman's face lit up by the glowing fires. Her lips trembled in a combination of fear and dismay as she hugged herself and rubbed her arms while her husband edged forward, on the defensive.

"Who are you?"

James stopped before he came too close, holding up his hands again. "I'm just a guy walking from the terminal where I was supposed to get on a plane to Florida. You all are the first group of survivors I've seen, that's all. What happened to you guys?"

Visibly relaxing, the man gave his wife a comforting nod and turned to address James. "We weren't supposed to be on a

29

plane, but we were heading to the terminal to pick up her parents." He tilted his head toward the teary-eyed woman as his gaze fell on the burning airport. "They were supposed to arrive this afternoon, but we don't know if they made it, and our phones aren't working." The man held up his cell phone and shook it, pointing to the glowing screen.

"Yeah, I can't get a connection either," James replied. "And I'm so sorry about your parents, ma'am."

"I can't believe this is happening." Her voice was barely more than a croak, and she coughed to clear it as she wiped tears from her eyes. "I just talked to my mom this morning, and she was so mad at Dad because he was making them late. I thought it was so funny at the time, because he's always been that way, waiting until the last minute to pack..." She started to say more but broke down, face pulled into a grimace, cheeks red as she sobbed and accepted a hug from her husband.

"I'm really scared for Grandma and Grandpa," one of the kids said, a little girl no older than eight, her tiny legs crossed in front of her as she colored in a book with ragged, scorched corners. "I saw a plane fall out of the sky, but I think it crashed."

James crouched down and gave her a comforting smile, the expression hard to hold as his own inner turmoil raged inside him. "I'm sure they're both going to be fine. Maybe they hadn't even left yet, like me."

The girl's expression was hopeful. "You really think so?"

"I'd say there's a *great* chance they're okay." James smiled and stood, locking eyes with the girl's mother.

"Thank you," she mouthed at him, wiping at her eyes again and leaned into her husband, gripping his arm as she continued to cry.

James gave the man a pat on the shoulder, squeezed it firmly, and nodded before he walked away. As he turned, he nearly ran into a young couple who were rushing up with excited faces.

"Sorry, sir," the young man said, taking his wife's arm and drawing her back a step. "We heard you say you came from the terminal, and we rushed right over."

"That's right," James said with a tired sigh as he pushed aside the recent memories of the underpass walk, the fiery wreckage and charred corpses that were burned into his vision. "I was supposed to get on a plane to Florida to see my family..." He gestured helplessly. "Clearly, there was no plane to get on."

"That's what we were going to ask you," the woman said in an excited voice, her light brown hair held back with a clip to keep it out of her face so it wouldn't brush the burn mark on her left cheek. "We were supposed to meet our friends coming in from Cincinnati. This was supposed to be a reunion vacation of sorts. We thought it would be cool to do it in the state capital." The woman laughed and gave a sad head shake, her voice cracking as she continued. "There's so much to do with all the memorials and statues and stuff. I just really miss my friends..."

The man leaned in with a pinched look. "What we really wanted to ask you was if you'd seen any planes land. You know, did anything come down without..." He glanced at his wife. "Blowing up?"

James stared at them for a long moment before shaking his head. "I'm sorry, no. Everything I saw went up in flames and smoke. Didn't seem to matter if planes were on the ground or in the air."

"That's what we thought," the man replied with a sincere frown. "Thanks."

The woman was instantly crestfallen, her eyes watering, bottom lip quivering as quiet tears rolled down her cheeks. The man seemed uncomfortable for a moment, his own sorrow buried deep beneath his stoic face. "Hey, do you want some of our water? You look pretty tired from your walk."

"Oh, no thank you." James waved a hand. "I've got some in my bag, and if I were you, I'd save every bit of that you can."

"Why do you say that?"

James nodded toward the city where the fiery color scorched the sky. "Judging from the damage, there won't be any emergency crews coming out to help any time soon."

The woman shared an uncertain glance with her husband. "You really think it's that bad?"

"Unfortunately, I think so. It's been hours since it happened and, well... no sign of anyone yet. I was coming over here to see if anyone else survived, and I gotta say I'm happy to see some other folks made it out." James raised his voice. "Does anyone know what caused this? Any news reports or anything at all?"

A tall man with wire-framed glasses walked by with his face smudged with dirt and the fringes of his T-shirt singed. "All I know is a bunch of cars exploded at the same time. I was in one. Barely made it out alive."

James winced. "Are there any cars left someone could drive out of here?"

A woman laughed morbidly, bordering on the fringe of hysterics as she gestured around at the parking lot. "Does it look like there are any cars left?"

James sighed in resignation. "No... no it doesn't."

Working his way through the crowd, James spoke to a few more people, several families with much the same stories as the others. One man sat alone off to the side, shoulders hunched where he squatted against a car bumper, the vehicle having already burned out, barely smoking and popping as it cooled.

"You okay?" James asked, leaning in but still giving the man room.

At first, the man didn't seem to hear, then he slowly raised his head and blinked at James with tearful eyes. "Huh?"

"I asked if you were okay. You look like you might be hurt."

"Oh, I'm not hurt at all," the man replied with a flash of shell-shocked emotion. "I was supposed to be on a late morning flight, and I didn't make it."

Confused at first, James shook his head. "Shouldn't you be happy you didn't make it on that plane? I know I'm glad I missed mine."

"Yeah, but so many other people died. They're all gone." With tears streaming down his face, he hiked his thumb back toward the airport, voice filled with strain. "That should have been *me* on one of those planes! Why did all those people have to die, and I didn't?"

"I know the feeling all too well. Been wrestling with that off and on since I made it to the underpass and hid from all the destruction."

"H-how are you coping?" The man wiped at his face and James leaned back, arching his back until it cracked.

"Guess I'm just focused on my family and figuring out how to stay alive until I can reach them." He swiveled to look the man in the eyes. "You have a family?"

"Yes. They're in North Carolina." He held up his phone and shook his head miserably, swallowing a sob. "But I don't know if they're okay. They could be dead... my whole family, *gone!*"

"But you don't know that, do you?"

The man deflated, slumping forward with his elbows on his knees. "No. I don't know anything."

"Then you're obligated to get off that suitcase and get home. You've got to get back to your family, no matter what. You have kids, too?"

"Yeah, two."

"Then that's it, man. Get up and get moving. Find a way to get there."

After a slight hesitation, a light clicked on in the man's eyes, and he stood and gave James a second glance. "Yeah, thanks. I think I'll do that. Seriously, thanks a lot."

"No problem."

With a pat on James' shoulder, the man scooped up his suitcase and went to join the others, asking questions to see if anyone else was heading to North Carolina. After watching the man for a moment, James turned and walked through the grassy field at the edge of the lot, wondering if he was strong enough to take his own advice. For starters, he had to pick a direction, and with no transportation, he had to stick close to Denver until he found some. Hands stuffed into his pockets, he put one foot in front of the other and made his way along the curving stretch of road skirting the city. Running down a list of his travel options, Florida was the top choice considering Alice and the kids were already there. Still, he knew Alice well, and if the same things were happening in Florida, she'd be taking the children to Michigan as quickly as she could, figuring that he'd be heading there since it was much closer. Even if she wasn't there when he arrived, at least he'd be working out of his home base for figuring out how to get to her or at least make contact, assuming he wasn't able to do so sooner.

So, Michigan it was.

Home.

After a long stretch of straight roadway with little burning on either side, James came to a warehouse district with buildings that were hundreds of feet wide and comprised of both storage and manufacturing facilities. National name brands were painted on the sides, and their rear lots had built in docks with rolling bay doors, most of them either up or blown off, leaving garbage and debris scattered across the pavement. Their lots were filled with cars, eighteen-wheelers and heavy machinery, all of which had succumbed to the same fate as every other vehicle James had seen. The explosions looked like a mix of car parts and commercial products, from office chairs and shelving to charred cereal boxes with corn-flakes strewn everywhere.

Among the destroyed materials and cars lay a spattering of corpses, many wearing burnt clothes while others were trapped in truck cabins, locked inside like human remains thrown into a barrel fire, the blazing orange tendrils torching them to the bone. Almost every building had been set ablaze or had received fire damage thanks to the vehicles parked at or near their dock doors, though James was far enough away that the flames didn't seem to pose an immediate threat. Sharp crackles and groans of metal echoed across the parking lots, and heat from the blazes came in waves to assault him, causing sweat to bead up across his brow and trickle down his back. Smoke wafted toward the street, not just from the fires themselves but from whatever chemicals the warehouses had been storing, the acrid stench burning his eyes and nose, forcing him to put the shirt back over his face to keep out the worst of the fumes. Gasping, coughing and choking, he jogged down the center of the road through the hellish landscape and up a gently curving slope to stand at the top of an overlook.

Below him, the street wound downward into some woods and a spattering of subdivisions that surrounded him on all sides. Off to the west, he gazed at the approach to Denver where every field and forest was caught up in the raging fires and forming a blazing line across his vision. The flames crawled over once verdant trees and brush, racing through parks and grassy areas to consume everything in its path. Back the way he'd come, the warehouses were an inferno of light and heat, the collective smoke flowing inward in a massive gray-black funnel that swept upward into the night sky. Gauging the wind, he realized it was blowing in from the south, pushing the fires behind him in a tight, impassable line that would consume him if he stayed where he was. Picking up the pace, he moved down the center of the road at a slight jog, slowing to a fast walk when he grew too tired, periodically glancing over his shoulder at the orange glow as it drew closer by the minute.

Approaching an intersection with several roads leading into various subdivisions, James stopped, took the shirt off his face and spat a wad of foul-tasting phlegm onto the pavement before having a look around. The streets in every direction were littered with wrecks and burnouts, though he spotted more congestion to the right and left, making his best option to keep heading north. Caught between encroaching walls of heat, James moved forward where there weren't as many distant fiery lights, and the woods seemed clear of conflagrations.

Dropping his duffel bag for a moment, he removed a bottled water, took a swig, and swished it around in his mouth before spitting it onto the pavement. Then he wet a second shirt and wiped his forehead and eyes clean of soot and dirt. His throat was on fire, rough and raw from his jog through the warehouse district after inhaling who-knew-what manner of chemicals.

Survival first, he chuckled to himself. *Mitigating long-term lung damage second.*

Putting his water bottle back, James slung his duffel bag on his shoulder and took a deep breath of what might be the last pure air he'd find for a long while. The road slanted at a downward angle where the open fields turned into a forested area with cool air that had a touch of woodsy green and he followed it downward, sticking to the left-hand shoulder. He skirted a burned-up van with its insides smoldering away, more blackened husks behind the wheel and in the passenger seat, forcing him to turn away and go around through the woods for a brief detour.

Rejoining the road, he pressed on, angling to the right to avoid another cluster of scorched cars that had run up onto the bank and exploded, slinging car parts across the pavement and into the woods. Puddles of oil and other fluids burned, and barbecued flesh stung his nostrils and turned his stomach. Several long driveways leading to houses sitting farther off the road passed by next, with smaller blazes in the yards and trees showing some signs that the fires were growing out of control after catching in the dry brush, though they hadn't yet grown to fully fledged infernos. Finally he came to another intersection with roads sweeping to the left and right, likely to other subdivisions where the fires were brighter, so he jogged to the one straight ahead and stopped to read the corner placard. *Cherry Ridge Estates.* Walking slowly through the entrance, he looked over the smoldering vehicles and garages that had gone up and sometimes consumed the attached houses, so much that in some places the smoke and cinders swept together, joining the burn-off from other homes to form small cyclones of fire and soot that corkscrewed skyward.

"This isn't the greatest idea I've ever had." His voice came out as a croak as a shiver of danger ran up his spine. When he glanced over his right shoulder, all he saw were clusters of woods and a wall of gray smoke underlined by the deadly orange glow. "Though won't be long until those forested areas fall prey to the flames. Any direction I go will be dangerous." James sighed. "Lovely."

Doing another complete circle, he saw that his way back had turned into nothing but gray haze with flickering shadows playing in the smog. Facing the neighborhood once more, he lowered his head and power walked forward, moving quickly between two houses on the corner that were still alight with the remnants of flames and giving off a heat that touched him in the center of the street. Parked cars on both sides burned brightly and the driveways were nothing but a clutter of exploded car parts and melted tires, leaving the surrounding grass smoking.

Taking the first street on the left, James searched for pockets of clean air, spots where the wind swept away the fog because of the natural configuration of homes along the shallow slopes and valleys. With sweat dripping from his brow and his shirt and mask both soaked through more with sweat than water, he wove within the smoke and wrecks, his path forward often cut off, forcing him into side yards where he climbed fences to other streets. Still, he continually worked his way north, moving toward an area where the damage was lessened. One sedan stood alone in front of a dilapidated house, both untouched by the flames. James jogged up to the vehicle, his hopes quickly dashed when he saw it was an older model car, a fixer-upper that hadn't been touched in what looked like years, with rust spots on the fenders and two flat tires with grass growing up past the rims.

"I find one car that hasn't exploded, and you're just an old relic that hasn't been driven in years." A sardonic grin struck him. "I'll bet the neighbors loved this piece of junk sitting out here devaluing the neighborhood."

Turning in a circle, wiping the sweat from his forehead, James sensed the fires pressing in on all sides, and the air grew even hotter and smokier, making it nigh-on impossible to breathe. "Crap. I need to get out of here now!"

Searching the haze, he spotted a path between the houses, lowered his head, and ran through the burned grass with his arms up to protect himself, warding off the occasional flames that licked at his coat and turned his jeans scalding hot. Bursting into the cooler backyard, he sprinted across the yard to a chain-link fence, hopped it, and jogged toward a house that sat in darkness. Stopping at the corner, he placed his hand on the warm brick, breathing the somewhat clean air, walking down the side to come out in a different street before stopping to look in every direction with firelight reflecting in his eyes.

"Most of these houses have gone up," he murmured, coughing and spitting before movement off to the right caught his eye. "Hey, are those people?"

Staggering down to the end of the driveway, he craned his neck and squinted, spotting a group of twenty or so hurrying on the left-hand sidewalk with jackets pulled over their heads.

"And I'll bet you know the way out of here."

James jogged after them, his lungs tightening and burning, agitated by the smoke. Thick mucus and saliva filled his mouth as his body responded to the overwhelming toxins being introduced to his respiratory system and he ran with a water bottle in his hand, sipping, gargling, and wiping at his eyes as he flushed out his eyes and mouth every fifty or so yards. The people ahead of him became mere shadows in the thickening haze, and soon it was so bad that the houses surrounding him became vague black shapes, the pavement barely visible as he stumbled through debris lying in the road.

Not for the first time, James considered he might not make it. His thoughts turned to Alice and the kids, likely trapped somewhere in Florida with everything going up around them and no way for him to reach them or help. With an angry sob, he growled and swept his arms in front of his face, only succeeding in whipping the smoke around as he picked up his pace and moved faster. Every step left him tripping and staggering, and every breath was pure pain as he turned his face toward any small, cool breeze that hit him. Stumbling blindly, he kicked something that was softer than a car part and glanced down to see it was a woman's charred corpse, tendrils of smoke seeping off her clothes and flesh, her scalp singed away to reveal the gleaming skull beneath. Sick but unwilling to take the time to throw up, James plowed ahead, figuring any step from there on out might be his last.

Giving up on pursuit of the people, he reeled in the other direction, limping back and angling off to his left where he thought he caught the hint of a cooler breeze and a tapering of the blazing blasts that had been assaulting his cheeks and forehead.

"If I don't find some relief soon," he croaked the words aloud to remind himself he was still alive, "I'll bake alive right in someone's front yard."

Lost and tromping through the brown grass, he stumbled over a plastic bike and plunged forward to land hard on his chest. Pure panic set in to light his brain on fire, and James lunged toward a house with dark, cool windows and bricks, leaning on it when he got there and earning a brief reprieve from the heat and smoke. Staying close to the brick side, he knocked open the gate and staggered through the backyard past the shadow of the swing set and an empty child-sized swimming pool. James gasped and reeled toward a fence line, where he thought he saw a cluster of trees with tall trunks caught in the hazy smoke but not yet aflame. The fence was nearly invisible as he came to it, slamming into it with his chest and rattling the chain-link all down its length. Grabbing the top bar, he attempted to pull himself over, but his body ached, starved of precious oxygen, and he fell back to the near side. On his second try, he lifted his right leg and caught the insole of his shoe on the top bar, using his momentum to fall over the other side and hit the ground hard, rolling several feet down a slope. The landing hurt, though he breathed his first fresh air in several long minutes, the cool breeze that slid over the grass bringing a touch of fall air with it, temporarily protected from the heat and smoke by the small rise he had crossed. Rolling to his stomach, James crawled into the woods, ignoring the sharp twigs and branches littering the forest floor and holding his face high as he searched for even cooler, fresher air. Climbing to his feet, he staggered through the brush with no trail in sight, just his arms sweeping sticker bushes and brittle saplings aside, crunching on piles of dead leaves as he angled for the darkness and kept away from the blazing light.

It was pitch black again, so he took out his phone and turned it on. A quick glance showed he had no network connection, and there were no messages from Alice, so he flipped on the flashlight function and used it to light his way. With exhaustion dragging him down, James fell to his knees several times and clutched trees to stay upright and catch his breath before plowing ahead once again. With a gasp and a burst of energy, he broke through the tree line and entered a wide park, which was only a carpet of scorched grass giving off thin drifts of rising smoke. The space was littered with blackened swing sets and trail entrances with signs that had already burned off, leaving just cinders and coals on the ground that glowed with a wavering intensity. Glancing up through the gray dinginess, James spotted a soft twinkle of starlight barely visible beneath the vaporous fog pouring in from the city outskirts and suburban areas.

There was a nearby restroom facility, and James held his shirt to his nose and angled in that direction, staggering against a bench corner and taking a sharp blow to his hip. Holding in a cry, he kept moving, tripping, and throwing himself forward onto a water fountain near the building. With a desperate gasp, he turned the knob on the side and stuck his face into the cold gush that poured straight from the spout. Blinking into it and ripping his shirt aside, he gulped mouthfuls of it, swishing it in his cheeks and spitting it out, sticking his eyes into it again and opening them wide to chill the burn. Glancing in every direction, exhausted from his run through the hellish streets, James straightened and staggered to the restrooms, pushing inside the men's door, sighing with relief when he found it unlocked. After pulling the door shut behind him, he placed his right forearm against the wall and used it to support himself as he shuffled to the sinks, testing the faucets to see they still worked. He dropped his duffel bag on the floor, reached beneath the spigot, and splashed cool water on his face again, gulping it down, his joy fading to despair when the flow began to taper off.

"No!" he gasped. Before the pressure could disappear completely, he took out every bottle he'd collected from the airport and quickly filled them up, placing them in a neat row atop the sink.

With the spigots off, he leaned against the wall and slid to the floor between a pair of electric hand dryers. Then he drew his knees up and placed his elbows on them, shutting his eyes as he listened to his buzzing limbs. His thighs quivered and his arms shook, but the worst part was his aching lungs and raw, burning throat, cursing him with a shortness of breath that no amount of water could fix.

But I made it. I survived.

Remembering that he hadn't turned off his phone, he held it up and stared tiredly at the screen, not surprised to see that there still were no messages from Alice and no connectivity. After turning the flashlight function off, he powered it down to conserve its battery life. With his phone clutched in his hand and his head thrumming with an intense ache, James rested his forehead on his arms and slipped into a frenetic dream of neighborhoods throttled with fire and shadows screaming toward the sky, choking as they died.

CHAPTER SEVEN

Ryan Cooper
Somewhere Outside East Lansing, Michigan

"Ryan, what's happening?" Helen paced across the dining room, lifting her coffee cup and taking a nervous sip as she ineffectually pushed buttons on her cell phone.

"I don't know." Ryan was standing in the foyer, one hand on his hip, the other holding his own phone to his ear and frowning at the series of beeps and squeals he was getting. "I wish I did."

"I've tried ten times to reach Alice and James." Helen hung up with a huff.

The pair looked at each other, and Ryan read the frustration in her eyes. "I can't reach our home phone or any of the neighbors in Grand Rapids either. It's not just one number; all the phone services are down."

"And I'm not getting an internet connection either," Helen replied, waving her phone like she wanted to send it through one of the windows or embed it halfway into the wall. "That means we probably can't get the news, right?"

"Not unless they have an HD antenna on their TV." Putting his phone away, Ryan rushed along the hall and into the great room, heading for the other side where a big-screen TV hung above the mantle. He looked along the mantle shelf where Alice kept tasteful knickknacks and family photos and when he searched around the sides of the television, he saw no sign of any HD wires, but he jumped back when the television flipped on to a burst of static, and he turned to see Helen standing there with a remote and an apologetic look.

She shrugged. "Sorry, I figured I'd try while you were searching."

"Best not give me a heart attack, woman," Ryan chuckled, "if this is as bad as it seems, you're going to want me around." He stepped back and watched her change the input to TV/Antenna on the screen using the remote's buttons.

"Nothing." She frowned, placing the remote on the end table where she'd found it. "What are we going to do? We can't reach anyone, and we're not getting any news. There's no way to know how far-reaching this is, and it's probably not wise to guestimate."

"Wish we could reach our neighbors in Grand Rapids." Ryan was dejected as he rocked back on his heels.

"We're cut off, at least communication-wise." Helen read his twisted expression and added flatly. "You're wanting to go to Grand Rapids and check on the house, aren't you?"

"Maybe not right away. It's not that far of a drive, but we've got a farm full of animals to take care of here, and we're late feeding them as is, so they'll be ornery. It's bound to be stressing them with all the explosions and all that smoke up in the sky." Ryan swallowed dry. "Let's go outside and get them fed before it gets too dark. We'll think about what we're going to do while we work."

Helen gave him a nod and the pair grabbed their jackets and headed out, strolling arm-in-arm along the dirt track to the first shed off on the right, a newer wooden construction with fresh red paint and a flower bed on the side facing the house. Using a thick ring of keys Alice had provided, Ryan opened the shed door and led Helen inside, greeted by the hearty aroma of feed that was kept in big tin cans along the back. The inside of the shed was quaint and functional, with a window on both sides, rows of shelves on the walls, and racks of basic garden tools and other implements everywhere he looked. Ryan held up his finger as if remembering something. "I'll go pull the wheelbarrow up if you can fix up some pails of feed."

"I can do that." Helen reached for a pair of leather gloves on a shelf to the right and slipped them on. After receiving a quick peck on the cheek, Ryan left the shed and went around the side where he'd parked the wheelbarrow after the previous day's feeding. Grabbing the handles, he brought it to the shed door but kept it parked a few feet away to give them enough room to work. He went inside where Helen had put together a pail of wheat and canola meal for the chickens, two pellet pails for the sheep, and a bundle of high-fiber barley straw for the donkeys. To top it off, she added a smaller bucket of dog food for Duke, Duchess, and Diana. Ryan helped her finish filling the last couple of pails, glancing at her as she worked, drawn by the angle of her jaw and neck.

She caught him looking. "Ryan Cooper, just what are you doing?"

"Just appreciating the woman I've loved for over fifty years," he chuckled. "And I'm not embarrassed that you caught me."

"As well you shouldn't be." Her smile grew wider as she turned with the last two buckets in hand, cocking an eyebrow at him before carrying them to the wheelbarrow.

With a light chuckle, he shook his head and brought some garbage bags and fence-mending tools with him. They'd packed the bed full, forcing Helen to rearrange things while spilling a bit of feed onto the ground.

After getting the buckets situated, Helen gazed at the sky, the worry deepening on her face as the growing clouds thickened and bloated above them. "The sky looks terrible. It's just getting worse."

While going for the wheelbarrow, Ryan had avoided looking up, part of him hoping it was just a localized event and emergency services would be coming in to help at any moment. When he faced toward the neighbors' houses, a sense of dread turned his already nervous stomach. From way down the road and to the south, the skyline was filled with dark clouds that lay thick over everything, fed by the smaller fires lifting from the surface. Shifting his gaze to the north, the township beyond the farmland and the highway just to their north was covered in black and gray, the dense fog barely stirred by the wind as it climbed higher into the atmosphere and threatened to block out the setting sun.

"And all the traffic has stopped, too." He pointed toward the highway just barely visible through the distant trees on the north end of the property where there were no cars or trucks visible on a day when traffic should have been heavy.

"I didn't even think of that," Helen said with a pinched look.

"I'm starting to think this isn't just local. No, this has spread incredibly far, as best as I can guess."

"What should we do?"

"The only thing we can do right now is make sure these animals are fed. My gut tells me this won't be over in a day or even a week. These animals are depending on us right now, so let's do what's within our control, then we'll figure out what to do next once we're done with that."

"That sounds like a plan."

Ryan wheeled the wheelbarrow north across the pasture, following the dirt track that wove out toward the chicken coops where the ground had been pecked to dust by the fowl. Several large wooden hutches covered in chicken wire stood beneath the shade of a pair of maple trees and he pulled up and set the wheelbarrow down and gestured to the feed pails.

"You can do the feeding, and I'll clean and mend the coops."

"Always the gentleman," Helen replied with a smile.

Helen grabbed a pail and walked off to the side as the chickens clucked and strutted around her feet. Ryan took his tools and garbage bags over to the hutch door, the cool fall air worming inside the gaps in his coat to chill his sweaty skin.

Before he went inside, he gave his wife a dubious glance as he caught her looking upward again. "Stop worrying, Helen. You're making me nervous."

Helen was tossing feed as she backed up, followed by the multicolored chickens and their bright feathers, who were in turn being pushed around by the larger guinea fowl in their spotted plumage, the entire lot clucking as they pursued her in a circle. "I can't help being worried, Ryan. That we can't get a hold of Alice or James or anyone from home has me really worried, and I just can't shake it."

With a dejected sigh, Ryan started scraping out some of the old hay at the bottom of the pen, disturbing the cranky hens who were sitting on their eggs. After filling one bag, he brought it outside and set it next to the door, tossing down his scoop and striding over to her.

Taking her in his arms, he squeezed until she was forced to quit feeding the chickens and let the pail hang loosely in her hands. "You just wipe that frown off your face, ma'am." With a kiss on her head and another hug, he held her at arm's length and fixed her with a firm look. "Alice and James are both extremely capable people. They'll be fine. We just need to make sure everything is okay on our end and trust that they'll know what to do."

"I know, but I just can't help it." Helen shook herself free from his arms and resumed her task, the chickens breaking around Ryan's feet in a wave of agitated feathers.

"I'll tell you what. When we're done here, we'll hop in the car and head home to Grand Rapids to check things there, then we'll come straight back. I'm sure things are fine over there, even if the phones are down. Maybe if we take a little action, we'll feel better."

"Do you think that's smart?"

"It's just a thought for now. Something of a plan, I suppose."

"Sounds good to me." Helen glanced up again, gazing from one side of the horizon to the other, frowning at the shifting colors that blended with the late afternoon sky. The distant fires were only growing, casting a tainted glow as greasy black smoke rolled upward to coagulate in the lower atmosphere.

"C'mon, let's finish feeding these ornery animals," Ryan patted Helen on the back.

"All right."

Ryan got back to work with renewed vigor, cleaning up the pens, checking the henhouse, and ensuring all was in order before he fixed a couple of spots in the mesh fencing where it was coming loose from its staples. Finished with the fowl, Helen put the pail away, and Ryan drove the lighter wheelbarrow out to the hutches and farmyard where the sheep were bleating and edging toward the gate in a jostling cluster. They were kept at bay by James and Alice's three Great Pyrenees, who barked and herded them back, their tawny coats ruffling along their well-muscled bodies as they stood guard.

Helen pulled the latch and shoved the aluminum gate just wide enough for Ryan to push the wheelbarrow through, and he wheeled over to a far section of the yard near a large gambrel-roofed barn painted bright red with white trim. He stopped and grabbed a bucket of feed, turning as the cluster of sheep and goats crowded in after him. Scooping up handfuls of food pellets, he backed up in a circular pattern across the front of the barn, tossing it left and right and drawing the animals out in a long line. As Ryan worked, Duke and Duchess each took a side, lingering around the edges of the herd, keeping the cluster tight, and voicing deep barks to make sure no one strayed. Duke was the more aggressive of the three, leaping and bounding after the sheep and goats, while Duchess remained in a sitting position and only moved when an animal got out of line. Diana stayed near the back, being the youngest and still learning from the older dogs, sniffing at the sheep and watching as the other two corralled them.

Helen took a larger bucket inside for the donkeys and the cow, Bessie, leaving the door open as she worked. Once Ryan was done and the goats and sheep had quieted down, he moved to the water trough and used a nearby scrub brush to clean algae that was growing along its sides. Once done, he returned the plunger and filled the trough with fresh water from a rain-catcher holding tank that was set up by the building. By then, he was sweating and panting, clutching and massaging his leg as he hauled the hose to its holder and wrapped it up without leaving any tangles.

As Ryan walked back to the barn door, he rubbed Duke's shaggy head, the great Pyrenees licking his chops proudly. "That's a good boy, Duke! Very nice work, though I do think Duchess is working a little smarter."

The dog gave a woof and padded by his side as Ryan peeked into the barn where Helen had fed the larger animals and was doing some cleanup with just an electric lantern for light as the sun faded.

"How's it going in there, honey?"

Helen glanced up as she finished raking out one stall into a pile of manure and hay. She placed the rake against the wall and dusted off her hands. "I'm pretty much done here for now. We can take this out to the compost pile tomorrow."

"Good." He rubbed at his leg again, trying to work out the muscle pains. "I'm wanting to get back to the house and sit down for a few."

With the sheep calmed down considerably, they fed the dogs, left the barnyard, and took the dirt track back to the storage shed. Ryan pushed the wheelbarrow ahead of them with Helen right behind him, grabbing some feed and tossing it to the peacock who'd spread his feathers and seemed less nervous about the gathering darkness above them. As Ryan parked the wheelbarrow by the shed, he caught himself glancing upward, blinking at the distant bursts of orange that reflected in the clouds and sky, still intense even hours after they'd first started, giving Ryan a sensation of being hunted by a looming evil. By the time they got back to the house, he was moving with a limp, face coated with sweat, his T-shirt moist with a salty ring around the neckline.

"I'm going to take some of these smaller tools into the garage in case I need them later. I'll meet you inside."

Helen nodded and entered through the back door as Ryan circled to the side of the house, pausing at the open garage door to stare at their electric vehicle where it was parked in the driveway, untouched by flames and smoke, with no signs of overheating, the white sedan sitting peacefully with its *EV* emblem on the edge of the trunk.

With a narrow-eyed stare, Ryan murmured, "That couldn't be it, could it?" When Helen had first approached him about getting an electric vehicle, he'd been skeptical, a view that had changed over the past year as he grew more impressed not so much with its efficiency but with the lack of maintenance he needed to put into it. Putting a hammer, screwdriver, and wire cutters back on James' tool bench, he entered the house, noticing the hall lights were dimmer and some rooms were completely dark.

"The main power is off," Helen called, "and we've switched to solar and battery backup power. They had it set to switch automatically."

"That's what I figured," Ryan replied as he entered the kitchen and met her at the breakfast bar where she'd poured herself a glass of ice water. "Do you want one, honey?"

"Absolutely! I'm dying of thirst."

He removed his jacket and plucked at his shirt to cool down. "James must have the refrigerator and furnace hooked to the backup power."

"Alice didn't get into specifics with me, but I'd assume so, yes. He always was very gung-ho about that sort of thing."

Helen opened the freezer and got him some ice, using the water dispenser to fill the glass with a crackling sound. Turning, she met him back at the counter.

"I'm just a little worried about the power output." He accepted the drink with a nod of thanks. "With those clouds overhead, there may not be a lot of sunlight over the next few days."

"You're thinking we might want to disconnect some of the unnecessary appliances?"

"Yes, but I haven't had the time to look at his setup yet." Striding over to the sink, Ryan leaned in and washed his hands. "Hot water. That means the water heater is on."

"I think the heater's on propane... the weather may get pretty cold over the next few weeks, so it's a good thing they've got everything hooked up, but I'd be worried about running out of propane."

"That's what I'm thinking." Drying off, he turned to Helen. "But we could get by without hot water. The furnace... eh, not so much. Space heaters are great for us, but a frozen pipe would be bad news."

Back at the counter, Ryan took a long drink to quench his parched throat, smacking his lips as he set his glass down and walked into the great room to have a look around. "Well, we've cleaned the house and fed the animals. That's about all we can do here for now."

"So, you think it'd be a good idea to go to Grand Rapids?"

"It's an hour there and an hour back, and we should have enough juice in the car."

"But do you think it's safe?"

"I can't imagine things are too terrible right now, and everything will be fine here in the interim with those pups they've got to keep guard. I promise, it won't take long to just do a quick check."

"I'll put together a little travel bag with some snacks." Helen gave a prim smile and went to the dining room to grab a carryall, bringing it back to the counter where she filled it with small packages of apple pouches and raisins. While she did that, Ryan placed bottled waters into a small cooler, using ice from the freezer to make sure they'd stay nice and cold.

"Are we ready to go?" he asked.

Helen slung her carryall on her shoulder. "We're armed with snacks and bottled water, and I threw in some travel pillows and blankets in case it gets chilly and we end up getting stuck somewhere. I think we're ready to go."

Gathering their things, they loaded them into the car before getting in and buckling up. Ryan started the electric vehicle with the push of a button and pulled out of their driveway in a smooth, noiseless motion. Even after a year of driving it, he still found it disconcerting when they moved without the ebbing and flowing thrum of an engine. At the end of the entrance lane, Helen got out and opened the gate while he slipped through and waited for her to lock up. From there, they followed the dirt road south past the neighbors' houses with vehicle fires in every driveway, some sitting off the road behind the trees where waves of ash and cinders rose and were carried off by the wind.

They wove along the dirt road surrounded by deep forest shadows and the stretch of fields, wooden fences, and an occasional stone wall, everything lit by intermittent flickers of light from the burning cars, the bright orange colors sharp against the saturated sky. Ryan caught glimpses of shifting vapors through the treetops and a few farmsteads that had gone up, along with more detached garages and sheds.

Helen glanced around with a defeated expression. "I hope people weren't hurt."

"Me, too," Ryan replied with a heavy sigh.

"Should we stop and check on any of them?" Helen's expression was full of growing concern as she glanced at a property where several large barns were still in the process of burning to the ground.

"What can we do for them?" Ryan replied. "We've got a few snacks and bottled waters, but not enough to feed what's probably..." He gave a flat scoff tinged with disbelief as he tore his gaze from the surroundings to focus on the road ahead. "Must be hundreds of people."

"Thousands."

"More than that, I reckon." He agreed.

Road dust danced in his headlight beams, and an added worry took root in his stomach, forming a knot of concern that was just hitting him. "We'll need to be really careful out here, Helen," he said in a low tone. "This is already looking worse than we thought, and people might get desperate, especially if everything they owned burned up."

As they rolled through the open fields, a large piece of farm equipment sitting alone shone with firelight, the big rubber tires on the back half melted by the flames, giving the chassis a sunken appearance. Close by were larger barns, some ignited by pickups and older farm vehicles parked around them, the wreckage bringing an unbidden clenching to Ryan's heart. Cresting the next hill ahead of them, the crowding trees gave way to an open sky, and Helen gasped as Ryan drew their vehicle to a halt at the top. The streets of a few sprawling suburbs in the distance were filled with charred vehicles, strip mall parking lots forming steaming metal pyres that gave off thick waves of burning rubber. Sharing a dark glance with his wife, Ryan eased down the dirt lane where the farmsteads were placed closer together, resembling country neighborhoods with their pink flamingo decorations and wind chimes on the porches.

Trees and brush were trimmed back to leave wide, grassy yards with backyard swimming pools and smaller fields off to the sides. Ryan cruised past them, gaping at the spread of debris littering the driveways and the dirt road, forcing him to bump over a tailpipe and weave between pieces of plastic and metal parts, wincing whenever he hit something hard. Several cars were nose-down in a ditch on the sides of the road, explosions having stripped off their panels and fenders, leaving bare frames of wire and scorched interiors, greasy-slick rubber fires burning off dark, stinking fumes. The roadside was littered with a spattering of corpses, people who'd escaped their vehicles-turned-ovens just as their bodies succumbed to heat and noxious vapors.

"This is *awful*! The smell is just...." Helen pulled her shirt up over her nose, looking at him with watering eyes.

"Oh, shoot. I should have switched the air circulation to interior only," he said as he turned a knob on the center console. "There. That should make it easier on us."

A quarter mile later, they took a right onto a paved road that wound toward the same subdivisions they'd spied from higher up, and soon Ryan spotted signs for I-69 approaching. On the left-hand side of the road, a pizza delivery car's back end had flipped up to land upside down in the branches of a big elm, the pizza delivery sign still blinking and flashing on top as the undercarriage baked in flames.

As they passed houses built closer to the road, Ryan spotted groups of families standing in their yards, watching their cars continue to burn while their homes remained powerless. Every window was dark, and only flashlights shined where neighbors gathered in the side yards, pointing and gawking at the destruction. Entering a more populated area, they passed burning subdivisions that cast cavorting shadows across the road. Fast-food restaurants and strip malls were completely dark, while others had become part of the fire chain, their lots engulfed in glowing cinders that set everything they touched ablaze. A group of people stood outside the neighborhood grocery store that had remained untouched with its lights still on, the patrons left scratching their heads as they stared at the surrounding destruction.

"Looks like they have some backup power there." Helen placed her fingers on the window. "I hope everyone's okay."

"At least that store will have some food available, short-term," Ryan replied. "Though judging from the size of the surrounding neighborhoods, there won't be enough to feed everyone for long."

"Do you think things are this bad back home?"

Ryan paused for a long moment. "I sure hope not."

Headlamps caught his eye and he stared at an approaching vehicle, the driver gripping the steering wheel tight, pressed up close to it with wide, unblinking eyes as they ran over debris, driving far faster than Ryan was, with a recklessness that betrayed their panic.

"Hey, that car isn't on fire." Helen watched it go by.

"Yeah, it's electric, just like ours..." Ryan watched the taillights of the vehicle as it passed, the driver barely registering their passing as he wove through debris lying on the road. Ryan turned his attention forward again, switching to the correct lane to enter the expressway. "Here's the ramp now."

Swinging into the right-hand lane, Ryan joined a sharp loop that curved down and around to the highway, slowing as he approached the bottom and got a good view of traffic in both directions. It was a mess of wreckage everywhere he looked. Back west, a long line of cars and trucks were piled up in every lane, with some dipped into the grassy median. A tractor trailer had flipped on its side, the bottom blown out as it had rocketed into the vehicles ahead of it, crushing their rear ends and causing them to swerve across the road in every direction. The explosive cluster had become a furnace of burning plastic and car seats, smashed glass, and bodies thrown out to hit the pavement rolling, clothed in flame where they'd come to rest. Shifting his gaze slowly to the east, Ryan stared at the same swath of destruction, miles of collisions and catastrophic wrecks, with some spilling off the shoulders in swerving sequences of violence. The mixture of impacts and intense heat had congealed along the road, turning it into the glowing backbone of a massive fiery beast as it curved ahead into the distance, looking for more material to consume with its flames.

"Oh, no," Helen gasped softly, one hand covering her mouth, scanning the mess with a terrified expression, her face lit by the orange-white fires that consumed everything as a realization dawned upon her. "I don't see anyone alive, Ryan... there's *no one* alive!"

Taking his hands off the wheel, he leaned across and wrapped his arms around Helen, drawing her in close, trying to shield her from the scale of the horror. "I... I know. This is bad."

"Bad? This isn't just *bad*, Ryan. This is catastrophic!" She pushed him away and gestured at the destruction, her voice rising in panic. "This is something we've never seen before, not in our whole lives."

Ryan let her go and shifted his attention to the outside once again, placing his shaking hands back on the wheel. "I know, but it's what we have to deal with right now. I wish I could make things different, but we have to try to make it to Grand Rapids, and I think I see a way through."

"Are we okay on battery life?"

"I'm pretty sure. We've got seventy-five percent left, and that should definitely get us there and back, but we'll use our generator to charge the car before we head back just to be safe. We... we need to just try to get there first."

Helen placed her hands in her lap and gave a firm nod. "Okay, if you think we can make it, I trust you."

His insides churning with waves of nervous tension, Ryan pulled onto the highway, weaving around one vehicle that had spun out at the head of the ramp, its entire undercarriage a blossom of flames. The people inside were silhouetted against waves of curling smoke that drifted up from the cracked floorboard and filled the cabin, turning everything black and charred. Beyond that, Ryan pushed them through a twirling cinder storm with bright particles that glanced off the windshield like fireflies. Past that, they found a patch of empty pavement with only a few small pieces of debris tossed into the road. Moving carefully, he ran over a taillight, the angular piece of plastic with its multicolored facets grinding beneath the wheel and bouncing off the bottom of the car, causing him to wince. They passed over the cleared area quickly and began swerving between the cooking traffic, baked off paint flickering away, swept upward by hot winds that roared across both lanes.

Next, they faced an eighteen-wheeler that had jackknifed in the road, the cab having imploded from simultaneous fuel tank explosions, pressed in as if two fists had crushed it, forming an I-shape of the sleeper section and engine block. The hood was flipped up and smoking, with the charred driver sprawled on the dashboard and the trailer had split along the middle, the front part shredded to pieces with black scorch marks while the rest of it had burst open, unrecognizable except for the writing toward the rear, the name of a national furniture store chain. Tables, chairs, and desks lay spilled to the sides, pallets of product sat wrapped in melted plastic, the wooden pieces it had been holding together forming a bonfire in the middle of the highway.

Ryan stopped and blinked. "Wow. This is insane."

"I thought you said you saw a way through, dear."

"I thought I did from back there, but it's worse now that we're right in the middle of it." Putting the car in park, he turned it off and looked over at Helen. "Give me a second. I'm going to check it out."

"Be careful."

Popping the door, he got out and shut it quickly to keep the smoke from entering, then he turned toward the burning furniture, scanning the wreckage for something easy he could shift out of the way to let them pass. The rig had pushed into the shoulder, so he went left toward the trailer, giving the heat and flames a wide berth. Ryan found that some of the spilled furniture wasn't on fire yet, and he grabbed a mahogany desk that was fully put together and still partly strapped to its skid and dragged it to the side of the road, dumping it off into the grassy median. There were more pieces he had to move, some disassembled and boxed up, heavier than they looked as he hauled and shoved them to the roadside and left them. As he worked, swaths of smoke attacked his face, stinging his eyes and assaulting his nostrils with the acrid scent of burning chemicals, plastic and wood, and the underlying stench of a barbecue that chilled him to the bone.

"Is that really surprising?" he chastised himself, grumbling as he worked. "You're basically standing in the middle of an oven, and it's not cookies that're baking."

Once he had cleared a path, Ryan walked back to the car and got in, shutting the door behind him as Helen waved her hand in front of her face.

"You smell awful," she said.

"I feel worse." Ryan chuckled, putting the car into drive and angling toward the opening he'd made.

The white sedan cruised through the sea of fire, which had become an obstacle course of volcanic magnitude where rubber burned and melted into puddles, corpses hung from windows or had splayed across dashboards beneath a shower of broken glass, their clothes and hair singed away to leave bare skin scorched down to the muscle and bone. The whole scene would have been more macabre had the bodies not been burned beyond recognition, a fact Ryan was silently grateful for as they passed a wreck where four consecutive vehicles had rear-ended each other, the entire thing shoved to the left-hand shoulder with the first three cars angled into the sloping median. Blackened forms smoldered in the front seats with smaller ones in the back, all barely recognizable. Ryan cursed softly and squeezed his eyes shut while Helen watched with a horrified expression, cheeks drained of blood, eyes glassy, gasping at every new horror she saw.

Their only relief came when the highway opened up, providing some breathing room for Ryan to pull off to the side and lower the windows so he could push back the overwhelming sense of panic. The fresh Michigan breeze blew through the cabin, cooling his nervous sweat and allowing him to regain his focus and he quickly turned to driving again, onward to the next cluster of wreckage, which came none too soon, forcing Ryan to pull to a stop thirty seconds after they'd started.

A moving truck had flipped on its left side, the flaming front end lying to the right with the rear split open and splaying its contents across the pavement. The amount of debris on the road forced them both to get out and start clearing a path through, dragging off tables, pieces of furniture, and a box of children's books with singed pages fluttering open in the breeze. Helen stopped working as she held a pile of the books in her hand, staring at them, thoughts of her daughter and grandchildren coming unbidden, and tears began to fall. Ryan dropped what he was doing and went to her, wrapping his arms around her and holding her close amidst a sea of fire.

"I don't think I can take this much longer," Helen whispered, gripping his shirt as she wept.

"Me either. Let's try just a little bit more before we give up."

With a brief nod, she wiped the tears off her cheeks, straightened her shoulders, and got back to work dragging a box of plates and silverware to the side of the road where she dumped it into the ditch with a clatter. With the major obstacles out of the way, they returned to the car and picked a path through for the next forty-five minutes. Ryan sometimes got out to clear debris, growing hopelessly tired, gasping and gripping at his leg as he gazed east into the hellish curve of firelight. When there was a lot of rubble, Helen got out and helped, though she too was fading fast as the evening stretched on and the sun drew lower in the sky. Her hair, normally light, had turned a dingy hue from the smoke and ash that had settled in it.

Face smudged with soot, Ryan cleared his throat, coughing up phlegm and spitting it off to the side. "I think we're done trying to do this, Helen. We're both so exhausted, and there's only thirty-seven percent battery life left on the car."

"Yes, I'd say that about does it for us," she agreed, following his gaze over the impossible obstacle course set before them. "This isn't ending anytime soon."

"Let's head on back."

Behind the wheel, Ryan made an arcing turn and followed the path they'd taken to get there, still hot and smoky but faster going since it had already been cleared. He tried not to look at the destruction surrounding them, though it was difficult to do when the carnage and raw gore were spread out before them like a nightmare come to life.

"What do you make of all these cars being destroyed, but ours hasn't?" Helen asked. "And neither was that one we passed before."

"It seems pretty obvious to me that it's the internal combustion vehicles that are affected by this... whatever it is. Other than that, I'm clueless."

"Could it be some malfunction of the fuel tanks? Or a terrorist attack?"

"I'd say the most common denominator would be the fuel itself. The gasoline and diesel. But diesel isn't as explosive as gasoline is, not normally. And with no evidence...." He shrugged and kept both hands on the wheel, moving faster as the vehicle's power trickled to thirty-five percent, giving him the first twinge in his gut, a warning to be very careful about their usage.

Once reaching the expressway exit, Ryan drove down the ramp and descended going the wrong way until they came back to the main road. From there, he took a turnaround lane, crossed to the correct side, and started for home with the scent of smoke coming with every breath. It was only when they passed the groups of people standing around the market-place that he switched off the headlamps and slouched a bit lower behind the wheel.

"What did you do that for?" Helen asked, squinting ahead. "Now we can't see anything."

"It just struck me that we're the only car on the road, and some people might see that as an opportunity."

"They'd steal it from us if they could, wouldn't they?"

Ryan was already nodding. "That's exactly what they'd do, so it's best we keep a low profile if we *must* be out driving."

They headed back through the blazing subdivisions, seeing a few new fires as more homes had been set alight, though soon they turned onto the dirt road and were driving past the neighbor's house, into the driveway, unlocking the gate, locking it behind them and headed up the gravel lane. The neighbors had a light on in the window, but weren't visible as Ryan drove past, the only noise being the crunch of rock beneath the tires. With a sigh of relief, Ryan slumped forward and shook his shoulders to loosen them up, but he didn't stop at the driveway, pulling around instead to the side and cutting through the grass around the large house.

"What are you doing?" Helen asked.

"I'm parking behind the house so no one can see our car from the road."

"Ah. Another good idea."

"We should keep a low profile," Ryan continued, feeling some of his energy return as their surroundings became more familiar. "If any more houses burned down, people will be looking to scavenge, and we'd be a perfect target out here by ourselves. The house still standing – and standing *out* on this little hill – is bad enough. No sense in attracting even more attention."

Finding a spot to park in the grass, Ryan turned off the car and got out, motioning to Helen. "Follow me. I want to check something out in the basement storage room."

The outside basement door was locked, and he moved aside so Helen could unlock it before they both stepped inside and he felt around in the darkness for a switch.

"Do you know where the light is?"

"I haven't been in here in a very long time. It's got to be over there, I'd think."

Ryan searched the drywall, finally finding the switch lower than he would have expected it, and when he flipped it on, the room stayed dark. "James doesn't have this room rigged up on the backup power, apparently."

Taking his cell phone from his pocket, Ryan held it up and turned on the flashlight function, bathing the area in a stark white LED glow to show a well-organized storeroom with shelves full of goods. There were old gardening tools, a few bags of topsoil, a big drill press from the fifties, and racks of electronics. Cobwebs hung from the ceiling, and the place had a deep musty smell that was a welcome relief after the highway. They stirred up dust as they walked in, sending particles swirling in his light, and as he dragged the beam across the top shelf on the right, he immediately found what he was looking for.

"Bingo! An emergency radio! Now, let's see if we can find out what's going on."

CHAPTER EIGHT

Alice Burton
Vero Beach, Florida

The sound of the beating surf reached them from off to the right where the foaming waves of North Beach swept up the sand and flattened it back down as the water drew away. Off to the left were trees and other beach houses, clusters of hotels and condominiums in the center of the tourist areas. While there were patches of undamaged buildings, flames consumed most of the structures, turning what should have been a nice Florida evening into a smoky, sweltering mess, coating Alice's forehead with a layer of sweat that dripped down her temples and cheeks. Head lowered, she hurried to get them away from a fire that had spread to several buildings on the edge of the sand.

"Aren't there any firetrucks?" Jake asked.

"There should be," Alice replied with a glance toward the seething structures that dominated the landscape. "My guess is the same thing happened to them that happened to the vehicles in town, and they probably went up in flames, too." She looked back to make sure Sarah was keeping up. "Come on, honey. Quit dragging your feet. I want to get away from this area as soon as possible. There are still a lot of people around, and the fires are dangerous."

Sarah shifted her colorful backpack on her shoulders, the one she'd intended to use every day on the beach, but instead of being packed with towels and sunblock, it was full of food, water, and emergency clothes. "My feet are killing me." She sighed and leaned forward, feeling as if the pack weighed a thousand pounds. Alice had made them change into more practical attire, which meant tennis shoes, jeans shorts, and T-shirts, anything that would give them protection on the road, in spite of how impractical it was in the heat and on the sand. Besides the durable clothes, they were carrying light backpacks, and each held a pool cue in their hands, Jake using his to bat at smoking debris as they passed by.

"It's only been two miles." Alice replied. "We'll find a place to rest later. There're still too many people wandering around, so I want to get up the road a little ways more before we stop."

Wherever she looked, people were milling around in the streets, scratching their heads and looking dumbfounded as they watched their beach houses or nearby stores and tourist attractions burn to the ground. Those who had reacted quickly enough were dragging personal items into driveways or yards with shirts and bandannas covering their noses to keep out the smoke. So far, Alice had seen no obviously dangerous people like the junkies who'd attacked them, though the magnitude of people gathering around put her mind more at ease.

"I'm kind of getting tired, too," Jake said.

"Have patience, kids. We'll get there soon enough."

"Where *is* 'there' though, mom?"

"Someplace that we haven't found yet. Just keep marching, kids, c'mon."

The trio strode past a highway sign that read A1A and they entered a quieter area with many of the homes and beach houses still standing, along with several private estates with generator-fed lights dotting the landscape. Some people stood outside their homes, but they held hoses, buckets and a few carried weapons as well, and all of them seemed more than eager to defend themselves from the flames, as well as any other threats that might come along.

Soon they left North Beach and the raging fires behind, and Alice closed her eyes as a breeze blowing in off the ocean cooled her hot skin. Slowing her pace a bit, Alice looked ahead where sporadic heaps of burned up vehicles still smoldered and smoked in a parking lot, stark against the backdrop of long beach grass and dunes that swept down to the water.

"I'm so hot," Jake said as his tennis shoes flapped on the pavement next to her. "I could run down to the ocean and jump right in."

"No way," Sarah replied. "Don't you know there are sharks out there?"

"There are *always* sharks out there, but they don't come in *that* close."

"They love to eat at night, and they come in close to shore to feed on the rays and other small fish. This is suppertime for them!"

Alice cracked a slight smile as she listened to the kids go back and forth about whether sharks would eat them if they went for a swim, happy for the momentary distraction. Coming up on the left-hand side of the road, Alice spotted a burning car, the detonation of which had shifted the nearby sand, half burying it in beach grass. The doors were blown open, and blackened car parts lay everywhere, with smoke pouring from the jagged maw where the trunk used to be. The edges of the hood had peeled upward and were leaking smoke with an orange glow pulsing in the engine block. Beneath it, antifreeze and fluid dripped down in a wide puddle, forcing Alice to look away as a thick cloud of sickly sweet vapor drifted by.

Jake tugged on her shirt and pointed fifteen yards up the road where a charred lump had been thrown from the vehicle to lie curled up and smoking on the pavement. "Is that a... dead person?"

"I think so." Alice hurried them to the right-hand side, using her body to shield them, though both kids tried to see around her, Sarah holding her nose as she grimaced.

They walked through the night into the wee hours of the morning, the kids grumbling and complaining the whole time, dragging their feet more by the minute. Distant fires loomed just a couple of miles away, and out on the beach, a pair of ATVs had flipped around, the riders' corpses illuminated in the fiery glow. With a sigh, she gazed out toward the deeper ocean, taking solace in the golden moonlight that spilled across the dark surface, a constant reminder that no matter what humans did, nature would march on. The moon would still rule the night sky, and the sun would still rise in the morning in spite of whatever was happening all around them.

After another hour of slow walking, and the kids' complaints growing to an annoying crescendo, Alice was forced to search for a place to rest for the night.

"You've got our beach towels," Sarah said. "Why don't we just lay them out on the sand and sleep there?"

"While I'm sure we can do that," Alice responded, "I'd rather find something a little more sheltered."

"Yeah, I want to sleep in a bed tonight," Jake said. "Not the sand."

"What's that up ahead?" Alice craned her neck and strained to see where a cluster of faint lights sat off the highway to the left. "That looks like a hotel."

"I thought all the power went out," Jake said.

"That might be true, but it's possible they could have a generator."

"Are we going to check it out?" Sarah asked, dragging her feet.

Alice guided the kids to the left-hand side of the road, where she got a better view of the hotel and a parking lot. As they drew closer, she saw it was a single-story, old-fashioned sort of place with a row of around thirty-five rooms and a hotel office at the near end. A big sign out front read *Majestic Beach Resort*, and there were palm trees interspersed throughout the lot and in clusters at the corners, with gardens stretching to the back. More lights in the back illuminated a pool area and some rooms she couldn't see, and out front people had gathered in groups, discussing the catastrophic events that had transpired.

Biting her lip, Alice said, "I have to admit, it looks safe."

"The only way we'll know for sure is if we walk up and see," Sarah said with a shrug.

"Maybe, but an even better idea would be for me to go first while you guys stay just out of sight in the beach grass." Without waiting for a response, she guided the kids into the tall grass, shrugged off her pack, and left them squatting with their pool cues in hand. "You know what to do with that if someone comes up, right?"

"Yeah, whack 'em." Jake held up the stick and gave it an experimental swing.

"Exactly. And I know you can do it, too." Ruffling his hair with a smile, she gave Sarah a squeeze on the shoulder and stepped out of the grass where she straightened and strode toward the hotel.

Hands at her sides, Alice walked in the general direction of the hotel entrance, angling toward the groups of people standing around. Beneath the light of the hotel sign, she saw a mix of tourists and locals in their work clothes, restaurant uniforms, and hospital scrubs. The visitors were easier to pick out, mostly families just like hers with beach style shirts and hats, and a nurse was applying bandages to a child's bumps and bruises while her family looked on anxiously. With a deep breath, Alice held up her hand and waved to a nearby family who had two small children sitting in lawn chairs. The father had a round belly and wore a loud, tropical shirt, holding a beer as he spoke to his wife. The woman was about Alice's age but with blonde hair clipped behind her head, her skin tanned as if she'd been out on the beach over the past few days.

She saw Alice coming and returned the wave. "Hello there!"

"Hi!" Alice called back as the father turned to her.

"Oh, hello there," he said with a warm nod. "Let me guess. Everything you own blew up, and you just walked all the way from North Beach or thereabouts?"

"That about sums it up," Alice laughed, feeling instantly comfortable. "This seems like a friendly crowd. Have you guys been here long?"

"The resort where we were staying caught fire." He nodded to the north where the distant fires burned bright.

"We were so tired after a day at the beach, we ordered room service." The woman gave an exasperated sigh. "No sooner had we put in our orders when the fire alarms went off. Bob said he could smell the smoke, and since we were up on the highest floor, we got out of there quick."

"Left everything behind," Bob confirmed with a nod. "Susan grabbed her purse, and I took my wallet, so we could walk here and book a room with Mrs. Smith."

"Thanks to her, we have a place to sleep tonight," Susan said with a nervous chuckle. "Otherwise, we'd be sleeping on the beach."

Alice held out her hand, shaking with the parents. "I'm Alice. And that's exactly what my daughter wants to do. Sleep on the beach."

"Daughter?" Susan asked, looking past her with a curious gaze.

"Oh, I had them stay hidden for a minute until I checked things out over here." With a glance at the friendly crowd, many of them grinning and laughing, Alice turned and waved toward the dune. Almost immediately, Sarah and Jake sprang up, carrying their packs and pool cues in a slap of feet and excited smiles.

"That was pretty smart," Bob said, staring curiously at the pool cues the kids were holding.

"Self-defense," Alice explained. "We ran into some... not-so-friendly people at the house we were staying at."

"Wow, that's not good." Bob took a sip of his beer.

"You poor babies!" Susan exclaimed, shaking her head at the kids.

"We're fine, um..." Jake said, shifting a look between the two.

"This is Bob and Susan," Alice gestured. "And this is Jake and Sarah. Turns out my son is quite the slugger."

Susan introduced their two little ones who were several years younger than Alice's kids and as they talked, a woman she didn't know approached with an arm full of bottled waters and handed them out. Alice thanked her and held the ice-cold plastic to her forehead with a pleased sigh.

Bob nodded. "You folks going to stay the night?"

"That's the plan," Alice confirmed, "but I can't imagine there are any rooms left."

"I haven't seen too many people swing in after us. I'd say most folks are either dealing with the fires, or they're..." Bob let the word hang there as he glanced at the kids.

"In that case, maybe we'll try to stay at least one night until the phones come back on and I can call my husband."

"You should talk to Mrs. Smith right away," Susan said. "You may have to stay here longer than just one night, so I'd secure a spot now if I were you. I can't imagine that they'll have the phones up soon."

"And I'm assuming most power backups are down, too," Bob said, then he quickly turned when an older woman with clipped gray hair caught his attention. She approached with a comforting smile, wearing a Florida Gators T-shirt with tropical shorts and sandals fleshing out her attire. Bob gestured. "Here's Mrs. Smith now. Hey, Mrs. Smith, these friendly folks here are looking for a place to stay."

"Is that right?" the woman replied, coming up and looking over Alice and the kids with bright eyes.

"It's looking that way," Alice confirmed with a friendly smile of her own as she held out her hand. "I'm Alice Burton, and these are my kids."

Mrs. Smith gave her a warm handshake in return. "Very nice to meet you all. Andrea Smith, owner and manager of this illustrious hotel. And it just so happens I've got around a dozen rooms left for struggling folks like you. If you'll just come with me, I'll get you situated."

"Yes!" Jake called, pumping his fist in the air while Sarah looked dour.

"Sarah wanted to sleep on the beach," Alice explained, "but Jake's opting for a bed, and I agree wholeheartedly."

Andrea laughed as she motioned for them to follow her into the office. With a smile, Alice took her carry-on bag from Jake and nodded for the kids to stay close. Andrea pushed through the door, causing a bell above it to jingle, then she held it for the family as they walked into a quaint lobby with two couches decorated in tropical designs. The interior was cool with a pair of high ceiling fans spinning at a slow pace and circulating air throughout the room.

"Quite a place you have here, Mrs. Smith."

"Thanks, and you can just call me Andrea." She laughed as she circled around the desk.

"It's amazing you're still operating with everything going on."

"We're always prepared for things like this." Andrea pulled out a ledger and raised an eyebrow. "I'll have to take your information manually since the computer network is down."

"Of course. You said you always have to be prepared for this? What did you mean by that?"

"The Majestic Beach Resort has been a mainstay around here for decades when it comes to taking care of locals during hurricane season. Whenever a disaster hits, we've always welcomed anyone who was put out of their home or business, as long as we've got enough rooms to take them in." With a shrug, she gestured toward the big front window and the crowd milling outside. "In this case, it – whatever *it* actually is - hit everyone hard, locals and tourists alike. Seems this disaster is pretty widespread, and I'm not sure everyone can just leave when the fires die down." She sighed sadly, looking out through the front windows at the crowd, "It's just terrible that everyone's stuck here."

"It looks that way for now," Alice replied as she gave Andrea her information, including her credit card number.

"Now, I can't charge you anything until the computers come back online, so just try to get the kids situated and keep them comfortable and don't worry about the bill. We run a safe establishment and pride ourselves on taking care of our guests, even at the worst of times."

"That's just... amazing." Alice felt a weight lift off her shoulders as she took the woman's hand in her own. "You're amazing for doing this."

Andrea's sheepish smile grew wider. "My husband, God rest his soul, built the hotel to withstand anything. More than once, it was the only place left standing for miles around. We've weathered every other storm and we'll weather this storm, so help me."

"Thank you."

With a smile, Andrea placed a pair of plastic cards into a device and punched keys on her keyboard to set their magnetic strips. "I'll put you in room thirty-one for now. Thank goodness the key cards don't need internet to run!"

"Thanks so much." Alice accepted the keys and followed the proprietress as she circled the desk and took them out the front door.

As they walked down the row of hotel rooms, she noticed more people had gathered in tight groups in the parking lot, many with coolers and card tables surrounded by lawn chairs. There were more than a few radios out, people leaning over them and tuning the knobs as they tried to get some information on what was going on.

"We have a kitchen and a few staff are around, too. There are snacks left out in the cafeteria, and you're more than welcome to those. We're working on the honor system, so just let us know what you take. There'll be a simple breakfast served in the morning with fruit, bagels, and juice... stuff like that."

"That sounds wonderful," Alice responded. "How do you power all this?"

Andrea waved her hand. "My dear husband was wise enough to install four generators out back. We haven't had to use them in a couple years, but I pay someone to keep them maintained and good heavens has that paid off every time a storm blows through."

As the kids carried on and jostled each other in good spirits, Alice walked next to Andrea and a man saw them coming and stepped away from his group to stroll beside them.

"We finally heard an emergency broadcast," he spoke dejectedly, "after hours of trying. Looks like this thing will be more far-reaching than we thought."

With a smile, Andrea turned to Alice. "Alice, this is Marty Ferguson, a local business owner. He's staying with us for a little while."

Alice reached across her and shook Marty's hand. He was a thin man, wearing loose shorts and sandals, and a shirt with cutoff sleeves. "Nice to meet you, Mr. Ferguson. I'm Alice Burton. Pardon me for asking, but... I mean, did your business..."

"Go up in a blaze?"

"Yeah." Alice winced.

"Not like most folks, thankfully. I run the Barbecue Shack just down the road. I lost a couple of storage sheds, but the main part of my business is still up so far."

"That's good news."

"It's okay for now, but as we were pulling out, at least six other places pretty close to us were burning bright, and those flames were kicking off some serious heat and cinders. We did everything we could to keep things wet around the exterior, and then the smoke simply got too bad and we had to leave. I doubt my place will be standing in the morning."

"I'm sorry to hear that. Really, I am."

"We have insurance to cover any losses..." He glanced north toward the bright orange horizon where hundreds of buildings blazed, voice lowering to a growl. "But I seriously doubt they'll fully cover all this damage. When Melissa blew through six or seven years ago, they pulled every dirty trick in the book to keep from giving full payouts."

"What did you hear on the broadcast?" Andrea asked.

"They're talking about this sort of thing happening as far away as Colorado, and most states are under a state of emergency."

"So, it's definitely not a localized event?"

"Doesn't seem that way, though it's hard to get specifics. Lots of stations are down, and it's hard to get a clear signal from the ones still operating. I'll keep monitoring the radio and keep everyone updated."

"Thanks, Marty." As the man walked away, Andrea turned to the door. "Here we are, Alice. Room thirty-one."

Alice slid her keycard in the slot where it clicked and turned green. Jake ran up and grabbed the door handle, pushing his way in with Sarah right behind him, both kids laughing as they tossed the backpacks on the bed and leaped in after them.

With a big smile, Alice turned and shook Andrea's hand again. "We can't thank you enough for helping us. I'm going to be honest..." A small part of the immense worry she'd been feeling slipped out, her eyes glassing over as she gave the proprietress a relieved look. "I really wasn't sure what we were going to do tonight. My daughter might just have gotten her wish to sleep on the beach if it wasn't for you."

Andrea gave a wistful sigh, holding Alice's hand and giving it a gentle squeeze. "Normally, that would be a nice idea, but not tonight... and not anytime soon. I'm just glad to get you and your kids off the street for the night. Please, get some rest and we'll see what things look like tomorrow. Remember about breakfast."

"Don't worry. We'll be up. Have a pleasant night, Andrea."

"You too, Alice. Good night, kids!"

"Good night, Mrs. Smith!" the kids called back, Sarah giving a wave where she sat resting on her elbows with her feet hanging over the edge of the bed.

Alice shut the door and leaned back against it, taking a deep breath of the freshly cleaned room, the carpet freshener and linens nearly overwhelming as she watched the kids kick off their shoes and roll around on the bed with Jake crawling up on the pillows and flopping down.

"I'm *so* tired," he said, kicking his feet on the mattress. "And this feels *so* good."

Sarah had her backpack on the bed with her, rifling through it before pulling out her e-reader. With a guilty look at her mother, she clutched it to her chest with one hand as she fluffed up the pillows behind her.

Alice scowled. "You weren't supposed to bring that with you."

"But it's super thin, and it fits fine in the front! I still brought all the things you wanted me to, too. Two changes of clothes, a flashlight, bottled waters and canned food, and even an extra flashlight." Clutching the e-reader with both hands, the girl gave her a plaintiff look. "Please don't make me leave it here when we have to go. I can't stand not to have my books with me. You know that."

"I know, honey." Alice stepped to the foot of the bed with her arms crossed, noting there were a handful of bottled waters sitting on the desk next to the TV. "But those things take electricity to run."

"But Andrea said they've got four diesel generators out back. And my e-reader doesn't take much power. It can run for weeks without a charge!"

"I'm not doubting that, but what happens when we get back on the road and try to get home?" Biting her lip, Alice gave her a smile. "Still, it *is* light and small, and I know you love your books. Just don't complain if it runs out of juice and you can't charge it."

"Thanks, Mom. I'll keep it in low-power mode and only read for an hour at a time once we get on the road. How does that sound?"

"Okay, but before you guys settle down for the night, let's get cleaned up. Jake, see if the water is on."

Jake bounced off the bed and into the bathroom as Alice grabbed a chair from beneath a table, turning it around and placing the back beneath the doorknob before pushing hard on the feet to jam it tight. A moment later, she heard water spraying in the bathroom for a short burst, and then a longer one before he came out with a wide grin. "Both sides are working, and there's hot water!"

"Perfect. No showers for now. Just use the sink to get your faces, arms and any exposed skin washed up, and that'll have to be good enough for now. I don't want us to be the reason for them being low on hot water – or water in general – given how nice Andrea's being. Also, change your clothes; they're covered with smoke and soot. Jake, you go first and Sarah can go second."

As Jake got started, Alice sat on the foot of the bed Sarah was lying on and called out, "Keep the water on low, and turn it off when you're not using it!"

"Okay, Mom!"

Taking the first comfortable breath in hours, Alice turned to her daughter with a wry smile. "How are you holding up, kiddo?"

"I'm doing okay," Sarah replied, putting her e-reader down. "But... I'm pretty scared."

"Me, too." Alice grabbed the girl's foot and gave it a playful tug. "We just have to hang in there and keep fighting. Who knows, everything might be cleared up in a few days or a week. One thing's for sure, clean running water will be in short supply soon, especially if this is as big as that Marty guy said. That's why we have to conserve everything we have, and any water we drink from our water bottles we'll refill from the sinks here."

"But where are we trying to go?"

"A big city, ideally. We need to see how bad things really are and try to find some transportation back home."

"What about Dad?"

"Your dad knows we need to gather at home base in case of an emergency, so I'm sure he'll abandon any attempts to come to Florida. I'd say he'll head straight home to Michigan, so that'll be our primary goal."

When Jake was finished cleaning up, Alice bade Sarah to go in next, the girl taking longer than her brother, coming out with her brown hair combed back and bundled in a soft ponytail holder, her cheeks rosy and moist. Alice entered the bathroom and checked herself out in the mirror, frowning at the smudges on her cheekbones, her long hair having come out of its clip to hang to her shoulders. Grabbing a lock of it, she leaned closer to the mirror, the ends curled and black from the proximity to the fires, and her cheeks had a rosy tint to them as if she had been sunburned.

"Note to self. Keep your face away from those fires."

With that, she let her long brown hair hang down and patiently combed it out before putting it back in a ponytail holder. Then she used wet wipes to clean her face, rinsing with a tiny splash of water and grunting in pleasure as it cooled her skin. She did the same with her arms and legs, washing off a surprising amount of dirt and soot, then she changed her clothes, tossing them in a pile with the kids' so they could take care of them later. Coming back to the bedroom, feeling a hundred percent more relaxed, she smiled at the quaint, tropical style decorations in the room, the bamboo desk and Calypso-themed wallpaper, the entire place neat and tidy with a fragrant ambience that made her sleepy. Sitting on the edge of Sarah's bed, she looked over their meager possessions, thinking about what they'd left behind at the beach house but trying her best not to get caught up in any negativity. They were alive and healthy and that's all that mattered.

"Good book?"

Sarah was sitting with her legs together and her feet crossed, toes wiggling in a pair of fresh socks. She looked up as if knocked from a trance. "Oh, yeah, it's awesome. This is one of my favorite series. I'm rereading it, since the ones I was working on are stored on the cloud."

"And you can't get those unless we have internet connectivity." Alice nodded.

"But that's okay. I've got dozens of books downloaded."

"Hours of fun filled reading!" they both shouted enthusiastically, mimicking an often-heard TV commercial as they broke down in giggles.

"Maybe you can let me read on that for a while," Jake said, head on his pillow and looking sleepy as he watched them.

"Oh, I know you're bored," Alice said. "For now, just try to get a little sleep."

"Okay." Jake yawned, climbed beneath the covers, and settled in.

"Mom, you can sleep with me if you want," Sarah said, scooting to her right and patting the side of the bed.

"That sounds like a good idea."

As Alice climbed beneath the covers, Sarah gave up one of her pillows, which didn't feel like a usual stiff hotel pillow, instead being exceptionally soft and large, and as soon as she put her head on it, the desire to sleep rushed in and pulled her to the edge of a tranquil slumber. Rolling on her right side, she watched her daughter for a while and appreciated how much they looked alike in the angle of their jawline and longish faces. They shared deeply shaded eyebrows and the same color eyes, a deep chestnut that gave their faces expressive appearances.

"Don't fight it, Mom," Sarah said. "Just get some sleep. I'll be right behind you as soon as I finish up this chapter."

With a wistful smile, Alice nodded and rested her hand against her daughter's arm, happy for the safety and being near her children. Still, as she faded from a doze into a deeper sleep, her dreams were plagued with hellish orange beds of flame, fingers of fire casting cavorting shadows through her mind.

———

A hard knock on a door outside jolted Alice awake hours later, and she opened her eyes to come face-to-face with Sarah snoring lightly with her e-reader still clutched against her chest. The knocking came again, and Alice rose with a start, head turning frantically until she realized it was coming from a few doors down. Sitting at the edge of the bed, she smacked her lips and rubbed her eyes, remembering they were in a quaint hotel room on Highway A1A, safe and surviving in the middle of a fiery catastrophe where every vehicle around them had blown up and set the landscape on fire.

"Not the kind of situation you want to wake up to in the morning," she murmured to herself as she got up and walked to the window.

Pulling back the blinds, she saw a rolling rack packed with baskets sitting outside the neighbor's door, and Andrea was conversing with whoever occupied that room. A moment later, the hotel owner came into view and waved to whoever she was talking to before the door shut with a soft bang, then Andrea was pushing the rolling cart their way and smiling when she caught sight of Alice in the window.

Pulling aside the chair and unlocking and opening the door, Alice stepped out and gave her a wave. "Good morning, Andrea. What's going on?"

"I like to bring around the morning's breakfast myself." The woman gestured along the row of rooms where several baskets sat outside the doors. "A lot of folks aren't up yet... but I'm glad you are. Here." The woman handed Alice a basket with pastries wrapped in plastic, three pieces of fruit, and some juice boxes and bottled water.

"Thank you." Alice turned and placed the basket inside on the table. "Jake... Sarah! Breakfast!"

Before Andrea could move on, Alice stepped back outside and folded her arms as she looked out across the parking lot, where a few people were already gathered with their radios to try and get a read on what had happened. It was a hazy, gray morning, and the air had a smoky tinge to it, reminding her of the times when neighbors burned their garbage.

"So, is there any news?"

Andrea leaned on her cart, stiff armed as she gave a dark glance toward the drifting haze. "We were up listening pretty late last night, and this is apparently a multinational thing. The feds and a couple of small news stations said that anything running on gasoline or diesel caught fire. I'm talking on a global scale."

Alice blinked several times in surprise. "I... I'm having trouble getting my mind around that... It had crossed my mind that it was a terrorist attack, but... globally?"

"That seems about right." Andrea shrugged. "Still, we've got to think there's some kind of conspiracy going on here. My generators still run, and they use diesel. Marty says his was working fine before he left, too. Now, tell me, why didn't those explode?"

49

"That's a great question," Alice replied as she scratched her elbow. "And it all seems so terrifying. I'm just thankful we could sleep with relative safety. Thank you."

"No problem at all. You folks have a nice morning. Come outside and mingle if you want."

As Andrea started away, Alice held up her hand. "Wait a second. When's the last time you fueled your generator?"

"Oh, it's been many months. We keep stabilizer in it for the off-season. You know, to keep it fresh and usable."

Alice bit her lip in thought. "That makes sense, and we do the same thing back home. Okay, well, you have a good day, too."

The hotel owner continued on, moving to the next door and knocking sharply. Alice stepped back inside where the kids had already gotten up and were digging into the food. Jake had a bagel in one hand and an orange juice box in the other, while Sarah had opted for a bottle of water and an apple. Slipping into a third chair with a sigh, Alice chose a water and a slightly bruised banana, peeling it and taking several small bites despite her ravenous hunger.

"Are we conserving food, too?" Jake asked, noticing her barely eating.

"I don't think so just yet. I guess I'm trying to think of where we can go next, and I should've asked Andrea for a map."

"There's one over on the wall," Sarah said, standing and walking over between the desk and television to grab a large picture of a map of the surrounding area that was hanging next to a painting of a sailboat. "I was looking at it when you were cleaning up last night, and I noticed it had all the beaches and highways on it."

"That it does!" Alice said as Sarah placed the map on the table and scooted it toward the center, shifting the basket out of the way. With her finger, Alice traced along Highway A1A. "Well, north of us is Palm Bay, which is the largest city in the area." She tapped on the spot. "That's the one we'll head toward. If we walk all day, we can reach Palm Beach by tonight and scope out a place to sleep. Who knows, maybe the damage won't be as bad. Folks here were pretty nice, right? Maybe there are more spots that weren't hit too badly. Spots like this one."

"I'm... kind of afraid to leave," Sarah said. "It feels safe here."

"I agree wholeheartedly, but this is just a small community on an isolated strait of beaches. I'd just feel better if we found some transportation to the mainland. Plus, we need to find a way to get in touch with your Dad, or at least get home to your grandparents and meet him there."

"Okay, but what about our clothes? Aren't we going to wash them?"

Alice looked out the window. "Ehh... after thinking things over, I feel like we need to get on the road sooner than later. Just pack the smoky clothes in a different compartment. We're going to be right back out and walking around in it, so it probably won't matter in the short-term."

Alice forced them to eat almost everything in the basket, and the rest they put in their packs. They rounded up all the bottled waters in the room, refilled the empty bottles and packed them with their things. While the kids finished stuffing their cases full, Alice pulled a twenty dollar bill from her purse and placed it in the basket. As they stepped outside, Andrea was just coming back with her rolling cart, and Alice put their basket on top of some others on the cart.

"Going so soon?"

"The kids want to stay, but I really want to get going. We've got a long way to go, and I want to try to reach Palm Beach before the evening."

"I understand," Andrea replied, then she saw the twenty and smiled. "You didn't have to do that, Alice."

"It's not much, but I just don't have much cash on me. I swear we're good for it on our card, though!"

"Don't worry about it. It's more than enough."

"Who knows where we would have been if you hadn't put us up for the night? You've been so kind. I just hope there are more people like you out there."

"I'd like to think so. Without kindness, who are we, huh?"

"That's so incredibly true. Thank you again."

Andrea gave her arm a gentle squeeze as she smiled warmly. "Have a safe journey, and look us up the next time you're in town. You know, after all this is past us."

"We will," Alice replied, eyes watering.

She led the kids across the parking lot, glancing aside at people gathered around radios, sharing food, and generally being surprisingly peaceful, all beneath a thrum of nervous tension. As they stepped onto the highway again, Alice gazed north and peered through a heavy layer of fog and smoke that lay like a thick blanket above them. Despite it being morning, there was no sun visible in the sky, and the fires were just faint orange glows off in the distance, providing no other hints of what dangers lay ahead.

CHAPTER NINE

James Burton
Denver, Colorado

A loud sound started James awake, either the sharp retort of a weapon or the snapping of a tree trunk, or just his imagination fleeing the deadly dreams he'd had all night. There was an intense charred flavor on his tongue as if he'd put his face over a barbecue and breathed it for an hour, and a flood of memories came back to him. Staggering through the suburban streets, trying desperately to find a way out as the raging inferno closed around him on all sides and he touched his cheeks, bringing a sharp, burning pain.

A nagging urgency flicked at his brain and he sniffed hard, coughing as he assumed the smoke had gotten thicker and denser since he'd entered the restroom, and it was trying to get in and suffocate him. Rolling to his left, he scrambled up and staggered on wobbly legs toward the door, bumping the doorframe as he threw it open and peered out into the pitch-black night. Slouching with relief, he saw there were no raging fires right outside the door, and nothing out in the woods, either. In fact, the smoke hadn't actually gotten any thicker; if anything, it looked as though it had somewhat dissipated.

Shutting the door, he went back inside and found his phone where he'd left it on the floor, powering it up and waiting to see if there was a connection, desperate for one line of text from Alice or even a hint of news. While the battery had plenty of life, the connection was still down, and there was nothing from Alice or any way for him to get information on what was going on. With a tired sigh, he flipped it off and stuffed it deep into his pocket. Going to the sink, he put his hand beneath the spigot and turned the water on, the trickle just barely enough to pool in his cupped palm so he could splash it on his face. Using towels from a dispenser, he wiped his face dry, wincing whenever he touched his cheeks. After tossing the wadded paper away, he packed up the refilled water bottles, shrugged on his duffel bag, then slowly soaked a couple of T-shirts in the sink to wear around his face, and exited the restroom.

Standing outside in the charred grass, he gazed west and south where the raging fires dominated the landscape and infused a glow into the black sky. Still, there were no lights from ambulances, firetrucks, or rescue vehicles anywhere, not that he'd really expected to see any. Based on the position of the flames through the distant haze he saw, he'd been able to get ahead of the destruction just long enough to stay safe.

"I was lucky to get out of that neighborhood," he mumbled, "thanks to those brick houses not going up like tinder."

Temporarily out of danger but still threatened on every side, James turned and strode briskly out into the park, heading eastward as best as he could tell and sticking to the city outskirts in hopes of running across a vehicle to transport him back home. Trudging through the blackened forest, his feet crunched over charred grass as he went past scorched saplings with their branches burned to cinders, feeling like an intruder on some distant world. A foggy haze pressed in and around him, reducing the visibility to next to nothing, though the lights from the fire and flashlight on his phone kept him oriented. The moistened cloth protecting his nose and mouth helped a great deal, and soon he was making good progress, having fully woken up from his nap and feeling slightly more energetic for having had it.

Thirty minutes later, he noticed the crunchy grass growing soft again and the trees looking less scorched, the leaves barely singed and still waving in cool breezes coming in from the north. Eventually, the smoke thinned enough to get a better view of his surroundings, and he blinked in surprise when he stepped out of a tree line and onto an empty, quiet street. In every direction, more neighborhoods burned, though he was far enough east to see plenty of cool, dark, unburned spots scattered around. He walked north a bit before the road swept him back east again where he entered a commercial area with wholesale warehouses, fast-food restaurants, and gas stations that still had enough material in them to be vigorously burning. On the left-hand side of the road lay a middle school where a line of buses were in a crumpled row, sunken in on themselves, their tops covered in smothering flames, and James sidestepped them, turning his head aside, certain his stomach couldn't handle what might be inside.

Moving back to the right-hand side of the road, he stuck close to the sidewalk for a while before angling right again into a lot where unburned apartment buildings stood, along with a few larger business offices and administration centers. The parking lots were filled with burning cars and delivery trucks, the road cluttered with fire-infused crashes. A tourist bus parked by a family restaurant had gone up with the people still inside, every window filled with crackling silhouettes shedding bands of smoke. Shadows of looters moved up ahead against the backdrop of firelight, running with items they'd taken from the strip malls lining the road, dropping boxes and bottles, more than a dozen on bicycles tearing across the street and screaming wildly.

Weaponless, James strode briskly to a pair of apartment buildings and slid beneath a brick skywalk that bridged the two, ears open for any threatening sounds and movement in the shadows. Stepping into the main courtyard, he angled right to cut between the bushes and the wall as he watched a group of people on the opposite side of the courtyard break a first-floor window and disappear inside. Nervous panic ticked up in his gut, and he tried to tell himself he wasn't carrying anything valuable enough to want to steal, but when he looked around at the darkened windows where a few shadowy faces peeked out in terror, it struck him that desperation was already setting in with the population, and it wouldn't matter how much or little he actually possessed.

Swallowing hard, James stayed low and kept moving. After circling the interior courtyard, he passed beneath a second skywalk heading north, jerking around when a glass bottle hit the ground a fair distance behind him. Seeing no one there, he spun back and rushed into a parking lot that stretched in front of several strip malls and three-story brick stores clustered on a corner, an older part of town where the buildings and signs were less uniform. The tall lampposts were dead and the shadows were deep and dark, though he saw openings between the buildings ahead of him and he dashed across the lot, kicking fluttering paper and debris until he reached the other side and ducked into an alley.

Creeping along the narrow alley with the towering buildings looming above him, he took his time so he wouldn't trip and fall or run into something hard. He moved aside a piece of office furniture and slipped past a mini dumpster with its top thrown up, the smell of rotting food pouring out of it, though it was a strange relief from the occasional wafts of charred corpses that sometimes struck from out of the blue, carried by a fell wind. He came to a narrow intersection and stopped, leaning forward to check the alleyways in all directions. With no one to his left or right, he continued straight across, stepping over debris and around stacks of garbage cans piled in his way. James expected to come out on a northbound street in hopes it would take him back to the main road heading east again so he could bypass any further dangers.

A trashcan fell over behind him with a clatter, but when he looked back, no one was there. Hastened by blind panic, he skirted a stack of barrel kegs from the adjacent bar and rushed along, ducking beneath a fire escape and almost bolting from the alleyway into the street. He held back just in time, throwing his shoulders against the right-hand wall and taking slow, careful breaths. Edging forward, he peeked around the corner to see a dozen people sauntering down the middle of the street from the east, wielding baseball bats and crowbars with sharp, practiced swings. Their flashlight beams swept back and forth across the street, lighting up torched vehicles and side alleys as they went along. Behind the main group, a few men and women were pushing grocery carts loaded up with food and water while a couple of others pulled wide, flat handcarts with big screen televisions, industrial-sized coffee makers, stacks of bakery boxes, and a host of other goods. There was a small dumpster in the alley with him and he crossed over to it, putting his left shoulder to the side to stay out of sight, watching as the group approached.

Across from him was a neighborhood hardware store with a beige brick storefront and a dark sign hanging above the door. Several individuals from the main group broke off and jogged over, using their weapons to break the wide front window, climbing inside with gleeful shouts as they continued with their raid. One man brought out two sets of power tools and threw them on a handcart, while another took an armful of something he couldn't identify. A woman exited with a chainsaw and swung it around wildly before she tossed it into one of the grocery carts with a clatter, earning her a curse from its driver. Once they were done with that store, they pointed to the one James was standing by, forcing him to shrink into the shadows as they sprinted across the street, smashed the glass, and ran away with canned goods, boxes of cereal, and gallons of water.

"Must be a grocery store," he mumbled to himself, watching as they returned another two or three times to fill their carts to overflowing.

Just when he thought they'd spend all night in the store, a voice from above him called out gruffly. "The wind's changing, people! Let's go!"

There came a clatter of boots on metal and a trickle of dust falling on his head and James looked up to see a man stomping down the fire escape, taking several steps at a time, practically leaping from one landing to another so his boots pounded on the grating. James edged backward and crouched in the dark corner between the dumpster and wall, watching as the man's feet slammed on the pavement, and he spun and rushed past James, heading into the street.

"The winds blowing eastward, not south like we thought," the man said, pointing back the way they'd come. "We need to go back! Everyone, go back!"

James edged forward, blood pounding in his ears as he watched the group turn their carts around with clattering wheels and shove them hard back toward the south.

Waiting until the group passed out of sight, James crept from his hiding space and stepped into the street, checking both ways through the misty haze of smoke before jogging across to the other side. Shoes crunching on shattered glass, he edged closer to the window and peered inside to make sure none of the looters were lingering. When he saw it was clear, he climbed inside and scanned along skewed rows of tools and equipment that had been knocked to the ground by the invading thieves. Their looting strategy had been amateurish at best, leaving piles of useful items behind while taking things they couldn't use, like power drills and battery-operated chainsaws.

"It's not like the power will be back on soon," he chuckled darkly.

Carrying his duffel bag in front of him, he eased along the middle aisle, stepping on boxes of spilled nails and screws, paint brushes and pans, and sandpaper discs that scratched the tiles under his shoes. At the far end of the first row were regular hammers and larger sledgehammers, neither of which were worth taking. Instead, he grabbed a five-pound mini-sledge from its U-shaped hook and placed that into his duffel bag, lifting it to judge its weight, trying to keep from over-burdening himself. Around the next corner, he stopped and stared at the wall with a widening grin. It was a small section of fishing poles, lures, hunting vests, and other basic sporting-goods, and along with those items were a set of light hiking backpacks with double stitched straps and plenty of pockets. Taking one off its hook, he placed it on the ground next to his duffel bag and began transferring everything over, grinning even wider when he slipped it on and the soft, cushioned straps gripped snugly around his shoulders.

"This will make things *much* easier. Still need to keep it light, though."

From there, he circled behind the counter at the back of the store to see if there was anything on the shelves below the register, but he found nothing but rolls of receipt paper and signs that someone had been looking for any small safes or hidden cash they could abscond with. Stepping to a doorway in the far back, he leaned both hands on the door frame and peered into a small office with a couple of vending machines with their fronts broken open and cleaned out of anything edible.

With a soft curse, James turned and was about to go back to the floor when he stopped at the counter, cocked an eyebrow at it, and walked back around to stare down at the messy shelves. He leaned over and started feeling around through all the clutter, shuffling around pads of paper, boxes of pens, and other clerical office supplies. Up near the register, he spotted a folded pile of newspapers with a jacket bundled on top. Curious, he slid the jacket aside and lifted the newspapers, giving a chuckle when he saw what was beneath it. A shiny, stainless-steel revolver with a polished wooden grip was tucked into a leather holster with an attached belt, and when he pulled it out and held it up, the engraving on the side read *Python*. Behind the gun against the back of the counter was a box of .357 cartridges.

"Oh, boy. You guys missed out on a gift."

While he was far from being what he'd classify as a 'gun nut,' he'd lived in the country most of his life and a 2 a.m. wakeup call that coyotes were trying to get into the chicken coop was enough to make anyone get a feel for a revolver or double barrel. The cylinder was already fully loaded with six rounds, and he stood and wrapped the belt and holster around his waist, buckling it tight and shifting his hips until it rested comfortably.

Stepping through the hardware store rubble, James made his way to the door, looking back into the street, noticing a slight increase in brightness coming from where he thought was west, though the taller buildings blocked his view. Glancing both ways as he adjusted the new, more comfortable backpack on his shoulders, James jogged across the street and up to the front of the grocery store. More glass was scattered around, and the doors were broken open and hung loosely on their rails. Jugs of milk and a few dozen broken cans of soda and beer lay splattered in the entryway, forming a fizzy, creamy mess. Stepping through it gingerly, he pulled out his phone and entered a pitch-black store, using the flashlight function to find his way to the back where a sign read *Pharmacy.*

"How could you guys have left all this stuff here?" he muttered as he scanned dozens of shelves still filled to the brim.

Leaping onto the counter, he slid across and landed with both feet down, approaching the shelves and shrugging off his backpack. He turned along the row, dropping in bottles of painkillers and a few broad-spectrum antibiotics whose names he recognized before heading back out onto the pharmacy floor where he entered an aisle full of nutritional drinks and snack bars as well as an entire row of first-aid kits. Taking some things out of his pack, he made enough room to stuff more supplies inside, making sure everything was organized before he flipped the flap shut and buckled it tight. His next deep breath stung his nose, and he glanced toward the front of the store where the gray haze had thickened to the consistency of soup. Breaking off his supply run, and with his backpack full to bursting, James slipped it back on his shoulders and crunched through the debris, stepping on snack bags and kicking aside crushed fruit juice bottles to come to the front of the store where he stood and listened, trying to remember what the man on the roof had shouted before he came down from the fire escape. He didn't want to follow the gang south... or was it east?

Confused, he shifted the backpack and turned to what he thought was north, marching past the storefronts with their broken windows and dark interiors. A deli, an insurance company and a cell phone store passed by in rapid succession, and as he crossed the next intersection, he found himself surrounded by thick walls of billowing gray smoke that hung in the air, creating an impenetrable haze that started to obscure the storefronts just a short distance away. He kept to what he thought was a northerly direction, staying in the shadows of the storefronts while his footsteps made soft echoes in the dense quietness. The fog and smoke seemed to absorb all sound but for the distant crackle of flames and the haunting shrieks of the occasional person caught in the catastrophic maelstrom. Hurrying his pace, he broke into a slow jog, the t-shirt wrapped around his nose and mouth becoming useless as the smoke continued to grow in thickness.

"Got... to get... out of this." The words came out as rough croaks, his voice not sounding anything like himself.

James's tennis shoes scraped across the rough concrete, kicking aside debris and he almost ran into a charred car that appeared out of nowhere in the gray haze. He circled it and kept moving over the rubble-strewn pavement and it quickly became apparent that he was crossing a six-lane highway that tapered into the haze in both directions. Stumbling across a median of grass, he choked and coughed as the wind picked up, staggering to the other side and climbing the guardrail where he leapt over a ditch and crawled up into a parking lot. The dark hulks of department stores and warehouses loomed in the distance, and the smoke began to thin a bit as he kept walking around the edge of the lot.

The pavement soon turned into gravel and he glanced upward as the buildings began to fade away, the smoke thinning to reveal him standing in a park area next to a pair of gnarled trees that looked like sentinels in an unforgiving underworld. Adding to the scene were a few bodies that had collapsed around a handful of tents and stacks of supplies that were scattered around as if the people in the area had gathered there to escape the growing catastrophe but had died from smoke inhalation while waiting for relief or a ride out. The canvas awnings were brightly colored but covered in layers of soot with holes singed in them as they flapped in a weak breeze, and James shuddered as he contemplated what his own fate might be if he didn't find a way out of the city.

Passing through the park, his feet once again dragged along the sidewalk as he took in the sight of a series of old-style buildings stories tall with exaggerated eaves and low-pitched roofs. Cinders drifted from the higher windows as fires still raged up the fronts of the buildings, leaving their façades ravaged as the fire methodically consumed all in its path. The lower floors were nothing but charcoal and shattered glass with smoke billowing from every opening into the sky and the flames had caught everything within the city block, giving the place a bombed-out look akin to an old WWII film. Bodies lay in shrieking repose around him, caught in various forms of escape. Larger people covered smaller ones or held them in their arms, many with their faces turned upward to the sky, their lips burned away to reveal white teeth shining from the gaping holes of their mouths. They were unrecognizable in tatters of charred clothing that fluttered in the hot winds produced by the smoldering grass. Cars lay twisted sideways in the road off to his right, and on his left in a side lot, they sat piled atop one another in a fusion of metal and cooking car seats.

"Must've been some kind of flash fire," James coughed beneath the shirt covering his mouth. "How did I end up here? I must be going west, not north. Damn!"

James angled right across another main road with only four lanes, the median just a thin strip of grass littered with wrecks and bodies tossed around in the smoking debris. When he reached the other side, he found himself standing amidst a long row of shops and he ducked into an alley between a blackened grocery store and a city administration building to come out in a back parking lot. Convinced that he was finally heading in the right direction, he held his head up, trying to feel for any sort of a breeze, letting it direct him to cooler patches that were somewhat clear of smoke and haze. Like they had in the burning neighborhood, his senses guided him through the worst of it, and he angled back toward the northeast where things had cooled off and he could breathe well enough to break into a jog.

Moving past a row of small two-family apartments where the buildings were still unaffected by the spreading fires, he caught his first sign of people not yet affected by the city blaze. Two stood on the high balcony, a man and a woman who surveyed the rest of the town and pointed at something off in the distance. The man gave James a dark look, but James ducked into an alley and squeezed past a set of trash cans, leaping a puddle formed from the waste dripping from leaking pipes. Stepping out from the claustrophobic passage, James stood in a relatively empty street. While several cars were burning and smoking, they were far enough into the street to keep from spreading the blaze to the buildings. Warm flickering candlelight glowed from a few windows, and a group of people had gathered around the stoop on the opposite side where they hunkered down around the concrete steps.

James turned left and walked past them, giving them only a slight glance to see two men sitting on the metal step nursing their wounds. One man wore a white bandage around his head as a woman leaned over him and inspected his arm, wrapping it in gauze that was stained a deep crimson. The air grew clearer with each block he walked and the growing fires faded behind him. More people had come out to stand in the street or gather on the corners, mostly keeping to themselves, though a few had formed up into small groups with stacks of supplies piled into children's wagons or carts as they stood and watched what remained of their cars burn in the street. At the next corner, two men had pulled out grills and were cooking right on the front stoop, serving a couple of families who looked homeless, judging by their soot-stained clothes and smudged skin. A little girl cried off to the side where she sat on a pink plastic chair as her mother knelt next to her and tried to care for a burn on her leg.

Keeping in the middle of the road and avoiding eye contact wherever he could, James finally caught a spot of sunlight in the east, a golden glow against the red-orange swells behind him where Denver burned and people died. Those he passed only spared him fleeting glances, too concerned with gathering and protecting their supplies or caring for others who'd come from deeper inside the city and had barely escaped death. The number of people that were gathered was shockingly low, far fewer than he would have expected, though given the number of bodies he had seen, it wasn't that much of a surprise. Many had pulled out lawn chairs or other porch furniture to sit on with almost everyone keeping watch back toward the South where the cities and suburbs had become one gigantic bed of charcoal and flame that was expanding outward. Men wearing firefighting uniforms dragged pieces of wreckage away from the front of a grocery store, and people stood by anxiously as they prepared to enter and gather whatever supplies they could find.

James was a ghost amongst them, keeping his hands tucked into his pockets, thankful for the heavy weight of the revolver on his hip. In the dark corners between the buildings, he occasionally caught sight of shadows, lurking figures that were no doubt waiting to prey on the vulnerable. Shifting to the other side of the street where there were less people, James didn't see the next group of shadows until he was right upon them. In an alley on his right, hidden in dark recesses, three men and a couple of women lingered in the shadows cast across the wall from a burning motorcycle, its frame twisted, the engine blown out. The men caught sight of James and shifted away from the boxes they were hovering over, flexing their arms as they stared at his backpack.

Before they could engage him, though, he cut back to the left toward a group sitting in chairs out in the open. As he crossed the street, he glanced back to see the men following swiftly behind him at first until he reached the other side, then they stopped to watch him with their hands on their hips, whispering to one another.

He drew even more looks on the left-hand sidewalk where families huddled protectively around each other, though being eyed with suspicion was better than the feeling he'd gotten from the group in the alley. Cutting back to the west and hoping he was far enough north to avoid the worst of the incoming fires, James ducked into a side street with cobbled pavement and tall apartment buildings crowding in on both sides. A handful of vehicles had exploded in the enclosed space, blasting the walls with scorch marks and leaving chunks of metal and polymer in his way. He leaped over small pieces of molding and plastic, circling the burning hulks and turning his face away at the potent scent of melted rubber.

The alley opened into a narrow lane with off-street parking and a row of backyards on both sides. At least one garage had been consumed by flames, though it was far enough away from any homes that the twirling cinders didn't reach them. Garbage littered the yards, and even more people sat out back with radios and grills, a few pulling resources together while one man stood guard over stacks of canned goods with a shotgun.

James passed by the last of the people without incident and crossed over into a warehouse district with long, quiet buildings and just a few trucks and cars smoldering in wide parking lots where the open space gave way to cleaner air. James pulled his moist shirt beneath his chin and took a long breath, the smoke still present, but greatly lessened. As he passed the buildings and circled the outskirts of what had once been Denver, a strange sound reached his ears. He stopped, turned in a circle, and tilted his head to the sky as a whistle blew a long and sorrowful note. It sounded again, louder, and when it stopped there came the grinding of a massive coal-fired engine and dozens of boxcar wheels clicking over their tracks.

CHAPTER TEN

Ryan Cooper
Somewhere Outside East Lansing, Michigan

A heavy night descended over the farmstead, the evening made darker by the rising smoke clouds and dense layers of haze that blotted out the starlight in nearly every direction. The fires from the township and neighborhoods gave the horizon an opaque sheen with a billowing belly the color of burnt tangerine, and Ryan stood at the bay window, peering through the blinds at the property where the road curved north along the fence line before disappearing into the distance.

"Psh." Ryan closed the blinds and shook his head, turning to the kitchen table where Helen had prepared two cups of green tea.

She was seated at the near end with the radio placed between them on the corner, only the appliance clocks lighting the room, and he turned up the electric lantern they'd brought up along with the radio. While the batteries had been dead on both of them, there was a stash of new and rechargeable ones in a kitchen drawer, enough to last them months if necessary.

"Do we really need to shut all the blinds?" Helen asked as she fiddled with the radio knob and tried to find a station. She wore a towel around her neck, her freshly washed gray hair falling around her cheeks.

"I think so. We're high enough on the rise to be perfectly visible from the highway, or the road out front. Anyone walking nearby would spot us right away, especially with most of the neighborhood being so dark. Except for the..." He nodded toward the window where the firelight shined through the blinds. "We'd be like a lighthouse beacon out here."

"At least we have the dogs to warn us if someone gets too close."

Ryan scoffed. "That would be all right if they didn't bark at just about anything that moves out there. They were going on all night last night."

"Well, have a seat and help me find something to listen to."

Ryan eased into his chair at the head of the table, holding his warm tea mug while patting the residual moisture off his face with a hand towel. Their clothes and skin had been covered in smoke after their adventure on the highway, and Helen had suggested they shower and change into some clean clothing. After scrubbing the layers of fumes off his skin, he'd put on a fresh pair of jeans and T-shirt and towel-dried his full gray head of hair.

"I feel a hundred percent better after that shower," Ryan said as he released a long breath.

"Well, I'm glad I suggested it then," she smiled. "I wanted us to be good and refreshed after all that... business on the highway."

He gave a nod to the radio. "So, what have you found out there so far? Anyone talking?"

"I can't seem to find anything." Helen leaned in and listened as the static faded in and out with sharp squelches and squeals.

"I'd imagine a lot of the radio towers will be out right now, plus anything that uses a backup generator is probably dead too, based on what we saw on the highway. Here, let me try."

Helen turned the radio toward him, leaving off with a shrug. "I've been up and down the tuning band. I can't find anything."

"The towers might come back online at any time if they have battery backups and someone switches them over." He increased the volume, rolling the tuning knob slowly with his ear bent to the speaker, listening for a voice buried beneath the static. He moved past one thousand on the AM dial and kept going higher, hitting the jackpot at around fifteen hundred when a man's robotic, monotone voice burst from the radio in a loud, clear tone. Glancing at Helen, he turned up the volume a little more.

"... emergency broadcast system. Please be advised a national emergency has been declared for what is believed to be a targeted bioterror attack against the nation's fuel supplies. Residents are urged to seek shelter indoors and stay away from sources of gasoline, diesel, jet fuel, and any machinery that utilize forms of refined petroleum for power. Stay tuned for updates from federal, state, and local officials. This broadcast repeats." There came a slight pause followed by a series of beeps before the message started over. "This is an alert from the emergency broadcast system. Please be advised..."

As they listened, the broadcast became spotty with more squelches and spits of static, ending in a long squeal that rose in volume and pitch until the channel cut off.

"What happened?" Helen winced at the bursts of noise coming from the speaker.

"I don't know," Ryan said as he pulled the radio closer and lowered the volume. "Whatever tower they were broadcasting from must have gone down, or..." He worked the knob a moment more before finally shrugging. "I just don't know. Whatever happened, we're not getting anything anymore. I'll turn it off for now to save battery life."

"Good idea."

The two sat quietly, Ryan's hand over Helen's as they sipped their tea and listened to the frogs croaking out front in the pond, loud enough to hear through the closed windows. The house itself held a tranquil ambience that allowed him to lower his eyelids and let the stress of the evening fade away.

"It's so peaceful," Helen said. "You'd never expect to hear about a national emergency on a night like this."

Ryan nodded and roused himself at the sound of her voice, pushing his chair back as he stood. Turning the electric lantern off, he grabbed the nearby flashlight and headed for the back door. With a quizzical expression, Helen got up and followed him as he stepped onto the concrete patio and got on the dirt track leading to the barnyard. Keeping the flashlight off, he strode urgently through the darkness with just the faint outline of the path ahead, the gentle clucking of the chickens greeting them as they passed the coop and pens on the way out. When they reached the barnyard gate, the sheep and goats were much calmer and didn't crowd them as they opened it and entered. The questioning barks of the dogs greeted them, though, their tails brushing back and forth excitedly as they bounded in circles, wanting to play. Ryan laughed and patted them on their heads, ruffling their fur and playfully shoving them around for a few seconds. Straightening to catch his breath, he strode over to Diana where she sat back on her haunches, tail sweeping the dirt, licking her chops as she tossed her head. After giving her some attention, they continued to the barn, fumbling in the darkness to remove the padlock off the door.

Helen lifted the latch, and Ryan grabbed the handle and heaved it open with a grunt, throwing it just wide enough for them to slip inside. Pulling the door shut behind him, he flipped on the flashlight and waved it around, lighting up dust particles as they drifted through the air. Sweeping the flashlight across the barn, he saw the donkeys standing quietly in their stalls and Bessie chewing some hay as she stared at them over her wall. Off to the right were a few stacked hay bales with larger bags of feed and another wheelbarrow. Tack hung from the wall along with an array of farm implements all in neat rows. From there, he shifted the light past the loft ladder and old wooden beams to where a tractor sat in back. Behind it, and a little to the side, stood a five-hundred-gallon diesel fuel tank bolted to the ground. Squinting at both the vehicle and tank, Ryan moved in on the left side, sliding past the orange tractor's hood, eying the engine compartment warily. The tires came to his chest as he moved past them and stood beside the fuel tank with its chipped black and spots of rust. Hesitantly, he gave it a few taps, not sure what he'd expected to happen, but there wasn't much echo, and the depth gauge showed it was about three-quarters full.

Turning to Helen, he shrugged. "It looks like the tractor and diesel supply here are fine. Totally opposite from what we saw out on the expressway."

"The emergency broadcast said we should stay away from anything that uses types of refined oil as power." Helen raised an eyebrow. "You sure you want to be in here?"

Ryan gestured to the tractor. "Clearly, some things aren't blowing up that probably *should* be. I'm not sure how thrilled I'd be about starting that thing up, though."

"Do you think the government is lying?"

"No, I don't think so. Look at the highway, or forget about that, look at the neighbors' houses. Everyone with a car has seen it go up in smoke. No... I think whatever this is, it only affected some fuel supplies." He scratched his chin, and placed his hand on the large diesel reservoir tank in the corner, running his fingers across the surface. "Maybe... when did Alice and James last fill this up?"

Helen shifted from one leg to the other and folded her arms over her chest. "Hm. I'm trying to think... but I just don't know. We can give Alice a call—" Laughing nervously, she corrected herself. "Oh. Right. But what about the ATV out in the quarter-barn?"

"Did they use it very much?"

"Off and on. Not a huge amount."

"Then it's probably the same thing. Whatever fuel is left in the tank was probably purchased months ago." Taking a step back, Ryan swept the flashlight across the tractor and fuel tank again, something from the broadcast bothering him. "They said it was an *attack*."

"Yes." Helen took a deep breath and let it out with a slight quiver.

Ryan stepped over and wrapped his arms around her shoulders, kissing her on the head and pulling her close. "Alice and the kids are going to be fine, and so will James. You know how much they love each other, and they'll be fighting tooth and nail to get home any way they can. Our Alice..." Ryan choked up for a second before recovering his voice. "Alice is a tough woman. That's how we raised her, and you know that."

"I know she is... they *both* are, but this seems like something bigger than anything that's ever happened."

Rubbing her back, Ryan acknowledged her concern with a nod. "I know, honey, but hey, look on the bright side, the government's out there trying to help us." He chuckled derisively. "So, it can't be all that bad." She smiled at him, but it faltered, and he patted her on the arm. "Come on. Let's get back inside and see if we can hunt down a receipt for the diesel fuel purchase."

"Why do we need that?"

Taking her by the hand, he led her to the doors and flipped off the flashlight, stepping into the darkness where the dogs were waiting to get more attention. "I'm just curious if I'm right about the age of the fuel and what else might have survived," he said. "Maybe some of the nearby farms might have stable fuel or even some vehicles that still run."

"And that," she said, wrapping an arm around him and squeezing, "is another example of why you're such a smart man, Ryan Cooper."

Turning and shutting the door, he checked the latch and lock, bending close in the darkness. "Well, it's not necessarily good news. I'm also thinking that if there aren't any stable fuel supplies around, this tractor might be one of the most valuable things in the area."

They gave the dogs some more attention before leaving the barnyard and strolling toward the house, and Ryan shot a glance at the quarter barn off to the left behind the coops and pens where James and Alice kept the ATV and its extra jerry cans of fuel. The barn, like the one housing the tractor, was fine, not a single sign of smoke or cinders, let alone fire. Aside from the distant orange on every horizon, the stroll back was peaceful, and they did it hand-in-hand, reminding him of the thousands of times they'd taken walks along old country paths and through quaint tourist towns while on vacation. A grin formed on his face, blood rushing to his cheeks as he choked up a little.

Helen smiled in confusion. "What's gotten into you?"

"Oh, I was just thinking how easy it is to walk with you anywhere. Even with all this going on, it's just nice to know that you're here with me."

"You're going to make me blush, you old softie," she replied, releasing his hand and locking arms with him. "Let's just get inside and get ready for bed. I'm exhausted."

"Me, too. Tomorrow we need to start thinking about how to conserve the kids' resources here. Everything, even the well water needs to be stretched to the absolute limit."

"I'll get some jugs from the pantry, and we'll use those to keep tabs on how much water we use for things like hand-washing and brushing our teeth."

"That's a great idea. We won't have to use them long-term, but I'd like to see how much water we each use every day, so I can figure out how much the well pump's going to have to run to keep us supplied."

They entered the house and got out of the cold, then Ryan helped Helen fill two plastic jugs with water and they carried them upstairs into the guest bedroom. They used the double basin sink to wash their hands sparingly and after changing into their soft pajamas, they fluffed their pillows and climbed into bed, lying shoulder-to-shoulder, holding hands as they stared at the ceiling.

"I was thinking," Helen said. "When we were driving to the highway, we saw a lot of houses on fire."

"Yes, probably due to them having vehicles in their garages."

"Sure, but there were some houses with no garages and no cars anywhere near them. They were on fire, too."

"Generators, I'd bet. The fact that the kids' house didn't catch on fire is probably because they installed a solar and battery-powered backup instead of a gasoline or diesel generator. That was a smart move in more ways than one, I've got to say."

"Well, you've said it before yourself, they're capable people. I just wish they hadn't taken that stupid trip of theirs."

"You and me both. The timing is... not good. But, for better or worse, I'm glad they had us house-sit for them. Can't imagine the state this place would be in without folks here to watch over it."

"You just like getting back on the farm, don't you?" Alice poked him in the side with a smirk.

"Yeah, I'll admit it's been enjoyable," Ryan chuckled. "And to make matters even better, James has that tractor and all that diesel out there. We're just lucky they didn't use it all that much."

"And now we'll have plenty of fuel for a while if we need it."

"Exactly. It'll also make us a prime target. If we were to start up the tractor or ATV, people could hear that and come to investigate. We have to be super careful, and if we use either of them, we'll have to do it as discreetly as possible."

"What if people come up asking for help? Like the neighbors?" Helen hesitated. "Shouldn't we try to help people if they really need it?"

"We'll burn that bridge when we come to it, but first and foremost, we have to defend ourselves and this property." Ryan took a deep breath, relaxing his shoulders as he exhaled, his mind still racing from the events of the day. "I'll look for some extra locks in the basement and sheds tomorrow, and I'll install them on the barn doors. We'll make sure the gates are doubly locked up, too, and we'll let the dogs roam at night, just in case." Helen nodded next to him, her eyes closed, already starting to fall asleep.

Propped up on his pillow, shoulders and back still sore from all the rubble and debris he'd moved earlier, Ryan tried to calm his mind and relax against the soft mattress. As he stared out the window at the continuous streams of smoke pouring into the sky and the fiery glow seething on the horizon, though, a pit of worry swirled in his stomach.

CHAPTER ELEVEN

Agent Alan Harris
Washington, D.C

The convoy of four Humvees tore through the D.C. streets as fast as the old pair of snowplows leading the charge could push debris aside. The vehicles at their disposal had been quickly assembled from a military salvage yard with the President ushered aboard the second one in line, Agent Harris sitting to his right with another agent on the opposite side. The driver was a Marine, and a White House staffer named Cindy Strode sat in the front passenger seat. The other trucks in the convoy were locked and loaded with fifty-caliber machine guns in their turrets and armored Marines clinging to the sides, sweeping their carbines across the shadowy streets.

They bounced along with the rough ride, running over car parts and pieces of buildings lying in the road, the detritus of the catastrophe that had consumed D.C. The rusty snowplows knocked everything aside, metal and glass exploding over the plows as they shoved the burnt-out cars and trucks out of the way in a crash of scorched parts, not stopping for anyone or anything as they pushed toward the Mount Weather facility.

Harris watched the President glance from the right-side windows over to the left, listening to the ear bending sounds of squealing metal scraping across the pavement as they swept wrecks aside. Pieces of buildings fell in chunks of smoking brick and wood, clumps of it rattling off the roof and hood, smaller bits falling like fiery hail. Scorched insulation and plastic gave off a dizzying reek, but what made him sick to his stomach were the charred corpses of people trapped inside the burning high rises and apartments that were slowly collapsing. The plows often knocked a car or truck aside so hard that it jostled loose the passengers, spilling blackened bodies onto the roadway in their twisted and agonized forms.

"Sorry about all this, Mr. President," Harris said as he picked up on Birk's discomfort. "It's a bit of a bumpy ride, and the scenery isn't too nice."

"Stop apologizing, Harris. We're damned lucky to have anything to use for transport, and I'm grateful for it." They hit something hard in the road that shook the Humvee and rattled its suspension, tossing Birk and Harris around. "On second thought," the President joked, "maybe walking would have been better."

From the passenger seat, Cindy Strode turned and handed Birk a tablet computer, the woman appearing exhausted, her sandy blonde hair stained with dirt and tied up in a bun. "Mr. President, here's some of the information you requested."

"Thank you, Cindy." Taking the tablet, Birk rested the device in his lap and began scrolling down the page and scanning through the material.

"It looks like the national intelligence agency is confirming this is some sort of biological agent," Cindy said.

"A biological agent?"

61

Harris' eyes widened as he watched the city streets, alert for any direct threats to their Humvee.

Cindy continued. "They're saying it's probably a bacterium that was introduced into oil refineries at some point."

"That isn't good." Birk sighed.

"I'm not an expert in that, sir," Harris spoke hesitantly at first, "but wouldn't the refinery engineers have caught that? Or, a better question would be, why did everything go up at one time?"

"Good question, Harris. Cindy?"

"The working theory is that the biological agent must have remained dormant until something set it off. A biological alarm clock is one proposed method, but we're still in the early stages of figuring all this out."

Birk had been given a thick military flak jacket before he got in the Humvee, and he wiped the heavy sleeve across his forehead as he gazed at his screen in disbelief. "It feeds on petroleum and crude oil in a wide variety of forms, both refined and raw to multiply. It's extremely exothermic to where virtually any fuel reaches its flash point within a few minutes, and because we keep oil and fuel in enclosed space..." Birk trailed off.

"Boom," Cindy said.

"Exactly." The President gave a heavy sigh of relief as he read the next part. "Well, it's good to know we're not the only country that was hit. I guess."

Cindy was nodding. "China, Russia, and several members of the NATO alliance, as well as Germany and a few Russian aligned satellite countries, are all suffering as much or worse than we are."

"Are we sharing information?"

"Everyone's waiting on your input on that once we reach Mount Weather. DHS wants to give their recommendations, too."

"Of course."

Harris was still watching the road as they broke from the thickest city congestion to enter the suburban areas where the detonations had occurred on a far smaller scale. Parks and woods were alight in the glow of spreading fires, and the shadowy figures of a few surviving residents ran through driveways and yards with buckets of water and hoses, desperately trying to tame the flames. The agent swallowed a lump in his throat and released a shaky sigh, quiet enough so that no one in the Humvee heard.

Cindy continued running down the list, apparently having committed the line items to memory. "Regarding our military, our subs and nuclear-powered ships are fine, and most of the carrier attack groups are in good shape. They were using fuel restocked before the biological agent was introduced into the military supply chains, much like these vehicles we're in now."

"That means we've got some assets we can use." The President rubbed his chin. "Good to know we can defend ourselves to some degree."

"Unfortunately, most land-based assets are dead. And..." Cindy paused. "We've lost Air Force One, sir, and over ninety percent of our Air Force. Our bases on the East Coast have gone up in smoke. Planes right out on the runway were going up like fireworks, and storage tanks of jet fuel were like bombs. We're still trying to gather the number of active forces who were killed, but we expect it to be in the hundreds of thousands, maybe upward of fifty percent or more. That number could change drastically up or down as intel comes in, but that's what we're projecting."

Harris stifled a curse as the President stared out the window next to him, processing the new information. The snowplows brushed through the last few suburbs, crushing through the smoking debris, their heavy metal scrapers sparking off the pavement as they swept rubble aside. Rolling Virginia hills loomed ahead of them as they left the embers of the city behind, and Harris got comfortable as he glanced back through the Humvee's hatch window. They'd pulled up the older model from the Marine salvage yard where it was very nearly ready for decommission before things had gone to hell in a bobsled. It was nowhere close to combat ready, much less fit to carry the President of the United States; the tires were bald, and the paint was flecked off the sides of the few bits of armor left and it was out of alignment, forcing the driver to work with the wheel to keep them on the road, a whistle of wind blowing through a crack in the floor and adding to the chill inside the cabin. Still, it was the best of the four Humvees they'd found, so the President had been loaded inside and whisked away as fast as humanly possible.

Cindy continued. "As I was saying, most of our land-based assets are dead."

"You say most. Any numbers on that?"

"About eighty-five percent, sir. The worst part is that our generators and backup systems were also hit hard, though thankfully we have enough in renewables so that small, isolated parts of the grid are holding up. We don't know how long that will last, though. The US power grid is…"

"A piece of crap, yes, I know." Birk finished scanning the information on the screen. "How many congressional members have been contacted so far?"

"It's not looking good, sir," Cindy replied with a glum expression. "Half were in the air or car on their way to their home districts when things went south, and they're confirmed dead."

The President's face darkened. "We need to figure out if the timing is just a coincidence or not. Because that is a *damned* odd coincidence if so."

"We're looking into that." Cindy continued. "Thankfully, several members who were in D.C. at the time have been located and are on their way to Mount Weather in a separate convoy, but that's it."

Letting the computer tablet rest in his lap, the President raised his head with a look of hope. "If we've got enough vehicles for two convoys, surely we can't be that bad off."

"This is all we have, sir. The two convoys we managed to piece together from salvage yards and repair garages are the sum of all of our running vehicles, civilian or otherwise. There's nothing else running in D.C. that we're aware of"

"I see." The President frowned, shifting his attention through the opposite window as the thick forests of Virginia rolled by, the highway winding higher with every mile as they headed for the Blue Ridge Mountains ahead.

Behind them, the city's inferno blazed on, adding dark layers to the sky as billions of tons of noxious fumes circulated through the lower atmosphere and spread like a tumultuous inkblot. Above the blue-tinged ridges, starlight shone down on the road to help light their way. The snowplows smashed through the last of the heavy debris, shoving it aside in a crash of shattered glass and smoking steel with bodies flopping around inside the cabins. Birk and Harris rocked back and forth as the Humvee rolled over fragments of trucks and eighteen-wheelers with their cargo spilled across the lanes and the plows took a hard right on Highway 601, Blue Ridge Mountain Road, where a forest of mighty elms, pines, and birches crowded the roadside, creating a canopy that blotted out the sky as the road wound upward in majestic curves. Harris watched the lead Humvee as it banked back and forth in front of their headlamps, the silhouettes of mounted machine guns and Marines hanging on the sides of the vehicle giving a fleeting sense of peace.

After a few more miles of driving, they reached the Mount Weather Emergency Operations Center, which was also the center of operations for FEMA. Having been briefed by Security Chief Westbrook well ahead of time, and having visited on multiple occasions, Harris already knew the layout of the extensive grounds, much of it underground with FEMA's training facilities on the mountain's surface.

The forested roadways gave way to concrete walls topped with barbed wire that flanked them all the way to the main gate. Behind the walls, gun towers guarded the road with Marines standing at the top and peering down with stony stares. The convoy roared through the massive iron gates and less than twenty seconds later, the doors swung open, and the plows and Humvees trundled inside where a cluster of Marines descended on the vehicles as the gates closed with a heavy clang. Harris popped his door and got out, holding it for the President and sticking by his side as Birk walked to meet other members of his staff. People from the President's cabinet and members of the Senate and Congress got out of the second convoy which arrived a few moments later, and Birk shook hands with everyone.

Harris activated his earpiece microphone. "Westbrook, this is Harris. Skylark is on the mountain. Repeat, Skylark is on the mountain."

"Confirmed. Make sure he gets into the bunker ASAP."

"Understood."

Harris pressed in behind the President and leaned in with a whisper, interrupting Birk as he was speaking with a senator. "Sir, we need to get you inside right away." Harris gestured to a concrete building straight ahead where four Marines flanked another steel door.

With a nod, Birk angled in the indicated direction and as they passed through the doors, Harris stayed close at the President's side, quietly guiding him deeper into the complex as they moved down a long hallway with ceiling lights that cast the drab green walls in a cold glow, and the doors behind them shut with a heavy bang, sealing them in the bunker's protective shell.

CHAPTER TWELVE

Alice Burton
Palm Bay, Florida

Every footstep drove a wedge of pain up through Alice's ankles and shins, leaving her knees sore and even her hips aching as the trio closed in on the outskirts of Palm Beach. They'd been walking beneath the canopy of pitch-black smoke for hours, the flat layer of clouds blending in with the sky as nighttime approached yet again. As Alice and the kids trudged along, Highway A1A grew more littered with wrecked vehicles blown apart haphazardly across the pavement. Countless others had left gaping rips through the rear bumpers and trunks, violently spinning off the road, hurling the passengers across the sand to turn the golden grains brown with dried blood. Vans and delivery trucks were often flipped straight over on their tops, leaving their drivers hanging from the windows with skin so charred it was impossible to tell anything about them except that they'd been human at one point.

She'd long ago stopped trying to shield the children from the gruesome mess, and though she often walked between them and the gory accidents, it did little good with as much violence as surrounded them. She sometimes caught Sarah's eyes lingering on a messy explosion with a flat, emotionless gaze while Jake mostly looked past the wrecks to the people sitting on the beach, clusters of them growing more numerous every mile they walked, their camps marked by glowing bonfires as the sun's heat waned. The kids still wore their backpacks, and Alice had her carryall slung over her shoulder, each of them carrying a share of their meager supplies.

"Mom, this sucks. My feet are killing me," Jake said as he plodded along on her left in a combination of slapping and shuffling feet across the pavement.

Sarah came up on her other side and nodded vigorously in agreement. "My feet don't feel so hot, either."

"And you think my feet feel great?" Alice replied with a smirk.

"Well, can't we stop to rest for a minute?" Sarah pressed. "We've been walking for miles now."

"Now you know why I had you bring extra pairs of socks and shoes. I figured there wouldn't be anything to drive."

"I'd give anything to ride in the worst clunker the world ever made," Jake sulked, swinging his pool cue at more wreckage in the road.

"Even one with two wobbly front tires?" Alice asked with a grin.

"*Especially* one with two wobbly front tires." He smiled back. "As long as my feet and legs get a rest."

Wherever there were small parking lots off to the side, Alice had been searching them for any signs of a single vehicle left untouched, but a majority of the seaside restaurants and beach houses had parking lots full of smoking debris, and there wasn't an intact vehicle in sight. Where there were clusters of still-smoldering vehicles, Alice avoided getting too close due to the still-brutal heat that had ravaged their skin and hair. It was only when they passed a pair of cars parked on the side of the road that Alice stopped her plodding to turn and investigate in detail. They were hatchback rentals with surfboards thrown on top, and at first glance they looked burned like so many other vehicles with scorch marks and tendrils of smoke rising from them, but she noticed something odd and stopped ten feet away behind the second car and stared at the mess.

"I thought you said we weren't supposed to get too close." Sarah held up her arm to shield her face from the heat.

"You two stay here while I check it out. There's something I want to look at."

Coming within about ten feet from the wreckage, Alice shielded her face and walked from the back of the second vehicle all the way around to the front of the first. The most obvious difference was that the lead car had suffered way more damage, its interior black with smoke rolling inside to escape through the shattered windows. The second car had some damage to the front end, though the rest of it seemed relatively untouched. The first car's detonation appeared to have broken the second car's windshield and caused some damage to the front end along with turning the paint black from the heat of its flames, but the second vehicle hadn't actually caught fire itself.

"All I've seen are what look like gas tank explosions." She stared at the second car with a curious tilt of her head. "So why didn't you go up with your buddy?" After staring at the pair of vehicles for a moment, she backed away and gestured to the kids. "Come on, let's go."

"What were you looking for, Mom?" Sarah asked as they continued their march north along Highway A1A.

"I'm starting to notice something interesting, but I can't be totally sure yet."

They were just passing a bait and tackle shop and a carryout seafood place nestled between two large sand dunes when, angling to the left-hand side of the road, Alice peered into the lot to see if she could prove her suspicions.

"Something with the fuel," Alice murmured as they trudged along.

Her heels were aching, and a sharp pain was developing in one of her knees, but still, she studied the cars and trucks they passed, growing more curious with each passing vehicle, observing the way some fires had raged in the high-traffic areas and picking out vehicles that didn't appear to have had their fuel tanks ruptured like most vehicles had, but had merely been in the proximity of others and caught fire.

With more traffic congestion came more poor souls who'd perished in the catastrophe; bystanders had been struck by flying debris and lay dead but unburned in the sand while some appeared to have died trying to help others from their burning cars. Each explosion was different, depending on the model and vehicle type. Lighter cars usually popped straight up or spun any which way while heavier trucks and vans rolled over or simply blew out in bursts of deadly debris to pepper unfortunate bystanders. The horrible reek of burning rubber, engine fluid, and fried fat made her want to gag, and she motioned at the kids.

"We need to get away from this," she said. "Let's walk on the sidewalk next to the beach."

Jake's voice was thick with emotion for the first time since they had set out. "But we wouldn't get away from any of this. Look, it's everywhere. Wrecks all along the road and everything smashed to bits..." He stopped talking, and when Alice glanced over at him, he was rubbing his eyes and cheeks to try and mask a few stray tears.

Alice stepped closer and gave him a hug, and the pair walked side by side for a while as she patted his shoulder and fed him words of encouragement. "We'll be far enough away from it on this side. See?"

Her words held true for a quarter of a mile, then the congestion on the right-hand side got worse, and the heat and smell forced them onto the sand to avoid the massive oval spread of debris that covered the beach and dunes in every direction.

"Okay, let's switch to sandals for a minute," Alice said, gesturing to a clear section of walkway near the sand where they could sit and exchange socks and shoes for something lighter.

"Can't we go barefoot, Mom?" Sarah asked as she dug out her sandals and sat next to her backpack where the sidewalk met sand.

"There's no way we're walking through this sand in bare feet." Alice shook her head. "There's bound to be sharp objects and glass everywhere."

"No way," Jake said as he sat next to his sister and took off his shoes and socks, dusting his feet off before slipping his pool flip-flops on. "That's got to be at least a hundred yards or more."

"You were standing right there when those cars exploded at the restaurant. What do you think?"

"Mm. I guess you're right."

After putting their tennis shoes and socks away, they shouldered their loads and began walking along the beach. It felt easier at first because the sand was much softer on Alice's ankles than the concrete, though it still radiated the sun's heat, and their progress went from slow to sluggish in no time flat as they struggled against the shifting sands. As they angled closer to the lapping waves, she focused on the tranquil sea as it continued its tidal routine and flowed in to lap at those who took refuge on the beach. The number of people had tripled since they'd first started seeing the bonfires and Alice tapped Jake on the arm with her pool cue, giving her weapon a wave to remind him he needed to use it if anyone bothered them, and he nodded and grinned in reply.

While many of the car fires had faded, the noxious fumes pushed the trio farther off the road toward the refugees. They caught snippets of conversations as families pulled together the supplies they had managed to salvage or listened to radios that blared that same emergency message repeatedly. Most of them ignored Alice and the kids, though others gave them sidelong glances either bordering on friendly or downright sour. There was a healthy mix of tourists and locals, judging by the number of backpacks and pieces of luggage lying around in the sand. Clothes were strewn everywhere, and propane camping stoves were set up on card tables and one man took meat from a cooler and cooked it on a charcoal grill like it was any old family beach party set against the peaceful backdrop of the ocean.

Alice kept the children to her left so she'd be between them and the refugees, though she caught a glance from one friendly woman who was sitting on a lawn chair with a half-consumed bottle of wine in her lap as she stared into the flames of their bonfire. Her husband was a burly man wearing flip-flops and swimming trunks with an old T-shirt beneath a button-up tropical print and he was walking around the campfire, tossing in pieces of wood and furniture they must've taken from one of the beach houses on the other side of the road. After he'd fed the fire, he used a stick to stoke the flames, jumping back with a grunt when the wind carried the smoke in his direction.

The woman looked up, struggling to focus on them at first before she gave them a wide smile. "Hey there, folks! Welcome to our little part of the beach."

"Hello, there!" Alice called, keeping her distance as she waved.

"You all from around here?"

"No," Alice and the kids stopped walking. "We were just coming from South Beach when everything went up in flames."

"Our place was right over there!" The man pointed back across the road with a sad smile. "Our car went up like everyone else's, and then our house did, too. I salvaged a lot of furniture so we could have a fire tonight, though. Why don't you guys join us?"

"No, that's okay," Alice forced a friendly smile. "Do you know of any places to spend the night, though? You know, someplace safe for kids? Like a motel or something?"

"Oh, I don't think you'll find any place around here like that," the man said with a glance at his wife, who only shrugged, her head wobbling from the effects of the wine. "I heard there might be a couple of places back south, but everyone's stuck on the beach for now... at least those who survived." A gust of wind blew his wispy hair around as he stared toward Palm Beach. "Most folks didn't, from what I hear."

"But do you know what happened or if the government is going to respond?"

"We haven't heard anything, have we, honey?"

The woman shook her head and tilted back her bottle of wine.

Alice frowned. "You haven't heard any radio broadcasts?"

He gestured to their packs. "Oh, we've got one, but it's just the same emergency broadcast message. There are a couple of radio stations that have been in and out throughout the day, but none of them have much information and they don't stay transmitting for long."

"I heard one of them." Alice nodded. "I think it was WFLA."

"That's the one." The man snapped his fingers. "He's doing the best he can to stay on, but they just don't have the power to do it."

"My only regret is that we didn't vacation on the Gulf side," the woman said, suddenly wistful as she stared at the dark horizon. "At least then we could've seen the sunset over the Gulf."

"That would have been pretty," Alice replied, taking a few steps in the direction they were headed. "Well, we appreciate the help. Thank you both."

"Oh, you guys can stay if you want to." The woman gestured toward the fire. "We've got some food and can probably share some."

"No thanks," Alice said with a smile. "We're trying to get north right now, but thanks so much for your offer."

As Alice and the kids left the couple, the woman gave them a faint wave before tilting the wine bottle up to her lips again. Moving on, they stepped between the bonfires and gatherings of survivors, some of whom had pulled up burn barrels and were pushing and jostling each other, blasting loud music from boomboxes as they acted like it was any other night at the beach. The very next fire was occupied by a younger couple with a pair of kids playing down by the surf. As they came up, Alice saw one child using the curved part of a taillight to scoop sand and move it to a larger pile where they were making a sad-looking castle. Next to a pile of broken furniture, their fire glowed bright and warm as the sun descended farther over the edge of the horizon, painting the night sky pitch black above the canopy of dark clouds. The Florida winds began stirring things around and bringing a bit of relief off the cool ocean waters. The man was squatting in the sand and stoking the flames with a metal pole while the woman stood facing the waves and watching the kids play.

Alice called out as she stopped ten yards from their fire. "Hi, folks! Hey there. Do you have a second?"

The man stood with his chest out and pole cocked back, fixing Alice with a dark stare at first before his hard expression faded when he saw her kids. "Sorry about that," he chuckled nervously and glanced toward the other camps. "I thought you were one of those troublemakers. Uh, hi. How are you folks doing? I guess that's a dumb question, right?"

"Kind of." Alice stepped closer with a hesitant smile. "It's still good to be congenial. It makes things seem a bit normal, right?"

The man laughed. "Sure it does."

The woman walked around the fire and approached Alice and the kids with a smile. "Hey there!" She was in her bare feet with a pair of cutoff jean shorts and a summer top. "Excuse us if we're a little on edge right now."

Alice looked around. "Did you run into some trouble or something?"

"Kind of." The woman gestured down the beach to the myriad of bonfires and laughing teenagers. "Some of the teens are getting too rowdy for us, especially since we have a couple of young kids. My name is Jeannie, by the way. My husband is Bernie."

Alice introduced herself and the kids before turning to glance up the beach. "They threaten you or anything?"

"Not exactly, but they're acting like this is just a great big party and not a major disaster. They seem to think help is going to come swooping in at any moment." She gestured to her husband. "But we've been listening to our radio, and we heard the emergency broadcast message. It doesn't sound like a minor emergency."

Alice nodded. "And it's definitely not a party."

"Exactly," Jeannie agreed. "That's why we've been staying away from them and keeping to ourselves. We've got a couple of suitcases of supplies, but we don't think it's going to last very long."

Bernie pushed his metal pole into the sand and leaned on it. "And judging from the state of Palm Beach, we're not seeing much help on the horizon."

"Were you staying in Palm Beach?"

"That's right. We'd been staying in town when everything just started... yeah. Every car in our motel lot just exploded. The place caught on fire pretty quick..." Bernie shook his head in exasperation. "We and a few other folks barely got out in time, but our rental car had gone up, too. All we could do was jam anything we could into our suitcases and roll them down the road to get away from the fire. It would've looked comical if not for other people doing the same thing."

"It was worse for a lot of people," Jeannie said sadly. "We saw so many people burning up and dying left and right, but we couldn't stop to help." The words came out in a sudden rush of emotion. "We wanted to stop... believe me, we did, but we had our kids to think about and had to get them out of there."

"I'm sure you did. What about the police and fire department? Were they helping anyone?"

"Cops? Firefighters? They're in the same shape everyone else is, I reckon," Bernie replied with an offhanded wave. "It's not like they could have helped, anyway." The man shook his head and glanced back at the smoldering city, his eyes hollow as his voice dropped to a near-whisper. "I've never seen or smelled anything like it. It was like a nightmare."

"I'm sorry you had to go through that," Alice looked at Jake and Sarah. "We've seen our share of horrors, too, and we walked a pretty long way to get here. The number of places that are actually intact is... pretty low."

"Not to mention those pair at the house who tried to rob us," Jake added, using his pool cue to swat at the sand.

"Aren't they afraid people will start looting businesses and stuff?" Alice asked. "I've always seen reports on the news when hurricanes hit the coast, and it seems like that's one of the biggest problems."

Bernie gave a sigh. "Hate to tell you this, Alice, but there's nothing really left to loot, and it seems most people are just happy to have a little food, water, and space on the beach for now." He shot the groups of younger kids a dark glance. "Except for a few people who have nothing at all. Those are the ones I'm watching out for. Otherwise, I guess there hasn't been any real need for law enforcement yet."

"Well, thank heavens for small favors, I guess."

"Heaven seems to have gone up in smoke with the rest of it," Bernie said, and the group stood in silence for a moment, watching the flames of the couple's fire.

"You folks have a good night, and stay safe," Alice said. "We're going to keep walking."

"You, too," the couple replied almost simultaneously. "Stay safe out there," Bernie added.

As Jeanie turned back to her kids to check them, Alice gestured for Sarah and Jake to keep up as she moved on, picking her way past more bonfires and burn barrels, heading for the lapping waves that reflected the orange flicker amidst their vast darkness. They got close enough so the cool waters washed across their feet, rinsing off the sand and heat of the day. As they moved up the beach, Alice fell into her own thoughts, staring at the sea of camps and fires along the shoreline, though the city's burning brightness was dimming fast in the coming night. It was only when Sarah came up and leaned against her that she snapped out of it.

"Can we rest, Mom?" the girl asked. "Jake is lagging behind."

Alice turned to see her son had fallen fifteen or twenty yards back, and she stopped and gestured for him to come over. "Yes, kids. I think it's time to find a place to settle in for the night. Not this close to the water though; we need to find somewhere sheltered."

Picking a path between the bonfires and groups of milling people, Alice guided the kids up the beach toward a row of sand dunes nestled together in a bed of tall beach grass. Delving into the nooks and sandy furrows, they searched for anything they could use to build a camp. Alice was drawn to an area where a few small families had gathered, the kids playing by the fires with their parents hovering protectively over them. Without bothering them, Alice used her pool cue to poke around in the tall grass and loose sand, calling for Jake and Sarah when she hit something metallic.

"Over here, kids. Help me."

Between the three of them, they pushed aside tall grasses to expose a rusted-out barrel half-buried in the sand. Jake used his hands and pool cue to dig it out, while Sarah found a curved piece of metal debris from a car door to help dig as well. After a few minutes, they had the barrel exposed and raised it onto its bottom edge, enabling them to roll it out of the tall grass and rest it upright.

Alice dusted off her hands and nodded with satisfaction. "You guys walk around and try to collect some driftwood for the barrel, but don't go far, okay?" Alice placed her pack down, knelt next to it, and took out a bottle of water.

"What are you going to do, Mom?"

"I'm going to see if I can make a trade." Turning, she pointed to the surrounding dune. "I'm serious, guys. If you can't see me anymore, then you've gone too far."

"Okay!" Sarah took Jake by the arm and guided him toward the darkening sand hills to swim through the tall beach grasses. Almost immediately, they snagged a couple pieces of driftwood and tossed them closer to the barrel.

While they worked, Alice turned away from the kids and meandered into the crowds of gathered families, glancing back at the kids as she went. Satisfied no one seemed to be bothering them or their things, she spun in a circle in search of a friendly face, finally spotting a thirty-ish man tending to his own fire with three young children under five years of age tottering around in the firelight. He wore bright red swimming trunks, brown sandals, and an old yellow T-shirt with a faded palm tree on the left breast. Every few seconds, he would stop to guide the youngest one off to the side to ensure she didn't get too close to the flames.

Alice approached hesitantly and called out from a distance. "Hello, sir!" When the man whipped around with a dark look, she held out her hands in a placating gesture. "Sorry. I didn't mean to startle you, but I had a question."

"Don't worry about it, ma'am." His scowl faded as he tried to smile. "I guess everyone's a little jumpy with the world going up like it has."

"Isn't that the truth? I was just wondering if we could get a piece of wood or some coals from you to help get our fire started." With a glance over at the kids where they were still searching through the beach grass, she gave him a smile. "We've walked so many miles today and could really use a break. I see your fire is going pretty well." Alice raised her eyebrows in question and held out her bottled water. "I can trade you a bottled water for it."

Following her gaze over to the dunes where the kids had a decent sized pile going, the man shook his head. "That's okay, ma'am. I'll give you a piece of wood, but I won't take your water."

"Are you sure? We've got enough for now, and you must have put in some time gathering what you have there. Surely one of your little ones can use this."

The man reached into his fire with his foot and kicked out a piece of dark driftwood that was burning on one end, and then he stooped to pick it up and hand it over. "Go ahead and take it, and don't worry about paying me. You've got kids, too, and you need to get a fire going before it gets too cold."

"Well, okay." Alice hesitantly accepted the piece of smoldering wood and held the burning end away from her face and hair. "If you insist."

"I do. It's just... I know how it is with kids, and not having my wife here to help has made things really tough."

"I know the feeling," Alice replied with an empathetic nod. "My husband is in Denver right now, and I wish more than anything he could be here with us. Is your wife...."

"She was at home when everything went ballistic. I had taken the kids for the day to give her a break." The man turned his attention back to the fire where he kicked some other pieces around to stoke the flames. "I have no idea if she's alive or not," he lowered his voice, "and I can't drag three kids through a burning city to find her."

"I'm so sorry... I can't imagine what that's like."

A smile broke out on his face as he leaned over and caught his youngest girl, who was toddling too close to the fire and guided her toward her siblings who were playing in the sand a few feet away. Straightening, he went back to kicking the wood before stopping to bow his head. "I'm doing the best I can to stay strong for them, but it's so hard..." A sob broke from his lips as his shoulders slouched.

Alice stepped closer and gave him a one-armed hug and a pat on the back. "I don't know you, but you seem like a good guy. I can't imagine being out here with three little ones. At least mine are somewhat self-sufficient. I'm sure your wife would be incredibly thankful to know yours are safe."

Shaking his head and rubbing his eyes, he swiped tears off his cheeks. "We can't even be sure we'll see each other again."

"Hey, it's okay." Alice gave him another brief hug, still holding the stick with her other hand. "Do you live close by?"

"About forty miles away in Lake Harbor. We've got a nice little place there, but it's a lot of work taking care of it. Marjorie does such a great job... The only reason we came here is to give her some time to herself. Now she's all alone, and my kids are cut off from their mother."

"Don't lose hope. As soon as some of this clears up, you'll have a clear path home. You'll be back in Lake Harbor before you know it. Look at us. We're not panicking too much, and we've got to get all the way to Michigan."

"That's a long, long way." The man wiped his arm across his eyes. "How do you stay strong?"

"I don't have a choice in the matter. Neither one of us does. So, take care of your little ones, and good luck."

"Thanks, ma'am," he replied with a smile toward Sarah and Jake. "Make sure you guys get some rest and stay safe."

"We will. And thank you so much." She waved the burning driftwood. "This means a lot. If you need anything, just let me know and we'll do what we can."

Leaving with a nod, Alice took the wood to their barrel and used her free hand to scoop up a few pieces the kids had gathered, tossing them in and shifting them around so there was room for airflow. After packing some dry beach grass at the bottom, she leaned in and dropped the blazing piece inside atop the grass. Soon, flames began licking up the sides of the barrel as the fire spread from the grass to the driftwood, giving off a vibrant warmth.

"How's it going, Mom?" Jake came up and stood on the tips of his toes to peer in at the glowing light.

"Pretty good, I think," Alice replied, using a longer piece to stir the wood inside the barrel a little more.

"Y'know, we, uh, could have just gone to one of the fires burning over there and gotten some wood started that way." Jake motioned further inland.

"But then we wouldn't have made a new friend to help watch our backs, now would we?" She winked at him.

Stepping away from the flames, Alice turned and inspected the pile of beach debris they'd collected, which included some nice thick chunks of driftwood and garbage. "Nice work on gathering all this, guys. Everything I'm seeing here should burn nicely."

Sarah stood from where she'd been leaning in the tall grass with a couple more pieces tucked under her left arm. "Do you think that's enough for now?"

"Yes, that's fine, honey. Bring it on over and we'll settle in for the night. Let's use some blankets from our packs to sit on."

Jake fell onto his knees in the sand and flipped his backpack's flap up to take out two small blankets. With Sarah's help, he got them spread out as Alice removed three plastic-wrapped bagels and a pack of cookies from her bag and handed them out. The three ate in silence, Alice's attention drifting to the thick layers of clouds above them, gazing up Highway

A1A to Palm Beach where the horizon was nothing but embers and smoke. When they were finished eating, Alice had them wash down their food with some water before splitting a juice pouch with them.

She gestured to their supplies, which Sarah had laid out. "What are we working with here, guys?"

"We've got three blankets and two of the smaller pillows from the beach house, but that's it as far as bedding stuff goes. We can probably bundle up some of our clothes to use as pillows, too."

"That'll work." Alice pulled her carryall closer. "As far as food goes, we've got quite a few bottled waters and a few snacks from the hotel."

"And the cans we took from those people who attacked us, right?" Jake added.

"That's right," she replied. "And I just found a side pocket in my bag with some candy bars and snacks I'd planned on taking to the beach today."

"Sounds like we're in okay shape, then." Jake said.

Alice frowned and rested back with her hands on her thighs. "For now. That's about it for the food, though. I've got a couple of battery packs to charge my phone, and we've got the pool cues for defense."

"We'll be okay, Mom." Sarah gave her a hug.

Alice smiled and glanced at the faraway blazes before crawling toward the kids and hugging them close. "I think so, kiddo. Are you two ready to hit the hay?"

"I've been ready for a while," Sarah replied, packing their loose items into their backpacks and spacing the blankets out a little more to give them some room.

Jake grabbed a pillow for himself and laid down between them, dropping back with a heavy sigh as he kicked his sandals off. Alice placed all their supplies at the edge of the blanket near their feet and close to the burn barrel, the sides of which were growing warm, helping to keep the night's chill away.

"All right then." Alice rolled up a couple of shirts to place beneath her head and turned onto her left side with her pool cue between herself and Jake. "This is it. Our first night on the beach. Not exactly how I pictured it, but it beats nothing, I suppose."

"Mom, can I read for a few minutes? I won't sleep otherwise."

Alice raised onto her elbow and saw Sarah sitting up with her e-reader in her lap. "Go ahead, honey. But just for a minute. I want you to be fully rested when we have to get up and start walking again."

"I will. I promise I'll be asleep in ten minutes."

"Okay."

Getting settled again, Alice stretched one arm above her head and draped it over Jake while curling her knees together as the soft sand shifted beneath the blanket. For the first few minutes, she couldn't stop her mind from racing through the events of the past two days. The explosions, smoke, and fires, and the blur of people they'd met along the way, some of whom had tried to hurt them. Those on the beach seemed nice enough, and Alice found her worry fading beneath the weariness of the day's travels. With her back and neck relaxing, she sighed as the stiffness that had gripped her spine all day evaporated. For a few minutes, the glow from Sarah's e-reader shone until she put it in its case and shifted on her side to snuggle against her brother. Not long after, the kids' light snores joined the steady lapping of the ocean waves breaking across the sand.

Alice fought sleep for a while more, trying to stay up and make sure they were safe, but with the families nearby and the lull of the ocean, she soon fell into a dreamless sleep. A long time passed before she stirred awake and heard someone rustling near her feet and she opened her eyes, expecting to see Sarah getting into the food for an extra snack, but her heart skipped a beat when she saw the man with the yellow shirt kneeling beside their packs, rifling through their things. He'd already found the candy bars and snacks in the side pocket and had lined them up on a folded blanket. Next to those, he'd placed most of their bottled waters and her portable battery packs. Too stunned and groggy to move at first, Alice watched him pack everything he'd taken into Jake's backpack, then the realization that most of their things were about to be stolen hit her with full force and she rolled over and leaped up with a cry, feet spread in a fighting stance as she brandished her pool cue at him.

"Hey! What the hell do you think you're doing?!"

The man glanced up and rose quickly, taking Jake's backpack and started to turn away. "Just go back to sleep, lady. Nobody needs to get hurt here."

Alice came around to flank him, nostrils flaring as she glared, raising the cue back in a hitter's stance. "One more step, and I'll crack this over your head! Drop the bag!"

The man snorted. "I doubt that. Just back—"

Alice lunged as he was mid-sentence, striking him in the upper shoulder with a loud crack. Staying on him, she hit him repeatedly, searching for soft spots and aiming for his legs. When he covered those, she struck high again, cracking sharp blows against his upraised arm and landing a few on his head as Sarah and Jake came awake with startled cries.

"Dammit, lady!" The man howled with pain as he stumbled around, trying to protect himself.

"Drop the bag!" Alice shouted, her blood boiling as she hacked at his unprotected body.

The man danced back, twisting through the sand and kicking it up as he tried to ward off her blows, finally dropping Jake's backpack and hopping away. Alice pursued him for another five yards, driving him off with sharp swings, the muscles of her arms bulging with tension as she carried out her attack. With a frustrated snarl, he lunged at her and snatched at the weapon, but she retreated and kept herself between the man and their possessions.

"We've already beaten two people halfway to the emergency room for trying to steal from us," she growled. When the man didn't immediately back off, Alice sidestepped, swung her hips around, and raised the cue above her shoulder. "Don't make us do it again!"

"I need that stuff for my kids!"

Alice's face contorted into a confused expression. "I don't get it. I already offered you a water, and I told you I'd help you, and this is how you thank me? By stealing from me?!"

"It doesn't matter now." He spat the words as he rubbed at his shoulder, the skin already turning a dark purple. "You were right. I've got three kids to care for, and they're younger than yours." Desperation filled his eyes as his pained grimace was replaced by a flat and resolute stare. "They can't take care of themselves like yours can. Mine need me, lady, and that means I have to do this now before things get worse."

"Do *what*?"

The man's hand slipped toward his pocket and a shiver ran down between Alice's shoulders, and she slowly shook her head in warning. "Whatever it is you think you have to do, just stop. You can still walk away from this."

Something changed in the man's eyes, his face turning into a snarl, and he pulled a four-inch pocketknife out and flipped open the blade, lunging at her with the sharp tip aimed at her belly. Alice began stepping into a swing, twisting her hips with every ounce of strength she had, but Jake flew in from the side and struck the man in the legs, bending him at the hip and buckling him in two, sending him tumbling face-first into the sand with his arms thrown wide. Adjusting her swing, Alice took a step left and brought the pool cue down on the man's wrist, striking it with a sharp snap of bone. The knife flew free as he jerked back and rolled away from her, avoiding a second swipe that nearly took his nose off. Switching the pool cue to her offhand, Alice dove for the knife and scooped it up before he could get to it, then she fell into a crouch and retreated as she held the blade out in front of her.

"Stay back!" she shouted. "Stay away from me and my kids. Leave us alone or I swear I'll *gut* you!"

The man started to get up and charge her again, but she lunged at him, driving him back to the sand as several people from other campfires began walking up, fathers and mothers keeping their own children behind them as they stared curiously at the altercation. One man stepped forward as if he was going to get involved when the attacker's kids came running up bawling.

"Daddy!" the oldest one screamed as she rushed forward, her voice echoing up the beach with her face twisted in panic. "Please don't hurt my daddy!" Throwing her arms around the man's neck, she fell against him as the other two stood close by, crying in confusion, looking on at their injured father. With a grumble, the man got up, holding his wrist that had an unnatural bend in it and stayed between Alice and his children. "Stay behind me, kids," he told them.

"What happened, Daddy?" the girl whined again, staring at Alice.

"Sorry, little girl," Alice said in a pleading voice, rubbing the knife against her pant leg to clean off the sand. "I wasn't going to hurt him, but your daddy attacked us."

"I had to," the man griped, backing his children toward their campfire with a scowl. "I have to do whatever it takes to survive."

Jake got up and dusted himself off, panting and out of breath from his take-down, ready to do it again if necessary.

"That's true," Alice replied with a snarl. "But I'd never steal food out of your mouth *or* your children's mouths. You should be ashamed of yourself. Especially after we *offered* to help you."

"You have no idea what..." the man spat, but when he noticed a couple of fathers and mothers stepping toward him, he stopped, gave a final icy glare at Alice, then guided his kids back to his campfire as the other families watched.

"What's wrong with him?" Sarah asked, coming around the burn barrel to stand at Alice's side.

"Nothing. He's just desperate and afraid and he picked the wrong people to mess with." Handing Jake her pool cue, she folded the knife and stuffed it into her pocket, then she picked up the dropped backpack and carried it back to the blankets as the rest of the families returned to their own spots on the beach. Turning to Jake, she gave him a brief hug and a kiss on the head. "Thanks again, Jake."

"No problem, Mom." The boy's eyes were glassy as his jaw worked back and forth. "There was no way I was going to let that guy hurt you. He was going to *stab* you."

"And you saved me." Letting him go, she turned and gazed out at the ocean, taking a deep breath as she watched the man get his kids settled in their own camp.

"Are we still going to stay here now?" Sarah asked, coming to stand next to her.

"Yes. We'll stay here for the night."

"After all that?"

"Pretty sure I broke his wrist, and he's not going to try anything again. Plus we can't guarantee there won't be similar problems if we go down the beach. No, we really need the rest, and we have as much of a right to be here as they do. I'll stay up and keep watch for a while."

Despite their uneasiness, Jake and Sarah went back to their blankets and settled in with Alice curled up next to them. She held the pool cue in one hand and the knife in her other, and while the kids soon quit their restless tossing and turning and fell into a sleep of comfort and light snores, Alice kept both eyes open, staring past their burn barrel and the other campfires to gaze out across the deep, dark ocean.

While Alice had tried to stay awake all night, the lonely sounds of the sea finally won out and pulled her into a dreamless sleep. She woke up a couple of hours before dawn to the sounds of seagulls screeching and diving for scraps along the shore. Jake was already up, sitting with his pool cue at the ready, keeping an eye on the man and his kids who were still sleeping. Alice patted his leg before she roused Sarah.

"Okay, kids. It's time to go."

Sarah sat up and rubbed her eyes grumpily. "It's not even morning yet, Mom. Do we have to go already?"

"While I'd love to sleep a couple more hours, I think it's best we got up and hit the road before anyone else. Go on. Get your things together."

Sarah tucked her e-reader and other items into her backpack, while Alice made sure they'd picked up all their wrappers and empty water bottles. She and Jake dusted off their blankets, folded them, and placed them neatly into Sarah's backpack. Hoisting their backpacks onto their shoulders, the kids started walking along the beach, but Alice caught their attention and tilted her head for them to follow her.

Working her way through the dwindling campfires, Alice watched the families dozing in the light of the glowing embers, still sleeping in spite of the devastation thanks to the crackling fires and sweeping rhythm of the ocean waves. When she reached the man in the yellow shirt and his kids where they were curled up on a meager blanket, Alice stopped and sighed softly at the sight. She took four water bottles from her carryall and placed them in the sand next to the man before gesturing at Jake and Sarah to quietly follow her.

Once they'd gotten a respectable distance away, Sarah kept pace at her mother's side. "What did you do that for, Mom? That guy tried to rob us and stab you. You didn't have to give him anything."

"I know, honey. Sometimes people do desperate things, but that doesn't mean they're bad people, at least not all the way to their core. I couldn't let those little ones suffer because of something their father did. As bad as what he did was, he was doing it for his children."

"You'd do the same for us, wouldn't you?" Sarah replied.

"Without hesitation."

"How does that make us better than him, then?" Jake asked.

"Oh, now, that's a tough one," Alice raised an eyebrow at him. "We'll always do our best to survive without harming other people. He could have asked us for help, or done any number of things other than trying to steal from – and hurt – people who he'd just met who tried to help him. We'll do our best to be far, far better than that."

Jake nodded, both kids contemplating what she said as they continued on, walking a good distance down the beach before she bade them move closer to the sidewalk and switch from their sandals back to their socks and shoes. Jake and

Sarah sat and brushed their feet off, and Alice joined them, using a washcloth to get the grains out from between her toes and passing it along to the kids to do the same.

"Make sure you clean your feet completely," she told them. "If you don't, you'll be grinding sand in your socks the whole way."

Once changed, they got started again, keeping close to the beach to avoid burned-out cars and people lingering on the road in the pre-dawn haze. Sections of Highway A1A grew more cluttered by the mile as they approached Palm Bay. The road was littered with strings of accidents Alice was certain were caused by gas tank explosions, though many engines were smoking and blown out with a haze still rising from the hot metal. As dawn's light fell across the landscape, the golden rays barely pierced the pitch-black clouds of smoke, a few meager sunbeams managing to break through and make shapes on the pavement that shifted as the smoke and clouds above roiled. The long road leading to the city was nothing but smoking dunes and refugees on the beach who were rising to start a new and dreary day. On the road, the charred bodies grew more numerous as they walked, and Alice steered away from them as much as possible. The once-gorgeous highway had been changed in the blink of an eye, transforming from a beautiful parade of beaches into a roadway of nightmares, death, and wreckage as far as the eye could see.

Still, there were exceptions to the wanton destruction, all seeming to depend on how many cars were parked near buildings and which way the wind had been blowing when the fires were raging full-tilt. Some blocks had caught fire for as far into the city as she could make out, and other buildings were still standing, miraculously spared from the destruction due to a change in the wind or their relative isolation.

Finally reaching a clear spot of beach off to the right, Alice took a deep breath of clean ocean air as a breeze came in and blew her dark hair off her shoulders. Glancing back to the left, she noticed a few small businesses, which included a coffee shop with a bamboo storefront and palm trees in front that remained untouched by the catastrophic infernos. In between them was a string of car dealerships and vehicle rental lots with a few blackened wrecks still smoking, though a few cars had somehow avoided going up like the rest. Angling to the other side of the road, they stepped past an overturned sedan with something inside still crackling with flames that belched smoke through its back end. The sidewalk was separated from a rental lot by a short strip of grass and several cars parked right up front were damaged, though it was just from the shrapnel blown off from other vehicles going up in flames on the road, leaving them with shattered windshields and hoods covered in debris and ash. A string of three were lined up side-by-side and left virtually untouched by the destruction, two sedans and an SUV with a small frame, their paint still shining and new.

"How come these didn't burn up?" Sarah asked as the trio paused in front of the vehicles, in awe of the find.

"That's a great question," Alice said. "Let's go check it out."

She crossed the small grassy section and stepped between the sedan and SUV, the brand familiar from some commercial she'd recently seen. Turning her attention to the dealership with its pristine white walls and navy blue trim, she noticed an italicized two-letter abbreviation in the bottom corner of the sign that focused her spark of a memory.

"I think I know what this is."

"What?" Sarah asked.

Alice pointed to the *EV* emblem on the side of the car that matched the one on the dealership's sign. "These are that new electric vehicle brand that just came out last year. I think your grandma and grandpa have one of these."

"Is that why they didn't explode?" Jake asked, running his hand along the slick hood before dusting off his hands with a sour expression.

"It seems so." Alice circled around behind the vehicles, took a few paces farther into the lot, and stood looking at the SUV with her hands on her hips.

"I've been thinking about this for a while now, what with all the blown-up cars and trucks and everything else, and it seems to me their gas tanks were the culprits, which leads me to believe this had something to do with the fuel. And it lines up with what Andrea was saying about her generators still running."

"Because they're running on older fuel?" Sarah asked.

"That's what I'm thinking."

"Does that mean we can get in one of these and try to drive it?" Jake looked up hopefully. "Since it's electric and not gas?"

Alice circled to the SUV's driver's side door and pulled the handle, surprised when it opened, then slid behind the wheel and took a deep breath of the new car smell. The seats were gray leather with a dashboard that included a large digital display in the middle and a sleek looking instrument panel. There was a single start button, but when Alice pushed it, the vehicle didn't start up. "Too much to hope for, I guess," she mumbled as she got out, shut the door, and stared at the dealership, which had an office section with a couple of maintenance bays around the side.

"I say we go inside and see if there's a key." The words sounded odd as they passed her lips. A week ago, she wouldn't have been caught dead contemplating stealing a car. With the world how it was, though, it seemed like less of a luxury and more of a necessity to their very survival.

The kids followed her through the lot as they passed a few other unburned vehicles and approached the large glass storefront where more models sat inside on the slick tile floors. There were no people inside that Alice could see, and when she pulled the front door handle, it opened smoothly. They stepped into a cool, quiet lobby with several desk-style cubicles where salespeople would sit with customers to go over contracts and leasing agreements. There was a waiting area immediately in front of them with a round desk, two rows of plain chairs, and a snack section with vending machines, a sink, and a simple coffee maker. Behind that was a wall with a mural that stretched in a high arc above some doors that led to the rear of the shop and maintenance bays.

"You guys hang out in that waiting area." Alice pointed to the rows of chairs. "Why don't you get a couple of snacks out and take a break while I look around for some keys?"

After the kids got settled into a pair of seats, Alice walked through the lobby area to a door that read *Sales Staff Only*. Inside were more rows of cubicles set up with all the desks covered in printers and stacks of papers and boxes. Immediately to her right was a corkboard with several key fobs pinned to it, each with a small tag with lot numbers and vehicle information written on the back.

Alice began going through each one, flipping the tags over and trying to remember what model it read on the side of the SUV. "I think it was a Jet Star," she mumbled, looking until she found the right one. Holding it for a moment, she shook off the momentary pang of guilt. "This is silly. Look at it out there. It's crazy, and everyone's dead or gone, so it isn't wrong to take one of these. No one's going to miss one little electric SUV at this point in the game. And we *need* it to get home."

Alice put the key fob in her pocket and walked back to the main lobby where Jake was out of his seat, looking at a brochure stand as he chewed. "Where's your sister?"

"Oh, she went through that door to check out the garage or something." He pointed to one of the doors beneath the mural and went back to his brochure-reading.

With a frown, Alice stalked toward the door, whipped it open, and stepped through to find Sarah out on the floor, walking between the empty bays and looking through the vast arrays of tools.

"Sarah!"

Her daughter flashed a smile. "Oh, hi mom. I was just out here trying to find something we could use."

Alice came up to her, sighing heavily. "I appreciate that, but you can't just wander off alone, okay?"

"Oh... right. Sorry. But I found something cool!"

"Which is?" Alice quashed her annoyance over Sarah's disregard for basic safety for the moment as her daughter pointed at a squarish looking device about as tall as Alice's knee with a big handle on the front and wheels in back, its gauges and plug-ins built-in next to a starter button.

"I think this is some kind of generator or something. You know, like the kind we took camping that one time so we could charge our phones? There are some solar panels to keep it charged up, too."

Leaning closer, Alice read the specs on a white sticker on the side, which showed information for amps and wattages. "Ohhh, no, this is even better than that. This looks to be a charger for these cars. Probably some kind of emergency kit, or something they use off-road."

"And look, there are some solar panels over here with the same brand name on them." Sarah walked over to another rolling bench where a stack of flexible solar panels rested alongside some neatly bundled cables.

The slim panels were each about as thick as a notebook, with one side filled with shiny solar cells and a cable coming out of their left and right sides. When she picked one up, it was light but felt durable, and the perfect size to slip into the back of the SUV.

"You struck paydirt, kiddo. You take the panels and I'll grab the generator."

"We're taking all this with us?"

"Absolutely. Don't forget the cables."

Sarah grabbed the stack of panels and tucked them and the cables under her arms while Alice grabbed the generator by the handle and wheeled it toward the door. When they stepped back into the lobby, Jake leapt up from his chair to come help.

"Whoa!" he asked. "What's that?"

"This is a generator we can use on our trip home."

"Does this mean…"

"That's right," Alice replied. "We're going to drive out of here in that SUV."

"Yes!" Jake gave a hop and spin. "Are we leaving now?"

"Nope." *In for a penny, in for a pound, Alice.* "We're going to get some food out of this vending machine first."

Leaving the generator by the chairs, Alice strode over to the vending machine, a slightly older model with a clear plastic front, about half filled with chip bags, granola bars, and a few packs of cookies. Not the most mom-friendly selection, but in a choice between cookies and starvation, it was a no-brainer.

"How are you going to get that open?" Jake asked.

Turning to Sarah, Alice said, "Honey, why don't you run back into the garage and grab me a nice heavy crowbar or hammer or something? Biggest you can carry, preferably with a really nice sharp point on one end."

"Sure, Mom!" She ran out to the maintenance area.

By the time Sarah came back grinning and holding a greasy crowbar, Alice had picked the best spot to hit. Taking the tool in a tight grip, she held it back and glanced aside.

"Okay, kids. Step back. I have no idea what this is going to do."

They moved away and gave her some room, and Alice pressed the end of the crowbar to the plastic front before she pulled back and struck hard, sending a reverberation through the entire machine. When it didn't break, she wound up again and swung repeatedly, slamming metal against plastic and ripping sharp lines in the weakening spot until, on the sixth strike, it shattered into three pieces and fell inward with a clatter.

"Nice work, Mom!" Jake shouted.

"Thanks," she replied, handing the crowbar to Sarah before she began carefully picking out the big plastic pieces, trying not to cut herself as she moved them aside and rested them against the wall. With the entire contents of the vending machine left open, she motioned for the kids. "Guys, bring over my carryall and your packs."

The kids brought them over, and Alice neatly packed everything she could pull out of the vending machine, taking a granola bar for herself to eat before they got on with the next phase of their plan. After a short break, they gathered up their bags, the generator and the solar panels and headed outside. Leaving the fresh air of the lobby, the smoke seemed particularly potent, though it didn't appear to have gotten any thicker. Approaching the SUV, she gave the key fob button an experimental push and the taillights blinked and the horn gave a beep in response.

"It works!" Sarah said, skipping to the rear hatch and popping it open.

"So far, so good," Alice pulled the generator up, looking around for any signs that others were watching, but the closest people were distant shapes walking the beach or milling in the dunes nearly a quarter mile away.

Together, the three lifted the generator and placed it in the cargo area along with their packs and the solar panels. Slamming the hatch shut, she went to the driver's side as the kids circled to the passenger seats and got in, with Sarah in the front and Jake in the back. Sarah pushed her long brown hair behind her ears, watching her mother anxiously as she sat with her foot on the brake and one hand on the wheel.

"Go ahead," Sarah laughed. "What do we have to lose?"

"You've got a point there, kiddo." She pushed the start button and the vehicle pulsed to life, the dashboard lights coming on in vivid colors.

"It's so quiet," Sarah said, gazing at her feet.

Jake leaned between the seats. "The dashboard looks like a spaceship."

"I guess it does," Alice laughed as she put the vehicle into reverse, backing it out of the parking space and switching directions, driving ahead to the exit, the vehicle responding with more force and immediacy than she was used to from a vehicle. With a grin at Sarah and Jake in the rearview mirror, she pulled onto Highway A1A and began driving north toward Palm Beach, weaving between debris on the roadway with the sun peeking through a clear spot in the cloud-filled sky.

CHAPTER THIRTEEN

James Burton
Denver, Colorado

On the outskirts of the suburban Denver streets, James hurried forward as fast as he could stand, his hands jammed into his pockets and his shoulders pushed forward to hold the weight of his backpack, glancing and turning in every direction to watch where he was going. There was never a more enticing beacon than the train's lonely whistle that guided him through the fiery night. Houses were lit in orange glows that cast eerie shadows into side yards and forested areas that were spread between the neighborhoods, the light making long shapes of mailboxes and light poles, casting their eerie shadows across the pavement and scorched grass. There were few survivors, a handful here and there that had gathered together in front of burning homes, quietly mourning the loss of property and life.

Occasional droning messages from the Emergency Broadcast System echoed out once in a while, piped in from old radios people had pulled from their basements, the signals mixed and filled with static. As far as he knew, he was moving west and a little north through an older part of town where the homes were made of brick and mortar and not vinyl siding like most new subdivisions. The brick exteriors had helped protect some of the homes from the raging fires out in the streets, but their roofs were still susceptible to embers that were starting to rain down with more intensity as the firestorm on the other side of the city approached in an unstoppable wall of flame. James ignored all except the sound of the train, homing in on it like his life depended on reaching it.

The horn cut long through the darkness due north of him, and James abruptly changed direction, cutting between a pair of houses where a dog barked unseen from behind a chain link fence covered in rusty pieces of sheet metal. He soon reached a patch of woods filled with elms, birches, and ashes that had remained unscathed and came out of the woods heading downward on a slope, which turned from dirt to gravel at the bottom where it then angled upward to meet a set of train tracks running from east to west. Stepping sideways down the hill, he glanced westward where a train was moving at a good clip, the last boxcar disappearing around a bend in the woods.

"Ah, damn!" Shoulders slumping, James climbed up to the tracks and stood watching as the last light from the rear end of the train faded from view. "It wasn't going my way, anyway. But at least *something* out there is running."

Turning east, he walked the tracks, listening to near silence and hopping from one sleeper slat to the next as orange light continued to flicker through the treetops. To keep his mind off the distant wails and gunshots that snapped off like crackling wood, he counted slats by the hundreds deep into the night until the cold light of dawn illuminated the torrid sky in a pale under-glow. After passing dozens of wilting neighborhoods and counting thousands of slats, an overwhelming exhaustion overcame him, and he stopped between the twin rails to catch his breath. With a heavy sigh he climbed off the tracks and squatted at the bottom of the bank, dropping his pack and resting back with his head on the gravel. He breathed into the moist shirt around his face as the faint chirping of birds reached his ears and lulled him into a light sleep and it was only when the tracks began to rumble and a train's shrill whistle split the morning light that he started from his sleep and sat bolt upright. Turning groggily one way and then the other, squinting into the pale sunlight, he rolled to his feet and stepped back to see a huge coal driven train creep by in a slow squeal of metal on metal.

James bent and grabbed his backpack, shrugging it onto his shoulders as cars rolled past him. He waved to the engineer, who was watching him from the locomotive's window, though the man didn't try to stop the train. Boxcars and massive flatbeds filled with crates and supplies rolled by. All along the tops of the boxcars, National Guardsmen peered down at him, though many gazed past him and into the distance at something he couldn't see. They sat on the edges of the cars with their rifles resting in their laps and their slack-jawed faces emotionless and blank.

James started climbing the rocky bank with his ankles twisting and knees buckling as he looked for a spot to jump on. Reaching the flat area next to the rails, he tried to snag a handhold but missed, tripping forward as his shoulders bowed beneath the weight of his pack, head leaning in close to the squealing steel wheels as they slowly rolled by. With tremendous effort, slipping and sliding, he hauled himself upright and broke into a jog along the railway ballast, turning to look over his right shoulder as the next car approached.

"Hey!" One of the guardsmen called from a boxcar roof as he walked along the edge to stay roughly even with James. "Just wait until the end... somebody will help you back there."

A woman in uniform with light brown hair pulled loose from its bun agreed with her fellow guardsmen and waved tiredly toward the rear of the train. James wanted to grab the next car, but the guardsmen kept waving and pointing down the line, so he stopped running and slowed to a walk beside the chain of groaning steel and wood, watching each boxcar as it rolled by with its fill of refugees and supplies.

James caught his breath from climbing up the bank and settled down, occasionally glancing behind him to see where a helping hand might come from. While most of the boxcars up front were painted army green or camouflage colors with big white labels on the sides James didn't understand, the cars toward the back were old flatbeds and rusted out boxcars with their doors thrown open. Inside were dirty-faced refugees wearing haggard clothing and haunted expressions, staring back at him with shell-shocked looks as they sat on crates of supplies or on the floor. The bit of light coming in through the cloud cover hit them from behind and cast their faces in shadow, more than a few weeping and holding each other as the train rumbled on.

James' breath caught in his throat when he spotted a girl clinging tightly to her mother, who sat cross-legged on the floor while the father stood by with his hand on her shoulder and swayed to the gentle rocking of the boxcar. The very next one that passed was relatively empty with just a dozen refugees inside, and he spotted a guardsman in full uniform standing watch at the door.

"Hello, sir!" James called out to the man, jogging along to keep up with the train. "I'm looking to hitch a ride. Can you lend me a hand?"

The guardsman shouldered his rifle and hustled over before James was passed by.

"Thanks, buddy." James reached up to clasp the man's hand.

"Just swing your feet up and catch one of those footholds," the man grunted, "and I'll pull you up."

Feeling his body already swinging in that direction, James kicked off and threw his foot up, catching his instep on the edge as the man stood and dragged him up so that he rolled onto his stomach on the dirty floor. James spat dust as he pushed himself up and brushed off his front with a nod.

"Thanks a bunch. Really glad to see some friendly faces."

"No problem." The Guardsman nodded at him. "You can have a seat anywhere in the train car, but don't bother anybody."

"Don't worry," he replied. "The last thing I want to do is bother anyone. Hey, if you don't mind me asking... what's your mission here?"

He shrugged. "All I know is that I'm guarding this train and helping anyone who looks like they're worth saving." With that, he took his rifle off his shoulder and returned to his former position guarding the door.

James nodded and rolled his own shoulder to work out a kink he'd gotten from swinging onto the boxcar deck as he slowly looked around. Finding a spot off to the side to get out of the way, he exchanged nods and friendly glances with those few people onboard. Up in the front of the boxcar, a large man guarded a family of five, the mother doting over her children and changing their youngest girl's shirt which was covered in blood and dirt. James spotted a white bandage on her upper arm before the mom pulled a fresh new shirt over her head. When the little girl gazed his way with a lollipop stuck in her mouth and tears glistening on her cheeks, James flashed her a goofy smile, hoping to make her laugh, but a dark glare from the father made him turn the other direction with a wince and an inward groan. As the boxcar shook and rattled its way along the tracks, James spotted a man in his mid-twenties with short-cropped blonde hair and an athlete's build. The man was on one knee, wearing fatigue pants and a black T-shirt as he dug around inside a military style backpack.

James approached but hesitated as the man glanced up with a scoff. "I don't have anything to give," he said. "I've only got enough for myself, sorry."

"I don't need anything," James replied. "I was just wondering where this train is going and if anyone has any news about what's happening."

The man gave him a second glance and saw his light backpack and rolled-up sleeves, and he shouldered his own backpack and stood. "I can't tell you much about what's happening except that it seems to be some kind of fuel malfunction – that's what I heard them calling it, anyway. As far as where this train is headed... it's just one of a few others coming through Fort Collins and Denver from the West Coast. Seems they're operating under the purview of the National Guard who are working with the train companies."

"What are they trying to do?"

The man shrugged. "From what I heard from the National Guard guys, they have a dual mandate to get critical supplies and survivors to relief camps farther east."

"I didn't know there were relief camps set up already," James said scratching at the stubble on his chin. "But as far as survivors go, the city's a nightmare. I was surprised to see as many people as I did. Doesn't seem like many made it to the trains."

"Whatever the hell this is," The man leaned against the edge of the open boxcar door, staring out at the remains of the city as they passed through another section that had already burned mostly to the ground. "It's like nothing anyone's ever seen before. You went through the city?"

"Came from the airport. I was about to board a plane when it all happened."

"Bet you've seen some things."

"I've seen my share," James said with a nod. "What's it like in the relief camps you mentioned? Can't imagine they're too nice."

"I'm hearing good things about them, actually. Probably the lack of actual survivors. People are being treated well and given food and medical supplies, as far as I can tell."

"That's a good sign, I guess."

"Yeah, but the thing that scares me the most is just how few refugees there actually are." The man smiled with a bitter twist. "Normally, a disaster like this would result in a tremendous amount of mob rioting and looting, but the chatter I've heard from the guardsmen is that they haven't seen much of it happening. Haven't seen any of that myself, but I hopped on the train in Wyoming and haven't gotten off since, so I don't really know."

"I've only met a few people so far," James confirmed, "but there were a few looters back in Denver. Just a handful, though, but I've been trying to outrun the smoke and fires. I've seen some other survivors, but not a lot, to be sure."

A second guardsman stepped from the shadows with his rifle held against his chest and a toothpick between his teeth. "Anyone still alive in the middle of the cities'll be dead inside of a day if they don't get the hell out." He looked James up and down. "I'm surprised to see you here. We haven't picked up many people from the city."

James nodded. "Yeah, I barely made it out of Denver International and managed to stay ahead of the fires. It's brutal out there, and I'm just glad to get a break from the walking."

"Well, rest easy. The train won't stop until we reach the relief camp at Kansas City."

"Thanks, sir," James replied with visible relief. "I really appreciate it. If there's anything I can do to help, let me know."

The Guardsman nodded and walked off, and James gave the man he'd just met a nod before turning and wandering toward the center of the boxcar, stepping to the opposite edge and leaning against the frame of the open door. Outside, the morning light was muted by a hard pattern of angry clouds that had reached the upper atmosphere and changed to gray around the edges where they were highlighted by sunbeams. The train had climbed to a slightly higher altitude, the trees parting to give him a wide-open view of most of Denver and across to the vague outline of the remains of the airport he'd escaped from. Above the tall buildings and miles of homes, a deep gray haze had settled like a poisonous gloom that was pressing down, threatening to suffocate anyone who was left in the city.

The wind patterns were erratic, with slow swirls of black clouds off to the west while swifter, tighter spirals corkscrewed up into the eastern sky, laced together from tendrils of smoke lifting off the edges of the city. In downtown Denver, the smoke was the thickest, and he wondered how the people left behind could breathe – let alone try to find and board a relief camp train. Out along the northeast part of the city, a huge swath of black marred the green forest, leaving charred woodlands in every direction, nothing left of the leaves and foliage except for pieces of flaky gray ash drifting off the forest floor amidst thousands of blackened sentinels, silent in the wake of their own personal apocalypse.

They passed a small town at the edge of the city at the foot of the hill with a cluster of two dozen homes, a corner store, and a single stoplight on the main road. The sounds of the train echoed through the hollow space, filling the silence of the town with its creaking squeals. Fire had devoured every home and left them collapsed inward on crumbling frames. The streets were riddled with the bodies of those who'd tried to escape, their charred forms wrapped in scorched clothing that smoldered and dripped off them, and some were fused to the pavement where they'd attempted to flee clusters of exploding vehicles and fireballs had left dark halos on the concrete for thirty yards in every direction.

The corner store was also a gas station with its entire lot split in several places where the fuel tanks had gone up, leaving massive gashes on both sides of the building. Concrete and dirt had peeled back and crumbled on the edges, huge chunks of it tossed for hundreds of yards to obliterate nearby structures like they'd been peppered with tephra. The town crackled and smoked with glowing embers beneath a swath of destruction for a mile or more until the forest gradually turned green again, and they were past it and moving away.

With a sigh, James turned from the endless sights of destruction and walked deeper into the car, finding a dark, isolated corner to sit and have a bit of food from his pack with some lukewarm water to wash it down. Draining the rest of the bottle, he washed out his eyes and swished some in his mouth to clear the soot, tucked his pack beneath his legs and finally rested his elbows on his knees and lowered his head until the next stop.

CHAPTER FOURTEEN

Ryan Cooper
Somewhere Outside East Lansing, Michigan

"Found it!" Helen said, holding up a crinkled piece of paper she'd taken from a set of metal shelves on the far side of the barn.

"Is that so?" Ryan called back as he used a power drill to drive the last screw into the second hasp he was installing on the side entrance to the barn to double-lock it as a safeguard from intruders. Looking inside the barn's shadowy recesses, he caught Helen standing in the faint glow of an electric lantern. "They kept those out here in that old desk?"

"Apparently so." Helen came outside to show him the receipt on its yellowed paper with its faded, purplish writing.

Turning it back and forth in the light, Ryan squinted at the words. "Yep. Says right here they purchased the tank refill a little over six months ago. I guess that settles it then." He handed the receipt back to her. "That means they avoided whatever was put in the fuel. That's a really nice find, honey."

Helen grinned. "Why, thank you, dear." Taking the paper to the desk, she returned it to its spot in the metal drawer on the shelf and shut it with a soft clang. "I figured they must have put the receipts out here since I didn't find them in James' office."

Ryan tested the hasp and saw it was secured well, and he went inside and crossed to the big rolling door in the wall near the desk Helen had been looking through. He'd already attached one extra lock on each side, and he gave them a tug to see that the padlocks were secure.

"That's about it for out here," he said. "It'll take any burglars a little extra time to get in at the very least."

Helen came up and admired his efforts, locking arms with him and giving him a hug. "Now that we know we have some of the only running vehicles for miles, it's really good you got the barn locked down."

"I'll add more locks on the other sheds later today," he rubbed his leg, "but I need a break for a bit."

"We've still got that tea I brewed up a few days ago," Helen replied.

"Sounds great, honey." Ryan gave her a hug and took the electric drill over to its case and placed it inside, putting all the bits into their proper slots. "Let's lock up first, then we'll head back up."

They stepped outside to the excited barking of Duke, Duchess, and Diana, the enormous dogs jumping around as they played with each other. Helen and Ryan laughed as they shuffled toward the gate, trying to avoid their bumping bodies as they leaped and ran around them.

"Okay, fine!" Ryan called, enticed by the Pyrenees' playfulness. When they reached the gate, he placed his drill case on the rail and turned to kneel so the dogs could get to him. Using both arms to hug them in, he wrestled them from side to side as they messed his hair up with their pawing and licking.

"Oh, dear." Helen came up and leaned in to ruffle Duchess's fur. "They're getting your clothes all dirty again. Need I remind you we're trying to save every bit of water and detergent we have?"

"It's okay, dear." Ryan laughed as the dogs bumped and pawed at him. "A little dirt never hurt anyone."

"You know, honey, I saw the Jones' down at their house earlier today."

"Oh, yeah?" Ryan shoved Duchess aside, and she snarled playfully and play-bowed in response.

"Yeah, and they were out in their yard. Looked like they were cleaning up after their garage burned down and all. Should we go check on them? What do you think?"

Ryan sighed as he grabbed Duke by his collar and gave him a playful shove. "I'd say they're probably doing fine, and I doubt they need much help."

"They weren't hurt in the fire, but it might be neighborly to check on them. We'd want them to check on us if we were struggling, don't you think?"

Ryan winced inwardly at the thought of paying the Jones' a visit, given that the neighborhood was in such disarray, but it was tough to argue her point. "I guess it's not a bad idea," he said with a nod. "Let's just avoid any talk about our car and the tractor and ATV."

"I totally agree. We'll just go down and make sure they're okay, and that's it."

"But after the iced tea, right?"

"Right!" Helen chuckled.

Rising and shedding the dogs off him, Ryan threw the gate latch and let Helen slip out, but as he tried to follow her, Duke plunged through before he could slam it shut. He started to open the gate again and call the dog back, but Helen threw up her hands and gestured at the massive beast as he bounded through the yard with his tongue lolling out.

"Oh, just let him come in with us," she said. "He'll be fine."

"I guess he won't hurt anything," Ryan agreed, and he clapped his hands and called out, "Come on, Duke. With us, boy!" Curling his lips over his teeth, he gave a low whistle, and the dog responded by turning on a dime and bounding back in their direction.

They walked to the house as a cool fall breeze whipped up, and Ryan glanced toward town where there were apparently still enough fires to bleed smoke into the sky in thick, towering columns that rose to join the massive clump of black drifting into the higher atmospheres and blotting out the daylight. Once inside, Ryan put the tools away while Helen fixed them both drinks, and they sat down for fifteen or so minutes, watching Duke sniff around on the front porch.

"You okay to go?" Helen asked.

"Yeah..." Ryan rubbed at his leg again. "I should be fine. Let's not stay too long, though."

Exiting through the front door, they strolled along the concrete path to the gravel driveway. Flocks of birds were silhouetted against the darkening sky, and the flowering trees and walnuts out front swayed to the restless winds coming out of the west. Moving briskly, they passed the gardens on their right with the remnants of the recently harvested rows of lettuce, tomatoes, and peppers that Alice had taken care of before leaving. The beautiful lane of red maples stretched out before them with their branches rustling together to send wide red, yellow and orange leaves floating to the ground at their feet. Out on the lake, the ducks and geese swam around nervously in the middle of the water, quacking and flapping their wings in agitation, acting as though they knew something was wrong with the world at large. Duke occasionally stopped to watch them, barking and running around the shore until Ryan called him to heel. Finally reaching the end of the lane and stepping up to the gate, he undid the padlock and latch and opened it just wide enough for them to slip through. After closing it back, he and Helen strolled down the driveway a short way before coming to the Jones' place.

"Oh, my." Helen pointed into their backyard which boasted a spattering of pear trees they'd planted in the last year, where another one of the Jones' sheds had gone up in flames along with several of the other neighbors' barns off in the distance. "Looks like they might have had some equipment out there."

"I can see where they had a small tractor inside," Ryan said, pointing. "There's the outline of the wheels right where the shed collapsed on it. I didn't even notice it yesterday."

"Poor people. I hope no one got hurt after we left." She nodded at two solar panels out in the middle of their wide backyard. "At least they have some power."

"I'm glad we're not alone on that front."

He angled them up through the yard and around the smoldering wreckage from before, though the smoke and heat weren't nearly as bad. As they were about to reach the porch, Ryan cocked his head to listen as a faint humming came from somewhere around the house, either from their basement, or around back.

"What is it?"

"Sounds like they've got a well pump going. Means they've got water, too."

"So we're not alone in that, either."

Reaching the walkway, Ryan cut to the porch and led Helen up the steps before knocking on the front door with three sharp raps. "Hello!" he called out, retreating a couple of paces while keeping Duke behind him. "Mike and Anita? Are you folks in there? It's Ryan and Helen Cooper."

A moment later, Anita cracked open the door before recognizing Ryan and Helen and opening it wide, giving them both a smile. "Hey. Good to see you again. Is everything okay up at your place?"

"Oh, sure." Ryan gave a faint wave. "We just thought we'd come down and check in on you guys and see how you're doing."

"That's so nice of you." Anita stepped out onto the porch.

"We were just happy to see that your house is still in good shape."

Anita chuckled nervously. "Yes, I couldn't agree more. Thanks to your help, we kept it from going any farther, but the garage and cars are all gone."

Ryan crossed his arms and grunted. "Saw your shed out back had caught fire, too. You had a tractor in there, right?"

"It was a riding lawnmower. We were keeping our tractor at the neighbor's place down the road, and it's gone, too."

"Oh, my," Helen replied, putting her hand over her mouth.

"Where's Mike now?"

"Oh, he's trying to get some old batteries set up to store power from the solar panels. You know, something to give us light at night when we need it. And, of course, with winter coming up, we're trying to get the furnace rigged up, too."

"Your solar panels..." Ryan asked. "They're not working?"

Anita sighed dejectedly. "Unfortunately not. We got them installed from some contractor who I guess didn't do everything right, so we're trying to fix them and get them wired into the house and it's just all a mess."

Before Helen could volunteer Ryan to help, he cut in. "Well, I know from what James has said, Mike is pretty great with that sort of thing. I'm sure he'll have those batteries up and running in no time."

"I hope so," Anita replied plaintively, her forehead creased with worry as she looked beyond the couple across the road at a burned-down home across the street. "It's just so frightening right now. Not only with what's happening to us, but what's out there in town. Have you been watching the smoke?"

"It's frightening," Helen agreed. "It's got some of our animals spooked, too."

"But not Duke, right?" Anita chuckled and gave the dog a wave. "I've always loved James and Alice's dogs. So beautiful and protective. I told Mike we should've got some animals to help protect the property, but I guess we just got too busy." She straightened and looked at Ryan. "What do you think is happening out there? Any clue?"

"Just what the emergency broadcast said. That we've been subjected to a terrorist attack on our fuel supply."

"That's what we heard, too. We even checked around a little to see if anyone has any working vehicles or tractors, but everyone's lost their equipment. Even the Willoughbys, who live a few doors down. They had dozens of farming equipment they leased to folks in the area. They're assuming it was a total loss."

Ryan's heart throbbed in his chest as he tried to navigate the topic carefully so that there wouldn't be any uncomfortable questions. "I'm really sorry to hear that... this has been so devastating."

"And it's going to be a nightmare for the insurance companies," Helen added.

Anita pointed at her and nodded. "I can't imagine how people are going to claim damage when *everything's* gone up in smoke. I'd assume the government would help with that, but I guess we're all waiting to hear more from them."

"That we are," Ryan agreed, glancing at Helen as he leaned down to pat Duke.

"If they can just get power back on, that would be a blessing," Helen gave a sympathetic nod. "It's like we're living in the stone ages. I'm sure everyone's got candles and things, but those will run out pretty quickly."

"Getting power back is going to be a tough prospect," Ryan said. "When you think about it, a big percentage of our power comes from coal, and with no vehicles to transport it, it's going to be a nightmare to get the power plants working again."

"I hadn't thought of that." Anita rubbed her chin. "What about trains? Don't they usually transport big loads of coal that way?"

"Either that or by barge, but any coal barges probably run on regular diesel fuel, although some might be coal driven." He shrugged. "I'm not an expert in that area, though."

Anita continued. "It just feels so strange being stuck here in our house with no way to go anywhere and no idea of what's going on in the bigger cities."

"I imagine if it's this bad here," Ryan gestured out beyond the porch, "it's bound to be ten times worse in the urban areas. If it was a terrorist attack on our fuel supply, like they say, just think of what it must look like in downtown New York and Chicago, or even Lansing. Any decently sized city would have gone up in flames by now, I figure, between all the vehicles and anything else that uses fuel."

"Oh, my," Anita replied. "I wonder when they'll declare martial law?"

"It'll be tough for the military to get around, too." Ryan rubbed his neck as sweat beaded up beneath his collar. "What are they going to do, march everywhere now?"

"Hey, folks!"

They all turned to see Mike coming around the house with his dark hair streaked across his sweat-soaked face, wearing an old greasy T-shirt and jean shorts.

"There he is!" Ryan called, shaking Mike's hand as he walked up onto the porch. "Anita told us you were working on batteries to store energy from the solar panels. How's that going?"

Mike nodded. "I'm almost there. Should have them all set up and filling with juice by the end of the day."

"That's wonderful!" Anita wrapped an arm around her husband.

"Do you folks want to come in?" Mike gestured to the door. "We can brew up a nice pot of coffee if you're up for it?"

"Thanks, but no, Mike," Helen replied before Ryan could. "We need to get back and tend to the chickens and other animals. Can't stop taking care of our kids' animals just because the world's falling apart."

"Don't we know it?" Mike stepped back and gave Duke a pat on the head before placing his hands on his hips. "What about you folks? You must be okay on power."

"I wouldn't say that," Ryan chuckled dismissively.

"Oh? I'm pretty sure James set up solar panels on the property. At least that's what he told me he was going to do last summer."

"Yeah... we do have some lights working, but I don't think it's enough to run the big appliances. I'm not sure James knew what he was doing when he set those up."

"I don't know." Mike wiped at the sweat trickling down the side of his neck. "James seemed pretty capable. And your daughter, too, of course!"

"I'll look into it a little more tonight," Ryan chuckled and shrugged. "But I'm not really an expert in any of that stuff."

"What about food and supplies? Are you guys stocked up on everything?"

"We have a small pantry with a few items." Helen interjected with a stammering tone. "We were supposed to go to the store and pick up some things so James and Alice wouldn't have empty cupboards when they got home from vacation. Other than a few cans, we've got some eggs. Ryan loves eggs."

"The doctor says I eat way too many." He forced another chuckle as he tried to steer the conversation away from where it was headed. "But I just can't get enough of them. I guess we'll be fine for a little while, but heaven help us when they stop laying so much during the winter."

"Heaven help us all." Mike glanced at Anita for a second time, Ryan catching some unknown look that passed between them.

Ryan patted Duke and started to turn around, taking Helen's hand in his. "Well, folks. We better get rolling. Lots to do before bed. Glad you're okay, and if you need any help, just ask."

"You too," Anita replied with a thin smile, stepping close to give both of them a hug. "You guys have a great night. All my love to James and Alice. I hope they make it back safely real soon." She squatted and reached to rub Duke's nose. "You stay safe too, big guy."

With the dog trotting next to them, Ryan and Helen strode through the rubble-strewn yard and angled back to their front gate. As Ryan turned to close the latch and lock up, he saw Mike standing on his porch with his hands on his hips, watching them. With a nod and a brief wave, the man turned and went inside.

The lengthening day grew no lighter or darker as Ryan and Helen strolled back into the house through the long, beautiful lane of red maples, while Duke chased the falling leaves, bringing them back to the couple before bounding off again. Ryan sighed as he walked, his mind lingering on darker subjects.

"I see what you mean." Helen spoke softly as she strolled to his left. "Seemed to me Mike was acting a little strange."

"More than a little strange," Ryan frowned. "Did you see those looks he was giving Anita?"

"I sure did." Helen locked arms with him and leaned against his side. "I didn't want to assume anything, but he seemed a little... I can't really put it into words. Uptight or suspicious maybe?"

"More like curious, if you ask me," Ryan replied. "He was really interested in finding out what we had in supplies."

"You don't think he was just concerned we had enough to eat and drink?"

"Maybe. But he was just a little too curious for my taste."

"What should we do?"

"No more neighbor visits, for one thing. And we'll make sure the dogs have free range over the property, just in case anyone tries to pay us a visit. Other than that, we'll just have to monitor things, and I'll keep bolstering the locks so if anyone wants to get at our stuff, it won't be easy."

"I'm so glad to be with you, honey." Helen leaned harder against him, her closeness and warmth putting Ryan at ease for a moment before his mind started racing again. "And I'm glad to be with you, too."

Wordlessly, and with a cold trickle of fear he tried to shake off, Ryan led Helen to the shed to gather their feed buckets and water pails before taking the wheelbarrow to the barnyard with Duke trotting at their side.

CHAPTER FIFTEEN

Alice Burton
Orlando, Florida

Alice wove the near-silent electric SUV through the debris strewn lanes, pushing through clouds of smoke and mangled automobiles that stretched as far as the eye could see. The pavement itself would've been easily navigable if not for the remains of other vehicles and big puddles of slick antifreeze and oil pooling in the road. The sky was invisible, locked behind a wall of clouds still so gray and black that they almost blotted out the sun, giving the late morning a dusk-like appearance and only allowing infrequent glimpses of rays of sunlight that managed to break through. They'd been moving slowly to avoid popping a tire or getting stuck, their lives caught in a surreal moment in time between earth and hell, a limbo with horrifying sights that would remain forever burned into her retinas.

What was worse was that she'd become used to the constant barrage of horrors. The blackened bodies with their skins slick with hot fat and whiffs of corpses that leaked through the Jet Star's vents despite her setting the air to recirculate seared themselves in her memory, coming faster and from a new vantage point thanks to the view the SUV offered. Sarah was sleeping next to her in the passenger seat while Jake was stretched out in the back, his feet kicking the door as he slept fitfully in murmurs and soft cries. At least Sarah snored softly at her side, her mouth hanging open and her head bumping gently against the window. With an endless line of destruction spilled out before her, Alice was gripping the wheel hard, her palms sweating as her jaw worked tighter and tighter until her molars were grinding and squeaking in her ears. Everywhere she looked, there was nothing but bodies and broken things, the highway to Orlando having turned into one massive graveyard, a monument to whatever it was that had happened.

Alice pulled off to the side of the road, allowing the SUV to coast to a stop as she bounced her head against the wheel in frustration. Her breath hitched in her chest as she wept uncontrollably, the tears bursting from her eyes, mouth twisted into a miserable grimace as the emotion of the past few days poured out of her in a flood. She tried to keep it in, but it flowed out like a faucet that wouldn't turn off and she sobbed until a gentle hand rested on her arm. When she looked over, Sarah was staring at her with sorrowful brown eyes and a fearful expression mixed with worry.

"What's wrong, Mom?"

"Just... all this." Alice gestured to the windshield and slapped her palm on the wheel, then she turned and looked behind her, pointing to the long line of scattered bodies and the broken-up rubble littering the road, the blackened skies and the still-burning buildings in the distance. "It's the end of *everything*."

Sarah's expression turned dark as she lowered her chin. "Mom, you're scaring me."

Jake woke up, rubbing his eyes as he leaned between the seats, instinctively holding Alice's arm. "Mom, is everything okay? Are we in trouble?"

"No trouble." Alice sniffed and sobbed again, turning in her seat and reaching for her children. Arms wrapped around them, she pulled them close, with Jake leaning between the seats, and hugged them tight, kissing each on their cheeks and breathing them in deeply. Just the scent of their skin grounded her in an anchor of family and love once again, and the horrible images faded into the background. The life they'd had before the world had gone to hell loomed large in her mind, and she gave them both one final squeeze before letting go and falling back into her seat.

"Sorry, kiddos." She sniffed and wiped at her eyes. "It just all feels so surreal." She chuckled. "It's funny. I always thought the end of the world... if that's what this is... would be filled with roving gangs of bandits or something, and not just a few desperate people trying to scrape by on a beach."

Alice took a deep breath to settle her nerves, smiling at the kids before she placed her hands firmly on the wheel and stared at the road ahead.

"Are you just going to drive straight home from here?" Sarah asked.

"That's a really good question," Alice replied. "I think we need to start thinking about the bigger picture here. We've got good transportation and a decent amount of supplies, but it's twelve hundred miles to home, and what we have on hand won't cut it."

"The charge on this car will eventually run out, right?" Jake nodded to the dashboard instrument gauges that showed how much power they had left.

"We should be able to recharge it off that generator and those solar panels back there, but I bet it's going to be painfully slow. Plus, what happens if someone takes the car, or it gets damaged? My priorities right now would be food, water, and making sure we can defend ourselves if we have to."

"Yeah I guess these pool cues won't last forever, huh?"

"We'll keep breaking them on people when they try to take stuff from us," Sarah added.

With a laugh, Alice pressed the accelerator and guided them from their spot on the side of the road and onto the crowded highway. So far, they'd been following signs for Orlando while picking the easiest path through. Alice was somewhat blind without her phone's GPS and mapping information, but A1A was a straight shot to get to the city where they could find what they needed to point themselves home. "I think Orlando will be our first stop. We'll hit the outskirts and look for some stores with supplies. From there, we'll play it by ear. How does that sound?"

"Sounds pretty good, Mom," Jake replied.

They hit a piece of plastic in the road, rocking the SUV and drawing a wince from Alice. "The roads are hard enough to drive as it is, but if we get a flat or run into any trouble, we need to be prepared."

"Is there anything we can do until then?" Sarah asked.

"Just keep your eyes open and let me know if you spot any stores that are still standing, okay?"

Sarah nodded and turned to her window, scanning the businesses just off the exits they were passing, gazing beyond the horrible wrecks for something that looked like hope. In the back seat, Jake did the same, sitting on the left-hand side of the SUV and peering into the deepening haze. With her two scouts on point, Alice squinted at the rubble, trying not to hit any sharp pieces of metal that could flatten a tire and stop them in their tracks. Beneath the smoke still drifting from the smoldering wrecks, though, Alice couldn't always see what she was bumping into, and from the number of dead lying in the road, that was probably a good thing.

―――――――

Hours later, she flexed her hands on the wheel, trying to loosen them from the tension of paying such close attention to the road. It was the constant turning and twisting through the haze and the smoke that kept her shoulders tense and her brain on edge, giving her no opportunities to relax, even for a few seconds. She was sweating from the effort, beads of moisture trickling around her eyes and down her face, unwilling to turn on the air conditioning due to the extra juice it would pull from the SUV's batteries. At one point, Sarah handed her a dry washcloth from their pack, and Alice took it with a smile and patted her forehead dry. As they approached Orlando along the Florida Turnpike, nothing changed on the road or in the air, and the landscape was a painting of destruction through her windshield. The amount of smog created by the fiery scenery had left it looking like a rotting wasteland, and the closer they came to the city the worse the smells became, the sweet reek of burning flesh sharp on their nostrils and drawing constant groans from both kids.

What kept her going were the constant signs for exits and stores, though whenever they got excited about a superstore coming up, they'd pull off only to see it was burned to the ground and trickling smoke into the sky with nothing left for them to take. The SUV hummed dutifully along, slipping through the wreckage, and as long as Alice didn't hit anything the ride was always smooth, its near-silence providing them with a low profile as they moved into areas that were potentially more populated.

The worsening congestion brought impossible crashes of scorched metal with cars stacked up and fused together from the heat. Bodies had been tossed from front seats or hung in burned strips of flesh from the piled-up steel like meat on clothes lines. They passed close to another SUV that had crashed into a smaller car, crushing it and then running up to settle on top. The impact had left a woman bent over the SUV's driver's side door, arms hanging down and her blonde hair scorched and smoking as tendrils of fire crept through the wreckage to set off anything that hadn't cooked yet.

"Sorry, hon," Alice said as Sarah caught sight of the dead woman and winced. "I should've gone the other way."

"It's okay, mom," she sighed. "We've already seen so much of this already. I just try to imagine it's one of those haunted houses Dad took us to last year."

"Yeah, that was pretty gross," Jake replied. "Not as gross as this, though."

"I don't think your father expected that to be so scary." Alice chuckled. "*And* so realistic. But I understand why you're thinking of it that way. It's better than believing it's real sometimes. Just keep in mind that these were people once, and I never want you guys to get numb to that."

"Yeah," Jake leaned between the seats and patted her on the shoulder. "It's just so..."

"Brutal?" Alice finished for him.

He swallowed hard, his voice cracking for a moment. "Yep. Worse than any horror movie I've ever seen."

"Exactly how many have you seen?" Alice asked with a cocked eyebrow as she glanced into the rearview mirror. "And did you have permission to watch those?"

"Don't worry, mom," he laughed. "They were all PG-13. Just ghost movies and stuff when I was over at TJ's a couple of times."

"Uh huh." Alice focused back on the road. "I guess that's okay then, especially considering we're in the thick of a, um..."

"Horror movie."

"Apocalypse, more like." Sarah added.

Alice swallowed a lump. "Right."

"Hey, is that something there?" Sarah asked.

"Where?" Alice glanced over to see Sarah pointing at a sign.

"It's one of the big chain sporting goods stores. I think Dad got me shin guards for soccer there."

"Can you see it from your window? Is it even still standing?"

Sarah shifted to peer through the glass from different angles before finally giving her an uncertain nod. "There's no smoke coming from it, and the roof isn't on fire or anything."

"Well that's the best news I've heard in a while. I say we try it." Alice pulled into the right-hand lane and drove along the edge of the road to the exit ramp.

Jake slid across the back seat. "I love that place. They have the best baseball equipment."

"Do they have guns or camping gear?" Alice asked.

"Hmmm... I don't remember. I just know Dad took me there to get a glove and bat when I played for summer league."

Alice vaguely recalled going into the store occasionally to pick up a last-minute thing for the kids before dropping them off at soccer or baseball practice. "Well, from what I remember, it's a pretty massive place, so I think they might have some survival supplies."

"It's worth a try." Sarah shrugged.

"It's the first really good place we've seen that might not be burned down, too," Jake added.

"Well, I don't see any people around," Alice said, "and no one is driving on the highway, so I think it'll be safe. Consider us there!"

Alice angled onto the exit ramp and wove between crashed traffic, sometimes stopping to wait until a cloud of smoke passed so she could see. At one point she had to back up and go around a tangle of wreckage to continue on to the end of the ramp, where she took a right and passed three gas stations that had blossomed outward in massive explosions that had torn them from their foundations and left pieces of pavement everywhere. Only one tall sign remained standing, though it was slanted so far to the side that it almost blocked the road. The SUV slipped beneath it and glided through the smoky haze, and for a moment, it seemed like they were drifting along in a dream. They slid between a pickup truck and a van on the right-hand shoulder and banked up a long road that led up to the larger department stores. Weaving up to the top of the rise, Alice guided them to the outer lane to circle the entire chain of stores.

There was a small garden shop and a picture framing shop off to the left with the larger sporting goods store on the right, its domed roof rising high above the others with a massive sign hanging over the double-wide front doors. The lane was clear of large chunks of debris, though a scatter of glass, plastic, and metal lay everywhere, and the SUV's tires crunched over it as she looked for a way in. The entire parking lot was covered from end-to-end with twisted car frames and the corpses of those who'd been inside them. Other people had been driving out of the lot or were walking to their cars when they were caught in the maelstrom and slaughtered where they stood. Thin patches of grass and ornamental trees protected the outer lane and had kept larger pieces of debris off of it, though one vehicle had spun through the air and caught in the low branches of the trees with its front end pointed to the sky and the rear end smashed into the grass. The entire lot between them and the store was a mess, the smoke thick and clinging close to the ground as it rolled in the listless winds.

"Phew!" Alice shook her head as she scanned the destruction, driving halfway around the store and approaching the rear. "It doesn't look like there's a good way to get in close."

"But look at the store," Sarah said pointedly. "It's completely fine from the fires. I wonder why?"

Alice raised in her seat and peered through the gray gloom. "It looks like there's enough sidewalk and pavement between the parking lot and store so there were no cars close enough to cause much damage."

Sarah was nodding as she rose to look. "That's what must've happened. I only see a couple of cars that blew into the store, but they smashed against the brick, so they didn't catch it on fire."

"Now if I can just get close enough so that we don't have to walk through all that mess," Alice growled, still looking. "I'm going to try around the back."

Giving the accelerator a push, Alice drove them carefully forward and soon they whipped into the rear lot where a handful of eighteen wheelers were parked off to the right in lined spots made for large rigs. They'd gone up like a row of dominoes straight down the line, their side tanks detonating, their hoods thrown off, the sleeper cabs crushed like tin cans, leaving a massive halo of black soot and still-burning parts around the damaged area. There were pieces of rubber, fan belts, hub covers, and exhaust pipes lying everywhere while axles were blown out and the tires were bent at odd angles so the frames sat skewed or flipped on their sides as they still smoldered.

Jake gave a low whistle, shaking his head at the sight, then he grew excited and pointed. "Hey, look! There are some trailers over there that don't look burned."

Alice followed to where he was pointing just past the rigs where a handful of companion trailers sat by themselves, resting on their landing gear with all the light and hydraulic hookups hanging in coiled cables from the front sections.

"They probably just dropped off loads of goods and are empty. Do you guys see an open door to the store anywhere?" Alice was looking for one as well, all while trying to keep from hitting anything. Off to the left were a series of dock doors with a few trailers parked in the empty spots, along with stairs leading to office doors. Jake shifted to her side of the car and was scanning every potential entrance, though most of the dock doors were rolled down and appeared locked. Just when she thought there'd be no way in, and they might have to break out a front window, Jake patted the back of her headrest excitedly.

"Right there, Mom!"

Alice let the SUV coast to a stop and squinted at where he was pointing. From where she was sitting, the door he was talking about was rolled up about a foot with the square glass window in the top section intact and undamaged. Alice waited almost a full minute to see if anyone would come out, but there were no signs of movement inside.

"Are we going in?" Jake asked. "It seems pretty safe to me."

"It's worth trying."

She turned the SUV in a tight circle, swinging it around by the stairs that led up to the door and pointing them back toward the road should they need to beat a hasty escape. Switching the car off, she shifted in her seat to face them. "I want you to stay close to me. The last thing I want to worry about is you guys wandering off. Is that clear?"

Both kids nodded, and they all exited the car and stood on the passenger side, staring up at the warehouse entrance where the door wasn't just opened, but someone had done some damage to it as well. The glass wasn't shattered, but there were dents around the lock, and the frame was cracked and bent. Moving cautiously up the stairs, Alice held one hand behind her to make sure the kids kept a respectable distance, and when she reached the top, she confirmed that the place had already been broken into. The paint on the door frame edge was chipped as if someone had taken a crowbar to it, though when she put her ear to the opening, she heard no one inside.

Holding up her finger to her lips, she slipped through without touching the door to keep from making any noise. Jake and Sarah came next, both copying her movements and squeezing in behind her without bumping the door. Once inside, Alice blinked into the darkness, about to reach for her flashlight when she noticed some dim emergency lights still running. They cast odd shadows throughout the loading area where skids of product stood stacked on one side of the warehouse, ripped apart and with packing peanuts and foam scattered across the floor. Nearby was a desk piled with invoices and lists of goods and Alice glanced at the desk as they walked by and then angled toward a doorway that led to the main part of the store.

When the trio came to the swinging doors, Alice gasped and stepped back. Smeared across the polished concrete floors were streaks of blood, swirls of boot prints, drag marks, and streaks of crimson sprayed on the doors. Swallowing hard, Alice paused and listened at the crack dividing the doors, staring through a small square window where the faint emergency lights filled the store's upper rafters and gave them just enough illumination to see by. Not seeing any bodies or hearing any noises, she glanced back at the kids and raised her eyebrows, gauging their expressions to see if they were ready to continue. Jake and Sarah nodded, so she went on through, pushing open the doors slowly and readying herself to retreat if they rattled or squealed, though they opened smoothly and noiselessly, and she held them and stood aside to allow the kids in before letting them swing shut.

A few steps in, Alice found herself in the camping section with the gear in front of her and a cash register and counter off the left. Alice froze and gaped at the surrounding mess. Most of the tents and pop-up canopy gazebos had been taken, and those on display were stomped and ripped apart and leaning sideways with broken poles and dented up cookware scattered everywhere. The sporting goods section was off to the right, and Alice spotted baseball bats, cleats, and deflated balls lying in the aisles with random pieces of catcher's gear thrown into the mix. Off to the left past the cash registers, racks of yellow hunting vests and camouflage coats lay on the floor, most of the stock cleared out with just a few jackets and hats left behind.

"This way, kids," Alice whispered, nodding toward the hunting section and pointing at the debris on the ground as she stepped over it. Moving to the left, they passed the glass counter where racks of shotguns and rifles had been wiped clean, the displays shattered, with no weapons or ammunition in sight.

Muttering in annoyance, Alice searched through the broken glass for something as basic as a knife, but everything had been taken, and not a single round was left anywhere. She turned Jake and Sarah in the other direction, and they walked toward shelves of miscellaneous goods where buckets of MREs lay spilled on the floor, the tops popped off and their contents looted. All that remained were a few plastic bottles, coolers, pots and pans, and random hunting gear. There was enough sporting equipment lying around to outfit a football team, though they had no use for any of it. They moved through the store, finally stopping beside one of the camping displays where the cardboard cutouts of a smiling family had been torn up and thrown on the floor. Alice turned a full circle and shrugged at the dismal pickings left for them to take.

"I guess there's nothing here, right Mom?" Sarah asked in a whisper, staying close to Alice's side as she gazed in disappointment at the trashed store.

"Still no signs of survivors," she replied, "but judging by the number someone did on this place, there are some people left alive."

"Are we going to leave or try to take some of this junk?" Jake asked with his chest out and his hands on his hips.

"There's probably nothing here we can use, but we should take a minute to go through it anyway. Never know what we might find."

"Should we still stick together?" Sarah asked.

"It's safe enough to spread out a little so we can cover more area. Just stay where I can see you."

The three broke apart and started going through the trashed store and what remained of the goods. After kicking some rubbish around, she found a large duffel bag and stuffed one hunter's coat inside it as well as a few pairs of goggles. There was a small first-aid kit she dug out from a pile of fishing lure boxes, and she tossed it in the duffel bag along with everything else. Sarah gave a low shout, and Alice looked up to see that she'd found a flashlight rolling on the floor and was holding it up to show her.

"Check to see if there are any batteries," Alice replied before going back to her own search. Jake wandered into the clothing section and returned with two pairs of track shoes and a pair of hiking boots, and she motioned for him to bring them over.

"What do you have there, buddy?"

"The hiking boots are kind of big but might fit you, but the shoes would be perfect for me and Sarah if something happens to ours."

Alice held open the bag. "Throw them in."

They searched the rubbish for another thirty or forty minutes but didn't find anything else worth taking, and loading up the SUV with useless dreck would just add to how quickly they drained the battery. Calling off the search, Alice gathered the kids around her and led them back through the warehouse area to the docks, where they stepped outside into the smoky haze.

"All that work for just a few little things." Jake sat heavily on the edge of the dock and kicked his feet against the concrete while Sarah sighed and leaned on the office door frame.

Alice stepped to the edge of the dock. "You guys want a snack?"

"I could eat," Jake replied.

"Me too," Sarah said.

Alice went to the car and dug out some snack bars and the remains of the bagel breakfast from Andrea's from their backpacks. They ate silently in the warm Florida day with a smoky gloom lingering in the air, though thankfully it wasn't thick enough to cause them to cough. The kids nibbled dejectedly while Alice paced a little but tried to relax as she stared across into other parking lots with more collapsed stores and a couple of small, wooded areas out past the burned-up rigs. There were outlets and strip malls off in the distance to her left and some larger warehouses mixed in, looking like charred and half fallen monoliths of another age even though they'd just been standing a few short days ago. That same haunted feeling of despair returned, and tears welled up in her eyes as hopelessness filled her chest like a hard lump. She was about to tell the kids to grab the duffel bag and throw it in the back of the SUV when she caught herself staring at the abandoned trailers sitting across the lot in front of them.

With a tilt of her head, she said, "Stay here just a second, kids. I want to run back inside real quick."

Alice stepped into the store but didn't go out onto the floor. Instead, she searched around the shipping area until she found what she needed over by a set of maintenance tools for the forklifts. A moment later, she came back outside with a crooked grin on her face and a pair of bolt cutters in her hands. As she traipsed down the stairs and over to the nearest trailer, the kids came behind her wearing curious expressions.

"Mom?" Sarah asked.

"It's a long shot," Alice admitted with rising hope, though she tried to keep her expectations tempered. "They're probably empty. But you never know."

Moving to the rear of the first trailer, she put the cutters to the lock and squeezed the handles, arms straining, tendons sticking out until the lock finally popped with the pieces clattering to the pavement. Handing the bolt cutters to Jake, she threw the latch open and grabbed both door handles, jerking them open and leaving the trailer's contents exposed. With a wide smile, Alice climbed up and stood on the edge.

"No way!" Sarah stepped up to join her mother with her eyes roaming over the skids of boxes and crates stacked almost to the ceiling. "What is all this stuff?"

Jake climbed in on Alice's right, going straight for the first skid and tugging at the plastic they'd used to wrap it all up. When he couldn't get it open, Alice took the knife she'd been carrying since the beach incident out of her pocket, flipped the blade out, and began cutting down the side.

Jake pulled the box out to read the lettering on the side, and he squinted at it with his eyebrows wrinkled. "This is… chicken pasta?"

"Not just chicken, honey. *Freeze-dried* chicken pasta in sealed bags!" Stunned, Alice turned and slid into the center aisle to the next skid. "And look, there's trail mix and freeze-dried fruit over here."

"Whoa!" Sarah climbed on one of the smaller stacks and reached all the way to several square plastic buckets stacked five deep with *Assorted Ready-to-Eat Meals* stenciled right on the side. "Are these the MRE things that are supposed to last forever?"

Alice laughed. "Not forever, but for a good long time." She turned in a circle and then stared into the back of the truck, overcome with delight at their find. Handing her knife to Jake, she turned to jump from the trailer.

"Where're you going?" Sarah asked as she tugged at the plastic around the MREs.

"I'm going to open up the rest of these trucks. You guys keep cutting supplies open, but take your time and don't cut yourself with that knife. Take some MRE buckets and a few boxes of those freeze-dried ones and stack them neatly beside the trailer. Then come behind me, and I'll show you what to add to the pile. And... hey, kids!"

They paused and locked their eyes on her.

"Keep your eyes peeled for any people snooping around. If you see a single person, come get me right away, okay?"

"Yes, ma'am!" Jake went back to work with the knife, sawing at the plastic and throwing it aside.

Alice hopped down and moved from trailer to trailer, popping each lock and propping the doors wide. The last one in the row was half filled with more camping gear, including cooking stoves and several sets of cookware with metal coffee cups and cutlery. She carried those to the edge of the trailer and set them down, then returned for more. There were backpacks and tents of all sizes, camping pillows, foam mats, and jackets and boots and she tossed out the softer items into the lot while placing the delicate supplies on the edge of the truck bed. The next three trailers turned up a proverbial horde of treasure, though Alice hit the jackpot when she found a stack of thin cardboard boxes with pictures of hunting knives inside. The label read *Kinsworth*, and beneath that in swooping letters, *Durable and razzzzor sharp!*

"That's exactly what we need." Heart racing in her chest with both relief and joy, she pulled off the top box and placed it on a shorter stack of goods. Peeling off the thick tape with her nails, she opened the cardboard box and pulled out an ornate wooden case with metal corners. She flipped two latches on the front and popped the top, revealing several light hunting knives, ranging from four inches to ten. Closing the box, she tucked it under her left arm and carried it out, stopping Jake and Sarah where they were gathering the items she'd tossed out and were lugging them over to some stacks they'd made by the first truck. She jumped down and raised her hand to get the kids' attention.

"I'm going to run back inside and check one thing, okay? But before I do, come here."

"What's that?" Jake's eyebrows pinched with curiosity, then his expression lit up when he saw it was a box of knives.

"The first thing we're going to do is get armed." She opened the box and handed a six-inch knife to each of the kids before taking a seven-inch knife for herself. Inspecting it for a moment, she held it up and grabbed the lever that flipped the blade out. "Just be very careful opening and closing these, because they are way sharper than the ones you have at home. They'll cut your skin like butter." Both Jake and Sarah stuffed their knives in their pockets, and Alice continued. "Okay. Take all the stuff we've gathered and start loading it into the SUV, but don't pile it too high against the windows, okay?"

"Yeah, we don't need to advertise the supplies we've got," Sarah replied flatly.

"Exactly." Alice patted her daughter's arm. "Don't worry. I won't be long, and we'll get right back on the road."

The pair grabbed a couple of food cases and lugged them to the car while Alice followed them over and unlocked the hatch before traipsing up the stairs to go back inside, angling for the hunting section and the counter with all the smashed displays. While they appeared stripped clean, there was still a chance the looters might have missed something and for the second time she scoured the counter case and used a piece of a broken fishing rod to stir the garbage and glass, hoping to score a box of bullets or even some shotgun shells. When the cases proved to be completely empty, though, she circled the counter and checked the shelves near the cash register, finding nothing but receipts, notepads, and cleaning supplies. Everything along the back wall had been wiped out, all the shotguns and rifles taken off the wall and hauled away, leaving the place seemingly empty.

Standing there with her hands on her hips, Alice kicked around loose debris before turning and wandering through a door to the back that read *Employees Only*, entering a dim room that smelled of gun oil and brass with a series of lockers and work benches along the right-hand wall. Alice headed over and stood in front of one bench which had a couple of gun-cleaning mats with some disassembled pistols and revolvers on them. There were plastic drawers full of bore brushes, woolen blend mops, slot tips, cloth patches, and other gun cleaning supplies, and cans of defluxer spray and bore cleaner stood in a line across the back of the table.

"Looks like a maintenance area." She stooped and began rifling through the drawers beneath the benches, pulling out old oily cloths and stained rags that smelled like chemicals and made her nose sting. Moving on from there, she found a box of gun cases off to the side and started going through them when a cry came from outside that made her heart drop clear down to her toes.

"Help! Mom! *Help!*"

CHAPTER SIXTEEN

Agent Alan Harris
Mount Weather, Virginia

The conference room was bathed in stark white light, the bright overhead lights casting everyone in a pasty glare while the old ventilation system rattled on in the background. Surviving members of various government branches and agencies had gathered together, deep under the earth at Mount Weather, to try and deal with an unprecedented time in their country's history.

Birk spoke with the few high-ranking officials of other member nations they could still get in touch with, trying to get to the bottom of why the tragedy had happened. Harris normally wasn't a coffee drinker, though he kept a large mug of it near his right hand as the data crunching and plans continued well into the night, and accompanying him were members of the Armed Forces and security staff as they took on multiple roles to fill voids left behind when the civilian staffers didn't show up.

As for Harris, not only did he have his regular responsibilities as the President's personal guard wherever he went, but he'd also been assigned to work as the President's personal assistant. It was probably better suited to a staffer who knew more about data organization than weapons and tactics, though Harris was doing his best. It was hard to complain when men like Colonel Crow, who sat just to his right, had been delegated equally menial tasks, from aligning guard duty and Marine provisioning to getting coffee for those in attendance in the secondary conference room. Even the President was no longer above getting his hands dirty, having helped a few Marines move crates of equipment out of a side room in the facility before working with them to set up a few dozen spare cots.

To Harris's left sat Major Jasmine Spencer who was reporting on casualty numbers that were pouring in while also taking direct orders from Colonel Crow once he'd doled out the assignments for the on-site Marine personnel, the light-haired, copper-toned woman wearing a serious, worried expression.

"Tactical assignments are in," Crow intoned in a stern, deep-voiced monotone that contradicted his thin frame. "Did you get that, Major?"

Major Spencer checked off things on her computer tablet with a matte black stylus. "Affirmative, Second detail will start at seventeen-hundred hours, including the changes you wanted made."

"Thank you, Major," Crow nodded, then shifted his hawkish gaze to Harris. "What's the status of the President, Special Agent Harris?"

"The President is secure in Conf-A, sir; I believe he's moved on to speaking with members of the House and the Senate that haven't made it on site yet."

"What about the President's family?"

"We've yet to find them, but when we do, they'll be transported to a secure location nearest to their location." Harris still wore his earpiece and was in constant contact with Commander Westbrook as the Secret Service scrambled to bring in their wards — both old and new — from the hellish chaos and into the safety of Mount Weather's concrete walls. "I'll keep you posted if anything changes, sir."

"Thanks, Harris." The man stood and leaned forward on the table with his long, thin fingers spread and the dark hairs of his arms standing out in the pale light. "We're just now getting in some real numbers, and we're piping them to your personal computer tablets now. Please take a look."

Harris watched as his tablet updated with a new item, and he clicked on it and read through the numbers being loaded in from USNORTHCOM. His mouth fell open as the first figure crossed his screen, exorbitantly high and rising steadily as thousands of data points reported in from across the country, audible gasps filling the room. The leadership stared at their screens, whispering and sharing glances of shock and horror. Harris blinked at the impossible numbers as a heat grew in his chest and crawled across his skin with an itchy uneasiness. Swallowing a hard lump in his throat, the agent wiped beads of sweat off his face with a napkin as one of the congressmen excused himself, his face pale.

New York Senator Rex Hernandez watched the man go before turning back to the table and falling forward onto his elbows with the computer tablet between his imploring hands, scanning the numbers on the screen before lifting his gaze to the Colonel. "Are these accurate numbers?"

"I'm afraid they are," Crow replied.

The senator sputtered in disbelief. "And this estimate you've given me, Major Spencer... it says two hundred million lives lost. Is that an accurate number as well?"

The sandy-haired Major nodded, her expression grim as she blinked at her own computer tablet as if she didn't believe the figures herself. "That's right, Senator. And the number of injured is up for debate amongst the disaster response teams, but likely in the millions, at least."

"This is just..." The senator shook his head and placed his tablet on the desk in front of him with shaking hands, clasping them so hard his knuckles turned white. "How can that be?"

Crow held his stoic visage, his voice remaining firm. "It comes down to massive fires sweeping through the major cities. As you know, petroleum-fueled machinery of all types caused those explosions. Any sort of engine that ran on refined oil fell victim to the bacteria. Of course, the damage is extensive—"

"*Extensive?*" Hernandez shook his head in disbelief. "This goes beyond *extensive*, Colonel. This is *catastrophic*! Over half the country is assumed dead because of fuel fires?!"

"Again, we can't stress how dangerous this situation is and how quickly the fires raced through the urban areas and even consumed many small towns." Crow strengthened his jaw as his eyes drifted across the room at the sickened expressions. "You must understand that while they were small fires, when spread out on a national – and even global – scale, they had the same effect of a weapon of mass destruction. The very machines we use to rescue people have been rendered inoperable, so our ability to respond to the fires has been wiped out. No one could have imagined this..." The Colonel's powerful voice finally cracked, and his breath caught in his throat. Then, with a deep intake of air, he propped himself up and stood straight again, throwing off whatever sudden weakness had consumed him as he stared at those in the room with a flat iron glare.

While Harris was a graduate of the ROTC and had fought through hundreds of tests and trials to become a Secret Service agent, the numbers he'd heard filled him with an anxiety that tightened around his throat and chest. Everything he'd trained to defend was vanishing in a massive storm of fire and ash, and the wound to his pride and sense of duty sent flashes of anger through his body. But there was nothing to hit, nothing to strike out at or take revenge on, leaving him helpless and weak.

"I don't understand," Harris spat. "We had no intelligence that pointed to anything like this. How could this have happened?"

"That's what we're going to find out." Crow replied. "So far, most cities have become tombs with handfuls of survivors, and suburbs didn't fare much better. Smaller towns and rural areas fared much better due to lower population density, natural fire breaks, and less fuel-based machinery." With a growl, he punched the table, sending a shudder through it that Harris felt in his hands and arms. "We've got a duty to protect this President and to save anyone still alive out there. We're all going to buckle down, ignore how many commas are in these casualty counts, and get on with our damned jobs. Is that clear?" While those at the table still looked sickened and pale, they nodded as they looked at him.

Harris straightened in his seat, taking the opportunity to jump in. "So, do we abandon the cities?"

MIKE KRAUS

"Not necessarily," Major Spencer replied. "We're currently pulling out some mothballed aircraft and drawing on our long-term fuel reserves that were old enough to avoid being affected by the bacteria. In combination with our electric drone fleet, we're flying recon missions in the cities, but we just don't have the numbers to cover a lot of ground. And, as you know, there are some wheeled vehicles that are still operational, though they're not in the greatest of shape."

"Yeah," Harris shifted, "I don't think the President's going to forget *that* ride anytime soon."

"Do you think the numbers will change the more information we get?" Senator Hernandez asked. "What I mean is, do you think those casualty numbers might go down?"

The Major shook her head. "Highly unlikely. IC's been bogarting the satellite infrastructure for defensive purposes, but we're working on a timeshare agreement with them, and they've carved off some analysts to help us look for any places that might have been spared, as well as plan supply drops and set up camps."

"That's a lot to chew on," Hernandez said. "We're not just talking hurricane or earthquake relief. We're talking millions of people who may be homeless and in need of shelter and supplies. I assume the supply chain is down?"

"Not just down, Senator. Obliterated." Crow replied. "But the problem isn't the supplies themselves, because we've got plenty of those in reserve — the big problem is getting the damn things *to* anywhere." The Colonel scoffed and shook his head. "I've never seen anything like it. Our few working vehicles can't cover a lot of ground, so —"

"Starvation is going to become a major issue." The senator stared at the table with vacant eyes as the wheels of doom turned in his mind. "We have enough food to feed everyone ten times over, but getting it to them is the hard part."

"Exactly," Crow affirmed. "So, we'll have to use what vehicles we have to rescue folks from fire-stricken areas while getting them the supplies they need for the short-term. There's one good thing, but..." Crow's words trailed off.

"What is it?"

"The experts are saying there will be no danger from diseases generated from the massive amounts of corpses left in the cities, because..." He shook his head. "The fires cremated most of the dead. While that seems harsh to say, it's good to know there'll be no epidemic on the horizon."

"A small favor," Hernandez nodded, smiling grimly.

"We'll keep everyone updated through the military network, straight to your tablets. If you have any questions about this, feel free to ask myself or Major Spencer, and we'd be happy to answer them."

"What about the efforts to refine new fuel?" Harris asked. "Has there been any progress there?"

Hernandez added, "And what about creating an antibacterial agent to fight any future fuel tampering?"

"Both good questions," Crow replied with a pointed nod. "We're working on the antibacterial agent, but the sheer amount of infrastructure destruction we suffered slowed our progress. Until we're one hundred percent certain that this threat is *out* of our fuel supplies, we're looking at coal-fired trains and electric vehicles as our primary means of transportation over the coming months."

Major Spencer jumped back in. "The USPS fleet can be repurposed fairly quickly, but finding manpower to drive them is a tough bet. And some areas are still working on the first gen electric vehicles, so their battery capacity isn't great. Many need to be re-outfitted before they can be put to any good use."

"What about civilian vehicles?" Harris asked. "I know the US hasn't exactly been on the forefront of EV technology, but we should have a vast fleet of civilian vehicles."

"You're not wrong there, Agent Harris," the Major replied, her light blue eyes regarding him seriously. "But unless they were isolated from the fires, not many are likely to have survived, and we may not have the people to drive them. Right now, trains are our best bet for mass transportation of people and goods."

Hernandez was already shaking his head. "That's a decent solution for now, but how many of those train engines are coal-fired? I know there's not a ton of those in New York."

The Major turned to the senator. "That's true, but we've got people working with the railroads — or what's left of them — to get what they have up and running. They'll bring them back online and put them to use right away. Some railroads have already got some older engines running and are on the tracks as we speak. And since the rail lines are still intact and weren't damaged as far as we've seen, things are at least stable on that front."

"Any further questions?" Crow asked. When no one immediately responded, he went on. "All right then. We'll turn to you next, Agent Harris. What's the President been doing?"

"As I've already informed everyone, the President is safe and in Conf-A, where he's busy talking with foreign leaders along with the Secretary of State and remote members of Congress."

"Any luck with that?" Crow asked.

94

"Yes, and no. The EU is in tatters because a variant of the bacteria that attacked us was apparently introduced into their natural gas pipelines, so you can imagine the damage that caused. The number of dead is... astronomical. To put it mildly."

Several at the table shook their heads, and another congressman sitting on Harris's right stood and excused himself from the room with a sickened expression, mumbling something about needing to try and make a call.

"In other news," Harris continued, "we can't reach Moscow, and North Korea is being their usual insular selves."

"What about China?" Crow asked. "Satellite images have shown no major military movements, which is something none of us expected. We figured the Chinese might be behind this and would already be moving to make headway in Asia."

"I think it's safe to say they're experiencing a similar situation as us." Harris used his fingers to shift some things around on his screen, checking the data points he'd been given earlier. "While China has expectedly closed themselves off, satellite imagery and leaks from our agents there confirm massive fires in their major cities, including Shanghai, Beijing, Guangzhou, and Shenzhen."

"Could it be a decoy of some sort?" Crow asked. "Something to make us think they're having the same issue?"

"They can't fake smoke clouds that big." Harris shook his head. "The explosions and subsequent fires aren't just for show, and much of the Chinese production capabilities and military strength have been debilitated. Like with us, anything they had in the air at the time of the bacterial activation fell from the sky and are now hunks of junk lying in fields or in the ocean." Harris let that point settle before he continued. "Canada's weathering the storm about as well as we are, and it's about the same in Mexico, though Mexico has a surprisingly high EV capacity, considering they manufacture most of what we drive in this country so they might be able to bounce back in some capacity even faster than we will. South America's been hit pretty hard, though. They're reporting tens of millions dead or missing, even more millions injured, and they have absolutely no control of the populated areas..." Harris shrugged. "They don't have much of an EV infrastructure at all to count on."

"Any word on the Middle East?" Senator Hernandez asked. "I'd imagine there are a lot of eyes focused there. Does anyone stand out as a potential perpetrator of this heinous crime?"

"There is no evidence yet. They're about as bad off as South America... worse in a lot of ways. No, the Middle East is not doing well at all. Dubai is in absolute shambles, and Amman is a bed of coals. Beirut, Cairo, Baghdad, and Tehran have all been devastated by this. As far as we know, every major military force in the world is at a standstill."

Hernandez arched his eyebrows. "Except for those of us who have nukes."

"Exactly."

"I just don't get how this can be happening," a red-haired congresswoman across the table from Harris spoke with barely restrained fury. "Are you trying to tell me that someone could strike at the heart of every major nation in the world and cripple them with impunity, including us?"

"That's what it's looking like right now, Congresswoman McMurphy. All in all, we're doing about as well as can be expected, both in terms of loss of infrastructure and loss of life, as sobering as those numbers are." Setting his tablet on the table, he winced inwardly as he gave the next figure. "Worldwide, estimates of deaths have reached upwards of three billion. That number is coming from Sharon Doherty's group, who are heading up the Disaster Recovery. As you already know, Sharon is an expert on this type of data, which is why the President is relying on her numbers as a fairly accurate statement."

The already dour expressions around the table deepened, and a sense of doom weighed on everyone's mind. The dread and magnitude of the disaster was palpable as Major Spencer and Colonel Crow sat quietly, and the assembled civilian leaders stared into empty space, their wretched silence a death knell in Harris's ears.

CHAPTER SEVENTEEN

James Burton
Topeka, Kansas

James slouched in the boxcar's corner, the gently rolling train having lulled him to sleep over the endless miles that passed beneath their steel wheels. Images of Alice and the kids filled his mind, and he briefly imagined he was home, sleeping in on a Saturday morning and waiting for Sarah or Jake to get him up. Those comforting thoughts were overlaid by visions of endless black clouds that battled in the sky above him, their billowing shapes plunging against each other, shot through with lightning streaks the color of rotted oranges. He tried getting back to those images of home; the farmstead, the magnificent open space and the barnyard where Duke, Duchess, and Diana watched over their flock of animals, and the gentle sway of their crops rustling in a soft spring wind as Alice's parents watched over it all for them until they returned.

When a bullhorn blared and shattered James' dreams, his eyes flew open with a jolt, and he grabbed at his pack. At the same time, a hand shook his shoulder, and he reached up and grabbed the man's arm to find a pale, dirt-smudged face staring down at him with soulful blue eyes, recognizing the young man with the bug out bag he'd spoken to when he'd first gotten on the train.

"Sorry to wake you up like that, buddy," the man said. "I just figured you'd want to be up for this."

"For what? Did someone try to take my stuff?" James was panting, heart thumping in his chest as he looked around frantically. His right arm fell across his backpack, fingers drifting over the revolver holstered at his side.

"Nobody tried to take your stuff," the man replied. "But something's going on outside, so you better get up."

The man backed away, and James shook his head, trying to orient himself. There were more people on the train than when he'd jumped on; the family with the injured little girl was off to his left talking to others who had their backpacks and personal possessions hanging from their shoulders while one father held a boy in his arms and a small girl clung to his legs. The National Guardsmen were standing near the doorway, leaning forward and peering toward the front of the train while others were trying to edge closer to see what was going on.

"Thanks, man," James replied with a nod, accepting the man's hand and allowing himself to be lifted off the shaky hardwood deck. "Much obliged."

As soon as he stood, the train gave a lurch and the squeal of steel that reverberated through the boxcar sent him stumbling. The man caught him as he started to fall forward, and together they steadied themselves until the braking let off for a moment. He turned and grabbed his backpack, shrugging it on his shoulders before leaning over to look out the open door. While the train had been moving slowly before, it was grinding to a near halt as trees and electric poles crept by outside. There was nothing but woods and forests visible from where he was standing as people continued crowding forward, eager to see what the guardsmen were looking at and James joined them, pressing into the curious throng, craning his neck to see between them or over their shoulders.

The train was curving to the left, and the forest was giving way to patches of greenery and some hillsides in the distance. He squeezed past the family with the injured girl and finally got a good view of what was happening outside. They were rolling through an open construction yard with piles of gravel, concrete and steel girders all around. A majority of the train had gone through it, though their boxcar was coming up on the railroad crossing where it met a paved road, and some of the National Guardsmen were jumping down to join several Army troops standing in the yard around a few APCs and Humvees.

The military vehicles weren't in the greatest shape, with dents in their armor, spots of rust, and pieces of plastic and duct tape on some of the windows. Army troops were greeting the guardsmen with waves and friendly shouts as the two sides conversed in the construction yard and the man behind the voice he'd heard yelling through the bullhorn from beside the vehicles joined a handful of the National Guard leaders and began gesturing to the train as it finally stopped. Someone jostled him from behind, and James turned to see it was the father who'd given him a dark look earlier. He'd left his family back in the boxcar and was shoving his way through the crowd to see better.

"Hey, c'mon," James said. "No pushing."

The man gave him a condescending scowl before leaning forward. "I'm just trying to see what's going on."

Another woman standing nearby craned her neck. "Is that the Army? Marines?"

The guardsman who'd helped James aboard the train, Les Frazier, glanced over his shoulder at her. "That's the Army, ma'am."

"What are they doing here?" the man behind James asked.

"Good question," Frazier replied as he continued peering into the construction yard. "This is the first time I've seen anyone from the Army since all this started, and I have to admit, they don't look like they're exactly well-equipped. Those Humvees look ancient."

"And those APCs aren't even in service anymore," one of the other guardsmen added.

"Well, they definitely are now." Frazier squinted at the vehicles but stayed calm.

"What do they want with us?" the woman asked him. "What are we going to do?"

"Nothing," the scowling man replied. "Unless you want to go talk to them and give up your seat on the boxcar."

"Does anyone even know where we are?" James asked as he stared out into the woods past the Army troops for any sign of their location, but he saw nothing to indicate their whereabouts.

"No idea," Frazier replied, and a few other guardsmen shook their heads.

James could only wait with the others as he watched the two sides gathering to talk for a while before coming to a conclusion, and Frazier's radio popped to life with a muddled sound. Before James could hear what was said, the guardsman turned and split the crowd until he stood toward the rear, stooping as he listened to his orders and replied with something unintelligible.

When Frazier was done, he stepped back through the crowd to stand near the edge of the deck, raising his hand and snapping his fingers. "Okay, folks, listen up!" The passengers quieted down and waited with expectant expressions. "Everyone is to stay in their cars for now. The Feds are commandeering the train." There were groans from the crowd, but the guardsman quickly added. "Don't worry, they'll still be taking you to Kansas City, where shelters are waiting. You'll still be given supplies and aid, but after that, the feds will take the train elsewhere to carry supplies, equipment, and manpower. They need it farther east."

Several passengers grumbled and complained, though there wasn't much they could do, and the National Guardsmen turned and motioned for everyone to step away from the edge and be careful so they didn't fall off and get hurt.

"Just be patient!" Frazier shouted. "This shouldn't take too long."

Soon after, the train started up again but barely edged forward until they'd gone another ten or twenty yards and one of the empty boxcars ahead of them sat right on the crossing where most of the Army troops had gathered with the National Guardsmen. James managed to squeeze through the crowd and sit on the edge of the deck with his feet dangling over the side next to Frazier, and he observed the Army troops as they drove their APCs and Humvees down a narrow lane toward the rear of the train where there were empty flatbeds capable of hauling the heavy machinery. The rest of the soldiers, which numbered a couple dozen, stayed where they were, some of them forming a line in the construction yard to hand up massive packs of supplies into the empty boxcars.

"I can't believe they made us stop." The angry father paced behind the crowd, sometimes leaning between people to look outside with a sour expression. "They're Army guys, and we're just civilians. This isn't a battle. We should get precedence on getting through to safety!"

"Why don't you sit down, sir?" Frazier shot a glance at the father, who merely crossed his arms and turned to the others in the boxcar in response.

"Who here agrees that these jerks should let us through?" After receiving a couple of halfhearted nods and a faint shout of encouragement from the rear, he faced Frazier with an emboldened expression. "Are you guys going to let those Army pukes push you around?"

"What do you mean?"

"It's *your* job to get us to safety, but these guys can just stop the train because they want to hitch a ride?" The father shook his head and stepped through the crowd to stand near the edge between James and Frazier. He scowled at the soldiers outside with sheer contempt, scoffing loudly before glancing at Frazier's rifle. "You know what we need to do, don't you?"

The guardsman turned and faced the man, squaring up to him. "No, what do *you* think we should do?"

A thin line of sweat dripped down the man's temple. "We need to shoot our way out of this. We've got them outnumbered twenty to one, so there's no way we can lose. If you give some of us your sidearms, we can help you."

Frazier's jaw dropped, and he re-gripped his weapon with his own scowl forming. "Are you crazy? These are *our* people, you *idiot*. The last thing we're going to do is point weapons at them!"

"You say that now," the man replied. "But you don't have a family on this train. Me and a lot of others don't have supplies at our fingertips like you guys. We need to get to that Kansas City camp as soon as possible, and these assholes are standing in our way."

James shifted and pulled his legs onto the deck, leveraging himself to his feet as he watched the father and guardsman argue. While Frazier had a rifle, the father was bigger, heavier, and itching for a fight.

"Sir, why don't you sit down?" Frazier asked, his tone still polite. "Just be cool, and we'll be on our way soon."

"Not good enough." The father's arms fell to his sides, chest sticking out as some civilians pressed in behind him while two other guardsmen took up positions behind Frazier. "I say we need to get moving right now so we can make sure we get to the camp and our families get food. Who gives a crap about a couple of Humvees and some army supplies?" He pushed forward, edging against the guardsman.

Frazier looked to the side as he clenched his jaw. "Step back, sir." He pointed the crowd toward the rear of the boxcar as other guardsmen backed him up. "Everyone... step back, *now*."

"Or else what?" The father stuck his chest out. "What are you going to do? Shoot us?"

"Sir, listen to me—"

"No! You listen to *me*, buddy!" The father pushed his finger into Frazier's chest, shoving him back and glaring at him. "We pay taxes, and you work for *us*! All this equipment you have..." He gestured around. "All these guns and uniforms and every damn ration you eat was paid for by me and the people on this train!" The man was shouting and glancing at the crowd where a few were nodding and jostling with the guardsmen while most of the others looked around warily.

James nearly reached out to help de-escalate the situation, but held back at the last second, unsure of himself. He was certain the guardsman could handle the angry father, but even as that thought crossed his mind, the angry man shoved Frazier, and when he pushed back, the father grabbed his rifle and began jerking it away, the two jostling back and forth. James started to reach out again to restrain the man, though he stopped yet again, gripped by fear and hesitation over becoming involved in the situation.

Within seconds the shoving match had turned into a full-on scuffle, with Frazier fighting against the angry father who was trying to twist his weapon out of his hands. The guardsman was thrown off balance and had to let go of his weapon or else topple off the train, and, snatching the rifle away, the father raised it and punched the stock into Frazier's face, bringing forth an instant fountain of blood before raising the rifle again and slamming Frazier across the chin. The guardsman tumbled off the deck and landed on the grassy bank next to the train, rolling a few feet before coming to his knees with a pained grimace, gasping for air from his bloody, bubbling nose.

The crowd flew back with startled cries as the remaining guardsmen finally reacted, unslinging their weapons and leveling them at the father. A strange look crossed the father's features as he held the rifle, and he glanced at his frightened family before leaping from the train and landing on the flat area beside the tracks. He pointed the gun at Frazier and tried to work the charging handle as people in the crowd yelled for him to stop. For a third time, James very nearly leapt to Frazier's aid, but held back, and another guardsman jumped off the deck and landed an elbow across the back of the father's head, causing the rifle to fly free as he went tumbling into Frazier. The angry, bleeding guardsman shoved him back, cocked his fist, and struck the man in the stomach to send him reeling backwards. Frazier finally found his full footing and connected with several more blows across the man's chin with sharp snaps, knocking him into the second guardsman, who grabbed the father by the arms and threw him into the grass.

Frazier snatched his rifle off the ground and turned it around, shouting, "Hands up! Right now, or I'll blow your head off!"

The man's wife pressed past James with her children clinging to her, screaming to keep the guardsmen from shooting her husband. "No! Don't shoot him! Please!" The father was lying in the grass with his hands up, panting heavily and shaking, chin quivering as he stared down the barrel while his wife begged for his life. "Please... don't shoot! It was a mistake! It was all a big mistake!"

The second guardsman's jaw worked back and forth, and he glanced over his shoulder as some of the Army troops and a few other National Guardsmen ran up and gathered around the grassy bank.

Frazier glared at the father and wiped his arm across his bloody face. "Cuff him. Put him with the other troublemakers."

A pair of guardsmen descended on the man, jerked him roughly to his feet, and began pushing him to the front of the train as he looked back to his family, eyes filled with panic as realization over what he'd done finally broke through.

The woman turned to James, panic in her eyes. "Please, mister. Can you help us down? I've got to get to my husband. They're taking him away! What are they going to do with him?!"

"I don't know, ma'am," James said, his gut twisting with guilt over not trying to stop the altercation sooner. "But I'll help you and your kids down. Come on. You go down first, and I'll hand the little ones down to you."

The woman was nodding as she sobbed, letting the children go so she could sit on the edge of the deck. James and another National Guardsman held her arms as she dropped safely to the flat part of the tracks. After that, James handed her a little boy and then the girl with the wounded arm. Once they were off, the woman snatched the children's hands and hustled up the tracks, chasing the guardsmen who were carrying her husband away. Frazier was brushing himself off and approaching the boxcar to resume his duties, and James kneeled at the edge and reached out to help him up. Between him and another guardsman, they got him back aboard where he stood touching his nose and wincing.

Frazier turned to James and glanced up the tracks. "Thanks, man. What a jerk, right?"

"That was a super-sized jerk." James nodded. "Here, let me help you get cleaned up." Taking off his backpack, he retrieved a bottled water and a first aid kit he'd taken from the pharmacy back in the last town. After hesitating too long to help Frazier before he was assaulted, James felt obligated to at least get the blood off the man's face. He wet a clean piece of gauze and motioned for Frazier to hold up his chin while he wiped delicately at the man's bloody lip and nose.

"Is it broken?"

James craned his neck to get a different angle. "I don't think so, man. It's not crooked or anything, so I think you're still handsome enough to charm all the ladies."

Frazier chuckled, wincing at the pain. "Thanks. I'll take your word for it."

James finished cleaning his face and started to open up his first aid kit when another guardswoman came up with gauze and bandages she'd retrieved from the rear of the boxcar, lifting Frazier's chin to get a better look at him. "I've got it! We'll just stuff some gauze up the old nostrils and you'll be good as new." She shot James a glance. "Your help is appreciated, sir. I'll take it from here."

Nodding, James backed off and took his backpack with him, his blood still pounding in his ears from the fracas, wondering if his inaction could've gotten a man killed. In the end, though, it was the father who'd been lucky to avoid lethal repercussions. He could've easily been killed if not for his wife having come in at the last second to save him.

James settled in the darkness with his back against the rear of the boxcar, sliding down the wall until he sat in a resting crouch once again, watching the others in the boxcar as they murmured and speculated.

"Do you think they would've shot him?" a woman asked.

"When you act like a lowlife," another sneered, "you deserve what you get."

"I guess so."

Still holding his bottle of water, James tilted it up and took a long drink, watching others do the same as they settled in to wait for the soldiers to finish what they were doing. Shouts rang up and down the line, and the Humvee and APC engines revved high, followed by heavy bumps that reverberated through the boxcar's deck. Feeling suddenly crowded by the others pressing in around him, James rose and walked to the doors again where the guardsmen were talking about what happened as they ribbed Frazier over the gauze packed up his nose.

Standing at the edge of the deck, glancing toward the rear of the train, James watched as the troops used folding ramps to load the Humvees onto the backs of the flatbeds. They'd already gotten one up, and the second flew up with its exhaust pipe spitting smoke into the air, the old vehicle's frame twisting and groaning, tires spinning and squealing as it got over the lip and hit the flatbed, turning sharply to nose in behind the first one.

"Not bad." James folded his arms and leaned against the edge of the door. "I doubt they've practiced that move too many times."

Frazier came up with a nod. "It's not every day you load Humvees and APCs onto trains."

"Where do you think they're moving them to?" James asked.

"I haven't the foggiest, but I'd say they're probably trying to save fuel by loading them up on those flatbeds and carrying them across the country that way."

"That makes sense."

The soldiers moved the ramps to the next flatbed and positioned the heavy APCs to board. As they cranked up the big diesel engines and drove them up the ramps, James winced as they clanked and shook on their old frames, their massive tonnage bowing the steel bridges to the point he thought they might break. They held, though, and the enormous vehicles rumbled aboard the flatbeds, turning on their six wheels and positioning themselves nose to bumper where the troops could chain them to the deck.

As they waited, a dozen more soldiers brought bins of rations and tossed them into the boxcars all the way down the line, responding to the shouts of thanks from the passengers with smiles and nods. James grabbed one left on the floor after everyone else had gotten one and sat on the edge of the deck, filled the heater bag with water and slipped the hot pack into the pouch next to the bag of chili mac. Soon, the train horn sounded way up front, echoing through the construction yard and earning murmurs of relief from the waiting passengers. A short time later, the soldiers jumped aboard some of the first few boxcars along with the National Guardsmen and, with everyone on board, the train began its slow, inexorable chugging, followed by the long groaning sounds reverberating up the tracks as the weight shifted and steel squealed.

"Here we go, people!" Frazier called out, and the passengers settled in again, resting back against the boxcar walls or sitting in circles and whispering.

As they pulled away, the low hills and construction yard gave way to wide open farmlands with rows of crops and the blackened remains of farm equipment. The fields stretched in every direction as far as the eye could see, and James caught himself thinking about their own crops and if Alice's parents had gotten the rest of the tomatoes and corn in before it got too cold. *I wonder if the house is even standing. Barns are probably gone by now, though....*

The train swung to the north, and James was distracted from his thoughts as he got a good view of the Rocky Mountains to the west where they stood tall against the billowing black and gray storm clouds that rolled over them. Flashes of lightning shot through them, illuminating the mountaintops in bright bursts of light, striking in comparison to the shadows that loomed like an evil omen closing in from the west. Squeezing the plastic fork so hard it began to crack mid-bite, he thought back to the man who had attacked Frazier, wincing at the remembrance of his own repeated inaction. Things had turned out reasonably well in the end, but his standing by and doing nothing, watching an attack happen that he could have easily stopped, was nipping at him like a dog, the guilt refusing to leave him alone. *I'll do better. Next time... I'll do better. I have to.*

James squinted up at the ominous clouds, happy to be moving again and heading eastward toward home, every mile that slipped beneath their steel wheels bringing him that much closer to those he loved. He couldn't imagine what was to come, and the uncertainty threatened to crush his heart with fear. Keeping in mind Alice's beautiful face and loving eyes, and the kids' playful voices echoing in his head as they ran around with the dogs out in the barnyard, he was determined not to allow despair to weigh on his heart.

At that moment, the train turned into a warm wind that ruffled his hair and caressed his face. With a thin smile, he dug into the MRE bag and stabbed some macaroni and processed meat chunks with his plastic fork, his nose wrinkling at the taste but forcing himself to eat it anyway just to get the caloric intake. Sometime during the ride, Frazier brought him a small cup of black coffee that tasted as bad as it looked, bitter and acidic, though he enjoyed every sip as he sat on the edge of the deck, the train picking up speed as James once again ventured into the unknown.

CHAPTER EIGHTEEN

Alice Burton
Orlando, Florida

Turning to the repair mats, Alice grabbed the parts of an S&W revolver and started putting them together, awkwardly at first, but eventually getting it mostly right. She slapped the chamber in place and spun it so that it locked. Without looking for any additional pieces, she sprinted from the back room and circled the counter, hitting the door to the warehouse section at a dead run, gasping as a groan worked its way up from her gut. Dashing across the warehouse floor, she hit the back door with her shoulder and almost slammed it shut before grabbing the handle and jerking it wide, leaping through and gasping at what she saw.

Three men had the kids trapped by the SUV and were menacing them with raised fists and sneers. Sarah was crouched by the back hatch, waving her hunting knife in front of her. Jake defended her by swinging his pool cue wide with his right hand while holding his blade close to his side. The men were grubby and wore frayed clothing in a mix of collared T-shirts, button-ups, and jeans. The man on the left had blood on his pants while the one in the middle wore an office shirt with the sleeves rolled up and tears on the side. Easily the widest and toughest of the three men, he lunged at Jake and tried to snatch the pool cue out of his hand. As the boy jumped back, he swung the stick with the heavy end cracking across the man's chin and sending his head jerking back with a curse.

"You better get out of here!" Sarah shouted. "My mom will be out here in a second, and you'll be in trouble!"

The leader shot a glance at a skinnier man on his left, and they both lunged for Jake's arms at the same time. Jake was quicker, cracking the skinny guy on the arm while whipping the cue at the leader's head with a shout. Having wised up, the bigger man jerked back before he got clobbered.

"Mom's here!" Alice growled as she flew down the stairs, brandishing the weapon and pointing it across the three men in a straight-armed grip, moving it just enough so that they couldn't tell it wasn't loaded. "Turn around and walk away! Go on, get out of here!" she shouted, her voice bordering on hysteria.

The man on Jake's left slapped his partner in the arm and pointed to Alice, edging toward her until she pointed the revolver at him, slowing him down before shifting it to the man on the far right. The skinniest of the three men skittered back with wide eyes, flinching as if expecting to be shot at any second while the other two men held their ground. Jake adjusted his hips to take a swing at the man who was backing away, striking him twice in the arm and eliciting a howl of pain before the man turned and sprinted through the parking lot.

"You better follow your friend," Alice snarled, spitting the words through clenched teeth as the last two slowly backed away, half tripping over each other as Alice's nostrils flared, neck straining, jaw clenching in raw rage.

Her expression and wild energy got the best of the men, and they turned and ran across the parking lot, following in their friend's footsteps. Panting heavily, Alice held the useless weapon on them for a few seconds more before lowering it, her blood pulsing in her ears as the surge of adrenaline began to fade. Finally, she let the revolver drop to her side, turning to Jake and grabbing him up in a quick hug before pushing him to arm's length to examine him before doing the same to Sarah.

"Are you two okay? You did amazing. I'm so proud of you both." Alice pulled them in for another embrace, gripping them hard as a few tears of relief rolled down her cheeks.

"What happened?" Alice asked. "Did they sneak up on you?"

"One came when I was trying to get more food from one of the trucks," Sarah replied with a sniff. "When I ran to get you, one cut me off from getting inside and another one appeared, so I just kept yelling."

"Good job," Alice smiled. "You did exactly as I asked. And you…" Switching back to Jake, she gave him another affectionate tap on the side of his head. "You defended your sister like a champ."

While Jake was still panting and shaking, a smile crept onto his face as his flushed cheeks drained to their normal color. He wiped the sweat off his brow and nodded, holding up the pool cue and staring at a new crack running along the side.

"Who were those guys?" Sarah asked, gazing across the lot to where they'd disappeared into a cloud of smoke.

"Drifters, judging by their clothing. I doubt they were even locals." Alice ran her fingers through her hair. "Come to think of it, that makes perfect sense. They probably wouldn't have owned a vehicle."

"Well, I hope we don't meet them again," Sarah said with a sigh.

Alice laughed darkly and held up the heavy revolver she'd barely put together in time to make a show. "They're just lucky I didn't have a working gun in my hand or they would've been in real trouble."

"It doesn't work?" Sarah gaped.

"Not at all," Alice chuckled. "I just grabbed one from their repair shop that looked like it was mostly assembled."

Sarah giggled. "I'm sorry, Mom. I'm not laughing at you, but the looks on those guys' faces when you came out were something else. You were pretty convincing."

"I wouldn't have messed with you," Jake agreed.

"I didn't even have to act. When I saw you kids in trouble…" Her words faded in a shaky sigh before she gave them another hug. "It doesn't matter now. Why don't you wait here another second while I run back in? I know what I'm looking for now, so I'll be quick."

Sarah nodded. "We've got a couple more boxes we can grab."

With a glance into the back of the SUV, Alice saw it was already filled with most everything they needed. "No. Just stay right here by the car. In fact, Jake you get behind the driver's seat and Sarah sit next to him. Here, let me show you how this works."

Resting the pool cue against the door, Jake circled to the driver's side and got in. After he was settled and had adjusted the seat to fit his shorter legs, Alice leaned in and showed him how to work the starter button and gearshift.

"It's super easy to drive, just like you practiced at home, except with a lot more oomph. If someone comes up again, or those men return, start honking the horn, put the car in gear, and run them over. Do you understand me? Don't hesitate for even a second."

Jake gave a somber nod. "Got it, Mom. They won't stand a chance."

"That's what I like to hear." With a ruffle of his hair, she nodded across the seat to Sarah. "I'll be right back. Hang tight."

Leaving the kids there, Alice re-entered the store and hustled back to the repair shop. Using a series of large, laminated guides taped to the wall above the workbench, she checked over the S&W revolver to make sure it was fully assembled before she dry fired it a few times, then she tucked it into the belt on her jeans. Moving to the next shelf marked with a hand-written sign that said *Completed*, she found a bolt-action rifle with a matte black finish and *Ruger* on the stock, freshly oiled and cleaned. Pulling it free, Alice tossed aside a rag that had been draped over it and held it to her shoulder while pointing it at the wall. After a snap of the bolt, she dry-fired it as well, then looked for ammunition. There weren't any new boxes on the bench, but with the rifle in one hand, she reached across the back of the bench and pulled open more of the plastic drawers that held more odds and ends. Finally, she found an oil-smeared box of .357 rounds and a dozen loose .30-06 rounds that she scooped up. Weapons in hand, she went outside and had the kids switch their seats so Jake was sitting on the passenger side and Sarah was in the back.

"Looks like you scored something." Jake accepted the rifle from Alice as she slipped behind the wheel, resting the barrel against the floor and holding the stock in between his legs.

"These are better than nothing, but I didn't get as much ammunition as I wanted. There's probably more tucked away somewhere in there, but I think we're pushing our luck by staying here for so long." With the box of .357 ammunition in her lap, Alice took out the revolver and loaded it, tucking the weapon under her leg before putting the box in the console between the seats. With a long, deep breath, she turned to Jake and Sarah. "Are you guys ready to go?"

"Yeah, let's get out of here," Sarah replied. "This place gives me the creeps."

"We didn't see any signs of those men again." Jake added. "I think we scared them off for good."

"Good for them," Alice said.

With the SUV packed full of supplies and weapons to defend themselves, Alice settled into her seat and, putting the SUV into drive, pulled straight out to cruise slowly through the rear lot past the blackened rigs and around the outer lane to circle the stores. In the back, Sarah had turned to rummage through the boxes of supplies they'd loaded into the car.

"This is incredible, guys," she said. "We went from having next to nothing to having enough to get home a couple times over!"

"That was a huge score!" Jake looked back.

"It's a lot, yes, but we shouldn't get too comfortable with all this stuff." Alice glanced at her daughter in the rearview mirror. "We need to be more on-guard than ever."

Sarah handed her brother a bag of trail mix out of one of the boxes. "Why?"

"We've got one of the only working vehicles in the area, and people will want to take it. And if they get a glimpse of what we have in the back, they'll be even more interested. Three easily-scared vagabonds will be the *least* of our worries at that point. Get me?"

Jake nodded solemnly. "Got you, Mom."

Sarah leaned forward between the seats and peered ahead through the front windshield. "After what just happened, I totally get it. This time, we'll be ready if anyone tries something again."

As they began their drive out of town, Alice got a different view of the surrounding area with its sky full of smoke above the scattered subdivisions. Almost seventy-five percent of the homes were nothing but beds of coal and ash that seeped tendrils of smoke into the blanketed sky while faint orange lights from gas fires continued to burn underground fuel lines that had ruptured and were blowing upward in a rush of purplish flames like welding torches cutting the air. Near them, the billowing smoke was the worst, turning the air noxious even inside the heavily filtered cabin of the SUV.

As they swung left to rejoin the highway, they passed a small subdivision with most of the homes lying in heaps, the surrounding palm trees scorched or having toppled on hapless houses to crush them beneath their thick trunks. One backyard had a burned-down shed and a doghouse with a peaked roof, and at the end of the tether lay the remains of a dead animal in the blackened grass with the owner sprawled nearby in a cloak of smoking clothes.

Wherever she looked were exposed beams and wooden framing, their tips blackened above piles of melted siding. A large financial bank slumped sadly with its scorched bricks and mortar spilled into the parking lot. The right side of the building was missing its entire section, and the second floor barely stood on charred columns as smoke bled up through broken skylights and holes in the roof. The wind picked up, making the ground seethe with glowing coals before grabbing a cluster of cinders and carrying them across the highway. Jake winced as the fiery embers gusted over the SUV, glancing off the glass and drifting in quick spirals across the hood. Alice gripped the wheel and pressed the accelerator, carrying them through the smoky haze in a burst of speed.

She slowed down once the embers faded, circling a crash around the entrance ramp where several vehicles had collided with a rig and trailer that had been hauling frozen food. The trailer had jackknifed and sat atop two columns of cars, and Alice squeezed the SUV around the trailer as fluid from its refrigeration units dripped on their windshield. Once through, they took a long, circular entrance ramp up to the highway and skirted the western edge of Orlando, twisting between knots of traffic and a sprawl of metal and fiberglass destruction. It was the same landscape they'd been driving through for hours, though Alice felt far less hopeless after loading up the SUV with supplies. If they could just get around the city and onto an open highway, they could finally make some progress.

The kids settled in while she looked past Jake out his window where Orlando was a massive ball of smoke and flames. Recalling a past trip to Disney World two years prior, Alice remembered it as one of the best times they'd ever had, and seeing it go up in such a terrible way made her chest ache with sadness. It was like whoever had attacked the country was trying to erase every good memory they had and wipe them from existence.

Jaw grinding against helpless anger, Alice took solace in that she was doing everything she could to take care of her kids in the present, and the only other thing she could hope for was to be back with James as soon as possible.

CHAPTER NINETEEN

Ryan Cooper
Somewhere Outside East Lansing, Michigan

In the subdued lighting of the basement, Ryan shuffled from one end of each shelf to the other, a notepad in his left hand and a pen in his right as he logged the supplies Alice and James had in stock. The faint light of an electric lantern illuminated the faded white labels on jars where Alice had written the names of the canned vegetables; there were tomatoes, corn, beets, carrots, artichoke hearts, and an abnormal number of green beans. To his left, on the south side of the room, was a small bank of batteries wired into the solar panels that collected energy all day long for discharge at night. Based on some testing, he'd found that the batteries recharged nearly to full during the day, but that was with power diverted solely to necessary appliances, and there was almost no tolerance for an overage unless they wanted to suffer an outage.

The supply room joined the old storeroom he'd been digging around in the day before where James kept his used oil, tools, and, in a word, junk. It was in vastly better condition than the supply room, though, meticulously clean and well organized with labels on just about everything and on the north side of the room were two rows of shelves with more supplies, from ready-to-eat meals to a few hundred gallons of water, more canning jars and other equipment, and boxes of dried noodle and rice meals that would keep for years if necessary. Next to those were several shelves of store-bought canned goods, including most types of vegetables as well as a decent supply of meat, from tuna to chicken with flavored ham thrown in. Alice had hung up small signs here and there, fancy pieces of wood with pudgy bears engraved into them, one with a smart-looking mouse wearing glasses and holding a clipboard, all of them reminding the kids to mark what they'd taken from inventory, and one quaint sign that read *Storage Room* posted near the foot of the stairs.

Ryan took a deep breath, catching the faint hint of a flowery fragrance that reminded him of his daughter and tugged at his heart. There were so many knickknacks and little touches she'd made throughout the storage area and the entertainment room on the other side of the basement. Alice loved woodsy artifacts and decorative pieces, and she'd done her best to get James to invest in a cabin-like aesthetic when they'd built the house, though her husband had pushed back, citing the expense of it and focusing on keeping their home functional. Ryan grunted in silent agreement with his son-in-law, though just sensing his daughter's essence in the room brought moisture to his eyes, and he stopped for a moment in the middle of his count to get control of his emotions.

Once he'd wiped the tears away, Ryan took a look back at the supplies, figuring they had a few months' worth of nutrition for the kids and grandkids together, but far more if he and Helen rationed and were the only consumers for a while. Stepping back to the canning equipment, he tapped his toe on the floor and leaned on the shelf, craning his neck to see several boxes of brand-new jars and a plastic bin of freshly washed ones from previous years. There were neat stacks of tops with meticulously scrubbed rubber seals, various tongs, holders, canning funnels, and strainers. Outside were several acres of produce that needed harvesting soon before the weather changed. If they could get that accomplished, and get a lot of it canned, they could increase their food supply by a lot, and ensure there was more than enough for when the kids eventually returned. *And they will return. If I know my Alice she's halfway home already,* Ryan thought as he completed his count, then moved to the staircase with its plain wooden finish and firm, smooth rail, calling up to Helen as he went.

"Helen! I'm all done with the inventory. Meet me in the kitchen, honey!"

Her faint response came from the top floor, and when he reached the hallway, he turned to wait for her.

They met at the kitchen table where Ryan sat in front of a cold cup of tea with his list of supplies while Helen sat next to him. "How's it looking up there?"

"I've got a pretty nice lookout going for myself." Helen smiled. "I've been using Alice's room at the back of the house to monitor things back there. I've got my favorite rocking chair, my tea, and plenty of memories of the kids to make me smile."

"But you're watching the front as well, right?"

"Yes. Every half hour or so, I do a quick round to check all the angles, and I watch the road coming up past the house. Haven't seen anyone yet, but I have caught glimpses of the dogs moving around out there, so I'm just relying on them to warn me if they see an intruder."

"Excellent." Ryan stretched his back. "You'd probably hear the dogs barking before you ever saw anyone coming, unless someone climbs the fence and the dogs didn't sniff them out right away. Still, I suspect they'd be found out pretty quick."

Helen locked her arm around his and gave him a squeeze. "I have to admit, it feels pretty safe with the dogs out there and you at my side."

Ryan chuckled. "Well, I don't move like I used to, so I'll be relying on the dogs to let *me* know, too. We'll handle any situation as it comes up, though, don't worry." He shifted the notepad in her direction. "In the meantime, I've got a list of all the supplies downstairs. Actually, I just used the list Alice already had and double checked against her numbers. They kept pretty good track of what they had, though there were a couple of snack bars missing."

"Oh, that was probably Jake sneaking around thinking no one would notice."

"I agree with you," Ryan chuckled. "The good news is we've got a few months' worth of survivability without having to leave the property. There's also plenty of canning equipment downstairs we can use on that harvest out there. A lot of that will be ready to come up soon, seeing as it'll be the last one of the year and all. We should probably walk the field and see how much work it will be."

"I agree. Let's do that after lunch."

"Deal." Ryan folded his arms and grew quiet.

Helen tilted her head. "What is it, dear?"

"I'm just not sure how we're going to get it all in. One quick glance tells me there's a lot out there. Alice and James were busy throughout the spring and summer, and we'll have to really be on the ball to get it all put away or canned… that's even if we have enough jars to keep it all in."

"The potatoes won't be a problem," Helen said as she got up and walked to the counter, opening the breadbox. "If we've got too many of those, we'll dry them out and make potato flakes for use later. Want a sandwich? We've got some of that tuna salad I made the other day."

"That sounds wonderful," Ryan nodded and focused back on the supplies, calculating calories and subtracting them from the list using his best guess.

He might've been a little conservative on his estimate that they had a few months of food, though it would be less than that unless they really stretched it, which made getting outside and inspecting the crops all that more important. They needed to know how much work it would take to get it harvested, canned, dried, and packed away, especially since it would just be the two of them.

"How about some vegetable soup to go with that?"

Ryan gave an affirmative grunt as he continued studying the list, murmuring to himself for a moment before he raised his voice. "No, we definitely want to pull that stuff in right now while we have the energy to do it. Folks will take shelter in their own homes, but soon they'll start looking outside their neighborhoods for food and other supplies, and we'll be a prime target with those corn stalks sticking up and those nice-looking tomato trellises sprouting up from the dirt." Ryan looked out the window and sighed. "This place is really nice-looking from a distance, being up on this hill, but I'm not sure I much like the downsides that offers in this particular circumstance."

As Helen stirred the soup on the stove, the liquid sizzled as it ran up on the sides of the pan. "That's a great idea, especially since the weather is still temperate enough to do that. I haven't canned anything in a few years, but it shouldn't take me long to get back into the habit of it."

"I haven't been the best helper in that regard," Ryan replied, "but you can count on me to be right there for you."

Helen waved off his apology. "I've got some incredible canning recipes you're going to love." She poured the soup into two bowls and brought them over to the table, setting them down before returning to a side drawer for the crackers. "This might be the first time those skills really pay off when we need them."

"Amen to that."

Helen made them a couple of sandwiches, scooping tuna salad out of the plastic bowl from the refrigerator. Ryan abandoned his list for a moment to brew them some fresh coffee and pour two glasses of water. When the table was set and ready, the pair sat and had their early lunch, eating quietly and exchanging an occasional smile. As they ate, Ryan thought about Helen's words and how she was right about things being more precarious than ever. While they'd always taken homesteading seriously, they'd never faced such a disaster. With the surrounding neighborhoods and cities on fire, and the expressways and highways cluttered with burning rubble, every decision they made, every action they took, would have a direct impact on their survival.

After they were done eating, Ryan stacked their bowls and carried them to the sink, giving them a brief rinse from a jug of water before setting them in the rack to dry. Joining Helen back at the table, they finished their coffee as Ryan tried to gather his energy for a long walk around the field.

She finally patted his hand. "I say we get on out there. No time like the present, right?"

Ryan chuckled and stood, and the pair retrieved their jackets and bundled up. Stepping out the back door, they walked west around the property where the field and its rows of crops waved beneath the boiling black skies. Duke sprinted from a copse in the south part of the yard, loping toward them with his tongue hanging out. Duchess and Diana yelped from somewhere on the other side of the property, but they weren't in sight yet. Ryan kneeled slowly and prepared for the big dog's affectionate onslaught, Duke barely slowing as Ryan caught him, leaning backward with grunts of laughter and throaty chuckles as the dog nearly bowled him over.

"Whoa, boy! That's a good boy!" He gave the dog a few hefty pats on his side, the barrel-chested animal swinging his tail around as he lapped at Ryan's face, play bowing and backing off as he spun in lumbering circles. Rising to his feet with a groan, Ryan rubbed the dog between his ears and rejoined Helen.

"Are you okay, dear?"

"I'm fine. I just need to be ready when he comes at me full bore like that. It's enough to knock a man down. What say we head out to the chicken coop first? I want to take stock of the situation out there."

"Sounds like a plan." Helen turned him in that direction, and the two marched up the path.

Duchess and Diana galloped over from the garage side of the house, barreling toward Helen and Ryan at full steam and banking away at the last second to chase Duke with barks and anxious yaps. The path led them up to the storage sheds with their pellet feed and grains, but they walked past that and moved straight to the chicken coop where Duke ran around like an obnoxious puppy, trying to play with the free-range birds and rooster, sending them clucking and flapping in agitation.

"Come on, Duke!" Ryan shouted. "Leave it!"

The dog bounded away with Diana hot on his heals, leaving Duchess to sit on her haunches and watch. With a smile, Ryan threw the latch up and entered the chicken run, gently nudging the birds with his boots as Helen slipped in behind him. Once they were in, he closed the door and stepped into the coop, the wood creaking beneath their feet as they ducked under the roosting areas and moved along the short row of nesting boxes where their twelve hens were bundled in and sharing the space. Ryan reached in and counted the eggs with his hand, calling out numbers to Helen as he went.

"These are more than enough eggs for us..." Ryan said when he'd finished. "I know Alice wanted us to collect them for when they got home, expecting the kids would eat them up. Until then, we'll have a huge overabundance."

"They'll be fine on the counter for a few weeks, a few months in the fridge, and indefinitely if necessary if we can get hold of some lime for water glassing." Helen nudged him jokingly. "I hope you're ready for a lot of scrambled eggs."

"That won't be a problem," Ryan chuckled. "If this stretches into the winter and they start molting, we may need to hatch some to help keep production up. We just have to keep that rooster healthy."

Helen was nodding. "They have enough here that I think we can definitely scale up or down as needed."

They stepped outside and exited the coop with Ryan making calculations in his head, glancing up toward the big barn where the donkeys and cow were kept. "All right. With Bessie milking regularly, we'll have plenty of milk and can even make some butter and cheese, provided we have enough to feed everyone long-term. Let's head down to the field." With a shout, he waved the dogs over. "Duke! Duchess! Diana! Come!"

As they turned down the path, the Pyrenees flew past them with renewed energy, banking sharply around Ryan. Circling the northwest corner of the house, Helen and Ryan strolled along a worn dirt path to the enclosed garden with its thin wire fencing held up by stiff wooden posts. Unlocking the gate, they stepped inside and walked slowly past the eastern side where three rows of corn stood tall, followed by trellises of tomato plants, several lines of green peppers, and tufts of carrots.

"We've got tons of tomatoes," Ryan said.

"A lot are still trying to bud, but some have fallen off and are beginning to rot."

"That's okay," he said, stooping to take a pepper in his hand. "We can deal with some losses." The pepper was vivid green with a soft outer texture.

Helen walked into the rows of potatoes and kneeled in the dirt. "Look here. The vines are withered and dead, so these potatoes are probably ready to go." To prove her point, she dug a few inches into the ground and pulled up a couple of mottled, knobby orbs, which she gave to Ryan.

Using his thumbs to wipe off the dirt, he turned them back and forth in his hands, nodding at the rough texture before Helen took one from his hand and gave it a sniff. "Like we figured, they planted a *lot* of potatoes. Alice and the kids love them. These'll be easy to process and store."

"Looks like an unlimited supply of mashed potatoes for certain." Ryan frowned. "We probably won't have much butter at first, though."

"You're probably better off without that." Helen gave him a playful elbow in the side before turning back to the crops.

Ryan looked across the rows with her. "All of this along with the eggs and milk — and we can always slaughter a chicken every now and again if we're building the flock — we'll have enough base nutritional items to get us through the winter easily."

"What about keeping the animals alive?" Helen asked. "Do we have enough feed out in the sheds?"

"I checked the barn loft, and there're plenty of hay bales to get the big animals through the winter. I'm not an expert on growing hay, and I'll have to look into which seed varieties we have on hand, but we could try growing some of our own. There's a lot to it, though. We'd have to harvest at the right time, dry it properly, and always be conscious of moisture levels and bale storage…"

Helen patted him on the arm. "We'll deal with that when the time comes. By then, Alice, James and the kids will all be back home and be able to help. We won't be alone."

"You're right. Sorry if it seems like I'm worrying too much."

"Another thing you haven't mentioned is that the pond is fully stocked with carp. Alice told me so herself. James and Sarah love fishing together, and that was one of their big goals when they built the place. That's an entirely different source of food that should resupply itself. We could even do some aquaponics if we need to grow fresh produce during the winter months."

"If we manage it successfully."

"We will, dear." Helen moved closer and rested her head on his chest before turning to look at the rows of vegetables. "We did this for years until we retired. Just because we've been taking it easy lately doesn't mean we can't farm the way we used to."

"It won't be the easy vacation we were hoping for, but we know what we're doing if push comes to shove." He smiled, recalling the earliest years and the simple recipes they'd used, and the taste of fresh fish and potatoes back when they were first starting their own farmstead and it was just a small house and a couple of sheds.

"We won't starve, that's for sure."

"No, we won't. We'll just have to get out here a little each day to maintain everything." Ryan was feeling better about the situation by the minute. "We can keep things going until Alice, James, Jake and Sarah get home."

Duke zipped into the field with Duchess and Diana right on his heels, chasing each other in the grassy swaths surrounding the field. The big Pyrenees started to angle into one row before Ryan shouted, "Out of the field, you mongrels!" Duke immediately turned left on a dime, kicking up grass and lumbering in a different direction with the girls right behind him. Ryan's grin faded as he continued walking past the line of crop rows to the southeastern corner. "I guess my only worry is if we need to fire up the tractor to get this done."

"You said we didn't want the neighbors to see us running the tractor."

"I did, and that's why we'll try to harvest all this by hand so we don't attract too much attention."

"Okay, but we need to be careful. While we may know what we're doing out here, we're not the spry youngsters we used to be. You especially."

"I know." Ryan shifted from one foot to the other, wincing at a slight bit of discomfort through his leg and hip, the result of all the walking around they'd done and the dragging of debris and clutter off the roads. "The last thing I want to do is hurt either of us."

"If it gets to be too much, promise we'll use the tractor?"

Nodding, Ryan encircled Helen's waist with his arm, fingers tracing along her belt line before giving her a brief but firm hug. "That's a promise I can make, ma'am. Like you said, there's no time like the present to get started."

CHAPTER TWENTY

Alice Burton
Madison, Florida

Having pulled off the highway the previous evening after a long day's drive, they'd parked the SUV in an empty spot behind the rest area near the vending machines. There were no other vehicles except for a trio of semi-trailer trucks on the far side of the lot that had fallen prey to the same fate as every fuel-reliant vehicle in the country. Aside from the halos of singed concrete and debris spread around the rigs, the rest stop was quiet and abandoned, an island of calm in a sea of destruction, the marshland behind the rest area stretching on seemingly for miles, interspersed by the occasional loblolly pine that swayed in the breeze. Alice stirred awake, shaken from sleep by a restless dream she couldn't remember, chasing after it briefly before realizing where she was.

"You dummy," she chastised herself. "You were supposed to be keeping watch this morning."

Glancing over, she saw Jake sleeping peacefully, and Sarah's light snores reached her from the back as she raised from her reclined position, staring out the front window as the sun tried to push through the ever-present gray clouds that had taken over the skies. The layer of rising soot had grown so black that the sun's golden beams barely poked through to give her light to see by. Reaching into the center console, she pulled out a bottled water, twisted off the top, and took a drink. It was lukewarm, but it washed away the sour flavor of sleep and helped her regain her focus. Jake stirred next to her and rose from where he'd been leaning against the door with the rifle tucked under his arm.

"Morning, Jake."

"Morning, Mom. I was so tired last night that I couldn't keep my eyes open. Where are we?"

Alice rubbed her eyes. "I can't be completely sure, but I think we're getting close to Tallahassee, right at the border with Georgia. The last exit I saw was for a town called Madison."

"I remember that," Sarah said from the back seat, where she stirred awake and sat up with a yawn. "I saw it right before I zonked out."

Alice recalled their trek up from Orlando following I-75 before being forced by the congested roads to take a detour. It was the worst wreckage she'd seen yet, making her backtrack all the way to the I-10 junction before exiting and finding a path west again. The kids had been drifting in and out of sleep the entire afternoon and evening and had missed most of the heartbreaking journey through what had once been a beautiful state.

"I'm so sorry for falling asleep." Alice rubbed the last bit of grogginess from her eyes. "I meant to stay up and keep watch, but I was just so tired."

"You need your rest, too," Sarah said. "You can't just stay awake for days and days."

"I know. That's why we need to start setting up shifts."

"You mean guard shifts?" Jake asked.

"Exactly. Next time we stop to rest, we'll start with me on duty first, then Sarah, then you, Jake. Does that sound good?"

"Sounds good to me," Sarah replied with a grin. "I'll get two sleeps."

"I guess you will," Alice laughed. "Hey, hand me a water out of our packs. What do you say we make some breakfast?"

"That would be amazing," Jake said. "I could eat a horse."

"Let's start with some of those MREs we have, then move on to horses if we have to. Are there any breakfast ones?"

"Yep," Sarah piped. "The emergency food bucket has breakfast, lunch, and dinner packets. I sorted through them last night before I fell asleep."

"Let's start with some cereal or granola... if they have any of that."

"Here's what we have," she held up a few packets. "Brown sugar and maple multigrain cereal, strawberry crunch, and regular crunchy granola."

"I'll take a strawberry crunch." Jake reached back as Sarah gave him the meal.

"I'll take a brown sugar and maple multigrain." Alice accepted the package from her daughter and read the instructions. "It looks like we just add a cup of water. We've got plenty of that."

"There are some plastic spoons in the kit." Sarah handed out the utensils before turning and sitting in the backseat with her own.

Alice poured water into her pouch and watched the freeze-dried food come to life as she stirred it around until it had a creamy texture. Her first bite was questionable, and she groaned at the wooden taste, but by the third or fourth bite, her hunger took over and she was able to look past the unique flavor profile. Jake finished first, holding his bag up with a grin as cream-colored moisture dripped to his chin.

"Can I have a granola bar, too?" He rolled up his garbage and put it in a bag they'd placed in the back.

"You've got something on your chin..." Alice pointed. "And we're pretty stocked up, so I don't see any reason to ration right away. We need to be conscious of how far we are from home compared to what we have to eat, though. The fewer times we need to stop to resupply, the better." Alice stirred the last bit of her cereal around and finished it. "And I want to remind you guys how serious we have to be when we're on guard duty. This will be a huge priority for us going forward, and if we screw it up, it could cost us dearly. You saw how fast those men came up on you."

Sarah agreed as she handed her brother a granola bar. "Yeah, and we might not have seen them if you hadn't told us to be careful. Don't worry. When I'm on duty, I won't go to sleep once."

"And no getting on your e-reader."

"Don't worry, Mom. You can count on me."

"Me too," Jake added as he unwrapped his granola bar Sarah had given him from the survival food bin and bit off a crunchy end. "Let's just hope we don't run into any more trouble, because *they* won't be so lucky next time."

Alice adjusted her seat and scooted forward. "Okay, kids. Get your garbage put away and let's get ready to roll out." She pressed the start button and watched as the dashboard lights came on, groaning when she read the battery level. Dropping her hands on the steering wheel, she sighed. "I should've noticed this last night, but I was getting so tired that all I could do was look for a place to rest."

"What's wrong?" Jake had pulled his seatbelt over his chest and buckled himself in.

"The battery is super low. We've only got another thirty miles before we have to recharge again. That'll barely get us to the next city, and I don't want to take that chance." Alice took a moment to look around at the rest stop. "You know what? I think we should stop here and try to charge the battery. This is about as good an area as we'll get, and we can spot anyone coming up the ramp before they see us."

"Do you want to use the generator thing?" Sarah asked.

"Yes. Let's get that out first and pull it around to the charging port."

Turning off the SUV, they exited the vehicle and circled to the back to pop the hatch. Between the three of them, they got the generator out of the cargo area and placed it on the ground, and Alice took the handle and rolled it around to the charging port on the left-hand side.

"Now for the solar panels."

They pulled out the ultra-thin flexible panels and began setting them up on the ground about fifteen yards away from the charger where they had the best view of the sky. It took a few rounds of positioning, but the clouds were drifting fast, and there were a couple of patches of bright, clear sky where the sunlight was bleeding through. Dividing groups of panels into sections, they covered a hundred square feet of ground, soaking up as much sun as they could get and, once positioned, they connected all the panels together with cabling and used one line to attach them to the generator.

Turning it on, Alice saw it was already seventy-five percent charged. "I'm not sure if we have the right attachment for this to connect to the car," she said as she examined a wound-up cable attached to the front of the generator.

"Right here!" Sarah was standing at the hatch, holding up several black metal and plastic pieces. "I found a bunch of different ones in a side compartment here. Would any of these work?"

"Bring them over and I'll check." Alice took the first one that looked like it might fit and after turning it around a few times, she connected it to the generator's cable and then plugged it cleanly into the port on the side of the SUV. "Okay, we're in business. I think that worked."

"Check the dashboard and make sure it's charging," Sarah said.

Alice leaned into the driver's side door and hit the start button, and the dashboard sprang to life. Where the total charge had been displayed previously, the charging status had replaced it, and a small number was slowly ticking down. Where it said *Time Remaining*, the numbers continued to change drastically from forty-seven hours to thirty-seven, fluctuating every few seconds as it continued to drop.

"Oh, no. I hope it doesn't take that long." After a minute, an alert showed on the dashboard, stating the SUV was in *slow charge mode* and had finally settled on a completion time. "Okay, thirteen hours is much better but still an eternity out here." Alice stepped back with her hands on her hips, turning in a slow circle to look in every direction at the mostly gray skies.

"That's actually not too bad." Jake winced into a patch of sunlight as he stared upward. "I mean, we have a working vehicle and infinite fuel to get us home. Thirteen hours isn't that bad, considering how hard we pushed things last night."

"Plus, the SUV wasn't fully charged when we got it," Sarah pointed out. "And it's just now morning time, so the sun is bound to get stronger in the afternoon and once we get away from the cities. And it may charge faster than we think."

"True," Alice replied. "We'll let it charge for three hours and then set off again. Hopefully that'll get us past the next city, and then we'll stop and charge it some more after that."

By late morning, they'd walked the entire parking lot several times, keeping the SUV in sight as they took turns watching the highway where it was mostly a field of debris and bent guardrails. Much of the burning had tapered off, leaving just smoke to drift over the carcasses of thousands of cars, trucks, and corpses. Dense woods surrounded the lot, bordering the marshes whose boggy smells were barely detectable through the smoke. There was no easy way to approach the rest area without being spotted, but Alice's paranoia ensured that they didn't dare let their guard down, constantly on the lookout for anyone who might wish them harm.

By the time they got back to the SUV, she couldn't help but check the charging level and let out an exuberant cry. "Hey, kids! You were right; it did charge faster! It's got an eighty-mile range now! Pretty doggone good for just a few hours of charging."

"That's great!" Jake leaned in to see the display for himself. "That should get us well past the next city, right?"

"Absolutely it will."

"It's probably because we readjusted the solar panels a couple of times," he said.

Alice looked up at the darkening sky where patches of light were still showing through but were too few to get a steady charge, and they'd spread the panels out more, trying to maximize their chances of catching as much direct light as possible. "Chasing that light was the best thing we could've done. I'll bet it charged twice as fast because of that. Otherwise, we could've been here all day."

"You sure you don't want to let it charge all the way?" Sarah asked.

"No, I'm good with this. Let's pack up and get ready to go."

They'd been in the process of re-arranging their supplies and had left some sitting outside the SUV, and Alice made them get their backpacks out and began stuffing each of them full of a variety of supplies.

"What are we doing this for?" Sarah asked with a long, slow sigh. "We've got a whole cargo area to keep this stuff in."

"If we have to abandon the Jet Star for any reason, we can just grab our backpacks and run. Gotta plan for the worst and hope for the best."

They started by packing several of the emergency MREs inside each pack along with most of the bottled waters and energy drinks they'd gotten from the semi-trailers. After that, a few thin blankets and small camping pillows went in, followed by a pair of sleeping mats. At the top, they put in more fragile items like calorie-dense snack bars, and in the side pockets they stuffed flashlights and batteries along with compasses and other odds and ends. Only when their backpacks were full to bulging did Alice agree they were ready to go. Placing everything in the SUV's cargo area, they tucked it all in tight and spread a few towels out so the supplies couldn't be as easily seen by anyone who happened to get a glance inside the vehicle. Finally, they gathered up the flexible solar panels, cabling, and generator and packed them into their spots in the cargo area, then they got back inside with Alice behind the wheel and Jake in the front passenger seat once again. With a glance up at the darkening sky, Alice started the Jet Star and pulled smoothly out of the rest area to jump onto a connecting road bearing north that looked far less cluttered than the highway.

She pulled onto the two-lane road where farmsteads and old-style homes stretched into the distance with wide, grassy fields surrounded by swaths of forests that were largely untouched by the disaster. The backyards were filled with barns and sheds and old farm equipment, and the smells of the Florida marshlands leaked into the SUV's cabin along with copious amounts of noxious fumes. Despite what should have been a beautiful view, though, the telltale signs of still-burning fires dotted the landscape, marked by thin smoke trails that drifted into the sky, with some corkscrewing upward in twirls of cyclonic winds. The smaller fires weren't as bad as the cities, though the ominous sky still loomed like a killer above them, an unnatural display that showed the true scope of the disaster.

"At least the traffic isn't nearly as bad," Alice joked as she drove around occasional wrecks and vehicles pitched nose-first into ditches. "Though this might be easier to navigate if there *was* traffic..."

Some of the vehicles had plowed into the trees or bushes, catching on fire and spreading their carnage across the road and into people's yards. On more than one occasion, cars were twisted in the center of the road, thrust together by detonations to create head-on collisions with no one surviving the fiery wrath. Alice had become an expert at navigating the tall SUV through the rubble, though, and where they ran into situations where the tires might be at risk, they got out and cleared the way by hand.

The farther west they drove along Highway 53 on their way toward Madison, the skies began to clear, the dark shades of gold and gray making a curved shape tinged with burning red light on the edges. Madison, Florida introduced itself with a green sign with a rainbow flourish beneath it, and Alice drove past the first exit, thinking she'd slip by until she stopped in front of a huge pile of steel and glass with twisted rubber tires and bent axles sticking out. Without stopping to investigate the twelve-car wreck, Alice backed up to the last ramp they'd passed and got off with a huff. At the bottom of the ramp, the first thing she noticed off to the right were strips of stores and three gas stations whose fueling pumps had gone up in a schism of concrete, dirt, and metal, with one of the underground tanks blossoming outward at the top in jagged steel petals. Things weren't as densely packed as they had been previously, though, and most of the vehicles had caught fire without causing much damage to things around them, though they still had to be careful of weakened pavement and loose debris.

"I'm going to try to find a back road to the next exit so we can get back on the highway again."

"It doesn't look like much burned up here," Jake noted, echoing her thoughts. "I mean, compared to the other places we've been."

As Alice pulled between the stores and up the main strip, she was surprised to catch fleeting images of human-sized shapes moving through the fog. After getting into the thick of it, she glanced eastward to see groups of them working hard around the storefronts, stacking boxes of cereal and diapers from a local grocery while others raided a hardware store and several other strip malls on the same block. It wasn't chaotic looting, but an organized layout of supplies into specific piles, everyone seemingly working together to get the job done.

"Finally, people!" Sarah shifted across the back seat. "They look like they've got it together. Should we stop and talk to them?"

"Absolutely not. I shouldn't have to remind you how valuable this vehicle is; we need to focus on getting home first and foremost."

As the SUV passed through a cloud of smoke billowing from a cluster of road wrecks, Alice gave a sharp tug of the wheel to avoid a woman walking across the street, startling her and causing her to jump back. Alice stared as they passed, seeing a dozen people digging in the wreckage and salvaging items from car trunks and back seats. Anything they retrieved was stacked in haphazard piles of charred clothing, suitcases, and other personal effects stained with soot and grime.

"Okay. We're out of here," Alice said.

Instead of continuing up the main road, she turned left and cut between the busy strip malls where people had noticed them and were walking closer to get a better view, a few of them pointing at the SUV. As they put the stores behind them, Alice caught sight of a man with a beard and cowboy hat striding parallel to them through a parking lot, following her path as they drove up a slight incline into several blocks of apartments. The hairs on the back of her neck rising, Alice drove them over the crest of a hill and out of sight, splitting the buildings and cruising down a lane crowded with elm trees, oaks, and a few pale ashes with long trunks that stretched skyward. Up ahead, the road grew thick with more wreckage where older neighborhoods left trails of smoke trickling into the sky and she had to slow down yet again.

The road wound up a series of curves and straight into a subdivision of newer homes, some of which had been ravaged by the fires, though most of the brick structures had remained standing thanks to their garages being separated from the main structures. Small groups of shadowy figures moved in the dim streets, gathering supplies or giving their SUV sideways glances as it passed by. While Alice tried to keep a good sense of direction and stay parallel to the highway, she soon got lost in a bevy of twists and turns where the houses started looking the same and the street names ran together. The SUV tore to the end of a cul-de-sac and was forced to turn around and go back the opposite way as Alice grunted with frustration. As she continued to navigate through the restless streets, there was enough rubble and wreckage to become a nuisance, clusters of it blocking them completely or too dangerous to drive through, and Alice didn't want to have to stop for fear of the local populace seizing the opportunity to try and take their possessions.

"This place is really creepy." Jake's voice rose from the seat next to Alice. "Can we get out of here?"

"I'm trying, hon." Alice ground her teeth as she ran up on a two-car pileup where an SUV had decimated a smaller economy car, leaving chunks of car parts scattered across the pavement and a pile of burned bodies lying in the grass off to the side.

"I mean, they can't be terrible people," Alice responded. "At least they're taking care of their dead. But I think you're right. We need to get out of here."

Two side streets later, and after shooting down a connector road, they entered an older subdivision where each home had a unique style with latticework gardens and add-on constructions. It still had a rural feel, but the houses were spaced far enough apart to avoid complete disaster, with wide backyards and clusters of woods between the homes, some with barns and sheds and in-ground pools. More shadowy groups of people gathered in side yards as they collected supplies and goods that hadn't gone up in flames, acting again not as looters, but as an organized force that was responding to a crisis.

"I am completely lost," Alice stated flatly as she rounded the next corner and stopped the vehicle. "I don't know where the highway is or how to even get out of here."

"Wish we had a map," Jake said.

"Even if we had one from a gas station, it probably wouldn't show any of these back streets and neighborhoods, and that's where we're lost right now." Looking up at the sky, she tried to gauge the position of the sun's glow through the thick canopy of clouds, guessing they were pointed just slightly south. With that basic direction in her head, she crept forward and gripped the wheel tighter. "We're just going to keep going till we find our way through to the highway. Once we get there, we'll be in good shape. Just... hang on."

At the next intersection, a wreck clogged the street where a food delivery truck had rammed an oncoming pickup head-on and the pair had gone up in flames with crushing force. The flying debris had broken out windows in the surrounding homes and had taken out stop signs and mailboxes, leaving the road filled with sharp, smoking pieces and giving off the impression of a bed of nails that could pierce her tires in an instant. Alice whipped the wheel to the left and skirted the wreckage, running over some lumpy debris and riding up into a yard to smash through a small garden in front. The grill mashed a bush to send purple flowers flying everywhere before they nosed down the other side and plowed over the sidewalk to get back onto the street. Still heading west, Alice pushed the Jet Star to its limits, switching the transmission to four-wheel-drive and churning straight through a series of yards. She wove between small gardens and scraped up against a retaining wall in front of a bi-level home, splitting a tree and a set of concrete steps in a grinding of grass and dirt beneath her tires before smashing over a sign that read *Welcome to our home!* with a heavy crunch. The SUV's electric engine offered full torque at an instant's notice, and they tore through the yards and gardens with ease, the tires spitting gravel and mulch, even taking out a small picket fence before they flew back into the street.

"Whoa, Mom!" Jake cried out.

Teeth grinding, hands gripping the wheel like a vice, Alice whipped them to the left, turning a corner with a screech of tires, the SUV's tail end swerving hard before straightening out with a jolt. Alice hit the accelerator and rocketed forward up a clear straightaway as she searched for an exit. "We've got to be almost through town," she said with a shake of her head. "Do you guys see anything?"

Sarah was sliding back and forth in the back seat, craning her neck before falling back with a frustrated sigh. "I can't see anything past these houses. There's just a bunch of woods and a few taller buildings to the north."

"That's not good," Alice said as she took her eyes off the road for a moment to look around herself. As they crested a shallow hill, she saw a corner store and some older strip malls in the distance, and she raced down the hill and back up again, hoping the heightened elevation by the stores would give them a good view of a way out. When they reached the top, there were more than just a couple of stores; several apartment complexes were nestled along the hill below them, and off to the right, a gas station smoldered atop a slab of ruptured pavement, though only a few small structures surrounding it had caught fire.

"This must be the center of town..." Alice looked around as they passed the empty Chinese restaurant with an *Open* sign still hanging on the door. "Maybe we're just slightly south of downtown."

"It's not exactly bustling," Jake quipped as he stared at a handful of burned-out buildings on the right, likely set aflame by the gas station explosion a couple of blocks back. "I don't see anyone — Mom! Look out!"

They were pulling into a bottleneck with the laundromat on their left and a driving school and liquor store on their right, and two dozen people were hauling two burned-up cars into the intersection by ropes, their arms straining as they quickly blocked most of the street ahead. The charred vehicles were useless, but their wheels were intact, and the two groups were able to drag them into position to block Alice's way.

From behind the buildings, another dozen people flowed from behind the wrecks and spread across the street and into the parking lots on either side, each of them brandishing a firearm or a blunt object. Leading the pack was the man she'd seen earlier with the cowboy hat and beard, striding into the middle of the street with a stone-cold glare. Hand raised, palm up, he shouted for Alice to stop, and those around him mirrored his glowering expression. Alice shook her head slowly, angling to the right as she searched for a way through the parking lot to get past them. Someone off to the side raised a pistol and fired it as their leader motioned for them to do so, and Alice and the kids ducked as the round flew harmlessly over them.

"Don't worry," she said with a growl. "That was just a warning shot."

"But they'll shoot us for real, Mom!" Sarah shouted.

"Just stay *down*!"

The man shouted louder, pulling a large silver pistol from a shoulder holster and holding it in the air. "You'd do well to stop, lady! Stop right now!"

"Don't stop, Mom," she hissed between the seats, her voice nearly squeaking with panic. "They're going to hurt us!"

"I'm not going to stop. Just hold on tight." Alice clenched her jaw and glanced both ways, looking for a way out. She'd let the Jet Star coast down the street, bringing them to within thirty yards of the people blocking them and when the man leveled his gun with their car, Alice punched the accelerator while jerking the wheel to the left. The move in the opposite direction surprised their attackers, and Alice blasted past them into the parking lot entrance and ran straight at the people standing in their way. A man and a woman leaped aside, barely avoiding her sweeping front fender. A gunshot ripped off from somewhere and missed, but the next one pounded the side of the vehicle with a heavy thud, causing her to jerk the steering to the right in surprise as she clipped a burned-up sedan with a jarring shudder. Crying out in frustration, Alice whipped the wheel back and forth and angled for another exit as more rounds popped off to the right.

As they bumped and rattled across the rough pavement, Alice misjudged a six-inch concrete curb around the exit lane and slammed into it, tossing them straight up into the air. Alice whipped the wheel left and then back to the right again as more shots were fired, and Jake threw his arms over his head as a bullet hit the side mirror and exploded in a shower of plastic and glass. Alice was already away, though, accelerating down the road to flee the marauders and their roadblock, the gunfire finally stopping as they swept left along a curvy lane and out of sight.

"That was way too close for comfort," Alice whispered, her heat racing as she kept glancing in her rearview mirror as they came down from the elevated part of town and the two-lane paved street turned into an old country road that guided them westward past more woods and farmhouses.

Jake rose from where he'd been crouched in the seat. "Geez, Mom. You weren't kidding about people trying to get our stuff!"

"I think they were focused on taking the SUV more than anything. But who knows what they would've done to us, and I doubt they would've let us keep our stuff if they were willing to shoot us."

Adrenaline was pumping through her veins, her heart racing in her chest as her breaths came in quick gasps, but the more the road slipped by beneath their tires, the better Alice felt, and she finally relaxed her hands on the wheel where she'd been holding it in a white-knuckled grip. For a quarter of a mile, Alice took her time and navigated through a short stretch of road rubble before noticing the SUV was responding sluggishly to both the steering wheel and accelerator.

"What the…" She looked around. "Something's wrong with the car."

Jake leaned in and pointed to the dashboard display. "Could it be that warning?"

A flashing red light next to a layout of the vehicle's battery system had appeared on the center display, and one of the batteries had turned red and had an X through it while the three others showed either yellow or blue.

Alice pulled the vehicle over to the right side of the road along a stretch of trees and tapped on the red battery icon to bring up a more detailed readout. "One of the main batteries is down, and we're only running at four percent capacity."

"What happened?" Sarah leaned between the seats.

"I bet one of those bullets hit a critical system component or the battery itself. They're all malfunctioning as a result."

Jake wrinkled his nose. "What's that smell?"

Alice tilted her head and sniffed, catching the acrid scent that was leaking up through the floor and creeping into the car, far more pungent than the ever-present smell of smoke and general burning.

"What are we going to do, Mom?" Sarah's voice teetered on the edge of fear.

"We're going to get our stuff out of this thing before it catches on fire. Grab everything you can out of the back and put it on the side of the road! Jake, get the rifle out and help your sister! Now! Go!"

Snatching the ammunition from the center console, Alice and the kids got out and moved to the rear, popping the hatch and taking the backpacks out to place them several feet away from the car. They continued grabbing bins of MREs and other food and set them at the edge of the road where the roadside brush swayed gently in a Florida breeze. Between the three of them, they got everything out in a couple of minutes and stood back, staring at the Jet Star as the acrid smell grew even more pungent and smoke continued pour out from underneath the bottom.

"Well, there goes our easy ride," Alice said.

"Yeah, that really sucks," Jake watched the car slack-jawed. "I thought we were going to be home free."

Sarah placed her fist on her hips and glowered over her shoulder. "We would've been if it hadn't been for those jerks shooting at us back there."

From inside the vehicle, a warning alarm blared in the cabin, followed by a polite female voice. "Attention, breach in main battery one. Emergency services are being automatically called. Please evacuate the vehicle and step away."

"They definitely hit a battery," Alice said. A sizzling sound started in the tail end, and she threw her arm out and guided the kids back. "Come on, guys. Get away! It's going to —"

A spark spat from the rear end, followed by a burst of them as the battery malfunction spread. The undercarriage crackled and groaned as the Jet Star's frame began to heat up, and popping sounds erupted from beneath it with flashes and flares as the batteries began to violently discharge all of their remaining energy much faster than they were ever designed to do so. Alice pushed the kids back another few feet and then dove to grab the backpacks, tossing them farther away from the hissing, spitting vehicle. Finally, a red flame licked up through the cargo area and more smoke began trailing from the back, followed by tendrils of fire that crawled up around the rear bumper to give off an oily, greenish smog that was far more foul than anything they'd smelled from other wrecks.

"Quick! Stuff whatever else we can into our backpacks." She grabbed hers and moved toward their stacks of supplies, waving adamantly at the kids. "Come on, guys! We need to load up."

"Why?" Jake asked, doing what he was told despite his deep frown. "We can still keep all our supplies. We just have to find something to put them in, like a wagon or another car or something."

"No time to go looking for new transportation around here. Those locals are going to see that rising smoke and come to investigate. The last thing they need to find is us three standing here next to a ton of supplies. Come on! Get to packing so we can get out of here!"

They tore through the supplies and picked out a few more MREs and stuffed them into their already overflowing backpacks. When they were done, Alice slung hers on her shoulders, groaning at the weight as her back bowed with the strain. They started down the road, but then Alice stopped and returned to the SUV. "Quick, guys, let's throw the rest of this stuff into the fire."

"Why would we do that, Mom?" Jake complained. "We could always wait here and see if the people actually come."

Alice was already shaking her head as she picked up a plastic MRE bucket and hurled it into the back of the SUV as flames licked around the opening. "No, because we don't want them to think we have anything valuable on us. We want them to believe it all burned up so they won't have any reason to try and come after us."

Jake nodded and grabbed some of the flexible solar panels and tossed them in with the rest. "Man... all this stuff is just wasted."

It took them less than a minute to get everything tossed into the back, and once complete, they retreated from the growing heat and watched the flames and smoke increase, kicking off a hot wind that stirred the nearby trees. Backing up and snatching the kids by the backpack straps, Alice pulled them along the road until they'd turned and were running away from the growing flames. The SUV crackled, sputtering fire as it gave off bursts of light and heat as more smoke rolled up from the chassis, green and black as it flowed up into the sky like a beacon for anyone watching.

Around them, flat farmlands and woods stretched out to either side alongside squares of perfectly plowed fields and the occasional burned down barns. A turkey vulture that had been circling the town banked around the curling smoke on its powerful wings and followed the trio as they fled Madison with backpacks bouncing on their backs. Their small patch of road stood alone in the middle of massive swaths of black clouds that stretched from east to west across the horizon, dots of distant firelight and hazy drifts plaguing the marshes, but when the smoke grew too thick, the scavenger banked upward on a crosswind of warm air and flew off in search of an easier potential meal.

CHAPTER TWENTY-ONE

Ryan Cooper
Somewhere Outside East Lansing, Michigan

The sun was just a bright blob in the sky, its sharpness diminished by layers of dingy gray clouds clogging the atmosphere and threatening to drown out any semblance of hope that things could eventually get better. Ryan tried not to let it affect him as he and Helen got busy harvesting the crops, pulling off tomatoes and peppers and digging up potatoes from the ground. They'd done a half a row of corn as well, twisting and breaking off the ears and tossing them into a burlap sack for Ryan to haul over to a pushcart they were using to transport the picked items to the house.

Ryan was sweating as the cool air chilled his skin, sending shivers through his arms as he hustled, mostly hauling sacks Helen had collected while doing some of the heavy digging himself. She was working her way between the peppers and carrots, diligently dusting each item she picked off and placing it in its proper sack. While it wasn't especially rainy, the moist soil was turning into mud by their constant stomping, threatening to suck their shoes off if they weren't careful. Waiting for Helen to have something for him, Ryan knelt in the potato row and used a small shovel to dig down a few inches and loosen vegetables in the ground. Once he had a good number of them ready, he plunged his fingers into the moist soil and lifted the tubers free, dragging the canvas sack behind him and filling it as he crawled. He'd fallen into a trance-like state, his hands digging into the cool earth and pulling sustenance from it, counting his blessings with every wad of dirt-covered balls that came free.

Once his sack was full, he called to Helen. "I'm going to carry this last one over and push the cart up to the house. I'll unload it and be right back."

Helen left her tools in the dirt and stood, wiping her arm across her brow before resting her hands on her hips. "I should have a couple more things for you when you get back. It's moving pretty quick, wouldn't you say?"

"We're doing well, but..." As Ryan turned and slung his potato sack on his shoulder, he teetered a moment, clutching at his leg briefly before standing straight and tall again. "We barely put a dent in this. I'd say it'll take us all day today and most of tomorrow to get it all up to the house." He wiped his arm across his forehead. "And while I love it out here, I could use a nap."

"No naps for us today," Helen replied with a playful smirk. "We've still got a *ton* more to do. You know the second we sit down we won't get up again."

Ryan's eyebrows raised in amusement. "I'd fall into James' recliner, and that's where I'd be the rest of the night."

He started to trudge back to the handcart, but he'd been standing for too long, and his shoes had become solidly stuck in the mud. As he put his right foot forward and tried to lift his left one, the mud clung to it and forced his hips to twist at an odd angle. There was a moment where he was caught between falling and staggering, straining to get his limb loose as the weight of the potato sack dragged him down.

"Oh, no!" he grunted with a windmilling arm, looking at Helen helplessly as his legs got tangled up.

At the last second, he jerked the upper portion of his left leg free from its prosthesis with a snap that made him wince. Off balance, he staggered into the next row, twisting and scowling as he fell. With two quick steps, Helen was there, grabbing his right arm and trying to hold on as he carried them both to the mud. Ryan landed hard on his backside with a pair of carrot tops jutting up between his legs while Helen collapsed on top of him, and on her knees and off balance, she inadvertently leaned on him, bowing his back and forcing him deeper into the mud. Gasping and straightening with a strained and worried expression, she held out her hands to check him for injuries.

"I'm so sorry, dear! I didn't mean to fall on you. Are you okay?"

Ryan was laughing as he helped her rebalance herself. "I'm okay. Seriously, I'm fine. This is just the last place I ever expected to end up."

"Let's get you up."

Helen stood and took him by the hands, squatting and using her weight to give him some leverage. Ryan leaned forward and got his right foot beneath him, coming straight up but gasping when he felt cool air down around the bottom of his open leg, and he clung to Helen rather than shifting his weight to his hobbled leg.

"Oh, no..."

"What is it, dear?"

"I lost my leg. It's gone."

Helen backed up and gazed along the plant rows. "I see it. It's stuck in the mud, honey. Come on. Let's get you over to the cart."

Leaning a good deal of his weight on her shoulder, Ryan hopped to the edge of the field on his right leg, slipping and sliding in the loose soil and mud, trodding on more than a few carrots and peppers along the way. When they reached the grassy edge, he bounced forward a few steps before grabbing the cart handle and anchoring himself there as he turned to spot his shoe with his prosthetic foot and leg still inside it stuck out in the mud.

Helen stepped back and squinted at the lost part. "I'm so sorry, Ryan. I shouldn't have made you lug all those heavy sacks."

Ryan shook his head. "No, we had the right idea, but we just executed poorly. The system is working great, but this mud is tough. Luckily, I thought something like this could happen." Turning so he faced the cart, he sorted through a couple of plastic trays near the handle, fishing out some strong twine before sitting on the grass. "Can you go grab my leg, please?"

"Of course. Be right back."

Helen shuffled out into the rows of crops and stooped to grab his shoe with the prosthetic foot still inside. She took it by its sides and wiggled it back and forth, pulling hard but unable to get it free. Finally, she reached for the shovel he'd left lying there, dug around the heel, and flipped it out.

After retrieving the limb, Helen held it up with a smile. "Got it!" Then she brought it over to him and waved it before handing it over.

Once in hand, Ryan flipped it over and inspected the inside where the prosthetic had cracked just beneath the socket. "Can you tell what's wrong?"

Ryan held the appendage out, sighing heavily. "Looks like it cracked where the socket attaches to the ankle. I won't be doing any heavy moving around with it like this, but there still might be enough suction to keep it on my calf."

Straightening the sweaty gel liner at the bottom of his leg, he slipped the prosthetic over it and put weight on it, taking a few steps before turning and coming back. "Yep. It'll stay on, but I won't be running any marathons. Maybe I can strengthen it a bit."

Using the twine from the tray, Ryan wrapped it around the top of the prosthetic and pulled it tight to bolster the suction he already had. He took a few more experimental steps, doing a full circle, hoping that it wouldn't randomly fly off just trying to walk.

"That's much better," he said with a nod. "I should still be able to get around with no problem, but it'll need a more permanent fix before I want to rely on it. For now, let's get this stuff up to the house." Turning and leaning against the pushcart handle, Ryan threw his weight into it and shoved it over the flat grass and out of the garden gate with Helen at the front, pulling a smaller handle on that side and working it back up toward the house with their reduced load. When the dogs came bounding up again, Ryan warned them off, too tired, sweaty, and aggravated to give them any attention. Leaving the harvested plants outside, they went in where Ryan stripped off his jacket and collapsed into a kitchen chair. Helen brought some wet washcloths to clean off the dirt as he removed the prosthetic and studied it to see if he could fix it any better.

"Is there anything else I can do?" Helen tossed the washcloths into a nearby laundry basket.

"A hug would go a long way. And maybe grab me the duct tape out of the junk drawer?"

With a smile, Helen fell against him and hugged his shoulder to her side, wrapping his head in a warm embrace. "Done and done." She shuffled over to the drawer, fished out the black duct tape, and brought it over.

After putting his prosthetic back on, Ryan ripped off a large piece of tape and wrapped it beneath his knee to cover the top portion of the prosthetic, then he wrapped a second one around the calf to see if he could reinforce the suction. Standing up, he took some more experimental steps and nodded.

"That'll do for now," he said, "but that mud is too much for me. I think we're going to have to use the tractor from now on. We'll just have to hope no one sees us working out here."

"While you do that, I'll grab the corn and anything you can't get with the tractor."

"That sounds like a plan. Let's get to work."

Donning their jackets once more, the two started to go outside when Ryan stopped. "Since we're going to be out here running the tractor, it might be a good idea to arm ourselves in case someone gets curious. Did Alice give you the combination to the safe?"

Helen nodded. "I tend to agree with you on that one. And yes, she did."

They went downstairs into the supply area and over to a small stand-up safe against the far wall, hidden behind the furnace and water heater. Helen punched in a code on the keypad, and they watched it turn green and click open a fraction of an inch. Grabbing the handle, Ryan leaned backward and pulled the heavy door wide to reveal the small arsenal James and Alice kept inside.

Ryan reached in for a rifle but held back. "I don't imagine we'll want to lug around anything too heavy out there. Just a couple of handguns will do us fine, okay?"

"Sounds good to me. You know what I like to shoot."

Ryan searched the hooks and found exactly what she wanted. "How about this one, honey?" He removed an S&W Model 642 and a small box of thirty-eight special rounds before scanning the top shelf and grunting in triumph. "Here's a quick loader for you, too."

"Perfect." Helen took the weapon and ammunition off to a side table where she began loading it.

"Let's see what you have in here, James," Ryan mumbled, scanning the hooks and cases in search of something with more power. He moved past several handguns and revolvers before settling on a pistol with a long barrel and fat grip, its stainless-steel glinting in the electric lantern light. "A Beretta 92FS. This'll suit me just fine."

Removing a box of forty caliber rounds and two holsters from the top shelf, he shut and locked the safe and then joined Helen where she was finishing loading her revolver. They clipped the holsters on their belts and tucked their weapons away, then they headed upstairs, exited the house, and walked to the barnyard with the dogs trotting next to them. The Pyrenees had worn themselves out over the past few hours and were getting back into their herd controlling habits, trying to nose the chickens and rooster around the coops before following Ryan and Helen out to the barn. Ryan unlatched the gate but wasn't immediately flocked by sheep and goats because they'd already fed them earlier. With no animals to hinder them, they strode out toward the barn, where he unlocked the double bolts, threw the latches, and opened the doors wide. The smells of manure and moist earth greeted them, and Bessie over in her stall lowed deeply in a haughty hello.

"We'll get you milked right after this, old girl," Helen called. She'd already milked her once that day and had stored the raw product on a shelf in the cool part of the basement with another six gallons they still had to pasteurize using the double boiler.

"We might want to do that before you head down and tackle the corn," Ryan commented.

"You're probably right." Helen patted his shoulder as they stepped up to the massive tractor. "You just worry about getting this tractor up and running, and I'll take care of that other stuff."

"Sounds good." Ryan stared up at the utility tractor. "It's not much newer than the one we had. I'm going to grab that trailer of theirs and the middle buster for the potatoes and get these doors open wide."

"Okay. Be careful."

Taking each step on his left leg with an abundance of caution, Ryan crossed to the trailer that was parked on the left side of the barn, grabbed the middle buster, and tossed it inside. As Helen prepared to milk Bessie, he threw the barn doors open wide and made sure they wouldn't close on him. The sky was still ominously dark, with its flat black clouds and gray edging, the sun's rays falling in sharp patches of golden light that sometimes broke through the foggy haze. The sight of it stretching over their heads like that filled him with a desperate worry, and he turned and shuffled back to the tractor quickly, climbing up and plugging the key into the ignition. He started to press the start button but paused with his finger hovering there, sweat trickling down his temples as he looked from the control panel to the fuel tank sitting against the rear wall that had mysteriously *not* exploded. While he was fairly certain of why that was, there was still a chance his theory was wrong and hitting the button could be what would ignite the fuel and blow himself and Helen both sky-high. But if he didn't at least try to start it, a lot of the crops would rot on the ground, and they all might end up suffering for it in the long run.

"Are you okay, honey?"

Ryan glanced over to where Helen was standing by the cow's stall with a couple of buckets in her hands. Ryan cleared his throat and pressed the button and the tractor kicked to life with smooth and effortless ease, the engine purring with diesel power followed by his deep sigh of relief. With a wave to Helen, he shut the cabin door and closed off the wall of sound, putting the tractor in reverse and backing out of the barn. Out in the barnyard, the goats and sheep avoided the noisy tractor and kept their distance, and the dogs instinctively herded them away from the rumbling diesel engine. Ryan got it turned around and backed in, angling to line up the hitch to the light trailer. Leaving the vehicle running, he climbed out and lifted the coupler, walking it a foot or so toward the hitch and dropping it on with a metallic *clack*. After connecting it, he got back in and pulled out carefully so he didn't clip the door frame.

Ryan quickly opened the barnyard gate, drove through, and shut it behind him, and by the time he got back in the tractor, he was sweating and panting hard from the urgency of getting things done quickly, leading to an increased risk of making mistakes. After the accident – and especially since there were no more medical facilities – those were risks that couldn't be taken lightly.

Tightening his jaw, he focused as he pulled through the field gate, leaving it open and driving around to the west side. Detaching the trailer, he hooked up the middle buster and drove up the well-placed vegetable rows, plowing through the hard-packed soil in three sweeps to upend them and leave potatoes sitting loosely, ready to be easily picked up. He did the same thing with the beets, carrots, and onions, the ripe and ready vegetables popping to the surface like bubbles in a lake, only a handful damaged in the process thanks to his skillful application of the buster. The big tractor tires moved swiftly over the mud and didn't get stuck once, their thick treads much better for handling the rough terrain than his own two feet. His last pass took him to the west side of the field, and he swapped out the middle buster for the trailer and then grabbed some burlap sacks they'd left from before. By the time he'd completed filling his second sack of potatoes and dropping it into the trailer, Helen came out from the barn, finished with her milking to join him in the field.

"Bessie was a little ornery, but she's happy now." As Helen slipped her gloves back on, she wiped beads of sweat off her brow with her jacket sleeve. "I put the milk in some sealed containers, so maybe you can swing by with the tractor, pick them up, and bring them down to the house."

"No problem." Staring out at the field with its upturned crops, Ryan gave her a smile. "It was a good idea to break the tractor out. We could've never gotten all this upended without it."

"Think anyone saw us?" Helen gazed toward the south side of the property, where the long line of red maples stretched to the end of the lane and partially blocked them from prying eyes.

"Honestly, I'm not sure. I haven't been looking very hard, but I guess I should've been." Ryan squinted at the front gate. "I was so excited to get these crops turned up."

"Don't worry about it. There's no one down there. If they were curious, they'd be standing down there by the gate watching."

Ryan shrugged and handed her one of the burlap sacks. "All we can control is how fast we bring this stuff in."

Nodding, Helen's expression grew serious. "I'll grab some more of that corn."

For the next hour, they worked quickly and efficiently, moving past the long rows of crops, dusting them off, and placing them in their sacks. The big trailer was more than enough to handle all of it, and they had it half-filled before too long. It was grueling, sweaty work, but Ryan was in his element, getting dirt beneath his fingernails and sweating up a storm, avoiding any of the labor that might cause a repeat of his earlier accident. Occasionally he'd glance out across the property to see if anyone was watching, his paranoia growing as the hoard of crops piled up and weariness set in. It was a veritable treasure trove right in front of them, more valuable than gold or silver, especially as the days grew shorter and the cold began to set in.

Neither Ryan nor Helen were used to going so hard at it, not since they'd retired from their farmstead when every morning had been a struggle to plant quickly, tend quickly, harvest quickly and get it put away or sold to the highest bidder. While Ryan's knees creaked and his back ached, there was something special about working with the earth. It was the moist aroma of an upturned field, the sense of accomplishment at bringing in what the soil had provided, and the pride of self-sustenance and hope even in the most dark and dismal times.

Soon, he and Helen fell into that familiar and steady rhythm, knowing exactly what the other would do or say in an unspoken language of two people who'd known and loved one another for over fifty years. Helen's strength and endurance was equally expected and pleasant, picking right up where she'd left off as a young wife working the family field to harvest their life-giving crops. She was relentless, and what she couldn't lift, she dragged through the mud, only rarely needing Ryan's assistance to get an especially heavy sack into the trailer.

At some point in their harvesting, the trailer became full, and he urged Helen to keep picking while he drove the entire load up to the house and unloaded every burlap sack near the back door in neat piles according to vegetable. By then, his shoulders and leg were aching, from the knee joint to the hip as he adjusted his movements to balance out the broken prosthetic. Its grip on his leg was growing looser by the hour, almost slipping off twice and forcing him to readjust it while he sat on the sacks. Back in action, he climbed in and returned to the field, where he hopped down and gathered up the sacks Helen had left at the ends of the rows. The day was deepening, and black clouds settled over the field, made worse by the setting sun to make it difficult to see.

"It's getting dark, hon," Ryan said as he lugged a sack of onions on each shoulder and dumped them gently atop the rest in the back of the trailer.

Helen stepped out of the cornrows, dirt on the thighs of her jeans and cheeks, her jacket stained and grubby. She wore a dazed, weary expression, but she nodded and raised a finger. "There's half a sack of corn in there. Let me grab that, and I'll be right out."

Ryan finished what he was doing and followed Helen into the tall cornrows. As she picked up her half sack, he took it from her and spotted another full sack she'd forgotten to bring out. He grabbed that too, and together they left the field, loaded the trailer, and climbed into the cabin where Helen sat on his lap.

Giving her waist a squeeze, he grinned and peered around her at the tractor controls. "Just like the old days, right?"

"A day out in the field, and I always got a ride back on your lap." She chuckled and held on to a handgrip built into the roof as he drove out into the field to get turned around. The gigantic wheels trudged over the loose dirt and mud to carry them out through the gate and back along the muddy tract to the house. The dogs caught up with him and bounded next to the trailer as they pulled up near the first stack of supplies, climbed down, and began unloading the sacks of produce. Ryan left the tractor idling, already feeling much safer with it behind the house and not in a direct line of sight from the road. With a huff, he dropped the last bag of carrots on top of the others and stood back by the trailer, gazing over everything they'd brought in.

Helen came to stand by his side and folded her arms as her grin spread. "This is quite a haul."

"Just like we were hoping. Those kids did a better job than even I thought they had in getting all this planted" Ryan rubbed the back of his neck as he marveled at what they'd done. "I'm not sure what came over us, but we really got into a rhythm for a while there."

"Like you said... it's just like the old days." Helen slapped her hands on her thighs. "I'll tell you what. I'm worn out and just about ready for bed."

"We can finish the bulk of this tomorrow." Ryan gestured to the tractor. "Do you want to come with me to put this away?"

"Absolutely!"

They climbed into the cabin and motored to the barn with Helen hopping down and opening the doors while he swung the trailer around. Loading Bessie's milk into the back, they drove it to the house where they placed the closed containers next to all the food, everything looking wonderful where it was laid out in a couple of neat rows. Corn, potatoes, peppers, onions, turnips, and a few smaller bags of herbs lay all across the back of the house, the fresh smells coming off and washing over them.

She rode with him back to the barn and got out while he attempted to reverse the trailer in. It took two tries to get it parked, and he climbed down and unhooked the hitch before pulling the tractor in a tight circle to put it back where he'd found it. The weight of the day rushed in on him as he powered the big diesel off and sat in the perfect silence with his body still throbbing from the noise and vibrations. With the satisfaction of having put in a great day's work, Ryan descended from the cabin and put both feet on the ground with his arms and shoulders shaking with weariness. He leaned against the tractor with parts of his leg sore and raw from the prosthetic's constant rubbing on his outer knee. The fix could come later, but there was nothing more he wanted to do than get cleaned up, put on a fresh change of clothes, and relax for an hour before bed. Taking a deep but resigned breath, Ryan pushed off the tractor and began walking slowly to the barn doors where Helen stood with one side half closed, her hand resting on the latch as she peered past the house.

Bessie lowed deeply and shifted in her stall, and Ryan laughed. "You're good for now, old gal. We'll be back tomorrow to collect some more milk, don't you worry."

Ryan's smile faded as he approached the doors and saw Helen's expression. As he watched, her head tilted slightly as she squinted into the growing darkness, the shift in her posture sending a spike of adrenaline through his veins as he moved quicker toward the door.

"What is it, Helen?"

"I don't know..."

"You don't know? I haven't seen that look on your face since last year when you wrote the check for the property tax bill."

"I guess... maybe I saw something down there."

"Where?"

By then, Ryan had reached the barn entrance and turned to see what she was staring at. From his position, he was looking straight past the sheds and play area to where their goods were stacked neatly behind the house. The EV was parked off to the side, but as he shifted his attention to the left, he could see past the red oaks and down the lane to the front gate. Everything was closed up nice and tight, and some ducks were crossing the lane from one pond to the other. The dogs were still sitting by the flock of sheep and goats on the west side of the barnyard, unaware of anything being off.

"I thought I saw a person down there."

"Was it one of the Jones'? Mike, maybe?"

Helen squinted harder before relaxing her shoulders with a shrug. "I can't be one hundred percent sure. It's probably nothing. The dogs didn't bark once."

"They might be too far away to notice." Ryan shook his head and glanced at Duke and Duchess, where they wandered around the edges of the flock with Diana somewhere on the north side. "Plus, they're so busy watching the other animals that they might be distracted."

Helen laughed and waved it off. "I'm sure it was nothing."

"Possibly, but we need to be vigilant. The dogs won't always catch everything right away even when we let them roam the yard freely. Let's not go anywhere unarmed."

Letting go of the door, Helen's serious expression faded to something more pleasant. "Agreed. What do you say we go inside and get cleaned up?"

"Then we'll team up for dinner before we work on pasteurizing that milk." The tension in Ryan's jaw released, though his eyebrows were still creased with worry as he glanced up at the dark sky. It had grown more ominous, with deep shades of billowing black and gray, the wind unseasonably nonexistent, leaving the sky with a stagnant, rotting look above their heads.

"Are you okay?"

He thrust his chest out and nodded firmly. "I'm fine, dear. But between those clouds up there and what you may or may not have seen, I'd be lying if I said I wasn't a little nervous."

"Me too. That's why we're going to set a watch tonight. You and I will take turns keeping ourselves safe."

Nodding slowly, Ryan grabbed the other barn door and brought it around to meet hers before they shut them together and locked up. Arm-in-arm, they strolled down the lane, past the sheds and chicken coops with a cool breeze ruffling their hair. With an end to the evening in sight, they stopped by the harvested food long enough to grab the containers of milk and take them inside to heat in the double boiler before putting it all away in the refrigerator.

Once in the house, Ryan put the last container on the counter and told Helen he was going upstairs to get a change of clothes. Stopping in the foyer, he cast a shadowy glance at the dining room window, and he walked over and pushed the curtain aside to gaze down the long lane to the front gate where Helen thought she'd seen something. He waited in the shadows for a good minute, scanning across the fence line and over to the Jones house in hopes of catching someone in the yard, but when nothing moved, he gave up his search and went upstairs to get cleaned up.

CHAPTER TWENTY-TWO

Agent Alan Harris
Mount Weather, Virginia

"These MREs really clog up the ol' plumbing," the President said with a slight strain in his voice.

"Yes, sir. Do you need any—"

"Relax, Harris. It's just a joke."

Agent Harris stood by the door of the bunker restroom with his arms folded as he leaned against the wall. The drab green colors, like everything else underground, were plain and simple with little decoration or stylish flare. It was solid brick, a full foot thick in every room and passage from the ground floor to subfloor three, where most of the meetings and global conferences were taking place with anyone they could reach through the spotty communications systems. President Birk was sitting in a stall with the door closed as he took care of business, chatting with Harris without a care for the awkwardness of the situation.

"Yes sir," Harris chuckled and shook his head, changing the subject. "As I was saying earlier, most of the civilian leadership and officers were terribly upset when they heard the numbers of those dead and missing, including myself."

"Sorry I couldn't warn you ahead of time about that. Those were just coming in during our global conference and the IC boys wanted to do some extra checks before we disseminated the news."

"That's okay, sir. Colonel Crow has been a true leader and kept everyone on track. Right now, we're still reeling from all this, but as far as I can tell, we're doing everything we can to reinvigorate the supply chain on both the military and civilian fronts."

"That's good to know, Harris. I know they're talking about hunting down all the EV's they can find."

Harris shifted and nodded as if Birk could see him. "We've got teams out scouring dealerships around the country for any and all vehicles we can find. Of course, anything we find will be taken by train to a consolidated location where they'll be divvied out according to their use and power requirements. Obviously, they can't be just driven across the country."

"But at least we won't be driving horse-drawn carts and wagons."

"No, sir, though that might not be a bad idea. I'd say we start collecting bicycles as well, though I doubt Crow will see the sense in that."

"A Marine battalion riding bicycles into battle." Birk laughed. "I've got that image in my mind now and I never want to let it go."

Harris smiled. "Sorry, sir."

"Oh, no. I'm not making fun of the idea at all. It might come down to that eventually, so it'd be a good idea to jump ahead on that one."

"Any news on what's happening around the world? If that information isn't classified."

"Most of it isn't to the high-ranking officials, and I certainly don't mind you knowing. Aside from some of the information on the Russians and Chinese, we just heard from South Africa, Algeria, and Botswana. They're holding things together but by the skin of their teeth."

"How did we even get in contact with them?"

"A satellite relay through our embassies in those countries."

Harris took on a pinched look. "And you say they're doing okay? I would've figured with Africa's constant economic and political strife, the disaster would've only made things worse."

"They're not as developed as most European nations, so ironically – is that irony? I always forget. Anyway, the impact locally has been more reserved than other places." Birk's shoes shifted inside the stall, sliding across the tiles. "The biggest shock to them will be from the global recession, but because they still have significant manpower, they could potentially pull out of this before anyone, provided they can pull together."

"Finally, something to cheer about."

After a moment's pause, Birk continued, his tone lower. "What about you, agent? Have you heard from your parents or sister yet?"

Harris felt his stomach clinch at the question. "No, sir. I haven't."

"They were in southern Virginia, right?"

"That's right, Mr. President. My sister was going to school at Virginia Tech, and my parents live in a suburb around Blacksburg."

"Have you tried to contact them?"

"I checked my phone when we had a brief break yesterday, but by then the phone systems were already down."

The toilet flushed, and Birk stepped out of the restroom to the sink where he began washing his hands. Something rattled in the vents, and Harris glanced up at the ceiling and its stark white light which gave the restroom an unwelcome and sterile feel marked by the faint scent of bulk-purchased cleaner and hand soap.

"Aren't you bothered by that, Harris? Don't you want to know where they are?"

"Yes I do. But I..." Harris choked on the words and swallowed a lump that had formed in his throat. "What I mean to say, sir, is that I have a duty to this nation and you, first. My parents are tough people, and so is my sister. If anyone could've made it through this, it would be them. I'm hoping they're alive and doing well, but I have to put them behind the needs of the nation. They'd understand that, and my dad..." Harris turned away, coughing as he fought against the welling emotions. "Well, my dad would rather me be here protecting you, as crazy as that sounds."

"I don't doubt you have a fine, patriotic family." Birk shot him a glance as he stepped to the hand dryers and punched the button, filling the room with a sudden wash of warm air as he rubbed his palms beneath the vent. "I know how you feel. They haven't found my wife, but she'd be saying the same thing." The President took on a lighter tone to mimic her voice. "Don't worry about me, Thomas. Take care of the nation, Thomas..." He shook his head and chuckled darkly. "It's tearing me up inside, but there's not much I can do. It's funny. Of all the resources of the United States military, and they can't find a single woman who was on a photo-op trip in Missouri to speak with members of the St. Louis school district."

"I'm sorry to hear that, Mr. President. I certainly hope they find her soon. Is there anything I can do?"

"I don't think so, Harris, but I appreciate the sentiment. They're doing everything they can, but there's a lot up to fate right now, for both of us." Birk put his hands against the wall and leaned there. "I just..." With a soft sigh, the President's eyes grew red around the rims. "I'll have a detachment sent to Blacksburg the next time they're in the area. We'll make sure someone's out there looking for your family."

Harris stuttered. "I-I sincerely appreciate that, sir, b-but that's unnecessary. There are other people, other places that need—"

"It's *absolutely* necessary that we take care of the people who are taking care of us."

"But we've got several members of Congress and the Senate still out there, and resources are incredibly thin."

"Don't tell me how thin the resources are, agent. I know more than anybody just how bad off we are."

"Sorry, sir. My point is that the people who need to be deciding things for us are more important than some Secret Service agent's family."

Birk came off the wall and turned to face Harris, folding his arms and raising an eyebrow. "I appreciate you trying to tell me my business, *Agent* Harris, but I'm pretty sure we'll have a few troops out that way handling other business, so it won't be such a big deal to have them swing by your house." When Harris didn't immediately reply, Birk gave him a wink.

"There are a lot of headaches that come with our jobs, but there are a few perks, too. One of those perks is having the leader of the free world's military telling you he's going to help you. I'm insisting on this, Harris. Is that understood?"

"Yes, sir. Thank you."

Birk's serious expression melted into a wide grin, and he slapped Harris hard on the shoulder. "Cheer up, Harris. We'll figure this out and do our best to help everyone. It'll be hard, but we'll do it."

Harris nodded, the knot that had been sitting in his stomach uncoiling, releasing days' worth of tension in just a few seconds. "I appreciate that, and I know my parents and sister will, too."

"All right then, Harris." Birk gestured to the door. "On to the next meeting. There's a lot to do before this day is through."

CHAPTER TWENTY-THREE

James Burton
Kansas City, Kansas

The sound of the train's whistle and a blast of steam cut through the night as James hopped from the boxcar into a holding yard about the size of a football field with tracks that ran along the south side. They'd come to a stop and the guardsmen were letting weary passengers off to stumble around sleepily as they gathered their meager possessions. The soft gravel and dirt parking lot was flat and bathed in stadium lights affixed to tall poles, and somewhere on the north side was the Kansas City camp that had been so long in coming. James was stiff and tired, groggy from several hours of a half-baked sleep, his rest filled with frightening dreams and uncertainties that never let him relax.

Turning back to the boxcar with his backpack firmly affixed on his shoulders and his revolver holstered at his side, he reached up to help a few people down, taking kids and setting them to the side, clasping hands with a mother of two and making sure she got both feet on the gravel without twisting an ankle.

After everyone was off, he called up to Frazier. "Come on, man. I'll help you down." Since the fight with the angry father, the Guardsman's face had swollen over one eye, and the skin around his nose was bruised and puffy. When the man hesitated, James laughed and gestured. "Don't try jumping down. You can barely see. You'll end up busting your ankle if you try it."

Frazier grinned in embarrassment but nodded, sitting carefully on the edge of the boxcar and allowing James to catch him as he hopped down. "I appreciate your help. You seem like a good dude. You want a job?"

"No thanks," James laughed. "I'm heading home, man."

"Roger that." The guardsman turned and grabbed his pack and rifle off the deck and shouldered both before looking down the line of boxcars where a mix of soldiers and guardsmen were getting off the train. Two soldiers were walking the angry father across the empty holding area toward the glowing lights of the camp, the man's family following close behind, his wife with a child in each hand as she tried to keep up.

"What do you think they'll do to him?" James asked. "They don't have a prison here, do they?"

"You've got me." Frazier shrugged. "I just got here."

James laughed. "Yeah, I guess you did. Hey, if I don't see you again, it was good meeting you."

"Same here. Maybe we'll cross paths again."

Others were getting out of the boxcars and passenger cars, some turning to their spouses or friends and pointing to the man who was being carried off, questions floating through the air about what had happened. James walked slowly across the lot, watching as equipment and supplies were offloaded by the Army and National Guardsmen, sometimes met by electric pallet drivers and small utility vehicles where they placed the crates and bins and drove them past the haggard throng to enter the camp. With no one to guide them, dozens of weary refugees milled around in clusters, pointing at other train tracks that swept in from all directions to meet theirs at a train station east of camp. On the passenger deck, bewildered civilians stood by what remained of their possessions, most of which amounted to a couple of pieces of luggage per person, at most. By the time James turned around, Frazier and the rest of the guardsmen had moved off and were heading toward the camp with a few people following listlessly behind them. Just when James was about to join them, speakers sitting atop the light poles blared to life.

"Attention, and welcome to the Kansas City Recovery Center. In order to receive the best possible aid, please follow the yellow signs into the support camp to receive lodging and food. We would ask you to move calmly and allow those who are injured to go first so we can process them efficiently."

The crowd began meandering in the indicated direction, following yellow signs that hung about twelve feet up on the light poles with big arrows pointing in the only direction they could go. James stepped aside to allow two men to carry a grimacing woman between them as she held her right foot off the ground and clung to the men's necks. He stayed in the back of the throng, watching as they filtered toward a series of checkpoints to the north. Slowing, James noticed more lights and movement to the east, where the train tracks converged and, curious, he shouldered his way carefully and gently through the crowd and arrived at a chain-link fence to gaze out at the train yard.

There were several massive engines with boxcars and flatbeds that swept in from every direction and many of the empty ones were being disconnected by Marine and Army units, replaced with cars loaded with big fifty-gallon and larger drums of what he assumed were oil and fuel, skids full of batteries, and crates of unmarked supplies. They connected flatbeds with gas powered machinery and electric loaders and transport vehicles, the organized chaos odd against the backdrop of the ruins of Kansas City. A little south of him, two soldiers were standing casually near the fence, sharing a cigarette as they looked around.

James meandered toward them, raising his hand and calling out. "Hey, guys. Chilly night, eh? You fellows doing okay tonight?"

The two shared a quick glance, and one with a thin face and bright blue eyes shrugged. "As good as we're going to get, I guess. All things considered."

"You guys on break?"

"That's right. You need something?"

James hiked his thumb over his shoulder. "I just got off a train back there after making it out of Denver International."

The first soldier took a drag on the cigarette. "No kidding? We heard it's a mess out there."

"You're telling me," James laughed. "There were airplanes falling out of the sky on my head. The airport was...." He trailed off.

The soldiers shared a glance and stepped closer to the fence. "Are you serious?"

"You didn't see anything crazy like that?"

The soldier shook his head. "We were training outside the city when some trucks blew up around camp. We got the fires put out fast, but we haven't seen much else. Heard a lot, but nothing like airplanes falling out of the sky. Did that really happen?"

"A jet engine almost hit me as I was trying to get beneath an overpass. Barely made it out with my skin intact."

"Sounds like it." The soldier frowned as he turned and stared east toward the city.

"I guess you guys already know all these explosions have something to do with bad fuel, right?"

"Oh, yeah," replied the first soldier.

The second soldier stepped closer and looked in both directions as if making sure no one was listening in. "You're right, but do you know why the fuel went bad?"

"Some kind of terrorist attack, based on what I heard on the emergency broadcast bulletin. I confirmed that with someone from the National Guard."

"It's not just that," the second soldier said. "It's a bacterial agent that's infected the fuel. Don't ask me how it all activated at the same time... but they did it, somehow."

James' mouth dropped open, his stomach twisting at the news about the deviousness of the attack, but it didn't change the question he had. He put his fingers through the chain-link fencing and pointed toward one flatbed stacked with blue barrels marked with danger and explosive signs. "I'm assuming that's fuel. Aren't you guys afraid of it going up? I mean, if everything's infected with the bacteria or whatever, won't it explode?"

"Nah, these are from the reserve stores we had in one of our underground bunkers. Stuff's been there for a while, so it wasn't infected with the bacteria."

"I guess that's why it's under heavy guard?"

"That's right." The first soldier nodded and blew a gust of smoke off to the side. "Good fuel is as valuable as gold these days."

"Yeah, I guess it is." James was about to ask another question when someone called out behind him.

"Hey! I need you to head into the recovery center, please!"

Glancing over his left shoulder, James spotted a soldier standing a few feet away from the main throng of refugees with an impatient expression as he waved.

James nodded to the men he'd been speaking with. "Thanks, guys. Stay safe."

"You, too!" The first soldier replied, while the second gave him a curt nod.

James turned, jogged to the waiting soldier, and hustled by. "Sorry about that," he said, though the soldier merely nodded and strode over to talk to the men smoking by the fence.

James followed the crowd of around two hundred people toward the camp proper, which was positioned just north-west of the rail station and illuminated by more of the same stadium lights which sat on shorter poles. The bright luminescence gleamed off the tops of the sea of tents, mostly green or black interspersed with white ones with red crosses on the sides. The first stop was a series of checkpoints set up across a fifty yard wide swath of vacant field where a few troops and administrative personnel wearing black or blue jackets covered the gates, hesitant smiles on their faces as they waved at the throng to organize them into lines.

There were only four lines, which was a small fraction of the available gates, and many of the workers stood by idly, shifting uncomfortably and gazing at the empty lot. As James slid into a spot between a couple of families, he rose onto his toes and gazed past the checkpoints to get a better view of the camp. The sea of tents went on forever with straight lanes dividing them into square blocks. Tent roofs were stretched taut over poles and held down with spikes and rope and most of the blocks had ducts affixed to small windows in the sides, and there were thousands of miles of cabling draped between poles with pipes running along the ground and leading to septic stations and water filtration units.

"Water and electric? Heating and air conditioning?" James shook his head. "This place is incredible."

Like the entry to the camp, though, there weren't many people walking the lanes which were flanked with bright white stones and gravel. Only a few groups of refugees milled around as rescue staff ferried supplies to and from larger storage tents which were colored orange or yellow. As James moved closer to the first checkpoint, a sinking feeling hardened in his gut, and a nagging worry pulled at his heart. The calculations just didn't add up. He figured there were only a thousand civilian survivors and double that in troops, far less than he would have expected there to be. His thoughts flew south to Florida, where he imagined Alice and the kids out there in a hellish landscape of fire and smoke and possibly in trouble.

The line moved quickly with so few people, and it only took him a moment to reach the front. "Where is everyone?" he mumbled, drawing a glance from a woman who had a couple of kids with her. After she walked past, he looked east to Kansas City where it lay in a thick haze of smoke with pulsing orange glows on the ground, creating an impression of a massive bed of coal. "Oh." He finished his thought. "That's where they are…. And that's why the camp is barely filled."

Instead of dwelling on the worst possible scenario, he stayed focused on the first checkpoint where two guardsmen sat at mobile tables with computer tablets in front of them, using a stylus to tap on the screen as they wrote in people's names and added them to a list. Army soldiers stood nearby, holding their carbines loosely or with them slung on their shoulders, seemingly not worried about any trouble from the crowd, likely because they outnumbered the civilians two to one and also due to the sheer lack of crowds. When James reached the table, he leaned forward so he could hear the woman as she addressed him in a stiff, professional tone.

"Welcome to the Kansas City Recovery Center. Can I get your name, please?"

"Yes. James Burton, ma'am."

"Thanks. Can I get your most recent address, date of birth, and social security number?"

James winced. "Do you really need my social security number to check me into the camp?"

"Yes, sir." Her expression softened. "It's just so we can verify who you are. There are a lot of people taking advantage of the current crisis for their own gains. We're trying to avoid any potential crimes."

"What kinds of crimes?"

"We have a refugee database so family members can be notified if someone in their family is found, and vice versa. If we didn't have some kind of confirmation process, an adult could claim children that weren't theirs, and that could lead to other problems. *Is* there a problem?" The guardswoman arched her eyebrow.

James was already shaking his head, anxious about the refugee database as he tried to peer over the edge of her computer tablet. "Not a problem, ma'am." He gave her his information. "And can you please put me on that refugee list?"

"Done."

"While we're here, can you check on my wife and kids, please?"

"Certainly. What're their names and socials?"

James gave her the information and waited patiently as she scrolled through something on her screen. After a moment, she winced and shook her head. "Sorry, sir. As of right now, we don't have anyone by those names on this list."

James frowned, and his shoulders sagged. "Thanks. Are there any camps in Florida?"

"I'm sorry, I don't have that information. I was at home when all this happened, and I got called in on the spot. We've been up to our eyeballs trying to get this place set up, and I barely got my own family here. But if you'll move on to the next checkpoint, you may find more information inside."

"Yes, thanks. I really appreciate that." James nodded. "Is that all? I thought there'd be more to it."

"That's it. Well, except for this." She handed him a small tag with a number on it. "This is your tent assignment. You'll have a single, though there will be some other family-sized tents nearby. Other than that, I've got all your pertinent information, and now you can move on through to the next checkpoint, where someone will help you get acclimated to the camp."

James held up the tag with a smile. "Okay, thank you so much for all your help."

"My pleasure." She was already looking past him to the next person in line. "Whoever's next... please step up."

James strode around the table to the stares of soldiers, guardsmen, and camp facilitators who were chatting quietly as they watched the refugees come in. The next checkpoint was less guarded, with over a dozen skids lined up and big cardboard boxes sitting on top. A guardsman stood on either side of the boxes, reaching deep and pulling out what appeared to be half filled duffel bags, which they tossed to passing refugees with nods and smiles. By then, the lines had trickled to almost nothing, and James was one of the last people through. He accepted a cheap, lightweight duffel bag from a young guardsman dressed in fatigues and wearing a light blue vest. As he stepped past, James unzipped it and peered inside, surprised to see bottled waters, a first aid kit, a water purifier, blankets and a camping pillow, and several bags of long-lasting rations.

Turning, James gestured to get the guardsman's attention. "Hey, thanks for the duffel bag."

The man faced James with a smile. "No problem, sir."

"I can't speak for everyone coming off the train, but I was in Denver when everything started blowing up. Denver International Airport, to be exact." He held up the duffel bag as if testing its weight. "I'm very thankful to have all this. It's... incredible. The past few days have been rough."

The man straightened, shaking James's hand. "I'm sorry for any hardship you might've faced coming out of Denver. I hear it was pretty bad up there."

"Not going to lie, but Denver and its surrounding areas weren't looking great." James shivered as a chill passed through his spine. "A lot of people didn't make it out of there."

"I'm sorry to hear that." The man shifted uncomfortably. "I don't have any relatives there—mine are all from Louisville —but I haven't heard a single thing from them."

James nodded to the young man. "I was just curious about something."

"What's that?"

"All this stuff." He held the duffel bag up again. "I'm thankful, but there's so much in here. I could live for days on this. Why're you all handing out so much?"

"Orders came out just yesterday that we're overflowing with supplies and to give people a week's worth of rations."

"I'm definitely not arguing, but I wonder what it means?"

The guardsman lowered his voice. "I don't think the higher-ups are expecting a lot of survivors."

"Have you heard anything? I mean, is there any official word on the numbers of dead and wounded?"

For the first time, the young man looked genuinely uncomfortable, and he glanced around to see that the other guardsmen had gathered a little way off and were whispering before he turned back to James with a hesitant sigh.

"Hey, I get it," James said. "You don't want to just blurt out official numbers, especially not to civilians. It's just that

I've got family in Florida and Michigan, and I'm desperately trying to put together some realistic odds in my mind on whether I'll ever see them again."

The man glanced around again and cleared his throat. "This is all pretty hush-hush, you understand…"

"Yes, absolutely."

"While I didn't hear this with my own ears, there are rumors out of NORTHCOM that upwards of…" Swallowing hard, the guardsman gave another look around, and after a pause he continued. "They're saying that upwards of two hundred million are dead in the US alone. At least that's the early estimates, but I don't have any figures on the injured or anything like that." Once he started speaking, the rest came out in a rush. "They're also saying that the cities got hit the hardest, and the rural areas have more survivors. The big problem is that we've got tons of supplies, but we just can't get them anywhere with no vehicles or fuel."

"Right." James started to thank the man, but he remembered that Alice's parents drove an EV and probably had it at the farmstead. "What about electric vehicles? Are you guys trying to seize any of those?"

The guardsman nodded. "Oh, yeah. Those are like gold now, and the government has commandeered all local civilian and government EVs, but we're lacking sufficient charging infrastructure with the grid down. There's just not enough chargers and charging stations."

"That's right. It's going to be hard to charge all those EVs when you can't get coal to the generators and three quarters of your infrastructure is burned to the ground."

"Not to mention the even *bigger* problem of the roads being covered in tons of debris. With all the wrecks and explosions out there on the interstates and highways, we just don't have the equipment to move it all very quickly."

James was nodding as the sheer magnitude of the disaster expanded in his mind. "It's not like you can just gas up a bulldozer and drive it down the middle of the road to clear it."

The guardsman pointed at him. "Bingo. And even though there are a few companies that make heavy electric equipment, a lot of that stuff is built in Mexico. There may be a couple of parking lots around that have some electric backhoes and dozers, but it's not enough for what we need to do."

James nodded and raised the duffel bag again. "I appreciate the information, and sorry for all the questions, but can you tell me a little more about the camp? The lady up there didn't give me directions or a time limit on when I needed to leave or anything."

"There should be a small map on your tag to get where you need to go."

Lifting the tag, James saw it was folded once, and when he spread it between his fingers and thumb, he saw a small map on the back with the different facilities and services around camp. "Oh, I see. It still looks a little confusing."

"The place is huge," the guardsman laughed, happy to be talking about something else besides the death tolls and the delicate state of the country. "The green tents are for civilians. You've got the smaller, single units and then larger ones where several families can stay together. Your tent is… let's see."

James flipped the paper. "Seven seventy-six."

The guardsman pointed out at the lot. "We're set up to hold a hundred times more than this. I just hope they can rescue more people out of the cities. Anyway, your tent will be towards the front of camp, and there should be a mess hall just north of you, along with toilets and showers and things like that. If you're hurt, just look for a white tent with a red cross on it and give your name to the person at the door. They'll check you out and see to you right away. We've also got a surgeon and an emergency surgery tent on the west side, but you don't look like you need anything like that."

"No, I don't have any serious injuries. I'm just tired." James held up his tag again and waved it. "I guess I'm just looking for a place to put my head down for a minute."

"Stay as long as you want, and you can head out whenever you want with no restrictions. If you do decide to leave, make sure you stop by one of the exit areas, or come back here, and you'll be given another bag of supplies."

James couldn't think of anything else he wanted to ask, and a small group of stragglers were coming up for their supplies. "Thanks for talking to me, I really appreciate that. And good luck in finding your family in Louisville."

"You too, sir. Have a good night." The guardsman flashed him a polite smile and turned to the newcomers, holding out more duffel bags.

James headed deeper into the camp, the start of which began at a soft gravel lane stretching from east to west with the first set of tents just beyond it to the north. Picking the first lane he came to, James walked north along the ten-foot-wide path past dozens of heavy tent flaps with large numbers stenciled in stark white next to the doorways. The piping and ductwork he'd seen from a distance were even more organized when viewed from up close, everything running along the edges of the paths and behind the tent walls in neat stacks and rows. The pipes stretched out to the edges of the camp where the water and plumbing were connected to large processing units with gleaming white domes. The tents themselves were made of thick canvas material and built solidly, the breeze coming through barely ruffling them. While the place seemed safe and well organized, it was a ghost town with just a handful of people walking around, minding their own business as they hustled from their tents to the mess hall or restrooms.

James allowed a moment of relaxation to pass over him as he stood with his bags in tow, taking stock of himself. His legs were weary, his back ached and a minor headache was forming at the base of his skull and squeezing his neck, leaving him feeling exhausted and numb. Despite that he'd finally made it to safety, the escape from Denver International and the subsequent trek through the blazing city had left his lungs raw and raspy, his throat still sore from breathing in all the smoke and fumes. The air in the camp had a tinge of smoke to it, but it was far clearer than it had been in Denver, and he realized just how desperately he needed rest before starting off again.

After passing two infirmary tents where emergency staff stood outside or sat on thin green benches near the doorways, James reached his tent, holding up his tag to double-check the number before pushing through the flap and stepping inside. A light switch hung on a wooden pole on his right, and he flipped it on to reveal canvas material covering the ground. On the far wall was a simple bunk bed, a small set of drawers beneath that, and a plain basin with bare pipes and water spigots next to a rack of white towels. It was spartan to the extreme, an easy structure to set up and tear down, but it was also clean and quiet, completely the opposite of what he'd experienced over the past few days.

A basic air conditioning unit rested on the ground on one wall of the tent, and he walked over and adjusted the temperature until the air coming out was slightly warmer. His first thought was to grab some hot food if they had it, and he went to the tent flap to see the zipper clasp had a lock on it with a key sticking out. James dropped his things near the cot and returned to the door, taking the key and stepping outside. From there, he turned and zipped the flap tight, locking the bottom clasp and pushing at the zippered edge to see if it would break or come open. Seeing it was a solid lock and there weren't enough people to warrant stealing his things anyway, James strode past his neighbors' doors and up the main lane, heading north and spotting the mess hall just a few blocks up.

The smells of cooking food drifted by, reminding him of his high school cafeteria when he was much younger, serving pizza and meatloaf and buffet-fresh foods. When he reached the extra wide tent with its tall, billowing, circus-like roof, he stepped inside to find a few families that had gathered, whispering as they ate. They were seated at one of several picnic tables laid out in front of a long assembly line of food trays with staff members standing on the other side, doling out helpings of whatever people requested.

"I haven't seen a buffet in ages," James mumbled to himself. "But the food smells doggone good."

He headed over to the start of the line, grabbed a tray and utensils, and stood behind a man and his young son who were going through and pointing at different things. The servers dished him something that looked like Salisbury steak and gravy then a scoop of macaroni and cheese and a huge helping of mashed potatoes, which they heaped onto one section of his plate, giving him enough for two people. With a thick layer of gravy spread on top, James took his tray and found a spot to eat on the far end, where he could watch the door and any newcomers who came in. He wasn't so much worried as he was curious about the people coming into the camp, still hoping there'd be an influx of more refugees at any moment. When the first bite of food hit his stomach, he closed his eyes and released a long, slow breath of relief.

Finishing every last bite, James stood and took his tray to a tub and spigot, using a splash of water to rinse the plate and put everything in its proper place. He exited and stepped into the brisk evening air, pulling his jacket tighter and headed to the bathroom, took care of his business and used the sink to clean his hands, then his face. Feeling somewhat refreshed but still tired, he returned to his tent, unlocked it, and entered the much warmer space where he stripped off his jacket and shoes.

Digging through his personal duffel bag, he found a change of clothes and tossed them on the bed as he undressed and used the sink to do a more thorough cleaning job with the washcloths and towels they'd left for him. With his skin scrubbed clean, James put on fresh underwear, jeans, and a thick pair of socks before sitting on his cot and resting back with a sigh. It was the first time he'd been able to lie down in a few days, and his entire body relaxed in a state of sheer relief. Sleep threatened to take him right away, and he had to fight it off while he thought about what he wanted to do next. Powering on his cellphone, he checked for a signal before shutting it off again, frustrated with his inability to find out any information about where Alice, Sarah and Jake might be – or if they were even okay.

Can't go down that road, he thought, putting his phone away and pressing on his eyes for a few seconds, trying to focus on the positives and what he was capable of doing, not what he couldn't control. Ultimately, he didn't expect Alice would want to stay in one place for very long. No, he was certain she'd be heading home even if she stopped into a recovery center to give the kids a break or avoid danger. He could leave a message for them to let them know he was on his way to Michigan in the event they showed up at a camp and checked for his name, but he had to keep moving. Survival meant movement – not just sitting around in a camp.

His thoughts of his family swirled for a few minutes longer, but his exhaustion was potent, and James soon fell asleep. Unfortunately, his peaceful slumber changed to dreams of fire and smoke and cinder swarms that rode gale force winds and chased him through an endless maze of dark city streets. While some images were vivid, and the sense of being hunted filled him with restless anxiety, at least it was still rest of a sort.

It was a real-life explosion, though, that tore him awake with a gasp, sending him jolting straight up, blinking into the darkness, heart thumping hard as a fading *boom* drifted across the camp, leaving just his faintly rattling ventilation system to occupy the next five seconds of silence. Gunfire began next, the staccato reports of automatic weapons and a few softer pops like fireworks in the night. They weren't right on top of him, so James quickly slid his shoes on, tied them tight, and strode toward the door, stooping to scoop up his duffel bags as he went. He unlocked his tent flap and unzipped it, then pushed it back to step into a waft of heavy smoke and a fluttering of embers as they floated by.

Waving his hand in front of his face, he walked into the gloom as the lights blinked on and off in several areas of the camp. He glanced at a family tent on the opposite corner and watched a few fathers and mothers step outside and turn to look back east while their children stood in the shadow of the wide tent flap in their pajamas. James started to grab someone's attention and ask them what was going on when a sudden burst of red tracer fire lit the sky. Standing in the intersection, he gazed over the tent tops as short blasts and long *brrrring* noises ripped through the night, followed by the sharp punch of two explosions that vibrated the ground beneath his feet. Several children screamed and ducked inside as two more fathers stepped out onto the lane and peered eastward. James stepped ahead to talk to them when a cluster of boots stomped up the western lane toward him, a contingent of soldiers with wild eyes, clutching their rifles hard, a few of them half-dressed with their helmets skewed sideways on their heads as if they'd just woken up.

As they passed, James waved to one to get his attention, running alongside him for a few feet. "What's going on?" He tried to keep up with the fast-moving unit. "What's happening?"

The soldier turned and walked backwards for a few yards, shouting and pointing at the tents. "It's an attack! Stay inside, please, and don't open your tent flap until the threat is cleared!" The soldier fell toward the end of his line and gestured at the parents standing around. "All of you! If you value your lives, get back inside *now!*"

James followed them a few yards as they stomped down the lane toward more sounds of gunfire and another explosion. A trailing whistle pierced his ears as a fiery piece of debris corkscrewed upward into the dark night before finally stopping its wild ascension to arc downward and fall on one of the tents. All along the side of the camp, tiny bursts of orange light erupted, soft at first and then quickly turning into miniature blazes with trailing smoke lifting into the sky. James looked south toward the camp entrance and back to the running soldiers, frozen with indecision.

CHAPTER TWENTY-FOUR

Ryan Cooper
Somewhere Outside East Lansing, Michigan

Ryan was drifting comfortably in a weightless sleep after a hot meal and a cup of milk, his belly warm and full, the body aches that had plagued him all day in the field kept at bay by a couple of over-the-counter pain pills. While he hadn't meant to fall asleep, the abatement of his pains and grumbling joints had pitched him headfirst into a deep slumber that was quickly filled with hot winds and cars bathed in flames, the vehicles clogging a long stretch of road that swept ahead into infinity. While he should've been anxious and terrified, the weight of his exhaustion made him feel like a listless voyeur in a world going up in a wicked cataclysm, looking on helplessly as the world was consumed by fire.

In the distance, somewhere beyond the flames, ferocious barking was just barely audible, though it quickly grew in intensity until it was enough to bring him out of his slumber, and he quickly realized that the three Great Pyrenees belting out deep-chested barks were no dream. At first, he blinked and groped around in confusion before he realized he'd positioned himself in front of the dining room window in one of the big chairs. Wincing, he reached for the M&P 15 Sport II rifle he'd brought up from the gun safe, standing and hobbling in a circle, disoriented at first until the dogs bayed and bellowed again. Figuring they were somewhere out back, he started down the hall to the rear of the house when he caught Helen's whisper from upstairs.

"What is it, Ryan? Is someone on the property?"

He backed up and rested his left arm on the stairwell banister, gazing up to see the outline of her form on the catwalk. "I'm not sure what it is, but it has the animals pretty worked up. I'm going to go take a look."

Helen was padding downstairs in her rubber-soled slippers, closing her robe with one hand as she came. Together, they moved into the kitchen, where Helen grabbed a large handheld spotlight from the kitchen table and stepped to the back door. Ryan parted the blinds with his fingers and peered outside. Two of the great Pyrenees — it looked like Duchess and Diana — were standing on the other side of the harvested food sacks, about thirty yards out, with their noses pointed toward the east side of the property as they growled and barked.

"There is *definitely* someone or something out there." Ryan unlocked the deadbolt with a clack of the tumblers and pulled it open softly, stepping out onto the concrete patio with Helen right behind him. The stairs leading to the storage room were on his left along with their electric car, but past that, they could hardly see a thing. Ryan had shut off all the motion detection lights on the barns and sheds, and around the chicken coops, because even though they required little energy to run, any sign that they had electric power would risk bringing looters like moths to a flame.

"Do you want me to turn on the spotlight?" Helen asked.

"Not right now. Follow me."

Ryan crept behind the sacks of supplies, sweeping his M&P 15 back and forth in the darkness. Stopping at the edge of the harvest stacks with the northeast corner of the house on his right, he paused to listen but could hear nothing over the sounds of the barking. He gave a low whistle, and Duchess and Diana immediately bounded over to them, whining and nosing at his hand as he tried to calm them.

Turning back, he glanced at Helen. "Let's go around to the driveway and check out that side of the property."

He guided them around to the driveway where it curved to the exit lane, and as he rounded the corner, the wind picked up in a low gust that sucked up the sounds of the dogs' whining. Duke's claws came clacking across the concrete from the south side of the house to join the other dogs, and Ryan reached to grab him, barely missing as the massive beast flew by.

Ryan bowed low and hissed. "Duke! Here, boy! Hey! Heel!"

The Great Pyrenees pulled up short, his big bushy tail sweeping back and forth as he looked behind him and then lunged forward again, shifting his shoulders toward something out in the trees. Ryan called him a second time, whistling low and sharp, and the dog turned and bounded back to them.

"Why don't you let the dogs go, honey?"

"I want to know what we're sending them after." Ryan growled, stepping onto the driveway with his head swiveling back and forth, keeping the M&P 15's barrel raised high. He paused where the driveway curved down to the lane, still looking east, standing another full minute in the silence except for the dogs who pranced and whined and kept their noses pointed toward the woods, where the tall spruces and pines stood like a thick green wall along the edge of the property.

No matter how hard he peered into the blackness, he finally shook his head and gestured for Helen to come up. "Go ahead and use your light."

Ryan grabbed Duke's collar while Helen flipped the spotlight on and aimed the light directly east into the trees. The bright beam cut through the darkness like a knife, settling on the cool ground where a slow mist was drifting and turning lazily in the wind. The spotlight reached the misty forest wall and penetrated several feet into the wooded area where dust floated in slow swirls. Helen moved it south along the tree line before coming back the other way, stopping once or twice and leaning forward as if seeing something, then she shifted it farther to the left to trace across the thick tree branches, bushes, and brush. Duke pulled him sharply north again, his head and eyes suddenly focused on something by the chicken coop, his whining yips growing sharper.

Duchess and Diana bounded forward but swept to the side again, looking back at Ryan and chuffing low but still restrained in their intensity, the pair barely able to keep from running off, their training holding them to Ryan's word. As Helen swept the light beam north, she caught movement out around the chicken coop where the birds were suddenly clucking and flapping as something worked them up.

Ryan leaned forward and gave a sharp command. "Go get him, Duke! Duchess! Diana... Go!" The three dogs leaped forward and bounded off, with Ryan and Helen shuffling quickly after them, the spotlight beam wavering and dipping as she tried to keep it straight. Clutching the M&P 15 to his chest with the barrel pointed upward, he focused on some movement, watching as a figure moved behind the coop where the bushes were thick. Panting, sides heaving, the three Great Pyrenees chased a rustling sound coming from the brush with their enormous paws digging furrows in the soft earth, pounding through the chicken yard and tearing around the corner of the coop, sending screeching birds flying everywhere with flapping wings and squawking beaks. A distinctly human voice gave a surprised yelp and a shout, and off to the right, a form burst from behind the chicken coops, feet flying as they sprinted toward the trees. Ryan pointed his rifle, taking aim as Helen pinned the man in her spotlight beam, but Ryan pulled the barrel up at the last second as the dogs burst from the brush, dragging branches and leaves with them as they shot across the yard in hot pursuit.

"Come on!" Ryan called as he gave chase, the short grass and well-manicured lawn making it easy for him to shuffle along without tripping and falling, his path taking him in a shallow arc in hot pursuit of the animals who plunged into the tree line and were gone.

Slow to get there, Ryan and Helen picked their way through the wall of spruces and pines, their sharp scent making them a world unto themselves, moist earth, mulch, and tree bark a background accompaniment. Helen's light gleamed off the tree trunks as she desperately searched for the animals, and they crunched over the debris-riddled forest floor with its deadfall and big clusters of clinging vines and sticker bushes with no real path to follow. Helen gasped, and Ryan turned to see that she'd gotten caught up on something and took her hand and helped her break free, keeping them always moving forward, but there was too much brush and too many low branches to really see with the shaggy pines and their thick layers of needles blocking their vision in every direction. It was only when they pushed through to the other side that they got a good view of what was happening. Past the trees was a narrow, paved lane that circled the property, more of a service road of sorts than anything, and beyond that was a wide swath of grass before the fence line. Helen's spotlight moved to the right and wiggled back and forth a second before she spotted a dark-clothed figure who was struggling to get over the fence. He'd caught his leg on the sharp barbed wire strung above the top rail, the barbs stretching and ripping his pants as he jerked and tried to get away. As the dogs ran up snarling and snapping, he broke free with a cry of pain and landed on the other side of the fence, staggering backward, sprinting off just as the Pyrenees got there and half climbed up the field fence, hopping on their back legs with their forelegs over the top, barking their heads off and foaming from their massive jaws.

"Whoa, Duke!" Ryan called, giving another sharp whistle, panting as he shouted for them. "Get back here! You're going to cut yourself on that doggone barbed wire!"

At first, Duke was too distracted to respond, but when Ryan crossed the narrow service path and whistled again, the massive dog reluctantly fell off the rail and gave Ryan an almost accusatory look, as if it was the old man's fault the dog wasn't able to go after his prey.

"Come on, Duke! Hey! Get over here, *now!*" Ryan whistled sharply again, the noise high and demanding as Duke came trotting back with the girls right on his heels. "Good boy, Duke!" Ryan started to kneel but swayed a little before he got his knee down, setting his rifle in the cold grass as the Pyrenees showed up, bumping and nuzzling him with affection. "Good dogs!" Ryan lavished them with praise and rubbed their heads as he stared at the fence.

Helen had Diana by the collar and was leading her along the edge of the path, holding the spotlight up by her shoulder and drifting it back and forth, shifting it out through the woods where the man had run off. Breathing heavily, her voice trembling slightly in the chilly evening air, Helen turned to him as she probed the trees with her light. "Did you recognize him?"

Ryan shrugged and stood with his weapon, worn out yet invigorated by the crisp evening air. "Your guess is as good as mine. Could've been someone from the neighborhood or someone randomly going by. I didn't see any cars..." He gestured toward the road, which they couldn't see from their position. "I guess one of us should've stayed back with the house."

Helen looked alarmed. "You think there are more people?"

With a glance at the dogs, Ryan shook his head. "The dogs aren't worried about anything back there. They're still hungry for the guy that ran away. Still, let's go back and check on the chicken coops. I want to see what he was up to."

The dogs circled them protectively as Ryan and Helen marched back to the coops through the deadfall and foliage, being more careful not to trip and fall than before. His prosthetic had held up pretty well, staying attached during the entire time, though it still felt loose and awkward, and he couldn't fully lift and rotate his leg for fear of it slipping off.

As they emerged from the forest, Ryan mumbled as he gripped his leg. "I need to work on this first thing in the morning. As it stands, it would take me a day to get to the other side of the property if I needed to chase someone out of here."

"That's what we have the dogs for, dear."

"I still need to get around a little better."

They soon reached the chicken coops, going around the bit of brush and a couple of small trees to reach the main structure with its plywood walls and chicken wire that formed a coop and protective run. The birds had calmed down, and were busy clucking gently amongst themselves, picking at the ground as if nothing had ever happened. Helen shone the spotlight at the white and rust-colored birds and the single rooster strutting around like he owned the place. Somewhere out in the darkness, the flashlight beam touched the peacock's feathers, though the bird quickly disappeared behind a bush as it made a few unhappy squawks.

"Can you tell if all the chickens are here?" she asked.

Ryan stopped for a moment and tried to count them as the light shifted around, but he finally gave up and waved it off. "There's no way we can count them out here tonight. Let's check everything for damage."

Sure enough, there was a broken latch and frayed chicken wire where the man had first tried to jerk the door loose and then cut his way inside the coop, scaring the birds out into the run and beyond in the process. Ryan and Helen slipped inside and did a quick head count estimate.

"He got it open," Ryan growled, "but I don't think we're missing any birds."

"Looks like those fur balls got here just in time to save your behinds." Helen spoke to the chickens as a few of them headed inside the enclosed section of the coop, then she turned to Ryan as she shined the light outside over the free-range birds. "What do you think he was trying to do?"

"Maybe trying to grab a chicken or two, or some eggs."

"We might've been in trouble if he'd grabbed the rooster."

Ryan's eyebrow went up. "We may need to think about expanding the flock a bit sooner than later." Moving back to the door, he played with the latch, giving a sigh when it hung loose and didn't catch. "First, I'll need to install a new latch and some additional locks on the door." He turned and gestured to a part of the mesh fencing that had been torn away. "And I'll reinforce this to make it harder for anyone to get in if they try again."

"Do you think they will? That guy seemed pretty scared when the dogs went after him."

"The dogs won't stop desperate folks." Ryan scratched his head. "Maybe I should have just taken the shot when he was stuck on the fence... well, it's too late now. I just hope it wasn't the tractor that got their attention."

"What do you say we free-range the birds during the day and keep them all locked up at night?"

Ryan was nodding. "I was just going to suggest that, but we'll never get them in there tonight. Best thing we can do is get some rest before we start processing all that food in the morning."

Helen let the spotlight sink as she released an exasperated sigh. "I was hoping you'd say that. I hardly slept a wink without you next to me, and I'm just about to fall out of my skin."

"Well, we're going to have to get used to sleeping apart for a little while." Ryan stepped closer and wrapped his arms around her, holding his M&P 15 well out of the way. He breathed in the soft scent of her hair as the chickens clucked and pecked at their feet, filling the cold evening with their soft sounds.

Finally, he let her go and gestured to the door. "You go on back to the house, and I'm going to get some wire and make sure this door stays shut."

"Don't be long."

"I won't."

They stepped into the yard, and Ryan accepted a peck on the cheek before he turned toward the shed to get some extra wire and search for a new latch.

Ryan woke once again, though instead of to barking it was to the sound of a rooster crowing, the shrill notes like nails being driven into his skull. He blinked his dry eyes and took a deep breath, staring at the pale white ceiling bathed in the dim glow of morning light. At first, he didn't realize where he was, but it quickly came back to him; the full day of harvesting followed by the dogs alerting them to an intruder in the yard. After the chase, he'd fixed the fence and locked the chicken coop door tight, then he'd come inside to Helen sitting by the dining room window with her revolver resting in her lap and a book on the table beside her. After she'd promised to pay more attention to watching the yard than her reading, Ryan had kissed her good night and gone up to bed for a bit of sleep while she kept watch.

He shook his head, because what he'd gotten was far from sleep. It was less even than a nap, merely shutting his eyes and then waking right back up again to the smudged daylight creeping in through the window. With a sigh, he swung his legs out of bed and put his feet on the floor, letting his body adjust to the grogginess before he attempted to get moving.

While he waited, he reached for a glass of water on his nightstand and had a long drink, then he slipped his prosthetic on and walked to the window, staring through the curtain at the dismal gray and black skies still stretching as far as the eye could see. The tendrils of smoke lifting off the neighborhoods and towns had dwindled somewhat, leaving drifting trails and wispy clouds to be blown around by the wind. Grabbing his Beretta off the nightstand, he started downstairs and was greeted halfway down by the aroma of freshly brewed coffee, and when he reached the bottom floor, he smiled to find Helen was sitting in the same chair as the previous night with a shawl on her knees and a book in her lap, positioned farther away from the window so she could reach her coffee cup.

Hearing the floorboards squeak beneath his feet, she looked up and grinned. "Good morning, dear. Did you sleep at all?"

"Not much, but that coffee smells wonderful."

Helen's grin broadened, and she winked. "Just brewed it fresh about ten minutes ago, if you want some."

"Woman, you are a lifesaver." While he wanted to head straight to the kitchen, drawn by the promise of something to drag himself out of his sleep-addled stupor, he crossed to Helen and gave her a warm hug. "Did you get much reading done?"

"More than I've done in quite a while. It's been forever since I pulled an all-nighter."

"Me too." He laughed and walked down the hall.

Next to the coffee pot was a small plate of Danishes with the sticky note on the plastic wrap that read, "Eat these first before they go bad!"

"Yes, *ma'am*!" Ryan pulled back the plastic wrap to grab a cheese Danish off the top, and with his coffee poured, he ate his breakfast at the kitchen table. Usually he would be looking for a newspaper or talking to Helen during breakfast, but they had problems to deal with, the thought that there might not be any more casual breakfasts for a long time a sobering reminder of just how serious things were.

As Ryan was finishing his breakfast, Helen came in and joined him at the table. "How was it?"

"Very good." Ryan licked his fingers as he chewed the last bite. Washing it down with some coffee, he put it aside and leaned forward to take Helen's hand. "I was thinking we could bring in a few sacks of vegetables for you to work on while I try to fix this dumb prosthetic."

"I'm way ahead of you on that." Helen nodded to the left side of the counter, where several canning jars were lined up with their tops stacked next to them. On the stove, she'd placed pots and canning tools resting on a towel next to them.

"I was so tired this morning, I didn't even notice," he sighed, rubbing his eyes. "How did you find time to bring that stuff up?"

"I did it in between walking my rounds through the house. I knew you'd be eager to get started right away. Do you have any ideas to fix your leg?"

He nodded downward. "I'm going to see what James has to work with downstairs, and maybe I can get this thing stabilized enough to not be a complete cripple."

Helen patted his hand as she smiled at him. "If there's anyone who can do it, it's you. While I'm working on the vegetables, I'll keep watch around the house and check at each of the windows to see if we have any surprise guests."

"It shouldn't take me long. Either James has something I can use to fix this or not. Either way, I won't leave you up here all day to slave away at this."

"Take your time, dear. I'm a little tired, but I think I'm going to enjoy this. Once we get used to taking guard shifts, we'll catch up on our sleep."

Ryan reached out and embraced his wife, her confidence and positivity lifting his spirits as much as the hot coffee and pastry. "Let's get started then. I'll grab some sacks of the veggies for you first."

Ryan stepped outside and grabbed a sack of carrots and potatoes, hefting them on his shoulders and carrying them up the short concrete steps and into the house where Helen was waiting by the table, gesturing to where she wanted them put down. Several trips later, he had fifteen sacks ready for her to can, all while she was at the sink and the stove preparing the water while laying out everything she needed, including a large bag of salt. Once she was settled, Ryan gave her a brief hug and went into the basement to search for something to fix his prosthesis.

At the bottom of the stairs, he turned right, away from the supply area and into a small workshop. Flipping on the light switch bathed the room in illumination, revealing more rows of shelving and a couple of workbenches on the north side of the room. Where James' other junk room smelled like oil and rust and was filled with old cans and lawnmower parts, the workshop resembled their supply space, kept meticulously clean and dusted with a set of shelves on both sides of the room.

On the workbench stood trays of screws, nails, and bolts, a pegboard with power drills, hammers, small sledgehammers, screwdrivers, and other odds and ends. Metal shelving on his right held more parts trays with labels like *Old Parts*, *Instruction Manuals*, *Circuit Boards*, and *Extra Wires*. Across from those were another set of shelves with old computer equipment, a few inkjet printers, and two bulky shapes covered up with dusty plastic. Moving to the workbench, Ryan looked at what he had to work with. There were plenty of tools, and on the right-hand side of the workbench were power tool batteries, all of them plugged up into a power strip screwed to the tabletop.

"And you're probably drawing some juice from the solar batteries." He unplugged all three chargers except the one for the drill, though he removed the battery and slammed it home in the drill grip, giving the trigger a squeeze, the drill turning sharply in response. "Okay, you work well enough. Let's see what else he has."

Based on his quick inspection of his prosthetic the day before, Ryan figured a clamp might be what he needed, and he returned to the shelves and looked through trays of PVC and copper piping, elbow joints, soldering equipment, and various plumbing and wood parts. On a lower shelf, he pulled out several trays of repair clamps, from light ones to heavy-duty stainless steel, and he gathered what he needed and took it to the workbench. Removing his prosthetic limb, he balanced on one foot and laid the limb on the bench to inspect it. The titanium tube jutting from the foot portion was cracked just beneath the socket, and the crack looked worse than the previous day. Any more wear and tear on it could pop the socket piece off and make the prosthetic impossible to wear.

Ryan searched through the selection of pipe clamps and picked an adjustable one that was exceedingly thick and wide enough to fit over the socket. Once on, he positioned it over the crack and turned the bolt so he could reach it with the electric drill. After a couple of trigger squeezes, he tightened the fitting and made the two pieces rigid together. Holding the repaired prosthetic high, he twisted the socket to inspect the strength. "A strong weld might help, but a complete replacement would be best."

He put the prosthetic back on and slipped the steel tip of the gel liner into the socket, using twine to tighten it around his calf and knee. After a few experimental steps, he concluded it wasn't a perfect solution but was better than before, and it would keep him from having to duct tape the thing to his leg every day. Still, he'd have to take it easy and be easy on it, lest the crack grow worse. With a temporary fix out of the way, he shifted his attention to the shelves on the west side of the room where the covered forms were resting almost eye level with him. Ryan walked over curiously, and he carefully lifted the cover off the first machine and blinked.

It was a contraption with a heavy base that sat between two metal columns, a bundle of wires running from a main control panel and winding beneath a thick steel plate and then up to a strange looking mechanical device that was mounted on two metal rods. Ryan studied it momentarily before shifting to the second bulky form, where he lifted the cover off and tossed it behind him to reveal a similar machine. It was enclosed in a stainless-steel encasement with the glass front that allowed him to peer in on a big metal plate and a half-finished form resting on it. Squinting, he made out the bottom half of a barn or shed, ten inches long and four wide, woven from a synthetic blue material. On the machine's front cover read *EZ Print 3D*.

"Well, I'll be..." Ryan scratched his beard. "These are 3D printers. I didn't know you were into that, James."

To his left were a laptop and a cardboard box labeled *Filament* with the lid half open, and inside were several spools wrapped with plastic fibers that reminded him of the kinds of spools he'd attach to the bottom of his electric yard trimmer.

"Interesting..." Ryan had some minor experience with 3D printing, and he briefly entertained the thought of creating a new part for his prosthetic, or at least repairing it. As he was popping the lid on the laptop computer to see if it had any printing software, the lights in the room dimmed for a second before flashing back to life and a moment later, Helen called down to him.

"Ryan, honey! Can you come here?"

With a reluctant grumble, he closed the laptop lid and walked back to the supply room, crossing to the stairs and looking up to where Helen stood at the top with a worried expression.

"What is it?"

"The freezers up here just shut off." She frowned. "I know you're going to ask what I did to break it, and the answer is that I plugged in the second freezer up here so we could have enough room to freeze some things we brought in. I'm sorry!"

He waved off her apology. "Nothing to be sorry for. You just overloaded the battery system, and it likely shut down the circuits that were drawing too much power. We're probably going to have to re-arrange some things. I've already shut off some things down here, but I'll check the circuit breaker and see if I can make some adjustments."

"Thank you, dear."

"Just give me a few minutes, and I'll be right back up."

With a flashlight in hand, Ryan found the circuit breaker against the wall where the HVAC and water heater were, and he opened both panels and looked inside at the meticulously labeled circuits. Part of the configuration was a built-in automatic transfer switch between the city power and solar battery system that was supposed to automatically switch them to the batteries whenever the city power failed, which explained why they'd not had an interruption in power immediately after the disaster. Looking at the battery side, he saw the freezer circuit had flipped off, likely when Helen had plugged the second one in, and Ryan figured James had a smart system that would automatically shut down any circuits drawing too much power.

"You're a wise man, James," he murmured. "This should make it easy to solve the problem. I'll just shut down everything and only turn on the things we need."

Ryan flipped every switch to the off position, killing all the lights before he turned the well pump, stove, freezers, and refrigerator back on. With those adjustments made, he crossed to the stairs and up to the kitchen where Helen was waiting for him at the table.

"Did I break anything?" she asked.

Ryan laughed. "No, dear. Nothing's broken. I've shut down power to everything in the house except the well pump, refrigerator, stove, and the two freezers. I figure we can use electric lanterns and flashlights to get around the house, and we can turn on the furnace and water heater for when we really need it. We'll just have to do without some luxuries for the short term until we tweak the system. While I'm sure we're getting *some* sunlight, those black clouds over our heads are going to put a real damper on that, so it'll be just the essentials for now."

When he was finished talking, she nodded definitively. "We've gotten by on less before. The food – survival – comes first."

"I figured you'd be on board with that." He sat with her at the table and pulled his notepad over, flipping through the inventory and adding some notes to a blank page in the back. "I'm going to make a list of things we need to do. I noticed James and Alice took our advice and have a wood-burning stove against the wall downstairs. There's no duct work hooked up to it, but I can probably run something myself with a fan, to keep the pipes up here from freezing if things get really bad."

"Must be the original we had from our old farmhouse," Helen said with a coy smile.

"I knew it looked familiar! I thought we got rid of that thing when we got our new one."

"You wanted to, but I told James and Alice they could have it, and James came and picked it up when you were at work one day." She laughed and shrugged. "I didn't realize they had it downstairs, but I'm happy to know it's going to come in handy."

"It'll come in handy for certain. It might just save our behinds. The only problem is that we'll need to cut more wood for it, which means another chore to add to taking care of the animals and processing our food. Another thing I saw down there were some additional solar panels, and we'll get those on the grid to add a bit more to our power collection capabilities."

"And there's still a lot out in the field for us to harvest," Helen's tone wilted as their list grew, Ryan scribbling madly to get it all down. "Are we even going to be up to all this?"

"If we can get to three quarters of it," he said, "we'll be fine." When she didn't respond right away, Ryan looked sideways at her and saw her watery eyes and a thin tear running down her cheek. Dropping his pen, he rested his hand on her back, fingers rubbing her spine with slow, gentle strokes. "Hey, honey. It's going to be fine."

"It's... overwhelming. Not just things here at the farm or even that we don't know where our family is or if our house or anyone we know in Grand Rapids is okay. Now we've got the neighbors to worry about, not to mention whoever was in the backyard last night and... everything."

"All of that's true, but we can only control but so much, so we have to focus all our energy on that alone. And I need you to stay strong to get through this. You're my heart and soul. You're what keeps me going, and I can't do this without your energy and flair. I need you to keep being positive for me..." He glanced at his empty plate which was still sitting on the table. "And feed me Danishes whenever possible."

Helen laughed and wiped the tears off her face. "I can't promise you the Danishes, but I might be able to whip up a batch of cookies."

"Perfect," Ryan beamed.

Turning in her chair, Helen took his free hand in both of hers and gripped it tight. "And I'm going to be as positive and strong as I can be. For you and me, and the kids and grandkids." She raised her eyes with a sad yet appreciative look. "Thank you, honey. Sometimes I need to know how important I am to you."

"And that's why it's easy for me to say it. I love you, dear, even more now. I know we're not as young as we used to be when we whipped every challenge that came at us, but we've got more than enough heart to see this through."

"You're darn right we do," Helen replied, the steeliness in her eyes returning as she sat straighter in her chair and gave his hand another firm squeeze.

CHAPTER TWENTY-FIVE

Jack Willoughby's Yard
Somewhere Outside East Lansing, Michigan

A quarter mile down the road from where Ryan and Helen were preparing for the worst, an enormous bonfire raged in Jack Willoughby's front yard. They'd thrown in pieces of firewood from the woodpile out back and had taken some pieces from the rubble of their home which had gone up in flames and collapsed a few days ago. It had all started when Jack's Ford F250 had blown up in the garage along with his motorcycle, riding mower, and his wife's Honda Odyssey. Almost every tool he owned had gone up with it before it had caught the rest of the house on fire, sending his family scrambling outside as they called the fire department in vain.

Between the Willoughby's and their neighbors, they had some basic supplies gathered, but they were still consolidating what they'd salvaged from their ruined homes. There were the Tillys, the Crenshaws and the Fosters, with wives, kids, and agitated fathers. They all shared a common misery in that they'd been driven from their houses by the explosions and fires, and everything they owned had gone up, leaving them dazed, confused, and then angry when no fire trucks came to help them.

The phones were down, and they were too far from town to walk anywhere substantial to get help for themselves. It had only been a short time later when Mack Tilly had found a radio in an old barn and brought it out to listen to the government's emergency broadcast that they realized what kind of trouble they were really in.

Jack's wife, Barb, sat in a lawn chair in front of the fire, planted deep in the seat with her feet firmly on the ground. She stared at the flames with a blank look, smudge marks on her cheeks and her thick brown hair pulled into a messy bun on top of her head, resting like a tired bird. Rita Tilly, a thin-faced forty-year-old with jet black hair and eagle eyes, stood across from her, stirring the bonfire with a metal rod and her husband Mack stood nearby wearing a flannel shirt over a ragged white T-shirt. The Crenshaws were rugged folks from a farm up the road, and Jack knew them from their kids playing ball together. The Fosters were smart, quiet people, a little older than the rest of the assembled group, with a massive farmstead that had gone up along with their tractors, cars, and extensive farm equipment. All of them wore the same dour expressions, down on their luck with no help in sight and no place to turn the sights of their growing disgruntlement.

A dog barked somewhere in the darkness and someone coughed from inside one of the tents they'd set up to keep them warm during the cool nights when the fire burned low. Whatever farm animals remained were out back in a small field, though many had perished or run off in fear into the surrounding woods, and trying to find them while exhausted and shell-shocked had been a hopeless cause.

Jack was standing near the fire's warm glow with his arms folded over his stained sweatshirt and a scowl on his face when a lone figure came running down the lonesome road, rounding a stretch of trees and cutting up through the neighbor's yard. Judging by his thin frame and quick feet, it was Mike Jones running and leaping over smoldering debris out in the yard, the pieces of someone's life burned beyond recognition and strewn about in the cold, wet grass. As for the rest of the neighbors, no one knew what happened to them. Their houses had gone up in flames before anyone else's, the sweltering smoke thickening in the street as boxes of ammunition exploded in people's basements like fireworks displays before they'd finally burned out. All that remained was the smell of scorched flesh and the first hint of the stench of decay.

Mike cut through the rough circle of tents and came to stand on Jack's left between him and Rita Tilly, panting and leaning over with his hands on his knees as he tried to catch his breath. Mike was an older man, but still young enough to run hard and fast, and smart enough to sneak into the Burton's backyard to see what they had on hand to take.

Jack nodded at Mike's jeans where the cuff of his right leg was completely torn and ripped up the back. "You're bleeding, man."

As if just realizing it, Mike sucked air through his teeth, wincing in pain and running his hand through his curly dark locks. "Yeah, stupid barbed wire caught me as I was climbing the fence. Had to hurry because their dogs were chasing me."

"Big ones?"

"Yeah. Three of them, and they were *huge*."

"Probably just a couple of Chihuahuas." Trace Crenshaw smirked and spit tobacco into the fire.

Loose chuckles danced around the circle as Jack rubbed his hand down his face. "Did you get anything? Guess that's a dumb question, right?"

Mike shook his head and winced again. "They've got a lot of chickens, but I couldn't get any. Looks like canned crap for us again."

Jack frowned. "It's not fair they have chickens while ours died in the fires."

"Ours too." Trace shot another spit into the fiery flames, causing them to sizzle and crackle. The Tilly's nodded and murmured to themselves, casting a glance back at their place down the road where their barn and house still smoldered and smoked throughout the night.

"At first, I didn't figure they'd have much," Mike continued, "but then I heard their tractor running earlier—"

"Wait a minute." Jack raised his hand to interrupt. "Did you say they have a... *tractor?*"

"That's right. I knew they had one but figured it must have blown up in the field somewhere since their barn's still standing. When I heard the engine, I figured out which yard it was coming from, and lo and behold I saw a couple of old folks putting it away out in their barn. Then I saw those stupid dogs running around and had to get back into the woods and wait till it got dark." Mike limped closer to the fire and held his hands out to the flames. "I guess it's just Alice's parents watching the property, and Alice and James still aren't back from their trip. I figured they'd put away those dogs after a while, but when I went out to grab us some eggs, the damn things started barking and chased me off before I could get away with anything."

Barb had turned away from the fire, her eyes eager. "So... they've got chickens and eggs and a tractor?"

"The chickens and tractor, yes, because I saw them with my own eyes. The eggs... I didn't actually see, but I'm assuming with all those hens they've got, there's got to be enough for all of us."

"Doesn't sound to me like they're too keen on sharing if they ran you off." Barb stood and turned to Jack with an arched eyebrow. The tough, weighty woman's eyes grew steely. "Jack, are we going to let them get away with not sharing?"

Jack shook his head and kicked at the fire. "*I'm* not going to." He looked around the circle at everyone else. "Are you people okay with that? One of our very own neighbors not willing to share what they've got with people who have it worse off?"

"I'm not," Rita Tilly said sternly.

"Oh, *hell* no!" Trace Crenshaw hocked up a big wad of spit and let it fly into the dancing orange flames where it exploded upward in a gust of hot steam.

"Then let's pay these old folks a visit," Jack said, cracking his knuckles, "and do something about it."

THE DESOLATION

CHAPTER ONE

Alice Burton
Greenville, Florida

The night sky loomed above like purgatory, sitting behind the canopy of trees, hiding the stars behind a thick covering of smoke rolling off the major cities as they smoldered and cooked off whatever was left to burn. Ash sometimes fell like snow in large flakes, bringing with it the smell of char drifting in on a breeze to make Alice's nose itch and wrinkle where she sat near their campfire.

The evening was warm and dry, with a faint murmur of birds and insects chattering around them to break up the eerie stillness. Sarah sat on a stump to Alice's right, and Jake squatted on a log across from her, all three with hands and arms covered in dirt from digging to make a Dakota campfire. Both kids were slumped over, shoulders hunched with exhaustion, Sarah with her head resting on her arms while Jake picked idly at a twig. The camping pot sat on a tripod grill about ten inches above the flames, the contents bubbling around the top in a rich brown gravy poured over canned stew, peas, and corn, everything thrown together because Alice was too tired and hungry to deal with any MREs. Savory ripples rolled off the pot and made Alice's stomach grumble with an intense hunger. Granola bars and junk food only got a person so far, and they'd burned through those empty calories on their trek from the outskirts of Madison to a wooded area much farther west.

"We have *got* to get a shovel," Alice said, breaking the silence.

"Three shovels," Jake added. "I didn't know digging with knives and your bare hands could be so tough."

"Well, it was worth it. This Dakota fire is good."

"It should be," Sarah grumbled. "We dug long enough to make it."

"I know it was hard work," Alice said, "but it was necessary."

"I think I broke a fingernail."

"You don't have fingernails."

"Not anymore. I just have some little ones now. See?" Sarah held up her dirt-encrusted hand, displaying chipped and broken remnants of her once well-trimmed nails.

Alice held up her own filthy and bruised hands with a smirk. "Sorry, but we needed to make sure we couldn't be spotted from the road by anyone in the area. That's why I picked this natural defilade, so we could dig a larger hole and pile the excess dirt up around it in a ring."

"Is that why we dug a second hole?" Jake's brow wrinkled.

"Yes, for the airflow intake." Alice nodded and pointed at the smaller hole set about a foot away that connected to the main one under the soil, moving her finger along it as she spoke. "The fire feeds off the air from the smaller hole, drawing even more through to make more intense flames. Not only does it burn better, but it will give off less smoke, and the ring we built up around it will keep the light leakage lower." When Jake only nodded, she continued. "Hopefully it helps keep anyone else from finding us. Last thing we need are more people like the ones from that town."

"Definitely." Jake tossed the twig into the fire and watched it crackle and burn as he leaned forward and rested his elbows on his knees. "I don't want to have to beat up anyone else with a pool cue."

Sarah giggled and dropped her head on her arms. "Yeah, Mom. Beating up people with pool sticks is getting a little old."

Alice allowed a mischievous grin and a chuckle to slip out before she sobered up. "I'm serious, guys. We've already had a few run-ins that have scared me to death, and I can't imagine you getting hurt because we weren't careful enough. We *have* to do better. Our lives depend on it."

"I know." Sarah reached over, putting her hand on Alice's knee to give it a playful shake. "I'm just slaphappy right now from being so tired. We're serious."

Looking deep into her daughter's dark eyes, Alice gave a satisfied nod and squeezed her hand. "You guys have done a great job so far. Helping to defend us and making camps, and not complaining too much. We just have to remember that just because there aren't many people left in the cities doesn't mean there aren't still a lot of survivors out here in the more rural areas. That last group of people who shot at us should be a harsh reminder of that."

"Where are we, anyway?" Jake asked as he itched his elbow.

"Well, according to the signs we've seen, and my vague memory of driving through here on a road trip once or twice *many* years ago, we're somewhere near Monticello, moving closer to Tallahassee." She jerked her head toward the west where an orange glow radiated from the distant city to make an eerie impression against the night sky. "You can kind of see it through the trees there."

Jake glanced away but turned back with a frown. "Great. More fires. Just what we need."

"I don't think they'll reach us out here, so I wouldn't worry too much."

Alice rose from the short log she'd been sitting on and leaned in toward the pot, taking a wooden spoon off a nearby stone and using it to stir the contents of their makeshift stew. Shifting the pot to a cooler part of the grill, she scooped some into two bowls and handed them to the kids before dishing some out for herself and retaking her seat. Before she'd even sat down, both kids were already blowing air around giant mouthfuls, trying to minimize the burning as they shoveled it in as fast as possible.

"Geez. It's like you guys have never eaten before."

"I've never been this *hungry* before," Jake replied between chewing and blowing on his food, a carrot missing his mouth, dripping off his chin and hitting the ground.

Sarah pointed at him with her spoon. "But you've never walked so much either."

As the kids talked between bites, Alice focused on eating, getting through the bowl quickly, filling it up halfway and draining it again before placing it aside and spinning around on the log to face their packs lined up behind her.

"You guys finish off the rest of the stew. I'm going to check our supplies." She'd traded in her old carryall for a decent backpack, and she hadn't checked their things since packing them hurriedly when their EV had caught fire.

Starting with Jake's pack, she dragged out a few blankets, a compass, a flashlight, his clothes, and some long-lasting rations and cans he'd gotten off the couple who'd broken into the beach house. Sarah's pack had her e-reader and her clothes, another flashlight, spare forks, spoons, and plates, and a good week's worth of meals and snack bars along with some clothes that gave off a waft of soot and smoke. As for Alice's things, she'd packed mostly food, including chip bags and MRE meals, and she also had a couple of first-aid kits, two small flashlights, a camp lantern, and a pair of blankets. The knives were in their accompanying sheaths, attached to their belts and ready to use at a moment's notice and they had the pool cues, too, though one had cracked and wouldn't take another strike without breaking. They'd been using them as walking sticks more than anything else, along with poking around at debris on the road as they passed. The rifle Alice found at the camping store rested against a tree nearby, and her revolver was tucked into the small of her back on the right side, both weapons having been checked by her multiple times in case they needed to use them.

"Well, we've still got a lot of stuff," she said, "but we lost comfort supplies like our tent and foam pillows and mats. The good news is that we won't starve for a while, though, and we've got light sources and weapons to defend ourselves. Despite everything, we're doing pretty good." She frowned, looking at the food. "We've got a lot of calories here in these meals, but like Sarah pointed out, we're walking an awful lot and will burn through these calories like nothing. If we were just sitting around, what we had would do just fine, but…"

"Our supplies will only last half as long as we think?" Sarah cocked her eyebrow, finishing Alice's thought.

"That's what I'm thinking. There's a good chance we'll need food with a bit more calories, and plenty of it if we're going to make it home."

"Do you think we'll have to walk all that way?" Jake asked with a wilting tone. "What is it, like six hundred miles or something?"

Alice turned back to face them and rested her hands on her lap. "Mm. Try a thousand."

Jake collapsed forward with his arms thrown over his knees. "Oh, man! My dogs are barking already!"

Alice chuckled. "Unless we find another awesome EV like we had, it looks like we'll be doing a lot of walking. Anyway, my point is, hunting may be on the horizon for us. But that's where your experience back on Grandma's and Grandpa's farm – and our farm – will come in handy."

"Heyyyy, that's right!" Jake perked up.

"It's been a long time since I've butchered a chicken," Sarah said. "I'm not even sure if I can do it anymore."

"Oh, it's been a while since I've butchered a pig or goat, but it's not a skill that you really ever lose. I think we'll just need a little practice and we'll be just fine. The real trick will be finding a big animal and bringing it down out here." With a mischievous glint in her eye, she looked back and forth between the two. "We might need to hunt a crocodile. Not only are those tasty, but we could make shoes, too. Even a couple of purses."

"Gross," Sarah grimaced. "Those things terrify me."

Alice laughed. "I was just kidding. I doubt we'll resort to that. I can't imagine standing at the edge of a swamp and trying to catch one."

"We can use Sarah as bait," Jake quipped with a sideways smile. "Just stand her near the shore while we sit back with the guns, ready to shoot."

"Hilarious." Sarah grabbed a pebble off the ground and tossed it at him.

While the kids laughed at each other, Alice sat back, the mention of her parents drawing her thoughts back to them, and then inevitably back to her husband. While Alice was constantly concerned about James and her parents back home, she'd avoided bringing up the subject, trying to keep from worrying the kids any more than they needed to be. But as the moments wore on, and they grew sleepier, Jake finally wadded up his snack wrapper paper and tossed it into the fire, sliding down off his log and sitting on the moist soil with his back against the wood.

"Do you think Dad made it home yet, Mom?"

"I've been thinking about him a lot, too," Sarah added, tossing her empty bag into the flames and dusting her hands off.

"Go on," Alice said.

"Well, Dad could be in a couple different places, right?" Jake mused. "Maybe he's stuck in Denver when his flight got canceled, or he somehow made it home and he's with Grandpa and Grandma right now. Or he could be anywhere between all that." Jake hesitated. "He could even be—"

"*Don't* say it." Alice cut him off before he could finish the thought, locking her jaw for a moment to get the emotions under control. "Let's just stay positive about him, Grandma and Grandpa, okay? If we start thinking negatively about this, we won't get very far."

When Jake only shook his head and leaned forward to stare into the flames, Alice continued solemnly. "Look, I won't sugarcoat things. You're absolutely right. He could've not made it out of the airport. Something could have happened to him when he said he was getting out." Alice swallowed hard as the idea of never seeing her husband again struck her like a punch in the gut. "It would be easy to think the worst. To give up. But your father's tough." Alice patted her chest. "I feel him in my heart, and even if it sounds dumb… I'd know if he was gone. You don't have to believe me, but—"

"We believe you, Mom." Sarah stared at her, her eyes gleaming with a hint of determination. "Jake's a little harder to convince." Gaze shifting to her brother, she raised an eyebrow in question. "But he knows Dad's okay, too. Right, Jake?" Jake only shrugged in response.

"He's probably in a dangerous situation, just like we are," Alice said, "but to count your father out for any reason would be a big mistake. What if he was standing right here on the other side of that campfire?" Alice pointed beyond the fire where smoke curled up into the trees. "What would you tell him right now? Would you tell him you gave up on him? That you didn't believe he'd make it?"

"It's... it's not like that," Jake responded with a pained grimace even as his gaze shifted as if he half-expected to see his father standing before him. "I'm just not sure how any of us are going to get through this."

"It's easy. We're going to stick together like we have been and take one step at a time."

"We need you to stay strong, Jake." Sarah spoke, putting her arm around her brother. "You're one reason we're even here right now. The way you defended us against not just one but *three* attacks was incredible."

"I'm proud of both of you." Alice patted Sarah's knee and shared a smile with them before letting her gaze settle on Jake. "Are we good?"

"Yeah, we're good," he replied with a slight smile.

"Okay. Let's get settled down for the night. I'll keep first watch."

Jake and Sarah dug around in their backpacks for blankets and some clothes to roll up and put under their heads, and they laid down between the logs and the fire, making a bed of soft grass and leaves on the already moist soil before bundling up to keep the mosquitoes and bugs off them.

"You'll wake us up, right, Mom?" Sarah asked. "Don't try to keep watch all night."

"We have to rest, but *you* need rest, too." Jake gave her foot a little nudge with his as he grinned up at her from under the blankets.

"I promise to get you up in a few hours, okay?"

With nods of affirmation, they pulled the covers to their chins and were soon snoring lightly along with the crackling flames. Alice stood with the rifle and made a quick round of the camp, climbing a short rise and gazing out across an open field of waving grass and rustling trees. Staring at the orange glow looming over Tallahassee and its surrounding neighborhoods, she swung around to the southwest and looked down on a narrow deer trail.

Her mind drifted to James and her parents, random thoughts and questions about where they were and what they were doing, wondering if they could ever imagine Alice and the kids in the Florida woods, camping out and fighting for their lives. After doing three or four rounds, swatting her way through the brush and collecting her share of stickers and burrs, Alice woke the kids up and took Sarah's spot on the blankets with the guns resting next to her.

"Do a few rounds," she instructed them. "And if you see or hear anything, get me up immediately."

Sleep came quickly and was as pitch black as the smoke-filled night sky, a heavy quietness that settled in her mind and kept her sleeping straight through the aches and pains that plagued her restless legs. The dreams came next; she was standing on an endless road that stretched ahead of them, the end shrouded in darkness and uncertainty, and when she turned to look back, there was only death and destruction, endless fires and soot filling the skies. Piles of corpses lined the streets and burned inside flaming vehicles, yet they weren't dead. The bodies moved and screamed in their metal incinerators, smearing the windows in melted fat and skin.

Alice awoke suddenly, roused by Sarah shaking her shoulder, the dreams evaporating into mist. She rose and blinked into a freshly stoked fire with light leaking over the edges of the dirt and radiating a warmth that drove away the vestiges of the dreams and the chill of the dark night. Telling the kids to lie back down, she got up and moving, slipping her shoes on and doing a quick round of the camp, slapping at her itchy skin and yawning until she finally felt alert enough to not immediately fall back asleep.

Groggy and hip-sore from yesterday's walking, Alice sat back in front of the fire and peered into the flames before digging around in their packs, pulling out a couple of packets of instant coffee. Using one of their pots, she boiled two cups of water and stirred in the dark grounds, sitting back on the log where she sipped the weak brew and savored its sour taste above having nothing at all. Slowly but surely, staring into the dying flames of their Dakota fire, Alice began feeling like something of herself again. Sometime around eight, she nudged the kids awake and bade them pack up their blankets, spare clothing, and any snacks and food they'd left lying around.

They started with a bit of stretching, Jake complaining about sore feet and Sarah scratching at several mosquito bites on her arm, before they gathered their things, buried the fire and got back on the road. Using a compass and going off the road signs, Alice kept them heading in a northerly direction, following country lanes lined with splayed hornbeams with their curved and weeping branches. Gnarled oaks anchored massive, swaying magnolias with leaves that rustled above their heads as they walked. As they shuffled along, shoes scuffing on the pavement, Alice told them to pick it up so they could make better time. Unlike before, when they'd been fortunate enough to find a working vehicle, there likely wouldn't be many EVs in the Florida backcountry, and every gas-powered vehicle they ran across sat crumpled on the road like a cast-off toy. Dead passengers filled the seats, having perished from the impact of the explosions or the resulting smoke and flames, and many bodies still smoldered and gave off the stinging reek of melted fat, hitting the trio with a zest that curled their nose hairs.

"I vote we stay away from people," Jake said when they saw a group of them gathered in a small church parking lot in the middle of nowhere, down a long gravel drive.

"I agree," Alice replied, keeping a wary eye on the group.

They cut across an open field with long grass and swaying trees bordering the edges where a clutch of crabapple trees stood in the center of the field. They rested beneath them, and had a quick brunch of MREs and some chips from the vending machine they'd raided. Alice almost could have imagined they were on a typical country hike except for the impossibly black-gray skies, burned-out farmsteads, and farm equipment still smoking in the middle of the fields. The weather was moist and muggy as they sat beneath the trees, finishing their lunch and watching the dark skies roll by.

"Which way are we heading, Mom?" Sarah looked around. "It's so hard to tell with all this smoke."

"Compass still says we're going North so we should be good."

"We've barely seen the sun at all." Jake stuffed his MRE packaging into a garbage bag and sat holding a bottled water between his knees. "I wonder if we'll ever see it again?"

"It *does* look kind of scary up there." Alice squinted upward skeptically. "If everything is burning, then it could be weeks before this stuff clears. At least it's better out here than it was back near the city, though."

Neither Jake nor Sarah looked like they believed her, but they cleaned up their site, packed up their things, and slung their backpacks on their shoulders once more. They moved through the field and entered a forested area with plants Alice couldn't identify and birds that flitted overhead, their songs seeming nervous and their movements erratic. Eventually, they reached an old fence with just three rails and no wire, and Alice picked a spot where the top rail had gone rotten and fallen, letting the kids climb over first before joining them. They moved down a shallow slope and entered another wide field of lush green vegetation where a small cluster of citrus trees had a few good-sized fruits waiting to be picked. There was a farmstead on the other side, with one barn trickling smoke, though the house was still intact.

"Kids, fill your pack up with two oranges each."

"I just want to point out, for the record, that this is technically stealing." Sarah reached for a couple of brightly colored orbs and tugged them down, turning and putting them in Jake's backpack before grabbing her own. "But we burned that bridge when we drove off with the EV."

"We're past calling it stealing." Alice was tight-lipped as she spoke, watching the nearby house for any signs of life. "This is about survival. Let's hurry and move on before we attract any attention."

They climbed a short hillock through a small patch of woods and jumped on another road, following it up to a high point with a break in the trees that allowed them to see miles in every direction.

Sarah brushed some strands of brown hair behind her ears. "What now, Mom?"

The road was running east and west, and she took a chance and took them west, uncertain if it would swing them north into Georgia or south toward Tallahassee where they'd be forced to go off-road again. They passed more farms showing signs of life where people had built clusters of tents and shelters beside their burned-out husks of homes. There were groups of refugees trekking through the fields, talking in indistinct murmurs with the occasional shout or a child crying. If anyone spotted them on the road, they didn't seem to care, though Alice encouraged the kids to hurry by quickly and discreetly.

"No staring or stopping," she said as they spotted a group walking along a tree line to the north. "Just keep on moving."

Alice constantly adjusted her rifle and backpack as her shoulders grew tired and the muscles at the base of her neck tensed. There was comfort in their weapons and supplies, though, as a deterrent against the shadows of humanity that lingered in the woods and on the lonely back roads and against nature itself.

They'd gone a couple more hours along forested lanes with wooden fencing and sometimes short brick walls when the road suddenly widened and swung them slightly north, bringing them to a spot of civilization where smaller farms and homesteads grew more frequent and closer together. A deserted strip mall sat off the road to their right, and a church with burned-out cars in the lot stood on the left. Beyond those were other small businesses and restaurants along the flat stretch of pavement, though there weren't any people that she noticed.

The trio stopped in front of a big sign on the road, and Alice read the sweeping green letters out loud. "Monticello."

Jake scratched his head. "I thought that was in Virginia."

"They have one here, too, I guess." Sarah pointed at a smaller sign just below the big one. "Home of the Kentucky Derby champion three years running? Hey... do you think...?"

Alice tapped her foot and reread the sign, eyeing the kids with a hint of hope.

CHAPTER TWO

James Burton
Kansas City, Missouri

Staccato bursts of gunfire ripped the night sky and blossoms of orange appeared on the eastern horizon where the city's outskirts sat a mile from the camp. A line of buildings and a business park that hadn't caught fire in the initial disaster still stood intact, and muzzles flashed from the windows and nearby trees as dark shadows crept toward the camp through the open fields. Fearful families fled inside their tents and zipped up the flaps as the military had ordered them, though even more were running away. Their boots kicked up dust from the dirt and gravel lanes as they flowed west against the onrushing National Guardsmen and soldiers rushing toward the danger and gunfire. Still groggy from sleep, James initially moved with the crowd, heading east with his packs on his shoulders but glancing back uncertainly as the military personnel rushed to face some unknown enemy. Jaw locked tight, he stepped aside and let one family pass before he started around the other way, slowly at first but picking up speed as his resolution hardened.

On the train, he'd held himself in check when an angry passenger attacked the guardsman who'd helped him, but standing by and doing nothing again was no longer an option. James ran against the flow as fathers carried children close to their chests, mothers towing them by hand, dozens of frightened faces hurrying past him as he focused on the green military uniforms converging on the main thoroughfares and gathering strength in numbers. The sounds of rumbling tanks with squeaky treads echoed through the encampment, and Humvees roared along wider lanes in the center of camp where they joined the Army infantry and National Guardsmen. A single mother with several children burst around the corner, the pile of them clashing with the military personnel, the two youngest taking a hard spill on top of one another in front of the rushing throng. James followed the military a few yards before he stopped and turned back to the crying kids, lifting a little girl and then a boy from the dirt, shooing them toward their thankful mother.

"Go on!" he shouted, handing them over. "Move east, but stay to the sides, or they'll get knocked down again."

The mother was nodding and gathering her children around her with sweeping arms, guiding them east and keeping close to the tents, ducking under tent strings as explosions and sharp cracks of gunfire ripped the air. With the family on their way to safety, James turned to chase down the Guardsmen to the far side of camp where they dispersed between the fenced-in areas and sheds and fell in behind a long row of sandbags, kicking up dust under a barrage of bullets. Ducking low and mirroring the movements of the guardsmen, James followed them to the sandbags, crouching low, scraping his knees across the hard dirt as tracers zipped overhead. A pair of guardsmen were setting up a large machine gun on a stand, pointing the business end into the darkness. An officer peeked over the sandbags and ordered the guardsmen to aim to the right and provide cover fire, then he turned to another who held a radio and carried a bulky backpack on his shoulders with an antenna sprouting from the top.

"Tell them we've got heavy incoming fire from the North! Skyscrapers and office park!" the officer yelled at the radio operator.

"Yes, Captain Ross!"

As the radio operator delivered the message, the Captain's eyes fell on James, and he shook his head and pointed east with a shout. "Go back with the rest of the refugees!"

"What's going on?" James called, edging closer but still crouched low with his insides quaking as rounds zipped over his head.

"Get out of here!" Ross bellowed. "We've got attackers hitting us from the ruins on the city's outskirts—"

They ducked as another explosion shook the air, vibrating the ground, stirring up dust, and James started to think that what he was doing wasn't such a good idea. Still, against the bombastic sounds and chaos, he stayed rooted to the spot.

"But who is it? Who's attacking us?"

Ross scowled in annoyance. "Either gang members or militia. Does that answer your question? Now, get out of here!"

"I want to help!" James shouted over the gunfire and cries of guardsmen and soldiers as they repositioned and began shooting back. "I can do something. Tell me what to do!"

Ross stared at him with a flat gaze before turning to a guardsman who was about to run off, grabbing his arm and holding him back. "Go with Corporal Stenson here and help lug ammunition."

"Thank you, Captain. I'm happy to help."

Corporal Stenson crouch-walked to him and took James' arm. "Stay low! Follow me!"

James nodded briskly and fell in behind the Corporal as he dashed past the fenced-in generators and water processing units and flew down a row of civilian tents. They angled north, turning into the main intersection where two massive Humvees rumbled by, washing the pair in a cloud of dust, James stumbling and falling as the old, paint-worn armored trucks trundled by, one of them nearly clipping him. The Corporal grabbed him and hauled him up, and together they jumped into the wide lane, only to leap back again as a bulky, groaning Abrams tank roared by with squealing tracks and an enormous turbine engine whining and cranking. James tripped on a tent string, twisted, and fell hard on his backside, eyes wide as another tank rumbled by, looming massively before him. Then he got his senses back and clutched the waiting Corporal's hand. Stenson jerked him off the ground again and led him two more tent blocks up, where a mix of Army soldiers and National Guardsmen were running everywhere, loading up Humvees that trundled off to the north through the narrow lanes.

"Over here!"

James followed Stenson to a sizeable concrete armory as military personnel came and went, carrying crates or rolling them toward the front line. The Corporal appeared and handed him a thick pair of safety earmuffs, and James thanked him and slipped them on his head to block out the worst of the bombastic sounds. A four-wheeled cart was pushed at him, and James grabbed the handle and dragged it out of the way of traffic. The pair then turned inside, and each took the end of a massive crate, lifting the heavy artillery and shuffling out to the cart with it. On a three count, they heaved it onto the top shelf and returned for some smaller ammunition that read .50 on the side.

Within a few minutes, James was sweating and panting, breathing dust and smoke as it drifted over the tents. The booming tank fire rocked the ground with a percussive jolt that rattled the hairs in his ears and set his teeth on edge. He and Stenson each took an end of the cart, dragging it through the dirt and gravel on its big rubber wheels, which enabled them to move swiftly through the crowds of running military personnel. With more heavy machinery flying by on the broader lanes, Stenson pointed to a side alley and shouted for him to angle that way, following another group of Guardsmen carrying artillery to the east side of camp. With a curt nod, James put his back into it and pulled the heavy cart in that direction, boots digging into the gravel and dirt and gathering speed as they rushed headlong toward the raging gunfight. Finally, the Corporal waved for him to stop, and they grabbed the larger case off the top and carried it into the firing area where three Humvees were lined up with their gunners carefully picking targets and shooting sharp bursts into the darkness.

"Over there!" Stenson bellowed. "First Humvee on the right!"

James switched hands and moved the heavy crate to the rear of the first armored vehicle where a pair of Army soldiers waited. As soon as they dropped the crate, the soldiers threw off the top and pulled out two big canisters of .50 caliber ammunition. They slammed it into the cargo area, and the gunner fired off his last few rounds before reaching back to grab it.

"Now, over here!" Stenson shouted and pointed in the other direction.

With the slightly lighter crate in hand, the two hauled it thirty yards to the next Humvee as an Abrams tank fired and knocked James off balance, legs wobbly for a moment until he straightened himself and kept moving. Stenson was grinning grimly as they fell to their knees behind the armored truck to serve canisters to the waiting soldiers who fed the ammunition to the gunner. James and the Corporal moved on, rushing to the third Humvee with a flurry of heavy rounds peppering the ground near his feet, zipping right in front of him and forcing him to pull up straight once as the crate cracked him in the back of the leg. With a pained grunt, James leaned forward and made it the last few yards, where the waiting military personnel took the rest of what they had.

Something whistled through the air as they ran with the empty crate back for more ammunition. Stenson dropped his end, grabbed James by the shoulders, and threw him down hard while landing on top of him. The tents to the west split open in a cyclone of kinetic energy, followed by a dense explosion that rattled James' teeth. The smell of burning canvas and flesh swept over them, punctuated by scorched plastics and other camp materials. Stifling a sneeze, James raised his gaze to see flaming tents and buildings with civilians and military personnel rushing in every direction. He started to run there when Stenson grabbed him and turned him back to the empty crate, and the two picked up their ends and sprinted out of the line of fire. Back at their cart, they hoisted their crate on top and pushed it again, jostling and bumping into other military personnel as they went. A generator building was hit, the explosion blossoming upward and riding a wave of orange flame and soot, the impact throwing James forward to fall against the cart. Sweating and covered in dirt and soot, he and Stenson reached the armory, picked up more .50 caliber ammunition, and delivered it to the Humvees on the front lines. When they returned to the arsenal for the third time, an Army Sergeant grabbed Stenson and shouted into his ear as he pointed at a tank fifty yards farther north, bathed in floodlights at the edge of the camp.

The Corporal turned to James and hollered over the noise. "We need to take some shells to the tanks!"

"Did they run out of shells already?!"

"A lot of our tanks and APCs weren't loaded yet," Stenson explained. "We've been so busy setting up the camps—" They ducked as another explosion ripped through the camp a hundred yards north of them. Once the dust and sound settled, the Corporal finished what he was saying. "We weren't expecting anything like this! They've got friggin' explosives, man!"

The Sergeant pointed toward the armory's west-side entrance. "The rest of you men get this ammunition out of here! The last thing we need is for this to get hit and this ammunition to cook off. Let's go, people! Move!"

James swallowed hard as he and the Corporal received a massive cart with even bigger crates already loaded. The lead officer patted Stenson on the back and pointed east toward the tanks. The Corporal nodded and shouted that he understood before gesturing to James to take the other side. Together, they wheeled the tank shells into the narrow lane and hauled them along with the traffic flow heading east, watching others return from the explosions and ricocheting bullets with shell-shocked expressions and dusty faces. Weaving the cart past the chaos, they angled it across the open space and fenced-in buildings as the tank fired another round into the night, the impact sending a jolt through the hull with dust flying from the tank's joints. The shot shook the ground beneath James' feet, his knees buckling slightly before he put his head down and dug in, dragging the cart behind him with Stenson pushing hard. They parked the ordnance by the armored hull, and the Corporal grabbed a phone on the back and called to the tank crew inside. A hatch flew open, and a crewman crawled across the turret, dropping onto the hull and rolling off to land between Stenson and James, all of them throwing themselves against the tank with a grimace as tracer rounds filled the night sky with color, and booms and crackles made it hard to hear.

"I'm the loader," the man said, clasping hands with Stenson. "Private Sepulveda."

"Great, Sepulveda," Stenson replied. "We've got some shells for you."

"I'd normally hug you, but we're having some problems up there."

"What's the problem?"

"The gun won't fire. We think the firing pin is jammed."

James uncoiled from his crouch to face the loader. "Can you fix it?"

"None of us can," Sepulveda said, "but we're trying to find a mechanic now."

James crouched lower and stared at the idling vehicle, shouting above the noise. "Let me give it a shot. I'm pretty good with things like that."

Sepulveda glanced at James doubtfully, flinching only slightly when a burst of rounds pinged off the tank's armor. When the shots passed, he shook his head. "A civvie can't help with this!"

"I've got a doctorate in mechanical engineering!" James bellowed above the battlefield noise. "Just let me look at the damned thing and see what I can do!"

Sepulveda stared at him a long time before saying, "Commander Halladay will tear my head off, but it's worth a try. Come on! We'll go through the loader's hatch!"

Waving him up, the Private climbed onto the hull and then atop the turret to holler into the tank. Finally, he gestured for James to come up, pointing and yelling for him to put his feet inside the hatch first. There was a moment when James was climbing up and felt naked and vulnerable, bullets flying overhead, a couple striking the armor with metallic pings, then he was slipping into the tank and falling as the gunner caught him. Sepulveda landed next to him and crammed into the tight space.

"This is Commander Halladay," Sepulveda said, motioning to a man buckled into a narrow seat above the crew, "and our gunner, Private Gutierrez."

"I'm James."

"How can you help us?" Halladay spoke flatly from his perch.

James looked between the gunner and the Commander. "I hear you've got a problem with your firing mechanism?"

"The pin is jammed," Gutierrez said, flipping out a small hatch on the gun barrel.

"Let me see." James leaned closer, taking a flashlight from Gutierrez and shining it on the mechanism. While there were some pieces in there he didn't understand, he saw the problem right away. "The firing pin is completely rusted through, and so is the activation mechanism."

Gutierrez shifted her gaze to Halladay. "They'd mothballed this damn thing for so long, and we didn't have any new tanks around. All the good ones went up in flames."

Halladay leaned in closer, staring hard but hopefully at James. "Do you think you can get it working again?"

James probed with the flashlight a little more, sweat beading on his forehead in the cramped quarters. The only thing keeping him from panicking was that they'd left the loader's hatch open, and if he looked up he could still see the night sky, tracers filling it with color. "I might if I had some tools."

"Right behind you," Sepulveda said, shifting in the tight space and showing him a bag of supplies hanging from the nest frame.

James rifled through the contents, shifting aside screwdrivers and wrenches before finally settling on a five-pound mallet and a can of spray lubricant. Turning back to the main gun, James asked Gutierrez to hold the flashlight while he shot the aerosol grease inside the mechanisms, using his finger to rub off the old rust and grabbing a rag from behind him to work around the firing pin and any other areas that seemed stuck. With everything greased, he used the mallet to gently knock on some pieces, using his left hand to loosen up the moving parts and get them moving again, and when everything was smooth and functional, he wiped off the excess lubricant and stood back.

"That might do it. You could probably give it a shot."

He switched positions with Sepulveda and squeezed against the wall while the crew cycled through their firing procedure, Gutierrez peering through her targeting sights and shifting the turret with a whining sound to move the barrel a foot to the left.

Sepulveda grabbed a shell from the cargo area behind them, locked the shell inside, and threw a latch upward. "Up!"

Halladay barked, "Fire!"

"On the way!" Gutierrez engaged the firing mechanism, filling the turret with a muffled *boom*.

The shot was like a blast of wind, and dust swirled in front of James' eyes as he swayed against the loader with a grin. "Well, that was something."

"Nailed it!" Halladay bellowed with his eyes pressed to his targeting periscope. "Took out that entrenched position in that burned-out building."

Gutierrez pumped her fist and slapped James hard on the shoulder, knocking him back as his smile grew wider.

"Great work!" Halladay called down.

"No problem." James laughed, still shaky with his neck throbbing from the concussive force of the fired shell.

"Now get up there and hand some more shells to Sepulveda!"

"Yes, sir!"

Holding his breath, wincing at every shot fired their way, James climbed out of the hatch and quickly rolled off the turret onto the hull. "Hand me a shell, Stenson!"

The pair formed a chain, Stenson passing shells to James, and James turning and climbing onto the turret to hand them down to Sepulveda. One after the other, they emptied the case, and James slapped the top of the turret and jumped off the back. The loader's hatch slammed shut, and the tank pulled off, firing again as it rolled, James shaking his head at the brutal force of each shot. Peering eastward into the distance, he spotted the building they were after, the second shell striking the front to send ripples through the structure, the brick façade shuddering before it collapsed straight down in a burst of flames and smoke.

"Very nice, James!" Stenson nodded, impressed.

"It was nothing! Just a rusted-over firing mechanism. Just glad I was able to help out!"

They each grabbed a crate end and put it back on their rolling cart, pushing it toward the safety of the rear lines. For the next two hours, James and Stenson ferried supplies and ammunition from the concrete armory to various units on the eastern flank, breathing exhaust fumes and smoke, ducking and sometimes diving to their bellies in the dirt when return fire ripped through the canvas tents and tore them apart. As they worked, the wounded were brought back to first-aid tents that had been reserved for the civilian refugees but had turned into trauma centers for the troops. James took orders and carried them out without knowing who was giving them, though he quickly got into the flow of the work as the heavy armor pushed off whatever mysterious forces were attacking. The two-man team ferried medical supplies or cleared entire areas of tents, putting out fires and pulling corpses from the wreckage to leave them smoking on the side.

At the city's edge, the business park was engulfed in flames, occasional rounds spitting from dug-in positions and aimed at the tanks pressing in. The tree line was blazing, and the smoke from the constant barrage of tank shells and incendiary rounds picked apart an enemy James couldn't see. His knees quivered, his back straining and aching from his previous journeying, combined with the lugging of heavy crates for hundreds of yards in every direction. When they got back to the armory, he leaned against the wall and squatted with his shoulders pressed to the concrete.

Coming around the corner, Stenson waved weakly and crouched beside him. "Hey, buddy. You look thirsty."

James swallowed dry, nodded tiredly, and gladly accepted the canteen the Corporal handed him. Unscrewing the lid and tilting the canteen up, James gulped, water leaking from the corners of his mouth and running down his chin. When he was done, he capped it and gave it back.

"Thank you," he replied with a gasp. "I needed that."

"No problem." Stenson leaned against the wall. "We should thank *you*. You never served in the military before this?"

"I'm not a career soldier," James laughed.

"Well, if you ever want a job, you're more than welcome back here."

The two stared at each other and then burst into laughter, Stenson swallowing hard from the canteen as the sounds of sporadic gunfire continued.

"So, what happens now?" James asked as a guardsman came by, handing out bottled waters from a backpack and tossing one to him.

"They'll send scouts out to ensure there are no more enemies in the vicinity, and we'll be on our toes from here on out."

"I'd be curious to know who the attackers were," James replied. "It would be nice to know what I'm dealing with when I get back on the road."

"You're not sticking around?"

"I've got to get to my family at our home in Michigan."

The camp was calming down, and hysterical refugees came back and were helping to pick up the mess after the northeast part of the encampment had been torn up. Medics and National Guardsmen took care of the dozens who'd perished, taking their bodies out of sight as an Army priest followed behind, speaking with a few of the civilians. Distant guns still rattled off as the military went after whoever had attacked them, and James used a wet rag to wipe the dust off his face and cool down. Once he'd gotten his wind back, he stood and offered his hand to the Corporal.

"Thanks for letting me help."

Stenson accepted his hand and allowed himself to be pulled to his feet, patting James on the shoulder. "Nah, it's all good, man. You chipped in and really made a difference. Now about that job..."

James laughed. "No thanks. I'll just grab my things and head back to my tent. I should probably rest up and eat something before I take off." James circled to the front of the Armory, excusing himself as he bumped into the milling guards who'd been placed at the entrance.

Having seen him around and working with the ordnance, they nodded and let him pass. James spotted his backpacks tossed in the corner on an empty shelf, and he picked them up and shrugged them on his shoulders. Stepping outside into the stark floodlights, James turned in a circle and tried to decide where he wanted to go. He started toward Stenson to ask for directions when a chorus of happy howls and cheers erupted from the wide truck lane east of them. A group of familiar Army soldiers were striding up, Commander Halladay laughing and patting Gutierrez on her shoulder, pointing past her at James.

"Looks like you've got some fans," Stenson said, coming up with a grin.

Sepulveda jogged up with his arms wide and a broad grin. "Leaving already, man?"

"I'm afraid so," James replied, leaning in as Sepulveda embraced him, broke off, and whacked his back.

"But you just got here," Sepulveda said.

"The Army could use a guy like you to help maintain our equipment." Gutierrez swung at him playfully and gave him a friendly shove. "You were amazing, man!"

"You got us up and running when we were dead in the water!" Halladay agreed. "We would've been sitting ducks if not for you. Man, that was incredible."

"And to think the captain wanted him out of here." Stenson shook his head and crossed his arms.

"You weren't so bad yourself, Corporal," Halladay said. "You got James acclimated in record time."

Stenson laughed. "He's a quick learner."

Other guardsman and soldiers smiled and nodded at the group appreciatively, enough for James to realize word must have gotten around about his repair of the tank's main gun.

Halladay glanced at Gutierrez. "Any recruiters around? We need to get this guy signed up."

"I'll run and get one." The gunner laughed and slicked back her dark, sweaty hair. "I'll get him assigned to our tank, and you can ride beside our driver."

"Just happy I could help," James replied sheepishly, looking for a place to escape the attention.

The group settled down, and Halladay wrapped his arm around James' shoulder. "Seriously, friend. Where are you heading next?"

"I'm heading back to Michigan," he replied gruffly. "Like I was telling Corporal Stenson. My family is meeting me there, so that's where I have to go."

"I understand," the Commander said. "If I were you, I'd be doing the same thing. Do you need anything?"

"Honestly, I could use a ride," James laughed.

"Wish we could help you with that," Halladay grinned, "but there's not a lot of available vehicles. Anything else?"

"I guess I could use a rifle, too. If you can spare one."

Halladay patted his shoulder again. "Are you kidding? We've got equipment coming out of our asses. What we're short on is people. You have a standing offer to join us."

Gutierrez beamed. "Are you sure we can't convince you to stay? The Commander would love to have a grease monkey on standby."

"I appreciate the offer, guys," James chuckled and shoved them playfully as they crowded around, "but I'm going to get a little rest and get back to my family."

"No problem," Halladay said and turned to Corporal Stenson. "Can you do me one more favor?"

"Just ask, sir." Stenson stood straighter.

"Go to the armory and find this man a rifle with a scope and some ammo. Let them know I approve it. Anything he needs, give it to him."

"Yes, sir," Stenson replied.

With that, James said his goodbyes to the jovial tank crew and followed the Corporal through the crowds of milling soldiers and guardsmen working hard to put the camp back in order. Somewhere north of them, they reached a small tent with a guardswoman sitting in the center at a table and a sign that read *Inventory Control*. Surrounding her were crates of ammunition and weapons on shelves, some with their tops broken open and piled on the side as the smell of oil lingered in the air. James' eyes grew wide at the sight of dozens of matte black rifles being repaired where they sat on rags, gleaming with oil.

"Evening, Corporal Jackson," Stenson said to the diminutive woman with her hair pulled tightly back except for a few frazzled ends that hung loose. "Rough night, huh?"

"It was unreal," she replied flatly, her gaze shifting between the men. "I take it we ran them off?"

"We're on their tails now," Stenson nodded.

"Ah, good. What can I do for you?"

"This is James." The Corporal gestured for him to step forward. "He's just a civilian, but he pitched in today and helped us win the fight."

"That's great." Jackson stood and looked him up and down. "Looks like they put you through the wringer."

"Nothing I couldn't handle. We lugged a lot of gear."

Stenson raised both eyebrows and leaned in. "*After* he fixed a tank's firing mechanism."

"Seriously?" Jackson asked in surprise. "How did you manage that?"

"I've got some mechanical experience," James replied. "The tank had been sitting for a long time and just needed a bit of elbow grease in the right place. It's nothing, really."

"Got it firing again so Commander Halladay could back off whoever was attacking us."

"Any word about who it was?"

Stenson shrugged. "I'd imagine we'll know soon enough. Anyway, Halladay wants us to load up James here with some supplies. We'll need a rifle, some ammo, rations, water, a good backpack, and anything else you can think of that might get him where he needs to go."

"Oh yeah? Where are you headed to?"

"Michigan."

"Phew," Jackson nodded appreciatively. "That's going to be a trek and a half. All right. I'll see what I can do."

After jotting a few notes, she stood and wandered around the crates, returning with a rifle with a scope and a pouch with a dozen magazines inside it. Jackson disappeared amongst the shelves once more, followed by the sounds of her jostling and bumping things in a clatter of tools and supplies as she filled a beige, camelback-style backpack.

"Wow, this is too much," James said as he picked up the rifle, adjusting the strap for carrying on his shoulder, and pulling on the charging handle to look inside the chamber.

"No problem," Stenson replied. "As Commander Halladay said, we'll hook you up with whatever you need. We owe you that much." The Corporal nodded at the weapon James held. "That's an M4 carbine with a smart optic scope. Do you know how it works?"

"More or less. Show me, though, so I'm not missing anything."

Stenson showed him the ins and outs of the weapon, and James adjusted the scope, then loaded a magazine. Jackson returned a moment later with the backpack full of supplies and set it on the table with a thump, its thick straps hanging from the curved frame designed to fit comfortably on the back for long stretches at a time.

"Try that on for size," Jackson said.

James put the rifle's safety on, set it aside, and belted on the ammunition pouch so it rested opposite his Colt Python's holster. He shrugged on the backpack and bounced it on his shoulders to settle the weight and after testing the fit, he nodded appreciatively. "This will work great. Thanks a lot."

"You should be loaded with a bunch of food and everything else you need for a long trek," Jackson said. "It might even be enough to get you to Michigan, if you ration wisely."

"Thanks, ma'am," he replied and shook hands with her.

"Do you want to keep any of your old supplies?" Stenson asked, lifting the two backpacks he'd dropped at his feet.

"Just the revolver and ammunition I have in there, but the rest you can keep."

Stenson dug out the Colt and holstered it for James as he held his arms out and then stuffed the ammunition into a front pouch on his backpack. Handing him the M4, the Corporal gestured for James to follow him outside. "I'll see you out."

Standing out front, they watched the military personnel come and go, stepping aside as two soldiers slipped into the munitions tent.

"Again, thanks a lot, James. I'm glad you stuck around for a while."

"Happy to help, Corporal. You all stay safe, and keep fighting the good fight."

After a quick handshake, James headed south through the camp, exhaustion looming over him, and he looked for his tent so he could get a couple of hours sleep before heading off on his long journey home.

CHAPTER THREE

Helen Cooper
Somewhere Outside East Lansing, Michigan

Packing the last of the eggs into a basket with a soft towel on the bottom, Helen smiled at the hens and bade them goodbye until the next day. She carried her bounty from the hen house into the chicken coop, gently shooing the white-feathered Brahmas and red Buckeyes aside as she headed for the door. With one arm weighed down by the basket, she fiddled with the replacement latch Ryan had put on after the coop had been broken into, grunting with annoyance as she forced it open. The door was skewed, and the temporary latch way off center, destined to remain that way until her husband had more time to fix the door properly. With one hand she lifted the latch and put her shoulder against the door, the wood squealing against the frame as she slipped through and closed the door twice before it would catch.

"Finally," she grumbled in agitation as she turned and shuffled toward the house, moving past the bins of vegetables they had yet to can and the EV parked in the grass at the corner of the house.

Beyond the car was the short field of solar panels that charged the batteries that helped deliver a constant supply of energy to the house's critical appliances. Ryan had placed several poles in the ground already, designing a framework to add more solar panels which would give them double the square footage and increase their power generation. The new panels were still in their boxes and resting against a cart, and Ryan was supposed to connect them later once he'd finished working on fixing up his prosthetic.

Squinting upward, Helen gave the sun a dubious glance, its golden beams shining down through cracks in the clouds that were mildly discolored by lingering smoke from clusters of homes and buildings that were still smoldering or had recently caught fire. At least it wasn't the glowing orange sky from the first night that still sent shivers of unnatural fear up her spine whenever she thought about it.

The big plan for the day was to start canning some of the massive amounts of potatoes they had on hand, and she'd already brought some inside, forming a path through the vegetables so she could get to the back door. Popping it open, she stepped inside and walked over to the far end of the counter, setting the eggs down and putting her hand against the refrigerator to feel its vibration. With a quick detour, she checked the laundry room to verify that the freezer was working, too. *Ryan must have tweaked the power so everything could stay up and running,* she thought.

With a smile of pride and affection for her husband, she turned to the stove and looked over the canning supplies, seven one-quart jars she'd already cleaned and left in neat rows, the lids and ringers, the jar lifter, and de-bubbling tools which comprised of a plastic spatula and a thin stick the diameter of a straw. She'd already filled the pressure canner and a side pot with water; all she needed to do was cut the pile of potatoes over on the cooking island. Helen was adamant about not only canning the food but making it look good, too, so she always peeled them, blanched them, and added a hint of lemon to help keep their bright coloration.

Before starting, she washed her hands and ventured into the basement to see what Ryan was up to. Down the dark stairs she went, avoiding hitting light switches that wouldn't work and shuffling across to James' workshop where Ryan had found some things to fix his prosthetic foot. The door was cracked with faint electric lantern light leaking out, and she could hear him moving around and mumbling to himself like he always did when he needed to focus.

"Knock, knock!" she called as she gave the door a double rap and pushed in to find him sitting at a low desk in front of a small laptop screen, the monitor light casting a bluish-gray haze across his chest and face and giving his white hair a glow. He'd taken one of the 3D printers and had it on the desk next to the laptop and was glancing up at it as she came in.

"Hello dear!" He swiveled in his chair with a wide grin. "How do the eggs look?"

"I filled a basket too full, so we may need to work eggs onto the menu in a big way."

"Not a problem. What about the extras?"

Helen stepped in farther and touched her index finger to her chin. "We could mix some eggs up with the dog food and let them have anything we can't finish. Supposed to be good for their hearts, anyway."

"What do eggs have that's good for a dog's heart?" Ryan pursed his lips and wagged his finger. "Taurine, right?"

"That's it, yes."

"What about milk? Can we give them some of that, too?"

"Mm. I don't think so, not unless you want to give them diarrhea or something."

"Negative on the dog diarrhea," Ryan replied as he turned back to the laptop and printer.

Helen stepped closer and crossed her arms, looking around the room at the single electric lantern and the printer's blue LED light. "I hate that it's so dark down here. You remind me of some evil scientist working on a creepy experiment."

Ryan turned quickly with a ghoulish expression. "It's alive! *It's aliiiiive*!" Both of them chuckled, and he looked back at the screen. "Seriously, I wish we could turn on more lights, but I had to limit our electric use so I could run the laptop and printer."

"Have you made any progress with the... whatever it is you're working on?"

"Actually, yes." He rolled his chair to the side. "Here, look."

Helen stepped closer and leaned in to peer at the pieces of his prosthetic placed in a neat row in front of the printer. "Is that the part?"

"That's it," he replied, pointing to one piece sitting off to the side with a clear crack in it. "I unscrewed the socket, and that's what I'm going to replace. This whole setup is pretty awesome, and I found enough PETG filament to print the replacement part. It might not hold forever, but it'll work for now, and if I need to make a new one, I should have enough filament for that."

"Whatever PETG filament is."

Ryan chuckled. "It's the thermoplastics the printer molds into whatever shape you program it into."

"I see." Helen looked at the laptop screen and studied the three-dimensional image floating in a slow circle. "Wait a minute... are you going to print a new leg?"

Ryan shrugged. "Maybe... yeah. This setup doesn't require much power, and James has a ton of filament. Given the circumstances, I doubt he'll care if I use it."

"How did you learn all this, anyway?" She rolled her eyes. "Well, I know your brain never stops, but what put you onto the idea?"

"How do you think I kept fixing up the machinery around the farm right before the end when we were out of money to pay for the parts?" With a laugh, he sat back in his chair and locked his fingers over his stomach. "I used my setup at home to make parts for things. I couldn't use them for engines or anything super high stress, but I could print clamps and fasteners and things like that."

Helen clicked her tongue. "My clever husband, multi-talented as always."

"Darn right. I'd rather be a jack of all trades than a master of one."

"Well, come on, Jack. I need some help with the canning upstairs."

"Meet you in twenty minutes? I need another ten to finish printing the part, then I'll get my prosthetic reassembled and working... hopefully."

Helen had finished peeling the potatoes and was getting the water heated in both pots when Ryan came up, moving swiftly in from the hallway to come up behind her as he wrapped his arms around her waist.

"Wow, honey!" she said, leaning to her right and planting a quick kiss on his lips. "I hardly heard you squeaking at all."

"I'm not." Backing up, he spread his hands and marched across the kitchen and into the great room before turning and coming back. "The printer made the piece perfectly, though I had to finagle some things to get the threads right so it would screw on properly, but it's on tight and completely functional."

"You're barely limping at all."

Ryan bent over, put his hand on the plastic prosthetic sleeve that rode up his thigh, and rapped on it with his knuckles. "And now that it's stable, I won't have to walk funny and cause it to rub my skin raw on the inside of my knee."

"That's wonderful, dear." Helen clapped him on the shoulder.

"Anyway, I'll test it more tomorrow when I work more on the solar panels. But for now, let's get canning. What do you need me to do?"

"I peeled the potatoes, and now we have to cut them into smaller chunks and fill up these seven one-quart containers I have."

Ryan turned to the cooking island where the potatoes were piled up, seeing a cutting board on each side and two small knives. "Sounds easy enough to me, especially after you did all the hard work to peel them."

"I'm just glad you got your prosthetic fixed and you're not in pain anymore," Helen replied, picking up a knife and potato, cutting it longways and slicing it crossways to make small chunks.

"It feels great." Ryan came over, grabbed a knife, and started helping. "Once we get the whole crop all canned up, they should last us a couple of years or so, I reckon."

"As long as we do it right and don't mess up the seals."

"I'll follow your directions to the letter," Ryan said as he focused on his cutting.

They quietly sliced potatoes as the water boiled, then Helen added a teaspoon of salt to each quart jar before using a wide mouth funnel to drop the potato chunks inside the first one. As Ryan finished filling the jars, she took the lids and ringers and soaked them in hot water. By the time she'd turned back to the cooking island, James had all seven filled to the brim.

"What next?" he asked.

"Now, we just need to pour hot water into the jars, leaving about an inch at the top."

"Leave that to me."

Ryan crossed to the stove, grabbed a couple of potholders, and picked up the smaller pot of hot water, bringing it back to the jars and filling them up.

"Thank you, dear. Just leave about an inch from the top. It's been a while since I've canned potatoes, but I'm pretty sure that's how I've always done it."

"You got it."

Ryan filled each quart jar as instructed and carried the pot back to the stove, setting it down and returning to the cooking island.

"Now we have to get out the air bubbles." Helen took her de-bubbling stick and pushed it to the bottom of each jar on the sides and in the middle, shifting the potato chunks so any trapped air would rise to the top and release. When she was done, she put the stick aside, and together she and Ryan put the lids on and screwed the ringers until they were finger-tight.

"Almost there."

Using jar lifters, they put the seven quarts into the pressure canner where the water was boiling about two and a half inches on the bottom. Helen put the cooker lid on and turned it so the seal was tight, then they waited for the pressure level to build. Once it reached eleven pounds, Helen set the timer for forty minutes and stood back with a flourish. "Voilà. All done. Now we just have to wait until they're done and take them out to cool. Rinse and repeat a few times, and we'll make a dent in these potatoes before too long."

Ryan glanced at the back door and wiped his hand across his face. "That's a lot of potatoes to can."

"And that's just the start of things. We've got tomatoes, carrots, and beans, too. Why don't you have a seat and try to find something new on the radio?"

With a pointed nod, Ryan sat down and turned on the radio, starting with the emergency channel and picking up the same message they'd heard before, moving on to find other snippets of conversations and music they couldn't quite make out. Helen got her book and read until the first seven quarts of potatoes were done. Using the jar lifters, they placed them on a towel to dry and cool and started peeling and cutting another batch of potatoes, bringing up more jars and cleaning them as needed until they were on a roll. Tomatoes came next as well as carrots, beets, and beans. While they said little to each other, their shared smiles and glances reminded her of why she was in love with him. They could chat as they worked or barely speak, simply enjoying the closeness and companionship. Helen didn't see the chores as hard but as more of a way to spend time with the man she loved. They canned well into the night until they had around sixty quart-sized jars filling up the counter space, cooling and drying as midnight drew near. Ryan was groaning by the end, sitting heavily at the kitchen table and gripping his leg.

"Is the prosthetic okay?"

"It's fine, but it's been a long workday."

After doing some cleanup, the pair decided that they'd had enough for one day. They slept well through the night, each taking a watch shift, and Helen was up and waiting for him in the morning with coffee, eggs, and fresh milk pasteurized from the day before. After lunch, they removed the rings from the jars, checked the seals, and began carrying the canned food downstairs to place on a supply room shelf. Back upstairs, they had a quick lunch with slightly stale bread and some sliced meat they had left, adding a dash of potato chips and water and green tea to drink.

"Well, that was a perfect couple of days," Ryan said, sitting back and sipping his tea, letting out a pleased sigh. "We just increased the kids' food stores by almost double. I have to admit, that feels pretty darn good."

Helen grabbed a cardboard box and placed it on the counter next to the jars, slowly unscrewing the rings and dropping them off to the side as she checked the seals.

"How do they look?"

"Great, actually. These are all sealed perfectly. Now they go down on the shelf downstairs with everything else."

Ryan rose from his seat and grabbed a second box they had lying around. "I'll help you with that."

Helen sniffed and smiled. "I've got another job for you, dear."

Ryan paused skeptically. "Oh?"

"Go out and bring in another couple of bins of vegetables." Smiling, Helen cocked an eyebrow at him. "And then get ready for round two."

"Oh, wonderful," he replied, scratching his head as he changed direction and headed for the door. "I really mean that, too."

"I'll bet you do."

Helen filled the small box, lifted it by its handles, and took it into the basement, heading almost straight ahead to the supply room on the north side of the foundation, entering and shuffling through the darkness to a small table off to the side where she dropped off the box. She found the electric lantern and turned it on, bathing the room in a dim glow that glinted off the canned goods already down there, illuminating the brand names on the boxed food ranging from noodle and rice meals to macaroni and cheese and pasta salads. Smiling at the cute signs Alice had posted around the place, Helen took a pair of cans from the box and walked to the north wall of shelves, placing them on an empty one she'd cleared up by consolidating some canned meat and boxed goods.

She formed several rows of potatoes, beans, and beets before filling the box up with more empty jars that would need cleaning and prepping before they could fill them with more of the harvested food. With a breathy sigh of satisfaction, happy to be working toward a goal in spite of – or, perhaps, because of – what was going on around them, Helen took the clattering jars upstairs and steeled herself for another productive night.

CHAPTER FOUR

Alice Burton
Monticello, Florida

With her feet begging for rest and cramping so much that every step was sheer agony, Alice stood at the end of a long gravel driveway, enticed by the potential of a safe place to settle for the night. The lane led west in a long curve, crowded on the right-hand side by a row of live oaks with limbs that swept to the left like windblown hair and formed a forest canopy. Beyond were fields of green stretching for acres to either side and at the end a manor house and massive farmstead with barns and buildings peeked through the trees.

Like most places, tendrils of dark smoke drifted upward from some unseen fire, curling lazily into the sky to join the smear of clouds above. The kids stood next to her, backpacks hanging off their shoulders, sweat cooling their pale faces as they looked on with expressions torn between exhaustion and hope. A simple gate blocked the lane with a four-rail fence made of dark wood that stretched to the north and south and ran parallel to the road. Fancy landscaping with small trees and shaped shrubbery surrounded by mulch all sat around the base of a large wooden sign, rustic in design with letters burned in along its face.

"Monticello Manor Horse Farm," Alice said. "Sounds fancy, and it looks fancy, too."

Jake leaned closer and read the smaller print. "Home of *Rare Breed* and *Rasta Runner*."

"I wonder if those were the Kentucky Derby winners?" Alice glanced at Sarah. "When you guys were learning how to ride, did your instructors ever mention this place or those horses?"

Sarah shrugged. "Mr. Scroggins wasn't really into horseracing, and it never excited us too much." She looked over at her brother for confirmation, and he scratched his head, shrugging.

"We never watched any races. We just rode for a few summers but never talked about Derby winners, breeders, bloodlines, or anything like that. I know some people take that stuff pretty seriously."

"It's a billion-dollar business, I'm sure." Alice blinked at the scene before them as birds flew in tight, almost nervous clusters across the fields and the insects chirped in the humid air. She gave the place a few minutes to weigh on her, looking for any sort of warning signs that they shouldn't go in. The remains of the house were barely visible, and there were some burned-out vehicles parked nearby, but in all the time they'd been standing at the end of the lane, there had been a complete lack of movement – surprising for such a large facility. When the hairs on the back of her neck didn't raise, and her stomach didn't squirm, she shrugged. "I think it's worth the risk. We'll skedaddle at the first sign of anyone

still being here, though it looks abandoned to me. If we can find a horse or three that were left behind, we'll ride them out of here if we can get them saddled. Got your weapons ready in case we need them?"

Sarah slapped her side and pulled up her smudged white t-shirt to show her hunting knife was fixed firmly on the belt of her jean shorts. "Got my knife right here."

"Mine, too." Jake mirrored his sister's move, lifting his black shirt to reveal a knife on his right hip.

Alice had exchanged her rugged button-up shirt for a blue camisole to give her skin room to breathe in the heat, and they were all wearing jean shorts and tennis shoes.

She shrugged. "I didn't even notice we weren't carrying our pool cues anymore."

"Those went into the fire last night." Jake shook his head. "They were all cracked and splintered, anyway."

"Probably for the best." Alice checked her rifle to ensure it was loaded and ready to go. "Okay. Let's go."

Alice reached over the gate and pulled the latch up, swinging it wide on creaky hinges as they slipped through and started up the soft gravel lane. Outside of the soft crunch of the rocks beneath their shoes, silence enveloped them in an eerie embrace. Still seeing no signs of life anywhere in the fields or in and around the buildings, Alice strode faster and got ahead of them.

"What if we find some horses?" Sarah asked. "Could we leave some food or something as payment? Or maybe leave our phone number if they want to reach us when all this is over."

"That's even if we find any actual horses here," Jake replied. "If the people who lived here were smart, they probably already rode them away."

Alice frowned. "And that's only if anyone survived the fires. Look there."

A dark cluster of trees surrounded the main property up ahead, and the smoke was worse, with branches and leaves smoldering on trees close to the buildings that had caught fire. Off to the left along the fence rail, an old-style tractor with a rusted red frame—something they might have seen at an auction—had gone up in flames with its frame warped at an odd angle and a lone figure slumped over the steering wheel, blackened to a crisp, smoke still coming off of it every time the breeze shifted.

Sarah waved her hand in front of her face and grimaced. "That's... awful."

"As morbid as this sounds," Alice said. "It's good news for us. If there were any survivors, I doubt they would have left someone out like that. Looks like this place took some damage, and I bet we'll find a lot more dead people. But here's to hoping something survived out in one of the barns."

"Right. I keep thinking it's still last week, before we had to *steal* to live." Sarah nodded, tone somewhere between sarcastic and sincere, still struggling to come to grips with their new reality.

"We're not barbarians," Alice replied, "and I would never condone hurting someone. But if there's something we *need* to survive – notice I said 'need' not 'want' – and it's right there with no one guarding it... it's ours."

"Finders keepers," Jake added.

"Not exactly," Alice rolled her eyes, sighing. "It's more complicated than that. But we need transportation north to reach your grandparents and father, and we're going to find some. C'mon."

She stepped within the circle of trees that surrounded the central grounds, and the remains of the building took shape in the shade. They passed a couple of small tool sheds at the front of the property, each still standing with the doors shut and decorated with flower beds with white gravel around their bases. There was a small barn with the name of the farm written on the side, and more fences sprouted up to section off the yard into training grounds with various paths that led to other parts of the farm.

The main house had once been a beautiful plantation-style home, two stories high with a single long roof and four chimneys, two on each end. Additional sections had been added to both sides of the manor, and white railings adorned every porch. Pathways split off from the front walk to the back of the home or curved through the gardens that sprawled in all directions, packed with well-trimmed bushes, rustic benches, and flowers of every color to give the grounds a rugged vibrancy.

Fire had ravaged the place, scorching the new white siding with soot and burning holes that still smoldered and leaked cinders when the wind breathed through. The middle section had collapsed on itself, forming a toothy-black grin, and the grand porches on both levels were just crumbles of wooden planks piled in on themselves to feed what must've been a raging bonfire. The foliage immediately around the base was wilted and brown, and the grass smoldered and popped with vivid heat. Only a few rooms on the left side were untouched by the worst of the flames, giving hints to what the grand structure must've looked like before its collapse.

Alice stopped at the stone pathway leading to what had been the front porch and scanned off to the left. "I see a few small buildings still standing over there, but those that burned down must've housed a generator or vehicles, and I bet that's where the fire started."

"There's a detached garage over on the right," Sarah pointed out past the barn to the east. "That went up, too. See the cars inside?"

Alice nodded at the sight of two cars mixed in with the fallen timbers and rubble, just husks of frames and smoldering rubber, greasy black smoke rising from the collapsed rafters into the sky. "Looks like they owned a pair of motorcycles, too."

Scanning back to the left, Alice spotted more shapes, and she gestured for the kids to follow. "Let's check around to the back where the barns are."

Leaving the main driveway, they took a soft gravel path off to the side that swept between flowering dogwood trees and well-manicured lawns with two large garden areas grown into the landscape. There were colonial-style benches, a fountain in one, and even a small graveyard on the right, closer to the home's backyard. A dozen or so gravestones hugged an oak tree that could've easily been a hundred years old or more judging by its thick, twisted branches and rough bark with deep, winding grooves thick enough to run her fingers through.

The path circled sharply to the right and behind the house, where it forked off into multiple tracts that led to smaller sheds and training corrals barely visible between the trees. One medium-sized barn had been razed to the ground, the husks of two tractors lying in the wreckage. A stall that appeared to have once held a diesel tank like the one they had back home had gone up in flames, leaving charred plastic parts scattered everywhere that might've once belonged to golf carts or ATVs used to maintain the property. Jake bent and picked up a piece of metal with a logo on the front, shrugging and tossing the scorched piece off to the side with a clatter.

"This place must've been amazing," Sarah said. "It reminds me of something I read in one of my books. I always wanted to live in a place like this."

"That's why we built the farm the way we did," Alice replied, allowing herself a wistful smile. "The ponds... the fields... we were just getting started, too. I sure hope everything is okay up there."

"I don't see anything that would have had horses here, Mom," Sarah said as she looked around at all the paths leading to different parts of the property before stepping toward a sign amid a scatter of rubble, knocked halfway over with the lettering on the front scorched as if hit by something that had been aflame. Picking up a shred of a feed bag lying nearby, she took hold of the sign and rubbed the soot off the front, revealing the word.

"Stables." Jake pointed to the arrow on the sign.

"Yeah, but it's bent." Alice was still peering down the paths, angling her head to figure out where it indicated. "I'd rather not head off in any old direction and end up wandering around this place more than we have to."

Jake grabbed the sign and twisted it upright into its original position so the arrow pointed down the left-hand path where it curved along a fence line mostly hidden by trees. When Alice peered through the flora, she saw a larger structure off in the distance beyond the wavering, smoke-filled treetops.

"Thanks, Jake," Alice said. "It's as good a start as any."

Clutching her rifle in both hands, barrel pointed down at the gray gravel, Alice led the kids through the charred and smoking ruins of the horse farm where anything within a few feet of a generator or a diesel engine had caught fire. Moving deeper along the path, Alice spotted two or three farm tractors smoking out in the field with the surrounding grass turning brown and off to the left, an ATV had plunged nose first into a tree with the driver thrown forward to land on the hood and crumple against the tree trunk. Alice instinctively moved to check on the man when she saw that the body wasn't burned like most, though she turned and kept walking when she saw the way his head had snapped backward at a sharp angle where the neck met the shoulders, angled in an unnatural position that no one could've survived.

"Keep walking, kids. Just keep your eyes up and feet moving."

After a few more minutes of walking, Alice spotted what they were looking for, a long, one-story wooden building with stall doors on the outside and a single passage running down the middle from east to west. Every six stalls, a fifteen-foot side-passageway cut perpendicular to the main one to create multiple intersections, and each stall had heavy latches with decorative trim that made it look like it was from the 1800s. The first quarter of the building had burned to the ground with pieces of the rafters and main beams charred and collapsed into a bed of coals. Dark lumps buried in the embers took the rough shape of a horse's haunches with thin legs sticking out of the mess. The near entrance had spilled onto the soft gravel path leading to it, and a ripe mixture of cooked and rotting flesh filled the stable yard. A half dozen fire extinguisher canisters were scattered around the edges, spent and covered in grime, and at the sight of them Alice raised her rifle and fell into a crouch.

"Careful, kids. Looks like someone put out this fire, and they might still be here." When no one immediately jumped out at them, Alice removed the S&W revolver from its holster and held it out for Jake. "Take this so you can watch my back, son. Remember what to do."

"Sure, Mom." Taking the gun, he shifted into a ready position and pointed the weapon away from his sister with his finger outside the trigger guard.

"Okay... follow me."

Alice stalked quietly along the gravel pathway, which widened between the smoking ruins and the tree-covered fence line. Smoke bled into the air, and she waved it away when they passed through a thick cloud to keep it out of her eyes. Nothing moved, and the only sounds were the gentle crackles of wood and the additional aroma of horse manure and hay as they got closer to the undamaged section of the stable. As she swept the rifle across the stalls, a shotgun boomed on her right, shocking her and she flinched and ducked. The slug struck a nearby tree to send bark dust flying with pieces hitting them even though they were ten feet away.

"Take cover!" Alice shouted, spinning and retreating toward the tree that had been hit, stopping to wave the kids behind it before ducking in after them.

The tree they'd taken shelter behind was a massive oak, wide enough for all of them to hide behind, and the bark was cool and moist when she pressed her palm against it and squinted into the gloomy ruins. Heart hammering and agitated at nearly dying, Alice peeked around the tree trunk before sweeping her rifle across the ruins where she thought the shot had come from. A crash of timber and boards smacking together came a moment later and a man's voice cursed loudly and incoherently.

After a few seconds, something heavy hit the ground, and rubble suddenly clattered and fell again as the man cried out in pain. Edging forward, she watched as more rubble fell, and the man shrieked in agony and cursed again. He was caught somewhere in the smoke and ash, and Alice shrugged off her backpack and turned to the kids.

"Stay here. Jake, only use the gun if you've got a good clear shot, okay?"

Jake gave a curt nod and gazed toward the stables, where the man was still crying out repeatedly in intense pain. Alice crept away from the tree with her rifle pointed at the pile of burned wood, craning her neck to see someone wiggling and squirming beneath the pile, gasping and panicking as he tried to kick the rubble off him. With a confused frown, Alice shifted the rifle barrel and traced the man's form in the darkness. He was on his back with one arm pinned beneath some fallen rubble that seemed to have trapped his legs, too, and he wore a pair of overalls with short brown boots that weren't moving. Groaning, head rolling back and forth, he clawed for a shotgun lying a few feet away, impossible to reach because of the scorched boards that pinned him down. Shifting to get a better view, she caught the man's face in a swath of light. White tufts of singed hair stuck out from the sides of his head, and his jawline was cleanly shaven with just a hint of a five o'clock shadow. His gasping and struggling stopped when Alice stepped over some fallen boards and pointed her rifle at his face.

"You grab that gun," she said, "and I'll shoot."

Gray eyes blinked up at her, and the hand grasping for the weapon stopped, fingers wiggling to show he'd given up. "Okay, you got me" His voice was scratchy and fierce with a touch of an Irish accent adding a lilt to his words.

"What about your other hand? Let me see it."

"I would, ma'am, but it's trapped under some fallen wood, and I can't move."

"Serves you right, shooting at me like you did."

"Hold on, now." He swallowed hard and gasped in pain. When it passed, he continued. "I only did that because I thought you were one of them bastards that's been poking around the place the last day. You're not from around here, though, I can see that." He groaned again. "Seems I hurt my shoulder when I fired that damn shotgun. Slipped and fell, and the boards fell on top of me."

"Good thing or that slug would have hit me. Good thing for you, too."

"Why's that?"

"If *you had* hit me, I wouldn't be obliged to help you get unstuck."

The man stopped squirming and blinked up at her. "Does that mean you'll help me?"

"Depends. I was just traveling north, saw your farm, and wanted to see if I might find a horse to carry me home."

"Where's home?"

"Lansing, Michigan."

"Whoa! Michigan's a good ways off, ma'am."

"I'm well aware of that. That's why I need a horse."

Despite the pain, he gave a weak chuckle. "Of course, of course. Makes perfect sense."

"Do you have one?"

"Let's say I do. Would that be enough to get me out of this mess?"

"It might."

The old man stared at her for several seconds before he nodded agreeably. "I've got horses, ma'am. I'll get you hooked up with whatever you need, gear and all, if you'll help me out of this little quandary I'm—"

The injured old man gasped sharply and fell back on the hay-covered floor, pieces of it smoldering and smoking near his head, his eyes pleading with her from a sweat-stained face. Alice hesitated, tempted for the briefest of moments to take his shotgun and find the horses herself, relying on the kids and her knowledge of riding to get them saddled up and ready to go. Leaving the old man to die, though, wasn't in her nature, no matter how brutal and cutthroat the world had become.

Alice shook her head and turned back to the tree line. "Come on, kids! I need your help over here!"

"Kids?" The man's pained expression changed to confusion as he struggled to speak. "Didn't... see any children when I fired. Then again, I couldn't see much what with the rubble and smoke."

"Yeah, you could've shot one of my kids, especially if you'd had buckshot."

"Bollocks. I'm sorry, ma'am," he stammered and gasped. "Swear I didn't know you had kids."

Jake and Sarah came pounding up the gravel path, stopping at the edge of the rubble next to Alice and staring at the injured old man.

"Is that the guy who shot at us?" Jake asked, keeping the revolver in a ready stance.

"Yes it is, son. We need to get him out of there."

"Why? He tried to kill us!"

"Remember the man on the beach?"

"Yeah..." Jake sighed as he lowered the revolver.

The old man squirmed and spoke apologetically from his awkward position on the ground. "Like I told your mother, it was a mistake. I thought you were some nasty buggers that've been creeping around the place, that's all, I swear."

"Just relax," Alice said, "we'll get you out, don't worry."

Alice gestured for the kids to follow her as they waded into the rubble, ducking and glancing up at the overhanging boards, some still on fire or smoldering while others hung loosely from a central beam that had collapsed at a downward angle. Alice snatched up his shotgun, took both that and her rifle outside, and leaned them against the side of the barn. When she returned, the kids were tugging at the boards lying on the man's legs as he groaned and languished.

"Hang on a second, kids," Alice said. "Let's grab this one here and shift it off first. It's holding the others down."

Alice was gesturing at a fifteen-foot-long piece of lumber lying across the cluster of others pinning the man's legs. Between the three of them, they found a safe place to step and took up positions on either side of the board, the kids squatting while Alice stood taller and gripped the board where it was about waist high. On a count of three, they lifted and shifted it in the kids' direction, but it slipped from Alice's fingers, and she dropped her end. The wood hit with a clatter, partially striking the others to cause the man to draw another cry of pain.

"Sorry," she murmured as they began lifting off scraps, one at a time, lightening the load on his body by fits and spurts.

With the heavy pieces out of the way, Alice shifted to where one of the stall walls had collapsed on his arm, about two hundred pounds of lumber keeping him from moving. All three of them squatted and lifted with their legs, raising the slab of wood high enough for him to jerk his arm back and hold it against his chest with a sob of relief. With his arm free, he was able to shuffle backwards with Alice's help, getting his legs free as well.

"Oh, thank you! Thank you, thank you!" He chuckled in pain, panting as he sucked air through his teeth. "I thought I'd lose the old limb for a minute there..."

With a nod to the kids to go back outside, Alice ducked between fallen lumber and stood near the man's head, kneeling by his right shoulder. "Do you think you can move? Is anything broken?"

"Don't think anything's broken. I can move, yes."

Alice lifted him into a seated position, and he patted his thighs and knees before smiling wide. "Nope. Nothing's broken, and I can wiggle my toes, too. Woo hoo!" Spreading his feet and moving his knees up and down, he proved they still worked. With a pleased expression, he held up a hand for her to shake. "Name's Wilford. Sorry again about... y'know."

"Alice." She nodded, returned the handshake, and then turned her head away from the drifting soot. "Okay, Wilford. Let's get you up and out of here."

Moving to his other side, Alice kneeled and squatted, allowing him to drape his good arm over her shoulder and turn his hips toward her. Feet anchored, she lifted him as his boots scuffed on the ground, finally getting his legs beneath him and holding his weight. She strained and leaned against him, her entire body a tight coil of muscle as they lurched to the exit and fresh air with his arm squeezing around her waist.

Realizing he was hurting her, he quickly loosened his grip. "Sorry, ma'am. Thought I was going to go straight back onto my bum again."

"I've got you." Alice coughed and turned her face away from a drift of smoke, then she nodded to the exit where the kids were waiting. "Come on. Baby steps forward until we're out of this."

"Baby steps. Right. Okay."

They cleared the debris and stepped through the dangerous rubble, slipping on plywood and kicking beams aside in a clatter of wood and charcoal. Jake came to Wilford's other side and put his arm around his waist.

"Wonderful, lad," the old man said. "Thanks to the lot of you. Sorry I shot at you... was a mistake. Ole Wilford isn't as sharp as he used to be. Not the best shot, neither, thank goodness."

"No problem... um... sir," Jake replied.

Despite his obvious pain, the man's jolly yet self-deprecating demeanor drew a grin from the kids. Alice flashed them a look and motioned to a soft spot in the grass next to the tree they'd been hiding behind. Sarah sprinted ahead, threw her backpack on the ground, and grabbed a blanket from the top, spreading it as Jake and Alice helped Wilford along. They turned him, eased him down, and left him sitting, rolling backward for a second before his legs kicked straight.

"Oh, thank you, young lady. That was quite nice of you. In case you missed the introduction, my name's Wilford. What's yours?"

"I'm Sarah, and that's my brother, Jake. What were you doing hiding in there? Don't you know it's dangerous to be in a burned-out building?"

"Indeed, I do. Especially now. Ah, thank you, young sir." He accepted a bottle of water from Jake, twisted off the top, and drank deeply as rivulets of sweat and soot dripped down his face. When he was done, he wiped his arm across his lips. "I guess I could've avoided all this if I'd given you folks a wave. Anyone out to rob the stables wouldn't have two fine children with them. Or be helping me now, would they?"

"Who are you?" Alice asked, standing with her feet spread and her hands on her hips. "Do you work here?"

"Indeed! I am the head groundskeeper for Monticello Manor, or *was* until the bloody thing burned to the ground."

"What's a Brit doing all the way across the pond, working at a Tallahassee stable? Not to sound rude or anything."

"Brit?!" Wilford looked indignant. "If you hadn't just saved me, I'd consider that an unforgivable insult! No, ma'am, I'm Irish. Been many a year since I've been back home, though." He sighed wistfully, then refocused on her, waving absently. "No, no, no. Not rude at all. Seems an astute question, given the distance between our two lands. I'm a quality groundskeeper, from my youth. Been working here for twenty, thirty years or so. Or, at least, I *was*. Suppose I'm not really one anymore, am I?"

"But you weren't a horse trainer?"

"No, no, but there's more to raising a competitive horse than just the training. It's the atmosphere... the *ambiance*, if you will." He waved his hand in a flourish. "I always kept the stalls spotless and knew every horse by name. I even had my afternoon tea with them and sometimes read to them."

"You read to the horses?" Jake laughed. "That sounds silly."

"It might seem that way, young sir." Raising his finger high, Wilford pointed at the boy. "But like classical music soothes the soul, hearing a calm voice reading the classics seems to comfort the horses and keep them in better spirits. But it's just a small thing I do, or *did*, around here." His jolly demeanor faded as he looked past Alice and scanned the ruins of the stables. "I couldn't save them all, but I did what I could."

Alice stepped aside and followed his gaze, frowning with a deep sense of sorrow. "Oh, gosh, Wilford. I'm so sorry you lost some horses."

His voice was low as he stared into the recent past. "I was out on the fence line calling some of the horses in to put them away for the night when the main house went up in a massive explosion. My quarters followed." A troubled frown spread on his face. "Thankfully, I wasn't in them. I spent the entire night fighting pop-up fires to keep the remaining stalls safe. I tried to create a fire line with some fire extinguishers to slow the flames down, but nothing worked. The fire simply beat me."

"I'm sorry to hear that," Alice said. "We were at a restaurant in Palm Beach when it happened there. Scared us to death. We're all lucky to have survived."

He nodded sadly. "Yes, I suppose we are."

"Again, we're sorry for what happened here..."

"But you're looking to get out of the state, not sit around and gab all hours of the day and night." He winked at her. "I might have something that would suit you." Wilford held up his hands for Jake and Sarah to grab, and they hauled the man to his feet, where he began shuffling and pointing toward the safe end of the stables. "They'll get you where you need to go and farther if you treat them right."

"We all have riding experience," Alice explained, "but we might need some help saddling them."

"Oh, no problem there," he replied with a wave. "I've set up new quarters for myself at the unburned part of the stables, at the end of the building."

"And you have no problem with us using them?" Jake asked.

"Problem? The problem around these parts is going to be feeding and caring for them all on my own, and keeping them safe from the limey bastards that've been poking around. No, no you folks've been nice to an old man who tried to blow your heads off. They'll be in good hands, I can tell."

"Great." Alice took her rifle and handed Wilford's shotgun back to him. "No hard feelings at all. And we'd greatly appreciate all the help you can give."

"Oh, yes. Of course." Waving again, he shuffled along the southern wall and the external stall doors, a big smile on his face as he angled off to the left, away from the burned structure toward a fence line hidden by trees and foliage.

"Where are we going?" Alice asked.

"Oh, just over here real quick to talk to a couple of friends. I hope you don't mind."

"You're the boss." Confused, Alice glanced at the kids and clutched her rifle tighter, following on his heels as he took a narrow path through the trees. The man moved faster than she would have expected after injuring himself, stepping between a cluster of bushes and leaving them behind as he disappeared into the green. The next thing she heard was his voice calling out, filled with pride and joy.

"Ah, there you are, my beauties. Peppercorn and Dawson. My handsome boys."

Alice and the kids emerged from the greenery to see Wilford standing next to the fence with his arms thrown around the necks of two massive stallions whose heads hung over the rail as they nuzzled him and nickered affectionately. The one on the left had a shiny, dark bay coat with a small dot of white on its forehead, while the other was a rich chestnut with a cream-colored patch running from his beautifully sloping forehead to his muzzle. "I'm so happy to introduce you to my friends," Wilford said, turning and grinning as the horses nipped at his hair, the great strength in their necks jostling him back and forth between them.

"Oh, wow!" Sarah rushed forward, Alice and Jake behind her.

"Careful, sweetie," Alice said, "don't get too close."

"Oh, no need to worry!" Wilford grinned broadly as he patted the horse's necks. "They're harmless. No need to be afraid. These are two of our prized stallions who were out running when the explosions happened. They were the ones I was trying to bring in. This one here..." He patted the darker horse on the left. "This one is Peppercorn, while his friend is Dawson." Wilford stepped back to let the kids in closer to pet them, leaving one hand on Peppercorn's jaw as he turned to Alice. "If we would've lost these two, I don't know what I would've done." He frowned and gestured back at the main property. "I just don't know what happened here. A few buildings are still standing, while most others burned to the ground. I tried to call for help, but there was no response from 911 or the bloody fire department."

"They wouldn't have come." Alice reached out, stroking Dawson's head.

"And why is that?"

"Because what's happening here is happening all across the nation. It has to do with a contaminated fuel supply." When Wilford only raised an eyebrow in confusion, she continued. "Anything that runs on refined oil has gone up in flames, or so it seems. The emergency channels say it was a terrorist attack on our fuel supply. Contaminated fuel... oil... *whatever* you want to call it."

"A *terrorist* attack?" Wilford stepped away from the horses, crossing his arms. "You mean like those planes what hit the Twin Towers in New York?"

"Something like that, but much, *much* worse." She briefly told him about their trip through Palm Beach and discovering that the fuel was the primary cause of the problems. "That's why only some of your buildings burned down while others didn't." Alice gestured at the smoking grounds. "Anywhere you had an ATV, lawnmower, chainsaw, gas-powered trimmer, or jerrycan of spare fuel probably would've gone up. We saw one place that had generators and didn't burn down, but it might have something to do with the age of their fuel."

With slumping shoulders, Wilford released a tired sigh of disbelief. "Well, that explains a lot. I appreciate you laying it all out like that, but it don't make it no easier to take. I was so distraught about everything that I leaped into survival mode... for the horses, but not for me. Didn't even think of looking for a radio right away. I spent the entire time making sure the horses were safe while trying to stop the fires from spreading."

"You did well, Wilford. I'm sure the owners will appreciate you saving all the horses you could. By the way... where are they?"

"Beats me," he shrugged. "Mr. and Mrs. Monticello were away for a horse conference, and most of the staff were also on holiday. There was a skeleton crew in the main house, but..." Slapping his forehead, he ran his hand down his face and let out a sob. "Would've saved them if I could've, but it was all over so fast." He gazed across the charred grounds. "The house was already up in flames when I got there. It was too hot, and I couldn't get in. I tried to call for help, tried to get someone out here, but the lines were busy. I'm as close to worthless as can be...."

"No, Wilford." Alice glanced at the kids as they gave the horses attention, the stallions gentle as they tolerated the children's petting, sniffing at them curiously. She took a single step forward and patted the groundskeeper on his gnarled, muscled shoulder. "You did the best you could with what you had. We all did. Things are tough right now, but we're survivors, and we'll make it through this. We have a lot left to fight for."

"Thank you, Alice," Wilford replied. "That takes a little weight off my soul to hear you put it that way, and it gives me hope, too." Gesturing back to the stables, he nodded. "You wouldn't want to come in for a spot of tea, would you? I've even got some biscuits I salvaged from the rubble of the main house. I know you folks want to get moving, but tea always puts the world in a much better light."

"We really should get going..."

"We've been walking all day, Mom," Sarah interjected, turning even as she hugged Dawson's brown neck. "Shouldn't we take a break before we leave?"

Jake agreed as Peppercorn strolled along the fence line away from them, seeming to have had enough of the kids' attention. "Yeah, just an hour or so, Mom. Please?"

Alice reluctantly nodded, giving in to her own exhaustion as much as she did to her children's pleas. "I guess it would be okay. After all, survival is a marathon, not a sprint."

"Yes!" Jake pumped his fist while Sarah gave Dawson a parting hug as the stallion followed his friend along the tree line.

"Okay, folks," Wilford waved as he got on the path. "Follow me. I've been living inside the safe part of the stables."

As they walked, Alice felt the intense weight of the disaster at the farm with its smoldering buildings and the faint scent of burned horse flesh, a sweet-cooked smell that reminded her of a mix between scorched leather and a fatty steak on the grill. Wilford moved past the burned-up section of the stables and through an open passage that cut across the main corridor, unblemished by flames to form an intersection. The groundskeeper had set up a camp of sorts, with a campfire in the middle and a tripod grill and teapots. Around the fire sat three plastic bins and a trio of lanterns hung from hooks on the vertical beams that anchored the stalls. The sound of horses and soft snorts drifted from the far end that had stayed intact thanks to Wilford's efforts.

"Ah, here we are. This is where I stay."

"Wow, this is close to the horses." Jake stepped in first.

"I love being close to them, and I wouldn't feel right living some posh life with my beauties all out here by themselves. No, I prefer living out here where it's peaceful and quiet." He winked at Jake. "The fact that my personal quarters burned up might have something to do with it, too."

"Impressive, Wilford," Alice said. "You've set up a nice little camp here. Where do you sleep?"

"I've been sleeping on the hay in one stall. I suppose they're just as good for people as horses," Wilford replied, heading straight to the grill where he stoked some coals, kicking up the flames. "I've always been near the stables in a bed, but now I'm right smack in the middle of them and bedding down in the hay where at least I can protect the remaining horses if I must."

"It's lovely," Sarah said, taking an air of primness as she sat on a bin, hands on her knees as she watched the flames grow. "What kind of tea are we having?"

Wilford snorted. "Given the circumstances, and since I don't have a lot of choices, I think a spot of Earl Grey for me. For you folks?"

"The kids will have some green tea if you've got it, and I'll take coffee if you don't mind."

"Oh, sure, sure." He gave her a mock salute. "Go ahead, Alice. Have a seat. I'll have something nice whipped up for you in a moment."

Nodding, Alice leaned her rifle against the stall wall, took the revolver from Jake, and circled to sit on the bin on Sarah's left while Jake took the one across from her. Wilford stoked the fire and poured water into a kettle, only an occasional drift of smoke wafting by to disrupt their limited view of the gardens outside the stable. The trees and fence line curved off into the distance away from them where the open fields of green were so vivid they almost hurt her eyes. Alice allowed herself to breathe for the first time in a long while, shrugging off her backpack and gesturing for the kids to do the same.

"So, you say you were in Palm Beach?" Wilford hung a kettle of water above the fire, stirring the coals with a stick.

"Vacationing. Ever been there?"

"Can't say I have. Never been much of a beach person, and I always had plenty to do here on the farm. Mr. and Mrs. Monticello always urged me to go on a trip sometime, but I only ever traveled back to Ireland to visit family and friends and see the old farms I used to work at."

"We walked about thirty miles up the coast until we found an electric vehicle to drive," Alice said. "That's when I realized what was happening with the explosions had to do with the fuel. Well, that and the emergency broadcasts."

"Very perceptive. Were you ever able to reach anyone on your cell phone?"

"Nope." She took the phone out of her pocket and placed it in her lap, powering it on then shutting it off again. "Still no connection."

"Based on what you told me about the state of the country," Wilford put loose tea into an infuser, which went into the kettle to steep. "Doesn't seem like anyone will get any help soon."

"That's exactly right. It's also why I can't be too hard on you for being protective and shooting at us. I'd have done the same exact thing."

"Still, it's something I regret, to be sure." Wilford started heating water in the second kettle. "But here we are, eh? At least we're friends now."

"That we are," Alice agreed.

As he finished making the tea and coffee, Alice told him a little more about their farmstead outside East Lansing and that her parents were busy house-sitting, but she didn't know if they were okay. She did the same about James, who could be anywhere between Colorado and Michigan, as well as the messages she'd received from him. Wilford responded with polite noises and gestures of affirmation to show he was listening, finally handing out the steaming tea to the kids.

"Sorry, but the coffee is just instant," he said apologetically, holding up a small can of coffee crystals.

"I'd take three-day old grounds at this point. Instant sounds wonderful."

When everyone was settled, he took some dry rags and poured hot water on them where they hung over a small rack, letting them cool a moment before handing them out. With one in hand, he wiped his face clean to reveal chaffed cheeks from fighting the fires, a sharp contrast against his wise grey eyes. Accepting a warm rag, she cleaned her arms and face, sighing as days of grime washed off.

Wilford flashed them a friendly smile. "There's sugar and cream for your drinks and spoons to stir with. Alice, here's your coffee. Again, sorry it's not gourmet."

"Some of the best coffee is the worst coffee," Alice chuckled, sipping hers black and nodding in satisfaction. "This is fantastic, Wilford."

"And now for the biscuits." From a bin, he dug out a plastic bag of biscuits, square and round shapes that looked more like cookies but with fancy designs on the edges.

Alice took one, finding it soft and sweet against the bitterness of her coffee. "Thank you."

Wilford remained kneeling as he passed some to the kids and met Alice's gaze across the fire. "They don't go too poorly with coffee, but better with tea for certain. The Monticellos always went out of the way to have some of these biscuits made for me. A few things from home. That's what set the Monticellos apart." Wilford bit into a cookie and followed it with a sip of Earl Grey, his eyebrows arching in pleasure.

"How many more horses do you have out there?" Jake asked as he chewed another biscuit and got close to the end of his cup of tea.

"After I got the initial fires under control... not full control, mind you, I realized I needed to get two mares and their colts out to the secondary stables right away, as they were too close to the lingering smoke and all. It was a tight fit, but we managed."

"Sounds awful," Jake replied.

"That's right, young sir," Wilford confirmed. "I was scared out of my gourd."

"How will you take care of them with everything burned down?" Alice asked with her cup held between her knees.

"We've got enough feed for now, and I can always put them out to graze around the fields if we need to, but there are a fair number of them for one person to watch over." The old man's eyes watered as he finished a chunk of a biscuit and washed it down with the rest of his tea.

"If you're willing to spare three," Alice said, "we'll take excellent care of them. Of that, I promise you. If you can't, though, I understand." Since getting to know the man, Alice's commitment to doing whatever was necessary had wavered ever so slightly. Forcing the old man – Wilford - to give up some of his charges was no longer as cut and dry as it had been when they'd first met him.

He smiled faintly, placed his cup aside, stood, and brushed crumbs off his hands. "Now that you fine folks have had a spot of tea, I'll show you what I'm thinking." He winked at the kids. "I'm positive I can come up with something to suit your needs. Yes, yes. Some fine animals for you to ride."

Finishing her coffee, Alice placed the mug down and stood, taking her rifle from where it rested against the wall and gesturing for the kids to follow Wilford as he shuffled outside into the bleak gray light.

CHAPTER FIVE

James Burton
Kansas City, Missouri

Someone shouted and waved at James as he walked through the east side of camp in search of his tent so he could lie down, and he returned the gesture, wondering who they were. After leaving Stenson and the tank crew, a deep weariness had set in, and his knees were wobbling even worse from the exhaustion, far worse than when he worked out or spent all day on his feet on the farm, and all he wanted to do was put his head down and close his eyes for a minute.

"There he is!"

James looked around and spotted some people rushing down the lane to meet him, moving past milling refugees still recovering from the camp attack. With an embarrassed heat rising to his cheeks, James stopped and waited as the two guardsmen he'd first met at the front gate approached; the female officer who'd checked him in and the man with the light blue vest who'd given him his extra supplies. Smiling, James half-waved embarrassingly.

"Hello, Mr. Burton!" the young woman called. "We were hoping to catch you before you left."

"Oh, I'm not leaving yet," James explained. "I had planned on getting a few hours rest before heading out."

The group stopped to shake his hand, the guardswoman stepping back with her hands clasped in front of her. "Well, good thing we found you because we are going off shift in a while and might have missed you."

"I didn't realize they gave going away parties for us refugees."

"It's not normally something we do," she beamed, "but one of the Army guys came by and told us what you'd done during the firefight last night. I remembered your name from when I checked you in, so I wanted to say thanks before we missed each other."

"Like I told Commander Halladay and Corporal Stenson...." James shook his head and made a helpless gesture. "I just did what anyone else would have done."

The other guardsman scoffed. "That's not true. No other civvies just ran in there during a firefight and offered to lend a hand. Everyone else either hid or ran away."

"Can't blame them. They had families to protect, and the soldiers told them to run. I just saw the threat and felt compelled to rush in." James kicked at the ground. "It could have ended up poorly, but that was a chance I was willing to take."

"We're proud of you," she said, "and we're glad we're the ones who checked you in. You ended up being a big part of defending this camp, and Corporal Stenson wanted to ensure you had everything you needed before hitting the road."

"I've got everything I need right here." James hiked his thumb at his backpack. "You all hooked me up pretty well."

Turning, she gestured to her friend, and he held out a package and a thick steel rod with a slightly rounded handle and a blunt end. "Well, here's a little extra for you."

"Thanks." James took the package and what appeared to be a metal walking stick. "What is all this?"

"There's some extra food and water purification tablets in the pack," he said, "and the stick thing... well, you'll see what it is. It's a combo tool, if you know what I mean."

James raised an eyebrow. "Oh, yeah. I've seen those before. Seriously, thank you so much for all this. I'm sure I'll put it to good use."

While they were talking, other survivors were walking by and giving them curious glances, his pack and rifle drawing a fair amount of attention.

"We've got to get back now," the woman said before holding her hand out.

James shook hands with both, thanking them for their hospitality, smiling tiredly, and nodding as they slowly broke off with wishes of good luck. Carrying his supplies, James searched for his tent, getting turned around once but quickly realigning himself based on the smoking parts of the camp. Finally, a part of one lane became recognizable, and two doors down was his own entrance. Unlocking and unzipping the tent flap, he stepped inside and stared longingly at his cot before setting down his heavy packs and rifle and sitting and unlacing his boots, kicking them off.

With the steel rod – more a stave than a true walking stick – resting across his knees, James grew curious and examined it. It was divided into eight connecting sections, about an inch in diameter with a total weight of roughly three pounds and at the top end was a compass and a lanyard to slip his hand through so he wouldn't lose it. Gripping two of the upper sections, he unscrewed them and opened them up to find an interchangeable screwdriver set. Continuing with unscrewing the rest of the sections, he discovered that every subsequent one revealed a new compartment with other critical tools that would come in handy on the road. There were several serrated blades, a can opener, a bottle opener, an arrow tip, and some fishing string wrapped around a makeshift reel. The bottom end of the stick had a thick steel point, useful for breaking glass, to help gain traction on slippery surfaces or as a makeshift weapon. Each part inside the tubes could be swapped out and reassembled in any order he wanted, and they were all encased in solid aluminum that felt strong enough to withstand practically any abuse.

"This is amazing," he murmured as he switched around the eight sections and organized everything the way he wanted. "This is probably the most valuable tool I have right now for getting home." He chuckled dryly. "I'm sure after several days of walking, I'll be leaning on this a lot."

Blessed by fate and thankful to have an impressive array of weaponry and supplies at his disposal, James allowed weariness to overcome him, and suddenly his simple cot seemed like a five-star bed. Placing the stave on the floor next to him, James tucked his revolver beneath his pillow and closed his eyes as a deep sleep gripped his mind and quickly dashed his exhaustion into oblivion.

———

James woke to a soft morning light filtering through his tent windows and the sound of fresh voices reaching him through the thin tent walls.

"We're so blessed," a woman was saying. "This place is a miracle."

"Yeah, they've got everything here," a man replied, "we should be safe."

A tiny girl's voice interjected with something James couldn't hear, but the woman responded, "That's a good question, honey. I don't know why those tents at the edge of the camp are burned down."

"It could be that something caught fire," the man chuckled nervously. "But they've got it under control. I wouldn't worry about it too much. Let's get you some breakfast."

Grinning at the new arrivals that had made it to safety, James swung his legs off the cot and placed them on the floor, leaning forward with his elbows on his knees, rubbing his tired eyes. He didn't know how long he'd slept or even when he'd fallen asleep, though the quiet warmth that filtered into his tent and the mentions of breakfast indicated it was sometime in the early morning. More voices passed by outside, the excited murmurs of weary people who'd found their first sense of safety and security in many days, and James' heart went out to them as he recalled his own similar feelings when he'd entered the encampment. While mysterious forces had attacked them the night before, with people in charge like Commander Halladay and Corporal Stenson, everything would be done to protect the survivors, no matter the cost.

With a yawn, he crossed to the tent flap and unzipped it, stepping out into the morning sunshine and smoky skies. There was a faint hint of ash in the air from the previous night's battle, and small crowds milled along the lanes, from military personnel to civilians. What appeared to be two dozen new families entered the camp, lonely figures with slumped shoulders and hopeful voices like the ones he'd heard coming in. While they seemed cautious, most were smiling and pointing out different parts of the camp with community showers, bathroom facilities, and mess tents. Almost everyone had a new backpack, bursting with supplies and comfort items courtesy of the guardsmen at the front gate.

A man shouldering a new backpack walked beside a young woman, likely his wife and, like many refugees, they appeared tired and road worn, their clothes stained with soot and mud, parts of the man's t-shirt burned on the edges, and the woman's thick mop of dark hair was tied up in a messy bun.

"There's not a lot of people here," the man said, glancing around at the sea of tents and refugees standing at the entrances like James, watching as the newcomers entered.

"We're lucky to be alive," his wife replied solemnly. "Bless these folks for taking care of us."

"No kidding. Who knows where we'd be if not here?"

Smiling, James tied the tent flaps back so his door stayed open, nodding at other people walking by. A small girl went by with her parents and he tried making a face at her, her open-mouthed laughter giving him a rush of relief and happiness. Going inside to his basin, he turned on the trickling faucet and filled it about halfway. Dipping his fingers into the cool water, he splashed it on his face with a sigh and washed up as best he could while refugees walked past his tent, some glancing inside as they murmured to each other and guessed at what their temporary shelters might look like.

He brushed his hair back with wet fingers, soot coming off it and his clothes like he'd been standing around a campfire all night. Promising himself to hit the mess tent for some coffee, James cleaned up and started putting his things together, tying up all the loose ends on his new backpack before sitting on his cot to re-examine his walking stick. Taking the pieces apart, he spread them on the ground at his feet, looked them over, and reassembled them into a single, long piece again. He stood and shoved the pointy end into the soft dirt and used it to leverage himself off the cot, taking experimental steps around his tent and swinging it like he was attacking someone.

"Nice moves. Nice stick, too."

James stopped thrusting, seeing an older man standing in his doorway, grinning and gesturing at James' weapon.

"Oh, thanks," he laughed at being caught swinging it around and held it up. "It was a gift."

"Multi-tool?"

"That's right." James used it to hobble up to the man. "Eight pieces, complete with a compass and a fishing pole."

"Nice," the older man replied, so tall he had to stoop to peer inside the tent, his gray hair parted on the side and wearing a collared shirt that was burned in spots and singed around the sleeves. "One of those would be worth its weight in gold these days."

"Yeah, I guess it would." James smiled in response, then walked over to his cot and finished putting his boots on. "It should come in handy where I'm going," James told the man, slipping his boots on and lacing them up. With his walking stick set aside, James gathered his new pack, slid his arms inside the straps, and rolled his shoulders to settle the weight.

"Whereabouts are you headed?"

"Michigan. What about you?" James slung his rifle and reached for his revolver beneath his pillow. "Where are you coming from?"

The man's eyes widened when he saw the Colt, and he nodded slightly in approval. "Nice piece. I'm from a mid-sized town west of here called St. Joseph. I was working at a local shipping hub when everything blew up." He shook his head dejectedly. "Craziest damn thing I ever saw. Nothing but fires and a lot of people —" The man swallowed hard and looked aside before turning back to James with a smile that sat uncomfortably on his face. "Let's just say it was bad."

"I want to say that I couldn't imagine that," James replied grimly, "but unfortunately, I get what you're saying."

"I guess you're heading out now?"

Nodding, James pushed past the man and stepped into the gray morning light, where the sparse refugees headed toward the mess hall or settled in their new tents. Faint tendrils of smoke still rose from the northeast side of the camp where their attackers had struck, though the emergency crews had done an excellent job dousing the flames and keeping them from sprouting up again.

"That's right..."

The man held out his hand. "Roger."

"Good to meet you, Roger. I'm James."

They shook, and Roger followed him onto the main thoroughfare leading through the camp. "Sorry we couldn't talk long."

"I imagine this is how it will be for all of us," James replied, glancing up into the morning sky. "Meeting people briefly before moving on is what I meant."

"I got your meaning," Roger said with a nod. "Until the military figures this out, I guess it'll be mostly camps for everyone for now."

"I'm afraid so," James replied. They stopped at an intersection and stepped aside to let a family by, exchanging nods and hesitant smiles as strangers walked side by side.

"I guess I'll be heading out now, Roger."

"Good luck to you, James, and I hope you get some use out of that stick of yours."

James laughed. "Me, too."

With a final handshake, James left Roger standing on the corner and went to the mess hall where he got a cup of black coffee and then went south through the camp toward the front gates. While the lanes weren't crowded, new people were coming in off the train and getting checked in by National Guardsmen at the tables, though James didn't recognize the ones who'd given him his new toys. Smiling at their kindness, James passed through with a wave and strolled toward the train tracks, where the locomotive was moving off with boxcars full of Army soldiers and other military personnel, equipment, and supplies. After crossing the tracks, James found a short road that curved south to the main highway, the pavement clear of blown-up vehicles, though scatterings of glass and plastic still littered the ground, and the burned-out hulks had been removed along with the scorched passengers.

Once past the light debris, James took a circular on-ramp and walked a short distance to join I-70 heading east. Smiling with the road clear ahead of him and nothing blocking him from getting home, he picked up his feet and moved faster. A breeze cut through from the south and ruffled his shirt, cooling his cheeks with the fresh forest scents of the surrounding woods and grassy plains, deepening his enthusiasm and confidence that he was on the right path to get home. Such breezes reminded him of the near year-round winds that blew through their crops and the field behind their house as he worked the farmland with Alice and the kids. The sun broke past a cloud bank above him, bringing golden rays across the clear pavement. An occasional military truck rolled past him with troops filling the back, rushing east or coming back west from some distant location, its mission critical enough to justify the expenditure of non-tainted fuel. Once, a driver gave James a friendly wave, and he smiled and returned the gesture, lifting his spirits and urging him forward with confident strides.

Hours later, the backpack was digging into his shoulders and his feet ached from the constant march, his knees starting to feel the strain after a thin night's rest. Yet, when he leaned a certain way to ease the pain on his lower extremities, his back pinched all the way up the middle section to his shoulders, and no matter how much he twisted and repositioned things, he couldn't get away from it. The pack was heavier than he'd first imagined, and as he stared into the distance, putting one foot in front of the other with his staff thumping on the pavement, the aches and pains began to wear on his resolve.

"I should have considered its weight before I left," he chastised himself, "but I wouldn't look a gift horse in the mouth."

When a sharp pain shot up his right foot, James winced and moved to the side of the road to sit on a concrete barrier along a construction site where they'd been working before everything had blown up. Slipping off his backpack and rifle, he slid them between his legs and relaxed with a sigh. He dug his phone out of his pocket, powered it on and dialed both home and Alice, not expecting anything and not surprised when all he received was an electric buzz and no connection link on the screen. Putting the device away, James looked up into the darkening sky, the afternoon slowly fading to early evening, the clouds filling the heavens with shapes against the crystal blue backdrop, shapes he and Sarah might have pondered together while out back playing with the dogs when the kids were done with their schoolwork and chores. While James often gave simple names to the cloud configurations, like cars or animals, Sarah always had some elaborate explanation for those odd formations up in the heavens, coming up with stories of castles and landscapes James could never see.

Standing up briefly, he wavered on his feet and looked around. "I need to make camp."

The median was wide with grasses and clusters of trees, but nothing else that looked good. James slung his backpack and rifle back on his shoulders and continued for another hour until he was far away from Kansas City and its desolate ruins. The military's reach was stunted so far from the base, and more burned-out hulks of cars and trucks sat off the roadsides along with their blackened passengers. He walked past it all with his eyes either on the ground or straight ahead, too tired to feel curious about the victims of the heinous attack on the country.

The stretch of woods crowding the highway on his right opened into a wide field of short grasses and a smattering of shrubs and trees nestled against the guardrail and partially covered road signs. Up ahead, a gnarled oak tree with twisted branches jutted upward and sideways, far enough away to keep him out of view unless someone was actively looking for him. Stepping over the guardrail, James strode to the oak and stood beneath its long shadow, shrugging off his backpack and rifle and setting them against the trunk's rough bark.

Digging through his pack, he pulled out a chicken and dumpling MRE, a bottled water, and the map Stenson had stuffed into a side pocket of his backpack. He leaned on the tree and slid down, sitting with his feet in front of him and the map in his lap. Unscrewing the bottle cap, he tilted it back for a long drink before setting it aside to start heating the MRE between his feet, then turned his attention to the map spread out across his lap. Tracing from where he thought he was on I-70 heading east, the Mississippi River stood out as his biggest obstacle. He had to assume the bridges were down, and he might have to cross by boat or other means. Moving his finger farther east, he traced a path to St. Louis and grimaced.

"I definitely want to avoid going there if I can."

Any major city would either be a pile of burning – or burned – rubble. Worst case, they could have people like those that had attacked the refugee camp and anyone willing to go to those lengths to survive in the cruel new world they lived in would see James as an easy target. Tracing ahead with his finger, James settled on a country road that would take him north to Highway 24 and then east again to a town called Hannibal.

He tapped on the spot bemusedly. "I wonder if there's a place called Clarice nearby. Mmm... anyway, from there I'll figure out how to cross the river and make sure I stay far away from Chicago. No way in hell I'm going near that place. It's bound to be worse than St. Louis."

Steam rising from the MRE between his feet drew his attention, and after a quick check, the main portion of the meal seemed sufficiently warm. He obeyed his growling stomach and opened the pouch, mixing up the contents and scarfing them down. After several bites, he stirred some chocolate beverage powder into a tin cup with some water, ignoring the grainy bits of undissolved mix as he rested his head against the gnarled tree. Along with the chocolate drink, he ate a cookie and then finished the main course, folding up the bag carefully and stuffing it into a side pocket where he planned to keep his garbage until some later point in time. It seemed silly to want to avoid littering with all the destruction and debris scattered everywhere, but the oak was old and deserved better. *Besides,* he thought, *even a silly routine'll keep my humanity and sanity both intact.*

Behind him to the south stood a small field of corn nestled in a gentle curve against the distant trees, and he shouldered his pack and rifle, picked up his walking stick, and strode through the shin-high grasses up the bank and into the cornrows. With a glance back at the highway, James stepped farther into the crops, off the beaten path and invisible to anyone passing by. Once he'd gotten deep enough so that he couldn't see the road anymore, he put his backpack and rifle down along with his walking stick and checked inside the pack to see what the Corporal at the supply depot had packed for him. Near the top of the pack was a one-inch pad rolled tightly inside next to a sleeping bag and, holding the MREs so they didn't spill out, James removed the bedding and found a flat spot to place it.

The mat went first, covered by the sleeping bag next, followed by James' tired form as he stretched out and allowed his back and legs to relax. With the end of the pack behind his head to act as a pillow, he stared up at the thinning sky through the waving cornstalks, lulled by their gentle swaying and whispering sounds in the quiet nightfall. The soft southern breeze that had been following him for hours returned and rustled the stalks even more, though it only deepened his weariness as homesickness crashed in upon him. As night came on, all James could think about was home, the last familiar place he remembered.

Soon, the sky cleared, and the stars winked at him from the heavens, filling his head with random dreams about sitting down to dinner with the family and discussing the next day's chores or how far the kids were getting in their schoolwork. Alice always had a sharp remark or an anecdote that would bring a smile to his face, and he wondered if she was out there thinking the same thing about him.

Despite the clearing sky and breathtaking view of the stars above, James' thoughts remained with his memories of hearth and home, times from before whatever it was that was going on. He quelled rising waves of anxiety with images of Alice and the kids who were no doubt waiting for him with open arms.

"Wherever you are, I'll find you. I promise."

The thought of hugging Jake and Sarah close to him and seeing Alice's smile filled him with hope and put James to sleep to the gentle song of rustling, brushing, and whispering cornstalks.

CHAPTER SIX

Ryan Cooper
Somewhere Outside East Lansing, Michigan

While the day had started off cool, the sun beat down on Ryan hard, and he wiped the layer of sweat off his brow and squinted up at the sun through his sunglasses. After a quick breather, he gripped the post-hole digger with his glove-covered hands and slammed it into the soil, grabbing some dirt and dropping it to the side where the pile was growing high. He moved about two feet before digging a second hole and then a third, using a spurt of energy to get through the chore quickly, finally straightening with a gasp as he held his lower back and tossed the digger aside. Resting for a moment, he watched the slow rolling clouds in the upper atmosphere pressed down flat as if he was looking at them from beneath a sheet of glass. Though their color was still dark, they were shades lighter than before, thanks to a lessening in smoke from the fires around town.

"At least nothing seems to be actively blowing up anymore," he murmured.

Grabbing a bag of quick-setting concrete, he poured it into the first hole, followed by water from a nearby five-gallon bucket. Ryan stirred the mixture until it reached the proper consistency, then placed the pole directly in the center, holding it upright and only letting go when it seemed stable. The concrete was quickly growing thick, but he didn't trust it to keep the pole straight, so he used a couple of stakes and twine to tie the top off and ensure it stayed level. He repeated the process for the rest of the holes, making sure each pole was straight with a bubble level before leaving them to set. The back door closed, and he turned to see Helen step around the bins of vegetables they still had to can with two cups of steaming coffee, handing one to him with a smile before admiring his work. "How long does that concrete take to dry?"

"It's the quick-drying stuff, so maybe twenty to forty minutes at most," he replied, taking a sip of his drink. "Hey, this really hits the spot. Thank you."

"With this weather going back and forth, it's hard to tell if it's hot or getting colder."

"Tell me about it." Ryan chuckled. "One minute, I'm burning up; the next, I'm freezing. I've been shivering all day." While Helen looked over the rows of solar panels, he caught the bags under her eyes and her heavy sigh. "You look pretty tired, dear. Is everything okay?"

Helen absently touched her cheek and chin. "Is it that obvious?"

"You're still my beautiful lady, but that doesn't mean you can't get tired like the rest of us mortals."

"Good answer," she laughed and then sighed again. "I guess I'm having trouble keeping up with the watch schedule.

Don't get me wrong. I love being there for you when you get up... we haven't had this many breakfasts together for a long time. I just miss going to bed with you and knowing you're at my side. And I'm just plain *tired*."

"Agreed. With just the two of us here, it's going to be hard to keep up with everything. It won't be getting any easier, either."

He shifted his attention north past the sheds and the fenced-in barnyard where the animals were, including the dogs, and the big red barn sitting behind them with its hidden treasure of the tractor and fuel.

Helen went on. "And worrying all the time about Alice and the kids is wearing me out, too."

"You're not the only one," Ryan admitted, stepping over and wrapping his arm around her shoulder to give her a comforting squeeze. "I think about them every other minute, and I'm constantly thanking James for all his preparation." Gesturing at the rows of solar panels, he said, "Aside from the printer and weapons and extra supplies and everything else we have on hand, they hit another home run with these. James found the perfect spot for the solar panels where the sun seems to hit all day regardless of the clouds."

Helen laughed. "I remember Alice telling me how much work he put in to get them installed. I'm glad it seems to have paid off."

"And they're so close to the house, too, which makes them easier to protect and less visible from the road."

They stood silent for a minute, quietly sipping before Helen glanced over. "Where do you think they are now?"

Ryan grunted and scratched his head, stepping away from her and doing a half-turn. "James is somewhere between Denver and here, provided he —"

"Don't even say it, Ryan Cooper." Helen fixed him with a stern look. "James didn't get on that plane. Chances are his connecting flight didn't even make it to the airport to pick him up. By then, he would've seen what was happening and got out of there." She spoke the last part decisively as she stared south along with him.

"I know... but the possibility is still there, and I don't want to give myself false hope." His face changed, growing darker before he forced himself to smile for Helen. "At the same time, I half expect him to come walking down the road any minute now."

Helen grinned. "Wouldn't that be a sight?"

"Indeed, it would." Ryan kicked the ground and shifted, taking a larger sip of his cooling coffee. "As for Helen and the kids, realistically... they've got a much longer journey with a lot of trouble between there and here. She's smart, and she'll keep them away from the big cities once she figures out what's going on. If she does that, they'll have a chance. Worst-case scenario, she finds a camp for them to rest in for a while. Otherwise —" Ryan fell silent as a lump grew in his throat, emotions overwhelming his entire body as he finally began to verbalize what he had been avoiding thinking about. Squeezing his eyes tight, a few tears ran down his cheeks, and he took several deep breaths, trying to calm himself and push the thoughts about his daughter out of his mind.

"Oh, hon." It was Helen's turn to come to him, letting her empty cup dangle from her finger as she wrapped both arms around his middle and squeezed hard until his labored breathing stopped and he patted her on the back, smiling at her.

"You still got quite a grip." He hugged her back and kissed the top of her head with tears dripping off his chin into her hair. "I suppose we both could use a little positivity, but it's just so hard. Just when we start to fall into a good rhythm, I fall apart."

Helen wiped her tears off her cheeks and tried to smile. "Have you seen anyone around lately, like the Joneses?"

Ryan was shaking his head. "I haven't seen anyone yet. That doesn't mean someone isn't watching us, though. I keep looking up and feeling paranoid."

"I can't blame you there, honey. After the chicken coop incident...."

"Yeah, I don't trust anyone right now," Ryan sniffled, "no matter how kind they were to us or the kids in the past. Situations like this bring out the worst in people for sure."

"They can also bring out the best. Though not this time, apparently. Should we... do something about them?"

Ryan looked south toward the fence and the front gate, past the row of trees and ponds with the ducks swimming around like the world wasn't rapidly decaying around them. "I don't think so. We just keep working, keep our eyes open, and stay armed at all times. You've still got your gun on you, right?"

Helen turned and lifted her blouse to show her holstered S&W 642. "I sure do."

"Excellent," he gave her another squeeze around her shoulders. "If someone comes on the property that isn't blood, I'm leaning heavily in the direction of 'shoot first and ask questions later,' no matter how hard that might be to do if it's someone that we or the kids know."

"I can't say I'm a huge fan of that idea, but I think it's probably necessary given... everything." She smiled up at him, her eyes misty. "I know what's valuable to me, Ryan Cooper. I won't let you down."

With an appreciative nod, Ryan turned back to his work, stooping to press his finger on the hardening concrete and using the bubble level to check that everything was still standing straight.

"How much do you have left to do here?"

"These'll be finished setting any time now, but I'm afraid I'll need some help lifting these solar panels and holding them in place while I attach them to the poles."

"I can help with that," Helen said enthusiastically.

"I don't think even the pair of us can manage it, unfortunately. These are a couple hundred pounds each, so I'll need to rig something up to help with that."

"Sounds difficult."

"Not really. I'll use the fork attachment on the tractor to hold the panels by rope so I can swing them in small degrees to where I need them." He frowned. "I don't want to use the tractor because it's going to make noise, but I'm afraid it's the only way."

"You want me to keep watch while you do it?"

"If you don't mind." He knelt down to check the concrete again and nodded. "Yeah, this'll be set enough to hold weight by the time I get the tractor out here. I'll get started now."

Ryan walked out to the barn, opened it up, and headed inside, greeted by curious bleats as animals gathered around. After half an hour of maneuvering the tractor around inside the large structure, removing the bucket and throwing on the forks, he was sweating profusely. He climbed inside the cabin and turned on the air conditioning, then drove it out through the rolling door and drove carefully around the animals to the barnyard gate, through it with Helen's help, and down to where he was setting up the panels.

Tying the rope around one panel in a series of loops to spread out the force the rope would put on the panels, he secured both ends of the rope over each fork, and gave it a few good tugs to ensure it was secure. Working the controls from back inside the cabin, Ryan lifted the first panel and moved it above the poles he'd installed, lowering it slowly until it hung just above the brackets on the poles, slowly rotating back and forth. He hopped out and untied the knot on one fork, letting the rope play out and pushing and pulling as one side of the panel fell into place. Tying off the rope again, he returned to the bracket, made a slight adjustment to the panel, and screwed it firmly in before repeating the process for the other side, then continued repeating the process for more of the panels. While Helen stood watch nearby in the yard with her hair blowing in the breeze, he finished working, going around to check that each connection was tightened, as even a single loose bracket could cause the entire structure to shake itself apart in the next strong windstorm that passed through.

"Looks great!" Helen called. "When will you know if they work?"

"I still need to wire everything up, but we should see the battery charging rate increase dramatically, along with the total daytime capacity we have. I'd say we'll know just how much more we're getting within a few hours, though, if this goes smoothly."

Hopping back into the tractor, Ryan drove it up to the barn and through the rolling door, removing the forklift attachment and quickly shutting and locking up. With a hop in his step, Ryan left the barnyard, closed the gate behind him, and hurried to the solar panels to connect the wires. Helen had gone inside, so he worked on the last steps by himself as midday faded. When he was done, he strolled west, away from the house, looking south past the field and driveway to the main gate. He turned back to check the angles on the solar panels when he did a double take at the entrance, seeing a figure moving down near the gate, leaning on a fencepost and staring directly at him, though it was too distant to make out who it was.

For a long moment, the two stared at each other before the man at the gate turned and walked out of sight to the southeast toward the Jones'. Heart rate pulsing, sweat dripping down his back, shoulders tense with anxious fear, Ryan shuffled inside and grabbed Helen where she was setting up for another canning session. Guiding her along the hallway to the dining room window, he parted the blinds and pointed to the end of the driveway.

Helen had followed him wordlessly, blinking at his pale face and hushed silence, though she finally spoke up. "What is it, honey? Did you see someone?"

"Yes, I saw someone down by the fence, and he didn't even try to hide. He looked back at me for a few minutes, turned around, and left." Ryan shrugged.

"Was it Mike Jones?"

"I don't think it was, but I can't be sure." He shook his head as his expression deepened to one of dark doubt. "And I can't tell if it was the person who tried to get our chickens, either. In any case, it's clear they heard the tractor and are getting damn curious about what we're doing here."

"Sounds like they're trying to sniff around."

"Undoubtedly." Ryan growled. "We need to be ready in case they decide to try something more drastic."

"I agree. I think we need to step it up. How far do you want to take things?"

"Well, the M&P 15 has a scope, and it's pretty easy to fire. You'll take that rifle, and I'll go downstairs and get the Winchester .308. That's got a scope, too, and we'll need them if we're doing long-distance shooting."

"Keep them at a distance," Helen affirmed. "Got it. Next?"

Ryan let the blinds fall shut and turned away from the leaking light into the dark dining room, pacing toward the hallway and back again. "Given the layout of the house and all the ways in, I think it would be helpful to board some of them up. We don't have to do it all the way, just enough to keep someone from getting in easily. You know, slow them down a little... make them make some noise that might warn us. And we'll bring the dogs down for the night. How does that sound?"

"Wouldn't it be better to let them roam the property like before?"

"For random interlopers on the property, yes." A shiver shot up his spine and down his arms as he entertained the nightmarish thought of several people flooding over their fences simultaneously. "I don't know why, but something tells me this isn't just going to be one person. They probably know a decent amount about the place – the dogs are obvious, but who knows if they're friends with the kids. Maybe they know about the guns, too?" Ryan was speaking a mile a minute, pacing around, tapping on his leg with nervous energy. "Doesn't matter. We'll handle whatever happens. But we need to get prepared."

"Sounds like a plan, honey. What can I do? Help you board things up?"

Turning to the dining room table, he picked up the M&P 15, checked to see it was charged, and handed it to her. "No, I'll grab the supplies from outside and start doing that. I want you to watch my back."

"You really think they'd try to come in the daylight?"

"I have no idea when – or even *if* – anyone will come. But we're done taking any chances. Upstairs gives you a vantage point on practically all the approaches to the house, so you'll be in a good spot up there."

Helen accepted the weapon, the large rifle looking strangely natural on her diminutive frame. "I've got you, honey."

With a brisk nod and a quick hug, Ryan exited through the back door, and rushed out to their smaller shed near the fenced-in barnyard where a wheelbarrow and scrap wood James had were leaning against the walls and sitting on a shelf on the right side. He picked out pieces of wood of varying sizes and loaded them into the wheelbarrow along with a dirt-covered cordless drill, long wood screws, a hammer, and nails, then he wheeled the supplies to the house, looking around in all directions, half expecting someone to come out of the trees or from the back of the property at any second.

Starting with the low basement windows, he screwed in pieces of scrap wood to the frames with at least one screw on one side and a nail on the other, wanting to make it as difficult as possible for someone to remove the wood. The high shriek of the drill motor caused him to wince at first, but then he stopped caring and screwed and hammered pieces until he was sweating and his joints ached from bending and stooping to cover the basement windows.

His knocks were loud and obnoxious as they echoed everywhere, a headache starting at the nape of his neck that spread upward around his head, but Ryan was on a mission and didn't stop until he had every bottom window covered with at least one piece of wood, two on the more oversized windows. Running back to the shed for a stepladder, he brought it back, enabling him to reach the higher ones out in the front. Paranoia crawled in his guts, filling him with a constant panic whenever he wasn't looking down at the gate or around him.

Once, when he was working on the dining room windows with Helen watching him from the inside, he thought he caught movement out of the corner of his eye and nearly slipped and fell off the ladder trying to draw his pistol. It was nothing, though, and he chastised himself as he returned to work and finished nailing a second two-by-four. Panting with exhaustion, shoulders aching, and the drill's battery dead, Ryan climbed down and put all the tools and stepladder in the wheelbarrow, pushing them back out to the shed and locking them inside. By then, the sun had faded entirely and was just a memory, the clouds dingy where they gathered in the east, leaving the sky overhead open with the first inklings of stars and moonlight filtering through the forest trees. Before heading back to the house, he strode out to the barnyard and let the dogs out, regretfully leaving the barnyard animals unguarded as he followed the excited, playful dogs to the back door.

Helen greeted them with a smile, kneeling in front of the wily Pyrenees as they pranced and ran through the living room with their massive paws and nails clicking on the hardwood.

"You're supposed to wait for us to wipe off your feet!" Helen called to Duke and Duchess, who'd taken off to leave Diana behind, obediently sitting with her tail sweeping across the floor and an eager look in her eyes. Ryan locked the back door, peeked outside, and turned to them with a smile. "She's the only one who obeys us."

"Oh, the other ones are okay, too. Diana is just an *especially* good girl." She said the last part with a smile, wrapping her arms around Diana for a big hug before motioning to Ryan for a moist cloth. "Get me something to wipe her paws, please."

Ryan crossed to the sink and moistened a washcloth, realizing how ridiculous it sounded, trying to pretend things were normal when they were far from it, though at the same time, the simple act of normalcy brought with it some temporary relief as well. After handing off the rag to her, he went to the basement to get the Winchester and some extra ammunition, the normalcy gone, replaced by the new normal once again.

An hour later they were sitting at the dining room table, the M&P 15 and Winchester lying within reach, each with a freshly brewed cup of coffee and caffeine thrumming through their veins. Duke and Duchess were in the great room while Diana obediently lay at Helen's feet. They'd put a small electric lantern way back in a corner where it shed a desperate, meager light across the room, just enough for them to see by so they didn't trip when walking around.

Ryan took another sip from his cup. "I'm so jacked up right now," he said with a laugh. "It feels like I'm using the restroom every ten minutes."

"Not near that much, dear, but I'm pretty wired, too. It's still pretty early, and I'd imagine they'll wait a while before they try anything, if they do it at all. Should one of us try to get some sleep?"

"I don't think either of us will sleep tonight. No, I'm afraid this will be an all-nighter for us. Maybe we should try to sleep during the day and sort of switch things around, if you know what I mean."

"Night shift," Helen nodded. "The first job I had in a warehouse was a third shift. Can't say I loved it."

Ryan leaned back with a sigh, glancing through the wide-open blinds where moonlight illuminated the treetops and glimmered off the ponds. The dark shapes of ducks floated by, one suddenly flapping his wings and rising briefly from the water before settling again, causing Ryan to sit up nervously for a moment before he purposefully relaxed his shoulders, letting them fall forward in a slouch. "At least we have clear skies tonight. There's plenty of moonlight and starlight to see by."

Helen glanced outside. "It's one of those weird nights that looks like near daylight."

"That's the full moon for you... but it also brings out the crazies, if you know what I mean."

"I do."

As the minutes ticked, Ryan continued glancing through the blinds and moonlit night, searching for shadows and movement but finding nothing. He got up and paced for a while to burn off some nervous energy until his back and knees ached, reminding him of the hard days' work he'd put in. Bleary-eyed and feeling paper thin, Ryan returned to his chair and rested his face in his hands, slowly drawing them down as if he could wipe the weariness away. When he saw the blinking lights at the far end of the driveway, it took him a few seconds to realize it was someone moving around, their light bobbing in the darkness. Snatching up his binoculars with a huff, Ryan burst from his chair, pressed the binoculars to the blinds, and peered through them.

"Are they coming?" Helen asked, turning from one side to the other as he moved past her.

"I think so... the idiots are using flashlights on a night like this." He snickered, watching the light, seeing at least one figure behind it as they worked their way along the fence line to the corner where they stopped for a moment, shining the light down at the ground as they climbed over and landed on the other side. Nostrils flaring, he cursed silently. "Damn people can't stay on their side of the property line."

Hanging the binoculars around his neck, Ryan went to the table and picked up the scoped Winchester, checking yet again to ensure it was fully loaded with a ten round magazine and one in the chamber. "I'm glad James had this in his safe." Holding onto the weapon with his left hand, he nodded to Helen and then at the M&P 15 she carried. "Do you have what you need?"

Helen was up and already reaching for the gun, checking that it was loaded and had one in the chamber. "I'm ready," she said, her voice shaking slightly.

With a calm breath, Ryan stepped toward her and gave her a quick hug. "It's going to be all right. Just go and watch my back from the upstairs window. Leave the dogs down here for extra protection and just try to keep me in sight."

"Okay. I will."

"They'll probably skip coming to the house and go straight toward the barn to see about the tractor. I may move around the house to track them, so you may have to switch to a back window. You can only see the side and front of the barn from that vantage point."

"If I lose sight of you, I'll assume you're circling to the backyard." Still trying to sound confident, Helen's voice faltered, and she fell against him. "Be careful, Ryan," she whispered.

With a nod, Ryan turned and went to the front door, unlocking the deadbolts and stepping outside, listening as Helen shut the door behind him and softly locked it. Half crouching, Ryan spun toward the quiet darkness and walked off the porch with his Winchester gripped tightly to his chest. The sounds of crickets and frogs were deafening, clashing with each other yet somehow forming a symphony in the soft night breeze. As his eyes got used to the darkness, Ryan moved along the front walkway, staying low against the short retaining wall and looking toward the southeast part of the property where he'd seen the man enter. Squinting into the night, huffing as he shuffled down the walkway, he searched for a sprig of light, the bobbing of a flashlight beam or lantern, or just a flash of movement which would give the intruder – or intruders – away.

Just as he reached the driveway, he caught sight of the intruder off in the distance, moving through the trees at a cautious pace. Sometimes he'd stop and point the light toward the house, though it was too weak to reach Ryan where he stood near the driveway, his crouched form blending in with the bushes and pines scattered around the structure. Glancing over his right shoulder, Ryan barely saw Helen peeking through the window with the curtain pushed aside a few inches, before he moved out of her line of sight.

Ryan forced down the butterflies in his stomach as he crept over the pavement and around the northeast corner of the house, stopping next to some vegetable bins and kneeling to calm his breathing. Still fifty yards off, Ryan focused on the shadowy form, watching as it slunk toward and behind the barn as he suspected they might. When he was sure of their direction, Ryan left the cover of the house and stalked after the figure, walking quickly but not putting too much pressure on his prosthetic. The last thing he needed was to break it and end up disabled in the middle of the backyard, a sitting duck for anyone with a weapon.

The dark shapes of the outbuildings grew more defined in the moonlight, and Ryan cross-stepped to his left, mirroring the man's movements, losing sight of him in the woods for a moment before his light blinked into view again. Ryan reached the first shed, paused, slipped along its front, and peeked around the corner to locate the man again, the sound of his own breathing and pounding heart impossibly loud in his ears. Judging from the man's direction, the intruder was more focused on what was in the barn than anyone sneaking up behind him, and Ryan grew bolder, hurrying past the sheds and chicken coop until there were only thirty-five yards between them. The intruder was still moving through the woods, blinking in and out of sight, then he crossed over toward the barn where he fell into the shadows.

Ryan shifted to the right and cut across some open ground, trying to swing around and come up from behind. Something shifted in his prosthetic, and it slid on his leg, causing him to lurch and Ryan fell forward onto the yard and laid flat in the grass. He raised his head slowly, spotting the sheep and goats off in the barnyard, clustered together in the moonlight and bleating in annoyance. Squinting, heart racing, Ryan searched the shadows but couldn't see anyone either along the fence line or in the woods. While he had the back of the barn covered, Helen had a much better shot of the side and front. He looked through the scope and then pulled away to peer into the darkness, watching intently, and after a stretch of anxiety there was a movement by the barnyard fence. Ryan's breath caught in his chest as he put his eye to the scope and tracked the man as he walked along the side of the barn toward the roll-up door. His flashlight was pointed at the ground, but the reflected light gave Ryan enough to see that he carried a crowbar in his right hand and wore a shotgun slung on his shoulder.

"The bastard means business," he growled quietly with annoyance.

While he couldn't be one-hundred percent certain, the man seemed too small to be Mike Jones or anyone else he knew from the neighborhood, though there were plenty of Alice and James's neighbors that he hadn't met. Eye pressed to the scope, he tried to breathe steady and track the man through the mesh between the fence rails, but his only clear shot was at the man's knees or waist, and the intruder was crouching in such a way that it would be a tough shot to take.

"Is there just one of you?" Ryan mumbled, his soft words coming out in puffs of moisture with each breath, the grass cool under his bare arms as he tracked his target, trying to decide what to do.

Ryan shifted his rifle to the right, searching the darkness for anyone else, glancing over his shoulder along the tree line toward the other end of the property but seeing no movement. When he looked at the upstairs windows of the house, he couldn't see Helen in any of them. Either she'd found a new target in a different location or she was keeping to the shadows to stay undetected. Turning back to his scope, he tracked the man past the roll-up door to the corner of the barn where he started prodding at the door with the crowbar.

Without knowing if there were more intruders, he was loathe to give away his presence or just open fire willy-nilly. Ryan groaned, adjusted his grip, and shouted. "Hey, asshole! Stop right where you are and drop your weapons!"

The man froze with a soft curse that Ryan heard from where he was lying, but the intruder made no move to drop either his crowbar or shotgun.

"I've got you in my sights!" Ryan shouted again, watching carefully for signs of movement from other locations around the woods or barn. "It'd be an easy shot. Drop it!"

Instead of doing what he was told, the man turned slowly toward Ryan with his hands raised, searching the darkness in vain for Ryan's position.

Looking back to the house, still seeing no sign of Helen, he shouted again. "Last chance! Drop the rifle or I shoot!"

The man's head ducked low as he continued looking for Ryan. "I just want to talk about borrowing your tractor! Why don't you come out, and we can discuss it?"

"We don't have a tractor to lend out," Ryan called straight back to the man in a low tone. "No more tal—"

As Ryan was speaking, the crowbar hit the grass with a soft rustle, and the shotgun whipped up, the man firing a blast from his hip in Ryan's general direction. Buckshot zipped by overhead as Ryan pressed his face into the grass, inhaling sharply in surprise. Another boom ripped off, and pieces of buckshot cut through the grass near his face, forcing his nose into the moist soil as he protected his head with his arm. The third shot was even closer, and he felt something hot pluck at the back of his shirt and glance off his boot before he'd finally had enough. Raising his rifle, he looked for the intruder straight ahead but he'd moved around the corner of the barn and was slipping across the front of the structure. Ryan tracked him and fired too quickly, missing as his round struck the barn wall in a puff of shredded wood and dust. The flash of his rifle muzzle drew the man's attention, and he swung the shotgun in Ryan's direction, about to fire again.

Helen's sharp rifle shots snapped through the night before the shotgun could, two rounds striking the barn wall close to where Ryan had hit, sending more splinters flying off. Showered with fragments, the man lowered his head and ran from the barrage as Ryan tracked him and squeezed the trigger in a clipped rhythm, but he kept missing and hitting the barn. A third round from Helen finally struck the man, and he jerked and grunted painfully, spinning and accidentally firing a shotgun blast into the ground. He slipped a couple of feet and sank to his knees, lurching forward and leaning on his gun, using it to support himself as he still tried to move forward. Another gunshot from Helen hit him in the chest and he fell back into the cool grass where he gurgled and rasped, squirming for a few seconds before falling still and quiet. Ryan rolled over and peered up at the house, seeing no sign of Helen except for a half-opened window in the bedroom she must have fired from. Waving upward at the house, her hand finally appeared as she waved back from the shadows.

Chest heavy and senses heightened from the rush of adrenaline, Ryan rolled onto his stomach and pushed himself to his knees, setting his prosthetic foot beneath him and stumbling to his feet. Gun raised, he limp-walked to the barnyard gate, keeping his rifle trained on the shape lying in the grass. By the time he got there, Helen was rushing down from the house with the dogs running ahead of her, tails sweeping back and forth, growling with their heads low and their eyes pinned to the downed figure.

"It's okay, Duke!" Ryan shouted as they came up. "Duchess... Diana. Settle down!"

Throwing the latch, he pushed into the barnyard, calling for the dogs as they broke away and ran straight for the figure, Duke spreading his paws in front of him, sniffing, growling, and barking as he tossed his head. Helen was next to him a moment later, and Ryan held out his arm. "Keep your rifle trained on him while I check him out."

"Already on it," Helen replied, voice shaking slightly as she leveled the gun.

Staying off to the side, Ryan stalked closer, taking a small flashlight out of his pocket and shining it at the bloodstained grass and up the barn wall where splatters of dark crimson stained the siding. He settled the beam on the still figure who wasn't moving or breathing as far as he could tell, but the shotgun was trapped under him, so Ryan shuffled over and put his right foot on the barrel before kneeling beside the man. Blood saturated his black jacket and formed a pool that was spreading across the soil, and the man's pale cheeks were stained with red smears, a soft hole caked with gore marring the side of his head in the temporal region.

Ryan started to touch it but drew back. "You got him in the chest and head." Taking the man's shoulder, he turned him over and stared into the man's blank eyes. "Yep... He's dead. Superb shooting, honey."

Helen was looking off to the side, her rifle barrel raised toward the sky as she avoided the sight of the man, her shoulders trembling as she tried to get her breathing under control.

"Hey, now. It's okay." Ryan shifted away from the dead man. "You saw what needed to be done and took care of it. Nothing to be sorry—"

"I don't feel bad about what I just did." Helen hissed venomously, not at Ryan, but at the body lying on the grass as she gestured at it and wiped away a tear. "No, sir. I don't feel bad about him at all. You, though... the bastard shot at you, and I could've lost you. And I'm worried he might have brought company with him, or they could be coming as backup."

The dogs weren't acting like anyone else was nearby, though Ryan stood and flipped his flashlight off as he scanned the yard for movement. While he saw nothing suspicious, Helens words had him back on the alert, a fresh rush of adrenaline causing his heart to race anew, and a lightness spread through his chest as he started to breathe faster, bordering on hyperventilation. Feeling unsteady, he took a deep breath, focusing back on the present, turning back to Helen, working his jaw back and forth as he slowly nodded.

"Judging by what he was going after—the tractor, based on what he said—that's not a bad assumption. Let's drag him out of sight and get back inside to regroup. We've got a long night ahead of us."

CHAPTER SEVEN

Alice Burton
Monticello, Florida

The four strolled west along a single gravel path with tufts of grass growing in the middle, curving to the left as the path followed a gentle slope downward. The woods grew thicker for part of the walk, crowding in on the sides except where they gave way to dirt trails that led to other parts of the property. Several small utility barns and sheds sat off to the right, the largest with its doors flung open and some groundskeeper's gear resting nearby. While the main grounds had pristine gardens and manicured lawns, the rear section was wilder and had grown out with waves of green everywhere, thick underbrush vibrantly colored with flowers sprouting on both sides of the lane.

"Normally, I'd take one of the ATVs down here, but..." Wilford let the words hang and continued after a pause. "Still, it's a lovely walk, and I loved bringing the horses down here. It'll be nice once I get it all rearranged and the rest of the horses moved."

Alice wasn't expecting much, figuring that the secondary stables were out of sight and mind for a reason, but when they came to the bottom of the valley where a building half the size of the main stable stretched out into the woods, its beauty was undeniable. The gravel lane led through a grassy yard and up to the east side of the structure, the space south and west clear of all vegetation and trees to leave a broad pasture with a training corral and light poles. The structure was extensive, with a big open front door topped by a raised roof and two beams that stretched its entire length. The wooden sides were painted what had once been bright red, its fade from time and wear giving the building a dignified appearance. While it was older than the other building, the grass was trimmed back and worn down to the dirt around the place, kept as neat as any other part of the property they'd seen. A single beige horse stood out by himself in the pasture and grazed and, hearing them approach, he raised his head and shook it, swishing his tail across his flanks in what Alice took was excitement over seeing his caretaker.

Sarah got out ahead of them, practically skipping on her way there, turning and smiling as she called back to Wilford. "How many more horses do you have in there?"

"You'll see soon enough, little miss. Just hold your horses." He chuckled happily. "Pun intended!"

Alice couldn't help but crack a smile as she and Jake took the last several yards with a hop in their own steps, something about the place – or the company – lifting their spirits. They entered the main corridor where a dozen horses stood at the stall gates and turned their long heads to take in the newcomers. A couple of them snorted and whinnied at the sight of Wilford as the group stepped inside the cool, moist corridor, the smell of manure and hay filling the air along with a heavy animal musk that reminded Alice of their farm back home and her childhood doing work on her parents' farm.

"You said you moved some horses down here already, right?"

"I brought down four more stallions and a couple of mares with their babies."

"But the stable looks only half full."

Wilford shuffled off to a side room near the entrance where a small desk and a workbench with hammers and tools butted the wall. "Well, these are where the grade horses are kept."

"You have other stables on the grounds, right? Ones with better horses?"

"That's right. We have many other facilities."

"Why didn't you take the mares and stallions to the other stables?"

The old man scoffed and waved off her suggestion. "Oh, no. Can't risk mixing the bloodlines, you see. We keep all of those separated around here." He sighed. "While we likely won't see much horse racing any time soon, I'd best stick to my duties and keep them that way."

"Ah."

"Besides, you'll not want to be taking any of the thoroughbred animals we have." Gesturing happily, he led them past several stalls with deep brown horses, curious equine eyes following them and whinnying whenever Wilford reached out to touch one of their noses or give them a pat on the neck. Sarah patted one horse and peeked over the stall at something else on the other side, and with a happy yelp, she turned and hopped up and down. "Mom, there's a colt in here. Look how small he is!"

"I call that little guy Mr. Clatter Hooves because he's always jumping around so excitedly. And he won't be a colt for long, as he's coming up on his first year when he'll be a yearling."

Alice moved to the stall door and peered over as the mare stepped aside as if showing off her son. The little chestnut colt was bounding around inside the stall, turning from one side to the other, prancing up on his back hooves to kick his front ones out playfully before tucking himself against his mother again.

"Boy! He's just itching to get out, isn't he?" Jake said, resting his arms over the stall door as Sarah laughed giddily at the colt's antics.

Sarah turned to Wilford. "Does he get to go out and run a lot?"

"As much as he can. I'll have time later to let him out before I walk the fence line."

Alice nodded and strolled toward the middle of the corridor, shifting back to Wilford as she peered at the horses watching them from their stalls. "Why wouldn't you want us to take any of the thoroughbred stallions? Not that we'd want to, with as much money as I'm sure they're worth."

"While those fellows are awfully pretty," he replied, turning away from the mare with a parting pat on her neck, "they're built for speed and grace, not for carrying people across the country. What you need is something hardier. Now, take these three fine boys here. They'd be perfect for you. They're geldings, and they can walk for miles without complaint. They're used to doing long treks and carrying loads the whole way."

Wilford walked over to some stalls on the left where three big horses stood, snorting and tossing their heads. The big cream one in the middle threw his lengthy forelock over his ears in a rock star gesture that made Sarah giggle again. The other two were much darker, and the one on the far left was a blood bay shade with a snip of white on his nose. His companion on the far right was a rich liver chestnut that shined in the light, with a stripe of cream from forehead to muzzle.

Wilford turned and clapped his hands, raising a mischievous eyebrow at Jake and Sarah. "Come on, kids. Let me introduce you to these burly fellows." Starting on the left, he patted each horse as he went down the line. "This first guy with the beautiful blood bay coat is called Stormy. The big cream-colored one is Buck, and this last handsome gentleman is Rocky." With a flourish, he ended the introductions, swept off to the side with a hop and a shuffle, and stood back to let Alice and the kids get a closer look.

"Now, they're not wearing shoes," Wilford added, "so they should be ridden mostly off-road and taken as slowly as you can, bar emergencies. If you take good care of *them*, they'll take care of *you*. Here... start with some treats. Get on their friendly side."

He handed them three large discs that fit into their palms. Alice fed Buck while Sarah and Jake greeted the other two, and the horses ate quickly out of their hands and snorted happily.

Stroking Buck's neck, Alice turned back to Wilford. "Are you seriously going to let us ride them out of here? You're so dedicated to their care... it seems wrong to take them from you."

"Well, you need them," he responded firmly. "You told me so yourself. And you didn't try to steal them from me, so why not?" His cheerful mask slipped for a moment. "I'm probably the only one left on the farm, and I doubt anyone will return. At least not anyone with good intentions."

Alice nodded slowly as Buck nuzzled her cheek, his lips pulling on strands of her hair as he examined her with deep curiosity. "Why don't you come with us, then?" The words came out without her meaning to say them, but she continued. "We're a long way off, but we have a decent-sized piece of property and plenty of space to keep your horses. They'll be fine with us, and we should have everything we need to take care of them."

Wilford almost seemed to consider the offer for a moment but chuckled sadly as he looked up the aisle at the horses staring back at him. Some shook their heads and nickered, while others merely blinked in what seemed like anticipation for their own turn at getting some food. "I appreciate the offer, but the racehorses wouldn't make the journey. It's simply too far for too many horses, and there are far too many risks, especially after what I've learned from you about what the world has become. No, I'll stay here and protect the rest of them while I can, hopefully better than when you showed up." His crooked sideways smile touched Alice's heart, and they broke into chuckles as she reached out and took his hand.

"Thank you, Wilford. You're far too kind, but I promise we'll take excellent care of these horses. When this is all over, I'll make sure they get returned to you."

"I know you will."

"How long do you think it will take to get the horses saddled and ready to go?" Alice asked. "Like I mentioned before, we've got some riding experience, but you'd be the expert there."

Wilford glanced toward the end of the corridor. "Beings it's getting late in the day, it might be best for you to stay here overnight and start your journey early in the morning."

Alice winced and started to protest, but Wilford stopped her. "I know you want to get home as soon as possible to check on your parents and be there when your husband comes home, but you don't want to start such a journey at night, especially when handling new horses for the first time on your own." He patted Jake on the shoulder and gave a hearty laugh. "And I'd be obliged to educate you on these particular horses. I'll make a maintenance list so you can care for them as I would."

Alice shifted, weighing their options as she looked over at the rapidly diminishing sunlight. "I... I can't argue with that logic, Wilford. I think it would be okay, provided you have the room."

"I've got several clean stalls to accommodate you, and we can ramp up the campfire for warmth before you all tuck in. It won't be a fancy stay, but I'll make it as comfortable as possible."

Alice turned to see both kids looking up at her expectantly as they stood by their respective horses, grinning while petting them. "Okay, we'll stay the night."

"Wonderful!" Wilford called out. "This will be just splendid."

"Are you sure, Wilford?"

"That I am, ma'am," the old man replied sorrowfully. "And if you don't mind me saying, I could use a little company for at least one dark and dreary night."

"Sounds good to me."

"Right this way." Wilford backed up as he gestured toward the exit.

They said goodbye to the horses, with Alice reaching up to pat Buck's big head and receiving a pleasing snort in reply. Wilford led them up through the forest on the old worn path, climbing back to the stable with its sheds and smoking ruins. Glancing at the ominous sky, she sighed with thanks to have another opportunity to rest after sparking a friendship with the old man. As for Wilford, he shuffled quickly along the right-hand track, occasionally looking down, but mostly looking toward the direction of the primary stable where it showed up around the last bend.

"We'll have a wonderful evening tonight. I'll start some dinner right away, maybe a pot of lamb with a side of oats and some greens I picked from the garden just the other day."

"That sounds wonderful," Alice replied. "I'm impressed you still have so much here after so much burned down."

"Aye, well, the Monticellos were nothing if not resourceful. There's a fair amount more food and drink underground that I don't believe the fires touched. Should keep me going for a long while, provided I don't have any run-ins with the locals."

"Is there anything we can do to help you? Preparations? Defenses?"

Wilford dismissed her with a wave. "No, no, no. What you need to do is let an old man take care of you for the night, and help me in return by taking good care of my horses."

Back inside the stable, they stepped past the first stalls, where Wilford showed them some spare ones that looked as clean as the day they'd been built. There was one for Alice and another for the kids, and together they stacked piles of hay with blankets over them and made pillows from their backpacks. On some of the vertical beams near the lanterns were pictures of historic horse tracks with owners Wilford had worked for over the years, the groundskeeper sometimes stopping to tell them a story about a particular individual who was hard on him, or another who had displayed exceptional kindness.

He stopped and pointed at an old black-and-white photo of a much younger Wilford standing next to a tall gentleman wearing a British-style vest and hat. "This man, Carl Button, was one of the greatest men I've ever worked for, aside from the Monticello's. His empathy for his animals was nigh-on unmatched. I stayed with them for two decades until he passed away five years back, at which point I came here and have been ever since."

"What was he especially good at?" Alice stared at the old image. "I mean, how did he show empathy for the horses?"

"Well, Mr. Button never went for the pretty ponies." Wilford grinned proudly. "He always saw a special thing about a horse that maybe ran a little sideways or was a little undersized. He picked out the ones with the most heart and brought out the best in them, making himself millions in the process. If I could sniff out talented horses like he could, I might have been an owner someday, but I knew my place in the world and have always been happy just caring for them."

"You seem to love your job," Alice nodded, glancing around as the kids laid out a change of clothes in their stall. "And it seems you have much more work to do, even if we take those three geldings."

"Come what may," he said in agreement, looking around the room wistfully before flashing Alice a wide smile. "If you don't mind, I'd like to get cleaned up. Tangling with that charred wood left me feeling less than presentable."

Alice laughed. "Of course. I'll do the same."

"There's a hose off to the side, and we can clean up using that."

"Great."

They stepped outside with some washcloths and towels Wilford took from a bin, and soon they were in their bare feet with the spigot going, the cool, clean water splashing everywhere as they wiped off their legs and arms and faces. Soon, they were back inside and resting on their hay mattresses with the sounds of Wilford banging softly around the fire. The kids' comfortable whispers from the next stall over relaxed Alice and she quickly fell asleep without meaning to, dreaming of James, the farm, and the sunny days after their last full planting that turned out to be the largest crop yield ever. The laughter and fun of placing those first seeds into the soil, and them standing on opposite ends of the field and watering everything down in a fine mist were some of the best memories she'd ever had.

The sense of safety was dashed momentarily when she woke to the dim light of dusk filtering into the corridor, her panicked gaze darting around the unfamiliar location as Jake and Sarah spoke unintelligibly nearby. Sitting bolt upright, Alice reached for her rifle where she'd left it leaning against the wall until she remembered where they were and relaxed, slumping against the stall and taking several deep, ragged breaths to calm her nerves. Wiping the sleep from her eyes, she put her tennis shoes on and holstered her pistol, exiting into the passage where the smells of boiled meat, potatoes, and green beans rolled off the fire.

"Mmm. Smells good." Alice smiled approvingly as Sarah and Jake were actively involved in helping Wilford around the fire as he pointed at things and told them what to do.

"I hope you had a good nap," he said, turning with a grin.

"Yes, longer than I needed, but it was nice. Are these youngsters bothering you?"

"Oh, no. Not at all. Young Jake helped peel the potatoes, and your wonderful daughter made the salads and peeled the carrots. Everything is boiling up now."

"What are we cooking?" Alice stepped closer to the fire, peering inside the largest pot.

"Well, it all started as one thing or another." Wilford scratched his head. "But it seems to be merging into a stew, of sorts. We'll have big chunks of lamb and biscuits." He winked and nudged Jake in the side. "And this time, it'll be the big fluffy American ones."

"I can't argue with that. Do you need any help?"

"Just sit down, Mom," Sarah said as she moved around Wilford to drop a handful of carrots into the boiling water and checked the pot next to it. "We've got a couple of minutes left on the biscuits. Never cooked them in a cast-iron pot before."

"Cast-iron biscuits are the best," Wilford tutted in mock disapproval. "How did your mother *never* make you biscuits in a cast iron pan?"

"Hey now," Alice snorted in amusement and sat on a bin, twiddling her thumbs as she watched them work. "With that kind of talk, I'm definitely going to just sit down."

"We've got it, mom!" Jake dumped a little more flour into the stew pot.

"That's it, young Jake." The old man stirred it in. "Flour to thicken things up." Wilford turned to Alice, his spoon dripping savory gravy back into the pot. "I suppose you'll want to talk about posting guards for tonight."

"Aside from learning more about the horses, yes."

"That's great news," Wilford's shoulders sagged with the release of built-up tension as he stuck the stew spoon back in the pot and gave the mixture another stir. "I've been going crazy trying to keep up on everything and staying up half the night with worry. The only sleep I've gotten since all this started was a couple of winks here and there when I couldn't keep my eyelids open anymore."

"We'll certainly help with that. The kids can take a shift, and I'll cover the rest. We'll make sure you get some solid sleep tonight, Wilford. It's the least we can do, after all of your generosity toward us."

Soon, they were all sitting around the campfire as the sun went down, the light casting along the stable's main corridor and spilling out the side exits. Wilford talked to them about the horses they were taking as they all spooned in chunks of lamb, potatoes and carrots, giving Jake pointers about Rocky being unruly and that he shouldn't shy away from commanding the horse firmly.

"If you don't show mastery of old Rocky," the groundskeeper pointed out, "he'll take advantage of you."

"It's just like one horse I used to ride when I was learning," Jake said with a nod. "Don't worry, Wilford. I'll be able to handle him."

"Just remember, horses are smart creatures. If you want to control them, you can't use force. You have to outsmart them."

They talked a little more about Wilford's time as a groundskeeper, all of his favorite horses, and the beautiful, expansive farms he'd worked for over the decades, most notably the Button Farm, the one he was most proud of. After dinner, he served green tea for everyone, and Alice's eyelids drooped several times while she was sipping hers, until she finally gathered herself together and drained the cup.

"I'll take the first watch." She stood suddenly and entered the stall for her rifle, forcibly shaking off the sleep.

When she turned to go out, Wilford was waiting for her at the entrance with a grateful smile, speaking softly to her. "I don't know you, ma'am, but I keep thanking the heavens above that I missed when I shot at you. Thank you for doing this."

Alice patted his shoulder. "Wilford, you don't have anything to thank us for. A bit of company is no trade for three strong horses, a bed for the night and a delicious meal."

"Ah, see, that's where you'd be wrong. Even in the best of times, that wouldn't be such a bad trade. In these times, though? It's me who's the lucky one."

"We appreciate it, Wilford. Thank you. Just make sure you put your head down for a few hours, okay?"

"That I'll do."

Bidding the kids and Wilford a good night, Alice stood by the fire for a moment and then strode into the dark evening to stop on the soft gravel lane. She turned to her left and right, the oppressiveness of the sky heavy above her, not even the quiet chirping of the insects putting her at ease. Turning left, she walked east across the grounds past the stables where dense areas of seething red-orange glows kept the air warm and brushed off cinders to flutter upward like fireflies into the night.

Alice wandered the grounds for hours, moving along the fence line in the cool evening, taking a vaguely circular path around the stable. Peppercorn and Dawson were awake out in the field, their muscular shapes comforting in the night as they stood stoic against the cloudy sky with neither moon nor stars to provide much in the way of light. Aside from her rifle and revolver, Alice had a flashlight they'd found back in the department store outside Orlando, using it sparingly, the bright beam cutting through the darkness whenever she got off a path or gravel lane. She went west again, back down to the secondary stables to look in on Buck, Rocky, and Stormy, smiling as the young colt pranced back to the protection of his mother after she ruffled his short mane.

Moving east away from the secondary stables, Alice walked up the track to a small garden near the burned-out farmhouse to sit on a wide decorative stone where she'd paused a few times during her rounds. Knees drawn up to her chest, she stayed in the spot for a couple of hours with her rifle beside her, cheeks chilly as the wind picked up. With no moonlight to measure the passing of time, she could only give her best estimate on when to return to the stables and wake either Jake and Sarah or Wilford for the next watch.

Before heading back, she began one more patrol of the premises, starting with the rear of the property where the tool sheds and other small buildings still stood. She briefly flipped on her flashlight to get her bearings, leaving the garden area and returning to the gravel path toward the stables, and faintly in the distance remnants of their small campfire spilled from the stable corridors, promising warmth and a few hours of sleep.

A strange noise from behind caught her attention, and Alice quickly turned and slipped toward a tree in one of the garden patches. Crouching and squinting around the tree, Alice spotted a brief flash of light near the main house. She tucked her flashlight away and retraced her steps, angling north into the more extensive gardens, creeping behind trees and partial walls of latticework and vines, operating more by feel than any sort of sight. Three lights winked up by the farmhouse, shining around the burned-up ruins with one splitting off and heading toward the sheds and smaller barn with *Monticello Farms* written in bold. Someone shouted in the distance, and two more flashlights flipped on and ran back to the first one, the three beams converging on the barn's lettering.

Alice crept across the grounds, stepping through the gardens she'd passed on her patrols, intending to circle around to get a better idea of who they were dealing with. A pair of voices burst from her left, followed by a flashlight beam cutting directly in front of her. Holding back a gasp of surprise, she retreated behind the trees, squatting by a cluster of bushes with cold sweat running down her face, hoping she'd moved quickly enough to avoid being spotted. The light beam passed over the bushes and toward the stables before shifting the other way and Alice peeked up to see two men walking by, their silhouettes showing them both with rifles in their hands. They stopped and turned back to the farmhouse, where their companions were going through the barn and sheds on the other side, speaking loudly enough for her to hear them.

"I don't know about you, Roddy, but ain't much we can do with a bunch of farm tools. We need food, water, and some basic supplies."

"I feel you on that," Roddy replied. "Got to be something around here, even if it's horsemeat."

"You think the owners are coming back?" the first man asked, his rifle swinging toward the fence where Peppercorn and Dawson grazed.

"Judging from the looks of that house, they're either dead or weren't here when everything went up in flames."

The first man chuckled. "Even if they'd planned to return, they definitely aren't now. Not unless they're *walking*."

Roddy laughed. "There's not much to come home to. Let's go get the rest of the guys and start working around the place. Got to be some horses or cows or something around here we can use."

Alice stayed crouched in her hiding spot until the men circled to the front of the farmhouse with their flashlight beams drifting across the gravel path before turning toward the burned-up house, lingering on spots where it smoldered and glowed with orange coals. Rising from her cramped position, Alice went back through the gardens to the stables to wake the others, moving as stealthily as she could to avoid alerting the intruders.

From a distance, the glow of their firelight was dim, though it still stood out like a sore thumb beneath the starless sky. Passing the burned portion of the stables, she stepped into a side entrance to the intersection where the kids had fallen asleep near the fire on their sleeping bags, not even having made it back to their stall. Wilford was lying opposite them, snoring softly to the snapping flames, and she kneeled between Sarah and Jake and shook their shoulders before shifting to Wilford.

"Wilford," Alice whispered, gently squeezing his arm while looking back in the direction she'd come from. "Wilford, wake up."

The old man grumbled and snuffed, shaking himself and blinking blearily in a daze. "What is it, Alice? Is something wrong?"

She glanced past the fire toward the exit. "Some people are up by the main house, and at least two have rifles."

By then, the kids had stirred mostly awake and had raised onto their elbows as they watched their mother curiously.

"How many in total?" Wilford asked as he rose, throwing off his blankets and looking for his boots.

"Probably half a dozen." Alice shifted toward the kids and gestured for them to put on their shoes. "I couldn't count them all, but more than just the pair, for sure."

"What are they doing up there?"

"I overheard two of them say they were looking for food, although most were out by the sheds and going through the tools."

"Blasted ruffians." Wilford jerked his shoelaces tight and tied them before standing and fuming. His face was growing redder by the second as he turned in a full circle, huffed, and grabbed his shotgun where it leaned against a nearby stall. "How dare they come onto the Monticello's property and rifle through their things without a care in the world? Spineless bastards need to be taught a lesson!" Checking that the shotgun was loaded, he cocked the firearm with a *clack* and fixed Alice with a stern look. "I'm going to head up there and give them—"

Jake and Sarah had already put on their shoes and were standing near the fire when two shots rang out, one hitting the siding at the edge of the entryway, sending wood chips and shrapnel flying as bullet fragments zipped by. The next one skimmed the soft dirt at Sarah's feet, causing her to yelp and dance back.

"Careful!" Alice jumped over their sleeping bags and pulled them out of the intersection and into the east corridor with the stalls. "They must have seen us! Stay down!"

Stepping between them, Alice stood at the corner and peeked into the south passage where three flashlights were splitting off to the west while two more stood in the trees near where Peppercorn and Dawson had been located a short time earlier during her patrol. Shots rang out, ricocheting off the pots sitting near the campfire, causing Wilford to jump into the western corridor across from her.

"Here, Jake. Take the revolver." Resting her gun against a stall door, Alice took out her revolver and an autoloader from her pocket, handing them to her son. "Sarah, do you still have your knife?"

"Yeah, Mom... for all the good it will do me."

Wilford watched the lights of the intruders across the firelight, nostrils flaring and eyebrows bushed up. He started to come across to join the other three, but Alice waved him off.

"No, Wilford," she said. "I saw some moving around to the west side, so we need someone over there. They could come in from the north, too."

With an expression of barely controlled rage, Wilford gave a string of curses, barely understandable through his thick accent, and retreated, glancing along the west corridor before moving to the near corner and looking up through the north passage. A second later, he jerked the shotgun to his shoulder and fired a blast into the night.

"You bastards better get off my property," he shouted, "or I'll sting your arses with buckshot!"

Curses and laughter replied, and Alice shared a worried look with him as the sound of footsteps grew louder around them.

CHAPTER EIGHT

James Burton
Fayette, Missouri

James' boots shuffled and scuffed on the rough back road as he wound through the Missouri countryside, the two-lane highway quiet but for the sound of the close-pressed trees waving in the wind and the cry of birds singing to one another in the cool morning shade. Telephone poles and power cables laced together a string of small, single-story farmhouses just off the road or nestled in the dense green fields. Many were burned to the ground with blackened walls and collapsed roofs, looking rotted and sore like scabs on the hillside. Still others were intact, quiet, old-style structures with porch swings and clotheslines in the side yards, pink flamingos, and tiny gnomes standing in overgrown gardens. James stayed away from them all, always conscious of the rifle on his shoulder and revolver on his hip, warily watching every property he passed, feeling unseen eyes on him the whole time though he never spotted a single person. He crossed short concrete bridges and passed alongside rusted guardrails for miles without rest, with only the occasional cornfield or farmstead to break up his monotonous journey.

There were spun-out vehicles on the roadside, twisted and incinerated in ditches with glass scattered on the shoulder, pieces of red and gold plastic, aluminum trim, fenders, and tires blown out and seared to leave the pungent odor of burned rubber lingering in the air. Occasionally, James ran across an explosion in the middle of the road, some old tractor or a pickup truck left there with the remnants of their passengers being picked over by avian scavengers. James passed them all with his head down, mind and heart numbed to the sight of so much death, the thoughts of his wife, kids, and home driving him onward. As the sun rose higher and the wind died down, James wiped the sweat off his brow, suddenly wishing he had asked the guardsmen for a hat to keep the sun off his head.

Ahead was a gas station and a few other structures nestled against the surrounding cornfields, the cornrows stretching off to his right, the ears still growing at the tail end of what would have been the last harvest of the year. Off to his left, a few gentle hills were covered in leafy green trees, thick clusters of oaks, maples, and spruce that grew right up to the first set of buildings, including a small motel with a row of rooms facing the road and some old concrete structures with signs on the front or up on poles.

The gas station stood on the right with its dirty signpost perched high above the highway, leaning precariously and blackened on one side. A mess of exploded vehicles and debris spread out in front of it across the road, partially blocking the way through. At least two cars had blackened sides, one a long Buick while the other was a pickup truck split down the middle by the detonated gas tank. As he moved toward the center of the road, he could see around the cornrows to a diner off to the right with a gravel parking lot filled with burned-up cars and an expansive front window with smudged, dirty glass. The closer he came, he picked up the nervous chatter of horses and loud, agitated voices.

Slowing his strides, James craned his neck past the lot to see a pair of black buggies nosed into a wide alley on his side of the highway between the gas station and diner. One was a smaller buggy that could fit a small number of people, while the other was a larger, sturdier wooden supply wagon, covered with cloth. An unseen voice rose into an angry shout, followed by another man pleading in a softer voice, and James clenched his jaw and eased to the right-hand shoulder. The arguing intensified with a second man's stern voice joining the other agitated one, threatening and growling as the tension thickened.

James slipped to his right into the cornrows, crunching through the soft-packed earth and dry leaves that had fallen off and weathered, heading eastward to get in behind the gas station where the field cut around the buildings. Stepping lightly and using his stave to brush stalks out of the way, James came even with where he thought the horses and buggies were and crept forward until he could see what was happening between the swaying stalks. The two vehicles were just in sight, the smaller a typical black Amish buggy with its red turn signals jutting from the frame and the larger supply wagon with its sturdier sides. Each was driven by a pair of well-maintained horses with shiny chestnut coats and smooth leather bridles. Three Amish men stood in front of the horses, an older one out in front with his hands raised while two younger ones held the horses' reins behind him and tried to keep them calm, looking nervously between themselves.

The Amish leader was arguing with a trio of gruff men dressed in jeans and boots, two on the right wearing hunter's flannels and holding rifles while the man on the left wore cream-colored long underwear beneath a black t-shirt, a gleaming stainless-steel pistol in his hand. The Amish leader gesticulated, frowning from a gray-white beard that hung midway to his chest and rode scruffily up his jaws, though his upper lip was clean-shaven in the traditional Amish style.

"Please, don't do this," he pleaded in a wavering voice. "At least spare our horses so we can drive our families to safety."

"Don't tell us what to do!" The lead hunter bristled in his red and black checkered shirt, a camouflage hat perched perfectly atop his otherwise bald head. "You're in no position to give anyone orders. You're nothing but a bunch of freaks from the Stone Age. Now, hand over what you've got and we *might* let you live!"

"Please, don't!" The Amish leader sidestepped to stay in front of the brutish hunter.

The man raised his rifle and acted like he was about to strike the Amish man with the weapon's stock, causing the soft-spoken man to flinch away with his arms thrown up as the trio of thieves laughed.

The hunter glanced at his friends, scoffing and chuckling before addressing the Amish leader again. "Next time you get in my way, I won't hold back. I'll crack you right across the head and knock that stupid hat off your head. I'm serious." When the Amish man only slowly stood back up and raised his hands again, the hunter nodded satisfactorily. "Now, let's see what's inside those carts of yours."

The man in the long underwear and shirt started to circle to the buggy door, but a younger Amish man with a black beard stepped in front of him and threw his hands up to shove him back while the other young man with light-reddish facial hair blocked the second hunter as he tried to get around to the right.

"Please, sirs," the leader spoke again, glancing back with a pained face. "We have supplies and will gladly give them to you if you let us pass. We have enough to fill your bellies many times over. You won't be —"

The leader stepped forward and did as he had promised, the butt of his rifle coming in low and punched the Amish leader's gut, doubling him with a stiff grunt and a gush of air. The man didn't go down, but backpedaled to the horses, reaching up to steady himself by grabbing a bridle as he wheezed, trying to get words out. Getting his balance back, he stepped forward and faced the hunter with a pained expression, gaze humble as he pleaded.

"Please... sir. I'm... I'm begging you —"

The second hunter laughed and kicked at the red-bearded Amish man, missing but following up with a shove from his rifle that sent him staggering into the horses with a cry.

"Let's see what they've got in here!" The second hunter circled past the horses to the buggy door.

The Amish man with the black beard started to intervene, but the thief in the long johns caught him by his jacket, swept his foot behind him, and shoved him to the ground so he landed with a grunt. The other young Amish, with the red beard, started to reach for his friend until he found the barrel of a rifle sticking in his chest, the leader of the thieves wagging his finger mockingly.

The second hunter threw the buggy door open, and a young woman's voice came from inside as she shrieked. When the Amish leader groaned and tried to get around the horses, the lead thief raised his rifle high and pulled it over the taller man's head, squeezing and trapping him with his arms pressed to his sides, dragging him backward away from the endangered woman as his wide-brimmed hat tumbled to the pavement.

"No!" the Amish man called with a choke and a gasp, swinging his tall form back and forth but unable to break the hunter's hold.

The second hunter pulled a woman from the buggy with several others shrieking in a sudden caterwaul of protest. He had her by the collar of her dress, pale blue in the morning light, her bonnet flying off and silky gray hair flying free as she struggled to get loose. For a moment she broke free until the man snatched a handful of hair and dragged her away.

James watched everything happen with a nervous fear gnawing at his gut. A part of him told him to move on, seeing as he'd be no match for three men with guns, and the commotion was more than enough of a distraction to allow him to slip by unmolested. The second hunter flipped the woman around and thrust her to her hands and knees and kicked her in the side, and she doubled over, clutching the back of her head and holding her belly with pained sobs. His rifle swung around and pressed to her temple, where strands of gray hair blew against the black metal.

"Please, no!" the Amish leader wailed, one hand thrown up and the other clawing at the rifle around his neck. "Don't hurt Clara!"

"Oh screw *this*," James growled. A group of people unwilling to defend themselves even in the face of being completely slaughtered was too much for him to bear. Rolling his shoulders, he shrugged off his backpack, laid his staff beside it, and took up his weapon. He stepped carefully between the cornstalks, aiming at the hunter who was bumping the woman's head with his rifle barrel.

With a pleading expression, palms pressed together, the woman begged, "Please, just take what you want and leave us in peace! I beg of you!"

The woman and children in the buggy whined in the background, though the trio of thieves only laughed and snickered.

"Wait, wait wait. Don't shoot her just yet, man!" The leader said. "We may need some extra hands to take with us. We'll have to do all the work ourselves if we shoot them all."

"You're right," The one holding the gun on the woman ran his tongue across his greasy mustache as he backed off and rested his rifle on his shoulder. "Pretty smart thinking."

"Get them out of there and line them up," The leader said. "We'll pick out the strongest-looking ones to take with—"

With the second hunter standing out on his own with nothing but the sky and fields of corn behind him, James fired a single shot that penetrated the man's skull above his left eye socket, exiting the back in a spray of blood and bone that splashed the Amish woman and cut off her shriek. The other two thieves jerked stiffly in shock, jaws hanging open as the man crumpled and hit the ground. The leader of the former trio of thieves released his captive, shouldering his rifle and spinning toward the corn rows to zero in where James was barely visible among the stalks. James didn't hesitate, squeezing the trigger twice, one round striking his target's left arm and tearing flannel and flesh in a burst of blood, the second round piercing dead center in the sternum, striking with the force of a hammer blow. The thief's rifle slipped from his hands and clattered to the pavement as his body weakened, and he glanced at the hole in his chest before raising his eyes to James, blinking once, and collapsing in a heap next to his companion.

The last man, wearing his long johns and a t-shirt, dropped his weapon as James strode out of the cornrows, rifle pointed at his chest. The would-be thief's smile slipped off his face as he backpedaled into one of the younger Amish men who stood aside and let him stagger and trip to the ground. James tracked him carefully as he strode ahead, and the man rolled over, flailing and screaming in fear as he scrambled to escape.

James stepped between the people he'd just rescued, not lifting his finger off the trigger or deviating his aim until the final thief was far away, sprinting toward the highway, flying to the other side and cutting between the buildings, diving into the fields and running beyond them. The Amish leader ran to the gray-haired woman who was kneeling and wiping blood off her face with her fingers. Stooping beside her, he got her on her feet while the younger men observed James. After getting an assured nod she was okay, the Amish leader rose from his crouch and turned to face James with an uncertain gaze, hands slightly raised.

With his heart still racing, James turned and smiled at the small crowd, lowering his rifle and approaching slowly with a half-wave. "Are you folks okay?"

"We are now, thanks to you." The leader glanced at the crying woman once more before gesturing to the man with the red beard. "Abram, go help your mother." Turning back to James, he took two hesitant steps forward. "You... won't use that on us, will you?"

James slung the rifle on his shoulder and held out his hand. "Not at all. Sorry about all of... that. Are you folks alright?"

"We are, thanks to you." The man shook James's hand and his shoulders sank slightly, one arm drifting to his bruised stomach as he winced. "I imagine things would've gotten far, far worse if you hadn't come along." He offered a hesitant smile. "I am Eli Bontrager, and the red-bearded fellow is my son, Abram. The other is Jacob Mast, my son-in-law." He turned and gestured at the crying woman, firmly nestled in Abram's arms. "And this is my wife, Clara."

James nodded at each of them in turn as Eli introduced them. "I'm James Burton. The folks in the wagons are your family, I presume?"

"One big one," Eli replied with a smile. "There's my wife and me, our son and daughter, and their spouses and children. The women and children are in the back, of course. We tried to shelter them from harm, for all the good it seems to have done."

Past Eli, the curtains were drawn behind the driver's seats so no one could see in. "I'm glad everyone is okay, Eli."

Abram turned and handed Clara off to a younger Amish woman with red hair who stepped from the buggy, her expression frightened and a cry lifting from her mouth when she saw Clara's blood-speckled face.

"Are you okay, Mother?" She rushed over and wiped the flecks off, stopping as if fearful of touching her.

"Yes, Esther." Clara held her crimson fingertips up with a look of exasperation. "It's just all this *blood*...."

Esther glanced back and gestured to someone inside the buggy. "Betty, grab a clean rag for my mother, please. She's got blood all over her."

Eli found his hat, dusted it off, and placed it on his head. With a heavy sigh, he stared at the two dead men and rested his hands on his hips, squinting with one eye at James. "That was some fine shooting there, friend. Praise the Lord that he kept us safe this day and delivered us from evil with our own personal guardian angel." Eli chuckled. "Thank you, sincerely, for your willingness to risk your well-being for strangers. Not many would have done that before this calamity, and fewer still after."

James moved a pace closer and shrugged. "I was just passing through and saw what was happening. Couldn't stand to let a few bullies get their way."

Exchanging a hesitant glance with his father, Abram stepped around the sprawled dead men with one hand out. "We are *truly* blessed to meet such a friendly face as yours on this dangerous road."

James accepted Abram's handshake, and Jacob stepped up last with a grateful nod and a firm shake, followed by patting James on the shoulder. "Thank you, my friend. You saved my mother-in-law's life."

"No problem at all," James replied. "Glad I could help."

A towheaded boy of about ten jumped out of the buggy and stared at the dead men, their blood filling in the cracks of the pavement and forming jagged crimson halos around them. "You shot them!" he shouted, his expression torn between horror and disgust. "You *killed* someone!"

"John, get back in the buggy!" Abram scolded the boy and turned to James. "I apologize for my son, John's, behavior. It's been... difficult for him."

"It's okay, Abram. Last week, I would've been shocked at having to shoot someone, let alone two, but as you say, things have been difficult."

Speaking about the pair of killings brought a sick sense of dread that gripped his chest and squeezed. He rolled his shoulders, loosening his upper body, trying to breathe evenly and calm the shakes in his arms as the remnants of adrenaline faded from his veins.

"You say you were just passing through?" Eli asked, his gray eyes piercing from a thin face filled with age and hard work. "Whereabouts are you headed?"

"I'm on my way to Michigan to get home... outside East Lansing, actually. How about you folks?"

"We have family out east in Indiana." Eli took off his hat and wiped his sleeve across his sweaty forehead, squinting into the eastern sky. "We knew the road would be long and tough, but we did not expect bandits like those to come upon us so quickly or violently."

Abram stepped up. "I just don't understand, father," he said. "We would have given those men whatever they wanted, but some devil got inside them and wouldn't let them see reason."

"There's a lot of reason missing from the world right now," James acknowledged with a sad smile, Eli raising an eyebrow and nodding imperceptibly in agreement.

"I am of the mind that people should work together and not against each other," Eli added. With a pat on James' shoulder, he nodded fervently. "Thankfully, you came along. A genuine miracle and angel sent by the Lord our Father. You rescued us from certain death."

Swallowing uncomfortably at the repeated praise, James nodded at the wagon, "Seems like you could've used one of those shotguns you have hanging in your buggy there. Why didn't you defend yourselves? Did they ambush you before you had a chance?"

Eli and Abram exchanged knowing looks before Eli explained. "Violence is not our way, James. The shotguns are for hunting and hunting alone. It goes against our beliefs to raise them against another human being."

"Not to disrespect your religion or yourselves," James said, "but you may wish to... revise your way of thinking given what's happening out on the road. I've seen far, far worse than this in the places I've been. Believe me, it's only going to get worse."

The Amish looked amongst themselves, sharing a confused look before Eli replied. "How could changing our beliefs help us? We should stand more firmly for what we believe in these trying times. The Lord always tests us, and how firm would our faith be if we turned our backs on it just because we have been threatened?"

"*Threatened?*" James couldn't stifle a chortle of disbelief. "Your family could have been slaughtered right here where those two dead men lay if I hadn't come along."

Eli glanced at the corpses, though instead of being alarmed by James' words, he merely smiled knowingly. "And that is a fulfillment of our faith, James. Our Lord has protected us with *you*."

Biting back a harsh retort, James lowered his tone. "I'm a man of faith, Eli. Not your... flavor of it, but I am a believer. And while I respect what you're saying, I still think you should reconsider your stance on self-defense. You may not always have a guardian angel waiting in the wings." With a nod, he started to turn away. "Well, folks, I'm happy to have helped, but I need to get back on the road. My things are just there in the cornfield, so I'll wish you good luck and be on my way. And I'd advise you to leave as soon as possible in case the guy that got away comes back with friends."

With a sharp inhale of surprise, Eli twisted to stare across the street where the escapee had gone, then he looked at his son. "James is right, Abram. I hadn't even considered that more men might come back to test us again so soon."

James returned to the cornfield and found his backpack, shrugging it on and adjusting his carbine, leaving the two men to talk while he prepared to get back on the road. Eli was gesturing at the highway and then at James, while Abram stood with his hands on his hips, shaking his head.

Grabbing his walking stick, James walked over to wish them a last farewell. "Okay, guys. I'm going to head out. Good luck to you all."

Abram looked as though he was going to speak before Eli held up a hand and turned, squaring up to James with a smile. "Why don't you come with us?"

"No thanks." James smiled thinly. "I don't want to be a bother."

"Won't you even consider it?" Eli gave an expectant glance at Abram, who seemed reluctant at first, but stepped forward with a more enthusiastic nod.

"It's the least we could do in exchange for your help," Abram agreed. "We have plenty of food."

James jerked his thumb at his backpack. "Thanks, guys, but I've got all the supplies I need right here."

Eli's brow furrowed. "That may be true, but we can also give you a *ride*. You'd fit in the front seat of my buggy beside me and could ride in comfort for a while until the Lord puts us on different paths."

The thought of riding brought back the memory of the train, the first time James had gotten a break since the airport. His long march through the Missouri back roads had done him no favors, his aching heels and arches, ankles and knees still sore from the previous day. On the other hand, riding with a larger group might prove even more dangerous, with the horses and clattering wagons drawing the attention of more nefarious souls.

Eli pressed. "Tell me, friend. Where are you going? What is your next stop? We'd planned to try and cross the river at Hannibal and head to Indiana from there."

James eyed Eli warily for a long moment before laughing and shaking his head. "You won't believe this, but Hannibal is actually the exact spot I'd planned on going next."

Eli grinned broadly, lifting his hands and tilting back his head. "Do you see? This is clearly an ordained meeting, my friend. Please... you *must* accept our invitation. We'd love to have our guardian angel travel with us, even if it's only for a short part of your journey."

James nearly declined the offer again, then changed his mind at the last second letting out a resigned sigh and a slight snort. "All right then… I'm not your guardian angel, mind you, but I'd be happy to travel with you folks for a bit. My feet could use the break."

Abram grinned. "Wonderful! Let me introduce you to our family."

"First, we should cover up these bodies," James said. "I'd rather not upset anyone else. They're…" He gestured at the corpses. "Not a pleasant sight."

Eli nodded and turned. "Clara, could you—"

"I'll get some old throwaway blankets." The family's matriarch had snapped out of her shock and was all business, grabbing Esther and taking her to the larger supply wagon.

A moment later, the women returned with blankets, which they lay reverently on the dead men. To James' surprise, the Amish women stood over the bodies and began to pray, with Abram, Eli, and Jacob joining them and affording their would-be thieves and murderers the same respect they would give any of their own flesh and blood. James stood off to the side as they prayed, watching their reverence, the weight of his rifle heavy on his shoulder and that same feeling of discomfort swirling in his gut. As soon as the prayers were done, Eli said, "Amen!" and turned with wide-sprung arms and a smile. "Let's introduce James to the family!"

Soon, the Amish were helping others out of the buggy and wagon, and everyone lined up to thank James for saving them and their supplies. Eli and Clara re-introduced their son, Abram and their daughter, Esther, a hardy woman with deep red hair to match her brother's beard. Abram was married to a golden-haired woman named Betty, and they had two children that shared the same expressive green eyes and shy demeanors, Sadie and John, whom James had met earlier. Esther was the wife of Jacob, and they had two young ones as well, each with dark crops of hair. All the children were within a few years of each other, ranging in age from ten to thirteen.

"Good to meet you all." James smiled and greeted each in turn, shaking each of their hands.

One moment the group had been on the verge of being wiped out, and in the next they were openly laughing and surrounding James with excited chatter, embracing him and patting his arms and shoulders

"You have a beautiful extended family," he said to Eli. "It seems pretty risky bringing them out here like this."

Eli cleared his throat as he adjusted his hat, lowering his voice as he spoke. "We came from a settlement near Hutchinson, Kansas when fires broke out through the settlement. We'd just been in the middle of some stormy weather, and high winds carried cinders and smoke from one farmhouse to the next in our tight-knit community. We were blessed to escape with our lives and a few possessions. Many others in the community were… not."

The women lowered their heads, joining hands with the children. Esther seemed to take it harder than the rest, and Clara and Betty descended on her, locking their arms with hers and leaning against each other.

"I'm sorry to hear that, Eli. Really, I am."

"Yes, well, I suppose that's just the Lord's way, and we're mere watchers in the storm."

James gave a non-committal 'hm,' doing his best to hold his tongue as Eli raised his voice and gestured at his sons. "I suppose we should move along now. Abram and Jacob, please get the carts turned around. After that, we'll unhitch the horses and use them to clear the blockage from the road."

"How can I help?" James asked.

"Please, James," Eli beamed, "Just rest, and allow us to show you what *we* can do. I promise we'll be on our way shortly."

With a nod, James walked to the street and found a bench in front of the diner, staying out of the way of the group and giving his feet a much-needed rest. The narrow lane was clogged by burned-up wreckage and had become an easy way for the thieves to trap people in the choke point. Depending on how quickly the trio had set up their ambush, the Amish group might not have been the first to fall victim to the trap, considering that both James and the Amish had both come down the route and had been traveling from two different locations.

After taking a few moments to discuss what they were going to do, the group sprang into action like a well-oiled machine, working as a team, driving the buggy and wagon back onto the road facing eastward. Abram and Jacob unhitched the horses and used ropes and chains to tether them to different parts of the wreckage, Eli standing by and pointing at places in the wrecks that would give them the most leverage. Within thirty minutes, they had all four horses ready to pull, and Abram gave a hearty slap on the horses' flanks to get them moving. With whinnies and snorts, the horses pulled mightily against the rope and chain tethers, hauling the charred hulks of vehicle frames off the road with grinding and screeching on the pavement.

The horses strained and snorted, tossing their heads as Abram and Jacob held the reins and encouraged them to bear down and pull. A long-bodied Buick ripped free of an SUV in a tear of metal and plastic, with more glass scattering across the pavement, its frame dragged away on the pair of wheels that worked while the others scraped against the ground, kicking up sparks and an awful racket. James started to get up and help remove some of the debris left over, but the Amish children scrambled from the shadow of the supply wagon and attacked the chore before he could stand, grabbing bits of plastic and metal and weather strips to carry them to the side of the road and place them in a pile. With the Buick out of the way, Eli stepped in and helped Abram and Jacob get the horses back in their harnesses, ready to pull the buggy and supply wagon through the newly-created gap along the road.

The children scrambled eagerly back into their designated seats, laughing and jostling with each other, their giggles a stark contrast to the death and destruction that lay around them. James smiled, the sounds reminding him of his own children, giving him hope that they – and his wife – had somehow faced down the odds and survived.

With the horses hooked back up to the wagon and buggy, Eli waved for James to come on up. Leaving his bench, James climbed up next to the Amish leader and sat on the seat, placing his pack behind him while Abram and Jacob sat together on the supply wagon to share the driving responsibilities. James placed his tactical stick on the floorboard beneath his feet and rested his carbine in his lap.

While Clara got the children organized and calmed for the next leg of their journey, Eli gave a light crack of the reins and a soft "Hup!" to the horses, and they were off, circling the SUV's wreckage and moving eastward into the warm afternoon sun.

James leaned out of the side of the buggy, glancing back, spying the two dead men still with blankets covering them and small bouquets of wildflowers resting on their chests, which the children and wives had gathered from the roadside. It was a simple gesture, understated, one of kindness in the face of brutality; a reminder that though the world might be teetering on the precipice, the actions of those in it still possessed the power to tip the scales.

CHAPTER NINE

Ryan Cooper
Somewhere Outside East Lansing, Michigan

Ryan was stretched out on the couch when someone gently shook him and he jerked awake, shifting in his awkward position where his back had gone stiff, rolling in panic on the cushions and looking up at the dark figure standing over him. Rubbing his eyes, he recognized the soft blonde-gray hair falling past the figure's shoulders and sighed with relief when she leaned closer with her hands clasped in front of her.

Relaxing back and wiping his hand down his face, Ryan said, "I'm sorry, honey. I must have fallen straight over and gone to sleep."

"It's okay, dear. You were only out for a few minutes."

"You shouldn't have to keep watch over me, too." Hauling his legs off the couch, he placed his feet on the floor and sat up with a groan that was half back ache and half disappointment at himself for falling asleep. "What time is it?"

"It's around six forty-five, and it's daylight now." Helen stepped back to show sunlight streaming through the cracks in the boarded-up windows. "We're in the clear for the moment. Want something to eat?"

"Absolutely."

Waving her off when she tried to help him off the couch cushions, Ryan stood and groaned, taking a few experimental twists to loosen up and checking on the state of his prosthetic before following Helen into the dining room. The smell of roasted coffee hung in the air, and daylight filtered in through the blinds where Helen had been keeping watch. The book she'd been reading was closed, and by the state of the bookmark she'd made little progress. A breakfast of Danishes, warm eggs, and coffee sat on the table, and he fell into the chair with a grateful nod.

"This looks great, honey. I could use an injection of coffee right into my veins."

"I've already been through half a pot myself," she sat at the head of the table to his right. "And these are the last of our Danishes, so I hope you enjoy yours. Might be a little stale."

"I'll take it." Ryan nodded to a tall glass sitting nearby. "And milk, too?"

"We've got more than enough, so drink it up. I figure we need all the energy we can get, so I'm officially letting you off your diet."

Ryan took a bite of his apple Danish, followed by a long drink of milk before speaking again. "How many times did we see someone out on the road overnight?"

Helen nibbled at her Danish, chewed, wiped her hands off, and leaned forward to consult her notebook. "Twelve times where we could see flashlights and figures." Reaching for her glass of milk, she pushed the notebook toward him.

Ryan craned his neck and scanned her notes. "But nobody crossed onto the property, which is good. Still, if that intruder we shot has friends, they'll be looking for him."

"Especially after all that gunfire." With a sigh, Helen closed her eyes and slowly shook her head, "What can we do now?"

Ryan put down his half-empty glass and placed his hand over hers. "Is something else bothering you?"

"It just seems so overwhelming right now." She shivered. "It feels like the predators are surrounding us, and now we're stuck behind these walls every night just to stay alive."

"That's partially true." Ryan leaned back in his chair and stretched his arms over his head, yawning and turning his head back and forth until his neck gave a satisfying crack. "But we have the defensive advantage here."

"That might be true, but what about the animals? They're just out there in the yard, and these people could pick them off one-by-one or make a big run for the chicken coop. If we lose that, we'll be hurting bad."

"They could go for the animals, but we've still got the car up by the house and a bumper crop of harvested food sitting right outside our back door." Ryan rested his elbows on the table, chin on his clenched hands as he mused. "And they probably think we have an arsenal of weapons here."

"Which we kind of do."

"Right. That's why they'll probably go for the house, instead. They can try the chicken coop and risk one of us taking potshots at them, but they'll have to be worried about their buddy, and they'll be hesitant to be caught out in the open. No, their target will be us. If they get us out of the way...." Ryan let the implication hang in the air.

"It would be a big step for them, with their houses likely burned down." Helen took it a step farther. "And with three working vehicles, taking us out would be like winning the lottery for them."

"Let's decrease their odds. What do you say?"

"I'm on board with that."

Ryan slapped his palms on the table. "Good. Let's set up some defenses and make it as hard for them as possible. If they're going to attack us, we'll make it an uphill battle."

"Okay."

"We'll start in the garage. We'll need a hammer and as many nails as we can find. Can you go out there and check?"

"Yeah, I can do that. No problem. What are you going to do?"

"I'm going downstairs to look for some wood scraps and other materials. There're probably some scraps out in the barn, too. I'll let you know when I head out there so you can watch my back."

Finishing his breakfast, Ryan crossed to the window for a quick look at the big red maples in the yard waving in a soft breeze. The ducks were all waking up, flapping and swimming around the ponds, oblivious to the upcoming battle, and when he didn't see anyone in the yard or down by the Jones' house, he turned to hug Helen and head downstairs.

"Do you want me to fix a thermos of coffee for you?"

He gripped her in an embrace but quickly let go and moved off anxiously. "That would be outstanding, honey. Thank you."

"Take Diana with you!" Helen called after him, the big dog's ears perking up at the sound of her name.

In the workshop with his flashlight to light his way and Diana trailing behind him, James found a few scraps of some building material, thinner pieces of wood that could be easily hidden beneath the windows and on the stairs. When he looked behind the door, he found a long box full of spare hardwood that matched the deep oak slats. With those under one arm and the scraps in the other, he exited the workshop. The big dog was cumbersome and bumped him excitedly as he went upstairs, and Ryan shoved her aside with his hips and snapped his fingers to get her out of the way.

"Come on, Diana," he scolded her. "You're going to kill me if you keep getting underfoot. How'd you like to read those headlines? Man with bum foot trips over dog on stairs... breaks neck. Then again, with no more newspapers, maybe you're the reason all this is happening." Ryan chuckled as he reached down and ruffled her fur good-naturedly. "Yeah, you big lug. You're the reason for all this, aren't you?"

Usually the quieter of the three dogs, Diana seemed especially agitated as she followed him around, though Ryan chalked it up to his own nervous tension rubbing off on her. Upstairs, the house was dim in the growing morning light, and he put the wood on the dining room table and opened the blinds. Duke and Duchess were quiet and still lounging around, not alerting to anything, and a quick scan of the yard through the cracks he'd left in the boards satisfied his paranoia, and he turned away and went to the garage.

Helen was waiting for him, lining up items on James' narrow workbench which stood against the back wall. She'd pulled out a couple of sawhorses with a single sheet of plywood resting on them, and Ryan placed his wood down and turned to the workbench.

"What do you have here?" he asked.

"I found two hammers, a mallet, and more nails and screws than we'll know what to do with."

"Good job. And a big thanks to James for being well-stocked with building supplies."

"What do we do with all this stuff?" Helen asked.

Ryan turned in a slow circle, scanning shelves with other tools he had to work with, letting thoughts flow over him as he mulled over some simple tricks that might buy them time should anyone attempt to attack the house. "We don't have a ton of time to get very elaborate, and we've already got the lower windows covered. I found some hardwood slats we could put some nails through and set up in the laundry room. We don't have to replace pieces of the floor but just lay them on top so that the wood grain matches. If someone comes through the garage and into the laundry room, they'll be stepping on nails."

"Ouch."

Ryan frowned. "The only problem is that we've gotta be careful because the dogs will be running around in the house, so we have to keep the laundry room door shut."

"Gotcha."

Something caught Ryan's eyes on one shelf, and he strode over to pick up a blowtorch, rolls of solder and some heavy-duty duct tape. Hefting them with a grin, he said, "We could solder razor blades to the outside doorknobs, and I've got an idea for the steps out there, too."

Helen made a disgusted face before it changed to a wicked grin. "That sounds terrible. Where did you get such awful, amazing ideas from, Ryan Cooper?"

"Remember when the catalytic converters were getting stolen every other day back on the farm and then the thefts suddenly stopped?"

"Ryan!" She gave him a slap on the arm, laughing. "You didn't!"

A sly smile spread across his face. "There was a *lot* of blood on the ground. The catcons stopped going missing, too. Funny coincidence, that."

"You're terrible. So, we need razor blades?"

"Yep. They'll be in small boxes where he keeps the box cutters, and there'll be some inside the knife handles themselves. While you look for those, I'll try to find some epoxy glue and stakes."

Helen had been looking through workbench drawers when she stood and fixed him with a narrowed eye. "Epoxy glue and stakes? What other torture devices are you thinking up?"

Ryan grinned. "Don't worry about it. Just find me those razor blades, and we'll be in business. I'll head out to the shed here in a minute, so keep a weather eye out."

In James' downstairs workshop, he found the epoxy in a bin with duct tape and other sealants and glues. Sticking the tube in his pocket, he went upstairs and out the back door, taking Duchess with him as he searched the sheds where they kept the garden tools. As he suspected, there was a bucket of wooden stakes, wire fencing, and wood scraps. As he carried them to the house, Ryan scanned their surroundings, checking for any signs of movement in the woods east of the property and out past the solar panels and field they'd recently harvested. Sweat was trickling down his sides as he returned to the garage, panting, limping and finally stopping to catch his breath.

"Found some razor blades!" Helen said, holding up a small box of them and gesturing at two box cutters she'd taken apart and gotten the blades from as well. "I say we have a good forty or fifty of them. You're going to put them on the outside doorknobs, right?"

"Exactly. If anyone tries to grab the doorknob in the dark and throw their weight around..." Turning sideways, he mimicked gripping a doorknob and throwing his shoulder forward. "They'll get a big surprise."

"Are you going to tell me what those stakes are for?" Helen faced up to him with her hands on her hips.

"Area denial barriers," Ryan replied flatly.

"And those are?"

"We've got those two red maples right out front and several in back they could use for cover if they approach the house, and I want to deny them that space." When Helen only looked more confused, Ryan explained. "I'm going to put these stakes in the ground in the blind spots around the tree trunks, pointing up. That way, if they try to run up to the tree and take cover, they'll have to move one way or the other, and they'll be in the open for us to shoot."

"Right where we can see them." Helen ticked her head to the side. "But these are just wooden stakes. They're dull, and someone could just step on them or kick them aside."

Ryan held up his finger with a grin and a wink. "That's why we'll put nails in strips of hose and wood and hide them around the stakes. The stakes will keep the dogs from running through those areas and getting hurt, and if a person tries to stomp on a stake, they'll get a nail in their foot for their troubles."

"That sounds awful! I love it. What about the epoxy?"

Ryan took the tube out of his pocket and held it up with a shake. "We'll use this epoxy to glue nails to the steps out front and maybe bury some around the window areas. They'll try to come in from the front because they'll think there's more cover there, but they'll find nothing to hide behind, and we'll keep shooting at them until they leave. If they get past us to try any of the doors... they'll pay for that, too."

"Bloody feet and bloody hands," Helen smiled back. "That's what they'll get for their troubles. I like it."

"Let's start with hammering some nails through these wood scraps and hose. Once we get everything built, we'll get out there and place them."

Side-by-side and throughout the afternoon, Ryan and Helen prepared their traps, drilling, nailing, and drawing a quick layout to mark where the pieces would go. They took breaks to make sweeps of the house, putting food and supplies in various rooms on all the floors in case they had to stay in one place for an extended period of time. By midday, they'd placed nail boards in the laundry room and closed the door to keep the dogs from hurting themselves and with rifles on their shoulders and a pair of binoculars around Ryan's neck, they walked out front with the dogs. They moved from one tree to the next, placing the wooden stakes around the blind spots behind the trees, held down by mesh fencing with nail boards and spiked hoses on top.

"The dogs should see the stakes and avoid all this," Ryan said, calling them over and letting them sniff at the area, telling them 'no' repeatedly before they turned and bounded away. "I hope."

"You don't sound too sure." Helen said.

"Well, I mean... I *think* they'll be fine. They should be inside or around the house with us, unless something unforeseen happens. But it's a chance we'll have to take. We can't have people hunkering down behind things and taking easy potshots at us."

They moved on to the next red maple and fixed up some areas at the rear of the house. With a few remaining stakes, they placed them at the shielded corners of the sheds, where people might try to take cover and fire around. In spite of his initial excitement over the idea, he'd grown a bit more leery over how well the plan might work, but looking back at how they'd anchored them and placed the nail boards and spike strips, he was convinced they'd be more than annoying.

"See how this works? When they come up to take cover behind the trees, they'll – at a minimum – have to deal with a bunch of sharp stuff that they'll either have to clear out or get punctured by. Either way, they'll be left in the open for at least a short amount of time."

Helen was placing the last stake through the mesh fencing, treating the dangerous areas like a garden, pushing clusters of grass together and sprinkling in some mulch so they covered the nail-ridden boards and spiked hose. Stepping back, she gazed over their handiwork. "Ryan Cooper, you may just be a genius."

"You can call me a genius if we survive the night." He gave her a quick side hug. "Now, I'm going to work on the door-knobs and start hammering up some more wood over the lower windows."

"Do you need any help with that?"

Ryan glanced up at the darkening afternoon sky. "We might be better served if you kept watch. If they're coming, it'll probably be soon."

"Sounds good to me." Helen raised an eyebrow. "While I'm in there, I'll whip up something for dinner. Omelet?"

Ryan laughed. "I'll take anything at this point. Keep the dogs close, and do us a favor and double check on the food and water we spread around the house on all the floors, just in case we end up having to stay in one spot for a while."

As Helen returned to the house and started on the food and her watch, Ryan adjusted the rifle on his shoulder and picked up the binoculars he had hanging around his neck. He did another quick scan of the property from the side yard, gazing past the red maples lining their driveway and sweeping across the east side of the property where the woods were the thickest, all the way back to the barnyard where the animals waited for their daily feeding. The chickens clucked loudly, annoyed at being penned up in the coop all day, but letting them wander was out of the question until things settled down.

With everything looking good, he returned to the house and gathered the hammer, nails, and spare wood they'd collected. Ryan nailed up more pieces over the windows next to the ones he'd placed the day before, leaving just enough space between them to shoot through, and by the time he'd started epoxying nails to the front steps, it was already growing darker.

"Even if they're watching," he mumbled, "they won't have a clue what we're doing." He carefully placed each two-inch nail and squirted drops of quick-drying epoxy all around them, testing each one to find them almost impossible to move, even when he kicked at them. "This is going to be better than I thought."

With a whole box left, he stuck some into the mulch around the windows and covered them. Next came the razor blades, which he attached to the exterior doorknobs just behind the knobs' curve so the sharp edges would barely stick out, and it would take a hammer or screwdriver to pry them off. In the dwindling daylight, he broke out his flashlight and checked his handiwork, pushing on the blades, finding them rigid all the way around. A shiver ran up his spine as he imagined grabbing the doorknob with his entire hand and giving it a turn.

"That's going to hurt," he chuckled darkly, taking one more look around the front yard before carefully turning the front of the knob with both hands and stepping inside. He grabbed all his tools, kicked any loose items off the porch, and shut the door behind him, locking the handle and the deadbolt. Helen stood by the dining room table, setting out some plates with cheese-covered omelets and home fries, her rifle lying across the table for ease of access.

"Dear, that smells wonderful."

"You all finished up?"

"I am now." Ryan dropped the bucket of tools with a clank and crossed to his usual chair, sliding into it with a wince as his joints and muscles cried out in pain, his lower back strained from stooping, hammering, and stretching all day. He took giant bites of his food, stopping only to sip at his drink and compliment Helen a few times, his body too close to the breaking point for him to do anything except put in fuel as fast as possible.

"You should stop making such good food," he chuckled around a mouthful of food as he finished the last two bites, dropped his fork, and sat back with a sigh.

"Don't count on it for too much longer... especially if we have a fight on our hands."

"No kidding."

"Is everything set?"

"We got a lot done today, and I think it'll work better than I thought it would." He shook his head and rested his hands across his belly. "Those are some solid deterrents for such quick work. You checked the food and water setup on all three floors, right?"

"We've got a couple of weeks' worth of food on every floor... some in the master bedroom upstairs, some in the laundry room and garage down here, and even more down in James' workshop. No matter where we are, we should be able to hole up and survive as long as we need to."

Ryan nodded. "I expect they'll come up from the front because they won't want to rile the animals and give us fair warning. Plus, they'll *think* there're more places to take cover behind."

"At least until they get there and find that they can't shoot at us from behind the trees," Helen replied smartly.

"That's why we have to guard the front and back at all times. If we can catch one of them out there..." Ryan closed his fist and bounced it firmly on the table. "We just need to discourage them from getting to the front door. If we can do that, we win."

"What if James or Alice and the kids come up?"

"If anyone comes up not shooting at us, we'll let one of the dogs go out and determine if they're our people. I'd imagine we'd know immediately, though, and we'll take them out if they're not. No negotiations, no waiting around, and no allowing anyone to gain the upper hand on us. I'm not getting sprayed at with buckshot again."

"Oh, now, it barely grazed you. Didn't even need a band-aid, you big baby." Helen winked at him as she finished the last of her omelet, washed it down with a drink of milk, and then picked up her cup of coffee. "In all seriousness, this sounds like as good of a plan as we're going to come up with on such short notice. Let's just hope we can win."

With a grim look, Ryan took his cup as well and they both sipped, his nerves wired beneath his exhaustion, stomach twisting with nervousness, hoping he could protect the woman he loved.

CHAPTER TEN

Alice Burton
Monticello, Florida

Growling at the intruders like a rabid dog, Wilford fired another shotgun blast from the north passage into the night. A handful of return fire answered the old man, the bullets driving him back into the main passage where he threw his shoulders against a stall as pieces of wood and dust flew off the corner. Alice caught his angry look in the firelight as a spattering of rounds came at them from both sides. Jake was next to her, ducking low and shooting around his mother south into the woods, firing slowly to conserve ammunition while Alice fired over the top of him at the same shadowy figures. While she didn't draw any pained cries, the figures ducked and weaved in the brush, leaving swaying branches in their wakes. Bark flew everywhere as she took chunks out of the trees, chasing them with curses and angry shouts. The return fire came hard and fast, bullets ricocheting inside the stables where the horses snorted in agitation, and one or two rounds zipped into the passage and hit the campfire to send chunks of wood and bright cinders swirling in the passage.

Alice pulled Jake back with her before yelling across to Wilford. "They'll have all the exits covered soon, and we won't have any cover. Any ideas?"

"I'm open to suggestions!" The old man jammed more shells into his shotgun's loading port.

"Kids, grab our packs," Alice said. The pair went into the stalls and came out with three backpacks, two of which they hoisted onto their shoulders. "We're coming over to you," she called to Wilford, shoving Jake and Sarah across the intersection, past the campfire, and into the west passage with Wilford, guiding them past the annoyed horses who whinnied and bumped the stalls as guns boomed.

"You folks, get on out of here!" Wilford sent a blast flying before shuffling behind them, chased by a barrage of return fire. "I can handle these ruffians!"

"No, you can't," Alice laughed darkly, stopping at the next intersection and peeking around the corner. She gestured for the kids to wait a moment and then leaped into the passage, firing south before nodding for them to follow.

"What are you doing, Mom?" Jake was silhouetted in the shadows with Sarah coming behind him and clutching his arm. They passed through two more intersections toward the western exit, and the attackers mirrored their movements, shooting into the passages and churning the air with hot lead, rounds striking the walls and flying out the opposite side.

They sprinted through the next intersection beneath the barrage of gunfire, Alice stopping them with a gasp and gathering them around. "Wilford, you're going to stay here with me!" Her gaze shifted to the kids. "You guys will slip out the west exit and head down to the secondary stalls where our rides are waiting."

"No way." Jake lunged toward the intersection behind them, swung his gun around a corner, and fired south, then turned back. "We're not leaving you."

"We'll keep them busy here... maybe take them back east a bit while you guys take the packs and get the horses ready, including one for Wilford. We'll be right behind you in a few minutes. Understand?"

"Are you sure, Mom?" Sarah asked, holding her knife in front of her helplessly.

"I'm sure." Alice bit her lip. "And if we're not down there in fifteen or twenty minutes, you've got to get away."

"No *way*, Mom!" Sarah grabbed Alice's arms and tried to hug her desperately. "We're not leaving without you."

"You won't have to..." Alice nudged the girl away with her rifle and stared at them firmly. "But if we're not down there soon, and the guns stop firing, that means we're gone and you need to run. Understand?"

The pale horror on their faces broke Alice's heart.

"Just *go*!" she growled, giving them both a hard shove. "We'll be down soon."

Jake paused with moisture reflecting firelight in his eyes, then he nodded. "Okay. We'll need a few minutes to get them saddled and tacked up."

"We'll hold them here. Just go before they surround us even more!"

The kids took the three packs and sprinted down the main passage out the west exit and into the night. Alice held her breath as they ran across the open space, finally breathing a sigh of relief when the kids reached the end of the gravel lane and disappeared into the woody darkness. After watching them go, Alice stood at the nearest intersection in search of lights and signs of movement to shoot at. She saw a couple and, without the distraction of worrying about the kids getting hurt, took an extra few seconds to steady her aim before firing at a shape near the tree line, finally drawing the cry of pain she'd been searching for.

"Okay, back the other way!"

Alice and Wilford shuffled east along the passage, shooting north and south at the moving figures and reloading as they went, drawing their attackers back east away from where Jake and Sarah had run. Stopping at the intersection with their scattered campfire, Alice slipped her Ruger around the corner and fired three times, chasing lights that sprinted across her field of vision, then she was out of bullets and retreated to reload with a scattering of rounds from her pocket.

Wilford stood at the corner across from her and peered into the north passage, his shotgun echoing as they tried to hold the junction against the tightening noose. The return fire was withering, shots zipping in like angry bugs, turning the air into a hornet's nest of hot metal and wood chips, cinders and charred wood flying up as they pulverized the campfire logs.

He turned to her with sweat trickling down his face in the orange campfire light. "Alice, you *must* go with the children! I will *not* let you stay here and sacrifice yourself when you've got those two to get all the way across the country to their father!"

Alice charged her weapon with a clack, raising it to her chest and getting ready to shoot when she crossed the intersection. "And I'm not leaving you here to get killed," she retorted. "We just have to hold them off a little while longer before we make a run for it. How many shells do you have left?"

"Three slugs and some buckshot and birdshot shells."

"You better save that buckshot for when they get closer," Alice said with a sideways grin that felt maniacal on her face, a sudden core of resolve hardening in her gut. "Jake and Sarah will get those horses ready for us. They just need a few minutes more!"

Wilford chuckled and nodded as he peeked around the corner and tracked the fluttering shadows that ran by, pulling back at the last second to address her gruffly. "You could die here with me. You know that don't you, lass?"

"I do," Alice replied, her eyes and nose stinging from the gunpowder, her arms shaking with weakness, shoulder sore from constantly firing the powerful rifle. "I'm going to give my kids every chance to get those horses saddled – for them as much as for us. If we don't make it down there, they'll know to take off. So just shut up and keep shooting."

Grinning madly with sweat trickling down his face, Wilford ducked low, swinging out with his rifle raised, firing another slug that elicited a sharp cry of agony and a furious flurry of return fire.

―――――――

Faint gunshots echoed in the night as Jake and Sarah hurried to get four horses saddled and packed up. An electric lantern gave them a soft light to work with, and the smell of manure and hay crept up Jake's nose as he tried to tack up Rocky in his stall with the door closed. Sarah had suggested readying them inside the closed stalls to keep them from getting spooked by the continuous gunfire, and while it was more difficult, it had kept the animals relatively calm.

The horse stood right behind him, and Jake was tucked under his neck, craning his body around to rest the bridle on his head as Rocky nuzzled him and shifted at his touch. The saddling had gone fast, thanks to Sarah, though she warned that the equipment straps might chafe the horses beneath their bellies.

"We can readjust them later once we're out of here," Sarah said, coming to his stall door and peeking over the top to double-check what he was doing. "Just keep in mind your horse might be a little grumpy from getting his skin pinched or if we saddled him too tightly." Watching Jake struggle for a second, she shook her head briskly and tore open the stall door, coming inside and taking the bridle out of his hands. "Watch me."

Jake stepped aside and rested his arm on the door to pull it shut, moving so he could see her better. Sarah got beneath the horse's neck and raised on her toes with the top of the bridle gripped in one hand and the bit in the other. In a quick motion, she slipped the bit between Rocky's teeth and pulled the top of the bridle over his ears, tightening the throat lash and noseband and used her fingers to measure the tightness between the leather and his head.

"And that's how you do it." She dusted off her hands, patting Rocky firmly on his neck and brushing her palm down his smooth fur to keep the horse calm as the distant gunfire continued to pop off. Pushing Jake through the door, Sarah said, "Okay, it's Buck's turn. Do you want to do him?"

"We're short on time," Jake replied. "You go ahead. I'll watch."

"No time for you to stand around, then. Check Stormy's saddle and make sure there's a little space between the girth and his front legs. Make sure it's not pinching them and that there's three fingers of space between the front of the saddle and his neck."

"Do we even have time to spare for all this?"

"No, but if we don't do it right, they could toss us right off their backs." Sarah finished getting Buck's bridle on and whispered soothing words as the horse shifted nervously. "We won't make it home with broken necks. Wilford and Mom will be here soon."

With his stomach turning, every gunshot driving a spike of dread deeper into his heart, Jake rechecked the saddles, ensuring they were comfortable and not pinching the animals anywhere. Stormy's was fine, but he had to loosen Rocky's and shift the saddle forward an inch to get it sitting correctly. Re-checking the fit, he found his fingers fit perfectly between the saddle and the horse's neck, and he ran his hand through the soft mane to keep the horse calm as Sarah burst from Buck's stall with a nod.

"Buck is ready to go now. Are the others okay?"

"I had to readjust Rocky's saddle a bit, but he's ready to ride, too."

"Okay, good." Sarah stepped to the edge of the electric light and stared into the night where the gunshots continued. "Sounds pretty crazy up there, but they should be okay, right?"

Jake scratched his head. "I think so."

"Do you think any of those jerks will come down here?"

"I don't know."

"Do you even remember how to ride?"

"Yeah, I do…" he scoffed, then grew nervous. "Well, I think so, anyway. It's like riding a bike, right? A big… living… bike." Coming to stand by Sarah, he stared with her into the darkness and winced at the constant crack of guns and bright flashes in the trees. "So, what do we do now?"

"We stay here and wait for Mom," Sarah nodded firmly.

"She said to leave if we don't see them in fifteen or twenty minutes." Jake grimaced as the gunfire picked up like bursts of popcorn.

"Only if the gunfire stops." Sarah gulped. "That would mean they're…"

"Don't say it," Jake replied miserably. "Just… don't say it."

Alice adjusted toward the flickering light from the sputtering campfire where pieces of it had been scattered by stray bullets from the attackers. She kicked embers aside and peeked around the corner, pointing her Ruger south. The enemy had stopped firing for a moment, and her heart was somehow racing *faster* than it had been when they'd been under heavy fire.

"Watch out, Wilford," Alice said. "They're going to rush us soon."

The old man racked a shell with a jerk of the shotgun's forearm. "I get that feeling, too. Want to break for the stables?"

"Yeah, we should--"

A man left the cover of the trees and sprinted toward the stables with a pair of pistols in his hands. Alice led him by half an inch and squeezed the trigger, her bullet zipping fast to strike him in the gut, twisting him, and sending him to his knees, guns dropping as he clutched his middle and kneeled there, screaming through blood-flecked lips. Another man rushed in behind him, shooting back at Alice, his rifle flashing in the darkness. Not bothering with the wounded man, she extended the Ruger, and fired it with a sharp crack. The man who had been rushing in screamed as his shoulder exploded in a red blossom that sprayed into the air with pieces of flesh flying off, his body twisting as he stumbled and fell so that he almost landed on his wounded companion. Consumed with pain, he clutched the remnants of his shoulder and squirmed on the ground as the other man stared at his bloody hands in disbelief, both of them screaming incoherently.

Barely noticing the caterpillar crawl of sweat down her face, Alice clenched her jaw and raised her rifle, putting another bullet into the man with the wounded shoulder to silence him for good. Wilford's shotgun boomed again, and Alice snapped around to see a burly man with shoulder-length hair stagger through the darkness at the edge of the camp-fire light, his chest smoking and torn open. After stumbling five steps, the man pitched to the ground and lay still, wheezing and groaning.

"Nice shot, Wilford!" Alice shouted at the top of her lungs as she whipped her gaze to the south where dark figures moved at the edge of the light. She hoped her gloating would discourage them, though judging by the gathering shadows, they were merely preparing for another charge.

Wilford hollered back in a ragged lilt. "Bloody right, Alice! I've got a shell for each one of these bastards. Let them come!" Glaring into the darkness, he shouted, "Come on, rats!"

As soon as the angry words left his mouth, he turned to her, whispering. "Let's go... to the stables!"

"Right!"

They began their slow retreat along the main corridor, swinging the rifle and shotgun back and forth along the passages where shadows loomed. The attackers cursed and barked commands back and forth as the wounded bled out on the gravel paths.

"I've got five bullets left!" Alice kept her voice low as she reloaded on the run.

"Three myself." Wilford huffed and shuffled hard to keep up as he loaded his last shells into his weapon.

"Sounds like more are coming, too."

"Could be they were nearby, heard the gunshots, and came to help their boys."

"We need to conserve our ammunition." Alice raised her rifle as they crossed the next intersection, spotting two men running toward them. She started to fire but pulled back at the last second, allowing them to reach the wall before turning to meet Wilford's gaze. "They're right outside the stables," she whispered sharply. "They're about to rush in. Get ready."

"Fire when you see their eyes," Wilford agreed with a snarl as he hunched over his gun and leaned around the corner to the north, looking like a soldier and not the groundskeeper he was.

Things grew quiet but for the fire still crackling in the darkness and the scuffling of boots and whispers beyond the firelight. The kids' faces entered her mind, and she wished that she and Wilford would have left sooner, but it was far too late.

"Climb on the backs of those horses and go, kids," she whispered to herself. "Don't wait to see what's happened to us. Just take what you have and disappear into the night."

Like an ill omen, Alice sensed the enemies were coming a second before they actually did. There was a sharp scuffle of boots, a barked command, and the attackers rushed them, but a clatter of frantic hoofbeats and heaving, snorting breaths grew louder, drowning out the sounds of the attackers. At the edge of the firelight, deep at the end of the stable, four horses came fast right up the main corridor, Jake seated on Rocky and bouncing awkwardly in the saddle, half twisted as he held the reins and tried to steer. Rocky tossed his head, nostrils flaring and snorting, eyes wide with raw panic under the withering gunfire. Sarah rode just behind him on Stormy, her pale face and skinny frame seeming to float in the air with the muscled beast blending with the darkness and rippling beneath her. Behind them came two more horses, each kid leading one by a tether, the corridor packed with charging horseflesh and snorts.

Alice charged across the intersection to get out of the way, throwing her left shoulder to the corner and raising her rifle. The men who'd made it to the stables were charging inside, the one on her right sliding along the wall with a pistol raised and getting a bead on Wilford.

"Wilford!" Alice screamed.

Alice and the man fired simultaneously, Wilford ducking and spinning away as her own round struck her target in the chest. The projectile went through the soft tissue like a hot poker through butter, spraying the far wall with red, and he gasped like he'd been gut-punched, blood trailing down him as he slid to the floor. The man coming along the inside wall on her side was on her, and Alice jerked back into the main corridor to avoid a pistol blast to the face, tripping and falling onto her backside. She tried to pull the charging handle to reload the Ruger, but the man rounded the corner and stood over her, looking surprised at his choice of easy targets, finally pointing the weapon at her face. Suddenly, the man launched forward with a bark of pain, his body sprawling, windmilling past her, the result of Rocky's broadside clipping him in the shoulder and back of the head. The man landed somewhere in the stable rubble, and for a moment, Jake and Rocky were silhouetted in the scattered campfire light flitting along the passage. The horse danced on his rear legs, his barrel chest heaving, forehooves pawing at the air, glorious mane flying as Jake hung on for dear life.

There came another shotgun boom, and the horses brayed in raw fear, drowning out Sarah's terrified cries. With her insides going cold, Alice finally chambered a round and turned onto her stomach, sighting the man who'd flown past her where he was getting to his feet again, holding the back of his head and snarling in pain and anger. Alice fired through his hand and skull without hesitation, painting the passage with bone and gore, then she rolled back the other way and somehow got to her feet, leaping past Stormy to the other side of the passage, joining Wilford where he was leaning against the stall wall covered in blood from another man he'd just fired upon.

He blinked once and wiped his arm across his face, smearing crimson across his cheeks. "You got the horses! Way to go, kids!" In the same motion, he reached up and took Stormy's bridle, whispering to the horse and girl as he held the shotgun pointed away from them.

The spare two horses for Alice and Wilford drew back down the corridor, almost pulling the kids from their saddles and Alice quickly grabbed the tethers from Jake and Sarah and wrapped them around their saddle horns twice. Jake was clinging to Rocky's back with his knees, one hand buried in the horse's mane, the other holding the reins too loosely. Alice placed her hand on his leg and squeezed hard to get his attention.

"Oh, Mom! That hurt!"

"Get control of your horse, son," Alice growled, shoving the hand holding the reins into his chest. "Remember the lessons!" Giving a quick nod, Jake took up the slack and jerked them to the right, steering the horse into the south passage so Alice could get to Buck.

With musk, dust, and the metallic scent of blood swirling in the air, and the other animals in the stalls whinnying and thrashing against the weakening walls, Alice grabbed Buck's saddle horn with one hand, jammed her foot into the stirrup, and said a silent prayer that she wouldn't launch herself off the other side and break her neck. Buck barely moved as she climbed aboard, tilting slightly to the right before pressing her tennis shoe firmly inside the stirrup. Righting herself, she drew the reins to her chest to keep control and get her bearings. There was a moment of dizziness at the sudden height, Buck spinning in place one time before Alice stopped him with a flick, all the riding training she'd done with the kids flashing in her head in a clash of congealing thoughts. The horses jostled and bumped each other in the enclosed space, and a thoroughbred kicked backward to crack their stall wall. She tried to guide Buck to the left, but his big shoulders knocked Sarah's horse to the side with an agitated grunt. Wilford swung his leg over his horse's saddle and angled him toward an exit.

"We'll be crushed in here, Wilford!" Alice shouted, trying to reach across Sarah to get the man's attention as shadows shifted in the flickering light, snorts and gunshots and curses blending into a cacophony of battle sounds.

Wilford had a wild look, squinting at an attacker and drawing a bead on them near the north passage. The old man cursed low before raising his voice in challenge. "Come on then, you bastards! You can't hide in the darkness from Wilford!"

He fired what might've been his last shotgun shell, and the blast set the horses leaping in every direction. Jake's horse turned and trounced over the fire, sending cinders and grating scattering. The pair slipped to the side, crashed into a stall wall, and charged into the south passage and into the night. Buck was right behind him, partially guided by Alice but more driven by his own sheer panic. Pure muscle rippled beneath her and launched her forward as two of the attackers stepped into view. One took Buck full in the face, the horse slamming him with his chest, knocking him to the ground and crushing him with stomping hooves. Alice hung on as Rocky sprinted west while Buck banked right and then left again to come up behind a man aiming a rifle at Jake's fleeing back.

Alice somehow got her weapon up, resting the stock against her hip, unable to remember if she'd chambered a fresh round or had any bullets left. With a desperate snarl, she squeezed the trigger, sending the shot flat from her hip, past Buck's head to strike the man between the shoulders and rock him forward. The horse panicked again at the closeness of the shot, and they were racing into the night, Alice helplessly holding the wavering rifle as she desperately tried to get Buck going left after Jake, inadvertently slamming into two more men and pitching one to the ground while the other tumbled into the bushes, both of them howling.

Molding her knees to his body, sitting upright and jerking his reins, she got Buck under control, guiding him in the direction she thought her son had gone, though through the darkness and scattering shadows it was impossible to tell. "Jake! Get him under—"

Jake flew out of the darkness on Rocky's back, holding the reins high as he half-stood in the saddle with his revolver raised. He fired a trio of shots at three men off to the left, the gun going off with sharp cracks, the flashes illuminating the boy's wild, rage-fueled expression. The men scrambled and dove away, one of them clutching some part of his chest before flopping into the bushes. Jake flew past her, his horse whinnying loudly, and she was pulling up on her reins, gasping in exasperation, getting Buck turned around.

In the chaos, faint hints of their campfire were scattered across the soft gravel lane, and Alice blinked as she tried to make out where Wilford and Sarah had gone. A terrified thoroughbred flew past her, trailed by a second one that broke toward the tree line and through the brush to scare out a couple of the attackers, then they jumped the fence and sprinted away into the field. Shoulders forward, Alice dug her heels into Buck, and he raced back toward the embers and past the broken stall doors while she desperately searched for a familiar face.

Reaching the end of the stables, Alice cursed and turned Buck around, releasing control of the horse long enough to raise the Ruger with both hands and check that there was still another round in the chamber. Moving forward at a more controlled pace, Alice trotted him along, scanning her surroundings as the wind whipped her hair behind her and dried the sweat on her chest and face. Reaching the burned-out section of stalls where she'd lost Jake, she put her head on a swivel, searching the darkness for the horses and riders. Someone moved in the tree line on her right, and she leveled her weapon and fired. The shot flew wide, but whoever it was turned and scrambled east down the gravel lane before diving into the tree line again. A moment later, she saw him leap over the fence and sprint into the field.

Swinging north around the front of the stable, Alice pulled Buck up short, nearly running into two riders circling from the other side. Wilford sat primly on horseback with his shotgun and reins in his left hand, keeping Sarah close as she hunched over Stormy's saddle and glanced around in fear, though when she saw Alice, her expression lit up, and she kicked her horse forward to catch up.

"Mom! I thought I'd lost you! I thought I was going to die!"

Getting as close as she could, she reached out and hugged Sarah, and the horses carried them past each other with Alice swinging Buck to come up beside Wilford.

"Did you see Jake?"

The old man gave a brief head shake and a snort. "I didn't see young Jake because I've been looking for the other bastards, but they've gone and run off like the cowards they are." Wilford grimaced. "Probably a good thing, since I'm out of shells."

"It's good they're leaving," Alice nodded, "but I've got to find my son."

"Right. Where did you last see him?"

"Behind us... heading east, I think." Alice glanced back. "He was shooting at someone as he rode by, but I lost him."

"Don't worry, Alice," Wilford said as he switched his shotgun to his right hand and flicked the reins. "We'll find him."

Alice and Sarah galloped behind him as they headed east through the grounds, around the gardens, and up toward the main house, a ride that took less than thirty seconds. Alice spied several shadows sprinting off to the east and down the exit lane, a couple climbing a fence with Wilford shouting after them not to return if they knew what was good for them. With the powerful horse under her, Alice felt herself come alive and swung the rifle one-handed out into the darkness, daring someone to challenge her. She shifted her hips for a more relaxed ride and fell into the normal locomotion of horseback riding.

She raised her mouth to the cool night air and hollered. "Jake! Jake! Where are you?"

Sarah and Wilford joined in, and soon their shouts and cries were echoing through the treetops, along with the soft clattering of hooves as they moved past the eviscerated mansion house. In the circular driveway where the husks of three vehicles sat with their insides blown everywhere, Alice turned Buck in a circle. "I don't see him anywhere. Do you think Rocky would've gone into the tree line and jumped the fence, maybe?"

"Now, Rocky is easily spooked, but I don't think he'd do that, not with a rider on his back. He's a smart horse, and he'd know better."

"We should split up," she said, "as much as I hate to do it. I think those looters have run off, don't you think?"

"Most of them have," Wilford nodded. "But I wouldn't put it past one to linger around for a while to see what they can swipe up from the scraps of our fight."

"Mom!" Sarah shouted and pointed toward the east. "Jake... I think that's Jake."

A lone figure on horseback was walking back to them, the thin figure holding his side, leaning forward in the seat. With panic rippling through her guts, Alice kicked Buck into motion and bolted down the lane toward her son. "Jake!"

When she got closer, Alice drew Buck up short, breathing a sigh of relief when Jake lifted his head and fixed her with a grin. Pulling Rocky to a halt, he waved with his offhand, revealing that he wasn't injured, but was holding his gun and the reins against his stomach in a relaxed posture, keeping his horse firmly under control.

"You're okay, son!" Alice rode closer, missed him, then spun Buck around to grab the boy's shoulder.

"Yeah. I'm okay, Mom," he laughed. "I just got caught up chasing one of those guys out of here... ran out of bullets." He held the revolver up and wagged it. "I even swapped out the autoloader while I was riding. Can you believe that?"

Sarah laughed with tears watering her eyes, waving as she came trotting up with Wilford. "You scared the heck out of us!"

"I guess I'm a cowboy," Jake replied with a delirious chuckle, as if he didn't believe it himself.

Wilford was beaming at the boy, reaching out to give his shoulder a good whack as he went by. "Good show, Jake. You did wonderfully!"

"We all did." Alice held up her reins to see her hands were shaking.

"That we did," Wilford said with a tone of determination. "But I need to check on those thoroughbreds in the stables. Once they're secure, I'll find any extra shotgun shells that might be lying around the place and go round up all the horses that got away. I'll bring Peppercorn and Dawson in, too. Especially with those thieves running around who said − and I'm sure I heard them talking about this − they wanted to *eat* them. Damned savages."

"We'll help you." Alice nodded and gestured to the kids to get in line behind Wilford and head back toward the primary stables.

"Nonsense, Alice. You three need to get going. No sense in sticking around here, especially with trouble lurking so close. Come, let's make sure you're squared away."

Once they returned to the campfire, Wilford got off his horse and tied it to a post by the building, scowling when Alice and the kids dismounted with him. With charred wood and coals scattered all the way outside, the four used their feet to kick the hot pieces into a pile.

"You can't be serious about staying." Alice shouldered her rifle and knocked a smoking ember in with the others.

Standing on the other side, Wilford swept more into the pile and shot fiery glances at the surrounding woods. His gaze drifted from the east lane to the fields where the thoroughbreds had jumped the fence. With flaring nostrils, he said, "This place is my home, and there's nothing that can drive me away from it. I'm sure you understand that."

"You shouldn't put yourself in danger because of your pride."

"It's not just about pride, Alice. It's about these horses and who will take care of them when the world's coming down around us. I'll certainly not stand for them being roasted on a spit!"

Alice swept some coals into the pile as Jake and Sarah picked up scattered bins and supplies and took them back inside to the stalls Wilford called home.

"Why don't you just let them all go?" Alice asked, hands on her hips. "They'd survive on their own just fine, I'm sure."

Wilford shrugged. "Maybe. Maybe not. Either way, I'm not abandoning them. I'm letting Buck, Stormy, and Rocky go only because of your gentle kindness and promise to look after them." Wilford stopped fixing the fire and mirrored Alice's stance, though he looked teary-eyed at the ground and his voice caught when he spoke. "If... if it hadn't been for you folks, and the kids' fancy riding, I'd be lyin' on the ground like these poor bastards and my horses would be chopped up for dinner. I'd be in awful shape if it weren't for you three, and you've won my heart for that. Now, I just asked you and your kids to get away safely. That's my last and final wish for you, and you don't need some old man and his horses slowing you down."

"You wouldn't be slowing us down. You'd be —"

"I won't hear any more about it." Wilford held his hand up in a halting gesture, fire flashing in his eyes. "And I won't take no more arguments from you, Alice. You're going to take the horses." He stepped over to the one he'd tied to the rail and patted the rope. "This one here is Hercules. He's a good, powerful draft horse and outdoes his brothers for hauling equipment. You're going to take him, too. He'll carry your packs and possessions."

In equal measures of gratitude and disbelief, Alice pleaded with the man. "You're beyond kind, Wilford. There's got to be some way we can repay you."

Sarah crossed to the old man and wrapped her arms around him, cheek pressed against his dingy shirt. "Please, Wilford. Come with us." The old man's lingering defiance and anger at being attacked by the thieves instantly deflated, and he grasped Sarah with one arm, the other still clinging to his shotgun. "You've already repaid this old man by saving his life and the lives of his friends, and you kept me company when you didn't need to. That's all the payment I could ever ask for."

They stood in silence and finished getting the fire going outside, surrounding it with rocks and piling more wood on it, then moved back inside to clean up after the gunfight, which had left several men dead. With tears in their eyes, they helped Wilford drag the bodies outside and leave them at the tree line where Wilford said he'd bury them later or feed them to the alligators in a nearby swamp.

"I'm glad you're taking the horses," Wilford went on as he continued his preparations, gathering wood from around the stable, beginning to fix the newly-created holes and shore up his defenses. "It's clear you know your way around them." With a gesture at the animals where they were tied up on the rail, he gave them an impressed nod. "You placed the saddles almost perfectly, though Rocky likes his a little lower on his back. He's got a long body, Jake."

"I'll remember that." Jake's voice was rough with emotion, and his eyes were glassy in the firelight.

"And you, lass." Wilford turned to address Sarah, who stood with her arms crossed, eyes filled with tears. "Stormy responds better with sweet words than harsh ones, if you know what I mean."

"I think so." Sarah wiped her arm across her nose and sniffed.

"Not like Buck." He pointed at the cream-colored gelding. "He's the youngest and needs a firm talking to at times." His gaze lifted, dark and sheepish. "Can you do that, Alice?"

"I can do that."

"All right then." Wilford nodded hesitantly at first, then firmly. He drifted down the side of the stable, walking backward and heading to the burned-up section to salvage more wood. "Remember what I told you before. The horses aren't shod, so you want to run them easy and stick mostly to fields and soft earth until you can get them home and shoe them properly if you need to." With a wave and a nod, he turned away. "You folks better get going. I'm going to collect some more scrap wood to get started."

Alice rushed after him and grabbed his arm, stopping him before he got too far. "You be careful, Wilford," she whispered.

"I will, ma'am." Wilford sniffed and averted his eyes as tears glistened on his cheeks. "Don't you worry yourself about old Wilford. I'll be fine."

With that, he gently broke her grip and shuffled past the closed stall doors, changed from a fighter into an old groundskeeper again with a portly belly and slumped shoulders. Wordlessly, he disappeared into the wreckage to leave Alice, the kids, and their horses to stare after him.

Alice waited a moment, then she turned to the kids and nodded. "Okay. Let's put our packs on Hercules and mount up."

They took all the kids' backpacks attached to Buck and Rocky, moved them to Hercules, and tied everything down tight. Alice found two Ruger rounds near the intersection where she'd dropped them by accident, and she stuffed those in her pocket with the other couple she had left. One big stallion had nearly kicked his stall door off its hinges, leaving shattered pieces of wood all down the corridor. Pots and pans, and the remnants of Wilford's bins that the kids hadn't managed to gather were dumped everywhere with food and tea scattered in the burning embers, and the pictures of Wilford's old stomping grounds had been shot to pieces with broken framing and glass lying on the ground.

"Well, kids. This is it. Let's go."

The kids nodded solemnly, Jake bowing his head while Sarah stood looking miserably at where Wilford had gone. Alice wrapped her arms around them, squeezed, and guided them outside to the horses. The three mounted up and walked the horses east along the gravel lane with tears streaming down their cheeks.

CHAPTER ELEVEN

President Thomas Birk
Mount Weather, Virginia

President Birk casually pored over reports while sitting at a plain metal desk in his side office away from the arguments and stress of the others, where the constant flow of updates shouted back and forth across the room had driven him to more peaceful surrounds. His office in Mount Weather was hardly built for comfort; its thick army green walls carrying vibrations from upstairs, heavy booms as massive doors closed and opened, the movement of equipment and materials throughout the facility that felt more like a prison than a refuge.

Still, it was a place of security where he had time to gather his thoughts and sit quietly until the next meeting as the best strategists they could find still living tried to come up with answers to the earth-shattering crises they faced. A single picture of himself and his wife sat near his monitor and was one of the few things he'd been allowed to bring from the bunker in Washington. The two of them were smiling with their arms around each other on a sunny California beach with the beautiful waters spread out behind them beneath the blue sky, on a vacation they'd taken before he'd been sworn in as President and began bearing the weight of the world on his shoulders. There was a terse knock on his hard steel door, echoing slightly in the room devoid of carpet and tapestries, just a single United States flag behind him with emergency communication gear nearby. He'd forgotten to ask if any other presidents had ever worked from the Mount Weather office, though even if they had, there was no doubt that *none* had faced a situation like his administration was facing. Still, Birk didn't complain, not even to himself as he perused reports and orders that constantly flooded down his screen.

With a sigh, he tore himself away from the monitor, straightened, and raised his voice. "Come in!"

"Excuse me, sir?" Staffer Cindy Strode pushed open the door and poked her head through. "May I come in?"

Between her strained smile and the tears standing out in her eyes, Birk gripped his chair in anticipation of bad news. "Yes, of course, Cindy. Step on in."

"Thank you, sir." The staffer entered quietly and shut the door behind her, wringing her hands as she came to stand before his desk.

"Please, sit down." Birk gestured to another chair just like his sitting directly in front of his desk.

"Thank you, Mr. President." The staffer lowered herself into the seat, her hands still trembling as she took a few deep breaths.

"What is it, Cindy? More bad news?"

She nodded wordlessly, caught in a terrible trap she couldn't escape. The hairs on the back of Birk's neck began to tingle, and he pushed away his keyboard, clasping his hands in front of him. "Go ahead. What is it?"

"It's... your wife, sir. She..." Cindy's voice caught in her throat.

The tingle was overwhelmed by nausea that washed over him, a dreadful vibration that moved to his chest, and his heart began to race uncontrollably as a wave of heat rushed across his face and head. With a slow nod, he swallowed, keeping his voice level. "She's... not okay, I take it?"

The staffer shook her head briskly, unwashed strands of hair framing her face where they'd come free. "No, sir."

"What happened? Where did they find her?"

"Her motorcade was located in Missouri, close to where she was supposed to speak. Her limousine—all the cars in the motorcade—were destroyed. By..."

He was already nodding, his jaw working, voice rough as the room contorted around him, growing smaller, the waves of heat and nausea growing stronger, making it difficult to think or speak. "The fuel. Yes."

There seemed to be so much more he was supposed to say, but the news had settled over him like a cloud of poison, squeezing his head in a vice, chest heaving, breaths coming shallow, heart thudding in his ears. He stared at the picture of him and Sue on the beach, her bright red hair blown back around her right temple by the ocean breeze, beaming at the camera as she clung to him. It was just them from the waist up, Sue with a summer blouse on and Birk with a button-up shirt, but there was so much more he remembered from that day. Her rolled-up jeans, bare feet on the warm sand, joking that she needed extra sunblock, being a redhead and all. The picture blurred, and Birk blinked to clear his vision, vaguely aware of the pair of tears running down his cheeks, suddenly wanting to leave everything behind and see for himself. The Marines who'd found her were wrong. They had to be. She hadn't been in the motorcade, but was stranded somewhere, still alive, well and waiting for him.

When he spoke, his voice was rough and wet, reality snapping back in an instant. "Are... they a hundred percent sure?"

Cindy seemed to have curled in on herself, afraid to look at him but raising her gaze to meet his anyway. "I asked the same thing, sir. They took DNA samples from a body in the limousine, and it... it's Sue's. I'm so sorry, sir."

He was falling apart, snapping into pieces, watching himself from outside his body when he grasped onto his years of training and practice, steeling himself, forcing his feelings into a box and closing the lid as tight as he could.

"That's okay, Cindy. Really. I know you loved her, too." His voice was barely audible in his own ears, nearly drowned out by his throbbing heartbeat. He took deep, raw breaths. In through his nose, out through his mouth. Tried to hold them in as long as he could to keep himself steady.

Sniffling, she took a tissue from her blouse pocket and wiped her nose, then she stood and offered him one. "I really did, Mr. President. We all did. I'll never forget my first day on the job. Sue was so gracious and kind, and she saw how nervous I was and got me through it. She was a First Lady like no other."

Birk nodded. "She was like that. Selfless, especially when she saw someone who needed help. I'm really going to—" He choked on his words and swallowed them down as his shoulders slumped. She really, truly was gone. He'd never see her again - hell, he wouldn't even get a chance to *bury* her. His own wife. Someone who was supposed to be protected, just like him.

Slowly folding over, Birk fought against another swell of emotion that suffocated him and pressed him into a darkness that threatened to consume him. He fought it, pounding a fist on the table and growling low in his chest, forcing himself to hold on and look beyond himself, shoving the box closed yet again.

"What about Agent Harris?" he changed the subject, clearing his throat. "Marines were looking for his family in Blacksburg. They have any luck?"

"They haven't done a DNA analysis yet, but there were skeletons in the house at the address Harris provided. I'd guess they're gone too."

"Has anyone told him yet?"

Cindy shook her head.

"Thanks, Cindy. You can go now. I'll let you know if I need anything. And... don't tell Harris yet, okay? Just give me a moment and I'll have you send him in."

Cindy got up and paused, staring down at him with her tear-streaked face, patting him on the arm before nodding and leaving the room, shutting the steel door behind her with a soft click. With the picture in one hand and a tissue in the other, Birk let the tears flow, silent as they streamed down his face, blinking them back several times and thinking them done before they came again, only stopping when his face was soaked. For a long time, he couldn't take his eyes off Sue's face, lost in the many wonderful moments they'd shared. After a while, he sighed deeply, put the photograph back - a few inches closer than it had been — and pressed a button on an intercom to his right.

"Cindy?"

"Yes, sir."

"Can you send in Agent Harris?"

"I will, Mr. President. I'm not sure where he is exactly, but I'll let Colonel Crow know you want to see him."

"Thank you."

Birk took a few moments to wash his face in a small metal sink in the corner, drying it as he stared at himself, his eyes still red, his face far gaunter than he could ever recall it looking. It wasn't long before another knock came at his door, and the President returned to his desk, calling for Harris to come in. The agent wore his same dark expression, a mixture of quiet strength and patience, always observant, always on the edge of action.

"You wanted to see me, sir?"

"Shut the door and sit down."

"Yes, sir."

Harris sat with his back straight and shoulders square, hands resting on the arm of the chair, neither relaxed nor tense but patiently waiting for the President to speak first. Birk reached into a side drawer and took out a bottle of bourbon and two glasses, inadvertently clinking them together as he set them beside his keyboard. The President leaned forward and pulled the cork, pouring two fingers of straight bourbon into each glass. Placing the bottle aside, Birk pushed a glass toward Harris before taking his own and sitting back.

"I don't drink, sir. Well, I do, but just a beer or two once in a while at a gathering."

"All the same," Birk said with a nod. "Pick it up."

Harris picked up the glass immediately, resumed his stiff position, and held it with both hands against his stomach. "What's the occasion?"

"Nothing good." Birk took a sip and jiggled the glass with a flourish as he grimaced at the burn that flowed through his mouth, liquid fire dropping into his belly. He picked up the picture of him and Sue, rested it gently on the desk, and pushed it toward the agent.

Curious but confused, Harris lifted an eyebrow questioningly.

"Go ahead. That's Sue and me out on a beach in California."

Harris picked up the picture and gave it a once over before setting it back on the desk. "I met her twice since you were President, sir. She's a sweet lady."

"*Was* a sweet lady," Birk said, sighing deeply and taking another drink. "Now, only in our memories. They found her with her motorcade in Missouri. Like everything else, the vehicles were blown up, but the DNA from the limousine was conclusive. It was her."

Harris froze, leaned forward briefly, then sat back heavily in his chair. After several long seconds, the agent spoke hesitantly. "I'm sorry to hear that, Mr. President. She was..." Harris shook his head. "She was a great lady." As if suddenly remembering he had a drink in his hand, he raised it in toast and took a sip, wincing at the sting.

"Yes, she was. Unfortunately, that's not all the bad news." Birk's shoulders slumped. "Take another drink, son."

Harris' confusion changed to flat misery, something dreadful flashing in his eyes as he slouched but lifted the glass again for another sip. "What is it? Is it my family?"

"I'm so sorry to have to break the news to you. The DNA analysis on the bodies found at the address you gave us in Blacksburg isn't complete yet, though the number of remains matched those you said would be there. Everything in the property was burned to the ground."

Harris twisted in his seat, face contorting through various emotions before settling into wide-eyed disbelief. Finally, he threw back the rest of his whiskey in a single gulp and slammed the glass on the desk a bit harder than he had intended.

"Can I have another, sir?" The words were strained, coming out through a grimace.

"You certainly can, agent." Birk poured two more fingers for Harris and then for himself, and they tapped the glasses together. "To our families."

Harris coughed and nodded, downing half of his glass before leaning back in his chair with a troubled expression. "I guess I'd been preparing myself for this for days now. It's not that I didn't have any faith in you, sir," he added, "but we've all heard the numbers and have seen what's been happening across the country. I wouldn't let myself be stupid enough to think my family wouldn't be affected. But still..." Harris trailed off, slapping his hand to his forehead, rubbing at his scalp

MIKE KRAUS

as if he could reach inside his head and rip the pain away. "I just didn't think it would take all of them. I figured my sister and dad would have made it out because they're always so prepared…"

"I wish they would've made it, Harris. You have my sincerest condolences. Your mom and dad raised a good man."

"Thank you, sir." The agent rose from his dejected posture. "And thank you for telling me yourself. Anybody else would've just given it to a staffer to pass along the news. It… means a lot coming from you. Especially with what you're dealing with right now."

"Cindy told me, but I wanted to be the one to let you know." Birk sighed and looked back into his glass, gently tilting it back and forth. "We get so used to wrapping ourselves up in our work that we don't stop to be grateful to those around us. I loved Sue deeply, but I didn't believe she could ever be hurt."

"Same here, Mr. President. I figured that once this initial wave was over and you were safe with no more threats, I'd beg a little time off to go see my family and they'd be fine." Harris smiled as his expression turned wistful. "Figured I'd come up in a Humvee with a couple of Marines and march up to the front door. Maybe the garage would be burned down, but the family would be fine. I'd go inside, and everyone would pile on with stories about what happened and I'd brag about how fancy I was hanging out with the President."

The two locked eyes before breaking down into sad chuckles, and Birk took another sip of whiskey. "This attack…" His voice grew cold. "Whoever did this had the obvious intention of taking everything from as many people as they could, but today it got personal."

Harris was nodding, one hand clutching his glass of whiskey while the other clenched his fist on the arm of the chair, squeezing, relaxing, and squeezing again as the sadness inside him changed to rage. "Me too, sir. I never imagined I could be so angry and numb at the same time…"

At a loss for words, Harris bent over his whiskey and let out a soft, raw, animalistic cry. Birk moved around the desk and put his hands on Harris's shoulders, feeling the man quaking beneath him, trying to hold himself together. Birk was about to call Cindy when a knock came at the door.

"Come in!"

It was Cindy, entering quietly with a folder tucked beneath one arm and a box of tissues in the other hand. Harris glanced aside as she stepped in and placed the box of tissues on the desk, backing away and nodding discreetly at Birk, who returned the gesture. Holding up the folder, she motioned at it. "We've got some new numbers for you to review, sir. No rush. Whenever you feel ready."

"Drop them on the desk, Cindy. I'll review them shortly. Thank you."

Cindy put them next to his keyboard and stepped out with a sorrowful glance at Harris before she exited. Once she had gone, Harris stood and put his empty glass on the desk, taking a deep breath and steadying himself. "I'll be going now, sir. I appreciate—"

"If you don't mind, I'd like you to stay." Birk swung back around to his seat, pulled the folder before him and flipped it open to the first page. When Harris didn't immediately respond, Birk gestured to the chair. "Please, agent. I could use a little company right now."

"I-I'm not sure if I can, Mr. President. Colonel Crow has a list of things for me to do—"

"A list of things that can wait." He raised an eyebrow. "Or did I suddenly cease being the Commander-in-Chief? Please. Sit." Birk gestured to the chair again before turning back to his documents.

Harris returned to his seat, and Birk pushed the whiskey bottle toward him, Harris pouring himself another quarter-glass full before leaning forward with his elbows resting on his knees, staring at the floor. Birk scanned slowly through the pages, hoping to find something positive but only seeing a lot of rehashed data.

"Still nothing much on the contaminated fuel," he sighed and gave a protracted exhalation of relief for something to focus on, something that helped to keep the compartmentalized box closed. "And we're now estimating the new global death toll will be four billion by the end of the week." Stopping, he took another drink and let the sting bring him back to the moment before chuckling darkly and pushing the glass aside. "I guess the good news is those numbers will slow once the urban areas… burn out. Most of the survivors will be out in the country where there's not a lot of heavy infrastructure."

Harris took a drink as well. "How are people going to survive out there?"

"They'll undoubtedly be more adaptable to life without modern infrastructure, especially in third world nations. In the western world, people will eventually run out of supplies, and if they don't tear themselves apart, they might form small communities? I don't honestly know; that's not my forte."

"It's none of my business, Mr. President," Harris said, "but what *can* you do to help people? Not you, specifically, but you know what I mean."

Birk rubbed his chin and took a deep breath as he studied the next page, full of highlighted highway corridors across the United States East Coast that he traced with a finger. "We'll keep up the supply distributions as best as we can. Heaven knows we have enough of the stuff to give out. If we don't have the trucks to deliver goods, or the people to drive them, we can set up supply drops at key locations near major highways and hope people can find them. We'll certainly get word to them as best we can through the emergency broadcast system."

"That sounds like a good plan," Harris agreed. "I believe that if you do it long enough, and consistently, people could migrate to these areas close to the drop-off points. I guess that would be a good thing, right? If people know where to go, maybe they can help each other out. Safety in numbers, if you know what I mean."

Birk shrugged. "I'm hoping it's a good thing. But whenever you put angry, displaced people together, things get pretty ugly. At least any trouble would be contained in certain areas, and those drop-off points would be easier to police." His eyebrows creased as he pushed the papers aside and took up his whiskey. "The crazy thing is that our biggest issue is having too many supplies spread across a few people. Anything perishable..."

"Will go to waste," Harris finished the thought.

"Exactly."

"Well, maybe they won't fight over supplies then. There'd be more chance of them working together if their bellies are full."

Birk laughed and nodded. "That's the idea. Make sure people are clothed and fed, and that they're safe. Figure the rest out later. Of course, we'll start with the camps we've already set up and continue supplying them while we stabilize the other drop-off points. We —"

Yet another knock came on the steel door, there was a half-second pause, and a second, more urgent knock.

"Come in," Birk called, putting his whiskey aside as he shifted his gaze to the door.

A young man in a wrinkled white shirt and tie pushed in, breathless as he held the door open with his other hand clinging to the door frame. "Sorry to burst in like this, Mr. President, but General Pulaski just arrived on horseback with some news."

"Horseback? Damn. Send him in."

Birk was motioning at the staffer to come in when Pulaski pushed past the man, bringing with him wafts of smoke and ash. A closer look revealed parts of his uniform singed around the shoulders and on his right side. Helmet and pair of goggles in one hand, he brushed back his mop of gray hair where it was burned in spots, only adding to the reek filling the room. Staggering slightly, he gave a stiff, pained salute. "Mr. President."

Birk and Harris both rose from their chairs, taking in the officer with wide eyes. "General Pulaski," Birk gawked, "you look like hell."

"It feels like I've been through it, Mr. President," he replied with a defiant growl. "I just arrived with Chief of Staff Sawyer on horseback, along with several members of our military and civilian leadership."

"Sawyer was carrying the encryption keys from the Pentagon." Birk nodded patiently. "Is he safe?"

"He's fine, and he's got all the encryption keys. We can connect via satellite to the Pentagon systems again." The General took a wide stance and grinned. "And we've got some big news. The analysts think they have a solid lead on where this damned attack originated from."

CHAPTER TWELVE

Alice Burton
Thomasville, Georgia

A day after leaving Wilford and Monticello Farm, Alice and the kids rode the horses along the center median of an expansive highway that stretched ahead into what she hoped was Georgia. The grass was long and thick, sometimes coming to the horses' knees and hiding dangerous shrapnel that could hobble them if they weren't careful. The roadway was a worse prospect in most cases, though, littered as it was with trashed vehicles. Trees crowded the roadsides with scorched branches and leaves, dozens sheared in two and left lying across the road. They weren't on fire anymore, but the lingering smoke burned her nostrils and drifted past them in sudden gusts with the horses tossing their heads in agitation.

Sarah sighed and rolled her shoulders, stretching back and shifting in her saddle. "There's junk everywhere. Stormy already stepped on a tailpipe."

"Keep looking."

"I am, but it's *impossible*."

"Look harder," Alice said flatly. "Do it for Stormy."

"I *am*." Sarah shifted forward over her horse's neck, patting him hard and giving him a brief hug, then she leaned to either side and continued searching the ground while guiding him safely through.

Jake and Rocky followed her, and Alice rode just to the right, a little ahead and beside them, keeping watch on the grass and pointing out larger pieces of jagged debris with Hercules coming behind her on his tether. There was a bit more convenience and enjoyment that came with traveling by horseback than in a car, and she was taking advantage of that by pushing them slowly and steadily north, constantly reminding herself it was a marathon and not a sprint. Buck barely missed stepping on a car battery, and Alice flicked the reins to guide him up the shallow, right-hand bank past a fender lying flat in the grass cast off from a nearby explosion.

"I suppose we could walk them along the highway if it gets clear enough, just for a bit," Alice said, glancing up at the roadway. "At least then we could see all the stuff on the ground."

"No way, Mom." Sarah kept searching the ground as she spoke. "You heard what Wilford said. None of the horses are shod, so we don't want to walk them on pavement unless it's absolutely necessary, or it could hurt their hooves."

Alice frowned and turned her attention back to the swaying grass. "I know. I'm just trying to decide what would be worse, walking them on pavement or having them get a piece of metal hidden in this grass stuck in their hooves."

For the first time all day, the skies cleared slightly, a mix of black and gray streaks stretched thin across the atmosphere, making it impossible to differentiate between rain clouds and smoke. The highway signs told her they were on Highway 19, somewhere between Thomasville and Omega, Georgia, though Alice couldn't say which they were closer to thanks to a lack of mileage markers for the cities. Going beneath an overpass, Alice guided them up to the next road and they crossed the intersection while avoiding a small scattering of debris from a nearby van explosion. There were bodies, charred remains that left the sickly-sweet scent of cooked flesh clinging to the air, and they moved back to the median as soon as they passed by. The morning shifted into the afternoon, and the weather grew muggy with moisture trickling down Alice's face. With her shoulders and back straining from hours of riding and craning her neck, she snapped her fingers and gave a low whistle to call Jake and Sarah who'd gotten a little ahead of her.

"Hey, kids. What do you say we stop here for a bit and take a break? There's a trickle of water down the center of the median the horses can drink from, and we'll dig around and see what we have left in our packs to eat."

"Sounds good to me," Jake said, swinging off Rocky's back and leading him down the slight incline to the shallow valley of the median where the stream ran south. The horse immediately bent and drank from the water while Buck nibbled at the surrounding grasses as soon as Alice was off his back. Sarah brought Stormy up and let him graze next to Buck as Alice and the kids moved up the bank a short way and took their packs off Hercules, who then joined the other three horses at the water's edge.

Alice nodded. "We need to keep an eye on them. We don't want them wandering off or getting spooked and running."

"What if we used some rope Wilford gave us to tie onto their bridles and around rocks or something?" Sarah asked as she looked up at the horses with her backpack between her knees.

"Eh, they should be okay," Alice replied. "It's pretty quiet out here, so they'll be fine now. We can hobble them properly later to keep them from walking off." Falling to her knees to start searching through her pack, Alice looked up the road both ways and shook her head. "We haven't seen anyone since those looters at Wilford's yesterday. The highway is completely deserted. It's weird just how few people are around."

Sarah took out a couple of blankets and spread them out, and the trio sat so that they were facing the horses. They opted for some freeze-dried meals, each with a package of macaroni and cheese with cardboard-tasting nuggets of meat mixed in. It was surprisingly spicy, and Alice nodded appreciatively as she dug into the plastic bag and shoveled the food into her mouth.

"This is probably the best one we've eaten yet." Jake wiped a smear of processed cheese off his chin.

"That's not saying too much." Sarah spoke in between mouthfuls of food. "But you're right. It's like...." She looked at the sky and thought about how to describe the taste.

"Like spicy cardboard?" Alice finished for her.

"That's exactly what it tastes like, Mom."

"And how would you know what spicy cardboard tastes like?"

"How would *you* know, Mom?"

They chuckled, finishing their food and sitting quietly for a few moments, enjoying the peacefulness of the place in spite of the destruction surrounding them.

"The horses are enjoying themselves," Jake said, watching the four as they walked slowly through the grass, eating as much as they could.

Buck and Hercules had wandered a little to the north, long necks bent down as they drifted, while Stormy and Rocky had taken to grazing on opposite sides of the trickle of water, one on each side. All four tails swished lazily in the midday sunlight, the odd colors of the clouds casting an eerie gloom about the place. After half an hour or so of sitting and resting, Alice groaned and got up, stretching and yawning before she lined up their backpacks and looked through them to take stock of what they had.

"We've got enough food between the meals and snacks to last us a few days at least, maybe longer if we stretch it out a bit." She raised an eyebrow. "Aren't you glad I made us stuff these backpacks full when our car was burning?"

"Definitely." Jake held his MRE up with the corner aimed directly into his mouth, finishing off the last few crumbs before he turned the package around and looked at the nutritional information. "That little packet was six hundred calories. Not bad."

"Yeah, we're going to be burning a lot more for the foreseeable future, though. All the walking and riding and general stress is going to have us burning them off like crazy."

"We definitely have to keep up our energy," Sarah nodded in agreement. "What are we low on that we should be stretching as much as possible?"

Alice took a bottle of water from a backpack and held it up with a shake. "We're running pretty low on water, so we need to think of something to do there." She frowned at the dirty trickle the horses were drinking from. "The horses will be fine, but we're sure not risking anything that isn't treated or boiled."

"Oh!" Sarah exclaimed, getting up and coming over to join Alice next to their backpacks, putting Jake's aside and taking hers to drop it in front of their feet. "It just so happens I picked up a couple of things from the items we were piling up at the warehouse department store." She dug in her backpack past the blankets, food packets, and snacks to some inner pockets that were zipped up. Sarah laughed. "It's funny because I'd put these aside in the SUV but didn't think we'd ever use them. They could easily have burned up inside it. But when you told us to throw stuff out, something told me to grab a pack of these and keep them just in case."

"And 'these' are?"

"These!" Sarah held up a handful of small cardboard boxes with pictures on them of extra thick straws about seven inches long with a drinking tip and caps on the ends. "Filter straws!"

Alice gave her a sideways grin as she reached to take one. "Well, aren't you the smart one?"

"Let me see one of those." Jake accepted one from Sarah and popped off the plastic caps to inspect both ends. "I guess we drink from this side and suck the water up... there's some kind of filter inside them?"

"Exactly." Alice nodded to where the horses were drinking. "This would probably make that water perfectly drinkable, but I don't know if—"

"I'll try it first!" Jake was already racing down the shallow slope before she could finish, giving Rocky a pat on his neck before squatting next to the small stream.

Alice started to protest, but they were going to have to use the filters at some point – and potentially on much dirtier water sources than the trickle – so there was no sense in stopping him. With a shrug and a tap on Sarah's arm, the two went down to join Jake where he was doubled up with the straw's fat end dipped into the water. Sarah kneeled on his left while Alice came to his right and watched as he took several mouthfuls and sat back in a resting crouch.

He licked his lips for a second, nodding his head back and forth, about to speak when his mouth twisted, and his hand flew to his throat, gripping it and he began making exaggerated gagging sounds. Sarah had been mere seconds away from drinking some herself when she stared at her brother in horror, her frightened gaze darting back and forth between his gagging face and the water. Alice raised an eyebrow and stifled a grin as Sarah began to panic, and after another few seconds of the charade, Jake's face shifted from pain to hilarity as he laughed and slapped his knee before pointing to his sister and her horrified expression.

"Oh, geez, Sarah! You should see your face right now!"

"Oh yeah, you're real hilarious, jerk," Sarah punched him in the arm, eliciting another howl of laughter. "I was trying to figure out how to save you from being poisoned, but I won't next time."

"I don't need saving," Jake said, holding up his filter. "It's perfectly fine. A little warm, but it doesn't taste bad at all... and it's not poisonous. I think the word would be... contaminated? I dunno, whatever."

"Poison or not, you know what they said about the boy who cried wolf." Sarah gave him another punch on the arm and bent down to drink, with Alice following suit, chuckling at Jake's antics.

She dipped the end into the water and sucked on the tip, but it didn't come out immediately. "This is like sucking an ice cube through a straw," she said. Stooping low again, cheeks sunken, she drew harder, and the water finally came through. The temperature was, as expected, lukewarm, but there was no taste, the filter doing exactly as it was advertised on the box. "This isn't bad. Nice work grabbing these, Sarah. They'll last us for... holy cow, a thousand gallons each?!" Alice looked at the packaging and grinned. "This is perfect!"

"What if we don't have any water around to filter?" Sarah asked, leaning down for another drink.

Jake shrugged. "We'll just fill up any empty water bottles with this, and when we get thirsty, we'll stick the drinking straws inside and slurp away."

"Easy enough," Alice agreed, retrieving a few of the plastic bottles that were running low and merging them into full ones before filling the empties in the creek, separating the dirty from the clean. "We've got four bottles of dirty water we can use with the straws and three clean ones we can drink from if we're in a pinch. It should be easy to tell them apart since the dirty water is a little cloudy, but we should mark them just in case."

"I know what to do," Sarah said, putting her drinking straw in her pocket and taking her knife out of its sheath. "I'll make grooves in the caps of the dirty ones that we can feel with our fingers. That way, if it's too dark to see or we drained one and aren't sure if it was filled with dirty or clean water, we'll be able to feel the caps."

"Smart thinking," Alice nodded. As Sarah was marking the dirty water bottles, Alice stood and stretched again, shaking off the exhaustion that was trying to creep up on her. "Okay, kids. Let's mount up and get moving again. I don't want to take another break till tonight if we can help it."

"Yeah, we've got about a billion miles to get home." Jake grabbed their packs and began fixing them to Hercules' saddle using rope and a combination of knots he and Sarah had learned as more parts of their lessons for riding and caring for horses filtered back into their minds.

The afternoon wore on as they traveled beneath the swirling skies, the flat Georgia landscape giving way to occasional hills and farmlands divided by highways and old country roads. There were sections of road with no wrecks at all, while at other times the clusters of debris and violent pileups were so thick they had to get off the horses and lead them through, picking up debris and tossing it aside to spare the animals from injury.

The forests around the highway grew denser, a press of woods like they hadn't seen around the cities and coasts, endless expanses of verdant green so vivid it almost hurt her eyes. All the wreckage against the world's natural beauty was a clash of imagery; smoking vehicles and half-burned woods, the winding highway stretching through the rising hills. At one point, they came to a bridge that crossed a shallow waterway, the roadway ahead going north packed with a single pile up in the center that had left a scatter of debris pouring over the shoulders. The twisted chassis of a dozen vehicles had fused with terrible impacts, leaving a few off to the sides and a single truck on the right-hand shoulder, hanging off the guardrail and balancing precariously over the water flowing below. The southbound lane wasn't much better with its share of still-smoking wreckage and spread parts, tires and tailpipes and twisted fenders, the remnants of human beings scattered through the mess, all of it shaken up and cast across the pavement. Forced out by the median coming to a close, they headed up to the road again, stopping at the edge of the bridge where Alice looked down and saw the sharply sloping land dip fifty feet into a fast-flowing river.

"Oh, what a mess." Sarah stared at the wreckage on the road. "Are we going to go through that?"

"The only other option is to get off the highway and cross at the water. That could take hours or even all day." Alice frowned and focused on the span ahead where it stretched two hundred yards to the opposite side. "No, we need to cross here. We'll only be on the road for a bit, and I see spots to get through the wrecks. It shouldn't be hard on the horses at all."

"It looks rough to me." Jake squinted. "I mean, that's a lot of dead people."

"I guess it is," Alice chuckled morbidly. "We've seen a lot already. Are you guys going to be okay? We can go back and look for another way through and —"

"No, it's fine," Sarah said as she stared straight ahead with slightly narrowed eyes and a frown. "We can go this way."

"Let's dismount." Alice swung her leg off and hit the ground on wobbly legs. "It would be better if we led them across. Less stressful on them, and easier for us to clear the way if necessary."

The kids dismounted to lead their horses and she tugged at her own pair of tethers and got them moving forward onto the bridge. At first it was easy going, but they soon reached the edge of the debris field and started weaving between pieces of wreckage; car tires were lying on their sides, splatters of oil and antifreeze created rainbow-tinted slicks and glass and plastic were scattered all around them. Alice gestured and guided their group to the right where things weren't quite so bad.

They passed the first wrecked vehicle, all four tires blown out and hanging from their axles with the chassis sunk to the pavement, ash blowing off of it as a breeze kicked up. Not a single window remained, and its once blue color had turned grey from the heat. The coal-black husk sitting in the driver's seat had a pair of stubs where the hands used to be, posed in a parody of driving. With a shiver, Alice kept them moving on a path that wound between the tangle of steel and past the dangling sedan hanging off the guardrail.

"I wonder if it'll go over if I give it a push..." Jake murmured.

"Please don't," Sarah said before Alice could, and he rolled his eyes at her as they continued on.

The reek of rotting flesh was ever present, mixing with cooked-off plastic and oil, and Alice's nose wrinkled as she waved her hand in front of her face. "Wow, that's bad."

"My nose is burning," Jake coughed and spat off to the side.

Alice was trying to look anywhere but the surrounding wreckage, though navigating the horses through the mess required far more of her attention than she wished to provide. Three-quarters of the way across the bridge, as they came around a particularly nasty wreck, she caught sight of something in the distance in a small field just off to the right side of the highway, and a smile spread across her face.

"Hey, kids. Have a look at that, would you?"

Sarah rose on her toes and grinned over the wreckage at sixteen animals grazing in the field. "Deer!" The deer heard Sarah's excited exclamation and jerked stiff for an instant, their long, smooth noses held high, ears flicking before they turned and dashed into the woods, white tails raised behind them.

"Darn it!" Alice frowned. "I was almost ready to get out my rifle."

Sarah shot her a glance. "What do you mean, your *rifle*?"

Alice shrugged. "We need to think about how we'll get food once our supplies run out." Nodding up the highway, she moved ahead and left her daughter frowning. "As Jake said, it's a billion miles to home, and we don't know if there will be ready supplies for us anywhere along the way."

"It's not a *billion* miles, Mom" Sarah offered reluctantly, "but yeah... I guess we will need to think about hunting at some point soon."

"Exactly."

"Shooting them is one thing." Sarah tugged Stormy ahead to keep up, "but what do we do with them after that? None of us knows how to skin and... *dress* is the right word, I think? We don't know how to skin and dress animals."

"Not true. When I was about your age, I helped your grandmother and grandfather butcher cows and pigs. I remember the basics and could probably fake my way through the rest. With a little practice, we could get pretty good at it."

"I don't know, Mom." Sarah's face twisted up. "Sounds kind of gross to me."

"It won't be so gross when you're starving," Jake pointed out.

Alice nodded. "No kidding. I'm pretty sure I could bring a deer or a boar down. I just need to get close. Then we can butcher whatever we kill and get a *lot* of meat off of it. Way more than we'll be able to eat. I know it sounds gross and bloody, but imagine the meat sizzling over a fire at our next campsite. I remember it from when I was a girl, and once you have that... you'll want to throw these instant meals away."

"Can't we just smoke or cure some of it?" Jake put his hand to his forehead as he searched the distant woods for any signs of the herd. "We don't have to eat everything we kill right away."

Alice chuckled lightly. "Kiddo, I don't have any earthly idea how to smoke, cure, or sun-dry meat to keep it for very long. I wouldn't trust it to sit at an ambient temperature for hours — let alone days — and still eat it. Plus, making jerky can take days, I'm pretty sure. I doubt we'll have time to stop any place for too long. We'll see what happens, but I'm just trying to be practical. Once we get home then we can figure out better methods of preserving extras."

Jake was nodding as he led Rocky off to the left, around a bucket seat that had been flung free from its vehicle. "Yeah, I guess you're right about that."

Soon, they'd cleared the worst of the debris and had reached the edge of the bridge where there was no more scattered glass or metal that Alice could see. "We're through, kids. Let's mount up and get riding again."

Jake mounted Rocky and went trotting out ahead while Sarah came next on Stormy's back with a swath of sunlight shining off his reddish flank. Alice climbed into Buck's saddle and gripped Hercules' tether firmly, giving a soft click of her tongue to nudge them forward back down onto the median and the soft grass. The strip of green was almost perfectly flat and short, likely tended to by highway road crews just before the world had gone up in flames. Relieved at not having to crane her neck and search for debris in the tall grass for a while, Alice relaxed back in her saddle and let Buck's natural motion carry her north.

CHAPTER THIRTEEN

James Burton
Hannibal, Missouri

The soft scent of forest green and honeysuckle drifted through the warm afternoon, the sky full of patchy clouds, pure white against stark blue heavens and a welcome relief from the streaks of black and grey. Sunlight shined down for long stretches in bright rays, bathing them in light and heat whenever the road turned so they weren't in the shade, though as soon as sweat broke out on James' forehead, a cool breeze would blow through like a sigh, relieving him of having to wipe his brow.

Eli was a quiet travel companion, the older Amish gentleman sitting straight in the seat with his feet resting on the footboard and his knees angled outward. The only movements he made were an occasional flick of the reins or a clearing of his throat. The man seemed fascinated with the beautiful sky and the surrounding landscape, preferring to focus on them rather than the continual destruction that he had to navigate around. In the back, Clara rode with Esther and the grandkids, and gentle screams, laughter, and squeals of delight came as they played games with one another. Along with the rhythmic hoofbeats and the smooth sound of rolling wheels, it made for a gentle, relaxing ride. A poke on his left shoulder made him turn, and Esther was behind him, leaning between the curtain with a piece of bread on a soft cloth cupped in both hands. What appeared to be bright yellow butter and thick maroon jam with bits of berries was smeared on top.

"What's this?" James asked.

Esther laughed. "It's sweet bread. Homemade, the last batch we made before we left the settlement."

"Oh, I couldn't eat your food." James shook his head, smiling appreciatively even as Esther's smile dropped. "I have plenty of my own; I don't want to take yours."

Eli grunted. "Nonsense, James. You can have all the sweet bread you want. Not only do we give it freely, but the girls don't want it to go stale and spoil. Please, you'd be helping us out if you had a slice."

With a reluctant sigh that vanquished Esther's frown, James accepted the bread. "Thank you so much. It looks great."

Turning to face the road once more, he rested the bread in his lap, picked off a corner, and tossed it in his mouth, the sharp sweetness of the jam and the light underpinning of dough a welcome relief from the packaged or bulk-prepared food he'd been eating. "Wow! This is amazing."

Esther nodded happily and disappeared behind the curtains, leaving the two men to chat.

"Seriously, Eli. This is delicious." James struggled to speak as he finished the bread before wiping his fingers and mouth on the cloth.

"My wife and daughters made this almost every day," Eli replied, "selling the best of it at the market in town. Little did I know it would become a commodity rarer than gold. I'll miss it when we can't make it anymore."

"I guess it's not something you can make on the road, huh?"

"Not without a good stove. We'll likely not get any more sweet bread made until we find a good wood-burning stove, which our relatives in Indiana should have." Eli cleared his throat gruffly and flipped the reins as he leaned back and turned to James. "You say you're heading home to your family?"

"That's right. My wife is Alice, and my kids are Sarah and Jake."

"Tell me about them, if you wouldn't mind. I would love to hear about your family."

James squinted into the sun. "Well, Alice is about as strong-willed as they come. She can work in a field all day long and still smile at the end of it. A tough farm girl, I guess. They called her a tomboy when she was a kid, but I don't really see it. There's such a sweet, motherly side to her no one else sees but me and the kids."

"The relationship between a man and his wife is truly a blessing," Eli nodded. "What about your children?"

"My son Jake is fourteen, and Sarah is twelve. But by looking at them, you'd think they were twins. Same dark hair and eyes. They're thin kids, but strong and wiry. They're still kids at heart. Haven't really seen much of the teenager-ness in them yet, thank goodness."

"Athletic, are they?"

"Not overly so. Well, they both play sports, but they're not superstars. They tend to anchor the team and try to be solid role players, mostly."

"They sound like excellent children."

"They are, and they're hard workers. We've got a little farmstead outside of East Lansing. Alice's parents are watching the property while we're away."

"You're both away?" Eli asked with a quizzical look.

"That's right. I was on a business trip to Denver, and Alice and the kids were in Florida, on vacation and waiting for me to get there." James took a deep breath and exhaled. "We had the whole thing planned out. Time on the beach doing silly stuff like making sandcastles and swimming, and I was going to rent a boat, too. I wanted to get the kids out in the ocean and let them see how big and beautiful it is. A whole week free of distractions, just hanging out together having fun."

"Why, that sounds wonderful," Eli nodded curtly.

"Have you ever been to the beach, Eli?"

"Oh, yes." He chuckled. "You probably think we Amish don't vacation, but we do. And, no, we don't take our buggies all the way there. Our elders allow us to rent buses which we take to popular vacation spots amongst the Amish. Being one with nature and all of God's creations is important to us."

James was nodding. "That makes sense. Anyway, they were waiting for me, and that's when everything went up in flames."

A forlorn look washed over Eli's face, and he patted James on the knee. "I am so sorry you were apart when this unfolded. I couldn't imagine being separated from my family like that, especially with the catastrophe that has befallen us. Do you think they're safe?" He gasped and glanced over. "My apologies, James. I didn't mean to speak so insensitively. Of course they're safe."

"No, you're fine. While I've tried to stay positive, there's a possibility they could be in trouble. It's... a simple reality that can't be ignored."

Aside from the occasional wreckage and decimated homestead, the rural landscape was astonishing, with sweeping hills, clusters of trees, and vine-covered fences running parallel to the road. Sometimes roadways and drives swept through harvested fields with an assortment of crops, though mostly corn prevailed, and he even spotted a handful of horses on a distant hill, casually grazing on the grass.

"Well, would you look at that," James pointed. "I'm glad to see some other survivors, even if they are four-legged."

The Amish man turned to look north and released an amused chuckle. "Indeed. What a beautiful sight in all this travesty."

They rode in peace for another few miles with just the clattering of hooves, the rolling wagon wheels, and the soft tittering of children to keep them company. It was only when James looked past the trees and spotted the hard corners of buildings with scorched siding that he stiffened in his seat and grabbed up his rifle where he'd placed it next to him.

"What is it, James?"

"I see a town up ahead. We need to be careful."

The Amish man only nodded and continued driving, where more structures appeared beneath the bright blue skies. There was a gas station on the right, followed by a pair of restaurants and a bookstore. Past that was a long, squat building with a steaming coffee cup for a sign that read *Jan's Books and Coffee*. On the left-hand side, the trees and hills cut away to reveal a few houses and then a series of stores weaving up a gently sloping hillside. There was a small grocery, a feed shop, and a strip with a hardware store, post office and an ice cream parlor. While several cars and pickups were wrecked on the sides of the roads and in parking lots, most businesses remained unscathed by fires. A few structures up in the higher hills attached to driveways had caught fire and were left in ruins, the surrounding trees burned brown by the infernos.

In the first two houses on the left, faces stared out at them from the windows, adults drawing their children away, leaving only the fluttering of curtains in their wake. On up where the road curved to the right into the embrace of encroaching hills, they could see more people inside the strip malls and stores. Shadows moved behind the glass storefronts, some flowing toward the doors, starting to come outside until James sat forward and stood up, leaning forward with the rifle in one arm, then they quickly backed up and slunk away. When James turned to look past Eli, he spotted a pair of boys peeking from an alley to stare at the horses in awe. A man with a fishing hat and a beard saw the carbine and immediately pulled them into the safety of the shadows.

"I don't think there's a need for that kind of posture, James," Eli said with soft scorn.

James sat back down, keeping the rifle conspicuously visible and shook his head. "If there was a time for looking intimidating, it would be right now."

"These folks just see us going by and are curious." He chuckled gruffly. "They probably haven't seen anything moving on wheels in a while."

"And they'd recognize you as Amish and could take advantage of your kindness."

"Fair point."

As the buggy and wagon continued rolling, more figures moved behind burned-down buildings and crept through parking lots where businesses once stood. From what James could see, some organized work was happening with crates of supplies and shucked corn taken off the stalks and piled atop spread tarps.

"We should stop and help these people," Eli said plaintively. "Perhaps we could pull over and offer to trade for something that might help us out, or even lead them in prayer."

James took his eyes off the curious faces and looked at Eli, raising an eyebrow. "That's an admirable idea, but the way things are right now, I suggest you focus on protecting the precious cargo in your wagons. And I don't mean your supplies."

Eli appeared troubled, his forehead furrowing in concentrated doubt. "While I understand what you're saying, James, the Lord would not be pleased if we did not come to the aid of others who desperately need it."

James shook his head and motioned off to the left with his rifle. "They're not in such terrible shape. Over there are grain silos and most of these buildings are still intact. Someone recently harvested the fields we passed. I'd argue the folks here will do just fine without your intervention, and it would only put you at risk of getting robbed."

Eli's concentrated expression flattened out, and he gazed from one side of the street to the other, seeming to measure up their surroundings a second time. After a moment of reflection, he nodded. "I see what you're saying. I don't see anyone starving, and there's no evidence of violence. Perhaps I should learn to assess situations like this more... critically rather than have a one-size-fits-all solution?"

"Exactly. Use a sniper rifle instead of a shotgun." James grinned and winked at him. "Unless you *really* need the shotgun."

Eli sat with a curious expression for a long moment, digesting the words before he finally broke into a belly laugh, shaking on the seat as his deep chuckling gripped him. After a long moment, Eli wiped amused tears from his eyes and sighed with cheerful satisfaction. "You've got a way of putting things, my friend. I get your meaning, and I'll be more discerning in the future. You're right about that precious cargo I carry. My children and grandchildren mean everything to me, and I would be nothing without them. Thank you for that bit of wisdom."

They neared the end of town where more of the damage was visible, three separate buildings burned to the ground with the bones of vehicles scattered around them, scorched to the springs from the flames. The remains of two people were being picked apart by the sharp beaks of turkey vultures, their rotting flesh strung out across the pavement and their bellies burst open in a gruesome display of scavenging. James shuddered at the sight, sitting back in his seat and lowering his rifle while Eli murmured a prayer as he urged the horses to hurry past the scene.

With the town finally behind them, and the curious faces fading from sight, Eli turned and parted the curtain to the buggy's rear compartment, nodding and speaking to the women. The Amish leader faced the road amid a bustle from the back, and soon Clara was reaching through between the men, a smile on her lips as she offered James something on a soft cloth. It was a darker, heartier slice of bread and several chunks of salted meat.

"Won't you take some?" she asked, holding up the food with a nod.

"I've already eaten from your stores." His gaze shifted from Clara to Eli. "I don't want to cut too deeply into your supplies."

"Nonsense, James. I'll warrant you have nothing but military rations in your backpack, which can't sit well with a man who likes good greens and meat. The bread and cured pork are packed full of nutrients. If you eat that, you won't be hungry for a full day."

"I appreciate the offer, but I just can't. Not when you have kids to feed."

Clara offered the food more forcefully, raising her eyebrows in concern as if James didn't know what was good for him. "While our supplies are limited now, wherever we end up, we'll use the land. It won't be long before our larders are full again, and the children will work hard to keep their bellies full. Please, James. Eat."

James chuckled. "Well, I can't argue with that." Accepting the cloth from Clara, he placed his rifle aside and set the food in his lap with his knees together. With his hunger already stirred after the snack from before, James ate greedily, tearing off a rough piece of meat that appeared dry, but was perfectly seasoned and chewable, the bread slightly sweet with the rich taste of grains and a hint of sugar. A moment later, Clara returned with a tin cup full of water, and James accepted it graciously, sipping to wash down the food.

"This is superb," James said. "This is what we hoped to make on our own, eventually. Alice was just getting to think about bread making, and I was seriously considering doing some hunting and curing my own meat." He shook his head and chewed slower. "We just... didn't have the time."

"The ways of the land take a long time to learn," Eli acknowledged, "but once the secrets are in your heart, they will keep you and your family fed forever, thanks to God's graces."

When he tried to hand Clara back the tin cup, she held it steady with one hand and poured a cloudy brownish liquid into it from a pitcher.

"What's this?" James sniffed at it and caught the scent of cinnamon and apples. "Smells good."

"Drink," she urged with a smile.

James did as he was told, taking an experimental sip from the cup as a burst of sweet tartness exploded through his mouth. "Apple cider?"

"Made by Esther," Clara nodded. "Do you like it?"

James took another sip, the taste more intoxicatingly delicious than anything he could recall in recent memory. "It's... *great*. More than great!"

"Thank you." Clara smiled and brought food up for Eli, and the Amish leader adeptly accepted it with one hand while holding the reins with the other, still driving while he ate.

Gesturing to his backpack, which he'd placed just behind the seat, James said, "I must insist that you take some of my supplies, too. At the very least, accept a handful of preserved rations and high-calorie energy bars."

Eli laughed. "Oh, James. I don't think we'll need any of that."

"Why not? You could run into another situation with the bandits on the road, and you may only be left with a few things. While I don't have a lot of these rations, just a few will give you and your family enough calories to survive days on the road." James pressed when Eli only laughed and popped a piece of cured pork in his mouth. "At the very least, try something. These are tried and true military supplies and would be good to keep on hand because they need minimal preparation."

"Hmm..." Eli turned. "Clara? Clara, dear?"

Clara pressed through the curtain. "Yes?"

"Would you help James retrieve something from his backpack?" His gaze shifted to James in question. "What do you recommend?"

"How about dessert?" James offered.

"A dessert?" Clara looked doubtful. "As good as our sweetbread?"

James chuckled and turned to gesture at his pack. "Not even close, but they taste like brownies, and they're filled with plenty of calories and will keep in their packaging for years without going bad. Go ahead, Clara. Get some out."

"You know, James, when we can food, it lasts for years as well." Eli gave him a bemused expression.

"We've canned as well, and you're absolutely right. Look, Eli... you're being far too generous. At least let me try to offer something in return. It'll make me feel better."

With an agreeable nod from Eli, Clara opened James' backpack and dug through his supplies, glancing up as if asking for permission.

"It's okay, Clara," James said. "Go ahead. That's it. Those right there. Those are the brownies."

There was a pack of eight in a large plastic wrapper, and Clara tore it open to remove four brownies in their individual packaging. She handed one to Eli and another to James, then she tried one herself, peeling back the plastic and splitting it in half. While James wished he had a glass of milk to go with it to counter the wooden flavor, he continued to sip at the cider, its tangy, homespun sweetness a sharp and welcome contrast to the military ration.

"Oh, mine has nuts on it!" Clara chuckled, covering her mouth, taking a few small bites.

With a sideways glance at Eli, James asked, "Well, what do you think?"

Eli was about three-quarters of the way done, and while his upper lip had curled on the first bite, he seemed to enjoy it more as he chewed. "It... is not pleasant on first taste. There's a sweet, dry texture. And heavy, too. The more I try, the better it tastes. Interesting... I do see what you mean by this being quite filling. Yes, very good." He smiled at James. "Not a substitute at all for sweet bread, but we'll happily accept some."

James nodded at the remaining brownies, feeling better about the arrangement. "Take those. And take some other snacks, too. There are some high-calorie granola treats that the kids might like. I know the taste is nothing compared to what you have here, but as an emergency backup, it couldn't hurt."

Clara called into the wagon, and young Sadie appeared with a hesitant grin. Together they rummaged through his things more eagerly, with enthusiastic fingers and curious smiles. James noticed Clara checking the military backpack, testing the seams and craftsmanship approvingly as she gathered a handful of snacks and took them back to the kids. Sadie reorganized everything in his pack in a polite and non-intrusive way before she zipped it up and disappeared with a smile.

"In spite of my initial declinations, I appreciate your insistence to trade," Eli said as he had another brownie bite. "You are truly the kindest and wisest person we've met on the road yet."

"I wouldn't call myself wise, but I'll take the compliment. You have a wonderful family, and I'm happy to share your company on the road." James relaxed against the backrest. "You mentioned being driven out of your community before."

"Not driven out, but split up by ill circumstances."

"What happened, if you don't mind sharing?"

Eli gazed into the sky, taking on a dark, dreamy look. "We were a wonderful community. A hundred and fifty of us, close-knit and working together in God's graces. The crops were plentiful, and we'd just finished settling another small family on the outskirts, building them a pleasant home on the hillside and raising their first barn with much joy, happiness, and hard work. We were mostly situated in a small valley surrounded by two hills we called the Twin Knobs. Beautiful, gentle, sweeping slopes filled with trees and farmsteads painted bright against the lush landscape." The Amish leader took another bite of brownie and chewed it slowly, his expression shifting through different emotions before settling on troubled and sad.

"When things went wrong, we were getting a delivery from some English in trucks. Normally, we allow the trucks to pull into the main lanes leading into the neighborhoods. Of course, some of our flock are – were – far too lenient for their own good. Trucks with lumber, feed supplies, and other goods we traded for from the world were allowed to pull up to our barns and warehouses until approximately five motorized vehicles had spread throughout the community. You can probably imagine what happened next."

"The trucks exploded and caught your buildings on fire." James' expression was blank as he stared at the road and recalled the insanity he'd witnessed from Denver to Kansas City - fires raging everywhere, explosions, people screaming, and planes falling from the sky.

"I awoke from a short evening nap to the sounds of Clara's screams, alarm bells ringing loud, and the roar of flames and smell of smoke." Eli cast his gaze downward. "Upon going outside and gathering Clara and the children to see what had happened, my eyes took in a sorry sight. Fires raged through the hillsides, infernos that appeared as though they could have been torn from hell itself. Many were trying to put out the flames, but they were unquenchable."

"Did you try to call the fire department?"

Eli was nodding. "We have one phone available in the entire community we can use for emergencies. When the elders tried to call, no one responded, and when I looked north from the heights between tossing buckets of water on raging flames, I saw the inferno burning everywhere, consuming parts of Hutchinson Township. That town contained the only means of our rescue." Leaving off with a heavy sigh, he used a finger to wipe at the corners of his eyes and sniffed.

"I witnessed things I couldn't have imagined. One of my cousins tried to rescue her son from their burning home, pulling the boy outside with their hair and clothes on fire. Abram tackled them to the ground, covered them with his jacket, and tried to put out the flames, but it was too late. To our heartbreak, he died smoking in her arms. Waves of cinders carried on harsh winds swept the fires through the field and trees, which have been dry this year because of a lack of consistent rains. It moved from house to house, sparing no board or human life."

Eli's expression grew more strained. "We continued trying to form bucket brigades, using spigots in our home and drawing water from a nearby well to attack the flames, but it was simply no use. Some of our bravest cousins perished, entering raging homesteads where their brothers, sisters, and parents cried for help, only to succumb to smoke inhalation and heat. I tried to stop my cousin Jed, but he was feverish with anguish, shook me loose, and sacrificed himself to save his wife and daughter. He disappeared into the smoke, and we never saw them again. Seeing there would be no saving our community and having already lost so many to the devilish conflagration..."

Eli's head dropped with sagging shoulders, and James patted him on the back firmly in solidarity, though the man's pain was beyond consolation. Finally, he took a deep breath and continued. "I had Abram and Jacob run to the other parts of our community and order them to load supplies while we did the same on our hill. We saved a few horses, this buggy, and the supply wagon and filled them with stores we had in our basement and larder, and we loaded up as quickly as we could to flee what I can only describe as an apocalyptic place. By God's good graces, we made it out."

"What about the others?"

"I'm afraid..." Eli shook his head, and his voice trembled. "Abram and Jacob returned to say the entry lanes into the other sections of our communities were consumed with fire, barring every pathway and trail up the slopes to thwart any reasonable rescue attempt." Eli shifted uncomfortably in his seat and grunted to clear his throat. "I must confess that I'm plagued with... uneasy feelings about what happened."

James was nodding. "Something like that happening to your people must be devastating. I can't even imagine what it must be like."

Eli's pained expression of anguish twisted his features into a grimace. "We should have had better warning systems and a better way to manage the fires. We should have done more to get people out of there. I should have —" The man choked back a sob, his attempt at a stoic expression failed, succumbing to horror at the memory.

"You should have what, Eli?" James asked. "What could you have done any better?"

"I should have saved them or..." Another sob broke from his throat. "I should have died with them." Clutching his shirt, wincing, he finally met James' gaze with bloodshot, bleary eyes. "The guilt plagues me terribly to this very moment. I don't know if it will ever leave me, and rightfully so."

"I've seen what those fires can do and witnessed entire *cities* burned to the ground. You're not alone in your grief, or your feelings. You did what you could, and because of it your family still lives."

Eli didn't seem to hear him. "For a moment back there with those bandits, I thought for certain it was the Lord's punishment for being weak and not doing more. At that moment, I thought I understood the Lord's will and realized my failings as plain as a blade of grass in the morning light."

James sat quietly for a moment. "And now?"

"Now... I'm not so sure. With your arrival and help, it seems God has changed his mind and sent an angel to us."

James chuckled as he patted Eli on the back. "I assure you, Eli. I'm no angel. I'm just a man who's a long way from home and wants to reach his family as soon as possible. I'm just happy I could help you out."

"Even if you're not an angel, at the very least, you are a blessing from the Lord himself."

"I appreciate that, and you are all equal blessings to me for your assistance. And, look, what you're feeling is a natural response to what happened. You lost so many you were close to." James chose his words carefully. "It could be something like survivor's guilt, and I doubt it's something that will ever truly heal itself. The pain will lessen, though, I'm certain of that."

Eli wiped his eyes again. "Perhaps by the Lord's graces, we'll find some kind of peace, though my heart will never be still after what I've seen."

James reached to pat the man on the shoulder, paused, then let his hand fall, squeezing Eli's shoulder, feeling his muscles tensed beneath his coat. "I wouldn't dare to compare my experience in all this to yours because you've lost so much. When this disaster started, I looked out the window at the airport terminal where jets were falling from the sky and maintenance vehicles were launching straight into the sky after their gas tanks blew. Fire rained down on us, and people were dying everywhere. It was so... I can't even explain it." His heart hammered with the horrific memories as the words came out, and he tried to steady his breath. "With thousands of people in sheer panic, I barely made it out by jumping on the back of a transport cart that an airport employee was driving." Wiping the sweat off his brow, he snickered sadly. "You should have seen the look on his face when I climbed into the seat next to them. Poor guy probably thought I was going to rip his head off or something."

Still drying his tears, Eli chuckled as James described the scene.

"From there, I fought my way out of the terminal and into the street where everything kept exploding. The entire parking lot was just one detonation after another, with fire raining on our heads and more planes falling from the sky, and... Eli, I'll never get the screams of those wounded and terrified people out of my mind."

Momentarily taken aback by his own story, James let his hand rise to his chest to quiet his racing heart, the sounds and smells of that day lingering strongly in his mind, images of the furious flames embedded in his brain forever.

"Yes, we both have similar feelings toward what happened."

James rested his elbows on his knees and leaned forward. "My point is, Eli. Out of everyone at that airport, I was one out of a few thousand or more, maybe, who survived that. I guess it would be easy to allow guilt and our emotions to overrun us, but I'll tell you the same thing I've been telling myself since this started. There's no room for guilt because this is about more than just us." He half turned and glanced into the back of the buggy. "It's about them, too. Our families are the most important things right now, and as long as there's a breath in our lungs, we must fight every step of the way." He stared at his rifle. "Even if it sometimes means stretching the limits of what we believe... or believe we're capable of."

Eli remained quiet, giving a thoughtful nod as he flicked the reins and leaned forward to contemplate James' words as they rode along the winding highway through a beautiful landscape as long, black clouds drew into sight on the horizon.

CHAPTER FOURTEEN

Alice Burton
Omega, Georgia

"Keep riding, kids! Make sure we've lost them!"

Four horses and their trio of riders burst from the thick woods and galloped into a wide grassy field that stretched before them. Around the edges were massive swaths of vibrant green and the distant shapes of fencing that helped define the border between the trees and grass. Alice glanced back with a ragged gasp, looking for any further signs of pursuit, waving for the kids to continue riding forward as she lagged behind, Hercules' rope lashed to her saddle horn to keep the riderless horse in line. Heading roughly northeast, they closed in on more trees that would provide cover, trying to keep Highway 319 on their left to avoid getting lost or losing their sense of direction.

Alice's heart was pounding after they had barely managed to get away from a group of would-be thieves along the highway, her mind filled with fear at the thought of being dragged out of their saddles and beaten and robbed – or worse. The horses were acting differently as well, their heads tossed upward, nostrils flaring and tails whipping as they ran hard. They'd been walking for most of the journey, barely breaking into a gallop for hours on end, and their pent-up energy was palpable as they sprinted toward the tree line. Buck's well-muscled body felt like a mountain beneath her, and the way they'd fled swiftly from their slower pursuers made her breathless where she perched in the saddle.

The shade trees fell across her vision, Jake and Sarah following each other ahead of her in perfect coordination as they picked a path and blew through clusters of bushes, leaping logs and turning on a dime to split between trees and cascading vines. Alice was more careful with Hercules in tow and fell behind, and by the time she caught up, the kids were picking their way down a shallow bank, working the horses right and left as they crossed a narrow stream, the water splashing up around the horse's hooves. Following in their tracks, Alice guided her horses across and flew up the next bank to enter another wooded section where birds shrieked and burst from the upper boughs, and small animals scattered in the brush as they thrust through.

They continued galloping for a while more, trying to gain as much distance as possible, staying together in a staggered formation. Alice was so focused on keeping Hercules with her she didn't see the tree line breaking ahead, and Buck suddenly leaped into another grassy field littered with bumps of deadfall and golden swaths of sunlight. Jake and Sarah were almost a hundred yards ahead of her and galloping fast, forcing Alice to whistle and shout to get their attention.

"Kids! Hey, kids! Wait! Hold up!"

Jake pulled Rocky up, breaking off to the left and swinging back the other way with a massive grin. Sarah slowed gradually, hair flying behind her as she turned Stormy slightly sideways before straightening again.

Alice huffed, pulling on her reins. "Whoa, big boy! Slow down, Buck. Whoa!"

She caught up with Jake and Sarah after another moment, and together they walked more leisurely, allowing the horses to take a breather after their escape.

"Man, we bolted out of there." Jake was still grinning, leaning forward and patting Rocky's sides enthusiastically.

"Good thing," Sarah replied. "Those people were *angry*. And the way they looked at the horses?"

"No doubt they would've loved to have them," Alice agreed. "But you guys rode like pros. There's no way anyone can stop us if we keep working smart like that. We can slip away as easily as you please whenever someone threatens us."

Jake drifted closer. "What was that last town, anyway? We barely started to get off the highway when they all came out of nowhere at us."

"I'm pretty sure that was Norman Park, Georgia. Good thing we didn't go through the town center, right?"

"Any idea where we are now?" Sarah stretched in her saddle, turning sideways while her hips and legs moved with Stormy's rhythm.

"I'm... really not sure. I knew we were circling Tallahassee before, and Highway 319 was just over there to the north. Maybe if we get back on it, we'll see some signs for some towns up ahead."

"We don't want to be *on* the road, though. I'd be scared to go back on the median again after seeing how fast they were coming after us."

"We can walk in the fields beside the road easily enough," Alice agreed. "Just keep an eye out for anything that might give us clues to what's coming up."

They angled the horses due north and soon reached Highway 319 where it crossed in front of them, separated by a wooden-railed fence. They walked parallel to it until they came to a break, passing through and moving along the grassy bank at the roadside. To avoid a crash on the near side of the road, they crossed over to the left-hand shoulder and started calling out pieces of debris that they saw, a chore that had become second nature to them.

A couple of miles along, Alice pointed. "And that's what we're looking for."

Jake leaned forward and squinted. "Omega, Georgia. Population, two hundred and ninety-five. That's a *small* town."

"Probably blown to bits like every other small town we passed," Alice said, though when she searched the skies above the town, she saw no signs of smoke or fires.

"Yeah, a lot of the towns will have been totaled," Sarah added, "but that won't keep people from wanting our horses."

Alice nodded. "That's exactly why I wanted to put as much distance between us and any populated areas as possible before we slowed down in that field back there."

"Should we get off the road then if we're getting close to this new town?" Sarah asked.

"That's a great idea." With a tug on the reins and a kissing sound, Alice guided Buck off to the right and pushed them forward to enter farmland populated with farmhouses, grain silos, and barns that sprouted up along the tree line. The farms were placed as far as a mile or two apart, with a few built right up to the roadside as they followed Highway 319's curvy path to the northwest.

"Stay close, kids. We'll stay near the highway for as long as possible, then circle the town and join the highway on the other side."

She took their silence as understanding and cut through several broad fields where a vast array of unharvested corn sat rotting on their stalks, slumped over with withered leaves, crowded with crows and other birds that flew overhead in squawking flocks.

"Oh, that's too bad," Alice winced. "That's a ton of food going to waste right there." The cornfield reminded her of home, where her parents were watching over the house and had animals to take care of and rows of crops that they might have brought in – if they were still alive. With a swell of emotion, she squeezed tears from her eyes and cleared her throat, turning Buck off to the right to guide him to a field of peach trees to try and distract herself from her thoughts. Much of the fruit had fallen off in the soft grass, chewed through, riddled with worms, or smashed flat, but there were still some hanging low on the branches that had yet to be found by insect or avian devourer. Riding up, she plucked a piece of fruit off a bending limb. Rubbing the soft furry skin with her thumb, she inspected it.

"Looks good." Taking a quick bite, the fruit exploded in her mouth and juices ran down her chin. Alice laughed, turning to the kids and gesturing at the trees. "Go ahead and try one. They're amazing."

MIKE KRAUS

They each took a peach and bit, Jake falling forward to catch an outpouring of juice as it ran off his chin onto his saddle.

Turning back toward Hercules, Alice reached for a plastic bag tied to the side and got a rag she'd kept handy, shaking it out and tossing it at Jake as he went by. He tried to catch it, but it flew past his open hand and bounced softly off his face, eliciting a cackle from his sister, who rolled backward in her saddle, clutching her stomach while holding her peach off to the side. They ate their fruit down to the pits and tossed them on the ground, then Alice pointed Buck back north across the farmland.

Sarah wiped her arm across her mouth to get the last bit of juice before waving. "Wait a minute, Mom! Those were amazing. Why don't we put some in our packs?"

"I guess you could try to wrap a couple up in a towel and carry them along. Just... don't let them leak all over everything and come crying to me if you get ants all in your food and clothes."

Sarah straightened. "Okay! I'll just take a couple... as an experiment."

Alice laughed. "God willing, there'll be a peach tree every few miles through the rest of the state."

"Hey, it is Georgia after all!" Sarah grinned.

Alice waited for Sarah to pack a couple of peaches into her backpack before kicking Buck back into motion, drawing Hercules behind her and galloping smoothly across the plain.

The following field over, almost a quarter mile away, Alice spotted a farmhouse sitting off the road with smoke trickling from its chimney and a couple of barns and sheds out back. It was a newer model, single-story house with a brick face and a wide front porch, and out behind the barn, sheep bleated noisily. A dirt track led from the home to the main barn nearby where they were riding, a big blue construction with a gabled roof and the front door standing wide open.

"Come on, kids," she called back. "Looks like someone's home. Let's hustle on past as quickly as we can."

The kids followed as Alice kicked Buck up a notch, circling around to the side of the barn, staying away from where a few trailers and bales of hay were stacked under a carport. Next to that, a large boat with a blue hull sat on a trailer with a cover over the deck, its back end blown out where the engine had been, though the damage was limited to the rear section, leaving most of it intact. As they moved past the wrecked boat and awnings, Buck suddenly snorted and pulled sharply to the left, causing Alice to grip him with her knees to avoid falling off, tilting forward and just catching herself.

A man came flying out from behind the carport, waving his hands and shouting for them to stop, and Buck pulled again. Getting him under control with a quick tug on the reins, Alice pulled her rifle from the makeshift scabbard she'd fashioned for it and swung Buck around, still pulling Hercules behind them. Whipping the weapon up, she leveled it at the man's head and tried to keep it steady as the horse walked to the left. Sarah had banked smartly away from the man, and Jake was backing Rocky up with quick steps, his revolver trained on the man's chest. Glancing between the rifle and pistol, the man skidded to a halt, raised his hands and retreated a few paces.

"Don't shoot!" he called, gazing across them fearfully. "S-sorry for surprising you. I'm not a threat! Please, I need help!"

Alice peered over the man in his dirty clothing and worn appearance, his overalls stained with dirt, beard scraggly and grown out and a red cap on his head above a pair of steely blue eyes that were shaded with an edge of panic.

Alice kept the rifle trained on the man. "Come on, kids. Leave him alone. Let's go."

The man lunged forward a pace, slapping his hands together, his voice growing more desperate. "No! You can't go. I need help. My *wife* needs help! Please!" He held his ground, yet still winced beneath the barrels of their weapons, taking a couple more steps in retreat before coming forward again, his whole body a ball of anxiousness.

"He's got blood on his hands, Mom," Sarah pointed out.

As the angle of the light changed, Alice spotted dark red smears across his palms and overalls. "Yeah, I see it. What happened? Did you hurt your wife?"

"No!" The words flew out of him in a torrent. "I wouldn't hurt a fly! It's my wife... my wife, Elaine, she's pregnant and giving birth." Swallowing hard, he waved at the house. "She's having a baby right now... but something's *wrong*! I was going to try to get to town for help!"

"If you're heading south to Norman Park, most of it burned down, and the people aren't too friendly, as we learned."

Against the barrels of their weapons, he came forward again, turning away from Jake and pleading to Alice directly. "Do you know anything about birthing? You're not a nurse, are you?"

"I'm not a nurse." She squinted at him. "Wait a minute... you live out here on a farm and know nothing about birthing?"

"We only moved here last year," he replied tremblingly. "We came out here to get away from the city. We wanted to

234

start a new life before the baby came. So, no... I *don't* have a lot of experience. With another kid on the way, we just wanted a fresh start away from everything. We were making good progress before... everything happened!"

"What did you do before you moved out here?" Alice asked.

"I was an accountant before," he said, the panic rising in his voice. "Look, lady, I don't know what to do. Elaine is in the house right now in a ton of pain. I can't help her. If you can't help us, please just let me go so I can try to get help from someone in town!"

Buck's head drifted a bit, so Alice turned him back the other way so she could keep her rifle lined up on the man's chest. His face was soft aside from the scraggly beard, and while his hands showed little sign of outdoor work, his clothing was well-worn in all the correct places. There wasn't much else rugged about him, and her instincts honed from the last several days warned her to take the kids and go... yet something in his eyes and the pleading note of desperation made her pause. If there *was* a young woman inside the house giving birth, Alice could never forgive herself for not helping.

Alice sighed with resignation. "Okay. We'll go back to your house and check on your wife. Hop on this other horse I've got and ride over." She raised the rifle and pointed the barrel at him. "But if you try anything funny, I won't hesitate to put a bullet in the back of your head. Got that?"

"Yes! I've got it! Don't worry. I'm telling the truth! You'll see how much I need your help!" As he was talking, he ran up between the horses until he finally reached Hercules.

"Hang on." Alice gestured for the kids to swing around and grab their packs off of Hercules, after which the man mounted the horse awkwardly, swaying in his seat, taking the reins and jerking them around like he'd barely ever ridden. They took off, and Alice looked back to see him riding Hercules like a clumsy beginner, spine stiff and heels kicking at the horse's flanks as he nearly tumbled off the other side.

Alice pulled tight on Hercules' line, settling the animal. "Easy there, boy. Hey, what's your name?"

"Nate. My name is Nate." He clung to the saddle horn with wide eyes, the reins loose over one arm.

"Okay, Nate." Alice shot the kids an uncertain look as they sped up, Hercules keeping up with her on the left thanks to some continued tugs from the lead. She glanced over at the bumbling rider. "Just focus on staying on; he'll follow next to me. Hercules is a big, strong guy, and if you don't pay attention you'll end up tossed on your head."

"Sorry!" Nate settled down, shifting in agitation as she guided Hercules toward the farmhouse deeper on the property. They were there in about two minutes, and Nate slipped from the saddle, almost getting his left foot caught in the stirrup before he hit the ground, still holding on as Hercules dragged him a few feet. Stumbling away, he made a break for the house.

"Whoa, whoa, whoa! Stop right there, Nate!" Alice slung her rifle up, freezing the man in his tracks.

Holding up his hands again, he turned slowly, expression falling into panic. "You don't understand! Elaine and the baby! They're in trouble! We've got to help her!"

"Sarah, Jake." Alice jerked her head at the house. "Go check it out. Jake, cover your sister."

They both nodded and dismounted, hitting the ground and dashing past Nate toward the house, stepping hesitantly onto the first porch step before turning to give Alice a skeptical look.

"Go ahead, Sarah." Alice leveled the rifle at Nate. "Your brother will cover you, and I've got Nate covered. Go on and check. Look through the window."

Sarah crept dutifully toward the house with Jake close behind her, pistol at the ready, their gazes shifting between their mother and the window with its blinds drawn tight. Sarah went to the top step, one toe at first and then leapt up, glancing back with a frown. When Alice continued nodding, she turned to the window, cupping her hands against the glass to peer inside. Sarah slid along it, rising and ducking to get a better view. Finally, she reached the spot where one of the blinds was broken off, and she froze in place, her entire body tense.

Before Alice could tell her to get away, Sarah exploded into motion, throwing a desperate shout back before sprinting to the screen door and ripping it open. "Mom! She needs help!!" Shoving her way inside, Sarah disappeared and sent Alice's heart shooting out of her chest. Nate broke into a sprint despite the weaponry pointing at him, hot on Sarah's heels for the door.

"Son of a..." Alice muttered, throwing her leg over Buck's flank and dismounting as she yelled at her son. "Jake, tie the horses up somewhere! Then stay out here on the porch until I call you, okay?"

She ran past Jake onto the porch with her rifle still at the ready, grabbing the storm door and throwing it open with her free hand, banging her shoulder against the half-open door as she charged in, instantly hit with the heavy crimson copper smell of blood. Looking around, Alice took in a living room coffee table, couch, and recliner shoved up against the wall. In place of the hastily moved furniture was a bright blue tarp spread out on the floor with a half-naked woman lying on top of it, bare from the waist down, her legs splayed open, thighs smeared with blood and birthing fluid. When she saw Alice and Sarah standing there dumbfounded, the woman dropped her jaw wide and unleashed a spine-jarring scream that sent Sarah retreating backward until her shoulders hit the wall.

Nate pushed past Alice and Sarah and fell to the woman's side, grasping her hand and shushing her with whispers. "It's okay, baby. It's going to be fine." He gestured at Alice with a bloody, shaking hand. "Ma'am, this is Elaine. Please... you have to help us."

Something moved on the opposite side of the room, and Alice lifted her rifle on pure instinct, lowering it immediately as she spotted a little girl with a dirt-smudged face and wide, frightened brown eyes. Her dark hair was greasy and unwashed, half-hiding behind a doorway as she blinked at the strangers who'd just invaded her home. Alice groaned softly and called for Jake, the urgency in her voice bringing him in an instant.

Handing him her rifle, she pointed. "Go over there and stand in that corner. Have a look outside and keep watch. Got it?"

Jake nodded and walked stiffly to the blinds, unable to take his eyes off the bloody mess in the middle of the room. The woman's constant groans and cries shifted from heady panting to high-pitched, mewling whimpers and, spinning to Sarah, Alice grabbed her daughter by her wrists and jerked her straight to shock her out of her wide-eyed stare.

"Sarah, we're going to help this woman, okay?"

"Yeah, Mom," she said numbly. "But how?"

"I need you to snap out of it right now, okay?" Alice tugged on Sarah's arms again, and she nodded and shifted her gaze to meet her mother's.

"Okay. I'm here."

"I need some things."

"What?"

"First, and most importantly, forceps. I don't care if you get them off the grill out back. You know, like tongs or something?"

"Yeah."

"Then I need scissors, towels, and a suture kit if you can find one." She whirled on Nate. "Nate, I need you to get up and help my daughter find the things I just mentioned. You'd know where they are, okay?"

Nate was nodding, but he wouldn't let go of Elaine's hand.

Alice clapped repeatedly, shouting at him. "Right now, Nate! If I don't have those things, I can't help. Go!"

Nate leaped up and brushed past her to take Sarah into the next room, and Alice fell to her knees beside the struggling woman, grabbing her flailing hand and clenching it tightly. Locking with Elaine's dark and faltering gaze, Alice could see the woman trying desperately to hang on, but she was beginning to fade. The miracle of life was happening right in front of Alice, but Elaine's life and the life of her child hung dangerously on the edge of a knife. A chill of determination shot up her spine, and she gripped Elaine's hand harder. Picking up a wet rag Nate had dropped, Alice began wiping Elaine's face clean of blood and grime and sweeping her sweaty dark locks away from her temples.

"It's okay, honey," she said. "I'm Alice. I'm here to help you."

"Something's wrong." Elaine spat through tightly pressed lips. "I noticed it almost immediately, but we didn't know what to do..." Her abdomen clenched tight, her belly undulating with throbbing and quivering spasms. She gripped her bloody t-shirt with her free hand as if she wanted to tear it off.

Alice blinked once and then turned back. "We're going to get through this, Elaine. We'll get that baby out of you, and it'll be fine."

"It's a *he*... a little boy." Elaine's voice trembled. "His name is Ethan."

Alice smiled tremulously. "Ethan. What a handsome name. Well, we're going to bring little Ethan into the world."

The little girl in the doorway had finally gotten past the arrival of the strangers and was overcome with fear, crying in quick gasps, her belly hitching dramatically before escalating into a full-on downpour of tears. With no one to comfort her, Jake rested his rifle in the corner and came to squat in front of the couch, calling to her from across the room.

"Hey, it's okay. Come over here." He waved her over, smiling through the moment's stress, trying to look friendly but only managing a wounded, panicked expression. Still, the girl saw something sweet in his eyes because she shuffled over with a glance at her screaming mother and fell into Jake's arms.

"It's going to be okay," he said, wiping off smudges of dirt from her cheeks as her crying faded into snuffles of uncertainty. Finally, he lifted her and placed her on the couch with a smile, talking in a soft, child's voice. "Just stay right here next to me, okay? Your mom's going to be fine, and my mom's here, and so is my sister, and we're going to be here for you, okay? Don't be scared."

The little girl's hesitant nods grew more confident by the second, and she rubbed her eyes and reached out for Jake's hand, taking two of his fingers and holding them tight. Nate and Sarah rushed in from the kitchen as Alice worked to calm Elaine.

"Here's the stuff, Mom." Sarah placed the scissors, some clean rags, and a dusty first-aid kit next to her. "There's a suture kit inside. It looks pretty old, though."

"It should be fine." Alice nodded firmly as she turned to go through the kit and take stock of her supplies. "If it has nylon threads, those probably wouldn't have weakened over the years. Did you–"

"We got some water boiling... two pans of it." Sarah shrugged. "I saw that on TV. I dunno what it's for."

"Good girl." Alice's gaze lifted to Nate. "We need as many clean rags as you can get. Use the boiling water to sterilize them if you need to, and do the same to the scissors and forceps."

Nate turned and showed her a laundry basket with several stacks of folded towels and washcloths. "We just did laundry before everything exploded in flames."

"Good. Put it down right there."

As Nate put the basket to the side and rushed off to sterilize the tools, Alice shifted her position to crouch between the woman's knees and gently lift her shirt. "I'm just checking things out, okay?"

Elaine was nodding. "Is Ethan okay? Is he going to die?"

"He's not going to die..." Alice replied firmly, surprised to find the tick of a smile touching the corner of her mouth as she leaned between Elaine's knees to see a round, peach-colored head pushing out already.

"Okay, this is going to be uncomfortable." Alice quickly slipped on a pair of gloves from the first aid kit and reached inside, gently pushing against the boy, feeling to see what the problem might be. "Dammit." Alice hissed. "I think the cord's around his neck."

"Around his *neck*?!" Elaine's words came out in a howl as another contraction seized her.

"It's okay. Just wait through this contraction, then I'll get it off of him. It doesn't feel tight, so I think he's fine."

"I... I can feel him kicking still." Elaine gasped.

"Good, that's excellent." As the contraction eased up, Alice used her fingers to slip around the baby's head and the cord, untangling it from what felt like his neck and shoulders. The space in the birthing canal immediately felt looser, and Alice pulled her hand out, leaning forward to look again.

"I think that... oh, *boy*! Here he comes! You're fully dilated, Elaine, and he's crowning! I think we're good!" Alice glanced around at the group as Nate came back in before leaning in and trying to see how she could grip the baby without hurting him. She took hold of Elaine's knee and squeezed it. "He's coming, but I need you to push with your next contraction! Can you do that for me, Elaine? Use the contraction and push *hard* with it!"

Elaine nodded, clenched her hands into fists, and tensed her entire, quivering form, legs and stomach straining, knees quivering, face turning bright red as she unleashed a harrowing, ear-piercing scream into the room.

CHAPTER FIFTEEN

President Thomas Birk
Mount Weather, Virginia

A Marine guard escorted Birk along a stretch of hallway in that same baked green color that was everywhere in the bunker, with Agent Harris right behind him and General Pulaski bulling his way forward at the front of the pack. They took a quick left-hand turn and descended a narrow stairway where the guard shouldered open a heavy steel door, allowing cool air to wash over them as they stepped into a well-ventilated chamber with the humming of computers and murmuring of military personnel. It was a well-lit space with blue system lights glowing from the darkness at the room's far end as techs walked between rows of servers, connecting fiber cables up to additional gear they'd just wheeled in. Closer were sections of communications staff who relayed orders to distant military units via satellite, radio, or even horseback if needed. The room was awash with the odors of strong coffee and perspiration, and Birk noted with some amusement that almost everyone – even the most prim and proper ones – had tossed their jackets off, rolled up their sleeves, and unbuttoned their uniforms to give them some breathing space.

Pulaski gestured for the President to follow him around a group he recognized as the strategic movement team who were poring over maps and charting paths through ruined cities and highways, with Major Jasmine Spencer leading them, her people jerking to attention when the President came in.

"Back to work people," Birk said absently, then he lifted his voice. "Everyone, back to work! Stick to the tasks at hand and keep working. Don't let me break the flow."

Spencer's group went back to work, hunching over their maps and pointing at a path from Baltimore and Philadelphia. Pulaski led Birk and Harris between busy groups who were planning on how to section off other parts of the Midwest and South, and a separate team with a placard on the table that read *California-West Coast* glanced up as he went by before returning to their work. The General led him to an oval table in the middle of the room with an empty seat at the head, which Birk took. Colonel Crow was on his right and Pulaski on his left. Before he addressed the group, Birk looked around for Agent Harris, nodding as the man quietly slipped in and stood behind him, hands clasped at his waist, constantly searching for any threats despite being in arguably one of the safest places in the world.

"All right, people," Birk started, "General Pulaski tells me we got some pretty good news. Ravi, tell us all about it."

The President's Chief Science Advisor, Ravi Anandan, stood five seats down on his right. The slight Indian man had a soft expression and his side-parted hair was combed back, looking as neat and well-groomed as if it were any other average day at work. Despite everyone bustling and bumping as they passed each other and sometimes called out across the room, the scientist spoke softly, barely getting his mouth open before Pulaski interrupted gruffly.

"Let me start, Dr. Anandan. I've got some initial information the President might be interested in."

"Of course, General." Ravi nodded. "And please, just Ravi will do."

The General grunted and raised his finger and circled at a handful of staffers around the twelve-person table, and they immediately swooped in with information packets that were spread to everyone assembled. "It's all in the report my team just handed out, but I'll summarize everything right now for you. Based on fuel samples Ravi and his team analyzed, cross-referencing data we had on existing weapons development across the globe, we traced it back to the Saudis."

"The Saudis?" Birk blanched. "Are you *serious*?"

"We think they'd been developing the tainted oil product to seize control of the global supply of oil worldwide."

Ravi stepped in. "The contaminant was supposed to lie dormant for decades and reproduce until a secondary catalyst, the bacteria, was introduced into the system. At that point, the two would interact and start the countdown to a thermal runaway situation." He gestured to the papers everyone had received. "The specific scientific data is in the information packet. Based on preliminary analysis of this catalyst bacteria, we can see they failed to account for a variety of mutations that led to a much sooner than anticipated thermal runaway situation."

"How do you know this?" Birk asked.

"Genetic markers pointed to three potential production sites outside the United States. Of those, records showed only two with the necessary supplies to create this sort of a bacterium, and only one – in Riyadh – employed biologists and genetics experts of sufficient training and skill to create such a bacterium.

"As for the mutations, there are at least five generations we have identified both in destroyed and select intact stock that have key genetic differences that show progressions between them. We believe that, over time, it became its *own* catalyst. It lit the match itself, in other words."

Birk flipped through the first couple of pages, blinking at the scientific explanations, the diagrams, and molecular mapping of the fuel components before looking over a layout of the various bacterial stages, all of which blurred together. He pushed the papers aside, shifting his gaze back to Ravi and the larger picture. "How did it happen at virtually the same time across the world?"

The scientist slipped his hands back in his pockets. "The original introduction of the bacteria must have happened long enough ago to infect the global supply. It could have been growing and changing for months, and apparently this self-immolating mutation was one most easily reached by the bacterium."

"Uh, excuse me, Dr. Anandan?" Harris raised his hand from behind Birk, the President swiveling to look at him.

"Just Ravi, please." The man smiled.

"Ravi. I'm... no scientist. But I remember my basic biology pretty well, I think. Most organisms mutate to better survive and thrive and beat out competition. Wouldn't a mutation that leads to the destruction of an organism be a pretty bad path for it to go?"

"Under normal circumstances, yes. But this is an engineered bacterium, designed from the ground up to eventually meet a violent end. Instead of waiting for a catalyst to be introduced to lead to that end, though, its mutations ended up creating the catalyst itself." Ravi paused, searching for the right words. "It took a shortcut, in essence. It was always going to be used for this purpose. But instead of waiting to be told to fulfill its purpose..."

"It did it on its own." Birk exhaled sharply, looking around at those assembled before settling back on Pulaski. "So they intended to hold the world hostage? And, what, selectively make country's fuel supplies go up in flames to squeeze more money out of them?"

"Appears that way, sir," Pulaski replied, "though I doubt it was ever intended to come to light like this. That's why we want to launch a counterstrike immediately. While our military is at a severe disadvantage, theirs is even worse. Our recovery time from this will be nothing compared to what it'll take to get them to form any kind of defense."

While Birk had experienced many emotions over the last few days, from sadness to rage at whoever had attacked them, the new information he was receiving softening any cry for retribution he might have considered.

He snorted. "Why? What would be the point of such an engagement now? It would only distract us from our own crisis and spread what little resources we have way too thin. They've suffered just as much devastation as we have – worse, it sounds like."

Pulaski made a fist and held it tight at his waist, chin shifting to the side as the tendons in his neck stood out with tension.

"But sir. Look what they've done to us. Look what they've done to the *world*. You've seen the casualty reports. Billions are dead, and that number is only going to increase. Even you..." The General caught Birk's jaw clench, and he stopped himself before he overstepped. Honing his focus, Pulaski narrowed his steel-blue eyes. "All I'm saying, Mr. President, is that they need to pay the price for what they've done. The world needs to know that this kind of blatant terrorism won't go unpunished."

Birk took a slow breath, leaned over the table, and rested his weight on his hands, the folders and information packets spread all around him, filled with disaster plans and reports that were assembled from a withering storm of data that was impossible to keep up with much less act on. Looking across at the faces staring back at him, their anger was raw, visible in scowls, hard glares, bleary eyes, and tear-streaked cheeks. It would be easy to lash out at anyone they assumed was at fault. The more challenging job would be to continue their dogged pace, trying to save what remained of the country and the rebuilding that would likely take decades of infrastructure repairs, and even more years of repopulating to get them even close to where they'd been. Ideas rolled through his head, but on a whim, he turned and nodded to Agent Harris, where the man was still looking everywhere *but* at the table until he finally realized Birk was watching him.

He stiffened and raised an eyebrow. "Do you need something, sir?"

A flat grin worked its way onto Birk's face, and he glanced at Pulaski before returning to the agent. "I'd like to get your opinion on this, Agent Harris."

Harris blinked and released his clenched hands, his gaze shifting from the President to the waiting officers. Firming up his slack expression, reclaiming his stoic stance, he interlocked his fingers then let his arms hang loose, unsure what to do with his hands with all eyes upon him. "Well, sir... I'm not a military expert, and I wouldn't know how to begin to address the situation."

"You're *not* a military expert, Harris. That's why I want your opinion right now."

Reluctantly stepping forward, Harris glanced at the maps and various packets lying all over the table, ignoring them and backing up to clasp his hands behind him. He stared at nothing and then seemed about to say something before shifting his gaze to the floor. Eventually, he met the President's eyes and responded.

"We should take a measured approach, sir. We could retask our satellites over their country and discover their capabilities. I'm sure the intelligence communities would love nothing more than to dig into everything about them, given this new information. If it looks like they're hiding something more, or like this mutation was a deliberate attack on the world at large, we strike. Otherwise... let's focus our resources on helping our people, not killing theirs."

Birk smiled as he chewed on the agent's words. "Take some time to gather more information before we strike. Makes sense. That's exactly why I wanted your opinion, Agent Harris." Turning to General Pulaski, he tapped his finger on the table with new confidence. "I want all eyes on the Saudis, General. I want to find out every piece of information about this weapons program, their original intentions, what went wrong, their future plans – everything. Peel back their cheeks and give them a rectal exam if you have to, but get me information."

"We'd be giving them time to build up, sir," Pulaski countered. "It's possible that this *was* their original plan, and they're feigning their injuries while they prepare to do something worse!"

"I understand how you feel, but I'm not about to sling ICBMs across the ocean without damned good reasons, and especially not without consulting our fellow nuclear powers. Last thing we need is to be burned, starving *and* irradiated. For now, we'll watch and study. Get me information ASAP. And General?

"Yes, sir?"

"If attack is the answer... we'll rain hellfire. You have my word."

General Pulaski nodded briskly, seeming satiated for the moment. "Yes, sir. We'll draw up a surveillance plan right away."

CHAPTER SIXTEEN

James Burton
Hannibal, Missouri

The town of Hannibal, Missouri rose gently in the distance to the soft clipping of horse hooves and the near silent spinning of the wagon wheels, the horizon scored by scorched building tops and smoke still trickling into the sky. The boyhood home of Mark Twain and a source of inspiration for many of his stories, the quaint farmhouses, lush fields, and woods surrounding them spoke of a quiet, peaceful town that had slowly stepped forward through the years. Remnants of a pizza shop stood on the left next to a flower store and an upscale coffee shop, and a corner entryway to a subdivision was demarcated with a brick wall with *Orchard Grove* engraved on it in golden script, half-covered in soot and ash.

Eli seemed intrigued as they arrived at the edge of town, the man leaning forward in his seat with a tighter grip on his reins as he squinted at the surrounding destruction. Entering by a road on the west side, the Hannibal hospital had once stood on their right, its parking spaces dotted with destroyed cars and pieces that had fallen off the building in piles of brick and steel. Bodies lay amongst the wreckage, shot through and cut up by the flying shrapnel, with wide-winged turkey vultures surrounding them and picking at the corpses with their bloody beaks.

"Oh goodness," Eli stammered, quickly averting his eyes.

James stared at the disaster with a cold, sad heart, taking in the building and looking for any signs of medical supplies they could scavenge, though the hospital was a pile of rubble, burned through with only parts of the corners standing. The rest had collapsed inwards in a pile of embers and broken floors, the layers pressed tight, forming an open pit where the hospital once stood.

"What a shame," James whispered. "I wonder how many were inside when it happened."

"Those poor souls." Eli's words dripped with sadness, choking on the words, reminded yet again of the destruction of his community. When the curtains parted and the riders in the back tried to look, Eli waved them back. "No, what's out here is too heavy for the heart. You don't want to see it. Please, go back inside."

As they entered a crowded main thoroughfare, heading for the bridge to cross the river, the initial fire damage became worse. All of the businesses had gone up in the conflagration, from small mom and pop stores to fast-food restaurants, a small hotel and a bed and breakfast across the street, and a local gym all changed into black rubble. Shadows of a few people were masked behind the drifting smoke, smudged faces of survivors living in makeshift hovels they had erected in open spaces away from the worst of the damage.

James gripped his carbine with the barrel tilted at a high angle just above the horses' heads, ready to swing it in any direction if someone attacked them. Eli, meanwhile, grew visibly nervous as their trek through town continued, the damage giving way to a blackened hellscape that was from a place far worse than his worst nightmares. Off to his right in the south, a short line of a dozen survivors marched, ranging in age from young children to shuffling adults, trekking along silently as black-winged birds circled overhead, waiting for another meal. With a grunt, Eli scooted to the edge of the seat, watching the slow-moving line as they trekked off toward the hills, seeming to want to say something or take the horses in that direction, his desire to help nearly overwhelming him. At a glance from James, Eli nodded and leaned back with his eyes pinned forward.

"I can't stop you from making the choice to help them," James shrugged. "I'd still advise against it. Your supplies aren't abundant enough, and they could easily overwhelm us. It's your choice, though."

"I know, but your wisdom is sound, and I see God's mission for me is to keep my *own* family safe from harm for the time being. We'll keep moving."

Things grew worse in the middle of town, and the horses shook their heads and snorted through the stinging smoke, parts of the woods to the north still burning in isolated fires that were slowly spreading through the thick greenery. They approached a bank of smoke drifting across the road, and Eli gave the reins a flick to drive the horses through despite their discomfort. Abram brought the supply wagon close behind them in a clatter of hooves, hurrying to keep up.

Covering his mouth and nose with his shirt and squinting, James peered into the gloom, barely able to see beyond thirty yards, searching the road for anything that might bar their path. Eli spotted a two-car wreck ahead and guided the buggy to the right to swerve around it, calling back without breaking pace. "Abram, up ahead!" The younger driver drew the supply wagon behind them until both vehicles broke from the fog bank into the clear midday sky with spots of blue sunlight peeking through the clouds.

James coughed and blinked to clear his vision, and the first signs of a bridge came into view ahead. "There it is, Eli. Should be our way across unless..." James' voice faded as they drew near, all sense of hope rapidly dwindling.

As they passed ruined stores and demolished neighborhoods, James kept his eyes on the bridge, its upper girders painted yellow with crisscrossing steel beams growing more twisted and bent toward the center where pieces of concrete hung by threads of tangled rebar over the Mississippi River. Guardrails connected the span on the left side, the pavement split and broken off, and they eased the horses to a halt near the start of the bridge, not daring to go any farther. James and Eli both half-stood in their seats, stretching out to look across the span where the ruins of a fuel truck and a cluster of blackened vehicles half hung over the rails with a few teetering on the edge of spilling into the river below them.

"That does not look promising," Eli said. "I don't see a way through."

"Yeah, this doesn't look good. There's no way we can cross here." James leaned out from the buggy to peer across the length, pointing to the left side where parts of the bridge were still barely connected. "I mean, we could probably cross on foot on the guardrails and sidewalks there, but it would be incredibly risky and we wouldn't get the wagons across."

"Then we must backtrack and go south to the next city to check if there's a bridge we can cross." Eli barely held in his disappointment. "I fear we may never find a good place to cross, though."

"Not so fast. Hang on a minute." James jumped from the buggy, reaching beneath his seat to grab his staff, checking that all of the sections were firmly attached before shouldering his rifle.

"Where are you going, James?" Eli asked.

Clara parted the curtains and rested her hand on her husband's shoulder. "Surely you're not abandoning us so soon?"

"No, ma'am," he said. "I'm just going to backtrack a little and walk down to the shore. Maybe I can find another way for us to cross. I'll leave my pack here, if you don't mind?"

"Of course, but why don't you let me come with you?" Eli started to rise.

James waved him off. "That's okay. It'll be quicker if I go by myself. You folks take a breather and get something to eat." He looked both ways along the highway, empty but for the gently drifting smoke, the survivors having opted not to follow their horses and carriages. "You should be safe here for a while. I won't be long. Give a shout if you see anyone, though, and I'll come running."

"Thank you, James. We'll have a hearty meal ready for you when you return, and we'll pray in the meantime."

After checking his revolver, James headed west for a hundred yards until he came off the raised highway. Soft voices came from behind, and he glanced back to see Eli and his family in a circle, holding hands with their eyes closed as they prayed. Stepping into the grass, he headed south toward a spread of neighborhoods and wooded areas near the shoreline. As he walked, James idly knocked aside debris from destroyed vehicles, taillights and steering wheels, parts of engines he couldn't identify, and oversized bolts lying in the road, the titanium and aluminum alloy staff easily swatting pieces of plastic and metal aside.

Searching the lurking shadows for signs of danger, James worked his way south until he came upon a concrete court-yard with a tall statue of two barefoot boys overlooking Main Street, one with his pant legs rolled up and holding a branch on his shoulder while the other wore a wide-brimmed hat and carried a walking stick similar to James'.

"Tom and Huck," he whispered, smiling as he reached out to touch the statue.

James turned south and took connecting paths alternating between gravel and pavement as he got closer to the river. Down a short, grassy slope, he found some railroad tracks running parallel to the waterway, and when he stepped up to the rails, the shoreline spread in front of him from north to south. All along the river were entry points for boats, small docks bobbing in the water and held up by floats with a few rowboats and fishing vessels visible, though anything with fuel onboard had capsized to leave only parts of their hulls jutting above the surface. As he scanned toward the south, he spotted a small port area that angled out into the water with sturdy concrete pillars and tie-up points for boats. A pair of tugboats had sunk just offshore, one lying half out of the water with its narrow bridge jutting above the surface where light reflected off the glass. From beneath, the bridge almost looked worse than it had from the road, as even the parts that were still intact looked like they could give way at any moment.

Leaning on his staff, James headed off the tracks and explored the shoreline, angling toward the concrete dock while constantly glancing at the tugboats and across the water where the river was split by islands of lush land with waving trees and tall grasses along rocky banks. On the opposite shore were sections of woods in every direction with just a spattering of recreational areas and parks. On his side, the river curved to the right, and he hopped off the concrete slab to land on a wide gravel lane that ran parallel to the tracks. Crickets and bugs chirped in the bushes that hugged the shoreline, and he listened to the slow tick of cool weather and soft splashes as he walked. After just fifty yards, James grinned when he spotted a long wooden dock structure made of planks that formed a shallow L-shape, the longer section running parallel to the shoreline.

Connected to it was a lengthy green barge with a single pile of sodden, moldy grain on its deck. The truck that had been carrying the grain had been propelled away from the barge when its fuel tank ruptured, sending metal shrapnel into the nearby crane, smashing it and leaving it twisted with the dead operator still lying across the control panel. Slowing as he approached, James scanned where a short, paved drive led from the parking lot to the dock. From there the lane wound up to the train tracks, moving beyond them and into the trees.

"If it's big enough for a grain truck to get down here, it should also be good for the horses and wagons."

Angling toward the barge, he took the short lane down to the dock where the long vessel was rubbing up against the boat fenders, the wood and metal creaking together as the boards beneath him vibrated with the ship's movement. Even with the pile of rotten grain heaped in the back, there'd be plenty of room up front near the pilot house where Eli and all his people could fit. While he couldn't see a ramp, there were clear markings on the barge rail showing it could be opened to allow goods to be driven up to the deck. Propelling it across the river would be a challenge, but it beat heading to another bridge and hoping that it was passable. With a glance across the river, James turned and moved up the lane to the lot and then north again along the gravel path, energized by the discovery.

When he got back to Eli and his people, they'd broken up their prayer group and had placed a wooden table in the road with foldout chairs all around. Red and white checkered tablecloths lay atop the table, their corners fluttering in the breeze. Plates of bread and biscuits, various glass decanters, more of the cured ham, and a basket of fruit kept the table-cloth from blowing away. As he came up, Sadie, John, and Levi were laughing and running around the group with pieces of sweet bread and honey or jam slathered on top. Abram, Esther, and their spouses, Betty and Jacob, sat along the table with Eli and Clara at the head, eating while they conversed. When Eli saw James coming, he waved and motioned to where a chair awaited him on Eli's left.

"Hello, James! Please, sit down and tell us what you found, anything to enlighten our hearts."

While Eli sounded jovial, his expression remained somewhat downfallen, not expecting much in the way of good news. James strolled over and sat with a smile, the handcrafted furniture firm beneath him, the slight curve to the chair back perfect to rest his weight as he looked at the spread.

"Thanks," James said, accepting a napkin with an assortment of food from Clara, who nodded and smiled and returned to her seat next to Esther. "This looks... amazing. Kind of a funny place to set up a table and chairs, though, right in the middle of the road."

Clara laughed. "These are special-built just for this sort of thing, James. When we're having a meal or even enjoying a break for tea or coffee, it's much more pleasant to use a table and chairs."

"Fair enough," James nodded, taking a bite as Eli and Abram looked on at him eagerly, and he began to tell them what he'd discovered. "I walked south along the shoreline for a while. A lot of boats were overturned out there in the water, and the bridge is impassable. I wouldn't even risk crossing on foot."

"That's a shame, but it confirms our fears," Eli sighed.

James accepted a helping of honey on one of his biscuits, nodding in thanks to Clara. "I did find a way to cross, though it may take some work to get over."

"Hard work is all we know." Abram smiled.

Nodding, James told them about his short trek along the shoreline and the concrete dock he'd found, and beyond that, the longer wooden one with the green barge parked there. "It looks like they were halfway through loading some grain when everything went to pieces. The crane is gone – not that it'd really be much use to us anyway – but there's a road leading from the dock and up across the railroad tracks. I didn't see where it connected or how we can get there from here but I'm sure there's a way if we look around a bit."

"Doesn't seem like a lot of work at all," Abram said.

James chuckled dryly. "Getting down there won't be the hard part. It'll be getting the horses and buggies up onto the deck. I figure we'll need to find the ramp or make one ourselves, then it's a matter of handling the horses well enough to get them on board."

"We've been handling these horses all their lives," Eli said, "and they have the utmost trust in us."

"I don't doubt that, but being on a barge will be a new experience for them."

"You leave that to us." Eli took a bite of pork, looking at both of his sons, who nodded in agreement. "At the very least, we can find our way there and check it out. If it seems an impossible feat, we'll only have lost a couple of hours, no?"

"It's worth checking out," James replied. "Here's the kicker, though. The barge doesn't have an engine – only reason it's still on top of the water instead of underneath. We'll have to pole-push the barge straight across to the other side."

"We have strong men here. Do you think we can win out against the current?"

"I think so?" James shrugged. "I think it beats going south or north for hours or days to find another way that may not even exist."

"Then it's settled!" Eli practically beamed as he turned to Clara. "I daresay that this task before us is the exact answer to our prayer!"

"Praise be to the Lord," Clara closed her eyes as she took Eli's hand.

"The Lord has blessed us through James twice in as many days," Abram slapped James on the back, grinning at him.

Their contagious enthusiasm brought a smile to James' face as he finished his food, dusted off his hands, and offered to help clean up until the girls leaped in and shooed him away.

"I guess it's a sign we'll be up and moving then," Eli chuckled and gestured to Abram and Jacob, who were taking care of the horses, hitching them back up and getting ready to move out.

The chairs were folded and put away, as were the table legs, so that everything could be loaded into the supply wagon quickly and efficiently. Within fifteen minutes, the group was ready to move, and they got turned around and started heading west up the highway to find a way to reach the barge. They took the exit ramp and swung around to Mark Twain Drive which cut southeast through town, dividing once massive Victorian-style houses that had burned to the ground. James went on guard again in the lead wagon, scanning the side streets and alleys and peering through dense clouds of smoke, eager to see if it was workable to get the wagons on board the barge. After traveling with them for a while, he felt a certain duty to keep the family safe when they weren't always looking out for themselves, and the pressure to constantly be on the lookout weighed on him.

What remained of Hannibal was quaint and had a small-town feel James expected from Mark Twain's hometown, with hints of old brick buildings, shops, and restaurants. A cool breeze came off the river, and Clara and the girls grew fidgety. They'd thrown the curtains wide open and were looking out at the town's ruins, growing somber at the sheer magnitude of the destruction. They were well suited for travel with their ability to efficiently store their supplies, tools, and horse care equipment, but the world had to be overwhelming them, especially in such a destroyed state, after spending most of their lives in an insular community.

They ran into several dead ends along Mark Twain Drive, forcing them to go around until they rolled past the Huck and Finn statue. "There's got to be a way down to the water," James said, standing and scanning the few businesses that lined the tourist district.

Coming to an open construction yard with several eighteen-wheelers and flatbed trailers parked together in a heap of dead embers made from the surrounding trees, James found a lane weaving between the warehouses and gestured for Eli to follow it. The lane wound them down into the dark areas south of the Mark Twain tourist spots, and the buggy and wagon rattled over the train tracks and swept into the parking lot where the grain truck had exploded and torn the crane to pieces. Eli took in the destruction before looking over to the barge, where it squatted low in the water and bumped softly against the docks with the rolling current.

"There it is," he said. "Isn't that a glorious thing?"

"I sure hope it is," James agreed.

They pulled the wagons around the debris and stopped at the path to the docks. James, Eli, Abram, and Jacob walked down to inspect the dock and the barge with James leading the way, all of them leaning out to grab the barge rail and trying to peer over, barely able to see the deck.

"Like I said, there're no engines, but they've got poles."

"The pile of grain is no good," Abram commented. "A shame."

"Yeah," James agreed, pushing himself off the barge and following along behind the man as they walked the entire length of wooden planks. "Looks like it's been sitting here for a while, wet and moldy now."

They ducked under the crane arm that was still half hanging over the dock, its bucket open with grain crusted on it, none of it salvageable.

"Such a waste of a precious crop and potential blessing," Eli said as he came to a stop and rested his hands on his hips. "But the true blessing is this barge, and I know it will carry us across." He patted James on the shoulder and gestured to his sons. "Abram, Jacob. Do you see a way we can get the carts loaded?"

Abram had stayed behind and had crossed his arms over his chest while stroking the scraggly beard on his chin. Deep in concentration, he studied the height of the barge compared to the dock and turned to look back up at the buggy and the supply wagon. "If there's not a ramp on the barge, we'll build one and run it up to the deck. We want to keep the climb less steep, so we could build it in sections, one short section angling out from the boat and then a second section running down to the dock, keeping the incline rather shallow, in an L-shape."

James was nodding. "That might work, provided you can get the horses turned up the ramp and onto the boat without getting spooked."

"We know our horses, James," Abram replied with a raised eyebrow. "They won't spook." With a grin, he jumped across to the barge, drawing a chuckle from Eli as he landed on a groove where the rail met the hull, grabbing the rail and balancing there. His momentum carried him forward, and he swung both legs up and leaped over to land hard on the deck. Walking the full-length, he grinned and pointed to the front of the boat behind the pile of grain. "Our work is lessened! I found a steel ramp," he called. "It has hooks to latch onto the deck."

James leaped over and joined him, and together they lowered the rail and dragged the ramp over, sliding it down to Eli and Jacob until the metal hooks caught on the deck. The latter pair lowered the ramp until it touched down on the dock, giving them a way to climb on and off the barge.

Rubbing his chin, James said, "That angle is pretty steep. We'll definitely need that second section to rest the ramp on. It'll make a shallower slope and be easier on the horses."

Abram studied the angle and began looking at how they could build the L-section. "We might build it from plywood and cinder blocks. There should be plenty of materials up in the ruins."

"Agreed," Eli said as he stood back and imagined the construction.

"What about the wagons?" James asked. "The horses won't be able to make that turn with the wagons attached."

"I think they will," Abram countered. "We just need to be ready with blocks in case we need to stop and keep the wagons from rolling backward."

"You're the bosses. Just tell me what to do to help."

Abram smiled. "I'll be in front and guiding the horses by their bridles, and the rest of you stay back and be prepared to help slide the rear of the wagons if necessary."

"That's what I was thinking." Eli affirmed.

"We just need to find those building materials," James said, looking around.

They removed some supplies from the larger wagon, and Abram took the driver's seat and got it turned around, running it back up to the burned-down warehouses in search of wood and blocks that had survived the fires. They dug through the rubble and found several pieces of plywood and a few two-by-fours which they put into the back of the supply wagon. Everyone helped except for the kids and Clara, who stayed with their offloaded supplies down by the barge.

While the rest focused on working, James helped where he could while he patrolled from the lot to the warehouse area, his carbine in plain view and a nervous pinch in his belly. They were vulnerable out in the open and – unlike when they had been eating – spread across several blocks, and it would only take a small group of armed people to attack and overwhelm them.

Eli seemed to adopt James' sense of urgency and oversaw the supply-gathering effort, hurrying everyone along. Between a section of warehouses were some small riverside homes burned and collapsed into piles, and Abram and Jacob looked for blocks while Esther and Betty dragged larger pieces of wood and stacked them in one yard. It was tough, grueling work, but the Amish wore broad smiles and called encouragement to one another, laboring without complaint.

Soon, the wagon was filled with supplies dragged from the burning ruins, and Abram drove it carefully down to the dock area with everyone else strolling beside it, their faces and clothing smudged with dirt. After gathering back at the dock, they unloaded the supplies, and the men began building the ramp structure by placing cinder blocks two high and packed close together. They laid the plywood and two-by-fours on top to make a shallow slope, giving plenty of room for the largest wagon to turn left. Once everything was set, Abram and James climbed onto the barge and dragged the metal ramp back into place, resting its edge on the platform they'd built, forming an L-shape up to the boat deck.

"It's going to be a pretty tight turn," James commented as he studied the construction and rubbed his chin.

"But you can see how much shallower the climb will be for the horses," Abram said.

"Yeah, it's barely an incline at all."

Abram ran up to the first landing and jumped up and down, his boots thumping and echoing across the water while James glanced around nervously.

"Now for the true test," James said. "Who's going to drive the first buggy up?"

Eli gestured to Abram. "I trust Abram to do it. He's been driving wagons and farm equipment since he was a child, and he's always been the best at it."

With everyone in agreement, Abram leaped into the seat with a grin and drove the buggy down to the docks and over the wood planks where the wheels made a loud clatter as they drew up to the ramp.

Abram climbed down and circled around to the front, taking the horses' bridles in hand. "You ready with the wooden blocks in case we falter?"

"Got them," Jacob replied, and he and James held up the wood and rocks they'd use.

Abram looked down at the width of the ramp compared to the width of the buggy, finally giving the horse's bridles a tug. They moved quickly at first, their hooves sounding hollow on the wooden ramp. When the front wagon wheels started up, the left-hand horse snorted and shook his head, pulling a little to his side to come dangerously close to the edge.

"H'yah! Come on now, Amber and Teakettle!" Abram shouted, grabbing their bridles and jerking them straight, talking to the horses and urging them to go. Still, they faltered to the left, one stamping in annoyance and chipping off a piece of plywood to send James' heart leaping into his throat.

"Come now, beasts. Follow me, by God's will!" Abram growled. At the last second, he slapped Amber on the neck and lunged backward, hauling the horses after him with a grunt. With quivering shoulders and heads hanging low, the horses straightened and moved up the ramp, pulling the buggy with them until they were standing on the first landing. Abram turned them hard left, and they drew the wagon forward until the front left wheel rode toward the edge. The other three men watched until the wheel was about to slide off, then they rushed in, gripped the rear end, lifted it a quarter inch, and scooted the entire rear of the buggy to the right until it was mostly straight and pointed toward the deck. In rushed shouts of encouragement, Abram hauled the horses to the top with thudding hooves and clattering wagon wheels, the buggy rocking back and forth as it surged over the lip and onto the deck.

"Whoa now!" Abram called in a low voice. "Whoa, Teakettle! Easy Amber!" Abram guided the horses slowly and carefully in a right-hand turn, getting the wagon up the rest of the way onto the deck and pulling toward the front of the boat. Everyone on the dock was cheering and clapping as Abram successfully parked the wagon and turned to them with a sweaty-faced smile.

"Well done, James and Abram!" Eli said.

"I can't take any credit for this," James replied. "It was Abram's idea. And what about that driving? You've got a way with horses!"

Abram blushed modestly, brushing off the praise and helping secure the horses and buggy to the deck, blocking it so it wouldn't roll out of control and cause them problems on the journey. They returned for the larger supply wagon with the same plan in mind, only its massive frame was far more difficult to manage, and it took them twice as long, having to block off the wheels twice and course correct until the big supply wagon was successfully on board and locked down. Everyone pitched in to gather all the offloaded supplies and carry them to the deck where they placed them down in an organized manner, not wanting to load the wagons until they got back on dry land again. They took a quick break on deck, drinking liberally from their water supplies, resting and letting the sweat dry. By then, the hard work had sapped much of the children's enthusiasm, and exhaustion was starting to set in.

Eli stood in the middle of the group as they hung their heads with weariness. "Steel yourselves, my people, for we have a long way to go. Have faith in the Lord, for he will see us to the other side."

After a collective "Amen," James stood and walked on sore legs around the deck while Abram and Jacob inspected the poles they'd be using to get across. He secured his own gear, with his carbine, backpack and staff off to the side so none of the children would get into them. Clara leaned on the rail and stared to the other side of the Mississippi River, watching the water flow by. Coming to stand next to her with his arms crossed, James gazed at the large island across from them and a little south. The tree line left a shady outline in the water, inviting and cool aside for the swirls of bugs buzzing on the surface. Clara was looking north toward the mangled bridge with its twisted girders still charred black from the fuel explosions near the middle, and spoke after a moment, her voice a whisper.

"So much terrible destruction. Seems impossible to survive."

"It *seems* impossible," James acknowledged, "but there's still hope for both of us. To the east lie family, and perhaps friends, for both your family and myself."

Clara turned her eyes up and patted his hand in a hesitant gesture, her smile as calm as the waters rolling by. "You're right, James. We've all been blessed, and it's those blessings we must continue to count and appreciate. We are very glad you came along."

James offered a tired smile. "Me, too. It won't be long until we're back on the road and you're closer to your people and me to mine. Just have to get across this doggone river first."

"Hear hear!" Eli said after overhearing James' words. "Men, grab a pole. Abram, let us embark!"

Jacob and Abram pulled the steel ramp back onboard, replaced the rail, untied the boat from its moorings, and coiled the ropes on the deck. The barge began to drift a little downriver, and the men spread to each corner with their poles as they eyed the depths warily. James held his in a two-handed grip, plunging the end into the water ten feet deep until it scraped across the silty riverbed. With James and Eli at one end of the craft and Abram and Jacob at the other, they pushed across the murky flow, fighting a gentle current that carried them south as they went. The poles got stuck on the river bottom and bumped awkwardly against the boat, almost jerking out of their hands before they could pull them out again. It happened to James on three consecutive shoves until he finally learned his lesson to keep the end of the pole angled out away from the boat and lift it free before it could get pulled away.

Soon, James and Eli had their end of the barge pointing eastward and slightly north as they fought the downward current. Clara and the girls kept the horses calm as the men bulled their way into a steady rhythm, James breathing hard as he used every upper body muscle to push the boat and keep from falling off. The water got deeper, seeming to devour several feet of their poles at one time until he estimated it was somewhere between twenty and thirty feet deep.

James shared a worried glance with Eli. "I hope the water doesn't get much higher."

Eli nodded. "If we can no longer reach the bottom, we'll be at the mercy of the current and swept far to the south."

Their fears disappeared when the water level stayed the same even as they approached the middle where the current seemed the strongest.

"Once we reach the other side, our journey will be much closer to its end," Eli said between gasps, the corded muscles of his shoulders bulging through his sweat-stained shirt.

"It's a straight shot to where you're going?" James asked.

"That's right," Clara said as she held a horse's bridle with one hand and the rail with the other, gazing southeast across the water. "Nothing but kindness and a second home awaits us just on the other side of these dark waters. The Lord is truly gracious and has blessed us this day."

"I wouldn't count your chickens yet." James grimaced as he shoved. "We've got a rough road ahead just getting *across* these dark waters."

"And we look forward to it," Clara replied with a fierce sidelong glance. "While the Lord may test us, our faith will win through."

James pushed against the bottom, taking a deep breath and straining his hands and shoulders as the boat moved swiftly through the water, gaining momentum until he was leaning over the side and exhaling as he jerked the pole back. "I certainly don't doubt your faith. Likewise, I feel blessed to have found you. It would've been a tough walk if not for you bringing me this far. Thank you. I just hope you all will be safe once you arrive."

"It is us who thanks you, James. And you needn't worry about us. The country out that way is sparsely populated," Eli broke in, "and we'll be out in the country and untroubled by folks who might harm us."

James nodded, unable to believe that was entirely true. "That's good to know. I truly hope it's greener on the other side."

Eli grinned at James and they continued their work, pushing the barge slowly but surely through the muddy brown waters with an occasional glint of sunlight reflecting across the ripples. James studied the opposite shore, where flocks of birds broke free from the tree tops and burst across the sky beneath the broken clouds. He looked at the island again, which had been just south of them when they started. "I don't think we're going to make the opposite shore right now, and we are all getting pretty tired," James said. "What do you all say we pull hard for that island and try to disembark there?"

"Will the way be any better for us there?" Clara asked.

Eli shoved at the bottom as he peered ahead. "Should we allow ourselves to drift as far as the river will take us?"

James was shaking his head. "I don't think that's a good idea, Eli. We don't know what's downriver. There could be a wrecked boat or something that might hurt us. While it seems safe right now, I'd say we try to get across as quickly as possible, or we risk damage to our hull or could be swept miles downriver, farther away from your kin."

"Point well taken." Eli raised his voice to his son and his son-in-law. "Jacob? Abram? Push hard for the island. We can rest there and further assess the situation."

With solemn nods, the young men put their backs into it and dug deep, jamming the pole ends into the silty river bottom. James pushed until his shoulders were screaming, and at one point Abram teetered over the water after overextending himself, Betty grabbing him by the waist of his pants to keep him from falling in. Esther rushed to help, seizing him and hauling him to safety where they laughed with nervous relief. Scouting the island's shoreline, it appeared that, at their rate of speed, they could easily land somewhere along the south side where the trees ended and a field of grass opened above the rocky bank.

"I say we head for the southern section there and drive right up to the bank," James said with a nod. "We'll ground the bow first and let Abram and Jacobs' end slide around to come parallel to the shore. A couple of us can jump out and tie up to those trees. We'll have to move fast, though."

"Did you hear that, boys?" Eli shouted.

When both young men nodded, all four put their heads down and drove toward shore to the cheers and encouragement of the family. Soon, they were cutting through the waters at a high rate of speed, and James saw the depths shrinking until it was only ten feet deep, then five, then three. Random deadfall and rocks scraped the bottom as they buried the bow into the riverbank with a crunch of wood on stone, the front end rising as it rode into the grass a couple of feet.

"Eli, come to my side and lock your pole beneath the boat!" James shouted, and Eli ripped his pole free, carried it across the deck, and shoved it into the ground. The current swung the barge's rear around until they were parallel to the shore and scraping on the bottom.

"Abram, with me!" James called, leaping from the boat and running toward a thin line of trees with grassy space between the clusters. He turned and held out his hands. "Throw me the rope!"

Eli whipped the coiled rope at James and tied his end to one of the cleats while James caught the other end and sprinted to the thickest tree he could find, wrapping the rope around it three times before tying a knot. The rope creaked, the tree straining as the bullish current tried to break the barge free, and with everything tied down, they stood back and waited to see if it would hold. The river gripped the barge's hull, wood creaking and groaning as it tried to move it, but the combination of ropes and being partially stuck on the silty shoreline kept it anchored.

"Nice work! Let's scout the other side," James said.

They pulled off a section of the deck rail and clambered to shore, disembarking from the barge and turning to help Eli down, the older man sliding off the deck to land in the grass where Jacob caught him and held him steady.

James, Eli, and Abram walked through the beach grass across the massive island they'd run aground on with the field and a forest full of pine and spruce, the dense undergrowth packed in tightly into a tiny area that was fed by the constant flow of water around it. They tested the ground on the way, James poking his walking stick into the mud and sand along the shore, walking out a few feet to prod and poke around.

"The opposite side is less rocky and covered in moist sand," James said, scratching his head. "It's only about fifty yards, but can the wagons be driven through all this?"

"It will be a task," Eli nodded, "but doable. The question is, how deep is the water on the other side?"

On the opposite side of the island, the water gurgled over boulders and deadfall caught in clusters, indicating that it wasn't very deep, and he pointed into the center of the channel. "I say one of us can take one horse across with a rope and tie it off to a tree on the other side. We get everyone else off the wagons and have them cross one by one. By then, we'll have a good idea if the wagons will make it. If it's too deep, we'll leave our people over there and find another place to take the wagons, maybe somewhere downriver."

"What do you think, boys?" Eli asked the other men.

Abram was rubbing his chin and chewing on James' words, finally giving a terse nod. "That sounds like a good plan. Not a lot of risk in that."

"Let it be done then," Eli replied.

Back at the barge, they climbed aboard and moved the ramp to the other side. It barely clipped the bank's edge, so they let it drop and used the plywood, cinderblocks and stones to bolster it to arrange something flat and stable for the horses and buggies to traverse. With everyone's help, they moved the first buggy around and carefully brought the nervous horses down the steep incline, James' heart rushing as the makeshift ramp sank into the dirt but finally held. The supply wagon came next, riskier in every way and almost causing the ramp to sink too far into the moist ground, though Abram whipped the horses to get them to pull the rear wheels over the sinking part to bring it safely into the shin-high grass. James had been standing off to the side and watching their progress with a nervous gaze, sweating, pulse racing every step of the way. With a relieved sigh, he helped Abram down from the wagon seat and patted him on the back.

"Nice driving," he said. "For a second there I thought you weren't going to make it."

With the wagons offloaded, Clara, Betty, Esther, and the rest of the kids disembarked in their dirty dresses and holding hands, looking around hesitantly as a flock of birds broke north above them. The Amish moved their supplies from the barge deck to the wagons, carefully driving them to the other side of the island and parking them in the grass. Unhitching Amber, Abram mounted her and started riding her across while everyone stood and watched.

He picked his way carefully at first, a coil of rope trailing off his shoulder with one end held by Jacob on the shore. Water reached the horse's knees, the slow but powerful current washing up the flanks and over its chestnut coat to drench her rider to the waist. With gasps from the women and James clenching his fists at his side, Abram had a clear and shallow path before dropping into a dip out toward the middle in which the water came to the horse's chest, Amber throwing her head and whinnying before finding her footing again, stepping over the uneven rocks and sand grasses to move up into the shallows. Soon after, Abram was grinning and waving from the opposite shore, then he dismounted and looked for a place to tie off the rope.

"This is going to be like the Oregon Trail," James remarked.

"I don't catch your meaning," Eli said in confusion.

Clara interjected. "He means when the settlers were traveling into the Wild West. A dangerous crossing, to be sure."

"That's sort of what I was getting at," James replied with a chuckle, "but... never mind. Let's just get everyone across."

Jacob tied their rope to a small tree that leaned over the water, and they began the long and careful process of transporting the children to the other side. Eli went first with little Levi in his arms, then came Clara right behind him. Betty brought Sadie and John, with Esther and James coming last and leaving Jacob with the wagons. With his left arm hooked over the rope and fighting the powerful current, James kept an eye on those in front of him and ensured no one lost their grip on the rope. The Amish held on tenaciously, crossing with their children hanging from their necks and strapped to them, always turning back to warn each other of slick spots in the riverbed, being especially careful in the deep area Abram had run into. The water was cold as it soaked James' clothes and splashed his face, though the current was not so strong that it threatened to rip anyone off the rope and send them rolling down the river. Soon they'd reached the opposite shore, hand-over-hand, straining to hold the rope, trudging through the wet sand in heavy pants and dresses, turning to help those behind them until they sat on the opposite bank and squeezed water from their sloppy clothing. Abram returned to the other side on horseback and re-hitched the mare. Climbing into the buggy's driver's seat, he slowly and carefully guided it down the sandy shore to the river, staring across at his father before edging forward.

Eli raised his voice. "Everyone, let's pray for Abram's safe crossing!"

Standing in a line and holding hands, the family closed their eyes and followed Eli's soft words of prayer as Abram started into the water, gripping the reins tight and crouching to see past the horses. James felt a tug on his wet sleeve and turned to see little Sadie staring up at him with big brown eyes. James smiled and held her hand as he watched Abram, who'd already made it about a quarter of the way across.

Water shoved against the buggy, splashing over the backs of the horses and up the side of the carriage, spraying Abram and filling the floorboard with an inch of muddy water. Still, Abram remained focused and drove the horses with a keen eye on the rope that lay just off to his left, correcting them so they stayed on track. The buggy jolted in shock as its wheels cracked across rocks and debris on the river bottom, and at the deepest part, it lost its traction and started to drift away.

Abram stood and snapped the reins hard with a hearty shout, "Yah! Come on!"

With a final burst of speed, the horses pulled up the sandy shore with the buggy wheels sinking into the moist sand and water sloshing off the carriage. At last, they reached the bank, and without giving the horses a chance to slow down, Abram drove them up the steep and grassy slope until they reached a level point and stood with heaving sides, water dripping from their quivering hides.

Abram leaped down and ran his hand along Amber's flank and patted it roundly. "Good work, Teakettle and Amber! Good horses, both of you! Well done!"

Clara gasped and pointed across the river to where Jacob was bringing the supply wagon, following in Abram's path as he started into the treacherous flow. Jacob moved slower as he was sitting on much more weight, and where the water hit him, it shot up the sides and onto the wooden top, rattling everything in the bed and sending Jacob lurching and rocking in the springy seat. The heavier wagon also held a slight advantage over the lighter buggier, as its weight kept it locked onto the riverbed, keeping it from being moved downstream by the water. He drove the nervous horses hard to the other side without giving them too much time to consider alternative options or allow panic to enter into the equation. They rushed through the deepest part of the water, dipping deeper, the horses' eyes bulging wide as their hooves scraped across the bottom, struggling for any sort of traction, the great weight of the supply wagon a challenge to pull.

"Prepare to take the horses by their bridles and help pull them across!" Eli called, gesturing at the struggling horses as James and Abram both rushed toward the water.

"Yah!" Jacob shouted encouragement to the straining animals. "Come on, Gentle! Yah, Bear!" He stood from his seat watching the horses as if willing them the rest of the way.

With a final lurch forward, the muscled beasts crashed ahead and pulled the supply wagon through the deepest part of the flow, finally hauling it out of the water and onto the sandy beach where James and Abram took the bridles, calming the horses and leading them up the steep grassy bank. The horses were even more tired than their predecessors, sides heaving and tossing their heads in agitation and weariness as they stared at the next hill. Not wanting to get stuck in the moist sand, Jacob drove the horses hard up the bank where they reached the slick grass made wet from their dripping coats.

"Abram and Eli!" James called. "To the back of the wagon. Let's help push!"

The men sprinted over, found a place to put their shoulders, and labored to shove them over the precarious lip. Faces twisting, grunting and grimacing, they moved up six inches at a time, with the horses jerking and lunging forward, legs straining, flanks quivering as they pushed over the soft ground, finally bringing the supply wagon with them. James was bent backward one minute with his face pressed against the tailgate, then they lurched forward, the three running up the hill and falling to their knees in the grass. Turning to each other, they laughed and clapped hands as they rose.

"Praise the Lord," Eli said with his arms spread as a ray of sunlight stretched across the tiny grove. The family broke into uproarious shouts of praise and thankfulness as they rushed forward and helped Jacob down from his seat, heaping congratulations and hugs on him.

Before they rested too long, Abram said, "I'll take Amber back across to untie the rope and bring it over."

"I'm tempted to leave it," Eli replied. "If anyone else needs to cross, maybe they'll find it helpful."

"Are you sure, Father?" Abram asked. "That rope is one of the best we have, and we must conserve all of our resources until we reach our people. Besides, how would someone reach the island without a boat anyway?"

Eli turned and looked across to the island, seeming to measure the value of the rope against his instinct to help others and desire to protect his family. With a confident nod, he said, "It's a dangerous crossing, and I know you can go over and back with no problems, son. But we'll leave the rope there if only to avoid that risk. And, if anyone else has a use for it, then good for them. Come on, let's move along the road here and see if it takes us to the highway."

With everyone still on foot, they dispersed deeper into the woods, with the softly flowing waters fading behind them. Soggy and exhausted, they walked slowly, heads down with the women and children holding hands, walking until a road came into view running north to south about a quarter mile away.

"There it is," James said, pointing. "We can probably stop and rest now if you want." As if on cue, the group stopped inside a warm ray of sunlight and basked in its glow, the family putting their arms around each other, weariness taking its toll.

Clara smiled, patting a few of the children on the back. "Come on now, everyone. Let's stay positive and keep those smiles and blessings coming. We're almost there. It won't be long now."

James headed off toward the highway by himself, both physically and emotionally drained, needing to take a moment to gather his thoughts and review what they'd accomplished over the last few hours. After going a good distance, James peered past the highway into a wide-open field with a scattering of homes and businesses on the other side, though clusters of trees blocked his vision to the north or south. With the sounds of children's laughter at his back, James stretched his arms above his head and took a refreshing breath, searching for any signs of people in the buildings.

The world was quiet, with the occasional fluttering of birds and insects and the flowing waters of the river behind him. Distantly, he heard Eli call for them to break out some food and drink and take a quick breather when another sound cut through the peacefulness. A motor – an actual *engine* – running from somewhere nearby, its coughing and sputtering echoing off the surrounding trees and throughout the broad river valley.

CHAPTER SEVENTEEN

Ryan Cooper
Somewhere Outside East Lansing, Michigan

Moonlight played across the front yard and the tops of the red maples, and the midnight glow captured the flowering trees in soft, golden light. The breeze had picked up, rustling the woods to the east while the patches of bushes and brush spoke whispers between the house and the front gate. The stars shimmered off the pond waters, and the steady thrum of frogs calling out to each other reached him as Ryan circled through the top floor of the farmstead.

They'd left all the upstairs windows open, and the house was cool and breezy. It might've been uncomfortable on any other day if not for his nervousness, continued movement and constant sweating. Ryan had changed into a fresh pair of jeans with his ratchet belt cinched tight around his waist and a black long-sleeved shirt to help blend in with the dark shadows inside the house. With his baseball cap turned backward on his head, he settled in behind the master bedroom window, moving from one side to the other behind the curtain.

The blinds were pulled up, and the room was quiet and dark with not a speck of light to draw attention. Raising the binoculars, Ryan craned his neck and peered across the yard, changing the magnification to scan the tree line and parts of the property where the moonlight didn't reach. Helen had taken the kids' rooms along the rear of the house, monitoring the backyard in case someone came up from behind, and they put up an old baby gate from the basement at the bottom of the stairwell so the dogs wouldn't go down onto the first floor unless they were let out. The Great Pyrenees were lying in the loft area near the stairs, except for Diana, who followed him through the house inquisitively.

With a sigh, Ryan lowered the binoculars and backed away from the window, stepping into the loft and across the catwalk overlooking the foyer to the other side where there was a spare bedroom. Pictures of the extended family decorated the walls in the room Ryan and Helen normally used when visiting, the guest room featuring lodge-style accents and thick bedposts, the bedspread soft and comfortable with an enormous pile of pillows by the headboard. The bed called to him, and though he yearned for a few minutes of quiet rest, there was no time for it, at least not until morning when they were out of the woods for one more night.

Over by the window, he eased into a chair and continued his search from a slightly different angle. The time between dusk and midnight had seemed to last forever, with his body aches untamed by the simple pain pills he'd taken. They didn't have anything stronger in the house, not that he would've taken them anyway. Pain was his body's way of telling him when something was wrong, and ignoring it would only make him careless and cause him more injury in the long run. Better to treat the root cause, he thought, than mask it.

It was quiet outside, and he felt like if more people were coming, it would be soon. They'd want to attack them in the deepest part of the night when they thought the darkness would conceal them, but the bright moonlight would work in Ryan and Helen's favor. Desperation would drive them, but Ryan and Helen still held the advantage in multiple ways.

"If they are desperate, it won't matter," he mumbled.

With a soft growl, he started to rise from his seat when a pair of blinking lights way down by the gate caught his attention. Eyes narrowed, he sank back into position, raised the rifle, and pointed it toward the lights, looking through the scope to see at least two people walking around with others following them as they spread out across the field approaching the house.

"Helen? We've got company!" His words were barely louder than a hiss, just enough to get her attention, and a moment later her soft footsteps came across the catwalk into the room.

"What is it?" She took a position on the other side of the window.

"Two lanterns down by the gate and making their way to the house. See them? They're spreading out across the property and coming up around the ponds."

"It's not James or Alice or the kids, is it?"

"I doubt it," Ryan shook his head as he shifted the scope from east to west, watching several dark shapes break away from the others. "There's too many of them, for one. And they wouldn't be spreading out across the whole front side of the property."

"No, definitely not them," Helen agreed with a nod, hefting the M&P 15 from its slung position on her shoulder. "I'll get the dogs settled at the top of the stairs and go over to the master bedroom and get ready. Come on Diana." Helen took the dog's leash and led her out of the room.

Ryan nodded, a grim hardness settling in his chest. "I love you, honey. Everything's going to be okay."

"Love you, too. Yes it will."

With Helen moving into position, Ryan tracked the intruders with his scope as they approached around the pond, keeping his focus on one with a lantern coming up on his side as he swung back toward the driveway. The light stopped at the row of trees bracketing the lane, the light partially hidden as they peeked around to scout the house. Whoever it was didn't seem satisfied to stay still, and after a moment of talking with another figure they broke cover and jogged toward one of the big red maples right in front of the house where Ryan had set up his first traps. Sliding from his seat, he kneeled at the window, resting his forearm on the sill and kept his sights pinned on the tree while the light bobbed in his periphery.

The man reached the tree and paused where the stakes were sticking up, holding up his lantern and leaning in to stare in confusion. Ryan started to take a shot, but the light disappeared, followed by a shouted curse as the man leaped and howled from the other side of the tree trunk, dancing in a circle and yelling in pain after having stepped through the spiked booby traps, his lantern swinging madly in his hand. Grinning, Ryan squeezed the trigger, and the rifle bucked against his shoulder, his round hitting the ground at the man's feet. The looter froze, twisting toward the house with his face illuminated in his lantern light. Heart pounding with rushed energy, Ryan growled at himself as he shifted his aim and squeezed the trigger again, the second round striking the man square in the chest and pitching him straight back into the grass where the lantern crashed and broke and winked out.

Sweeping his rifle around, he tracked the other group by their lights, and he was about to fire upon another rushing shape when the lantern suddenly went out and cast the backyard in darkness again. He'd been looking so hard at the light that it took a few seconds for his eyes to adjust, though he didn't stop searching for more figures across the yard, squeezing off another pair of shots before they disappeared behind the flowering tree and maples.

He backed away from the window and called softly through the door, hoping his voice reached her. "Helen! There are four more! Move to the top of the stairs with the dogs in case I don't get them. You're our last resort if they get inside!"

"Okay!" she replied, her footsteps shuffling through the house, with the anxious growls and low barks of the dogs straining on their quick-release leashes where they were tied to the rail at the top of the stairs on the catwalk.

The clouds parted, casting the yard with the most light he'd seen all night, and he caught sight of figures moving through the tall weeds. They hadn't quite made it to the maples when they fired at the house, bullets snipping the brick with sharp cracks and puffs of mortar dust. The group off to his right ran toward the red maple, still unaware of the area trap he'd set. Waiting for them to fall for it like the other man had, he waited until another figure passed in front of the sights and he fired, his gun bucking again, punching his shoulder and forcing out a groan. The pain was offset by his second round hitting his target, though the person continued running, holding their left arm as they somehow squeezed behind the red maple despite the spikes.

Ryan grumbled. "Just winged him. You've got to do better than that, you old fool."

"Are you okay?" Helen called from the stairs.

"I'm fine," Ryan growled with his ears ringing in spite of the earplugs he'd hastily jammed into them, "but they're going to reach the house."

"Do you want me to let the dogs loose out through the front door?"

"No! I don't want to risk them getting shot out there just yet. Besides, they'll be better in close quarters. Just —"

The sharp report of a gun broke their conversation, and the window shattered above him, glass flying everywhere as he jerked away and fell against the bed. When no followup shots immediately followed, he slipped to the floor and crawled out on all fours, rifle in his right hand as more bullets struck the brick front and zipped over his head to hit the opposite wall. Outside the bedroom, he fell to his belly and crawled into the loft area, glancing back at the stairs where Helen was keeping the dogs, all three animals straining their muscled shoulders to head downstairs. More gunshots rang out, one punching neatly through the foyer's front glass and striking the ceiling somewhere above him, but when the intruders realized no one was shooting back, they stopped firing and the house fell quiet once again. Ryan sniffed, catching the faint whiff of drywall dust and the cool outside air through the new holes in the house before he crawled to the rail overlooking the foyer and brought his rifle to bear. When soft voices reached him from the yard, he quit moving, cocked his ear to the side, and listened.

"... do now? They hit... he's down, and so is—"

"Shut up," a man hissed. "Stay down, or... damn head blown off."

"... a plan, or we're just sitting ducks out here."

"You take Trace around back... Rita and... take the front. Get in any way you... that?"

Things grew quiet again, and Ryan prepared himself for another assault. He couldn't hear the people circling to the back, but the ones in front crossed the walkway and stepped into the landscaping along the front of the house, shuffling around for a minute until a woman yelped in pain and slammed her fist against a plank of wood he'd nailed up across the dining room window.

"Damn! Be careful, Jack. They got nails spread out in this mulch! Went straight through my boot!"

They went silent again as they pulled on the boards over the windows, then a shriek burst from the rear of the house, followed by a rising scream that echoed through the night. "My damn fingers!" A man shouted from the back door in an ascending wail of agony. "Oh, sonofabitch! I lost fingertips!"

"I hope you lost more than that," Ryan mumbled with a grin, crawling onto the catwalk where he stuck the rifle barrel between the rails and peered down at the front door, a view of the dining room on his left and part of the great room behind him.

Squinting down over the foyer, he shifted his gaze from the front door to the dining room windows, watching the shadows move between the gaps in the boards as the moonlight revealed their every movement. Tongue jutting out of the corner of his mouth, Ryan angled the rifle barrel down toward the window, listening as they continued bumping around and trying to pull off the plywood. Making his best guess at where they were standing, he squeezed the trigger five times, making an arc from the top left portion of the window down to the bottom right, hoping to get at least one of them.

Rounds shattered the glass and punched through the scrap of wood he'd nailed up, a woman screamed, and a shadow shifted in the cracks and fell into the mulch, howling with more pain as she landed on the nails. A second form swore in a pained, raspy voice and hauled the woman out of sight before Ryan could try to take another shot. The two out back came back around, more shadows moving across the yard, and Ryan fired several shots into the dining room windows, shattering glass and piercing the boards he'd put up, filling the air with gunsmoke as the intruders rushed to aid their fallen friends. There were harsh whispers from below, anger and pain flooding their voices, then a man's voice said, "We'll be okay! Just get in there! Stop letting them take potshots and just flush them out, now!"

Heavy hammers pounded on the wood, sledgehammer blows like a lumberjack hitting hard, Ryan wincing and cringing as the boards split. A hammer claw wedged between the cracks and began tearing pieces of the wood free, letting moonlight spill inside through the shattered windows. Ryan aimed his rifle and pulled the trigger, but groaned when nothing happened.

Stupid, stupid old man! He chastised himself as he ejected the spent magazine and reached for a new one in his pocket. Hurrying his shaking fingers, body twisted so his jeans were tight against his upper thighs, his position made it almost impossible to get it out. He shifted, pulled his pants up, and jammed his hand deep into his pocket to rip the magazine free. As he was bringing it up to slam the magazine home, it slipped from his fingers and clattered on the hardwood toward the edge where it rattled between the rails. Reflexes kicking in, he slammed his palm on the magazine and pinned it down.

Loading the magazine into the well, he snatched the charging lever, loaded a round into the chamber, and aimed down at the window where the intruders had already torn a large hole. He fixated on the shadowy movements where the hammer ends were pounding around the edges, fired once, then again. A second later, he ducked and threw himself flat on the catwalk as hands with guns slipped into the gap and shot wildly upward into the foyer. Rounds peppered the catwalk, glanced off the railing with wood chips and splinters flying. The floor vibrated as some struck the hardwood and penetrated all the way through while others hit the ceiling and struck the chandelier to send crystal shards raining on his head.

Ryan ducked and buried his head between his arms, covering and keeping out of the line of fire as best he could. Something pinched him painfully below his knee, and he cried out and flinched, curling up as more rounds penetrated the floor and spat pieces of hardwood and carpet fibers into the air.

Putting his rifle down, he reached for his leg and felt warm blood seeping into his blue jeans and running onto the floor. When he touched his calf, a lancing fire shot up his leg, and he slammed his knuckles to his bared teeth to stifle a scream of pain. Grimacing in agony, Ryan felt the punctured flesh where the bullet had gone through, shifting his hand around the wet denim to the other side to put his finger to the exit wound with blood running into his palm and down his arm. He started taking off his shirt, jaw locked, forearms straining as his wet hands tried to grip the cloth and shred it into a long enough piece to make a pressure bandage.

The firing stopped, the air suddenly quiet but for the dogs' barking and the violent swirl of dust and smoke, the trickles of drywall from above sprinkling his sweaty face and arms and clinging there like a batter. There was bumping and kicking of glass from the windowpanes as the remaining pieces of wood were ripped from the dining room window. Leaving his half-torn shirt aside, Ryan grabbed his weapon and aimed between the rails as a pair of dark shadows darted through the house, one diving into the dining room and the other sprinting across the foyer and to the great room. Ryan tracked the last one but bumped a rail as he fired, hitting the foyer floor just a foot behind them as they disappeared deeper into the house.

Crawling backwards a few inches, resting on his left elbow with his rifle clenched tight, he glanced back to see Helen at the other side of the loft, crouched in the shadows with three massive shapes straining at the ends of their restraints. When she raised her eyes in question to see if he wanted her to release them, Ryan vigorously shook his head no, grateful when she nodded and kept the lunging, whining dogs at bay with both hands on Diana's leash, keeping her balance low to the ground and hissing at her to stay put. The banister creaked as the animals jerked, howled, and lunged madly to get after the attackers. Duke had lost his mind, barking and snapping as he tried to get down the stairs, straining against his harness and rising with his paws flailing above the stairwell.

"Hush, Duke!" Helen hissed, looking worriedly at Ryan as if wanting to go to him but forced to hold her position.

Feet shuffled downstairs as the intruders repositioned themselves, and Ryan rose and glanced left and right, shouting, "What do you people want?"

There was a pause, and a gruff voice replied. "That's an easy one. We want what you have."

Duke growled deep in his chest and punctuated it with several throaty barks, cut off when Helen jerked the dog's leash and whispered harshly in his ear. Ryan glanced back to see if she still had things under control, though she was struggling. Ryan tilted his head, homing in on the man's voice, which seemed to come from off to the right. The problem was that the dining room and great room connected the house in a full circle with access to the basement stairs, so anyone could get behind them and attack from the rear. They could even stand beneath them and fire up through the floor all day if they wanted to. Smaller rounds probably wouldn't penetrate, but larger ones could do more of what they'd already done to his calf. Still, holding the high ground gave them an advantage, and they still had a trump card he had yet to play.

"There's nothing here you need," Ryan spat back.

"Don't lie, old man. We've been keeping an eye on you, and we know you have a tractor and crops you just brought in. We can see them plain as day in the bins outside your back door, and we're curious about the car you've parked back there. If you just share with us, we'll leave in peace and won't hurt you. If you make it hard, there's going to be bloodshed!"

"The only blood that'll be shed is yours!" Ryan kept his tone low, fighting to keep the pain out of his voice as it continued to radiate out from the penetrating gunshot wound to his leg. He gave in to rage, letting fury and resentment explode through him. "How dare you step into our sanctum and make demands?! How'd you like it if we did that to you?"

The man chuckled darkly. "We'd be mad if we had any homes *left*. Put your gun down, old man. Make the right choice."

"Turn around and march right out the way you came. I won't shoot you in the back."

"That won't work. We've got mouths to feed out here. A lot more than what you have. You can't just *not* share!"

A wave of dizziness passed over Ryan, and the warm blood pooling on the carpet down his leg reminded him he needed to get it taken care of soon. Quietly, eyes streaming pained tears, he picked up his makeshift bandage and started tying it just below his knee, wrapping the thin material twice around the top of his calf where the wound was located to try and stem the flow of blood, wincing and taking long breaths to keep from groaning.

A pause followed, then a woman spoke, her voice ragged and dripping with pain. "What about Mack? What did you do with him?"

Ryan shook his head. "I don't know anyone named Mack."

"We sent him up here yesterday to do some scouting, and he didn't come back. You people got him captured in the basement or something?"

Ryan realized she was talking about the man Helen had shot out by the barn. They'd dragged him inside and locked the door, so the intruders wouldn't have seen him or known that he was dead, and Ryan broke the news to her. "We shot *someone* trying to steal from us last night. I take it your Mack was a thief? Because that was probably him."

The woman wailed, her anguished shriek echoing through the house, gripping Ryan's ears and piercing them as she held out a long note until it settled into hiccuping cries and then an angry growl that set the dogs barking louder. Something shuffled below and behind him, deeper in the house, maybe someone in the kitchen crossing into the dining room. Hushed voices whispered in the darkness, the pair downstairs arguing and Ryan catching pieces of it.

"No, Rita," the man implored. "Not yet. Listen to me."

"But they killed Mack," the woman cried. "They've got to pay for that."

"I know, but stay with me now, you hear?"

Helen grunted behind him where she crouched in the shadows, her face anguished in the trickles of moonlight filtering in from the upper windows. "Are you okay?" she whispered, her voice barely audible over the dogs and the people shuffling downstairs.

Ryan gave her a thumbs up in reply and returned to tying his bandage, pulling it tight and double knotting it before he shifted back to his rifle. Reaching deep for every ounce of strength he could get, he lowered his voice and gave their attackers one last warning.

"This is your last chance. Get out of this house and you live. Stay, and you join your friends!" The woman cursed him and cried out, and Ryan grinned, her position revealed to be opposite of where she'd been just a minute ago with her voice coming from the great room. "And before you blame us for Mack's death, remember one thing. He shouldn't have been on our property to begin with. You should never have sent him, so his death is on *you*, not us!"

"You'd let our kids starve?" the man shouted back. "What kind of heart do you have?"

"I would've shared some things with you bastards if you'd have asked instead of sneaking around and trying to steal from us! Could have gone about this differently, and maybe we could've worked something out."

"Yeah, well, we're past that! I've got a lot of angry people with me who will come at you even harder for what you've done!"

"Well then, let them come and try!" Ryan's voice thundered through the house.

There was a pause, more whispers, and shuffling from downstairs and Ryan looked back along the hall at Helen, who stared at him across the loft. He gave her a macabre grin, nodding slowly as he looked at her, then the three dogs. She nodded back, reaching for their leashes, and he gripped his rifle tight in his bloody hands, gathering his strength for a decisive end to the conflict – one way or another.

CHAPTER EIGHTEEN

Alice Burton
Omega, Georgia

A baby's wail cut through the room, its ear-splitting warbling wail music to Alice's ears as she held the trembling child up after pulling him free from the birth canal. His cherub face was squashed and compressed, colored purple and red as he squalled, and a shockingly thick tuft of wet hair lay curled over his head.

Turning with the infant, she called to Sarah. "Bring the clamp, quick! Yes, that's the one. Now, get in there and clamp off the cord near the baby's naval, a few inches out. Perfect! Put the other clamp an inch away from that. Great, Sarah. You're doing outstanding. Now, Nate, use the scissors to slice the cord. Come on, hurry up!"

Nate leaned over Elaine's knee, sweat trickling down his cheeks as he placed the scissors against the delicate cord.

"Go ahead! I assume you've done this before?"

Nate gave a nervous half-smile. "I nearly passed out with the first one so the doctor cut the cord."

"Well, you're doing this one. Go ahead, keep cutting. Perfect!"

Nate clipped the cord and took a step back next to Elaine. The next squalling cry from the shaking, shivering baby brought a wellspring of tears from Alice's eyes, forcing her to blink quickly to clear them.

She turned to where Nate was holding Elaine's hand and hovering with an expectant expression. "Go ahead," Alice said, wrapping the baby half in a towel offered up by Sarah. "Take your son and give him to Elaine. They need as much skin-on-skin contact as possible."

Nate gulped and stared wide-eyed at his son as the infant shivered, kicked, and squalled, still slippery from head to foot. Elaine was trying to reach for the infant but couldn't, and her weak gasp of joy forced her husband into action. He took the baby from Alice and shifted him to Elaine's waiting arms, resting him on her chest where they'd cut her shirt away.

Shifting to Sarah, Alice gestured at the tarp beneath the woman's legs. "Hold up the edges of the tarp. Got them? Good. Now, Elaine, we need you to keep pushing, honey. Just keep pushing as hard as you can."

"I don't think I can. I'm so tired."

"That's okay. I'm going to help you." Alice placed her hands on the woman's abdomen and leaned forward to add pressure with her shoulders. "On a count of three, I want you to push hard. Ready?"

Elaine nodded and took a deep breath, still holding her baby with Nate's help. As Alice finished her count, they pushed together, Elaine groaning as spittle flew from her lips. When she finally ran out of air, she collapsed backward and cried in exhaustion.

"What are we trying to do, Mom?" Sarah was on edge as she held the corners of the bloody tarp.

"We still have to get the afterbirth out." She shifted back to Elaine. "One more time, honey. You've got so much strength left, and I know you can do this. Ready?"

Elaine stared at Alice in disbelief and exhaustion, seeming like she might try again but shaking her head. "I can't."

"I'm not accepting that." Alice raised her voice. "You can *do* this!" Leaning closer, jaw tightening, she gave Elaine a firm but appraising look. "One more time. This is it, and it's the last thing I'll ask you to do today."

Elaine closed her eyes, breathing hard, giving a faint nod in response.

"Come on, girl!" Alice hissed. Without waiting for a response, she counted down again and pushed. Elaine joined her, coaxing a steady groan deep in her chest and squeezing her trembling body tight, digging for some impossible inner strength.

Fist clenched on her leg and her entire body quaking, Elaine gave a gut-wrenching cry of pain, and the afterbirth came out in a splash of fluids. Sarah instinctively pulled the tarp from beneath her, wrapped it up, and carried it away while Alice quickly replaced it with several layers of towels, leaving Elaine shivering in sheer exhaustion as she looked on at her child with unfaltering love. Nate propped Elaine up and placed pillows beneath her, piling them up so she could sit upright and hold the baby more comfortably. Alice sat back on her haunches, watching the doting parents stroke the baby's cheeks as his cries softened and he began to look around, blinking, coughing and snorting. A sort of numbness passed over Alice, shell-shocked at being thrust into such a situation at the drop of a hat and with a sigh, Alice backed up a little more, holding up one hand to see it shaking uncontrollably.

Elaine craned her neck to peer over her baby. "What's your name again, ma'am?"

"I'm Alice, and these are my kids, Jake and Sarah." Alice nodded at the kids in turn, noticing for the first time that Jake was sitting on the couch next to the girl. She'd stopped crying, and her tears had been replaced with an awe-filled smile at the bundle her mother was holding.

"Hi, little one," Alice whispered. "Introduce yourself to your little brother, Ethan."

The young girl blinked at Alice before losing herself in the loving light of the squirming baby, who'd already latched onto his mother and was trying to start feeding.

"Ethan?" the girl asked shyly as she tugged at the bottom of her dirty shirt.

"That's right." Elaine grinned. "It's your new baby brother. Come closer. Don't be afraid."

"Go ahead." Jake urged the girl off the couch.

She hopped down and approached haltingly, falling to her knees beside her mother, leaning closer to the swaddled child, and grinning softly. "Hi, Ethan. I'm Missy. Nice to meet you."

Alice turned to Jake. "Looks like you made a friend, too."

Jake shrugged, unable to contain a slight smile. "I guess so."

"Is there anything else we need to do?" Nate asked, looking up.

With arched eyebrows, Alice turned her attention to Elaine's bottom half, shifting some covers around and peering at things below. Finally, she nodded and shrugged. "I don't see any excess bleeding, and there were no tears, so we don't need the sutures." She clenched Elaine's knee and gave her a gentle shake. "You're like elastic down there, girl!"

The new mother laughed as her pain seemed to fade beneath the glow of her child. "I just can't believe it." Her tone was soft and loving. "He's finally here... we did it."

"You sure did." Alice turned her sober gaze back to Nate. "We'll want to keep an eye out for clots that might pass, especially large ones that would indicate an issue."

"What if we find something like that? What do we do?"

Alice shrugged. "To be honest, Nate, I don't know. I'm just going off what I remember when I gave birth...." She glanced at Sarah and then across at Jake. "Every minute of that is seared into my memory."

"Mine, too," Elaine sniveled and chuckled.

"From what I can recall, the nurses kept kneading my abdomen every once in a while, pushing out any clots that were forming and making sure none of them were large. We can keep doing that for a bit, and go from there."

With things under control and the baby feeding well, Alice turned to Sarah. "Come to the side and bring some clean rags and a bowl of clean water, too."

Alice held out her hand, and a clean cloth appeared and together Alice and Sarah worked around the parents and wiped slick fluids off Ethan's arms, finally wrapping him in a fresh towel as he continued feeding. They dabbed gently at Elaine's belly and legs, cleaning her up and making her comfortable, then handed Nate a towel, which he used to wipe Elaine's forehead and neck to keep her from shivering.

"Nate, make sure she's got enough cushions and pillows beneath her. We want to keep her elevated."

Nodding, he adjusted Elaine's position, shifting the bedroom pillows and couch cushions beneath her shoulders and back and helping her rest higher so she could look into Ethan's beautiful face.

"That's it, Nate. Perfect."

Alice and Sarah finished cleaning her up and tossed the dirty clothes into a bag, and Sarah carried it into the kitchen, then they covered Elaine in towels and blankets until both mother and child were resting comfortably. After a few minutes of everyone fussing over her, Elaine finally gave them a loving but exasperated look. "I'm okay now, guys. Thanks so much. I just want to lie here for a little while with Ethan."

"Okay," Alice laughed. "But we're right here. If you need *anything*, just ask."

"I will."

The wind gently stirred outside, rattling a loose gutter as everyone sat down, taking a short breather while they listened to the baby suckle and feed with soft grunts of satisfaction.

———

An hour later, the house was silent, the afternoon's chaos long past, leaving Alice with a sense of accomplishment and no small amount of pride. Standing by the blinds, she watched as Jake stood on the front porch, acting as both guard to those inside and monitoring the horses while they figured out what to do next. Alice and Sarah had cleaned up around the house, washing the dirty bowls and soiled towels as best they could, so they didn't leave the place in a mess. They'd put back most of the furniture and made sure Nate and Elaine had plenty of water before the mother finally fell asleep on the floor with Missy curled up at her side.

"I've got a generator out in the shed," Nate said from where he sat in a recliner on the opposite side of the room, gently rocking with Ethan in his arms. "I'll hook it up later and make sure we can run the washer and dryer for a little while."

"Your generator still works?"

"Yeah. I heard on the radio this has something to do with fuel, right?"

"You might say that, yeah." Alice chuckled.

"Our generator's pretty old, and the gas has been sitting with stabilizer for several months. I guess it was old enough to not be affected. My truck, on the other hand..." He groaned. "I just worry about what we're going to do. I mean... a new baby? In all of this?"

Alice patted his arm. "Keep that generator secret and safe... lots of people out there would love to get their hands on it. And don't worry too much. As long as you have plenty to eat and drink, that's the most important thing. Elaine and the baby'll both be fine. You've still got a house here, which is more than a lot of people."

Nate's eyes watered with tears. "Thank you, Alice. I don't know what we would've done...."

"Oh, you would have figured something out, Nate," she replied, raising an eyebrow and struggling to hide a bemused smirk, "but I'm not sure trying to run to town was the answer."

"That's what I'm talking about," he laughed. "I would've been in the next town like an idiot while Elaine was trying to have the baby alone." A shudder passed through him. "That would've been disastrous. I'm just glad you all didn't shoot me, and were able to help."

Alice laughed. "I'm glad too, Nate." Her smile widened at the sight of little Ethan in his arms. "We've had some bad run-ins with folks along our little journey, but also some good ones. I'm glad this has been one of the good ones."

With a heavy sigh, Sarah came in from the kitchen and dusted off her hands. "The kitchen is all clean. Boy, I'm beat." She turned and fell onto the couch near where Alice was standing, and Alice circled and plopped down beside her, feeling the tension in her neck and back loosen as she relaxed for the first time in hours.

"I'm just glad everything worked out." She smiled, placing her hand over Sarah's, and winked proudly.

"There's got to be something we can do to repay you," Nate said. "Anything I can do to make it up to you for getting you off track, I will. Do you want to rest here for a while?"

Sarah shrugged. "What do you think, Mom?"

"It *is* getting late in the day, and we should probably take care of the horses and find a place to bed for the night." Alice looked at Nate. "If you had a barn or something we could sleep in... and a spot for the horses, that would be great. We've got food but having a roof over our heads tonight would be icing on the cake."

"Absolutely not," Nate replied flatly, breaking down and laughing at Alice's surprised face. "Sorry, I'm so tired! What I meant to say was.... you absolutely will not stay in a *barn* when we have plenty of room in the house here. We've got a guest bed and the couch, and you're getting the best dinner you've ever had."

"So, you're the cook in the household?" Alice asked with skepticism.

"It just so happens I *am* in charge of the cooking around here." Nate gave a broad grin. "I even slaughtered one of our pigs last week before all this nonsense started! If you stay, I'll make pork chops, potatoes, green beans, and the last bit of our store-bought bread and butter."

"What about the horses, Mom?" Sarah asked.

Nate laughed. "They can use the barn. We've got some space out back and freshly cleaned stalls for those boys to spend the night in. I promise they'll be nice and safe, tucked away with the rest of our animals."

"How can I turn that down?" Alice asked with a smile. "Of course, we'll stay the night – *if* I get to hold the baby for a few minutes."

"Are you kidding? We're going to make you his Godmother at this rate! Besides, Elaine is down for the count, so if I'm going to be in charge of whipping up dinner, I'll need some help with the little tyke." Nate's gaze lingered on his wife and children, and he shook his head in disbelief as emotion struck him out of nowhere, and a pair of tears streaked down his cheeks.

"Let it all out," Alice said warmly. "Treasure the good moments as often as you can. It's so nice to hold them in your arms... the emotion can be overwhelming." With an elbow to Sarah, she snorted. "At least until they get old enough to argue back with you."

Sarah poked Alice playfully in the side as Nate laughed, and Alice's heart swelled with something like pride, relief, and love, an intertwining of emotion that brought back the feelings she'd had giving birth to Sarah and Jake so long ago.

"Well, let's get started on things," Alice said. "How about I take the baby while you take Jake and the horses out to the shed and get them settled? I'm assuming you have some tools to brush them down properly?"

"Yes, I do. No worries there." Nate swung himself up from his chair and tiptoed around Elaine where she still lay on the floor with a foam mat beneath her, leaving her there until she was strong enough to get up and move onto the couch or into the bedroom. Without hesitation, he held little Ethan out, and Alice took the baby from him, holding him close to her chest and bobbing him up and down.

She nodded to Nate. "I've got him. Go out with Jake, and we'll start getting things ready here."

As Nate stepped outside and called to Jake, Alice motioned for Sarah to clean up more around the living room and then pulled her into the kitchen. It was a small area with a four-person table and a stainless-steel stove with plenty of counter space to work with. Back in the laundry room, Sarah had hung the washed clothes and towels to dry on the wire shelves, and Alice told her to take them outside and use the laundry line, which was tied between two trees.

Sarah rolled her eyes good naturedly. "Suuure, you get to hold the baby while I do all the *hard* work."

"We'll take turns, of course," Alice said, kissing Ethan on the forehead, "but I get to hold this little one first." She winked at Sarah then headed to the kitchen window, watching Sarah hang up the drying laundry as a beautiful swath of sunlight streaked across the backyard. Any concerns she had about Nate and Elaine had fallen by the wayside after spending some time around them. Plus – a small, cynical voice in the back of her head whispered – there was no way they'd try to do anything nefarious to her or her children with her holding Ethan.

The property stretched for a few acres off to the left, where half the crops had been harvested with many corn stalks still standing and rows of greenery down low to the ground waiting to be picked. Off to the right, clusters of sawtooth oaks, pines, and lush vegetation rode up a shallow hill to disappear into a growing haze, though Alice wasn't sure if it was lingering smoke from the city fires or simply a fog rolling in. Two sheds stood side-by-side out past the patio, and Missy's swing set stood between them, simple but clean, looking like it had been purchased within the last few months as rust had yet to set in.

The big barn sat at the end of the dirt trail off in the distance, with the wide doors facing them and a loft bursting with hay above it. All the buildings looked like they had either been newly constructed or had special care paid to their upkeep, from the barn to the farmhouse, the boards barely creaking beneath Alice's feet as she paced softly across the floor with Ethan resting comfortably in a blanket in her arms. Sarah came back inside, and Alice handed Ethan to her.

"Support his neck and head."

"I know, Mom."

"And make sure to keep your arm wrapped around—"

"Mommm... I know! I promise, he's fine."

Turning and backing carefully into a kitchen chair, Sarah sat with one leg crossed and one eyebrow raised at her mother. "You should check on Elaine and Missy and see what food we have to work with. I heard Nate say something about potatoes, and there's the basket of them over on the counter needing to be peeled and cut."

"Mhmm... you take the cute baby and leave me with the hard work. I see how it is." Alice snickered and shook her head, leaving with a grin as she checked on the mother and daughter where they slept on the floor, curled up and snoring lightly. With the sun going down, Alice opened the blinds to get the last bit of warmth she could, then she returned to the kitchen, sorting through the potatoes and washing them. As she worked, Nate and Jake exited the barn, with Jake carrying two backpacks on his shoulders and Nate with their spare supplies and several paper-wrapped packages of meat clutched against his chest. When they got inside, they all pitched in to get dinner started, dicing potatoes and tossing them into a pot of boiling water. Nate explained that he'd turned the generator on outside, and it was okay to use some appliances sparingly for a few hours.

"We've been holding off until a little later to use the lights and stove at night or in the early morning," he said, "but we can make an exception this once if only to celebrate the birth of our new boy."

Smiling, Alice popped open the refrigerator to find two total gallons of whole milk inside, a couple of tubs of store-bought butter, and a few other perishables that would've gone bad if not for the generator power. Soon, dinner was on, with Alice stirring the potatoes while Nate seasoned the pork chops and took them outside to grill them over charcoal. Sarah continued cleaning up, getting things ready for Elaine and Nate that they'd need most over the next few days. Missy woke up from her nap and started helping Jake break off the ends of the green beans, and soon the two were laughing and throwing the discarded pieces at each other before Alice laughingly told them to stop.

The smells of cooking food filled the air, and when Nate brought in the pork chops a few minutes later, it set Alice's stomach growling, reminding her of just how long it had been since they'd had a proper, home-cooked meal. Elaine woke up last, and they helped her get to her feet and rest on the couch with piles of cushions and pillows underneath, and a glass of ice-cold water by her side with Ethan bundled up in her arms and fresh towels pushed under her midsection. Dinner trays came out last, everyone standing in line to get a plate of food, Nate bringing one to Elaine before sitting down next to her on the couch. Alice pulled in a kitchen chair and sat at the end of the couch next to Nate while Sarah, Jake, and Missy sat on the opposite couch in front of the window, Ethan sleeping in a crib the next room over.

"I want to thank you again," Nate said around a mouthful of food. "If it weren't for you folks, who knows what kind of trouble we'd be in?"

"You'd probably be in town by now," Sarah pointed out, "and maybe in a *lot* of trouble."

"No kidding," Nate laughed. "You guys mentioned being on your way home before. Where were you coming from?"

Alice raised her fork, finished chewing, and answered. "We're on our way back home to Michigan from a vacation down in Palm Beach. It's been a long trip so far, to say the least."

Alice launched into what had happened after every car in the parking lot at Seafood Jack's went up in flames, scattering bodies and leaving wrecks everywhere. She told them about the junkie couple and how they'd had to run them off before hitting the highway. There was the man on the beach who'd tried to take their things, and the stop at Andrea's hotel, then came the sad story of the EV dealership and taking an electric SUV, a generator, and flexible solar panels, only to lose them a short time later. And then there was kind, old Wilford and the looters who'd tried to kill them – and nearly succeeded in the process.

"After we got away from the people in town right down here, we came across you." Alice laughed. "I gotta say, you scared the daylights out of me, running at us like that."

Nate gave a low whistle, his eyes wide from her story. "No wonder you almost blew my head off. I'll be a lot more careful from here on out." He reached for Elaine's hand. "We knew things were bad, but we haven't really been out in the world, like you, and nobody's been by here. We didn't realize it was so cutthroat."

"It definitely is," Jake sighed.

Alice went on. "I think Andrea's was the first place where we started figuring out what was going on. There were radio reports of a terrorist attack on the nation's fuel supply."

"We'd heard the same thing on the radio." Nate swiped a piece of bread through the sauce left from the noodles and potatoes. "But it's only happening in the fuel that's been more recently processed, like in the past few months."

"Agreed. That's the conclusion I came to shortly after we were at Andrea's hotel. She mentioned her generators were running great when everything else in the area went up in smoke."

Elaine sat up a little straighter, propped up on the couch with a half dozen thick pillows and blankets. "That electric vehicle you drove for a couple of hundred miles is even more proof it's the gas, wouldn't you say?"

Alice nodded and set her plate to the side. "That's what I noticed after walking through a lot of the wreckage. The EVs had only been destroyed near vehicles that had exploded. They had burned down, yes, but they looked like that had happened from the fires started from *other* vehicles. It's a real shame we lost that thing... I doubt we'll see another one for a long time."

"That EV was an awesome ride." Jake stabbed at his potatoes and meat and shoved the last few bites into his mouth.

"Tell me about it," Sarah sighed from where she sat on the other side of Missy. "I'm not complaining, though, because our horses are awesome, too. And they don't have to recharge in the sun."

"And you diverted through the farm here because of the locals?" Elaine glanced at Nate. "That doesn't sound good for us, hon."

"I'd say they were after the horses more than anything." Alice finished her glass of water, turning it over in her hands. "Any kind of transportation out here will be worth its weight in gold. Horses, electric vehicles, tractors or farm equipment that hasn't been refueled recently. Generators, too. Really any machinery that still functions is going to draw people like flies to... er, like a moth to a flame."

Nate grinned as he looked over at Missy, then glanced at Elaine before coming back to Alice. "That makes sense because we've got a little farm tractor out back that didn't go up like the rest. I'm not the best farmer in the world yet, but I knew to keep some extra fuel on hand, and I had them fill up a tank out back almost six months ago. That's what we put in the tractor. We don't have a ton of it, but there's a few more refills' worth in it."

"You're lucky then. If you want to keep it very long, you've got to keep it out of sight. Only use it in absolute emergencies."

"The tractor is out behind the barn and covered up. No one will see it unless they intentionally start searching around."

"But you've got a generator too," Jake pointed out. "These lights we have on now? They'll make you stand out like nobody else. You'd be better off keeping everything pitch black and maybe spending all your evenings in your basement, where there's no chance of light leakage."

Alice was already nodding. "My son's right. We've already met so many bad people on the road, so you should focus on keeping a low profile. Do you have any weapons?"

"I've got a shotgun and a few shells, but we've never had to —"

"Get it out, clean it, and get ready to use it. No, *plan* on using it." Alice leaned over, gripping his forearm hard so that he got the message. "I'm serious, Nate. If an intruder gets inside your home, there won't be anyone to save you. You've got to be ready to defend yourself. Not only that, but you need to make sure your family is in a safe spot while you're doing it. Understand?"

Nate was nodding, looking over at Elaine, her jaw hardening as she nodded at him and looked back to Alice.

"We'll do everything we can to prepare. There's a junk room downstairs, but we can get it cleaned out."

"Set up beds and sleeping quarters in the far back. It wouldn't hurt for Elaine to have a weapon, too. So, go out and scavenge one." Alice glanced at her rifle, which leaned against the wall by the door. "I'd give you one of ours, but we've only got two, and we're desperately low on ammunition."

"That's fine," Nate said. "I'll go out tomorrow and start looking for something. Just brief trips to some neighborhood farms that might be abandoned or burned down... nothing that would put me at risk. I'm pretty sure I know a few who have some weapons and aren't... around anymore."

"The Batemans?" Elaine asked.

"Yeah, they were out of town and I'm pretty sure I saw a lot of smoke coming from over there."

"Just be careful when you're out there." Alice looked around at their small farmhouse. "You've got a nice place here, and you should focus on keeping and defending it as long as you can. As soon as Elaine is able, you'll want to set up watches, too."

"We will, for sure."

"I'll be back on my feet in a couple of days," Elaine quickly added, then groaned and chuckled. "Well... maybe a week or two."

Alice laughed. "Uh huh. Definitely a week or two or longer. You have Missy; you know what it's like."

"I know, but..." Elaine raised her chin in defiance. "If it means protecting our home, I can at least sit by a window and keep an eye on things."

"That's the spirit."

Sarah was the first one up to clear the dishes, and Jake joined her with Missy tagging along to help.

"Thank you, dear," Alice said to the little girl when she took her plate off the TV tray and tried to carry it into the kitchen before Jake scooped it from her hands.

"You can help us wash the dishes, Missy." Taking her hand, he led her into the kitchen where plates clattered, and the kitchen faucet turned on.

Relaxing back with a sigh, Alice said, "Have you checked the radio recently? Is there anything new?"

"Let's find out."

While the kids cleaned up, Nate picked up a small, one-speaker radio. Resting it in his lap, he flipped it on and tuned it until he found the emergency broadcast message. There was little change except for the additional mention of camps the government was setting up in Georgia, Florida, and elsewhere across the US, and Alice vaguely wondered if her husband could be in one of them.

"Are you guys going to try for a camp?" Elaine asked. "Or just head straight home?"

"We want to get home, check on my parents, and wait for my husband. Don't get me wrong, I'm glad there're camps people can seek refuge in, but we wouldn't go to one unless we had to."

"I understand that," Elaine replied. "Honey, why don't you put on some music instead of that government rambling?"

"On it." Nate picked through a stack of CDs on a shelf and found one with soft music, setting it to play on a small sound system under the TV.

As the quiet sounds drifted from the speakers, things almost felt normal, and Elaine fell asleep almost instantly, going from energetic and lucid to wiped out all over again, and Missy soon followed suit. The early evening soon turned into late night, and Alice walked to the barn to check the horses one last time, finding them in stalls with clean hay and plenty of water. Alice spent a few minutes brushing Buck and talking to him, then she went back inside where the kids were hanging out with Nate at the kitchen table, speaking quietly so they didn't disturb Elaine. They were sipping water, and Alice found some tea bags in a cabinet per Nate's direction and brewed them some warm, comforting cups of tea that steamed and gave off an earthy scent.

"I don't think anyone could make tea like Wilford." She put a cup in front of each of them. "But it'll do in a pinch."

Alice sat with them for a while, talking in low voices about the country's state and what the future might bring. It was only when Sarah leaned on the table and put her head down that Alice realized how late it had gotten.

"It's time for bed, kids," she said, then turned to Nate. "If you don't mind, I'd like to put the kids in the spare bedroom."

"Absolutely," he replied. "They can go in there on the king-sized bed. Should be plenty of room."

"As long as Jake doesn't kick me," Sarah added.

"I'm sure he will," Alice smiled. "Go on, guys. Get cleaned up and in bed, and I'll be in to check on you in a few minutes. I want to make sure you get some solid sleep before we head out."

Alice helped clean up the kitchen and checked on Elaine, seeing Nate had taken her advice and shut off the living room lights, leaving a single electric lantern in the corner turned to low. The blinds were covered with blankets, and mother and son were resting, Ethan in the crib Nate had rolled in from the other room. Going to stand beside it, Alice watched the baby sleep for a few minutes before shuffling down the hardwood hallway to the guestroom, where Jake and Sarah were lying side-by-side. Sarah's face was lit up by her e-reader while her brother was already snoring away. Alice started to say something about the light leaking outside when she saw Sarah had draped a blanket over the blinds to block everything.

With a smile, she circled to Sarah's side and pulled up a chair. "Still working on the same book?"

"I'm almost done with this one." Sarah yawned. "I had the entire series downloaded before we left home so I've got plenty of stuff left to read."

Alice sat, put her knees together, and leaned in. "Is there still battery life in that thing?"

Sarah shrugged sheepishly. "When I heard Nate say he turned the generator on to the house, I plugged it into a socket and charged it up."

Alice laughed. "Smart girl. I'm glad you brought that along with you. It's... good you're reading with everything that's been going on. If only I could unplug from the world like that right now."

Sarah held it out. "Do you want to borrow it?"

"No thanks." Alice smiled. "Keep reading. Just go to sleep soon."

Jake suddenly shifted and rolled over, his face half buried in a pillow, blinking at his mother with a yawn.

"Oh, I thought you were sleeping."

"I was only half asleep. My legs are sore and restless from riding."

"Good thing you'll be able to sleep in a bed tonight, right? Otherwise, we'd be camped out in the woods, getting eaten alive by bugs."

"It was crazy what happened today, huh?"

Alice shook her head and leaned forward with her elbows on her knees. "I certainly didn't figure we'd be delivering a baby today... not the first thing I imagined us doing when I woke up, especially after everything we've been through."

"I thought it was awesome." Sarah rested her reader on her chest and looked up. "It was crazy to see little Ethan come out, and it was a lot more painful than they show on TV. Poor Elaine."

"Which one of us was more painful to have, Mom?" Jake stretched out and put his hand beneath the pillow.

Alice tilted her head in thought. "You were both pretty tough to deal with, just like now." She squeezed Sarah's arm and grinned. "But seriously, I'm pretty sure Jake was the toughest, but I wouldn't have changed it for the world."

Jake laughed softly, then whispered. "Yeah, I'm glad you put up with me. Hey, Nate and Elaine are pretty cool people, huh?"

"Yes, they are. And they've been through a lot. I'm glad we could help get them through it."

"It could have been a major disaster," Sarah said.

"I'm sure us coming along made a big difference. Even though Nate is green about things, he's not as bad as he thinks. He's learning and adapting a lot, a lot faster than he probably ever imagined he'd have to."

"We have to adapt if we want to survive," Sarah replied flatly.

"That's right, honey." Alice drew her daughter's blanket to her chest and patted it, earning her an affectionate smile.

"I keep thinking about Wilford," Jake said. "What do you think he's doing right now?"

Alice shrugged. "Probably still chasing horses around the field."

Sarah laughed, but Jake pressed on with a worried look. "Yeah, but he's an old guy. What if those people come back?"

"He was setting up defenses when we left. And, c'mon, the guy tried to take our heads off when we walked up." Alice chuckled. "Don't be fooled by his accent and white hair, he's tougher than nails."

"He's one of the good ones," Sarah whispered. "And he's so different from other people we met out there. Like that guy on the beach who tried to take our stuff."

Alice snorted. "Well, I wouldn't be too hard on him, dear."

"But he tried to hurt us," Sarah countered. "You said we should defend ourselves against people like that. That means hurting people like the ones who attacked us at Wilford's."

Alice shifted in her chair and tilted her head as she struggled to explain. "People don't fit into just two categories. They didn't before all of this, and they don't now. It's not like people are just good or just bad. Some are good, but desperate."

"The guy on the beach," Jake stated flatly.

"Yes, at least that's what I believe. While he showed us kindness initially, panic and desperation changed him somehow. He lost a bit of his humanity because he was worried about his kids. I can't blame him for that, but he tried turning us into his enemies, and that was a big mistake."

A dark look passed over Sarah's face, and her eyes narrowed in the light of the e-reader. "Good people can become our enemies, right?"

"I'm not sure *enemies* is the best word, but regardless, it doesn't mean everyone is our enemy." Alice sat back and blinked, their experiences over the past few days hitting her hard. "But even those people in the last town that were looking at our horses? They probably weren't *really* our enemies, but more like the guy on the beach. Scared, hungry, and probably a little paranoid, too. And, just like him, we handled them well by cutting and running."

"I guess we're learning fast, huh?" Jake asked.

"We absolutely are, and I'm so incredibly proud of both of you for responding so quickly and doing exactly what I asked at all times. Both of you."

"Thanks, Mom," Sarah smiled.

"We're proud of you, too, Mom." Jake sniffed and blinked, coaxing up a smile. "We always knew you were a great mom, but I guess we didn't..." He buried his face in his pillow.

Alice pressed her mouth tight as his emotion touched her heart. "What is it, Jake?"

With a sleepy blink, he drummed up the words. "I guess you always did stuff for us, but we took it for granted. Seeing you deliver that baby today and how you jumped in there and took over... I was so scared, and you just got in there and nailed it. You sounded just like a doctor or nurse or someone who does that kind of thing every single day."

Alice smiled. "Thank you for saying that, but I was shaking, too." She touched her fingers to her stomach. "Inside and outside... My hands were trembling, and I wasn't sure I was doing the right thing. But I had to do *something*, or we would've lost Ethan or Elaine. Maybe both. Sometimes you simply have to *act* and figure out the details along the way. Make sense?"

Jake nodded, and Sarah stared at Alice until she finally smiled in agreement. Leaning down, Alice gave Sarah a quick peck on the cheek and then blew a kiss to Jake before leaving the room. She was taking the first watch over the farmstead, glad to give Nate and Elaine a peaceful night's rest, quite possibly their last for a very, very long time.

CHAPTER NINETEEN

James Burton
Hannibal, Missouri

The forest trees moved by in a blur as James guided Amber between them, riding bareback, knees clenched against her sides, leaning and clinging hard to the reins. All of his strength and energy went into just holding on, fighting against gravity and his body's attempts to overcorrect his balance. The few riding lessons he'd taken with Alice and the kids had come back in full force, though he never imagined his joking question to the instructor about 'how hard is it to ride bareback?' would come back to haunt him.

"*Way too hard.*" He muttered, imitating the instructor who'd laughed at his question. "*That's why we put saddles on them!* Bite me, you old coot."

Above Amber's heavy breaths and the thudding of her hooves on the soft woodland floor, the engine continued coughing and sputtering, growling and hitching and sometimes running for a few seconds before it died again. The noise emanated from somewhere along the highway to the north, and James headed directly for it, reaching the roadway and galloping along a ditch still hidden by the tightly packed woods.

When he thought he was close enough, he dismounted, tied Amber to a tree, and stalked up to the roadside where he climbed a short bank and peered across to the other side. About fifty yards up at the corner of a field was an intersection with a lane heading east. A small group of people were gathered around a makeshift vehicle, more of a contraption than a car, with an oversized engine and stripped-down frame, the roof missing and the rear end attached to a pair of large tires. The seats were bolted in, too, and there was no trunk he could see, merely an open gas tank with lines that ran beneath the frame up to the front. The four standing around it were gesturing and arguing with each other, and James crept closer, crouching behind some bushes as he came within twenty-five yards of them to hear what they were saying.

"That's not where it goes, idiot." A tall man with shoulder-length brown hair and a grimy t-shirt on took a rag out of his pocket and slapped it against the engine block. "I told you to fasten the clamps better before we left, and now we've got a leak."

"Sorry, Len. I thought I had it tight."

"You thought wrong!"

The two men were opposites from each other, the leader tall while his partner was shorter with a greasy baseball hat on and a blue bandanna tied around his neck.

A woman with dyed blonde hair and numerous tattoos on her bare arms stood next to the taller man, Len, as she smoked a cigarette. "You're the mechanic here, Len," she said. "You shouldn't have let Jerry touch the damn thing if you thought he'd break it."

"I don't want to hear it from you, Marge," Len snapped.

"You're going to hear it from me every time we get stuck out here trying to drive this thing around!"

"If it wasn't for me," Len growled and leaned farther over the engine, touching hot pieces of metal with his rag-wrapped fingers, "we wouldn't have gotten this far. You should be thanking me."

A second woman wearing jeans and a gray tank top stood on Jerry's right, and like the others, she wore a pistol on her hip in plain sight. "Let's say we stop arguing," she said, "and figure out how to get this piece of junk moving again."

"It's not a piece of junk, Jess." Len growled harder. "This is a masterpiece, the one thing that's going to get us where we need to go. If you don't have anything good to say about it, then you can walk the rest of the way."

The shorter man frowned. "Hey, man. Don't talk to her like that."

Ignoring the remark, Len backed out from beneath the hood and stood at his full height, glaring across the lot of them. "I pulled parts off just about every go-cart, sedan, truck, and lawnmower I could find to get this thing running. I built it, and I'll get it to run again... trust me."

"Just tell us what's wrong," Jess said, peering deeper inside the engine.

"Back up. I'm still working on it."

Jess turned and slapped her leg as she guffawed, her gaze sweeping right across where James was peeking from the brush, sending his heart leaping into his throat as he ducked and let his carbine slide off his shoulder.

"Trust you?" Jess cried. "Put up with you, maybe. Trust is stretching it."

When James raised up and peered between the branches and over the road, he saw Jess walking away, hands on her hips and shaking her head in exasperation.

"It's got to be a part you put on wrong." Marge stepped back and crossed her arms.

"It's not any of the parts," Len replied with a glance. "Most likely, it's the gas Jerry filled the tank with. Stuff was probably sitting around for a few years or more. Stabilizer only works for so long, and from what I can tell, it's caused one of the fuel injectors to seize up. We're screwed until we can get another one."

"What do we do?" Marge asked, squaring up to the taller man. "Are we just going to walk now?"

Mimicking her posture, Len leaned in. "We're going to find a new fuel injector. That's what."

Jess gestured at the field right next to them. "So, is a fuel injector just lying around out here somewhere?"

"Not in the *field*, dummy. Good grief you're stupid. Up there by those buildings, or from some of those wrecks down the road there." Len turned south and pointed down the highway, and James glanced that way to see the remains of several vehicles spread along the road all burned up and beaten, their hoods thrown open, trunks blasted out with car parts scattered everywhere.

"Let's all spread out and start walking. Jess and Jerry, you two head south while Marge and I head up to those buildings. I see some wrecked cars in those rear lots, and I'll bet I can find something that will fit in my baby here."

Len used his rag to shine the contraption's grill, grinning broadly at the others, who only rolled their eyes and began meandering in different directions to search for a car with any sort of engine that was marginally intact. "And watch out for other people," Len called out to his group, "if anyone heard the engine, that might draw them in. Easy pickings for us!"

James watched Jess and Jerry laugh as they broke away and moved south past his position, panic flooding him as they inched toward the service road where Eli's family was located. Retreating quietly and slipping his rifle off his shoulder, James turned into the woods and slunk off, staying well hidden behind the layers of trees and brush and doing his best not to make a sound as he crept back to Amber, untied her, and walked her through the woods. Once he'd made it about fifty yards away, he swung his leg over her back, almost slipping off the other side before righting himself again.

With a soft, "H'yah," James flicked the reins and galloped back to Eli and his family. The Amish leader was still squeezing water from his trousers when he glanced up to see James approaching, and he stood from his crouched position and shuffled up the service road to meet him.

"What is it, James?" Eli asked.

James drew Amber to a halt, threw his leg over, and dropped to the ground. Breathlessly, he explained. "There are people just north of us up the road. They've got guns, and they are trouble with a capital T."

Eli's face darkened. "Oh, that's not good. That's not good at all."

James glanced over his shoulder. "Two of them are walking down this way, looking for a part to fix a cobbled-together vehicle they built. They'll be by here in a few minutes. You need to get your things together and go *now*."

"Perhaps they're friendly, and we can talk to them," Eli pleaded as he glanced back to see Clara and Betty looking concerned while most of the others hadn't yet noticed their conversation.

"No. We've got to go! They've got guns, and they are *not* friendly!"

Something in James' eye shook Eli, and he turned and waved to grab Abram's and Jacob's attention. The family started to gather around him, but he motioned toward the wagons.

"Everyone, back in the wagons now. We must go!"

"Why, Father?" Esther asked, her long, dark, wet hair dangling in her face.

"James says bad people are coming," he replied, taking her gently by the shoulders and turning her toward the buggy. "And we don't want a repeat of what happened before, do we?"

While they prepared to go, James jogged down the lane about forty yards, crouching and ducking, peering through the empty spots in the trees to see Jerry and Jess strolling toward them casually, stopping at a burned-up hulk in the road, leaning beneath the hood and checking the engine. James reeled and sprinted to where Abram was leading Amber away, patting his shoulder to stop him and waved his other hand to get Eli's attention as he climbed into the buggy seat.

"They're coming fast, Eli. Can one horse pull this buggy? Or do you absolutely need two?"

"One horse can pull the buggy fine." Eli's expression changed to confusion. "Why do you ask?"

James hesitated, torn between self-preservation, the desire to keep traveling with the family, and the certainty of what would happen if he didn't go through with his plan. "This is going to sound crazy... but if you let me take Amber, I can ride her past the group to draw them away from your family." James turned to where Abram was holding the beautiful chestnut mare, the bottom half of her coat still wet from fording the river. "While I distract them, you can turn south on the road ahead and get back to your people."

Eli's eyes grew wide. "I don't know about that, James. I do not wish for you to take any more risks for—"

"We don't have time to argue about it." James looked over his shoulder, still not seeing Jess and Jerry. "We got maybe five minutes before a couple of armed and nasty people show up at the end of that road. They're going to see your horses and wagons, and they're going to want them. Two I might be able to take on, but their friends will hear the gunfire and when that happens, we will be royally screwed."

Face torn with indecision, Eli glanced toward the end of the road and back to James. "Are you sure?"

"Look, Eli," James said, circling to the buggy seat to grab his pack and staff. "Your family won't commit violence to protect yourselves, and I can't handle a group that large on my own. If we don't do something now, we'll be shot and robbed... or worse. Do you want that for your family?"

Eli squeezed the reins and slowly shook his head. "No. No, I don't." With an urgent grunt, he motioned to Abram. "Son, get the saddle out of the back and get Amber ready for James immediately. We're going to split up."

Clara stepped over with a frightened expression as Abram handed her Amber's reins and ran to get a saddle. The woman gestured fitfully and turned to Eli and then James. "Do we really have to split up? Things were going so well."

James disassembled his walking stick and put it in a front pouch on his backpack, buckling the top flap and swinging it on one shoulder. "I'm afraid so, Clara. I won't risk them finding you and chasing you down. You'll have to flee south while I draw them away." Rifle in one hand, he gently squeezed her shoulder. "If I get the chance, I'll circle back and try to find you, but it might not be possible."

"I hope so," she said worriedly and handed over the reins with a sob. "Regardless, Amber is a great horse, and she'll treat you well."

"I know. And I'll take care of her as best as I can."

Abram appeared from behind the supply wagon with a lightweight saddle in hand, jogging it over and putting it on the mare's back, circling to the other side, saying, "James, can you feed me the strap?"

"On it." With a glance up the road, expecting to see Jess and Jerry at any moment, James reached beneath the horse's thick belly, handing Abram the leather strap, which he began buckling tight, checking that there was enough room between the front of the saddle and Amber's neck.

"You should be ready to go now, James," Abram said as he circled, teary-eyed and patting the chestnut mare's neck. "I'm going to miss you, girl." With a last hug, he nodded firmly at James. "Take good care of her. She's a fine beast."

"You can bet I will," James replied. "I'll treat her like she's my own, and I'll bring her back to you if I can."

The rest of the family had climbed into the buggy and supply wagon, watching from the back, blinking away tears as he mounted Amber and shifted in the saddle, his heart sinking even in the panicked rush to leave.

"Clara, give James some food for his trip." Eli gestured to the girls behind him. "Some sweet bread for James, please."

Betty turned to get it even as James shook his head. "I appreciate that, Eli," James replied, glancing back and turning Amber toward the road. "But I need to get moving."

Before he could get too far, a small satchel filled with food appeared, and Betty handed it to Clara, who used a leather strap to secure it to the saddle. With a gentle pat on his knee, Clara looked up with bleary red eyes. "You take care of yourself, James. Don't forget us."

His gaze lingered on her warm, motherly expression before he turned and blinked away tears. Eli sat proudly in the driver's chair with his face strained with worry, almost anguished as he watched James on Amber's back, stepping sideways down the road. Kneeling at the front of the carriage, Betty held Sadie against her right hip while young John, with his mop of brown hair, was blinking at him from around her other side. Abram was backing up toward the supply wagon and waving, and Eli stood from his driver's seat, holding his wide-brimmed hat and saying goodbye with a slow, somber nod.

"I am afraid, James." Eli's voice wavered. "That this may be the last time we shall see you."

James fought against the lump forming in his throat. "I'll do my best to circle around to you, but your safety is most important to me right now, so I'm going to draw them north and keep on riding. If we don't see each other again, I won't forget you all, Eli. Please, take care of yourselves. Ride hard and fast, and stop for nothing and no one."

Before James could turn Amber toward the highway, Eli stood and held one hand out, head shaking and voice filled with emotion. "It is you we should be thanking. Go in peace with the love of the Lord. May he protect you and bless you for your kindness to us."

James nodded, his expression grim as he pleaded his case one final time. "Eli, please, listen when I tell you that the world has changed, and you must change with it. I know your beliefs are sacrosanct, but self-defense is not murder. Just think about it, please. For your family's sake."

For the first time, Eli's response was hesitant. "I... will think on your words, James. Your friendship won't easily be forgotten. Go forward in the Lord's light, and may your journey be safe."

James nodded, then flicked the reins and turned Amber toward the highway, steering the horse with his left hand while swinging his carbine up in his right, partially resting it on his thigh. As he rode from the cover of the trees, Jerry and Jess came into view, finished with the car they were searching and walking south in his direction. The two caught sight of James and gawked before shuffling back to the edge of the road. James turned Amber north up the highway and kicked her flanks so she leaped forward with a strained snort and flex of her rigid spine. Jess and Jerry went for their guns, Jess pulling hers hesitantly, giving James time to shoot first.

The carbine swung up, and he aimed from his hip, squeezing the trigger three times as the weapon bucked in his grip. Two shots missed, but the last one clipped Jerry in his left shoulder, the powerful round spinning him with a yowl as he stumbled and fell to the ground. Jess was caught between firing at James and going to her man's aid, deciding on the latter and falling to her knees next to him. James gave them two parting shots, his bullets spitting dirt and gravel around their knees and Jess sprawled backward on her backside, drawing her weapon and firing wildly after him, the rounds passing harmlessly into the woods. She shouted something at his back, but James was already too far away to hear and focused on the next intersection where the makeshift vehicle sat stalled on the corner.

Len and Marge were sprinting toward him from where they'd gotten about halfway to the homes and businesses they were going to search, Len jogging up ahead with his gun out, watching James race down the road on the galloping horse. He glanced at Jess and Jerry, both of whom were up and running, firing at James' back, rounds flying past him as he half expected to get hit, though he was already forty yards away and gaining speed by the second. Amber's form was pure muscle beneath him, hooves crashing on the pavement as he hunkered low over her neck and urged her on with sharp commands.

"H'yah, Amber! Let's go, girl! Show me what you've got!"

Len and Marge had stopped and were walking slowly toward James with their pistols raised, firing at him until he raised his carbine and shot back, sweeping the weapon in their direction and squeezing the trigger a handful of times, not expecting to hit anything, but scattering the pair to either side of the road. He was past them in a flash, Amber's hooves clattering on the pavement as they rode up a hill, her metal shoes sparking over the hard surface, flanks heaving beneath James' knees. In the space of thirty seconds, he'd ridden out of range, and he drew Amber to a trot with a gentle flick on the reins.

Len and his friends were rushing up the road behind him, shouting and gesturing obscenely. "I'm going to kill you, you bastard!" Len bellowed, firing one more time. James fired back at them, sending them diving and causing their attention to focus entirely on him. More wasted rounds flew in his direction, but they finally stopped shooting as James moved Amber into cover, taking potshots back at them to keep their attention focused on him.

Back at the far intersection, the Amish buggy and supply wagon were barely visible from the top of the hill as they pulled through and angled south in a rush of clopping hooves and quaking, bouncing carriages. Faces peered from the backs of the wagons as they swayed on their springs, then they turned around a bend and kept going south, driving hard and drawing Eli's family and their precious cargo out of range. Shouts from Len's group drew closer, yelling about killing James and taking his horse, and he grinned at the success of his distraction, faced forward again and continued riding north away from his allies.

He began to slow Amber down another half mile up, preparing to turn back east and south when movement caught his eye, several people alerted to the gunfight running toward him down a side street, each of them brandishing a firearm, and he sped up again. After three more attempts to stop and circle around, and three more sightings of people who had spotted him and the horse, he gave up and kept riding until he was well out of the urban area. Two miles later, with no signs of people nearby, he slowed Amber to a trot, his anxiety fading as he spoke confident and loving words to her and patted her neck. "Good girl, Amber. Good, good girl."

They'd reached a series of farmsteads, some still smoldering from old fires while others remained standing and unchanged. James ignored them all and kept moving north along the desolate highway, walking the mare between burned-up hulks of vehicles stranded in the road, squatting in a sea of car parts and scattered debris, nothing to salvage and no one else around but corpses. Hoping that he was out of danger for the moment, James slung his rifle on his right shoulder and relaxed, reaching back to dig his canteen out and take a long drink. He didn't know where he was except that he was north and slightly east of Hannibal, but he kept riding north until he hit I-72.

Once on the expressway, he checked his compass to see that he was going northeast, and he settled back and reached for a side pouch on his backpack that held his map. Getting it open one-handed, he spread it across Amber's neck. After some finagling, he traced his finger to Hannibal, Missouri and then followed miles of major highways and smaller ones to the northeast, looking for the best way back to the south and east, but failing to find a route that wouldn't take him directly back through the urban areas he'd just escaped.

"Son of a gun..." Amber snorted beneath him as he muttered to himself, her neck tickled by the edges of the map, and he patted her side as he looked around at the farmland and back at the road he'd taken to get to I-72. "Sorry, girl. It looks like we're going to be riding together longer than I had hoped."

With Eli's family having successfully escaped, James' primary objective was done. Returning Amber to them was important, but less so than his own survival – particularly with very few options left to him to try and deviate south as well as east to try to link up with them along the road.

Giving a light flick to the reins, he got Amber trotting forward, searching the map for any sort of alternate route as he continued to talk to himself. "Maybe... Peoria? We can divert around there I guess? I don't know.... I'm not exactly loving any of these options, quite frankly."

Putting the map away, James pushed forward, reloading his carbine before re-shouldering it, trying to ignore the nagging feeling that things were about to get a lot worse for him. A gunshot rang out to his right, the round impacting on a nearby vehicle, and he pushed Amber into a gallop as he looked over, seeing a pair standing on a hill near the expressway, one of them with a rifle trained on him.

"Hiya, Amber! Let's go!"

James flew like the wind, leaving yet another set of would-be attackers behind, his confidence in himself – and the world, thanks to Eli's family's kindness – rapidly shrinking as he realized that his path would not be dictated solely by himself, but by others around him, both good and evil.

THE RUINATION

CHAPTER ONE

Ryan Cooper
Somewhere Outside East Lansing, Michigan

Jack Willoughby stood in the old couple's dining room, annoyed at how long it'd taken him and his group to get inside. As they were breaking in, the old man had shot at them through the plywood-covered windows, drowning the intruders in wood shrapnel and bullet fragments. Jack had been led to believe it would be an easy fight, but the old man and his wife were much tougher than he could've imagined. Mack Tilly had been the first casualty of their little war, when they'd sent him to scout the barnyard the evening before. He'd never returned, leaving Jack wondering what the oldsters had done to him. That should've been the first warning sign.

The second should've been all the traps that had been set up in the yard, starting with the spikes hidden in the grass, keeping them from taking cover behind the trees as they were approaching. As a result, the old couple had shot Tommy Sloan dead and wounded Jasper South with a shot that would probably end up killing him slowly and painfully.

He had the old people trapped upstairs, but Jack didn't know how to get to them without incurring even more losses. The old man was an excellent shot, and the barking dogs sounded big and nasty. If he gave up, though, he wouldn't get to their supplies, and walking home empty-handed would lead to a lot of complaints, and it wouldn't be long before he lost the support of the other neighbors. Barb would never let him live it down.

A table took up most of the dining room, and a cabinet rested against the east wall along with a tall chest of drawers next to it. The cabinet was covered in school books, notebooks, older children's toys and various odds and ends, and for the briefest second a twinge of guilt passed through Jack. Rita Tilly stared back at him across the foyer from the great room, a question in her eyes as dust and smoke from the shootout drifted through the moonlight, and the twinge was gone. Ron Jenkins crouched near her shoulder with the same dumbfounded look, the last to charge the grounds and the weakest of the bunch. It was doubtful if he'd even used the pistol he carried – or if he'd be willing to if push came to shove. *Cannon fodder has its purpose, I guess,* Jack mused, the macabre thought lifting his spirits a bit.

Across from the kitchen and dining room, the great room had a TV mounted on the west wall above a gas fireplace, and a leather couch sat in front of the massive display with a pair of recliners on each side. The modest arrangement of common household goods was a fortune compared to what he and Barb had left after all they'd owned had burned to the ground, along with two barns and most of their feed and supplies. If he didn't come through with something soon, they'd be hard-pressed to survive long out there.

"Hey, man. Are we going or not?" Trace Crenshaw whispered as he peered around Jack and tried to see up into the loft area.

He'd wrapped his right hand up in a rag after grabbing the back doorknob covered with razor blades, the cuts so bad he couldn't hold his pistol, the blood soaking heavy through the cloth and running down his arm. He tried to get around Jack, but Jack pushed him back, chiding him.

"Just hang on a minute."

"What are we waiting for?"

"We need to think this thing through. We've already got some people down, and running out there like idiots will only get *us* killed too."

"What's there to plan?" Trace hissed back. "I'll step out there and give you some cover fire while you and Rita rush up the stairs."

"Yeah, we'll take on those dogs by ourselves."

The dogs hadn't stopped barking, the timbre of the notes deep and chesty, giving the impression that they were huge, slavering beasts of war waiting to be unleashed. He remembered seeing Alice Burton walking her dogs one day and thinking how massive and shaggy they were. They'd seemed friendly and dopey as they trotted beside her, but if that was them upstairs, they were more akin to monsters than big, playful household pets.

"Just shoot the damn things." Trace grabbed Jack's shirt with his bloody hand. "Only dogs a bullet won't stop are pit bulls, and those ain't pit bulls."

"Are you crazy? Those're *big* bastards, and it'll take more than one round to kill them!" Jack edged toward the threshold, peering up into the loft through the chewed-up rails, seeing no one before he eased back. "I wonder how bad the old man is injured? I think one of us got him."

Trace shook his head and pushed past him. "Let's just get on with it, man."

"Wait!"

Trace shoved him back with his forearm and crouch-walked into the hallway, glancing up the stairwell before scanning up along the catwalk. "No dogs up there I can see."

"It doesn't mean they're not there. Listen to them!"

Trace slipped into the hallway, staying beneath the catwalk, slowly moving toward the great room, neck craned to look above. As he cleared the edge of the loft, the old woman's voice cried out, and a second later something massive and white flew up and over the catwalk's rail, plunging into him in a blur, paws slamming him full in the chest, knocking him backward, and sending his gun flying as they hit the floor. The shaggy, bear-like dog snarled and flashed its teeth, clamping on his throat, pushing him back toward the front door. The animal was ripping and jerking its powerful head back and forth to tear out a sizeable chunk of Trace's neck and windpipe, the bloody muzzle whipping upward in a spray of blood, Trace's pulsing jugular vein spurting red in a high arc that coated the door like paint.

Jack took a step back in shock and horror, mouth dropping open, fumbling with his pistol in shock, barely catching it before it fell to the floor.

The old woman shouted again from the loft, clearly enough for him to hear, and his blood ran cold. "Attack, Duchess! Attack, Diana! Attack!"

The growls and barks were replaced by paws pounding down the stairwell and another massive beast hit the hardwood foyer with a grunt. Almost a perfect twin of the animal gnawing on Trace's neck, the second one swung its heavy head to the right toward Rita and Ron, who were backing into the great room, gaping at the bloody mess developing in the foyer.

In a scrabble of claws on wood, the dog launched itself, knocking Ron aside and enveloping Rita in one bound. They tumbled into the great room, the dog pinning Rita to the back of the couch, jaws snapping at her arms and face. The dog's enormous frame shook back and forth, shaggy fur rippling as blood sprayed the floor and walls and splattered Ron. Rita shrieked repeatedly, gurgling and gasping in between bites while Ron dropped his weapon, screamed, and dashed into the foyer toward the broken-open window, running headlong into a third dog as it too hit the foyer floor in a tumble of fur and snarls. Legs swept from beneath him, Ron went down on the floor chin first, bone against wood with a sharp crack, then the dog was on him, snapping, grabbing the back of his jacket and jerking backward, tearing its head back and forth.

Jack woke from his surprised daze and took two steps forward with his gun raised. At first, he aimed at the dog attacking Trace, but his friend was gone, so Jack shifted his aim to the beast across the hall destroying Rita. Its paws were spread, its powerful shoulders low to the ground as its maw did its work, and Rita could only cover up with one arm as she punched and kicked weakly at the massive, enraged Great Pyrenees.

Ryan had been crouched back off the rail, holding in a groan from the pain radiating up his wounded calf when Helen clicked the dogs' quick-release leashes and shouted for them to attack. Duke and Duchess spun in a frenzy, almost surprised to be let loose. With Duchess taking up the space around the top of the stairs, Duke bounced off her, reeled, and rushed toward Ryan, jaws snapping. In two bounds, the dog leaped on the rail, his massive claws scrabbling, slipping, pawing at the wood as he propelling himself over, plunging out of sight before Ryan could even think to stop the beast's movements.

A moment later, Duchess flew down the stairs, hitting the hardwood floor in a scrabble of nails. Screams ripped through the house, guttural sounds of raw terror, followed by canine grunts, snapping teeth, and snarls. Ryan came out of his crouch and stepped toward the rail with his rifle raised while Helen finally got Diana turned down the stairs to follow the others, then came to join him.

Curses, exclamations of horror and the primal sound of death itself sent a shudder through Ryan. Soft flesh tore, and the gurgling shrieks of a woman fountained in his ears as at least two people downstairs received the brunt of the Great Pyrenees' rage. Hundreds of pounds of muscles, teeth, and claws unleashed a storm of violence upon the intruders as the dogs did exactly what they were born to do: protect and defend.

Still, even with the dogs turning the tide of the battle, Ryan and Helen had to take advantage of the situation while they could. He nodded to Helen, and they flew to the rail with guns aiming downward, looking for targets. Ryan shifted his barrel to a man wearing a red flannel shirt about to shoot Duke, the dog holding a man against the front door, paws spread, massive body pinning him, jaws clenched on his face. Squeezing the trigger too quickly, Ryan pulled his shot and clipped the man's gun hand, forcing him to flinch with a cry and lose his weapon to clatter on the hardwood.

Helen shot multiple times at a different man crawling across the foyer floor, trying to escape Diana, her shots hitting him in the shoulder, punching through to the floor, and he spasmed and ripped free of Diana's jaws. Flying through the swirling dust, he slammed into the man in the red flannel, the pair shouting and cursing as they tried to get away. Ryan and Helen peppered the intruders, their weapons lighting up the darkened foyer like a fireworks display as Diana crouched, barking loudly.

In the darkness, Ryan couldn't tell who he hit because the men were bunched together and stumbling, though the one Helen was firing on collapsed to his knee with a sudden, crippling weakness. The man in flannel dragged his wounded companion to the broken window while Ryan kept shooting at them, his bullets finding flesh, drawing cries of shock and curses of anger and pain. They fell backward through the window, taking out glass shards and broken wood before landing in the bushes.

"Come on!" Ryan called, turning and hobbling toward the stairwell, wincing and growling as his calf cramped. He fought it, slamming his teeth together, grinding through the pain as he hobbled down the stairs and into the foyer to stand in the middle of the bloody scene. Duke was still locked onto his prey, and Duchess had the woman's neck in her jaws, pinning her to the floor, snarling deep in her throat but holding tight even as the woman's last gurgling breaths bubbled from her lips.

"Get the dogs, Helen! I'm going to chase these bastards off!"

Ryan angled toward the window, limping, slipping on the bloody floor and finally falling to his knee at the sill. Sticking the barrel outside, he tracked the two men stumbling through the yard, the larger one helping his friend stay upright, both of them somehow still able to walk, their adrenaline fueling their escape. He popped off two more shots, missing both times but sending the men into a frenzy to escape. A third squeeze came up dry, and he ejected the magazine and took a second one out of his pocket, almost dropping it from his blood-slick fingers, finally jamming it home. Charging his weapon, he aimed at the fleeing men, slowly lowering the barrel as they got to the gate and clambered over it, the man in the flannel working hard to get his wounded companion up and over before they staggered off into the night.

Helen had set her rifle down and pulled Dutchess off her prey, taking her by the collar and kneeling between her and Diana. Duke was ignoring her, still with the man's face in his jaws, panting through his open maw, growls rippling from his throat as his sides heaved.

"He's not listening," Helen said with strained frustration.

"Come on, Duke!" Ryan shouted at the dog, crossing the foyer and stopping a couple of feet from it. His white coat was stained dark red around his chest and jaws, with streaks along his flanks where the man had tried to beat him off.

Duke rolled his eyes and looked at Ryan with animal ferocity, though a hint of recognition showed through, and his tail, previously low, swept back and forth, and he loosened his hold slightly.

Ryan shouted, "Come on, Duke! Let it go, boy! Let it go!"

Duke's tail wagged a little harder and his chesty growls tapered off, though he still had a firm grip on the man's mangled face, fangs puncturing his cheek, the flesh shredded away to expose his bone-white jaw and bloody insides of his mouth.

Equally disgusted and thankful for the animal's effective response to the intruders, Ryan used the Winchester to support himself as he knelt on one knee, wincing at the extreme stiffness gripping his calf muscle. "I said, let it go, Duke! Let it go, *now*!"

The stern note in his voice cut through the animal's instinct, and Duke dropped the man's face, letting the skull hit the hardwood with a thump. The Great Pyrenees turned, tail wagging as he licked his chops, sniffing at Ryan's outstretched hand before shifting to Duchess and touching noses with her. Diana was the most curious, her aggression having been raised but not fed, and she sniffed at her parents with her ears perked up and her tail wagging.

Ryan patted Duke's side. "Good boy, Duke! Real good boy. You, too, Duchess. You're such a good girl!"

Hauling himself up using the Winchester, Ryan turned slowly, gaping at the bloody mess around him. Bullet holes and empty cartridges peppered the floor and there were jagged holes torn in the sidelights, window frames, and even parts of the ceiling. Blood streaked the hardwood and soaked the gray carpet in the great room where the dead woman lay, and arcs of red could be seen halfway up the walls. Some spatters reached as high as the foyer window fifteen feet above them, the red slowly dripping down across the walls. Stepping closer to the big dogs, he gave them hearty slaps on their sides, rubbing their heads to put them at ease as he looked over at Helen who was stepping gingerly toward him.

"Are you okay, honey?"

With a half-smile, she said, "I think so. I'm a little shaken up, but I'll live. What about you?"

Ryan shook his head. "I'm afraid to look. I got hit in the calf."

Helen glanced down and blanched. "Oh, no, Ryan! I didn't even notice you were hurt... everything was moving so fast!"

"I can hardly feel it, though I imagine it'll hurt like hell here soon, once this adrenaline wears off." Ryan held up a hand, watching as it gradually began to shake faster with each passing second.

"Come over to the dining room table. I'll get the first aid kit and take a gander at that."

"That's okay, dear. I'll be fine for now. Let's get these bodies out of here while I can still stand."

He leaned his Winchester against the wall and stepped through the pool of blood to stand next to the dead man. Unbolting the locks on the front door, he opened it a few inches but stopped with a frustrated sigh when the door stopped with a thud on the corpse's head.

"We need to move him first," Helen said, swallowing a nauseous gulp.

"Right. Let's drag him away from the door."

They each grabbed a foot and pulled the body into the hallway, leaving a smear of blood behind. Ryan returned to the door, popped it open with a tug, and returned to the man. In the same fashion, they dragged the man in a circle, his arms hanging wide, face chewed to bits as the curious dogs crowded around and sniffed at him.

"Hey! Get back!" Ryan hissed.

Duke sat at the edge of the pool of blood with his head tilted to the side and his tail sweeping in the smears. Duchess and Diana paced in the hallway, the younger dog trailing behind her mother and sniffing at the blood on her fur. Bumping their shoulders against the door frame, Ryan and Helen got the dead man outside and dragged him off to the side of the front porch, wincing as the man's head thudded and scraped across the hard concrete.

"This is just terrible," Helen said in a trembling voice.

"Would've been smart of them to just back off when they first stepped on those traps out near the trees." Ryan winked at her. "This pair of old folks wasn't quite as easy to take out as they thought we'd be."

Helen only sniffed and nodded, tears glistening on her cheeks as she gripped the man's foot and kept pulling until they had him out in the yard.

"I'm sorry it came to this, dear." Ryan dropped the man's foot and went to Helen, squeezing her tight. "If we could've done it any other way, we would have."

"Oh, I know. I don't blame you for any of this. They pushed us hard and got exactly what they deserved." Her voice dropped for a moment. "*Bastards*."

"Except the part where I got shot, I'm a little surprised at how well it all worked. Thank heavens, though... the way they were coming at us, there's no way they were going to just let us live. The dogs were our trump card, though, no doubt."

"I know." She held him at arm's length. "Could you imagine Duke and Duchess could cause so much damage to someone? I'm shocked at what they did – and I remember what our Shepherds would do to the odd coyote or possum that came after our chickens back in the day."

"They're powerful animals. Pretty well-trained too. The kids did a good job with them."

Back inside, they moved into the great room and stood over the dead woman, her face unrecognizable, red staining her white tank top, and small pieces of her lying around.

"Oh, Duchess," Helen sighed. "You really put her through the wringer."

Each taking a leg as they had with the previous corpse, they dragged the woman through the foyer and got her outside, laying her next to the man and dropping her feet in the grass.

"There's at least one more in the yard," Ryan said, gesturing toward a lump out in the grass. "We should bring them over, too."

"No. I want to see to that leg." Helen wiped her hands disgustedly. "I don't want to look at dead people anymore. They'll be fine out here."

"Fair enough." Ryan winced as they went back inside. "Besides, this calf is really starting to stiffen up."

"Your pant leg is soaked in blood. Come on, into the dining room with you."

Ryan shuffled through the foyer and angled toward a dining table chair, then altered course and sat on the floor, stretching his legs out in front of him and lying back to rest his hands behind his head. Helen shuffled off to find a first aid kit as the dogs came up, wanting to lick at him with their bloody maws.

Laughing and more than a little disgusted, Ryan pushed them away. "Not right now. Go on, now. Get away from me."

"Not sure if they'll be hungry after all that," Helen called from the kitchen, "but maybe I can distract them with some food."

A moment later, the sounds of a food bag shaking got the dogs' attentions, and their ears perked up as they trotted away, Duke moving with a noticeable hitch in his step. Helen poured a heavy amount of food into their bowls and joined Ryan in the dining room with the first aid kit, a pair of scissors, some clean hand towels, and a big bottle of saline. With everything bundled in her arms, she crouched slowly, her hips reaching a breaking point before she fell onto her backside. The items she carried fell into her lap, and she leaned against the wall with her hands resting at her side.

"I'm getting too old for this, dear," she said.

"You and me both."

"Okay, let's see the damage."

Ryan rolled onto his left side and scooted closer to Helen, lifting his pained right leg and resting it across her knees. "Here you go. One missing leg and one shot-up leg."

Helen groaned at the sight of all the blood caking his lower pant leg and seeping into his shoe, then she took a pair of scissors and cut the surrounding material, laying it open and leaning closer.

"It's kind of hard to see," she said.

"Wait. I've got a flashlight."

Ryan unclipped the flashlight from his belt, flicked it on, and shined it across his leg, for the first time getting a good look at the damage. The hole had gone through the thickest part of his calf, not quite the center, but toward the back. The hair around the wound was soaked in blood, and the edges were dried and crusty.

"The bleeding seems minimal," Ryan said. "Probably nothing to worry about."

Helen pressed around the wound on his calf, forcing blood to ooze from the entry wound, drawing a wince from Ryan when her finger circled around to trace the exit hole. "Sorry, honey," she said sheepishly. "Oh, my. The bullet went right through, for sure."

"It did? Good. At first, I wasn't sure. Did it nick an artery or anything?"

"It's bloody, that's for sure," she replied, "but it couldn't have hit anything vital or we'd see a lot more blood. I do wish you would have let me look at this before hauling those bodies outside, though."

"Oh, no," he said. "Not sure I'd be able to at this point." He held out his hand, which was shaking noticeably more than it had been before. "Pain's kicking in more now, too."

"Is it a lot?" Helen asked with a raised eyebrow.

"Heck yeah, it is." Ryan tried to get comfortable. "What do you recommend, Dr. Cooper?"

"I'll grab some water to go with some pain meds."

Ryan held out his hand. "I'll swallow them dry."

After giving him two white pills and two green ones, Helen took a towel in one hand and squirted saline on the wound where it drained onto the carpet, Ryan wincing and grinding his teeth.

"Oh, shoot. I should've put something down. Now the carpet is ruined."

Ryan laughed. "If anything, I think you just made a clean spot. I wouldn't worry about it too much. There's a lot more to deal with than just some stained carpet. Probably best to just cut it out before it dries into the padding."

"Alice might have some good stain remover that'll get the bloodstains out. Let me work on it before we go cutting."

"Well, we'll worry about it later. Most of the blood's on the hardwood, and we can soak up the big puddles tonight, then actually clean tomorrow." Ryan winced as she continued dousing the wound. "Do you think I'm going to need stitches?"

"That's a definite yes on the stitches. Alice has a suture kit downstairs with their supplies. I should probably go get it before I get too deep into this." Duke walked up, blinked at the two, and laid down with his legs stretched in front of him, licking along both sides of his upper jaw, dog food crumbs caught up in the bloody fur. Helen sighed. "And before I pass out from exhaustion."

After Helen had shuffled away, Ryan laid next to Duke, reaching over to rub the clean spot between the dog's shoulders, the dog stretching his mouth wide in a yawn and resting his head between his legs.

"We certainly got ourselves into a brawl, didn't we, boy? You did so well protecting us. Alice and James are going to be so proud. Might make up for destroying half their house... I hope."

Duke's tail swished back and forth.

"And I hope you're up for a bath tomorrow because the two of you are going to get soaked. And I don't want to hear any fussing about it." The tail swished harder, sending droplets of red flying back and forth. "We're not going to worry about that right now. I'm the one who's going to be howling in a few minutes as soon as Helen puts the stitches in me. Not sure if that makes you feel any better."

Duke emitted a low whine and rolled on his right side toward Ryan, craning his neck to lap at Ryan's face.

"Whoa, boy!" he jerked, setting off an ache that coursed up the back of his leg. "You almost crushed me."

The pair lay there for the few minutes it took for Helen to come upstairs with the suture kit, and when she got there, Ryan was nearly passed out with Duke snuggled by his side, his arm thrown over the big, red-stained dog.

"Are you ready for this, dear?"

Ryan's eye opened, and he gave a slow and tired nod. "I guess so. Are you any good at this?"

Helen sat down in her previous position, pushing Duke aside to make room. With a towel covering her lap, she motioned for Ryan to put his leg back and turn so she could see the wound, and he complied by rolling onto his stomach and resting on his elbows.

Helen prepared the needle. "Well, there was that time I stitched Alice's finger myself during that big winter storm when we couldn't get to the hospital. Do you remember that?"

The memory hit him hard; Alice in her brown pigtails sitting at the kitchen table, sniffling, cheeks wet with tears as she rested her arm on the table with her index finger sticking up. The cut ran beneath the second knuckle from where she'd been playing out on the farm with her cousin and cut herself on glass in a pile of junk out at the back of the property.

Ryan grinned wistfully. "I told her and her cousin not to play in that pile of junk."

"But they did it anyway," Helen nodded. "Never was one to be locked inside the house."

"She had the whole farm to roam, but they chose that damnable pile for some reason."

"It was mysterious to them. I'm going to spray some topical anesthetic on this. It'll feel a little cold." There was a hiss as the cold spray hit his leg. "Okay, first stick coming right up."

"I'm ready for it." Ryan squeezed his fists tight. "Are you going to count down - ouch!"

"That's the first one through," Helen replied with a frown. "Sorry, dear, but if I'd counted down, you would have flinched."

"True." Ryan sucked air through his teeth as Helen continued stitching. The pain medication he'd taken, plus the topical anesthetic, took the edge off, but the needle's sharp tip sent pinpricks of pain through his leg regardless.

"Now shift a little to your left so I can get the exit side of it."

"Okay." Ryan clenched his teeth, eyes squeezed shut all the way through until the last stitch was placed.

"That exit wound needed an extra pair." She gave him a light tap on the back of the knee. "I'm all done, but I'm going to clean up a little more and get some antibiotic cream on it."

"You're the doctor."

"Back to your previous point. Remember the time when Alice's cousin cut her knee on a creek rock? Well, I stitched that, too."

"Your brother was so mad at you for letting them play in the woods unsupervised."

Helen shrugged. "We were always allowed to roam the neighborhood, but it was different times back when we were young. You didn't have to worry as much about things. I was just trying to give Alice a place to use her imagination and play with no boundaries."

Ryan looked down as she finished cleaning the wounds and putting bandages on top, smoothing them out with her long, graceful fingers. "And that's why you were such a great mom."

Helen scoffed. "I did the best I could. We both did."

"All done, Doc?"

"All done," she replied and started putting things away, rolling up the towels to put in the laundry bin and giving Ryan's leg back. "I don't know about you, but I could go for a cup of coffee right about now."

"I'll brew it up." Ryan started to roll to his feet.

Helen got up as fast as her sore legs would allow. "You'll sit at the kitchen table, and I don't want to hear any arguments."

Ryan got up with her help, limped in a circle, and hugged her. "Great work, honey. My leg's as good as new."

Helen chuckled and took his hand. "Quit goofing around and stop putting so much weight on it."

"I'm not," Ryan complained as she guided him into the kitchen. "Well, maybe just a little."

Leaning against the wall in the kitchen, Ryan looked out into the great room and under the catwalk at the mess that lay before them. Helen was humming next to him, quietly heating water, pouring it over grounds in a French press, and pulling out some milk from the refrigerator. A dejected sigh from Ryan drew her attention, and she slipped up next to him.

"What's wrong?"

"Just… all of *that*." He gestured at the mess. "It's a *lot* to try and think about dealing with, on top of keeping watch and everything else."

"You want to work on it some tonight?"

"Kind of, yeah. Mopping up the worst of the blood, maybe getting some vinegar on the carpeting and using some towels to get some of the stains mopped up." He groaned. "Laundry's going to be a pain in the butt, too."

Helen wrapped an arm around his waist, pulling him in tight. "It'll be okay. We're through the worst of it. At least for today."

"I hope so."

"C'mon. Let's have some coffee and catch our breaths. I'll get to work on the worst of the blood while you figure out a way to keep the door closed for the night and get some plywood over that broken window. An hour of work and then we'll get some sleep and get back at it first thing in the morning."

"What would I do without you?" Ryan smiled at her, giving her a kiss on the forehead before she turned to pour the coffee, adding a splash of milk to each mug.

"Still have a hole in your leg, probably. Can't imagine you stitching that up yourself, you big baby." She gave him a wink and he laughed, the stress, tension and shakes from the fading adrenaline beginning to melt away. Relaxation was a distant goal, but safety, a loving companion and a cup of something hot to drink would be good enough for the time being.

CHAPTER TWO

Alice Burton
Omega, Georgia

Alice walked outside to an unusually brisk morning with groups of birds landing in the yard to hunt for insects and seeds before flocking to a tree or another part of the yard. There were two rockers on the front porch to sit on, though she ignored them in favor of standing at the edge and rocking on the balls of her feet as the rich aroma of freshly brewed coffee drifted from her cup.

"I've just about got the horses ready, Mom," Jake said, coming around the corner and dusting his hands off.

"We just woke up and you're already dirty," she replied, reaching to wipe a smudge from his cheek.

"Hey," he said, drawing away. "I like getting dirty!"

"The work suits you." She stared admiringly at his shoulders, which seemed to have grown several inches since their whole ordeal had begun. "You've come a long way since we left the beach house."

Jake shrugged noncommittally. "Let me know when you want me to bring them around front."

"Give me a couple of minutes."

"You're the boss." Jake stepped toward the front door. "Just let me know. I think I might have some coffee too, in the meantime."

Alice smiled and turned her attention back to the Nielsen's property. She'd only learned their last names at breakfast the day before, and they continued to be the consummate hosts. On the previous two nights, Nate had relieved her early, insisting Alice and the kids had a long road ahead, and they'd need all the rest they could get. Nate and Elaine had talked the trio into staying for an extra day, as well, and while Alice had argued at first, the hospitality, delicious meals and rare opportunity to relax were too much to pass up.

In return, everyone doted on Elaine and little Ethan, helping out around the house with chores and cooking while Elaine and Ethan recovered. By then, Elaine had gone into the master bedroom with him, leaving the living room remarkably peaceful and giving Alice the best couple of sleeps she'd had in days, free of bad dreams and constant worries about James and her parents. While they had a long way to go, the road seemed a little less dark and foreboding thanks to the Nielsen family.

The front door opened and Sarah stepped out, hands wrapped around a big blue mug of coffee, mirroring Alice's grin. She'd found a brush somewhere and untangled her brown hair so it fell halfway down her back, covering her thin neck and shoulders.

"What are you grinning about?" Alice asked with an elbow nudge.

"I guess I'm still giddy after the other day. The baby is *so* cute."

"He is, isn't he?" Alice's smile spread. "I'm so proud of you, Sarah. You were so strong throughout the whole thing. Didn't even flinch when things were touch and go there for a minute."

"I saw how you handled it and wanted to be the same way. I'm so happy they're both healthy. They're going to be okay, right?"

"Baby's perfect as far as I can tell, and Elaine's in the clear, I think. They'll be fine, especially with a guy like Nate looking after them. He has a lot more skills than we figured. Great cook, too."

"Are you kidding? Scrambled eggs, leftover pork chops, bacon... biscuits and butter." Sarah took a deep breath of her coffee's fragrant aroma and smiled. "I'm almost tempted to suggest we stay here forever."

"Uh huh. Nice try, but we need to get back on the road. Your brother has the horses ready."

"I know we have to get home to Dad and Grandpa and Grandma. I can't wait to see them, but I'll never forget this place. Maybe after all this is over, we can come back."

"Maybe." Alice wrapped her arm around her shoulders. "Right now, two days is more than we can afford, and it's important we don't lose sight of where we need to go and what we need to do to get there. It was a nice rest, but it's time to move on."

"I'll get our things and put them on the porch. Then I want to say goodbye to little Ethan."

Alice nodded and let her go, taking a deep breath of the fresh morning air, watching as the sun rose across blue skies for the second day in a row. "This is the perfect time to go. It's a nice day, and I've got a good feeling about it."

Finishing her coffee, she called for Jake to bring up the horses and nodded at Sarah when she came back out. They placed their packs in a row across the porch and reconfigured things to ensure their supplies were stowed properly, and Jake brought the saddled horses around.

"They're all ready to go," he said. "I saddled them up just like Sarah taught me."

"Good morning, Stormy." Sarah patted the blood-red horse's muzzle, getting a pleased snort in response. "Look, Mom, he's bonding with me! They're *so* great!"

"Probably because they know we love them. I'm sure they appreciated getting brushed out last night."

"Oh, they loved it," Jake agreed with a pat on Rocky's neck. "I can't wait to get riding again."

Nate stepped out. "I'm truly sorry you folks have to go. You're welcome to stay as long as you want. Heaven knows we could use the company."

"We really appreciate that," Alice replied, "but two days was perfect. We rested and got to help around the house and snuggled with Ethan. You guys make a fine family."

"Thanks." Nate held his hands clasped in front of him, eyes glassy with emotion. "We're going to miss you guys."

"We're just glad we could help. I'm pretty sure you all are going to be okay."

"We will. Elaine will be fine, and Ethan is pretty strong for a little guy." The storm door came open, and Nathan turned. "Hey, honey. We were just talking about you. You shouldn't be out of bed, though."

Elaine stepped outside, her shoulders wrapped in a coverlet with baby Ethan in her arms, swaddled tightly as he cooed and grunted. Nate gazed lovingly at his son and put his arm around his wife, hugging her close and kissing her on the forehead.

"I'm weak, but I can't let you all leave without seeing you off. I hope it was all good talk," Elaine laughed.

"It was," Alice grinned back. "And let me say, you're positively beaming. You look beautiful."

"Thanks. I feel a *lot* better, in spite of everything." She released an exasperated breath. "That's the second hardest thing I've ever had to do – well, besides giving birth to Missy, of course. The hospital and epidural made it a lot easier on me, though."

They stood in silence for a moment with Elaine bouncing Ethan gently on her chest, staring sadly into the expansive front yard and their gravel driveway that stretched way down to the main road. "I wish you guys didn't have to go."

"Us too," Alice stepped forward and hugged her, then cooed at the baby, smelling deeply from him, reminded of the way Jake and Sarah had smelled when they were newborns. "Thank you for sharing the gift of this little guy with us."

Elaine blinked back tears. "And thank you for spending so much time with us and rescuing us. You didn't have to, but you did. Not many people would've done that. At least not from what you told us."

"It's been a hard road," Alice agreed, "but we've met a few good people. Enough to keep hope alive. You're part of the proof of that."

Alice backed up as Sarah hugged Elaine and Ethan, kissing both, sniffling, and wiping away tears. Jake gave Alice the horses' reins and jumped onto the porch to say his goodbyes, shaking hands with Nate before the older man wrapped his arms around Jake in a strong embrace. Alice and Sarah hugged Nate as well, patting his back as tears flowed down their faces.

"You're going to do great, Nate," Alice told him. "Remember what we talked about and do the best job you can. It's all any of us can do."

He nodded assuredly. "I will. And, before you go, we've got some gifts for you."

"Oh, that's not —"

"Nope, no arguing!" Nate turned and held the door open, reaching and calling to Missy. A moment later, they both stepped out holding pillowcases with the bottoms bulging.

"What's this?" Alice asked.

"Just a few supplies to see you on your way. It's not much. Some canned food and water you can put on Hercules there."

"We can't take this stuff." Alice drew back. "You've got two little ones to feed. That's no small task, especially with things how they are."

"Believe me, we've got plenty. The biggest problem will be protecting it, and you gave me the right advice. I'm heading out today to look for weapons at some houses that I know are abandoned. Should be able to scrouge up something."

"Be careful, Nate, okay? It's not just you who you need to worry about."

A faint smile tugged at the corner of his mouth. "Yes, ma'am."

"Bye," Missy held Nate's hand and waved. "I'll miss you."

"What do you say, honey?" Elaine asked.

"Thank you!" Missy grinned sheepishly. "Thank you for my little brother!"

Sarah laughed and kneeled to hug her, and Alice swooped in and wrapped her arms around both as Jake came up and tousled the little girl's hair. "I'll talk to you later, you little knucklehead."

"You're the knucklehead," Missy said with exaggerated toughness before breaking into laughter.

Jake leaned down and tickled her sides, sending her retreating behind Nate in fits and giggles, peeking around his leg. Disturbed by the commotion, Ethan made a soft mewling sound and began stirring in his mother's arms, his face going red, mouth coming open as he shook and squalled.

"Welp, he's getting hungry," Elaine sighed. "I better get him inside and feed him. Y'all take care, okay? Be safe. I mean it."

Alice nodded while Jake sniffled and led Rocky away by his bridle. Nate was holding the door open for Elaine when Sarah suddenly rushed forward and embraced them one more time, planting a soft kiss on Ethan's head. With a half wave, she mounted Stormy, turning away to wipe away her tears. Elaine watched her go with a loving look, a smile, and a tear racing down her cheek as well, then the door swung shut as she and Nate headed back inside, leaving Alice and Jake standing with sad smiles.

Alice nodded to the backpacks and sacks of food on the porch. "Jake, help me get these loaded onto Hercules."

They had their supplies loaded in less than a minute and were mounted up when Alice handed Jake his tether. "Take Hercules, would you?"

"Sure, Mom."

While Jake and Sarah began trotting down the driveway, Alice patted Buck's neck, watching the shadows of Nate and his small family walking around in the living room. With a faint smile, she nudged Buck and turned him toward the road, kicking him into a gallop to catch up.

After catching up with the kids, they joined the main highway heading north, moving along at a leisurely pace on the roadside, seeking soft grass for the horses to ride on, looping far around the first two wrecked vehicles they came across and keeping their eyes peeled for chunks of debris. The skies were still blue, and the sun cut brilliantly across the sky, coating everything in a vivid brightness. A two-day break had been more of a delay than Alice wanted, but she couldn't argue with the results. She felt more invigorated than she could remember, and her mood and motivation to get home were sky-high.

"I'm so stuffed." Sarah held her belly. "I think the food was just about as good as that baby of theirs."

Alice laughed. "It didn't seem like you ate all that much."

"Are you kidding, Mom?" Jake snorted. "She was sneaking bacon the whole time. Ate darn near half of it!"

"I did *not*, Jake," Sarah replied in mock offense, then stretched back with a yawn. "Now the biscuits and butter maybe...." When Sarah finished her yawn and stretch, she took on a more sober demeanor. "Where to now, Mom?"

Alice reached into a saddle pouch and pulled out some maps Nate had given her, old dogeared things he'd pulled from an old cabinet from before the age of phone apps and built-in navigation systems. She unfolded one and put the others away, holding Buck's reins in one hand as she spread the map and held it steady. "The general idea is to head north but let me see where these roads lead... Can you tell where we are now?"

"No idea." Jake scanned ahead. "This is just some old country road. We could be going anywhere."

Sarah held up her compass. "But at least we're going north."

"This might be Omega Road we're on," Alice said as she traced the stained map with its many interconnecting highways. "But this thing looks old. They could've built it out over the years. I guess we'll just have to keep following this and hope it takes us somewhere we can use to get a better sense of location."

"As long as it keeps going north, can't we just keep following it?" Sarah angled Stormy off the road into a long stretch of soft green grass. Flat woodland pressed in around them, with crowded clusters of saplings standing or leaning against each other, vines hanging from the high boughs like brown drippings. Hooves crunched on the deadfall and forest debris, nuts and twigs, and small branches lying everywhere, and the rustle of small creatures in the trees and undergrowth was constant as they scattered from the approach of the four horses and their riders.

"More or less." Alice folded the map and put it away, straightening, and sighing. "We'll keep going until something makes us turn off. It's a beautiful day, but let's not be lax. Keep your eyes open, especially along the highway."

They rode for most of the morning, leaving Omega Road only when they had to. One large section was covered with a tremendous car crash, several vehicles smashed in a metal lump with sharp debris scattered across the pavement and lying in the grass and woods on both sides. Not long after that, they passed a burned-down farmhouse with twisted vehicles blown to bits in the circular driveway, parts having rained down on the road, forcing them to divert around through a clearing.

Returning to the highway, they rode more miles past edged fields with beautiful straight and curved patterns cutting into the reddish-brown dirt. Some land had been harvested before the disaster while other areas suffered with rotting, drooping crops, and Alice kept a wary eye on every farmhouse they passed, on the lookout for anyone who might leap out as Nate had done, only with different intentions. They swept over more miles, the horses walking with a sense of purpose after two days of rest and near constant attention.

Eventually they passed beneath Highway 82 running east and west, and from their position on the road Alice saw spots of wreckage in the distance. Blown-out glass and metal shards glinted in the sun, smoked-out car interiors with matte black soot stains on the hoods sitting like ancient relics of some bygone time and Alice tried to imagine what they'd look like in five or ten years.

Omega Road branched into Cottle Road, though they kept riding straight ahead to stay on a northerly path, passing through the front yard of a still-standing home with no signs of people anywhere. Dogs barked in the distance, a frantic sound beneath the bright blue sky and off to the northwest, storm clouds loomed, big round puffs of billowing darkness suspended in the sky. They avoided the main roads for the rest of the morning, opting to take back roads and country byways. Stretches of straight gravel roads cut between pure green fields with waving grass while at other times they were on curving avenues crowded with sturdy oak trees and tall white pines that broke up the winds and left only soft breezes fluttering through the branches.

They crossed bridges over thin, trickling streams that smelled like mud and wet moss, vegetation growing thick up to the road, making the horses work hard to cross the soft areas. When things became too swampy they ventured into the fields where the dirt was firmer and the horses steps surer. Farther north, they saw their first people in a lonely patch of low hills on a farmstead in the middle of a broad curve of trees, the family out in the front yard working gardens with ripe tomatoes glinting in the sun and long stalks of corn stretching as high as the tallest child.

"What a beautiful setup," Alice commented as they rode on the edge of the woods outside the tree line.

"It looks peaceful," Jake replied. "Let's hope we have something like that to look forward to when we get home."

"If I know your grandparents, things will be well taken care of. I bet they've got the place looking beautiful right about now."

In the farmstead yard, a girl spotted them and pointed, and an older child stepped in front of her and fixed Alice and the kids with a stare, lifting his shirt to reveal a pistol on his hip before shouting something over his shoulder. A few seconds later, their father rushed around the corner of the house and the front door flew open, and the mother came out to stand on the porch, wearing an apron and wielding a shotgun, studying Alice and the kids.

"Come on. Let's get out of here." She flicked Buck's reins and galloped along the tree line with the kids behind her, putting the farmstead behind them.

A deer path cut north through the woods, and she turned Buck onto it, grinning as he quickly took the sharp dips and sudden twists in stride, flying through cascading vines and brush until they came to another stretch of green. Somewhere up near Tifton-Worth County Line Road, they spotted a few businesses still set up, a simple vegetable stand with three people on guard with shotguns. They waved at Alice and she waved back, but she and the kids still continued on with haste.

By midday, the road was getting long, and when they came upon a glimmering pond secluded in a forested area, Alice called for a lunch halt. They dismounted and let the horses drink at the water's edge while they sat on a grassy slope and broke out their provisions. Sarah stuck to peanut butter-flavored snacks while Jake removed an MRE and put the main course in a heating pouch and Alice went to her favorite meal, a brown sugar and maple multigrain package.

"Can you believe we still have some of these old rations?" Alice opened the package and poured a measured amount of water inside, chuckling at herself. "Look at me, calling this stuff 'old' as if we've had it for more than a week."

As they ate, the storm clouds she'd seen earlier appeared above the treetops, and a brisk gust of wind blew through to rustle the leaves. The tree branches arched over them, protecting them from the drizzle that made ripples on the lake and caused Buck to shake his head and look back at Alice in annoyance.

"Hey, don't look at me," she shrugged and fed herself a spoonful. "If you want to stay dry, you'll have to come up here away from the water." The horse snorted and lowered his head for another drink.

Lunch passed quickly, and as soon as they were done, they stowed their garbage and mounted up again. Checking her compass, Alice guided them around the pond to find another deer trail continuing northwest. They picked up the pace, and she began sweating as the drip from the forest canopy trickled on them. The woods went on longer than she'd figured until the trail ended at the top of a rise overlooking a vast field that was littered with rusted farm equipment and the remnants of old barns and sheds long forgotten. At the bottom of the slope was another highway and small blocks of farmhouses burned to the ground. They sprinted past the charred ruins, letting the horses run hard through fields and glades, searching for some sort of path running north.

Slowing to a walk, Alice hunched over the saddle and tried to protect the map from the raindrops, tracing the multi-colored lines with her finger. "There should be something up ahead. If we keep heading north, we'll cut right between Macon and Columbus and hopefully avoid both those two towns."

"Should we pick up the pace a little?" Jake asked.

Alice looked upward. "I'm tempted to, but we don't want to run the horses too hard. We've still got a *lot* more miles to go. A little wet won't hurt us."

Jake stood in his stirrups and twisted in his seat to stretch his back. "That's probably the smart way to do it, but I just want to fly so fast on Rocky. I can feel he wants to run."

She self-consciously pushed Buck to go faster, getting well ahead of the kids and forcing them to catch up, feeling the mountain of muscle moving beneath her. "They do seem like they want to run a bit, huh? We should save their energy for when we're in trouble and need to move fast, but I guess a few minutes wouldn't hurt!"

As the shadows grew long and night began to fall, the drizzle finally stopped and Alice called for a halt, catching sight of a tall, dilapidated structure way off in the gloom surrounded by clusters of waving trees. She angled Buck to the right, leaving the highway and cutting across a short field to reach the old, disused barn.

"This old place should do us just fine. Let's tie the horses out back and give them enough lead so they can graze on some of this long grass."

Alice dismounted and gave Jake her reins, then circled to the other side to inspect the place. It was of moderate size, the original color blue by the looks of things, but weather had stripped the wood bare and much of it was broken off or rotten along the bottoms. The roof was intact for the most part, though, and aside from one wall looking particularly rickety, it seemed in decent enough condition to serve as a temporary shelter. Alice leaned in close to peer through a crack in the boards and a field mouse squeaked and dashed past her feet to burrow through the brush and disappear into a hole.

Alice put her hand to her chest. "Jeez! You scared me, little guy."

She met Jake around back, where he found a short section of old wooden railing to tie the horses to. "You think they'll be okay out here?"

"We'll let them graze for a while and bring them in before we get some shuteye." She gestured to several puddles on the gravel lane and overgrown yard. "They've got plenty of water to drink."

Once they had the horses tied up, Alice explored the rear barn opening, but it was packed with stacks of old rusted machinery. They circled and entered through the wide entrance, where a mud puddle spread about ten feet inside. The smell of old musty hay filled the air, touched with the remnants of horse manure and something – or somethings – dead. Alice flipped her flashlight on and shined it around from left to right, illuminating old crates, wood and iron farm implements, tractor hitches, and field tools.

"Wow, this place is a museum," Sarah said.

Jake jumped over the puddle and walked past the thick wooden beams holding up the roof. "What's with this stack of stuff?" he asked, using his own light to highlight the pile of junk blocking the rear exit.

"No idea, but this back corner looks pretty dry and clean," Alice said, following them inside. "There's some decent-looking hay lying around we can make into beds. Hey, there's an old lantern over here, too." Alice stepped between the piles of rust to the back corner where the crates and boxes formed an L-shape. On one of them sat an oil lantern, and she gave it a shake, hearing the splash of liquid inside. "I'm going to light this."

"Someone's been here," Sarah said, stepping in and pointing to a soda can and discarded chip bags and candy bar wrappers, all of them covered in dust and dirt.

"Could be some local kids used this as a hang out before. In any case, it looks like a decent spot to spend the night."

"It's not nearly as good as Wilford's stable or Nate and Elaine's place," Sarah chirped as she stood in the middle and looked around. "But we can make it work for a night."

"You read my mind," Alice replied. "Jake, go grab our stuff, and Sarah and I will clear a spot for us to lie down for the night."

Together, the two got the place straightened out, making soft beds from the non-moldy hay and moving the boxes and crates to create a barrier to help keep them protected in case someone wandered in. When Jake returned, she found a lighter and lit the oil lamp, grinning as she set it in the corner and brightened the place with warm, ambient light.

"That'll draw some attention," Jake said.

"If anyone's even out here, yeah, but we need some light to see by and I'd rather use this than try to start a fire in this old place. The lantern's enough of a fire risk as it is. We'll just have to hope it's gloomy enough outside to keep us hidden."

"It's getting pretty foggy out there. I think we're safe." Sarah said, peering through a crack in the wooden walls. Outside, a heavy mist had descended over the area, filling the cracks between the trees with soupy gray. The sound of frogs and crickets intensified in the fog, adding to the eeriness of the place and sending a shiver down her spine. "As safe as one *can* be when you're in an abandoned barn in the middle of nowhere...." She mumbled as she turned back to her mom and brother.

They broke out their blankets and placed them over the hay beds, patting them down and making pillows out of rolled clothes, then sat cross-legged, with Sarah facing Alice and Jake. Packs in front of them, they pulled out some food, and the sounds of packages tearing replaced their talking.

A weariness passed through Alice as she ate, the food settling in her belly to make her eyelids droop. "Wow, that was our first really long hard ride. I'd say it was a resounding success, though. We kept out of trouble, stayed hidden as much as we could, and generally did a great job of moving with both speed and stealth."

"Creeping around sure takes a lot out of a person," Sarah sighed.

"You should eat something more than just those candy bars."

"You said they were high calorie, though."

"It's the nutrition part I'm talking about," Alice said. "Those things have tons of sugar and not much else, so get a meal, please, Sarah."

"Okay, MRE mac and cheese it is."

Alice rolled her eyes and sighed. "Good enough. I'd cook some canned food, but, well... that lantern is making me nervous enough as-is."

"Hey, this is why we have these," Sarah broke open the package and placed the components on the blanket at her feet.

She read the directions, took out the entrée, and put it into the heating pouch, then she poured water in and sealed it. While it heated up, she examined the other contents of the MRE, brightening and holding up a bright red pack of multi-colored candy. "Score!"

Alice shook her head and laughed. "I tried to get you to stay away from sugar, and you still managed to find it."

"There's some beef jerky, crackers, and jalapeno cheese spread here, too," Sarah said. "Never know what you're going to find in these things."

Alice had a strawberry-flavored multigrain meal, the contents filling enough, though the watery milk-like drink didn't quite substitute for the real thing. "Jake, you should be eating, too."

He shrugged. "I'm going to finish some of this jerky. We've got a bunch of bags of it with crumbs and stuff. I'm not that hungry; I just want to get something in my stomach and get some sleep more than anything."

"Fair enough."

Jake took a bite of his jerky and gestured toward the front door of the barn. "How far do you think we got today?"

Alice grabbed her map and placed it in front of her. "I was keeping a close eye on the signs as we rode, and it seems like we're somewhere between Macon and Columbus, closer to Columbus, though we're heading a little too far west for my taste."

"Take an immediate turn north?" Jake asked.

"Yeah. We'll get back on this highway in the morning and take the first left-hand turn we come to."

Sarah opened her package of mac and cheese began to eat, dripping cheese sauce down her chin. She caught it with her finger, then licked it off. "This is great, Mom. Thanks for the suggestion."

"Oh, yeah, sure. I've got plenty more recipes where that came from," Alice replied dryly.

After they'd finished eating, they put their garbage away, curled up on their makeshift beds and whispered about what might be happening back home and what Ryan and Helen were up to.

"I bet they're having a movie night or something," Sarah said.

"Definitely taking it easy," Jake added.

"I can't wait to get home. I'm going to hug Grandma so hard when I see her."

"I'm going to hug everyone," Jake said, his voice growing sleepy, "especially Dad."

Just before drifting off, Alice woke up, picked up her rifle, and stepped outside into the cool evening. She went out to bring the horses inside, tying their leads to some of the heavy metal pieces at the back of the barn, removing their saddles, and brushing them down. In between caring for the animals, she walked outside and took in some air, leaving churning eddies of fog as she passed.

The highway crossed west to east, framed by fields of long grasses and gnarled trees beneath a misty, green-tinted sky. Nothing moved, no lights blinked, and there were no shouts in the darkness. A glowing ambiance bathed the place in full moonlight, though its round shape was merely outlined in the puffy cloud cover. As the light passed through the fog, it created a brilliance that illuminated the ground and even cast shadows across the field. Alice turned and circled the barn, slowly counting down the hours before she had to wake Jake up to take his shift.

The following day came swiftly with the distant crowing of a rooster, then another and another after that. Sarah woke up Jake and Alice and the trio had a quick breakfast, then gathered their things with little fanfare. The fog still surrounded them, though the morning sun was rapidly burning it away. Jake got the horses saddled up, and they soon found a pleasant strip of soft grass along the roadside to travel on. Alice guided them northwest, looking for a satisfactory route to turn north on, the miles passing beneath them as they moved from one side of the road to the other, using grass and fields whenever they could, depending on the amount of debris and junk in the way. Every intersection was clogged with destruction, though, and campfires and house chimneys trailed smoke through the treetops, making her leery about going offroad.

"Are these actual neighborhoods or something, Mom?" Sarah asked.

"Some of them might be," Alice responded, "but I'm not interested in wandering into someone's backyard to ask them about it."

The farther they rode, the more the side roads seemed to be purposefully jammed, with piles of garbage and appliances dragged out and stacked up to form obstructions. Poorly cut trees stretched across the road with construction materials thrown on top, spilling onto the shoulders.

"Shouldn't we be turning north soon, Mom?" Sarah asked with a nervous glance.

"Yeah, probably best to get out of here as soon as we can, but I don't see a spot where we can get north very easily. I was hoping to stay out of the deep woods today, but we may need to cut through some fields."

"Too late for that." Jake pointed at the black railings running along the roadsides. "Unless you want to jump the rails, we have to go forward or back."

It was a detail Alice hadn't thought much of, as such fences usually ended after a mile or so, and there were often breaks. The ones they were riding along, though, stretched as far as she could see, and any potential breaks were filled with unnaturally stacked piles of debris. She cursed silently for not seeing it sooner. "You're right, guys. Something doesn't feel right about this."

"Mom, we need to get out of here," Sarah sat stiff in her saddle, head on a swivel. "How about that street up ahead? It's mostly open."

The lane's entrance was conspicuously lacking any obstructions, and narrowed into a series of driveways that wound downward into a side yard. "No way. That looks like a trap to me... heck, *all* of this looks like some kind of trap. Let's ride on through as fast as we can. There's bound to be something up ahead."

Jake moved off the left-hand shoulder and onto the road, kicking Rocky into a gallop. Alice and Sarah came right behind him, raised in their saddles, searching for a way through the fencing ahead when an engine revved, sending growling echoes over the treetops, causing chills to shoot up Alice's back, punctuated by a tailpipe backfire and *boom* that startled the horses enough to make them whinny and rear up. A cloud of smoke rose into the air from off to their right and behind them, and something massive moved toward them behind the trees, angling in their direction, trundling on wheels that sounded as though they were crushing everything in their path.

Alice swallowed hard and gathered her breath. "Ride, kids!" she shouted. "Ride hard!"

CHAPTER THREE

James Burton
Frankfurt, Illinois

Rain fell in fat drops that struck the brick walls and cobblestones in rhythmic sheets, hammering everything in their path, feeding rivulets that fed streams that in turn fed large torrents of rushing water. It flowed along the alley's edges, dumping its crimson-stained liquid into wide puddles that eventually poured into sewer grates. Garbage had half-blocked many of the grates, and with no one around to unblock them or monitor and maintain the complex sewer system, the tainted water was at risk of becoming a full-blown flood.

Beneath the towering buildings in a back alley reeking of wet trash and urine, splashing through puddles and tripping over wet cardboard, James Burton fought for his life. Amber lay a few feet away, a bullet hole in her head, her sides heaving one last time, a final breath before expelling a long, quivering exhale and lying still, James unable to give her even a second's attention as the life bled from her and mixed with the rushing water.

He took a punch to the gut and staggered back two paces, straddling the dead man at his feet who was bleeding out from several head wounds James had inflicted with his aluminum staff. The remaining assailant – a tall, sinewy man with sores and scars on the insides of his arms – looked like he weighed eighty pounds soaking wet, but fought like a demon, shoving James back and going for a revolver tucked into his waistband. James swung his staff one-handed, grunting as he aimed for the man's head, gore and bits of flesh whipping off the end of the stick before it struck the man in his rising forearm, cracking hard and drawing a pained grunt, but not stopping him from getting the gun out.

With his free hand, James lunged and seized his attacker's wrist, keeping the gun pointed at the ground. The man jerked backward to escape, but James went with him, stumbling forward and digging his fingernails into the man's wrist, pressing with his thumb and nail into his tendons to make him drop the gun. His staff flailed as he nearly lost his balance yet somehow remained on his feet, staggering, throwing himself backward, staying upright at all costs.

The assailant screamed with rage as rain poured off his nose and chin, his lank black hair plastered to the sides of his temples. James held on, pulling him closer to gain more leverage even as the man punched him in the face with his left hand. James grunted and returned the favor by cracking his staff into the man's ribs, and as he was drawing back for another strike, the assailant twisted frantically, his limbs like rubber, breaking free, grinning as he raised the gun to fire.

James was already swinging, his stave cracking the man's gun hand, knocking the weapon off-course as it popped off with a muzzle flash and a bang that echoed through the alley, the smell of gunpowder immediately washed away by the torrential rain. James' backhand sweep with his staff caught the man in the jaw, a glancing blow that snapped his neck hard enough to buckle his knees, and James charged in with his head low and feet driving. Just before impact, he held his breath and locked his jaw, shoving the man's arm aside, planting his head on his hip, and tackling him with his right shoulder. Driving forward and lifting, James picked the slighter man off the ground, held him suspended in midair, then slammed him hard on the wet pavement.

The man landed with a grunt, air shooting from his lungs. James lost control of the man's gun arm and felt it angling in to shoot him in the side, but he caught the skinny arm and pinned it to the ground. Keeping the wiry man from squirming beneath him, James raised the staff to strike, but he was too close to get any sort of momentum built up. With the man wiggling like a wet fish, James tossed his staff aside with a clatter, balled his bloody fist, and struck the junkie across the jaw. The man shook his head and grinned with bloodstained teeth, his drug-fueled glare filled with undaunted fury—he had nothing to lose.

The rain picked up in a rush, lightning cracking overhead bathing the dark alley in a sudden burst of light. James was slipping and sliding on the cobblestones as he tried to balance atop the squirming man, and for a moment the two were grappling like awkward, exhausted wrestlers. The attacker clenched a fistful of James' jacket and shoved him, almost flipping him off onto his back, but James leaned into it, thrusting his right arm and grabbing the loose material of the man's hoodie around the shoulder area, leveraging him to the ground with a strained groan.

They stayed locked that way for a long moment, James' bruised ribs aching as he gasped to get his wind back. The attacker was weakening, his body shaking, grasp slipping as he tried to angle the gun toward James' head. In a quick shift of balance, James slid his hand down to grip the man's wrist with both hands, and he slammed the pistol on the concrete multiple times, trying to knock it free. Seeing he was losing, the junkie let James go and tried to roll beneath him, bringing his arms together against his chest and curling up on the ground. James found himself mounted on the man's back, and he sank, using his weight to keep the gun arm trapped and pointed at the brick wall. With a frustrated growl, the man fired twice, the bullets cutting deep into the brick, sending a spray of debris that the rain carried away.

Twisting and leveraging himself, James slipped his right shoulder in and got both hands on the attacker's gun arm again, one clenching his wrist, the other grasping his forearm. The man had worked himself into a twisted shape, turned face-first into the pavement with his gun arm stretched beneath him, losing his tenacious hold on the weapon. James pressed his thumb hard into the man's bloody wrist, adding his body weight to it, dirty nails digging into flesh and separating the tendons painfully.

The man groaned and whined, the sound morphing into a strangled wail that grew in volume and intensity even as his fingers loosened on the revolver. With a final smash against the pavement, James knocked the gun free, pounced on it and grabbed it with both hands. The attacker exploded into movement beneath him, punching, kicking, and grasping to hold James back. Once James had secured the weapon, he threw a right elbow backward, hitting the man's jaw with a sharp crack and dropping him backward onto the pavement. Gun in hand, he staggered to his feet and fell against the alley wall where rain cascaded down in a waterfall from the roof above, splashing over his shoulder and into his face. His vision swirled in front of him, water dripping off his eyebrows and down his face, the junkie just a blur as he wailed in frustration, the sound slicing through James' ears. He raised the pistol as the man tried to roll into a crouch but slipped in the water and collapsed onto his backside, glaring up like a wounded animal. James stumbled over with a pained grimace, and when the man tried to rise, James planted his right foot onto the man's chest and pushed him to the ground, pinning him.

"You... killed my... horse." James' voice was ragged as he struggled for breath.

"Never... was... your horse." The man spat blood as he wheezed out a response. "No one owns... anything out here anymore."

"It was given to me."

"Nothing is given, you fool," The man leered. "It can only be taken away. Even if you kill me, someone else will take my place. You're going to die out here, man. You're going to –"

James squeezed the trigger and the man's head rocked back as red sprayed across the cobblestones, quickly washing away into the cracks and crevices. The man fell back with a thud, his body convulsing weakly as some still-intact part of his brain fired off signals to his extremities, his eyes rolling back in his head. James nearly shot him again, but hesitated as there were only three rounds left. While the would-be killer's blood was carried away by the raging torrent, James crouched and found a box of bullets in the man's front pocket, transferring them to his jacket.

He fell away from the dying man, putting his shoulders against the wall, sliding slowly downward until he was squatting in the couple inches of water, gasping for breath as the adrenaline surge ended, staring straight ahead. He listened as he tried to calm himself, trying to pick up any motion, footsteps or changes in the pattern of rain that would tell him that his pair of attackers had a third partner around somewhere, but the only sounds above the rain were distant cracks of gunfire and shouts that echoed through the narrow city corridors.

It had been three days since he'd left Eli's family on the road, and he'd lost almost everything. His M4 and Colt were gone along with half of his supplies, not to mention poor Amber. James stood over the remains of the most recent group who'd attacked him, walking over to kick the other man in the shoulder to make sure he was dead. Rain dripped from James' chin and ran down his jacket as he inspected himself for injuries, finding several cuts on his neck, some facial abrasions, and pains in his knee and hip. His ribs ached from being punched and kicked, and he was probably at risk of infection from whatever was in the water swirling around his feet, but other than that, he was fine.

He retrieved his staff, wiping the last of the gore off on the dead man's shirt, giving him a final look of disgust before staggering away to his former companion. Amber's massive form lay unmoving on her side in a pool of blood, so much of it that the water swirling around her was still bright red. The pair of attackers had shot her point-blank during the ambush, a single round to the head that had sent her crashing to the pavement and thrown James off. He stooped over to ensure she was dead, prepared to end her misery if she was somehow still alive, but the round had gone all the way through her head, her chest wasn't heaving, and her deep black and brown eyes were bereft of life.

"Bastards." James choked out the word, sinking to one knee and stroking the horse's head and snout. "You were a good girl, Amber. Such a good girl. You did so good, carrying me so far and keeping us safe for so long. Rest easy now, girl." He turned his face to the sky, letting the cool rain wash his cuts and sores, sputtering, spitting and crying as guilt flowed through him.

"I'm so sorry, Abram. I'm sorry I got your horse killed. She was the best gift you could have given me and I'm so, so sorry." Squatting lower, falling to his knees, he rested his head against her neck and hugged her one last time, breathing deep of her wet, musky smell before standing back up.

James retrieved his backpack where it had fallen when he had been thrown during the ambush, then tried to get his other supplies, but Amber was lying on them, and it was impossible to get them free no matter how hard he tugged and pulled at the straps or tried to move her heavy, water-logged body. Gunfire came, a staccato burst, and James stiffened, crouching low and pressing himself against the wall, pulling his pack toward him and hefting the revolver he'd taken from his attacker. After a moment, and several more shots, it became clear that they weren't nearby.

Shrugging on his pack, James stood and listened, trying to pinpoint the location of the gunfire and shouts echoing through the city through the noise of the rain, needing to find a spot to rest and gather his wits about him. Checking the compass on the top of his staff – cracked, but still functional – he turned due east, creeping beneath creaking fire escapes and past dumpsters filled with garbage and things that smelled of death, his boots splashing through puddles and clanking on metal sewer grates. The sky was virtually nonexistent thanks to the roiling storm clouds, moonlight piercing through them every once in a while with a glow that gave the city a purgatorial appearance.

Lightning and thunder cracked, the sounds reverberating through blocks of cold brick and empty windows, lightless and filled with shadows moving inside, either from the shifting light or from figures that were hiding from the rain and violence. James felt eyes on him, fearful denizens crouching beneath porch stoops and in alleyways as he staggered past with his jacket tight around his shoulders. Revolver held against his waist, ready to shoot anything that moved, he crept through the alleys in the dripping rain.

What he thought was a small town or the outskirts of something larger, had turned out to be more dangerous than he'd expected. Refugees from Chicago were everywhere, overrunning the town and spreading into whatever buildings could provide shelter. Every nook held potential danger, and shadows swept through the streets to disappear into alleys and narrow lanes. The streets were congested with the remnants of vehicles and flame-ravaged buildings. A strip of small local shops had been defaced, their front windows blown in, glass and brick glinting on the wet sidewalks with the smell of wet ash coming in waves as the water poured over the blackened structures. James was lost in it all, the compass nearly useless as he kept having to change directions in the concrete jungle, unable to follow it while he was wounded, disoriented, and desperate for a safe place to catch his breath.

He went several more blocks, hoping to stumble into a highway that would get him out of the mess and into a more rural area where he could find a secluded place to hide, but the city streets continued with no end in sight. James spotted a small office building wedged between a pair of old warehouses with no lights in the windows and he took slow steps across the street and into an alley, turning to search the street and make sure he wasn't being followed. Satisfied he was alone, he looked upward and spotted a glinting iron structure about halfway down the alley, a fire escape leading to the upper floors. Standing beneath it, he leaped up and pulled down the ladder with a loud creak that set his teeth on edge. Anyone nearby would undoubtedly hear it and come to investigate, so he climbed quickly, drew the ladder up behind him, and continued his ascent up the winding stairwell to the third floor. Flipping on his flashlight – one of his few possessions still *in* his possession – he pointed it through the window to reveal a warehouse room full of junk and machinery with odd-shaped arms that jutted out from their steel bodies.

When he tried to open the window, it stuck, so he put his flashlight down, slipped his fingers beneath a pair of metal tabs, and jerked it upward with a groan of painted wood. Iron shavings and dust swirled past his face as he climbed in and slammed the window shut, cutting off both the rain and the sounds of the dangerous and dying town. James turned off his flashlight and stood next to the window for a good five minutes, staring into the alley, waiting to see if anyone had noticed him or his light, until finally he was satisfied he hadn't been followed.

With a heavy sigh, he turned and faced the floor of machinery, boxes, and crates. It was some manufacturing plant that turned out machine parts and other odds and ends he couldn't identify. In the center of the floor was a massive cargo elevator he assumed led downstairs, though it – like the rest of the city – didn't have power. On both sides of the warehouse were stairwells leading down, and he locked the deadbolts to each, checking through the square windows for signs of people. Satisfied the floor was relatively secure, he continued exploring until he found a side office at the front side of the building with a desk and a plush office chair. James locked the door behind him, shrugged off his pack, and dumped it on the desk next to a dead computer monitor. He took off his jacket and hung it from a coat rack in the corner behind the door before going to the window and checking the street through a crack in the thick curtains, his high position affording him a view across the surrounding buildings' rooftops. It was difficult to make out anything in the torrential rains, but there was an occasional shadow that ducked and moved along the alleys, thin shapes huddled beneath tarps and pieces of vinyl that flapped in the wind, refugees covering themselves from the rain as they sought shelter from the inevitable violence that lurked around every corner.

James exhaled deeply, feeling – at long last – some measure of safety. "Should be okay here for a while. Got to catch my breath... figure out what to do next."

James placed the revolver and staff on the corner of the desk, along with his flashlight turned to the lowest setting. He stripped off his shoes and socks, draping them over chair backs and filing cabinets, followed by his wet jeans and underwear. His skin was clammy cold as he stood there naked, but he found a dry towel tucked deep down in his backpack and patted every inch of himself dry, drawing the cloth down his face with a wince, smearing it with blood from some cut or scrape he'd just reopened.

Tossing the towel on the desk, he put on a loose gray jogging bottom, sweatshirt, and a thick pair of socks he'd gotten from the refugee camp. The garments were too big for him, but their warmth and comfort made his eyelids droop. Shaking the weariness off, he dug out his first aid kit and took care of the wounds on his hands and forearms, the result of the first of the alley attackers who'd pulled a knife on him and got a couple of swipes in before James had managed to use his staff to put a sizeable dent in the man's skull. One cut on his left arm could have used stitches, but he settled for cleaning it out with some antibacterial cream and used several butterfly bandages to press the wound closed before wrapping it in gauze and medical tape.

His knuckles were raw and bleeding from punching the other man's jaw and getting scraped on the cobblestones, and he cleaned those with some wet wipes and applied antibacterial cream and bandages to the more significant cuts while leaving the raw spots alone to save on supplies. As his body began to warm after being out in the cold rain for so long, he started feeling better, and after finding a small mirror in one of the desk drawers, he rested it against a brass lamp, and attended to his facial wounds, covering the end of the flashlight with a sock to further mute the glow.

The man looking back at him had changed. His face was thinner, his eyes dark and ringed with bruises and bags, and a grayish-brown scruff was growing around his jaws and neck, creeping up to his cheeks. He attended to the cuts and scrapes as best as he could, trying to avoid thinking too hard about where each one had come from. He couldn't guess at the miles he'd fought across since Denver. At times, it seemed like fate was giving him a reprieve, but the majority of the time seemed as though it was throwing obstacles in his way on purpose, tripping him up every step of the way, pushing him two steps back for every one he took. *Especially the last few days*, he thought. *What the hell is the world even coming to?*

When he touched an especially bruised spot on his cheek, pain blossomed through to the bone, and he sucked air through his teeth until it began to fade. As James worked against the pain, he thought of Alice and the kids, trying to remember what their voices sounded like. Every wince was soothed by Sarah's laughter, and the burning cuts cooled by Alice's touch. The deep, aching bruises that made him want to quit were eased by one of Jake's jokes or encouragement.

Staying positive wasn't for him – it was for them, that simple truth hardening his resolve. No one would stop him from getting home and finding them, even if the entire world conspired to try and foil his plans.

He finished cleaning up and collapsed back into the office chair, listening to the rain and the soft drip of his clothes on the office carpet. When he felt energized enough to stand again, James got the box of bullets out of his jacket and placed them next to the revolver. The box was only three-quarters full, giving him about thirty-five rounds to work with. His staff was still in good shape, though, and he used the already dirty rag to clean the dirt and bits of gore that were stuck in the small gaps between its sections, recalling how many times over the last three days the simple tool had saved his life. The pack had some tears and was covered in dirt, water and blood but was none the worse for wear, and he lined up what remained of his supplies on the desk: another change of clothes, some dry socks and underwear, a pair of boots he'd found in his size, a half-dozen MREs, and a well-used water filtration straw. The first aid kit, a box of assorted bandages and gauze, and a small bottle of pain pills rounded out his medical supplies. As he put everything neatly back, a low growl of hunger rumbled through his guts, and he reached inside for an MRE.

He tore the package open, ripped the inner bag, and placed the contents in a neat row in front of him. He started with the oatmeal cookie, liberating it from its pouch and taking a bite, eyes closed as the sweetness overwhelmed him. After two more bites, he put the beef and beans packages into the flameless ration heater, poured a small amount of water inside, and sealed and shook it, setting it aside.

James contemplated not making the orange drink because he didn't want to waste his remaining water, but he'd been going on empty for days, and the calories of the powdered beverage were sorely needed. Plus, with it raining out, he could stay hydrated with his drinking straw until he found a new source. He mixed a half bottle of water and the orange powder and drank it as he walked around the room with the sock-dimmed flashlight, looking over the generic office paintings, curiously drawn to a display of framed maps showing various parts of the city including marked business districts and famous restaurant spots.

Something familiar piqued his memory, and he squinted at a map of the warehouses. "Hey, I remember a few of these streets. I passed them on the way here."

James placed the beverage pouch down, took all of the map pictures off the wall, turned them over, and removed the backings. He spread them on the desk, taking up the entire surface area, and dug around in a drawer for a pencil. Using his flashlight, he marked the spots he remembered and traced his location to a warehouse on South Winton Street, right in the middle of the warehouse district that stretched several blocks in every direction. The vast spread of buildings that surrounded him was disheartening, but knowing exactly where he was felt like progress, and the trapped feeling lifted from his shoulders as he began tracing potential paths out of the area.

James ate his meal with the maps as companions, chewing absently as he focused on two paths that could keep him off the main streets and out of trouble. He looked them over again and again, checked any potential side routes and marking off odd-shaped corners that might have stores or gas stations. While those spots would likely be destroyed, it was possible there could be some food left lying in the streets or ruined husks of buildings – or perhaps they hadn't gone up in flames at all. *Just need to get out of this damn city,* he thought. *Then I can reassess my situation.*

After he finished his meal, James sat back in the desk chair with the maps in front of him, resting his eyes for a few moments, the time creeping past with nothing but the rain coming down in sheets and the soft sounds of the creaking building as if ghosts roamed the halls.

CHAPTER FOUR

Ryan Cooper
Somewhere Outside East Lansing, Michigan

Ryan wore thick leather gloves as he picked up the last piece of broken glass from the floor and placed it in a bucket along with the rest. He pulled shards of the windowsill off as well, big chunks split by bullets he and Helen had fired down at the intruders the prior evening. A cool breeze blew into the wide-open dining room, whistling through the cracks between some of the boards that he had yet to pull off, blowing his graying hair around his head. An enormous pile of bloody rags sat heaped on the floor, used to soak up the crimson pools that had been on the hardwood, the crusty parts scrubbed off with soft cleaning brushes. The vacuum and wet vac sat to the side along with bottles of cleaner, floor polish, and a bucket of Helen's homemade cleaning formula they had soaking into the carpet.

"I can't believe how much damage we did to the place," he spoke as he put the glass aside and picked up the plywood piece he'd cut to replace the window. "I'm almost tempted to look around town for a new window in some of those ruins."

"That sounds way too dangerous, dear." Helen replied.

"Nah, I'm just kidding. We'll settle for plywood and an apology to the kids when they get home. This is a *lot* of damage to the place."

Helen was repairing the walls with patching plaster, filling in the bullet holes and using a putty knife to smooth them out. "It seemed way worse from where I was standing. So much noise with the gunfire and dogs barking." She wiggled her pinky finger inside her left ear. "If I wasn't hard of hearing before, I certainly am now."

Ryan laughed. "My ears are still ringing, too. Those earplugs we used sucked." Most of the furor of the battle had worn off for the dogs, and they'd gone back to lying on their dog beds after receiving baths in a big tub in the backyard. While Duchess and Diana rested in the living room, Duke got up from his bed and went back to patrolling with a heavy limp, watching the front door and windows, licking his mouth where faint traces of blood still stained bits of his fur.

"Poor Duke," Ryan said. "Big guy hurt his shoulder pretty bad last night. He must've landed wrong."

"Well, he did go flying off the foyer rail and land on that man. I'm surprised he's not got something broken."

"I wonder if we should wrap his leg or something?"

Helen shrugged. "I don't know. He came running when I made him a special breakfast with eggs and extra gravy mixed in with his dog food. I don't think he's as hurt as you think he is."

Ryan gave the dog a skeptical look. "Is that true, boy? Are you just pining for attention?" Duke chuffed and wagged his tail. "I wouldn't put it past him," Ryan chuckled. "He must really think he's a hero after all that."

"He's definitely a hero. And a ham, too."

Ryan picked up the large square piece of wood and fitted it where the window used to be. He put his left shoulder against it to hold it in place, then drove screws in with a power drill through the wood and vinyl sides of the windowframe, moving from the top right corner all the way around, placing twelve screws in total.

"That should just about do it," he said, pressing on the wood.

"It'll be nice to keep the draft out. Been chilly this morning."

"I'll kick the furnace on and get the house warmed up a bit once we finish up. Isn't it absurd that we're sitting here patching bullet holes after everything that's happened in the world?"

"Well, we've always said we should leave a place better off than we found it." Helen focused on the last couple of holes, working in the patching plaster and smoothing it as perfectly as she could. "I'd never forgive myself if we left the house a mess for Alice and James to come home to."

"I think they'll understand if we don't have everything in tip-top shape." He raised an eyebrow. "I think we'll get most of it in order, but these windows are hopeless."

Helen laughed. "I wonder what replacement ones would cost?"

"Insurance'll cover it... well, if there's even insurance left at all."

Helen fell quiet for a moment, her expression turning worried.

"What's on your mind, honey?"

"I'm just... thinking about all the changes we'll be making in the coming months and years if this really as bad as it seems. Especially when all we used to talk about was our retirement, savings, and medical coverage in our golden years."

Ryan took off his gloves and embraced her, pulling her away from the wall and holding her close against him. She put her cheek on his chest and wrapped her arms around him, squeezing him hard as he replied.

"We shouldn't just assume all that's gone now. The world's been turned upside down, but never underestimate the ability for human beings to rebuild. It's just going to take some time. There'll be organization again. I mean, shoot, if anything, you can count on taxes to never go away. Just wait till the IRS wants their money next year... they'll find a way to fix things up, you'll see."

Helen smiled at him, then sighed. "It just seems impossible to salvage anything good in all this."

"I don't care about any of that other stuff anyway." Ryan gave her an extra squeeze. "As long as I'm still here with you, I'm happy. We'll figure the rest out."

"You're right. I'm sorry. I'm usually the positive one."

"We pick each other up, Helen. That's just what we do. Are you okay?"

"I am now." Breaking away from Ryan, she went back to patching, finishing the last hole and shaking her head. "Did you expect the neighbors to attack us so hard like they did?"

"I was a little surprised that they didn't give up after we shot a couple of them. They certainly were tenacious. I guess it's easier when you're attacking strangers. Makes me wonder if we shouldn't have gotten to know the neighbors around here a little better." Ryan scratched his head and glanced toward the front door. "Kinda hard to do that when we only come by for visits once in a while, though. The two dead ones I pulled out of the yard this morning... I've never seen them before."

"Me neither. I guess I expected them to be more like Mike. He seemed appreciative that we helped his family put out that fire in their garage, in spite of how he was watching us. Who knows where they got off to? He wasn't with the ones who attacked us last night, was he?"

"I didn't see him," Ryan shrugged, "but anybody's got the potential to be nice or mean. They can be sneaky and even deadly when a situation goes south." He pointed toward the patched bullet holes that would eventually need sanding and repainting. "And we've got the damage to prove it. Let that be a lesson to us never to underestimate anyone."

Helen stooped to pick up the pile of bloody rags lying off to the side. "Well, I'll take all these dirty rags into the laundry room and start washing them. Do you think we'll have enough power to do that?"

"Let me limp downstairs and switch off the freezers and refrigerator circuits to be sure. The food will be fine in there for a few hours. Should give you enough time to run a few loads through the washer, and I'll hang them up to dry later."

Ryan headed down to the breaker box, with Diana getting up to follow him like usual. Once he'd switched off the freezers and refrigerator, he came back upstairs, wincing with every step as lancing pain shot through his stiff calf. He met Helen in the laundry room, helped her separate out the stained rags, and put in the first load, the washer starting up without any issues.

"It looks like our power plan works pretty well, but I need to get the rest of those solar panels up today. If my napkin math is correct, another row will give us all the power we need to run more things during the day."

"Well, shouldn't we conserve power, anyway? Keeping the refrigerators and freezers off at certain times of the day would be okay, wouldn't you say?"

"Eh, once we've got the extra panels up, we should only have to turn things off at night. They should eliminate power lags or losing it completely when we least expect it."

Helen looked out through a narrow window in the laundry room as they sorted through the rest of the rags and some garments at a long laundry table. "Do you think they'll attack again?"

Ryan laughed morbidly. "After the ass-kicking we gave them, I doubt they'll be by again for a while."

"And you said we shouldn't underestimate people."

"The drubbing we gave them should give us time to rebuild our defenses for when they *do* try again. Replacing or covering all the windows with wood would be a lot better. If I can find enough scraps, I might just do it. It's probably unnecessary right away, though. Another thing..." Ryan stopped sorting and gazed upward.

"What is it?"

"No matter how much we bolster the lower-level windows, they could still climb up and enter through the top floor if we ever had a slip-up in our watch rotations. A nice tall ladder and someone could sneak in and we'd never see them coming."

"Oh, my," Helen raised an eyebrow. "I hadn't thought of that."

"If we have time and materials, I may try to do something there. In any case, I'll head to the barn to get the tractor out and finish hooking up the solar panels. And we've still got to finish a few chores out in the yard before the day is through."

"Should we do something about the bodies soon?"

"Do we have to?"

"Yes, we do. We have to give them a proper burial."

Ryan scoffed. "It just doesn't seem necessary."

"What's not necessary?"

"People come on our property to die, and suddenly it's our responsibility to bury them *proper*?"

She slapped him gently on the shoulder. "Oh, Ryan. I know that, but we have to do it. It's the right thing to do, no matter who they are."

"We'll do right by them," he nodded, "but they take second priority to us keeping the place running. Speaking of which, the animals need to be fed. Can you handle that while I work on the panels?"

"Of course. Let me get this mess sorted, and I'll be right out."

"Thanks." Ryan rested his forehead on her shoulder and hugged her waist. "I appreciate everything you do. We make a great team, and I'm proud of how we fought last night." He sighed sadly. "I'm not happy we killed people; I feel it weighing on my soul already. But they pressed our backs to the wall, and we had no other choice. I'm confident that in my heart of hearts, we did the right thing."

Still with stained rags in her hands, Helen half turned and kissed him on the cheek. "You're my rock, Ryan. I don't know what I'd do without you."

With a lingering smile, he returned to the dining room for his jacket, rifle, and magazines. He'd cleaned the blood off everything, putting one magazine into the gun and the other into his right pocket. His pistol was still holstered, and he carried two spare magazines for that in his left pocket, giving him plenty of ammunition to handle any trouble in the yard. Exiting through the back, he walked past their EV and sacks of harvested food, testing his weight on his injured calf which still radiated a deep ache despite doubling up on pain medication and trying his best to favor it as much as possible.

In the barnyard, hungry animals harried him in expectation of being fed. "It's not my job today, guys," he grumbled, stepping past the bleating sheep and goats who tried to follow him inside the barn. "Go on! Get out of here! Yah!"

Bessie lowed in greeting as he stepped in, and he promised her Helen would be out to milk her soon. Ryan reattached the forklift to the tractor, then backed it out slowly, waiting for the animals to meander out of his way, then headed through the barnyard gate and closed it behind him so the animals didn't follow him down to the house. Halfway there, Helen came out, carrying her rifle and pistol, her light grey hair pinned back in a tight bun.

"Oh, aren't you a sight?" He called over the steering wheel as she strode by with Duchess on her heels.

She grinned and waved as he pulled up slowly to the solar panels and lowered the forks, then climbed down and grabbed the box of extra panels where they leaned against the house next to the post hole digger and quick drying cement. Taking up where he'd left off the previous day, he spaced out spots to dig more holes, filled them with cement powder and water, mixed it all up, and used tension strings to hold the poles in place.

After a few hours of dirty, sweaty work, he was ready to mount the panels. Helen was still working out in the barnyard, talking to the menagerie as she finished tossing feed to them before giving him a distant wave and going inside to milk Bessie. While the last of the cement dried, Ryan did a quick walk of the grounds, patrolling around the house past the harvested fields where the stalks and vegetation they'd pulled out lay brown and wilting. He strode out front to the trees where he'd placed the area traps and kicked up several spiked pieces of wood and hose with blood on them where the intruders had trampled.

Gathering up the pieces, he placed them back on their respective spots and lifted the wooden garden stakes so they were pointed up again. The attackers knew where the traps were, and Ryan figured they'd try from a different direction next time, but any chance to inflict pain on those trying to harm him and his wife was worth taking. For the next attack, he'd make sure to cover the sides and more of the backyard as well. The only true weakness he saw was that someone could try for the animals first to lure them out into an ambush, and it might behoove them to keep the animals locked up inside the barn at night, unless, of course, that just gave someone an opportunity to get at the animals when they were in a confined space, in which case....

Ryan took a deep breath, trying to stop the torrent of thoughts and what-ifs that kept surging through his mind. "First things first. One thing at a time."

He paused at the front of the house where the four dead bodies were piled up, pale faces staring at the sky; at least the two with faces *left* were staring at the sky. The pair Duke and Duchess had torn into looked like something from a horror movie, flesh flayed off their heads, chunks taken out of their arms and hands from trying to fend off the dogs. Ryan couldn't look at them for too long without feeling his breakfast trying to come up. They were already attracting bugs and starting to give off a foul scent, so he'd have to do what Helen asked and bury them soon. *Course, if I had it my way*, he thought, *I'd put you all on stakes at the front gate to show the neighborhood what we do to thieves and would-be murderers.*

With a sneer at the cluster of corpses, he circled the house and returned to the solar panel work, using the forks to raise each panel into place, finally bolting them to the frame. Once set, he pulled the pin beneath each one, adjusting the angle so they lay in a flat layer with the others, and locked them tight. Stepping away, he checked that they were perfectly level then used the levers at the end of the rows to shift them forty-five degrees toward the south and east and then back flat again, which gave him the ability to angle them as the sun arched through the sky.

Ryan got the bag of cables and crawled beneath the panels, plugging the cables in and running them along the frame system. He clipped them neatly into the wire holders and wiggled on his back, repeating the procedure until he reached the far end and plugged them into the unit's control box. Ryan crawled from beneath the panels, stood, and dusted himself off, then hurried inside and went into the basement to James' workshop with Diana jumping on his heels. A small door built into the west wall led to the cramped battery room, watertight and filled with stacks of batteries against the north wall. A cabling conduit branched up from the batteries and angled to the right where it connected with the main line in from the solar panels. Using a multimeter and a specialized controller James had set up on the battery rack, Ryan tested all the terminals for incoming current and grinned when the indicator shot through the roof on every single one on the very first try.

"That's more input that I thought we'd ever get, girl," he told Diana, who watched him curiously from the doorway. "There should be more than enough juice to keep a solid flow to the batteries. Let's go tell Helen, okay girl? C'mon!"

Helen was just coming in from the chicken coops with a basket of eggs and Duchess by her side when he got upstairs. "The solar panels are looking pretty good. Are we drawing any more power?"

"Absolutely." He grinned. "We'll need to let the batteries charge for a while so we've got power for tonight, but we'll be able to run the fridge, freezers, and lights, and have limited heat through the HVAC, too. And, shoot, it's cloudy out right now. Imagine how much power we'll generate on sunny days!"

"Oh, that's wonderful, Ryan." Helen's grin widened as she stared at the solar panels from the doorway. "Does that mean we'll be able to take some hot showers too?"

"The pump on top of everything else'll push things to its limit, and we do need to conserve the propane unless I can somehow source an electric water heater in the future... but yes, we should be good. Do you need any help with the chores?"

"We could use the tractor or ATV to bring down the milk, but other than that, I've got everything done."

"Great. Want to have a late lunch before we finish up?"

"I'd *love* that."

Before lunch, Ryan went downstairs to turn on the water heater, grinning when the flames popped on and the metal casing ticked as it heated up. Back upstairs, he got cleaned up as Helen got out a pan and a can of soup from the pantry, heating it up before starting on a pot of coffee as Ryan went over his list.

"Here's what I want to do," he said, holding up the notepad. "Bolster the upstairs windows so we have some concealment in case we're shot at again, set some more area traps around the sides of the house and barn, and start putting the animals inside every day."

"Anything else?"

"We'll start with burying those would-be thieves the first chance we get. They're starting to attract bugs and probably animals soon. The last thing we need is coyotes running around here gnawing on the bodies. Wouldn't be good for the chickens."

"And it's the right thing to do."

"Yes, exactly."

"I'll help, of course." Helen finished heating the food and brought two bowls and utensils over to sit across from him. They ate vegetable soup and stale crackers, then Ryan ran the faucet in the kitchen sink, smiling back at Helen as the warm water hit his sore hands.

"Heyyy, we have hot water again, honey."

She rose and squeezed his shoulder. "Thank you so much."

"Don't thank me. Thank James and Alice for having such a great setup. Those two picked a prime spot to settle down on with the well, and they've got a great well-pump." He gave Helen a brief hug, then gestured. "You go ahead. Have yourself a shower. Not a ton of hot water in the heater yet, but it'll be better than ice-cold sponge baths or shutting off half the house just to run the well pump for an ice-cold shower."

"I don't care if it's just lukewarm; a shower sounds like Heaven to me," she replied, kissing him on the cheek and heading for the master bathroom.

Ryan made a quick trip to the barn while she was inside, firing up the ATV to bring the milk down where he placed it just inside the door on the kitchen's gray tiles. Then, he put all his tools away and drove the ATV back to the barn. With gloves on, he dragged the man Helen had shot the previous day to the ATV, straining as he lifted the body and laid it across the cargo tray.

Helen would no doubt be mad at him for not letting her help, but there was no way he wanted her to have to suffer with the images of the mutilated, bloating bodies any more than she already had. As soon as he could, he'd dig the holes for them and drop them in. Helen could help with the finishing touches if she wanted, but he'd spare her the worst of it, if he could.

Ryan drove the first body to the east side of the property and dumped it at the edge of the woods, then went for the others. Soon, all five were piled up next to the woods, and Ryan put the ATV away and walked back to the house with a worsening limp, his calf stiffening and tight.

Back in the kitchen, he poured himself a cup of coffee with shaking hands and sat heavily at the table, a wave of nausea hitting him deep in his gut, more strongly than he'd ever experienced. His whole body was shaking, and he nearly spilled the coffee three separate times as he sipped on it, breathing deeply to try and return a sense of calm. After a few moments, he returned to his notepad, going over his list of things to do, crossing off a few he'd completed and bringing new ones up as priorities, trying to forget the bodies and their gruesome faces. By the time Helen finished with her shower, Ryan was wired from the caffeine and feeling better.

"How was it?"

"Heavenly," Helen replied, moving to the coffeemaker and pouring herself a cup. She'd laid a towel around her shoulders, and her wet, gray hair lay over it. "Water pressure fluctuated off and on, but I could get used to regular showers again."

"Mm... might need to tweak the power, then, if the pump's shutting off a lot." He gestured at his list. "In the meantime, I'll be able to knock a few of these things out before dinner."

She sat across from him with the steaming cup. "First thing we need to do is get you a shower and change that bandage. Trust me, honey, it's worth every second. The warm water will do wonders for your joints and muscles."

"Mm." He continued looking at the notepad. "I don't doubt it."

Helen reached across and placed her hand on the notepad, turning it around to look at it before pushing it back.

"With everything we've gone through in the past few days, you should settle down and rest a bit. I don't know about you, but I barely got any sleep last night."

Ryan frowned and tapped his pen on the table. "I didn't sleep that well either, but I can't help but keep working on this stuff."

"We've got plenty of food and water for now," Helen insisted. "*Hot* water, too."

"Warm," Ryan countered. "And that might not be for all that long unless I can do something to convert from propane to electric."

"That's what I mean, hon. Instead of worrying about the hard things that could take days or weeks or months, why don't you think of one or two things we can do together *tonight* before we start our shifts? Nothing too hard or strenuous. We need to take a bit of a break. I feel beat to heck, and I know you do, too."

"Okay," he sighed, shoulders slumping. "I'll take it easy tonight."

She took his pen out of his hand. "Trust me. You'll feel a hundred percent better, then we can talk about what to do next."

"It might be nice to make it safe to turn on lights in the bedroom. We'd need to put some coverings over the windows to keep any light from leaking out."

Helen smiled and patted his hand. "I'll look for some curtains and blankets while you get cleaned up. Now, get on up there. I'll watch things down here."

Ryan shifted in his seat, unable to give up on the list of responsibilities he'd made for himself, reaching for the list again, though Helen pulled it out of his reach.

"Go, mister. Upstairs. Now."

"Oh, all right."

Ryan finished his coffee, stood, and went upstairs, peeling off the old, sweaty clothes he'd been wearing for days, tossing them in a basket and heading into the bathroom. A mist still clung to the mirror and shower door, and it smelled like shampoo and soap. Ryan peeled off the bandages he'd accumulated, wincing when he pulled the one off his calf, bringing some hair with it. The bullet wound was puckered, pink, and clean, and showed no signs of infection, Helen's stitches still holding strong, but the muscles were stiff, the skin tender and bruised all the way around.

Stepping into the shower, he turned on the hot water and raised his face to the sharp spray, abrasions and cuts stinging as he washed away the dirt and grime, trying to scrub away the memories of barking, snarling dogs, gunshots, and the torn-up, shot-up bodies lying on the east side of the property.

CHAPTER FIVE

Ray Sider
Paris, France

Smoke rose above the streets of Paris, congealing in a thick, desolate fog the midday sun could not penetrate. The once beautiful city, the cultural heart of Europe, bled like a burst abscess, its edges black and oozing dirty water from broken pipes, creating a sludge that spread over everything, clogging the sewer system and giving off a reek so foul that not even scavengers wanted to go near it. The city's buildings lay split open and bombed out by strings of explosions thanks to an endless supply of delivery trucks, public transport vehicles and cars that had crowded the streets. Though most of the two million residents had perished in the flames, the ruins crawled with small groups of survivors, scavenging for morsels to keep them alive.

In the Saint Germain neighborhood, Ray Sider and his new companions were picking through the husk of a restaurant, digging up the rubble beneath an open sky, turning over corpses, checking pockets, and looking for anything edible that might've survived the explosions. They were a mixed group of American and Japanese tourists that had been on a walking tour, along with several French citizens who'd been fortunate enough to make it out alive when the end came.

"Anything, Jiro?" he asked.

Jiro stood from the rubble of a server's station with a broken cash register and a partial wall of shelves. He responded in Japanese and shook his head helplessly, shrugging and holding his hands out.

"I'll take that as a no," Ray replied, looking around as Gemma and Sara picked at what appeared to be a buffet bar with a wilted plastic cover. They were Americans, like Ray, missing a father and husband who'd lost his life when a piece of debris had smashed through a café window and embedded in his face.

Ray walked over, smiling at little Sara as she picked up a metal serving tray and flipped it to reveal a pile of charred biscuits that had turned to charcoal. She looked up at him with smears of soot on her face.

"Not much there, huh?"

"Nope."

"You're standing in mud," Ray said. "Here, give me your hand."

He helped Sara out of the mud and gave her to her mother. "Here you go."

"Thanks," Gemma laughed. "She can't seem to stay clean around here."

Ray gestured at his soiled tennis shoes and smiled hesitantly. "None of us can. No matter how much we try."

Gemma wiped the smudges off Sara's cheeks, stood, and frowned. "We've been at this for hours and have barely found a thing to eat."

"Well, we have to keep trying," Ray replied. "There's nothing else we can do until help gets here."

Gemma rolled her eyes. "It's been days, Ray. There won't be any help coming. The entire world is like this."

The complex Parisian architecture of a church across the square was gone, the lines of gothic arches and stained-glass windows blown to pieces. Pews inside had burned like kindling, spreading glowing cinders for blocks in every direction and helping lay the city aflame. The sharp spike of the Abby of Saint Germain des Pres two blocks away had split, its top half crumbled, leaving a sliver of concrete and stone jutting up.

Tears brimmed in his eyes as Ray stared at the damaged ruins. "I was just there with Julie the day before everything went up. She loved that place. She... loved all the gothic churches. We were supposed to be here another week."

"I'm sorry about your wife," Gemma said.

"And I'm sorry about Steven."

"Ray!" Another voice cut in.

Jiro was standing on the other side of the restaurant with some of their new French friends. Beside a decorative fountain were a pair of lopsided swinging doors leading to the kitchen, hanging crooked on their hinges. Jiro said something in Japanese, and when Ray only shrugged, he frustratedly mimed putting food in his mouth and pointing at the doors.

"Okay, sure. Bound to be something to eat in there."

Jiro climbed over some garbage to join Paul, pressing on the door but only getting it to move an inch or two.

"Is it stuck?" Ray asked, coming over. The section still had a ceiling, and the walls were intact but crumbling. He didn't see another way in unless they wanted to go around.

Jiro gestured, and Paul said something in French, but pounded his fist against his palm and nodded toward the doors.

"Yeah, yeah. We need to break it down. Stand back." Ray waved them away. "Give me some room."

Ray was bigger than the two men by a foot and a half and fifty pounds, with meatier shoulders and an overall larger frame. As the members of their group gathered around, he laughed. "I was a lineman in high school, and I blocked guys way tougher than these doors."

Jiro and Paul shared a confused look while Ray prepared to charge.

"Don't hurt yourself, Ray," Gemma said.

Yua shook her head, seeming to agree with the gist of Gemma's tone, and Paul and Anna held hands and watched with concern.

"I won't. Don't worry about old Ray."

Ray launched himself at the doors, striking them, knocking whatever was blocking them back a good three inches. He held his stinging shoulder, walking away from the doors while giving them a side-eyed glance. "One more time should do it."

On his second attempt, he gave it his all and slammed the doors hard, plowing the blockage aside so the doors swung fully back, knocking into a cart and banging against the wall. Jiro pumped his fist and grinned, and the rest of the group followed Ray in as he rolled his arm, rubbing it and looking around. It was like any other kitchen he'd ever worked in, except it looked as though a fire-laden tornado had torn through the place.

Toppled shelves and garbage lay everywhere, most of it at least partially burned up, but there were several untouched cans of tomato sauce, olives, and moldy cheese lying around. Paul held out his sack, and Anna started putting things inside while the rest spread out and kept searching. Ray continued to hover near Gemma and Sara, their shared language and country of origin making it far more comfortable to communicate with the pair over the hand signals and charades with the others. Checking in another area of the kitchen back by the walk-in refrigerators, he grabbed one handle and tried to jerk it open, but it was stuck. Bracing himself with his foot against the edge, he tried again, yanking it wide and releasing a belch of fetid air that singed his nose and twisted his stomach with nausea.

"Oh, that's disgusting," Gemma said, waving her hand in front of her face. "Smells like rotten food."

Ray shined his flashlight inside and swallowed hard, shutting the door as they came up. "Uhhh... yeah, that's what it is. Just a bunch of rotten food. Nothing else. Nothing to salvage."

"We should go through it anyway," Gemma insisted, reaching for the handle. "You never know what we'll find."

Ray winced. "You *really* don't want to go inside. All that rotten *food*. Trust me on that."

Gemma mouthed "bodies" at him questioningly and he nodded, then she quickly pulled Sara in the other direction.

"Yeah, you two go over there," Ray said, "and I'll check the rest of the walk-ins."

"Bingo," Jiro called from a pantry area, pointing at a box of crackers Yua held.

Yua dug open the top, frowning as she pulled out a small bag with just a few broken crackers and some crumbs at the bottom. She shook it sadly, then poured the remaining crackers in one hand, crossing the kitchen to Sara, kneeling in front of her and holding them out.

"You don't have to do that, Yua," Gemma said, though she didn't try to stop Sarahwhen she reached for the crackers and ate them hungrily while everyone watched with sad smiles.

"Eat all, please," Yua said in broken English.

Gemma wiped some crumbs off her daughter's chin. "There you go. See, things aren't quite so bad now! What do you say?"

"Thank you!" Sara looked up at Yua as she spoke, cracks of clean skin showing through the thick layers of dirt as she smiled broadly in thanks.

Across the room, Paul and Jiro found several trays of expensive-looking cutlery, stashing them in their pockets and handing Ray the steak knives. He put them in an extra-thick sack they'd picked up specifically for collecting sharp objects and tucked one under his belt. Plates and bowls had spilled across the floor, but they ignored them, having more than enough dishware back at camp.

After a while, they finished picking through the restaurant ruins and were standing back outside again where gray clouds crept across the sky, a distant scream or the sound of an explosion or gunfire occasionally punctuating the city's silence, sounds they'd gotten used to over the past several days. They were only worth worrying about if they got too close, and if that happened Ray had promised to form up a defensive team to go investigate and run off any would-be attackers.

Ray scratched his head and pointed to the sky. "Come on. The sun will be down soon, and we don't want to be out in the dark."

They packed up the meager supplies they'd collected since starting their scavenging earlier in the morning and prepared for another long walk. Ray's legs and shoulders ached, head throbbing from sadness and worry, yet he held it all back behind a grim face. He told himself it was for the others, playing the part of the big dumb American brave enough to run off marauders and show leadership when the others broke down. In reality it was for Julie, the memory of her, and knowing she would want him to keep going in spite of everything, just to help those around him.

Ray was walking point, as he always did, as the sun began to set over the ruins of the city, bringing another deep night when the real predators would come out, the ones that couldn't be frightened off by screaming at them. They were the ones who'd practically gone feral and would stab you and strip your body while you were still breathing for nothing more than crumbs and the fun of it.

"Hanging in there, Ray?" Gemma asked, suddenly next to him with Sara walking beside her.

"Yeah, absolutely." He nodded and smiled, blinking back a wave of emotion and moving faster to get ahead of them as their faces were suddenly replaced by those of his wife and child.

Halfway home, Ray spotted another group encroaching from the west, about the size of their own, but with several big men standing on the periphery as the rest scavenged through the skeleton of a building. He'd seen the group before, skirting the edges of their territory and eyeing their camp in the park. As they learned over the days, attacking a smaller group was not a guarantee of success, and fights had left the combatants bruised and beat up. With basic medical supplies difficult to come by, two people had already died from scratches that had gotten infected. A simple cough could turn into pneumonia, and eating rotten food could bring stomach illnesses that could put someone down for days – or permanently. It was best to avoid confrontation altogether and only attempt to steal or scavenge from another group when the odds were heavily in their favor.

Still, Ray put up a bold front, and he stood in the middle of the road with Jiro and Paul, each wielding splintered sticks or pieces of sharp metal, knives tucked into their belts, glaring at the other group as they stared back, the two parties keeping a respectable distance. Ray was reminded of an old stray cat he and Julie used to feed off their porch for five or six years. They'd cared for the cat as best they could, named him, and got him neutered and kept him well-fed. Still, every night Old Man would come home from roaming the neighborhood with scratches, patches of fur missing, and infections Ray had to get treated and stitched at the vet. Whenever a possum or another tomcat came around, Old Man would stand at the edge of the patio, mewling, hissing, and spitting until his challenger finally gave up. Ray was feeling a lot like Old Man, a beleaguered, beaten-up old tomcat guarding what little he had left in the world, protecting his people and their meager supplies by appearing tough.

It worked, though, and they passed the other group without incident as they walked the Parisian lanes, twelve grubby adults and a couple of kids, carrying sacks of what they'd collected that day over their shoulders, heads down, slouching, feet shuffling beneath the gray skies. Ray took them a different way home to avoid seeing the other group again, and in the narrow cobblestone lanes they stumbled upon a small French market that had escaped most of the burning. The shelves were stripped, and most of the nonperishable goods were gone, but still they spread out through the store while Ray and Jiro kept watch out front. Jiro pointed to the sky with a worried expression, putting his hands together and spreading them.

"I know, man," Ray said. "It's getting late, and we probably should get home. It looks like they're finding a lot of stuff, though. Might be worth sticking around a few more minutes."

Jiro shook his head and formed his arms into a hugging shape, opening and closing the circle, muttering more Japanese.

"Right. We've got to get back to the others soon, or they'll be undefended. I get it, friend." Ray patted him on the shoulder. "Just a few more minutes. It might be the last chance to scavenge this place. We brought in three more mouths to feed, remember?" Ray held up three fingers, and Jiro threw up his hands frustratingly and nodded.

"Ray, look!" Gemma said, coming outside and flashing him a can of expensive French canned meat.

"Fancy." He grinned and held open a sack. "Drop it in. Hey, how much longer do you think you'll be? It's almost dark."

"Just a few more minutes, and we'll call it a day." She went back inside.

Someone found a box of stale animal crackers, which automatically passed to Sara, who ate them on a countertop, grinning and swinging her legs. Just when Ray was starting to worry, his people came outside with the bottoms of their sacks weighted down, smiles on their faces as they finished chewing on bits and bobs they'd found inside, their relief over the found supplies nearly palpable.

Ray had them pick up the pace, marching through narrow alleys and backstreets to reach Rue de Vaugirard. The main thoroughfare circled a massive series of parks and greenery in the middle of the city, the backyard of Luxembourg Palace with its fountains, gardens, tennis courts, and quaint fields of greenery divided by paved walking paths. Turning down Rue Guynemer, they stayed on the left-hand side of the road, where trees grew right up to the road and the brush was over-growing the sidewalks. Ray watched the thick clusters of apartments and hotels to the west as the last vestiges of sunlight dropped below the horizon, leaving fractal rays of light scattered across the buildings and streets.

Lanterns and flashlights were forbidden for safety's sake, so they took known paths they'd cleared of wreckage and were known to be clear of obstructions. Ray knew the way by heart, and at a certain point, he stepped into the brush, putting his big backside against the rough branches and squeezing them back to give the others room to get by. Jiro led them deeper into the park, and after the last person passed, Ray stayed where he was for a few extra minutes, watching the streets and making sure no one was following them. He dipped inside and took a narrow trail to the main camp, guided by twin points of candlelight up in the tree branches that marked the entrance to their base. If the lights were on, the camp was safe to enter, but if they were out, it meant the camp was jeopardized, and it would be time for Ray and his people to move on. They'd relocated twice before, carrying their supplies to new spots, slipping deeper into hiding each time, starting over and over again.

Ray passed beneath the tree, nodding to the guards in the bushes, drawn by murmuring voices and occasional chuckles. The adults seldom laughed, though Sara and the other children did, the youngest showing incredible resiliency in the face of disaster. Still, the evening's haul had put smiles on everyone's faces, and a giddiness spread through the group like a bolt of lightning in a storm. He hugged and shook hands with several people on the way in, working toward the center of the clearing, the night sky looming over them, the hidden moonlight casting an ambiance that didn't seem hostile for once. Tiny fires dotted the camp, illuminating the field of tents and tarps hanging from poles, raggedy shelters offering a degree of privacy.

They'd opened the sacks and spread them around the camp's central fireplace, a large, circular pit that they made sure kept a low fire going at all times, where they gathered to exchange stories, make plans, and slowly learn each other's languages. A French cook, Gemma, and Anna rifled through the collection, stacking canned goods, separating out powdered meals and giant cans of tomato sauce and processed cheese, and fussing over what to make in the pot. Ray accepted a bottled water from Paul, and the two stood and watched as the meal came together like it often did, most everything going into the single pot, with the French cook standing over it and sprinkling in spices.

At first, Ray had thought there was no way the process could give them edible meals, but the mélange had often made the meal filling and flavorful when the broth was thin and chunks of meat and vegetables were hard to find. Wood went into the fire, and the flames kicked up, bathing the surrounding faces in a warm glow where twenty-five of them sat on old lawn chairs, seats stripped from theaters, bedrolls, bins, stones, and logs. Smudged faces beamed with renewed hope as cans were opened and dumped into the pot and the French cook stood over it, coaxing the flames, bringing the meal to a boil, and stirring it with a big spoon as she sprinkled her spices and worked her magic.

Gemma approached and crossed her arms, keeping watch over Sara as she played with the other camp kids. "We've got a nice little place here for now."

"Yes, we do."

"But we've had to move twice already because bigger groups moved in. What'll we do if they try and come in on this one?"

"We'll keep moving," Ray nodded. "Whatever we have to do to keep everyone alive until help... ah, never mind."

"Do you really think help will come?"

"I have to think the cavalry is coming," Ray grinned hesitantly. "Otherwise, why keep going on?"

"Because it's the only thing we can do?"

"That only gets you through a few days. After that, we need more hope, and we have to get angry and want to do it for those we've lost. Your husband, my Julie..." Ray clamped his mouth shut and pushed away the emotion. "We have to imagine a future where we're not living hand to mouth, and that's all there is to it."

While he hadn't asked her age, he was probably fifteen or twenty years her senior, her like a daughter to him than anything else. She locked arms with him and rested her forehead against his shoulder.

"Thanks, Ray. Sara and I... We can't thank you enough for taking us in."

"Don't mention it," Ray replied, patting her on the arm.

"Water," Jiro spoke hesitantly in English, pointing to a satellite dish in the middle of camp connected to a central pipe that ran to a barrel. Off to the side were several containers they'd filled, though a lot of them were empty, and it hadn't rained hard in a few days. "More buckets."

Paul came up, adding his thoughts in broken English. "Radio says rain."

"Yes, we need some more containers to save water in," Ray agreed. "I saw a bunch of those on the outskirts of our area..." As Ray talked, he made gestures with his hands, using his fingers to draw a perimeter and point to the edge. "Very dangerous past there. We have to be very careful."

"Careful, yes," Jiro nodded, clasping his hands behind his back. "Careful."

"We've been thinking, Ray," Gemma said. "I mean... some of us have been talking."

"Yeah, about what?"

"About what we can do next. You know, the next steps in all this."

"Safety," Jiro nodded in agreement and gestured around.

"Isn't survival enough?"

"It's great, of course," Gemma said, "but some of us wonder how long we can sustain this."

Ray nodded, in fact, had been prepared for such a discussion. "I don't know. This is a pretty good spot. We've got protection and plenty of prime scavenging spots. That's not something we want to give up lightly."

"But people are encroaching on us every day," Gemma pressed. "We keep seeing that same group, and they're getting bigger and bigger. You and I know it's just a matter of time before they attack us."

"We don't know that. We could try to reason with them, join with them."

"Conflict is inevitable, Ray. You know this."

Ray crossed his arms and watched the pot come to a boil, the chef pointing and lining up people to get their share. "Okay, what are you thinking?"

Gemma and Jiro exchanged a look before Gemma continued. "Well, wouldn't the rural areas offer more shelter?"

"Maybe it'll be worse out there."

"It can't be worse. The pickings are getting slim around here."

"Farm," Jiro said, making a square shape with his fingers. "Grow."

"So, you guys want to pick up, head to the country, and start building farms? That tells me you've given up on any chances of rescue."

"Not at all. Look, none of us have a chance of getting home. We haven't seen an airplane or helicopter since all this started. The radio hasn't been helpful at all. For all we know, this thing could stretch on for months or even years. We need to plan for the long haul, not just camp out in the city streets, hoping for a break. We need to make our own breaks."

Ray sized up their expressions of determination, finding an equal measure in all. "All right. Maybe we should get out of the city and find a quiet spot in the country to set up. There's bound to be less competition for resources."

"Farm," Jiro said.

"Right. There's bound to be some good farmland outside the city, but that will be fiercely guarded, too."

"But there would be more of it, and we could use the land to protect it. Hills and valleys and things." Gemma nudged him with her elbow. "Come on, Ray. We could get out in the fresh air and show what we're made of. I grew up on a farm myself, and Paul told me about his family's farm."

"So we're all farmers now?"

"Not farmers yet, but we know enough to get started. You wouldn't have to do anything different. Just keep an eye out on things. Protect us."

A long line had formed, reaching from the big pot to the edge of the woods, the kids all together in a bunch, fidgeting and jostling and laughing with their bowls and spoons clanking. They were happy for the moment but deserved a lot more, and Ray imagined them in a different place, perhaps a barn with a big fire out front, land to play and run in, woods to let their imaginations run wild.

"We'd be packing up and moving everything."

"We know."

"Our supplies are low, so we'd need a lot more to make a journey like that. Possibly thirty or forty miles."

"Fifty, by Paul's estimation. That would put us outside the city and in the surrounding farmlands."

"More danger and more risk."

"You'll protect us."

"You really want to do this?"

"Yes. The parents have all discussed it, and everyone understands what's at stake. We're ready to go."

Ray flexed his arms and shoulders, stunned by the revelation that they all put so much faith in him, concerned he might not have what it would take. "All right. If everyone agrees, we can move to the outskirts. We'll build that farm you want, Jiro."

Jiro nodded and grinned. "Build farm."

"And, who knows, maybe we'll find peace until all this blows over." Looking out across the dilapidated city, Ray had to concede that Gemma was right. It could be months or years more before anyone with any significant resources or power came to help out the people of Paris, and meanwhile the thousands of tourists and residents who had survived would slowly starve and die. "Let's form up a few scavenging groups. We'll need to pull double time if we're going to gather enough food and water to make the trip."

Gemma was beaming at Sara as she came up with a bowl of stew, almost spilling it over the edges before Gemma took it. Around them, other families had taken their food to their seats, sipping on the watery mix of meat and vegetables.

"How long until we can leave?" Gemma asked.

"Inside a week, but we shouldn't wait any longer than that. It's going to get colder before too long, and our chances of making it through this go way up if we find a place before winter hits."

"Sounds awesome, Ray. Thank you." Gemma had a bite of stew and nodded to the French chef appreciatively. "Wow, this is good. I can't wait to start growing our own food. It's just... liberating."

Ray accepted a bowl of stew from another person who held it out to him and they stood in a semicircle, watching the line continue to move.

"All done with mine, Mama," Sara said, holding out her bowl. "Can I have some more?"

The soup spoon was already clanking against the bottom of the pot as the last few people moved through the line, and Gemma shook her head. "Mm. I don't think so, honey. There won't be any seconds today."

"Aww. That's okay," Sara said, lowering her bowl.

Jiro smiled and stepped over to Sara, dumping the bit he had left into her bowl, and the others followed suit, every adult in the group picking a child and offering what they had. Ray took two bites of his own, downing a couple of meat chunks before giving the rest to a little boy sitting off to the side who'd lost his parents.

"Here you go, son," he said, scraping the last bit into his bowl. "Eat up. You're going to need your strength."

CHAPTER SIX

Alice Burton
Columbus, Georgia

The engine roared, its exhaust pipes bursting with smoke, belching, choking, and rumbling with diesel fury, but Alice couldn't tell from what direction. Jake and Sarah had already gotten ahead of her, breaking the horses into a sprint with the wind whipping Sarah's hair around. Leaning forward, balancing her weight on her hips and legs, Alice rode hard after them, Buck's hooves pounding the pavement, searching for a way north. She almost missed the service road coming up, hidden as it was behind a thick cluster of brush.

She shouted to the kids before they shot past it. "Jake! Sarah! There's a service road on the side... it's open!"

Alice angled Buck toward it as Sarah yelled at Jake to stop, and they both turned to fall in behind her. Alice turned up the narrow lane and kicked Buck faster toward the curve ahead, hoping to outrun whatever was trying to cut them off. Movement erupted from the tree line to the right where something massive trundled toward them. A white cab with a bright yellow stripe along the side flashed in the trees, followed by a wide steel frame and a big, flat front windshield. Surprised faces stared back at her from the cab as it rounded the bend and cleared the trees, pouring smoke from its exhaust pipe. The street sweeper had two arms with massive round brushes stretching from beneath it, spinning furiously to sweep stones and dirt beneath the frame with a raucous clatter. Large workbaskets had been welded to the sides with four men standing in them, two holding shotguns while the others clung with one hand to crude handrails while brandishing blunt instruments.

She pulled Buck up and rested back in her saddle as the sweeper bore down on them, simultaneously stupefied by the appearance of a working internal combustion powered vehicle and confused that it was a street sweeper. Only the sounds of Jake and Sarah riding up fast broke her from her terrified trance, and she threw her arm out to stop them. They hadn't seen the street sweeper at first, but when they did, they drew their mounts up with surprised cries. The driver and passenger seemed just as surprised to see the four horses as the trio was to see the vehicle, but the driver didn't alter course at all. If anything, he accelerated and turned right at them with the rollers spinning harder, the clatter of stones and pebbles loud in the carriage. The men in the baskets erupted into gleeful cries, pointing at them and slamming their palms on the cab's roof in encouragement. Alice guided Buck to the right, but the driver followed them, barreling down just twenty yards away, the vehicle surprisingly fast.

"Back the other way! Come on!"

Alice turned and raced back to the main highway, cutting hard right onto the road to go west again. Wind blasted her face and blew her hair back, strands whipping across her eyes as the kids rode furiously on her tail, Jake clinging to Hercules' tether where their backpacks and supplies bounced on his sides. In a burst of dust and flying rocks, the street sweeper banked hard onto the highway behind them, its tail sweeping around and throwing the men on the baskets around, the spinning brushes sweeping back and forth, knocking chunks of rubble and debris aside, scattering pieces everywhere. Alice slowed to avoid a pileup, weaving Buck between husks of car frames blocking their way, hooves pounding on the pavement as Sarah and Jake caught up with her, keeping well in front of the churning truck as it rushed toward them.

"We've got to get off the road, Mom!" Jake shouted. "Rocky is having a hard time on the concrete."

"Stormy, too!" Sarah called, breaking left around an economy car.

"I know!" Alice took a sharp angle to avoid a bucket seat in the right-hand lane with a corpse still slumped in it and Buck's hooves slipped and sent Alice's heart leaping into her chest.

"We're heading toward the city, Mom!" Jake shouted. "Shouldn't we stay away from there?"

Alice nodded, catching sight of an opening off to the right. "Follow me!"

She kicked Buck hard and rode him off the shoulder, leaping a ditch to land hard on the other side, shoulders thrown forward with the impact. Falling back into the saddle, she kicked Buck again and crashed through a thicket with a clatter of snapping brush and whipping branches, ducking a split second before a big one almost took her head off, jerking her face aside when a switch cut her chin. She dodged between a pair of massive tree trunks, leaped a log, and burst into a park with circular patches of artificial turf and jungle gyms all around. The grass was soft and green and overgrown, and they trotted across the vast field, angling northwest with the street sweeper's engine fading off to the left.

"What was their problem?" Sarah asked, moving up to her right and galloping smoothly ahead.

"They want to run us over," Jake said exasperatedly, "that's their problem."

"Well, they can't drive through all those trees to get to us," Alice said with relief. "Our best bet is to keep heading north and away from that infernal machine."

She snapped the reins and rode ahead over a baseball field, sprinting through the infield and exiting on the first-base side to head through a parking lot full of debris. Buck leaped part of a dashboard lying on the ground, landing smoothly and trotting by a baseball glove and several aluminum baseball bats sitting amongst the wreckage. They reached a road stretching west to east and stopped to check both ways, Sarah and Jake riding past her, turning their horses in a circle as they helped her search, Jake getting Hercules' tether wrapped around him.

The roar of the street sweeper's diesel engine jolted her stiff in the saddle, and the machine burst from between two city maintenance buildings on the left, turning up dust and pebbles, flying into the road and swerving as it drove right at them. A man in one of the baskets fired a shotgun blast into the air while his partners yelled at Alice and the kids to stop.

"Mom!" Sarah cried as Stormy whinnied and reared on his hind legs, touching down and leaping back the way they'd come on his own, running out across the parking lot toward the baseball field again.

"That way, Jake!" Alice shouted, leaning low over the saddle and urging Buck to go. "H'yah, Buck. Come on!"

The horse snorted and leaped into motion, Alice squeezing her knees as she tried to stay in the seat. Jake did an extra turn on Rocky to get untangled and raced right behind them, flying fast and guiding Hercules with quick tugs on the tether and reins. Another shotgun blast went off, followed by more shouts and whistles for them to stop. Alice ducked as they thundered across the baseball field, thinking they'd gotten away, but the street sweeper turned off the road and into the grass, churning up dirt and mud from its tires as it raced after them.

"Come on!" she growled. "You can't *possibly* follow us this way."

The massive vehicle continued onward, though, bouncing and jostling the men in the baskets as the driver angled across the walking path and rode the sloping hills up into the park, trying to cut them off. By then, Sarah had gotten control of Stormy and was glancing back for instructions and Alice rode up, trying to stay calm as another shotgun blast rocked the sky, the truck's horn bleating at them as the driver screamed out of his window.

"Should we split up, Mom?" Sarah's hair whipped around her head, cheeks rosy-red from the rush.

"No! Let's lead them off that way... to the southwest. Get them caught in some brush and woods, then turn around and run right past them. We can get back to the service road and fly north if we do that."

"Okay, let's go!"

"Stay with us, Jake!"

Determined, Alice leaned low over the saddle and fell into Buck's rhythm, pushing him hard around the edge of the park, flying across walking paths, cresting shallow slopes, and dashing past tennis courts to the wooded area on the other side. The street sweeper stayed nearby, the spinning brushes tearing up grass and dirt and throwing it high into the air, rocks and deadfall sweeping beneath it to rattle around in the undercarriage before spitting out the sides and back. More shotgun blasts chased them into the wooded patch, buckshot striking the trees and shredding leaves to pieces.

The brush was thicker the deeper they went, though, and soon they were forty yards inside, Alice pulling Buck up for a moment, drifting sideways as she watched the truck approach the wooded patch at breakneck speed. The men in the baskets were slamming their hands on the side and top of the truck, yelling for the driver to stop, but the diesel engine only revved louder, the broad front grill plowing right at them. It hit the first line of vegetation with a crunch, one sweeper arm catching a sapling and breaking off with the vicious jolt to the truck's frame, nearly throwing the men out of the baskets. Bushes and brush slapped the front windshield and rocked them back and forth, but the driver was so focused on Alice that he didn't see the magnitude of his predicament.

"Now, kids!"

She leaned forward and kicked Buck all in one motion, clinging to his back as he sprinted away from the high-throttling monster chasing them. They burst from the woods and flew around the tennis courts, heading due east toward the service road again. She raced on, willing Buck to fly faster, hooves pounding the ground in a flowing, powerful locomotion. Wind whipped into her eyes, forcing her to squint and turn her head to the side as his heaving chest worked like a massive furnace beneath her. They were a quarter mile distant when the truck finally reached the edge of the woods, rocking, tires spinning with big chunks of logs and deadfall caught up in its undercarriage, dragging along and slowing it to a near crawl.

A slow smile spread across her face as they flew past the swing sets and kept heading east, working their way through a stand of yellow poplars, weaving around a restroom facility and some basketball courts with the nets torn down. Bursting through the tree line, Buck leaped a shallow ditch and landed heavily on the service road, with the sounds of the other horses' clopping hooves right behind her.

"Whoa, Buck! Are you guys okay?"

Jake flew by without stopping, Hercules trailing behind with his tail flying in the wind. "Yeah! But why are we stopping? Those guys are trying to kill us!"

With a snap of the reins, Alice leaped forward and caught up with Jake, and they galloped north past city buildings, recycling dumpsters, municipal waste management, and the sanitation department. Gravel pathways branched out all around them and wove between the structures, many of them reduced to jagged sections of wall and the vague outlines of foundations to show they'd been buildings at all. At the city mechanic's shop, police vans and cars lay shattered and ripped apart by fuel explosions, parts of their flashing lights strewn across the road. Garbage, scraps of foam seating, and ash skimmed the pavement in front of them as the wind picked up and clouds moved in overhead. They slowed to a trot past the repair shop and came together in a straight line, the horses' sides heaving, heads tossing, snorting and twitching like they wanted to keep running.

Alice turned to an exasperated Sarah who was still panting and clutching her chest in disbelief. "Are you okay, honey?"

"I'm fine! Can you believe those guys, Mom!?"

"We're not out of the woods yet." The distant sound of the sweeper truck revved high and loud. "Come on, this road is turning east, so let's jump into that field there. H'yah, Buck!"

Alice nodded straight ahead and slightly left, angling Buck toward the field. The pavement turned to gravel and then dirt again as they pushed into a low stand of brush, the thin understory tugging at them as they squeezed through. Vines crawled up the tree trunks like they were massive trellises, and the scent of honeysuckle and sharp, bitter vegetation touched their noses. As soon as they were through, they broke into a gallop, crouching in their stirrups as the rain caught up to them and began to drizzle.

The shallow slope took them to a ridge line, giving them a decent view of their surroundings for miles. Alice glanced toward the road, half expecting the sweeper truck to come flying through the trees, dragging sticker bushes, ferns, and bits of deadfall behind them in relentless pursuit, but after a minute of catching their breath and letting the horses walk in peace, Alice turned Buck down the other side.

"Let's get out of here," she said. "The more distance we can put between us and those lunatics, the better."

They continued for another two miles, trotting into the rain, cooling the sweating horses and Alice's burning hot face. Finally, she drew Buck up, turning, laughing nervously as the kids came up behind her. They walked the horses up a moderate slope with spots of brush dotting the landscape as far as they could see and the sun came out through the clouds, golden rays bursting across the fields, turning the rain into a glowing mist.

"Look, Mom," Jake said. "A rainbow!"

Off to the left beneath the clouds, an arc of color spread from one end of the horizon to the other, orange, blue, purple, and green, vibrant against the saturated gray skies, the sweet smell of rain blotting out the ash and smoke as they crested the hill where wide plains stretched all around them. By the time they reached the far side, they were soaked, and Alice guided them into the tree line where they took protection beneath the tree cover.

"Why don't we rest here for a while?" Alice said, halting Buck and dismounting.

As Sarah and Jake got down, she noticed a red spot blossoming on Jake's back. "Son, come here. You've been hit."

"Wait, what?" Jake asked, tying the horses up to an oak branch while he glanced back. "I felt a sting, but it barely hurt."

"Sit down over here."

Alice knelt behind Jake as he took a seat on a rotten log, rolling his shoulder and wincing. "Ow! I guess I did get hit. Is it a bullet?"

She put her fingers through the shirt tear and tore it open, spreading the material and looking at the bloody wound beneath. "Not a bullet. Buckshot." Sliding her fingers over his slick skin, she found where the round pellet was embedded.

"Ouch!"

"Sorry, son."

"It's okay. Is it deep?"

"No. We should get it out as soon as possible and get this cleaned up, though. Sarah, get a first aid kit for me, please."

"On it."

Spreading the kit out next to her, Alice found a large tweezer and some saline rinse, which she sprayed on Jake's skin to reveal the silver lump just beneath the surface. It had made a small crater in his skin, like a miniature comet, the wound puckered and bruised around the impact site.

"Hold a flashlight on it, would you?"

Sarah stood behind her with the light, Jake sucking air through his teeth as Alice sprayed saline on the wound and picked at it with the tweezers. Plucking the piece out, Alice held it up for a moment and tossed it aside, then cleaned the wound more and spread some antibiotic ointment on it. Sarah handed her a bandage, and she dried the wound with gauze before covering it and pressing down with the bandage.

"There you go," she said. "Easy as you please."

"Thanks, Mom," Jake said, standing, rolling his shoulder with a mild wince. "Give me a minute to change my shirt and I'll be ready to ride."

Alice checked out their surroundings as Buck and Stormy found a pond-sized puddle near the trees and put their heads down to drink. "Like I was saying, why don't we just rest here for a while? The horses can drink and graze for a bit, and we can catch our wind."

They stayed just within the tree line, sitting on a couple of logs that were still dry, Sarah getting some snack bars from their packs and handing them out. Jake changed into a black T-shirt, one of their articles of clothing they'd washed during their stay at Nate and Elaine's. Once settled, they sat on the edge of the forest, listening to the rain fall around them with a soft patter on the leaves, drops hitting the forest floor with the shifting of branches and the sighing wind.

"Doing okay?" Alice looked over at her son as he winced and touched his shoulder.

Jake nodded. "It just stings a little. I'll be fine."

"We just need to keep an eye on it and make sure it doesn't get infected. Sarah, you're on duty for that. Make sure your brother gets his dressing changed at least once a day and tell me if it starts looking red and inflamed. You know he'll forget."

"I'm on it," Sarah replied. "Where do you think we are now?"

"I'd guess we're a few miles north of Columbus by now. Hopefully through the worst of it for the time being."

"Yeah, no more people, I hope." Jake snorted.

"No more people with street sweepers," Sarah added.

"What even *was* that?" Jake chuckled. "If they hadn't been shooting at us, it would have been funny. Running a street sweeper offroad and with a bunch of guys hanging off the sides."

"Making use of what they could find that still worked, I guess." Alice looked back in the direction they'd come from, the rain starting to lessen. "They were certainly no Wilford, Nate or Elaine, that's for sure."

After a short break, when the rain finally let up, Alice called for them to get moving again, and they mounted up and headed north along the tree line where birds chatted in low warbles and the staccato hammering of woodpeckers echoed through the woods.

CHAPTER SEVEN

James Burton
Chicago, Illinois

Holed up in the office on the third floor, warm in his soft camp clothes and with a blanket over his shoulders, James took stock of his position again, referencing the maps spread on the desk surface. It had taken an hour, but he'd finally relaxed, shaking off the shudders and shivers that had been constant at first, then tapering off as his cold bones warmed. Rain poured in sheets that were often too thick to see through, sprinkling off the brick, tinkling on the metal fire escape, splashing against his window, and running down in rivulets. There were sharp cracks of lightning, followed by lengthy waves of thunder that rolled lazily on for several long seconds. It was more rain than he'd experienced in a long time, giving the city a feeling of cold, dreariness, and hopelessness.

Sighing, he pulled his blanket around his shoulders tighter and chewed on a high-calorie double chocolate bar he'd found in his backpack, courtesy of the corporal in the refugee camp. The pistol he'd taken off of the man in the alley was beneath all the maps spread in front of him as he tried to develop a plan for where to go based off of where he'd been and where he was.

As best as James could tell, he was somewhere on the south side of Chicago, not a place he'd wanted to be, but driven there by fate and circumstance. Like Denver, the broad warehouse district and surrounding neighborhoods were a mix of intact and burned down, a twisting wasteland of buildings, wreckage, and decay. For the hundredth time, James traced a line from Hannibal to his current position with his finger, dismayed at what it had taken to get so far and what he'd lost along the way.

In circling Springfield, Missouri, he'd run into a sudden horde of refugees fleeing the city. The thousand bedraggled denizens had spotted him on his horse, and a group of able-bodied men had given chase, forcing him to kick Amber into a full gallop to get by, only to run into more people who'd grabbed at him and his supplies and Amber, trying to stop him and pull him off the horse. He'd run them over, fired on them with his rifle, and fought through the throng as they slashed and cut Amber on her flanks and shoulders with knives and machetes. After fording a wide creek south of the city, he'd lost the crowd and sprinted away, camping several miles east along the highway and well out of sight. Amber had grazed in a field that night while he slept outside in the moonlight and a sky full of stars with just a soft bed of sticks and fir branches beneath his bedroll.

He had next run into trouble in Decatur, Illinois, when he'd tried sleeping in an old, abandoned-looking barn only to find it was occupied by people when they returned late in the night from a scavenging run. The small group blocked his way out and demanded James give up Amber and his supplies, but he'd shot two of them after figuring out that they had no firearms, driving them back enough to hop on Amber and flee. They threw bottles and rocks at him, striking him and Amber both a few times before he got away.

He'd reached Champaign, Illinois and circled to the north after seeing massive glowing fires in the central and southern portions of town, and a motorcycle gang caught him on a strip of road between fields. Six of them on a combination of street bikes and dirt bikes chased him along the strip with roaring engines, and he barely made the next field before they overtook him. The dirt bikes pursued him through the rolling pastures and foothills, following James as he raced toward the nearest hill where he'd hoped the gullies and thick woods would be too rough on their machines. But the drivers kept coming, their faces impossible to see in the darkness as they throttled their bikes, spread out, and chased him. They could go almost anywhere he could, forcing him to drive Amber up a steep hill covered with loose deadfall, logs, and a ground full of stiff saplings. One bike had tried to follow him, misjudged a tree, and was knocked off by a branch to send him tumbling down the hill with his bike flipping on top of him. The other two met James at the top of the hill, and he turned Amber past them, narrowly avoiding being shot as a rider went by.

The motorcycles raced along the ridgeline with their engines spitting and sputtering, revving in increasing degrees of volume and pitch as they tore after him. They'd found James waiting atop the hill in a construction lot where several half-built new homes stood on the hillside. He had room to turn Amber and swing his rifle up, and when they flew up a dirt service road into the lot, he unleashed on them, missing the first man completely but hitting the second, first sending up sparks on the steel frame and then landing shots to the man's chest, causing him to fall off the motorcycle. The remaining driver sped to the end of the lot, turned, and stopped to pull out a radio. James assumed he was communicating with the riders on the road, and he fired at the man again, scaring him off and down the hill, dropping the radio under the wheel of his motorcycle in the process.

James had stayed around the construction neighborhood for the next few hours, Amber resting while he patrolled the area with the bit of ammunition he had left. Rain poured in a constant shower that lasted all night, turning the neighborhood into mud. Throughout the evening, motorcycles echoed through the hills, their engines revving as they closed in on him and formed a constricting ring to trap him. Abandoning his position and the temporary roof over their heads, James avoided the dirt road and carefully guided Amber downhill with only sporadic lightning bursts to illuminate the treacherous landscape. He discovered a deer trail leading him into a valley with a creek where Amber drank and rested and for the next hour they kept close to the stream and finally reached the road, using the compass on his staff to stay north, hoping to find an intersection to take him east again.

Two miles later, though, a burst of light came from nowhere out of the trees, and a powerful revving engine exploded to life, followed by the squealing of tires. James flew north again, and Amber's lagging response and heaving breaths told him she'd nearly reached the end of her endurance. After a mile-long chase, the other motorcycles joined in, cutting him off at the next intersection and sending him into the wilderness again, where the man on the dirt bike continued to harass him.

The rest was a blur of maneuvering, circling back on animal trails, flying fast, and sometimes hiding, all in the cold mud and rain as the headlamps pursued him. As Amber had continued to flag, James pushed her to a close cluster of storm-shrouded warehouses and neighborhoods at the edge of the woods. Seeking refuge in the town was pure desperation, but it was all he could think of, especially since the forests were failing him. Unfortunately, the decision had been one that had cost Amber her life in a dark back alley between the buildings. Finger sliding across the paper, he took in a deep breath, trying to fight back the tears as he traced his path one more time, trying to remember the signs he'd passed, the images blurry in his head as he had ridden in mindless panic. *Yeah, I'm in Frankfurt. I'm sure of it.*

Sitting back, he finished the last bite of his MRE, wadded up the packet, and tossed it into a nearby waste can. He hadn't noticed at first because of the boxes of papers and stacks of books on top, but a small couch rested against the east wall, the cushions comfortable and plush, if not threadbare from years of use. He made a bed out of it, putting down his bedroll and using some wadded-up clothes as a pillow. Standing and stretching his aching body, James took one last look through a crack in the blinds before he closed them and shuffled over to the couch, seeking refuge from his guilt and exhaustion.

There was no way he wanted to go out in the pouring rain, so his best bet was to stay inside for the night and possibly try to leave the next day or night, depending on what it looked like. Daylight travel could be safer in some ways and dangerous in others, and the night hadn't proven to be his friend, though he'd be less of a target without Amber. It would be a longer and more challenging road ahead, going on foot, but if he could stay beneath the radar and blend in with his surroundings, he'd still be able to make it. Appearing like someone too down on their luck to have anything of value would help, though would-be predators might not care.

He laid back on the sofa with a long groan and drew the cover over himself, then rolled onto his right side and stared at the dark and dismal room with the flickering shadows of rain on the walls and the slow drips like spiders dropping from strands of silken threads. His plan had always been to avoid entering cities, and he'd largely done that, at least until he was forced to do so – to his and Amber's detriment. Still, with as bad as his situation was, the last place he wanted to go was into Chicago proper and make things a magnitude or three worse. Of all the byways and highways, the cross-sections and adjoining roads, one stuck out in his mind, a long stretch moving west to east a few miles north of him: Highway 30. That was the demarcation line he'd decided meant the difference between being in Chicago and not in Chicago, and he promised himself he'd stay south of it at all costs.

With weariness dragging his eyelids downward and outweighing his frustrations and guilt, he let his eyes fall shut, brought his knees up, and curled up, pulling the cover tight and clenching his arms to his chest as a final shiver ran through him. Alice would tell him to be thankful for what he had. A quiet, warm room. Two exits should he need to escape. Food, maps, and water at his fingertips. Yes, he'd lost a lot of his supplies and he'd lost a fine animal in Amber, but he was still alive, and James wouldn't soon forget Amber or the kindness Eli and his people had shown him. The world had gone mad, but there was still kindness and hope left. Squeezing his eyes tighter only sent tears dripping onto his rollout mat, so he sighed and tried to listen to the rain, hoping it would lull him to a quick and dreamless sleep.

A smattering of distant gunshots and shouts woke him, and he laid still, blinking and listening in the quiet room to the slow drip of water outside his window, the stillness in the drifting dust, the tiniest sliver of gray light of day capturing the motes as they swirled in front of his face.

Another gunshot rang out, followed by two more in rapid succession. A shout of pain came afterward, then one of rage and anguish, causing his heart to beat a couple of paces faster. Swinging his legs off the couch, he sat and took several deep breaths, getting his mind around his situation, remembering where he was and that he was safe for the moment. James gathered his things, feeling his wet clothes to see they'd mostly dried out. The bathroom sink wasn't working, so he relieved himself in the toilet, then scooped out several handfuls of water from the tank to drink, then the rest went into a couple of plastic water bottles from his pack. Avoiding the mirror, James returned to the office and opened the blinds a crack, checking the dreary street with deep puddles everywhere, water glistening off the pavement as a low mist clung to every surface.

There were no signs of movement and had been no gunshots in several minutes, just a drizzle of rain that kept the rivulets on the windows fresh. With an uncertain shake of his head, he returned to the desk and began poring over the maps again. His next choice might be the difference between life and death, or failing to reach his family. He closed his eyes and thought about Alice, her beautiful dark hair running through his fingers like silk, her weight in his arms, and the smell of her body lotion. If she were there, she'd tell him to keep going no matter what and that it wouldn't make a bit of difference if he traveled during the day or night because every second of the road would be fraught with danger. The most important thing was to keep moving, to keep forcing his way through with each step carrying him closer to home.

With his mind made up, James got out of his soft, dry camp clothes and put on his travel gear, still soggy but tolerable. The second he put on his shirt, an unpleasant shudder ran through him. He circled to the maps again, memorizing the surrounding streets, studying the faint marks that were back alleys and the places he could hide if he got into trouble. While it had seemed like a vast city before, it was only a small suburb of Chicago and not the metropolis itself. He could get through it if he kept his head down and moved.

Maps folded and tucked securely away, James held his staff in one hand and tucked his newly-acquired pistol in his outer coat pocket along with the box of ammunition he'd gotten. He listened at the door for a moment, just to be sure no one was rooting around through the building, then quietly opened it and exited the office through the manufacturing floor. Descending the east stairwell, James paused at the bottom to peek through the square window. It was dark on the other side except for small streams of gray light spilling in the warehouse glass, and there were no signs of movement.

He stepped out of the stairwell and walked down the central aisle with machine equipment all around him as he crept to the south side of the building where he found a loading dock in the back, and exited through it to avoid the main street. Off the alley was a small patch of grass, and he suddenly changed course, walked over, squatted, and dug some of the moist ground up, smearing it on his coat and stick and then wiping it on his face. He'd cleaned himself up too much back in the office, he realized, and cleanliness would make him stick out like a sore thumb. Better to be dirty again and blend in than risk catching the eye of some lowlife.

Sticking to the narrow back alleys, James crossed from one block to the next, heart racing, breaths shallow as he kept one eye on the higher windows and one on the shadows. Dumpsters provided hiding spots whenever he caught a suspicious sound or something flitted at the end of the alley. He ran out of large buildings and jogged through back parking lots of still-standing warehouses, sprinting past those that had burned to their foundations.

At one of the corners he'd marked on his map, he found a gas station with its tank bays ruptured, the concrete split and peeled upward, the jagged edges of stone and metal jutting up from the ground. There was a minimart attached to the property, the front end scorched sideways across the brick front, glass shattered, insides gutted. James approached it with his head on a swivel, checking the dark shadows as rain swept in sideways, blown by a sudden gale tearing through the streets. He stepped inside through the blasted front door, searching the empty shelves for scraps of food. Everything had been stripped, but he fell to his knees and looked beneath the shelves, sweeping out several packs of potato chips, some wafer cookies, and loose hard candies. A few bottles of old milk rolled around in the bottom of the refrigerator, long gone bad, but his persistence was rewarded when he found a bottle of apple juice and several bottles of water in the bottom.

He drank the apple juice, the sugar surge giving him a burst of energy within a few minutes of finishing it. After collecting a few more items from the store, he topped off his backpack and started out the front door until two shapes flowed out of the shadows and slipped toward him. Turning quietly on his heels, he slipped out the back door and into an alley, circling back and going east again before they had a chance to pursue him. James stuck to the ruins like a rodent, becoming one with the husk of a city, keeping to the shadows and listening as another spattering of gunshots fired off to the north in counter to the closer ones.

Leaving the warehouse district, he entered smaller neighborhoods with strip malls and smaller buildings and businesses, and he kept to the rear lots and connecting streets to stay out of sight. A burst of violent gunfire ripped from the south, the echoes bouncing off the wet pavement, echoing across the buildings, distorting both the direction and closeness of their origination. The combination of bad weather and urban surroundings confused his ears, and for a moment he imagined being stuck in the city's grip forever, hunted by violence, unable to find a way out. Picking up the pace, James left the cover of a bank drive-through and sprinted for the next corner, seeing the first signs of trees and open fields in the distance.

When gunshots sounded again, they were much closer than before, so close the ricochets off the brick and the shouts of the combatants as they hurled obscenities at each other were crystal clear. When the sound of several pairs of running feet came down the street behind him, James fled the bank and ran for the next corner. Past the rubble of another gas station was a wide-open road leading out of town with the crowded buildings tapering off to subdivisions in the distance. Sensing freedom, he got out ahead of the throng, creeping quickly and quietly, glancing back repeatedly, losing the group in the misty morning streets.

James came to a corner of an intersection, a four way stop with the streetlights hanging from wires, the signs bent sideways from nearby explosions. In front of him, the sidewalk had cracked and fallen in, exposing the sewers beneath the street, raw sewage splashing around the edges as the broken and battered sewers overflowed from the recent rains. A different set of gunshots came from a southbound street, shadows shifted in the gloom, and muzzle flashes flickered in the corners of his vision. They were moving parallel to him but edging in his direction, laughing, cursing and firing their weapons – though at what, he could not say.

The groups would soon converge on one another and James would be caught in between them if he didn't move quickly. In a desperate race to get off the road, James flew across the street and past a strip mall to a grassy lot with a ditch running along the side. With catcalls and whistles behind, James ran hard and jumped into the ditch, which turned out to be a grassy culvert embankment. Raising his feet, sliding down on his backside, he grabbed the edge of a concrete wall and flipped over to land in six inches of water flowing through the culvert pipe. With the violence closing in around him, James quietly squelched toward the circular opening and ducked, huddling on a narrow concrete lip just above the water's edge, waiting to see if the shooters would pass him by.

CHAPTER EIGHT

President Thomas Birk
Mount Weather, Virginia

Agent Harris stood at the door of a side conference room away from Mount Weather's bustling staff. Inside were President Birk, General Pulaski, Marine Colonel Crow, Marine Major Jasmine Spencer, and staffer Cindy Strode. Missing a central table, it was more like a gathering of people about to watch a football game, with their jackets off and hanging from hooks on the walls, sleeves rolled up, ties loosened, sitting in foldout chairs arrayed haphazardly around the screen. Two urns of coffee and a modest assortment of snacks sat on a table against the rear wall.

The mood in the room was upbeat after the news about the Saudis, relief rippling through those in the know over the fact that they'd found the source of the attack, giving them a target for their anger and dismay. Pulaski used a remote to filter through several images on the screen, settling on a couple and discussing something quietly with Colonel Crow. Cool ventilation and the distant rumbling of some generators were the only noises audible outside of the room, reminding Harris of just where they were, deep underground with tons of earth, cement, and steel resting on their heads.

Harris took a step to the side and sipped on a styrofoam cup of tepid coffee before resuming his stiff position with his hands clasped in front of him. His job deep underground in a secure facility was nothing if not boring, and his thoughts turned once again to the loss of his family, filling his heart with warring emotions that clashed with his sense of duty. The few moments he'd had alone in his tiny quarters were a slight reprieve, and he used that time to reflect on his life with his family and shed his tears over their loss.

He'd loved his parents with all his heart. They'd provided him a wonderful atmosphere to grow up in, challenging him to do better and *be* better, supporting his interests as they'd changed over the years. His father had beamed when Harris had told him about being accepted as a Secret Service Agent, and while his mother hadn't been impressed about her son's new job, she warmed to it in the end, encouraging him to find a nice girl to date in Washington, get married, and make her a grandmother as soon as possible.

Losing his parents stung, but it was his little sister's death that cut him the deepest. Even when he was a senior at UVA, Veronica was the person who he spent the most time with, the scrappy tomboy who picked fights with the older boys in the neighborhood, played tackle football in the snow, and hit the gym hard. When he told her about his new career, she'd immediately asked, "When do I get to meet the First Lady?"

"It doesn't work that way, sis."

"Then what are the perks of being your little sister, bro?"

A smile touched him, and his eyes turned glassy as a dozen such conversations ran through his mind, then he shook his head to rid himself of the haunting thoughts lest they draw him deeper into a pit of loss and despair.

"Hey, Harris. Get over here."

Harris stiffened and blinked as the President waved him over and patted the chair next to him. "Come on, agent. Have a seat."

"Pardon me, sir?"

"Sit, please. I want you in on this."

"Are you sure?"

"I'm sure. It's better than standing by the door all day."

"That's my job, sir. I—"

"I'm still the President, Harris. Park your ass."

The agent nodded and stepped briskly to the chair, circling it and sliding into the seat in one smooth motion. General Pulaski and Colonel Crow shot him odd looks but didn't argue with the President.

"What am I looking at, sir?"

"These are satellite feeds over Saudi Arabia we picked up over the past twenty-four hours."

"Don't we have an agreement with Saudi Arabia to refrain from aerial surveillance of their country based on a recent arms deal?"

"That," Birk laughed, "wasn't exactly ever adhered to."

"Mr. President, are you—" General Pulaski started to interrupt, but Birk put up a hand before he could continue. "Harris has my complete trust, General. Relax. Anyway, prior agreements wouldn't mean diddly squat anymore anyway. We need to be positive they're not readying some attack to take advantage of this situation." Birk pointed to the screen. "And these images will show us exactly that." He nodded to General Pulaski. "Go ahead, General."

"Yes, sir."

The heavyset man edged forward on his chair and gestured toward the screen, which showed a saturated image of an area marked *Saudi-Iraqi Border*. All Harris saw were a bunch of crisscrossing highways, the vague outlines of large buildings, and miles of sand. Pulaski flipped through several similar images with unique structures and digital markings Harris figured were for some sort of internal, unknowable processes.

"What you see here is the border between Saudi Arabia and Iraq. Now, if they were readying for some kind of attack or preparing to send forces to aid their allies, you'd see a lot of buildup here, here, and here." Pulaski leaned forward and touched different parts of the screen where major highways seemed to intersect. "But we're not seeing any of that, which leads us to believe the Saudis aren't planning an offensive."

"They *aren't* planning one?" Birk asked, "Or they *can't* plan one?"

"I… wasn't ready to believe it, but we believe it's the latter. They don't have the mechanized divisions or air power to do it." The General clicked through pictures of what appeared to be urban areas with more buildings and streets clustered into sections and dark stains obscuring parts of the city. "This is Riyadh."

Birk gaped. "Is that smoke, General?"

"Yes, sir. It almost completely covers parts of the city and most of the outskirts. It's the same with Jeddah. We reached our embassy in Riyadh, and they've been locked into their buildings with basic communication cut off except for our ultra-secure satellite feed the Saudis aren't aware of. Our people described explosions and chaos in the streets, and we even received some shaky footage from a staffer in a second-floor window."

"What about the border between them and Jordan?"

"No activity whatsoever. These images were taken over two days, sir; we had to reposition some satellite assets after it became clear using strictly visible spectrums would be next to useless thanks to the cloud cover. We would've picked up any minute troop movements after that. There were none. We have images of every Saudi base, from Aziz Air Force Base to Riyadh, and there are clouds over all of them and no signs of armored units moving anywhere – or even left intact. The whole place is a dead zone. They were hit just as hard, if not worse, than everyone else in the world."

Harris raised his hand hesitantly.

"Go ahead, Harris," Birk said.

"I was just wondering. If they created this biological agent, why couldn't they keep it out of their fuel supply?"

"We asked ourselves the same thing," the General replied. "It could be they had a mix-up in their supply chain, or someone sabotaged them from the inside. Analysts are working on it, but between a lack of information plus the general situation in the world at large, we may never know."

"They're in worse shape than us," Birk whispered as he sat back, resting his coffee on his knee and shaking his head. "While we'd all love to exact some revenge for what they've done, I'll not authorize an attack. No sense in wasting resources on bombing a place that looks like *that*."

"I agree with that, sir," Pulaski nodded. "Glad we took our time and looked into it."

"Cindy?"

"Yes, sir?"

"Let's have Secretary of State Lewis reach out to the Saudis through our embassy. I want to set up a meeting with King Nayef and members of his staff to see if they need our assistance in any way. I want to keep our lines of communication open with them without letting them know we're on to them. I want to lean on them *hard* – any chances we have to get intel while keeping the moral high ground are ones I want to take."

"I'll talk to Secretary of State Lewis right away, sir," Cindy said, standing and leaving the room.

Birk turned back to Pulaski. "What about the Russians and Chinese?"

"Shitshows." Pulaski switched the screen view to a coastal region. "This is the East Coast of Kamchatka, where the Russians have several bases we're not supposed to know about. This is their biggest one, and all I see is a smoke cloud. Right there on the edge of the lake."

"Is that the Mengon Air Base?" Birk asked.

"The one and only, or what's left of it that's still burning. And look at this..." The pictures shifted south along the coast into what Harris recognized as China, Japan, and Taiwan. A red dot marked a spot southwest of Hong Kong. "This is China's Yulin Naval Base, which appears to be burning like the rest of the surrounding cities. But look here at these outskirts. See these lines along the highways near the hardest hit areas?"

"What are those?" Birk squinted at them. "Are those military convoys?"

Pulaski shook his head. "We thought so at first, but no." The images magnified with incremental clicks as the lines grew more pixelated. "Those are people and carts. Hundreds and thousands of them, pulled by humans and animals alike. None of it appears to be military."

"What are they doing? Trying to get away from the cities?"

"We think the Chinese government has enlisted the general population to clean up from the disaster. With most of the country being rural and living in what we'd consider to be squalor, they've got a lot more survivors than we do. Many don't have cars or trucks, and they move from village to village on foot or on pack animals."

Harris stared at the image.

"A built-in workforce," Birk said, with no small amount of awe. "And they look exceptionally well organized."

"Because they've been conditioned to be that way for generations." The General snorted. "Most wouldn't bat an eye if they were ordered to switch from farming to clearing rubble in a single day."

"So, the major players don't appear to be taking an aggressive stance?"

"It doesn't appear that way, sir. What we're seeing is a complete breakdown across the world."

"So, the Saudis screwed up," Birk said, "and the rest of the world has to clean up the mess? At least there're no threats from other nations, leaving us to focus on things at home."

"Looks that way."

Birk rested his elbows on his knees and looked across the room. "Alright. In light of this, I want the lion's share of our efforts spent here at home with minimal focus on surveillance of these other countries. Is that clear?"

The group collectively nodded, some referencing their notepads and jotting things in them.

"We're taking too damn long helping our people, and I want us to quadruple our efforts. Some of the reports from the cities have me scared out of my damn mind, I don't mind telling you."

"Law and order is exceptionally difficult right now, sir."

"I don't care." Birk began to stand up. "We're the United States of America. We're *not* going to sit around with our thumbs up our—"

The screen died, the images Pulaski had been showing snapping off in an instant as the lights faded, blinked, and flipped back to full power again. A slight rumble rippled through the walls, and a faint trace of dust trickled from a ventilation duct in the ceiling. Mumbled confusion filled the room as the group stood.

"What's going on, General?" Birk asked, turning as Harris stood as well, moving closer to his ward.

"I don't know, sir, but I'm going to find out." Pulaski took a radio from his belt and spoke into it.

Knuckles rapped hard on the metal door, jerking Harris to attention as he spun, hand resting on his pistol. The door flew open, and a Marine sergeant stuck his head in, face frantic, beads of sweat on his brow.

"Sorry to interrupt," he said. "but we're under attack."

Birk stood and pushed past the General. "What? Who's responsible?"

"I don't know, sir. They sent me to find General Pulaski, and to tell Agent Harris to get you to a safe room immediately."

Harris exchanged a look with Pulaski, and the General grabbed Crow and the others and cleared the room, jaws set as they rushed upstairs. Left alone with Birk, Harris gave him a quiet nod and gestured at the door.

"Right this way, sir."

CHAPTER NINE

Ryan Cooper
Somewhere Outside East Lansing, Michigan

"Can't we put them farther inside the tree line?" Helen panted, leaning on her shovel, wiping her arm across her brow.

They were out on the east side of the property with the five bodies stacked where Ryan had left them the previous day. He was waist-deep in a square pit he'd been digging all morning, sweating, arms and shoulders sore, hands sore in his thick leather gloves. The first two graves were completed, four feet deep and perfectly square on the edges. Ryan had made two more roughly shaped holes where Helen was standing, using the tractor's middle buster to churn up the soil and make it easier to get started, and Helen stood next to the pile of dirt he'd made, taking a break from her turn in the hole.

"I thought about it," Ryan replied, "but I want people to see these graves if they come onto the property again."

"But we can see them, too. Every morning, a reminder of what we did."

"A reminder of what we *had* to do, to defend ourselves," he corrected her gently. When she only glanced at the corpses with a sad frown, he slowly climbed out of the pit and put his arm around her. "I know it's not perfect, and it hurts to know we actually took people's lives, but these graves also serve as a different reminder."

"Which is?"

"It could easily be us instead of them," his tone darkened. "And if you think these people would have given us half the respect we're giving them, you'd be sorely mistaken. I imagine they would've just thrown us out in the woods along with the dogs after they put them down."

Helen's frown deepened. "That's a terrible thought."

"That's why I'm leaving the graves out here as a reminder. To their friends of what we'll do to defend ourselves, and to us that we must always be vigilant."

"I... this world. I don't like it, Ryan. I don't like what it's become and what it's turning us into."

He kissed her forehead and hopped back into the grave, staggering a little on the loose soil before plunging the shovel tip into the dirt and leaning on it. "Best way I know of to deal with it is to just keep digging."

"Move over. I want to keep helping."

It was Ryan's turn to frown. "That's not necessary, hon. I'd hoped to get this all taken care of before you even noticed it."

A tear streaked down Helen's cheek as she leaned her shovel against the tractor. "That's awful sweet of you, but we're equal partners in all of this, both the good times and the bad, the rewards and the burdens."

Ryan stared at her for a long moment and then nodded. "Fair enough. You can start moving that loose dirt out of the other two graves. Just drag it over to the main pile, and I'll use the tractor to push it over top of them after we lower them inside."

The next two hours were a grueling exercise in hard, unforgiving manual labor, digging being the hardest work he'd ever done, even more so than the farming, and by the time they had all five graves carved into the earth, Ryan was beyond sore, his wounded calf aching beyond belief, his arms and shoulders weak and shaking. Helen's white T-shirt was covered in dirt, the front of her jeans stained dark, her once white tennis shoes turned brown. The sun crept higher above them, filling the increasingly blue skies with light and glinting off the majestic red maples lining the lane. Birds kept them company as they labored, and the trees seemed reverent in their gentle rustling as the constant breezes ebbed and flowed to soothe their sweat every time they popped their head out of one of the holes.

"Why are you grinning?" Helen asked, stopping to lean on her shovel, wiping the sweat with a dirt-stained sleeve.

"Don't worry about it. It's silly."

"No no, I want some of that positivity you've got going on."

"Well," he smiled, "I couldn't help but think how fast the batteries are charging right now and how much juice we must have in the house."

Helen smiled and looked up, shielding her eyes with her hand. "It's a beautiful day. Prettiest one in a long while. Makes me want to just sit out back and relax, if we didn't have so much to do."

"We should be finished here soon, then we can get back on with what we *need* to be doing. Plenty left to get done so we're ready for when James, Alice, and the kids come home. I want them to be shocked by how well we've kept things here."

Helen nodded, winking at him. "The bullet holes will be a real shock, I'm sure."

Ryan laughed and the pair got back to their work, Helen clearing the last grave, then Ryan jumping in and digging deeper with the shovel, finding a rhythm to the work, fighting through the pain and discomfort, plowing through the last foot of dirt quickly and thoroughly. Finally, he leaned on the side of the grave with a groan.

"Are you okay, dear?"

"I'm fine," he replied, climbing out, unwilling to let himself rest. "I just want to finish with this and move on. Let's put them in now."

Ryan's shirt was soaked with sweat, and with both of them out there, he didn't bother using the tractor to lower the bodies in. Instead, he took their arms while Helen took their feet, and together they moved them to their respective graves, stooping to lower them as far as they could before dropping them in. Ryan avoided looking at their faces and thinking about who they'd been before everything had happened, people with families, hopes and dreams who'd made enough bad choices to wind up being buried on the edge of a field.

He started up the tractor and used the bucket to shove the dirt over the graves, filling them to overflowing, then ran across the graves with the tires and bucket to tamp them down until there were five neat mounds sitting side-by-side, deep and covered well enough to keep the smells buried so that scavengers wouldn't be able to dig them up. After getting out and surveying their work, Ryan threw the tools in the bucket and started to climb into the tractor when Helen gently grabbed his arm.

"I... think we should say something, don't you?"

"We've done a lot for them already," Ryan said, pausing. "We could have left them for the coyotes—"

"But we didn't, because that's not the kind of people we are. They were our enemies, but they've passed beyond this world now. It's still our duty to try to be the better people, in some form or fashion. "

Ryan backed out of the tractor and eyed the graves warily. "I'm not sure I'd know what to say to them."

"You'll think of something. Anger, forgiveness, something in between... whatever it is you have to say, we shouldn't leave this unfinished." She took his hand in hers and squeezed gently, and he nodded and stepped over to the graves.

"I... know where I'm headed when I die, and I sure hope you all knew, too, because it's too damn late now. Ya'll might have been good people before all this started, or maybe not. This sort of a thing'll turn a good man bad before he even realizes it. But either way, I forgive you for trying to kill myself and my wife and take what belongs to our family." Ryan's throat constricted as the tumultuous emotions flowed through him. "And I hope and pray with every fiber of my being that we never have to kill like this again. I'll do my best to keep it from happening. But if we have to – we will. May God have mercy on you and keep your families from harm."

Helen was nodding by the time Ryan stopped speaking, and whispered quietly, barely loud enough for him to hear.

"Amen."

Ryan followed Helen from the chicken coop down to the house and into the kitchen, with baskets of eggs in their arms, faces and hands dirty from the digging, feeding the animals and doing some general cleanup. They placed their baskets on the breakfast bar and washed up, turning and smiling at one another as they dried off their hands and leaned against the counter.

"Another day's work done," Ryan said, crossing his arms. "And here I was thinking that we were done with farming when we retired."

"Just when you thought you were out, they pull you right back in." Helen laughed. "We've still got to bring down the milk from the barn. You'll have to run that ATV every day to bring those containers down. That'll make a lot of noise."

"I'll use the wheelbarrow from now on."

Helen frowned. "Oh, I wasn't saying that. You do not need to be straining those legs of yours, and if that means I need to help out or you need to use the ATV more, then do it. It's not like the gasoline is going to stay good forever, after all."

"Still... better to draw less attention. And the leg is feeling better, too; I should be able to walk them down without too much hassle."

"You're not as young as you used to be, Ryan Cooper," Helen crossed her arms. "You've got to let yourself heal. A *bullet* went through your *leg*. Even if it didn't do any permanent damage, it's still no minor injury."

"I'm not as young as I used to be, but I'm at least twice as tough."

"Tough? Ha!" Helen laughed. "Stubborn, you mean."

"Another truth," Ryan grinned before sobering. "But I can get the job done without running that ATV. The best thing we can do is to keep a low profile. If it means me going through more pain to do it, I will."

Helen wrapped her arms around him, resting her head on his chest. "I know you will. But don't overdo it. It won't do either of us any good if you run yourself into the ground. If you start hurting too bad, either use that ATV, or tell me so I can help you out, okay?"

Ryan hugged her and breathed in deep as she squeezed him back. "I'm glad the tough work is done... that was rough, seeing them like that."

"Sorry again about where we put the bodies."

"No, it's like you said, we want anyone else who tries to come out here to think two or three times before they pull anything. Still... doesn't make the process any easier."

Ryan turned to the sink to get a glass of water. "I'm glad we did it. When this all blows over we might have some explaining to do to the authorities, but, well... better to be judged by twelve and all that."

Helen nodded. "And, in cheerier news, my secret concoction got the bloodstains out of the carpet. It looks almost brand new."

"Whatever you used worked, though I won't easily forget what that woman's face... sorry." Ryan shut his mouth and took a sip of water. "Trying to get off the subject just brings it back around."

"The dogs did their job. It's all we can ask for from them."

"That they did. A little *too* well, maybe. How's Duke been?"

"Still limping, but more when he wants a treat."

"He knows how to play you. Don't fall for it."

Helen laughed. "I don't mind, really. He deserves it after what he did to help save us. Speaking of food, what would you say to me fixing us a snack? We need to finish up the leftovers."

"Only if you'll let me help make it."

They re-heated two half-eaten omelets from earlier and a large bowl of a boxed tuna meal they'd made the previous evening. Arms full, they took everything to the dining room and set it down, going back for cups of water and freshly pasteurized milk. Before they sat, Helen walked to the window and peered through the plywood pieces, gasping at something outside.

Ryan was chewing a bite of his omelet when he looked at her. "What is it, honey? Is something out there?"

"Not something, some*one*. But..."

Ryan threw down his fork with a clatter, grabbed his Winchester off the table, and kicked his chair back. Joining her at the still-intact window, he spread the blinds wider and glared into the yard through gaps in the wood. "Where are they?"

"At first, I wasn't sure." Helen tapped the glass. "Then I caught the movement way down by the fence."

"What in the world?" Ryan had been looking at the woods on the east side of the property but shifted attention to the driveway. "Is she waving a white flag?"

"I think so. Grab the binoculars?"

Ryan swept the binoculars off the table and pressed them to the window, focusing them in on a tall woman with brown hair down at the very end of the driveway, one hand resting on the gate and the other waving a stick with a white rag tied to the end.

He handed over the binoculars. "Any clue who that is?"

Helen checked. "Nope, I've never seen her in my life. Might be one of the neighbors from down the road."

"She looks young, maybe late twenties, but I can't be sure from here. Looks like she's alone, but impossible to tell with the tree cover."

"What are you going to do?" Helen asked, then shot him a skeptical look. "You're not going down there, are you?"

"Are you kidding? I'm absolutely not going down there. That's a trap if I ever saw one." He hefted his rifle. "I'll take the shot with the Winchester from the front porch."

Helen's eyebrows went up. "Wait a second. There's no need to shoot her."

"Isn't there?"

"How do you know she's with the group who attacked us? And you can't just shoot someone waving a white flag. What if she really needs help?"

Ryan pursed his lips and sighed in annoyance. "You know what I'm going to say to that."

"That we can't trust anyone, I know. So let's watch her for now. Just hold off on doing any shooting until she comes onto the property, okay?"

"I..." Ryan's mouth opened and closed a few times before his shoulders dropped. "Okay. We'll do it your way." He set the rifle and binoculars on the table, grabbed his plate, and moved back to stand near the window, watching the woman as he ate.

Helen brought him a scoop of tuna, and he finished eating while on guard, occasionally putting his fork down to raise his binoculars and check on the woman. When they were done with lunch, Helen took their plates into the kitchen while Ryan remained vigilant, his frown growing with every passing minute. The woman continued her flag-waving, switching arms when one grew tired, her expression hard to read from such a distance. Ryan watched her head movements to see if she was checking for any accomplices waiting off to the sides behind the trees, but she seemed singularly focused on their house and getting their attention. Helen took his place for an hour while Ryan cleaned up around the house, but when he came back to check, nothing had changed, except that the woman was swapping the flag between hands more frequently and the waving was done with less intensity than before.

"If she wants to stand out there all day, let her," he fumed. "It's nothing to us. Maybe she'll drop out of exhaustion."

"We won't get anything done standing here," Helen replied. "Why don't you get the milk from the barn, and I'll keep watch."

"We can't be sure they're not waiting to take a shot at us. And in case you didn't notice, I'm not exactly Flash Gordon these days."

She placed her hand on his shoulder. "It's the middle of the day, and if they were going to attack us, it would have already happened. Take Duchess to the barn with you. She'll sniff out anyone lurking in the shadows."

Ryan frowned and rested his hand on his rifle. "You know what? You're absolutely right. We can't let them scare us into hiding. We've got animals to care for."

"That's right. Go on, and I'll keep an eye on her. Why don't you take one of James' radios, too? I'll keep the other one with me. "

"I'll grab them." Ryan went into the kitchen where the radios were charging and brought them back, giving one to Helen while hooking the other on his belt. "You know what to do, Annie Oakley."

Helen gave him a bemused salute, and Ryan called for Duchess, attaching her leash and taking her out to the shed along with the wheelbarrow. The woods were still, a heavy silence settling over the farm as the breezes died down, making the woman down at the gate an even more ominous presence. Up at the barn, he picked up the containers of Bessie's milk and brought them to the house, setting them inside the door. By the time he returned to the dining room window, he was tired and sweating, and the expression on Helen's face told him the woman still hadn't left.

"She's still out there," she said, confirming it. "Hasn't moved and keeps waving her flag. I have to give it to her, she's got some endurance. My arms would be dead tired if I did that."

"That's it," Ryan snapped. "I'm going down there to run her off once and for all."

"What about the trap?"

"You can cover me, but this is getting on my nerves and needs to be put to a stop."

"You want me upstairs?"

"Watch me from the upper floor with your gun, just like before. I'll take Duchess with me in the back seat of the EV."

"You're taking the car?"

"They already know we have it, and it'll enable a fast getaway should I need to make one."

Helen looked back at the woman through the binoculars. "Promise me you'll at least hear her out, okay?"

Ryan groaned, starting to roll his eyes, then relenting. "Yeah, I guess I'll listen. If I don't like what she has to say, though, I'll run her off."

"Fair enough." Helen nodded while Ryan took Duchess outside and walked gingerly to the EV, putting the dog in the back before climbing behind the wheel.

His right calf was stiff, forcing him to put the seat back a few inches so he could stretch. The EV still had a twenty-five percent charge, an alert on the dashboard reminding him to charge it soon.

"Better plug it into the house soon. Doubt we'll need it charged all the way up, but better to have it and not need it." Ryan glanced back when Duchess whined. "There's a good girl. We're just going for a quick ride. Don't worry, it's not a vet visit."

He pulled around through the side yard and onto the driveway, rolling down the gravel road between the statuesque trees, a group of ducks fluttering out of the way from where they were crossing over the gravel. Ryan slowed and checked for movement in the woods and in the brush crowding the fences, but all was dark and quiet. Thirty yards from the gate, he pulled right into the grass and made a complete circle, staring at the woman as he passed. She'd quit waving the flag and stood there with both hands on the top rail, expression neutral as she watched him.

He'd been right about her age: late twenties, maybe early thirties, with dark hair, brown eyes, and a face full of fear and hope all at the same time. There were bruises on her arms and one of her eyes looked darker than the other; someone had put her through the wringer, or perhaps things outside the farm were even harder than they seemed. Once he had the EV pointed back toward the house, he paused and took stock of his surroundings, using his binoculars to check that Helen was sitting quietly in the second-floor window.

With a grunt of discomfort, he slowly got out and stood still with his gun in hand, hesitating another moment to listen and watch along the front fence and tree line. He popped the back door open, ordering Duchess to stay but giving her a way out if he needed her. The woman seemed vaguely familiar as he approached her, though he couldn't put a name to her face or say where he'd seen her before. Ryan came ahead with his rifle in both arms, keeping it loose and at the ready, stopping fifteen yards from the gate and the woman standing behind it.

"Who are you, and what do you want?" He was overly gruff, intentionally so, and pushed back the guilt over his impoliteness.

An uncertain smile tugged at the woman's mouth, and when she turned her head, he could see the remnants of a deep, old bruise on her left eye. "Glad you came out. I was getting tired. You'd think a stick wasn't all that heavy, but —"

"Who the hell are you, and what the hell do you want?" Ryan growled, looking around and still seeing no signs of subterfuge.

She stuttered. "I-I'm Sandy Crenshaw. W-wife of Chase. We live just down the road and—"

"Was Chase one of the men who attacked us the other night?"

She glanced away for a moment, hesitating, then the words came out in a rush. "I... yes. Yes he was. Look, sir, I've got a sick child. He's in a bad way and needs antibiotics, if you have any. I don't have anywhere else to turn—"

"Oh, that's rich," he laughed, genuinely amused at her brazenness. "Oh, you've got a lot of nerve, *Sandy*. Why should we help you when you attacked us?"

Sandy rested her hands on the rail, pleading with him. "I... what he did was wrong, okay? But I swear I wasn't involved. He was... I told him not to go, not to trust Jack, not to try and steal from other people but he did anyway and... I can guess what happened to him. He never came home, and my child is sick. I can't..." Her eyes turned glassy as emotion welled in her chest. "I can't lose him. He's a good boy, he's not like his daddy – I hope he never turns out to be like his daddy, truth be told – and he doesn't deserve to die like this. Please, if you've got any kind of heart..."

Ryan's curled lip slowly lowered as he listened to her, the mention of the boy short-circuiting his planned retort to the woman's begging. "Your son's sick?"

"Yes."

"Son of a..." Ryan groaned and sighed heavily. "What's his name?"

"Stephen."

"What are the symptoms?"

"He won't eat but a little soup and water. Cold even though he sits close to the fire and he's got a temperature pushing a hundred and one. Hasn't been this sick since he was a baby."

"Sounds like an infection. Could be viral, but how long's it been going on?"

"A few days now. Keeps getting worse."

"Probably bacterial, if I had to guess." Ryan rubbed the bridge of his nose. "And you say you live close by?"

"About six houses down."

"There a reason you came to us instead of friends of you and your husband's?"

"I-I didn't know what else to do. The others are... they're all bickering and fighting and don't have much in the way of supplies. Plus, I figured since Chase didn't come back, that ya'll were still standing."

"Bold of you to come seeking help from the people your friends and family attacked and tried to steal from."

"I—"

"What makes you think we'd help you after what your people did to us?"

Sandy's expression dropped. "I-I just thought I'd come down and ask nicely. Not for my sake. For my son's."

Ryan's resolve cracked, just a bit, and he searched her eyes for any signs of a lie before sighing. "All right, Sandy. Meet me here tomorrow, and I'll see what I can do. I'm not promising *anything*, understand me?"

Sandy's eyes widened at Ryan's unexpected response. "I understand. Thank y—"

Ryan bristled, his frustration boiling over, with Sandy the only person to direct his anger toward. "Your people – your *husband* – shot at us. Tried to kill my wife and me! Shot clear though my damned leg!" Ryan took a deep breath and released it slowly. "I should just put a round through your head to keep more problems from coming up." Sandy gulped, taking a couple of small, shuffling steps back before Ryan rolled his eyes and held up a hand. "I'm not going to. Just... I'm pissed off, understand, Sandy? If you people had come to talk *first* then we could have been working together from the start instead of dealing with this bull!"

"I'm sorry for that," she replied softly. "I can't make up for what my husband and the rest did. What he did..." Her voice dropped as she rubbed absently at her bruised arm. "Please, if you can, I'm begging you to help my son."

Ryan started to step back, shaking his head. "Not now. I need to think this over some more. Tomorrow morning, be at this gate, and come alone. Bring something to trade, and I'll try to see what I can do."

Her whole person melted in gratitude. "Thank you, thank you! Stephen and I both appreciate it. You bet I'll be here. Thank you again...."

"Ryan. And listen, Sandy? Just one more thing." Ryan spoke the words through clenched teeth, holding the butt of the rifle against his shoulder. "If I even *think* you aren't alone or that you're trying to pull something, I'll shoot you before you can make a move, and I'll bury you next to the rest of the assholes who tried to kill me. Got it?"

Sandy nodded as tears broke from her eyes. "Yes, I-I mean no. Yes. Of course. Thank you! I'll see you here first thing in the morning."

Turning and nearly tripping as she went, Sandy quickly walked back the way she'd come with her flag stuck in her pocket, up the road past the neighbor's house where she disappeared out of sight around a bend. After she was gone, Ryan closed the back door of the car, got in, and drove back to the house, swinging around the rear and parking between the solar panels and harvested crops they still had yet to process. Inside, Helen greeted him excitedly as the smell of fresh-brewed coffee began filling the air.

"Well, what did she say?"

Ryan leaned on the counter and released Duchess from her leash. "*She* is someone who claims to be named Sandy. Said her husband was involved in the attack on us. Said his name was Chase Crenshaw. Ring a bell?"

"Nope."

"I figure we must have buried him because he never came home, according to her."

"Well, what does she want?"

"She said her son is sick. Sounds like an infection. I'm guessing bacterial because it's been getting worse and worse, or so she says."

"Mm. Alice stored some broad-spectrum antibiotics upstairs in the hall cupboard. Could spare a few."

"True, but those are valuable pills, and we might need them someday."

"Fair. What'd you tell her?"

Ryan unslung his rifle and set it on the breakfast bar. "I told her I'd think about trying to find something her son could use, but it wouldn't be free. Thinking about it more on the way back up to the house... I figure she'll have to make us a great deal if she wants them."

CHAPTER TEN

Ricardo Braga
Rio de Janiero, Brazil

Sprawling favelas ran up the hillsides, brightly colored homes standing atop one another, filling in every nook and cranny both low and high, with terraced verandas jutting from the upper floors to peer out over the ocean. The skies were dark, yet the city was alight with both electric bulbs and candlelight that bathed the slope in a golden ambiance and glinted off the waves.

Boats out in the harbor had burned and sunk, the warehouses having gone up in flames or were already looted, many in the lower favelas living like despot kings. Along the shoreline, taxis, cars, and delivery trucks had caused raging blazes that had devoured entire sections of the city, leaving almost a million dead with fires still occasionally turning the skies orange several days later as some new source of fuel went up in smoke. Unlike those in western cities, the citizens of Rio de Janeiro had largely come together to keep the fires at bay, working in shifts to carry buckets of water up from the ocean and reservoirs, fighting tooth and nail for their homes and lives. Communities had absorbed displaced citizens even as the hotels and tourist spots along the shoreline curled with smoke and flames.

The worst had seemed to be over, but when the more affluent people living in the heights demanded harsh punishment for a poor boy who'd stolen from them, it kicked off a clash between the citizens. Underlying class tensions roared to the forefront, fights broke out, and genuine fear rippled through the city as it straddled a fine line between order and chaos. Unruly citizens overwhelmed the high-rise homes out on Irmaos Point, looting, destroying, and putting them to the torch while the surrounding favelas remained unspoiled, Christ the Redeemer standing atop Mount Corcovado, overlooking the city with outstretched arms.

Ricardo Braga and his family sat in their home around a small kitchen table with modest decorations on the walls, a large wooden crucifix, and an image of Jesus above the doorway. Lanterns burned in the corners and sat on the windowsill, filling the room with a warmth that contrasted with the soft sounds of the ocean in the background. Marcia stirred a big pot of barbecued beef and corn, the rich smells drifting through their home. The short, dark-haired woman stood over the pot and sprinkled a few spices across the top, stirring, tasting it again, finally giving a sharp nod.

"This is ready, my loves," she said, using a pot handle to grab the cast iron pan and moving around the table to serve each one of their five children heaping spoonfuls of it, stopping at Ricardo's plate and dishing him an extra amount.

"Take some back and divide it between the children," he told her. "This is too much for me."

"Nonsense," she said with a smile. "Look at these round bellies. Everyone is eating well, thanks to you, Ricardo. Such a good and loving husband." She held the hot pan away, leaned in, and kissed him on the cheek before heading back to the stove and setting the pan down with a clank.

Ricardo's heart swelled with pride, watching his three daughters and two sons eat. "It is only by God's grace I have the strength to take care of my loving family. There is nothing I wouldn't do for you. Let us pray."

Ricardo gave his heartfelt thanks to God for their good fortune, their health, and the meal they were about to eat. With an "Amen,' he picked up his fork and ate while Marcia turned up the radio, and an official-sounding government voice filled the room.

"... Brazilian government continues to request all citizens stay indoors, shelter in place, and report any looting to the local authorities." Ricardo scoffed. "Looting of any sort will not be tolerated, and President Manuel has declared the act of stealing punishable by death..."

"Could you please turn that off, Marcia?"

"Why?"

"I can't stand hearing them prattle on about what *we* should do and all the promises they make to protect us. They only want to control our lives."

"It was a terrorist attack, Ricardo. No one could have seen this coming."

Ricardo scoffed louder. "But they should stop making empty promises. Nothing will change, and our people will always be exploited... more so now than ever!"

"I need to know what is happening. I need this radio on, Ricardo. Please?"

"Very well. Maybe they will say something worth listening to soon. But we would be fools to expect someone to come and rescue us. They will only try to save those at the top of the mountains first, while the rest of us are on our own. That's okay, because we don't need them, anyway. We're doing just fine."

"We're holding on by a string," Marcia reminded him. "And there are rumors of a mass relocation."

"Why would we move? We have everything we need right here."

Marcia shrugged. "They are only rumors."

The kids finished their meals and were excused from the table, and Marcia called after them to clean their rooms before they went to their cousin's.

Ricardo ate his last bite and started to get up to clean his plate when Marcia bade him sit. "I'll clean up. Rest a few more minutes before you leave."

"Thank you." He folded his hands in front of him as Marcia poured him a half cup of water from the jugs they kept in cool storage in the floor.

"I'll stop by the market today and buy a week's supplies if the prices are still low."

"The markets will continue to stabilize, and the vendors will have things under control again soon. The ships can't run, but we can do without imports. They've switched to local farms now. Beef will still be quite high, but pork will be cheap. Buy more of that until the price for beef comes down."

"I'll look for it," Marcia nodded, "and plenty of fruits and vegetables, too. The cost of corn has actually gone down. Can you believe that? I thought people would try to take advantage of the situation, but everyone has been so kind in the markets. No lines, no fighting, and everyone getting what we need."

"It is a testament to our people. We go through so much, but we always persevere."

"My only concern is the value of our money. What if the Real becomes worthless?"

"The vendors at the market will honor it still, out of pride. If not, we still have the valuables beneath the floor."

Marcia stood by him with her arm resting across his shoulders. "Heirlooms and things I'd rather not part with."

He patted her hand. "It should not come to that, dear. Ah, it's time for me to go." At the door, Ricardo hugged and kissed her. "Keep an eye out, dear. If you see looters, let Lucas know. He'll know what to do."

"I will. Have a good day."

Ricardo said goodbye to his kids, laughing as they all stormed in and hugged him, then he was out the door, descending the winding stairwell, crossing a short bridge to another landing, and smiling at the family sitting on their porch. He climbed down a steel ladder that creaked and groaned under his weight and at ground level he jumped off and landed on the cobblestone street, staggering a bit before heading along the winding lane to the construction site where they were clearing debris from a badly scorched collapse.

Dogs barked and citizens shouted up into the heights, and the distant sound of music came warbling in on the wind from the direction of the market area, filling him with a sense of peace he couldn't explain. People pushed carts packed with goods, carried baskets, and traded on street corners. They'd turned small warehouse buildings into hospitals where the injured could receive care. Nearby parks bustled with children and mothers. *It's truly a miracle,* he thought.

Ricardo moved with a hop in his step, entering the lower levels along the shoreline where the smell of char stung his nose and eyes. Around a bend in the hill where the tourist restaurants used to be, the scene opened to a blackened hillside with a spillage of bricks and steel, glass and furniture in an ever-shifting pile of junk. People stood on the outskirts with gloomy faces, watching and waiting and hoping beyond hope for their lost family members to walk out of the rubble. Workers just coming off shift dragged their feet as they left the work site, smears of dirt on their masks, their gloves pitch black, some bleeding from cuts and scrapes.

Ricardo waved to Darius and Miguel, took an air filtration mask from his foreman, and joined the work. As he entered, men stepped past him carrying timbers, scorched furniture, and sometimes a corpse on a bloody, filthy gurney, a thin sheet or piece of tarpaulin draped over the still forms. He fell into line with all the others, grabbing an enormous chunk of stone and handing it to the person behind him. More debris followed, an endless conveyor of rubble, winding like a snake into the thickest part of the collapse. While the bulk of the workers concentrated their efforts on one spot, others climbed over the hillside like insects, using blunt objects to bang on things, seeking out survivors and testing the stability of the structures.

Panting in the stifling mask, face hot even as the breeze off the ocean cooled his neck, Ricardo fell into a trance-like rhythm, becoming one with his fellows as the foreman guided them to new spots to dig. The head of the line turned upward, and Ricardo found himself on a steep part of the hillside with his feet spread apart, balancing as he handled heavy rubble, his hands sweaty and blistered inside his work gloves. After another hour, he was ready for a break, throat parched and desperate for a single glass of water. An explosion of noise and shouts filtered down, and word reached them that someone was buried alive in the hillside. All eyes shifted upward, sweaty faces hoping for a miracle. The second it was confirmed, workers ran up the treacherous slope, forming a new line where the foreman was pointing. Men with sledge-hammers, axes, and a jackhammer turned large chunks into manageable pieces, and wheelbarrows were brought up, filled to overflowing, and wheeled down on plywood ramps.

Ricardo worked his way up the hill, loading, carrying, and dropping big chunks of debris into the wheelbarrow until his hands were raw and bleeding even under his gloves. Off to the right, a group of people cheered and shook their fists as a woman was pulled from the wreckage, clothes torn, her face covered in dust, knees shaking as they led her to the waiting medical staff. Exhausted and applauding, Ricardo thought they were done, but workers raised their hands and flocked to another section as more soft bangs came from the rubble. Laughing giddily in disbelief, Ricardo stepped out of line and climbed up to be with the lead rescuers. An entire house had crumbled on the slope, spilling on top of several others, forming a bubble of wooden beams, chicken wire and steel rods they used to reinforce the structures, with bricks, mortar and dust everywhere.

The main body of workers stood off to the right, scooping aside big chunks, gesturing for more wheelbarrows to be brought up. As the minutes wore on, the workers grew impatient, throwing up their hands in frustration. Ricardo had worked in the caves and deep in the hulls of ships, and he knew how sound traveled. It could be tricky, and reverberations in steel and stone were difficult to track. He remembered searching through an entire ship for a half day before locating the origins of a mysterious pinging noise ringing up through the decks, narrowing it down to a steel shaft coming off the rudder.

He drifted off to the left by himself, staggering on weak legs, finding a flat spot in front of the spill, kicking random rocks and debris out of the way, falling to one knee, hands settling on the stones. Resting, breathing quietly, he prayed that whoever was stuck in there would strike something and make a sound that would reach him through all that rock. When it did a few seconds later, he could hardly believe it, the faint *clink* barely audible above all the rest of the din.

Whipping off his gloves, he rested his blistered fingers on the stone, whispering a prayer, begging them to hit it again. The next clink vibrated through his fingertips, metal on stone, the strikes weaker than before, and something deep within him told him time was running out. Ricardo worked his way back and forth across the ruins, touching different places and getting a feel of where the knocking was coming from. He fell to his knees and crawled beneath a lip of dangling stone, spotting the top half of a window frame, glass hanging off in jagged shards, the area beyond it pitch black beneath tons of rubble. There was only a foot of space, but he used a stick to knock out the sharp glass and thrust his head and shoulders inside.

"Hello! Is anyone in here?! Can you hear me?!"

The clanking came again, repeated whacks, Ricardo's heart leaping as he crawled in farther until his waist squeezed through the window frame and dust trickled on his head. He hollered again, but his air filtration mask muffled his voice. Lying on his belly, squeezed between tons of rock, he tried to get it off, but the space was too confined, and he had to back out and whip the mask off before diving forward again.

"Hello! Are you in here?" Remembering his flashlight, he unhooked it from his belt, flipped it on, and shined it into the darkness. A maze of piled stones stretched out ahead of him, just a few feet of space in any direction, shards of wood and steel jutting everywhere. "Hello? Answer me if you can!"

"Yes, I'm here," came the weak reply, a boy's voice filled with pain and fear. "Help me? *Please!* I'm here!"

A sudden rush of adrenaline hit Ricardo. "Are you hurt?"

"There's a rock on my leg, and Mama... she's dead, I think."

Ricardo's heart sunk, both for the boy's mother and in doubt that they could get the child out with a stone resting on his leg.

"Okay, I hear you. We're coming to get you. Don't move."

Despite the slim odds, Ricardo backed out of the hole, got to his knees, and stood. By then, a crowd had gathered around, the foreman grabbing him by the shoulders and shaking.

"Did you find someone?"

Ricardo embraced him and grinned wider. "Yes, there's a little boy in there. He's alive and talking."

The crowd roared with joy, and hands slapped his back.

"He is alive," Ricardo repeated, "but he has a rock on his leg, and his mother is in there with him, dead."

The foreman's face went ashen. "He's been in there the whole time with his mother's corpse? Poor boy. We must get him out."

The foreman stepped up on a tall stone to address the growing throng with a loud, booming voice. "This rubble has a rounded shape, so there must be some support below it. We will pull pieces off the top and try to lighten the load. Let's get to work!"

They attacked the hill of debris in a swarm, rolling off huge rocks, tossing the smaller ones way off to the side, leaving the longer beams jutting up to keep the support structure intact. From the air it would have appeared as though the mound took on a life of its own, the pieces of rubble shifting, the people groaning as a large section collapsed and fell in. Everyone stopped working, staring at each other until the mound finally settled into stony silence.

Ricardo fell to his knees and crawled in, shouting beneath the window frame. "Are you still with us? Are you there?"

After a painful pause, the child's voice graced his ears. "Yeah, I'm okay. What was that noise?"

"It was the rubble shifting. That was our fault. It won't happen again. What is your name, child?"

"Rafael."

"Okay, Rafael. Don't be afraid. I'll be right back." Ricardo stood. "He's okay, but we shouldn't move any more rubble. Someone must go inside and pull him out."

The foreman nodded and drew in some people around them, leaving Ricardo standing by the opening, eyeing it, shifting from one foot to the other as he measured up his chances of reaching Rafael. Someone ran off and returned a moment later with a diminutive female worker who barely weighed a hundred pounds.

"This is Rosa," the foreman said. "She is the smallest of us. She volunteered to go inside and save the child."

Rosa stepped forward and stripped off her mask and gloves, staring at the narrow entrance with a determined expression. Workers behind her gathered some rope and started tying it around her waist, but the fear of crawling into the enclosed space - into the darkness beneath tons of rubble - finally got to her and tears began streaming down her face.

Ricardo grabbed the rope and took it off her, turning, tying it to himself. "I'll go inside."

"Ricardo, no," the foreman said. "You won't fit."

"I am no large man," Ricardo replied. "I've seen what it looks like inside, and I can fit. Plus, large stones might require my strength to move." He turned to Rosa. "Thank you... bless you... but I will do this, Rosa. Just remember to pull me out when I tug."

Rosa smiled and nodded, and as Ricardo faced the opening, the workers patted his back and shouted words of encouragement.

"Come on, Ricardo."

"You can do it!"

"We'll pray for you. God will go with you!"

Taking deep breaths like he was about to dive into a pool, Ricardo laid on his belly and flipped on his flashlight. The twisting curves of rubble looked the same, passages cutting into the pile of loose debris, like the tunnels of an anthill. Before fear and doubt could overtake him, he crawled inside, advancing past the window, wiggling ahead, pulling himself over tiny mounds of stone and squeezing beneath a wide beam of wood, stopping to shine the light around.

"Rafael, can you hear me?"

"Yes, I hear you," he called back with a whimper. "Are you going to get me out now?"

"Yes, I'm coming in now. No more delays. By the way, my name is Ricardo."

"Okay, Ricardo. Thank you."

Ricardo shook his head, admiring him for remembering to be polite despite the fact that he must be shaking with terror. As they talked, Ricardo had been tilting his ear, trying to pinpoint Rafael's direction, sensing he was off to the right. "Okay, son. I need you to keep talking to me so I can tell where you are."

"What should I talk about?"

Ricardo started crawling to his right with sounds close around him, trickling pebbles, the smooth sifting of sand and dust and a larger, deeper rumble reverberating beneath them, the shifting hillside, a tomb for the living and the dead. Shaking the terrible thoughts off, Ricardo crept along in increments, trying not to think more than a few seconds ahead at a time.

Have to keep moving... have to work deeper before you freeze completely. Talk to him... talk to Rafael.

"Tell me about your Ma —" He caught himself. "I mean, tell me about your brothers and sisters. Do you have any of those?"

"Yeah," came the timid reply. "I have one brother... Antonio. I have a sister, too."

"What's her name?"

"Emila."

"Oh, that's a pretty name. Where are they?"

"They were staying with my cousin when our house fell in."

Ricardo breathed a sigh of relief. "Well, I'm sure they're safe, Rafael. What is Antonio like?"

While Rafael talked, Ricardo focused on his voice, tuning out his fear and claustrophobia, imagining God's hand holding up the massive pile of stones above his head to soothe his mind. Where he crawled, he bumped and bruised himself, shoving rocks out of the way as he pushed on. With two more turns, Rafael's voice grew louder, somewhere off to the right, bouncing off the stones. But no matter how much he shined his flashlight around, he couldn't find the boy anywhere, and then he arrived at a dead end, forcing himself to wiggle backward until he came to a junction and took a hard right, chin brushing the ground as he edged into a wider space that gave him room to breathe and speak.

After a few feet, Rafael called out. "Is that you?"

"Yes! Do you see my lights?"

"I see it flickering. You're close."

"Keep talking to me... Tell me about Emila, and let me know if my light is getting brighter."

"Okay."

Ricardo estimated he was thirty or forty feet inside the rubble pile, the tunnels running deeper and farther than he could've imagined. Choking on dust, blinking particles out of his eyes, Ricardo reached the narrowest spot yet, forcing him to turn sideways, stick his arms through and suck his stomach in to draw past the sharp steel and concrete scraping his skin.

"Hi, Ricardo."

The voice was right by his ear, and Ricardo twisted, shifted, and sighed with relief when a pale face blinked back at him in the flashlight beam.

"Hello, Rafael!" He crawled a little farther and grasped his hand. "I found you. Now, let's see how you're stuck."

"It's my legs." He was sitting up but slumped over with the low ceiling atop his head, a large piece of concrete or stone covering the lower half of his body.

"Okay, let me see."

In the tight space, Ricardo worked around the massive slab, its shape roughly rectangular where it sat on a bed of smaller stones. As he worked his way around, his stomach sank, seeing how impossible it would be to move the rock without causing more damage to his legs. Coming around the other side, Ricardo stumbled upon the mother's body and jerked back, hitting his head on the ceiling with a sharp crack that sent waves of nausea through his stomach. Her entire left side was stuck inside a wall, her face covered in ash and dust, one eye staring past him into the darkness. He'd been so caught up in getting Rafael free, he didn't smell the rot until he was right on top of it, and he waited for the nausea to pass before he went on.

"Mama is dead, isn't she?" The boy's voice held the slightest bit of a tremor.

"I'm afraid so, Rafael," he replied, working on clearing the loose stones from beneath the slab. "And I'm sorry about that, son, but we need to get you out before we shed any tears for your sweet mama. Do you feel any pain right now?"

"No, no pain at all."

"Can you wiggle your toes?"

He thought about it and nodded. "Yes, I can wiggle them."

Shaking his head in confusion, Ricardo kept working, moving stones, unable to understand how Rafael could still feel his limbs. Soon, it became clear that the large slab was resting on the piled rocks, and the boy's legs were trapped at an awkward angle, but thankfully not crushed.

"I'm almost there," he said hurriedly as he cast more rocks aside. "Just a few more minutes."

"Okay."

Ricardo soon cleared enough stones to see the boy's shorts and his legs where they were trapped, feet spread where the rock had pinned him. More determined than ever, Ricardo finished maneuvering and reached to take Rafael's lower leg gently.

"Can you feel that?"

"Yes."

"Good. Now, we're going to pull that leg out first, and I want you to tell me if it hurts."

"Okay."

Tugging Rafael's leg and then his knee, Ricardo worked the limb free, making him shift to his left side and start backing out so that the other leg came, too. After some scraping and head bumping, with trickles of dust falling on their faces, Ricardo had him free.

"Excellent, Rafael. You're free. Can you move your legs?"

"I... I think so... yes..."

"We're not out of the water yet, son." Ricardo used the flashlight to inspect the boy's small form, finding some scrapes and bruises, but otherwise Rafael was unharmed.

"I'm so thirsty," Rafael said.

"Me too. I don't have any water with me, but there's plenty outside. Now, let's get out of here."

Ricardo gave the boy room to let him slide past, but Rafael paused to touch his mother's arm, her pale face bathed in the stark flashlight glow. Ricardo had tried to keep from shining it in her face, but in the enclosed space, there was no getting around it.

"Bye, Mama. I love you." He turned to Ricardo, his gaunt, dirty face holding more bravery than Ricardo had seen in his life. "Okay, I'm ready to go now."

With a nod, Ricardo gestured toward the rope. "I've got this rope attached to me. I want you to go out ahead of me and follow it to the exit, okay? I'll be right behind you."

The pile shifted as they started to move, dirt trickling more intensely, the low grumbling of stone vibrating through his whole body and jaws and teeth. Entire sections of the wall slid five or six inches, rocks clacking on the floor, voices outside calling in for them to hurry. The next few minutes were a blur, with Ricardo shoving Rafael out ahead of him, pushing on his backside and ignoring his complaints and cries as he bumped his head and elbows. Finally, with stones falling on him, Ricardo removed the rope from around his waist and tied it to Rafael, taking up the slack and tugging hard two or three times.

"Hang on to the rope, son! They're going to pull you —"

Rafael shot through the twisting passages, feet kicking, leaving a trail of dust behind him. Suddenly the boy was gone and Ricardo was alone. He shoved a pile of falling stone out of his way, fighting, spitting dirt, directionless. He slipped to his right where the ceiling dropped, clambering over it and sliding down the other side, cracking his head on a lip of rock before he was moving once more, elbows and knees propelling him like a lizard through the dust.

Crawl, man, crawl! For Marcia and the kids. By God's good grace, crawl!

Stones fell like rain, trickling in his hair, the dust so thick he could barely see in the dim light. A cool breeze touched his left cheek, and he turned toward it, pointing the flashlight ahead of him and pushing ahead. The window frame was five feet away, the clearance having shrunk by several inches since he last entered. Still, he crawled until his legs were pinned to his sides, and all he could move were his arms. He clawed at the rocks as the weight of the hillside pressed on his spine. Creeping the last inch, Ricardo tried to call out, but his throat was choked with dust, and the words died on his lips. He thrust his hands through the opening to the sounds of cheering and celebration, but it wasn't for him, it was for Rafael.

Ricardo coughed and choked on his last breaths with a smile on his face, his last moments of life given to saving someone else's. Then firm hands gripped him by the wrists, tugging and pulling, inch by inch, freeing him from the mountain's hold. The cold air was a slap to the face as the workers hauled him free, and he slid another two feet, turning on his side and curling up his legs as the debris pile gave a final belch of dust and collapsed on itself.

Hands lifted him and patted his back, knocking the dust from his lungs, water sprayed his face, and someone thrust a bottle into his hands. He put it to his lips, drinking, washing out his mouth, spitting it to the side, then swallowing the rest. His legs were rubber, his back aching, bleeding from a hundred cuts and scrapes, but he turned his smiling face toward little Rafael where the crowd carried him around, cheering with joy. Rosa threw her arms around Ricardo, squeezing hard as tears streamed down her dirty cheeks and the foreman gripped his shoulders and hugged him, holding up his arm and shouting to the crowd.

"Cheers to Ricardo! Cheers, my friend!"

"Thanks," he said weakly, hand shaking as he took another bottle of water, drinking from it and spitting mud.

"God is truly good, Ricardo. The people will remember you for this."

"One thing, foreman."

The foreman leaned closer. "Yes, my friend?"

"It is good that Rafael is safe, but his mother…" Ricardo glanced toward the settling pile. "She's inside there and gone. He will need a place to stay, someone to care for him."

"Don't worry about it, my friend." The foreman patted his shoulder. "The boy will be well taken care of. Go home to your wife and kids."

"But I'm not even halfway done with my shift."

"Go get your day's pay from Juliana at the office. She will know what happened by now. Do not worry about it, Ricardo. Take your pay and spend it at the market. Take something good home for your family."

"Are you sure?" Ricardo asked, thankful when the foreman nodded and ushered him away.

He stumbled down the hillside, tripping over rocks and rubble. Hands took his arms and helped him until he stood at the bottom of the hill, and he turned to watch the workers crawling over it, still searching for any living souls. After collecting his pay, he passed through the favelas where savory scents drifted and music filled the air, the people still cheerful in spite of the dire situation. His dirty face and clothes showed where he'd been, and news of Rafael's rescue had spread throughout the favelas. People stared and smiled, grandmothers hugged him, younger women pointed and grinned and men clapped him on the back and shoulders.

At the market, a meat vendor threw in an extra cut of beef with the chickens, and another gave him a bag of candy for his children, expensive chocolate truffles for a fraction of their normal cost. By the time he left the market, he carried a basket of goods and a bouquet of colorful wildflowers and roses for Marcia. He made his way home, rounding the bottom of the hill where things were normal once more, music playing on the beaches, people dancing on a balcony way up high in the upper favelas. With his arms full, he climbed the steel ladder, crossed the bridges, and ascended the stairwell to his family's small apartment. He didn't mask his entry, putting down the packages of meat, vegetables, and candy on the counter with a loud thump. Footsteps came down the hall and turned into the kitchen, Marcia with a worried look that fell away when she saw it was him.

She clutched her chest. "You scared me, Ricardo. I didn't expect you home so early. Your shift —"

"Isn't even halfway over," he nodded. "They sent me home early."

"Oh, no, dear," her expression fell. "Did something happen? Did you get fired?"

Ricardo laughed tiredly. "Oh, nothing like that. Everything is fine. Well, I guess something happened…"

Marcia spotted all of the packages on the counter and her jaw dropped. "What is all this?"

"I received my full pay and made a quick trip to the market. Some kind people gave me some extra."

Marcia shook her head as she walked over, finally getting a good look at him, gasping as she reached out to touch his face. "Ricardo, what happened? You've got scratches and cuts… You're bleeding."

He nodded, remembering Rafael and the darkness beneath the rubble pile, the tight passages, the twists and turns and the rumbling stone, shuddering at the thoughts. "It's… a long story."

She took him by the hand. "I want you to tell me all about it. I'll get you a beer and take care of these cuts." She gestured to the things on the counter. "You didn't happen to pick up some bandages, did you?"

"In the bag."

Marcia checked. "There are bandages and antibiotic cream." She turned and held a tube up. "This is expensive, Ricardo. We cannot afford this."

Before she could go on, he pulled her close and hugged her tight. "Don't worry, Marcia. I didn't pay for that either. In fact, I got almost everything for free. I still have my day's pay. Here it is."

Bills and coins hit the counter, and Marcia blinked at the packages and her husband's grimy face. "Well, I expect this will be quite a story."

Ricardo shrugged. "Just another day on the job. When will the kids be home? I would very much like to hug them."

CHAPTER ELEVEN

Alice Burton
Talladega National Forest, Alabama

Water trickled over stacks of stones that dipped southward into the valley below as Alice and the kids stood on a flat piece of land just before a steep drop-off, the trail running parallel to it for a time before cutting back east the way they'd come along the hillside. The horses drank deeply at the creek's edge after their long ride through the beautiful, bug-infested woods, their tails swatting at the gnats and flies that had followed them out of the foliage. Red, orange, and gold leaves streaked the distant treetops like splashed paint on a canvas, and the slopes around them were covered with muted color as the changing season worked its magic on the flora.

The air was cooler than it had been during their trip through Florida and Georgia, though the sun still stood high and cast rays of golden light through breaks in the trees as it cut across the landscape. They'd entered an area of sloping forest-land covered in low brush, crowded with hardwood saplings and prickly bushes, though the forest's denseness wasn't all that thick, and was interspersed with small meadows like the one they were taking a breather in while they waited for the horses to finish drinking. They could have ridden through the woods directly, but had come across animal trails that were much more accessible, three-foot-wide paths they'd been following for the entire day with no sign of humans, only the sharp hammering of woodpeckers, falling acorns from unseen squirrels and the snorts and chuffs from animals as they passed by.

"Would you look at that?" Jake stood a bit down the trail with his hands on his hips as the misty valley opened up at their feet.

"It's beautiful," Alice agreed. "We could live here if we had the right gear."

"No way!" Sarah was crouching near the horses, working on preparing an MRE. "There're way too many bugs up here. Almost as bad as Florida. Jake, can you find the bug repellent?"

"Coming right up."

Alice sat on the soft grass next to her daughter and opened an MRE. "Hrm. Beef patty and jalapeno pepper jack."

"We've been avoiding these," Sarah frowned, "but we're all out of everything else. Now we don't have a choice." She popped her beef patty into her heating pouch, poured in some water, sealed it, and shook it up, placing it on a rock beside her where it could cook, then she lifted a pack of crackers with a flourish. "And while that cooks, Chef Sarah will prepare the jalapeno dip for proper eating. Note how the chef breaks the crackers into bite-sized pieces *before* opening the packet." She smashed the package between her fingers, crunching the saltines inside, then broke the pack open and dug out a piece. With a squeeze of cheese spread on top, she ate it, shrugging. "Chef Sarah is not entirely displeased."

"We're getting pretty good at this MRE stuff," Alice smiled.

"Oh yeah. I've opened my share of MREs out here." Sarah spoke with a swagger as she chewed. "It's rough on us soldiers, but we'll get through somehow."

Alice laughed and got her MRE sorted out in her lap. There were crackers, a chocolate chip cookie, multicolored candy bits, and powdered chocolate drink. "Someone pass me some clean water."

"We need to conserve that in case we need it." Sarah held up a filter straw. "Today, we drink from the creek."

"Not for the chocolate drink." Alice groaned. "Please, tell me I don't have to use creek water for my chocolate milk. I know, it's filtered and just as good as the fresh stuff just... please."

Sarah eyed her. "You look desperate, mom. Fine. For you, a bottle of fresh water we got from..." She looked thoughtful as she handed over a bottle. "I'm not sure where we got it, but it's clean."

"Thanks."

"Found it!" Jake backed away from the horses and held up a can of bug spray. "I thought we might've lost it, but someone put it in one of Hercules' saddlebags."

"That was me," Sarah said. "I wanted it to be handy since I've been using it just about every day out here."

Jake walked over and tossed it to her. "Mosquitoes must really like you. They hardly ever bug me out here. Pun intended."

Sarah rolled her eyes and stepped away from the pair to stand back on the trail where she sprayed chemical mist all over herself.

"What about you, Mom?" Jake asked, sitting next to her. "Do the bugs drive you nuts, too?"

"I've been bitten once or twice," Alice replied, sealing her beef patty inside the heating pouch. "Not as bad as your sister."

"I'm not sure why they like her so much." Jake mocked. "She can't be that tasty...."

Sarah held up the bug spray can and threatened to throw it. "You want a dent in the side of your head?"

Jake laughed good-naturedly, holding up his hands. "Sorry, sis. I'm just playing around. I'm sure you're *extra* tasty to the bugs."

A moment later, after Jake had caught the flying bug spray can with a laugh, they were all sitting in a semicircle with the creek trickling nearby. Jake had filled their "dirty" water bottles with creek water, and they sipped from them with filter straws. The minutes passed lazily as they ate in silence, enjoying the peace and quiet, Alice wishing it was back home in the woods outside their house where they sometimes practiced camping on weekends.

"Your father would love this place," Alice said. "I miss being home, but that view is incredible."

"I wonder where we are?" Jake asked.

"It's hard to tell. After those guys chased us off the road, we could be anywhere. Feels like we've been following animal trails for ages."

"I'm not complaining about that," Sarah replied. "It's much easier than going through the woods blind."

"That's why I picked the trails," Alice nodded. "Much easier on the horses and us."

Sarah dipped her last cracker in her cheese and ate it. "Who do you think those men were back there? They were driving around a street sweeper. Can you believe that? They wanted to run us over so badly, but they didn't start shooting at us until we were about to get away."

"I wish I had an answer for you, honey. The way the world is now, I can't imagine what's running through people's minds. We'll never know what motivated them to be so mean. This is happening all over the place.... Society is messed up, and the survivors are a mix of good and bad."

Jake threw a pebble into the creek, where it bounced off another rock and splashed. "Mostly bad."

"You can't say that. What about Wilford, Nate, and Elaine? Those are all great people, and I'm sure we'll meet more like that on the way home. Need I remind you —"

"We've got a long way to go," Sarah finished for her.

"That's our motto, right?" Alice said. "We've got a long, long way to go."

"And a short time to get there," Jake added.

Alice finished her meal, folded up the empty packages, and placed them in a small plastic bag sitting between them. "Okay, guys. Let's get going."

They slung their packs on Hercules and mounted up with Alice leading the way north along the soft dirt path. Occasional tree roots cut furrows in front of them, and the trail edges grew steeper as they parted ways with the creek and entered the deep woods. The hillsides were bursting with pine and hardwood trees, purple flowers, and ivy scaling high up the tree trunks. The sharp scent of decaying leaves was turned up by the horse's hooves, and massive slabs of bedrock wore through the soil in great strips of gray. Other trails intersected with theirs, and she did her best to keep them moving north, but the trails inevitably wound west again, cutting through an endless expanse of wilderness as far as she could see.

After an hour, Sarah looked worried. "Are we even getting anywhere?"

"It's a trail, so I'd think it'll lead us *somewhere*, but these are pretty deep woods, and we haven't seen a house or a person anywhere for miles."

"And all we have is basic camping gear," Jake added. "No thermal blankets and stuff. It could get pretty cold out here at night."

"Keep looking, kids. There has to be an end to this. I'm only certain we're farther west than we wanted to be, and I hope we're not lost in the Appalachian Mountains somewhere. Those trails go on for hundreds of miles."

The next hour passed slowly, feeling like they were moving at a good clip but not getting anywhere. Cresting a rise, Sarah saw something and pointed, and they took the horses along the flat section of trail running smoothly into a gravel lot. A trailhead stood on the north end with a big sign next to it, and a few vehicles sat around gutted by explosions, leaving chunks of debris scattered everywhere.

"I think that used to be a camper." Jake pointed to a pile of junk sitting on its side with a long silver roof charred with fire marks.

"I think you're right," Alice replied. "And look past that... there's a service road that probably leads to a highway or main road."

"Should we take it?" Sarah asked.

"Let's go see what this sign says."

They turned their horses toward the sign across the lot, but Sarah got there first. "Talladega National Forest," she called out. "Okay, where is that?"

Alice frowned. "Alabama."

"Alabama?"

"Yep. I hate to say it, but we're off course." Alice started rummaging through one of her saddlebags. "But at least we know where we are, and I have a map that might help."

"Can we course correct?" Jake asked. "I mean, does this road lead to where we want to go?"

"Give me a second." Alice unfolded the map and placed it in her lap, pinpointing the Talladega National Forest. "According to the map, this main trail will take us through the hills and down the other side to another group of branching highways. It looks like a long shot, so we might have to do some camping."

"In the middle of nowhere?" Jake said. "Do we have the supplies for that?"

"We've got the supplies, though it might be a little cold. Still, we'll have access to all the firewood we'd need, and the road hasn't been too good to us lately anyway. Might be nice to go off-road for a while." Alice looked at the sign and then up the trail. "These trails are bound to be amazing, and the horses will have plenty to drink with all the creeks and streams running through these hills."

"But the bugs, Mom."

"You're going to get bugs no matter where we are, honey. Don't you want to avoid people?"

"And street sweepers?" Jake added.

"Ugh," Sarah groaned. "Okay, I guess going through the woods would be better than being on the road. And it would be better for the horses, too."

"It's settled. Let's go."

Alice walked Buck past the sign and onto the trail with a gentle breeze ruffling the low brush as birds chirped in the rustling trees, casting a peaceful calm over the forest. Off the trail on both sides were a spread of clearings, with iron grills jutting up and stone fire circles filled with pieces of charred wood.

"Looks like this place was busy at one time," Sarah said.

"This is probably for casual campers," Alice replied. "You know, those who didn't want to hike very far."

They rode for almost a quarter of a mile, spotting multiple campsites right off the trail. Abandoned, half-collapsed tents stood in a few places, flapping in the breeze, one spot with camping equipment strewn everywhere, blackened by flames, the edges of the clearing shredded by shrapnel. A handful of charred corpses lay sprawled around a squarish object with its top blown open and peeled back.

"Geez, what happened there?" Jake asked.

"A gas generator, I'd guess," Alice nodded. "Come on. Don't look at it." She picked up the pace and trotted up a short hill, popping over the other side but drawing up with a surprised cry.

A man popped out of the brush, stepping toward the trail with his hands up and waving. "Hey there! Hello!"

Alice grabbed her rifle as the kids rounded the hill behind her, pulling their mounts up short but pressing Buck forward with their collective bulk.

"Stop!" Alice said, training her gun on him. "Back the hell up!"

"Hey, no need for the gun, lady!" The man raised his hands straight up and took several paces back, bumping into a woman who'd stepped out of the brush behind him.

"Stay back!" Alice snapped, keeping her rifle pointed at the man's chest, holding the reins and controlling Buck as she did so. "Don't step onto the trail."

"I won't, I promise. The trail's yours."

Alice started walking Buck forward. "Okay, we're going to pass you, so don't try anything."

Glancing at the woman, he laughed. "Who's going to try anything? We saw you coming up the trail from our campsite and thought we'd say hello."

The man looked normal, early thirties with tussled brown hair and dark eyes, wearing a button-up denim shirt and jeans. The woman was short, with blonde, shoulder-length hair, wearing worn and dirty jeans and a light blue hoodie.

"Hello, and goodbye," Alice said, gesturing with her weapon barrel for them to move away.

"No need to be like that." The man's smile persisted. "We've been looking for good people out here for a while, and you seem like a nice family. That's why we came out of hiding to say hello. Can't... really say the same for others who've passed us."

"My name is Christine," the woman blurted and stepped forward. "And this is my husband, Mark. We're the Hubbards and we've got a couple of young ones, like you."

When they didn't move away from the trail but kept smiling, Alice said, "If you know what it's like out there, you wouldn't be walking up to armed strangers."

"I didn't know you had a gun until you pulled it on me," Mark replied.

"Surprising people on the trail like that is a good way to get yourself shot."

He swallowed hard. "Well, luckily you're good people because I'm still alive."

"Saving my bullets," Alice responded flatly. "Come on. Step back."

Mark did the opposite and stepped onto the trail in front of them, never dropping his smile. It only grew wider, and he lowered his hands to rest them on his hips. "I'm sorry, but we would be terrible people if we didn't offer you weary travelers some food and a warm fire to sit by."

Christine stepped to her husband's side. "Seriously, we could use some news if you have any, and Mia and Hunter are craving a little company. They haven't seen another kid in days." She gestured to Jake and Sarah. "It would do them wonders to talk to some other children for a change."

"We're not children," Jake replied.

"Well, you're close enough." Christine laughed. "They've been staring at our tired faces for the past couple of weeks." When Alice didn't immediately respond, she pressed on. "Stay for a few hours, please, we'd be thrilled just to have someone to talk to. There's plenty of food, and we could use the company." She gave Mark a sad glance. "A group passed the other day, but they didn't sound too nice, so we stayed away from them."

"Real rough-looking bunch," Mark said. "Big guys with guns and dogs. We hid down by the creek, hoping the dogs wouldn't smell us."

Alice backed Buck up a few paces and whispered to the kids. "What do you guys think?"

"We've got a long way to go to reach the other side of the woods," Sarah said. "We've been riding all day and... we could probably use a break."

"I guess it would be okay." Jake kept his voice low and didn't take his eyes off them. "And if they've got some kids, maybe we could help them out. Who knows, they could be like Nate and Elaine. Let's just be real careful, mom."

"Mhmm." Alice nodded and turned back to the couple. "Okay. We'll take a load off at your camp for a bit, but we're only going to stay a few hours before we get ready to ride through to the next highway."

"Great!" Mark said.

Christine smiled. "Oh, that's wonderful. The kids will be so happy, and they'll love the horses."

"Uh huh. Just... keep your distance for a while. Trust is hard to come by these days."

"Absolutely. Understood." Mark backed up a few feet and nodded understandingly.

"Where are you folks camping?"

"Oh, just right over here," Mark said, edging into the woods and pointing behind him. "Just forty yards off the trail."

"Lead on."

They followed the pair at a cautious distance, still staying on the horses as they went through the woods, picking their way along paths between the thistles and brush, finally coming to a clearing. Like the rest of the campsites, it was a circular area of about forty square feet with trails leading into the woods and a stone fire ring in the middle. Two large foldout chairs and two smaller ones sat around a modest fire with soft blankets thrown over the backs and bottles of water in the drink holders. A big blue tent and a smaller green one sat side-by-side close to a cluster of trees with their flaps open, thick covers and pillows folded inside.

On the far side of the camp, a boy and girl of around six played with an assortment of toys. Buck chuffed as he entered the campsite, and the girl dropped her dolls to stand and stare in awe, eyes wide as the four horses circled and stood at the edge of the encampment, keeping their distance from the couple. The boy gaped and clutched his toy cars, where he'd made a small town of ramps and roads in the mud, using rocks and stones as buildings.

"Hey, kids, we've got some guests," Mark said, gesturing to Alice as she dismounted cautiously and looked around, still holding her rifle, ready to use it at a moment's notice. "They haven't told me their names yet."

"I'm Alice. These are Sarah and Jake."

Christine walked straight across the campsite, turning as she got close to the children. "And this is Mia and Hunter. Kids, say hi to our new friends."

Jake and Sarah waved, but the new children only stared slack-jawed at the massive horses where they towered over everyone.

Christine laughed the kids' shyness off and gestured at the fire. "Mark, do we have any chairs for our guests?"

"We'll sit on some logs while they take our chairs."

"No thanks," Alice replied, handing her reins to Jake. "We'll pull up some logs. Don't want you folks to be put out."

Jake tied the horses up close by, while Alice, Sarah, and Mark dragged up some logs and spread them out opposite the chairs. After they had everything situated, they sat around the warm flames, Alice keeping herself and her two children on the side of the fire closest to the horses.

"What's cooking?" Alice glanced at a pan sitting on the grill over the fire.

"Just some country beans and ham I brought from home." Christine sat in one of the chairs and stirred the beans, moving the pan away from the center of the flames. "Have some."

"That's okay. We ate a little while ago." Alice gave Jake and Sarah a quick look, raising an eyebrow.

"Don't mind if I do." Mark found a bowl and dumped a couple of spoonfuls in, then grabbed a fork off a small table near the tents and sat in the other chair.

"You folks want some iced tea?" Christine asked. "There's plenty left."

"Yeah, I guess that would be okay," Alice replied.

"No thanks," Sarah said with a sidelong glance. "I'll just drink water."

Christine bent between the chairs, pulled up a large pitcher and some cups, and poured Alice, Jake and herself half a cup each. "It's unsweetened. I hope that's okay."

"It's fine." Alice put the cup to her nose and sniffed. "No offense, but you wouldn't mind drinking first, would you?"

Christine took a long drink while Mark chuckled next to her. "There's really no need to be so suspicious, I promise!"

"If you'd traveled the roads we have, you'd understand."

Mark sobered and nodded. "No, completely. I get it."

Alice took a sip and nodded, shoulders relaxing a bit for the first time since encountering the couple, hand slipping off of her rifle as she leaned forward on the log. "Thanks, Christine. This is good."

Jake sipped his and nodded in thanks while Sarah crossed her legs and put her hands out to the fire, watching the younger children who'd resumed their playing. Mia was fashioning clothes for her dolls out of twigs, grass, and wildflowers while Hunter drove his cars around the muddy freeways he'd built out of the knob of dirt. All four of them looked like they'd been at the campground for a few days at least, lending credence to Mark's and Christine's story. They also seemed to have more than enough supplies, and her worries over them potentially trying to rob her, Jake and Alice began to wane.

After a moment of silence, Alice gestured around at their camp. "So, what are you doing way up here in the woods?"

Mark finished his bite of beans. "We're from Ashland, about ten miles from here. Had a nice ranch house in the suburbs."

"It was a really great neighborhood," Christine said with a sad smile.

"After everything went to—" Mark looked at the two children, lowering his voice, "*hell*, we lost our house and most of our neighbors. A lot of great people died there."

"How did you survive the initial explosions?" Alice asked.

"Pure luck. We were out for a walk when it all happened."

"It was my day off from work," Christine said, "but I'd been doing housework all day. I was feeling pent up and wanted to get out for a little while. Know what I mean?"

Alice nodded.

"We were on the swings — I remember that so vividly — when the cars in the neighborhood started going off." Mark glanced at Mia and Hunter. "It scared the living daylights out of those two. Things were flying everywhere. People were screaming. We wanted to protect them, so we stayed put."

"That sounds terrifying," Alice said. "I can relate."

Mark shook his head. "It *was* terrifying, and I know you must have gone through the same thing. Anyway, we helped a couple of neighbors who were hurt in the explosions. We tried to dial nine-one-one, but all the emergency services were down. We stayed as long as we could before Christine suggested we get home. Our place was a few blocks from the people we were helping, and I saw it burning before we even got there." He took Christine's hand and squeezed. "There was nothing to salvage except a storage shed with some boxes of old clothes and stuff. I couldn't even get within twenty feet of the house until all the flames died down. Everything we had was taken away in an instant. We were destitute."

"I'm sorry to hear that," Alice said.

"I appreciate that. But you know something? It didn't seem so bad compared to what others had gone through. Not only had they lost their homes, but they lost pets and family members. From there, it took a while to adjust. Wasn't a single hotel standing in our area, and only a few barns, but we quickly learned how to survive. We scavenged, found places to sleep and stay warm, and somehow survived. We're working our way north to get to our family members up near Fort Payne. Figured the easiest way would be to take the forest route to keep away from people. Lord knows we've run across some bad ones."

"You're telling us," Jake snorted.

"We've met our share of bad folks on the road," Alice said. "Been in some pretty wild fights ourselves."

Mark took another bite. "Took us a while, but we hiked up here to the park and found the place all... well, I guess you saw all those cars down in the parking lot?"

"We sure did."

"And that site down there?" Christine clasped her hands on her knees and leaned forward. "It looks like it just blew up all the people. Must've been a generator or something."

"That's what I figured," Alice said. "They didn't stand a chance."

Christine spoke in a hushed tone. "We walked through there to see if we could scavenge anything, but I couldn't stay long. It was terrible."

"The reception isn't so great up here," Mark said, "but we tried to call the police. No response from them. Then a text came through from my brother up north – I guess before all the cell towers went dead – telling us to stay where we were and that everything had gone south in a hurry. We turned on our radio and heard the emergency broadcast system, but they've just been repeating the same thing for days."

Christine frowned. "Some kind of terrorist attack on our fuel, they said. Sounded pretty scary, so we decided not to take the kids out in that. We've been up here ever since."

Alice nodded and glanced at the little ones. "It was the best decision you could've made. There're still some good people out there, but there's a lot of danger, too. Having young ones like that makes it even more difficult. It seems safe up here, at least, which is good. What are your plans from here?"

"Still heading north, but we're giving it a couple of days to cool down. It's going to be tough, but we'll figure it out. The kids can walk fine, but not for very long."

"We've seen people struggling so hard with their children." Alice shook her head. "I can't imagine what it must be like to have to travel with little ones so young."

"Especially without those horses you have," Christine said. "Where'd you get them, anyway?"

"I promise we don't want to take them!" Mark held up his hands, chuckling.

"Oh gosh, no. We don't know two things about horses." Christine laughed. "

Alice smiled and recalled the events leading up to finding Monticello Horse Farm, including the man who'd tried to take their things on the beach and their short stint at Andrea's hotel. There was the shocking moment getting shot at by Wilford, who they'd eventually befriended, and talking about Wilford filled Alice with unexpected emotion, and she swallowed a hard lump, recounting the wild ride through the farm, shooting at people, and being shot at. "When it was all said and done, we've probably been forced to defend ourselves and shoot a half-dozen people and could've died several times over. Luck has been on our side, and the horses have made all the difference."

"What a crazy story," Mark said. "All those horses, and that old man trying to take care of them all by himself."

Alice gestured to the four horses tied up a short distance away. "That's why he offered to give us these to help us get back to Michigan."

"He turned out to be a pretty good guy," Christine said.

"He reads to his horses to relax them and stuff," Jake said. "I thought it was weird at first, but he's like a horse whisperer or something."

"And he can cook, too," Sarah added. "We had some great meals while we were there."

"We're going to miss him a lot," Alice said. "And we hope he's doing okay."

"Is that where you're headed?" Mark asked. "Michigan?"

"Yep. We've got a home outside East Lansing, and we'll hopefully meet my husband there. It already feels like we've been on the road so long, and we've got a way to go."

"We've got a *long* way to go." Sarah echoed their motto, and Jake grinned at the inside joke.

"Good thing we're only going as far as Fort Payne," Mark said. "That's a short distance compared to where you're going."

"Will the kids be okay walking that far?"

Mark chuckled and put his empty bowl aside. "We can get them pretty far, and we'll carry them for a while if we need to, at least until we find a vehicle to drive."

"That's easier said than done," Alice replied. "The only cars that work are electric ones. We had one for a little while—"

"Until someone shot it and made it catch on fire," Sarah finished for her.

"Oh, no!" Christine gasped. "You poor folks have been through a blender."

"It feels that way sometimes... but there were good moments, too."

"Like with Nate and Elaine," Sarah said, launching into what had happened at their house with the delivery of little Ethan and the night they'd spent there. Christine looked over at Mark with wide eyes when Sarah got to the part about Ethan popping out. "Mom was holding him, and I got to cut the cord. It was the most beautiful thing."

"That *is* beautiful!" Christine said. "I wish I could have been there to see it."

"You folks have quite the stories." Mark nodded and gestured toward a pack sitting at his feet. "Do you need any snacks or anything? I've got some jerky and cashews."

"Jake, would you get some of those granola bars from Hercules, and we'll trade the Hubbards for some of their snacks."

"Just not the peanut butter ones!" Sarah blurted, then looked around apologetically. "Sorry, but those are our favorites."

"Don't worry about it," Christine laughed and fell to a whisper. "We're not giving you the honey-roasted cashews, either. Only the plain ones."

Sarah chuckled and Alice grinned, feeling more at ease with their new friends, and by the time Jake had returned with the snack bars, she'd made up her mind.

"Hey, listen... sorry about the hostility earlier. It's been tough out here."

"Don't even mention it," Mark replied.

"If you're going to Fort Payne, why don't we travel together? Your kids are worn out, and we'd be happy to carry them, and you."

"That's so kind of you," Christine said, "but we couldn't impose like that."

"Nonsense. It wouldn't be a big deal. You can ride on the horses with the kids, and I'll go bareback with the equipment on Hercules."

"I hate to say it, Alice." Mark frowned, "but we'll have to turn you down. You folks have been through way too much to be put out like that. Those horses are about the most valuable thing out here now, and you need to treat them like gold."

"It won't hurt to share them until we reach Fort Payne. We'll drop you off and get right back on the road."

Mark and Christine shared a look before Mark finally broke down and smiled. "Well shoot, I guess if it's not too much trouble, we'll take you up on that offer."

"Then it's settled," Alice said. "When do you want to leave?"

"I guess we should go as soon as possible." Mark glanced at the sky. "It's getting pretty late now, though. Maybe we should hold off until first light?"

"That sounds good," Alice said. "We'll get a good night's rest, let the horses graze a little, and Jake... can you look around for a stream they can drink from?"

"There's one right over there," Christine pointed. "We've been taking water from it and boiling it."

"Perfect."

After slinging her rifle on her shoulder, Alice took their bedding off the horses while Jake and Sarah unsaddled them and led them to the creek to drink. Alice placed their bedrolls on the ground opposite the tents and prepped them for the kids, spreading blankets on top of them and rolling up old clothes to use as pillows.

"I hope you're good with that," Christine motioned at Alice's rifle as she bustled with some other chores. "I'm pretty nervous about guns around the kids."

Alice rested her hand on her pistol. "Gotta get used to it from now on, unfortunately. Chances are, you'll need one to protect yourself. You don't have any weapons?"

"Nothing at all." Christine sighed. "We've always been... against firearms. No offense to you or anything. I'm kind of rethinking that stance right now."

"Yeah, I can imagine. These are an absolute necessity out here with how things are right now. I'm shocked you didn't look for one before you left your neighborhood."

"Seemed kind of impossible since everything was burned down." She shrugged. "We just wanted to get out of there." Christine sidled up closer, lowering her voice. "And you've actually shot people?"

Alice nodded. "I didn't want to, but I had to defend us, and I'd do it again."

"I wouldn't want to mess with you guys."

Alice only smiled and marched up the slope a few paces to greet the kids coming up with the horses. "Did you find the creek?"

"Right where they told us it would be," Sarah said. "It was a little like the last creek we were at, and boy, were the horses thirsty. I think Buck drank my weight in water."

"Good. I want to make sure they're fed, watered, and rested before we move on. They'll have more to carry for a little while."

"There's a little field south of here a bit," Jake said. "Want us to take the horses down and let them graze?"

"That's a good idea, son." Alice turned back toward the camp and watched Mark and Christine talking to the kids quietly over past the fire and out of earshot. The woman bent low, speaking firmly to Mia as she brushed the dirt off her cheek, and Mark knelt in front of the brother, gesturing to him, also speaking too quietly to hear.

"Aren't they nice?" Alice asked.

"They're almost like Nate and Elaine," Sarah replied. "A little older, but their kids are cute."

"Quiet, though," Jake said. "I thought they'd be more curious about the horses. They haven't said two words to us since we've been here."

"Maybe they're just shy, or scared." Alice shrugged. "Anyway, it's nice to have met such nice people again. Helping them out feels good, and it's nice to be helped as well."

"I could get used to helping people," Sarah agreed. "Come on, Jake, let's let the horses graze for a while, then we'll brush them. Maybe Mia and Hunter will want to pet them when we get back."

Alice watched them go with a wry smile. "Don't go too far, and if you need me —"

"Just yell!" they called back.

Sarah walked Buck and Stormy away from the fire, a satchel slung over her shoulder as they picked their way carefully through the woods. Christine was still speaking with Hunter and Mia, leading the kids by their hands and sitting them behind the chairs. Once out of earshot, Sarah focused on getting down the hillside, and they followed the creek down to a small clearing that was relatively flat where the water gathered in a pond before continuing its run over the bedrock. The forest was thick, but gaps in the canopy allowed sunlight to pour in like warm honey over the water.

"This place is incredible," Jake said, letting go of Hercules' and Rocky's reins, standing close by in case they started to wander.

"Yeah...." Sarah replied, guiding the horses over and letting them graze in the thick, vibrant grass. She strode to the edge of the woods where the forest floor was covered in moist deadfall and squirrels scampered up tree trunks to pause and watch them, insects singing in the shade, a rich chorus of sound that washed over them like a blanket of peace.

He came to stand next to her with his hands on his hips as he admired the sloping forest and the gray stones showing through the mossy ground. "What's up with you, sis?"

"What do you mean?"

"Well, you've gotten quiet."

"I'm always quiet."

Jake laughed. "No, you aren't. At least not for long. Come on, what's on your mind?"

"I'm not sure. Probably nothing."

"Is it something about Mark and Christine?"

"I'm not sure... I can't put my finger on it. Maybe it's because of all these abandoned campsites around, especially the one with the dead people. Maybe that's just creeping me out or something."

"Are you serious? After all the dead people we've passed on the road? I'd think you'd be used to it by now. I am."

Sarah scoffed. "I'll never get used to it, and I never *want* to get used to it. You'll be the first to know if I figure it out."

"Okay. What do you say we brush the horses out?"

"Yeah, sounds good."

They took the brushes from the satchel and brushed down the horses, working up a sweat, talking about Nate, Elaine, and Wilford, wondering what − and how − they were doing before switching to the topic of their missing family member.

"What do you think Dad's doing right now?" Jake asked.

Sarah shrugged. "It's funny. I can imagine what Wilford's doing, and even Nate and Elaine, but when I think about Dad... I can't think of anything. All I see is danger and...." Sarah trailed off with a whisper.

"Yeah, I know what you mean," Jake said. "Sometimes it's hard to remember what he looked like. I mean, I can't think of the last time I saw his face."

"Probably the morning he left for his flight to Denver. I barely told him goodbye. If I could have that moment back, I'd hug him and never let go."

When they were done, and the horses' coats glistened in the sunlight, they led them back up to camp where Alice sat across from the Hubbards with a rifle resting across her knees. The unsettled feeling in Sarah's gut returned, but Mia came running up with a smile and asked if she could pet Stormy, and the unease was dashed as the girl broke her silence.

Taking Mia by the hand, Sarah led her over, lifting her so she could reach up and pet the horse's beautiful, dark snout. It wasn't long before Christine came over with a smile, taking Mia from Sarah's hands and guiding her back to the camp, where she put her back with her dolls to play behind their chairs. Sarah watched for a moment, then she patted Stormy on the neck and hitched her to a tree branch with the others.

CHAPTER TWELVE

James Burton
Frankfurt, Illinois

Water trickled through the culvert pipe and swirled into the stagnant basin before flowing over a row of raised stones to race down the other side in a fast stream. James stood in six inches of the rushing water, pressed against the extended stone wall, grabbing the edge and pulling himself up to see who was coming down the road. It wasn't long before a group strolled into view; they were a rough-looking bunch, a couple dozen strong, men and women dressed in clothes that were too clean to be anywhere except from freshly looted stores. Tattoos decorated their bare arms, some with indigo blue markings visible on their necks and faces, undoubtedly members of a gang tuned to the streets who knew every shadowy alcove and back alley.

They pushed and shoved each other roughly, laughing, grabbing looted items from shopping carts and throwing them at each other. One man drew a pistol and took potshots at the remnants of the gas station, cracking rounds off the awning and then at one of the ruined pumps. Another man fired a shotgun at a building on the other side while a laughing woman kicked a chunk of debris and sent it sailing toward the culvert. James ducked as it skittered on the pavement, rolled down the hill, and plopped into the basin. Pressed to the cold, wet concrete, he waited for someone to notice him, ready to run deeper into the sewer system if necessary.

When no one came, James pulled himself up and peeked over the edge, rainwater dripping down his face. The gang was moving quickly and would be right on top of him before long, and James started to let go to get back out of sight but paused when someone shouted from down the road. Six figures jogged from a building behind the gas station and spread across the street, all of them big men, barrel-chested and wearing leather jackets with the arms cut off, symbols and emblems painted on the front in rough white and red scrawl, their heads shaved, beards hanging long from their chins. Taking up the width of the road, they gesticulated and flashed rude gestures at the much larger gang, one man casually swinging a chain as the others kept their hands close to weapons hanging from their belts. The potential confrontation heightened as the larger group turned to face them, spreading out two lines deep and brandishing more crowbars, pipes, golf clubs, pistols, and shotguns. The man with the chains shouted a challenge, and the leader of the larger gang, a lanky man with long dark dreadlocks that fell to his waist, turned and stared them down.

"Looks like some fools wandered into our territory!"

The big man wielding the chain stepped forward and spat. "Can't be your territory if you're dead."

"What d'you want?" The man with the dreadlocks barked.

"Everything," The other replied. "Just drop what you're carrying and step away, and you can live."

The man with dreadlocks turned to the people behind him, saying, "They want our supplies. Can you believe this?"

The others laughed and snickered, a few glaring at the smaller group.

"Just leave all the carts and backpacks," The man swinging the chain bellowed again, his smile growing wider. "It's pretty simple."

Dreadlocks scoffed and grinned before going dead serious. "We're not giving up anything, man. Tell you what. We'll give you ten seconds to beat it, or we'll beat *you*."

The smaller group's leader continued swinging his chain around casually, twirling it over his head and down at the ground where the heavy links bounced off the pavement. The rest of the group glanced at each other with crooked smiles, and James got the feeling there was something else at play.

The man with the dreadlocks had been counting down quietly, but then shouted the last part, "Three, two, one!" and started moving toward the other group. Before he made it two steps, figures rose on the roof of the building the smaller group had run from, rifles resting on the brick edging and aiming at the first group. Others appeared on top of the apartments across from them, and James shrank back as gun barrels flashed in a rapid-fire procession from rifles and handguns alike. Bullets struck the ground, ricocheting everywhere, a couple zipping by a foot above James' head while another snapped off some blades of grass on the embankment as it burrowed into the soil.

Rounds punctured flesh, peppering the larger group in a flurry of lead, and a handful of gang members screamed, clutching their chests, arms, or stomachs as they buckled over and collapsed to the ground. Others drew their weapons and were immediately targeted, guns clattering to the pavement as they gripped themselves and cried out in pain. Pinned between the two buildings, they took fire from both sides and only got off a few shots in retaliation. They jerked and spun, crying out, ducking and covering, running into and bowling over their carts as they sought cover.

Supplies spilled onto the pavement, and two cans of green beans rolled across the road to stop just a few feet from James. He was tempted to reach out and take them, but the shooting intensified, and the leader of the larger group grabbed a gun from a fellow gang member and started firing at the rooftops from behind cover, sending the attackers ducking back and giving his still-living comrades a brief reprieve. He ran out of rounds after a few seconds, growling and throwing the weapon aside, turning to glare at the man in the street as he still stood where he had before the gunfire started, swinging his chain with a slow smile plastered on his face.

Standing in the middle of his decimated group, the leader started gathering survivors to him, getting the wounded up, shouting for them to move or they were dead. The head of the smaller group put his hand up, and the incoming fire halted. He gestured, and his people walked forward, preying on the downed group, beating them as they crawled and held their hands up, ignoring the cries for mercy. A crowbar struck a man's temple, leaving deep crimson splatters on the pavement and another man with a leather jacket kicked a woman in the side as she tried to stand, knocking her to the ground before swinging his ax in a brutal, overhanded blow.

The two leaders met in the middle of the bloody street, the chain whipping through the air, the one with the dreadlocks absorbing the blow on his arm, allowing the chain to wrap around it, grabbing it tight. Jerking his enemy toward him with his own chain, he swung a spiked bat at his opponent's side, sinking two inches of nails into his ribs with a thud.

James watched the engagement with a sinking feeling in his gut. If he stood, he'd be visible to the people atop the buildings, and when the winners of the brawl started picking up the loose supplies, they'd undoubtedly check the culvert pipe for survivors. Heavy objects struck ribs and jaws cracked as the groups descended into hand-on-hand violence, one battling for vicious, violent supremacy, the other for survival, both groups becoming more absorbed in the almost ritualistic fight.

It's now or never, he thought, slinking to the opposite side of the culvert entrance and starting up the moist embankment, staying low with his face pressed close to the ground, doing his best to hide in the knee-high grass and reeds. He made it ten and then fifteen yards, catching the end of the fight as the man with the dreadlocks took a punch to the side of the head, spun, and went down to the cheers and raised fists of the victors. Bodies lay everywhere, the rain carrying blood into the cracks in the concrete and washing it out in a pinkish flood.

James was just ten yards from the next block with two small buildings, scattered dumpsters, a telephone pole, and a length of collapsed fencing covered in vines he could hide behind. Across the street, the crowded city blocks stretched ahead, more warehouses and buildings with narrow alleys and big stone stoops, old signs above the doors that were too weathered to read.

The victor raised his bloody chain at the people on the buildings, waving it as they cheered and celebrated their victory over the larger force. James was about to make a run for cover, but he caught sight of a grocery cart at the top of the ditch with its front wheels on the edge of the road. Inside were some food boxes and several gallons of water sitting in the basket. He started to move past it, then felt the light weight of his backpack resting on his shoulders with only a day or two of food remaining and no real way to get reliable, clean drinking water.

His decision-making and weighing of risks took a split second, then he was scrambling up the embankment, rising from the cool, wet grass, and grabbing the cart handle to push it down the road. The wheels made a clattering sound, louder than the rain but not as loud as the man waving his chain around as he bellowed and motioned to his group, receiving cheers and shouts in response. Stepping over to the man with dreadlocks lying in the street, he kicked him in the side, roaring at his people in victory as the rest of the gang laughed and picked up the supplies that had spilled in the road. The group above on the rooftops cheered louder, their collective shouts raucous as they celebrated their victory and spoils.

By then, James had made it almost a block away, shaking hands trying to keep a grip on the cart handle, his shoulders hunched over, shuffling at a steady pace to try and keep the wheels from clacking, but the sound was obnoxious, and it wouldn't go unnoticed for long. He winced when a shout rang out, and the cheering stopped, replaced by rumbles of surprise and faint laughter. James sank lower, staying as small as possible, trying to be invisible, a speck on the street. But the gang had spotted him, their curiosity roused into a growing murmur, six pairs of eyes staring at him from the street with others up on the roof reloading their weapons and taking aim at his back.

The man with the chain punched his fist in the air, bellowing, "Stop right there, man! I said, stop!"

James did the opposite, putting his head down and pushing hard, angling the rickety cart to the left as a spattering of bullets struck the asphalt behind him, the wobbly cart wheels making even more of a racket on the rough pavement. Pulling back on the handle, he got the front wheels on the curb and crashed up and over, pushing past another apartment building and warehouse as the gang gave chase, their feet pounding through puddles and kicking aside rubble as they ran, laughing and shouting as they yelled out what they were going to do to him when they caught him.

Adrenaline flooded his body and James tuned out their words and barreled ahead, looking quickly left and right, shoulders tense in expectation of a round to the spine. The gang closed on him, one woman with dyed blonde hair out in front, her skinny legs pumping, tongue sticking out from the corner of her mouth, a streak of violent glee in her eyes.

James banked hard left into a narrow alley, ducking as bullets shot past him, and as he rounded the corner too quickly, he hit a cobblestone surface that caught the cart's wheels, flipping the backside up. The handle hit him in the chest as it sent him tumbling, the contents of the cart spilling everywhere. He landed on the cobblestones, arms pinned beneath him and chin smacking the ground. Stars shot through his vision as scuffling feet and shouts came closer, and the images of what he'd seen them do to the other gang flashed through his mind.

He forced himself up, starting to wholly abandon the cart and its contents, but stooped to grab a few cans of food in one hand and two-gallon jugs of water in the other. He ran for it after he'd picked them up, swinging the heavy jugs and tucking the cans in his arm like a halfback. The alley's length stretched on with no end in sight and no intersections to sidestep into and the gang reached the spilled cart a few seconds later, some laughing, while others continued the chase with growls and catcalls.

"Hey, buddy, you forgot something!"

"Come back, man... you left all this food back here. I'm gonna jam it down your throat until you choke!"

"Don't let him get away!" The leader bellowed, a cold streak of malice running through his voice.

Heart pounding in his chest, stomach sinking, James ran as hard as he could. The wind blew back his hair, and he considered throwing the jugs and cans down but stubbornly hung onto them. Finally, he reached the end of the alley and dashed to the right, sprinting headlong into a crush of dilapidated buildings that had caught fire, collapsed, and crashed together to fill in the alley with bricks and charred wood. He started to go back the other way but saw a path through, darting to the left between sections of piled rubble, ducking beneath toppled beams, jumping a crushed washing machine, and hopping through an ankle-twisting field of burned boards, wires and piping.

His knees and hips bumped sharp objects as he breathed in the stinging scent of ash and burned plastic, circling the piles to keep as many physical barriers as possible between himself and his pursuers. Shouts of frustration chased him as the group reached the end of the alley as well and saw what they had to go through to get him. Curses echoed off the buildings and into the neighborhoods beyond, and shots ricocheted off the rubble, though they were fired in frustration, and had no chance of hitting him, so he paid them no attention. Keeping his head down, he stayed low and ran hard, holding the water jugs and food in a death grip, trying to keep ahead of those hunting him.

While several tried to follow him through the ruins, others ran the edges, working to get around so they could cut him off once he came out the other side. James leaped and ducked and worked his way deeper into the moist soot-covered darkness, finding an old stairwell leading down into a basement, gently pushing aside the wet hanging flaps of insulation, reaching the subfloor, and seeking cover inside a darkened hall. He crouched behind a pile of drywall and wood, smoke drifting by, the softly glowing coals of smoldering materials stirred by the wind of his arrival, the smell acrid and nearly causing him to sneeze. He buried his face in the crook of his arm as footsteps reached the top of the stairs and stopped.

"Do you think he could've went down there?" a woman asked.

"Could have," the man responded, "but do you really want to go down after him?"

"Boss won't like it if we come back empty-handed."

"The boss won't know we didn't check every nook and cranny. Ugh, do you smell that? I ain't going down there and breathing that stuff in. Probably asbestos mixed with who knows what."

James kept his face covered, breathing through the moist material of his jacket, closing his eyes against the fog drifting through the hall, the broken pipes that had once been filled with who-knew-what creating a haze of fumes that mixed with the smoke. Feet appeared on the top step and descended a few paces, paused there, someone stooping and looking down the hallway past James and into the darkness. A flashlight's beam appeared suddenly and James held still, eyes shut tight as he tried to control his ragged breathing and keep from jostling the bottles and cans still in his aching arms. The figure seemed about to come down and look, but her shadow shook its head and headed back up.

"Yeah, you're right. It's pretty nasty down there. Let's head back with the others."

James waited until the footfalls faded far into the distance before he crept from his hiding spot, moving to the stairs, peering upward and half expecting the pair to be hiding somewhere just outside, waiting for him to poke his head up like a rabbit from its hole. At the top step he checked in every direction, creeping out of the condensed haze lightheaded and dizzy, stumbling ahead a few feet and ducking beneath part of the upper stairwell that had fallen and remained intact. He still caught the faint scent of fumes from the stairs and, beneath that, a more pungent sewage stench that was offensive but probably not nearly as dangerous to breathe as whatever was being churned up underground.

He remained there half the night, hugging himself, cold and shivering beneath the broken concrete, water dripping incessantly on his hood and off the front of his jacket. The gang moved through the shadows of the city around him ceaselessly, cries and whistles cutting through the chilly air as they searched for him but eventually gave up, their voices fading as late night turned into early morning. James fell into an uneasy, dozing state between sleep and consciousness, his head filled with flashes of dreams of Alice and the kids, their faces, mannerisms, and laughter shining through the murky fog like rays of sunshine. Eventually, James fell into a deep sleep, hungry, thirsty and yearning for home.

CHAPTER THIRTEEN

Ryan Cooper
Somewhere Outside East Lansing, Michigan

Ryan and Helen sat at the breakfast bar, each with a cup of coffee resting in front of them after finishing their chores for the day, going so far as to dust in nooks and crannies and even vacuum the floors. They'd taken their time, trading off shifts and listening to a bit of music on a CD player Alice had in the master bedroom. Soft rock, a little country, and even some old hits Helen had found in her carry-on she'd brought from home. The mundanity of the work was refreshing, bringing a sense of normalcy to the couple, and with the day's tasks done, they sat quietly, sipping the hot drinks tempered with a touch of fresh cow's milk and sugar.

"Those dogs eat as much as two people." Ryan snorted and took a sip from his cup.

"Good thing we have more eggs than we know what to do with."

The appliances hummed comfortably in the background, giving the place a sense of safety and security, but the feeling of sanctuary was only skin deep. The unpainted patches on the walls, broken dining room windows and damage to the loft were all direct reminders that violence could visit them at any time.

"The railings were chewed up by bullets," he said, looking up at the loft area, "and James doesn't have a lathe to make new spindles. We could search for some in another house, when it's safe to go out. Or we can just patch them up and do something more pressing. Personally, my vote's for that."

Helen ran her thumb along the smooth side of her plain white mug. "I'd like to get the place as close to normal as possible." She scoffed and shook her head sadly. "But I know that's not reality."

Ryan rubbed his leg nervously. "I would've expected Alice and James to be home by now. It's been too long."

"Don't you start worrying about them. You'll get me to worry, too."

"No, no. It's just hard not hearing from them, especially the longer this goes on, and with knowing what kind of people are out there and what they'd do to capitalize on an opportunity. Alice is alone with the kids...."

"Competent kids," Helen corrected him.

"That's true. But the world out there..." Ryan glanced at the blinds covering the rear bay window. "It's worse than it's ever been."

Helen grabbed his arm and squeezed. "See, now you've got me worrying again."

"Sorry, honey. I hate to sound pessimistic, but sometimes I wonder how long we can keep this up."

"Listen to me, Ryan Cooper, you've kept me going through all this, and I won't let you fall into despair. Can't afford for that to happen. Do you understand me?"

"Yes, honey." He sipped his coffee. "I should probably keep some things to myself, eh?"

"Not at all." Helen rested her head on his shoulder. "I always want you to be honest and let me know how you feel. But never forget – we've made it this far, and we'll keep making it just fine."

"We're just doing what we need to do to get by," he replied with a shrug. "Like with that young woman I'm meeting tomorrow. If she turns out to be a fraud, she'll pay a hefty price. I warned her I'll put a bullet in her head if she tried anything, and I think she understood. Still, I'd be surprised if she showed up at all."

"I thought you said you got a good vibe from her."

"Ugh. I'm basing that on my feelings about people *before* all of this. Who knows what's good or bad anymore. I'm trying to reserve my judgment for when I go meet her tomorrow."

"You think she'll bring anything worth trading?"

"That's the least of my concerns. I doubt she'll have much we need. No, I'm more concerned about her honesty. She seemed genuine, but that doesn't mean this isn't another tactic for them to get at us. A direct assault didn't work, so maybe they're trying something else."

"If they wanted to ambush you, they would've done it this morning."

"Maybe. Maybe not. I suppose it doesn't matter. If her intentions are false, we need to know exactly what we're dealing with here. She seemed to imply their group wasn't as tightknit as it had been, but it just takes one desperate person to rally a group of people to do some bad things."

"You should ask her more about that. Maybe she knows..." Something caught Helen's attention, and she raised in her seat and craned her neck.

"What is it?" Ryan asked, turning to his left to see she was looking through one of the windows on the rear side of the house.

"I thought I saw a flash of light out there."

"In the backyard?" Ryan pushed his coffee cup away and grabbed the Winchester, turning and popping out of his chair.

"I don't think so. It's out in the distance in the woods." Helen squinted harder. "On the highway, I think. You can just sort of see it through the trees."

"I'd wager someone's creeping around out there." He threw on his coat. "I'll take Duchess and check."

"Well, I'm going, too." Helen took her coat off the back of the chair and slipped it on.

"You don't have to. Might be best if you stayed here with Duke and Diana."

"Nonsense," she said, picking up her rifle and hanging it from her shoulder. "If it is those people again, you'll need some backup. We'll leave the dogs here to guard the house. Let's go."

Ryan got his boots from the foyer and sat on the stairs to put them on, and when he returned to the kitchen, Helen was standing at the window with her hand on the glass, looking through a pair of binoculars.

"Are they still out there?"

"I still see lights, yes. There's a lot of them flashing through the trees, but it doesn't look like flashlights. Too much greenery on the trees still to tell what it is, exactly."

"Now I'm more curious than ever," Ryan groaned. "If it's not the neighbors trying to circle behind us for another attack, maybe it's another threat. Can we not get a day or three's respite, please?"

They exited the house and walked to the barnyard gate, through the yard with the curious goats and sheep staring out from their enclosure, though not hungry enough or curious enough to come out and follow. The night was cool, their footfalls crunching on cold, stiff grass as the lights glared in the distance past the trees.

"You're right about them not being flashlights," he said. "They're all sitting at one level, not jostling around and pointing in different directions like a person would do. They're not moving around all that much. Looks like cars to me. Sounds like it too. Maybe somebody *is* out on the highway, like you said."

The sky was still cloudy gray, with the moonlight filtering through the gaps and giving them a little light to see by. Ryan kept his flashlight off until he reached the rear gate, using it in brief flashes to see in front of them. There were no trails to follow, only the forest floor covered with dead leaves, twigs, and deadfall big enough to tangle them or cause them to sprain an ankle. Thirty yards into the woods and his calf was stiffening again, the punctured muscles sending a deep ache up through the back of his knee to his hamstring, forcing him to favor it heavily. Approaching the end of the trees, they stooped and parted the bushes in a rustling of dry brush to reveal the short stretch of field and the highway beyond.

Humvees, APCs, and flatbed semi-trailer trucks with long tanks sat on the highway forty yards distant, moving west to east in an armored convoy that stretched out of sight. Off in the distance to the right, a Humvee with a wide plow on the front broke through the wreckage at a steady speed, shoving it off the right-hand shoulder with a crash of metal as it cleared a path for the line of military trucks following behind. Bathed in the glare of headlamps, the vehicles were a hodgepodge of old equipment riddled with dents and rust spots, broken windows with new pieces of plastic taped over them, entire sections of armor refitted and welded together. Old troop transports held the shadowy outlines of soldiers sitting in the back and three long, tubular fuel trucks brought up the rear, their seams rusted and worn but with bright new warning stickers plastered on the sides.

"I wonder where they're going?" Helen whispered.

"Somewhere East... maybe Detroit? Or heading to Washington eventually?"

"How do they even have the gas to move all those?"

Ryan shrugged. "It could be they've ramped up the production of new fuel. They've got a fair number of people in those trucks. Armed to the teeth, too."

"Protecting their fuel." Helen shivered. "Can we head back now?"

"Yeah. I'd rather not get spotted and have to answer uncomfortable questions." Ryan backed out of the bushes, guiding them back toward the house.

As they passed through the barnyard, Helen gestured toward the enclosure where the sheep and goats lingered. "We need to spend more time with the animals. Here, come look at something."

Changing direction, Helen led him over through the pack of animals and rested her hands on their heads as she passed them. "I noticed one of the female Southdowns was limping a little. Where are you, girl... ah, there!"

She guided Ryan through the bleating throng, the smell of manure thick in the cool night air. Finally reaching the trembling female Southdown in the middle of the herd, Helen nudged the others out of the way and crouched, holding the sheep steady with one hand while lifting her front right leg. Ryan shined his light on it and saw a series of short red cuts above the knee, the agitated animal kicking before Helen let her go.

"Might've gotten that wound on the brambles overgrowing the fences on the northeast corner. Darn it, I'd wanted to get to that earlier."

Helen stood and wrapped her arm around his waist. "We've been dealing with so much lately. You can't blame yourself for not getting to that. Besides, it's not that big of a deal. I think the bigger takeaway is if we don't start spending more time with them, we're going to miss when more serious problems crop up."

"No kidding... I'll take care of that brush now. Do we have any supplies to take care of more serious injuries?"

"Alice has some things in a cabinet in the barn. Just some antibiotics and gauze in case of an event like this. We've got her veterinarian's phone number, too, for all the good that'll do."

Ryan snorted. "Yeah, not like we can call it. This brings us to another problem - how to get veterinary care for the animals. I guess we're on point for that, too."

"We never used vets much when we were just starting with our farm. We got by on what we had. If I remember correctly, you kept our farm animals in pretty good shape back then, mostly with bandages and antiseptic cream."

"Yeah, but without wormers, vaccines and professional help things could turn sour if we get some kind of disease that blows through the animals. But I guess we'll just have to deal with the situations as they come." He patted the sheep's head. "Well, no sense in letting her be uncomfortable. How about you bandage her up and I'll go cut down the brambles."

While Helen went inside to find antibiotics and a bandage for the sheep, James grabbed the rake, pruning shears, and a small hand ax from the shed. With his tools in the wheelbarrow, he rolled out to the northeast corner of the property where bushes and vines had overgrown the rails, creating a tangle of stickers and thistles the Southdown had likely gotten caught up in. He went to work on the top of the greenery, cutting away the longer switches and branches, dragging the prickly vines off the rails with a ripping sound, and using his axe and shovel to cut out the more extensive roots that had embedded themselves deeper in the ground.

It took him forty-five minutes to get it all pulled, the strain in his back noticeable as he balanced his weight to keep it off his injured leg. He tossed the loose pieces over the fence to be burned later and got ready to go back. Wiping the sweat off his brow, he packed his tools back in the wheelbarrow and returned to the barn where Helen was checking out the other sheep, the Southdown with the injury easily noticeable by the bright white bandage wrapped around her leg.

"How are they looking?" he asked.

"Oh, most of them are fine," Helen said. "I found a few more scratches and cuts here and there but took care of those."

Ryan shook his head. "Just goes to show you how things can get away from us if we're not maintaining things daily around here."

"Did you get the brush all cleared?"

"It's taken care of. I dropped it over the fence so it'll be out of the sheep's way. I'll wait for it to dry and then drag it over to James' burn pile. Come to think of it, I should probably clear more of that brush that's been building up over the past few weeks and burn it, too. I reckon that's why a lot of the land around here burned so readily after all the fuel went up in smoke. Too much kindling everywhere." He nodded at the sheep as they wandered into and around the barn. "How much more work do you have to do up here?"

"I'm basically done, but I wanted to look at a few more animals before we went inside."

"I'll put the tools away and help you."

As the light faded, Ryan and Helen examined the remaining sheep, checked their hooves and coats, and inspected their eyes for any signs of injuries. For the most part, the animals appeared fine but for a few who'd gotten scratched up in the bushes.

"I'm kicking myself for letting that grow past the fence line," Ryan told Helen as they knelt beside one sheep and examined her legs. "I've heard stories about sheep getting strangled by vines. Not exactly the smartest of animals."

Helen shook her head. "I asked Alice why they'd decided on raising sheep, of all things."

"Ha, wouldn't catch me dead raising the things. Except now, I guess."

"Alice swears up and down by them. They were producing enough meat and wool sales to make it worth it, plus they clear the grass well enough that they didn't need to do any mowing. After getting more experience with them, Alice said they wanted to purchase some dairy breeds and expand the farm." Helen looked around. "At least we're not having to wrestle a whole herd of cattle between the two of us."

"That is very true. We should be able to manage what they've got so long as we don't need a proper vet."

"Alice has a few books on sheep-rearing." She nudged Ryan and winked at him. "So much for that retirement, huh?"

"No kidding. Let's hope they're home sooner than later and can help. Looking at my growing list of chores is starting to get intimidating."

"Maybe if we can smooth things out with the neighbors with that woman's help and get some trading going, we might not have to work so hard to defend ourselves."

"Don't count on it. I'm pretty sure we're the only place that's mostly intact after what happened. House, vehicles, the whole nine yards. I think we'll be on guard for the long term."

Helen put her hands on her hips and stretched her back. "What do you say we get back inside?"

"Yeah, sounds good."

As they cleared the wandering sheep from the barn and locked up, the lights of the military vehicles continued blinking through the trees at the back of the property as they left the barnyard and returned to the house.

Helen held his arm as they walked. "I guess if we ever want to find out where those troops are going, we could follow the path they're clearing."

"I hope it doesn't lead to more highway traffic out there or people walking along. The last thing we want is more folks going by and noticing us."

"Time to tighten up the coverings on the rear windows."

"And I have to be careful not to run the tractor at night, and if I do, it's with the headlamps off." Ryan opened the back door and let her in. "Lights will be a death sentence if we're not careful."

Helen stepped past him and gave him a peck on the cheek. "I hope tomorrow won't be a death sentence for you when you meet that young woman."

Following her inside, he said, "I'll be careful, I promise. Besides, you'll keep an eye on me from up high."

"Absolutely, I will," she replied with a smile. "Want a warm-up on your coffee?"

Ryan shut the door behind him and took off his coat. "Absolutely."

The rising sun had yet to illuminate the horizon and Ryan and Helen stood by the back door, getting him ready for another trip to the gate. Belly full of coffee and breakfast, he finished slipping into his boot and Helen helped him shrug on his heavy coat.

"Do you have everything?"

He patted his belt line and jacket. "I've got my radio, flashlight, and pistol, and my rifle is out in the car with Duchess already."

"Don't forget these," Helen said, grabbing a small bottle from the breakfast bar and shaking the two dozen pills inside. "They've expired, but assuming he's got a bacterial infection, I'd guess they'll work, but make sure to emphasize that we're not promising anything."

"Thanks, honey," Ryan replied, putting the bottle in his pocket. "Don't worry, I will."

Helen squared up to him. "Let's go over the plan again. You go down there like yesterday...."

"And turn the car to face the house in case I need to make a quick escape. I'll keep the back door open so Duchess can come to me if I need her, too, same as before. Any signs of Sandy having a weapon or even the faintest hint there's anyone else nearby, I'll shoot her and make a run for the car. But as long as she's honest, I'll make a deal with her."

"Perfect. Be safe, okay?" Helen gave him a brief hug before stepping back.

With a confident nod, Ryan went outside into the brisk morning, his breath condensing into clouds of mist. The yard was quiet but for the occasional bird call from the woods or the chickens in their coop, scratching and clucking in the predawn light as glints of it began lighting up the yard. He zipped up his coat and walked to the car, climbing into the driver's seat and activating the vehicle. The dashboard lights illuminated Duchess' shaggy form in the backseat, her head tilting as she watched him from where she was sitting.

"We're taking another short ride. Ready?"

Duchess whined, licked her chops, and danced back and forth on her front paws. "Okay, let's go."

The EV rolled around the side of the house and down the driveway with its lights off, the gravel crunching beneath the tires the only sound the vehicle made as the electric motor propelled it forward. He turned a full circle in the grass down near the gate, then got back on the drive and pointed the front end toward the house. Once the vehicle was powered down, he slipped out with his rifle and moved to the passenger side, where he opened the back door a few inches and reassured Duchess with a confident pat on the head.

"Good girl. Stay here. This will be over before you know it."

The dog lowered herself with a whine and shake of her shaggy fur, showing no signs that she'd noticed someone hidden nearby, only staring at him with her big eyes as she whined again over being left behind. He scratched her between the ears and moved to the left-hand side of the gate where a drainage ditch ran along the fence line. It was only four feet deep, a mixture of moist clay and rocks along the sides which he slipped down, then he crouched and moved slightly closer to the gate where he'd have a good view of anyone coming up the road. Duchess stood in the back seat, watching him through the rear window as Ryan squatted in the darkness, the cold seeping through his jeans and jacket, calf stiff and tightening up, forcing him to reposition himself every few minutes.

As the first light of dawn crested the horizon and brightened the treetops to the east, the ducks began to make noise off toward the pond, and birdsong became louder and more varied. It wasn't much longer before a figure appeared out on the road, huddled in a thick coat, hands in her pocket, a plastic grocery store bag hanging from her arm. Duchess growled softly in warning, then louder, ears perked up and alert as the woman slowed her approach. Sandy stopped ten feet away, neck craning forward and searching for Ryan inside the car.

"Ryan? Are you there?"

Still crouched, he turned his head and called, "I'm here. What did you bring to trade?"

With hesitant steps, Sandy approached and rested the bag on the gate. "Batteries. We had a lot of spare batteries we weren't using, so I brought them. It's a mixture of double A and C... We're using the D ones in our lanterns, or I would've brought those. I also have some needles and thread in case you need to repair some clothing. I... I hope it's enough."

There had been no other movement on the road behind her, and the tree line to the east held deep shadows that shifted in the early morning light, though none seemed out of place. Duchess, too, was only fixated on Sandy, and showed no signs of having caught anyone else's scent, so he shouldered his rifle, rose and climbed from the ditch with his pistol in one hand and radio in the other, walking slowly toward Sandy as he thumbed the transmit button.

"Helen, do you see anyone hiding?"

"No. I haven't spotted any movement in the trees on either side of you, and there's no one in the road or around the Jones' house."

"Thanks. Keep watching. If anyone so much as sticks their heads up, you know what to do. I'll make sure this one gets it, too."

"Got it."

Ryan put the radio back on his belt and approached the gate, slipping his pistol back into his pocket and gripping his rifle in both hands.

"You don't have to threaten me like that," Sandy said, taking a few steps back. "I came alone. There's no one hiding anywhere."

"Trust comes hard, Sandy, especially with what happened the other day."

"Believe me, you did a number on them... on us. They've been licking their wounds and no one wants to mess with y'all ever again."

"Good, though I highly doubt they never want to try something again. If they get desperate enough, they'll come again... and I'm sure you can guess what'll happen if you're part of that."

Sandy gulped nervously. "I just want to help my son." She returned to the gate and put the bag back, expression flat yet hopeful as she awaited his judgment.

After another once-over of the surrounding area, he pulled the bottle of pills from his pocket and put them on the gate, stepping back and nodding at them. "These are expired, but only by a few months. Should be plenty potent. Obviously I have no idea if they'll work, but they're broad-spectrum and I'd think they'll work assuming this is a bacterial infection. Two a day for ten days is what's on the instructions."

Sandy glanced at the bottle before taking the bag off the gate and holding it out to him. "Here are the batteries and sewing stuff."

Ryan shook his head and turned away, walking back to the car with a slow gait.

"Wait, don't you want this stuff?"

He stopped and turned at the back of the car. "Of course I do. Given what's going on around here, I want all I can get my hands on." He glanced at his leg and let out a deep sigh. "I'm old, my leg hurts and what I really want, at the end of the day, is just to be able to work together with the folks around us. Trust, Sandy. That's what I want. This is a good first step, you coming to meet me like I asked. Keep your supplies – you and your son probably need them more than we do."

Sandy took the bag and grabbed the pill bottle, staring at the label and turning it around to read the instructions. With glassy eyes, she held the bottle and bag aloft and shook them in his direction. "Thanks for this, Ryan. I'm... I'm so sorry my husband was—"

Ryan shook his head and waved her off. "Yeah, yeah, I don't need to hear it again. And you're welcome. If you want to keep building on this trust, meet me here again in the morning after you've medicated your son. I'd like to know how he's doing and if the meds are helping him or not."

"Absolutely. I'll be here in the morning. Thank you so much," tears streamed down her cheeks as she clutched at the bottle of pills. "I won't forget you for this."

Ryan nodded and muttered an 'mhm', shut the back door, and climbed into the car, watching Sandy hurry down the road. Before she passed out of sight, she broke into a jog, flying with her hair bouncing on her shoulders. Duchess whined and leaned over the seat to nudge and lick his face.

"Good girl," he laughed and rubbed her ears, then he turned on the car and crept back up the driveway.

Helen met him at the back door, letting Duchess in and joining him at the kitchen table where she warmed up his coffee and sat across from him.

"Well, what happened? I saw you let her keep her bag of whatever she brought."

"It was a productive exchange, I think." Ryan related the conversation, describing how appreciative Sandy was of the antibiotics, and how he'd refused to take what she'd offered and why. "I couldn't bring myself to take her supplies given how much we've got here."

"You could've taken it out of principle."

"Maybe."

"What's your angle, Ryan?" Helen's eyebrow went up.

"Like I told her, I want trust." He thumped his fist on the table, growling in frustration. "I'm tired of being on guard twenty-four seven. Even one more person we can trust would do wonders for us, and for them."

"Will we be able to trust any of those people, after what they did to us?"

"I doubt it... but you know me, always holding out hope."

Helen reached across the table and patted his hand. "You've made some pretty good decisions, and I trust you've got a solid plan."

"The important thing now is to keep working hard and maintain our patience, both with ourselves and the neighbors. And you know that's something I run thin on sometimes."

"I'll help you with that," Helen smiled. "Are you ready to go do some work?"

"Yeah... let's fill the thermoses with coffee first. It's going to be a long day."

CHAPTER FOURTEEN

Sarah Burton
Talladega National Forest, Alabama

A rustling near her head brought Sarah out of a deep, dark sleep, the exhaustion of riding all day on the slanted forest trails leaving a deep soreness that penetrated her hips and lower back. She blinked wearily at the campfire, the flames having died down to orange and gold flickers as grogginess clouded her head. All around her, insects chirped and the brush rustled, the wilderness crackling and snapping to the light snores of those lying around the fire ring.

Christine and Mark were across from her with Hunter between them, three bundles mixed in with a variety of blankets and red and blue sleeping bags. Jake was at Sarah's feet with Mia near her head where the rustling had come from, the young girl behaving restlessly all night and struggling to sleep.

Mark and Christine had kept the two children busy, making it hard for Jake and Sarah to spend time with them, but at least Mia still hadn't been worn out enough to sleep out of pure exhaustion. Sarah closed her eyes again, clinging to the grogginess, hoping to get a few more hours of rest before Alice woke them up to get packed up and move out. Just before she drifted off, a light tapping on her shoulder brought her out of it, and she stirred back awake with a subtle flicker of alarm in the back of her head. Sarah pushed her sleeping bag down and started to turn when a small hand gripped her shirt and a soft, timid sound came into her ear.

"Sarah? Are you awake?"

"Yeah, um..."

"Please, help us." It was Mia, her request urgent, voice barely above a whisper. *"Please."*

"Wha...?" Jolting awake, Sarah got her elbow beneath her and turned, expecting Mia to be right next to her, but all she saw was a rustling of blankets and a small form shifting, rolling over, and disappearing in the folds near Mark, Christine and Hunter. She started to say something, but Christine and Mark were up and moving across from her, whispers passing between them. Christine got up, checked on Hunter, then crawled around the fire in the opposite direction. Sarah sank into her sleeping bag, closed her eyes, and pretended to be asleep as more covers shifted and rustled near her head, then Christine whispered something Sarah barely made out.

"Be good... understand...?"

Mia responded in a quiet, tiny voice. "Mm hm."

Christine stood and circled the fire to lean over Mark. "I'm going to help Alice keep watch. I'll be back soon. Keep an eye on things here."

"Okay."

After Christine had gone, Sarah tried to recapture the grogginess of before, but an irritating nausea clung to her stomach, and she only half dozed to the forest sounds that had suddenly grown cold and sinister for reasons her sleep-addled brain couldn't quite figure out. When she finally slept it was fitful, with explosions and angry faces chasing her through her dreams, weapons firing from the darkness and shapeless forms trying to drag her and her family off their horses. A short time later, the sun crept above the trees, casting a fragile glow over the campsite and making it impossible to sleep.

Alice appeared a few moments later, shaking her and Jake's shoulders. "Come on, guys. It's time to get up and get moving. We'll help them get their bedding and tents packed up and buckled to Hercules, then we'll divide up the riding between the other three horses. Sarah, make sure your brother gets up."

"Okay, Mom," Sarah replied, pulling herself out of her half-sleep and slipping her boots on, hips and back feeling even worse from lying on the hard, uneven ground.

She went to wake Jake, but he was already up and moving, shoes on and kneeling by his sleeping bag, slouching as he rolled it up and tied it into a firm, round bundle. When she turned back the other way to find Mia, she'd gone off with Mark and was busy gathering the toys she and Hunter had been playing with the day before. With a grunt, Sarah rose and got moving, rolling up her sleeping bag, stuffing it into her pack, and buckling it to Hercules' saddle with automatic movements driven by exhaustion. A few minutes later, Mark had stoked the fire and had something cooking on it, the rich aroma helping to drag her the rest of the way out of her sleep.

"What *is* that?" Jake said, heading back over to the fire. "It smells amazing."

"Just a few leftovers from the week," Mark said. "The ham and beans from last night and some sausages packed in tinfoil. I just toss them into the fire along with onions and peppers. Let them cook for about ten minutes and you've got a meal."

"That sounds delicious, Mark," Alice replied. "It's good to know we found some more new friends with cooking skills."

"Oh, we do a lot of camping, so I guess I've learned a thing or two."

They ate off tin plates, Sarah sitting on her log with her knees together, head down as she focused on eating when Jake sat next to her and nudged her with his elbow.

"What was all that about this morning?" He kept his voice low, and Sarah checked to see that Mark and Christine were standing by the horses, where Alice was helping them strap their tents and campfire equipment to Hercules.

"I thought Mia might've whispered something to me, but it feels like a dream."

"Whatever she was doing woke me up," Jake said. "What was she whispering?"

"I think she said..." Sarah shook her head slowly. "I think she said she needed help, or maybe her brother did. I can't remember right."

"Maybe they both did." Jake gave a pointed nod to where the kids stood off to the side, holding hands with toys tucked under their arms. "They seem way too quiet to me. You should tell Mom what you heard."

Sarah took a deep breath. "I'm... I'm really not sure if I heard anything, but something doesn't feel right about the situation. I'll tell Mom as soon as—"

"Sarah. Jake. Let's get moving. Please help Mia and Hunter onto the horses. They'll ride with you on Stormy and Rocky, and I'll let Christine and Mark ride on Buck."

"That's unnecessary, Alice," Mark said. "We're more than happy to walk beside you guys."

"Seriously, I don't mind. Do you know how to ride? If not, I can help you."

"Absolutely not, Alice." Christine took her arm. "We wouldn't think of making you walk. It's enough that our little ones will be off their feet and up high where it's safer. We've seen snakes around, and there are predators everywhere, so we'll help make sure the horses don't get spooked."

"I heard a story about someone's kid getting snatched while they were up here," Mark said. "A mountain lion had dragged them several yards to the woods when the father finally caught up with them and shot the darn thing. The kid, though...well. It was a tragedy."

"Oh, that's terrible," Alice raised her eyebrows. "I think we're strong enough in number to keep everyone safe, though."

"We appreciate that," Christine said, then turned to Mark. "Come on, honey. Let's grab our packs, and we can get moving."

Sarah kneeled in front of Mia and held out her hand. "Come on, honey. You can ride with me."

Mia nodded and allowed herself to be led to Stormy, and Sarah mounted and held out her hands for Jake to lift the little girl. After Mia was situated in front of her, and while everyone else was busy, Sarah whispered in her ear. "Are you okay?"

Mia nodded.

"What did you say to me this morning?"

Mia shook her head.

"But—"

Christine stepped past them, glancing up with a smile.

"Is this your first horse ride?" Sarah asked Mia, matching Christine's smile.

"Yeah."

"Are you scared?"

"Yeah." Sarah's heart nearly broke as the word came out in a small, soft whimper.

"Well, hold on to the saddle horn in front of you. I promise I won't let you fall off."

"Okay."

"Stormy would feel better if you petted him. Want to pet him?"

"Okay..."

"I'll hold on to you, and you can just reach down and pet him. Go ahead."

Mia put her hand on Stormy's muscular neck, stroking his sleek coat and when he snorted, she snatched her hand back and giggled wildly.

"Did you like that?" Sarah laughed.

"Yeah."

"See, this'll be fun!"

Mia's giggle cut off when Christine stepped over and held Stormy's bridle, drawing an annoyed grunt from the horse. She gave Mia a lingering look before shifting to Sarah. "What a beautiful horse. Is he gentle?"

"Oh yeah, Stormy's great. I promise I'll take good care of Mia. I've got a lot of experience riding now."

Christine's smile faltered before the corners of her mouth lifted with a nod. "Good. Now, Mia, stay in the saddle with Sarah, and do exactly what she tells you, okay?"

Mia nodded back and settled against Sarah, and Sarah hugged her and took up the reins, staring at Christine as she joined Mark up front with Alice and Buck. Soon, everyone was ready to go, and Alice, Christine and Mark took the lead, walking slowly through the thickets that crowded their pathway, kicking up a dust cloud as they headed back toward the trail.

Alice swayed on Buck's back as the seemingly endless trail wove over a string of spurs that skirted the southern tip of the Appalachian Mountains. The path cut north again along the edge of a narrow ridge that gave them astounding views of the sweeping valleys, with bright pink coloring the horizon, and the sun glinting across the treetops, countless trees standing at attention like spears pointed at the sky. Conifers were standouts in the forest as many of the other trees' leaves were beginning to change color, the pines growing thicker where creeks ran through the flatlands and becoming thinner up on the valley walls. Wide streams wound down from the heights, pouring over cold stones to the bottom where they cut through pastures filled with tall grasses.

"Oh, check it out!" Sarah pointed into the valley at four specks lumbering alongside a narrow creek.

"Are those bears?"

"I think so," Sarah replied.

Jake shielded his eyes from the sun. "It's a mother and some cubs I think."

"See them, Mia?" Sarah asked with hushed excitement.

"Yeah, whoa!"

"They're pretty cute," Alice said. "At least from this distance. Won't be so cute if we get between mom and her cubs, though."

"Yeah, Mom," Jake said, and Sarah chuckled.

Alice smiled at Mia seated in front of Sarah, hanging on tight and wearing a wondrous expression. "How's she doing?"

Sarah forced a smile. "Pretty good, I think. At first, she was a little scared, but she's enjoying the ride now."

"The kids have never been around horses before," Christine said, walking up quickly and patting Stormy on the neck. "They might act a little weird until they get used to it. If she starts to bug you, let us know, and we'll get her right down. That goes for you, too, Jake."

"We're good back here," Jake replied.

"And Mia's doing fine," Sarah said, "right, honey?"

Mia nodded faintly and looked in the opposite direction, her tiny mouth forming a thin line.

"Are you sure you don't want to ride?" Alice asked Christine. "Seriously, you can ride with me on Buck. You and Mark can take turns."

"We're fine walking," Christine replied, looking back at Mark.

"Yeah, don't worry about us," he added from where he hiked beside Jake and Hunter, having drifted back from the lead.

"Have it your way." Alice shrugged and faced forward, focusing ahead as they descended a deceptively complicated switchback that hooked them south and then north again, pulling them deeper into the valley where the slopes rested in the dark, cool shade of the trees and mountains above.

Acorns fell with sharp cracks, and the woods creaked around them as unseen creatures scurried through the branches above and the undergrowth below. Flocks of birds launched high and turned in perfect synchronization, painting the sky in moving shadows before alighting in the treetops. A squirrel ran across the path, dodged back and forth through the thickets, then scampered halfway up a tree to stop and stare as Alice and Buck slowly ambled along. She gave the woodland creature an amused half wave, and it shot up into the higher branches at the movement to disappear into the leafy vegetation.

They walked endlessly, taking only brief breaks to rest or drink where the trail was wide and flat, coming upon ample creeks and small ponds where the horses could refresh themselves. By the third hour, Alice noticed Mark and Christine panting and sweating as they all ascended a treacherous incline, barely able to lift their feet, leaning against the horses and nearby trees for leverage.

The soil crumbled beneath them in places, thick roots stretching across the trail that stood inches above the dirt, easy to trip on for anyone not paying attention. At the top, they reached a shoulder of the hill with a massive stone monolith, its chiseled gray walls towering over them. The path wound around it to the north and continued on the other side, and Alice waited for everyone to join her at the top while she looked out across the extraordinary view.

"Are you sure you guys don't want to swap and ride for a while?" Alice asked Christine as she stumbled to the top, stopping to lean over with her hands on her knees.

"No... it's... fine." Sweat poured down her face as she sucked air, and it took a good minute to catch her breath. "We're doing fine."

"It doesn't look like it." Alice mumbled as she turned Buck away to give the others more room to fit on the shoulder.

Sarah and Jake joined them, leading Hercules up with Mark coming last after falling behind. He took the same position as Christine, leaning over and holding his side.

"I'm fine," he waved. "Just have a cramp, is all."

"We'll rest here for a minute. It looks like the trail winds around this big outcrop and continues down the other side. It's going to be just as hard going down as it was going up, maybe harder. So, let me know if you want to ride." Christine and Mark stood to the side in quiet discussion but didn't accept her offer. Sarah and Jake dismounted with the younger kids and started to give them water, but Christine and Mark pulled them to the side and gave them some from their own supplies. Alice allowed them a few extra minutes to rest before calling for everyone to mount up again. She gave up on offering Mark and Christine a ride but watched them as they descended the hill, half staggering over rocks and branches, forced to grab the horses' saddle straps or harnesses to stay close to the kids.

"You're going to get yourself stepped on if you keep that up," Alice warned them, but they paid her no mind and stuck to the horses' sides, checking on the kids every few minutes until Sarah finally looked at Alice with a helpless expression and got a shrug in response.

It took them an hour and a half to get down the hill with the midday sun brutally beating down on them, and Alice was sweating just watching the others try to keep up. After a tricky descent, they reached a floodplain that sloped straight to a crystalline lake surrounded by a stand of pines above a windswept forest floor. Alice marched them to the edge of the lake where Mark and Christine stooped over with their hands on their knees, gasping and beyond winded. Sarah started to help Mia down when Christine came out of her tired stance and snatched the young girl out of Sarah's hands.

"I can get her..." Sarah said, exasperated. "And I was going to ask my mom if we can rest in the shade for a while."

"Yep, that's what she needs," Christine said. "Come on, Mark. Let's take the kids in the shade and let them rest a while."

Mark and Christine took the kids and sat them on the shoreline where the trees arched over the lake, handing them their toys and some water and sitting tiredly next to them. Alice slouched in her seat, sliding off Buck and staggering a couple of steps, leaning on him so she didn't fall.

"Good boy," she said, leading him to the water's edge. "Come on and get yourself something to drink."

Sarah and Jake brought their mounts over to stand in line and cool off in the shade, then together they gathered lake water in bottles and drank it through filter straws, standing around quietly while a soft breeze blew through and dried their sweat. Alice went to the shoreline, stooping and wetting a rag to place against her cheeks and neck while Jake and Sarah squatted by the water, glancing over at Mark and Christine as they came up.

"Those are pretty cool," Mark said. "Are those filter straws?"

He'd taken off his heavy coat and looked miserable and wet, his sweaty clothes hanging off his shoulders, pants loose on his hips. Christine walked up behind him, a ring of sweat around her T-shirt, beads of it trickling down her face, strands of lank hair clinging to her cheeks.

"Yep," Alice replied. "We got them a long time ago from a warehouse just before someone tried to rob us."

"I guess you don't need any of our waters," Mark said, holding up an unopened one.

"No, we're fine. The straws work well."

Christine pushed a strand of hair behind her ear. "That's got to be a pain, having to suck on the straw so much."

"Eh, it's not hard, especially when you're thirsty," Alice smiled, watching Jake and Sarah strolling over to the kids, Jake side-arming tiny stones so they skimmed across the water. "You two seem to have plenty of supplies for people who've been up in the mountains for several days."

"We used Hunter's toy wagon to haul our supplies up here," Mark said. "Saved our butts."

"Until the wheels fell off," Christine said, accepting the wet rag Alice offered and going to the edge of the lake.

"We started out with a few cases of water and have less than one now," Mark said. "I guess we should have picked up some filter straws, too."

"Camping supply stores would have them. Before we leave you at Ft. Wayne, we'll look for some."

"Oh, wow. We'd really appreciate it." Mark wiped off his forehead with a rag. "Maybe you could give us a list of stuff in general to pay attention to."

Alice patted Buck's flank. "I mean, it's good to have an idea of where you're going and what supplies you have on hand and need, but most of the lessons we learned out here are from experience. We were never what you'd call preppers or anything like that, but we've adapted and just rolled with the punches." Alice crossed her arms and laughed. "The world doesn't care about lists or plans."

"But you've done well compared to a lot of people we've seen.

"Well, you haven't seen the kind of people *we've* seen if you've been up here so long."

"No, that's true. But we survived."

"Don't get me wrong," Alice crossed her arms. "You made the right decision coming up here, especially for your kids. But off these trails, the world is a different place."

Mark turned his face away and rubbed his chin. "Yeah, well, um... I'll pick your brain a little before we get out of these woods if you don't mind."

"Sure, maybe on one of these breaks—"

"Hey, kids! Get back here!" Christine shouted as she got up and started around the shoreline where the four kids were sitting together. Sarah was stooping by the water and using a stick to poke around at something while Hunter and Mia were nearby, leaning on Jake, watching, and smiling as he spoke quietly to them. Christine rushed over in a panic, snatching Mia up and taking Hunter by the arm, turning them roughly back to their original spot and sitting them down hard, leaving Jake and Sarah standing there gaping.

"I-I was just showing them some tadpoles," Sarah stammered confusedly. "They weren't even close to the water."

Christine reeled on Sarah, fist clenched, her eyes flashing with anger briefly before the look faded, and she shook her head and smiled thinly. "I'm sure they were fine, but I just don't want them that close to the water. Neither one of them can swim... so, please just keep that in mind."

"Yeah... okay... sorry again," Sarah replied in confusion.

"Oh, my..." Mark put his hand to his forehead and started to walk away. "Sorry about that, Alice. Christine is super protective of the kids."

"That's okay," Alice frowned. "I totally understand. I'll make sure my kids don't take yours too close to the water. Jake. Sarah. Over here please."

"Mom, we didn't do anything," Sarah whispered, coming over with Jake as she defended herself. "They were three feet from the water the whole time, and Jake was right there next to them!"

Alice gripped Sarah's shoulder. "I know, honey. I saw them. You're fine."

Sarah's aggravated look faded into bewilderment. "I thought they were nice people, but... they're starting to annoy me."

"We're all under some stress from being on the trail. Tell you what, just stay away from them for a little while and let them cool off a bit. In the meantime, let's check out the horses for cuts and abrasions. We passed through some pretty rough thickets growing up on the trail. And remember what Wilford said about scratches. If you see any breaks in the skin, we have to use that antibacterial ointment he gave us to gently clean them. Just report anything you find to me before you try and treat it."

"Yes, ma'am," Jake said with a brief salute, while Sarah stared across at the Hubbards for a long moment.

"Mom, there's... something else."

"Hm?" Alice pulled Buck away from the others and moved down each leg carefully, running her hands along his forearms and knee, all the way to the hooked pastern, remembering what Wilford had told her about pale legs being more susceptible to sun damage and chaffing. "What is it?"

"It's the kids, they're just...."

"I know, hon. Mark and Christine are an odd pair."

"No, I mean... I had this... nevermind." Sarah sighed and headed off to tend to another one of the horses.

Alice watched her go for a long moment with a raised eyebrow before finishing up her once-over of Buck. "Looks like you're perfect, boy." She patted his hip and had a handful of cashews from their pack, watching the Hubbards closely where they sat off to the side, Mark and Christine crouched on the lakeside, talking quietly amongst themselves, occasionally gesturing to the children who continued to nod in response.

Not long after, Alice cupped her hands over her mouth. "Okay, folks. Let's move out. This time we'll keep going until it's dinnertime. We're talking a good three hours or more of tough terrain. Mark and Christine? Are you going to be okay? Sure you don't want to ride?"

"Oh, yeah," Mark called, standing and stretching his arms over his head. "We're good. Looks like it'll be flat forest trails from here on out."

The trail followed the lake shore to the north and cut eastward through the trees again. "It looks that way," Alice nodded, keeping her voice positive. "Just let me know if you need some help."

"We will."

They mounted up the same as they had before and walked along the glimmering shoreline to where the trail cut east, stepping into a narrow tract of sun-baked dirt with few roots or stones in the way. Mark was right about the area; the path was broad and flat, with thin stands of pines and good visibility for forty or fifty yards in any direction. Mark jogged ahead, confidently calling out spots where the trail dipped or turned and once out of the woods, they descended even deeper into a valley, moving along the edge of a pine forest with vast, sweeping grasslands off to the right.

"Mom, can we stop for a bit?"

Sarah and Mia were riding close behind them, and Christine had fallen back a little to talk with Hunter, resetting him in his seat and shaking her head as she spoke with him.

"I said we're riding through to dinner."

"I know," Sarah winced, "but we really need to stop now."

Christine had let go of Hunter and was shuffling ahead, catching up with Sarah and Mia.

Jake chimed in, "Seriously, Mom. My legs are killing me from being on this horse all afternoon. If we could rest a few minutes so I could walk it off, that would be great."

"Yeah, Alice, a short break for the kids wouldn't be bad!" Christine called out.

"I was hoping to get farther," Alice replied, "but we can take a quick break. Hey, Mark, we're taking a break."

He'd gotten about twenty yards ahead but came jogging back, hand raised and nodding. "Sounds good to me!"

Pulling the horses off the trail and a few feet into the woods, they tied them up so they wouldn't wander and sat on the leaf-covered trail edge. Christine and Mark took Hunter and Mia off to the right, sitting them a few yards away from the group, speaking and gesturing to them as they had been throughout the trip. At some point, Hunter said something loudly and punched Mark in the arm. Mark's face turned red with anger, and he drew back his hand but let his arm fall at the last second, chastising him quietly instead. Alice watched the exchange closely, eyes narrowed, sipping on a bottle of water.

"Jake, let's get some snacks," Sarah said, and the two stood beside Hercules and rifled through his saddle bags for some high-calorie protein bars. The pair talked quietly for a moment before Jake wandered off a few yards to the right near the Hubbards and the horses, eating his protein bar while staring into the woods.

Sarah sat heavily on Alice's right, head low and whispering. "Mom, we've got a problem."

"What's going on?" Alice accepted a protein bar and tore open the package. "Besides how those two treat their kids, I mean."

Sarah shook her head. "Whatever you do, don't look over at them, okay? Just try to be natural."

Alice stiffened slightly but nodded. "What is it?"

"Mia and Hunter? They're not their kids."

"What in the world are you talking about?"

"Mia and Hunter aren't theirs. I had my suspicions last night when –"

"Hey, Alice, do you have any extra snack bars?" Mark was walking over, smiling at her.

"We've got some here." Jake swept in and cut him off, turning him toward Hercules and their saddlebags.

"Jake's running interference so I can talk to you." Sarah's voice dropped another octave, and her words came out in a rush. "Last night, Mia tried to tell me something, but Christine interrupted her. I was so tired I thought it was just a dream but I'm sure of it now."

"Is that what you were trying to talk to me about earlier?"

"Yeah!"

"What did she say?" Alice asked, picking up a twig and twirling it between her finger and thumb as she sipped from a bottle of lake water.

"She said, '*help us.*'"

"Help us?"

"Yeah. I was confused at first, but now it's making a lot more sense. The way they've been overprotective of the kids but being just awful to them. And every time I try to talk to Mia about *anything*, Christine is right there, interrupting us."

Alice smiled as if Sarah had told her a joke. "I wonder why she's doing that?"

"Well, she's looking at us now, so don't look."

"I won't. Go on."

"When we first met them, Christine *seemed* friendly, but her smile creeps me out now."

"I won't lie, I've been watching them a fair amount since the lake... something definitely seems off."

Mark and Jake walked over with a handful of snack bars and gave one to Christine, and the three stood talking together.

"Jake is keeping them busy," Sarah said, "so we have to talk fast. What have you been noticing?"

"Everything, now that I've been paying attention," Alice replied. "They won't ride even when they're near to keeling over, and ever since the lake, Mark really seemed to know the trails. A little too well, if you ask me..." Alice shook her head. "But... why?"

"I don't know *why*, Mom. I just know something's wrong."

While Jake was talking with Christine, Mark stepped away and had turned to watch Alice and Sarah. Alice and Mark locked eyes, and Alice saw something sinister in them, something she hadn't quite picked up on herself, not until Sarah had made them stop, not until she'd colored in some lines and asked a few more questions of herself. Mark's eyes shifted as he glanced toward Buck, and Alice's heart sank as she saw him shifting to move toward the beast, realizing that she'd made a horrible, terrible mistake in letting her guard down.

Her rifle was no longer in her arms, but was instead strapped to the side of Buck's saddle.

She leaped up and launched herself toward the horses, slipping on the loose leaves and almost going down. Buck was in the middle of the horses, forcing her to skirt around Stormy's flanks and circle to the right side where the gun was sheathed. She squeezed between Buck and Rocky and lunged for the weapon, but Mark was already there, hand on the stock and drawing it free from its sheath.

With a desperate gasp, Alice grabbed the gun barrel and tried to shove it back down into the scabbard while simultaneously reaching for her pistol. Mark saw what she was doing and struck out awkwardly with his left fist, landing a weak blow, though it caught her on the jaw, sending stars spinning through her head as she fell and rolled beneath Buck. The horse shifted his massive weight above her, hooves stomping close to her head and Alice rolled to the opposite side, grabbed Stormy's stirrup, and hauled herself up, wrestling her pistol free.

There was a scuffle near the trail, and Alice slid in that direction, gun pointed at Christine where she struggled with Jake, pushing, pulling, twisting with grimacing faces as they each tried to gain control. Gone was the timid, seemingly friendly woman of before, replaced by a wildcat who glared and snarled at Jake, the tendons in her arms and hands standing out as she wrestled with him. Sarah rushed in screaming and flailing, striking Christine in the head with a wild punch, then hit her again, knuckles cracking hard across her neck and shoulders and arms, but unable to knock her off of Jake.

Unable to fire unless she wanted to hit one of her kids, Alice shifted in the other direction, looking for Mark when the butt of her rifle flew toward her face, smashing her in the side of the head, sending her staggering to her right, twisting, tripping, and falling on her backside at the trail's edge. Rocking backward and then forward, she swung her gun up, focusing on Mark's blurry form, and firing half-blind, barely holding onto the weapon. The pistol's kick threw her off balance as the rifle butt sailed by two inches from her nose, and her head cracked the dirt hard, sending arcs of light shooting through her skull all the way to her eyes, clenching her head in a fist of pain. She brought her gun to bear for one last shot, but through the blur in her vision she realized she wasn't holding it anymore. Before she could scrabble around for it, Mark was on her, his knee in her chest, pinning her to the ground while she gasped and gripped his leg, squirming and kicking weakly.

"Knock it off, Alice!" Mark growled, putting the rifle barrel against her forehead and pushing back to the ground. "Knock it off, or I'll blow your head off!"

Alice gave another kick, and the rifle barrel slipped to her cheek, pressing the side of her face against the dirt.

"I'm *serious*." She heard the safety tick off. "Settle down right now, or you *and* your kids will get it!" He half turned. "Christine, you got things under control back there?!"

"I've got them," she said. "Just give me a second to get them tied up!"

Mark stepped aside enough for Alice to see, and a slow-burning anger grew in her chest and twisted her guts with hatred as she stopped struggling, blinking away the dirt in her eyes. Christine had a gun pointed at the back of Jake's head, forcing him to slump forward where he sat on the trail. Sarah lay on the ground nearby, holding her stomach and nursing a bloody nose and lip while glaring at Christine with revulsion.

Christine's hair sat in a tousled bun, strands hanging loose from their clips to frame her red, puffy face as she panted and screeched at Sarah. "You come at me again, you little bitch, and I'll put a bullet in the back of your brother's head!" Forcing his arms behind his head, she used a piece of rope to bind him, eying Sarah the entire time, daring her to try something.

"I... I don't understand," Alice murmured, each word like a gong going off in her head.

"Of course, you don't." The rifle barrel pressed harder into her cheek as he laughed. "Because you're stupid. Hurry up, Christine."

"Almost there."

Brandishing Jake's pistol, Christine walked toward Sarah, who'd gotten to her knees and looked like she was about to lunge. Christine lashed out with a kick and Sarah cried out in pain as she tumbled over, holding her face as blood poured from her nose. Jake tried to move toward her, but Christine side-stepped him and pistol-whipped him, sending him tumbling over next to his sister.

"Now, y'see, that's the kind of foolishness that's gonna get you all in trouble." Christine tutted, wagging the pistol at the pair. "Let me go over the rules real fast. *We're* in control now, and we got the weapons. If you do something stupid, I'll put a bullet in you both and your mom, too. Play nice, and you'll get out of this just fine. We don't want to shoot anyone if we don't have to. You're no good to us lame or dead."

"You're... you're liars! I knew it!" Sarah stammered as drool and blood dripped from her chin, her face smeared with red.

"Ohhh, come on now. We're not *that* bad. If we wanted to just shoot you and take your things, we'd have already done it. Now, the pair of you get up and come over here. Sit down nice and easy together."

"Jake... Sarah..." Alice croaked, "Just... just do what they say."

"That's right," Mark purred. "Even your mother knows when you've lost. Come on now. We don't have all day. This charade has put us *massively* behind schedule."

Emotions battled behind Sarah's eyes, her jaw working back and forth as tears streamed down her cheeks. Finally, she looked at Jake who had rolled over onto his side and the pair nodded and she helped him stand, then they moved over to where Christine had indicated.

"Now, put your hands behind your back," Christine said. "Good girl. I'm going to put the gun down for a second, and I know what you're thinking, but if you make so much as a twitch to try and get it, Mark'll put another hole in your pretty mommy's head. Are you going to make any trouble?"

Sarah's whole body sagged and she bowed her head and shook it.

"Fantastic. See? We *can* get along! One second, hon."

While Christine bound Sarah and tightened Jake's rope, Mark removed his knee from Alice's chest, gesturing with the rifle barrel. "I'm going to need you to flip over, too."

Hatred flashed in her eyes and she glanced over, trying to find her pistol, gauging how long it would take her to lunge for it. Mark chuckled and shook his head.

"Your gun got knocked about ten feet in that direction. If you think you can get to it before I shoot you three or four times, well, I mean hey, try it and see where it gets you."

"Don't do it, Mom," Sarah rasped. "They said they wouldn't hurt us. You won't hurt us, will you?"

"Of course not." Christine's words were saccharine as she finished with Sarah and Jake and came to assist Mark, getting on her knees, rolling Alice over, and binding Alice's hands while Mark stepped back. Taking her by the shoulder, she flipped her back and retreated a few paces to survey her handiwork with Mark.

"Dang, Christine," Mark laughed. "We finally got 'em. That rest break was perfect. Kudos to you kids for insisting on it."

Christine whooped and slapped him on the back, waving the pistol around in Sarah's direction. "I wasn't sure we could do it. That little bitch is pretty strong, but an elbow to the gut was all it took to knock her down."

"C'mon, let's get Alice over by the others." Together, the pair took Alice by the arms and lifted her, half dragging her to the kids, and throwing her down next to them.

"Now, let's see what they've *really* got on them." Before he stepped away, he aimed the gun at Jake's face. "Don't try anything stupid, you hear? Your kids will suffer the consequences of your mistakes. Ya get me?"

Alice clenched her teeth, taking a long breath and nodding before Mark and Christine went over to Hercules and began rifling through their bags.

"Are you kids okay?" Alice spoke softly to them, and Sarah sniffed and nodded.

Jake leaned forward, glaring intensely, jaw flexing. "I'm going to kill them, Mom."

"I heard that!" Christine called, taking the nearly-empty bug spray and two used water filter straws and tossing them over her shoulder into the woods.

"I'm just glad we don't have to put on that act anymore," Mark snorted. "Took forever for the bitch to let her guard down."

"Right?" Christine replied. "Maybe we should just shoot them all for annoying us so much."

"Now, you know we can't do that, so don't get too excited. We've still got a way to go. But, hey, we just doubled our workers for the camp up north. Want a snack bar?"

"Sure do. What about the brats?"

Mia and Hunter sat quietly a few yards away with their heads low and holding hands, Mia clutching a doll to her chest, both of them avoiding even a wayward glance in Mark or Christine's direction.

"They can go hungry for all I care," Mark shrugged. "They nearly gave us away anyway."

Tears stung Alice's eyes and ran burning down her face. "How can you say that?"

"We can say – and do – what we please." Mark stepped away from Hercules and stood in front of Alice with his feet spread, mouth twisted in a contemptuous grin. He stared at her for a few seconds before raising the rifle and pointing it at her chest. "Or are you deaf *and* stupid?"

"If you lay a finger on any of their heads," Alice spoke through bared teeth, "you'll wish you didn't live to regret it."

Mark's smile dropped for a moment, his eyes opening nervously for a few seconds before he dropped the charade and laughed uproariously. "Nah, Alice." The laughter ceased without warning and there was a slight *click* as his finger ticked the rifle's safety off. "You won't be doing a damn thing about *anything*."

Alice's eyes registered the briefest flash of light from the end of the rifle's barrel, though both it and the ear-splitting boom were instantly cut off when a meteor struck her chest and sent her flying backward into a pit of darkness.

CHAPTER FIFTEEN

Raj
Industrial Area, Doha, Qatar

Dawn broke over the city of Qatar, the sun's rays streaming across the rooftops and the telephone poles, seeping in through the window to give the first glimpse of the day's heat. Raj finished his morning tea in the one-room apartment he shared with fourteen other men, the workers packed in on cots lining every wall, the bathroom only a bucket in the corner, leaving the room soaking in a perpetual reek that choked his lungs. Foremen outside shouted for the workers to get up and moving, their voices booming above the quiet din, eager to force their workers to get back to clearing Qatar's streets and rebuilding what the flames had destroyed. Once rolling in gas and oil money, the ultra-rich city had been brought to its knees just like the rest of the world by the explosions that had broken out in its refining factories and neighborhoods.

The slums where the workers stayed had been spared the worst of the explosions since they couldn't drive vehicles or operate gas-powered machines. But the ruling class of Qatar - the business owners and foremen who owned the workers' "contracts" - were determined to keep them moving every hour of the day in constant, grueling shifts. Several men in the room were on their knees in the middle of the floor, praying as a voice from a radio chanted softly beside them, while others poured themselves tea from a small stove in the back, burning scraps of lumber they'd picked up from the previous day's shift.

Bali, an older man who'd been in Qatar for three years, sat up in his bed and held his feet, gently touching the blisters covering them. "I don't think I can work today."

"You must keep working." Akash, a younger man who hadn't been in the country working for long, leaned against the bunk pole, "or you won't get fed."

"What does it matter when all we eat is dirt and water?"

Raj couldn't disagree with the older man. The food, which had already been bad before, was more rotten and bland than ever, and regular supplies of rations had dwindled. The men in his work crew were withering away more each day, losing muscle mass, energy, and the will to live. Tea in hand, he walked over to talk to Bali and Akash.

"It doesn't matter what you feel or think," he said. "If you do not show up at the roll call, they will come looking for you."

"What are they going to do?" Bali replied. "Beat me more?" He turned to show long open sores across his bare back and shoulders.

"I understand, my friend," Raj said, trying desperately to find something to motivate the man. "But if you don't get up, you will lose the money you've made, and they'll send you home."

"What money? They haven't paid us for weeks – and the pittance from before? Barely worth it anyway!"

"Perhaps they will make it up once we're out of this." Akash shrugged and gestured. "How can we expect them to pay us when everything has crumbled?"

"Then how can we afford to work?" Bali continued. "If only they would send us home." He grabbed Raj's arm. "And why don't they send us home, you wonder? Well, I know. It's because they can't. The planes no longer run and even if they did, we are nothing but slaves to them anyway."

"You don't know that," Akash said, shooting Raj a doubtful look.

"I do know that, in fact," Bali replied. "The company office burned to the ground. That's where they kept our passports."

"Is this true, Raj?"

Raj shrugged. "I don't know. And we may be slaves, but at least we have a place to sleep and some kind of food to eat. What can we do but keep working?"

Bali squeezed Raj's arm harder. "We could fight back. They were strong before, too strong for us to fight against. Now, though, we may stand a chance." He broke down, his expression twisting miserably. "As it stands, I may never speak to my wife again, much less see her. They promised us so much, and lied about it all, but now...." His words trailed off into sobs and tears.

"All of that may be true," Raj said, the first stirrings of anger and resentment welling up inside him, "but all we can do is keep going. They cannot abuse us so badly that they lose their workforce! They could get more of us before, but they can't now!"

"Yes, that's right," Akash agreed. "They must take care of us."

"Oh, they don't care." Bali fixed them both with a glare. "There are so many of us here already. It doesn't matter. Where one of us falls, another takes his place. We're going to die here, my friends, and I will be the first."

"Hush, old man," Akash said, noticing others in the room watching them, a danger if one of them was spying for the company. The mere hint of a complaint or workers making demands would bring whips – or worse – down on their heads. "Come on and get up. Raj and I will help you."

Raj was nodding. "That's right, old man. We'll help you get there, but you're on your own from there. Here, now. Where are your shoes?"

They got Bali dressed, fed him some tea, and helped him walk outside to the booming voices of the foremen. Workers formed lines in the two-story apartment slums, marching like zombies to the staircases and into a wide lot where foremen tapped heads and called names, ensuring everyone was on hand to work. The reek of so many unwashed, sick bodies clung to the air, burning Raj's nostrils and filling him with hopelessness.

Raj's story was like so many others, lured from India by a recruiter who promised a fine contract to come to Qatar and work for a company, though as soon as he arrived, they'd taken his passport and swapped his contract for a new one, extended by an extra year with only three-quarters of the promised wage. Raj had been warned of such practices before he signed up, but with no jobs in India, he'd had to take what he could get and hope things wouldn't be as bad as people claimed. But it hadn't turned out the way he'd wanted, and life had become more dismal with every passing day, only compounded by what had happened to the fuel supply.

"What kind of work will it be today?" Bali asked as they reached the ground floor and shuffled across the court where a smoky haze covered everything.

"The same as yesterday," Raj replied, "We will clear rubble until that is gone, then we'll rebuild their city."

The foremen counted the marks on their arms drawn in permanent ink, checked off their lists, and waved them through. They walked east along a boulevard toward downtown Doha, the once pristine high-rises glowing in the desert sun turned to tall spikes of char still giving off clouds of soot. The sun crested the horizon and bathed them in its warmth, the temperature reaching close to a hundred well before noon. On the way, they were handed lukewarm bottles of water with broken seals and at another line, workers gave out bowls of cheap, fatty pork and oatmeal, a combination that tasted like lumpy sawdust to Raj, though he forced himself to eat it anyway. By the time they reached the work camp, Raj was sweating, his stale clothes moist, and the several men walking near him were barely shuffling along, shirts pulled up over their heads and shoulders slumped.

Under the watchful eye of a few Qatar guards in their clean brown suits, the line moved between husks of buildings that had fallen in on themselves, narrow paths cleared through the streets so they could trek deeper into the ruins. Their worksite was a block of shorter office buildings, fourteen floors, most of them collapsed into a pit of rubble like a tooth rotted to its root. Raj fell in line with other workers picking up debris, dropping it into wheelbarrows or sending it down a conveyor run by men turning cranks. There were no trucks or heavy machinery to move anything, just a few hastily constructed pulleys to lift the bigger pieces, shifting them to large trailers to be pulled away by more workers.

Foremen shouted insults and threats to keep the pace up, and the workers hurried at first, but their energy quickly faded by midday when the sun's glare spiked temperatures upward of a hundred and seventeen degrees. Despite the thousands of workers picking away at the pile, things moved at a painfully slow pace, the dent in the building's side slowly carved out to reveal the guts of the place; its stairwells, pipes and wiring were all cut into smaller pieces, rolled up, and stacked in trailers for reuse.

A little after noon, the first man collapsed on a pile of bricks and was carried away by some other workers, but instead of calling a break, the foreman pressed them harder, using belts and sticks to whip the men and keep them moving as they slowly cut through the rough mound. Only a few wore gloves they had been able to find, Raj not being one of them, and his hands were soon raw and aching, not even the calluses he'd built up offering any protection. The workers wore rags on their heads and shoulders, glistening bodies sweating and dusty beneath the sun's heat, clustered beneath patches of shade at every possible opportunity to keep cool.

A short time later, two other men collapsed from heat exhaustion, adding to the murmurs of disgruntlement. The worst injury of the day occurred when a makeshift pulley failed and dropped an I-beam on a worker's head, instantly breaking his neck and drawing cries from the men until the foreman amplified the threats and abuse, forcing everyone back to work. They continued their grueling labors, working beneath the cruel sun and the foreman's whips and curses. Raj wiped the beads of sweat off his forehead and stayed close to Bali and Akash, the two younger men watching over and helping the older one as he picked up huge chunks of rock, turned, and shuffled over to the wheelbarrow to drop them heavily inside. He was a robot, expression slack, eyes blank as he trudged on until, finally, they came to their first break of the day.

Carts were pushed up with dozens of water bottles stacked on top, the seals broken and the liquid cloudy, but it didn't stop the workers from grabbing them and drinking them in two or three gulps. A few splashed the last bit into their faces, washing away the sweat for only a moment before it came back twice as strong. Raj and Akash helped Bali over to the cart of water, but he was mumbling, hands shaking, eyes rolling back into his head.

"Here you go, old man," Raj said, taking a bottle for himself and Bali, opening it and feeding him so it dribbled down his chin. "No, Bali. You must get it in your mouth. Don't spill it." Bali felt blindly for the bottle, almost knocking it from Raj's hands. "There you go, man. Drink."

Raj opened his own bottle and drank deep, his nose curling at the dirt and grit and the faint whiff of sewage.

"All right, men! The break is over! Back to work now!"

Raj turned as the foreman grabbed the water cart and shoved it to the side. He held a belt wrapped around his fist, and he glared bloodshot at the group as he pointed to the pile of debris he wanted moved.

"Can we get some good water?" Raj asked.

The foreman turned his gaze in Raj's direction. "What is that? Who spoke?"

"It was me," Raj replied, holding up the bottle, particulates floating inside. "I asked if we could have some good water. This is dirty."

The foreman stared at the bottle for a moment before snatching it out of Raj's hand. "Oh, I am sorry your water is not adequate for you. I would hate to have you drink poor-tasting water."

With a widening grin, he turned the bottle upside down and drained it into the road to the groans of the workers.

"You didn't have to do that," Raj said. "I just wanted —"

"No, no, no!" the foreman cried, throwing the bottle into the air and raising his hands. "This man has exposed a grave injustice. We will only have the *best* water for you from now on. We will immediately send back all the water planned for you on the next break and dump that into the sea. Then we will look for the best water in the city for you. It might be a couple of days until we get the pipes working again, but I'm sure you will be fine holding out until then."

The crowd groaned even louder, and someone shoved Raj from behind as the members of Qatar's official guard laughed and nudged each other behind the foreman, who spoke louder, addressing the crowd.

"Do all of you feel the same? Do you want fresh spring water in a few days after you've died of thirst, or are you happy with what you have?"

Many shouted apologies to the foreman, begging for forgiveness and to allow them to get back to work, though a few voices cried out in dissent and cursed him.

"Who said that?" The foreman's eyes widened with rage, spittle flying from his mouth as he screamed. "All of you will pay for the remarks of a few! No more water until the evening for all of you!"

"Please," Raj pleaded. "There is no need for all this."

"No need for all this? You are the one who is causing problems, and you're disrupting everyone's work."

"I wasn't —"

The foreman slapped him in the face, the sound cracking above the murmuring workers, their voices fading as they stared. Raj touched his hand to his burning cheek, mystified at his own swelling rage, a volcanic pit of lava rushing from his stomach and up through his chest. Shoulders rising on a sharp breath, Raj flexed his fists, surging with strength, opening his hands so they formed claws. Before he knew what he was doing, he lunged forward and wrapped his hands around the foreman's neck.

Growling, the foreman grabbed Raj's arms and tried to remove him, but the grip was too tight, some unfathomable power coursing through Raj's fingers, digging into the man's neck to squeeze off the airway. His only satisfaction would be killing the man who'd made his life a living hell, and no one tried to stop him as he dug his thumbs into the foreman's windpipe and crushed his voice box with a sharp snap. The foreman crumpled, eyes bulging, cheeks turning red, gasping as he dropped to his knees and slipped from Raj's grasp, collapsing on the hot pavement where he kicked weakly, clawing at his throat for a moment before he lay still.

Raj stood straight, staring at the foreman and then at his hands, flexing them as strength still surged through them. Squeezing out tears, Raj waited to be shot or dragged away immediately, but the crowd had fallen dead quiet, hundreds of men standing in the rubble who'd seen Raj strangle the foreman. The two guards came forward, their rifles sliding off their shoulders and into their hands before they paused as if sensing a change in the air. There was a moment of calm, a pause between what had happened and what would happen next, Raj's life already gone in a blink, nothing left to lose and everything to gain.

One guard moved to help the foreman while the other pointed his rifle at Raj's chest. "Kill them," Raj spat, his voice rising on a quivering note of rage. "Take them and kill them! Do it now, or we'll all die here and never see our families again."

No one moved, the weight of their servitude heavy in their minds, the idea of rising up such a foreign concept that it seemed impossible to grasp. Uncertainty flashed across the workers' faces as they glanced between the guards, Raj, and the foreman on the ground. With the foreman dead and his whip silenced, something shifted in the crowd. Eyes narrowed, bodies tensed, and fists flexed like Raj's, the sentiment among the workers shifted in the face of the guards' hesitation, wanting to punish the people responsible for their misery.

One guard pressed the barrel of his rifle against Raj's chest and started to squeeze the trigger, but hands reached in, grabbed the weapon, and pushed it upwards. Two shots fired into the sky before the crowd dragged the guard down and took his rifle, viciously striking and kicking him until he no longer moved. They turned the other guard's gun on him, shooting a quick burst of rounds to his stomach, blowing blood across the hot pavement as his agonizing screams were muffled by the bodies pressing in around him.

Men raised the rifles into the air while others lifted the dead foreman's body, tossing him back and forth, cheering as they punched and kicked him before throwing him into the pile of rubble, his body impaling on twisted rebar jutting out of the ruins. Raj grinned grimly as the crowd swept forward to the next worksite where the confused guards and foreman came running up only to be overwhelmed by the throng, who beat them, stomped them, and took their guns before they could open fire. More guards in spotless brown uniforms were trampled in the flood, and one soldier fired back, killing two workers before he was disarmed, the smell of blood enraging the throng as they spilled into the streets and tore apart anything left standing, showing no mercy. Raj turned and found Akash, clasping his hand and pulling him close.

"What did you do!?" Akash cried. It wasn't an accusation, but a question of wonder as he grinned madly into the rage-fueled faces shouting and cursing their masters. "What did you do, Raj?!"

"I have set us free!" Joy and bewilderment rushed through Raj as they were swept away in the sea of humanity.

The crowd squeezed into empty streets where there'd been no fire or destruction, quickly overwhelming the guards before breaking into the foremen's apartments, taking fresh bottled water and food, liberating them of the fancier pieces of furniture, snatching up their clean clothing and carrying their spoils above the crowd, cheering as they celebrated. They rushed over to long tankers with clean water sloshing inside, at first taking turns at the spigots, but in their haste to drink, breaking them off so that everyone squatted to get hit full in the face, gulping what they could as they washed off their filth and sweat.

Raj and Akash were shoved forward into a gush of fresh water that hit them in the chest, splashing, cooling their heated skin but not the flames of their rebellion. Laughing, Raj pushed his way to the front and took several gulps of the foamy spray before he was knocked out of the way. The throng finally began to settle, men milling around, raising their fists and cheering for their victory.

When the loudspeakers erupted with a foreman's voice demanding the rioters stand down and return to their hovels, they grew quiet, cowed as the inevitability of their servitude weighed on their minds once more. When a new group of guards and mercenaries in black riot gear ran in, Raj gritted his teeth, jumped on a trailer, and swept his arm at them.

"Take them down quickly, or they will kill us. Do it now before it's too late!"

The crowd shifted uncertainly toward the guards, fists raised and shouting but not attacking, merely forcing them back with threats and curses. When a nervous mercenary fired a burst of rounds into the throng, dropping a handful of workers, the flames rose again, hotter than before. Teeth gritting, heart pounding, Raj encouraged them with sweeping motions, yelling words that seemed to come from another person, not himself.

The first few mercenaries were trampled, and the rest quickly dropped their weapons, turned tail and ran for their lives, begging for mercy and receiving none. The crowd swept on, growing to almost ten thousand angry voices, spilling into elite Qatari residential neighborhoods that had been spared the destruction, dragging family members of the guards and foremen from their homes, beating them in the roads and leaving them bloody and bruised. Workers leaped atop expensive cars that were fresh from the factory, devoid of fuel and thus having survived the devastation, jumping up and down on the hoods and violently tearing them down to their individual components.

As the Qatari citizens got wind of the uprising, they fled their homes, rushing to escape the angry throng, men defending their families with rocks, knives, and sometimes guns, only to be consumed by the hungry mob. Akash thrust Raj atop a shining white car, and thousands packed in the narrow street, raising their fists to him, shouting encouragement, and waiting for their next orders. Raj lifted his hands and motioned for quiet, then a foreman's bullhorn was pressed into his hands, and he turned it on with a squeal of feedback.

"My fellow workers, we have been slaves too long. They lured us here with false promises, lying contracts, and slave's wages. They have treated us worse than animals!"

The crowd cheered as one, the sound so deafening Raj was sure they could hear them back in India.

"They made our fathers, mothers, brothers, and sisters promises of a better life only to grind them into the dirt beneath their heels. They would do the same to us if we let them. It's time for the tables to turn! Show these monsters what we have lived under for far too long! To the docks!"

Like a sea of humanity breaking upon the stones of injustice, the crowd shifted and followed intersecting lanes to the Qatar dock area, where ships lay sunken in the bay, a graveyard of passenger boats, cargo vessels, and tankers. They were cracked open, capsized, their hulls blown out and breached, and the oil and fuel that hadn't burned slicked the waters in giant black patches that had captured fish, seagulls, and garbage in the glistening rainbow waves.

The people who had been driven from their homes were pushed to the docks, squeezing to the edge, turning to face the rising swell of workers who swarmed after them. Raj's people chased hundreds of them up to the heights where tall cliffs loomed above rocky shores, where a simple waist-high stone wall was all that helped to keep people from straying out and falling to their deaths. Still, the press of the throng pushed some too close, and they were shoved over, windmilling into the open air to crash on rocks that crushed their bones and cut off their screams in an instant.

The workers jeered at them, sticking and poking them with weapons they'd fashioned out of rebar and pieces of wood. Grim-faced men stood in front of their families, yelling back while women with silken hair and well-manicured fingernails crouched behind them, holding their children close as they were pressed to the edge. At the docks, the workers surged forward, shoving hundreds into the bay to splash and flail, their oil-covered faces searching for their loved ones in the brackish mess. A worker threw a lighter into the bay, and flames arose with a tremendous whoosh that swept across the waters, consuming everything in its path, screaming mouths sucking in the flames as they gasped for air.

On the cliff, Akash grabbed a man and pulled him away from the wall, and the workers behind them threw him to the ground and beat him. A woman fell in front of Raj, hands pressed together, begging for mercy as more plunged from the heights in a chorus of howls. Raj could only see the friends and family who'd died for the benefit of the rich, his brother, father, and many others worked to death, lied to, and cheated by the Qatari government, her pleading eyes and prayers doing nothing to quench his simmering rage.

Raj grabbed her hand and helped her to her feet, the woman's expression changing to gratitude until Raj stripped the golden rings off her fingers and the jewel-encrusted bracelets from her wrists, then shoved her toward the edge. She hit the wall, flipped back, and went over, flailing as she plummeted, striking the sheer cliff face twice before smashing against the rocks below.

The ocean crashed over the dead in a blood-oil spray, patches of it aflame as it consumed thousands of bodies, the waves clutching them and dragging them out to serve their endless sentence in the cold and ruthless sea.

CHAPTER SIXTEEN

James Burton
Frankfurt, Illinois

James cowered beneath a pile of wreckage, a cold concrete slab that had fallen from some upper floor looming over him, supported by stacks of rubble, protecting him from the storms rippling across the city. It was drizzling, and the pipes in the building were gurgling as water passed down through the ruins, finding every nook and cranny it could to escape into the sewers. He held a can of peas on his knees, one from the spilled cart, using a can opener from inside his collapsible stave to open it. The jugs of water sat by his side, and he'd already drunk and spat back out half of one of them to wash the smoky particulates from his throat.

The food went from can to mouth automatically, shoveling it in with his fingers, so focused was he on the edges of the ruins and the shadows that lurked there that he disregarded the fact that the food was cold. People wandered out in the gloomy early evening, faint movements out in the fog, though none had ventured toward him, held back by either the thick smoke drifting around the ruins or the potential of the whole place to collapse at any moment. While he hadn't heard anything from the gang, he wasn't out of the woods yet; escaping the congested and violent city was paramount. Shoving the last handful of peas into his mouth, he chewed them into mush and swallowed them down, then had one final swig of water, stood, and packed everything up.

He shrugged his pack on and picked his way through the wreckage, crouching to sneak between the rubble and fragmented walls, squeezing through cracks and ducking when he heard sounds on the perimeter. Near the edge, he got on one knee and waited, listening, observing the darkness before rushing into the night. With his stave in his left hand, he used the compass end to stay heading east, breaking into a narrow alley and stopping at the end to look both ways. When he didn't see anyone, he sprinted to the other side, barely catching a glimpse of the street sign as he flew by. He couldn't remember Rosen Street from his map studying back in the warehouse district, so he continued slinking through the darkness, his footsteps hidden by the sounds of pattering rain and grumbling thunder. Whispers and the occasional shouts bounced off the brick walls and old wooden siding of the surrounding buildings, making it impossible to know where they came from.

He slowed to check each street sign, not recognizing any until he came to a major intersection with Dixon running west to east, a street that was far too close to the Highway 30 demarcation line for his taste. Going by his compass, James angled south by southeast, heading toward a long block of wooded areas cut by winding lanes and a spattering of buildings.

When the road turned back to the north, he went off-road and passed through a vast park with children's play sets and slides. The soft pink padded turf under the swings and slides had been burned and melted, the surrounding grasses turned brown, and the treetops stripped bare of leaves and healthy branches by a firestorm that had swept through.

He pointed his flashlight toward the parking lot off to the left, which had been turned into a field of hot slag by explosions. Bent car frames littered the pavement in a scatter of shredded metal and parts, already showing rust spots and decay from the intense rains. Bodies had fused to the seats, crushed and burned, hair lank, skin hanging loose off their bones, organs liquefied into thick puddles that mixed with the rain. A reek of death lingered in the air, and James wrinkled his nose and moved on through the park at a steady clip, cutting between two buildings that had collapsed in a mountain of black coals. When he shined his light across the rubble, he gasped, stomach churning at the pile of dead bodies around the doorways turned to charred sludge.

Clamping his teeth to hold down the rising bile, James bent his head and continued, keeping his flashlight pointed at the ground and searching for a path through the darkness. With no trail in sight, he pressed past the brush and pushed between sticker bushes, tripping over chunks of black wood and crunching dead leaves and twigs. The gray mist rose off the forest floor, reflecting his flashlight beam into a glow so bright it forced him to turn it off in order to keep moving. Stumbling into the darkness, he came to a patch of thinning trees and moved from one to the next, touching his palms to them as he passed to keep his balance through the unsteady, mucky terrain. On the other side of the woods was another park with a pond in the middle, rain sprinkling the surface where the remains of a half-dozen bodies floated at the edge of the water, surrounded by burned branches, the details of their forms mercifully too obscured by darkness to make out.

James came to a street heading due east and south, taking it despite the distant cracks of guns echoing from ahead. Soon, the squarish forms of buildings stuck out above the treetops, and he entered another small township on the edges of the larger city. The storm had started to pick up, whistling between the buildings, howling in gales like ghosts trapped in a concrete limbo, destined to haunt the shadowy stoops and darkened windows forever. Rain struck him sideways without warning, forcing him to put his hands in his pockets and slump forward, head low as he stared at the pavement slipping by beneath him. Water gathered in his hair and dripped off his chin, creeping down his neckline and getting his semi-dry shirts wet once again while the eyelets on his worn boots leaked like sieves, and soon his feet were wet and cold as well.

James kept to the center of the road, walking with a wide stance to stay balanced as the wind punched him like a prize-fighter. He stopped looking for signs and focused on staying upright, squeezing between piles of junk and spilled bricks, stumbling toward a line of sawhorses stretched across the road, covered in tarps and flapping in the breeze.

Sandbags stood in stacks on both ends, like a military checkpoint, though it appeared abandoned, with no lights or soldiers anywhere. When he reached the barrier and tried to squeeze through, though, dark figures rose from behind the sandbags, water dripping from their helmets, green ponchos fluttering in the breeze, a half-dozen guns pointed at him.

"Got another banger!" someone called from the left-hand side, aiming a rifle at his face. "Stop right there!"

James had frozen at the first signs of movement, and he threw his hands up when he saw the soldier's finger slip beneath the trigger guard. "Don't shoot! I'm not a—I'm not one of them! I'm just passing through, I swear!"

Another soldier grabbed the rifle barrel and shoved it down, the tall, cowed figure stepping forward to get a better look at James. After a second, he nodded. "Hold your fire, people. I recognize that stick he's carrying. They give them out at the refugee camps." Shifting his attention to James, he said, "Okay, buddy. Who are you?"

He stood in the cold with his hands up and water dripping down his arms. "My name is James Burton. I'm coming from Denver, Colorado, heading to East Lansing, Michigan. Yeah, I got this from one of the refugee camps back west."

"I guess I shouldn't have mentioned that," the soldier replied. "You could've stolen it from someone leaving those camps. Show me your arms and neck."

"My... arms and neck?"

"Tats. Do you have any?"

"No." James rolled up his sleeves as a flashlight beam cut across him, then he unbuttoned his shirt and moved back and forth, exposing his chest and neck.

The light flashed across his face and moved back and forth before lowering.

"Okay, you're not in one of the gangs. Or if you are, you're the only one I've seen who isn't all inked up."

"Definitely not. Is this a military checkpoint?"

Chuckles rose from the group as they lowered their weapons and relaxed.

"Some might call it that. Some might call it hell on earth." The tall figure rested his hand on a sawhorse. "We're the remnants of a group from the Illinois National Guard. I'm Captain Fred Lister, and the young woman who almost shot you is Lieutenant Dawn Washington."

James put his hands down. "Thanks for not firing, ma'am."

"You're very welcome," Washington replied. "You should be more careful next time walking headlong into a checkpoint like that, though, especially with it being so dark and rainy out."

"Yeah, that's my fault," James chuckled nervously. "It's been a hell of a week, and I'm just trying to get out of the city. I hadn't meant to come this far north."

"None of us did, man," Lister replied.

James shivered and put his hands in his pockets, hugging his coat tighter around his waist. "How long have you guys been here?"

"Way too long. You said you came from a camp back west?"

"Outside of Denver."

"Any news?"

"I'd ask you the same thing about conditions to the east. I've got a long way ahead of me. Maybe we can trade information."

"That sounds like a good idea," Lister replied. "Come on through."

The guardsmen parted, and James stepped past the barrier, nodding respectfully to Lieutenant Washington before following Lister onto a sidewalk along a series of dilapidated buildings. One of the older apartments gave off muted light from the covered windows, and the captain guided them up a set of stone stairs and through the front door to stand in a large foyer area with a raised ceiling and an old chandelier hanging above them.

Without taking off their coats, they entered a side room with a table, chairs, and a short stack of supply bins with more empty ones sitting on the side. An electric lantern rested on the old wooden windowsill and gave off a dim light, barely enough to see by. Near the window, which was cracked open a couple of inches, a two-burner propane stove sat on a table with a pan on one side and a coffee pot on the other.

"Have a seat there." Lister gestured at the chair nearest the window. "You hungry?"

"I could eat something." James nodded and sat. "If you've got any of that coffee left, I'd welcome it. Haven't had anything decent in me in days."

"I'll get it," Washington said, shouldering her rifle and heading that way. She was a squat, burly woman with ink-black locks stuck to her cheek.

The captain sat across from him, falling heavily into his chair and pushing back his wet hood to reveal a sharp-eyed young man with a troubled brow, face smudged with dirt, taller than James by a few inches, and lean under his bulky National Guard poncho. He ran a hand through a dark buzz cut, whipping water onto the floor.

"I'll have a cup of coffee, too, if you don't mind, Lieutenant."

"No problem."

Lister sat back with a sigh and gestured at James. "I'll let you go first. I'm sure your story is a lot more interesting than mine."

James shrugged. "It started back in Denver; I was waiting for my airplane at Denver International, to fly down to Florida to meet my family for a vacation. Everything started exploding on the tarmac... planes, fuel trucks, just everything. It was a horrible, bloody scene."

Lister leaned forward. "How did you survive all that?"

"It was insanity trying to get out of the gate. People were screaming, and chunks of debris fell on our heads and crashed through the windows. I hitched a ride on an employee cart, got to the concourse, fought my way downstairs, and got outside. It wasn't much better there; the parking lot was one big ball of flames, and the debris was hitting everyone and cutting them to pieces. I saw..." James shook his head, remembering the people taking luggage out of their trunks when their vehicles exploded. "Just a lot of stuff I never want to see again as long as I live."

"I'll bet. Obviously, you made it out of there."

"Hid beneath an underpass with planes falling from the sky. A jet engine almost hit me."

"Damn," Washington said as she set a cup of black coffee and a bowl of what appeared to be chicken noodle soup in front of him. "Sounds like a war zone."

"It felt like one. I was just trying to get away from it all. There were fires everywhere, and I talked to some folks on the way in who were supposed to pick up people on incoming flights. Don't think they made it." He picked up a spoon and took a bite of the soup, which amounted to a thin broth with a few noodles and small chunks of chicken. "Anyway, I made it through the city and hitched a ride on a cargo train heading east. It was actually your people running the train, at least for the first stretch."

"Colorado National Guard?" Lister asked.

"Not sure if it was Colorado or not, but they were a good group of people. We stopped once to pick up some Army troops and vehicles, then continued until we reached a refugee camp outside Kansas City. Couldn't tell you exactly where, but it seemed to be a train junction somewhere."

"Maybe the Sims Junction camp," Washington said, bringing the Captain his coffee. "We call it camp ten-twelve."

"Sounds like it. Thank you, Lieutenant."

"Not long after I showed up, the place fell under attack —"

"Attack?" Lister leaned farther forward with concern. "What kind of attack?"

James shrugged. "Couldn't tell you who it was, but I jumped in and tried to help them out. I followed a corporal around for a few hours and helped lug ammunition to the tanks and Humvees."

"So, they found some armored vehicles that work," Washington stated, standing beside the table with her arms crossed.

"Equipment they'd gotten out of the junkyard motor pool. The tank crew mentioned they were old machines on the verge of decommissioning."

"You talked to the tank crew?" Lister glanced at Washington. "How'd that go down?"

"I sure did." James slurped the rest of his soup. "Helped them fix a firing mechanism problem in their tank. While I was inside, they mentioned all that."

The Captain and Lieutenant exchanged another look. "Seems like you were pretty involved over there," Lister said. "I'm not sure how you fixed a mechanical problem the crew couldn't."

"I've got a doctorate in mechanical engineering and tinker heavily at home, and their mechanic was indisposed. Not a complex problem, but easy to miss and not know how to fix."

"I'm sure they appreciated the help."

"They loaded me up with some good gear, including an M4 I lost somewhere around Champaign. Luckily, I still had my walking stick." James motioned to where he'd leaned it up against the wall. "That thing has saved me more times than I can count. Probably the only reason why I'm still alive."

"Yeah, they've been handing them out at all the camps, last I saw."

James settled back and sipped his coffee, the hot brew warming his belly and sending a chill up his back. "Other than that, I met some nice Amish people and hitched a ride to Hannibal. We pushed our way across in a pole barge, and that's where we split up. Took a horse all the way here, getting chased and harassed the whole time. I'm surprised I made it this far. Amber – the horse – didn't."

"Sorry to hear that," Lister said, leaning back in his chair. "That's quite a story."

"Now, I'm just trying to get back to my family. My in-laws are in East Lansing and I'm hoping my wife and kids will be able to make it up by the time I get home, otherwise I'm going to have to go searching for them. I've got a homestead with some supplies that might carry us through this, but if not, I've got some farmland I can work to keep us going."

"Your wife and kids are down in Florida?" Washington asked.

"They *were* down in Florida, waiting for me to meet them for a vacation when all this started. Couldn't say where my family is or if they're even safe. I signed up for some database thing back in Kansas City, but they weren't in it."

"Most communications are down or spotty at best. Everything except for military radios and some AM-FM channels."

"I guess I just have to hope they're on the way, then." James sighed, finishing the soup before continuing. "How about you folks? How'd you end up here? Shouldn't there be more of you?"

"We're the remnants of a group sent into Chicago to search for survivors," Lister sighed wearily, "back at the start when finding survivors was a priority. We were supposed to meet up with another group at O'Hare International Airport. Didn't make it past Oak Lawn. We got cut off by fires — boy, the city was blazing — and had to seek shelter nearby. We were holding our position and helping people where we could when a gang attacked us out of nowhere. They overpowered some guards on the perimeter, took their guns, and wreaked havoc on the rest of us. Took down half my damn squad before we could get out of there."

"We've been heading south since then," Washington added, "hoping to link up with a rail line. We've got some wounded in the other room. Things are slow going what with the rain and injured, plus having to deal with bangers coming out of the woodwork."

"I believe it. The rail lines are the way to go, and I wouldn't mind finding one myself, especially after seeing the people running around these neighborhoods."

"I take it you ran into some gangs?" Lister asked.

"Ever since I showed up in this area. The first people I ran into were a couple of junkies, and the next day I ran into the gangs while trying to get out of town. I was stuck in a ditch while they fought." James shook his head and released a low, whistling sigh. "I'll tell you what, the people living in these streets are as violent as they come. Slaughtered each other right in front of me without a care in the world. Small group ambushed a big one and took them down like it was nothing."

"Yeah, numbers have very little meaning anymore," Lister said. "The stronger are getting taken out just as easily as the weak."

"It's a madhouse," James agreed, "and it's hard to find hope in any of it. But getting home to my family is what's keeping me going. It's the one light I cling to."

"So, how'd you get away from the gangs?" Lister asked.

"Ah, they spotted me when I tried to grab some food they'd abandoned during their fight. Almost caught me, too."

Washington chuckled. "Hear that, Cap? James here tried to steal supplies from right under their noses."

Lister grinned. "That takes some balls, for sure."

James laughed. "Turns out it wasn't such a great idea. Almost got myself killed over a couple gallons of water and some cans of peas, but I hid in the ruins until they lost interest. I wandered around for a few more hours trying to find my way out of the city until I found you guys."

"Look, James," Lister said after a pause and a slight nod of agreement from Washington. "We're getting out of here soon and heading south. Want to come with us? We could definitely use the help, and it sounds like you've got some experience under your belt."

"I'm no soldier," James replied, "but it sounds like you're heading my way, and I can hold my own, so yes. Absolutely."

Lister slapped his palm on the table. "Good man. We'll leave first thing tomorrow morning. Until then, you can take a bunk in the next room and get some rest."

James was already shaking his head. "No way. I'm way too hopped up, especially after the soup and coffee. If you don't mind, I'd like to take a watch, maybe help relieve someone here? I can handle a firearm, but as I said, I lost my rifle a few nights ago." James removed the revolver he'd taken off of the junkie from his pocket and set it on the table. "I took this from one of the folks who attacked me. It's all I've got as far as weapons go, but I'm happy to use it."

Lister gave James a nod. "All right, friend. Washington, go get Rodriguez."

"Yes, sir."

The Lieutenant stepped out and came back with a haggard-looking woman who staggered in and gave a weak salute, water dripping from her helmet and poncho.

"You wanted to see me, sir?"

"Get this man a weapon and get some shut-eye."

Rodriguez stiffened. "Get him a weapon?"

A mischievous smile played across Lister's mouth. "James here is the man we heard tell about over in Kansas City, Rodriguez."

"The tank man?"

"One and the same."

"Wait a second," an eyebrow went up as James looked at the trio. "You knew who I was? Why all the questions?"

"Sorry, not sorry. Had to make sure you were who you claimed. Not every day a civvie fixes a mothballed piece of armor and helps save lives. Your name was passed around by a few folks who said to keep an eye out for you should you pop up. Said you were good people. Anyway, Rodriguez? James'll take your shift until morning."

The guardswoman looked at James with uncertainty.

"Trust me. Hit the bunk. You've been up forty-eight hours straight, and I don't want you shooting your foot off or letting some banger sneak up from behind and shank you because you're exhausted."

"I... thank you." Rodriguez's shoulders sagged as an untold weight was lifted from them, then took off her helmet to shake out a thick mane of soaking-wet black hair. Without another word, she walked into a back room and disappeared into the shadows, briefly reappeared with a rifle, then vanished once again.

James checked the weapon over, taking a couple of extra mags from the captain, then slung it on his shoulder and gave a brief salute. "Private James Burton, reporting for duty."

"Very good, James," Lister and Washington both laughed. "Follow the Lieutenant, and she'll show you your assignment."

James started after the Lieutenant before she turned and handed him a long poncho. "Put this on," she said. "It'll keep you dry, mostly."

James thanked her and put it on, buttoning it tight around his neck and pulling it down to cover his midsection and upper legs. From there, he followed Washington outside and marched to the barrier, crossing the street to the left-hand side where two guardsmen squatted behind the stack of sandbags.

Washington spoke loud to be heard over the pouring rain. "This is your spot for the night with me, Wiseman, and Pugh. Wiseman and Pugh, this is James. He's sitting in for Rodriguez tonight."

"Are we still moving out in the morning?" Pugh asked, the dark-eyed blonde squinting beneath the brim of her helmet, not bothering to question the unusual arrangement.

"That's the plan," Washington replied. "We'll get Rodriguez up in eight hours so you two can get some shut-eye before we move out."

"Righteous, Lieutenant." Pugh pulled her helmet lower and leaned against the wet sandbags.

"Appreciate that, ma'am." Wiseman nodded and took up a position next to Pugh. James and Washington squeezed in on the outside, and James peeked around the sandbags into the wet, dismal streets. For the first time in days, his heart settled, his mind stopped racing, and a sense of peace rested on his shoulders.

He turned to Washington. "I'm sure glad I ran into you, Lieutenant. It's good to be among friends."

"It's good to have you, James. As Captain Lister said, we can always use the help."

"You know how to use that thing?" Pugh asked with a glance at his M4.

"Well enough," James replied. "The Captain said you ran into trouble around Oak Lawn."

"It was a rough and tumble for a while there," Pugh replied. "We got called out of a training session to kill fires at our motor pool. Half our training buildings went up in smoke and there was nothing we could do about it. We were standing around in the rubble, pissed off about losing some of our buddies, when we got the order to head to O'Hare. I guess the Captain told you how that worked out."

"Lots of fires and gang trouble?"

"Yeah, we were on fire control the whole way there, trying to work with some local departments to save some city buildings and the police station. We were dragging hoses through the streets and trying every hydrant we came across." She laughed sadly. "We had a little water pressure for a while until the treatment plants lost power and the pressure stopped. All we could do after that was run away."

Wiseman grunted. "The fires were moving fast, and we got surrounded pretty quick and had to get out of there, but some of those firefighters hung around and kept fighting. Don't know what happened to them, but by the time we got north of the area, it was nothing but an orange fireball everywhere you looked."

"Not a pretty picture," James frowned.

"Not even close," Wiseman replied. "I guess we finally wised up and got our butts out of there. Wandered south for a while, tangled with the local gangs who'd somehow survived. Then out of nowhere, it started raining. Damndest thing."

"That was a miracle," Pugh said. "One minute, we were breathing smoke and ash, the next minute it was clear. I used to hate the rain. Not anymore. Well, maybe not so much now that it won't let up. Can't keep my socks dry for the life of me."

James recalled his ride through the back woods and hills, barely escaping the motorcycle riders before ending up in the torrential rain in the city where he'd lost Amber. "I can't say I love it so much, but I can see your point. It's certainly a blessing in a lot of ways. How about your families? Have you heard from them?"

"Not a thing," Pugh replied, while Wiseman only shook his head. "My parents are in Ft. Wayne, and Wiseman's people are in Columbus. I tried calling my mom and dad every ten minutes at first but gave up. My phone ran out of juice days ago. How about you?"

"I was supposed to meet my family in Florida for vacation. In fact, I was about to board a plane just before everything on the tarmac blew up. If things had happened ten minutes later, I would have been aboard and wouldn't be kneeling in the rain with you fine folks."

Pugh grinned. "Lucky you, James."

"Yeah, welcome to the club," Wiseman added.

James nodded and sat back on his heels with rain falling on his poncho, the moisture somehow seeping in around the neck. Lightning cracked and illuminated the bottom portion of Washington's quiet visage, jaw firm as she searched the gloom with the other guardsman standing vigilant. With a heavy sigh, his worries muted for a little while, James hunkered down and guarded against the night and their enemies.

CHAPTER SEVENTEEN

Ryan Cooper
Somewhere Outside East Lansing, Michigan

It was early afternoon, and Helen and Ryan were out in the chicken coop after feeding and tending to the rest of the animals. They'd milked Bessie and wheeled the containers to the house, placing them just inside the door to pasteurize later after they went in. A brisk breeze rustled the treetops, sending leaves and pieces of garbage skimming across the yard. The flying garbage had been a steadily growing sight over the last few days, growing as it was caught up along the fence line and in the woods, and Ryan grumbled as he pointed at it.

"I haven't seen so much garbage blow around in all my life," he said.

Helen narrowed her eyes. "No more garbage collection and lots of places burned down... it'll probably get worse before it gets better."

"Yup. I imagine this stuff is being carried for miles across the town, especially with the kinds of winds we've been seeing." He sighed wearily. "Just more things on the to-do list. I'll get to it later if I can. It might be a good idea to walk the fence line anyway and ensure there's no funny business happening."

"Well, let's get the eggs and get back inside. My hands are freezing."

"This whole not having weather forecasts anymore kind of sucks."

Helen chuckled and poked his side. "You used to complain all the time about how wrong they always were!"

"Yeah, well... you don't know what you've got till it's gone and all that jazz."

When Ryan opened the chicken coop door, the birds rushed at him, clucking and squawking to get past his feet and he stepped aside and let them go flying out into the yard where Duchess and Diana were chuffing and loping around playfully.

"You not feeling good or something?"

"Hmm?"

"You just let all the birds out, or are you so caught up in thinking about trash you missed that?"

Ryan grinned at the chickens running around as they circled to the right and settled down to peck at the grass and dirt. "Eh, I figure we can start letting them out again and feed them out here."

"You sure about that? Someone could still run up and snatch them."

"Well, given all that happened, I kinda doubt that'll happen again, but we can put them back up in the evenings. Regardless, they need some fresh air and running around space."

"Agreed."

"Hey, look at that," he said, pointing to Duke who was sitting and watching as the other dogs ran around with the birds. "Duke really must be hurt if he's not chasing them. Hey, Duchess! Leave the rooster alone!" Ryan shook his head and went inside, nudging aside the lingering birds and heading for the roost.

They put their rifles down so they didn't bump things in the confined space and Ryan reached in to get the eggs in the top row while Helen knelt and got to the bottom. Soon, their baskets were filled with golden brown eggs, and they were ready to head back.

As they left, Helen checked the lock. "Way to go on the latch; it's still holding up strong."

Ryan smiled and nodded, and they walked back to the house, with Ryan taking a detour over to the solar panels. He handed Helen his basket and kneeled at the end of the row, checking them for evenness and angle, ducking beneath them to verify the wires and cabling were still firmly connected and the poles hadn't shifted in the recent wind.

"Everything looking okay?" Helen asked.

"So far, so good." Ryan looked at the sky. "The clouds are staying away this week, and we're getting plenty of sun. The batteries are nearly full, and the appliances are running just fine."

"I'll need a nice hot shower to chase the cold out of my bones." Helen shivered. "It seems like it'll be a frosty winter if it's this cold already."

"Let's hope it evens out," Ryan nodded, taking his basket back and gesturing toward the house.

He gave a low whistle. "Come on, you old mutts. Get over here."

The dogs came running, except for Duke, who walked behind them, still favoring his shoulder with a slight limp. They piled through the back door, dog claws scratching on the hardwood, slavering and nosing at the egg baskets, causing Helen to turn away.

"Shoo, you nosy animals," she said, "or you won't get any of these in your food tonight."

The dogs gave up on Helen and turned to torment Ryan. "Oh, no you don't," he said, gesturing to his right. "Go on. Now!"

After the dogs went off, Ryan and Helen placed their baskets on the breakfast bar, leaning forward and looking at each other bemusedly.

"Those animals have the energy of five-year-olds."

"Someone around here needs to have some energy," Ryan replied, "because mine's running low."

"Me too." Helen paused reflectively. "I was thinking about what you said about Sandy today. Don't get me wrong, I'm glad it all worked out, but you're so dead set on getting something in return, then you just let her keep what she had. Sometimes I don't get you, Ryan Cooper."

"I'm a man of mystery."

"Seriously," she frowned. "What was your goal with all that?"

"Well, the way I see it, whatever this is..." He gestured all around and at nothing in particular. "It isn't going away anytime soon. If anything confirms that, it's the damn military trucks we saw."

"That much is true. We've seen no signs of any aid coming from anywhere, nor power coming back on – have we even seen a plane in the sky?"

"Nope. And aside from some bruises from the brawl and a little nick in the calf, we managed to survive just fine. We've proven to everyone left around us that we're strong. At the same time, showing some generosity to Sandy will go a long way to show that we're not total assholes and that we can work with other folks as long as they respect us. With any luck, that'll lead to folks wanting to work with us and not against us."

Helen grinned. "Smart man. Look at you, playing the long game."

Ryan winked. "Of course I am. When don't I?"

"You want some dinner?"

"I'd love some dinner." He smiled warmly. "I'm enjoying our meals together again. Not the best situation to make it happen, but I'm very grateful."

Helen circled the breakfast bar and moved to the refrigerator, resting her hand on the handle. "We've tapered off a bit over the years.... You had so many projects you wanted to work on, and I had my shows. But we always had dinner every night."

"That's true, but it's nice starting the day with you again. I missed it." Ryan shifted uncomfortably. "What I mean to say is, I love you. I always have, and I always will. I wouldn't want to go through this with anyone else."

Helen's expression reflected his love, her eyes glassy as she returned to his side, wrapping her arms around him and resting her head on his chest. "And I'm just as in love with you as the day we met. I'm so proud of you, Ryan Cooper. I'd be helpless if it weren't for you."

Ryan hugged her tight and smiled in the still moment. "What we taught the kids enabled us to be here when all this happened. I just wish they were here with us."

"They will be. Soon." Helen selected a boxed meal from the pantry, noodles and a parmesan sauce. "This is supposed to take chicken. Want to go dress one?"

Ryan laughed. "Not right now, but I've got another idea."

Helen got some water boiling while Ryan took a handful of eggs out of the refrigerator, cracking them, scrambling them, and slowly cooking them in a pan, stirring frequently. Once the noodles were done, Helen put in the sauce mix and Ryan chopped up the eggs with his spatula and dumped them in the pot, stirring everything up in a rich mixture with the garlic-parmesan aroma drifting through the house.

"Not bad," Helen nodded. "Good use of the eggs."

"We need to put the blasted things in everything, so I figured hey, why not try it."

By the time the pair had nearly prepared their food, the dogs had all lined up in the great room, ears perked up, used to hearing eggs cracking before going into the gravy and dog food mixture they'd been getting for dinner.

"I guess I should feed these monsters, too," Helen said.

Together, they fixed the dogs their bowls and put them off to the side, then Ryan stewed tomatoes from their harvest and made mashed potatoes with butter and milk, salting them lightly.

"How are we doing on spices?" he asked.

"We've got plenty of salt and pepper and some other odds and ends. But we'll have to find some more eventually."

"I can't imagine life without them," Ryan agreed. "Let me add them to my list, though I don't have a clue where we'll get them long term without coming across a stash or something." As he sat down with his plate, Ryan pulled his notepad over and wrote *salt and pepper*. "At least we've got our own garlic bulbs and rosemary. That stuff grows fast."

"We can grow the garlic all year round, but the rosemary and other leafy spices will struggle if it drops below twenty."

"Garlic is my favorite anyway, so I'll be fine if we keep our supply up." Ryan wrote garlic on his list. "You know, Michigan is one of the largest producers of salt in the country." He tapped his pen on the tablet as he thought. "From what I remember, there are salt companies in St. Clair, Manistee, and Detroit."

"I know we had a lot of salt companies in the state," Helen said as she brought her plate over and sat next to him, steam rolling off of it. "But I didn't realize we were one of the biggest producers."

Ryan shook his head absently. "I remember reading it somewhere, but that's something to think about if we talk about gathering resources. Salt is critical for us to live, so it might be worth a trip over to the east to look around. Maybe we can do that after we check in at Grand Rapids once the kids get back."

"Oh, you're talking big quantities, huh?" Helen said, talking around her food. "I was thinking an easier way would be to scavenge from some local markets or homes in the area. Could get a lot of essential spices that way."

"We can start there, but it's hard to say where all this will take us, so I'm going to put that idea on the back burner. Think about what we could trade for salt if we had enough. Also, we'd need it to make butter, which we need to start working on soon.

"Speaking of Grand Rapids, I'd hate to think what would've happened if we were back there when this all took place...."

———

In Grand Rapids, Michigan, the skies loomed cloudy and gray, flat and elongated as if pressed against a glass tabletop. There was no sun like in East Lansing, a bitter cold layer of cloud cover floating in off Lake Michigan to keep the temperatures down. Miles of destruction stretched in every direction, vast patches of scorched neighborhoods and smoking warehouse districts with just a few clean-standing buildings and homesteads glowing like diamonds in a box of coal dust. Around many of those oases stood people with shotguns and crowbars, pieces of rebar and knives, guarding what few supplies remained, the lone survivors of the vast waves of fires that had swept through the region.

Dogs barked throughout the ruins as they meandered, ratty-eared and skinny through the rubble, dragging out food scraps and nibbling on cooked corpses, roaming in small packs as the former pets slowly turned feral. Turkey vultures swooped in big lazy circles overhead, diving, gathering in flocks to pick bones clean, tearing through char and ash to get at rotting flesh underneath. Shouts rang out to chase them away, and a sporadic shotgun boom sent them flapping and squawking.

In the middle of a field straddling two properties was a wide, brown barn where light peeked through cracks in the walls. Off to the side, a few crates of supplies were stacked beneath tarps held down by bricks. Shopping carts with bottled water, canned vegetables, soggy boxed meals, and two-liter soft drinks were parked in a neat row under an awning with backpacks lined up next to them. Inside the barn, lanterns stood in every corner, filling the room with a dirty yellow light, wind howling through the barn windows. The place had a dusty, musty feel thanks to the years' worth of accumulations of old hay and manure. Around a dozen farm folks with graying hair, scraggly beards, and oil-stained overalls had gathered, rugged people who hunted and farmed, all of whom wore camouflage jackets, flannel shirts, military coats and hats and thick leather and rubber work boots.

Women locked arms with their husbands, all wearing mixed expressions of determination and frustration. One man threw back a shot of whiskey while others drank from a five-gallon water cooler against the north wall, or picked at the small tray of crackers, cheese, and beef jerky. All of them were quiet, their attention focused on a tall, older man standing on a platform on the south side of the barn floor. He wore a long-sleeved shirt with a camouflage fishing vest over it, blue jeans and work boots, and a pistol on his hip. A neatly trimmed white mustache sat above his thin upper lip, and his face was long and lean with weathered features that betrayed the number of years he'd spent out in the sun.

"Settle down now, folks. We're about to get started." Red Fletcher motioned, waving his hands as the crowd noise faded to murmurs and grumbles. "Now, I'm not going to waste everyone's time. We know from the government broadcasts that this is some kind of terrorist attack, and it's been more devastating than we could have ever imagined. We've all lost something. Even Martha and I lost..." A sob hiccupped from his chest, but he quickly controlled himself. "Well, you all know we lost a son and daughter-in-law and two grandbabies. Sorrow runs deep in all our hearts."

Any remaining mumbling fell dead.

"Now, we've managed to survive thus far by pulling our resources together with what remained after our properties burned down and doing what we had to do in that regard. And we've scavenged everything we can from the ruins of the surrounding farms, even harvested some crops. But the fire has claimed almost everything and left us with next to nothing. Jed Reese slaughtered the two cows we had left, and we thought that would help get us through the winter, but most of that was stolen by those sons of bitches a few nights back. And they killed Jed, too. Good news is we got three of them —good shooting Reynolds and Hansen—but the rest got away with our meat. Chasing them down is going to burn more resources than we could retrieve so we're going to leave that particular avenue unexplored.

"We've got some supplies left, but they won't last us long. I've talked to all of you, and none of us has any other family around. That means no help unless we come by it on our own, by peaceful means or violent ones." He paused and rubbed his forehead. "The bottom line is that we're in trouble, down on supplies, and things aren't going to get any better. We need to find someplace permanent to go if we're going to get through this."

Murmurs ran through the crowd, followed by nods and affirmative whispers.

"What I'm saying is, we need to leave this area. There's nothing for us here but trouble. Bigger gangs are moving in all around us and, well, we're crafty – but they've got numbers on us."

"Why don't we join up with one?" Jim Brunson spoke from up front, a former Army grunt with a firm jaw and slicked back white hair.

"Really? You think they want more mouths to feed? Especially older folks like us?"

"What about planting crops in the spring?" Nancy Likely asked, a tough, wiry farmer who owned what remained of the next property over. "We've got two or three fields ready to go, and if we start early in the spring and don't get any days of frost, we could be well stocked up by the middle of summer."

"That's just it, Nancy," Red replied. "We don't have that much time. Everything we've got is right here, and it ain't much. Martha and I estimated we've got maybe a week's worth of food, tops, and barely any ammunition after that last fight we had to secure a couple days more food. I figure we can use what we've got to get someplace better rather than sitting here and starving."

"What about the shopping plaza downtown?" Tyler Reed asked, raising his hand. "That place is packed with stuff."

"I'd warrant they're the same people who took our cows, too. I can't prove it, though. You think they're going to help us? Or that we've got enough ammo to neutralize them?"

Angry murmurs rippled through the crowd, mostly between Tyler and the two other retired Marines he had in his group. Tyler conferred with them a moment before turning back to the front, red-faced and angry. "Well, maybe we do! Why don't we march down there, shoot the bastards, then take our stuff back?" A few people cheered and clapped.

"That would be great," Red conceded, "but they've got us outnumbered ten to one, *and* I heard they raided the police armory right after everything went south. I reckon there are about a hundred people in that camp, most of them heavily armed and a hell of a lot younger than us. We go walking into a place like that, we'll last about ten minutes. Our advantage is being smart, not numbers or brute force."

The crowd grew quiet and shared uneasy looks, then Tyler broke in again. "Okay, let's be smart about it. We come up with a plan, sneak in, and steal what we need."

"Okay then," Red snorted. "Who here's the fastest of us?"

The aging crowd measured each other up before frowning and shaking their heads.

"That's right. We've got three people in their forties, and the rest of us are older than that, a couple of us with one foot in the grave. We've got joint problems, bum legs, and more than a few hip replacements."

The response gave way to a ripple of grumbling laughter from the crowd, and most nodded in agreement with Red's assessment. He'd taken on the role of de facto leader near the start of the whole debacle, his neighbors coming to him right away as his reputation for being a man of action put him head and shoulders above most. He'd accepted the position with some reluctance at the start, taking responsibility for their failings and accomplishments with a firm jaw and a willingness to learn from his mistakes.

"What do we do then?" Tyler asked, thumbs hooked into his belt.

"Well, like I said. We move to a better place."

"That's bound to be a lot of walking. Maybe shooting, too."

"Any way you measure it, yep. I figure we've got a week to get wherever we need to go, and we may be able to stretch our supplies if we scavenge along the way. Take what we need from anyone who we see along the way. Put 'em down if necessary."

"Where are we going?" Jim asked. "Is there some kind of Garden of Eden no one knows about?"

"I don't know about that, but there is a place close by that might give us a lead."

"*Might* give us a lead?" Tyler spat. "A lead doesn't get us anything, Red. A lead sounds like pissing in the wind to me, not a permanent roof over our heads."

"A lead will get us to that place, Tyler. We sure won't find it around here."

"What's your lead, then?"

Red glanced at Martha. "I know this guy named Ryan. A friend of a friend. Play – played – golf with him from time to time, and he lives just a few miles away in a townhouse with his wife, Helen."

"He got a farm in that townhouse, Red?" Tyler asked, a few in the crowd smirking.

"There's not a farm in his townhouse, Tyler, but they *were* farmers their whole lives, just like us, and they've got relatives not too far away who have property. Just last week, he told me about how they'd be spending a few weeks outside East Lansing to house sit for their daughter's family. Apparently it's a big, nice farm on a solitary road, shared with just a few neighbors. Sort of place that might have survived the fires, much like this building we're in."

Tyler spread his hands in a helpless gesture. "And what makes you think it's still standing?"

"I'm not saying it'll be standing for sure, but Ryan made it sound like his daughter and son-in-law were real sharp folks. Not preppers, but homesteaders, if you know what I mean. They've got supplies, farmland, and animals. Even some kind of backup power system or something that could keep appliances running for a good long time."

"Sounds like a great place!" Nancy said.

"Sign me up!" Another person in the group shouted.

"Unless they're Amish, they drive cars like the rest of us," Tyler smirked, looking around. "That means their in-laws house probably went up, too."

Red shrugged. "They're house-sitting. Means the daughter probably drove their car to the airport and left it parked out there. And I happen to know that Ryan and Helen have an electric car. Now, an electric car wouldn't have blown up, would it, Tyler?"

Arms crossed, and a few people rubbed their chins while others whispered excitedly among themselves at the prospect.

"Okay, you got me, Red." Tyler shook his head. "It sounds like a nice place, but risky. Why can't we find something like that around here?"

The crowd broke into mumbles and disagreements, uncertainty and dismay as they gestured and discussed the predicament heatedly.

"We'll be in deep shit in a week if we stay here." Red raised his voice to quiet them again. "And you know as well as I do how good the prospects around here have been looking. The way I see it, this is our shot. If we find something good on the way, so be it, but if not...."

"You know where the farm is?"

"No, but I bet if we go to Ryan's house and see if there's anything left of it, we might find a clue. It isn't that far, so if it doesn't pan out, we won't be that much worse off. Folks, this is our best bet at getting to a solid place. In fact..." He paused and looked grimly across the group. "This may be the last walk we ever take. We'll need to keep going right on through. No stopping for anything unless we come upon a good scavenging spot. We take what we need, even if it means killing everyone in our way – well, so far as our ammo holds out, anyway. All right, I've spoken my peace. Let's hear how you feel about it."

Red stepped back and waited for the mumbling voices to discuss what he'd proposed, and after a few long minutes of debating, Tyler stepped through the crowd in his red coat and scruffy, brown-gray beard.

"Okay, Red," he said. "Most of us agree with you. You've shown some darn good leadership so far, so we'll go."

Red smiled and glanced at Martha, then shook hands with several people in the front row as the buzz of excitement rippled through the group.

"All right, everyone, there's no time like the present. Let's get packed up and head out. We'll need everything we can carry, in case we find somewhere between here and there that looks suitable to stop in for a while. Load up the carts and wagons and let's get a move on."

The group packed up the food and water that was inside the barn, put out the lanterns, and stepped out into the cold. Carts were loaded up, tarps folded, ropes gathered, bundled, and put away. Red and Martha took the lead, pushing their carts ahead of them on a dirt track with all the possessions they had been able to rescue from the remnants of their home: a motley collection of canned goods, a backpack with a couple of changes of clothes, their shotgun, a box of shells, two jugs of water, and some odd pieces of camping equipment. The lack of extra firepower had been Red's greatest regret from his house fire. A stockpile of gasoline and a generator had been near the outside of the house directly opposite the interior wall where his gun safe had been, and the conflagration cooked off the ammunition and caused catastrophic damage to every firearm contained inside the safe.

Reynolds and Hansen were near the front with Red and Martha, the pair of retired Marines each carrying a shotgun along with backpacks with some pistols and the bulk of the remaining ammunition. Tyler slogged behind the group with an oversized backpack on his shoulders and a pistol on his hip, leaning forward, arms hanging forward to balance his weight. The others pushed carts or pulled small brush or firewood wagons behind them, rusty things with wobbly wheels, packed with goods and held down with bungee cords.

More than a few of the group were already walking with limps, having long had problems with their hips or knees or not being in the greatest shape to begin with. They all wore the same haggard expressions, a tired and worn-out bunch, but as they turned east on the main highway and left the burned-out husks of their homes behind, an energy overtook them. Hope and desperation both drove them, each knowing they had to be strong if they were going to reach their destination. A woman wept and staggered along, crying about everything they were leaving behind, her husband replying that they weren't leaving anything behind because there was nothing left. Miles passed by swiftly to the jangling song of wobbly wheels and rickety aluminum, shadows moving with the huddled forms of people still around, stray dogs getting bolder, and people watching warily from porches of half-torched homesteads.

"Reynolds, Hansen, and Tyler," Red pointed. "Go on up to that string of houses there and see if they have anything worth taking."

The men nodded, checked their weapons, and went on up while Red and the others formed a perimeter around the carts. People ran from the first two houses, and Red's men brought back a couple of garbage bags full of canned goods and assorted supplies.

"Not bad," Red said, nodding for them to give the bags to Martha. "How about those other houses? I'll go with you this time."

Checking his pistol, he led the three men up to a house with a burned-out garage that had taken part of the house with it. It was a small ranch model with aluminum siding and a small garden and porch. Red went up first while the men went to the front windows and put their hands to the glass.

"Anyone home?" Red asked.

Tyler shook his head and tried to look through the cracks in the blinds. "I don't see anything—Wait! Yeah, I see someone inside there. They just ran to the back."

Red backed away from the door. "Were they armed?"

"Unknown. But if we're going in, we should go now."

Reynolds stepped up to the porch, hauling his two-hundred and sixty-five pounds with him. "Step back, Red. I'll knock it open."

Red came down off the porch with a glance at the others, then he got his pistol out and held it at the ready. Reynolds held his shotgun in his right hand and opened the screen door, putting his ear against the door for a moment before rearing back and slamming his foot against it. The frame cracked and bowed but didn't break, then on the second try it exploded inward, and Reynolds ambled inside, followed by scuffles and something crashing, glass breaking, and a grunt and shout. Tyler and Hansen flew inside next, but Red came up slower, taking his time to enter carefully as shadows fought and staggered across the living room, smashing a table and hitting the wall with a thud. Reynolds pinned a man half his weight against the wall by his neck, shotgun in his right hand as he pressed his bulk against the homeowner while Tyler was laughing and Hansen grinned with his shotgun half raised.

It was an open floor layout, and Red saw into the kitchen where several cardboard boxes sat filled with supplies. He went straight over, nodding to Reynolds to hold the man still while he put his pistol to the stranger's head.

"We just want your supplies, not your life, though we'll take that if we need to. Just quit struggling and you'll get out of this more or less intact."

The man relaxed his grip on Reynolds' arm, though there was little else he could do with the larger man's forearm pressed to his chest and pinning him to the wall.

"That's all the supplies we have," he wheezed and struggled weakly. "You take those from us, we'll starve and die. Please, don't."

Red was struck by how guiltless he felt, wondering when those vestiges of humanity had slipped away before he shrugged off the thought and pushed the weapon the harder against the man's head.

"Settle down, son. You're young. You can find more supplies us old farts can't. Hey Tyler, check in back, would you? Don't want any surprises."

The man gasped, struggling a little to break free but stopping when Red raised an eyebrow. A long hallway stretched to the rear of the house, and Tyler started down it but was drawn to the kitchen table where the boxes were, picking through them and pulling out some canned goods, rice packets, flashlights and batteries.

"Hey, man. There's some good stuff in here." Tyler flipped a can and caught it with a laugh.

Red growled. "Tyler, would you do what I told you and —"

A thin woman in a white T-shirt slipped from the hallway, crouched low and dashing past Hansen to grab Reynolds' gun, jerking it out of his hand, fumbling with it, but getting it to her waist as she backed into the kitchen. "Let him go!" She shouted at Reynolds and then swept the gun menacingly from Tyler to Hansen. Red shook his head at Hansen, who looked about ready to make a move, and held his hands up.

"Hey, lady," he said. "No one needs to get hurt."

"You've got no right coming in here, threatening us and taking our things, you damn thieves." She spat every word, her dyed blonde hair striking a contrast to her angry red cheeks.

"We don't want to hurt you," Red said, "and we won't take your things if you put down the gun."

She scoffed. "You think I'm stupid? No, y'all get your asses out of here now! I swear I'll shoot you!"

Reynolds loosened the pressure on the man's chest enough for him to slide down the wall and stand unsteadily on his own two feet. The retired Marine looked back and forth between the woman and Red, one eyebrow arched in question at his leader.

"Why don't you put down the gun first, lady," Red said, "and we'll just—"

"No! We've been told that before and still got robbed! Took us three days to get what's on that table, and we won't have it taken again!"

"Honey, why don't you put the gun down?" The man licked his lips nervously as he looked at the men standing in his home, undeterred by his wife flailing a shotgun wildly back and forth. "Maybe... maybe we can work something out."

"See, your man's got a good point there. He can see you're outnumbered and —"

"No!" she snapped. "I won't let it happen again! I just won't!"

She jerked the shotgun to her shoulder and got a bead on Reynolds, squeezing the trigger, though Reynolds dove out of the way faster than his age would have suggested him capable of. Hot buckshot hit the woman's husband in the chest and he slumped against the wall as blood drenched his shirt and the wall both. Red raised his pistol without hesitation and fired four times, each round hitting her square in the chest. She fell to the floor still holding the shotgun across her lap, gaping at the crimson stains spreading throughout her shirt. She tried to say something but slumped flat onto her back with a sob, and Red fired once more into her head, sending a spray of blood across the wall.

The room hung in silence for a few long seconds before Red wheeled on Tyler with a snarl. "Man, you were supposed to check the hallway!"

Tyler stared at the dead people and shook his head. "Sorry, Red. I, uh, —"

"Just do what I say, when I say it, and things will go smooth. This did *not* go smooth. Do you not realize that every round counts? That's six less than we had before, dammit! And who the hell knows who heard all that commotion."

He shook his head as Reynolds used the kitchen table to get back to his feet, feeling across his shoulder and back where a few pellets had grazed him. The rest of their group outside were shouting, and Red crossed to the door to see Jim Brunson and a few others coming up into the yard with their guns out while Martha stood on the sidewalk looking concerned.

"Everything's fine," Red waved. "It's all under control. Y'all just stay there, and we'll bring out some supplies in a minute." When everyone relaxed and milled back to the street, Red turned back to those left inside. "You okay, Reynolds?"

"Yeah, Red. Just a few scrapes. Better'n those two."

"I was wrong about you," Red nodded. "You move pretty damn fast for a big boy. Okay, let's get this stuff loaded up and get out of here before those shots draw more attention than we bargained for."

They packed everything up and took the five boxes out, Hansen and Reynolds each carrying two while Red and Tyler got the rest. Outside, they handed the supplies to the others who started putting things away in their carts.

"It won't last us very long," Red announced, "but every little bit helps."

Martha took his arm and pulled him aside, whispering. "What happened?"

"That got ugly, but nothing we couldn't handle. It's all good now."

Martha fixed him with a lingering look, and Red nodded firmly. "I said it's all *good*."

"Is it? I heard a woman in there yelling."

Red's eyes narrowed. "Martha. You and I've had this discussion before. It's a dog-eat-dog world now, and we've got to play hard if we want to survive this. You know it."

She stared at him for a long moment before nodding and gripping his arm harder, marching onward down the road out of town.

"Reynolds and Hansen," Red called as the convoy got back underway. "Walk the edges and watch for anyone moving in. Shoot first, ask questions later. You know how hard and fast things can turn."

The two men nodded and took up their positions, shotguns at the ready while others spread out and lingered on the edges of the group, protecting the supplies and one another as they moved through the midday gloom. They passed once vibrant neighborhoods decimated by fires, looking like they'd come under attack from bombers, guts of houses and cars strewn everywhere, leaving only a few beams or brick walls standing.

The recent rains had turned everything into a dark sludge that carried debris to the sewers which had quickly clogged and created wide, swirling black ponds that covered the streets. The water was dank and gave off a pungent, rotting reek, and Red shook his head and picked up the pace, moving out ahead of the group. He stayed out in front for a quarter of a mile, surprised when he turned and saw that the group was keeping pace with him.

"It won't be long now," he called. "Just another mile and a half past the golf course where we played."

The group chatter picked up, and a few smiles showed as they helped each other along. There was a hardness about the members of the group, the kind of toughness that only came from living and fighting through hard times their whole lives, sharing wounds, tragedy, and victories and bearing hardships that would have killed anyone weaker years prior – say nothing of the last few weeks.

A sudden swell of baying, barking and yelling pulled their attention to the rear of the group, all eyes on Tyler where he was lying on his back, legs kicking, reaching to punch at a pack of dogs as they tore at his backpack and thick jacket. Reynolds and Hansen moved into position on either side, Hansen closing and squeezing his shotgun's trigger as a dog spun and snarled at him, the shot removing the animal's face and scattering it across the pavement. Reynolds fired at another dog that looked like it hadn't eaten in weeks, hitting it square in the side, causing it to break off and crawl for a few yards before lying dead on the pavement. The pack took off as others in the group came forward and began swinging hand tools at them, yipping and howling as they fled down the street in a scrabble of claws. Reynolds fired again at the pack, hitting a few of them in the backside, stinging them with birdshot as they hurried after the group.

"Hold your fire, dammit!" Red yelled. "Save the ammo! Are you okay, Tyler?"

"I'm fine," Tyler replied, getting up with help from the others and brushing himself off.

Red glowered at him, his voice low and serious. "You need to get frosty quick, Marine. I'm serious. That's two times you've screwed up and almost got someone else *or* yourself killed, and two times I've overlooked it. There won't be a third."

Tyler's normally brusque expression had turned soft in the face of the reprimand, and he replied softly. "I hear you, Red. I'll do better."

"Damn straight you will." Red glared at him and turned to address the group as a whole. "He's lucky it was just a few mangy old dogs. Next time, it'll be people, and it'll be a knife in your back or across your throat, and you'll be left to bleed out in the street while the rest of us carry on. I'm telling you, folks. Be on the lookout and ready to act instantly." He shrugged. "Otherwise, you're just going to die, and the rest of us will have more food as a result."

Martha came and walked next to Red as they marched on, taking him by the arm to the front of the procession, and the group continued their march east past the golf course with its expansive, overgrown greens and unblemished woods, still remarkably beautiful with their gold and rustic red colors coming with the weather change.

Soon, they'd gone farther away from their neighborhood than they'd been since the disaster, the protective ring around their supplies growing tighter, their gazes warier, senses elevated and on the alert for any threats. Beyond the golf course were more neighborhoods, and Red stood at each intersection ahead of the group, trying to read the signs and figure out which road would lead to his destination. Everything was unrecognizable, though, the houses and townhouses having turned into darkened squares beneath the gloomy skies and fog, the streets hardly streets anymore but riverbeds of wreckage and murky puddles.

They came to one neighborhood Red recognized, and he moved up the lane, shuffling out ahead of everyone else, heart pounding with the expectation of failure since there was hardly a house left standing, and those that were had fire damage to their exteriors or had been broken into.

He superimposed what he remembered about Ryan's townhouse over the wrecked area and stopped at the end of the street before it curved left, standing in front of a line of five homes with the remnants of garages and stoops marking each one. The foundations were placed so close together it made a single long structure with fire breaks between them, though they had made little difference since almost all the garages held the remains of gas-powered vehicles, their burned-out frames half covered in collapsed roofs. The smoke grew thicker on the far end of the street, clinging to everything, swirling through the gaps with every uptick of wind.

"Are you sure this is it?" Martha asked, coming up next to him.

"I'm positive." Red gestured to the left. "I remember because when I dropped Ryan off, I turned around in that driveway over there to get back out to the main road. His house would've been..." He stepped to the middle garage and front porch and held both hands up perpendicular to the ground to frame what would have been the townhouse's sides. "Right here. They were right here."

"Doesn't look like they're here anymore, boss," Hansen said. "What should we do now?"

Frowning, Red growled. "I figured they wouldn't be here, on account of them visiting their daughter's home. But there's a fair amount of wreckage to look through. We should dig through it, see if we can find any kind of—"

"Red?" Hansen's demeanor changed, and he turned, gesturing with his shotgun pointed at the far-left end of the homes. "Looks like we've got company."

Shadows approached through the gloom, slinking between the piles of rubble and an engine block lying in a driveway.

Red stepped back and unslung his rifle, hissing to the rest of the group. "Anyone with a gun, get up here. Form a defensive line."

The defenders moved into position with their weapons raised, keeping those who were unarmed behind them with their supplies. Red placed his hand on Hansen's back and stepped to his right, tracking a figure coming toward them.

"Best slow up and show yourself before we open fire!"

A man rushed to them from the ruins, hands up, weaponless as far as Red could see. "Please! Can you spare some food? Please?!"

"Step back, mister," Red growled when the man kept coming, seeming to ignore the firepower arrayed against him.

The firing line moved a couple of paces backwards, waiting for Red's orders, all except for Hansen who took a step forward, lining up a shot. Still, the man was undeterred, and he hurried across the stretch of burned grass separating the driveways where Red and his people were standing. He wore ragtag clothing, a chewed-up poncho that hardly kept the rain off, his pants soaked and dirty, stomach lean and wide bloodshot eyes stark against his gaunt frame. Others moved behind him, forms creeping through the shadows with flashes of loose garments, and Red felt a ball of nervous tension creep into his gut.

"I said stop!" Red took a step forward, leveling his pistol at the man who refused to heed his warnings. "Stop or we will fire!"

Hansen's shotgun barrel flashed in a blast of smoke and flames, buckshot spraying the man's face and chest, tearing his plastic poncho to shreds as he screamed in agony. He staggered to the edge of the grass and fell to his knees, blood dripping from his wounds, then more gunshots flashed as the defensive line continued what Hansen had started, firing at the remaining shadows in a barrage that made them dance and cavort until the three or four shapes pitched backward into the driveway, falling motionless to the ground with cries of pain.

Martha ran forward, her flashlight sweeping across the downed figures, screaming, "Stop shooting! Stop it!"

The gunfire sputtered to a halt, and she rushed through the clearing smoke to the fallen man, but it was too late. He was lying in the grass, body twitching and arching upward as he breathed his dying breath and fell flat. Red rushed forward to her side, his near-empty pistol still trained on the bodies farther away, kneeling next to Martha as she touched his neck to try and find a non-existent pulse.

"Dead... they're... they're all dead." Martha stammered, moving past him and shining her light on a mother and children who were lying dead beyond the person Red presumed was their father. The woman was face down in the driveway, reaching for a smaller, curled-up figure off to the side, and another child, a teenager, lay against an old piece of furniture near the mother's feet, hair hanging lank on her shoulders, staring at nothing, body slack. Blood soaked the driveway, running through the cracks, over the side, and into the street.

Martha knelt between the mother and first child, looking back and forth before turning to Red. "It was a family, Red," she gasped. "We... just killed a family."

Red stiffened, working his jaw for several seconds before turning back and giving Hansen a near-unnoticeable nod. "It's a damned tragedy, but they should've stopped. We warned them and they kept coming. It's just how it is."

Martha broke down with a sob. "Don't say that, Red! These were kids and a mother, unarmed and innocent! We didn't have to kill them in cold blood!"

"Sorry, Martha," Hansen said, watching Red as he spoke, "but your husband's right. I didn't want to shoot him, but who knows what they would have tried to do. Been on enough tours to know that kids are just as dangerous as adults."

"Don't give me your war bullshit, Hansen!" Martha choked out the words, hissing at the pair of men before turning back to the fallen figures. "These people... we didn't have to do *this*."

Red placed his hand on Hansen's shoulder. "You did good. We *did* have to shoot, and we'll have to do that a lot more if we want to survive this. They could have been anyone with any number of intentions. Hell, there's no way to know if they even *were* innocents. They should've stated what they wanted from a distance and not rushed us..." He shook his head. "No, my conscience is clean."

Red stared at the girl pinned in Martha's flashlight beam, resolve hardening his heart, a stone wall growing over the tender muscle, the pulsing beat clenched in a cold hand. It had been a crying shame, but the worst of it was the disapproval in Martha's eyes, and he had to turn away or be consumed in it.

"We can't show anyone any quarter," Red announced, speaking louder to the group. "No one showed *us* any. Remember that." He nodded and wiped the moisture off his nose with the back of his hand. "Now, let's start going through these ruins and see if there's anything we can find to help us. Look for supplies, but more importantly, look for things that might tell us where Ryan went. Letters, address books – anything. Got it?"

Turning away from the bodies with murmurs of agreement, they approached the house, the right side of which looked like it had almost melted and broken away, leaving some of the left side intact. They wandered through the rubble, picking through pieces of Ryan and Helen's lives with the soggy black furniture, fallen ceilings and part of the second floor hanging off the stairwell which was crushed and twisted.

"No one goes upstairs yet," Red announced, standing at the edge as the others went inside. "Let's check this floor and the basement first. Check and triple check what someone else searches. Leave no stones unturned. Canned goods and supplies are likely down in the basement if they've got one."

Red stepped into the living room, feeling his way around with the tip of his boot, making sure the floor was still stable before he went on. He shoved a couch aside, clearing a path for those coming behind him and working toward the kitchen. The kitchen table was still mostly intact with debris piled on top, and the cooking island was covered in wet drywall and wood. He was about to start checking the cabinets and drawers when Hansen called out.

"Over here, Red! I think I found the basement."

"Martha, can you check the drawers, please?" He forced himself to speak softly to her, trying to undo some of the damage from earlier.

"I'll... I'll do it now," she confirmed with a nod, barely looking at him.

Red worked his way out of the kitchen, stepping over a chair and coming around to where they were gathered by the door. Hansen tugged at the door, and it came open, grating against the floor. The steps had collapsed in a few places, though they could see the basement at the bottom.

"Want us to go down?"

"I'll go," Red said. "I won't ever ask any of you to do anything I wouldn't do myself."

Flashlight out and shining toward the bottom, Red led a couple of people down, bringing sacks with them, stepping precariously and calling out stable footholds and holes in the wood. At the bottom, he walked across the carpeted floor of the basement, shining his light around what had once been a comfortable living space, though its walls were covered with soot and black mold, the floor wet from water still dripping from the pipes. Working his way around, he found a small bar with some whiskey and soft drinks, gesturing for one of the people behind him to collect them while he went through another door on the far side of the room. His smile grew wide as he shined the light around at a couple of shelves with some canned goods stacked on them.

"It's not a lot," he told the person behind him, "but it makes this trip worth it, at least."

Red and his helper filled up their sacks and left the basement to the excited murmurs of everyone upstairs. He stepped into the kitchen, holding up his sack. "Not quite the goldmine I was hoping for, but we got something, anyway. A couple of cases of corn and green beans, some baked beans, and tomato sauce."

His helpers held their sacks up, one saying, "Whiskey, soda, and a few boxes of spaghetti and pasta, too."

The group nodded appreciatively, though all eyes had turned to Tyler and Martha, standing in the kitchen with all the drawers pulled open, papers and pens and drawer junk strewn everywhere.

"That's great," Martha said, coming to the kitchen table with a thin smile, still avoiding meeting her husband's eyes. "But I think you'll be happier to see what I found stuck to the side of the refrigerator."

Red put his hands on his hips. "Well, do tell. What did you find?"

"This." She held up a half-burned, soggy piece of paper and waved it at him, and Red stepped over and took it, reading it with a confused expression that faded into pleasant surprise.

"Well, I'll be. An envelope. This what I think?" He took the remnants of a red card out of the envelope, flipped it open, and read it. "A birthday card for Ryan, signed 'Your Loving Daughter.' Hmmm..." He threw the card on the floor and looked at the envelope again. "The half with the address is burned off, but... ha!" Red's smile broadened and he chuckled wildly as he grabbed Martha's stiff form in a bear hug.

"What're you so excited about, Red?" Tyler grumbled. "No address on it, so it's useless."

"Are you kidding me?" Red gawked at Tyler. "I swear, you need your head looked at." Holding up the envelope, he pointed to the postmark. "It's postmarked Elsie."

"What's that mean?" Hansen asked.

"You idjits... you'd think you hadn't ever been farmers in your whole life before." Red rolled his eyes. "It's a farming town, just outside East Lansing! And the card was to *Ryan* from his *daughter*, who...."

Hansen and Tyler both looked at each other, their looks of confusion slowly vanishing as realization dawned.

"Now you're getting it," Red laughed as he tucked the envelope into his front pocket, his aches, pains, emotional distress and exhaustion melting away. "Ladies and gentlemen – we have what we came for. It's time to get a move-on!"

CHAPTER EIGHTEEN

Agent Alan Harris
Mount Weather, Virginia

Harris guided President Birk through the bunker's inner passages, the long concrete hallways painted green with bold white markings. Military personnel hustled by, running to their posts while alarms blared throughout the facility, a voice booming from speakers in the walls, ordering various groups to different locations. A distant explosion rippled through the building, the concrete trembling ever so slightly from the blast, dust trickling from the ceiling vents as Harris instinctively grabbed Birk around the shoulders.

"Right this way, sir," he said, still moving, gesturing for the President to turn. "The safe room is at the end of this hall."

As they walked, Harris received updates from Security Chief Westbrook over his earpiece. "Attention all security teams. Hold your positions. General Pulaski is sending Marine units into the woods in a hard formation to scatter the attackers. I'm patching everyone in."

A Marine's gruff tone cut through the line along with scattered bursts of gunfire and a distant explosion. "Enemy units have struck the comms tower, and Bravo and Charlie teams are moving into the woods to counter."

"Who's hitting us?" Colonel Crow asked. "Saudis?"

"Negative, sir," replied the Marine. "They appear to be civilians."

Harris let go of his earpiece and turned to Birk. "I'm hearing it's a group of civilians, and they've taken out the comm tower, which explains the disruption in our feed."

"Civilians?"

"Seems to be. They're hitting us around the perimeter. Hold on a second... I'm listening in." Harris walked and listened as the spotty feed filled his ear with static and bits of transmissions. "Okay, Colonel Crow has sent Alpha team led by Sergeant Timmons around to the east wall...."

"Colonel Crow, this is Alpha team. We're halfway along the east wall and found a box that used to hold explosives. It's some heavy stuff the civilians shouldn't be playing with. We'll leave it by the fence line for someone to secure."

"Roger that, Timmons," Crow replied. "They may be trying to distract us before attacking the gate. Get your asses moving."

Harris leaned closer to Birk. "They've found some explosives and dead civilians, so they think they're trying to rig up something to take down the gate."

Harris and Birk reached the end of the hallway, a door guarded by two armed Marines who saluted and stood aside.

Birk stooped and punched in his keycode, and the magnetic locks popped the door open. Harris pushed through and checked the room over, a small space with a stripped-down bathroom, a desk with a computer on the north side, and a few sparse pieces of furniture and crates of supplies on the east wall.

"Can we hold out?" Birk asked as they entered the room. "This place is hardened as far as I know."

"Assuming they don't breach the entrance, then yes. The barriers around the facility were mostly chain-link fencing and barbed wire when we got here," Harris replied. "They put up a few more barriers since then, but that's clearly not deterring them. And the hardening on the entrance isn't anywhere near the level of more robust facilities."

"Is that supposed to make me feel better?" Birk chuckled as he slipped into the computer chair.

"No, sir."

Birk pressed a key, and the computer screen lit his face in its glow. "Well, I appreciate the honesty, Harris. I'm tapping into the communication channels now." He read the display and rolled backward a foot. "I don't get it. We've been making supply drops all around the country. Why are they coming here and attacking us?"

"Good question. I'd say..." Harris hesitated.

"Go ahead, Harris. Speak freely."

"In my opinion, people are pissed at our response to what's happening. The supplies were a good first step, but people are looking for long-term answers. At least, that's my best guess. I think they're here to vent their frustrations on whoever's in power."

Birk snorted. "Well, they could've just knocked or filled out a complaint card or something. We don't have *that* many people here, but they can't imagine that getting to the President is going to be easy, can they?"

"No clue, sir. Hold on, there's more coming in..." Harris touched his earpiece and listened. Timmons was panting over the line when it suddenly opened up to the Sergeant's entire team.

"What's this, Sarge?" a Marine asked.

"It's explosives, rigged to blow," a female Marine replied. "But I've never seen it set up like this before. Looks demented."

"Will it work?" Timmons asked.

"You got me. It's a clusterf—"

"Focus. Can you disable it?"

"No way, Sarge. Not without a lot more time to trace this mess of wires... and we've got fifteen seconds left, if this alarm clock is the timer."

There was a brief pause, then Timmons' next words were shouted into his radio between him running and panting. "Back away, now! Colonel Crow! Brace for detonation. I repeat, brace for deton—"

Harris nodded to President Birk. "This doesn't sound go—"

An explosion rocked the facility, far greater than the one before, sending light fixtures rattling and the floor shifting beneath them as a brief swell of claustrophobic panic ran through Harris' brain. He forced himself to settle down, breathe deeply, and remember that the facility – while not built to NORAD specifications – was still designed to withstand an enormous amount of firepower. Next to him, Birk gripped his desk, grimacing until the rumbling and dust had stopped.

"Are you okay, sir?"

"I'm fine." He chuckled and raised an eyebrow. "Whoever they are, they sure know how to introduce themselves."

A few minutes earlier...

Sergeant Timmons stood behind a wall of sandbags on the north fence line of the Mount Weather facility, pacing and watching the murky tree line with its shifting shadows and fog. The sky was cloudy, with an ambient glow clinging to the soft edges and spreading halos across the Blue Ridge Mountains.

"You sure the attack is going to come from this direction, sir?" Private Tori asked, the assistant gunner squatting in a corner while she finished wiping down their M249 SAW.

"It doesn't matter what we think, Private. Our orders are to make sure nothing comes over that hill."

"They'd need to be mountain goats to get up here," Private Ramakrishnan replied derisively. "Or birds."

"Birds, mountain goats or flying unicorns – I don't care. Shut your traps and focus!"

Where the hill bent toward the north, the ground became treacherous and rocky, with only about twenty yards of flat space before it dipped almost straight down, with trees and foliage clinging to the hillside. Their visibility wasn't much better, made worse by the sweeps of floodlights from the towers, only serving to fill the woods with an impenetrable glow where shadowy branches waved. The insects were particularly loud as well, forming a chorus of chirps and creaks that echoed all around them, blocking out any hope of picking up potentially important sounds, except for the occasional order bellowed from loudspeakers set atop poles.

Timmons spoke after a long pause. "Colonel Crow's orders are to guard this piece of fence line, and that's exactly what we're going to do."

"I know, Sarge, but —"

"I said *that's exactly what we're going to do.*"

"Yes, Sarge."

The small group was part of the squad guarding the Mount Weather perimeter, run by Colonel Crow from inside the command center. Sergeant Timmons paced inside their small four-by-twelve-foot barricade, which sat just outside the fence line with a gate right behind them and more guard towers spaced along the three-hundred-yard length. Through gaps in the woods, the faint orange glows of fires pulsed across the valley and spurs. Smoke drifted by, the byproduct of cities and towns long since burned to the ground, leaving a fog that carried across the miles with no signs of dissipating.

"How long do you think those fires will rage, Sarge?" Tori asked.

Timmons stopped pacing. "Your guess is as good as mine and worth about the same, too."

Samson took the rag from Tori and finished drying off his weapon. "With no firefighters around, the fires from the cities will probably carry on for weeks. Probably have to wait for everything to burn itself out."

"That's going to destroy...everything," Tori replied.

"Yeah."

"Do you think it's this way everywhere, Sarge?"

"Oh, it's everywhere. At least that's what they said at the last officer's meeting, but they're keeping things under wraps. They want us to focus on our jobs, and that's what we'll continue doing until someone comes to relieve us." Timmons raised an eyebrow. "But since you all seem so bored and chatty and unable to focus, let's do a complete equipment check. Right now."

"Yes, Sarge," Tori sighed and received grumbles from the rest of the fireteam as they found their equipment packs and began going through them.

They hadn't gotten more than a few moments into their check when an explosion erupted from the west side of camp, drawing surprised cries from the team and causing them to stagger back in surprise. A fiery plume crawled over the high fencing and rolled up into the sky, billowing black and orange flames pluming upward with blasts of sparks flying off to the sides. The buildings just inside the fence line blew apart in the explosion, and the shrieks of the dying followed close behind.

Marines from other sections sprinted toward the fires as a smattering of machine guns erupted from the corner positions, lighting up the night with tracers in brilliant flashes of red. The communications tower, a one-hundred-foot-tall steel construction with heavy beams and crossbars, satellite dishes, and antennas jutting from the top squalled as the metal twisted and bent. The structure continued groaning as the top third cracked in slow motion, broke downward, and finally toppled to the ground. Marines dove out of the way as it crashed and threw flames and debris into the sky, the heat rolling across the grounds.

His Marines started to leap the sandbags when Timmons grabbed them and pulled them back behind cover. "Get back here!"

"But, Sarge!" Sampson argued. "They're getting hit hard!"

"Sit down, Marine!" Timmons jerked him by the arm. "We don't move unless we're ordered to."

Grabbing his radio, he crouched down, speaking quickly into it. "Central, this is Sergeant Timmons on the north fence line. We've got an explosion on the west side, multiple casualties, incoming enemy fire and a breached perimeter. Please advise."

Flaming debris rained across the grounds, and more gunfire was exchanged, shrapnel and stray rounds flying in their direction, pinging off buildings and poles, zipping by like hummingbirds in the darkness. His radio erupted in a spattering of commands, cries for help, and requests from other units for direction until Colonel Crow came on the line and barked orders for Bravo, Charlie, and the reserve units throughout the facility. Marines gathered and charged toward the west side of camp in a flurry of running boots, and while Timmons expected the gunfire to fade and stop, it only grew more intense, the rat-a-tat of small arms fire chattering with machine guns, and two heavy thumps he took to be grenades.

"Who the hell... get ready, Marines," he growled, hand on his rifle. "I have a feeling—"

"Alpha team..." The rest of Colonel Crow's order was lost in a flash of white noise, a hiss, and a crackle of static.

"Say again!" Timmons shouted at the radio.

Puffs of dust erupted all along their sandbagged position as rounds embedded themselves in the barrier. The Marines instinctively ducked, falling flat as the nearby tree line sparked to life with muzzle flashes that deepened the approaching shadows. Forms ran between the trees in a surprisingly organized fashion, stopping in staggered formations to shoot at them from behind the thick trunks, keeping them pinned.

"Suppressing fire!" Timmons howled, wincing as rounds zipped above them. "Give them something to think about!"

"Yes, sir!" Sampson called, crawling to his M249 sitting on a crate, the barrel pointed out at the woods.

He slid up to the weapon, put the stock to his shoulder, and ripped off a return barrage, sweeping the barrel from left to right in a burst that sent their attackers ducking, diving aside, or flying back. The forest blossomed in high-pitched screams as a few of the rounds found their marks, and a spray of wood chips and shredded foliage erupted into the air. Tori and Ramakrishnan flung themselves against the sandbags on either side of the machine gunner, dispersing fire to the edges in a withering response, keeping their attackers pinned down.

"Colonel Crow!" Timmons shouted into his radio. "Alpha team is under attack at the north gate. Say again, we are under attack at the north gate. Small arms fire coming from—"

A spark of flickering light flew from the tree-line, arcing through the air, falling just short of their position, glass shattering and releasing its flammable liquid in a splatter of fire and heat that ran up the front of the sandbags and billowed skyward. The Marines flinched and pulled back for a few seconds, waiting for the wave to dissipate. They quickly resumed shooting at the tree line, though the break in suppressive fire had given the attackers time to scatter, making them too hard to pin down.

Timmons tossed his radio to the ground and crawled to Tori's side, resting his weapon across the sandbags to join in firing at the running figures moving along the tree line. Another arcing firebomb flew at them, hitting the ground five yards away and spreading liquid flames right at them, a potent concoction that stuck to the sandbags and kept burning.

"Is that gasoline and Styrofoam?" Timmons yelled, rising to the sandbags, firing bursts through the flames. "These assholes are dropping homemade napalm on us! Don't let it get on you, whatever you do!"

"Incoming!" Tori shouted, and the Marines dropped again as another bottle soared into the air, flying over them and tumbling end-over-end where it crashed into the gate and erupted in a ball of flames that crawled up the fencing, rolled around the barbed wire and licked at the sky.

"Damn that was close!" Samson shouted.

"Suppressing fire! Do not let them throw more of those!" Timmons ejected his mag and slammed a new one home, crouching back down behind the sandbags as the SAW began to fire next to him.

Samson picked out shapes along the tree line and opened up again, sending more bodies jerking and rolling back in the thick foliage. "Got two, Sarge! I need another belt soon!"

Bringing all their firepower to bear, shooting long bursts with their carbines and the SAW and alternating to swap out mags, they turned the treeline into mulch, cutting limbs to pieces so that they crashed to the forest floor, dust and smoke billowing up in plumes. The attackers fled the tree line in the face of the onslaught, and the muzzle flashes faded until there were none left.

"Bastards!" The last of Samson's ammunition rattled off in a rain of brass casings, the 249 clicking dry.

Tori was beside in an instant, loading in a new belt, then Samson slammed the cover over the feed assembly before pulling back the charging handle. He knelt back down, sweeping his weapon through the smoke and dust still filtering through the air, finger resting on the trigger guard as he squinted, looking for any hint of movement.

"I think... did we get them all?" he asked quietly.

Only silence answered from the tree line, and as their adrenaline began to drain, the dark edges around their vision lightened, and they began to hear other noises from around the camp as they filtered in. More Marines and various Army units were pouring from the bunker doors through the breach in the fence line, heading into the western woods where muzzle flashes flickered like fireflies.

"Alpha team, are you there?"

"I'm here, sir." Timmons fell to one knee. "We're all present and accounted for."

"Sitrep?"

"We engaged a small force of maybe two dozen armed with light arms and Molotovs and repelled them."

"Were they soldiers? I need identification."

"It was too dark to make them out, and we haven't swept the area yet, but my impression is they were civilians. Well-trained, but still civilians."

"Did you get a bead on what kind of weapons they were using?"

"Pistols and AR-style rifles, sir."

"Did you hear any automatic weapons?"

Timmons glanced at the others, who all shook their heads. "Nothing we could hear."

"Very good, Timmons. I want you to bring your team to the south gate, via the east fence line."

"Sir? That would leave this area unguarded."

"We've got some reserves coming up to take your place. We need you to make haste toward the south gate and hold that position until told otherwise. Understood?"

"Absolutely. On our way." There was a squelch from the radio, and Crow began addressing other teams as Timmons strapped the radio to his hip. "You heard the man," Timmons told the team, who were already packing up their gear. "Grab ammo and get your asses moving."

"I need another belt," Samson said, taking a belt of ammunition for the SAW from Tori and looping it around his neck.

As he wound a strap for the SAW around his shoulder, Tori and Ramakrishnan got their remaining magazines stuffed into their vest pouches and inside a duffel bag, and they slung all they could carry on their shoulders.

"Let's go, Marines!" Timmons straddled the sandbags and climbed over. "We're already late to the party."

He cross-stepped along the fence line, using the flashlight on his barrel to sweep the area as his team trailed behind him. Blinking and flashing lights from broken light poles flickered behind him, combining with the burning buildings to cast an eerie orange glow over the area. Bodies lay at the edge of the woods, some caught in brambles and thick brush, all of them with tattered clothing and gaping wounds after being hit with Samson's M249 and the others' carbines.

"Ramakrishnan, get up ahead. Watch the fence line and we'll cover the woods. Double time."

Wordlessly, the scout swept past them and got out in front, nearly jogging to the northeast corner as the others watched the woods. When Ramakrishnan fired in three bursts at something up ahead, Timmons broke into a run and caught up.

"Use your words, dammit! What do you see?"

"People running down the hillside to the east; I gave them some parting shots. Should we pursue?"

"Negative. Stow the gunfire unless I say. Just keep moving."

They crept along the east wall, getting farther away from the main battle, which seemed to have gone deeper into the hills to the west. Fires were spreading, and thinly-manned emergency crews were trying to put them out, but Timmons stayed focused on the tree line. It was flatter on the far side, with sparse clusters of trees and brush, the moon bright behind the clouds, its sparse rays that broke through the cloud cover highlighting a rise that swept south and curved out of sight.

"Watch that little valley. If there was any place for an ambush, that would be it." Timmons' shoulders clenched as he jogged, sweat dripping down his neck and back as he waited for someone to hit them.

Tori followed close behind him with Samson, the squat woman carrying the heavy duffel bag full of ammunition over her left shoulder with her carbine resting on her hip. The privates worked as one, sweeping their weapons across the trees, focused and silent as they searched and moved. Halfway along the eastern fence line, Ramakrishnan stopped to squat over a pair of dead Marines and Timmons swept his flashlight across the sprawled bodies, illuminating the gunshots and blood-stained fatigues.

A pair of civilians in jeans and dark jackets lay a short distance away, one with a shotgun, the other with an older Winchester rifle lying in the grass nearby. Spotlights from the near watchtowers swept in and stopped on the Marines, and Timmons turned and waved, then the lights moved on.

Tori kicked one of the attackers. "Must've been a militia or something."

"I wonder what they were trying to do? They lost a *lot* of guys." Samson leaned over, looking at the bodies.

"The answer might be right there." Timmons nodded to a plastic bin lying on its side, the lid thrown off, its contents spilled across the grass. "Have a look, Tori."

"On it." She circled smoothly to the bin and knelt. After a moment of rummaging, she held up a block of gray clay. "This is not good, Sarge."

"What?"

"Take a look."

Timmons moved where he could see and shined his light near the spilled contents, which amounted to more gray blocks, timers, wires, and switches. "Son of a... that's C4. Civvies wouldn't have that."

"If they raided an armory, they might," Tori replied. "Plenty of 'em left to raid, I'm sure, especially if they're a militia. Whatever they're up to, it can't be good. I wonder if this is what they used to destroy the guard positions on the west side."

"Bigger question is – is there more of the stuff?" Timmons shook his head, lips pressed firmly in a tight line. "Put all that in the bin and set it against the fence, out of sight."

"Yes, Sarge."

While Tori worked, Timmons got his radio. "Colonel Crow, this is Alpha team. We're halfway along the east wall and found a box that used to hold explosives. It's some heavy stuff the civilians shouldn't be playing with. We'll leave it by the fence line for someone to secure."

"Roger that, Timmons. They may be trying to distract us before attacking the gate. Get your asses moving."

Ramakrishnan led them to a section of the perimeter reinforced by concrete walls and higher fencing. The air was still, the sounds of fighting growing distant, the cracks of rifles, the sharp *pop* of pistols drawing the Bravo and Charlie teams away. Wind blew gusts of smoke past them, Timmons feeling vulnerable out in the open with their backs to the wall, chasing shadows that flitted at the edge of the darkness.

Near the southeast corner, Ramakrishnan stopped again. "What's this, Sarge?"

Timmons moved past Ramakrishnan and shined his flashlight at a blind spot along the wall where groups of gray blocks were lined up at three-foot intervals, connected with wires and small junction boxes. Tori dropped her ammunition sack and strode over, feet spread as she took in the configuration with a glance. "It's explosives, rigged to blow. But I've never seen it set up like this before. Looks demented."

"Will it work?"

Tori shrugged. "You got me. It's a clusterf —"

"Focus. Can you disable it?"

Tori took out her flashlight and examined them closer, tracing the path along the cables to reach a junction box with glowing red numbers. "No way, Sarge. Not without a lot more time to trace this mess of wires... and we've got fifteen seconds left, if this alarm clock is the timer."

Timmons sidestepped and watched five seconds tick down, brain trying to process what he was seeing before he grabbed Tori and threw her toward the sweeping lowland, clutching Samson and Ramakrishnan next, shoving, pushing, and screaming at them to take cover. As he ran, he snatched his radio off his belt and shouted into it. "Back away, now! Colonel Crow! Brace for detonation. I repeat, brace for deton–"

The explosion came with a sharp thud so thick and deafening that it sealed out all sound around him, filling his ears with throbbing pain and high-pitched ringing as his ear muffs were ripped off by the force of the blast. Pieces of dirt, rock and concrete stung the back of his neck as his body was picked up and hurled through the air by a blast wave of heat. His rifle and radio flew out of his hands, stomach doing somersaults as the world rolled around him. He defied gravity, windmilling his limbs until he met the ground feet and knees first, then rolling, arms and legs limp as he flailed and tumbled.

Chunks of concrete zipped past him and thudded like lobbed softball pitches, an enormous cloud of dirt and smoke filling the area. His mind was numb, lungs heavy as he gasped for an elusive breath that refused to come. Flipping onto his back, panting, he blinked at the sky as a column of fire and smoke swelled high above the complex, its top rounded and oozing across his field of vision. For a moment he clung to consciousness, then darkness claimed him, sealed his eyes, and dragged him down to a world of black silence.

CHAPTER NINETEEN

James Burton
Frankfurt, Illinois

James woke up on the cold, hard floor with a thermal blanket over him and a backpack for a pillow. The room was chilly and musty, and two wounded soldiers were lying head to foot against the north wall, stirring awake as well, stretching and groaning in pain.

Washington stood over him. "Come on, James. It's time to go."

James nodded, threw the cover off, and swung his legs around. His body was not only sore from the previous day's chase through the streets, but he'd slept awkwardly, and a stinging pain radiated up the right side of his neck.

"Ugh," he grabbed his neck and massaged the spot.

"You good?" Washington asked.

"Yeah, just a crick in my neck. I'll be fine."

"We move out in fifteen. Did you want to help carry some of these crates out?"

James had left his boots untied but still on, and he leaned forward to tighten the laces. "Yeah. I'll start bringing out some crates. Do you want everything?"

"Leave anything marked 28B. That's all camp gear. We'll be moving fast, so we want ordnance, food, and water. Start with the MRE bin over there against the wall." The Lieutenant nodded to the south side.

"Got it. No twenty-eight bravo. Start with the MRE bins."

James stood and stretched his arms over his head, then bent and touched the ground, swinging his upper torso back and forth to loosen up his stiff muscles as one of the wounded guardsman sat up against the wall.

"Tough sleeping on the floor, huh?" she asked dryly.

James nodded. "Probably doubly so for someone with a wounded leg. Got shot?"

"I wish. Sprained my ankle carrying equipment with this genius." She rolled her eyes and jerked her chin toward the soldier at her feet, who was getting up.

"We were carrying our crates through the ruins," he said. "Could have gone around, but Cap wanted us to go right through." The guardsman shook his head and raised his arm, which was in a sling. "Plenty of places to get hurt. Bunch of stuff fell on us. Oswell hurt her ankle, and I busted my arm up."

"Good thing we're not taking all the stuff," James said.

"Screw the gear. I just hope we get out of this damn city soon." Oswell winced as she kept one leg straight and edged up the wall. "This place has been a death trap since the day we entered."

"You got that right, sister," her partner said.

While a pair of soldiers came and helped their wounded comrades, giving the woman with the hurt ankle a makeshift crutch made from an iron rod, James started carrying out the MRE crates and set them outside where the guardsmen were gathering. The troops began emptying them and stuffing everything they could into their backpacks, readying their carbines and ammunition pouches. James' breath plumed in the cold misty morning and he yawned repeatedly while trying to force his sluggish body into action, but the dozen guardsmen seemed energetic, eager to escape the crowded and violent city. Back inside, James adjusted his pack, organized his remaining supplies - which weren't much - and grabbed his pistol and walking stick before joining the troops. Lister was rounding everyone up and climbed onto the hood of a car to address them.

"Okay, people. Listen up. We're getting out of this town ASAP. I want Washington and Witkowski on point and the rest to keep good spacing and know where your friends are. I want eyes on the rooftops and searching every nook and cranny. Let's not get caught with our thumbs up our asses. Any questions?"

The guardsmen all stood silent, feet spread, expressions focused; twelve, plus the two wounded, and James. Grubby, wet, and cold, they stared nervously at the imposing streets as if expecting something to leap out of the shadows and strike.

When no one spoke, Lister hopped down. "All right, people. Let's move out."

Washington took point with Witkowski, a broad-shouldered redheaded man with stern gray eyes. They fell in line, marching up the right side of the street, leaving behind the sandbags and tents, assorted crates of camping equipment, and an old radio with the parts stripped clean. Every step they trekked south, away from James' self-imposed demarcation line, left him feeling a little better. Still, the township stretched around them with old buildings and architecture from another age, a block of warehouses with bold writing. James lingered toward the rear with the wounded as they marched, the man with the broken arm holding his carbine in his left hand while his companion hobbled on her crutch, already breathing heavy but focused ahead with a set jaw.

"I'm glad to be getting out of there," James said. "I didn't want to get any closer to downtown."

"No kidding. Never got your name, by the way. I'm Oswell." She held out her left hand. "Emily Oswell."

"James Burton. Good to meet you." James started to ask a question, but she was panting and struggling with each step, looking for a place to put the end of her crutch and careful not to fall.

"You want a hand?"

"It's all good," she said with a head shake. "I can handle it. Just don't want to fall and break the other ankle. Cap would never let me live it down."

The crew traversed narrow streets and moved through an endless field of wreckage, where blown-out vehicles and piles of bricks mixed together. Where he could, James walked ahead of Oswell and knocked chunks aside with his staff, doing what he could to make it easier on her. It had stopped raining, but everything was still dripping and wet, the buildings glistening and stained, dark scorch marks up the sides wherever fires had licked at them. Boots splashed through puddles and crunched across shattered glass, kicking bricks and garbage aside as Rodriguez walked up ahead with Pugh and the ever-quiet Wiseman.

The line suddenly stopped, Washington and Witkowski standing in the middle of a major intersection with the corner buildings shattered and fire-scarred, car parts and metal strewn across the cracked pavement. Stock still, rifles shifting to the east where fog choked off their visibility, they searched the gloom as echoes of kicked rocks and scuffling feet came from that direction.

Captain Lister pointed to three guardsmen, and they rushed to where a pair of cars sat sideways in the middle of the street. James circled to the right-hand car and stood by the trunk where a taillight dangled loosely by its wiring. Rifles flew up when a group of people strolled from the fog, dark figures led by a massive man James recognized, one with a wide chest and huge gut, his clothes bloodstained from his fight – and victory – over the man with dreadlocks and his gang. A chain dragged the ground behind him, the links stained red with chunks of hair and flesh, held in a huge hand with bruised and scraped knuckles.

The leader's hair hung limp, beard smeared with blood, eyes filled with malice as he walked straight toward Washington and Witkowski. The guardsmen backed up, carbines raised to their shoulders, fingers slipping within the trigger guards, bodies clenched as the rest of the gang filtered in behind him. They'd grown since James had last seen them, numbering two dozen or more, and their piggish eyes sized up the soldiers before catching James where he was hiding, turning his insides to liquid beneath their malicious grins.

"Stop right there!" Washington shouted. "Don't come any closer or we'll blow you away."

The leader growled from behind bloody lips. "I like our odds."

"It's not just us," Washington said. "I've got another dozen rifles pinned on you assholes. One wrong move, and you're dead."

As if noticing the guardsmen crouched down behind the cars for the first time, he only snickered. "I still like our odds."

James slipped around the car and walked to where Lister was about to step out and confront the man. He grabbed him by the arm. "Wait a minute, Captain. I've met these people before. It's one of those gangs I told you about."

Lister ducked back under cover. "What can you tell me?"

"Up there." James nodded upward. "They'll have people up on the buildings ready to ambush us. I watched them pick apart an entire gang from up there. They're a lot smarter with their tactics than they look, trust me."

Lister pointed at Rodriguez and Wiseman and then at the rooftops, the two guardsmen splitting off and moving down the street with their guns sweeping the heights. The Captain stepped from cover and strode out to stand next to Washington, sizing up the gang leader and the dozen people behind him, their own hands bloody evidence of their violent rampage.

"I'm Captain Lister of the Illinois National Guard. Stay where you are, and we'll move through this intersection without any problems. Make any sudden moves and we'll put you down. Get it?"

The leader stared at Lister for a moment before his thick tongue came out and licked his lips as he glanced in James' direction. "You got a man with you who stole from us. We've got no beef with you, but with him... that's another story. Give him up, and y'all can pass."

"Can't do that," Lister said. "Everyone with me is going to pass through this intersection, and you're going to take your people and move back. This isn't a request. It's an order."

"If you won't give us our man, then you'll have to pay full price to cross... in bodies."

Lister's finger slipped inside the trigger guard. "Back the hell up, or I'll open up that fat belly of yours! We've got people watching the rooftops; you won't even get a chance to try your bullshit on us! You *will* lose this fight! Now move back!"

The gang leader watched Lister closely for a long moment, seeming to contemplate the weapons arrayed against him and his odds of winning when he finally backed his people up several steps, holding his hands up in a mocking gesture, the chain scraping against the pavement. "Go ahead, soldier boy. Go on by."

Lister didn't move his eyes off the gang leader or his finger off his trigger as he called to the rest of the guardsmen. "Move out. Single file. Let's go."

Pugh went first, stepping between the vehicles with the remaining guardsman following. James gestured for Oswell to go next, and she hobbled out ahead quickly with him right behind her, his insides curling as he locked eyes with the gang leader and noticed the thin woman who'd chased him into the alley standing nearby, snickering loudly.

"That *is* the slimeball who got away from us," she said with a malicious grin. "He's going to pay first."

The leader snickered. "They'll all pay in the long run."

"Shut up," Lister growled, backing up with Washington and Witkowski as Rodriguez and Wiseman filed in behind them, crossing and slipping onto the right-hand sidewalk, heading east and continuing their trek through the wreckage.

The crew navigated the foggy streets with Washington and Witkowski on point, the Captain and James guarding their rear, and as they tried to pick up the pace, it was clear where their weakness was; Oswell was hobbling in an upright position, rifle swinging by her side, unable to keep up with the guardsmen who moved faster and were able to better stay in cover, with a full range of movement.

Sounds echoed around them, drawing James' attention everywhere and nowhere: every dark alley, every cross-section of narrow lanes, and up above where the enemy might shoot from the rooftops. A breeze blew from an alleyway ahead in a burst of fog, and a shape rolled out in a clatter of plastic wheels. Washington and Witkowski stopped and raised their rifles to fire, and the rest of the troops hit the walls, only for the mist to clear to reveal a small gray wagon packed with dolls and kids' toys.

"What the hell is this?" Lister stepped to James' side. "IED?"

"I think it's just... toys. These people are kind of messed up in the—"

A brick hit the ground two feet in front of the pair, breaking in half and scattering shards. The guardsmen pressed harder against the walls or threw themselves behind piles of junk and then another brick fell, then another, high-pitched whistles and cheers from above shrieking through the gloom to accompany the bombardment. A rock bounced off the back of Rodriguez's helmet and knocked it crooked on her head, and when she looked up, another landed directly on her uplifted face, crushing her nose and cracking her teeth, sending blood flooding down her front. She fell against the wall and dropped straight to the sidewalk in silence, a single burst from her carbine firing into the sky. James slid next to her as bricks rained around them, striking the ground, one glancing off his forearm as he tried to protect himself. Flipping Rodriguez over with one hand, he winced at her bloodied face and crushed forehead, blank eyes staring up at the sky.

"Lister, s-she's gone" James' face was pale.

"Son of a *bitch*!" Suppressing fire, *now!*"

Washington was the first guardsmen to start returning fire, aiming upwards and dispersing several bursts toward the rooftops, chewing at the brick and sending more shards raining on their heads. Soon, the air was filled with dust, and the guardsmen cursed as they searched for targets while a seemingly limitless supply of bricks dropped on them, all without a solid angle to return fire on their attackers. To the west, the leader of the gang and his people jogged after the group, taking their time as they took up positions behind the cars and piles of fallen concrete and brick.

"Lister, we've got a problem," James called out as Lister knelt over Rodriguez's fallen form.

Lister saw where James was looking. "Keep moving forward, people," he called ahead. "Someone help Oswell. James and I will cover our retreat."

James held up his pistol. "I've only got a few rounds for this thing."

"Take Rodriquez's rifle. Ammunition pouch in front. C'mon, man, hurry up!"

The weapon had become tangled in her arm, and he had to lift her and slide the strap off her shoulder, setting it aside and trying unsuccessfully to unhook her ammunition vest. With a grunt of frustration, he grabbed several magazines from it and stuffed them into his pockets. Bullets cracked the brick above his head, shots coming from the west forcing James lower, crawling, pulling the M4 across the pavement, staggering to his feet, and throwing himself onto a pile of debris next to Lister. The sputtering of the Captain's rifle set James' teeth on edge, and he raised his pistol and emptied six bullets into the shadowy mist, draining the weapon.

"Aim for the fat one," James called. "Take their leader out and they'll crumble!" He stuffed the dry pistol into a pocket and brought the M4 to bear, picking out targets, clutching tight to the bucking weapon as he fired in bursts, trying to keep the shadows at bay. Where one fell, though, two more took their place, barrels flashing in return, thudding into their cover and sending fragments of brick bursting into James' face. He aimed directly at the flashes, catching one man as he sprinted from one car to another, knocking him off his feet while Lister pinned a second man against the brick wall across the street.

"Let's go, private!" Lister patted James' shoulder, shoved himself off the brick, and chased after the moving guardsmen.

James got up and staggered behind him, past the toy wagon someone had kicked over, stumbling, turning, and firing west to keep the gang on the street pinned down honest. As he spun back to follow the Captain, he nearly tripped on Pugh who lay sprawled with her helmet crooked, a fragment of something embedded in the side of her face. He stooped to grab her ammunition, but the pack had already been taken, and Lister was urging him onward.

"No time, James!" he growled. "We're all dead if we don't move!"

Bullets pinged and sparked off the metal husks of cars, ricocheted off the walls, and zipped by, a horde of angry hornets with deadly stingers. Ducking and scrambling, he kept up with the Captain to the echoes of laughter and high-pitched whistles, bricks and bullets plaguing their retreat. Finally James and Lister caught up with the main group and they pressed on, sidestepping, sweeping their weapons upward and back with Washington calling out possible escape routes and angles of future attacks. James ran up beside Wiseman, who was helping Oswell hobble along, grunting and groaning whenever her sprained foot struck something.

"Are you guys okay?"

"We're good," Wiseman mumbled. "Just watch our backs."

Lister surged ahead with Washington, leaving James alone to guard the rear. The gloom closed in behind them in slow swirls of smoke with no moving shadows or signs of pursuit, and his hopes began to rise that they'd gotten out of the worst of the trouble. It was only when Lister shouted and a flurry of bullets sprung at them from the other direction that

James shed that hope. He fell to his knees instinctively as chaos exploded in front of them, the guardsmen retreating from a group who'd cut them off. Two were shot before they could get to cover, spinning and running into each other before toppling onto the pavement, their uniforms shredded and dripping red.

Washington and Witkowski crouched in the open, spraying bullets at shadows rushing at them in a horde of shapes, cutting them down even as incoming fire flew at them. A round struck Washington in the shoulder and another hit Witkowski in the leg, and he collapsed to his good knee as he ejected his spent magazine and jammed a new one home.

"Into the alley!" Lister called. "Come on! Washington, Witkowski, let's go!"

Guardsmen angled into the narrow passage, one struck in the neck, clutching the gushing wound as he hit the corner and bounced to the ground, dead before James could try and reach for him. James got behind Oswell and pushed her and Wiseman toward the opening when Wiseman's head rocked back, and he collapsed beneath Oswell's arm. Another guardsman was there to take his place, and the two disappeared into the passage. James and Lister reached it, waving the other troops inside and waiting for his point men. They were backing up, firing in alternating intervals, Witkowski somehow staying on his feet as rounds hit him in the arms and chest.

"Come on! Let's go!"

Witkowski turned, stumbled, and took another handful of rounds in the back, his face a mask of pain as he collapsed to his knees and hit the pavement. Washington sprinted past them, and James followed Lister as they dove deeper into the passage, dodging rocks and stones still falling from above but escaping the withering gunfire that had cut them to pieces. He stayed on Lister's heels, weaving between the garbage piled in the alley with aluminum trash cans and dumpsters everywhere. One lid flew up, and a man jumped up like a jack-in-the-box to fire on Oswell and Lister, the wicked thuds of lead plunging into flesh, bits of fabric and blood popping off Lister's body as he collapsed against the wall. James aimed at the figure with his arms stretched over the edge of the dumpster but his aim was off, and he shot the side of the dumpster before raising the sights and burying a string of rounds in the man's chest and face, rocking his head back.

Oswell wasn't where she'd initially fallen, but had kept hobbling ahead into the narrow passage. Lister was tumbling backward, and James switched his rifle to his right hand and caught him, bearing his weight for a few steps before pushing on. Staggering, clinging bloodily to each other, they pitched forward into the gloom as it rained rocks, bricks, and garbage from high above their heads. Something light struck the back of James' head, and a heavier piece crashed on Lister's foot, causing him to yowl in pain. Through the smoke and chaos, light appeared ahead at the end of the passage where the rest of their group ducked and fired in wild, panicked bursts. Bricks and bullets rained on their heads, and the forms ahead staggered and fell with waving, windmilling arms as they were taken down.

"Stay with me, Lister!" James shouted. We're almost there—"

The Captain jerked in his grasp, slipped to his knees, and took them both down. They hit the ground, James crawling from beneath him and rolling him over. Lister was spitting blood, gasping, seizing James by the shoulder and squeezing as he tried to say something. James leaned forward to hear the whispers sputtering from his mouth, but the racket was too much, the calls and whistles and shapes closing in on them, finishing the guardsmen and stripping them of their weapons, ammunition, and the few supplies they carried.

When the light left Lister's eyes, James laid him gently on the ground and faced the onrushing figures surging toward him, who were so caught up in their assumed victory that they had ceased firing. Clenching the M4 to his shoulder, screaming at the top of his lungs, James fired through them, putting three-round bursts back and forth to shred their flesh, drawing howls and curses as he cut them to pieces. James turned the narrow alley into a kill box of their own creation. His scream ended as his magazine emptied, and he quickly exchanged it for a second, leaping bodies as he ran, firing with abandon, continuing to fire until he reached the other end of the passage and stopped. Part of him wanted to keep going, to keep shooting and cutting them down for what they'd done, but as the heat of the battle fled along with the adrenaline, James lowered his weapon and slowed to a halt.

Spinning, he sprinted back down the passage, leaping the dead, reaching the end where the rest of the guardsmen had perished. He glanced around at the corpses helplessly, checking them for signs of life, tears stinging his eyes as he found no one left alive. Operating on pure survival instinct, he got on his hands and knees and collected spare magazines, stuffing them and an extra pistol into his pocket. When he was finished taking all he could, and with the worry of the attackers gearing up for another assault on his mind, James started to run but stopped when he heard a groan nearby.

"Oswell?" James called, rushing to a dumpster with its lids flipped open and hanging over the cobblestones. Behind it, Oswell had taken cover, a rifle in her lap, her teeth grinding in pain. James kneeled next to her, checking her for wounds. "Are you okay, Oswell? What hurts?"

"In the hip," she replied in a pained voice, face twisted in agony. "Leg, too."

James bent closer and parted the torn material of her fatigues, unable to see the entry point between the blood and swollen flesh. He searched the dead bodies, tearing off a guardsman's belt and wrapping it around Oswell's leg directly on the wound, double cinching it tight to her pained groans.

"I can't do anything about the hip, but maybe the pressure will help stem the bleeding in your leg. We need to get you somewhere safe. Come on."

Getting beneath her arm, he started to lift her but stopped when she clenched his shoulder with a red-stained hand, shaking her head, distraught, tears running down her face in despair. "No, it's no use."

"What do you mean? Come on, Oswell. We're the only ones left, and we've got to get out of here before they come back."

Oswell dropped her weapon, grabbed James' jacket, and pulled him close. "I'm not going anywhere. It's because of me all this happened. We couldn't move fast enough. Everyone had to wait on me."

"That's not true and you know it."

"No..." She shoved him away. "I didn't want them to take me. I should've stayed back there at the camp and let them go ahead. Now, look at them." She stared at the corpses, familiar faces turned lifeless and dead. "I went through basic with these guys. Saw them every weekend. I don't deserve to be alive when they're all —"

"Shut your mouth," James growled, grabbing her and trying to lift her again. "There'll be time for self-pity later. We've got to go. Come on!"

"What's the point?" she whimpered, settling like dead weight. "What's the point in any of this? Everything we had is gone. I don't know where my family is... they're probably dead like everyone else. And these animals in the streets..."

"Get a grip, Oswell! That's not true at all. I've met good people since airplanes were falling from the sky in Denver. And I know there's more, including my family and yours. We're going to get out of here for *them*!"

Oswell shoved her rifle into his chest and started taking off her ammunition belt. "No, James. You've got a family to get home to. You don't need me slowing you down. I won't have it. I have nothing to fight for anymore, but you do."

"How do you know what I have to fight for?"

"I heard you talking to Lister and Washington. About getting home to your family in Michigan. I know you'll make it, but not with me in tow. Now, take the gun and ammo and go. I'm gonna bleed out here soon anyway. Just go!"

James crouched with the equipment lying at his feet, the sounds of shuffling boots coming from behind them, dust trickling on the metal dumpster lids as their enemies prowled the rooftops. They shouted back and forth to each other, hunting for their prey in the smoke and dust, reinforcements looking for their fallen comrades and those responsible for the slaughter. If James and Oswell weren't gone by then, there'd be no repeating his victory; they'd be dead. He picked up the belt, buckled it around his waist, shouldered her rifle, and stood over her, watching her sob quietly with the pistol resting in her lap.

"When they come for me, I'll be ready," she said. "I'll take a few of them out before they get me or I bleed out." She wiped tears away. "Go on, man. Get out of here. Get back to your family."

James nodded gently and started to turn, then stopped, fist clenched at his side and heart torn with indecision. He recalled his time on the train, at the camp, and then with the Amish and wondered, for the hundredth time, what might've happened to them, hoping they were okay. All of his regret over the train, his pride over having helped at the camp and the advice he'd given Eli and Clara about making hard decisions to stay alive, even if it went against their religion, came back to him in a flash.

Oswell was right, of course. It would be a suicide mission to assist her and think he could escape unscathed; the gangs were fast and knew the streets too well. He'd be a sitting duck, slow and helpless, likely getting them both killed, and ruining his chances of being reunited with his family.

"Son of a...." Sighing, shaking his head, he kneeled by Oswell.

"What the hell are you doing?" Her breaths came hard as she struggled to focus. "Every second you waste is —"

"Shut *up*, Oswell," he snapped. "Listen, you're probably right. I stand a much better chance of getting out of here alone, but I *won't* do it. Getting back to the people I love is important, but it won't mean anything if I leave a friend behind. Survival has to be for... something more. More than just living. And if I don't walk that walk, then there's no point in *any* of this."

Oswell glowered at him, but James chuckled darkly. "If you won't get up off your ass, I'm just going to sit down next to you and we'll see what happens. I'm putting the choice on you, like it or not. Now, make it."

Her jaw tightened as she considered his words, finally shaking her head and snatching her weapon back. "*Asshole*. Help me get my gear back on."

"That's the spirit."

Stooping, he got under her arm and used the dumpster to leverage her to a standing position, laying the ammo pack over her shoulders and buckling it around her waist. She leaned against the dumpster as he did it, putting her weight on her left foot and wincing at the slightest movement.

"I can't find my crutch."

"It's right here." James stooped and snatched it up, handing it over and waiting for her to rebalance. "You got it?"

"Yeah. I should be able to go on my own."

"Great. I'll provide cover." James rested his hand on her shoulder. "We're going to get out of this. Or take a *lot* of them with us."

Oswell nodded, set her lips in a firm line, and gestured for him to go. James stepped into the passage, swinging his rifle in both directions, mimicking a soldier's crouched firing stance he'd observed from the guardsmen.

"Okay, follow me."

They moved south, getting only a few yards before someone on the roof spotted them and shouted. The shots were sporadic and off-target, though, the rounds merely peppering the pavement nearby. A moment later they were at the end of the alley, staring across an expansive open dirt yard with several large buildings behind it. A dilapidated crane with a leaning arm loomed above a bloody battlefield in the yard with dozens of people on both sides, knives flashing and pistols rattling as they fought and died. Their gang colors were indistinguishable from one another in the fracas and their methods were beyond barbaric. Combatants waved knives and lunged while others swung bats and crowbars like cavemen, smashing bones and cracking skulls, spilling blood on the dirt.

"Are they the same gang?" Oswell grunted.

"I don't think so," James said, jaw dropping as a man stalked a woman with slow, deliberate steps, arm extended, pistol firing only when he was on top of her and she turned on him, backpedaling when he shot her, staggering a few more paces before pitching onto her back. "It's another group... these people are crazy."

"See what I mean?" Oswell shook her head. "We've got insanity behind us and in front of us. We'll never get away."

James followed a trail of old cars, most of which were rusted out and stripped down, not blown up or burned like he was used to seeing. They were parked nose to tail, forming a lane leading into an enormous junkyard with rows of crushed vehicles stacked ten high as far as he could see.

"I see something. Follow me. Quick."

"Quick ain't in my vocabulary at the moment, in case you forgot," she replied with a grunt, shouldering her rifle and grabbing the loose pant material of her right leg to help keep it elevated enough to walk on the crutch.

They moved west, keeping close to the brick wall, rushing for the next crushed vehicle to hide behind, casting glances back at the battle. James stepped away from the building, exposing himself as he got a better look at the yard and how they could get just a hundred yards down and across the street.

"What are we looking for?"

"See the junkyard? I think a couple of people could get lost in there pretty easily."

"Yeah, I see it now. Good call."

"It's as good a place as any. We have to cross the street, though. Let's go. Quickly!"

Angling between a pair of cars and leaving their cover, they crossed to the other side of the road and moved west, then south along the junkyard's curved dirt lane. James cringed at every shout and gunshot, expecting them to turn on Oswell and himself, their luck finally turning somewhat when no one fired on them or gave chase.

They hobbled toward a corrugated aluminum wall, rusted and flimsy with wide-open gate doors hanging from their hinges. The place was massive, a cityscape of towering stacks and heaps of metal atop each other with smoke loosely drifting above the top layer. The gravel path through the yard was filled with puddles, pieces of car parts and old oil slicks that clung to their boots and pants as they shuffled along. Oswell was practically dragging her leg behind her, grunting as she gripped her pants leg to keep it elevated, every step pure agony.

"Just a little farther, Oswell." James kept watch behind her, rifle at the ready. "Just keep pushing!"

They made it to the first row when their luck finally ran out and the first bullets struck the metal car frames with sparks and dings. Lead ricocheted with sharp whizzing noises as rounds buried themselves in crushed engine blocks and doors and shouts and curses followed them, boots pounding pavement as the gangs gave chase, the victors of the battle looking for more blood to shed. James and Oswell moved deeper into the rows, cutting left to get lost in the massive stacks that were quickly turning into a maze. The smells of oil, antifreeze, old gasoline and grease clung thick to the air, and they splashed through rainbow-colored puddles, hurrying to find a place to hide.

Taking Oswell's arm so she could lean on him, James' back strained to keep her upright, grunting and panting with every step as he searched for a place to go, anywhere to hide from their hunters. James stopped them at an intersection with nothing but rows of crushed and dismantled vehicles stretching in every direction, massive towers of rusted hulks with hoods thrown open, their parts stripped out and sold. Several stacks appeared ready to fall, the top layers leaning precariously atop the groaning steel, water from the recent rainstorm still dripping from the fenders and off the chassis to add to the greasy puddles around them.

"They're still coming," Oswell said, looking back. Something zipped through the air and exploded behind them, sending flames climbing a stack in tendrils of orange and dark smoke, the heat gusting against their clothes, blowing their hair around.

"We need to get lost *real* fast," James growled. "Come on… this way!"

CHAPTER TWENTY

Ryan Cooper
Somewhere Outside East Lansing, Michigan

Rays of golden sunlight bathed the frosted ground, burning off the moisture into a fine haze that covered the property, spreading to the high boughs where robins and sparrows huddled and waited for the coming warmth. Some flew in agitated patterns, flitting across the treetops, bickering with the others in sharp chirps and piping warbles, chasing each other from one tree branch to another. On the ground below, sheep and goats bleated for their breakfasts, crowding Ryan as he pushed the wheelbarrow to the gate and entered, each trying to be the first to get their morning meal.

Despite the chill, Ryan had worked up a sweat after collecting eggs with Helen and making another minor repair to the fencing where it had separated from the frame. A couple of chicks had escaped in the process, and he and Helen had spent a few long minutes chasing them around, a process made much more difficult with his wounded calf. Ryan had kept stooping and grabbing at the running balls of yellow fluff, only to have them slip out of his hands at the last second. When Duchess cut the lightning-quick birds off and sent them flying back in his direction, he'd managed to catch them and put them back in the coop.

"Ryan, one. Chicks... twenty-two," he mumbled as he wheeled the wheelbarrow up to the barn and popped the front door open.

Taking a bale of hay from inside the door, he dragged it to the enclosure and dropped it into a hay trough, the barnyard animals surrounding it and nibbling at the roughage. For additional nutrients, he took a bucket of feed and spread the pellets around the yard in wide tosses to keep them from crowding the barn entrance, where he hoped to pull out the tractor and perform some maintenance. Once everyone was fed, he walked inside and took care of Bessie, refilling her trough with fresh water and leaving her a good portion of hay to eat.

He patted her side. "Helen will be out in a little while to milk you, old girl. Hang in there."

Bessie lowed in response, and Ryan took that as an "okay," after which he pulled the tractor out in the yard, cutting the engine off to kill the noise. Taking a folded piece of paper out of his pocket, he looked over the list of maintenance items to prepare the tractor for colder weather. James had maintained the tractor well, but the battery terminals were caked with potassium carbonate, and he used the terminal cleaner to scrape them off before reattaching the cables. The oil had a dirty sheen, so he changed it, started up the tractor, and let it run for ten minutes to spread the oil throughout the engine block. One fan belt was dry and cracked, and the tires looked like dry rot was just starting to set in on them.

"Hopefully these get us through this next season, but we'll have to look for some new ones in the spring."

Hands and arms smudged with grease, Ryan began to wipe down the tractor, cleaning it from the dirt and grime that had caked on over the last several days. The woods were quiet around him, the shadows still deep in the early morning light and fog, and the robins flitted actively in the warming air, coming down to pick at pieces of feed the sheep and goats didn't eat. Duchess chased a few before getting bored and lying in a patch of sunlight, her furry tail swishing back and forth in the grass. In a sudden jerk of movement, the dog twisted to her feet, head high and ears perked up, nose pointed at the front gate.

"What is it, girl?" Ryan reached for his rifle sitting in the wheelbarrow. "Do you see someone?" When he got to the barnyard gate, he saw the reason for Duchess' distress. "Someone at the gate, eh? Looks like Sandy again. Wonder what she's doing here... c'mon girl, let's go back to the house."

Ryan waved to let Sandy know he'd seen her and then slipped his coat on, squeezed through the barnyard gate with Duchess, and headed to the house.

"Back already?" Helen stood at the stove, canning the remaining produce they'd harvested. "Or maybe you're looking for something else to eat?"

"Food sounds great," he replied, ignoring his groaning stomach. "But that's not why I came in. Sandy's down at the gate again."

"Were you expecting her?

"Not today." He shrugged. "At least not that I remember. I'll go down and see what she wants."

"Well, take Duchess and Diana with you. Diana is fidgety today and has been driving me crazy. Are you going to take the EV?"

"Not today. I'll walk them down. Do you have a sec to watch my back?"

"I've got jars in the pressure canner, so I've got nothing to do for another forty minutes. I was thinking about milking Bessie, but she can wait a little longer."

"She looked fine when I saw her," Ryan agreed.

After Helen went upstairs with her rifle, Ryan left through the front door and walked down the long driveway, passing the majestic maples as they swayed in the gentle breeze. The warm smells of decaying leaves and mulch drifted by, and the ducks quacked as they floated on the ponds, flapping and flicking water off their wing tips at the sight of Ryan and the dogs.

Reaching the gate, Ryan nodded curtly. "Sandy."

"Hi, Ryan."

"What brings you here this morning? We didn't plan to meet today, did we?"

"No, we didn't. I'm sorry about dropping in like this, but it's not like I can text you or anything."

Ryan allowed a slight smile. "You certainly can't. I don't have a problem with you stopping by as long as you stay behind the gate."

"Fair enough," Sandy brushed a lock of dark hair behind her ear. The haunted look in her eyes from the last two meetings had been replaced by something like relief, a smile tugging at the corners of her mouth. She held up a small plastic bag. "I brought this for you."

"What's in it?"

"A dozen eggs... and a thank you letter from my son, who's recovering very well right now, thanks to those antibiotics you gave me."

"Oh, that's good. Let me see." Ryan opened the bag and unfolded the note written in blue-crayon scrawl, which he read out loud. "Thank you for the medicine, Ryan! You're the best!" Chuckling, he held up the note and waved it. "That's awful sweet of him. I assume he's doing much better?"

"Miles better. His fever broke overnight, and he had a gigantic appetite this morning."

"Well, there you go. That's wonderful, Sandy. I'm happy to hear he's doing all right."

"The antibiotics really kicked whatever he had in the butt."

Ryan nodded. "Make sure you keep taking them for the full regimen of ten days. You don't want it coming back stronger."

"Will do. It's amazing how a little thing can go so far." Sandy gestured to his leg. "I saw you limping. Is your leg healing okay?"

"It's a little stiff, is all, and it'll be that way for a while. The bullet penetrated clean through, though it didn't hit any arteries, thankfully."

Sandy covered her mouth. "Oh, my. I... I didn't realize that. Is there anything I can do to help?"

"Unless you've got a spare leg, not much." Ryan pulled up his other pant leg to show her his prosthetic. "I mean that literally."

Sandy gaped. "Is it just your foot, or is it cut off higher? If you don't mind me asking."

"Foot and a bit more. Came off just above the ankle, but the prosthetic rides all the way up to my knee. Gives it a little more to hold on to, if you know what I mean."

"How'd that happen, if you don't mind me asking?"

"We were farmers back in the day, and accidents are a way of life. This one happened to be bigger than most."

"Well, I'm sorry that happened to you. It's got to be hard getting around with your legs injured like that."

"I'm tougher than I look," he chuckled. "I get by. What about you? What's your story?"

Sandy raised her eyebrows and sighed. "I was a teacher at the middle school, and my husband was a plumber. When everything happened, he was on a job site, and I was at school. One minute things were fine, and the next the parking lot was a wall of flames. The windows blew out, glass sprayed everywhere, the kids were crying and screaming... we thought it was the end of the world."

"Close enough," Ryan nodded and rested one arm on the fence.

"Anyway, we watched out the windows for a short time, thinking it was some terrorist attack or something. I just wanted to keep the kids safe and away from the windows. The fire spread pretty quickly to the building, though, and that's when everyone started panicking.

"I packed the kids into the hallway to join some other evacuating classes. The smoke was so thick, and everyone was choking and crying. I've got to tell you, Ryan, my heart was racing like it's never done in my life." Sandy's eyes turned glassy as she dove deeper into the memory. "We'd gotten to the end of the hall, and kids were filing down the stairs. I thought we were home free, then I heard crying from back the way we'd come. I went back to look for them —"

"How did you keep from suffocating on the smoke? That stuff can kill you in just a few minutes."

"No kidding. It took me about a week to recover. I used my shirt to cover my mouth and stayed low like they say in the fire videos. Didn't take long to realize that the boy crying was my Stephen."

Ryan's eyebrows went up. "Your boy?"

"Yes. Ryan, I... I've never felt fear grip me like it did then. A list of class schedules ran through my brain, trying to remember which room he'd be in. I ran straight for Mr. Westerly's class and got halfway there before remembering he'd taken a study hall at the end of the day, which started a couple of months ago. I rushed to the end of the hall, but it was all one big blur. I don't remember any details, but I eventually found Stephen under a desk with another little girl. Smoke was much thicker in the hallway, so I checked the windows to see if there was a way to climb out from there, but there were no fire escapes on that side, and it was a three-story drop. I took my shirt off, ripped it in two, and covered their mouths, then I snatched them by the arms and took them back into the hall. Luckily for us, the stairs were right there, and we joined a bunch of other people trying to leave. We made it out but..." She shook her head, smile fading as tears began to fall. "I heard later that most in the preschool building didn't make it."

"Good heavens." Ryan used his finger and thumb to rub his wet eyes. "That's horrific."

"It was hell. We waited for emergency services but obviously they never showed up, so we helped as many people as we could, then walked home."

"So, you're all by yourself with your son now?"

"Sort of. A few of us have gotten together, had communal meals, and traded with each other. At least until Trace got involved with Jack and his buddies... we're kind of on the fringe now, just staying nearby for safety's sake but not participating with the group very much. It's complicated."

"I can imagine."

"It's just one more tragedy in a string of them." Sandy looked past him to the farm. "Nobody's fared quite as well as you all have, though. Especially since you have that tractor."

"I reckon that's what's got people worked up."

"That's part of it, for sure. You've got what nobody else has... a tractor, dogs, plenty of farm animals, a standing house and barn...."

"Well, none of it's mine, remember. It belongs to my daughter and son-in-law. And, listen... I won't promise we'll be best friends, but I wouldn't mind contributing to a potluck of sorts, if that's the kind of thing you're doing."

"That'd be nice." The smile returned. "I'll tell the others you're amicable to something."

"No, no, no. Hold on a second. I want to take it slow with everyone after what they did to us. Despite you and me getting along fine, I still don't trust most anyone these days."

"No, I understand."

"And I triply don't trust anyone in a circle of folks who tried to steal from us and kill us. It could just as easily be us in those graves we dug."

"I understand completely."

"Let's keep these meetings going for a few more days and continue sharing information. If I'm comfortable with what you say, and you're comfortable with what I say, we'll see about joining in for a meal together and maybe even working together. If that goes well, we can see about talking to the other folks, too. I like to help folks and I'm open to the idea of second chances, but I won't take any unnecessary risks."

"I can't disagree with you there, Ryan. And I think I speak for the group – well, the few who I talk to from time to time – when I say we all understand that. They know you're not to be trifled with."

"Good."

"Tomorrow morning, then?"

"I'll be here. Is there anything else your son could use?"

"No, I think we're okay for now."

"I'll figure something out to return the favor for the eggs."

"Great. Until tomorrow."

"Tomorrow."

Sandy waved, turned, and headed back down the road with a hop in her step. Ryan watched her for a long moment before calling the dogs to him and heading back to the house, contemplating the conversation and hoping the tightrope he was trying to walk wouldn't end up backfiring on him. When he reached the front yard, he waved up to Helen to meet him around back, where she shrugged on her coat as she came out the door.

"How'd it go, dear?"

"Better than I expected." He showed her the bag's contents and handed her the note. "She gave us a dozen eggs, and this is from her son.

"Isn't that sweet? Not that we need the eggs, but that's very kind of her." Helen read the note with a growing smile. "This is so great, Ryan. It really feels like we're making some progress here."

"Seems that way. Do you want to go up and take care of Bessie now?"

"I'll just take the cans out of the pressure canner real fast."

Helen hurried off, then locked arms with him a few minutes later as they walked. "What's Sandy like?"

"Seems nice enough. A teacher, apparently, or she was. Been through a lot, just like everyone, I guess. She almost lost her son twice."

"How so?"

Ryan told her about what happened at the school and how Sandy had heard Stephen crying from a classroom down the hall, recalling the smoke and flames she'd mentioned. "A place like that with the generators gone and the sprinkler system not working would go up like kindling. Sounds like she saved those kids in the nick of time. Feel awful hearing that there were a lot who couldn't be saved, though."

"Oh, my."

"I have to say, I've got a good feeling about her, and she seemed genuinely remorseful about her husband's actions."

"So, you trust her?"

"Hell no. For all I know, she's playing the long con. Good feelings don't get you far in my book these days. We'll see, though. It'd be nice to have an ally."

They reached the barnyard gate and slipped inside with the dogs, Duchess and Diana walking toward the sheep and goats, barking low, cutting them off when they tried to get around them, and herding them away.

"I'll put the tractor back, and you work on Bessie. We'll use the ATV to drive the milk to the house; my leg's sore after all this walking."

They finished the day's chores with Ryan pulling the tractor inside the barn and fetching the ATV. He straightened up around the place while Helen collected a single large five-gallon container of milk, ready to be pasteurized. Legs tired, calf stiffening from the day's work, Ryan brought up the ATV and pulled it to the barn entrance where Helen waited.

"Do you need help with anything else?" she asked.

"Afraid so. Today's chores wore me out. I could stand for a night on the couch with a movie."

Helen put her hands on her hips. "Are you suggesting we skip guard duty shifts tonight and enjoy a night together?"

"Not really, but you know, with the dogs around and the neighbors appearing to be kept in line, we can probably afford a couple of hours of semi-relaxation. I'll go through Alice and James's DVD selections and pick us out something good."

Helen grinned. "Feels like ages since we've had a good movie night."

Ryan grabbed the five-gallon container handle and started to lift it when the sounds of engines caught his ear. "You hear that?"

"Yep." Helen scanned the treeline. "I think it's coming from the north side of the property."

"Someone's on the highway again."

"The military?"

"I don't know, but we should have a look. We'll drive out this time. I don't feel like walking that far."

Climbing aboard the ATV, Ryan drove it up to the barnyard rear gate where Helen got out and let him through, and he waited for her at the edge of the woods. Once she was back in the passenger seat, he moved ahead, sticking to the thin patches of birch saplings and avoiding the heavy undergrowth where they could get stuck. It was a bumpy, jarring ride, and working the pedals with his injured leg sent aches running from his knee to his hip, but he finally pulled to a stop about three-quarters of the way through the woods.

"C'mon, let's walk from here."

They got off and trekked the rest of the way, crunching over the deadfall as nuts hit the forest floor and the high boughs rustled. At the edge of the tree line, roughly in the same spot as before, Ryan spread the stiff branches to reveal another line of armor moving on the highway, wide APCs and Humvees with mounted guns manned by military personnel. The convoy stretched far to the west, a hundred units long at least, more of the same older equipment and gas tankers.

"This one's even bigger than the other one," Ryan said.

"More fuel and supply trucks, too."

"I count seven fuel trucks so far... they either have a cache of older fuel, or they're refining it."

"Should we try to talk to them?"

"I don't think so," Ryan shook his head. "But we should start monitoring the radio more often. If they've got a way to make fuel, or at least transport it, then maybe they're attempting to try and start some recovery operations."

"That'd be nice – a bit of potential good news would be welcome."

"Exactly." Ryan pulled back from the bushes. "Let's go."

Ryan drove them to the barn, taking his time and easing them over the bumpy terrain, tired from the day's work and mulling over the situation with Sandy and the military's recent movements. The situations left him with mixed emotions, fear and uncertainty clouding his thoughts, pressure to make the right decisions intensifying as things continued to progress around them.

At the barn, they teamed up to get the milk container back onto the ATV, Ryan grunting as he bore most of the weight, his calf screaming in pain by the time he got it situated and dropped it into the cargo tray.

Helen noticed his discomfort. "Let's get you inside with some warm compresses on that leg of yours."

Ryan climbed into the driver's seat and went to start it up, then paused when the hairs on the back of his neck stood up. "Did you hear that?"

Helen got in next to him and tilted her head to listen. "What?"

Ryan shook his head, still listening but only hearing the wild woods and fluttering birds, the soft bleating of the barnyard sheep, and the gentle gusting of wind across the yard. "I thought it was an engine...."

"The convoy?"

"Pretty sure they're gone by now. No, it was loud and clacking, kind of like a diesel truck." Ryan raised his head and gazed into the distance. "Sounded like it was coming from the west."

"More people who got older vehicles running, maybe."

Ryan stood still for another moment, then shrugged and chuckled. "Or maybe it was nothing at all. I'm old; hearing things is what I'm supposed to do, right?"

Starting up the ATV, he drove them back to the house beneath steel gray clouds pressed flat and stretched thin, with sunlight coating the edges in bright highlights. Ryan took it as an omen of an uncertain future, a reminder to remain vigilant in a world torn asunder.

CHAPTER TWENTY-ONE

Dappled sunlight filtered through the towering boughs of the loblolly pines, casting warm patterns on the humid, dank undergrowth below them. A trio of songbirds, unbothered by the cares of the outside world, chased each other from branch to branch, swooping beneath each other with elegance unmatched by fighter pilots, their tittering warbles their own miniaturized version of gunfire. The sight of a few insects skittering across the pine needles of the forest floor distracted them from their rivalry and they dove low, landing and devouring their food, hopping back and forth in search of more. A low groan emerged from a misshapen lump near the songbirds and they scattered, not knowing what had made the noise, driven by pure survival instinct back into the trees where they sat silent for a few moments, watching the forest floor with newfound caution.

Death wasn't supposed to be painful. A warm loving embrace, a release from life's pain and an eternity somewhere better, yes. Side-splitting chest pains, sore arms and legs and a headache to beat the band, no. For several long, agonizing moments, she lay still, trying desperately to return to the dark sleep where pain receded to some back corner, her mind fragmented and unthinking of anything except the physical pain until one tiny tendril emerged. A single thread that, when tugged, unraveled the curtains and sent Alice Burton bolting upright, the lightning bolt of agony ignored as she forced words from her dry, ravaged throat.

"Jake?! Sarah!?"

THE DARKNESS

CHAPTER ONE

Alice Burton
Talladega National Forest, Alabama

Alice gasped and tried to rise but her chest throbbed in pain and her whole side was a massive cramp that squeezed her breath away and knocked her back into the dirt. The sky was pale blue and fading to dusk, and it seemed to pulse as her heartbeat throbbed in her ears while she lay in a bed of pain where every breath was a new agony. The sharp discomfort left her disoriented and confused, and when she tried to roll over, her side spasmed and forced her down again, leaving her feeling like she'd just been hit by a car, then run over by a train, then kicked by a mule for good measure. Groaning softly, Alice let her head rest against the hard ground, struggling to catch her breath, occasionally wondering if she was still alive, concluding each time that she must be, because death couldn't bring so much raw pain.

Flexing her hands, she checked herself for injuries without getting up, starting at her stomach and working her way upwards, feeling tender and sore over every inch of her skin. Alice expected to find blood at some point, but when she reached her ribs where the pain was it its apex, she felt no warm slickness, just the pain like a stab to the chest from the slightest touch. She pulled her hands away and blinked at them, relieved and perplexed they were dry with no signs of blood.

"How...?" The word came out in a whisper, pain lancing through her chest.

Something heavy was caught in her shirt pocket, which had spread open and was hanging down off her side. She dug in the front left pocket and pulled out her cell phone, pieces of plastic and glass falling away, the case almost crumbling in her hands. The facing was still intact except for a diagonal crack, and when she tried to turn it on, it wouldn't work. The backing was snapped and broken, and her fingers traced a rounded divot in the titanium plate. She flipped it over and picked off pieces of the case and ceramic cover until all that was left was the shiny rectangle of metal with a perfectly round indention in it. Bits of her memory returned, and she recalled the last thing she saw. The sleek, matte black barrel pointed at her, the flash of light, the punch to the chest, then darkness. She'd been shot... by... who was it? Alice shook her head and tried to remember through the scrambled shock, but nothing came to her.

"Come on, get up."

Her throat was scratchy and raw, head throbbing as she tried to tuck her right elbow beneath her and roll over, grimacing, gasping, and spitting. Everything was less painful on her right side, but it still took several tries to flip onto her stomach. Elbows pressed into the hard dirt, she walked her knees beneath her, fighting chest spasms with every tiny intake of breath, gritting her teeth until she was on her knees in a tight ball.

She expelled the air she'd been holding and held still, drawing the next breath slowly and carefully, testing the limits of the pain. Sweat trickled down her face and neck, and tears dripped from her cheeks into the dirt. Palms on the ground, she pushed herself up and settled back on her heels, resting with pain radiating through her body in waves of dizziness. It was easier to breathe in that position, and she almost took a full breath before gasping. Doing an experimental twist, she found that if she leaned the right way, the ache faded slightly. Lifting her shirt, she revealed a deep yellow bruise spreading from her breast to her waist, and a stinging, intermittent cut streaked down her left side to her hip.

"The bullet... must have ricocheted off the phone and grazed me somehow. How on earth...."

Alice picked up the ruined phone and pulled aside the dented piece of titanium, still partially attached to the circuit board with tiny screws and epoxy, a few small components falling down across her shirt and onto the ground. The battery on the opposite side of the plate was still intact, somehow, and still epoxied directly onto the titanium.

Scowling through hot tears, she started to toss the remnants of the device into the woods but she couldn't let it go, couldn't throw away the last connection to James. She clutched it against her right side and wept for a full minute, finally putting it in her pocket in case she could find a use for the battery later. It had grown darker since she'd been... *shot*.

Wait... yes, someone had shot her. She vividly remembered they'd been in the woods on a trail. The sky had been clear, the sun hot. She'd been on a path of some sort, walking... no, *riding*... riding Buck and holding the leather reins in her hand.

"Sarah? Jake?" she called in a raspy whisper, the memories of the pair coming back into focus. "Sarah! *Jake?*"

Birds chirped and fluttered through the treetops, and the slow swell of buzzing insects rose and fell like a tide through the humid air. Alice forced herself to her feet, lurching side-to-side before stabilizing on shaking legs. She tried to take a few steps and almost stumbled off the path but put her right arm out for balance, pushing off the rough bark of a nearby loblolly pine.

"Sarah! Jake!"

The woods were an undisturbed wall, nothing on the trail nor in the woods in front of her to indicate where her children had gone. Turning on wobbly legs, she faced pines with the branches stretching above the humid, moist undergrowth and casting shadows across the trail. A scuff in the dirt caught her eye - the ground was disturbed, the grass smashed in spots, a cluster of footprints in the dirt at the trail's edge.

"Sarah! Jake!" Her voice carried louder through the woods and echoed up the trail but no one replied.

Her unanswered calls brought a slow swell of dread that sent her pulse racing, breaths coming in desperate gasps as more details of what happened filtered back. She'd been riding on Buck with the kids right behind her when someone shot her - no, not when she was riding but when they'd dismounted to rest.

Alice saw the gun again, then the man standing behind it... *Mark*. The memory was accompanied with white-hot heat and pain, and she flinched back and almost fell. She stood with her head down, eyes shut and drawing the scattered threads of her memory together, weaving a tapestry of faces and voices to match. Something formed, a short stitch of a conversation just before the flash of the gun.

"*If you lay a finger on any of their heads,*" Alice remembered saying. "*You'll wish you didn't live to regret it.*"

"*Nah, Alice. You won't be doing a damn thing about anything.*"

"Mark." She spoke the name with growing fury. "Mark and... *Christine*. That's right. And Hunter and Mia weren't even theirs...."

Fuming, blinded by watery eyes, Alice's rage overcame her pain, and she took two staggering steps up the trail, the rutted path stretching, curving out of sight, lost behind the towering pines and tangles of brush.

"Give me back my kids!" Alice tried to scream, but it came out as a breathless choke, and the next breath twisted her insides with a dagger's point.

Shuffling to a stop, she sobbed and slumped over, clutching her left side as a wave of pain started in her chest and wrapped around her back with spasms thrown in for good measure. When the agony finally passed, she took short, steady breaths to calm her shaking hands. The bullet might not have penetrated her chest, but given the level of pain she was in, she undoubtedly had at least one or perhaps two broken ribs. Rushing forward without taking some time to orient herself would just lead to further injuries, and then she'd never get Sarah and Jake back.

Alice turned and hobbled back to the edge of the trail where she'd been shot. The horses were gone – including Hercules with the extra packs and provisions, Mark and Christine leaving nothing but garbage... and something hanging from a cluster of thick sticker bushes.

"My pack," she whispered.

Alice came off the trail and shuffled over to the pack, picking it off the thorn branches where they'd tossed it. She opened the main compartment and took a quick look inside, her stomach dropping in disappointment when she found nothing. She threw it down and started up the trail but stopped and returned to the pack, slowly crouching and falling forward onto her knees as she lifted the front flap. While the main compartment didn't have anything in it, there was something about the weight of it that made her think twice about throwing it away before checking all of the small pouches and pockets it had on the outside and inside.

Her search was not in vain. The side pockets yielded a pocketknife, two crushed water filtration straws, and a few bits of trash. A smaller front pocket had a full, sealed MRE, and the backpack itself was intact but for a few small snags from the sticker bushes. Looking around at the trash that had been left behind, she spied several lengths of orange string lying in the grass along with some empty water bottles, and she gathered everything up and put it in the pack with the rest. When she tried to sling it on her shoulder, pain rippled up her side, the pain nearly too much for her to walk without doubling over.

Alice laid the backpack back down and removed the pocketknife – one of the small ones she and the kids had taken from the trailer outside the sporting goods store so long ago – then slowly crept forward into the underbrush in search of a tree branch. After finding nothing but sticks and brush, she checked some nearby saplings, measuring their diameter, settling on a sturdy, straight one she could grip firmly in one hand. With her pocketknife, she began sawing around the base about six inches up off the ground, angling the blade downward and then cutting across, brushing the shavings out with her fingers. The task required every bit of mental and physical energy she had, taking her mind off the pain as she drew steady breaths and focused on Sarah's and Jake's faces, clinging to a thin thread of hope that she could somehow find them, if only she continued pressing forward.

Sweat trickled down the sides of her face and into her eyes, and the fingers of her right hand began to cramp, but she kept doggedly sawing through the sapling. She took several breaks to catch her breath, settling on her heels and staring up where sunlight dribbled through gaps in the canopy and flowed like water across the forest floor. After a moment she'd go back to work, shaving the sapling down, shoving it back and forth to loosen it up before cutting some more. Finally, when she was nearly through it, she grabbed it and used her weight to push it over, breaking it so it fell into the underbrush and dragged vines and branches with it.

Holding it up to get a gauge of what height would be the most comfortable to walk with, she began sawing on the opposite end. When she was halfway through, Alice tried to snap the top of the sapling off, but flexing her arms merely brought her more pain in her chest and a deeper, wrenching cough that left her bent over double, gasping for air. When the fit ended, she drew her hand away from her mouth, relieved when there wasn't any blood on her fingers.

"Guess I… didn't puncture a lung. Small favors."

Unable to break the stick clean, she was forced to finish cutting all the way to the very last fiber until it fell free. Alice then went to work stripping the twigs and offshoots away, breaking some with her hands and sawing off the thicker ones until the stick was relatively smooth and easy to grasp so that she could put some of her weight onto it.

She put the knife in her pocket and slowly shouldered her backpack, clenching it to her side as she put the end of the stick into the ground to test walking again. Alice took several trembling steps, gritting her teeth against the fiery agony ripping through her chest. Rising to her full height, she turned and hobbled back to the grassy area near the lake, better balanced and with less pain in her side.

Alice checked over the footprints and trampled grass but couldn't tell which direction Mark and Christine had taken the kids without further scouting. Leaning most of her weight on the walking stick, she moved up the shallow bank to the trail, the effort leaving her breathless and panting. She searched the trail again, putting the pieces together, trying to recall what Mark and Christine said as they were rifling through the packs. There was something she couldn't quite remember, something about more workers for a camp up north.

"That's the way we were going…" Turning back in the direction they had been heading originally as a group, Alice hobbled up the trail and finally found hoof prints that continued on up the path.

"I see where you went, you bastards." She croaked. "I'm coming… I'm…."

Swallowing dry, she sniffed and wiped the sweat from her forehead, her eyes stinging from the salt and sunlight. With no other choice but to keep moving, she stared up the trail, ignoring her growling stomach and aching chest, clinging to her walking stick in a white-knuckled grip, desperation and determination the only things driving her forward.

CHAPTER TWO

James Burton
Frankfort, Illinois

James trudged through a short stretch of woods with a box in his arms, ducking and running as he fled the intense gunfire that had erupted behind him as the remnants of the city tore themselves apart. The sky was hazy and dark, no moon or stars in sight, with tailwinds driving tatters of pale fog through the trees like ghosts. The occasional stray round zipped overhead, snipping leaves and branches, urging him to keep moving and dodging, glancing over his shoulder at the wavering flashlight beams, muzzle flashes, and screams. Breath gusting in plumes of steam, James ran for the tree line, pushing through a cluster of bushes, climbing over a fallen log and landing with a huff on the other side. Three more steps carried him to the edge of the woods where one heel slipped from beneath him and sent him sliding down a hillside on slick leaves and grass, water shooting up his back all the way to the bottom.

"Ugh!" He was soaking wet and covered with mud, but the box was still in one piece and relatively clean.

Rolling to his left, he pushed against the hillside to get up, jogging east past a long stretch of blocks with scattered buildings and wooded spots, a few old brick warehouses dripping wet with dark windows watching him in the gloom. James reached a massive curbside storm drain and stooped to set his package down, then stood over the grate. Reaching his fingers through the bars, he hauled it up with a groan, and tossed it aside with a clang.

There was a shuffling from down in the drain, and Private Oswell's pale face appeared, dark eyes staring at him, thick strands of brown hair clinging to her cheeks. She was looking worse than she had been when he'd left her earlier, having been shot clean through at least once and nicked several times in the hail of gunfire they'd run through back in the warehouse district.

"Did you find anything?" she asked in a pained voice.

"Yes, I did." James handed the box down and climbed in next to her, grabbing the grate and hauling it toward him with a grinding sound until it half covered the opening, then took hold of it from below and slid it into place with a clang. Their breaths were close in the darkness, squeezed in beside each other on a sloping, seat-like curve in the center of the pipe with water dripping on all sides.

"Busy out there?"

"It's insane." As if to emphasize his point, several shots cracked, mixed with the smooth rattle of automatic weapons, going silent for a moment before breaking out into another feverish racket. "It's like the Fourth of July out there." James situated himself on a dry part of the pipe, pulling his backpack between his feet and resting the package in his lap. "I found a couple of first-aid kits."

Oswell nodded with a wave of pain. "Where at?"

"Restaurant a couple of blocks back. Most of it was burned down, but beneath they had a few first-aid kits in the kitchen." He opened a bag to reveal two plastic boxes with red crosses on the front. "They're just basic ones, but they should have some gauze and antiseptic ointment to keep your wounds from getting infected." James switched positions and put the first-aid kits on the seat while squeezing in between Oswell's knees. "Okay, let's see what we're dealing with here."

Oswell's dog tags jangled as she shed her coat to reveal a camouflage T-shirt over long-sleeved undergarments soaked with blood. She pulled it up, exposing a pale stomach smeared with red, the outline of her abdomen muscles and hipbones defined even in the darkness thanks to a steady lack of nutrition and constant stress for days on end. James searched for the bullet hole, only to feel warm blood seep between his fingers.

"I can't see a thing. I'll need to use my flashlight." He dug it out of his backpack and put a sock over the end before turning it on, shining the light directly on the wound. "The entry wound is small, but let's see if there's an exit wound." He reached behind her, feeling beneath her shirt, his fingers sliding over her cold, clammy skin, but not finding an exit wound of any kind. "Must still be in there."

"Wonderful." Oswell's sarcasm was thick. "Just what I wanted to hear."

"We can keep the bleeding down, but we need to get you out of this bacterial hellhole and to a doctor. Let me check the leg." A few inches below the makeshift compression bandage, James found another bullet hole with a trickle of blood that was slowly leaking down her leg. "This one went through at least. And the good news continues – nothing's bleeding too badly. I should be able to get you patched up." He opened the first-aid kits and found packages of painkillers in a side pocket. "Do you want something for the pain? Dumb question, huh?"

Oswell nodded briskly as she sucked air through her teeth.

James took one of the gallon jugs he still had in his backpack, the plastic dented from running with it in his pack, and handed it over. She grabbed the pills and water and downed four NSAID pills while he sorted through the other supplies.

"I'll start with your leg." He tore her pants leg open with the help of a knife, used a cloth and saline to clean the wound, applied antiseptic to the gauze, and packed it in, slapping on an oversized bandage on top to seal it. With an old rag, he wiped the area dry and ensured the bandage was sticking to her skin. "Now, the exit wound. I'll need you to twist around so I can get to it."

Oswell groaned as she grabbed her pant leg and pulled her right knee to her chest, shifting so she could lay on her left side and expose the back of her leg to James. He found the entry hole in her pants but couldn't locate the actual exit wound. "There's a lot of blood back here, and I can't—ah, there you are." The material was tough to rip, but he grabbed two handfuls of it and tore it wide enough to get a good look.

Oswell clenched his arm and squeezed hard, her bony fingers digging in. "Is it bleeding bad?"

"Not terribly. Besides, if they'd hit a major artery, you'd already be dead."

She nodded as he went to work cleaning and binding the wound, then taking care of two nicks on the side of her knee and calf.

James shook his head. "You must have walked into a spray of buckshot or something, because I'm seeing small cuts all over you."

"Feels like I'm on fire," she said, grimacing with every wave of pain. She gripped him harder as he cleaned and patched her up. "We'll leave the tourniquet on for now. Let's have a look at that hip."

Oswell brought her leg up straight, settled back, and lifted her shirt to check her shot hip. When James pushed around the puckered bullet hole, there was no blood at first, but pressure from a different angle forced a teaspoonful of warm red fluid to bubble up and drip down her side, revealing a quick flash of metal beneath the blood.

"You know what? There's something right there beneath your skin, maybe caught in the muscle or something. I can try to get it out."

"Are you sure?"

"I'm no expert, but it's near the surface, and if I can get it out, we might avoid an additional infection vector."

Oswell looked doubtful for a moment but nodded. "What would you use to get it out?"

"My staff's got a couple of blade attachments. I could sterilize one and sort of pick at it and try to squeeze it out. It wouldn't be like taking out a splinter... it'll hurt."

413

She nodded and took a deep breath, wincing at the movement. "Yeah, it's hurting and I don't want an infection, so let's do it."

"Okay."

James opened the section of his collapsible staff to find a long serrated blade. He affixed it to one of the sections of the staff to act as a handle, screwing it on tight and testing the balance. It was oversized for what he needed it to do, but it was the smallest thing he had – and it was sharp, to boot. Using a small bottle of isopropyl alcohol from a first-aid kit, he sterilized the blade and cleaned around the wound again as Oswell bit her lip, trying to keep from crying out.

"You'll have to hold the flashlight on it."

Oswell took it and shined it straight down while James worked on the piece of metal, pushing it toward the opening of the wound through the skin while picking at the edge of the hole with the blade. Each time he touched her, Oswell sucked air between her teeth, cursing softly, gripping his shoulder with a white-knuckled grip.

"You're doing great, Oswell. Just hang on there."

"I'm going. To break. Your shoulder." Each word was accompanied by a wheeze.

"That's okay. I've almost got this thing out."

The blade tip clinked against the metal, and she clenched her teeth to hold in a howl of pain as James pushed the bullet between the blade and his fingers from beneath a flap of skin, the edges of the metal jagged as they clung stubbornly to her flesh.

"This looks fragmented, like it might've ricocheted off something and hit you... that would explain why it didn't go very deep."

"Lucky me," Oswell seethed and gasped, sucking another breath of air and holding it as he caught the underside of the bullet with the blade and flipped it out into her lap.

"Got it!"

With a tremendous exhalation, Oswell collapsed back and rested her arm on his shoulder. "Ow, that hurt like hell...."

"You did great." James worked on cleaning the wound, packing gauze into the opening, and pressing a wide bandage on top.

"Ow! Jeez."

"Sorry. I have to pack this really tight. I'd trade anything to have your backpack. Probably would've had some coagulant powder for gunshot wounds."

"Yeah, that last fight we had was rough... had to leave almost everything behind."

James pulled her shirt down over the bandage and nodded at the pistol at her side. "I'd say we're both lucky to be alive and with anything left to defend ourselves. It's a blender out there."

"Yeah, I guess so."

Patting her uninjured leg, James repositioned himself so that he was sitting next to her, looking up through the dripping sewer grate. He wiped the moisture off his nose and spit into the darkness at his feet, listening to the distant gunfire.

"How can they be fighting so long?" he asked. "You think they'd run out of steam by now trying to kill each other so hard."

"They're savages... no humanity left inside them." Oswell chuckled painfully. "If only they'd stop fighting long enough to pay attention, they'd realize they don't need to kill each other... at least not over supplies."

"What do you mean?"

"They're dropping enough supplies on the highways to feed the survivors for ten years or more. There're radios, clothing, and survival equipment. Tons of good stuff they're missing because of... what?"

"Some people thrive on conflict and drama. You can't expect them to go docile in *the* most intense situation, ever."

Oswell put her pistol in his lap, but he pushed it back into hers. "You keep it. You'll need it more than me, plus I have my staff."

"I can't shoot the way I'm shaking. Even if I had my rifle, I couldn't hit the broadside of a barn. Can't believe I lost my rifle and ammunition back in that junkyard. Or that we're *back* in *another* sewer." She let her head fall back against the damp wall, taking a deep, shuddering breath. "No, you're the one who has a steady hand. Take the gun."

James slipped it into his coat pocket. "Okay, but it's right here if you need it." He grabbed his backpack and pulled it closer, unzipping it and rifling through the contents. "We've got some canned stuff left in here if you're hungry."

"What is it?"

"We've got corn, peas, and baked beans. Breakfast of champions."

"Ugh. No thanks. I'll wait till I'm really desperate."

After searching through some more, he brought out a package of twisted black sticks still in its crinkly packaging and gave it a shake. "I forgot I even had this."

Oswell read the label. "Licorice?"

"Yeah, I had it in a side pocket. Can't stand the stuff, but calories are calories. Want some?"

"I'm not big on candy, but licorice is pretty good."

James ripped open the package and handed it to her. "Go ahead, it's all you."

She pulled out a piece and chewed while James used the knife from his staff on the can of baked beans, getting the lid open just enough to peel it back and begin pouring the cold, sugary sauce into his mouth.

"It's not a gourmet meal," he said between mouthfuls, "but it'll do."

"Beats nothing," Oswell agreed as she chewed the tough candy. They ate in silence for a few minutes, listening to the rain fall and the distant battles rage on. It was comfortable in their little nook, a tiny parcel of peace and quiet amidst the chaos. The smell coming up from the sewer pipes wasn't pleasant, but the tremendous amount of recent rainfall had washed much of the usual foul odors away, allowing them to eat without gagging.

"So, what should we do now?"

"We'll get you out of here, somehow."

"Not sure how that's going to work, but sure. We'll figure something out." She wiped her hand down her face, shaking with constant tremors that ran through her body.

"Here..." James scooted closer and wrapped his arm around her, hugging her so that her head rested against his chin. "Geez. You're freezing."

"F-feels like w-winter," she replied with chattering teeth.

"Well, you've lost a fair amount of blood. And it has been getting colder as of late. You're cut all to hell and back but holding up well. You'll make it, Oswell."

Her body relaxed, slouching against him, clinging to him and letting her head fall to his chest. "How long till we move out? I'm exhausted just thinking about it."

"We should probably stay here for a few hours and rest, then try to leave. Maybe the gunfire will have moved away by then."

"I could stand to get a little rest and..." Her voice was soft, slurring slightly as her eyelids drooped. "And the pain pills are starting to kick in. My hip doesn't feel too bad right now."

"Where are you from, Oswell?"

She grunted softly. "A little farming town outside of Peoria. Mom won't be happy when she finds out I got shot. She never wanted me in the Guard, but I followed in Dad's footsteps. He'd be proud of me. Mom just always worries."

"Probably made for some intense dinner conversation."

She chuckled softly and coughed. "They're usually too busy with my younger sister to notice what I'm up to. They realized long ago I was the kind of girl to make my own way. At least, I *was*..."

"You're not done yet, Oswell. We've got a long way to go, but we'll get there."

They sat quietly for a few minutes before James spoke again. "Hey, I'll keep first watch. Why don't you try to get some sleep?"

She nodded. "Sounds good."

James tried to stay awake for a while after she drifted off, but her steady breathing lulled him into a restless slumber filled with twisted, angry faces shouting at him and chasing him through the back alleys of Chicago. The flash of gunshots exploded behind his eyes, and echoes of cries rang in his ears, sometimes starting him awake until he drifted off again. The writhing images followed him in every dream and not even thoughts of home with Alice and the kids could drive away the darkness.

A distant shotgun blast was what finally jolted him from the torturous slumber, and he squeezed Oswell's shoulder tightly. "You still with me?"

Oswell woke up and pushed herself back, dazed and blinking. "Huh? Yeah... I mean, unless this is hell. Seems pretty close to hell."

"Not that lucky, I'm afraid," he chuckled.

"Is Alice... is she at home, still alive?"

James hesitated. "She's alive. I'm sure of it. And so are my kids." He tilted his head and listened. "It sounds like the gunfire has moved away."

"Sounds like it."

"Then it's probably a perfect time to go."

James packed up what little they had, putting the first-aid kits back together and placing them into his backpack. He pushed the grate to the side and climbed out, reaching for his things, tossing them aside, and holding his hand out for Oswell to grab. Using the edge of the sewer hole, and with James' help, she climbed out and got to her feet, wobbling a little but leaning against him until she had her balance.

"Can you make it?"

"I think so, yeah."

"Take my staff to support your right side, and I'll support your left. We'll keep as much pressure off that right hip and leg as we can."

"Okay."

He handed her the staff and shouldered his backpack, and together they started down the road heading east, hobbling past brick buildings that dripped with moisture and rust, water stains forming dark patterns on the walls. Drizzle sprinkled across the tin gutters and car roofs, and a couple of inches of water stood in the grassy areas and weed-infested yards. Remarkably, a pair of streetlamps remained on, likely solar-powered, sputtering off and on intermittently in the early morning as dawn crept closer.

Oswell grunted softly with each step, staring hard at the ground, favoring her right foot and keeping it elevated as much as possible. It didn't take long before they'd fallen into a good rhythm and were taking longer strides, though, with James shuffling beneath her arm to keep her weight supported. Twin puffs of breath escaped into the cool morning air and billowed up to join a rising mist stirred up by the rain.

"Looks like we made it out of there, eh?" Faint gunshots were barely audible behind the pair as Oswell gestured with her head in the direction of the city.

"As long as we keep going east, I don't care. You have a destination in mind?"

"I wouldn't mind making it to the National Guard outpost in La Porte. That's just south of the Michigan border."

"I'm familiar with the area. As long as it's closer to home, you won't get an argument from me. You set the pace, Private."

Oswell huffed and puffed, teeth clenched as she swung her right leg forward to give momentum to her strides. The blocks passed swiftly, moving from corner to corner with James watching for people, ready to reach for his pistol at a moment's notice. At the next intersection they came to an industrial building on the right with a big, sagging sign on the corner that read *Packard Candle Company*, and James broke their rhythm and drew them to a stop.

"What is it?"

James paused to listen, trying to triangulate on the sounds echoing off the buildings. "I hear voices."

"I don't hear any... wait. I hear them now. What direction?"

"Maybe somewhere in the next block or two. Let's keep going, but slower."

They walked across the street with James' head on a swivel as he checked the dark stoops and alleys for signs of movement, but the shadows continued playing tricks, making it difficult to spot any potential trouble lying in wait. The voices got louder up toward the next corner, though, and as they got closer, he let Oswell rest against the wall and held his finger to his lips. She nodded in understanding, and he left her there and approached the corner slowly, taking his pistol from his pocket and craning his neck to look off to the left. When he saw no one to the left, he crept ahead and peeked around the corner to his right.

The next block was a short string of stores with signs he couldn't read, and a car was backed up to one door and four people were hauling supplies out from the store and into the car. They carried out jugs of water, armfuls of cans and glass bottles, crinkling bags of snacks, and other assorted items, hurrying to load them into the trunk. They whispered quietly as they worked, one person pacing around the vehicle, on guard duty with a rifle in his hands, though he spent more time walking back toward the store than he did keeping an eye out, pointing inside and giving instructions. All of them were younger, looking like they were in their twenties or early thirties, though none wore clothing or bore tattoos that identified them as members of the gangs who had battled through the streets back in the city proper.

Their vehicle wasn't idling, nor did it have any fire damage; an EV for certain, which very nearly tempted James into confronting the group. Before he could follow that train of thought any further, though, the vehicle pulled noiselessly away and drove smoothly down the road, heading south. After watching them for a few moments, he turned back to Oswell and took her by the arm.

"Who was it?"

"Just some people in an EV, looting from a store."

"An electric car? We could've used that."

"I know, but there were four of them, and we need to pick our battles carefully. Let's just keep walking and keep our heads down."

"Okay."

They plodded along the lonely road, never entirely leaving the city, passing through one small township after another with darkened signs that read *Dyer*, *Hartsdale*, and *Schererville*. There were stretches of fields in between the small cities with wilted crops where dirt washed across the road, low spots forming pond-sized puddles they splashed through, their feet soon soaked and chilly. Oswell's teeth chattered, and James' stomach grumbled loudly when they passed a lone pizza restaurant with a deal for a large pepperoni for six ninety-nine painted in bold red letters on the front window. Twenty minutes later, they began slowing their pace as Oswell's injuries and general weakness took a toll on her. She leaned on him harder, putting a strain on his shoulders and back, forcing him to deal with her injuries while bearing through his own. Their boots shuffled on the pavement as they trudged on, and a quarter mile later at the edge of another small township, something caught his eye. Across the street stood a string of burned-up specialty stores with scorched signs that were barely legible; a coffee shop, a bookstore, and one that caused him to angle Oswell across the road.

"What is it now?" she asked as they crossed.

"It'll be worth it, trust me. Head for the store on the far right. It's burned up pretty good, but maybe we'll find something inside."

A moment later, they stood in front of a bike shop with most of the brick front spilled onto the sidewalk, the door hanging crooked and shattered from its frame. The inside was a blackened mess with a few sparkling pieces of chrome standing out amongst the char. James left Oswell leaning against a beam and stepped inside, his footsteps crunching over the burned wood and fallen brick. The ceiling had fallen, burying almost everything except for a few bikes hanging on the wall and some handlebars jutting up from the floor. He started picking through the wreckage, dragging out a couple of children's bikes with the spokes split and the frames bent from the intense heat.

"I like where you're going with this, James, but riding won't be any easier for me."

"It's worth a look around."

James picked through the rubble some more, pulling out a decent looking ten speed and a mountain bike, walking them over to a clear place, checking out the tires, and resting them against the wall. If he'd been alone, the mountain bike would be perfect to hop on and go, and it would only be a few days before he was riding up the gravel driveway to his house.

Oswell read his mind. "Hey, listen, if you want to take one of these and go, I wouldn't blame you."

He shot her a dark look and rolled his eyes. "Shut up and rest, would you?"

"Yes, sir."

He fiddled around with a couple more half-buried bikes and then worked his way toward the middle of the shop, stepping beneath the drooping roof that dripped sooty water, pieces of ceiling tiles, and insulation. The place was a dangerous mess, the slickness made worse in the darkness. He pulled out his flashlight and checked over his shoulder, but there was no one around, and the gunshots had faded out. Flipping the flashlight on, he stepped deeper into the store's recesses, kicking pieces of trash and debris off to the side, dragging out bike frames that had burned up in the fire. He was about to give up when a strange boxy shape caught his eye, a flat cargo tray with rails and two smaller wheels.

"Hey!" He put the flashlight to the side and tossed chunks of wood and charred ceiling aside. "Check this out."

"What is it?"

"It's a cargo trailer of some sort."

"Need some help?"

"No. Stay there. Give me a second." Breaking through the debris, he grabbed a handlebar and pulled a mountain bike frame from the wreckage that was still attached to the cargo trailer. Both the bike and trailer were covered in dents and scratches, but had been spared from any serious damage thanks to the thick layer of bricks that had fallen atop them from the nearby wall.

"Is it broken?"

"No, it looks like it's in decent shape." James stood it up, put the kickstand down, and grinned at Oswell as her eyebrow went up.

"You think that thing can carry me?"

James bent and looked at the label attached to the side of the cargo tray. "It's got a two-hundred pound maximum capacity. How much do you weigh?"

"Not two hundred pounds," she replied in mock offense.

James was already unhitching the cargo tray and guiding the bike over the rubble to bring it to the front of the store. He brushed off the dust and debris, checked the chain, lifted the rear end, and spun the tire so that it rotated smoothly.

"Seems functional."

Heading back for the cargo trailer, he finished clearing off the rest of the debris resting atop it and jostled it free, dragging it over to the bike and hitching the two. Kicking the kickstand up, he walked the bike and trailer back and forth, grinning at Oswell.

"Smooth as silk."

"Looks like we've got a new ride. C'mon, let's get you settled." James held out his arm.

Nodding in thanks, she handed over the staff and James walked her closer to the cargo trailer. With his backpack against the rear rail as a cushion, he had Oswell straddle the trailer hitch and ease down until she was sitting inside with her knees hooked over the front rail.

James stood with his hands on his hips. "Is that comfortable enough?"

She shifted back and forth, settling in and gripping the side rails. "I think so. There's plenty of room to move around."

"It'll keep your injured leg and hip elevated somewhat, but it won't feel the best what with the bar pressing on your legs. If we find some blankets or cushions, that should help a lot."

"Thanks, James. Even if I had to sit on a bed of nails, it'd be better than walking the whole way. And I appreciate you not taking off on me."

"Oh don't you worry," he laughed, "it's crossed my mind a few times, but you're just too good of company to leave behind."

"It must be my glowing personality," she winced as she shifted around, trying to get comfortable.

He chuckled and put his flashlight and staff away. "Something like that. Okay, let's give this a try. I sure hope I remember how to ride a bike."

"Oh, now you tell me." Oswell closed her eyes and gripped the side rails of the cargo trailer. "Maybe I want to walk after all..."

Throwing his leg over the top bar, James put the bike in first gear and used his heel to push the kickstand up. With one foot on the pedal, he rose and put his weight into it, moving them forward a few feet on the sidewalk, shakily turning the front wheel back and forth to keep his balance. After a moment they picked up speed, reaching the corner, and banking sharply into the street where he switched into second gear with a sharp click. The bike's tires spun smoothly, wheels ticking softly as he wove between clusters of debris, hit a couple of bumps, and found a long stretch of wet, glistening pavement ahead. As they picked up speed, he glanced back to check on Oswell as she clung to the side rails, keeping herself steady.

"You good, Oswell? Need me to slow down for you?"

"Just keep pedaling, James," she growled.

James grinned, a rush of elation hitting him as they sped over the pavement with the tires devouring yards of road, looted storefronts and burned-out buildings zipping by faster than they had in days. Shadowy figures looked up from the wreckage to watch them pass, the bike quiet enough to not draw attention until James and Oswell were already well past anyone who might want to pursue them. He continued changing gears as the road got smoother and easier to navigate, and as the pedaling got easier, the strain in his back and shoulders faded as they raced eastward beneath the coal-colored clouds.

CHAPTER THREE

Alice Burton
Talladega National Forest, Alabama

Alice attacked the path at a feverish pace as clouds of swarming bugs buzzed in her face, bit her, and stuck to her sweaty arms and neck until she brushed them off. As the day grew longer, humidity seeped in from all around, the sweltering heat settling on her like an electric blanket, making her feel thirstier the wetter she got. Her shirt hung off her shoulders, damp and musty from lying in the dirt, and sweat trickled down her back, collecting at her belt line where her jeans soggily clung to her hips. She swallowed dry, yearning for a single sip of *anything*, dreaming of crossing a cool clear stream to drink from, though leaving the trail to search for one would undoubtedly lead to her swift demise. The forest stretched on all around her, endless and lonely without Sarah and Jake's company, the sounds of their voices, their laughter and the way they teased each other, all of which had made the whole journey bearable.

Alice was alone, a desperate wanderer on the sweltering trail with only hoofprints to follow and an occasional piece of garbage tossed off to the side to encourage her that she was heading in the right direction. The trees pressed up against her, the path overflowing with pine needles and sticks, forest refuse that crunched under her feet and gave off a floral musk that agitated her throat. She wouldn't consider resting, never stopping once, drawn along an invisible thread she was driven against all odds to follow.

The trail wove back and forth up strenuous inclines that pit her will to go on against her body to see which would give out the first. At the top of a ridge, Alice paused above a curved valley shaped like a bowl to catch her breath, the slopes below her swept with pines and birches, their needles and leaves glittering in the sun. Flocks of birds flew across the open spaces while a lone red-tailed hawk called out as it drifted in the upper wind currents, searching for its next meal.

She walked the treacherous ridge line where the path was wide enough for a single rider, the stones embedded in the soil worn smooth by horses and tires and hiker's boots. Swaying under the sun's heat, Alice came off the ridge and entered the woods again where the ground leveled out. The whole time she limped along, she kept her head down and focused on the horse tracks, counting them by the thousands until they suddenly weren't there.

Alice stopped and blinked, checking the brush on both sides of the trail but finding no clue as to where they could've gone. A hill butted up against the trail on her left, dense with trees and foliage, but she doubted she could climb it if she tried, and the horses certainly couldn't have traversed it without leaving some sign of their passage. Broken branches hung off the bushes on her right, and sticks lay cracked and smashed in the dirt. She shuffled off the trail through a patch of short grass, prodding at the debris with her walking stick, finally stopping at the forest's edge. Something fluttered in the breeze, and she reached and plucked a tuft of beige horsehair from a branch that jutted out into the trail.

"Buck?" she rasped.

A barely perceptible trail cut through the bushes and saplings, and something – or some*things* – big had pushed them aside and trampled them to get through. The path curved about thirty yards into the woods past flat clearings like the campsites she'd seen when they first met Mark and Christine, public spots for campers with iron grills and stone campfire pits spaced reasonable distances apart. Spots of sunlight touched the forest floor where gray squirrels scampered, and insect clouds grew thicker, and Alice rubbed the horsehair between her fingers and stepped amid the campsites, edging sideways past branches and sharp thorns that curved like shark's teeth.

The first pair of campsites showed no signs of recent activity, with the remains of fires weeks old and covered with scatterings of fallen pine needles. Moving across the camp area, she rediscovered the horse tracks in the moist earth and followed them up through the woods until the sound of trickling water reached her ears.

Picking up the pace, she climbed to a tall bank that loomed over a lazy, narrow stream. Trees hung over the water, sometimes butting heads, the roots running deep and clinging to the steep banks. Alice found another campsite forty yards up the trail to her right with logs pulled up around a ring of rocks, the remains of the fire inside giving off a small trickle of smoke that drifted into the upper boughs. Alice hurried over to the fire, prodding the ash and coals with her walking stick until the remnants turned red and released a fresh gray tendril of smoke that curled upward before being torn apart by the breeze. Buried in the ash were a few wrappers that might have looked familiar if not for their scorched edges and indiscernible labels, but the more she churned the coals and ash, the more pieces of trash turned up. One she flipped over revealed black writing on white packaging, an MRE wrapper like the ones she and the kids had been carrying.

Footprints encircled the stones and logs, the soft ground and a few water bottles stomped flat by several pairs of feet. Near a low-hanging branch, she found a cluster of horse hooves, and she tracked them through the bushes and down to a larger creek where a rush of clear water broke over a V-shaped spill of mossy rocks and poured into a wide basin in a spray of foam. It dispersed lazily in bubbles and swirls, spreading out in tiny waves to lap at the muddy bank. The hoof prints were clustered at the water's edge, so compounded that she couldn't count them, but it had to have been Buck and the rest of them. That meant Mark and Christine had made camp there and then went on. Between the fading fire, the trash and how she felt, Alice must have been lying on the trail, in the hot sun, for several hours or perhaps even a full day.

"No, it couldn't have been a whole day," she croaked. "That's impossible!"

With her phone broken, though, she had no sense of time, and as she looked around at the tracks, the stream, and the dying campfire, the long period of time started to make more sense. Digging her walking stick into the mud, she climbed the bank to the camp, panting, her sides aching, feet throbbing, every breath bringing a sharp sting to her lungs. Her foot caught a raised root, and she stumbled and almost fell, saving herself by thrusting the walking stick at the ground to keep from falling. Stabilizing herself, she stood frozen, staring at the trail. If she kept going at her current pace, she'd quickly push her already fragile body far past what it could take, which would do no one – neither herself, nor her children – any favors.

As much as she wanted to trudge ahead without stopping, her body and mind demanded a break, to take a few moments to think things through, recoup some energy and think through what her plan should be going forward. The campfire coals she'd stirred up were fading to gray, the smoke trailing up faster as if on its last breath and she shuffled over and used her walking stick to stir the coals around again, drawing another flicker of red from the ashy heap. Dropping slowly to one knee, she scooped up twigs and leaves from around the stones and logs and tossed them atop the coals, stirred them up to get them alight, then got another handful, picking up a few larger sticks as well and dropping them on top of the leaves and pine needles in a pyramid shape, making several shaky trips until the flames licked up the sides of the wood.

By the time Alice was done, she was panting again, sweating, gripping her walking stick with both hands, arms quivering and barely hanging on. She backed away from the raw flames, the heat too intense to stand by, yet the light gave her hope, and she slipped off her backpack and laid it by one of the logs. With slow, shallow breaths, she very carefully sat on a log, taking a minute to find a comfortable position and catch her breath as she stared into the blaze. The crackle and pop of the wood cast cinders upward and lulled her into a trance-like state of exhaustion.

Alice swallowed dry and rubbed her neck, the thirst gripping her again out of nowhere, throat raw after breathing dust and pollen and eating enough gnats to make a meal. It was tempting to simply go down to the creek, cup a bit of water in her hand, and drink her fill, but getting sick on top of her aching chest would devastate her chances of finding the kids – if she survived at all.

You can only go about three days without water, she thought, *and the way you're sweating, you can cut that number in half*.

Unzipping the backpack, she pushed her remaining MRE aside and took out the damaged water filtration straws. One was merely bent with some plastic tubing inside stretched and cracked and bits of filter media trickling out. When Alice bent the pieces back straight, it seemed like it might still be usable, and she put the straw in her left pocket, climbed the staff with both hands, and made her way to the creek.

Getting on one knee at the water's edge was agony, but she was getting faster, learning which movements brought her more pain and avoiding them whenever possible. Gasping and holding her breath, Alice held the straw straight and bent toward the crystal-clear flow, the air lifting off the water to cool her face. It took a painfully long time, but she touched the end of the filtration straw to the water and sucked on the tapered tip. Nothing came right away, so she sucked harder, waiting for a hint of moisture to reach her lips. The teasing agony of refreshment at her fingertips but being unable to taste it made tears run down her cheeks as she put every ounce of energy into the simple task of drinking. A cramp pinched the left side of her neck, and she backed off the straw for a moment before trying again, sucking with all her strength until the faintest trickle of water seeped from the tip, the cool taste touching her tongue and encouraging her to keep trying. Cheeks sunken, she got a trickle going and filled her mouth, then tilted her head back and swallowed, the cool water hitting her stomach like a block of ice, sending a shiver up her back.

"Oh, that was good," she gasped, bowing back toward the water and drawing another mouthful, then another. By the time she finished the third mouthful, her sides and cheeks were aching too much to continue so she sat on her heels and allowed her chest to decompress, taking deep breaths, still dizzy from the lack of air. In spite of the soreness, the small amount of water she'd taken in had transformed her, and her senses grew sharper as life returned to her body. The straw was infuriatingly difficult to use in its half-broken state – but it worked, and that was all that mattered.

After a short time, she drenched her hands, arms, face and head in the water to cool herself off, then slowly rose and headed back to the fire. It was still blazing, its heat more comfortable as the heat of the day was replaced by a cooler breeze, the smoke helping to drive back the endless swarms of gnats. Alice sat on the log next to her pack, stirring the coals a bit and throwing in a few nearby pieces of wood to keep the flames high. She leaned the walking stick beside her and picked up the last MRE, with *Beef Patty and Jalapeno Pepper Jack* written on the front. The water had ignited her hunger, her stomach gurgling loud enough to be heard over the roaring fire. She tore open the package and stuck her hand in, moving past the beef patty and drawing out the cracker and jalapeño cheese sauce.

Remembering Sarah's instructions to break the crackers up first to save from losing any crumbs, Alice opened the packages and selected a large corner piece of cracker, spreading the spicy cheese on top and popping it in her mouth. Chewing slowly, she finally swallowed and deemed it the best cheese and crackers she'd ever eaten. One piece at a time, she got through the pack, hot tears burning her cheeks as she thought of the kids, where they were, and what they could possibly be doing. Already, the food was clearing her mind, seeds of ideas turning in her head, possibilities taking shape and fading out just as quickly. When the crackers were gone, she tilted the package up and dumped the crumbs in her mouth, then squeezed out the last drop of cheese. She felt... *decent* by the time she was done, but exhaustion was settling in on her heavier than ever. Her feet were sore — she couldn't imagine walking another step — and her eyelids were drooping as she fought to stay awake.

While she had no idea what time it was, judging by the dwindling light and chirping insects, it was late afternoon or early evening. The air had a heavy, drab feel to it, opposite of early morning when the sun beamed through the treetops and made everything glow. She'd been walking for hours, then, nearly a full day, and going farther wasn't a matter of willpower, but of physical ability and energy expenditure. The moon had been full one or two nights ago, so maybe she could sleep for a couple of hours and hit the trail early in the night, using the moonlight to guide her. If she was lucky, she might catch up with Mark and Christine at the next campsite. Tracking them had been easy enough; they were sloppy travelers, leaving tracks and garbage everywhere, and they most likely thought she was dead, which gave her a distinct advantage over them. They'd never see her coming.

But not right away, not with her body on the verge of failing her and the weight of exhaustion draining all her energy, forcing her down into a deep den of sleep. As she sat by the fire contemplating what to do next, dozing without realizing it, shadows fell over the forest and the sound of insects swelled in announcement of evening. Small flocks of bats flitted wildly between breaks in the trees as a breeze rode in on dusk's cooling cloak, while leaves and twigs crackled out in the thick of the trees, like something big was creeping by – deer, most likely, or something that preyed upon them. A caterwaul sounded in the distance, though between the fire close at hand and the source of the sound being far away, she wasn't immediately concerned.

Getting back to her feet, Alice gathered a pile of pine straw and leaves, using it to make a bed for herself near the fire. She used her backpack as a pillow and took her time lying down, slipping from her seated position on the log to her knees, rolling onto her right side and slowly to her back where the campfire warmed her shoulders.

After several minutes of shifting and moving to reduce the number of pine needles jabbing her in the back, Alice finally found a comfortable position and rested her head down with a shallow sigh. As she drifted off to sleep, all she could see was an endless trail ahead of her that cut through vast swaths of forested hills and mountains. She was racing along it at forty miles per hour, her body free of pain, easily bounding up slopes as she navigated the switchbacks and narrow trails with graceful ease. In that moment of pure control and transcendence, she fled her pain and worry and drifted into sleep.

CHAPTER FOUR

Ryan and Helen Cooper
Lansing, Michigan

Ryan stepped into the kitchen, knees still sore but the rest of him moderately refreshed from a good night's sleep. They'd forgone taking watch shifts in the name of getting some serious rest, relying on the dogs to watch over the house. Duke slept in bed with them, playing up his shoulder injury the entire time to win enough sympathy from Helen to be pampered and brushed before they'd gone to sleep.

The first thing on Ryan's mind was coffee, and he grabbed the pot from the coffee maker and went to the sink to fill it up. The flow of water was normal for the first couple seconds, then the pressure dropped as the pipes groaned and the flow quickly dropped to a mere trickle.

"Oh, what is it now?!" He put the pot in the sink and shuffled to the basement door, pushing his hair back, his agitation over a lack of coffee only compounded by the thoughts of whatever might be causing the issue.

Helen was coming down the hallway when she stopped and watched him walk by. "What's wrong, dear?"

"Water's not working. No coffee."

"Any idea what it is?"

"That's what I'm going down to find out."

Diana followed Ryan as he headed downstairs and over to the circuit breaker panels, opening the boxes and reviewing the various switches, reaching the one for the well pump and flipping it off, then back on. Turning a spigot on a nearby utility sink, the water flowed for a couple of seconds before it too sputtered out to a trickle.

Great. So it's the pump. Phenomenal news. Turning the circuit off, he grabbed an adjustable wrench, a piece of rope, and a flashlight from James' workshop.

"You find the problem?" Helen asked as she stood near the stairs, watching him.

"Yep. Pump's dead or there's something wrong with it," he replied as they headed back upstairs and he put his boots on by the back door. "That's a pretty serious issue. No more *hot* water... well, no more water, period."

Helen leaned on the cooking island. "Can you fix it?"

"I don't know. We'll have to see what the issue is." Ryan glanced at her as he opened the door. "Can you take care of the chores today while I work on this?"

"Of course, dear. Do what needs to be done; I'll handle the other stuff."

"Thank you." He leaned forward and gave her a peck on the cheek and a hug before heading out the door with a weary sigh.

The morning was bright and crisp, and he quickly shut the door to keep the dogs in and walked past the EV and over to the well head, which stuck up several inches from the ground in the rear corner to the side and behind the house. Using a wrench, he loosened the cap and pulled it off along with a bundle of wires, which he placed off to the side. Tying a rope around the flashlight, he lowered it until it shined on a shoe fitting that connected the pump to the pipe running into the house.

Twenty minutes later, after poking around in the basement and two of the sheds, Ryan finally found a T-bar and put the long end into the hole, and threaded it into the shoe fitting. Once connected, he began wiggling and pulling on it, feeling it give a little but working it harder until it popped free from the junction, and he hauled it to the surface. He tossed the T-bar aside, grabbed the hose and wires, and started drawing up the pump itself.

The back door opened, and all three dogs shot out of the house with Duke trailing behind, looking up at Helen as he exaggeratedly favored his leg.

"How's it going out here?" Helen asked, coming up behind him.

"Perfect timing. I could use your help for a second."

"What do you want me to do?"

"Grab that bundle of hose and wires and such and walk away while I draw out the rest so they don't get all tangled up. I have no idea how deep their well is; there could be twenty feet or a hundred feet of hose down there before the pump comes up."

Helen dragged the hose and wires through the yard as Ryan kept pulling, shaking his head after forty feet came out but with no pump. Ten feet later, a thunking noise came from below, and a moment later a cylindrical metal object about eighteen inches long clanked against the top of the pipe and popped out.

"Got it!" Ryan grunted as he lifted the heavy object, carrying it over to a patch of gravel where he laid it down.

Helen brushed her hands on her jeans as she rejoined him, squatting down next to him as he poked at the pump. "How does it look?"

"Not so good; it's definitely the problem. This thing is completely rusted out, and the seals are all rotted. Motor's probably been on its last leg for a while now. It's amazing this thing even worked."

"It's probably the original one... maybe twenty years old?"

"Absolutely." Ryan looked over at the solar panels. "If I had to guess, it's the constant power fluctuations that finished the motor off."

"Can you repair it?"

"Nope. Pumps like this are designed to be replaced, not repaired, and even if I had the parts... no, I can't fix it, so we'll have to figure something else out, and soon."

"I'm sure there's something we can do."

"Not unless James has a second well pump lying around." Ryan snorted as he stood up, kicking at the broken piece of machinery idly as he wiped his brow. "Anyway, this will have to wait. It's about that time; let's go see if Sandy's here."

Walking around the side of the house, they both shaded their eyes from the intensity of the morning sunlight, spotting in quick order two figures – one smaller than the other – standing down by the front gate, both of them waving at Ryan and Helen, who returned the gesture.

"If you want to go ahead and start with the chores," Ryan said. "I'll go down and talk to Sandy. Then I'll see what I can do about getting us some water."

Helen waved toward the barnyard. "The animals can wait to be fed. They're not going to starve."

"You want to watch my back? Think she might be trying something?"

"Actually, I'd like to finally meet her. See if I can't get a feel for what's going on myself, too."

"Perfect. I wouldn't mind some company, either."

After grabbing their rifles, the pair exited through the front door, Duchess running around the side of the house and joining them while the other pair hung out down near the fence line surrounding the barn.

"Settle down, girl," Helen laughed as Duchess bounced around her and Ryan. "You need to burn off some of that endless energy."

As the trio approached the gate, Helen and Ryan waved to Sandy, who was wearing the same jeans and boots she'd been in the last couple times she had met with Ryan, along with a leather coat and scarf smudged with dirt and ash.

Stephen stood a little behind her, gawking as the massive Great Pyrenees bounded up to the fence with her bushy tail wagging.

"How's it going, Sandy?" Helen called with a wave.

"Oh, not too bad, all things considered. You must be Helen?"

"The same. Ryan's told me a lot about you."

"I'll bet. Probably how much he mistrusts me."

Helen laughed and took off her gloves, reaching across to take Sandy's hand. "There was definitely some of that at first, but I think he's starting to warm up to you."

"Well, I appreciate that." Sandy nodded at Ryan as he stood a few feet behind Helen, keeping a watch on things. "I wanted you to meet my son, Stephen, who you helped so much. Stephen, come and say hi to Helen and Ryan."

Stephen stepped from beneath his mother's shadow, eying the Great Pyrenees warily as she sat near Ryan, tail wagging furiously in the gravel.

"Hello there, Stephen." Helen smiled, turning to Ryan. "I think you've probably heard about Ryan from your mom, and that's Duchess."

"Hi." He spoke softly, waving at Ryan and Helen as Ryan stepped up to the gate, smiling at the young boy.

"I'm glad to see the antibiotics worked for you, Stephen. Your mom told me you were in pretty bad shape."

"Yeah... my stomach was hurting and I felt like I was burning up. I feel pretty good now though."

"I'm glad to hear it." Ryan looked up at Sandy. "Just be sure—"

"Yes, he's still taking them. And thank you – again."

They stood in awkward silence for several seconds until Helen looked over at Ryan with a raised eyebrow and he nodded almost imperceptibly. "Hey, why don't you come in?" Helen looked back at Sandy. "There are some benches and chairs right over there by the pond and we can sit and talk for a spell."

"That... sounds good," Sandy said haltingly. "Are you sure that's okay, though?"

"Like we talked about before," Ryan unlocked the gate and pushed it open wide enough for the pair to step inside, "next steps in this little thing revolve around trust."

Sandy and Stephen walked through the gate, watching Dutchess warily as Helen held the dog's collar and Ryan locked the gate back up. "Stay, Duchess," Helen said and walked over to her guests, shaking both their hands and touching their arms. "You both must not hang around the folks who came over to the house the other day, otherwise she'd be a lot more aggressive."

"No... I'm glad for that." Sandy held Stephen's shoulders as Ryan turned and patted his leg.

"Come here, Duchess. Come, girl." Duchess obeyed, treating the newcomers with indifference as Ryan rubbed her head. "Good girl. *Very* good girl. Well, Sandy, I'd say you both passed the dog test. If you want to pet her, go ahead."

Stephen reached out but jerked back when Duchess sniffed at him, though his action didn't dissuade her, and she came right up and licked his arm, sending him into a shy fit of giggles as he held Sandy's hand. Duchess continued, snuffling and snorting at him until he finally patted her head and let his hand slide along her shaggy neck.

"Yep, passed with flying colors" Helen grinned and gestured to the pond. "Okay, follow me." Duchess leaped ahead as they walked over to the larger pond where Alice and James had placed stone benches and seats at some point in the past. "Back before all *this*, we'd come down and feed the ducks."

"It's a beautiful property," Sandy said. "I came over a couple times in the past, but not very often. They've changed it a lot since then."

"They've done a nice job with the place, I have to say." Ryan stood in silence for a few moments, watching the sun standing high in the sky, angling above the trees and casting warm rays across the pond's surface with sparkles of glimmering light. The sky was bright below thin, tattered clouds that appeared pulled apart at the edges.

"Ryan, how about if I go up and grab those sandwiches I made for lunch today?" Helen said, stepping between a pair of rich red maples and down to the shore, gesturing at the benches near the water. "I'd say this little get-together could use some food, wouldn't you?"

"Oh we couldn't possibly im—" Sandy started, and Helen dismissed her with a wave.

"Don't you *even*. I'll be back in two shakes."

"Thanks, hon." Ryan eased himself onto a bench, rubbing at his legs as Helen hurried back up to the house. Sandy and Stephen sat down nearby, watching the ducks paddling across the pond, dipping their heads down every few seconds, occasionally coming up with a minnow or strands of grass from the bottom. A few moments later, Helen shuffled up with a basket and blankets draped over one arm.

"Back! Spread the blankets out on the grass or seats if they're dirty. We haven't had much time to do cleaning of the non-essentials lately."

"Oh, Helen, you didn't have to do all this," Sandy got up, helping Helen with the basket and spreading out a blanket on the bench to sit on.

"It's nothing, really. We're both happy to have someone to share some food with." Helen sat on a bench with Ryan next to her while Sandy and Stephen took a pair of seats to her right. "I hope you don't mind vegetable and egg sandwiches on stale bread, though."

Sandy laughed. "Vegetable and... egg sandwiches? I don't think I've ever had one."

"Oh yes, it's the latest fashion. No, we ran out of deli lunchmeat a while ago, but veggies and eggs are still in good supply, so...." Helen brought out two sandwiches wrapped in paper towels and handed them to Sandy. "They're honestly not bad. Tomatoes, lettuce, peppers, scrambled eggs and a little vinaigrette dressing."

"You know what? That actually sounds pretty good."

Sandy gave one to Stephen and opened hers up to show leafy pieces of lettuce hanging out and thick slices of tomato piled high between the bread. "This is *fresh*. And cold, too. Do you have a working refrigerator?"

Ryan shot Helen a glance and responded. "Nah. We moved our perishable items down in the basement where it's cooler."

"Oh, I see. Smart thinking."

"We've had to make a lot of adjustments in how we live," Helen added, changing the subject. "What about you two? How are you getting along?"

"Well, about the same as when Chase was around. He was a good man, back in the day, but lately... well, I told him not to join that group, and he did it anyway. Ended up being more trouble than it was worth. Got him...." She shot a glance toward the burial mounds on the east side of the property.

"Killed." Stephen spoke softly, Sandy wrapping an arm around him while Ryan watched on with a pained expression.

"If you'd like to visit his grave, you're welcome to. I'm sorry it went down the way it did, but—"

"It wouldn't have mattered." Sandy wiped a tear from her eye. "You had to defend yourself, and I understand that." Sandy handed the remnants of her sandwich crusts to Stephen, encouraging him to feed them to the ducks. Her eyes turned glassy as he trudged off. "Stephen is... to be honest, things haven't been going so well the past few years. Chase took to drinking more often than not, and did what he wanted no matter what I asked. He even started to, well..." She rubbed at her arm again, where the faint outlines of a bruise were still visible. "He'd been going in on me for a while now, and looked like he was going to start on Stephen. So you can imagine that him not returning wasn't *entirely* unpleasant."

"Oh, hell's bells." Ryan growled as Helen put an arm around Sandy, pulling her tight.

"I'd be happy to walk over with you if you'd like," Helen whispered. "Or we can stay with Stephen, whichever you prefer."

Sandy nodded her thanks and they sat silently for a few minutes, as a brisk breeze rushed in, clacking the treetops and sending the tall grass whipping back and forth like waves on the ocean.

"How close are you to that group?" Ryan cleared his throat. "The ones Chase was involved with?"

"Jack and Barb Willoughby? I can't say I like them much... they're both blowhards if you ask me, but they're convincing enough to get people to stick around and follow them."

"People still follow them?"

"The Joneses are with them, and so are the Fosters, but they're a little older and aren't too keen on fighting. A few others from the end of the road have joined since they attacked you. There's Tommy and Joyce Coleman. Mitchell Ward and his son, Greg. A few others."

"So, at least a dozen?"

"Something like that. They've pulled together some RVs and campers out in the Willoughby's backyard. New folks are bringing tents and supplies... they won't let you in unless you have supplies to contribute."

"That makes sense," Ryan nodded.

"We're still at our house – or what's left of it. Our back porch survived mostly, and it's got a cover on it. Plus we had camping equipment in the shed."

"Have the Willoughby's been talking about us, or what happened?"

"I couldn't really say. I hear them in the field playing music and talking sometimes, but they're almost a quarter mile away from us. We've traded with them some, but ever since it happened, they've been pretty standoffish."

Helen nodded. "Did you know our Alice very well?"

"We weren't best friends or anything, but she's one of the few people in the neighborhood I liked. We always said hello to each other at the grocery store, and we planned a food drive together a long while back for the high school. She and her husband always kept to themselves for the most part, and seemed content that way just... doing their thing out here. But she was always friendly anytime our paths crossed."

"It's nice to know you two got along."

"I'll take friendly casual acquaintance over enemies any day of the week," Ryan agreed. After a while more of sitting, talking and watching the ducks in the pond, Ryan looked over at Helen before speaking to Sandy. "Would you like to go see..."

Straightening her back, she nodded. "I suppose so."

They got up and walked along the southern edge with the ducks swimming next to them, turning onto a small dirt path between the berry bushes and fruit trees, drooping branches brushing against their shoulders, coming out at the east edge of the property where Norway spruces dominated the tree line, forming a wall of green along with the oaks and white pines.

Sandy stood in front of the mounds. "Which one is his?"

"I, uh... didn't really check for IDs on them. I'm sorry."

"No, it's... I understand. Thank you."

Helen and Ryan turned and headed back to the pond while Sandy and Stephen stood near the mounds, heads down as they spoke quietly to each other. After a few moments the pair returned, Stephen's face a mask of silent contemplation while Sandy wiped a few tears from her cheeks.

"Thank you again for that. We should be getting on home. Do you want to meet again tomorrow? Is there anything we can bring in trade?"

"Actually, there *is* something we've been wanting." As they walked back to the gate, Ryan chose his words with care. "We'd appreciate it if you could find some information on a pump."

"A... pump?"

"A well pump. I figure that since you're from the area and would know of any suppliers or well diggers... or maybe someone has one lying around in a shed or something."

"I can check around. Why do you need one?"

"I want to put a second well out back for the animals. I'm thinking about digging one by hand, and I'd like to have a pump for it if we can get some reliable electric going."

"I might know of a well-digger outfit that's still standing, based on what some neighbors said. How much would one be worth to you?"

"What do you need?"

"Food, weapons, ammunition; the usual."

They reached the gate, and Ryan stopped and rubbed his chin. "Something like that would be worth a couple of hens, at least. It'd be a good start to a flock, and you wouldn't have to rely on your neighbors so much."

Helen opened the gate while Sandy faced Ryan and crossed her arms. "What about three hens, if I were to find a way to get you the pump itself?"

"*Three* hens... hoo, you drive a hard bargain." He looked at Helen, mulling over the idea for a moment before nodding. "Tell you what. *If* you can find me a good, high-capacity well pump then we'll do two hens, plus two chicks when we get our first hatching."

Sandy thought for a moment before extending her hand. "It's a deal, Ryan. I'll see what I can find and get back to you."

They shook hands, and Sandy took Stephen through the gate.

"Bye, now," Helen called. "Same time tomorrow?"

"We'll be here."

Helen smiled and watched them walk hand-in-hand past the Jones' old home and out to the street, disappearing behind a stand of trees. Helen and Ryan turned and strolled up the long lane to the house with Duchess trotting next to them, tongue lolling out and exhausted from all the running around she'd done while playing with Stephen.

"She seems like a nice lady," Helen said.

"She *is*, so far as I can gather, and she knows how to drive a bargain. But we still need to be careful."

"At least she can tell us what the neighbors are up to."

"Knowing where they're living — I think the Willoughbys are about six farmhouses down, if memory from a few years back serves me correctly — is incredibly valuable. And knowing Sandy and Stephen are just a few houses farther down is helpful, too."

"Do you think we could..." Helen paused and shook her head. "Never mind."

"What is it?"

"I was going to say, what if she could work her way in with the neighbors and find out what they're up to?"

"You mean *spy?*" Ryan put his hand on his cheek and gasped dramatically.

"Oh stop it. We wouldn't ask her to lie or anything. But she could ask questions when they come around to trade and tell us what they said."

"Information is just as good as anything else to trade. We need the well pump first, but if she's amenable to helping us further, that'd be a smart thing to ask from her. Nice thinking."

He wrapped his arm around her shoulder as they moved up the front walk and into the house, letting Duchess in first.

"I'll get back on the chores then." Helen picked up an apron she'd laid over a kitchen chair and started putting it on. "Do you want to help, or do you have something else to do?"

Ryan put the basket on the kitchen table, folded the blankets, and laid them neatly inside the basket. "Actually, I've got an idea for a manual well pump that I want to try. The reserves of water we've got will only last for so long, and I don't want to count on Sandy coming through for us."

"You'd best get to it, then. Holler if you need anything."

"I will."

Helen gave him a peck on the cheek and went out to feed the chickens and gather eggs, leaving Ryan to grab a notepad and pencil and head down into the basement, ideas swirling in his mind.

CHAPTER FIVE

Alice Burton
Talladega National Forest, Alabama.

Sometime during the night, Alice started awake as the echoing crack of a branch or stick somewhere nearby in the forest jarred her from her sleep. She sat up quickly, but immediately regretted the sudden movement when her chest muscles spasmed in painful fits. Leaning to the right, she waited until the spasm passed and took several gasping breaths until her wind returned and the pain receded. Whatever had made the sound had darted off into the thick of the darkness, scared by her movement and sound into beating a hasty retreat.

"Nice alarm call," she croaked, leaning forward and putting a hand to her forehead.

While she felt like she could sleep for another dozen nights, Alice forced herself to roll to her right and climb up on the log to sit for a few minutes, yawning, wincing, and blinking back tears at the unbelievable pain searing in her chest. Once the worst of it passed, she woke up a little more, her senses sharpening and coming alive. The woods were vivid in the greenish-gray light, illuminating the leaning trees surrounding her, the tangled brush connecting them, half-broken branches hanging under the weight of vines and deadfall.

Her lifeline – the fire – had nearly gone out, and she stirred it, throwing a few more sticks on along with a handful of pine needles to feed the flames. Hunger gnawed at her insides and a desperate thirst raged in her throat, more than it had the previous day, as her body continued trying to adapt to what was happening.

With the help of the blossoming firelight, Alice shuffled down to the stream, kneeling in the same spot as before and using the half-broken filter straw to drink, getting five or six mouthfuls down before the wrenching cramps in her side forced her to quit. With water dripping from her chin, she eased back on her heels and watched the light glimmer off the surface of the stream, the mixture of white from the moon and orange from the fire churning in the bubbles. She was about to get up when the thirst returned, a craving for water unlike anything she could remember, her body desperately needing to fulfill a primal desire.

Alice very nearly bent down and drank straight from the water, but she resisted and continued to use the straw filter instead, settling into a semi-comfortable position with her weight resting on her right arm and leg, working through the pain and discomfort, each mouthful of the liquid providing the motivation she needed to keep going for a couple dozen more mouthfuls. When she finally stopped and tried to get up, nothing worked, and she had to push hard on her thighs to sit back on her heels and gasp through the pain and stiffness.

Wiping the moisture off her chin, she grabbed her walking stick and leveraged herself off the muddy bank to face the opposite woods, freezing suddenly when a pair of eyes stared back from the dense foliage. An unwitting gasp caused her side to ache, and she winced, backing up as she clutched at it, trying to circle around to the fire. As she moved, a shadow turned and leaped away, a vaguely deer-shaped bit of darkness crashing through the brush, a veritable freight train in the relative stillness of the forest.

Alice laughed hoarsely, shaking her head with relief. "Good grief, you scared the crap out of me. Last thing I need is to become mountain lion scat...."

Alice made her way back to the campsite, sitting by the fire for a few moments before kicking dirt onto it and packing her things away in the backpack. With it on her shoulder, she held fast to her walking stick and hobbled back the way she'd come to the main trail. She assumed Mark and Christine had taken the same track after stopping at the campsite since there were no other paths leading anywhere else nearby, and the main trail had – based on her foggy memories – been what they'd tried to stick to the entire time before, as well.

"You can do this," she told herself, setting her jaw and walking with a lurch and a sudden burst of unexpected energy thanks to the food, sleep and intake of water. Judging by the uptick in her awareness, she must have slept at least a couple of hours; more than she had wanted to spend, but just enough that she could continue her hunt.

Alice focused on the ground as she trod along, searching for tracks, trash or other indications that her children's kidnappers had taken the path as well. Flashbacks of old movies and books where prisoners dropped a trail of clues for rescuers to find went through her mind, but Jake and Sarah most certainly thought she was dead when they had been taken, and they wouldn't intentionally be leaving any traces for her to find.

The dirt was hard-packed and rocky, and while the moonlight illuminated the path, it was darkened by passing clouds and masses of fog, making it too dark for her to see any possible details in the dirt. She briefly considered constructing a torch, but she'd already put out the campfire, and it wouldn't last long without fuel or materials to keep it burning. There was also the matter of her only advantage being that Mark and Christine didn't know she was alive, and carrying around a torch would negate said advantage.

Far from the light and heat of the fire, the forest came alive with a cacophony of sound. Cicadas, crickets, and katydids sang in the night, a nocturnal chorus as they searched for mates while large creatures occasionally moved through the trees, just far enough to be out of sight. Just when she was starting to wonder if Mark and Christine had taken Jake and Sarah along another route, she spotted the wide curvatures of hoofprints in a muddy section of the trail, and she knelt to run her fingers along the shapes.

"Oh, I've got you now," she whispered.

Gripping her walking stick with both hands and leaning on it to support as much of her body weight as possible, she trudged on with an automatic locomotion that had far too quickly become second nature. Jab the staff and take a step, then repeat ad nauseum. Jab and step, jab and step, onward into the night as the path stretched far and away, curving slightly by degrees. Her chest ached with each breath, her legs burned and her feet ached, but she lowered her head and kept marching, more machine than woman, treading a path that not even death itself could keep her from.

The forest trail soon leveled out and transitioned from rock and hard-packed soil to looser dirt, and the hoof prints stood out in the moonlight, imprinted in soft earth higher on the slope. She continued for another half mile, looking down occasionally to make sure she was still following them, until – without warning – they vanished.

Backtracking slowly, Alice found where they'd left off, appearing to just disappear into thin air. Slowly lowering herself down to her knees, she crawled around, leaning one way and the other to get out of the moonlight's way, tracing the hoof-prints with her fingers off the dirt and through the grass as they veered to the left on a side trail. She got to her feet and squeezed through the dense brush, barely able to see a foot in front of her, taking careful steps as she tried to adjust to the change. The path turned into hard-packed dirt covered in mulch and sticks, and she had to feel around with her boot, sometimes getting on her hands and knees until she found the tracks again.

Thorny branches swatted her arms and legs, the barbs digging into her skin. Alice winced and put her head down, shoving the brush aside with her stick and plowing through it with her shoulders low. Her breaths got deeper, and something wheezed in her chest, a sick whistling sound that told her, in all good sense, to stop. She trudged on with a defiant grunt, swinging her feet forward, untangling herself only to get caught again. With a final burst of energy, she lunged and broke through, stumbling forward, windmilling with her walking stick and free arm, almost pitching off a rocky ledge to plunge into unfathomable darkness.

Alice found her balance and took two steps back, kissed by a cool breeze coming up from the cliff she'd nearly fallen off, her hair whipping around her shoulders as she took hold of a nearby sapling as she took in the view. An expansive valley aglow with moonbeams stretched out in front of her, a pair of curving spurs sweeping up from the valley floor to meet where she was standing to form a horseshoe shape. The trail followed frighteningly narrow ridges downward both to the left and the right with dark, rocky slopes dropping off both sides, and silhouettes of trees clung to the hills with their waving tops shimmering in the moon's light.

She caught her breath and took a few steps in both directions, but the path was too rocky and didn't show any hoof prints or human tracks no matter how close she looked. Cursing softly, she slammed her staff into the ground, seething resentment for fighting all the way to the top only to be left with nothing. Her next decision would be no more than a mental coin flip, a simple guess as to what route to take. But she was unprepared to possibly make the ultimate mistake that would take her farther away from her children. Her vision blurred, but she blinked away the tears, shoulders sagging until, off to the left, deep within the valley trees, a sharp orange light flickered and cast a faint glow that painted the surrounding trees a soft shade of red.

A.. campfire?

It had to be them. It *had* to. She could almost see Sarah and Jake sitting around a fire with Mark and Christine watching them, holding her own rifle on them, putting them down or even hurting them. Before she could start second-guessing or falling into despair, Alice took the left-hand spur in that staggered gate she'd adapted — *jab, step... jab, step* — glancing repeatedly at the orange spot in the trees, measuring it against where she stood and how far the trail curved to the valley floor, figuring they were at least three miles away, maybe a little more. Distance didn't matter, though. She had a bead on her children and clung to the faintest flicker of hope that she could reach them before morning came and they took off again.

She bore through the pain, wincing and grunting with every step, forcing herself to keep moving through the cool night. She tripped and almost fell multiple times as she clambered across stones and circled large gray boulders perched on the trail amid spills of rock. Breezes crawled up through the pines and spruces, blowing her hair around, and driving away the sweat by sending chills up her sides.

Alice picked up the pace, easing down a sharp descent that forced her to turn sideways, body twisting and stomach lurching every time she slipped and almost fell. Scrub-covered fields blinking with fireflies rose to meet her descent, and soon she was moving through the valley toward the end of the horseshoe shape she'd seen from higher up. The woods grew thick again as she got off the side of the mountain, and a fog spread upward where bats banked sharply through swarms of bugs that swirled in the moonlight.

The path leveled out but became rockier for a stretch, and Alice had to slow down and lift her feet higher with each step to avoid tripping on obstacles hidden in the darkness. The moon had shifted halfway across the sky when she came to the first source of water since coming down off the mountain, the trickle luring the ravenous thirst inside her. She found two stones to straddle and knelt to drink, sealing her cracked lips around the filter straw. A steady flow of water eventually trickled through, and she held the position in defiance of her screaming ribcage, making sure her belly was full before getting back on the trail.

Stomach growling, sore heels pounding the rocky earth, Alice began to make progress, readjusting to the shortness of breath and stabbing pains, holding her left arm against her side to discourage unnecessary movement. She began eating up the scree-covered trail yards at a time, the pain growing into one constant ache that pulsed throughout her body, warning her that if she didn't stop, it might be forced to take matters into its own hands. Sweaty strands of her hair clung to her face, and she hardly felt the insects crawling in her sweat, attempting to bite her and crawl up her nose. Only two things mattered: Jake and Sarah.

Alice could swear she could see the orange glow several times off the sides of the trail, nestled in a woody depression or behind a stone, but when she blinked, the color was gone, an illusion of hope in the vast wilderness. She tracked her time by the moon as it slid through the clouds, the puffy shapes breaking around it in feathery wisps that turned yellow when the light hit them. After what must've been an hour, she came to another stream that sat low in the landscape, forcing her to traverse a steep bank to reach the water's edge. It moved slower than the other with a stagnant, pond-sized depression off to her left. Alice stayed off to the right where the water ran quickly across the rocks, pausing again to drink all she could until her stomach couldn't hold any more. It was getting harder to draw it through the straw, a sure sign that the damage it had suffered was contributing to its rapidly diminished lifespan. Taking off her pack, she dug inside for the two empty plastic bottles and went to work sucking up more water, but instead of swallowing it, she spit mouthfuls of it into the bottles until they were full.

Screwing the caps back on and stowing them in her pack, Alice moved on in spite of her body's protests, baffled that she still had yet to come across the fire. Hoofprints were still occasionally visible on the ground, so she was on the right track, but the distance must have been farther than she originally thought. Up on the ridge, it had seemed close, not easily attainable but certainly closer than the length of trail she'd been walking.

Occasionally she stopped for a few moments to lean against a tree to catch her breath, her gasps so shallow she was sure her lungs would collapse at any moment. Sometimes she sat on a stone with her head in her hands, waiting for the cramps in her feet and calves to go away, the guilt growing with each moment that she stood still. As soon as she could, Alice got back on her feet and kept moving, losing track of the moon as the sky changed from a deep shade of night to somewhat of a fainter pale blue. As the sky's tint lightened, Alice grew worried that she might not see the fire and walk past it altogether, but with the morning light came a better view of the trail where the hoofprints were still clearly visible.

As the sun's first rays finally crested over the distant hills, Alice was beyond exhausted, skin scratched and itchy, bleeding from a few dozen different cuts. She could hardly walk anymore, resorting to dragging her throbbing heels along by the bowed walking stick, her right foot turned inward to keep her weight on the outside. She'd slowed to a near crawl, uncertain if another breath would come or whether she'd collapse on the trail and slowly decompose.

When she spotted a tendril of smoke rising off the right-hand side of the trail, it didn't register for several seconds, and she merely stood, staring at it until her brain finally caught up with what she was seeing and her body lurched into action. With a desperate grunt, she launched herself into motion, hobbling fast and reaching a flat circle of packed dirt with a large campfire still smoking in the center. Alice glanced over her shoulder, looking up to where she'd stood on the ridge hours before, confirming that the campfire was the same one she'd spotted from so far away.

Like the other campsite she'd come upon, a few logs had been drawn up for people to sit upon, and hoof prints and shoe prints cluttered the dirt and mud. Pieces of half-burned garbage sat in the bed of coals and ash, the packages singed but discernible enough for her to recognize that they had come from Sarah's and Jake's packs. With a delirious, choking sob, Alice turned in a circle, angry tears streaming down her cheeks as she clenched her fists in frustration.

"I barely missed you by..." she shook her head and sent tears dripping from her chin. "A few hours. At most. Dammit!"

Exhaustion and disappointment washed over her like a wave, and she struggled as a vision flashed through her head of the kids walking out of the forest with big smiles on their faces, hugging her and telling her they'd somehow gotten away from Mark and Christine. But, as much as she hated to think about it, the fact was that they weren't free, and were instead most likely tied up, barely being fed, and suffering under the same abuse that Mark and Christine's supposed children had already suffered.

"I've almost got you, you bastards," she growled, hardly recognizing the raspy, guttural sounds that came out of her throat. "You're going to be..." She coughed and gasped, swallowing a lump. "... so damn *sorry*."

Alice jammed the walking stick into the ground and started to get back on the trail and push on, but her wobbly legs betrayed her, threatening to drop her on the spot after taking two steps. She could barely move, much less walk who knew how many more miles.

Mouthing curses at her feeble body for failing her, she set her backpack on the ground and worked on the remnants of the fire, adding kindling to the coals and stirring them to life with her stick, then shuffling around and finding pieces of deadfall around the edge of the camp to toss in. Soon, the flames were flickering high as the wood crackled, and she again saw Sarah and Jake's faces. Tears broke free and stung her dirty cheeks, then a sob hitched from her throat, bringing with it a new wave of pain that rocketed up her side and locked her chest in a single, conjoined spasm that stole her breath away.

"Damn you..." Alice gasped, holding herself, grimacing as she sank onto a log.

When the spasm stopped, all she could imagine was doing unspeakable things to Mark and Christine, making them experience pain and anguish a thousand times over, letting them recover – and then starting all over again anew.

Licking her dry, cracked lips, Alice slouched and took an inventory of her injuries. There were more scratches on her arms than untouched skin, and when she touched the sore spots on her face, her fingers came back covered in bloody smears. Lifting her shirt, she was horrified to see the bruising had turned even darker, stretching across her entire chest. Pulling the backpack closer, she fished out her water bottles and popped one open, tilting it back, draining half of it in a few gulps.

She sat on a log sipping at the water for several minutes, letting the pain in her side recede a little, trying to calm herself and think straight, but there was nothing left to think about. She was so close to the kids she could practically feel them in her arms, but opening her eyes revealed only the fire and emptiness around her.

For the first time she could remember in days, her bladder needed relieving, and she went into the woods to spend several painful minutes trying to find a position that didn't feel like someone was sticking a knife into her chest. When she was done, it took her a full two minutes to wiggle into an upright position and get her pants buttoned, then she slowly hobbled her way back toward camp. By the time she was back, the sun had fully risen and was casting rays into the upper boughs, the shade recoiling as the light advanced across the forest floor. A group of three squirrels involved in some sort of squabble dashed through the campground, paying her no mind as they fought and squeaked before running off through the brush and up into trees to chatter at one another.

She sat there for some time, considering eating more of the MRE to bolster her strength, but ultimately deciding to leave it in case she – or one of the kids – needed it more later on. Without bothering to gather any pine needles or leaves, Alice slipped to the ground and laid down with twigs and stones poking into her back, her need for sleep smothering the faint desire for some comfort. As she lay and stewed in misery, Alice tried to remember the times from back on the farm with James and the kids, when they would bring in some crops or perform simple chores like mending fences or feeding the chickens. But her mood was too dark to change with some simple memories, and her thoughts came back to one simple point, obsessed with thoughts of things she wanted – no, not just wanted, but was *going* – to do to the people who'd stolen her children and tried to kill her.

"N-no mercy for you," she choked out. "No mercy, and no forgiveness. Nothing for you two. Y-you're going to die... and you d-don't even know it."

With a shuddering sigh, Alice fell into a troubled sleep as, deep within her a monster grew, rising from the pit of despair and anguish, sharpening its claws and gnashing its curved teeth as it awaited the moment when it might finally be unleashed.

CHAPTER SIX

James Burton
Merrillville, Indiana

James pedaled smoothly down the road, squeezing the spongy handgrips as he switched to a higher gear, leaned back on the seat, and cruised faster than he had since he'd ridden atop Amber to escape the motorcycles. The wind whipped past him, cool against his face as it pushed his hair back, energizing him and pushing him to greater speeds. The skies were still dark and cloudy, and gutters dripped with stagnant water but the rain was finally ending as the temperatures dropped from a cold front blowing through the region. A month prior, such a front would have been predicted down to the hour – or less – but weather forecasts of rainfall and cold fronts, while important, were the least of most peoples' worries.

James glanced over his shoulder as he cleared a field of debris with a slight bump, checking on his passenger. Oswell looked pale where she rode doggedly in the cargo wagon, her legs padded by a heavy jacket where they hung over the rail, her back supported by a small couch cushion they'd found in a dumpster. Her face was a constant grimace as the small cargo trailer bounced and swayed ceaselessly, its suspension not nearly as robust as the bike's, and James called out to her.

"How are you doing back there?"

"It's not my proudest moment." Oswell clung to the rails, resting on her left side on the pillow to ease the pressure on her hip. "How about you?"

"Doing great." James grinned. "This is a little like... well, like riding a bike. I feel like a kid again."

"I feel like an old lady." Oswell countered. "Everything is achy, especially my hip."

"Any change in the bleeding?"

"Not much since we changed the bandage. I'm surprised, what with all the bouncing back and forth."

"Don't worry. I'll have you in La Porte with your people in no time." James pointed at a sign coming up. "Look. Merrillville, ten miles."

"Can it be ten seconds, please?"

"Hang on. There's a straightaway ahead; I'll pick up the pace a little."

Oswell groaned and gripped the sides of the trailer harder, bracing for the uptick in bouncing and swaying as James put his head down and raised off his seat, switching into fifth gear and began pedaling harder. The wind swirled against him and howled in his ears, whipping his coat around his back. Highway 30 was a straight shot, with hundreds of roads interconnected to towns like Hartsdale and Schererville. It was a mix of big-city and small-town designs, peppering in new constructions with buildings that could have been a hundred years old. They all shared one thing in common, though: the charred remnants of vehicles flipped on their roofs, twisted sideways or buried in storefronts.

Tomb-like buildings rolled past them at breakneck speeds, tires zipping over the asphalt. An occasional shout or gunshot from the ruins broke the steady sound of the bike and trailer, cutting the dead air and reminding James that they were nowhere near safe, and he had to keep pedaling hard and fast. His legs were holding up remarkably well thanks to all of the walking he'd been doing, but the real test was starting to come down to calories and endurance, and he was burning through both of them trying to get to La Porte as fast as possible.

He'd been snacking all evening and into the morning on packs of honey-roasted cashews they'd found in a corner store, and kept eating a mouthful every fifteen or twenty minutes to keep his energy boosted, but his back was stiff and his legs had a deep, mild aching buzz in them. Oswell was in far worse shape, though, the jostling ride not doing her injuries any good, but her resilience had been on full display as a barrage of sarcastic quips continued to mask her pain.

James felt around in his pocket for the last bag of cashews, slowing down as they passed through an open space between buildings. After tearing the corner of the bag open, draining half of it, and swallowing, he grabbed a bottle of fruit punch from his other pocket, switched hands, and twisted the cap off with his thumb and index finger. He took two swallows and finished it off, tossed the bottle in a high arcing shot that landed in the backseat of a blown-up car.

"Look at this guy," Oswell laughed from behind him. "A regular Jordan!"

"I'd rather be Armstrong right now!"

"With or without the doping?"

"Ha!"

Highway 30 turned into Schererville's main thoroughfare, Joliet Street, and the roadsides grew thick with businesses. Restaurants flew by in large numbers, and he was tempted to turn in to one to see if there was anything left to eat, but any that were left standing had been ransacked several times over. As a chain hotel came by on the right, he thought about stopping to try and find a mattress to load onto the trailer to make Oswell more comfortable, but the doors on the bottom floor were broken in with bedspreads and pillows pulled out and strewn across the parking lot. TVs and drawers were lying broken and scattered amongst the fabrics, and mattresses had been dragged out and left to soak in the rain. When a man stumbled out of a room with a bottle of whiskey in one hand and a pistol in the other, James stood up and pedaled faster, blowing by him as he shouted and fired haplessly, missing the pair by a country mile.

"Did you see that guy?" Oswell called up.

"How could I miss him? Looks like he turned over every room in that place."

"I wouldn't mind lying down in a real bed." Oswell drew ragged breaths, speaking in a hitched, halting tone. "My hip is really screaming."

"We'll rest soon, maybe somewhere past Schererville, okay?"

"Wherever's safe; you're the boss."

The highway split in two, leaving a thin grassy median between the strips of asphalt. Around them spread a concrete jungle with restaurants, hotels, and shops, their parking lots brimming with piles of wreckage and corpses that had soaked and liquified in the rain, turning into streams of charcoal runoff.

A massive department store appeared on the left, the lot swarming with dozens of refugees – the most they'd seen since the gangs – who were gathered toward the front. People dragged suitcases behind them and wore wet backpacks on their shoulders, bouncing children in their arms or holding their hands as they looked at the two big green military tents with *Indiana National Guard* stenciled on the sides in bold lettering.

"Hey, Oswell. You see what I see?"

She hung over the side rail and squinted. "Yeah, I see it."

"Are those your people?"

"I don't see any trucks, but maybe they pulled them around back. Or maybe they got stranded somewhere like my group did."

"Want me to pull up and check it out?"

"Yeah, it might be worth a look."

James pulled through the intersection, cruised to the turn-in, and cut between two restaurants, hoping to come out up front on the right side near the tents. Thirty people stood in the entry lane, marching along like zombies, glancing at them as they went by, most with dead expressions except for a couple who saw the bike and edged in their direction. It wasn't until James was almost up to the end of the lane that he saw the poor shape of the facility. The hastily constructed tents were torn and sagging, and most of the security ropes and chains had been cut or pushed to the side. Men with guns stood at the entrances dressed in blue jeans and leather jackets, more than a few wearing motorcycle helmets with dark visors pulled over their faces. Whatever was inside the tents, they guarded it with force, a few of them shoving a pair of adults to the ground, threatening them, and cracking them in the faces with their gun stocks.

A man at the back of the line in front of the tents pointed at James and Oswell and tapped another man in the chest. "Hey... hey, we can grab that bike and make a trade! They'll give us food for that, I bet!"

Dozens of eyes turned in their direction, measuring them up, edging toward them to cut them off and a man and woman trotted toward them while the first two men shoved them back with a shout. "Hey, the bike's ours! We claimed it first!"

Oswell slapped the side of the trailer and James shouted back at her. "I'm on it!"

James did a quick turnaround, blowing by a few curious people who'd stopped to measure their chances of knocking him off and taking the bike and their supplies. Others flew at them outright, feet pounding the pavement behind them as James bore down on the pedals, a panicky burst of adrenaline fueling his legs as he shot past them back toward the entrance.

"Stop him!" A woman jumped in his way and tried to grab the handlebars, but James growled, sticking out his left foot and driving her back.

"Out of the way! Oswell, watch out!"

A man rushed in from the right and grabbed the cargo trailer rail, jerking it and trying to tip it over. Oswell punched and scratched at his arms, knocking him off so he toppled over on the pavement. The man's weight had slowed them down, though, and James swung back and forth, leaning on the pedals to get them moving again. A half dozen more people were coming in from the sides, crouching to grab the handlebars, hungry to knock James off and take the bike for their own.

James plunged his hand into his pocket and pulled out his pistol and the first man he aimed at threw his hands up and backed off, but someone on the left stepped right in front of him, a big man with a ghoulish grin, teeth bared and sneering as James sped toward him. James shifted his aim and fired when they were ten yards apart, sending a round through the man's shoulder with an ear-splitting report. The man stood in dumbfounded shock, but he didn't move, and James fired again, hitting him in the breastbone, the man's grin wiped clean as he staggered and fell to his knees, pitching sideways right in James' way. He swerved the bike over at the last second, barely getting by, Oswell clinging to the rails and throwing her weight around to keep herself from tipping.

James sped across the turnaround lane, spitting gravel beneath his tires as he tried to turn east onto the highway. People sprinted to cut them off, so he altered his course and stayed south on a road that connected several major stores. The pavement tilted downward, allowing James to sit back and catch his breath as he put more distance between them and their pursuers who finally stopped chasing them and gestured rudely instead, cupping their hands over their mouths and shouting obscenities at them. Breathless and pumped full of adrenaline, James followed the road to where it connected with Wicker Avenue, flying through the junction and welcoming the sight of abandoned businesses with no crowds once again.

"Nice pedaling, James," Oswell said.

"Nice fighting," he replied breathlessly. "That went south pretty quick."

"It's almost as bad as the city was."

"Yeah, no kidding. From now on, no more crowds or main highways... and no towns. The back roads take longer, but we'll stick to them from now on. Hey, check the compass and let's make sure we're still heading east."

Oswell pulled the top portion of James' staff from beneath her and held it aloft, keeping the knob on the end with the compass in it steady against the bumping and swaying of the trailer. "We're heading due south right now. I'd say take your first left, assuming it looks safe."

"Does anything really look safe these days?" James laughed as he turned onto a street, entering a long straight lane of neighborhoods.

A desolate landscape of houses and shells of burned-up vehicles stretched before them, a sight he was growing uncomfortably used to. Large oaks dotted the lawns in front of the remnants of the houses, most of them blackened all the way up their trunks, with a smattering of leaves still intact on some of the upper boughs. There were no signs of people, though, the residents either hunkered down inside their houses or having moved off to other areas – like the shopping area he and Oswell had just vacated.

On a section of flat, empty road, James relied on the natural balance provided by the attached trailer to remove his hands from the handlebars and reload his revolver from a box of bullets in one of his pockets. When he was done, he clicked the cylinder shut, stuck both the gun and bullets back in his pocket, and relaxed with his hands on the handlebars and his head on a constant swivel. The next two hours were primarily flat riding, alternating between hard peddling and coasting as they maneuvered through desolate neighborhoods which turned into farmland as the miles progressed. Soon, they'd left Schererville behind and entered quiet country roads with woods and farms surrounding them.

Oswell moaned and grimaced with every tiny bump, clutching her stomach and side, looking pale with discomfort, sickly and feverish, and on the verge of throwing up.

"Are you okay back there?"

"My leg and hip are just *killing* me…" She gasped. "I've never hurt so much in all my life."

"Let's stop, then." James was already looking for a place off the side of the road. "We'll get you a couple of hours' rest and try again later."

Oswell shook her head. "No. We said we'd go until night. I'll be fine until then. It's just pain. I'm not bleeding."

"Are you sure?"

"Yeah, I'm sure. Keep pedaling, James. You watch the road, I'll try to tamp down on the groans."

"I'm on it. You let me know if you need to stop, though, understand?"

Oswell nodded but stayed quiet, bearing through the pain with only a grimace and an occasional readjustment of her position to betray what she was going through. While James appreciated her courage, he was beginning to worry about her, questioning whether she had sustained internal injuries that she wasn't telling him about – or was unaware of herself. Still, he kept his head down and pedaled faster, ignoring his own aches and pains and focusing on making progress.

Soon, after miles of farmland, he spotted a church at an intersection on the right. It was an old building with a red brick front and sides and a peaked roof that had burned up and collapsed, the rectory a mere skeleton of blackened beams and framing. Parked behind it was an ancient Dodge Ram van with its windows shattered and scorch marks wrapping up around the roof. The fire's path was clear, leading from the van to the rectory and over the church's spine, leaving destruction in its wake. Only the front of the building and bell tower survived, the red brick standing up to the flames and suffering a few singe marks and crumbling mortar.

The worrisome matter was the congregation gathered outside, a dozen people kneeling in the mud, heads bowed as a preacher stood at the top of the front steps, his suitcoat and white shirt stained with sweat and dirt, sweating as he shouted and gesticulated.

"Repent, repent! I'm here to call you all to repent. Know that it was God who brought down the world. It was *He* who did this. We are witnessing the downfall of a sinful world where the wicked once ruled and are now being punished!"

As James drew closer, he spotted several bodies of men, women, and children with suitcases and belongings scattered around them lying in the front parking lot of the church, near the parishioners. Their clothes were bloodstained and their scalps crusted with bloody hair that covered gashes and cracked skulls, evidence of some sort of brutal treatment. James pumped the pedals harder to try and skirt around the place, but the preacher heard the whirring of wheels and the low clack of the cargo trailer's axle as they clattered up, and he met James' eyes over the distance.

"Not good," James muttered.

The preacher waved the Bible in their direction and screamed at the top of his lungs. "There are more of the *sinners*! There they go in defiance of God! Get them and bring them to their knees!"

The congregation turned and struggled to their feet, confused at first, haggard faces twisting with anger, tortured eyes glaring with malice and violent hatred. When they saw it wasn't two people on foot but riding on a bike and cargo trailer, they went from walking to running in an instant. Surrounded by fences, ditches and trees on both sides of the road, James had no driveways or side lanes to take, and no escape from the quickly closing mob.

"Here we go!" James called back. "Get ready, Oswell."

"Can you turn around?"

"There's no time for that! I'm going straight past them! Hang on!"

James strained against the pedals, forcing them forward, clicking up two gears to grab every bit of torque he could. While the crowd came at them with bared teeth, they ran slow and flatfooted, unable to efficiently close the distance across the church yard and parking lot to cut them off. The first group missed him but lunged for Oswell, and she swung the top portion of his staff at the reaching hands, breaking fingers and knuckles with the crack of metal on bone, forcing them back with yowls and curses. James swerved wide to the left, tires crunching on the narrow shoulder and barely getting around the woman who'd been in the lead as she dove for them. Oswell punched the top of the staff into the woman's chest and redirected her behind them, tripping her up and causing her to fall face first on the asphalt, skidding along on her palms and face. James checked his side mirror as the crowd milled into the road, the preacher filtering toward the front, raising his Bible, pointing, and shouting something James couldn't hear.

He turned back to the road just in time to brace himself as they plowed through a debris field, the bike tires cracking over pieces of plastic and metal, crushing a headlamp before swerving to avoid hitting a fender. The cargo trailer shook violently, rattling Oswell and almost tipping her over twice, then they were through the worst of it and back on smooth pavement again, pedaling hard to put distance between themselves and the church crowd. The handlebars were wobbling, and James craned his neck to see a slight bend in the front rim that was rubbing against the brakes.

"You okay back there?"

"Yeah, I'm fine..." Oswell gasped as she readjusted in her seat, pulling the backpack in behind her for extra padding and settling back with the upper section of the staff resting across her lap. "They weren't kidding when they made these things. Should've given 'em to us, too, not just you civilians."

"When we get to that outpost, I'll ask for another one and get them to engrave it for you."

"Bite me, Burton."

James chuckled. "Speaking of, are we still heading east?"

"Yep."

"It's getting late, and my legs are killing me. I'll find us a place to stop soon. Just hang on a little longer, okay?"

"Thank heavens. I'm pretty sure my hip is about to fall off of me."

James adjusted his grip on the handlebars and pedaled on, devouring the miles slowly but surely as the land faded into Indiana backcountry. It was getting dark when the country road wove them between close-pressed woods with only a few homesteads and barns sitting off the roadside. Before long, the moon had risen enough to pierce the gaps in the clouds and light the road, shining on the telephone poles and wires that hung low to the ground. After passing a few run-down farmsteads, James spotted an old barn off to the right with faded sides and a roof riddled with holes and rotting wood. He banked onto a dirt path overgrown with weeds, pedaling over ruts and rocks out past a rusted tractor with its wheels buried in the mud.

"Are you trying to finish me off back here or what?!"

"Sorry!"

A minute later, James squeezed the brakes and brought them to a stop in front of the barn. Out behind it was an old fence with rusted wire and rotted rails, entire sections of it broken and overgrown, and built into the barn walls were windows with broken glass and two collapsed stalls at the end.

"Give me a second to check it out. Stay here."

James put his kickstand down, took the revolver and flashlight out of his pocket, and moved off to his left around the first corner. Virginia creepers crawled up the side, and long grasses grew high along the base. There was a wide-open entryway with no door, and he shined his flashlight inside to reveal a dirt floor, stacks of hay bales, and a glimpse of barrels lined up in rows. A rusted cage was outside along the back of the barn divided up into several sections with food and water bowls and leashes half-buried in the dirt, and the last portion of the barn had a few dozen wooden slats lying on the ground with rusted nails sticking up.

Coming back around to the front of the structure, James found Oswell curled on her left side with her head bowed, and he hurried to her side, looking around as he spoke. "Hey, hey, you okay? What happened?"

"Well," she laughed haltingly. "I finally found a comfortable position is what happened."

James laughed. "I hate to get you up, but I think this place looks good. I saw some hay bales we can use as bedding, and there's plenty of dry wood around to start a fire. Come on, let's get you up. I want to look at that wound as soon as possible."

Oswell nodded, taking James' hand with an iron grip as she struggled to stand, and a moment later he was supporting her weight and turning her toward the barn. They walked up to the main double doors and stood in the entryway, and James flipped on his flashlight and shined it around. Off to the right were three barrels with loose, rotting hay bales sitting on top while farm implements hung from hooks, and dusty piles of refuse were scattered around on the floor or hanging crookedly from nails and hooks on the walls. A pile of decorative stones, boxes of tiles, and smaller barrels with rusted hoops sat off to the left, and James motioned to where one hay bale had fallen over, broken apart, and spread across the floor.

"Come on, let's get you laid down on that, then I'll use those stones to make a fire circle so we don't burn the place down."

He guided her inside and left her leaning against a pole while he grabbed their things. Putting a blanket and clothes over the spilled hay, he helped her sit and turn over into her comfortable position before hauling stones over to create the fire circle on the dirt floor. Using wooden planks, he formed a pyramid shape with hay for kindling in the center, then he removed the flint and one of the knives from his staff, squatting beside the stone circle, leaning in, and flicking the pieces together to shoot sparks into the dry hay. Soon, a bit of smoke drifted up, and he blew on it harder to coax out some flames. After a few moments of work blowing between the slats, he got the fire going in earnest, tendrils of orange licking up and caressing the wood and giving off a wave of heat.

"There we go, Oswell. Come on and get closer, see if you can get yourself dried off some."

She scooted herself closer, with James spreading more hay around and adjusting the blankets to make a soft place for her to lie on. Oswell stretched out on her left side, resting on her elbow and keeping her right leg straight.

"You okay there?"

"Best hospital I could imagine being in, Dr. Burton."

James snorted, sitting down to start unlacing his wet, mud-caked boots. "I never was one for being called 'doctor' so don't you start giving me any lip. C'mon, get your boots off so we can see how bad our trench foot is."

"Feels like I've been walking around in sacks of water for days now." Oswell tried to reach her boots but fell back with a frustrated gasp and a groan of pain.

"Just sit back and stop aggravating your wounds. I've got the boots."

James unlaced her boots and tried to pull them off, but they were stuck to her feet, forcing him to jiggle them until they came off with a wet squelch. He placed them next to the fire while she peeled her socks off and swung her feet around to put them in front of the fire.

"That feels amazing," she sighed. "No sign of trench foot, either."

James sat opposite her with his boots and socks off, rolling back and putting his heels up to the fire while he checked his toes and bottoms of his feet before sighing wearily.

"Same here. They look like prunes, but I think we're in the clear." Groaning, he sat back up and scooted closer to Oswell. "Before you get comfortable, though, I need to check your wounds."

James got the first-aid kits out of his pack and brought them around, pulling up Oswell's shirt, wincing at the bloody bandage which was leaking all down her side. He gently peeled it off, the flickering firelight showing the puckered entrance wound with a bit of yellowish fluid seeping out.

"You've got an infection in your hip wound." James sat back and shook his head.

"That's what I was afraid of." Oswell leaned over, trying to get a look at it. "It's been hurting too much to just be from the ride."

Shifting to her leg, James inspected the entrance wound where the tourniquet was still wrapped tight, keeping the bleeding to a minimum. When he removed the bandages and rolled-up gauze, he didn't find any puss or signs of infection, and a bit of scabbing was even taking place around the edges of the wound.

"Looks like we were lucky with the leg but not so much with the hip. Thankfully it's only a few more hours' ride to La Porte, and then we'll get you some real medical attention. In the meantime, I'll clean these and re-dress them, and you can take a couple of pain pills and aspirin to help with any fever that might come.

Oswell nodded and turned over, gritting her teeth as James rifled through his things to get the medical supplies out. "Thank you, again. You didn't have to do this."

"The heck I didn't." He chuckled and began setting aside pieces of gauze, bandages, a rag, saline, and antiseptic cream. "How do you think I'd look my wife and kids in the eye and tell them I abandoned someone to die just to save my own skin?"

"They'd probably tell you you were being smart. You could be home by now."

"Yeah, well, the right thing is rarely the easy thing. Doesn't mean we shouldn't do it. Hold still, I'm going to open this up, see if I can't get some of this puss out." James squirted some saline into her infected wound, squeezing and pulling on it to wash out the yellow fluid.

Oswell ground her teeth together, fists clenching and unclenching as he worked. "Good *grief* that hurts like a—"

"Sorry. Should be better now." He tossed a stained rag into the fire and applied a heavy dose of antiseptic cream inside and around the wound, then piled on gauze and taped everything up. When he was done, he gave her a gallon jug with a bit of water swishing around and had her take a couple of NSAID pills and aspirin.

"Thank you. I feel better already. And look, right or wrong, I really do—"

"Oswell, I get it. You're welcome, okay?" James laughed. "Now simmer down, try to find a comfortable position to rest in and stop telling me how much you appreciate being alive before I jam a stick into that hole in your side."

As Oswell chuckled, James took his socks and boots and set them to dry next to Oswell's, then he sat opposite her on a rock and put his feet up on the stone circle to let the flames warm them. They sat in silence for a short while, listening to the crackling wood and letting the heat radiate around them. When the fire got low, James gathered more dry rotted pieces of the barn's walls and ceiling, talking as he worked.

"Ideally we'd rest here until morning, but I'm worried about letting that infection go for that long. Let's rest for a few hours but get back on the road before morning. If we push hard, we can make it there by daybreak."

"That's fine. I just need a few hours outside that cargo trailer, and I'll be fine. If there's such a thing as an *anti*-suspension, that sucker has it."

James grinned and placed more wooden planks in the fire, stirring the coals with a tire iron he'd found among some rusty tools hanging from hooks in a corner. "It's not a Cadillac, that's for sure."

Once the flames were roaring again, he wrapped his arms around his knees and stared into it. "This is a great fire. I only wish we had some real food to cook over it. We have only a can of corn and a bag of honey-roasted cashews. Hardly fine dining, but—"

"Wait a second..." Oswell grabbed for her jacket and opened a side pocket, pulling out a can and waving it triumphantly.

"No way! Where did you get that?"

"I forgot to tell you, but I found it in the same store we found the cashews. I put it in my pocket and kept looking for other stuff but didn't find anything."

"Well, toss it over."

She did, and James caught it and read the label. "A pound of cooked ham, with maple flavoring. Not bad, Oswell. Not bad at all. I officially nominate you for a Medal of Honor."

Great," she laughed. "My parents will be so proud."

James searched for something to cook it on, finally settling on a thin piece of aluminum he found over by the farm implements. He gathered more stones and stacked them opposite each other on the circle, placing the metal sheet on top so the flames licked up around the sides. After a few moments, he flipped the sheet over and scraped off the burned residue to make a semi-clean surface, then used one of the knives from his staff to open the cans and put them on the new cooking sheet, then settled back and waited for them to warm.

"What will we eat with?" Oswell asked.

"I think I saw something over by the tools." James went over and picked out a couple of slim pieces of scrap steel about four inches long and two inches wide. "I'll clean these off and sanitize them in the fire. We can probably use them like spoons... sort of."

"Sounds good to me."

James used a rag and a little water to clean them off and rested them on the edge of the stone circle with the eating ends pointed inward over the flames. After a while, when the liquid in the cans began to bubble and steam was rolling out of them, he used his semi-dry socks to protect his hands as he moved the cans and utensils and set them aside to let them cool. Oswell took one of the pieces of steel and the can of corn and tried to eat from it, but the steel was nearly useless, and she was only able to get a few kernels in at a time.

"Maybe just eat directly from the can? Tilt it up and scoop it in your mouth? I wouldn't drink the juice, though; that stuff's salty as all get-out."

Oswell nodded and ate half the can, handing it over to him before moving on to the ham. James finished off the corn and threw the empty can into the fire, then broke out the last of the cashews. He ate his portion and traded her for the ham, the meager amount of food more than enough for them to fill their shrunken stomachs.

"That's the most food I've had since I was with the Amish," he said, tossing the second can into the flames along with the cashew packet.

Oswell slowly moved back onto her side, grimacing as she stretched her legs back out into a comfortable position. "I bet you ate like a king with them, eh?"

"Yeah, it was crazy how much they had with them even though they were on the move."

She chuckled and shifted on the hay bed as a drizzle started up, pattering gently on the roof and raining in through the holes, the droplets sparkling in the light of the fire as the smoke curled up through the same holes the rain entered.

"Go ahead and get some rest," James said. "I'll keep watch for a while."

"Don't worry about keeping watch," Oswell replied, unsuccessfully stifling a yawn. "No one's coming out here in this rain. We're a million miles away from anything."

"Maybe, but I don't want to take any chances. We're so close, and I don't want to screw it up by taking our foot off the gas, or the bike pedal." He grabbed the tire iron and stirred the coals, coaxing out more heat. "Once I get you settled in at La Porte, it shouldn't take me long to get back home. I just hope..." His eyes watered and he choked up for a moment. "I just hope my wife and kids made it back."

"If they're anything like you," Oswell yawned, her words slurring slightly as her eyelids drooped. "Then they're doing just fine."

"From your mouth to..." A snore cut through James's words, and he smiled and shook his head. "Okay, I'll stop talking."

He stood and walked barefoot to the front double doors, squeezing between them and checking outside. The road was empty and the fields and trees swayed in the wind and rain, the area filled with a quiet peacefulness that showed no sign of hidden malice. There were too many entrances into the barn to guard, though, and no string or rope available with which to set alarms. Still, he cracked the front doors and wedged a pair of stones on top so that if someone opened them, one or both would hopefully drop on the intruders' heads. It might not hurt them much, but it would at least wake him up.

James went outside through the side door, gathering some loose nail-filled boards and placing them beneath the windows with the nails pointing upward. Rolling a barrel over to the side door, he blocked it and piled random pieces of wood and tin on top to make it harder for anyone to get in. If they tried, they were bound to knock something off and wake him up with the clatter – an imperfect solution, but the best he could do given the circumstances.

Standing in the middle of the barn with the crackling fire and glistening drizzle, he inspected his traps and nodded in satisfaction. He gathered up some hay and placed his coat on top, making a bed for himself opposite Oswell. Gun in hand, he laid down and stared up at the smokey rafters, listening to his body's complaints about his sore legs and aching back, a slight headache and a runny nose adding to the weariness he felt down into his very bones.

But his belly was full, and the fire had driven back the cold chill that had gripped him all day. Most of all, he was so close to home he could practically feel Alice in his arms, the kids buzzing to tell him what they'd been doing, and Ryan and Helen smiling with relief that the family was reunited once again. The thoughts couldn't hold a candle to his exhaustion, though, and the next time his eyes closed he was gone, succumbing to the sleep he so desperately needed.

***

James woke to a gentle roll of thunder and the steady *tink* of water dripping onto the aluminum sheet, then sizzling away into nothingness. He rose to his elbows and blinked at the moonlight filtering in through the gaps in the roof. The barn was dark, and the fire had died down to glowing coals that gave off a steady warmth without the accompanying light of a roaring fire. He rolled over and got to his knees, groaning at the soreness in his legs and back. Back home, before everything had gone to hell in a bobsled, a long day of physical labor would be wrapped up with a dose of painkillers to help reduce inflammation and soreness. Such niceties were mere memories, though, as any medication they found would have to be saved for dire circumstances, not the relief of muscle aches.

Around him, the shadows in the barn were quite different in the moonlight, casting strange shapes that stood in the corners or behind the hay bales. The barrel, pieces of wood and the stones above the main door still stood undisturbed in the side entrance, and there were no other sounds but the steady drip of rain and the rustle of leaves and grasses outside.

Shifting positions, James grabbed the tire iron and stirred the coals, throwing a few pieces of wood in amongst them and kicking the flames to life to chase away the dark shapes around him. Oswell lay where he'd left her, still on her left side but looking paler, with a glistening sheen of sweat covering her face. He went over and placed his palm against her forehead, shaking his head at the heat coming off her.

She stirred, moaned, and blinked up at him. "James?"

"Yeah, it's me. Everything's fine, but you've got a fever. Feels like a bad one."

"I...was hoping... that wouldn't happen."

"How do you feel?"

"About... about the same..." She started to get up but fell back with groan. "Actually, I'm not feeling so good at all."

"We've got to go now, then. We need to get you to La Porte ASAP." James took two of the pain pills he'd been tempted to consume from the first-aid kits and handed her those along with the water jug. "Take these and drink the rest of this."

Oswell accepted them wearily, then paused mid-drink. "What about you?"

"Don't worry about me. We need to get fluid in you to keep your strength up. Stay here a minute, and I'll get the cargo trailer packed up."

"But—"

"Zip it; I don't want to hear any arguments."

James stuffed the first-aid kits into the backpack and folded the blankets, pushing open the front doors and watching the stones he'd placed on top thud to the ground. Outside, he arranged everything in the cargo trailer to make the ride as comfortable as possible for Oswell. As he worked, Oswell coughed and hacked inside the barn, her lungs rattling with phlegm. The bike's front rim was still warped, and the fork had a slight bend in it, though there wasn't much he could do about it but ride as gingerly as possible to avoid any more damage. All packed up and ready, James returned to get Oswell, helping her up, and giving her the assembled staff to lean on, guiding her outside. She moved sluggishly, tripping and leaning all her weight on him, climbing clumsily into the trailer before falling heavily into her seat with a grunt.

"Thank... you," she slurred, eyelids fluttering as she tried to keep them open.

"Don't thank me yet. We've still got a ways to go."

James pushed the bike along the dirt driveway until they reached the road, then he swung them east and hopped on, pedaling and clinging to the trembling handlebars. They rode through the moonlit darkness, bypassing Valparaiso by skirting south around the city and striking northeast on Highway 2. The streets were quiet, the rain light and cool as it sprinkled on them, though the bike's wobbling progressively worsened with every mile they rode.

Soon, James struggled to pedal, forced to put twice the energy into it and stick to the higher gears. Oswell wasn't faring much better, her coughing growing worse, rattling her chest with every fit that gripped her. Along one stretch of road, she stopped coughing altogether, and James pulled over to check on her, finding that she'd passed out while clenching her fists beneath her chin, shivering, teeth chattering like it was the middle of winter. Her forehead was on fire, and James dampened a rag in a nearby puddle and placed it on her head to try and cool her down before rearranging the blankets to keep her stable and secure.

Back on the bike, he kicked off again and pedaled even harder, the handlebars rattling his arms and shoulders and nearly shaking out of his hands. The bike was shifting and shaking as the rim rubbed the brakes, and the front end got wobblier and looser, then something clattered in the chains, loud and obnoxious as he winced, hoping the thing would hold together and not attract any unnecessary attention.

"Hey, Oswell," he said, pointing to an upcoming sign. "You with me?"

"I... think so..."

"Check it out. La Porte in three miles."

"Gr... Great," she said and coughed.

"Can you direct me to the outpost from here?"

Oswell shifted into a sitting position and wiped at her face, trying to clear away her bleary-eyed confusion. "Where are we now?"

"Highway 2, heading northeast."

"Just stay on Highway 2, and that'll get us there. You'll... see signs... I'll... try to help... watch..."

She trailed off, and James nodded, focusing on the road again. "Take it easy, Oswell. I can do that."

The highway curved to the right past wide-open fields and farmland, the wind sweeping the drizzle around to form a spray that soaked through his clothing and chilled his legs. As the aches in his body grew, he bore down harder over the handlebars, keeping his eyes pinned to the straight line in the center of the road, fighting with the bicycle's shaking and rattling for control.

Without warning, there was a metallic snap and the bike chain flew off, his legs suddenly spinning out of control for a few seconds with the resistance of the chain removed. Something in the front wheel gave out afterward and the front end collapsed, pitching him forward and nearly throwing him over the handlebars, the pull of the trailer the only thing keeping the bike upright. They ground to a halt in the middle of the road and James hopped off, whispering a prayer of thanks that he hadn't painted the road with his face. While he was no bike mechanic, a quick glance revealed that the front tire had broken in three places and the wheel was sitting loose between the spokes, impossible for him to fix without a new front tire. Even if he'd had a replacement, though, there was still the problem of the broken chain that dangled from the rear tire's gears, chewed up and missing a few links.

"What's wrong?" Oswell asked in a shaky voice. "Why... why'd we stop?"

"It looks like we're in trouble." James put the kickstand up and let the bike lean to the left. "The front end is screwed up. The tire's completely broken, and the chain snapped too."

"I guess... we're walking."

"Sure looks like it. Can you make it?"

"No choice. How many... miles do we have left?"

"We were at three miles a little while ago. I think it's maybe three-quarters of a mile away from here?"

"I can... make it. Help me up."

Stuffing the blankets and extra clothes into the backpack, James shouldered it and held out his hand for Oswell, pulling her from the trailer. She fell against him and clung to his neck with barely any strength left.

He rechecked her forehead. "Yep, you're burning up. We need to get you there *now*."

James reached inside the cargo trailer and got his staff, handing it to her and making sure she could keep some semblance of balance before they moved down the road. They started slow and stayed that way, Oswell's boot on her injured side scraping the pavement in a steady, agonizing rhythm. After fifty yards, she was barely holding her weight anymore, bowing him over and dragging him down.

"S-Sorry, James," she murmured.

"Don't be."

"I am."

"We'll make it."

"You should... leave me."

"Shut up and focus. One foot in front of the other. You didn't come this far just to fail everyone."

"E-everyone?"

"Captain Lister, Lieutenant Washington... Rodriguez, Pugh, Wiseman, Witkowski. Their sacrifices won't mean jack if you don't make it. And the only way you're going to make it is if we get to the outpost. You hear me?"

"Yeah... I hear you," Oswell replied, her left arm strengthening around his neck, back stiffening as she got her foot off the ground.

They picked up the pace and soon reached a La Porte National Guard sign indicating the outpost was just ahead. Off to the left, the La Porte County Fairgrounds stretched out in a wide-open area divided up by multiple roads. On the right were neighborhoods, motels, and a church, all having suffered heavy fire damage. The outpost was on the left in the middle of a large parking lot with the remnants of a few vehicles and scattered debris and the gatehouse building was a dark squarish shape with two tall flagpoles in front, the brick wall stretching thirty yards to either side before turning into fencing with barbed wire strung on top.

"Do you see anyone?" Oswell asked.

The moon had fled behind gathering clouds, obscuring everything in darkness and gloom, forcing him to squint to see anything as they stopped at the edge of the lot.

"There aren't any lights on, and I don't see anyone out back. Looks like no one's home. Come on, let's go check it out. Maybe there's someone inside who can help us."

"I don't... don't think so..."

"Just come on. If nobody's home, we'll figure it out our own damn selves. Move your ass!"

They hobbled up to the gate which stood partially open with a guardhouse off to the left. James stepped through first and helped Oswell slide in, walking her inside the guardhouse and placing her in a chair. Papers and forms littered the floor, and a table had been turned over, spilling radio equipment and equipment everywhere.

"Stay here for a minute and rest," he turned the table back up, pushing it close to her. "I'll go look for help."

Oswell nodded and slouched forward, breathing heavily as she laid her head and arms on the table. James stepped outside and jogged into a courtyard surrounded by the dark shapes of buildings and flat concrete lots with smaller squares that might have once been armored vehicles parked in them.

"Hello?!" he called. "Is anyone here? I've got a wounded guardswoman who needs medical attention immediately! *Hey!* Anyone home?!"

No one responded, leaving James standing in the middle of the lot with his hands on his hips, unsure of where to go to keep searching. The cloud cover shifted a few seconds later and moonlight broke through to spread across the outpost, chasing away the shadows and exposing the true horrors of the devastation around him.

Out of a dozen buildings, at least half had been destroyed by fires that left scorch marks on bricks and skeletons of crossbeams and two-by-fours. The worst sight was the bodies, though, sprawled out around the buildings and across the open spaces, some on their backs but most face-down on the pavement. All of them were surrounded by dark patches of what he assumed were blood, a mix of green and camouflage fatigues and civilian street clothes, and all riddled with bullet holes or showing signs of having been burned alive, leaving the stench of death drifting on the wind.

"Oh, no." James whispered, his stomach twisting into knots, reaching for his pistol as he half-expected some monster in the darkness to spring out upon him, adding his body to its collection.

After calming himself down with a series of slow, deep breaths, he started walking amongst the bodies, searching for any signs of life. Pallets of supplies sat in random spots around the lot, plastic torn off of them, their stacks of goods long since raided. The largest cluster of pallets sat in front of a pair of warehouse bay doors that had been rolled up to reveal more provisions inside, though those too had not been spared.

Most of the buildings that hadn't gone up in flames had their doors hanging off their hinges and windows shattered, with garbage and supply packaging scattered inside and out. The trash fluttered as the wind kicked up, the haunting sounds eliciting the feeling of a ghost town – albeit, one with a much higher chance of actual ghosts than most. Remembering Oswell, James turned and jogged back to the guardhouse where she still lay across the table, her breathing erratic and the edges of her lips starting to turn blue.

He straightened her and gently slapped her cheeks. "Oswell? Still with me, Oswell? Hey..."

James started to lift her into his arms when the chair shifted and nearly rolled out from under them.

"It's got wheels? Thank heavens for small favors." He gently placed her back in the chair and adjusted her so that she slumped to one side with one foot tucked beneath her.

Getting behind her, James pushed the chair through the guardhouse door and rolled her across the pavement as the wheels creaked and groaned over being taken across such inhospitable terrain. After slamming over ruts and almost tipping Oswell out of the chair twice, James angled into a central lane that cut between the buildings toward the back of the compound. Taking his flashlight from his pocket, he flipped it on and shined it at the burned-out ruins in search of anything that might have medical supplies, but the buildings were looted clean. At the end of the lane, his flashlight beam fell across a brick building with a tall metal flagpole and a US flag whipping in the wind where a sign on the front read *Indiana National Guard Administration, La Porte, Indiana.*

"The glass is still intact. Maybe it's got something we can use." He rolled her up the walkway to the glass double doors, turning her, and pushing his back against the doors to shove them open.

Leaving Oswell in her chair, he shone his light around the lobby area, which had a front desk and chairs lined up along the walls. Slipping behind the desk, he rifled through papers and checked cabinets, finding two large metal flashlights that dwarfed his. When he popped one on, the light was bright, cutting through the gloom. James continued his search and found two first-aid kits in a drawer, placing them on the counter before moving into a hallway with several doors, one labeled as a restroom and another a supply closet.

He pushed into the closet and rifled through shelves of cleaning products, orange cones, mop buckets, and boxes of forms and paperwork. His flashlight beam lit upon a separate cabinet hanging from the back wall with a big red cross on the front, and he rushed over and popped both doors open to find a pair of thick, oversized medical kits with dozens of pockets and a big central compartment. James grabbed one and hauled it off the shelf, the weight almost ripping it from his hands. Heading back to Oswell, he found her still slumped over in the chair, sprawled with one arm hanging over the side.

Sitting her up straight, he put his ear close to her nose to ensure she was breathing and tried shaking her lightly to wake her up. "Oswell... are you with me? *Oswell!?*"

When she didn't respond, he grabbed seat cushions from the waiting room chairs and placed them on the floor behind the front desk. He wheeled her around, lifted her from the chair, and laid her down, then swung the trauma kit and his backpack onto the desk and dug out the blankets and extra clothes to elevate her head and cover her up. The first-aid kit held a huge array of supplies: rolls of gauze and cloth tape, isopropyl alcohol wipes, antibiotic ointment, and cold packs. Grabbing a cold pack, he shook the contents and rubbed it vigorously before placing it on her forehead.

"Now, we need something for that infection."

He rifled through the kit for antibiotic pills, but instead found an IV bag filled with clear fluid and labeled as *Cefazolin* along with a brief explanation that it was a broad-spectrum antibiotic. Digging around a little more, James found some tubing and an IV needle and started setting up an IV for her. James placed the flashlights upright on the floor for illumination and taped the IV bag to the counter, then attached a drip chamber to the fluid bag and unrolled the rest of the tubing, clamps, and ports. After putting on some gloves from the bag and sterilizing Oswell's arm, he opened the cannula package and felt for a vein beneath her elbow on the inside, following the guide written in large print on the side of the cannula packaging. When he couldn't find one right away, he tied a disposable tourniquet to her upper arm and tapped gently around the vein to get it to pop.

Holding the needle close to her skin, he took a deep breath and released the air slowly, leaning in and inserting the needle tip into her vein, waiting for blood to fill the cannula tube. When it didn't, he withdrew the needle and wiped the sweat off his forehead, gathering himself to try again as he re-read the instructions. On his second attempt, blood filled the cannula tube, and he released the remaining breath he'd been holding and slumped forward to calm his shaking nerves. After taping the tube and needle to her arm, James flushed air from the IV line and connected the rest of the tubing, checking the drip chamber to ensure there was a steady flow of fluid.

When he saw it was working, he collapsed against the cabinets, drawing his legs up and wrapping his arms around his knees. His head throbbed, body vibrating with echoes of the wobbly bike handlebars, and he hadn't realized how fast his heart was racing until it finally started to slow. With Oswell's fate out of his hands, there was nothing left to do but wait – and sleep.

CHAPTER SEVEN

Agent Alan Harris
Mount Weather, Virginia

The walls shook and faint dust trails trickled from the ceiling as another explosion went off in a nearby corridor. A shudder ran through the Mount Weather complex where Special Agent Alan Harris, President Birk, and a handful of Marines were sequestered. The President's office within the building, buried deep underground on level three, was more than likely the target of the invaders who'd breached the outer walls and were beating their way past the Marine guards outside. It was impossible to tell for sure, though, since there'd been no answers to attempts to contact the attackers throughout the ordeal.

Birk was pacing near his desk, jacket off, tie undone, with his shirt buttoned down and his sleeves rolled up, communicating with his military leaders through a speaker on the desk. His computer screen flickered every time an explosive went off in an adjacent passage, and Harris cringed at the closeness of the walls, the ceiling suddenly too low, the walls too weak, ready to collapse on their heads at any moment. The walls were double-reinforced steel and concrete and could withstand much more than a few pipe bombs and grenades, but facts didn't hold up very well in the face of the overwhelming assault.

"We crushed their last attempt to get deeper inside, sir," General Pulaski said in his deep baritone, voice steady without a hint of strain. "But they've got that main hallway locked down."

"Where are you currently located, General?" Birk asked.

"We're at the foot of the main corridor, and Colonel Crow is holding the B1 passage ahead of us. We've got most of the rooms barricaded and secure halfway up the hall."

"And *we're* just off C1 in the secured Presidential suites. We're actually closer to the bastards than you."

"You should stay right where you are, sir. Don't try to reach the main corridor through C1. They're about three hundred feet up the passage at the top of the stairs and they've got control of the elevator shaft and stairwell. Anyone emerging from C1 will be turned into minced meat. We've already lost most of Marine Units Two and Three, and Unit One is divided between myself and Colonel Crow, sir."

"Why can't we break through that position?"

"There's a curve in the hallway, and they've got barriers set up far enough back that we can't hit them with weapons or grenades. They can't get a direct sightline on us, either, but they can roll grenades and IEDs down the stairs at us."

"A stalemate then."

446

"That's right, sir."

Harris had changed into combat fatigues, and the Marine guards had brought in crates with carbines, pistols, and ammunition from a small stockpile they kept in an adjoining storage locker. The equipment had been there for a few years but it was still in good shape thanks to regular maintenance and testing. Harris had chosen a standard-issue Beretta pistol and an M4 carbine, strapping on an armored ammunition vest stuffed with several spare magazines.

"Do we have anything better than grenades?"

"There's an armory just up past where C1 intersects with the main corridor," Pulaski said, "right in the middle of no man's land. We got the codes to get inside, but we haven't been able to get close much less hold a position there."

"But the armory is stocked?"

"RPGs, ammunition, rifles."

"Any ideas on how to get to the armory, General?"

"I combined the remnants of Marine Units Two and Three into their own support unit and sent them through the ventilation system to an adjoining hallway up ahead of C1. They don't have the numbers to attack, but they're on standby... Wait, sir. I've got the fire team leader of SU coming through now. I'll patch him through. Go ahead, Green."

The line spit and sputtered before falling into the soft hum of background noise. "Yes, sir, General Pulaski. This is Sergeant Green, sir." The Marine's voice was barely above a whisper. "We just showed up and are in position but be warned there are a dozen tangos moving down the main corridor, headed in your direction."

"Did any of them enter C1?"

"Negative. They're skipping adjoining rooms and hallways and are coming right at you. They're carrying riot shields, too."

Birk stopped his pacing. "Where did they get those?"

"Could have been from a local police armory," Harris said.

"General Pulaski. What can we do? Should we head to the next level?"

Pulaski's heavy breathing filled the speaker and consumed the silence as the seconds ticked painfully on.

"General Pulaski?"

"I'm here, sir. Just... considering options. The riot shields offer them some protection from small caliber fire, but they aren't going to hold up under a steady barrage if it comes down to it. No, we can beat them. Green, we'll hold them here at the end of the hall and keep their attention. Sporadic gunfire, nothing too heavy. You'll creep in behind them along the walls to avoid any crossfire from us. On your mark, we'll stop firing and take cover while you hit them hard from behind. Crow, you'll stand by in support of all units."

"Yes, sir," Crow said.

"Orders received, sir," Greene replied.

"Green, stay quiet and out of sight. If they see you, retreat to the ventilation system and head back our way."

"Yes, sir."

Harris, the President, and the Marines stood quietly in the room, cycling through equipment checks, the Marine Captain pacing as they listened to Pulaski report on the attackers approaching up the main corridor.

"We've got movement through the smoke," Pulaski whispered, still somehow sounding like a bellow coming from the deep-chested general, making Harris cringe in expectation of the violent clash.

"Incoming!" a Marine shouted, followed by the brisk pop of explosions and flying debris, the screams of multiple people and a roar of gunfire that clipped the speakers in a single wave of unrecognizable noise.

Harris had stopped to face the desk with his rifle clutched against his chest, sweat trickling down his cheeks and moistening the neckline of his undershirt as they listened to the communications chatter.

"Coming, General," Greene said in a clipped and quiet tone.

"Down, Marines," Pulaski hissed, "Get down."

One barrage of gunfire was replaced with another, less intense but no less deadly. Distant screams cut through the din, filling the speaker with living agony and Green's steady, heavy breathing as his carbine belched fire and smoke. Suddenly, he grunted like he'd gotten punched in the stomach, sucking a big chest full of air and letting it out in a clipped sigh.

"I'm hit..." he said, voice fading quickly. "Medic..."

"Crow!" Pulaski called, and more gunfire erupted in the hall, a confused mess of sound Harris could barely make out.

Birk listened for several long moments, hands pressed hard on the table and leaning over the speaker. "Crow? Pulaski? What's going on?"

The firing continued, men and women screaming and suddenly falling silent, and Harris released a quiet breath when Pulaski came back on the line.

"Sir, we're checking the hall now," Pulaski said. "Green is down... most of his unit is down. We're abandoning the forward halls and consolidating all units to the foot of the main corridor."

Birk closed his eyes and shook his head. "Damn."

"The security cameras being down screwed us, sir. We had them, but they kept an eye on their backs and caught Green and his team coming in. We beat them, but we lost too many. They got away with their wounded, and they still hold the head of the corridor."

"Understood, General. Do we have anyone left to assault them?"

"All we have is remnants of Unit Two's Alpha and Bravo teams, and Unit One's Charlie team. Nine Marines, sir. Eleven if you count me and Colonel Crow. We've got another half-dozen wounded, but most aren't capable of fighting."

"Stand by, General." Birk hit the mute button on the speaker and turned to Harris. "What do you think, Harris?"

"I'm not a battlefield tac—"

"Did I ask?"

"No sir. It's not looking good," he replied flatly. "They've got the superior defensive position and we have no idea how many reinforcements they can muster. Do we have any backup?"

"None who can get here quickly enough. Any other suggestions?"

Harris lowered his weapon and stared at the ground as he thought, then he met the President's eyes. "The key is the armory, sir. Heavier, overwhelming firepower's what we require."

"The bastards have a solid defensive position and eyes on the armory, though. They'll see anyone coming in and cut them to pieces before they can even get inside. Even if someone gets access to it, we'll lose too many in the assault."

"Those riot shields gave me an idea."

"You heard Pulaski. They won't stop bullets."

"I'm not suggesting using scavenged shields, sir. But we have some *damn* thick metal doors and tables around here...."

Birk's eyebrow went up and he grinned wickedly. "Say no more. I'm sending you out there to lead this."

"Me?" Harris stiffened. "I'm not a soldier. And besides, without me, you'll be completely on your own. I think we're pretty safe in assuming that you're their target – and even if you aren't, you will be as soon as they figure out you're here."

"Are you implying that I can't handle myself, Agent?"

"No sir, but—"

"I served two tours; I can handle myself. Get me a pistol and magazines. It's big boy pants time."

Harris hesitated for a long minute before his shoulders slumped. "You're not going to take no for an answer on this, are you?"

Birk winked at him, unmuting the line. "General Pulaski, I'm putting Agent Harris on. He's got an idea."

"I'm all ears."

"General, I'll take the President's Marine guards through the hidden corridors to C1. I'm pretty sure I can get into the armory."

"It'll be a suicide run, Harris."

"It *won't* be. I've got an idea to make this work."

Pulaski's tone changed, pleading with Birk. "Mr. President, are you sure about this?"

"Harris has my full support, Pulaski, and at this point we're running out of time and people."

Pulaski paused but finally consented. "We'll be there, Harris. This better be a damn good plan."

"Meet you there in fifteen minutes, sir." Harris hit the mute button and retrieved a pistol from one of the Marine guards outside the President's office, handing it and two spare magazines to Birk.

"Kick some ass, Harris."

"I won't let you down, sir."

The President grinned. "Make sure you don't." He let Harris go and gestured to the Marines. "Follow this man's orders to the letter. Bring us back a victory."

The Marines saluted the President and turned to follow Harris as he exited the room, guiding them through back hallways and side passages that he had spent the last few hours studying on Birk's computer. When they reached a small hatch, he punched in a code and the door popped open with a *clank*, revealing a narrow, closed corridor leading off into the darkness.

They shut and locked the door behind them, and Harris jumped back in front and jogged to the end with steaming pipes hissing above his head, the faint flicker of emergency lights barely lighting his way. At the end of the corridor stood a door with another keypad, and they popped that open and stepped into a small, bare room with a single door on the north side.

"Alright, gentlemen. On the other side of this door is the C1 hallway. We need to get across that hall to Pulaski. Can you help me do that?"

"Yes, sir," they replied in whispered unison.

"Okay. Here we go. Slow, steady and quiet is best, but be prepared to lay down suppressing fire."

His fingers danced over the keypad buttons and the door popped open softly. Harris pushed with his shoulders and stepped into the C1 corridor, suppressing a gagging cough as a swirl of smoke and ash hit him square in the face. Swinging his rifle left and right, he moved to the other side to give the Marines room to flank him, and once they'd all filed out, Harris led them down to where Crow, Pulaski and the remaining Marines were at the backside of the hallway, barely dodging a spattering of gunfire that zipped past them down the main corridor.

"Colonel Crow." Harris nodded. "General Pulaski."

Crow stood tall, arms held out with his carbine in one hand, helmet tilted on his head. Pulaski was a bull, taking up the space of three men, rifle looking small where he held it against his wide chest.

He pushed Harris down the hall, thick eyebrows narrowing over steel gray eyes. "This better be a damn good plan, Harris."

"Frankly, sir," Harris shouldered past Pulaski and through the Marines to peek around the corner, surveilling the armory door and the slight right curve of hallway that blocked their view of the enemy. "I'm surprised you didn't think of it already."

"What *is* your plan, Harris?"

Harris turned and strode back along a junction of C1 past the annoyed General, who followed right on his heels. "These doors." Harris gestured to the doors. "They're three-inch thick reinforced plate steel. You'd need a wad of C4 like they used on the entrance to get through them."

"What's your point?"

"Shields, General. I say we take two of them off their hinges, turn them sideways, and march straight down to that armory. The second an IED comes rolling down the hall, we drop the doors and hunker down behind them until the danger has passed, then keep moving. Unless they've got a big ball of C4 or an RPG, they won't be able to do anything to get through them."

Pulaski stared at Harris for a moment before walking down the hall, putting his hand on the door to a barracks and slapping it with a heavy thud. "That... might work," he said. "Son of a... you're right. I *should've* thought of it myself."

Harris shrugged. "No offense intended."

"Plenty taken," Pulaski's relief at the possibility of a viable plan was palpable as he winked at Harris. "Okay, gentlemen! Let's get a couple of these doors off!"

The Marines got to work, using tools to attack the hinges, knocking out the pins, jerking the doors free, and dropping them with heavy *clangs*. One brought up a set of ratchet straps from a storage locker which they wound around the doors, providing handles that would allow them to keep their fingers safely behind cover. After things were set up, Harris and the Marines dragged them across the floor, tilted them sideways, and carried them to the end of C1 where it intersected with the main corridor.

"Put them together, side-by-side," Harris pointed. "We'll use the straps to slide them along the floor like shields so that our whole bodies are covered, then if we hear a grenade or something coming, we angle them and brace ourselves. It'll be like a rolling barricade. You get what I mean?"

The group nodded, a couple of Marines enthusiastic as they knelt behind the doors, keeping their shoulder pressed against the heavy steel and clinging to the doorknobs and straps to prevent them from sliding. The others followed suit, crouching, seeing how many they could fit behind each door.

"We'll have a second wave coming in behind you guys," Harris said. "Myself, General Pulaski, and Colonel Crow. As soon as we reach the armory, we hold that position and go inside to find something to take them out."

"Oorah," a Marine growled, nodding and grinning, the others joining in, slapping hands and shoulders, jaws firm and resolute.

"Okay, let's do this." Pulaski directed six Marines to sling their weapons and carry the doors to the intersection. At first, they moved awkwardly, bumping their knees against the doors and almost dropping one, but they quickly fell into a rhythm and marched to the intersection.

Crow got in behind the door on the right with a few more Marines, and Pulaski took the left with his group. Harris brought up the rear, forcing himself to breathe steadily as smoke drifted up the hallway. He was used to surveilling a crowd, picking up the fine details and determining who might be a threat to the most important man in the world. The act of charging down the hall in an attack formation was utterly new to him, but Harris tried to turn his brain off and let his instincts take over.

"Okay, Marines," Pulaski said. "Let's move!"

The Marines carried the doors out into the hallway, turning left and shuffling through the debris where the smoke was thick, and shadows played tricks on their eyes. From the end of the corridor, an enemy shouted and fired, and a round pinged off the steel door and hit the wall to his left. More shots came in, the doors slipping lower as the Marines instinctively ducked, and Harris faced the incoming flashes, ducking down as something hot whipped past his ear.

Pulaski boomed, "Brace!"

The doors slammed on the tiles with a *clang*, and the Marines ducked behind them as a pair of grenades bounced off the steel before throwing a wave of heat and shrapnel out into the corridor. Harris crouched and pressed himself into the packed group of Marines, the smell of sweat, blood, and smoke surrounding them. A barrage of gunfire came with sharp concussions that vibrated the doors, the rounds careening off in every direction, taking chips out of light fixtures and tiles to send a trickle of dust on their heads. The Marines held firm, though, and not a single projectile or piece of shrapnel got through.

Pulaski called out. "Let's move!"

The troops lifted the doors just enough to slide them along the floor and moved forward again, taking more small-arms fire as they progressed down the hall. Harris peered over the doors, shifting to the side and watching the curling smoke as shadows charged down the corridor at them, quiet through the haze, the sharp profiles of their rifles stark against the gray light.

"Here they come, General!" Harris shouted.

"Marines, let's have some cover fire!"

Marines lifted their carbines high and fired over the doors, cutting into the charging enemy formation, sending them flailing and windmilling through the smoke. A couple threw themselves against the walls, ducked, and came ahead firing wildly, doing everything to disrupt the Marines' slow but steady progress up the hall. A Marine holding the door on the right cried out and stumbled, a huge gash taken out of his leg by a ricochet off of a nearby doorframe and he took three more steps before letting go of the ratchet straps and crashing to his knees.

The door nearly tilted over to expose the rest of the people behind it, but two Marines rushed in and replaced him, lifting it level in time for a heavy barrage of gunfire. Rounds flashed and ricocheted off the steel, and Harris winced, desperately wishing he had more ear protection than a simple pair of earbuds used for communications.

"Right here!" Pulaski bellowed as they came level with the far edge of the door leading to the armory. "Hold fast!"

The Marines dropped the doors just as a round of pipe bombs came hurtling down the hall as the attackers retreated. They exploded, shards of nails and quarters *chinking* off the doors and zipping overhead like a swarm of angry yellow-jackets.

"Hold this position," Pulaski growled. "Get that man's leg tended to. Harris - we're stuck. They can sit here and hammer us all day, but we can't do much back to them."

"Let's see what we've got to work with in the armory," Harris replied, crawling to the armory door keypad and punching in a code. The door hissed and popped open to reveal a pair of rifle barrels pointed outward, the guns brandished by a pair of wounded Marines, one leaning against a shelf packed with bins and the other sitting on the floor with his legs spread, the front of his fatigues covered in blood. The latter glared at him wide-eyed, nostrils flaring, hand shaking with his finger on the trigger.

Harris held up his hands. "Whoa! We're on your side! Pulaski, we've got survivors in the armory!"

"You guys finally made it?" One of the Marines inside the armory asked as smoke poured into the room through the half-opened door.

"There aren't a lot of us left, but we made it." Harris glanced at Pulaski as the general crawled up next to him, the pair inching their way inside the armory before standing up. At the sight of Pulaski, both Marines lowered their rifles and attempted to salute until he waved them off.

"How long have you been in here?" The man's typical growl softened as he knelt down next to the injured Marine on the floor.

"We got hit first." The Marine gasped and swallowed dry. "Me and my four buddies got inside and locked the door... two of us didn't make it."

"Excuse me, sir." A Marine slid to her knees next to the wounded soldier and pushed Harris aside, breaking open a first aid kit.

"You did good, son. Take it easy." Pulaski stood up and turned to Harris. "Good work, Harris. Time to make these bastards pay."

Harris nodded and spun into the aisle, facing crates of grenades, ammunition, and weapons on ten racks that stretched the length of the room. At the end, an array of automatic machine guns and RPGs hung from hooks on the wall. A pair of Marines lay side-by-side on the floor in a corner with their hands resting on their chests, their appearances peaceful in spite of the blood and gore that surrounded them.

"Santa just came down the chimney, Harris." Pulaski came up behind him and scanned the wall, grabbing a couple of M4 carbines with M203 grenade launchers affixed beneath the barrels. "I'll hand these out and get some counterfire going. It'll give them something to think about. Grab a couple, would you?"

Pulaski carried the guns away and Harris reached for a pair of M4s but stopped, instead stepping to the right and taking an RPG off the wall, reading the designation as an Akeron MP anti-tank weapon. "Since when did we start importing these?" Harris mumbled to himself.

He had trained with stingers, javelins and similar launchers outdoors on target ranges but had never fired one in closed confines. While the M203s were a boon, any progress up the corridor would be hard-earned and bloody even with grenades on their side, but a missile could swing the odds in their favor. He pulled it off the wall, found the box of rockets, and took one from its foam bedding. Stomach twisting with reckless intent, Harris loaded the weapon and checked the safety and firing mechanisms. He started to walk away but paused beside a case that read *30x-M67 Fragmentation Grenades* and hooked four on his vest.

Skin crawling, sweat trickling along his back and sides, he grabbed the rocket launcher and trudged down the hall, stopping at the door where the battle was raging and Pulaski and Crow were shouting orders, coordinating the Marines' firing. Harris stood by the door and held the tube aloft shouting to get Pulaski's attention.

"What's the arming distance on this?"

"Say what?" Pulaski turned to him, eyes widening when he saw the launcher. "You've got to be joking, Harris."

"Seventy-five meters." The answer came from the wounded Marine behind Harris.

"Damn. Too far." Harris turned to the man. "Is there a way to reduce it to, say, twenty-five or thirty meters?"

The Marine nodded weakly. "It's a prototype unit. There's a selector dial on the side. You can reduce it to twenty meters but the blast radius—"

"Don't worry about it." Harris swiveled back to Pulaski. "General, we're never going to break through with rifles and grenades. They've got high ground and can lob stuff around that curved hallway till the cows come home. But with this..." Harris hefted the launcher.

"You want to destroy the hallway?" Pulaski shook his head. "Are you insane?"

"Are you a NASCAR fan, General?" Pulaski stared blankly for a few seconds before Harris continued. "Neither am I. But my dad is – was – a huge fan, and told me about this driver, Ross Chastain, who—"

A weak laugh came from behind Harris as the wounded Marine held his side, grimacing in pain. "You're crazy. But it'll work. Reduce... reduce the arming distance to thirty-five meters. Fire it along the wall. If the curve is too steep, it won't destroy anything. If it works, though... thirty... thirty-five meters is enough to take those son of..." the man's head slumped and the Marine tending to him checked his pulse, working harder to treat his wounds.

"I have no idea what either one of you are talking about, but you got us this far, so if you have a smart idea, make it happen." Pulaski went back to the entrance to the armory, shouting at the Marines to prepare to lay down cover fire.

"Hail Melon," Harris muttered as he twisted the dial on the safety selector knob, "don't let me down."

He stepped outside to the thump of an M203 round bursting from its barrel and skipping down the hall, bouncing off the walls and out of sight before it exploded, sending shrapnel and smoke back at them. Shouts and cries of pain rang out from down the hall, followed by a cluster of molotov cocktails skittering across the tiles, glass clinking, breaking, bursting in a gush of flames that rolled over the steel doors. A new burst of outgoing fire came from the Marines behind the doors, and Pulaski drew up next to Harris, shouting over the din.

"Do it, Harris! Kill the bastards!"

CHAPTER EIGHT

Ryan Cooper
Lansing, Michigan

In James' workshop, Ryan lined up pieces and parts with the hope of designing a manual well pump. The basic function of the device rolled around in his head: draw the water into a main chamber with an upstroke, trap that water with a one-way valve, and on the downstroke pump it out a side spout that would feed the house. So far he'd managed to assemble a long, two-inch piece of PVC pipe as the main housing, a one-inch pipe converted into a plunger, a homemade check valve made from a bicycle tire, various couplers, and a jar of PVC cement. Most of the supplies had come from a shed out back, but the other parts had been on the bottom shelf of James' workbench.

Ryan measured eighteen inches on the longer PVC piece and cut off the excess, using some sandpaper to smooth the edge. On one end, he plugged in the check valve and on the other he placed a T-shaped connector with one opening pointed off to the side which would form the spout, then capped the top.

There was a soft knock, and Helen stepped inside. "How's it going down here?"

"Well, I've got my pieces together, and I'm trying to work out how to make them fit so they'll actually work. How'd the chores go?"

"Everything's done, but I left the milk to you."

"I'll pick that up as soon as I'm done with the pump."

"Explain to me how this will work?"

"The first thing I did was make a check valve." He took out the check valve and held it up. "That's this piece here."

"It looks rough."

"Yeah, well, I built it myself. I drilled holes in a standard plug and screwed a piece of rubber to the inside. It'll allow water to enter the pump housing when you draw up on the pump but won't let it fall back into the well. This spout here is where it'll come out on the downstroke of the pump. I fixed it so we can screw a hose on it for whenever we need to get it to places." Ryan put the check valve back on. "It really all depends on how well this check valve works."

"Where'd you get the rubber for it?"

"From an inner tube and hose." He gestured to where he'd tossed the spare pieces off to the side. "I've got everything ready, but I need to put it together and test it. I've got a five-gallon bucket for that, but I need water."

"I'll get that for you," Helen said, heading out of the room.

Ryan inspected the one-inch pipe he was using as a plunger, hoping it was wide enough to do what he needed. He held the pieces together, sliding the plunger up and down and testing the smoothness until Helen returned with two gallon-sized jugs taken from the basement storage room.

"Where do you want it? In the bucket?"

"Yup, just pour them in there while I connect this piece of hose to the spout... okay, good. Now, we'll just put the end of the hose into this jug. Ready?"

"Yeah."

Ryan twisted the housing, trying to keep it together with his hands. "Okay, let's see if this'll work."

He pressed the plunger to the bottom and drew it up, bringing some water into the pump housing. Ryan continued to work the plunger up and down, watching as more water filled up the housing until it reached the spout and gushed through the hose into the bucket on the next downstroke.

Helen grinned. "Looks like that was a success!"

"Yeah," Ryan raised the plunger and pressed it down again, forcing more water into the jug and stopping when it was almost full. "There you go," he said, drawing his arm across his forehead. "It'll be tough, but I bet we can get a couple gallons per minute. I just need to attach a hose to the bottom of this going down deep enough into the well and we can draw out as much as we have the arm strength to muster."

"When will you hook it up? They have enough bottled water here to last us a couple days, if needed."

"Nah, won't take me that long. I want to make some adjustments first, then cement everything together. I have to draw water up fifty feet of hose, so I need to make sure everything is super tight and can actually handle the pressure."

Helen stepped over and kissed him on the cheek. "I'm so proud of you, dear. There's nothing you can't build. Can I entice you upstairs for a snack before you finish up?"

"No, ma'am. I'm going to cement all the pieces together now and get it ready to test outside. I figure we can use one of James' five-hundred-gallon water tanks he's got stacked out behind the barn. We can bring that up to the house, set it up on bricks, and connect it to the water filter in the basement."

"Will that give us enough pressure?"

"It'll probably create enough pressure to use the downstairs shower once it's filled. Now, filling it is going to take some muscle but maybe later on I can figure out how to get a motor running on it." He grinned determinedly. "Anyway, we'll burn that bridge when we come to it. I'll have this up and working by dinner."

"Let me know when you're going to test it and I'll come out."

Ryan nodded as Helen left the basement, then took everything apart and spread it out on the workbench, carefully using the PVC cement to glue it all back together, fitting the pieces tight, ensuring the check valve was in place and that the hose attachment for the well was firmly affixed to the bottom. The job he'd had running on one of James' 3D printers wrapped up a short time later, and he picked up the part he'd designed to keep the pump from falling into the well. It was a circular, star-shaped piece with one open end and spikes sticking out from the sides and he slid it onto the bottom of the pump housing and tightened it with a pipe clamp.

Excitement brewing, Ryan took the entire contraption upstairs and showed it to Helen where she was working at the stove, and together they went out to the well head. Ryan connected the well hose to the bottom of his new pump and handed the pump to Helen to hold while he fed the hose back into the well. Once it was all fed in, he dropped the pump in gently and rested the spiked stopper on the top of the well head, allowing everything to sit level in the pipe.

"Okay, this is the moment of truth."

"You built it. It's going to perform phenomenally!"

Ryan put the plunger into the pump housing and started working it up and down with long, smooth motions. Gurgling, slurping sounds came from the hose, and after a full five minutes, he finally had to quit because his arm was hurting and nothing was coming out.

"What's the problem?"

"The hose must be deeper than I thought... the end of the plunger needs to be bigger. That might give me more suction to get the water up." Ryan fished around in his pocket and brought out a small screwdriver and several plastic chips. "I used the printer to make these in case I needed to try different sizes. The one I have on now was an inch, but this new one is an inch and three-quarters." He used a screwdriver to remove the old plunger and put the new one on, then resumed pumping.

After two minutes of continuous pumping, water showed up inside the pump housing and Ryan kept going, drawing more up each time until it gushed from the spout and splashed his feet.

"Awesome work, honey." Helen wrapped her arms around him, and he lifted her off her feet and spun her before putting her back down.

"We've got water!" He pumped his fist and sighed, rolling his shoulders. "That's a load off my mind."

"I never doubted you."

Ryan continued working the pump to see how much he could get out, the water coming out the spout sporadically in fits and spurts, spilling through the opening until the ground was muddy. "I mean… it's not perfect. We'll have to stand here and continuously pump to keep the flow going, and it's going to take a lot of energy to get this out. But I can also make even bigger plunger tips, accurate down to the millimeter, to help make it as efficient as possible. I'll have to experiment with that a bit, but I'm sure I can make it work a lot better." Ryan put his hand out, caught a palm full of water, and had a taste. "Ugh. Tastes like licking an iron bar. No wonder they've got the softener."

"I'm assuming we can't pump it fast enough by hand to give it enough pressure to go through the softener?"

"Nope. We need a new well pump, or one of the tanks we were talking about. If we fill it high enough, we can probably get enough pressure to get some kind of flow through the softener. Even a trickle'd be better than sucking on iron day in and out. I think James has a skid of old garden bricks he used to make the retaining wall out front. We can use those to get it up a few feet and level it off."

"You need help getting that all up here?"

"I don't think so." Ryan sized up the EV. "I'll use the car to drag the tank down and a piece of plywood to get the bricks. Shouldn't be too hard to get the tank on the bricks, I don't think."

"Sounds easy enough." She gave him a wink.

Ryan laughed. "Not easy, but workable. I do worry about what will happen when other things start to fail around here, though, like the furnace and stove."

"I suppose we'll deal with that all if – or when – it happens." Helen locked arms with him as a cool breeze blew in off the barnyard, carrying the smell of hay and animals as it brushed a gray lock of hair into her face. "You're not a young man, though. You can't push yourself to do *everything*."

"We'll do what we must because we must." Ryan patted her arm. "And as soon as the kids get home, we'll have some real muscle around here to get things done."

"Hopefully sooner, rather than later." Helen stood next to him for a moment as they looked out over James and Alice's property, the stiff breeze wicking away their sweat as it blew the long grasses in the yard and field to and fro.

Ryan squeezed her arm and started walking toward the EV. "Honey, I'll take care of this if you want to continue the chores. I'll try to get done fast enough to help you."

"Don't worry about it, dear, I can manage everything but the milk myself. Just do what you have to do."

He got in the EV, powered it up, and drove it carefully up through the barnyard gate and around back where five big rain collection tanks sat unused. They were all made of white polyethylene, dirt stained on the outside but in perfectly good shape otherwise, with a small opening on the top and a hose connection on the bottom. James had several chains hanging from the barn wall, and Ryan grabbed a thirty-foot-long segment with hooks on each end and secured it to the car frame beneath the back bumper, then wrapped the other end around the tank. Hopping back in the EV, Ryan drove slowly, dragging the tank behind him, constantly checking his mirrors and ensuring he didn't dent or damage the tank, waving and shouting to get the curious barnyard animals out of the way.

Down by the house, he swung in a wide circle and dropped off the tank, throwing the loose chain in the trunk and driving back up to the barn for a piece of plywood upon which he loaded a hundred and fifty garden bricks. He drilled a quick hole in the plywood and put the chain hook through, then dragged the bricks down to the house near the tank and well head before parking the EV.

Helen waved from the kitchen window, and he waved back before starting to stack bricks close to the house, using a level to keep things fairly flat, purposefully ignoring his penchant for making things perfect in favor of making them workable first and foremost. Once the stack was five bricks high, he placed the plywood on it to make a ramp, tilted the tank up on its bottom edge, and rolled all one hundred and fifty pounds of it up the ramp until it sat atop the bricks. After a short break to catch his breath, Ryan kicked the plywood piece out of the way then connected a standard hose to the tank spout, putting the other end through a gap in the wood covering the basement window.

Ryan hurried inside and headed down to the basement where he opened the window and grabbed the hose end, pulling it through and looping it over a nail near the water filter. A hose coming in off the PVC pipe from the well was attached to the filter, and he used a wrench and some liquid lubricant to loosen it up and get it off before he connected the new line to the water filter. His fingers were sore, arms and back aching as he finished, and he dragged himself upstairs to fall into a kitchen chair with a huff.

"All done?" Helen asked, bringing him a glass of water.

"Everything is done except for pumping five hundred gallons of water," he chuckled, wiping the sweat off his forehead. He took a long drink to wash down the dust of the day, putting the glass on the table with a nod of thanks.

Helen sat across from him. "Are you ready to call it a night, dear?"

"I don't want to, but it's not that important for us to get a shower tonight... we know it works and can get water up out of the well, and that's all that matters right now. I'd still like to have a new pump, though."

"Hopefully, Sandy will come through."

"I'm not counting on it, but maybe she will. It would make things a *lot* easier."

"We've still got plenty of water in the jugs," Helen spoke sympathetically, reaching across the table to hold his calloused hands. "Why don't you take the night off? We'll make a nice dinner and listen to some music. Maybe we can take a walk around the property later. You know, take first shift together."

"That sounds like a productive and romantic evening with the woman I love." Ryan turned his hand over and held hers, running his thumb across it. "I have to remember that this is a marathon and not a race. Whether we pump that water tonight or tomorrow won't make a difference, although I was hoping I could get you a nice hot shower tonight."

"Don't worry about me," she smiled. "I'll be fine. What do you say we heat some of this water and take a nice warm sponge bath, though? We don't have to clean ourselves all the way, but your face, dear... well. You look like a little boy who's been playing in the dirt."

Ryan chuckled before standing on sore knees and gesturing toward the kitchen. "I guess we better get started. If I sit down for too much longer, I won't want to get up again."

Helen got a large pot from a cabinet and heated water from a few gallon jugs while Ryan collected two sponges and dry towels from the laundry room. When the water was warm enough, Ryan brought it over to the table and placed it on some oven mitts she'd put down. After peeling off his shirt, boots, and socks, he rolled up his pants legs and removed his prosthetic limb.

Helen popped a CD into the player but paused before pressing the power button. "Do you want me to turn on the news? Maybe there's something new on?"

Ryan started to say yes, but he shook his head and snickered. "Nah, it'll just be the same thing they've been preaching all week; stay inside, looting won't be tolerated - isn't that a joke - and here's a list of refugee centers, updated as of this morning. I'd rather listen to music than that bunch of useless crap."

Helen laughed as she started the music, then the pair got to work with the sponges, cleaning as much of the sweat and grime off as possible, squeezing the dirty water into a bucket next to the table. When they'd reached the limit of what they could reach on themselves, they took turns washing each other's backs and Helen helped Ryan with his leg, paying particular attention to the cracks and crevices around the scar tissue.

"Thanks, hon." Ryan gave her a hug as she handed him a fresh shirt, both of them slipping into clean clothes. "Not as good as a real shower, but I'll take it."

"Oh, come on now. I could get used to getting my back scrubbed by you." Helen winked at him and they both laughed, taking some small measure of joy from their brief reprieve from the horrors of life.

CHAPTER NINE

Alice Burton
Talladega National Forest, Alabama.

Alice was back on the trail after a few hours of restless sleep, never truly resting but instead turning and shifting ceaselessly as she tried to get comfortable. Eventually she gave up, the combination of forest floor and never-ending distracting thoughts about Jack and Sarah too much for her to ignore.

It was early afternoon when she sat up and staggered to her feet, the glaring sun bright across the treetops as it cut onto the trail, threatening to bake her where she walked across the hard-packed earth. She was huffing and puffing on the hot, humid air, digging in and trudging hard to make up for the time she'd lost during her much-needed rest. High above, the screech of a hawk echoed as it circled under the blazing sun, spiraling in lazy circles, giving no care to the ways in which the world around it had changed.

Alice had taken off her jacket due to the heat and used it to cover her head to keep her neck and ears from burning as the tree cover began to wane around her, though she had nothing for her arms, and they were starting to ache from an impending sunburn. The forest trail had smoothed out and swept straight down from the heights, flattening out with a layer of loose gravel and weeds on top. The hills rose around her like shoulders, with stony slopes to her left and rolling lumps of brown and green to the right as far as she could see. To the northeast, a radio tower sprung from the trees, standing out in the wilderness with its steel girders and communication dishes clinging to its sides. The staccato hammering of a red-cockaded woodpecker echoed through the valley, and the thin chirps of black-throated green warblers sang from the deeper woods. Other birds swept through the trees in flocks and choruses, background noise to the raw wheezing in her chest and the repeated stabs of pain every time she moved.

With only a couple of hours of fitful rest to fuel her, she felt like a shambling corpse with only a few coals in her gut. She still had a little water left in one bottle and pulled it from her waistband, the plastic crinkling as she tilted it up to drink. Dropping the empty bottle from her aching fingertips, Alice stared down at the hoof prints which continued diverging onto other paths but still maintained a northerly course. The grass grew thick and tall, sometimes as high as her shoulder, crowding the trail so it was almost impossible to see. Honeysuckle clung to saplings and brush, spiderwebs woven between them with their fat-bellied makers perched in the middle, awaiting a meal. The air swam with pollen and dust, floating on warm breezes that occasionally were enough to cool her skin, though the high humidity kept that from happening for the most part.

With each turn she made, the paths grew a little wider, some with gravel spread across them as if someone had put it down to even out the rough spots. After a hundred-yard stretch of dirt tract, she came to a wide path almost fully covered in gravel with the grass cut away on both sides, not quite a road but not a trail, either. She stood there as her feet throbbed and ribs ached, the tenderness and swelling having grown increasingly more agonizing since she'd set out. No matter how much she leaned on her walking stick or changed her posture, the pain was always there. The discomfort had become part of her, embedded in every breath and heartbeat, yet still inconsequential compared to her tenacity and drive to find her children.

Turning back and forth, Alice stared back up the trail to the south, wondering if she might have missed a turnoff where the horses had been taken. She very well could have, but their tracks were still right in front of her, ending where the gravel road started. There was only one direction to go, so she continued up the trail at a snail's pace, checking to both sides, trudging ahead as the trail strayed like a loose ribbon, twisting back and forth but never once branching off.

The faint scent of smoke took a few moments to register in her sleep-addled and injury-riddled brain. It was the smell of burning logs and cooking meat, an aroma that sent her stomach into a fit of grumbles. Memories of hot dogs and hamburgers sizzling on a grill sprang to mind: Fourth of July parties, summer cookouts filled with laughter and play, a big bowl of potato salad and homemade, crinkle cut French fries. It took several minutes for her to realize the significance of the smell, and she paused where she stood, sniffing deeply, trying to decide if the smoke was real or just some hallucination.

After an hour of weary walking, Alice swayed on her feet and could barely lift her chin. The fire inside her – the only thing keeping her going - demanded her legs move faster, but her whole body was shaking, and she could barely hold a breath much less force hours more movement from her tortured body. Still, she forced herself to go on. There was no choice; death hadn't conquered her, and she was therefore obligated to continue on no matter what her physical condition demanded of her.

It was only when her shoes touched the edge of a paved road that she stopped again. The blacktop stretched east and west in front of her, with more tall grass and woods beyond on the other side. Heat, unbearable in its intensity came off of the blacktop in waves, adding to the discomfort from the sun above and the humidity all around. There were no more hoof prints or tracks to follow, just an empty road going both ways and the path back to where she'd started. With a frustrated, weak sigh, Alice stood barely moving, frustratedly locked in indecision over which way to go and lacking a coin with which to spur her decision.

The campfire smells hit her again, and she lifted her eyes and spotted a sign on the side of the road. Shuffling over, she stood in front of a wooden plank with the words *Swimming Hole* painted in bold yellow lettering and an arrow pointing off to the east, roughly the same direction she thought was the origination of the smoke. She forced her feet to move in the direction the sign indicated, her walking stick making soft thuds on the pavement, each footfall more a drag than a fall. The road meandered eastward, and soon she was walking through a wooded lane where the brush was cut back, but the surrounding trees stood fifty or more feet high, their canopy stretching out to cast a blessed shade across the burning pavement.

A hundred yards along the road stood a rough building next to a circular field of grass with a rail fence. The structure was a half-barn, a skeleton structure, held up by wooden beams with a single rail stretching along one wall. Half covered by faded, rotted wood, every tiny gust of wind caused it to groan and creak. Alice approached it with narrowed eyes, spotting movement between the loose boards. Tied to the inside rail stood a line of horses, snorting and nickering softly in the shadows. Checking to make sure there were no people, Alice walked up and slipped in through a rear door, standing on a floor of hay and manure, a cloud of dust swirling in the dappled sunlight that squeezed in between cracks in the roof.

"Buck?" Alice gaped at the beige gelding, who tossed his head and snorted at the sight of her. "Oh, Buck!"

Alice flew to him and threw her arms around his neck, resting her cheek on his flank and taking a deep breath of his musky coat, accepting his nuzzles and affectionate snorts. On his other side stood Stormy and Rocky, both curious, tossing their heads and pulling on their tethers.

"I can't believe I found you guys!" She kept her voice to a whisper as she clung to Buck's neck, looking around to inspect the dusty barn. "How did you get here? Where are my kids?"

There was a short ladder leading up to a loft, and saddles and bridles hung on the opposite wall along with some tools and blankets. At the end of the stall stood two more horses she didn't recognize, both chestnut mares eating and drinking from a bucket and trough beneath their noses.

"And where are all the people?" She patted Buck one more time and retrieved her walking stick, walking from one end of the stable to the other, finding a tool chest and a small farrier station that was well-used, though she saw no sign of the kids' backpacks or personal items.

Another draft of campfire smoke carrying rich scents of cooking food swept by, but the smoke was the only sign that anyone else was nearby. Figuring there must be a camp at the end of the lane ahead, Alice headed for the exit, groaning as her trail-beaten body protested in a spasm that traveled down her side and left her doubled over and leaning against the door frame.

Spitting and gasping, she waited until her body stopped cramping and her shallow breaths fell steady again. Finding the horses meant that she had nearly reached the end of her journey, but even that excitement wasn't enough to convince her battered and broken body to keep carrying on. She was still bone weary, beyond exhausted, and she needed some rest. Resting, though, while they suffered who-knew-what tortures at the hands of Mark and Christine was antithetical to everything she believed in both as their mother and a decent human being. She stood at the edge of the doorway to the barn, swaying, trying to psych herself up enough to continue forward, but after a few minutes of almost falling over, she had to concede defeat. She needed a moment of serious rest, some place where she could rest her body, get her head on straight and formulate a plan of attack.

Turning away, Alice shuffled over to the ladder and looked up into the loft. Pieces of hay stuck out over the sides, big bales of it stacked up in various states of condition and stages of decomposition. She used her left hand to grab a rung and anchor herself while reaching up with her right to take the next rung up. Taking a deep breath, Alice started her climb, trying not to drop her walking stick, ignoring the inevitable pain and ascending two or three rungs before she had to stop and rest. After another moment, she got to the top and tossed the stick into the hay, then she finished her climb and crawled into the loft, her good hand slipping forward on some dry hay so that she fell forward, striking her chin on the wood.

Alice swallowed dry and waited for the shock to pass, then rolled over onto her back and scooted farther into the hay. She fell slack with relief as spasms and cramps faded, replaced by the shortness of breath that came after any excess exertion. Stretching her right arm above her, she shifted and tried to relax, blinking at the old wooden roof, water stained and dry rotted, the stifling heat at least fifteen degrees hotter than it was out on the trail, lingering in the rafters until Alice thought the heat rather than the humidity might suffocate her.

A breeze stirring through the bottom level rose into the loft, cooling the sweat on her arms and face, and with that little bit of relief she crawled backward on one elbow until she was partially leaning against the barn wall. Slipping off her pack, she sat it next to her, digging out the MRE and the last water bottle. She put the beef patty in the heating element and added a bit of water to get it warming, then opened the chocolate drink package, squeezing the package into a funnel shape and pouring its contents through into the bottle, recapping it, shaking it, and setting it aside.

She ate the cookie in small chunks, feeding herself slowly, her body responding with a surge of alertness, her vision sharpening as she surveilled every detail of the loft, every knot in the plywood walls, even the pieces of straw she'd broken trying to climb up. It was quiet inside and outside the barn as she mixed the meat sauce in with the beef patty and ate it out of the pouch, the meal hitting her stomach like a brick, and her eyelids began to droop, her thoughts growing sluggish and detached as the temporary alertness wore off.

Alice finished every bit of the MRE she'd saved, downing the rest of the lukewarm chocolate drink and turning the cookie packaging inside out to get at the last few crumbs of chocolate. With her shrunken belly feeling more satiated than it had in days, she rolled onto her right side and shifted in the straw, finding a low pile of hay to hide behind, using her backpack as a pillow and grabbing handfuls of hay to stuff beneath her left side for extra comfort.

In the few seconds it took for her to fall asleep, guilty thoughts of Jake and Sarah passed through her mind, but she pushed them back. A shambling half-corpse would only result in failure, no matter what was going on with her children. No, she needed the sleep and to let her stomach digest her meal to fuel her body and mind both. The horses were there in the barn, so the kids would be close, and she would get them back. *Would*. There was no other option.

CHAPTER TEN

Red Fletcher
Ionia, Michigan

Red Fletcher reached into a bucket, grabbed a wet rag, and climbed up to the truck cab, trading Martha his clean rag for a bloody one and receiving a disgusted look in return.

"This... *stuff* is everywhere, Red," Martha said. "It's all over the seats and floorboard."

"It'll be fine, Martha. Let's just do this and move on."

"But we have to drive in this, Red. You're really okay with sitting up here with all this blood?"

Nancy Likely was inside the truck with her, the women cleaning out the bloody cabin after Red's people had liberated it from two National Guardsmen a few hours earlier. The passenger window was completely gone, and spiderwebbed bullet holes dotted the front windshield. The remaining glass on the driver's side was splattered with red, and the late afternoon sun shined through the patterns of blood in a macabre mockery of stained-glass.

They'd reached Ionia that morning on bicycles and handcarts they'd found near Lowell, making much better progress than they had initially on foot, and the salt truck about to be driven away by the National Guard was too good to let slip away.

"We'll put down blankets to cover the blood," Red said, his voice taking on a malicious edge. "Stop whining about it. This is huge for us."

"How long will it take us to get there?" Nancy interjected herself into the conversation.

"Hard to tell." Red cast one last glance at his wife before addressing Nancy. "The roads are bound to be congested, but Ryan's place is only about twenty minutes east of Lansing."

Reynolds came up and scratched his head. "That'll be about an hour, hour and a half from here."

"Sounds about right," Red nodded. "Like I was telling Martha, we won't be in this truck very long."

Hansen came up with a lopsided grin and his rifle clacking against his hip. "Don't blame us for all this blood, Martha. Those a-holes should've just got out like we asked and not tried to drive off."

"That wasn't a smart move," Reynolds agreed. "They got *themselves* shot. You're mad at the wrong people."

Martha looked over the two men, both in jeans and heavy coats over flannel shirts, combat boots with their pants tucked in, blood caked beneath their fingernails from dragging the bodies out of the truck. Red glanced at the two guardsmen lying by the dumpster, stripped of their weapons, ammunition, and packs. When they'd failed to respond and tried to drive through his people, they'd fired on the truck, striking from two sides and taking them out before they could return fire.

The truck had suffered minor damage when it lurched off to the side out of control and hit a car where it stuck and roared like a dying beast until the driver's foot was removed from the accelerator. The important part was that it had been a quick ambush and they hadn't suffered any casualties, a moment of great pride for Red. It was the first time they'd worked together cohesively as a unit rather than a motley collection of neighbors, moving in on the truck, flanking it, offering the guardsmen a way out but showing no quarter when they wouldn't comply. From there it had been easy enough to check for any other guardsmen in the area before pulling the bodies out of the truck and calling the rest of the group on up from where they'd been keeping out of sight on the road.

Red climbed down and went back to check on the others where they'd pulled their bikes and handcarts up to the truck bed to have them loaded on. "How's it going, Tyler? Is everything going to fit?"

Tyler nodded. "It'll be tight, but we'll make it work. Those guardsmen had already loaded the few barrels of fuel that were stored here, so we're covered on that, too."

"And the truck is full," Red slapped the back. "Should be enough to make it to Lansing and then some. Can you handle the rest of this? I want to take Reynolds and Hansen inside and give it a thorough once-over."

"No problem. I'll put a couple of people down by the road to stand watch, and we'll get this thing loaded up in about twenty-five minutes."

"Perfect. I'll meet you back here then. Reynolds? Hansen?"

"Right here, Red," Hansen said, jogging up.

"Follow me, fellas. Let's check for supplies."

The salt storage facility was in a fenced-in area with a standard brick city building with four thousand square feet of offices, a motor lot out back and a dome-shaped building filled with salt and dirt. They followed the sloping driveway to the rear where the first signs of destruction appeared behind the office building.

"Looks like all the cop cars went up," Reynolds said. "Too bad."

The lower parking lot held about a half-dozen police cars, city maintenance vehicles, and white vans, all blown to pieces with their insides strewn everywhere. Parts of the main building had burned down as a result, and one bay door hung open, knocked off its rollers with chunks of steel, wood, and fiberglass hanging from the frame.

"Maintenance bay for the city vehicles," Red said. "I doubt there's much by way of supplies unless we want salt." Red nodded to where the door to the salt storage facility was sitting halfway open.

"You can eat that stuff, can't you?" Hansen asked.

"It's for the salt truck," Reynolds replied.

"Still, it's just salt."

Red laughed. "You go ahead and try it. It's not food grade, for one thing, and probably has a bunch of rocks and chemicals and crap mixed in. You let us know how it tastes." Hansen grimaced and Red rolled his eyes at the man. "Come on, let's check this place out." Ducking and stepping through the bay door, Red murmured, "Looks like a shotgun blew this place apart."

Several toolboxes were knocked over, and the tang of oil and metal lingered in the air mixed with dripping antifreeze, though it was all overshadowed by the stinking rot of death. Two men in coveralls lay sprawled on the empty bay floor, hats flung off, engine parts penetrating through their torsos. Red kicked one man over to see a six-inch piece of metal sticking out of his sternum, his cold, rotting hands still clinging to it. Reynolds checked the other man out, fiddling with a large sliver of glass that had pierced his orbital cavity, jerking it back and forth to give the corpse an animated appearance.

Red scowled. "Leave it alone, Reynolds. Come on."

They stepped over parts of the engine block, the manifold, and scorched gaskets, entering a storage area that smelled of burning, the stench so acrid and sharp they almost couldn't stand to be in the room. Shelves had toppled over, and the remnants of oil and gas cans littered the floor where they'd caught fire, and there were scorch marks on the walls where flames had ignited portions of the building.

"I guess it's in the oil, too." Red covered his nose with his sleeve and gestured to a set of stairs going up.

"Or the oil caught fire when the gasoline went up." Reynolds kicked one of the cans across the room.

"Mm. This way." Red started to get out his flashlight and go up, but Hansen flipped on his tactical light and shined it up the steps.

"We haven't checked up here yet, Red," Hansen said. "Best be careful."

Red clutched a pistol in one hand as he climbed the stairs carefully, making sure not to step on anything weakened by the fire, popping a door open at the top and entering a long hallway that ran most of the building's length. The air had an acrid, smoky sting, riding a breeze drifting from the burned-up part of the building where the hallway opened to the sky. He gestured for Hansen and Reynolds to follow him, and they slowly made their way through conference rooms and filing rooms filled with dusty cabinets and records no one would ever see again.

"Those guardsmen came from somewhere else, looking for transport I'll bet." Red holstered his pistol. "Ain't nobody left around here. Place'll be ancient ruins before too long."

"Already looks that way to me." Hansen moved to the next room with his rifle held to his shoulder, knocking the door open with his boot and sweeping his weapon back and forth.

"Stop being a jackass, Hansen," Red said, following behind Reynolds.

"Just practicing," Hansen busted into the next room with a grunt, hammering the door so hard that it slammed back against the wall. "My Marine training is coming back to me."

"Great." Red gestured to the next hallway, the longest corridor yet. "Make sure you yell 'clear' just like you did when you sat at a desk all day in Germany."

Hansen fell into a half crouch and crept to the end of the hall with his barrel pointed toward the open door. "Looks like a break room in here," he whispered back. Wait... I see vending machines." His voice dropped even lower. "They're broken open, but there's stuff still inside. That doesn't make any sense."

Red moved to the right to see past him where faint daylight spilled into the room, casting shadows everywhere – and caught sight of some of the shadows shifting imperceptibly. Hansen was about to kick open the doorway when Red reached past Reynolds and grabbed his shoulder.

"Wait!" Red hissed, but the man was already lunging toward the door. It slammed in Hansen's face with a bang and was swiftly followed by the scraping of furniture across the floor, dragged into place on the other side of the doorway.

"Get it open!" Red growled as Hansen threw his shoulder into the door but only budged it a quarter inch. Someone on the other side slammed it shut again and pushed the furniture up with a squeaky scrape.

A man called out. "Go away! Leave us alone."

Hansen was about to ram the door again when Red grabbed his jacket and held him back, calling out, "Who's there?"

"None of your business! Go away!"

"Oh come on now," Red said, "we're just looking for some supplies and help on our trip."

"Like hell you are! We saw what you did!"

"Then you know what we'll do to get what we need," Red spoke with an ominous note. "This doesn't have to end poorly."

"We've got weapons, too. Come in here and see!"

Red was about to confer with his men down the hall when Hansen threw his shoulder against the door one more time, bouncing back and raising his rifle as the people on the other side shoved the furniture back in place. As soon as he heard the squeal of the wood he squeezed the carbine's trigger, spraying rounds through the door, furniture, and flesh. Screams and curses erupted from the other side, drowned out by the gun's chatter as Hansen emptied the entire magazine, ejected it, and slammed home another, then rammed the door open an inch, hitting it again and breaking it open enough to slip his broad shoulders through.

Hansen's actions were a blur that Red barely had time to process, and before he could stop him, Reynolds bowled his way inside on Hansen's heels, weapon raised and sweeping back and forth. Baseball bats flew in with heavy strikes from survivors of Hansen's initial assault and the man screamed and grunted as he and Reynolds both continued firing until both the shouts and gunfire abruptly cut out. Blood hammering in his ears, heart racing, uncertain of what he'd find on the other side, Red stepped in and almost tripped over a dead woman before swinging into the center of the room where Hansen and Reynolds stood with their rifles pointed outward, barrels smoking, bloody bodies sprawled on the barricade, nearby tables and the floor.

Hansen rolled his shoulders, his curly brown hair matted with blood above his right temple and trickling down the side of his face. Reynolds was breathing hard and scanning the room with wide eyes, taking in the half-dozen people lying twisted and bloody, filled with holes, all dead except for one man moaning off in a corner somewhere. Bullets had chewed up the counters, and gun smoke and the tang of blood hung heavy in the confined space.

"What the *hell* Hansen?!" Red growled.

Hansen shrugged and walked over to the smashed vending machine, grabbed a candy bar out, ripped the wrapper off, and shoved it in his mouth. Red shouldered his rifle, took two strides across the room, snatched Hansen by the hair and slammed his face into the open face of the machine, rocking it backward and sending candy bars and bags of chips and crackers flying everywhere. Before Hansen could get out a protest, Red swept his feet from under him and jerked him backward, slamming him to the ground with a thud before planting a boot on his neck. Hansen gasped and choked, startled and out of breath with the candy bar jutting from between his lips and chocolate smeared across his cheeks. His eyes flew wide at the sight of Red's rifle pointed at his nose, and he grabbed at the gun to sweep it aside, but Red dug his boot heel into Hansen's neck and lashed out at Hansen's nose with the gun barrel, forcing his head back down onto the bloody tiles with a wet smack.

"You call yourself a Marine?" Red jerked the rifle to the side, fired several rounds into the floor and then pushed the hot barrel into Hansen's chest, leaning on it, snarling as the metal sizzled through Hansen's shirt and into his skin. "You're a piece of shit, Hansen. You get me? You are *nothing*. I will *end* you right here and right now and sleep sounder for having done it."

Hansen's breathing was jerky, his eyes searching back and forth for an ally, but Reynolds stood across the room, quietly watching. "Y-y-yeah, sure, R-Red."

Red took the rifle barrel off Hansen's chest and leaned in closer to the man's face. "Let's get one thing straight since you were too busy chewing on crayons earlier, '*Marine*'. *I'm* in charge of this operation. You don't do anything, not even take a *dump*, unless I tell you to. You got that?"

"Y-Yeah, Red. I got it." A trickle of blood ran out of Hansen's nose and mixed with the chocolate smeared across his cheeks. "Whatever you say!"

"That goes for you, too." Red whipped his rifle up and pointed it at Reynolds, still leaning heavily on Hansen's neck. "If we're going to get through this, I need people who will do what I *need* them to, not what they *want* to do. Charging in and shooting up people who we could have recruited or pumped for information is *not* what we need to be doing unless *I* give the order. Get it?"

Reynolds held his hands up, taking a step back in deference. "No problem, Red. Whatever you say goes."

"Damn straight it does." Red looked down at Hansen for another moment before shaking his head and addressing Reynolds again. "Get him up. Put all the food, supplies and weapons in a bag, and let's get out of here. It stinks."

While they were largely in his imagination so far, the malodorous scents of death had already begun to fill the room, and Red found his stomach beginning to turn in spite of his attempts to ignore the carnage. He started turning over bodies, checking through pockets for keys or weapons but not finding anything except doubts about what they were doing, which he brushed off as quickly as possible. Reynolds helped Hansen up, the big man wiping the blood and chocolate off his face with a paper towel, throwing a fearful side glance at Red.

"There's not much here, boss," Reynolds said quietly as he stuffed the rest of the food in a sack, tossing in a few rolls of paper towels he'd found above the refrigerator.

"If Hansen hadn't decided to go all Rambo on these people, we could've questioned them to see if they had any *other* supplies." Red stood and walked over to a closet, opening it to find it completely cleared out. "I bet there's nothing in the cabinets, too." He gave the room a skeptical sweep, observing how the furniture and filing cabinets had been dragged in from other rooms to make the barricade. "This could've even been a trap... lure people in with the vending machine snacks before beating them up."

"Why didn't they try to lure us in?" Reynolds asked.

"They watched us kill the guardsmen and probably decided to play it safe once they saw what they would be up against. 'Course we'll never know because brainiac over there came in shooting like Yosemite Sam, and now they're all dead."

"Sorry, Red," Hansen whispered, shouldering his rifle and holding a few paper towels to his bloodied nose.

Red walked over and stared up into his bloody face before sighing wearily and patting the man on the shoulder. "It's okay, Hansen. We've only been in a couple of real combat situations. The first one went well. This one... we've simply got to do better."

"Right. I understand. I'll remember my old train—"

"No." Red squeezed Hansen's shoulder tighter, eliciting a grimace from the man. "What you'll do is remember to listen to me. Get it?"

"Got it, Red."

"Good. Now let's get everything and head outside. I'll do the talking. Don't need Martha crawling up my ass again."

They gathered up the supplies and walked out the front door, taking the sidewalk to the salt truck. The rest of the group waited apprehensively by the truck, forming a defensive position behind it with their guns out and ready to shoot.

Martha saw Red and broke cover, hesitating when she caught sight of the blood on Hansen's head and face. "What happened, Red? We heard gunshots."

Red turned her by her shoulders and walked her back toward the truck. "Found some people holed up inside, and they attacked us. Had to defend ourselves. We're fine, though, and we got them all."

"More people dead?"

"They attacked us, Martha."

"But—"

"They. Attacked us. Martha." Red's voice dropped an octave and she stood still for a few seconds, staring at him as her jaw worked back and forth before finally giving him a disgusted look and changing the subject.

"What did you get out of whatever really happened?"

"Not much. Some packaged food from a vending machine. Looked like they were running low themselves so they were probably hoping to steal from us." Red gestured at the two people they'd designated as medics, one combat-trained and the other a former EMT. "Hey, can you take a look at Hansen's head? Took a bat to the nose and back of the head. He's bleeding a bit."

"Yes, sir!"

Red handed off Hansen with a knowing look, then met Tyler at the rear of the truck, where everything had been loaded up but a couple of bikes and handcarts.

"Are we about ready to go?"

"Yep. We've got all the supplies and bikes in the middle," Tyler said, "leaving the rest open for people to stretch their legs or lie down if they've got to. We secured everything with bungee cords and rope, so nothing will tip over or fall out."

"Excellent. I'd say we're about ready to roll out, then. Martha and I will take the front seat with Reynolds. Get everyone else in back."

The last of their things were loaded into the back of the truck in short order and everyone jumped inside and put up the tailgate with a clang. Red got behind the wheel and started it up, the engine's powerful vibrations a welcome relief beneath his feet after so much walking. Martha got in on his right, with Reynolds riding shotgun, and the latter held out a folded, dog-eared piece of paper.

"I found this, boss."

"Boss?" Martha arched an eyebrow, but Red ignored her.

"What's this?" He took the paper from Reynolds.

"It's a map I found on one of the guardsmen. Looks like it's marked with National Guard locations, ones you'll probably want to avoid, especially now."

"Martha, dear, will you be my navigator?" Red held out the map and she took it from him, nodding quietly as she spread it out in her lap.

Red revved the engine, put the salt truck into drive, and pulled out, whipping onto the road, easily knocking aside a vehicle frame and smashing over a smattering of debris with the truck's massive tires.

"Oh, this is good," he patted the steering wheel and threw the truck into a higher gear, smiling as it plowed through yet another burned-out vehicle. "This is *really* good. We're going to *eat* those miles up!"

CHAPTER ELEVEN

Alice Burton
Talladega National Forest, Alabama

It was the middle of the night when Alice woke from the most restful sleep she'd had in days. Instead of being overheated and sweating as she had when she'd collapsed in the hay, though, she was shivering, and it took her a moment to realize that there was a breeze blowing through the rafters, wicking away the sweat from her skin. She lay still for a moment and listened to the horses making soft noises below, and when there were no sounds of people along with them, she got up on one elbow to perform a self-check and look around.

Her right side was stiff from sleeping on it so long, her right pinky finger tingling with pins and needles as the circulation returned and her chest still ached with every breath – but the pain was duller than it had been previously. There was no moon visible through the cloud cover by which to estimate the time, but based on how much better she felt, she guessed that it must've been a few hours at least.

Despite breathing easier, her chest still hurt terribly, the primary ache having shifted from her sternum area to the left side, muscles twitching beneath her scapula and down her spine. She sat up in a slouch, stretching her neck in both directions, cracking it, testing the pain level to see if anything had gotten any better. She couldn't tell if things *were* better, but she had more energy and felt like she was dealing with her injuries well enough that she could climb out of the loft and have a look around.

Alice grabbed her backpack and started scooting toward the ladder when voices approached from the east along the road out beyond the barn. Carefully and quietly she slid back to her spot behind the hay pile, getting her knife out and ready, heart pounding in anticipation of some kind of confrontation with the kidnappers of her children. As the voices came near, Alice peered through the cracks in the wall, watching as a pair of flashlights moved across the road and swung up toward the stable, flashing across the wooden slats and doorway into the structures, and she sank back down.

"Can't we get one of the hands to do this?" an older man said in a gruff voice. "I'm getting a little too old for chores."

A younger man chimed in. "We've got work hands, but that doesn't mean we don't have to do a thing or two, especially when the brats are so busy. At least we get the choice of when to do this, and I'd rather do it at night before we go to bed because I like sleeping late."

"That's because you're lazy, Charlie."

"I'm not lazy, Carl. Just smart."

"Whatever, man," Carl chuckled. "I'll fill the water troughs if you want to grab the hay from the loft."

"Sounds good to me."

The pair stepped inside and clanked around with tin pails while the horses chuffed and snorted in anticipation of being fed. One man set his flashlight on the rail, illuminating a large circle on the ceiling and flooding the loft with light. Alice clenched her pocketknife, staring at the ladder with wide eyes and then moving a few inches to the left where her walking stick sat in plain view. In a rush, she raised up, drew her legs beneath her, and stretched to grab it just as Charlie clasped the ladder rung and started climbing. She reached with her left arm, compressing her ribs on that side and sending streaks of agony pulsing up to her neck. Teeth clenched against the gasp of pain wanting out, she wrapped her hand around the stick, lifted it quietly off the hay, and brought it to her chest.

Charlie's hand came over the edge and felt back and forth until it landed in a small pile of hay a few inches from her leg. He grabbed a handful and pulled it off, stuffing it into a sack before reaching for more. Alice held her breath and froze, holding the stick in her left hand, knife in the right, ready to use them if the man ventured further into the loft. When Charlie ran out of hay in the spot he had started in, he reached farther, with his fingers brushing her leg as he grabbed some more. Alice rolled the other way, her movements masked by the sounds of him stuffing hay into the sack and he took one last handful before climbing down, and Alice released the breath she'd been holding.

"How long until the next delivery of workers comes in?" Carl dumped feed out into a trough for the horses, who chuffed and snorted as they jostled to get near enough to eat.

"Another week, probably. They sent more folks out yesterday. Gonna take a day to get out of the park, few days to acquire them and a day or two to get back." Charlie replied with a snort. "They're worth the trouble, though. Things are easy with them doing the hard labor for us. And the best part is, if they screw up, you can give them a little business for it. What're they gonna do, fight back?"

Alice's jaw clenched as she imagined Jake and Sarah in the clutches of what was obviously a larger group of people, operating side-by-side with others as a slave labor workforce for whatever the pair of men were involved with.

"I guess that's one good thing." There was a splash of water as Carl transferred it from the bucket to another trough, and the horses began to munch on the hay and drink. Alice stayed tensed in the quiet, barely breathing as the men went about their work and finished stacking the pails in the barn.

"Well, this should be good enough," Charlie said.

"Yeah, doesn't need to be perfect," Carl agreed. "You ready to head back?"

"Yep. Let's go."

A flashlight that had been left shining at the ceiling was picked up and the light blinked out as the pair moved through the rickety door and slammed it behind them, but it hit with enough force to bounce back open.

"Damn latch is still busted."

"Whatever. We'll put it on the list of stuff to get. Not like it matters, though. They're all tied up."

"Yeah, but what if someone..."

As the voices, footsteps and flashlights faded, Alice left her backpack behind and quickly crawled to the edge of the loft, swung her feet over, and climbed down the same way she'd come up, keeping her left arm mostly locked against her side. Boots down, she brushed past the horses and went for the door, which was a loose construction of planks connected by two cross pieces, and pushed it open. The latch was rusted, but the hinges were quiet, and she leaned out and watched the distant glow of flashlights as they crisscrossed in front of the men. Before she could think better of her actions, Alice forced herself to move out from the barn and through a swath of grass before reaching the edge of the road, staying off to the side, matching their footsteps, keeping the bushes near if she needed to crouch down somewhere and hide.

The night was alive around her, insects singing in thick swells that were loud enough to mask her movements, and a gentle breeze provided a natural rustle that her footsteps blended with. Up above, bats flitted in the darkness, chasing bugs in wild acrobatic moves, and the moonlight was bright without much cloud cover to hide it. After a moment, the sounds of rushing water came through over the insects and wind and she heard splashing and more voices.

Across the road was a large wooden sign held up by a pair of thick posts, though she was too far away – and it was too dark – to see what it said. The faint orange glow of campfires washed over Charlie and Carl and stretched their shadows to where Alice crept stealthily behind them. She caught more distant conversations, and when the campfires came into view she married the voices to about a dozen people gathered around a wide open space in the trees. Picnic tables dotted the area at the edge of the light, and two people sat eating at one while others stood and sat farther away. Off behind the group were small buildings with wooden siding, screen doors, and big porches with awnings that faced the fires, and many of the windows and screen doors held a soft glow of inhabitation behind them.

The breeze changed directions and Alice was hit with the smell of cooking meat. She spotted a man leaning over campfire grills, grabbing something with a pair of tongs, and flipping it in a burst of flames as another person stood near him, pointing at the fire and speaking something unintelligible. Alice stepped off the road and into the brush, letting Charlie and Carl go as she crept deeper into the bushes between a pair of large trees, moving to the south side of the camp area where the view was better.

Pulling down a slim branch, she stood up slightly and looked around, still too far to hear any meaningful snippets of conversation, of which there was a copious amount. She was close enough to observe that the men and women were poorly dressed, with many of their shirts and pants ripped and covered with dirt and other stains, indicating that they had been out in the forest for quite some time. Some of the men had a borderline junkie look to them, though a few rippled with muscles and carried themselves with an air of surety not possessed by the others.

A group of four women stood by the nearest fire, each wearing long flannel shirts or T-shirts, tight jeans, and beers in their hands as they talked and flicked ashes from cigarettes. One man grabbed another by the shoulders and shook him, the other grabbing him back, the pair wrestling a moment before breaking down in laughter and slapping each other's shoulders. Beyond the fires, she spotted both candlelight and electric lanterns glowing from within the buildings, the three largest structures shaped like bunk houses while the other smaller ones could've been out houses or storage sheds.

"Reminds me of summer camp," Alice whispered. "Maybe it *is* a summer camp."

From the woods, a pair of shorter forms appeared – the first she'd seen since observing the camp – their chains jangling faintly and each with a bundle of sticks and deadfall in their arms. The two boys slouched as they stepped into the clearing, carrying their burdens over to the farthest fire where the pair of men had been wrestling a moment earlier. The adults, laughing, slapping the kids on the backs of their heads, the smaller of the two falling into the other, both almost going down until the men snatched their arms and held them up right. That gained them another slap, and one man pointed to a spot next to the fire where the kids staggered over and dropped the wood with a clatter. One man grabbed the larger boy by the arm and shook him, gesturing at the pile and explaining something, then the boys fell to their knees and gathered what they'd dropped into a neater pile, picking up any scraps that had fallen off the side and placing them on top.

"That's how you do it!" the same man shouted loud enough for Alice to hear, clapping mockingly at the pair and patting the larger of the two children on the back so hard he almost tripped over the woodpile and toppled into the fire.

The man grabbed him again, by the neck, hauling him backward before shoving him toward the smaller boy, the two slamming together and grasping each other to keep from falling. The other man came up and gestured at the pair of children with a hatchet, and the boys flinched in response, grasping each other in terror. The man burst out laughing at their fear, flipped the hatchet around, and held the handle out, shouting at them. "Go get some bigger pieces! Cut it down if you have to!"

"Yeah, none of this small crap." The first man pointed at the wood pile. "This stuff burns too quick! We need bigger logs to make a real fire. Go on, now. *Go!*"

The bigger boy took the hatchet and grabbed his friend, and the two chain-bound laborers staggered off past the fires and laughing people into the woods about thirty yards from where Alice was standing.

"And don't think about trying to get away!" One of the men called after the children. "Remember what happened the last time!"

Alice scowled and slid deeper into the brush, stepping carefully in the dry leaves and pine needles as she moved in the direction the two children had gone. It didn't take her long to find the kids, the larger boy hacking on a sapling while the other dragged a log from a short distance away, bound together by their short length of chain. Alice stood in the shadows for a moment, catching her breath and studying the two children for a moment while she tried to decide on the best course of action. When she finally stepped from the trees, both boys jumped back in surprise, the bigger one – probably twelve or so – raised the hatchet while the smaller boy dropped his log and stood with a quivering chin.

"Hey, kids." Alice's held up one hand. "Hey, don't be afraid. I'm..." Alice stepped closer, leaning on her walking stick as she took a breath, her chest aching from the bit of movement she'd been doing.

"We're getting the wood like Stan told us to," the bigger boy said. "We're trying to go faster, I swear!"

"No, no, no." Alice gestured. "I'm not part of this... whoever these people are. I've just been watching from the woods here."

The boys shared a look before the bigger one pushed the smaller one behind him. "There's no need to test us," he said. "We won't run. We couldn't if we wanted to. We know that."

Alice shook her head harder. "No, boys. I'm not here to test you or punish you. Look, my name is Alice, and I came from... it's a long story. I'm not with these people, though, I swear." As Alice spoke, the pair only stepped back and shared another frightened look.

"I was with my kids a few days ago. Jake and Sarah... you might know them? Anyway, a couple of... real jerks tricked us and took our horses and guns, and my two children. They shot me right here, too." Alice pulled down her shirt to reveal the bruise and touched the spot on her chest a little too hard, wincing in pain.

The bigger kid shifted his grip on the hatchet and stepped into the light. His face was soft and round with hazel eyes, and he was fairly broad in the shoulders, a tough looking kid, but he wore an expression of mistrust mixed with intense, overwhelming fear. Both boys didn't appear physically older than twelve or thirteen, but there was a look to their eyes that added several years to each of them.

"You got shot?"

"Yeah, right here."

"If you got shot, lady," the smaller boy piped up, "why aren't you dead?"

"I had my cell phone in my pocket, and the bullet hit it and ricocheted down my side. Here." She lifted her shirt enough for them to see the line of scrapes and where the round had glanced off her hip. Moonlight penetrated the upper canopy and shined across her stomach, exposing the dark bruising all along her front, causing both boys to open their mouths in shock.

"*Wow*, you really did get shot," the bigger boy said.

"Yeah, I did. And you know what the worst part is?"

Both boys shook their heads.

"The jerk shot me with my own gun. Now, what are your names?"

The bigger kid jerked a thumb at himself. "I'm Ricky, and this is Colton."

"Nice to meet you boys. How long have you been here?"

Ricky shrugged, nervously looking at Colton. "I don't even remember. Maybe a week or two?"

"I was here before him," Colton said, stepping closer. "Like, forever, when they first started it."

"What is this place?"

"I guess it used to be a summer camp? Reminds me of the ones my mom used to send me to," Ricky said, "but it's not a camp anymore. These people took it over."

"All I see them doing is sitting around the fires and partying."

Ricky looked at Colton again, his eyes darting around nervously. "Yeah, they do a lot of that but they make stuff, too."

"Make stuff?"

"Yeah, in one of the back buildings. It's a lab or something. I don't know... I was never in there for long. I just deliver stuff for them..." He gestured. "And get wood."

"Are they cooking drugs?"

Ricky thought for a minute. "The stuff they make smells really bad, but some of them use it in pipes and stuff. I think they trade some of it too, but mostly they just make it and stash it in one of the buildings."

"What about your parents? Are they around?"

Ricky sniffed and wiped his arm across his nose. "Nah, Mom and Dad didn't make it. Colton's didn't either."

"Did these people..." Alice trailed off, unsure of how to finish the sentence.

"No," Ricky replied. "Colton's parents were in a car, and mine were in a building that burned down."

"I'm sorry, boys," Alice said, "I'm so sorry this happened to you."

Ricky nodded, and Colton pulled a sleeve across his eyes.

"Do they feed you?"

"Yeah," Ricky said, "but not like home."

Alice wiped her eye with her shirtsleeve. "Is it the same group of people here all the time?"

"Nah. New people show up sometimes. They keep sending people out on supply runs and stuff. I don't know half of them, but it makes it kinda easier."

"Easier how?"

"Well, sometimes they can't remember all of us, and we can sneak extra food when nobody's looking. Or get extra break times."

Alice nodded knowingly. "I see. Say... have you seen anyone new around here? New kids, I mean."

Ricky considered the question. "They bring in new kids all the time these days... I guess a lot of people are dying out there.

"You could say that. The ones I'm looking for are mine, though."

"Yours?" Colton's eyes widened. "They don't take kids from parents who are *alive*."

"Well, they did shoot me. And I think my kids and I might have spooked them or something, when we ran into them in the forest a couple days ago."

"What do they look like?" Ricky asked.

"Jake is about yay high, fourteen, with short brown hair... well, I guess it's grown out a little bit now. Sarah is a little shorter, twelve, with long brown hair. She'd probably be wearing it in a ponytail or clip or something."

"Oh, yeah," Ricky said, looking at Colton again, who nodded in confirmation. "Must be the newbies that came in this morning."

Alice nodded. "Yeah, that's about when they would have showed up. Can you tell me where they are?"

"They moved them to the other side of the camp," Colton said, "near the river. They got them hauling water and food. They've got them on cleaning duty, too, mainly because they're not doing what they're supposed to."

"What do you mean?"

"Well, the girl slapped one of the guards, and when he knocked her down, the boy tried to punch him."

Alice smiled. "Those're my babies all right."

Ricky glanced toward the fires. "Look, uh, Ms. Alice... if we don't get this wood back, we'll get in trouble. We've barely cut anything, and Stan will be expecting us back soon." He stooped to gather up some of the bigger pieces Colton had dropped and put them back in his outstretched arms.

"Wait, kids. I know you're chained up, but you've got a hatchet. Why don't you try to run away?"

Ricky shook his head and kept working. "A couple of kids already tried to get away, and they got ripped for it."

"Ripped?"

"You don't want to know." Colton spoke softly as he and Ricky exchanged a look. "But they treat you okay as long as you do what you're told. We need to do what we're told!"

"Okay, kids," Alice said. "I'll let you get back to work, but I promise to help you get out of here."

"Yeah right. Nobody's gonna do that."

"Still. I will, I promise. Can you do me a favor?"

Ricky nodded and let Colton squeeze by with his stack of wood.

"Can you get word to Jake and Sarah that their mother is alive and coming?"

Ricky picked up some larger logs and tucked them under one arm. "If I see them, I'll tell them. But I probably won't see them, though. They work on the other side—"

"Of the camp, yes. That's good enough. Thank you. Stay safe, kids."

"We'll try."

The two figures shambled away, dragging their chains through the brush with arms full of wood, getting snagged on forest debris and tripping, finally disappearing from sight. Alice moved north along the tree line, buried in the brush, moving closer to the bunk houses after they left. She stopped when a man and woman walked by half drunk and stumbling on a dirt path, pushing each other playfully before coming together and locking arms. Once they'd passed, she surveilled the bunk houses, getting a good view through the windows. There was at least a half-dozen adults in one directly in front of her, and more in the other two, their shadows silhouetted in soft lantern light. Smoke rose from the double chimneys of the building, and there was the smell of some other sort of food being cooked inside the buildings.

Alice walked the length of the entire camp, hidden by the darkness and the depths of the forest as the breezes picked up, cooling her sweaty face. There were more bunk houses near the river, a few campfires blazing high with people gathered around them where a radio played and a few women danced drunkenly, spinning and almost falling into the fire, pulled to safety by their partners and laughing in their arms. Others were working, carrying plastic-wrapped packages or wood for the fires, kids mostly, hunched over and cowering beneath the heavy hands of their jailers. Men and women alike shouted and cuffed them across their heads, shoving them down steps when their tasks were complete or sending them running with their packages.

The hairs on the back of Alice's neck rose at the sight of children being treated as they were, but she continued onward, staying well within the tree cover and counting buildings and people as she went. Soon, the sound of rushing water grew louder and, remembering what Ricky had told her about Jake and Sarah she trudged eastward, moving slowly and carefully to avoid crunching too loudly on the dry forest scatter. She avoided rocks and logs, sometimes poking at the ground like a blind person with her walking stick, using her left hand to grab saplings and clutches of vines to keep herself from stumbling. Bugs crawled across her skin, and she swatted away the ones on her face and neck, too sore and focused to bother with the others as they slowly ate her alive. Leaves and branches brushed her arms and legs, grabbing at her jeans and sometimes bare skin to add more cuts and scrapes. Alice paid the minor annoyances no heed, though, instead pushing through the tangle of woods until she finally reached the river and looked down from the bank at the water's edge where firelight glinted off the river as the water rolled by.

A grassy field swept north along the riverbank with more buildings and campfires, more people, shouts and laughter, and even more drinking and partying. Pairs of kids walked around the camp, many of them chained together like Ricky and Colton had been, delivering wood and fetching food and other items around the campgrounds. Cooks dished out food from large, homemade grills where flames leaped high and grease sizzled and snapped. The smells hit her hard and her stomach twisted in agony, her body suddenly coming to the realization that it *desperately* wanted food.

Alice stopped where the bank cut sharply toward the water, moving back the other way, craning her neck and squinting through gaps in the brush at the children, finding it impossible to tell if any of the prisoners were Jake or Sarah. In the firelight and shadows all of the smaller figures looked the same; younger kids and teenagers both, all marked by their shuffling movements and clanking chains.

At one grill, what looked to be a girl of about ten held out a plate with shaking hands, and when the cook slapped a piece of meat on it, the dish tilted down, slipped off, and the food hit the ground. The man smacked his tongs on the top of the grill with a clang, drawing glances and laughter from those gathered. He stood with his hands on his hips, glaring at the girl who remained rooted to the spot with her arms still held out and the plate dangling from her fingertips.

The cook snatched the piece of meat off the ground and dropped it back on the grill, scraping dirt off and brandishing the tongs with a furious shout. "Get down and eat some dirt," he growled. "Go on. Get on your knees."

The girl dropped to the ground and stared up at the man in question.

"Get a handful of dirt. There you go. A little more. Perfect. Now eat it."

She knelt, trembling, with a mound of dirt in her palm, shaking her head, her sniffles and sobs audible even to Alice.

"You know the rules, girl," he said. "If you drop something, you eat dirt."

"I wasn't ready for it," she cried. "You dropped it too-"

"Shut up." The cook pointed his tongs at the ground. "This'll teach you to be ready next time. Now eat!"

With shivering shoulders, the girl drew her hand to her mouth, and it was all Alice could do to hold fast to the sapling she was leaning on and not burst from the trees and plunge her knife into the man's chest. "Easy, Alice..." she murmured to herself under her breath, swallowing hard. "Can't save Jake and Sarah if you're dead, now can you?"

"That's it," the man said. "Swallow it. Good girl. Now get out of here."

The cook gave her a parting smack with his tongs as she leaped up and ran away, her chains jingling through the crowd to their laughter and mocking sneers. Alice shook her head and took a deep breath, the sharp pain in her side a reminder of the poor condition she was in. Even if she could locate Sarah and Jake, there was zero chance of her being able to take on the entire camp by herself.

"Gotta think of something else... gotta be sneaky somehow." Alice continued her peregrination along the treeline, her teeth grinding and her clenched fists white with rage as she witnessed other abuses as they happened in real time. Ricky and Colton's insinuations of what went on hadn't prepared her for the slaps, shoves, shouts, denigrations and – in one case – full on beating with a switch torn from a nearby tree, leaving the victim's shirt in tatters. In between the mistreatment and rampant partying, both the children and adults labored, the former operating as the manual labor while the latter performed other tasks, such as cooking and – along one building – constructing what looked like a small supply shed.

A figure caught her eye at the edge of a campfire, a flash of chestnut hair in the light, a tall boy with a messed-up mop of brown hair, shirt off, sweat glistening on his chest. He was chained at the feet with another figure like Ricky and Colton had been, each with a rope over their shoulder, leaning forward and straining to drag a tarp covered in stacks of bricks. The tarp had been loaded so high that some of the bricks wavered and toppled into the grass. A foreman stormed over and pointed at the pile while shouting at the pair and both of them dropped their ropes, held their fists out and hollered back, their voices raspy and raw and brimming with pain – but still unmistakable.

"Jake," Alice whispered. "Sarah... my babies."

The foreman and Jake went back and forth for a moment before the man shook his head and delivered a hammering backhand to Jake she could hear from where she stood. The next one was for Sarah, a slap across the cheek that rocked her head back and sent her flailing backward, nearly cracking her head on the pile of bricks.

"You son of a...." Alice growled like an animal, starting to come out of the bushes but forcing herself to remain crouched against every instinct she possessed.

Jake turned and shoved the foreman, grappling with him before the man balled up his fist and struck him across the jaw, the blow knocking him on his back atop the pile of bricks. Sarah, who had barely gotten to her feet, threw herself over Jake, covering him with her body, glaring up at the foreman and shouting something at him that Alice couldn't make out. It was a nightmare scenario; her children were being beaten in front of her, and any move she tried to make would mean certain death for them and her both.

"Stay down, Jake," she whispered. "Just stay down. Come on, son, be smart about this!"

Jake pushed Sarah off him but remained on his back, and the foreman nodded in satisfaction and gestured to the bricks, then pointed the other way. Other nearby children who had been watching in slack-jawed fear jumped back to work as more of the adults stopped their carousing and came around, yelling and slapping them. Jake and Sarah helped each other up, both of them in obvious pain, and the two began picking up spilled bricks and re-stacking them in rows while the foreman barked another order before walking off laughing.

CHAPTER TWELVE

James Burton
La Porte, Indiana

The morning sun crept across the sky, sending a ray of light between the blinds in just the right location to fall squarely on James' face. He flinched and blinked, turning away from the brightness and warmth and putting his hand up to shield his eyes. Rolling to his left, he slipped off the cushions he'd been lying on and got to his knees as the events of the last day rushed back to him. The ride into La Porte, the bicycle breaking down, and finally – "Oswell?" he asked, mouth dry and lips chapped.

When no one replied, he crawled to his jacket, grabbed it and got up, feeling every inch of soreness from the bike ride – and uncomfortable sleeping arrangements – through his back and legs. Half staggering to the counter where he'd last left Orwell, he rubbed the sleep from his eyes, but she wasn't there. There was no sign of the IV drip, the tubing, or the guardswoman. The cushions were still there, though, and the jackets and blankets had been tossed aside along with the bloody gauze he'd used to clean her wounds, but she herself had vanished.

"Oswell?!" he called again, turning toward the front doors to see if she'd gone outside.

A soft bang echoed through the building's hallway and James whirled and crouched, taking his revolver out of his pocket and tossing the jacket on the cushions. Another bang came from somewhere down the hall, not urgent or violent, but casual, inasmuch as a strange noise in a strange, empty building could be called casual. Still dizzy and dazed, sore from almost two days of non-stop pedaling, James limped down the hallway, pausing at each door to listen for sounds, finally reaching the end where he rested his hand on the doorknob and waited. From inside came shuffling and clanking, and he gathered himself before slamming into the door with his shoulder, raising his gun up and preparing to fire.

"Oh, hey, James!"

James blinked several times before lowering the pistol, letting out an exasperated, relieved sigh. "Dammit, Oswell, I nearly shot you! Didn't you hear me calling?"

Oswell sat at a break room table with a big bowl of cereal in front of her, her spoon clanking as she took another bite, nonplussed by James' unorthodox entry into the room. "Sorry, I didn't," she said around her chewing. "I was so hungry that I couldn't wait to eat. I found cereal and some powdered milk. Not as good as the real stuff, but it gets the job done." She pointed to a box and pitcher filled with white liquid with her spoon. "C'mon, have some."

James laughed in bewilderment and relief, sat across from her, and put his revolver on the table. "Sorry about that... I just woke up and saw you weren't there, then I heard some noises. Scared the hell out of me, what with all the bodies all over the place."

"Oh, yeah, that was me getting dishes out. I got up about... eh, fifteen, twenty minutes ago and saw this hooked up to me..." She raised her arm to show the cannula still in her arm and a fresh fluid bag hanging from an IV stand with wheels. The color had returned to her face, the dark circles beneath her eyes had faded, and her expression was bright and alert. She'd combed back her greasy hair and put it in a ponytail, and while her face had been scrubbed clean, her clothes were still dirty and ragged. "I figured you must've done it. I would've thanked you but you were sleeping, and I didn't want to wake you up. So, thank you. You saved my life, Burton. *Again*."

"You're welcome. You look like a new person."

"Thanks. Found a sink and some water and cleaned up a little bit, then I got to eating. I feel a thousand times better, and I woke up *hungry*."

"Honestly, I'm shocked to see you up and moving around. You were pretty bad last night. The infection had a grip on you. I didn't think the antibiotics worked that fast."

"Oh, they don't. I'll feel a hell of a lot worse later."

"What do you mean?"

Oswell laughed as she poked at the IV bag with the handle of her spoon. "This ain't just antibiotics. It's a cocktail of antibiotics and painkillers and narcotics they use to dose people up during field triage. I'll feel like crap later, but I feel amazing now."

James chuckled. "Well, sorry... and you're *welcome*. Hey, I didn't find this room before. I see we've got a couple of vending machines and a sink."

"The spigot works, too."

James grabbed the bowl and spoon and poured some sugar-coated flakes and reconstituted milk into it. After the first tentative bite his hunger took over, and he finished the bowl in two minutes, then had a second bowl and ate that one almost as fast.

"Slow down. You'll get sick."

"I didn't realize how hungry I was." He replied between bites. "Is there anything else?"

"Nope. We've got powdered milk, water and cereal. Nothing else in the cabinets except a box of stale snack cakes, some coffee, and filters. All the food in the refrigerator is rotten and the rest looks like it was ransacked."

"Well, maybe there's something else around the outpost. Have you been outside yet?"

"Not yet. I was waiting till you woke up to venture outside, just in case there're any neerdowells lurkin about."

James took a slower bite and nodded to the IV stand. "Where'd you find that?"

"Storage room on the other side of the building."

They finished eating, and James took their bowls to the sink and dropped them in. "Can you walk?"

"I can with your handy dandy walking stick," she said, lifting it from where it leaned against her chair. With shaking arms, she used the staff and table to leverage herself up, fell off balance for a second, but recovered and stood straight.

"Not bad. I'll help you down the hall."

"No, I've got it. Just get the door for me, please."

James crossed the room and opened the door, waiting for her to pass and staying close in case she lost her balance again. They made it to the end of the hall and then into the lobby, and he held open the front doors as she stepped into the warm morning light that cut across the outpost, revealing the full extent of the death and destruction.

Oswell frowned and shook her head. "I just... I can't believe it. It's all gone. The whole thing... just gone. Who would *do* something like this?"

James squinted at the rotting bodies and twisted metal of armored vehicles, buildings reduced to rubble, and garbage everywhere. The smell that had been previously dampened by the cool of the night and a slight wind was ten times worse in the daylight, and the rotting stench would only grow more pungent as the day warmed and the sun climbed to its zenith.

"What do you suggest we do?" James asked. "I think if there was anyone left here, they would have found us by now."

"Yeah, agreed." She shrugged. "Honestly... I don't know what to do at this point."

"Are there any other bases or outposts around?"

"Not within walking distance... there's a training camp outside Shipshewana, Indiana, but that's sixty or seventy miles away. I'll never make it on foot."

"Yeah, we'll need a ride," James said, surveilling the remains of numerous rusting armored vehicles lying around the outpost like chunks of coal. "Let's look around. Maybe we'll find something."

With a flashlight and pistol in hand, James guided them away from the administration building and they walked the long lane leading to the main four-way intersection. They'd only gotten about twenty yards when Oswell's foot started dragging, and she quickly fell behind.

"Hold up, James," she huffed, slumped over with her arm shaking on the walking stick. "I can't walk fast enough to keep up. This isn't going to work."

"What if I help you?"

"Nah, you'll only wear yourself out. You'd be better off going by yourself."

James scratched his chin, then motioned back to the building they'd just left. "Is the armory close by?"

"Yeah, why?"

"Why don't you look around for some weapons and ammunition while I see if I can find us a ride? Just stay close to the administration building."

"Hey, good idea. I can limp around for a while, for sure. I'll grab your backpack and load it up with whatever I can find."

"Good. If you run into any trouble, just holler. And use that office chair if you're getting worn out – that's what I brought you in on last night."

"Ha!" Oswell chuckled. "So *that's* how you got me into the building. I wondered why that chair was covered in blood."

While Oswell hobbled off, James walked along the lane toward the main intersection. The first two buildings lay in burnt, rained-on ruins, and while the next few stood intact, their front windows were broken and the main doors had been torn from their hinges. More guardsmen lay sprawled on the ground and around the buildings, their weapons and ammunition vests stripped from their bodies. One guardswoman hung halfway out of a ground floor window, her knuckles resting on the grass, bullet holes puncturing her back and a thick, reddish-black puddle covering the ground beneath her hands. Others showed signs of having been beaten bloody, dead eyes staring at the sky, faces mottled with purple and black bruises. Three people not wearing uniforms – some of the attackers, James assumed – had been cut down in the yard, their bodies shredded, painting the grass red.

"How on earth did they take this place so unawares?" James muttered to himself as he reached the intersection, turning left where more armored vehicles were strung out along the road.

He passed warehouses with delivery trucks parked by the loading docks, their gas tanks having exploded and setting the rest of the buildings on fire, and any goods left intact had been dragged out into the parking lot, though only their outer packaging and wooden pallets remained. He found a couple of intact, half-melted water bottles rolling among a pile of destroyed ones and put them in his pockets. Several boxes of uniforms had been tossed aside with jackets and fatigues hanging out, fluttering in the breeze. Helmets and air filtration masks, folding chairs and tables, range targets, stuffed dummies, and other training supplies lay scattered around, but the food and water had either been destroyed or hauled away.

James came across a small brick warehouse about three buildings down on the left with two doors rolled up and a half-dozen guardsmen in a rough semicircle around them. They'd been overrun, their helmets twisted on their heads, skulls crushed, stripped of their weapons and armor. At least five times their number of civilians lay dead in the front yard of the warehouse, their stench making his stomach twist, and he began to regret how much cereal he'd eaten.

"This where you boys and girls made your last stand? Looks like you took a fair number of these a-holes with you, that's for sure."

Picking through the soldiers' corpses was a grim and unproductive task, yielding only a smattering of wallets and cell-phones that he left on the ground next to the bodies. He was about to give up his search and move no to the next building when he saw a pair of boots sticking out a nearby doorway, with the rest of the soldier's body lying back in the shadows. Curious, James walked up and shined his flashlight over a man partially covered in a strip of plastic that had likely come off a supply skid.

Tossing the plastic aside, James saw the man had been stabbed in his stomach with the butcher knife still stuck in his gut, but whoever had killed him left his M4 carbine and ammunition vest. Inside were two full magazines, and the gun had a half magazine in it as well. James gingerly stripped off the bloodstained vest, put it on, shouldered the rifle, and moved on up the road.

Humvees, armored vehicles and troop transports littered the streets and parking lots as he moved deeper into the outpost, each and every one destroyed well beyond anyone's ability to repair. James' hopes lifted, though, when he spotted a building bearing the label of *Maintenance Depot* at the end of the lane with its doors thrown up and dark, rectangular shapes inside. Jogging up, James flipped on his flashlight to reveal several Humvees in various states of repair, one tilted toward the ground at an awkward angle after the hydraulic lift it had been sitting on had failed. None of the vehicles had been destroyed by the blasts, but neither were any of them in any shape that could be considered drivable. Still, James walked from one to the next, checking under the hoods to see what conditions they were in, finding a lot of major components missing, some with their transmissions or engine blocks hauled out and hanging from chains.

"Well, shoot. This'd take weeks to cobble together." he murmured as he picked through the scraps and checked out the tools and workbenches along the walls.

A lone Humvee, nearly overlooked due to its position, sat back by the rear doors of the building with a jack next to it and a new tire leaning against the passenger door. The hood was up, and he looked inside to find the engine was mostly intact, unlike all of the other vehicles in the depot. A battered fuel pump and alternator sat nearby on a workbench, covered in oil smears, and the new parts sat nearby, still fresh in their boxes with paperwork on a clipboard bearing signatures of guardsmen who'd been working on the Humvee.

James picked up the clipboard and scanned over the papers, looking back inside the Humvee to verify that the paperwork matched the vehicle. "They must've been in the middle of fixing this one when the civilians attacked. Dang. It's... basically intact."

Pushing back against the hope that he so desperately didn't want to have dashed, James opened the driver's side door and checked the fuel gauge to see it was half full, and there were three more red jerrycans marked *diesel* standing against the wall. He circled to the front of the vehicle, carrying over the new parts, leaning in, pushing aside wires and hoses to see if the vehicle truly needed as little work as it seemed like it did.

Tapping his hands on the frame, he nodded with growing excitement. "Holy crap. I think... yeah. This might work... this might be *perfect*."

Leaving the garage, James jogged back down the street and took a right at the intersection, catching up with Oswell where she was hobbling toward the administration building with his backpack on one shoulder and an M4 slung on the other, carefully rolling the IV stand next to her.

When she heard his footsteps, she turned and lifted her shoulder bearing the rifle. "Hey! The armory didn't really make it. I think somebody ignited the ammo and it went to hell in a bobsled. I found a rifle, pistol, and some mags someone had left behind. Well, I don't think they left it behind, exactly... they were shot trying to run off with it. What about you? Oh, hey, you found a rifle too. Nice."

"Yeah, forget the rifle. That's not the best news."

"Try me."

James panted with excitement, pointing back down the way he'd come. "There's a Humvee in a repair depot with a few missing parts, but the replacements are right there and I'm pretty sure I can fix it quickly."

"Okay, that sounds promising. What about fuel?"

"The gas tank is half full," James said with a pointed grin. "It must be from some old stock. And there are some jerrycans of untainted diesel nearby. It should be more than enough to get us where we need to go."

Oswell couldn't suppress a growing smile. "Are you sure you can fix it?"

James laughed. "Are you kidding? I fixed a *tank*, Oswell! Of all the things I've done that I never thought I could, this is one thing I *know* I can do."

CHAPTER THIRTEEN

Ryan Cooper
Lansing, Michigan

A cardinal sat on a post thirty yards down the fence line, watching curiously with a tilted head as Ryan and Helen leaned against the rail and waited for Sandy to show. Duchess and Diana were lying in the grass on the left-hand side of the driveway near the fruit trees, their tails wagging lazily in the morning sun. The heavy fog that had lingered throughout the morning was scattering, and the skies were a brilliant shade of bright blue without a hint of clouds. Birds bustled and came alive in the treetops with chatters and chirps, and the ducks fussed and quacked in the pond, shaking their feathered bodies and diving for minnows and grasses.

"She's late. Seems unusual."

"Yeah." Ryan squinted and shielded his eyes to see farther up the road. "This is odd. Oh, well. Maybe something came up."

"Maybe," Helen replied unconvincingly.

"Let's wait a few more minutes. I don't want to come back down here in a few minutes if she shows up."

Ryan found a stick nearby and tossed it to the dogs, watching them race to grab it, bring it back, and drop it at his feet. He threw it a few more times before they got bored, and stopped partway back to him to chew on it instead of bringing it back to him.

"Well," Ryan stretched, "Looks like Sandy's not coming, so we might as well get back up to the house."

"Hey, do you want to have a cup of coffee with me before we get started this morning?" Helen asked as they walked back up the long driveway toward James and Alice's home.

"Nah. I want to get that well pump going properly as soon as possible. I've still got a little work to do on it."

"Well, go ahead and take care of that, and I'll feed the animals."

"You sure?" Ryan asked. "You did all the farm work yesterday, and I don't want you to have to do it all today."

"Nonsense," she replied as they reached the garage. "I've got it down to a science. Besides – we can't do much without water."

"Still, I don't like you being out there alone with no one to watch your back."

"Alone?" Helen chuckled. "Don't be silly. I've got the dogs – well, Duchess and Diana, anyway – and I'm armed to the teeth."

"Are you sure?"

"Absolutely."

They reached the back door where they'd stacked a few vegetable bins filled with rotten or deformed vegetables they'd use to make compost later and Ryan stopped Helen before she went in. "Do you know where they keep the bleach?"

"They've got plenty of it in the laundry room. Why?"

"I want to shock the tank and the well. The cap's been off all night, and the hose running down there isn't exactly sanitary anymore. It's a fifty-foot pipe at least, and I don't know anything about the well itself so I'll have to guess how many cups to use. But still, the last thing we need is coliform growing in there."

"Ugh. I'll bring that out to you before I start with the animals."

"Perfect. Thanks."

They kissed, and Ryan checked on the five-hundred-gallon tank, lifting the lid to find it in good shape with a bit of dirt inside. He used vinegar and water to clean it out, then left it to dry while he found some rubber tubing in James' workshop and ran it from the manual pump to the tank, letting it hang inside through an intake flap. By the time he'd turned around, three bottles of bleach and a thermos of coffee were sitting on the patio with a note from Helen that read, *Have a good day. I love you, dear! Your heart, Helen.*

Grinning, Ryan watched her walk to the barnyard gate, pushing her wheelbarrow of feed with two of the dogs trotting by her side, facing a horde of hungry barnyard animals that bleated and clucked for attention. His grin faded as he thought about their remaining feed and hay. He hadn't been able to check on the hay to ensure it hadn't rotted or had any mold infestations, though James and Alice had enough feed stored to last for several months if they were careful about rationing it. Still, if they ran out of either, it would be tough on the animals. They could graze during warmer months, but they'd already overgrazed part of the barnyard, and keeping an eye on them if they were allowed to roam the rest of the property would be difficult, to say the least.

"One problem at a time...." Ryan pushed the thoughts aside and got back to the tank, double-checking the connection into the basement where it fed the water filter and softener.

With everything looking as good as he could manage, he grabbed a five-gallon bucket and returned to the well pipe. Pouring several cups of bleach into the bucket, he put it under the pump's spout and started drawing up water with slow easy motions. Slushing and gurgling sounds came up with each stroke, and after a few minutes of steady pumping, liquid showed up in the housing and soon sloshed into the bucket. The chlorine smell burned his nostrils, forcing him to turn his head away as he worked, and when the bucket was almost full, he stopped pumping and poured the mixture directly into the well head, repeating the process twice more, introducing about a gallon and a half of pure bleach to the well.

With the well disinfection sorted, Ryan capped the well head and walked out to feed the chickens, letting them wander the yard for a bit and tossing their feed into the dirt. When he was done there, he put up the feed buckets and walked out to where Helen had just finished milking Bessie and was capping the container.

"How's the old girl doing?" Ryan asked, patting the cow on the rump.

"She's great," Helen said as she started dragging the container out of the stall. "Without this girl, our lives would be a lot less enjoyable."

"That's for sure. Here, let me get that." Ryan grabbed the container and hauled it out into the shade for pickup later.

"We could give some of this to Sandy and Stephen for trade. I bet they could use it, or trade it themselves."

"I've been thinking of tossing a few gallons in if she comes up with an actual well pump. It'd be more than worth it."

"And we can't really drink it all." Helen rested one hand on his arm and the other on her hip, wincing as they walked to the barn entrance. "At least not till the kids get back."

"You okay?" Ryan asked, patting her arm.

"I'm fine. It's back-breaking work, but I'm thankful to have it."

"Amen to that. Unfortunately, it won't get any easier."

"Why do you say that?"

"We still need to fill up that water tank."

Helen sighed. "Can't it wait until after lunch?"

"Absolutely. The bleach needs to dilute into the well anyway."

They walked down to the house, taking in the afternoon midday breezes as they swept through the grassy field and barnyard. They put together a light lunch of berries and stewed tomatoes, followed by two glasses of milk from the refrigerator. Eating quietly at the kitchen table, Helen sat with her legs crossed to the side, mixing some olive oil and vinegar in as she ate. Ryan cut himself a couple of extra slices of tomato and ate them at the window with the plate in his hand, cutting them with a fork and popping the pieces into his mouth.

"What do you think about fried potatoes tonight for dinner with bacon bits and cheese?" he asked.

"Oh, that sounds good. I'll make one of those boxed pasta meals to go along with it." Helen laughed. "I'll pull out some recipes to spruce things up. You know, your doctor would be happy knowing you aren't eating fast food anymore."

"Dr. Sander can kiss my butt," Ryan said in mock offense, "But I guess that *is* one upside to all this." He patted his gut. "I've lost ten or fifteen pounds already."

"And you're looking good."

"I feel like hell, but thanks for the compliment."

"How's your calf feeling?"

"Awful – but less stiff every day. I'm getting used to ignoring the pain as much as possible."

"You should still take something for the inflammation."

"Yeah, I will if it gets bad. You ready to go out and try the pump?"

Helen rose from her seat. "As ready as I can be."

After dropping off their plates at the sink, they walked outside to the pump. "First, let's do some flushing, and see how badly I chlorinated the water." He removed the spout tube and grabbed the five-gallon bucket, getting back in position and pumping the plunger. Soon, water was sloshing into the bucket, filling it slowly but surely, and he quietly counted each stroke until the bucket was full.

"Smell that?"

Helen put her face near the bucket, sniffed, and turned away disgustedly. "Ugh. Yep, that's bleach."

Ryan grabbed the bucket, took it over to the edge of the field and dumped it into the dirt before returning and starting the process again. Each subsequent bucket smelled less like chlorine until, after twelve times, he scooped out a bit with his hand and tasted it.

"Okay. This is... well, it's not *great*, but it's decent. And the chlorine will evaporate pretty quickly, too, especially at this dilution. I think we're good." He reconnected the pump to the tank. "The bad news, though, is I figure it'll take about two thousand cycles of the pump to fill that tank. We'll have to take turns, if you're up for it."

"Just let me know when you need a break and I'll get my pump arm on."

Helen retrieved her sun hat, put her sunglasses on and sat in a nearby chair, looking across the property with her rifle sitting on her lap. Occasionally she got up and circled the house or walked over by the graves, checking the tree line, watching to see if the dogs gave any indication there were people around. Each time she returned and shook her head at Ryan before sitting back down.

Ryan kept working, alternating arms, keeping the flow going and the water moving through the tubing and into the tank, listening as it sloshed around inside, slowly, inexorably filling the giant reservoir. Helen retrieved another folding chair from the basement once his knees ached too much to keep kneeling, and he sat as he pumped the plunger, sweating, elbow and shoulder hurting after a couple hundred cycles.

"Okay, I'm ready for a break now." Ryan panted as he spoke to her. "Feels like both my arms are about to fall off."

Helen left her rifle leaning against her chair, coming over to take Ryan's place. At first, she struggled with it, trying to get comfortable on the chair while cycling the plunger up and down, finally standing to get a better angle on it.

"This is awkward," she groaned.

"I know," he replied. "If you stand, it puts pressure on your lower back. If you sit, it puts pressure on your upper back, and if you kneel your knees are going to feel like crap. Can't win for losing."

"This *really* makes me hope Sandy comes through with that pump."

Ryan laughed. "You and me both. I'll take a quick walk around now with the dogs. Holler if you need me."

"I will." Helen pulled the chair closer and straddled the pump, looping the hose over her left knee. "Ah, that's much better."

"There you go," Ryan nodded. "Whatever works, works."

Calling Duke and Duchess to him, he grabbed Helen's rifle and walked west toward the tree line, sighing at the sight of all the cleanup they had left to do in the field to prepare for the next year. It would've been done already – albeit by James and Alice and their kids – if not for the world blowing up in everyone's faces.

Reaching the tree line, Ryan turned south and strolled along the rustling barrier of white pines and Noble Firs bordering the property. Everything smelled sharp and sweet and sappy, tainted with the slightly rotten-egg stench of the pond. He walked up to the shore where bald cypress trees clung to the edge with their roots buried deep around the water and ran his hand down the rough bark of one of them, feeling the knots along the trunk and taking in the serene sounds of fish splashing near the shore.

Ryan continued his stroll, walking over to the berry bushes and fruit trees, grabbing some late-developing raspberries off the branches and trying them with an approving shrug. James and Alice had already harvested most of the fruit and had either eaten, canned or sold it at the local market, but next year, they'd have another abundance of apples, pears, peaches and more, a welcome bounty in a trying time. Ryan gave the graves a passing glance and derisive snort on the way back to the house where he found Helen leaning forward, focused on the well pump, working the plunger aggressively.

"How's it going?"

"Tougher than I thought," Helen said, easing up and glancing back. "Once you get used to it, it's not too bad, I guess. I'm ready for a break, though."

Ryan walked over to the tank and stepped onto the brick platform, flipping up the lid and looking inside. "You did good. It's a quarter of the way full."

Helen let out an exasperated sigh. "Just a quarter? I feel like I've been doing this all day!"

"It starts to feel that way, doesn't it?" He set the rifle back against the far chair and gestured for her to switch positions with him. "It's a beautiful day. I walked down around the ponds and through the fruit trees. Boy, when spring comes..."

"We'll have such a harvest. I'll make so much apple and cherry pie, you and the kids'll be sick of it."

"Never."

Ryan started the cycling motions again, watching water rush along the clear tubing and into the tank. He became lost in his thoughts for the next hour as his shoulder ached and his back muscles spasmed, sweat pouring down the sides of his face as he was forced to breathe deeply, trying to keep pace with the repetitive motions.

"Just let me know if you need a break," Helen called.

"I'm just thinking. We'll only use a little bit of this water each day, but we need to keep it topped off to keep the pressure in the house up."

"We could top it off in the morning after we make coffee and wash up, then again after we're done with chores at the end of the day. That way we'd have decent pressure throughout the day. It sure would break up the monotony."

"Please, give me some monotony."

"Any way to make it easier without a well pump?" Helen asked as she walked to the corner of the house and surveilled the property.

Ryan's expression deepened as an idea clicked in his mind. "Well... maybe I could use the car."

"Repeat that, please?"

"Well, I could pull the EV closer, jack up one side, and strap something to a wheel to cycle the pump up and down. I'll have to think about that one. Or maybe James has an electric motor inside I could rig up somehow...."

"That sounds like a good idea... uh, Ryan, dear?"

"Yeah?"

"Come over here a second."

"If I stop pumping, the water will settle back into the well, and I'll have to work harder to get it primed again."

"Ryan." Her tone changed, and the hairs on the back of his neck began to stand on end. "You need to see this."

Ryan stopped pumping, regretfully letting the plunger go, then he grabbed his rifle and joined her at the corner of the house.

"Is that Sandy? What's she doing down there at this hour?"

"I don't know," Helen said as Ryan raised his rifle to peer through the scope and sweep it across the woods on both sides.

"She doesn't have Stephen with her. That's... strange. And she seems... weird, somehow."

"What if she needs our help with something?"

"I don't know," Ryan's voice dropped an octave. "Something seems off."

Helen touched his arm. "She could be in *trouble*. We should at least see what it is. Come on, Ryan, we'll take the dogs down with us."

Ryan huffed but nodded. "All right. We'll see what's up, but if I say to go back to the house, we go back."

"Of course."

Ryan took a few steps out from the corner of the house and raised his arm high to Sandy, and she raised hers back and waved. He whistled, and Duchess and Diana raced from the west side of the property where they'd been lying in the grass, and Duke came over from the chicken coop, nosing around with the other dogs.

"Ready to go?" Ryan asked grimly, clipping a trio of quick-release leashes to the dogs' collars.

"I'm ready. Let's head down."

They walked down the driveway with the dogs straining on the ends of their leads, heads raised, ears up and alert. When they got close, Ryan slowed up and gave Sandy a brief wave. "Hello, Sandy. You're a little late today."

Sandy stood with her hands on the rail, her thumbs fidgeting, fingernails picking at the old wood, back stiff.

"Where's Stephen?" Helen asked.

Sandy smiled awkwardly and jerked her thumb toward the road. "Oh, he's back at the house."

Ryan raised an eyebrow. "The porch, you mean? He's not sick again, is he?"

"No, he's... he's doing fine. He was just tired and wanted to stay home."

"Well, what can we do for you, then?" Ryan asked.

"I came down to tell you that I found something out about that well pump you were asking about..." Sandy glanced over her right shoulder and her voice dropped to a whisper. "I'm... I'm sorry, Ryan...." She retreated from the rail and took several long steps back.

Ryan gently pushed Helen behind him, and the dogs all stopped sniffing around and came to attention with their broad heads pointed to the trees off to the left, growling low in their chests. A broad man with a gray-brown beard and a black sweatshirt stepped out from behind the trees, followed by a heavyset woman with her brown hair pulled into a messy bun. Others followed them, all people Ryan didn't recognize except for Mike Jones, and all of them advancing slowly toward the fence line.

Ryan handed the leashes to Helen, raised his rifle, and faced the approaching crew, who stopped a few yards from the fence. "I know you, Mike Jones. And I know *you*, too." He nodded to the broad-shouldered man. "You were in my house a few days ago, trying to kill us. The hell are you doing showing your face around my property? Remember what I said? I told you not to come back or I'd shoot you!"

"I'm not on your property, old man." The man held out his hands. "You wouldn't shoot me just for standing here, would you?" He looked as though he weighed two hundred fifty or three hundred pounds, and standing next to him was a woman who glowered at Ryan and Helen.

"You must be Jack and Barb Willoughby."

"That's right," the man replied.

"Good." Ryan ticked off the safety of the rifle. "I like to put names to the faces of thieves before I kill 'em."

"Hey, asshole." Barb stepped around Jack and pointed at him angrily. "We ain't thieves."

"S'cuse me?" Ryan kept the rifle pointed at Jack's chest. "How the hell do you figure that, you dumbass?"

"We have a proposition!" She replied indignantly. "We *thought* we had to take things from people, but we figure now we should all unite if we're going to make this work."

"Oh, sure. Unite. Now that you figured out you can't take what you want, you want to work together? Screw off. Maybe we could have worked something out earlier, but not anymore." Ryan kept the gun leveled at them as the dogs growled low, several hundred pounds of muscle and fangs behind him, giving him the confidence to hold his ground.

Helen tried to hold the dogs in place, but they were dragging her forward, growling low, foam dripping from their jaws as they lunged for the fence, recognizing the people who had invaded their home, desperate to do their jobs.

Jack's confidence wavered ever so slightly in the face of the slavering beasts and he stayed next to his wife as he addressed Ryan. "Look, why don't you have your wife march up to the house and come back with some eggs and vegetables for us? Help us out a bit, eh?"

"You don't have any right to them," Ryan replied flatly. "If you got something to trade, I *might* be willing to do that, but—"

"No, no, no... no trading. You'll hand over some food, and you'll do it now. We're not going—."

Ryan steadied his stance, shifted the rifle a hair to the right of Jack and Barb and fired twice, making the whole group flinch, then he swept the barrel across the lot of them. "Yes. Yes you are going away, or my wife and I are going to be digging a *lot* more graves. Your choice, assholes."

Mike Jones and three others retreated, fear in their eyes as the dogs behind Ryan fought harder to get off their leads, Helen barely able to keep a hold on them.

"Don't be afraid of him," Jack smirked with mock bravado, lifting his sweater to show a pistol holstered on his hip. "We've got guns, too."

Sandy was backing off over to the side, her expression panicked as she looked helplessly back and forth between Jack and Ryan. Ryan glared at her briefly before directing his rage at the others. "Well then, try it! If you think you can take us, come on and try!"

"Look, I didn't come here to fight." Jack held his hands up again. "But the way we see it, you owe us for killing some of our friends. Rita and Mack were good people, and Trace was, too. And how do you think Sandy feels about you killing her husband?"

Ryan shot Sandy another dark glare. "She knows the score on that, and you do, too. Screw off with your bull – what exactly do you take me for here?"

"Someone who's willing to defend his property," Jack said, his tone growing less aggressive and more desperate. "That much is obvious. But, c'mon, man. That's three people we lost, plus Ron who's shot up bad and still in bed. Can't work, can't help us scavenge... you cut our workforce in half, and—"

"There's that word again, 'you.'" Ryan shook his head. "You all know damn well it was *you* who chose to attack instead of work together. I didn't cut anything, *you* did."

Jack started to approach the fence when Duke's lead finally snapped and he threw himself against the gate, barking and snarling at the group, sending them a few steps back as Helen tried to keep the other two in line.

"I'm not arguing anymore!" Ryan bellowed. "Helen, let them go and cover me!"

Two men in the group who had been reaching for their own pistols froze as two more massive dogs joined the third at the gate, the metal structure groaning and vibrating violently as the Pyrenees tried to get through. Helen unshouldered her rifle in a flash and fired a shot into the air, sending the dogs into a further frenzy.

"Back the hell off!" She shouted as Ryan slowly backed up next to her, both of their rifles scanning the crowd, watching for anyone who might try to go for their gun.

"Duke! Diana! Duchess! Come! Heel!" Ryan hollered at the dogs and, miraculously, they obeyed, backing up toward him while still barking and snarling at the group beyond the gate.

Barb stepped out from behind Jack, moving toward the gate, and Ryan fired at her husband, the Winchester bucking against his shoulder, a round slamming through the man's arm, twisting him to the ground in a howl of pain. The men around him retreated further, and Ryan addressed Barb directly.

"I'll put the next one in his fat belly," Ryan screamed over the roar of the dogs. "With no hospitals around, it'll take a week for him to die! You want that?!"

Jack fixed him with a hard stare, his fingers slick and red, then he got to his feet, turned and waved to the others to put their guns down, his wife clutching to him as the group slowly edged away from the gate.

"We're not going away, old man!" Jack shouted at Ryan and Helen as his group moved away down the road. "We're neighbors! And we have nothing better to do than wait you out till you want to work with us!"

"You'll be waiting a long damn time!"

Ryan and Helen continued backing up, putting as much distance between themselves and the fence as possible, giving the pair a distinct advantage with their rifles. Sandy was the last of the group to leave the gate, and she stood at the tree line wearing a pitiful expression, raising her hands and mouthing something Ryan couldn't make out. His lip curled and he spat at the ground, then he, Helen and the dogs quickly retreated back to the house as fast as they could backpedal. When they reached the front porch, Ryan followed Helen and the dogs inside the house and slammed the door shut, immediately heading for the dining room blinds and peering through a crack in the plywood, rifle at the ready.

"Looks like they're gone,"

Helen was standing to the side, bent over with her hands on her knees and panting heavily as the dogs moaned and grunted around her. "What... in the world... was that?"

"A weak attempt to extort and threaten us. I should've put a bullet in all of them, dammit." He shook his head and pounded his fist against the wall. "Damn you, Sandy! I should've never trusted her!"

CHAPTER FOURTEEN

Alice Burton
The Past

Alice held a pair of chickens by their legs, walking stiff armed with them back to the trailer to lay them with dozens of others already piled in a bloody heap. Her gloves were bloody, and she had smears on her forearms and flannel shirt she'd rolled up to the elbows. She'd put her hair in a ponytail after being repeatedly reminded to, though her eventual acquiescence was due to the threat of an extra-long bath, and not because of the gore getting into her hair.

Scores of chickens lay dead in the trailer, some of them in pieces with their wings or heads torn off, and a half-dozen sheep lay on the other side, savaged beyond belief by teeth and claws, though nothing was eaten, just destroyed and left to rot. It was a nightmare, a ruthless slaughter Alice could never have imagined. Her mother and father were collecting what was left of the sheep, Ryan's shoulders broad and stout and Helen's hair a lighter shade of brown, curly and pulled back in a bunch like Alice's. Her mothers forearms rippled as she lifted a dead yew and brought it over from the field to place it in with the others, and her father joined her, carrying a few more chickens he'd found who had been trapped in a corner of the fence.

The night was dark and cool, and they'd just about collected all the living sheep from across the field where they'd tried to escape, though few had actually been successful. Some of the younger ones had died by the chicken coops, and Alice was gathering those while her parents did the heavier work. A pair of electric lanterns gave them light to see by, one hooked to the back of the trailer and one on the ATV, keeping the darkness at bay, but all Alice could think about were the monsters that had torn the animals to pieces; flashes of yellow eyes, snarls, and growls out beyond the safety of the light. Every time she blinked the terrifying sights and sounds reappeared in her mind, leaving her heart racing and her blood pounding in her ears.

"Damn pack of dogs did this," Ryan grumbled with a plume of warm breath as he stood by the trailer and measured the surrounding darkness.

"A pack of dogs, Ryan?" Helen said, fists on her hips. "How can this be dogs? I'm thinking coyotes."

"No, coyotes would have stripped the sheep, left nothing but the head and backbone. This was dogs. Probably came from the Loomis' farm when it shut down last year. They never did control the animals, and the damn things probably went feral." He pounded his fist on the trailer rail, sending a shudder through the frame, and Alice turned and went back for more chickens, stooping to pick up a wing here, a leg there, a handful of feathers and a head, listening to her parents go on.

"Well, somebody's got to pay for this." Helen gestured to the dead animals. "This cuts into next year's income something *bad*. These hens were giving us dozens of eggs a day, and our roosters are gone. That's not even counting the sheep. It'll take two or three years to build this up again."

"We've got the money to replace them." Ryan's low tone resonated with rage. "We'll recover."

"We *don't* have the money, dear," Helen replied in exasperation. "We spent the last of it on this year's feed and equipment. We were supposed to expand next year, and that's not going to happen unless we march right up to City Hall and demand reparations for this. If it was those dogs, Animal Control should've gotten them before they got out of hand." She turned in a circle and shook her fist. "It took us so long to make it here, and all we have left are these bloody corpses. Ryan, they ripped this place to *shreds*!"

"That's what we have insurance for."

"But it won't pay out for everything, and it won't bring back the momentum we had."

Ryan sighed wearily. "We'll go down and talk to the city in the morning."

"And if talking doesn't work," Helen snarled, "we'll sue. We have a friend who knows a good lawyer in New York. One word and he'll bring hell down on them."

Alice dropped the chicken parts in the trailer with the rest and went back for more, stepping into the bloody battlefield where every square foot was covered in blood, crimson stains smeared on the coop door frame, feathers stuck in the fencing, eggs smashed on the ramp to the hen house with yolks dripping on the cold ground. Alice didn't understand a lot of what her parents were saying about the city, insurance, and next year's income, and she'd only known one of the Loomis kids, having gone to school with her for a little while before they had to move. There was only the blood and feathers, the matted wool, the way the trailer shook when they dropped another dead body on the pile. Her parents' anger was real, too, and while her mother's was outward, she sensed something deeper inside her father, a familiar silence that sometimes overcame him when he got really mad, to the point he could knock a person over with a look.

She found Rooster Bob just outside the hen house door, dead on the ground with his wings spread, a patch of hair on his talons, the poor bird not near big enough to put up a real fight. She picked him up by his legs and grabbed the last hen, taking them back to the trailer and dropping them on top with tears forming in her eyes thinking about all the times she'd woken up to his crooning – though those times were far gone, never to return. She wiped her gloves off in the grass and stood by the trailer, and Helen and Ryan turned to her with strained smiles.

"All done, honey?" Helen asked.

"Yes, ma'am. Rooster Bob was the last. He's…" A sudden sadness gripped her heart, not only for Bob but for the fears she could not see, things adults talked about that she couldn't understand. Her face got hot, and she wiped away a gush of tears with a clean patch of her sleeve. "He's the last one. There's still a lot of blood and hay, but I can rake it, I guess."

"We can get that tomorrow," Ryan said, his hands gripping the rail, shaking slightly, his shoulders bulging beneath his shirt, the straps of his overalls tight with restrained fury. "Are you okay, sweetie?"

"I guess I am." Alice started to wipe the tears away with her other arm but stopped, and she realized she'd only smear blood across her face. "What are we going to do, Dad?"

Ryan knelt down, embracing his daughter for several long seconds, then held her by the shoulders at arm's length. "We're going to set up a little trap and kill them, hon. We're going to kill them all."

Alice crouched by her father thirty yards from the chicken coop at the edge of the woods with the forest at their backs. Ryan had spent the day mending some of the fencing the dogs had torn apart and put a couple of hens inside along with a pair of sheep staked to the ground out front, the animals grazing on grass and feed they'd scattered around, oblivious of what their true purpose was.

Ryan lifted his radio and whispered into it. "Anything yet? I thought I heard some barks."

"Oh, yes. I hear them coming," Helen replied, the radio slightly staticky due to her distance in a nearby blind. "They're noisy as all get-out. Alice, you do what your father says, you hear me? Ryan, I swear to you, if she—"

"Helen." Ryan's voice was weary. "We've beat this horse to death. She'll be well away from them, and I can't handle this by myself. We need her here."

"She only goes after the stragglers, Ryan Cooper. You take care of my baby."

Alice wore camouflage pants and jacket but without the orange vest she normally wore when she and her father hunted. She'd rolled her sleeves up and had her long dark hair pulled back with a green cap perched on her head, sitting so tight it smashed her ears down. She held her thirty-aught-six rifle and had a small pistol holstered at her hip, and Ryan was dressed similarly, holding his rifle and staring eastward toward the old Loomis farm. A full moon was hiding behind wide strips of clouds that allowed most of the glow through, illuminating the wide fields and forests so well that they didn't need flashlights to see by. A nervous tick had been stirring in Alice's belly ever since they'd left the house that afternoon and her father explained what they were going to do.

"It's going to be bloody," he said.

"I know, Dad," Alice replied in a broken voice.

"Are you okay? You can go back to the house, you know. Lord knows your mother would prefer that."

"I'm fine. I *am*, Dad. You know I can shoot."

Ryan allowed a thin smile to cross his lips. "That you can, girl. Okay, be ready."

The radio crackled, and Helen piped in again. "I just saw several dogs pass *right* beneath me, heading straight for you, but I've got a bead on them."

"Don't shoot yet. We want them grouped up when I hit them with the buckshot."

"Roger that."

Ryan gave Alice a firm, flat look. "You ready, honey?"

"Yes, sir," she replied, trying to keep her voice even. "I'm ready to go."

"Safety off?"

"Safety off."

"Let's go. Just like we talked about. Pick off the strays only. Stay far away from the pack. C'mon."

Before Alice could answer, Ryan was up and jogging from the tree line, angling to the left to get a good view of the coop while Alice leaped up and moved to the right, staying near him, lifting her rifle and aiming toward the rear corner.

"Remember, take your time with your shots."

Alice swallowed dry to loosen her tightening throat, adjusting her grip on the weapon to keep her arms from shaking. "Okay, Dad."

"If you get into trouble, stay calm, get up in a blind and don't hesitate to do what you have to do."

"I will."

Pounding paws drew nearer, running through the woods, accompanied by yips and yelps and a chorus of barks. The chicken wire shook, and scraping sounds like nails on wood came from the other side of the coop. The chickens scattered and flapped, clucking excitedly, and the sheep flinched and scrambled back, jerking against their tethers.

The radio crackled, and her mother's voice piped through. "The dogs are at the coop, Ryan. Did you get that?"

"Got it. What are they doing?"

"They're on the opposite side of you, trying to dig under the wire."

"Okay, don't fire. We're spread out over here. We'll take care of them."

"Roger that."

"Alice, I'm going to take the first shots as I move around. Stay behind me."

"Yes, sir."

Ryan crept forward with his shotgun in a tight grip and the stock nestled into his shoulder. "Stay back a bit and remember to watch where you're aiming."

"Okay, Dad," she replied nervously, adjusting her grip on her rifle.

From the corner of her eye, she saw him cross stepping to the left, flashes spitting from the barrel, the electronically-amplified sounds coming through her ear guards cutting out with each *pop, pop, pop* of his shotgun.

Alice jolted and gasped, trying to stay steady as pained howls cut the air. Teeth snapped and the dogs snuffled and yelped as they crashed against the chicken wire, sending the birds into an insane frenzy, the dogs fighting with one another as they sought out the source of their pain and misery.

"Alice! Eyes open, girl!"

A pile of claws and fur and gnashing teeth bolted around the corner, mottled mutts rushing around the far side of the pen toward them, but they cut back toward the coop. A couple angled for the sheep while the others went for the door where they'd broken in before. Hardly thinking, her breath trapped in her chest, Alice whirled and fired, hitting one dog in the ribs and sending him skittering sideways into the chicken coop, bouncing off the wire and crashing into the other mutts. One dog snarled at him, leaped back off balance, then rushed Alice and Ryan, saliva flying from its jaws and its sharp canines snapping.

She was already pulling the charging handle and loading another round, lifting the weapon and firing before her father could, taking the dog square in the head and dropping it several yards away. She backed up but more canines appeared, frenzied, wounded and dying from her father's buckshot, and she fired three more rounds in rapid succession, hitting a dog in the side and a second in the shoulder, the hounds yelping and howling as they scattered in every direction.

As her father fired at the main pack, they started to break, but one on her side, a massive black and white mix of German Shepherd and Bulldog, shot right at her, those around it following like a flock of birds, coming together and charging her as one. A cold spike of terror struck her spine, and she was caught between freezing and running. Her father's words came back to her.

"Take your time with your shots ... do what you have to do."

His voice soothed her while she continued backing up, putting distance between her and the raging hounds. Fear left her, and she responded with calm, deliberation. She fired once, striking the lead dog in the shoulder, spinning him with a vicious yelp, then she sidestepped and loaded another round, forcing the pack to come around a tree to get to her. A pair tangled in the protruding roots and crashed in a heap, and Alice shot one through the side, dropping it instantly. Still backing up, lifting her feet high so she didn't trip, Alice charged the weapon and fired again, then again, shooting by instinct more than aim, putting down one dog and sending another spinning and snapping at its rear leg where she'd grazed it.

Eyes as wide as saucers, breath coming in shallow gasps, Alice loaded the rifle yet again in automatic movements that had possessed her limbs. A shaggy white dog appeared in front of her just as she squeezed the trigger, her round striking the dirt and blasting it into the beast's face. It yelped in surprise and leaped back, and the rest of the animals stopped charging and dashed off several yards back toward where her father was, barking and snapping, running in confused circles with frantic yips. A nigh-on palpable wave of fear rippled through the pack, and when Ryan came around in front of the chicken coop and started firing on them, the dogs broke in every direction, some flying right by her, bumping and knocking her legs as they sprinted by. The big German Shepherd Bulldog mix she'd hit earlier blasted from the center of the pack, charged through a tangle of brush, and crashed into her, sending the rifle flying out of her hands. The dog leaped again, trying to get by but only slamming into her and knocking her to her knees. Fangs snapped at her face, driven by deep-throated, panicky snarls, the sharp scent of iron-hot blood and animal musk in her nose.

She jerked back as the gnashing teeth snapped within an inch of her nose. Throwing up her left arm, she blocked the next bite from tearing her face off, holding her arm against the animal's neck, her whole body shaking as she fought against its weight and strength. She swung her left leg out to anchor herself, right hand reaching across her waist to grab the four-inch knife sheathed there, just an afterthought when she'd strapped it on, wanting to mirror her father. Whipping the blade free, she swiped at the dog as it latched onto her sleeve, barely missing her arm, though she missed with her blade as well.

With a strained grunt that hardly sounded human, Alice hauled the dog back in her direction and swept in with the blade, jamming it into its shoulder close to where she'd shot it. The knife came free in a spray of blood, but the dog still dragged her forward, pulling her off her knees. She went with the momentum, using her weight to drive the animal into the roots at the base of the tree, knocking it off its feet. She stabbed again, a deep thrust to the neck, drawing the blade back across the folds of skin, slitting its throat in a gush of blood. Throwing herself on the animal, she pinned it against the tree with their faces inches apart, the dog's sanity lost in its feral frenzy as it snarled and squirmed. Alice screamed as she plunged the knife into its eye socket all the way to the hilt, collapsing on top of it, lying on it, panting, chest heaving, twisting the knife until the dog kicked and shivered and finally, mercifully grew still.

"Alice!" Ryan came around the tree, squeezing off multiple rounds at the few retreating dogs that still lived. In the wake of the scattering pack, he threw the shotgun down and grabbed the rifle slung on his shoulder, firing into the woods with heavy booms, swinging one way and the other, picking off the beasts as they tried to retreat, thinning their numbers so that any survivors would no longer be a threat.

Once they'd gone, he ran back to Alice and fell to the ground next to her. "Alice! Are you okay, honey?!"

Alice rolled off the dead dog with her knife sticking out of its eye socket, her sleeve still stuck between its teeth. All she could do was blink in numb disbelief, tugging faintly on her arm to get it free from the locked jaws. Ryan slung his weapon and grabbed the animal, prying open the jaws and pulling her arm free. Pain from having been jerked back and forth came a moment later, a sharp radiating sting that began to pulse, bringing a gush of tears to her eyes.

"Oh, honey. I'm so sorry... Oh, baby girl."

"I'm... okay, dad." She held up her arm, covered in blood and certain to blossom with bruises, but mercifully free of any breaks in the skin. "It only got my jacket."

Ryan embraced her, tears streaming down his cheeks. "I'm so sorry, baby. I'm so, so sorry. They were heading around the front, I thought there were just a couple around on your side so I went after them and—" A few shots rang out from the direction of the blind, and Ryan looked up. "You sure you're okay?" She nodded, and he helped her to her feet. "Come on, then. Some must have run your mother's way. Let's finish this. Stay close to me."

In the chicken yard, eight or nine dogs lay dead, their blood turning the dirt to crimson mud, snarls silenced. A few were crawling away, and the terrified sheep stood pressed against the mesh wire, bleating and shivering as they shifted, unable to run. Part of the remaining pack had indeed broken around the coop and to flee back toward the Loomis' – right into Helen's hands. Ryan grinned coldly as the sound of her Mini-14 popped off rounds in twos and threes, each report followed by sharp, pained barks and yowls that echoed through the woods. Alice stayed close by her father as he moved through the remains of the feral pack, searching for any animals that had been wounded and putting them out of their misery with cold, workmanlike efficiency.

When he was done with his bloody work, he turned and embraced her again. "Are you okay, honey?"

"Did I do okay?"

"You did amazing. I'm so darn proud of you. I'm just so sorry you had to do that."

"Mom's going to kill you, y'know." Alice forced a smile, which turned genuine, then Ryan laughed, the slow leak of tears from their eyes turning into a flood, and Alice sobbed and threw herself deep against him, wrapping her arms around him and clinging to his hunter's jacket as if for dear life.

"I'm sorry that I got knocked down. I'm sorry I almost ran away. I-I tried to hold my ground."

"Oh, honey." Holding his rifle out in one hand, he returned the hug even harder and kissed the top of her hat. "You did great. You held your ground just fine." Ryan looked at the dead animals all around them, "It's my fault for bringing you out here tonight. I should have listened to your mother. I had no idea it was going to be like this. I'm the one who's sorry."

"It's okay, dad, really. We did what we had to do."

Ryan's eyes glistened in the moonlight as he stared at his daughter proudly, nodding at her. "We did, sweetie. We did good."

Alice lay in the brush at the edge of camp with the moonlight blanketing her in an eerie luminance, clutching her knife in one hand and her walking stick in the other. The whites of her eyes glowed brightly amidst a face covered in river mud, spread across her cheeks and neck, ears smeared with it inside and out. She'd rubbed it over her arms and hands and into her clothes, heavy and wet and grungy as the garments clung to her clammy skin. Her hair was bound with an orange piece of string, also covered in mud, with a sprinkling of dirt and twigs all around to help her blend in. Just a shadow in the darkness, she lay still with her stomach turning and anxiety pecking at her brain, terrified at the wheezing coming from her chest and the stabbing pain in her side that had only grown worse.

As she looked across the campground, though, the fear and anxiety melted away. The people in the camp carried on their evil deeds and the abuses continued, the kids— *her* kids — suffering malice and cruelty for reasons she couldn't comprehend. Every slap, every shout, swelled her anger until it eclipsed all the pain and the fear and the rage and at the end there was only one question remaining in her mind, a singular focus into which every ounce of her strength and rage was poured.

What are you going to do, Alice?

Her father's words came back to her.

"Kill them. Kill them *all*."

CHAPTER FIFTEEN

Agent Harris
Mount Weather, Virginia

Harris crouched with the rocket launcher on his shoulder as smoke filled the hallway from the guns, grenades and fuel-filled bottles that had exploded up and down the corridor. His nose stung and his eyes watered, but he tuned his ears to the sounds of the battle, the exchange of gunfire as one side opened with a barrage only to duck and reload, giving the other side a chance to respond. General Pulaski grabbed his Marines and pulled them to the floor, shouting orders for them to get down, drowned out by another pipe bomb explosion that rocked the steel shields and sent fire reaching for the ceiling.

Harris waited for the flames to pass before he rose and aimed the round-tipped Akeron toward the enemies, standing exposed for a handful of precious seconds while he hugged the tube resting on his shoulder. He cycled through the launch sequence on the keypad, a target screen flipping out and magnifying the hallway. Everything became massive in the viewfinder, and he settled the crosshairs where the hallway curved right and swept upward out of sight. Taking a deep breath and holding it, he kept the crosshairs aligned as dark shapes moved into his line of vision through the drifting smoke, muzzles flashing as hot rounds zipped past his ear, rattled the steel doors, or hit the wall near his head, showering him with bits of hot metal.

"Fire the damn thing, Harris!" Pulaski bellowed. "*Now!*"

"Clear!" Harris released the breath he'd been holding in one long gust and at the end of it, he pressed the firing mechanism.

Air hissed beside his right ear as the rocket shot smoothly from the tube and a fresh plume of smoke flushed through the corridor as the round headed toward the enemy, glancing off the intersection between the wall and floor and miraculously not stopping, but curving around the bend and up the stairs. Harris dropped behind the Marines, slamming his hands over his ears and gritting his teeth before an explosion like no other rocked the air, followed by screams and shrieks of agony.

A pressure wave shoved the steel doors like a giant hand, pushing the Marines backward and knocking Harris on his back. A wave of heat and flame crawled toward them after the pressure wave, hitting the doors and exploding upward to roll across the ceiling, and Harris could only gape at the curtain of orange-red tendrils that devoured the ceiling tiles, sending embers of insulation and old paint flickering down like fireflies.

Marines hit the floor with their hands over their heads next to him, but Harris rolled to his left and crouched against the armory door, waiting for the wave of heat to pass, half expecting the hallway to come crashing down on his head. An eerie silence fell over them, punctuated only by a few scattered moans and cries from somewhere far down the hall ahead of them. Harris opened his eyes to the flickering overhead lights as the Marines slowly uncovered and crawled to their knees.

With a grenade in hand and his pistol at the ready, Harris stepped forward, creeping toward the sounds of trickling water and pained groans. Smoke rolled along the floor, cutting his visibility in half, though the worst of it was the sudden smell of scorched flesh that wafted over him, and no matter which way he turned his head, he couldn't escape the sweet, blackened reek. The toe of his boot bumped something, and he swept his hand to clear the air, catching a glimpse of someone's arm lying on the floor, skin scorched, one of the fingers twitching as the nerve was somehow stimulated even after amputation. He stepped into a slowly spreading pool of blood that was cascading down the stairs and moved quickly through it, stumbling over more bodies and stepping on bits and pieces of flesh, boots slipping on the slick tiles.

A sudden current of cool air floated through the corridor, stirring the fog and pushing it past him toward the Marines. The walls were splattered with blood, bits of flesh and clothing stuck to the scorched brick, smoking in tendrils that twisted to the ceiling. Every step he took revealed more carnage; someone's torso off to his left, another unidentifiable limb to the right and bits of viscera stripped of skin, singed and smoldering. Up ahead, where the missile had finally detonated against a pillar in the wall, wires and cabling drooped and water pipes had burst, the trickle mixing with the blood and gore. Harris clamped down waves of revulsion, holding his stomach and leaning against the wall as he clenched his teeth tight to hold back the bile rising in his throat. He forced himself to look, to take a quick count, somehow cobbling together twelve deceased attackers just by the number of limbs lying around.

Turning back and stepping into the center of the hall, he waved. "Come on up, Marines!"

Seconds later, running boots reached him, Marines appeared through the smoke, falling into crouches as they crept around the corner, undeterred by the carnage that lay before them.

Pulaski ambled up with them, whispering orders. "Tight formation, Marines! Keep your eyes forward on that far stairwell! Move! Move!"

The troops pulled together and pressed on, and Pulaski stopped next to Harris. "The fools must've been stacked up here right around the bend, taking turns lobbing their pipes and grenades at the wall to bounce down the hallway at us. Your rocket bounced right past them before detonating, wiping out every damn one of them." Pulaski's heavy hand fell on his shoulder. "Damn fine shot, Harris."

Harris nodded and wiped at his mouth as if he could get rid of the taste of death surrounding them, then he fell in behind Pulaski and a couple of lead Marines as they shuffled past the worst of the butchered attackers, ducking beneath the dripping pipes and coming out on the other side. The elevator doors were leaning heavily in their slots, the elevator car tilted dangerously as well, and wall panels were askew inside of it. The stairwell on the near side of the elevator had collapsed in spots, concrete and bricks piled up on the bodies of dead attackers, sharp rebar jutting through their chests. Mortar dust drifted by, and Harris got a breath of it, turning his head to cough it out.

"Sweet Mary...." Pulaski murmured, nudging a dead attacker with his boot before joining Crow and the rest of the Marines by the intact stairwell. Crow took two Marines to the first landing and ducked beneath buckled concrete to peer up the shaft. Gunfire peppered the steps, and the Marines jerked back and came down to gather around Pulaski and Harris.

"There are two, maybe three attackers on the landings above us." A spark of malice flickered in Crow's eyes. "We can take them... kick their asses out of here once and for all!"

Pulaski's spine stiffened, and he glared at the group gathered around him.

"All right, Marines," the General said. "We're heading up in teams of three. Alpha Team, go with Crow. Bravo and Charlie, with me." As the troops formed up, Pulaski took out his radio and put it to his mouth.

"Mount Weather Command, this is Pulaski. We've cleared the main corridor and are heading up to the first level to continue clearing the base. You're clear to send medical personnel up to this level to see to the wounded."

"Excellent news, General," Birk replied. "Keep us posted."

"Yes, sir."

Harris started to join the ranks of Marines when Pulaski grabbed his arm. "Harris, I want you to go back and see to the President's safety."

"Are you sure?"

"We can handle this. You've done more than needed, and we can take it from here."

The General pushed through the Marines and nodded for Crow to go ahead. The Marines hit the first landing, one covering the others while an automatic machine gunner squeezed by with his M249 and continued up, firing a long burst up the shaft that sent dust and debris trickling down. The attackers tried to return fire, but the Marines outgunned them and filed up the stairwell in crouched stances, shooting in alternate fashion, pushing up two flights until the last Marine disappeared. Harris turned and jogged back through the ruined, smoking hallway, past the flames and carnage to the armory where he found the two wounded Marines resting against the ordnance shelves. The man with the wounded chest held a tourniquet tight around his right leg, nostrils flaring as he clung to life while the other lay unconscious on his side, though his chest was moving in rapid, uneven breaths.

"Did... it work?" the Marine asked with a scratchy voice.

"It did. Better than I could have hoped. Thanks for the instructions."

"No problem. I'm... just glad you... got the bastards, but..." He swallowed hard and glanced down at himself. "I... don't think... I'll live... to celebrate."

"We've got medical personnel coming up. Just hang tight. I'm going to pick up some of your buddies and bring them in here, okay?"

The Marine nodded and Harris jogged up the hall, looking for the wounded men they'd left in the corridor, finding them sitting shoulder to shoulder, pale and sweating with blood splattered on their shirts and pants.

"Come on, guys," Harris said, kneeling next to them. "We've got medics on the way, but we should get to the armory where it's safer."

As he finished the sentence, pieces of the hallway fell, brick and concrete cracking on the tiles where water trickled in red-stained streams. Wordlessly the pair started to get up, and Harris gestured for the man with the wounded hand to get on the other side of his comrade. Together they helped him down the hall and into the armory, and Harris got them against the wall with the others. The Marines had left a couple of first-aid kits, and Harris grabbed one, popped it open, and lined up some bandages, wraps, and antiseptic. Kneeling in front of the Marine with the finger stumps, he removed the bloody bandages, rewrapped the man's hand with gauze, and added a thick layer of self-adhesive wrap.

When the Marine's eyes fluttered and he leaned to the side, Harris sat him straight and slapped his cheeks. "I need you to stay with me, Marine. You got that?" Harris retrieved a tourniquet from the first-aid kit and applied it to the man's upper arm, twisting it tight and securing it, taking him by the chin, shaking him, trying to keep him consciousness. "You've lost a lot of blood, but you'll make it. Help's on the way."

The Marine's head lolled forward, but he mumbled something and nodded. Harris moved to the man with the chest wound, taking over his bandage, tightening the windlass rod on the tourniquet surrounding it to apply pressure and locking it in place. "Are you with me?"

"Yes, sir." The Marine's voice was sluggish, eyes rolling upward in their sockets.

Harris parted the man's shirt and cleaned the wounds, sprinkling clotting powder into them and packing bandages on top, but it was a mess he was unqualified to treat, and all he could do was hope and pray for medics to arrive soon.

"Going to stitch me up, too?" the man chuckled.

"Sorry, Marine. Not much I can do about this chest of yours. Looks like something chewed you up and spit you out. Guess you didn't taste too good."

The man laughed harder, and he leaned forward and coughed, Harris catching him by the shoulder and keeping him upright.

"Take it easy, man. Just sit back and wait for the doctor to get here."

"It's okay if I don't make it," he replied. "It's the end of the world anyway, and my brothers... they kicked ass. We stood tall... to the end."

Harris took the man's chin and lifted it, looking him in the eye. "You're not going to die. You *can't*. Who else is going to tell stories about some fool who fired an anti-tank missile in an enclosed corridor?"

"True," the Marine chuckled and nodded. "I'll try to hang on just for the story alone."

"Good man—hey, here they are." Harris stepped back as a few medics and a doctor swung into the armory, pushing Harris aside as they fell to their knees and started working on the wounded Marines.

With nothing left to do, Harris backed into the hallway with water trickling around his boots, still tainted bright red in the stark, blinking overhead lights. The sounds of fighting were still prominent in the distance, though the M249 was the loudest, indicating the Marines were winning. His pulse was still racing, heart thumping in his chest as he trudged along the main corridor to C1 and then into the narrow passage leading to the President's bunker. As he stepped out, voices reached him, and he headed toward them to find President Birk, Major Spencer, Cindy Strode, and others standing in an intersection.

"There he is," Birk waved him in. "The man of the hour! Agent Harris! Your insane plan worked."

"It was touch and go there for a minute, but we broke the sons of bitches." Harris shook hands with the President, accepting the uneasy smiles and congratulations from everyone, recounting – at Birk's insistence – what they'd done to recapture the main corridor and deal a fatal blow to the attackers' hold on the complex.

Cindy stood with her arms crossed, shaking her head, but Birk grinned and slapped Harris on the back like it was another day at the office. "Doesn't surprise me, Harris. Excellent work. How about I promote you to Second General after all this?"

Harris laughed. "I was just thinking outside the box, sir."

"Yeah, *way* outside the box." Birk patted his shoulder. "Major Spencer, do you have any updates from Pulaski?"

Spencer held up a radio and turned up the volume. "I've been following along, sir. Our Marines have broken through the main entrance and are taking the fight to the attackers. Still waiting for a fresh update from General Pulaski. Until then, we are advised to stay put."

"I want to go outside. I want to know *who* did this to us."

"With all due respect, sir," Harris replied, "we should wait for an all-clear from the General."

Birk accepted Harris's advisement with a roll of his eyes and took Cindy off to the side to have a conversation while staffers brought bottles of water and passed them out to everyone. Harris gratefully took one, twisted off the top, and downed the entire contents in a few long swallows, washing out the dust that caked his throat. A few people gathered around Spencer, each with a radio, a couple with headsets as they coordinated the remaining forces scattered throughout the underground complex, bringing them up to the main corridor.

After ten minutes, Pulaski's loud baritone broke through Spencer's radio. "Spencer, let me talk to the President immediately."

Birk took the radio. "This is Birk. What do you have for me, General?"

"Thanks to Agent Harris, we cleared the main corridor and fought to the first level."

"That's what I heard. What else?"

"We've pushed the attackers outside the complex grounds and rescued several of our people. We need medical support right away, but the area is clear, sir, and we're currently chasing the bastards out of the area."

A cheer went up among the assembled, Birk pumping his fist and howling the loudest before grabbing the radio. "I'm coming out, General."

"I wouldn't advise that right now, Mr. President."

"Don't worry. I'm in good hands. I've got Harris with me, Major Spencer, and a few Marines who are meeting us in the main corridor." Before Pulaski could protest more, Birk handed the radio back to Spencer and gestured to Harris. "Let's go. All of us. We're going outside to breathe some fresh air."

With Birk leading the way and Harris and Spencer keeping up, they trekked toward hall C1 with distant alarms still blaring and warbling through broken speakers, the emergency lights flickering with fluctuating power.

"Spencer, does anyone up top know who or what the group was who attacked us?"

"Not yet, sir."

"Harris, you were up there. Did you get any indication of who it could be after you drove them back with your rocket?"

"No."

"And why not?"

"Well, sir... I..."

"Go ahead, Harris. Speak plainly."

"Well, they were unidentifiable, sir."

"Unidentifiable?"

"Yes, sir. The rocket had an... *effect*."

"An effect."

"A... prejudicial effect, sir."

"I see."

"The larger issue is that the base was breached at all," Spencer jumped into the conversation.

"We should have been ready for an attack like that."

"We were, Mr. President, as ready as we could be. We just didn't have the personnel on hand that we should have."

Birk shook his head as they came out in C1, and Harris jumped out ahead and guided the group to the main corridor, stepping back to give them room while also checking ahead for any dangers. Bloody water pooled around their feet and flooded the hallway, the flow growing heavier as the weakened pipes continued to leak.

"The armory is up here, sir," Harris said, splashing through it and up a few doors where the medical team were still tending to the wounded.

Harris gestured toward the steel doors lying in the hallway, their fronts scorched with fire, nicked up and pockmarked with bullet and shrapnel impacts. "These are the doors we used to make it to the armory."

"Brilliant idea." Birk shook his head at the scattered glass and shrapnel lying everywhere, blood streaking the floor in long smears. "We would've never made it without that, Harris. Kudos again."

"It was a team effort, sir. Once we'd established our position, we worked out a second phase of attack and pushed them back."

Birk gestured down the hall where the fires had gone out, but the flickering corridor lights illuminated a scatter of bloody debris visible through the lingering haze – the first few body parts at the edge of the light.

"That smell." Cindy waved her hand in front of her face. "Is that –"

"It gets worse, ma'am, I'm sorry to say. We'll get to that next, but I thought you might want to stop at the armory first."

Harris held his breath and directed them inside, pushing the heavy steel door open, bracing himself for the men he'd helped to be dead. Instead, the Marine with the chest wound was sitting up, his shirt cut open and a massive cluster of bandages plastered to his side. When he saw Harris he smiled, but when the President stepped in behind Harris, the man's jaw dropped, and he attempted to salute.

"At ease," Birk said. "All of you. Thank you for what you did today. You did an amazing job. Rest up, get well and get strong so you can rejoin the fight."

"I'll be back up and fighting as soon as they let me, sir!"

"I'm sure you will. Do you have everything you need, Dr. Wesley?"

A tall doctor with short-cropped, curly black hair and wire-framed glasses stood and nodded. "A couple of these men need serious work. We need to get them downstairs and prep them for surgery."

"Marines will be here in a minute. You'll take four as orderlies."

"Thank you, sir."

"Hang in there, people," Birk lifted his voice and stared at each Marine in turn. "We're going to take good care of you."

Birk and Harris stepped back outside where the staff were talking, and Birk grabbed four and directed them into the armory to help the medical staff. With the wounded situated, Birk gestured that he was ready to continue, and Harris once again led the way, crunching over shrapnel and debris and picking his way toward the dark stretch of hallway where the rocket had done the most damage. Taking out a flashlight, he shined it ahead, purposely keeping it pointed upward and letting those behind him know whenever they were about to step on something distasteful.

"Body here, sir. Be careful... there's an arm ahead of you, ma'am. It's a little slick over here."

"I want to see them," Birk said. "Spencer, your flashlight."

Spencer slapped a flashlight into Birk's hand and the light flicked on and moved around their feet, illuminating the charred and blackened forms twisted into impossible shapes from the rocket's detonation, the sheer pressure and heat from it having flash-cooked multiple attackers instantly. The humid reek of burned bodies rose off the tiles, the group members struggling to keep their expressions stoic as the color drained from their faces. Cindy groaned and pressed her hand to her mouth but walked on through to join Harris midway down the hall where they waited for the others to catch up.

"You weren't kidding when you said the rocket had a... what was it?" Birk asked.

"Prejudicial effect, sir."

"Prejudicial effect, my ass. There's nothing left of them."

"Sorry to have to take you folks through this, but—"

"Don't be sorry," Birk said grimly. "Just lead on."

"Yes, sir."

With the images of the dead, twisted forms burned into his mind yet again, Harris led them to the end of the hallway near the elevator, and Birk shined his light down the cracks between the elevator and the shaft into the darkness.

"Elevator's out. We'll have to take the stairs, sir," Harris said.

"No kidding," Birk chuckled and followed him up to the first landing, ducking beneath the collapsed stairwell, climbing up toward a break of daylight illuminating the exit hall. On their way up, they stepped over the bodies of several attackers and one dead Marine.

"Careful," Harris said. "The stairs are slick."

Birk and Spencer stopped and knelt next to an attacker, Birk shining the light on the man's bloody, bearded face while Spencer rifled through his pockets. With a sigh, Spencer sat back on his heels. "They look like regular civilians. No uniforms. No identifying marks. Nothing."

"Hrm." Birk stood and motioned at Harris. "Let's go."

Harris held his pistol at the ready as they wound up the stairwell and approached the first landing, turning off his flashlight as daylight filled the shaft, illuminating more dead bodies but, thankfully, no friendly casualties. At the top they stepped into an intersection of halls with a single short hallway leading to the main blast doors. The main doors were in shambles, having been blown off their hinges and collapsed on their corners with vaguely human shapes lying around them. As they passed, Birk stopped to look at a woman sitting up against the doors wearing a rain-resistant jacket, bullet holes peppering her upper torso, her rifle still resting across her lap.

"What would've possessed them to attack us like this?" Birk spoke to Harris, who remained doggedly at his charge's side. "Don't they know we've been trying to help them?"

"I guess not, sir. Why don't we check with General Pulaski before we —"

Birk suddenly stood and squeezed between the broken-down doors, and Harris hurried to follow him into a brisk Virginia wind that hit him like a slap in the face, sweeping away the stuffy heat of the corridors. The sky was cloudy, though even the mild gray daylight forced them to squint and protect their eyes.

The bunker entrance faced the south, where the main gates had been torn off, and there was fencing down everywhere, the watchtowers barely standing, smoking with their spotlights dead and Marines hanging from their twisted walls. The group circled to get a better view of the compound where sheds and buildings smoked and smoldered like coal beds while groups of Marines guarded the perimeter in every direction, more than a few with bloody bandages on their arms or wrapped around their heads.

Dead Marines and attackers lay everywhere, most with bullet wounds or showing trauma from explosions, but some had died together in the throes of hand-to-hand combat. Off in the distance, down the hills around the facility, the gunplay continued, and a Humvee rumbled to life and pulled around to the west side of the compound, its mounted machine gun armed by a Marine who pointed it out toward the woods, scanning for enemies.

"Over here, sir," Harris said, striding to a near wall where the reinforced concrete had bulged inward and spilled into the yard. Spencer joined him as they knelt next to a blackened chunk of rock where the remnants of wires sprung from a fractured control box.

"This confirms the transmissions," Spencer said. "They used C4."

"Where would they have gotten that?" Birk asked.

"They could've pilfered it from a military stockpile somewhere. Heaven knows we probably have plenty lying unguarded."

Birk stepped to where a group of attackers lay in a cluster of bodies and knelt next to one man, rolling him over, rifling through his jacket pockets, then his jeans. He shook his head and stood, speaking to Spencer. "Still no identification, not a single damn thing to tell us who these people were."

"It could very well be a one-off incident, sir. There's no immediate indication that this was part of some larger sort of operation."

Harris' earpiece popped to life, and Chief of Security Westbrook chimed in for the first time in hours. "Agent Harris, do you copy? We just reestablished communication with Mount Weather."

Harris turned and saw that Pulaski and a group of Marines had established a command tent with scraps of tables and chairs brought up and maps thrown down. A radio team was about finished setting up replacement antennas and dishes for long-distance communication, their lights blinking steadily across the tops of the mini towers.

"One second, sir," Harris said to Birk. "I've got Chief Westbrook on the line."

Birk nodded. "We'll be over here with Pulaski."

"The President is secure," Harris said, stepping away from the others. "I see Radio Control has some equipment humming right now."

"Thank goodness for that." Westbrook let out an audible sigh at the news that Birk was still alive. "What the hell's been going on over there?"

Harris got the security chief caught up, starting with the cut communication lines, the attack on the complex, and the damage done on the surface, ending with the defense of the bunker and how they'd ultimately pushed the attackers back in a bloody battle that had cost many lives.

"So the complex is secure?"

"Not yet, but the Marines have routed the attackers from the grounds and the remnants are being dealt with. It's as secure as we can get for the moment."

"Good work, Harris. For now, you're the only agent I've got, so you're officially in charge of things until I can get more people to you. Your next task is to work with General Pulaski and facilitate a transfer of the President to Site R in Pennsylvania. Pulaski should be receiving similar orders from NORTHCOM as we speak."

"Understood."

"A second part of this transfer will include survivors from the Pentagon and critical equipment and supplies moving in from DC."

"Will we meet them at Site R?"

"That's up to you, the military staff and the situation on the ground. You can either meet them there or re-route them and have them pick you up on the way. Whatever you decide, we'll need reports from you every thirty minutes. Is that clear?"

"Yes, sir."

"Talk to you soon, Harris. Good luck."

Harris muted his earpiece and strode over to where the command center was quickly coming together, the officers gathered around a detailed map of the Eastern United States spread atop a long table, staffers bustling around, and Marines carrying out crates of ammunition and supplies from the armory.

"Excuse me," Harris said, circling the table. "Did you receive the orders to transport the President to Site R in Pennsylvania?"

"They just came through," Pulaski confirmed. "We're establishing communication with the convoy coming out of DC now. Once we figure out where they are, we'll have them meet us here and drive to the site together. Seems like the safest course of action to me."

"You read my mind, General," Harris nodded.

Staffers worked in the background to make everyone comfortable, bringing up supplies from the lower levels, their faces blanched after passing through the corridors, but going about their business with stoic professionalism as they brought up blankets and first-aid kits, tending to the mildly wounded and handing out rations and cups of coffee.

"Colonel Crow is handling the defense of our perimeter until we solidify our plans." Pulaski ran his hand through his dirty hair, face smeared with soot and blood. "We're not expecting another attack anytime soon, but we weren't in the first place, so I'm not about to get caught with my pants down twice."

"Casualty reports?" Birk asked.

"We lost seventy-five Marines. Half that number again are wounded. Attackers lost two hundred and ninety at last count. It'll be well over three hundred by the time we're done counting."

"Not the best trade-off we could've asked for. How the hell did they field that many if they aren't part of some organization?"

"No idea, sir. For now, though, we're treating them as an enemy force and taking an offensive approach. We have strike teams hunting down the remainder of the enemy forces."

"I concur with that," Birk replied.

A radio control operator came over and saluted the President and General. "General Pulaski, we've got Mongoose One on the line, Colonel Rachel Kane."

"Patch her through now," Pulaski replied.

The radio controller handed out headsets, and everyone put them on and activated them, the line sparking with static and feedback squeals.

"One second, sirs," The controller ran to a tower console and made some adjustments. "Okay, you're on with Colonel Kane. The feedback should be gone."

"Colonel Kane?"

"General Pulaski? This is Kane." The colonel spoke in a clear tone with the thrum of diesel engines in the background. "I'm reading you loud and clear."

"You received your orders from NORTHCOM?"

"Yes, sir."

"I've got the President and his staff with me on the line, and we're trying to figure out the best way to reach Site R while keeping President Birk safe. What's your current status?"

"When all this started, my people secured decommissioned vehicles from the DC and Reckord armories and started piecing them together. Some of them went with you to Mt. Weather right away, and since then, we've pieced together another six dozen working vehicles and a small convoy of rigs and tractor-trailers."

"Excellent work," Pulaski said, leaning over the map with his arms spread wide.

"Thank you, sir."

"So, you're well on your way to Site R?"

"We're currently on I-270 between Gaithersburg and Frederick."

"Given our valuable cargo, the best strategy would be for your convoy to swing by Mount Weather and pick us up."

"We'd be honored to escort the President and his people to the new site. We'll plot a route to you."

"Excellent. Report back on your planned route and your ETA."

"Roger that, General. Give me fifteen minutes. Kane, out."

"How long do you think it'll take them?" Birk asked.

"Depends on what the roads look like and the resistance they face. If there are more of these civilian attackers trying to take control of the roadways, we could face more trouble."

"We noticed the attackers had no insignias or markings, but having such a large group almost forces me to assume they're part of something bigger. Any thoughts?"

"It's hard to tell, sir. We have to assume they're part of a larger group, and all we can do is prepare for the worst and hope Kane gets here quickly. It'll be a race to bring up our supplies and equipment from the sublevels before they arrive."

"What do you propose?"

Major Spencer stepped up. "If you don't mind, I have a suggestion."

"Go ahead, Major."

"Well, I've already been working with the civilian staff and supplies. That includes medical supplies for the medical teams. I know where it's all stored and can have that brought up and stacked outside the front gate in half a day."

"Good," Pulaski said. "I can have Crow do the same with the munitions and military gear. I'll collect the remaining troops, transports, and trucks and begin forming our portion of the convoy."

Birk stood back from the table. "Will everything fit?"

"I doubt it. I'll get with Kane to see how much extra room she has, though I doubt it will be much. We may need to leave some things behind. We can make sure it's... *prepared*, though, in case some enterprising a-holes come across it. Sir."

"All right, people," Birk clapped, patting his officers on their shoulders and offering a grim smile. "Let's get started. You all know your assignments."

Pulaski echoed him and took Crow off to the side, pointing at the west end of the compound where Marines were returning with weapons and packs. Birk walked toward the north end of camp with his arms folded, plumes of breath rising as the Virginia woods rose before them. The mountains stretched across the horizon through gaps in the trees, the forest-covered spurs descending into narrow valleys dovetailing north into the lush green hills of West Virginia. Brushes of soft clouds streaked the bright blue skies, marked with drifting smoke from the fires left to burn so every resource could be thrown into the evacuation. Harris followed a few steps behind Birk, instinctively watching the woods, unable to believe that things were actually safe.

"We shouldn't wander so far, sir," Harris said. "The Marines are stretched thin."

Birk shrugged. "Meh. I want to savor a bit of fresh air before they pack me into a Humvee and carry me away. We were in the bunker way too long... it's not natural."

"Yes, sir."

"Would you look at that view?"

"It's wonderful," Harris replied, trying hard to look past the bodies, the chunks of burning debris, and the signs of violence everywhere. "It's... good to find some beauty in all this."

Birk patted Harris' shoulder. "We have to, or we'll go crazy living in constant fear, stuck inside bunkers for the rest of our lives."

"I understand that, but it's important to be cautious. I'm just looking after you, sir."

"I know." Birk patted him on the shoulder. "Congratulations on stopping those attackers. We couldn't have done it without you."

"It's what I get paid to do, sir."

Birk laughed. "I hate to inform you, Harris, but your next paycheck might be a *bit* delayed."

Harris couldn't quite suppress a grin. "Understood, sir."

Birk joined him in sharing a hearty chuckle, and the two men stood transfixed by the beautiful landscape, the Marine units bustling behind them, the convoy coming together by degrees.

"Might I ask, sir, what's waiting for us at Site R?"

"No idea. Never been there, never bothered to ask about it. Too many meetings and responsibilities to check out the cool bunkers and all that. What do you know about it?"

"I've never been there, though it's obviously a high-security site. I think they have a nuclear reactor on hand, for power generation."

"Well, it'll be a learning experience for us both then."

A group of Marines strode up carrying their carbines at the ready, the fire team leader stepping up and saluting the President. "Sir, can you follow us inside? It's just temporary. We need to run some patrols around the perimeter until the convoy arrives."

"Back in the bunker we go," Birk said, patting Harris on the shoulder and turning him toward the massive blast doors that hung crookedly off their hinges.

CHAPTER SIXTEEN

Ryan Cooper
Lansing, Michigan

Ryan scrubbed the shower wall hard, removing the last layers of grime and mold to expose clean white tiles underneath. Judging by the scum around the drain, it hadn't been cleaned in a couple of years and was used primarily to wash the dogs and dump dirty water. The spare bathroom stood outside the workshop near the furnace and water heater, four walls with no ceiling and a view of the joists and pipes. Dunking a cup into the five-gallon bucket, James splashed it on the wall and washed the gray water down the drain. Bleach and surface cleaner hung heavy in the air, and the small fan he'd set up to help ventilate the room did nothing to keep him from constantly sneezing.

Backing out of the shower, he collected the scrub brushes, the bucket, and cleaner, and set them at the foot of the stairs, then walked over to the water filter and checked the pressure coming in after they'd filled up the five hundred gallon tank to the top. The gauge read forty-five psi. Not great, but not terrible, either. It was enough to draw water from the spigots on the lower floor and use the toilets, and get low-flow trickles upstairs as well. Not long after they'd started pumping water into the tank, Helen had kicked one of the water heaters back on, both of them excited by the potential of a hot shower in the not-too-distant future.

Heading back to the bathroom, Ryan put one hand on the glass door and the other on the faucet handle, giving it a turn and waiting as the pipes groaned and shivered, the nozzle spitting and sputtering until a bit of water sprayed out and dwindled to a trickle. The next pulse came in a spray about half the intensity of normal that rained on the shower floor, settling into an airy but steady stream. Grinning and turning the temperature to hot, the pressure shifted but remained steady until hot water was running out steadily, steam rising up and bringing the lingering scent of bleach with it.

"That's what I'm talking about," he said and turned the shower off.

The basement door came open, and Helen called down. "Ryan, dear?"

"Yeah!"

"Sandy's at the gate."

Heat flashed through his cheeks. "Shoot her. The shower's working and putting out hot water, too. It's not blasting, but plenty good enough to get clean from."

"That's wonderful, but... Sandy doesn't look so well. I watched her through the rifle scope. I can't completely tell from here, but I think I saw blood and bruises, and she keeps looking over her shoulder like she's nervous."

"You know what I'd call that?"

"What?"

"A lame try by Jack and the rest of them. Let me know how the shower works tonight, would you?"

"I will, and I appreciate you doing this for us. But if you could just come up and have a look at Sandy for yourself, *please?*"

Ryan shook his head and shut off the water, moving to the foot of the stairs. "It's just another trap. I'm not sure what you want me to do, go out there and get shot at?"

"No, just come up and see," Helen replied imploringly. "It'll only take you a minute."

Ryan put the cleaning supplies down and stomped upstairs in a huff, annoyed by the very thought of Sandy. "The best thing we can do," he said, moving past her toward the front window, "is to ignore them. I've been thinking about it all day, Helen, and we just don't know what they might try. Distractions? Tricks? Or another all-out assault?"

"I'm not entirely sure Sandy was involved in the incident yesterday," Helen said, following him into the dining room where he picked his Winchester off the table.

"Sandy was *with* them," he replied, spreading the blinds.

"I've been thinking about it all day, too, and I heard what Sandy said to you."

"Yeah, that she'd found out about a well pump, which was a *lie*."

"Not that part. The part where she was sorry."

"I doubt she was sorry," Ryan snorted as he pulled the front door open and put the rifle barrel through, leaning against the doorframe to steady his aim as he adjusted his scope.

"What... what if, maybe, they *forced* her to draw us out."

"And why wouldn't they do it again if it worked the first time? I'll tell you, Helen, I'm not ready to deal with any more bullshit from these people. I'd rather just shoot them all and call it a day."

Helen ignored his anger. "Look at her. You see what I mean?"

Ryan studied Sandy through the rifle scope as the wind blew her dark hair around her shoulders. She wore the same shirt as the previous day, an old flannel over a gray camisole, blue jeans, and boots. Squinting, he tried to pick up on what Helen had seen.

"Yeah, she doesn't look great," he said. "Her shirt's all torn up on her shoulder, and I can see some shadows on her face. I guess those could be bruises." Ryan lowered the rifle as a shudder of disgust swept through him, torn between feeling sorry for Sandy over her condition and wondering just how far Jack, Barb and the rest of them were willing to go to trick Helen and himself.

Helen rested her hands on Ryan's arm, speaking softly. "We should go down and check on her."

"No way." Ryan glared down the driveway. "We're not going down there. It's just another trap."

"I don't think so, dear. My guess is that someone must've seen her going back and forth to our place and making trades with us, and they tried to use her to get to us. I don't think she meant to hurt or trick us – she was forced to."

"It doesn't matter." Ryan raised the rifle to his shoulder again, taking a deep breath and letting it slip out slowly. Even if Helen was right, they couldn't risk letting their guards down for one second.

Helen squeezed his shoulder. "If you don't go down, *I* will."

Ryan lowered the gun and shut the door, staring Helen down for several seconds before finally relenting.

"Oh, all right," he huffed, "have it your way. We'll leave the dogs at the house this time as a rear guard in case this is some kind of diversion, and you'll cover me but stay back quite a ways."

"That sounds acceptable. Thank you." She smiled and gave him a quick hug.

They armed up and Helen grabbed a first-aid kit and some soft, clean towels. Ryan led the way down the driveway, checking all directions for signs of movement at the pond or the edge of the woods. With the dogs back up at the house, they were protected from behind, but Ryan was taking no chances. When they came to around fifty yards from the gate, Ryan turned to ensure Helen was keeping her distance, then he finished his walk, stopping fifteen yards from the fence and looking everywhere but at Sandy.

"I'm sorry for what happened," she said, the words rushing out. "I didn't want to do it, but they made me... Jack and Barb."

When everything looked clear, Ryan fixed her with a hard stare, swallowing dry when he saw the damage to her face up close. Her left eye was blackened, her cheek on the same side was swollen, and blood had splattered on her shirt from what looked like a fierce nosebleed, confirmed by her crooked nose.

"I'm listening," he grumbled. "If this is some kind of diversion, though, there're three furry friends who'll take care of anyone who you might have sent up to the house."

"I—what? No, I swear this..." Sandy stumbled over her words and started again. "Look, I just wanted to apologize because I should've fought them harder, but they started threatening to hurt Stephen if I didn't go along with them. I thought about running away, just picking up and leaving, but what little we have is in the house, well, on the porch, and—"

Ryan snorted. "You did your job, leading Helen and me into a trap. Why would they beat you up over it?"

"When their plan failed, they took out their frustration on me." She shook her head and wrung her hands, the tears around the rims of her eyes breaking free and racing down her cheeks. "I had to at least let you know I was sorry for what happened and for breaking your trust."

Ryan lowered his rifle and kicked at the ground, turning back to Helen and jerking his head toward the gate. Helen rushed up with the first-aid kit, reaching the fence and stopping with her hand covering her mouth when she saw Sandy's face.

"Oh, dear. What did they do to you?"

"I'm so sorry, Helen," Sandy said. "Will you forgive me for bringing those people back here?"

Helen scolded her softly. "There's nothing to forgive. You're the one who was abused, not us." She put the first-aid kit on the fence, opened it, and placed gauze and bandages on the rail. "Now, come here and let me have a look at you."

Sandy stepped closer, but instead of stopping at the rail, she reached for a hug through the wide bars, and Helen put aside her things and embraced her, squeezing hard and rubbing her back.

"There, there," Helen said soothingly. "I can't imagine what it must be like living out there next to those animals."

"I tried to mind my own business and keep Stephen away from them, but they kept coming over and making threats, and when they told me what they'd do to him, I just... I broke down."

"I wouldn't wish that on anyone." Helen glanced back at Ryan who ground his teeth together, looking around, still half-expecting an ambush.

"Here," he finally, begrudgingly said, pointing at the gate. "Come on inside. No sense in standing out there."

"No, I can't stay long. I've got to get back to Stephen. He's at the house alone, and if they find out I came here, they'll do something to him."

"Let me see your face," Helen said, patting the rail. "Put your elbows here and lean in."

Ryan kept an eye on the tree line and road, watching as Helen cleaned up her cuts and abrasions and applied some antiseptic. She started to put bandages on, but Sandy gently pushed her hand away.

"No, no, don't do that," she said. "If they see I've been fixed up, they'll know I was here."

"Then take this first-aid kit with you and tell them you found it and put them on yourself." Sandy nodded and allowed Helen to put the bandages on her cuts and abrasions.

"They didn't do anything else to you, did they?" Ryan asked. "I mean, do you have any sprains or broken bones?"

"I don't think so. Well, one of them kicked me in the side, but it's just sore. I don't think I have any broken ribs or anything."

"That's good," Ryan grumbled. "Those people are animals. I'm glad you're not hurt too badly, but I don't think that's the end of it."

"What do you mean?" Sandy asked as Helen placed a bandage above her left cheek.

"Well... assuming you're telling the truth—"

"Ryan Cooper, you stop that!" Helen whirled on him and he put his hands up in defense.

"Hey, I'm just saying! If she is telling the truth, then I think they'll use her to get at us again." He looked at Sandy. "What I mean is, they'll use *Stephen* to get you to do their dirty work."

"I'm never helping them again."

"It won't matter. They know where you stay. A little bit of leverage and you'll be dancing for them."

Sandy raised her chin in defiance. "All I care about is making sure my son is safe. I'll leave the area if I have to. I'm sure we can find somewhere else to eke out an existence."

"That I sincerely doubt. Trust us, we were out and about at the start of all of this, and it's not fit for anyone, much less a mother and a young boy."

"I hate to agree with Ryan right now," Helen said, giving him a wry smile, "but he's right."

Sandy shook her head, absently touching the bandages on her face, her expression brightening with an idea. "Could you... put us up? I'd be willing to work or do whatever it takes to earn our keep."

Ryan was nodding with one arm resting over the rail, watching off into the distance down the road. "I'm thinking that we could arrange something like that. If you can source that well pump for us first, of course."

Sandy started to reply, but Helen held up her finger and gave her a forced smile. "Hang on a second while I talk to my husband?" She took Ryan's arm and drew him out of earshot before socking him in the arm. "Ryan! How could you say something like that? This woman clearly needs our help, and you're forcing her to trade?"

"We need that well pump, Helen. In case you hadn't noticed, I still don't trust her farther than I can throw her. And if she's not going to be talking to that group anymore, well, this is the best thing she can do for us. It's simple mathematics. We'd be going through more water with the two of them here, requiring us to pump more."

"Stephen and Sandy will do all that, and they can do the chores that are too hard on us. We've been wanting help—"

"All that's true, but it won't be enough. We need the pump, and she needs to be the one to get it. Bottom line? If she does that, then I'll trust her. You and I are too old and slow to go out there scrounging around for something like that, especially when it's something we *really* need. That jerry-rigged pump... it'll only get us so far."

Helen stood with her arms crossed, tight-lipped as she stared out at the woods. "I don't know, Ryan. It seems down-right mean to put her in this position."

"We're *all* in this position, Helen, whether we like it or not. Let her prove that what happened before really was coercion and that she had no choice by doing this one difficult task. If she does it, we open the gates to her and her son and welcome them in."

Helen reluctantly nodded. "All right. We'll do it your way, but this is her only entrance fee. We won't ask her to do anything else after this, agreed?"

"Agreed."

They walked back over to the fence, and Ryan looked at Helen as he spoke to Sandy. "Helen and I talked, and we want to invite you and your son onto our property to stay with us. You'd be safe here, and wouldn't have to worry about much. Let's just say we have more here than we're letting on."

"That doesn't surprise me at all. I don't know what to say except thank you."

"Yeah, well, don't thank us yet. We still need something from you first."

"The well pump."

"The well pump. If you can get us that pump, you and Stephen can stay. No other conditions or anything else. I mean, you'll both have to work hard, obviously, but consider that pump your entrance fee – and your way of showing us that we really can trust you."

Sandy thought about it for less than two seconds before nodding enthusiastically. "I'm not sure how I'll do it but thank you so much for giving me a way out. We were sinking... but I'll figure something out, and I'll get you that pump. Shake on it."

"All right." Ryan smiled and shook her hand.

"I'll come back as soon as I find something... it might not be tomorrow morning, exactly. Just look for me to be here over the next few days, okay?"

"We will." Helen reached across the fence to squeeze her hand. "And you be careful, dear. Don't put yourself in harm's way if you can avoid it."

"I'll try," she said. "But harm's way is a way of life these days."

"True enough."

They watched her jog to the road and disappear behind the tree line and Helen locked arms with Ryan, and together they walked up the driveway with the sun bearing down on them and warming the rising breeze.

"I take it you aren't mad with me anymore?" Ryan asked.

"As much as I'd like to be... no. We were both right about things here. Me, about checking on her, and you about the pump. As much as I'd like to let her in now and try to get the pump later...."

"We could have, but I still don't trust her. This'll be a good test, to let us know her true intentions. If she wants her son to eat... if she wants to get away from those thugs at the Willoughby's place, she'll have to pay a price. I don't think it's too much to ask."

"She's a strong, smart young woman," Helen said, sounding like she was trying to convince herself of the fact. "She'll be fine."

"She'll have to be if she wants to survive out here."

CHAPTER SEVENTEEN

Alice Burton
Talladega National Forest, Alabama

Alice crept through the dense woods, moving from the river toward the forward bunkhouses, creeping along the tree line, waiting patiently for a chance to strike. An hour went by, the moon drifting across the sky above the clearing clouds, the stars peeking out in pinpoints of light. Most campfires dimmed and died as the adults' parties wound down and they went back to their bunkhouses, but a couple of campfires near the river raged on with a few who twirled and danced without ceasing. The child workers were taken north through a small clearing to another set of bunkhouses where guards stood silhouetted in the window lights.

A lone woman stepped away from a campfire and walked up a side path toward the tree line, heading toward the bunkhouses with her arms crossed, hugging herself in the cooling evening. Alice followed her for twenty or thirty yards, creeping softly through the brush, waiting for a moment where she could ambush the woman. She'd just about given up when a pair of shadows came out of the darkness and walked right toward her. Heart skipping, Alice sank back into the foliage, knife up and ready to fight.

A man raised his hand to the woman. "Had enough for one night, Shiela?"

"Yeah." She turned and walked backwards, still hugging herself. "I'm done for tonight. Got a big day tomorrow."

"Can't hang with the big dogs, huh?"

She rolled her eyes. "Yep, that's what it is. Anyway, have fun, guys!"

"Oh, we will."

The men stepped into the woods, swaying slightly as they each found a tree, unzipped, and sprayed the foliage with a pair of urine streams. Alice stood less than seven yards away, crouched behind some brush, body tensed to pounce.

"What do they have you doing tomorrow?" the first man asked.

"I gotta hitch up that giant horse they brought in yesterday and get a load of building materials from the other camp."

"Hercules," Alice thought.

"That's hard work, man."

"Yeah, I've got to earn my keep." He laughed. "Not like you. It must be tough smacking kids around all day."

"Don't let them fool you. Those damn kids are nightmares. They're lazy, they back talk and they try to escape every time you blink. I didn't join this outfit to be a full-time babysitter."

"You just gotta know how to handle them. If they get out of line, take 'em down a notch or two."

"Yeah, but the bosses don't want broken bones or even bruises, so you're damned if you do, damned if you don't."

"I guess so." The second man finished his business and zipped up. "All right, I'll see you back at the fire."

"All right, man."

As he walked away, Alice kept her eyes pinned on the man still standing by the tree, tensing her body in anticipation of what was to come. When he finished and was about to zip his pants back up, Alice gathered her strength, pushed her pain to the back of her mind, and took two long steps from the bushes, not bothering with stealth. Before he could turn, she leapt on him, locking her left arm over his shoulder, clinging there and drawing the knife blade across his throat with the cutting edge angled inward and upward to tear through flesh and sinew, biting into his spongy windpipe and carotid artery and ripping clean through them.

He jerked straight and stumbled backward, gasping, gurgling in surprise as hot blood rushed over her arm and down his chest. Alice's feet swayed as he spasmed, her toes brushing the forest floor, struggling to keep hold of him as he thrashed. Alice stabbed him twice more in the side of the neck before she released him, but she was late jumping off, and his elbow caught her in the right shoulder and sent her staggering and falling at the base of the tree.

The man gurgled, clutched his throat, and tried to scream but only pushed air bubbles between his fingers, blinking and mouthing soundless words at her in shock and terror as blood gushed down his shirt. Alice scrambled to her feet, transfixed by what she'd done, feeling like a stranger in her own body. The man took a step toward her, then staggered back toward the campfires and buildings, taking two steps before crashing to his knees and falling flat on his face, a final shudder signaling that his body had lost too much blood to continue fighting for life.

Alice leaned against the tree trunk, catching her breath before walking over to stand over the man. She put the knife away and grabbed his feet, dragging him backward, breathing hard as her chest was rocked with waves of agony. The body slid easily over the dry leaves and brush, but it was impossible to get him through the thicker foliage so, finally, she took some branches and leaves and covered him up so he was just another lump of deadfall on the forest floor. Breathing heavily, hands on her knees, expecting to be crippled by pain, Alice was surprised to find herself invigorated. Yes, the nagging body aches were still there, and waves of pain still cycled through her chest, but adrenaline and a sense of purpose suppressed most of it.

She resumed stalking the tree line like a tiger, sticking to the shadows, waiting patiently for opportunities. At the river's edge, she took a drunken man out in the same manner, coming up behind him as he urinated into the river, the act covered by darkness and the sloping bank. Her blood-slicked knife plunged in repeatedly as she clung to him, using her body weight to drag him down into the floating branches and refuse that bobbed along the shoreline, ripping through brush as they went. Like the other man, he spun and tried to throw her off, then tried to punch her, but she'd already gotten away, crawling on her backside up the riverbank, watching flat-faced as he finally toppled backward and splashed in the water. He died face down as well, his body snagged by stones and wet brush, so Alice got up and shoved him with her boot so that he drifted lazily out into the river's flow, turning slowly as the current carried him away.

By the third kill, it was almost effortless, though her hands and arms were bathed in so much blood she had to wipe them – and the knife – off with leaves so she could maintain her grip on her weapon. On her way back to the bunkhouses where she'd taken her first victim, a woman with a rifle slung on her shoulder stepped away from the campfire and came to the edge of the woods.

"Artie! Are you out there?"

A flashlight sprung to life and flashed right past her, and Alice pressed herself closer to a thick oak tree as the light beam moved back and forth.

"I'm not kidding, man. If you're out there and trying to scare me, it's not going to work. Plus, it's a great way to get yourself shot." She stepped into the woods and shined the beam deeper, sweeping it across Alice's tree, though the trunk was twice as big as her, and she remained well-hidden. Alice anchored herself with her left hand against the trunk as the crunch of the woman's boots came even closer.

"If you blew off your shift and went to bed, I'm going to kill you." The flashlight beam found the spot where Alice had dropped the first man and stopped, drifting slowly across the lumpy form where bits of his flannel shirt and boots poked out.

"Artie?!" The light jerked as the woman slipped the rifle from her shoulder and held it in both hands, still gripping the flashlight in her offhand, the beam trembling ever so slightly.

"Artie?" She stepped closer and nudged at the body with her boot, dislodging leaves and sticks. "Artie? Oh, no. Artie!"

Alice stepped in front of her, taking advantage of her shock to wrap the woman in a one-handed hug, squeezing her close and trapping the rifle between them. Burying her face in the woman's hair, Alice punched rapidly upward with the knife from stomach to neck, the blade flashing in and stabbing her stomach, between her ribs, then the soft, fleshy parts beneath her chin, slicing her trachea and arteries to bits, hugging her tighter and dragging her backward into the woods. Blood spilled between them, the hard iron scent rushing up Alice's nose as the woman burst into a frenzy of movement and wet grunts, shoving back with the rifle, head-butting Alice in the jaw with a sharp crack, finally knocking her away and getting enough separation to raise the rifle.

Face stricken with blind panic, eyes blurred with tears, choking and gasping as she tried to breathe and swallow, the woman got off a shot, firing blindly into the darkness and missing her target. Alice came around the tree behind the woman, grabbed her by her hair, and jerked her to the ground, finishing her off with a couple of quiet stabs and putting a hand over her mouth as a mewling groan stretched from her mangled throat and faded to a feeble last breath.

The camp flew into an uproar, shouts of surprise and alarmed cries ringing out orders, flashlights springing to life and shining across the tree line. Alice rolled the woman over, grabbed her rifle and moved west toward the stables, angling deeper into the woods, throwing glances back as people rushed over from the campfires. The bunkhouses came to life, lights flipping on and people bursting through the front doors. They stood around, scratching their heads, finally seeing the gathering stretched along the trees near the river and running to see what the fuss was about.

Meanwhile, Alice was slowly and quietly slipping away, though a dozen or more flashlights searched frantically through the foliage, and it wouldn't be long before they found the woman and Artie. They were all on one side of the camp, though, giving Alice an idea. She left the cover of the trees and moved quickly across the campground past the first set of bunkhouses, slipping between dying campfires and into the woods. More bunkhouses and buildings stood farther off, interspersed between clutches of trees and brush. Fires burned low, and guards milled toward the south, stopping and scratching their heads, pointing toward the commotion.

Alice hid behind a wide birch tree surrounded by a spattering of saplings, rubbed her jaw and took stock of herself, trying to ensure that the blood covering her body from head to toes all belonged to other people. Her chest hurt but the pain was tolerable, her legs were okay, and her breathing wasn't bad despite the scuffles. Swallowing dry, she pushed off the tree and led with the rifle, circled off to the left to get closer to the buildings, drawn by the lights shining from the smudged windows.

Small shapes moved around inside, kids peering out the windows, though they seemed to not notice her creeping through the trees toward the first row of bunkhouses and past an archery range. She glanced repeatedly at the adults a short distance away, six or eight of them who weren't paying attention to her direction thanks to the commotion happening on the other side of camp. More buildings stood off in the distance, and she assumed there were more guards around every corner so she swiftly moved across an open area to the north, stopping to crouch behind a set of aluminum garbage cans. She was maybe twenty yards from a small bunkhouse with its screen door closed and shapes moving inside, but some adults were nearby as well, ten feet south of the building, so close she could hear them talking, questioning what was going on as they shook their heads.

A cry went up, followed by shouts and flashlight beams shifting as people ran toward one spot along the tree line. The lights pointed down and then out at the woods, and a man bellowed. "Slick, bring your guys over here, now!"

The guards took off running in the indicated direction, and Alice slipped ahead, coming up the front stoop, drawing the screen door open, and stepped inside to find four kids sitting on bunks, chained to the rails. Two of them had enough slack to reach the south-facing window and were watching the men run away, but when Alice entered they turned to her with wide, terrified eyes, the two at the window jumping back and sitting back down.

It was a standard camp-style dorm, musty and dusty with a few small pieces of furniture around and some old posters half hanging off the wall. A stack of plates sat tilted over in the center of the room next to metal cups and a pitcher. Alice looked down at herself covered in gore and mud, rifle in her bloody hands, red caked beneath her fingernails. It was in every conceivable crease in her clothes and skin, and the kids stared at her like she was the angel of death.

"Oh, no." Alice stepped inside and held one hand up. "It's not what you —"

"You're the outside lady," the little girl said in a tiny voice.

Alice shook her head in confusion. "The outside lady?"

"Yeah, Ricky and Colton told everyone about you. You're looking for Jake and Sarah."

"Yes!" Alice noticed that she was framed in the window, so she stepped closer and lowered her voice. "Yes, that's right. I met Ricky and Colton outside, and I got to talk to them. They told me you guys were prisoners in here."

"We're in jail," the little girl said. "Where they put bad people."

"Oh, you're not a bad person." Alice replied sadly, barely able to restrain herself from reaching out and taking the girl's hand. "The people who put you in here are bad. They're looking for me, now. That's what all the commotion is about over there."

"We thought one of our friends tried to escape again," the girl said. "We thought they tried to run away, and that's a big no-no. You can get in big trouble for that."

"I know, and I'm sorry for stirring things up. Hey, the guards will be back soon, and I need to find Jake and Sarah right away. Can you tell me where they are?"

The boy pointed to the east. "Yeah, they're a couple of buildings over, the big one with all the smoke coming from the chimney."

"Is it a cafeteria or something?"

"No. We used to eat there, but now that's where they make drugs."

"Yeah, it smells so bad," a second boy on a window bunk said. "You can smell it from here if the wind's wrong."

Alice inhaled deeply, catching the faint whiff of ammonia and something else she almost couldn't describe, an acrid reek of chemicals burning. A boiling rage grew in her gut, drawing her jaw so tight she could hardly speak.

"I do smell it. Those.... *people* have Jake and Sarah in a drug den. You say it's that way?"

"Yeah. But be careful, lady," the girl said. "If they catch you, they'll hurt you really bad. They're way worse to adults than they are to kids."

"Yeah, they'll do horrible things to you if they catch you." The second boy's voice was shaking, and he glanced outside at the crowd searching the woods.

Alice grinned maliciously, her white teeth glowing from her muddy, bloody face. "Don't worry about me, kids. It's *them* who need to worry." She put her finger to her lips and softened her tone slightly. "Don't tell any guards I was here. I'm going to do my best to get my kids, then see if I can't figure out a way to make a distraction for the rest of you to escape."

"We won't," the girl replied, the boys nodding in agreement. "And thank you."

"Awesome, guys. Thanks a lot."

Alice waved at them, her motherly smile fading as she backed to the door and stepped outside. Seeing the coast was clear, Alice slipped around the side of the building and caught the kids watching her through the windows, the little girl giving her a faint smile and wave as she went by. Alice clutched the rifle to her chest, stopping at the back corner to wipe away a tear, the sadness over the abuse of the children eclipsed by a rage that bubbled from her stomach to fill every ounce of her body. The drug-making building was across an open space ahead with dead fires and empty benches all around it. It was a long, lodge style structure with a single peak running its length, black shingles and faded red siding that looked gray in the moonlight. The windows were dark, boarded over, the double doors in front shut tight.

Alice stormed straight across the grass, glancing left and right, expecting someone to challenge her, but none did. The camp stood empty and still with only a symphony of chirping crickets making swells of noise, the adults having all vacated into the trees on the far side. The stench of the drugs grew, stinging her nostrils and turning her stomach and as she rushed between a pair of smoldering campfires and marched up to the front doors, teeth bared, rifle charged and ready to shoot anyone who stood in her way. She tried the doorknobs and found them unlocked, ripping one open and shouldering the door inward.

A long hall stretched before her like in the other bunkhouses, wooden planking and walls and a pair of doors at the far end bracketing a hearth with a blazing fire and a big pot boiling and gurgling on a metal grate. Two sets of benches stretched the length of the building, pieced together from picnic tables and office desks, cabinets, and doors placed across sawhorses. On the benches sat a combination of science-looking equipment and every day cookware: glass beakers with rounded bottoms and curls of smoke drifting up, plastic soda bottles, pots and pans with modified lids, darts of flame shooting straight up the side of burners cooking bubbling substances, all the pieces strung together by hoses and copper piping.

In the center of it all, tied to a pillar in the center of the room, were Jake and Sarah, gagged and blinking in shock as she crept toward them. Sarah made a muffled noise, her eyes flying wide in disbelief as she squirmed and tugged on her restraints.

"Jake! Sarah!" Alice kept her voice low as she rushed over. "I can't believe I finally found you!"

Alice kneeled between them, resisting the urge to hug them, instead taking out her knife, putting the rifle on the floor and leaning in to start cutting at their bonds. Sarah had a bruise on the left side of her face, and Jake's right eye was black and blue, but instead of seeming happy she was there, they both squirmed and shook their heads, mumbling into their gags and blinking in wide-eyed fear. Alice paused with a confused expression and pulled Sarah's gag off.

"No," Sarah hissed. "It's a trap!"

"What do you mean?" She leaned forward and started sawing at Jake's bonds.

"No. *Stop*! You've got to get out of—"

The front doors burst open, and three guards charged in with guns and scowling faces, spreading out across the room with the barrels leveled at her.

CHAPTER EIGHTEEN

Ryan Cooper
Lansing, Michigan

Ryan worked the well pump one handed and tried to pour coffee from a thermos with the other, his shoulders shifting, hand shaking as he attempted to keep the majority of the frothy liquid inside the cup and not on the ground. When it was half full, he gave up and placed the thermos down and sipped, watching as the morning sun rose high over the trees, distant and misty behind a wall of clouds drifting off to the east.

Helen was finishing up with the chickens, watching them spread out across the yard and running free with Duke on guard while Diana and Duchess sat a way off to their left, intent on something small and noisy moving in the tree line. Letting go of the plunger, Ryan raised from his lawn chair and looked down his rifle scope for trouble, but the dogs' ears settled, and Duchess laid down with her tongue lolling out as whatever small animal it was finally vanished.

There'd been endless false alarms and scares throughout the night, Ryan endlessly paranoid about Jack and his people trying to pull a fast one, and after dinner he'd expanded his area traps on the north sides of the shed and chicken coop, layered with debris and nail boards. That had taken the rest of the hose and more scrap wood from the barn, and his hands were sore from hammering half the night, but he felt somewhat better for being slightly more prepared.

Helen drew some chickens off with a handful of feed before she shuffled back the other way in an evasive maneuver with the big rooster and hens giving chase. Laughing and calling to them, she finally turned and tossed the feed off to the left, and the birds broke on a dime toward it.

"I could live out here the rest of my life," she said, coming over, panting, smiling, and wiping sweat off her brow.

Ryan sat back down and resumed pumping, getting the water flowing again and listening to it splash in the tank. "I'm glad you're having a good time. Meanwhile, I'm being reminded of why we decided to leave this and head for a townhouse..."

"The townhouse was Alice's suggestion." Helen picked up the thermos and another cup and sat in a lawn chair next to him.

"And it was a good one," Ryan nodded. "Selling the farm was the right decision. Couldn't expect the kids to take care of their farm *and* ours."

"I guess it's something everybody has to think about at some point."

"Getting old sucks."

"Beats the alternative."

Helen took a sip of her coffee and leaned forward with her knees together, gazing toward the sun. "You know, I've barely thought about the townhouse since we've been here."

"I'm sure it burned up like everything else," Ryan replied with a grunt. "I haven't thought about it much, either. Doesn't much matter, though, what with all of this going on. We're both safe – *that's* what matters."

Helen smiled. "I love you, too, dear."

"I just wish Alice and James and the kiddos were here with us to enjoy it."

"They'll come home. I just know it. And it'll be great having Sandy and Stephen here with us. We could use their energy."

"First thing I'm doing is having Stephen get that milk canister from the barn every day," Ryan chuckled. "The thing about tears my shoulders off when I try to carry it."

Helen laughed and gestured to the pump. "Is it my turn yet?"

"Yeah, take over for a bit while I take a walk around and check up on things."

"Switch seats?"

Ryan got up and shouldered his rifle, stretching and pulling at his arms and hands to work out the kinks. "Thanks, hon. I'll be back in fifteen or twenty minutes to finish topping it off."

"Okay. Be careful."

Ryan walked out to where Duchess and Diana were sitting, petting them, rolling his shoulders, working out the stiffness that had settled in since he'd started pumping water almost an hour ago. The previous evening they'd used the water liberally, each showering before they refilled the jugs and spare plastic water bottles, putting some in the refrigerator to chill. It had only taken the tank down about a quarter of the way, and the pressure in the kitchen spigot had decreased from a moderate flow down to a slow trickle. The basement shower, on the other hand, wasn't an issue, and the pressure was solid even after the usage.

"I don't see anything out there," he told the dogs. "But we might as well walk out and see."

Ryan strode off with his rifle in hand and the dogs trotting behind him, getting distracted by little things like helicopter seeds and leaves drifting in the wind, early signs of fall's approach with the promises of chill winds and rain. They still had to prepare for winter, which was hard to do when he had to worry about people like Jack Willoughby around every corner.

He continued circling the property, sometimes walking along the tree line, other times stepping deeper inside the woods both for a change of pace and to make sure nothing untoward was going on where they couldn't normally see. The spruces and firs stood tall, sticks and nuts clattering on the forest floor, and the heavy-sweet scent of forest musk and dead leaves filled his head. Beyond the trees, the ducks were quiet on the ponds as the sky darkened and storm clouds rolled in fast and low. A distant sound stopped him in his tracks, the faint growl of what first sounded like thunder, but continued on long enough that he realized it was an engine, throaty and deep. Staring south toward the road, he half-expected a truck to pass by, but when the engine's roar faded to silence, he hurried back to Helen, placing his gun on the EV's hood.

"I know that look," Helen looked up from her pumping. "Is something wrong?"

"I heard an engine again. This time from the south. Definitely a truck. Diesel."

"Is it the same as the one you heard before?"

"Nah, this one is much bigger. Sounds like someone out there was able to cobble together some working parts."

"Isn't that a good thing?"

"Ehhh. The military guys showing up was probably a good thing, but I don't know if I trust some random person out there who has the resources to put together a truck."

Helen kept pumping. "Might I remind you that we have *three* working vehicles?"

"You've got me there," Ryan laughed. "Still, this doesn't sit well with me."

A bright flash of lightning lit the western sky, followed several seconds later by a peal of thunder that rolled over them, a rumbling vibration that rattled the windows of the house and car. The skies had changed considerably, dark shapes sweeping in across the blue, the clouds deepening in color as more lightning ripped through them.

"Storm's coming in fast." Helen looked over her shoulder. "Looks like a big one."

"I have an idea." He walked over to the water tank and lifted the lid to check how full it was. "Hey, can you help me with something?"

"Sure," Helen dropped the plunger and stood. "What is it?"

"There are several more of these tanks out behind the barn, and Ryan never set them up."

"Rain catchers?"

"Exactly."

"That's a great idea. It'd be a perfect backup if Sandy can't get the well pump."

"That's what I'm thinking. I just hope I can get them setup before the rains get here." Ryan grabbed the ramp he'd used to drag down the bricks and hooked the chain to it.

"If we can't catch this one, we'll catch the next."

"Yeah, but the faster we set it up, the better. Give me a hand?"

Ryan attached the chain to the EV's frame, and they got in and drove up to the garden shed, grabbed another two hundred bricks, and stacked them on the wood. Ryan hauled the bricks up to the barn with Helen getting out and shooing away the curious animals to make way. Together, they rolled two five-hundred-gallon tanks onto the layer of bricks and rested them upright.

Constantly checking his rearview mirror, Ryan slowly drove the bricks and tanks down to the house, wincing as the tanks slid around on the bricks but didn't topple. As the first kisses of drizzle fell from the sky and thunder fell on their heads in claps, they rolled the tanks off and put them aside,

"If you clean these out, I'll stack the bricks next to the main tank."

"Okay," Helen used the remaining disinfectant mixture to scrub out the tanks while Ryan stacked the bricks three levels high. The sprinkles of rain got heavier for a moment but faded just as fast, the wind kicking up, gusting, then falling off again.

"Let's roll these up and let them catch what water we can today." Ryan took the lids off and set them aside, holding out his hands to catch a few raindrops. "Might get an inch or more if we're lucky and this storm lasts for a while."

Together, they got them into position and stood back and admired their handiwork, and Ryan gestured. "I'll chain these two to the main tank, but I want to get one more tank, position it at the corner of the house, and run downspout extensions to it. We'll get everything that runs off the back of the house, but it'll have sediment, bird crap, and whatever else is up there. The animals would be fine with it, and it'll save us from having to pump water exclusively for them. Let's go up to the barn and grab the last tank."

Helen called to the dogs and put them inside while Ryan waited for her in the car, and as soon as she got in, he drove up past the chickens who were huddling in the coop, seeking shelter from the coming storm.

"I swear I'll only be gone for a little while, Stephen. Summer will be here with you the whole time."

"But I don't *like* Summer," Stephen complained where he sat on the floor with his book in hand, staring up at her.

The pair had been camped out in the living room since the fires had claimed all the bedrooms, the damaged section of the house completely blocked off with plastic and tarps. Sandy slept in Trace's old recliner while Stephen took the couch, using coverlets and blankets from the hall closet to stay warm. They still had the kitchen, though nothing worked, no electricity or gas, the stove and refrigerator as good as useless. She'd been cooking their food on the porch with a camping stove taken from the attic and had brought down some sleeping bags for especially cold nights.

Five-gallon buckets served for washing up and as restrooms, and she emptied the dirty water and waste each evening in the bushes far from the house. The faucet had worked for a few days, but they were on city water lines, and soon the pressure from the nearby water tower had run out, forcing her to haul water from a nearby creek and boil it on the camping stove. For a while, they'd been okay, gathering supplies from the basement and attic and trading them with Jack's group, but they were running out of things to trade, the cupboards were bare, and she was running out of material to burn to boil water. Her only hope was to get Ryan and Helen the well pump they needed and join them on their farm.

"You met Summer before. She's a nice lady."

"She reminds me of those other people..." Stephen sighed. "Jack and Barb. They hurt you, Mom."

"Yes, they did." She brushed his hair back. "But we're going to change all that. I just have to get *one* thing, then I'll be home right away."

Stephen was ten, but he was a sensitive and perceptive boy, and his father's death and their unstable living conditions had sent him into a tailspin of fear and neediness. It hadn't helped when Jack and his friends had stopped in to threaten them and then followed up by giving her a brutal beating.

"You're going to leave and never come back," he said with wide, teary eyes.

"That's not true. I'm just going down the street to do a little scavenging so we can have something to eat." She gave him her best mom's smile. "And when I get back, all this will change."

"What do you mean?"

"I can't explain it right now, but don't say anything to Summer, okay? It's just between you and me."

Stephen nodded. "Okay. I can keep a secret."

"I know you can. That's why I'm trusting you with this. Be a good kid for Summer, and I'll be back before you know it with something *really* special."

"Is it toys or something?" he asked skeptically.

Sandy laughed. "I can't tell you. If Jack and any of those others come around, just tell them I'm out scavenging for food. Got it?" She held up her fist.

"Yeah." Stephen knocked knuckles with her and grinned.

Sandy raised and looked out the window where the skies were dark. "There she is now. Bye, hon."

She kissed Stephen on the head, stuffed her feet into her rubber boots and grabbed a black poncho off a hook, stepping outside and nodding to Summer, who came up to the porch in a yellow sweater.

"How long do I need to stay?" Summer asked as a drizzle fell.

"I'll only be gone a couple of hours. Three, tops."

"You're not going to that farm with those old people, are you?"

Sandy scoffed. "Absolutely not."

"Because Jack told everyone not to go there, and he'll blame me if I'm here watching your kid while you're doing that."

"I talked to Jack, and he wants me out there scavenging. He gave me a whole list of things he needed. So you helping me helps Jack."

"Oh," Summer said. "I guess that's okay."

Sandy took her by the arms and smiled warmly. "Look, we've been friends a long time, and you know how Jack is. I'm not working against him or any of them — I really want to help, but I'm *not* okay with them after what they did to me. That's why I'm asking you. Please, just watch my kid for a few hours, huh?"

Summer gave her a crooked grin and nodded. "Yeah, no problem. Maybe we'll find a game to play or something."

"He's got a stack of board games, and he loves the one with the warships."

"Okay, no problem."

"Thanks." Sandy gave her arms a squeeze, turned, and walked off past the junk lying in the yard, the old boat covered up and forgotten, a half-assembled motorcycle beneath a blue tarp, and other reminders of their past life when the family was much happier – or at least appeared happy on the surface. But Trace was gone both for better and worse, and it was up to Sandy to come up with a solution to feed Stephen and herself and help them survive.

Beneath ominous clouds and increasing winds, she strode briskly up Kirby Road past widespread farmhouses and fields, their doors hanging open, houses burned to the ground, firebombed vehicles resting crooked in the road or in folks' yards. A quarter mile down, she turned left on Hawkwood Road and walked another half mile before going right on Kellerman, where many of the town's small construction businesses were located. The bigger lumber supply stores were farther down Hawkwood, but she didn't have time to go into town, so she'd have to hope she could find the well pump somewhere on Kellerman. She'd driven past the area many times, had seen vans and tractors drive in, but had never gone down it herself. Trace would've known where to look since his company helped service the community's septic tanks and plumbing lines, but he'd gotten himself shot and wasn't doing anyone any good buried in the Burtons' backyard.

The paved road turned into gravel, and signs came into view... *Evans Sand and Gravel, Mitchell's Plumbing and Accessories, 67 Lumber* and many others. In their parking lots, construction vehicles of all types sat crumpled with their bucket arms gnarled and twisted, the cabs exploded, parts scattered for a hundred yards in every direction, though some of the businesses were, mercifully, intact. Sandy stopped in the middle of it all and turned in a full circle with no idea which building might have a well pump. The plumbing store looked like it sold faucets, pipes and other general supplies but well pumps were a different matter entirely.

"There's got to be one around here somewhere," she said, walking farther down the road, shining her flashlight into the growing darkness.

There was a shadowy sign at the end of the road, one her light couldn't reach, so she walked the last thirty yards until it was revealed. *Majestic Septic & Well Service* was written in large letters, with a company logo beneath it that was too worn away by age and poorly-applied paint to make out.

The building was medium sized with an office on the left and a small warehouse on the right, the glass entrance still intact and reflecting both her flashlight and the distant crackles of lightning. She checked the office building first, shining her light through the window at the water tanks on the sales floor, hose and tubing hanging on the walls, shelves full of chemicals, filters, and what appeared to be well-related components in the back.

The front door was locked, but Sandy found a brick in the landscaping and smashed the window, using a stick to knock the sharp shards from around the sides. She stepped in and went straight to the back, checking out the signs for the various types of well pumps that were available with pressure readings and gallons per minute posted on their labels. Choosing a pump that seemed about the middle of the road of what was on display, she pulled it off the shelf and dropped it on the floor with a *clank*.

Dragging it a few feet, she tried to lift it, but dropped it again. It must've weighed a hundred pounds, and there was no way she'd be able drag it home – let alone to the Coopers – by herself. She left it on the floor and headed toward the back and through to the warehouse via a pair of swinging double doors, the dark quietness of the warehouse and constant pattering of rain sending cold fingers dancing up her spine.

Sandy found a handcart in the warehouse and pushed it to the front of the store just as a flash of lightning exploded and drizzle came down hard before backing off again, teasing, threatening to dump a flood outside. She put her flashlight and poncho down and tried to lift the heavy pump, resting part of it on the cart and using her knee to shove it the rest of the way on. Shrugging on her poncho, she gripped the cart handle and pushed it outside, peering up at the sky where the clouds settled in dark shapes. She started pushing the cart up the gravel drive, but it got stuck on loose scree. Turning it around, Sandy pulled it backward, jerking and muscling it across the lot, keenly aware of the rapidly passing time. After fifteen minutes of struggling, she wrestled it onto the paved road and spun it around, leaning on it as she pushed. The wheels clacked and clattered, sometimes catching fast and almost dumping the pump, but she held onto it with a white-knuckled grip and kept it stable.

She ran the cart down the middle of Hawkwood as the rain alternated between heavy drops and drizzle, using her flashlight to catch gleaming metal and scraps in the road to avoid them. Turning onto Kirby, Sandy paused there and caught her breath, leaning on the cart and running her fingers along the smooth, wet well pump. The rain and darkness, though a bane to getting it back home, would shield her from prying eyes and allow her to hide the pump temporarily until she could gather Stephen and make a break for the Coopers.

Head down, she got behind the cart and pushed it a quarter of a mile until she came around the curve to her house. With a sudden gasp, she jerked the cart to a halt and drew it back behind the cover of the trees. Leaving the cart there, she followed the tree line, keeping to the shadows and watching them from the bushes near her driveway. Fifty yards past her driveway a dozen armed people were squared off, half of them Jack's group, the others strangers. A massive dump truck sat on the left-hand side of the road with several strangers clustered around the front of it and more people crouched in the dump bed with rifles and shotguns aimed at Jack's group.

Jack and Barb had set their guns on the ground while Mike Jones and the others were in the process of lowering their weapons as well. The leader of the group of strangers appeared to be a thin, older man with a mustache dressed in a military jacket, rifle in his hand and speaking to Jack. The two men flanking him were huge, wide-shouldered, and big-bellied, though they stood in soldiers' stances with their fingers outside their weapons' trigger guards, barrels pointed at the ground. When Jack didn't give the leader the answer he wanted, one of the big men shouldered his rifle, stepped in faster than Sandy thought possible and grabbed Mike, twisting his arm behind his back and sending him to his knees. A pistol appeared and pressed against the back of his head and Sandy crept closer, struggling to hear what they were saying over the rain and thunderclaps.

Mike held his hands up and begged. "Please, man... don't shoot me. Jack told you already, we don't know any Ryan or Helen... or *any* Coopers!"

A short, compact man stood behind the enemy leader in the same professional pose as the others, but his head swiveled slightly as he scanned the area for any more of Jack's people. When his eyes slid in Sandy's direction, she gasped and dropped down again, crouching and peeking through a gap in the branches.

"... ask you one more time," the leader said. "Tell us where the Coopers are."

Jack put his hands up and spoke in a low, soft tone. "I told you, man. We don't know any Coopers. Never heard of them. This is *our* neighborhood, and there isn't much left for you to take. So, you'd be wasting bullets if you--"

The leader flicked his chin at the one holding Mike, and Mike's head suddenly exploded, blood splattering the pavement in a V-shaped pattern before he dropped like a log. Sandy put her hand over her mouth to keep from yelping, backing away, staying out of sight and slipping back to the tree line where she'd parked the cart and pump.

She grabbed the cart handles with shaking hands, fear coursing through her body, the image of Mike's blood and brains splattering the pavement burned into her retinas.

"Stephen." Sandy wanted to hide the cart and get inside her house, but she paused, hearing the leader's voice in her head.

"*Tell us where the Coopers are.*"

If the strangers caught Ryan and Helen unawares, she and Stephen's last hope for a safe haven would vanish, and they would be left alone to fend against the evils of the world. Sandy turned the cart around and pushed it back up the road, running for the only people who could help her.

CHAPTER NINETEEN

James Burton
La Porte, Indiana

James leaned inside the Humvee and tightened a few bolts on the fuel pump, tugging on the lines to ensure the clamps were tight. He backed out from beneath the hood and wiped his hands on a rag, squinting into the sunlight that bathed the motor pool's rear parking lot. The skies were blue for the first time in days, and he was working out back to avoid the worst of the field of corpses in the front and middle sections of the outpost. The repair shop shielded them from some of the stench, though an occasional draft would come through the bay doors or around the structure, carrying the scent of rot.

Oswell lay on a cot in the shade with her left leg hanging off and her right leg straight, the only comfortable position she could find. She'd removed her IV and was solidly on the upswing, getting stronger by the hour, her color returning to her face and neck. Her eyes were brighter and more alive, her grins and jokes more frequent between the pained groans as she continued to get through the downward swing from the cocktail of drugs in her original IV.

"Thanks for helping me pull this Humvee around," James said, walking up, wiping grease off his fingers.

Oswell waved a hand dismissively. "All I did was steer. You pushed."

"I got the fuel pump in. I'll install the alternator next, then I'll need your help putting the new tires on."

She swung her legs off the cot and leaned into the sun, covering her eyes with her hand. "You're a pretty handy guy, you know that? First tanks, now Humvees. You a grease monkey in a former life?"

James chuckled. "No, never. I've got a degree in mechanical engineering and I like to tinker."

"What'd you do before all this?" She waved her hands in circles in the air.

"Eh, corporate gigs. Boardroom stuff, research and development, stuff like that. My real love is maintaining our farm. I set up our solar panels and charging system for the whole house, fixed pretty much every electrical and plumbing system in the place twice over, stuff like that. Replaced a few transmissions, swapped a few engines, overhauled our tractor…"

"Since we're on the subject, how exactly *did* you fix that tank?"

James smiled and grabbed the alternator from a table, searching for a ten millimeter socket. "'Fix' is an exaggeration. The firing mechanism was jammed, that's all. Some grease and a good whack got it working again. Plus, I mean, there were other tanks – fixing one didn't make or break that situation."

"No, no. You're the hero of Kansas City, full stop."

"Yeah, well, right now, I'd settle for the hero of La Porte."

Leaning in, he worked the part into place, but the angle was off, and the compartment was crowded with hoses and other components. He grabbed a rubber mallet and twisted the cylindrical alternator in as far as it would go, hammering lightly on the metal frame to get it to snap in place. James finger-tightened all the bolts, used a socket wrench to get them tighter, and connected the wires, then worked the belt into place, grunting and straining to get it on the pulleys and tightened.

"All right, all done." He wiped off the alternator and backed out. "Now to get this tire changed."

James jacked up the front right side and applied spray lubricant to the lug nuts of the old wheel, then he and Oswell rolled the new tire over next to the vehicle.

"Hold up a second, let that lube loosen the lugs up a bit. How are you feeling?" he asked Oswell. "You good, or you need to sit down?"

"Much better. I'm still a little sore and nauseous from the medication, but it's a night and day difference from before. I changed my hip dressing earlier and it's looking clean, no infection."

"Fantastic. As soon as we get this tire changed, we'll be good to try and fire this sucker up and see what else needs fixing."

He got back to the tire, and with the help of a breaker bar finally got it off, then Oswell helped him put the new one on, finger-tightening the lug nuts before he finished them off with the breaker bar once again. Tossing the tool aside, he circled to the driver's side door and got in.

James paused with his finger over the start button. "Moment of truth."

"Why didn't you test it before we put the tire on to make sure the parts worked?"

James pushed the start button and the engine thrummed to life, settling into a smooth idle. "I didn't need to. 'Cause I'm *good*!"

Oswell laughed. "I guess so!"

"Okay, let's get packed up and get the hell out of here, eh?"

"Ready when you are!"

James circled to the back, flipped open the hatch, tossed his backpack inside. Oswell had rounded up some food from the vending machines, a few MREs and a dozen bottled waters they'd found scattered through the ruins. He added the extra flashlights, first aid kit, bedrolls, foldout cots, pillows, and blankets from the barracks and they had several magazines of M4 ammunition, two rifles, and a service pistol each.

"Hopefully, we won't need any of this stuff. Something tells me we will."

"Yeah, no, I suspect we will too" Oswell shuddered. "You never know what can happen out on the road."

"You've got that right." James slipped on his jacket and ammunition vest, checked his weapon to ensure it was charged, and slammed the hatchback closed. "Okay, I think we're ready."

"I'll take the first driving shift."

"Negative on that, Oswell. You're still hurt."

"And *you've* barely slept. We didn't come all this way for you to fall asleep behind the wheel and wreck us. Step aside, Mr. Mechanic."

James started to protest, but her mention of his state of exhaustion brought it to the forefront of his mind and his whole body sagged as he leaned against the Humvee. "Fine," he relented, "I'll ride shotgun if that's what you want. But let me know if your leg or hip starts bothering you."

"Don't worry. I will."

They got in and Oswell buckled up, put the Humvee into drive, and headed around the mechanic's lot where several vehicles sat off to the side, quietly rusting in the sun. She navigated the debris-filled streets, easing between the corpses and garbage, sometimes with no choice but to run something over, then pushed through the gates, breaking the chain and spreading them wide. With the highway opened to them, they turned left on Highway 2, heading northeast, no longer limited by the power of their legs.

James settled back with his rifle on his lap, surrounded by armor and bullet-resistant glass, finally able to rest without *having* to do so. He took a few gulps of water and leaned forward, painfully aware of the cuts and bruises all over his body. Rolling up his pants legs, he traced some purple spots along his right shin, tender to the touch, then picked at his socks which were grubby and brown, boots grass-stained and muddy. He had an ache in his knees that had been there for a while due to the endless hours of pedaling and running, and he was covered in scrapes and bruises from fighting, running and hiding. Settling back, he flexed his hands and noticed the tiny cuts in his fingertips from fixing the truck, his fingernails caked with dirt and grease. A coating of sweat and dust covered his arms, face, and neck, and the bags under his eyes could hold an elephant each.

"You okay?" Oswell asked with a glance.

"Yeah... no. Probably not," he sighed. "Feels like I've lost twenty pounds or more, and I'm more beat up than I realized. If there're people at this training camp, do you think they'll have some medics and a shower?"

"What happened to ladies first?"

Look, I know you're worse off than me, but I wouldn't be surprised if I have some low-grade infections I'm fighting at this point. Plus, I *reek*. Oh, son of a... I should have showered back there!" James groaned, slapping his forehead and sinking lower in the seat.

Oswell howled, more full of energy than she'd been since she'd been wounded. "Relax, Burton, you were too busy saving my life and getting us on the road. And yes, they'll have showers."

"Any chance they'd let me keep the Humvee so I can take it the rest of the way home?"

"*That* I can't promise. I'll ask, but you know how strapped they are for vehicles."

"Yeah, yeah. It was the same story back in Kansas City." James rolled his eyes good-naturedly. "I'm just good for fixing y'all's stuff."

The road passed beneath their wheels, near-silent but for the rolling of their tires and the constant thrumming of the big diesel engine, slow and steady, eating up the easy miles. The slight bumps and swerves lulled James into a half sleep, head back on the hard seat with his hands resting in his lap. His aches and pains were many, but the weariness of the road grabbed him and pulled him down into a gentle and welcoming darkness and a few moments later, he nodded off to sleep.

James came to suddenly, drawn from the depths of slumber by Oswell's gentle shaking. He reached for his rifle out of habit, looking around in a panic for a few seconds before Oswell's words reached him.

"James. Hey..." Her words were hushed but urgent. "Get up. We're here. We made it."

He blinked and groaned. "What? We're here already?"

"Yep. We made it to the outpost, and everything is fine." She gestured through the front window.

James sat up, placing his rifle aside as a contingent of National Guardsmen came running up to their vehicle, rifles at the ready, one soldier knocking on his window and motioning for him to get out, but he was still groggy, shaking his head and rubbing sleep out of his eyes.

Oswell popped her door open, putting her hands up as she spoke. "Easy guys. I'm Private Emily Oswell of the Illinois National Guard. We just came from La Porte."

"Private, Oswell," a guardsman said, "we need you to step out. Please get out and step to the front of the vehicle."

"I need a hand. I'm injured and can't walk very well."

Hands reached in and helped Oswell out, guiding her toward the front of the Humvee as she gestured and explained things. James popped his door and pushed it open, then hands reached in to take his rifle and pistol, disarming him and pulling him out at the same time.

"Hey, guys. I'm on your side. Take it easy."

"Relax," a guardsman said. "Just follow directions and you'll be fine."

"I understand. Just... hey... go easy on the Private, okay? She really is injured."

"Mm."

James waited until they finished frisking him and lowered his hands, allowing himself to be guided to the front of the truck where a stocky guardsman with short-cropped hair stood with his hands behind his back. The outpost was much like La Porte with a wide courtyard and straight lanes leading off to other parts of the complex. Troops were hustling back and forth as orders blared from speakers, and more than a few people stopped to watch them.

"You say you came from La Porte?" the stocky officer asked.

"That's right, Sergeant Piker," Oswell replied. "The outpost was overrun. The armory and most of the buildings were burned down and looted."

"We lost contact with them almost a week ago. Did you find anyone alive?"

"Negative. There was a mix of civilians and troops there, but everyone was dead. James Burton," She gestured to

James. "Fixed this Humvee, and we topped off the tank and drove it on over. Let me tell you, Sergeant Piker, you guys are a sight for sore eyes."

Piker looked from Oswell to James and back again, still eying them with a healthy dose of skepticism. "Glad you made it. Are either of you hurt?"

"I was shot in the leg and hip, and I had an infection for a while, but I'm past the worst of it."

Piker gestured to a medic. "See to Private Oswell."

Oswell waved the medic away even as she grimaced and rubbed at her hip. "Can you see to my friend here first, please?"

"You've been shot, Oswell," Piker said. "My orders are to see to military personnel before civilians."

"With all due respect, Sergeant" she replied, "James is the *only* reason I made it out of Chicago with news about La Porte. Please, he's been taking care of me the past few days, and he needs medical attention more than I do."

Piker started to protest, but Oswell shook her head. "Sergeant, you don't understand. This is James *Burton*. He's the hero of Kansas City."

"Pardon me, Private?" Piker asked, the other eyebrow going up. "You mean the tank guy?"

"Yeah, *that* James Burton."

"Hey, we heard about that," the medic said. "Something about a jammed firing mechanism he repaired. Got that tank firing again and they lit up those attackers like it was the Fourth of July."

Piker's stance relaxed ever so slightly as he looked over at James. "Is that right?"

"I mean," James shrugged. "The story is slightly exaggerated, but I did get that tank firing again. I'm no hero, though."

A few guardsmen standing around relaxed along with Piker, a couple of them whispering amongst themselves as Piker nodded and spoke to the medic. "Corporal Whitaker, take Mr. Burton to the medical tent and get him checked into an examination room."

"You got it." Whitaker replied. "Come on, Mr. Burton. I've got an ATV over here."

"Thank you, Corporal. Sergeant Piker. You too, Oswell. Catch up with you later?"

"No problem, James, you're in good hands now. I'll catch up with you in a bit."

"Sounds good."

Whitaker was a short woman with short-cropped brown hair, and she moved with an urgency, guiding him to an older green ATV with a red cross on the front, helping him into the passenger seat before getting behind the wheel. She started the ATV and drove them in a tight circle away from the crowd of guardsmen who were listening as Oswell continued detailing what had happened to her to Piker.

"A civvie fixing a tank?" Whitaker asked, weaving past a group of marching soldiers and taking the first right down a lane of barracks placed side-by-side along the route. "Y'know, when I heard that, I thought it was just some BS story. You really do that?"

"I have a background in mechanical engineering and it was really just a simple jam. The crew would've fixed it eventually."

"Nah, don't sell yourself short," she said. "From the way I hear it, you basically saved that place single-handed."

"Ha, hardly!" James chuckled, gripping tight to the handholds on the ATV as it swerved around a group of people. "How have you folks been holding up here? Things were bad at La Porte, but it seems like you've been holding up okay."

"Things have been calm for the most part. We've been sending crews out to help other outposts and have taken in a few refugees. Sad to hear about La Porte, though. I knew some people who were stationed there."

"Yeah, it was a messy sight. A real tragedy."

"Where are you hurt, Mr. Burton?"

"My side, knees, ankles... everywhere, I guess. It's been a long couple of weeks."

"We'll start with some x-rays to see if you have any broken bones or sprains."

"Thank you. That would be great. Honestly, I think a shower and some sack time will help the most."

"I think we can help with that. Okay, here we are."

Whitaker drove him up to a two-story brick building where nurses and guardsmen bustled to and fro, and two medics stood outside the doors, talking quietly. They parked in a side lot, and Whitaker circled to help him out.

"I've got it, thanks," James said, climbing out with a tired groan.

Whitaker took his arm anyway and guided him through the front doors, grabbing a wheelchair as soon as they got inside and gesturing for James to sit in it.

"The wheelchair won't be necessary."

"It's standard procedure in case we need to take you down to radiology."

"Well, okay. If you insist."

Whitaker wheeled him up to the front desk to talk with the check-in nurse, a prim-looking woman with her hair pulled into a painfully tight bun. She gave him a quick once over and turned to type something into her computer. "First and last name?"

"James Burton."

"Age."

"Forty-two."

"Birthday?"

James gave her all the required information, and the nurse typed it in rapidly, glancing up at Whitaker when she was done. "Put him in room fifteen. Dr. Agarwal will be in to see him shortly."

Whitaker pushed him past the desk and down the central hallway, turning into the room and placing him near an examination table, then she gestured to a folded gown. "You'll want to strip down to your underwear and put this on. Just…" She looked him up and down, gesturing at his filth-covered clothes. "Fold those up as best you can and put them on the chair there. We'll get them washed for you. After you get changed, you can have a seat on the examination table."

"Honestly," James chuckled and stood. "If you've got something better, I'll take it. I've been wearing this shirt and pants for *way* too long. They might start walking and talking once I take them off."

"One thing we've got plenty of is clothing," Whitaker flashed a smile. "I'll see what I can do. Just to let you know, Corporal Moody will be taking care of you, and I'll be busy running errands the rest of the day. If I don't see you again, good luck, Mr. Burton. Real pleasure meeting you."

"You too, Whitaker. Thanks a lot."

"No problem."

Whitaker shut the door as she left, and James undressed, taking off his jacket and T-shirt, his old dirty boots and socks, then peeling off his pants before putting on the soft, warm gown. As he finished, a nurse with shoulder-length hair entered and set a clipboard on the examination table.

"Hello, James. I'm Corporal Moody, and I'll be assisting you today. Dr. Agarwal will be in shortly, but do you have any injuries that need immediate attention?"

"Hi… um, nothing critical, I guess. Mostly just general wear and tear all over."

"You look pretty beat up," she said, stepping closer, looking him over. "Geez, looks like you've been through the ringer."

Moody got all his vitals and updated his chart before stuffing his dirty clothes in a bag and taking them outside. A moment later, a tall Indian man entered with a thin smile, introducing himself as Dr. Agarwal. He went straight over to the chart, picked it up, and had a look, talking as he read.

"All your vitals look good. Are you having any pain?"

"A little everywhere, Doctor, but mostly on my left side."

Agarwal finished reading, put the chart down on a nearby desk, and started to put on his stethoscope to examine him, nonplussed by James' rough appearance. "Who did you tangle with?"

"Feels like just about everyone. It's a long story."

"There are a lot of those these days, it seems."

Agarwal examined him, starting from his head and working his way down, noting each injury and marking them on his sheet. When he reached the deep cut on James' left shoulder, he murmured to himself and pressed around the wound, drawing a wince from James.

"You'll need some stitches. What happened there?"

"Could've happened during the fight in the alley with the junkie." James tilted his head, staring off into space. "Or it could have come from a piece of flying shrapnel when Oswell and I were trying to escape an alley. They were shooting at us and dropping bricks on our heads."

"Mm-hmm. That would do it." Agarwal clicked his tongue at the sight of James' scraped knuckles and the large bruise on his right elbow. He stopped to mark those down and checked his heart rate and breathing with a stethoscope. "Your heart sounds good, but I'm picking up something in your lungs." He walked around to stand behind James, parting his gown and running his finger from his scapula to his waist. "You've got some pretty severe bruising and intramuscular contusions on this side."

"Yep. That's the side that hurts."

"What about when you breathe?"

"A little."

"We'll get chest x-rays." Agarwal circled back to face him and pulled up his gown. "Your shins are marked up pretty badly, and you've got some swelling on this right knee." Leaning forward, he felt around the area, drawing another hiss of pain from James. "Tender there?"

"Yeah."

"Hard to tell if this is a result of trauma or overuse, but I want to get an x-ray of this, too."

"You're the doctor."

Agarwal stood and marked a few more things on the chart, nodding pointedly. "You mentioned shrapnel. That would be consistent with many of these scratches. Looks like you survived a small war. You're a lucky man."

"Don't I know it."

Dr. Agarwal tapped the chart and moved toward the door. "I'll have Corporal Moody take you down, and I'll see you right after with the results."

Agarwal exited the room, leaving James sitting in silence for a minute, feeling groggier and in more pain with each second that passed. Moody returned after a short time, helped him into the wheelchair, and rolled him through several hallways, past the bustling skeleton staff, and into a door labeled *Radiology*. She briefly discussed something with the radiologist and had James stand inside the x-ray machine, arms down, arms up, then turned to the side. Afterwards, they had him sit on a table to get a better shot of his knee from different angles, and Moody wheeled him back to the exam room.

"Thanks, ma'am."

"No problem, Mr. Burton." She parked him closer to the exam table and got out a suture kit, salves, gauze, and bandages. "I'll stitch you up and clean your abrasions while we wait for those x-rays to process." She pulled out a chemical cold pack from a drawer, shook it up, and handed it over. "Here, put this on your elbow."

James held the cold pack to his elbow while enduring a series of sharp stings as Moody thoroughly cleaned his cuts and scrapes, applied antiseptic, and covered them with waterproof bandages. She had an efficient touch and had him patched from head to toe in less than thirty minutes and after numbing the deep cut on his shoulder with lidocaine she poised with a needle above his skin.

"Are you ready?"

"I hate stitches," he said and released a long breath.

"It won't take long."

"Yeah, go for it. Can't be worse than anything that's happened so far."

Moody put the stitches in over the course of a few short minutes, leaving him sweating and tense. "All done." She smiled and handed him some pills and a cup of water from the sink. "These first two are for the pain. Nothing too heavy." She waited for James to wash them down and gave him a bottle. "This is a regimen of antibiotics. Two a day for ten days. It'll knock out any infections you might have."

"Perfect, thanks." James popped the top and took the first two right away.

"I'll let Dr. Agarwal know you're done, and he'll go over your x-rays."

"Thank you."

"You're welcome. As soon as the doctor is done with you, I'll take you to the showers where you can get cleaned up."

"Do you still have hot water?"

Her smile widened. "Yes, we do."

"Oh, hallelujah. That'll make all this worth it."

Moody left and a moment later Dr. Agarwal entered with a manila folder in his hand. "Well, you've got a fever on top of your cuts and bruises, and I was right about your side." He walked over to the x-ray viewer, flipped it on, and slid the x-rays into their clips, lining them up.

"Oh, yeah?"

"I'll start with the knee. No major sprains there, and the ligaments are all intact. The fluid buildup is from overuse, so I suggest taking it easy for a few days. You've got a small fracture on your right foot on that fifth metatarsal bone. Has it been tender to walk on?"

"Yeah, but I must not have noticed, we were so desperate to get out of Chicago."

"You'll need to take it easy on that as well... no running, et cetera. Now, your side is another story. As I mentioned, those intramuscular contusions were a dead giveaway, but the x-ray shows you've got three cracked ribs on that left side."

"*Cracked?*"

"Indeed." Agarwal stepped toward the viewer and traced the minute cracks with his finger. "See here?"

James leaned forward and squinted. "Yeah, I see."

"Any idea how that might have happened?"

"Probably happened when I fell off my horse."

Agarwal's eyebrows rose, the doctor showing some measure of surprise for the first time. "Your... horse?"

"It's a... long story. Again."

"Somehow I'm not surprised. You're not having trouble breathing?"

"A little, but I hardly noticed."

"The ribs will heal in a couple of months on their own, but do try to take it easy and not get into fights... or fall off your horse again."

"I'll try not to," James laughed. "It might be easier said than done."

"Pay attention to your breathing. Make sure you're taking deep breaths. Shallow breathing can lead to pneumonia."

"Oh, I didn't know that."

"Most don't, and it's admittedly rare, but I've seen it happen." He stepped over to shake James' hand. "That's all I've got for you, Mr. Burton. I'll send in Corporal Moody to help you get cleaned up. Welcome to Shipshewana."

Moody returned, and with Dr. Agarwal's blessing James was allowed to forego the use of the wheelchair. James and Moody walked down several long hallways to the rear of the facility where there were spare sleeping quarters for the staff, a locker room, and a shower and restroom area. The mirrors were still steaming from a recent shower and the smell of lightly scented shampoo filled the air.

Moody handed him some shower sandals, a couple of bottles, a washrag, and an oversized towel. "There's shampoo and soap. Just toss your gown into the laundry basket there by the sinks, and I'll have some fresh clothes waiting for you on that bench there."

"Thanks, Corporal. Seriously – thank you.."

"No problem, Mr. Burton. When you're done, just come outside and find me at the end of the hall at the administration desk. I'll take you to see Colonel Hawkins."

"He runs this outpost?"

"Yes."

"Okay, thank you. I'll be in and out in ten minutes."

James slipped on the shower sandals and stepped into an open shower area with twelve spigots along the far wall. He hung his towel from a hook, took off his gown, and tossed it around the corner into the basket. Over at the last spigot, he adjusted the water to warm and ducked his head into the spray, letting it splash over his shoulders and down his back. The water hit his few unbandaged cuts and abrasions, stinging his skin, but James only cranked it hotter, washing his hair, dragging his fingernails along his scalp and removing all the grease and dirt. He sighed with relief as suds rolled down his chest and pooled around his feet, the heat sinking into him as the bone-weary cold relinquished its hold on him in a single shiver.

He scrubbed himself gently but thoroughly, watching the dirt and suds run down his legs and swirl around the drain. Hot soapy smells filled his head and banished the lingering scent of corpses, and by the time he was done, his skin was red and flushed with color, and he felt like he'd been entirely reborn. After drying off by the bench he found the fresh clothes Moody had put out for him, some standard-issue National Guard gear including a new set of boots, green pants and T-shirt, and a light, weather-resistant camouflage jacket. He looked for Moody and found her at the administrative desk, speaking with another orderly and nurse.

She turned to him with a smile. "Feeling better?"

"Absolutely. I can't thank you enough. Look, I uh... I don't want to seem impolite, but is this Colonel you talked about the man to speak to about how I can get going?"

"Already? You just got here. Don't you want to rest for a few days?"

"It's tempting, but I've got to get home."

"Colonel Hawkins wants to see you first, but I'm sure it won't take long. Right this way."

Moody guided him back down the hallway, taking a right at the first hall and walking into a set of offices. She stopped by the conference room door and knocked.

"Come in," a man called from the other side.

Moody held the door for him, and James stepped inside to find Private Oswell sitting across from an officer with an intense stare that assessed him in an instant, piercing through him and divining all of his secrets, or so it felt.

"Hold on a second, Oswell," the man said and shifted to James. "Hello, Mr. Burton. I'm Colonel DeAndre Hawkins, and I run this outpost. Please, have a seat."

"Thanks, Moody." James nodded at Moody and slid behind Oswell to take the chair on her left.

Hawkins interlocked his fingers. "Continue, Oswell."

"Like I was saying, sir. The outpost was in ruins when we showed up. Half of it was burned to the ground, and there were bodies everywhere."

"Signs of a fight?"

"Yes. All indications were that the civilians had attacked the outpost. It looked like our people put up a good fight but couldn't hold out, I'm sorry to say."

The Colonel grunted. "I'm not surprised. We've heard similar stories from other outposts. Some are holding out, but too many others have gone offline, and we figure they've been hit as well."

Oswell sighed wearily. "Are there *any* outposts left standing?"

"Most are barely holding on. And our orders... let's just say we're holding tight until we can build up enough manpower and machinery to start bringing some law and order back to the cities."

"Understood. Anyway, once we arrived, James got an antibiotic drip going for me that probably saved my life, the way that infection was going. We stayed through until the next morning and by the afternoon, James had a Humvee up and running. From there it was a surprisingly straight shot here to you. No more trouble to speak of."

Hawkins' eyes flicked over to James, his jaw seeming perpetually locked. "The things I've heard about you are impressive, Mr. Burton. You have our thanks."

"Please, just call me James. And, it's nothing, really."

"Far from. Oswell told me about you helping her get out of Chicago. What you did for Lieutenant Lister's group is impressive." He let out a small breath, clenching his jaw. "I'd known Frank for a long time, and I'm... sorry to hear they were overwhelmed by enemy forces. How you conducted yourself, aiding Private Oswell when you could've left her, is admirable."

"I'll admit that I was tempted to cut and run, but I couldn't do that, Colonel," James shrugged. "No way in hell."

Hawkins nodded. "And then you dug that bullet out of her hip and got her here on a bike and cargo trailer, no less."

"We improvised where we could."

"Well, we are incredibly grateful." The Colonel shuffled a few papers on his desk, leaning back in his chair. "I'm not sure what your plans are after this, but I'd like to offer you a job. We're short on mechanics and could use the help of someone with your skillset."

James gave him a serious stare. "I'm very thankful for that, Colonel Hawkins, but all I want to get home. Is there any chance I can take that Humvee I fixed up?"

"I understand you want to get home. And I'd love to give you that Humvee. Truly, I would. But it's already been shipped out along with almost every other vehicle that would run."

James put aside his disappointment and nodded. "I can make it on foot from here. It's only another hundred miles or so."

Hawkins toyed with the papers as he thought for a moment. "Mr. Burton—"

"James."

"*James.*" He glanced over at Oswell, then back at James, his stiff, no-nonsense demeanor dropping just a bit. "Half my squads were barely a week into training when this all went to hell. Most of my mechanics don't know a monkey wrench from their ass and we're supposed to be fixing up every mothballed engine we can lay our hands on. Could I persuade you to stay and help us – just for a short while – and offer you an alternative means of transportation by way of thanks?"

"What do you have in mind?"

"Do you know how to ride a horse?"

James stared at the hard-nosed Colonel with a straight face, then a tickle of laughter grew from his stomach, curling up into his chest to become a full-fledged belly laugh that wouldn't stop. His cheeks and eyebrows crunched up and tried to meet as tears sprang loose from his eyes, and he laughed until it hurt to even breathe.

CHAPTER TWENTY

Alice Burton
Tallahassee National Forest, Alabama

The two adults spread out, their rifles tucked tightly to their shoulders with Alice pinned squarely in their sights. A tall woman wearing hunter's boots, jeans, and a drab green military jacket strode in behind them.

"Leave the gun where it is!" she barked. "Pick it up, and you're dead."

Alice's left hand rested on her rifle, pausing as the men charged up on either side of her, making it impossible for her to dive for cover without putting the kids in the way of crossfire. The woman leveled a pistol at Alice's head, glaring from deep-set eyes below a protruding brow line, her blonde hair tied back into a tight ponytail.

"I'm serious," she growled in warning. "Leave the gun, or I'll drop you on the spot!"

As beads of sweat trickled down her dirty face, Alice weighed her chances of grabbing her rifle and squeezing between the tables to take cover before being shot multiple times. She couldn't do it under the best of conditions much less with her injuries, so she lifted her hand off the gun.

"Good. Now stand up."

Alice grabbed Jake's hand's, clinging to them for a long moment before touching Sarah's shoulder. "Sorry, kids. Hope you find a way out sometime."

"No!" Sarah struggled against her bindings, tears streaming from her eyes.

"Get up!" The woman gestured with her pistol. "*Now!*"

Alice stood and backed up with her hands up. "Okay. I'm up."

"Get her."

The guards shouldered their rifles and moved in, one holding her arms while the other circled behind, pinning her hands behind her back and tying them with a length of rough rope. The one behind her grabbed her bindings and jerked hard, digging the ropes into her skin and Alice grunted in pain, breaking free for a second before he snatched her back with a growl.

"Quit screwing around."

"You're *hurting* me."

"You're not in a position to complain." The woman gestured to a chair with her gun. "Put her down there."

The guard hauled her backwards and shoved her toward a seat near a table of nasal decongestant, glass beakers, and small baggies wrapped with rubber bands. The guard slammed her into the chair, grabbed her shoulders, and straightened her, then backed off. The woman holstered her pistol and regarded Alice curiously, stepping closer and lifting Alice's camisole to see the one massive bruise on her abdomen and the scratch down her side.

The woman's curious expression deepened as she shifted back to Alice. "That's some wound. Did you get run over by a bull?"

"Shot."

"I don't see any blood."

"Had a phone in my pocket. It deflected the bullet."

"That's some luck."

"Incredible luck, yes."

The woman placed her hands behind her back and paced. "Did it happen on the trail?"

"Yeah."

"Who did it?"

"Don't know. I was traveling alone, and someone ambushed me from the trees. Took most of my supplies and left me for dead."

"How'd you find this place?"

Alice swallowed dry. "I was coming off a horseshoe-shaped rise and smelled the campfires and food."

"And you thought you'd swing through and steal from us?"

"I wasn't stealing."

"But you broke into this building. With these two kids."

"I was tired and hurt. Just looking for a place to sleep. Found these kids here and thought I'd be a good Samaritan and break them out."

"A good Samaritan, huh? You could have come up and introduced yourself."

Alice shrugged and the woman stared at her for a long moment. "Well, my name is Riley, and I run this place. This is my home and my business, and I don't like when people break into my home and business for *any* reason. Now, who are you?"

Alice stared ahead, ignoring the question.

"You go deaf all the sudden?" Riley leaned closer with her hands on her knees. "Who are you, and why are you *really* here?"

"Let me go." Alice squirmed in her seat and tugged at her bonds.

"Are you with Charlie's group? Did he send you to spy on us?"

"I don't know anyone named Charlie."

"What bout Reese Maddox? You with her group?"

Alice only shook her head. "Like I said. I found this place after I got shot. Wanted a place to put my head down. That's all. Just let me go... you won't see me again."

Riley chortled. "Look, you come into our camp and killed our friends."

Alice feigned surprise. "I didn't kill anyone. How..."

"You're a terrible liar," Riley laughed. "I mean, seriously. You *literally* have blood all over your hands. And judging by you picking *this* building, you wouldn't be here if it wasn't important. Could it be..." She crossed her arms. "That you've come here for some *children*?"

"What would I want with children?"

"Not just any children. *Your* children."

"Mine? I don't—"

Riley laughed and jerked her thumb over her shoulder. "Oh, sweetie, I know these are your kids. I even knew you'd come to rescue them right here, because that's how we planned this to go. See, your mistake is that you're too trusting. And you're a terrible liar. Did I mention that?"

Alice shook her head in confusion. "Too trusting?"

"Yeah, you shouldn't trust anyone. Especially little bratty kids. They like to tell on people, you know?"

"What does trust have to do with anything?"

Riley stepped back and crossed her arms. "Ricky. Colton. Come in here a sec, boys."

The boys walked in through the open front doors with their hands in their pockets, Ricky barely meeting her eyes while Colton only stared at the floor. Alice sighed and shook her head as the pair stopped next to the guards.

"Really, guys? You snitched on me. Not cool."

Ricky shrugged. "Sorry."

"That's right, Alice," Riley said. "Not only do these two cuties work for me, but they're quite good tattletales. Helps keep the other brats in line." She patted their heads a bit too hard and ruffled their hair before pushing them to the side. "As soon as you finished talking to them, they came to the guards and let them know we had a criminal in our midst."

"I'm not a criminal."

"Looks like it to me. You killed our people, broke in, and were about to kidnap my two newest workers."

Alice slumped more, eyes squeezed shut and burning. "I just wanted my kids, that's all."

"Bit off more than you could chew, didn't you? You didn't realize we've established a tight-knit community here. All you managed to do is survive being shot and then get caught."

"That's not true," Sarah shouted from behind Alice. "She's a good mom! The best! It was *your* people who took us, Mark and Christine! *You're* the criminals!"

"I don't question my recruiters. Out there..." Riley gestured all around. "It's a zoo. I don't care."

"I watched you hit them. I watched you hit my *kids!*" Alice rose, but the guard shoved her back into her seat with a thud.

"Oh, please. Spare the rod and all that. We hit them because we have to," Riley said. "It's all about discipline, and that's how we keep things in order around here. It's a small price to pay for safety and security. Sarah and Jake will come to understand this after you're gone."

"You better not hurt my mom," Jake replied with a cold stare. "If you do, I'll kill you and tear this place—"

Riley spun and backhanded Jake in the face in one smooth motion, knuckles cracking across his jaw and rocking his head to the side.

Seething with rage, Alice tried to rise only to be shoved down again, landing so hard shock waves of pain rocketed up her side as she spat and screamed. "Don't touch my children, you *bitch!*"

"Oh, tsk, tsk. Language, Alice. And they're *my* kids now, Alice. Not yours. They work for me, and they'll fit in real good around here. Right guys?" Riley ruffled Ricky's hair.

"Yeah..." Ricky nodded slowly. "We'll show them the ropes."

"I guess..." Colton added in a soft voice as he stared at Jake's bright red cheek.

Riley leaned over with her hands on her knees. "Hey, boys. How about a reward?"

"That'd be cool," Ricky replied, but Colton only wiped his arm across his nose and sniffed.

Riley jerked her chin at one of the men. "Give these guys the rest of the night off."

"Yes, ma'am. You heard the boss. Let's get you back to your bunks." Ricky went straight for the door and Colton threw an apologetic look back at Alice before following his friend outside.

Riley turned to Alice, arms crossed. "See, that's what I do here. If you work hard and act right, you get rewarded. If you kill my people and try to steal my laborers, though..." Her tone dropped an octave, and her glare dripped with scorn. "Then I string you up by your own intestines and burn you alive in front of your kids at first light."

Riley spat at Alice's feet and nodded to the remaining guard before turning on her heel, giving her instructions as she walked out of the building. "Check her for any more weapons, then tie her up with them. Let's give dear old mommy one more night with her preciouses."

"Yes, ma'am."

The man lifted Alice from the chair, shoving her over to Jake and Sarah, grabbing her shoulders and shoving her down between them. Alice hit the pole hard and slid down, landing on her tailbone, the shock of white-hot pain so terrible she forgot all about her anger and fury. The guard circled and patted her down roughly, nodding once he'd found nothing else, then leaned between Jake and Sarah, snatched Alice's bound hands, and retied them to the pole over Jake's. As he jerked the bonds tight, Alice grimaced, fighting in vain against tears of agony streaming from her eyes.

"You're hurting her!" Jake twisted his hips and swung his left leg around, kneeing the guard in the side. The guard turned and backhanded Jake in the jaw, knocking his head against the wooden pole with a thud.

"No!" Alice squeezed the word between her teeth, bucking and snapping, trying to break free, but his hand flew in from behind and silenced her with a hard slap to the side of the head, her cheek erupting in fire, white noise exploding in her head.

"Settle down, lady, or getting burned alive'll feel like a gift."

The other guard was just stepping back in and laughed. "Yeah, he'll hit you so hard, you'll wake up in the next century."

Alice sat in a daze, barely able to move or think, much less break free, and her back ached with agonizing pain, shoulders stretched to their limits at an awkward angle.

The second guard circled to face Alice and squatted down in front of her. "Normally, I wouldn't have to say this, but I think it's important." He leaned closer and glared from Jake to Sarah. "Don't try anything stupid. Stupid will get you killed."

"I'm already dead," Alice gasped.

"Yeah, but your kids aren't. Do something stupid, and Riley will hang them right next to you... *after* they watch you die. You don't want that, do you?"

Alice merely glared at him, and he nodded in approval. "Okay, good. We have an understanding then."

He stood and joined the other guard by the entrance, and they paused to watch Alice and the kids before slamming the door behind them and latching it tight, leaving them to contemplate their fate.

CHAPTER TWENTY-ONE

Red Fletcher
Lansing, Michigan

"For a one-horse town," Red said, "This is taking *way* too long to find these a-holes."

The salt truck trundled beneath the turbulent skies, the powerful diesel engine growling higher as he shifted to a lower gear and slowed, turning sharply onto Kirby and pushing the accelerator so they lurched forward. The clouds had been growing more ominous by the minute, big voluminous shapes rolling in like a tide, riding lightning bursts and peeling thunder.

Red's group had driven up and down the streets in and around Elsie, winding past neighborhoods, burned-down stores and hundreds of acres of fields in forest, but had come across nothing that would indicate where Ryan and Helen Cooper might be.

After a good minute of driving slowly down yet another road, Red pounded his palm on the steering wheel. "Ah, this is no good! Most of the mailboxes had been knocked over and scattered, and half the homes have burned to the ground. We don't have the fuel to check every friggin' driveway and lane that might have a home at the end of it!"

A half mile down another long country road they found several houses still standing, some with soft lights glowing from the windows, setting an almost cozy scene in the stormy landscape. Red stopped the truck in front of a black chunk of a farmstead with a massive, burned-up tree lying across the roof, its gnarled and blackened limbs buried in the heart of what had been the house. What had once been a sprawling property with a three-car garage, sheds, and wide, screened-in porches was gone.

"That next house up has lights on, and the one behind us does, too," Red said. "I say we get out and do some knocking. Someone's gonna know where these old farts are."

"Look there." Reynolds pointed up the driveway of the burned-up farmstead where two people stood. As soon as they saw the salt truck, one slapped the other in the chest, and they both ran in the other direction, disappearing into a field where distant lights glowed.

"Might be trouble," Martha said quietly, her voice barely audible over the roar of the engine.

"Yep," Red agreed flatly.

"Want us to hit them first?" Reynolds asked, his hand lingering on the door handle.

"Nah. Let's get out and play it low key." He looked over at his wife. "Unless, of course they give us a reason to play rough." When she didn't respond or look at him, he rolled his eyes. "Martha, stay here, please."

Red and Reynolds got out and circled to the back of the truck where the others waited in the truck bed, expressions grim, rifles in their hands.

Red gestured to Tyler. "Tyler and Hansen, step out with us. The rest of you stay low until I give the command for you to make your presence known."

Several nodded and squatted against the railing, staying out of sight. With a satisfied nod, Red walked into the street as a group of people strode from the field, led by a heavyset man and woman with a bunch of hair piled atop her head, each of them carrying shotguns on their shoulders and flanked by another half-dozen men with handguns and blunt weapons.

"Here we go, boys," Red said and moved to greet them with Reynolds and Hansen flanking him and Tyler staying a few paces back.

Red scanned over the group. They were all haggard, younger than his people, wearing tattered clothes that were ripped and grubby. And, most crucially, none of them was Ryan Cooper. The leader wore a baseball hat and flannel shirt stretched over his wide chest, and while he wasn't as big as Reynolds or Hansen, he wore a confident grin.

"Howdy, folks!" Red called with a wave. "How are you this fine..." He glanced at the sky. "Well, I wouldn't call it a *fine* day."

"Not at all." The leader brought his group up to stand a few yards off the street. "My name's Jack, and this is my wife, Barb. These are my people."

Red turned and gestured. This is Reynolds and Hansen. Tyler's the one behind me. I'm Red Fletcher."

"Good to meet you, Red. Now that we've got introductions out of the way, what do you want?"

"I promise we won't be long," Red assured him, looking across the group, studying each one and judging them to be lacking. None were hardened or former soldiers and none looked like they'd ever shot at another person in their lives. "I'm looking for the Coopers. Any chance they're in your camp?"

Everyone in Jack's group shook their heads and threw puzzled looks around.

"We don't know any Coopers," Jack replied with a shrug.

"Well, you probably wouldn't mind if we searched your camp and around the area, then."

Jack smirked, and his grip on his shotgun tightened. "Hell *yes*, we'd mind. I'll tell you what. Why don't you toss us the keys to that truck and take your boys on down the road."

"Don't be stupid," Red chuckled darkly.

The big woman with the hair piled on her head stepped forward with a smirk. "There's three of you an' seven of us."

Red stared at her a moment, smirked, and raised his hand, and the people in the truck bed rose in unison, their rifles pointed at Jack and his group. Barb's smug expression melted as she stepped behind Jack, who'd suddenly gone as pale as a ghost.

"Like I said. Don't be stupid. Now, put down your guns so we can get what we came for and get out of your hair."

"Go ahead," Jack swallowed hard and nodded over his shoulder. "Everyone put your weapons down."

"I want to see everyone's hands," Red said. "That's right. Good. And don't try anything funny. Now, tell us where Ryan and Helen Cooper are."

Jack balked. "I swear that we don't know any Ryan or Helen Cooper. We've never heard of 'em."

Red nodded at Hansen who shouldered his rifle and grabbed one of Jack's men out of line, twisting his arm behind his back and forcing him to his knees. Hansen whipped his pistol out and put the barrel to the man's skull.

"Please, man... don't shoot me," the hostage said, hands up and shaking. "Jack told you already. We don't know any Ryan or Helen... or *any* Coopers."

"Last chance," Red spoke with indifference, idly picking at one of his nails. "I'll ask you one more time. Tell us where the Coopers are."

Jack put his hands up in an attempt to pacify Red. "Look... we honestly don't know any Coopers. Never heard of them. This is our neighborhood, and there isn't much left for you to take. So, you'd be wasting bullets if you—"

Red sighed deeply and Hansen's pistol popped with a sharp crack, followed by a spray of blood on the ground in front of him and the soft thud of the man's body hitting the ground.

"What the—" Barb threw both hands to her mouth and hid behind Jack. "You shot Mike! You bastards killed Mike! Why'd you shoot him!?" The rest of the group jolted and backed up, shocked and gaping as their friend's blood soaked into the pavement.

"You'd be wise to stay right where you are," Red warned them.

A ripple of thunder tumbled across the sky and shook the ground, emphasizing his words.

"Just answer the question," Red smiled pleasantly, "and you can go about your day. Where are those old bats hiding? If they're up in your camp, and you're lying to us, though, you'll all die."

Jack's face worked through several emotions—confusion, concern, and fear—before something finally clicked. "Wait, did you say *old bats*?"

"Yeah, a couple of old people. Ryan and Helen Cooper. I might have mentioned them."

"Do... do you mean Alice Burton's parents?"

"Ryan has a daughter named Alice." A thin smile spread across Red's face and Jack deflated with relief.

"Geez, man. Why didn't you just say that? You didn't have to kill Mike! Yeah, we know where they are."

"So, where's the house?"

Jack pointed up the road, and both men turned. "Last house at the end of the road, up a long driveway. You can't miss it, but I've got to warn you they're a couple of mean old coots. They killed five of us and wounded another when we were just trying to get some help from them."

Red chuckled, taking a step forward, causing Jack's entire group to flinch. "Help, huh? You mean you were trying to steal from them?"

Jack's shoulders slumped. "They shot first. Hell, man. We didn't expect him to put up such a fight."

"You say they killed five of you?"

"Yeah."

Red's eyes narrowed. "I assume some of you are hunters, so you must know how to shoot, yes?"

"Most of us, yeah. We know our way around guns."

"And Ryan and Helen kicked your butts? What the hell happened?"

Jack glanced at Mike, still lying in a big round pool of blood. A soft crack of lightning broke across the sky, and thunder boomed once more, grumbling like a distant, hungry stomach while the houses stood silent and dark.

"We... didn't think about them at first. Most of us didn't even know James and Alice had gone on vacation. Then everything happened, and most of us lost our homes. Supplies got tight. Mike said a couple of old people were housesitting up the road... Alice's parents. We figured they'd have some things we could use. We tried to scout them, but their damn dogs kept us from getting too close. One day, we heard a tractor on their property, so we snuck up and watched them harvest all the food they had." Jack scratched his head. "They have a chicken coop and were bringing in eggs every day. Cow milk, too. They've got *everything* up there, man, and we were getting desperate. We tried to scavenge in town, but everything was crazy there, and we got run out. We thought about going to one of the government camps, but those are too far away."

"So you decided to attack the Coopers?"

"Yeah. We tried to steal some eggs, but the dogs chased our guy out. Then we sent Mack Tilly to get a count of how many sheep and goats they had, but we think they killed him 'cause he never came back. Rita, Mack's wife, lost it and demanded we go up there and attack them head on. We got together and rushed right up the front yard, but that old man had traps behind the trees." Jack spat, tone shifting from fear to anger as he related what had happened. "He picked off two of us, but we finally made it to the porch. That's when we stepped on the nails, and one of us got cut up trying to open the back door."

"Nails? Cut up?"

"Yeah, they put razor blades on the doorknobs and glued nails on the steps. Hurt us bad. We eventually made it inside, and that's when things went *really* bad."

"How bad?"

"They sicced their hellhounds on us. Killed three of us... mangled us to pieces. Ron and I barely got out of there with our lives."

"What kind of dogs do they have?"

"I don't know what they're called, but they're big, white shaggy things. Probably weigh about two hundred pounds each easy."

"Two hundred pounds?"

"They're Great Pyrenees," Barb chimed in from behind Jack. "I've seen Alice walking them on the road sometimes."

"Yeah, those get pretty big," Reynolds said. "Used to own a couple when I was a kid. Real protective animals."

Red sighed and stared up the road for a long moment before holding up a finger to Jack, smiling broadly, and taking Reynolds by the arm.

"'Scuse us for a minute, folks. Don't go anywhere." He and Reynolds stepped back toward the truck, and Red whispered. "Those old codgers might put up a real fight."

"Looks that way, boss. We're up for it, though. You know it."

"Traps and big dogs are what await us up the road," Red mused. "We've got weapons and numbers, but it sounds like Jack and his people made Ryan and Helen be *more* prepared, and they'll likely be ready for an attack. This won't be easy. Thoughts?"

"It's up to you, boss. You led us here, and if you think it's too big a risk, we'll back you on that." Reynolds' big shoulders shrugged. "I don't know where we'd go from here, though. Everyone's been looking forward to this."

Red's jaw worked. "You're right. We've come a long way, and we have to see this through." He and Reynolds walked back to Jack's group and Red resumed the prior conversation. "So, you gave up after you got your butts whipped?"

Jack shook his head. "We regrouped and talked about attacking them again, but no one wanted to get shot. We were about to give up when we found out Sandy Crenshaw had been playing nice with them, trading and talking to them like regular buddies. We convinced her to lure them out and tried to get them to see things our way, but they didn't want to listen to nothin'. Almost shot us up *again*. Nah, man. We're not going anywhere near that place again."

"What are you going to do?"

"We're thinking of moving out of here. Trying to find greener pastures."

Red rolled his eyes. "Everything you needed was at that farm, but you couldn't man up and just take it?"

Jack placed his hands on his hips and looked at his wife. "Yeah, that about sums it up."

"You mentioned you got this, who was it... Sandy? To lure them out? Where is she now?"

"I don't know..." Jack shook his head and turned to look at a house about forty yards up the road. "She lives right there."

Red squinted. "Is that her standing on the porch?"

"No, that's Summer, a friend of hers. She's probably watching Sandy's kid."

Red smiled and waved, raising his voice to be heard. "Hey, there, Miss Summer. Why don't you come on down?"

The woman standing on the porch was youngish with light hair and a round, frightened face, and when she saw Red was talking to her, she shook her head and backed up toward the door.

"Look, young lady." Red beckoned for her again. "Don't make me send one of my boys up there to get you. You don't want to end up next to ol' Mike here, do you?"

Summer looked from Red to the dead man lying in the road, and her resilience broke like a wet paper bag. She came down the steps and strode over briskly, stopping at the edge of the yard with her arms crossed and her eyes averted.

"Now, don't be shy. I won't bite unless you make me. Come on over. That's it." Summer hugged herself harder and walked the last few yards until she was standing right in front of him. "That's better. Jack here says you're a friend of Sandy's?"

"Yeah."

"Where is she?"

"She went out scavenging."

"And she left you to watch her house?"

"She wanted me to watch her kid while she was away."

A boy of about ten stood on the porch, watching them with big, scared eyes. Red smiled at Hansen, and they both turned their grins on the boy.

"Well, hello there, son," Red said. "What's your name?"

CHAPTER TWENTY-TWO

Alice Burton
Talladega National Forest, Alabama

As the doors slammed shut and the guards' footsteps faded, Alice tested her bonds by tugging at them but found them so tight that she could barely wiggle her wrists. "Are you kids okay? Jake, did you…"

"On it."

"Mom?" Sarah's voice trembled. "What *happened* to you? I saw you get *shot*."

"We thought you were dead." Jake grunted as he spoke. "We saw Mark shoot you right in front of us. I…" He shook his head and leaned over to brush her shoulder with his. "I can't believe you're alive."

"Easy, son. I'm still hurting pretty bad."

"You're not a ghost then?" Sarah asked.

"Takes more than a round to the chest to put me down." Alice winked at her daughter. "Believe me, I'm as surprised as you are… turns out I had my phone in my breast pocket, and the bullet ricocheted off the titanium plate and down my side. Didn't kill me, but I'm pretty sure I've got cracked ribs and then some."

"Oh, Mom." Sarah laughed and cried all at once. "I'm just glad you're still alive."

"We couldn't even think straight the last couple days, Mom," Jake said, his voice gathering strength. "I wanted to hurt them so bad for killing you. Well, hurting you."

"We'll worry about that later, sweetie. Give me the rundown on this place?"

"It's some kind of work camp for junkies and drug dealers," Sarah said. "From what I heard, this place was abandoned a few years ago so they've been making drugs here part-time for a while. Then when everything happened, they decided to move here full-time and take advantage of free labor.

"Children," Alice snarled. "Disgusting."

"Yeah. They've been working us really hard ever since Mark and Christine left us here. We got thrown in here out of nowhere, though, while we were working outside."

"I saw you from the woods not long after I talked to Ricky and Colton… I didn't think they'd tell on me like that."

"You can't trust anyone around here," Jake said. "It's not really the kids' fault, though. They're doing whatever they can to survive."

"I had no idea why they threw us in here," Sarah added, "but I guess we know why now. *You're* the reason."

"I saw them slapping some kids around, and then you got into it with that foreman. You okay?"

"Yeah, he's a jerk." Jake shifted positions, his hands shifting back and forth behind his back. "Most of the kids are orphans – I mean, I think maybe all of them are? I guess this is better than starving, but...."

"But what?" Alice cut in. "Never excuse evil just because there's tragedy."

"I wasn't mom, I was just saying—"

"I know—I'm sorry." Alice's head sagged. "We need to get out of here, and fast."

"Wait, what about the rest of the kids?" Sarah asked. "Don't they deserve to be saved, too?"

Alice hesitated. "I'm... I don't know how to do that, hon."

"So evil gets to be left alone just because we don't know what to do to stop it?"

"Point taken. But I'm not doing so hot, and it'll be a minor miracle just to get us three out of here."

"*Mom.*" Sarah stared at her, and Alice groaned.

"Okay. Yes. I will do everything I can to give these kids a chance to escape. We can't take them with us, though... we can't just kill all the adults here, and there's no way us three can lead all the kids out of this forest."

"A chance is all they need." Sarah looked at Jake. "I think if there was a big enough distraction, something that really showed them they could fight back, they would."

"I'll do my best to make sure we can give them that chance, sweetie. But right now, we've got bigger problems. This is a life and death situation, and death is coming for me at first light, apparently. How are you coming with that rope, Jake?"

"Not too bad. I'm about halfway through it. The blade's pretty dull. What'd you *do* to it?"

"Oh, the usual. Sawed some trees, cut some throats, stabbed some chests." Alice chuckled darkly. "Sorry. It's been a long couple days."

Sarah looked confused. "Wait, what? What knife? What's Jake doing?"

"I gave him my knife earlier when Riley and her goons came in." Alice winked. "Pretty bad acting I put on there, wasn't it? Worked pretty well to distract them."

"It was *awful*, mom." Jake grunted as a piece of rope snapped. "I didn't know what you were doing at first."

"Wait..." Sarah's brow furrowed, then her eyes grew wide. "Did you seriously?"

"Yup. And, for the record, it takes a good actor to pretend to be a bad actor."

Jake rolled his eyes. "Uh huh. Give me a couple more minutes and I think I'll be done here." A minute later, something snapped, and Jake rolled to his knees and started working at Alice's bindings. Alice felt the tight, rough ropes start to loosen and she pulled her hands free, rubbing her wrists, sucking air between her teeth while she waited for another bout of chest spasms to pass.

"Help me, son," she said and held out her hands.

Jake took them and gently pulled her to her feet, putting his arms around her in a light embrace, whispering into her ear, "Glad to have you back, Mom." He broke away with tear-filled eyes.

"Go free your sister," Alice nodded and shuffled along the nearest row of countertops where the demented science experiments bubbled softly. Smoke spilled from the beakers down the sides, and the acrid scent got stronger, making her nose hairs curl. She turned away as Jake finished loosening Sarah's ropes and helping her to her feet.

Sarah rubbed her wrists. "What now?"

"Just stay there a minute. I want to check something." Alice walked to the front door, listening for a moment before creeping to the window to her left. The cold campfires in front of the building were dark, and the surrounding woods were still bathed in eerie moonlight. Off to the left at the edge of the yard, Riley and her guards guided a handful of kids who were dragging a pallet of jugs and cans in the general direction of the bunkhouse, Riley motioning for the children to hurry. The kids were leaning forward, straining against the ropes and giving it everything they had to drag the wooden sled across the grass and gravel. They got it within ten feet when Riley told them to stop and gestured for them to take some of the items inside.

Alice, who'd been peeking around the edge, jerked away and hustled toward the wooden pole, pointing. "Quick, kids. They're coming back. Get down in the same positions you were before and act like you're still tied up."

"Crap, crap, crap," Sarah groaned as she rushed to the pole, sitting and fiddling with the ropes.

Jake guided Alice over and helped her sit, waiting for her to put her hands behind her back before he draped the ropes on her wrists and tied them loosely.

"I'm good," she whispered. "Sit and do yours."

The latch rattled and the door swung open just as Jake hit the floor, and Alice leaned a little to the right so whoever was coming in wouldn't see what he was doing. Ricky and Colton walked in with canisters in their hands, moving all the way across the room past Alice and the kids, staring straight ahead as they placed the supplies at the end of the row and turned to get more.

"Speak of the devil," Alice said dryly. "I thought you two were getting the night off?"

Ricky kept walking, but Colton slowed, glancing at her guiltily. "Riley changed her mind."

"What a shock."

"Shut up," Ricky muttered.

"Colton? Why did you tell on me? I just wanted my kids back."

They'd reached the door, Ricky stepping outside, and Colton turned and held his hands out plaintively. "We had to. It's not like we wanted to."

"You don't *have* to do anything if you don't want to, Colton. You can help us —" Colton shook his head and turned away, about to follow Ricky, when Alice hissed softly. "Colton. If we escape – if we find a way – you have to take advantage of it. Understand? You kids need to get out of here and find help!" The young boy froze, a deer in the headlights with his hand on the door as he looked back at Alice for a long moment, then headed through the door.

"Mom, seriously?" Sarah whispered. "They *betrayed* you!"

"Colton clearly doesn't want to be here doing this. It was Ricky who told them about me, I'm sure of it."

Ricky and Colton returned with more supplies, four metal containers with no real labels except for some permanent marker scrawled on the sides, looking heavy as they bumped against the kids' legs.

"What is that stuff, anyway?" Alice asked.

Ricky shrugged. "I don't know. Some kind of chemicals they use to make all this stuff. Quit asking questions."

Alice bristled. "You've got quite the mouth on you, you know that?"

"Only to stupid people who get themselves captured," Ricky said, scowling at her and slamming the cans down hard next to the others.

Colton kept his face averted as he followed behind the bigger boy to the end of the counter and waited to put his canisters down.

"Those're the last ones, Colton," Ricky said, dusting his hands off. "Let's get out of here."

"You can still do the right thing," Alice said as they walked by. "Set us free. Hey, kids... look at me when I'm talking to you. Ricky... *Colton*... they're going to kill me in the morning. Is that what you want?"

When they were just a few feet from the door, Ricky turned, his cheeks red. "Shut up, lady! Just 'cause you're in trouble doesn't mean you need to ruin it for us, too!"

They stepped outside, and the door slammed shut, the latch locking hard. "I don't know, Sarah. Even if they have a chance to escape this, they might not actually *do* it."

"Can you blame them?" Sarah leaned forward, resting her elbows on her knees. "They've lost their parents, and this is the only stability they have, as cruel as it might be."

Alice pulled her arms out slowly and slouched in the only position that stilled the ache in her side. "I don't know what to do for them."

"Hope that the older ones take charge for themselves when we give them the chance," Jake answered, standing up and offering a hand to Sarah. "And when we get to something resembling civilization, tell someone with authority about this place and what they're doing."

"I guess that's the best we *can* do," Sarah sighed and helped Jake get Alice to her feet.

She embraced them as hard as she dared. "Sarah, go check the windows and report if you see anyone coming, but be careful. Don't let anyone see you."

Sarah nodded and moved off while she and Jake had a look around, casting shadows across the floor from the glowing burners.

"Let's check these out first." Alice shuffled over to some cabinets against the back wall. "Look for any kind of weapon we can use. Sarah?"

"The two guards are standing on the other side of the dead campfires, but they're walking in the other direction."

"Good. Stay as low as you can. Don't let your shadows betray you."

They reached for the cabinets and opened them, checking inside but only finding hazmat suits, N95 masks, and boxes of latex gloves and heavier rubber ones. "Do you see anything, Jake?"

"Just a bunch of hazard gear and boots. Do we need any of that?"

"No, just keep looking."

They spent the next five minutes going through the cabinets, gently opening and closing the doors, finally giving up and shutting the last one. Alice walked over to Jake with her left arm held against her side and her right hand on her hip, squirming to find a position that didn't make her teeth clench in pain. The fighting and sneaking around had worn her body down, and she was struggling to continue forcing it to function. Alice took deep, steady breaths, looking around, trying to clear her mind.

"What's this here?" She walked over to the containers Ricky and Colton had brought in. "Hand me one of those, please."

Jake picked one up and set it on the counter, tilting it back to read the black marker scrawl. "*Dethyl ether*. What's that?"

Alice shook her head and chuckled softly. "Well, well, well... this is a meth lab, kids."

Jake's eyebrow went up. "How do you know that?"

"I watched a lot of *Breaking Bad*. Bottom line is, this stuff is really flammable. Like, explosively so. If we set a fire near these cans..."

"The place would go up like a bomb?"

"A *big* bomb."

"Think we could use it to mask our escape?"

"Yep, and Riley and the others would think we were dead and wouldn't even come after us. Might take a few of them out, if they're close by."

"So how do we do it?"

Alice walked along the counter and eyed the instruments and burners. "We could probably just open the containers and run, but I want to be a hundred percent sure this works. Find me something to make a wick, like some cloth or something, and let's get this show on the road. You too, Sarah."

Sarah nodded and searched along the other counter, checking boxes and shifting things around. "What about after we blow it up?"

"I'll explain it as we go. Just hurry and find something."

Alice stooped as far as she dared, checking beneath the counters and tables but only finding more glass beakers and other chemicals, endless packages of cold medicines still in their boxes, jugs of water, and canisters of butane.

"What about the kids, though?" Sarah asked. "What will happen when this place goes up?"

"Hopefully they take advantage of the situation to either escape or take a little vengeance out on their captors."

"We can't help them any more than that?" Sarah pleaded with her.

"Hon..." Alice rubbed her eyes, wracking her brain, but finding nothing. "Like I said before, I'm barely hanging on by a thread. Between the three of us, we're going to be lucky just to get out of here. The kids are...."

"Mom's right." Jake spoke as he checked the other cabinets. "We *want* to help them, but we aren't capable. Best thing we can do is get out of here and try to send help for them later, if we can find anyone to help."

"At the end of the day, we just need to make sure *we* have each other. You kids are the world to me, understand?"

"We love you too, mom," Jake replied. "But are you sure this is even going to work?"

"Oh, I'm pretty sure it will."

"Will this work?" Sarah was holding up two rolls of paper towels. "I was thinking we could unroll these and twist them up like a long rope."

"Hey, that might just do the trick. Jake, move the cans of dethyl ether closer to the back door. Sarah, unroll the paper towels and I'll start twisting them together."

They worked at the end of the counter next to trays of clean white powder, scales, and baggies. Alice took the line of paper towels and twisted them tightly, stretching them out to make a sort of delicate rope, building it until they had twenty feet coiled on the floor.

"Okay, all the cans are in place," Jake said. "I checked out the back window, and I didn't see anyone out there."

"Great. Let's lay this strip of paper towels from the cans to the door. We'll leave one can open to put the end of the paper towels in, slip outside, and light the wick, then we'll run like the wind."

"Run where?" Sarah asked as they carried the coiled paper towels over.

"To the river, then circle south to the horses."

"You found the horses?" Sarah gaped. "I thought they killed them for meat or something!"

"All but Hercules. I heard someone say they were hitching him up to get supplies, so I don't know if he'll be around." Before Sarah could protest, Alice said, "Okay, let's do this."

She grabbed a butane lighter near the edge of a counter, and they moved to the back door with the dethyl ether containers, placing them in a cluster about ten feet from the door. Jake unscrewed one top and set it aside while Alice put the wick inside the opening, bunched it at the top and on the floor, then led the rest to the door.

"Hurry, kids. I think just the fumes from this stuff alone will make the place go up, and we don't want to be near it when it does."

"Are you sure this is going to work?" Sarah murmured as she stood by the door with her hand on the latch.

"One way or another. Okay, open the door."

All was dark in the backyard with empty boxes and crates stacked up alongside garbage cans and other waste. The forest stood wide open beyond that, and Alice wanted nothing more than to hide deep within it, but they had one thing left to do if they wanted to get away properly. Sweeping winds came in from the west, rustling the treetops and drawing thick clouds over the moon and stars to bathe their surroundings in darkness.

"Okay, everyone outside. As soon as I light this, you run like crazy to the woods. I'll follow a minute later. No questions. Ready?"

The kids came out to stand on the back porch of the bunkhouse, nodding nervously as they looked around. Alice flicked the butane lighter on and lit the end of the paper towel line. Pieces crumbled off, but the flame ran swift and true, devouring the knots in seconds and flying through the room.

"Oh, that's fast; come on, get going!" She held out her right arm and the pair came down off the porch and rushed through the backyard, angling north into the woods, crunching over the dry debris.

Alice dashed back inside the building and flung open the front door, putting on her best high-pitched, young-girl voice and screamed at the top of her lungs. "They're escaping! They're escaping!!"

Without looking back, she slammed the door shut and dashed past the paper towel fuse, which was already uncomfortably close to the open drum of ether. The cool air soothed Alice's lungs, clearing her sinuses of the chemical smells and once she reached Jake and Sarah, they slipped behind a thick tree, clinging to the rough bark as they waited for the meth lab to explode.

Shouts came from across the camp, and several individuals she couldn't make out raced across the open space between bunkhouses, disappearing around the front of the chemically-laden one. The trio heard the front door being thrown open and there were shadows of figures standing around inside, along with shouts and pointing.

"Mom, did you seriously?" Sarah asked, staring at the figures as they appeared to make no effort to leave the bunkhouse.

"Yep. Told you I'd do what I could. The fuse was already under the table so I'm just hoping they don't notice it before it goes off... come on already!" Alice averted her face slightly, wincing, expecting an explosion at any second, but when none came, she deflated and shook her head.

"I thought for sure it would work. Maybe our wick failed, and the fumes aren't concentrated enough."

"Or they found it and snuffed it out. Should I get closer, see if I can hear what they're saying?" Jake asked.

"Absolutely not. That's a powder keg ready to explode. And if it doesn't go off, then we'll have to—"

A whoosh of glowing light blossomed in the windows, making them gleam for a split second before they exploded outward in a fiery gush. The roof lifted off the building, bubbling in the middle, breaking into multiple pieces as the walls bent outward under the force of the massive, orange blossom. Alice grabbed Sarah and pulled her closer, all three of them pressed to the thick tree trunk as shrapnel zipped by, taking off chunks of bark and slicing through the foliage around them.

CHAPTER TWENTY-THREE

James Burton
Shipshewana, Indiana

"Sorry, Colonel. I can explain." James' laughter finally petered out, and he wiped the tears from his eyes.

Oswell sat back in her chair, a petrified look on her face, and the chiseled Colonel's eyebrow was arched yet again. "Please, enlighten me, Mr. Burton."

"It's just... I had a horse. She was loaned to me by some Amish folks I traveled with for a while. But she was killed in Chicago when I got jumped and knocked off. I'm pretty sure that's how I cracked my ribs."

"Ah. I understand."

"Yes, I'm sorry about that... I'm pretty punchy at the moment."

"Indeed." Hawkins leaned forward and fixed James with an intense stare. "Look, if you can help us get a few more of our Humvees fixed up, I'll make one of the horses we have on record for logistics and transport disappear off the books, and you can take it. It's a lot easier to make an animal vanish than a Humvee – the former don't have serial numbers, if you catch my drift."

James couldn't answer quickly enough. "A horse would be perfect. How long will you need me to help you?"

Hawkins spread his hands. "It depends on how fast you can fix the Humvees. Get four or five up and running for me, show the idiots how to do some basic repairs on their own and you'll get that horse."

James shook his head. "It depends on what they need. Replacing transmissions will take a while..."

"We don't need transmissions replaced. It's a lot of small things needing done. Fuel pumps, wiring jobs, fuses, welding cracks in frames. We don't need perfection. Just enough to get them up and running."

"If it means transportation, then it's a deal, Colonel."

The two shook hands, and Hawkins stood. "Fantastic. I'll have someone show you around the outpost. By the way, all your gear is in barracks storage, but Oswell held onto this for you. Said you'd appreciate having it back sooner than later." The Colonel leaned back, plucking James' staff from where it rested in a corner, handing it over to him.

James patted the titanium composite stave with an affectionate grin. "She wasn't wrong. Thank you, I was hoping to get this back. We've been through a lot together."

"No problem."

"What about you, Oswell?" James asked. "What will you do?"

She grabbed a crutch that was leaning against the table and stood. "I've got an appointment with Dr. Agarwal, then I'm hitting the showers."

"You're in for a treat. Almost makes me forget the sewers."

"Sir?" Oswell looked at the Colonel and he nodded.

"Dismissed. I'll show you out. Wait here a moment, Mr. Burton." Hawkins and Oswell left the room, but Hawkins returned a moment later with a guardsman he introduced as Corporal Church, a red-haired young man with blue eyes and freckles dashed across his cheeks.

"Corporal, I want you to take James Burton to the motor pool and introduce him to Sergeant Peterson and Specialist Diaz. Tell Peterson to put him to work on the Humvees. Mr. Burton is in charge – they are to follow his instructions and do everything in their power to absorb as much information from him as possible. Is that clear?"

Church saluted. "Yes, sir. Mr. Burton, if you'll follow me."

James stepped out with Church, followed him down the main hall, through the hospital lobby, and outside. They took a quick right around the building to a row of electric golf carts painted green with numeric designations on the sloping front hoods.

"If you get in the passenger side, sir, I'll drive you over."

"Sounds good."

James got in and waited as Church hopped behind the wheel. "Where'd you get all these carts, anyway?"

Church hit the accelerator, and they whipped out of the lot and turned left, heading deeper into the outpost. "Golf courses all over the area, from Elkhart to South Bend. Hawkins sent us after them shortly after things went south. It's an easy way to get around and transport officers and guests to different parts of the outpost. We use the generators and solar panels to charge these and keep the hospital running, mainly... oh, and the mechanic's shop. The rest is on staggered electricity while they try to run down more solar panels and batteries."

The sun stood at its zenith in an empty blue sky, the heat feeling doubly good on James' face as they hummed past a vast training ground where guard units were taking target practice with carbines. Six troop barracks buildings lined both sides of the road with a few guardsmen seen strolling through the campus.

"Everyone seems pretty busy."

"We're only at half capacity, but Hawkins keeps everyone hustling, especially since a lot of our people weren't anywhere close to being done with their training. When we're not running patrols and scavenging for things we need, we bolster the outpost's defenses."

"Have you had much outside trouble yet?" James asked, thinking of La Porte.

"Groups of curious citizens mostly, and we direct them to the nearest refugee camp, which is close. Sometimes we give them supplies to take if they're in bad enough shape."

"Doesn't seem like you're lacking ammunition or supplies."

"Got plenty of supplies, though fuel has been an issue. We keep hearing about new shipments coming in but haven't received any. Ah, here we are."

Church pulled into a massive lot filled with a dozen rows of armored vehicles, giant hulks parked from smallest to largest toward the back. They passed lightly framed trucks that resembled old-style Jeeps, some more like ATVs or go-carts with weapon mounts in the back.

"These are all light strike vehicles and desert patrol models. We've got a few advanced strike vehicles Hawkins wants to get repaired pretty quickly, but mainly he wants the Humvees running. They're stripping some down to repair others, and that's what you'll be doing."

Dozens of bulky three-ton Humvees sat in a row of rusted armor and broken headlamps, hoods thrown up, engines stripped of their parts. They, in turn, were eclipsed by even bigger vehicles encased in thick armor and resting on tires and tracks, dwarfing the golf cart as they drove by.

"These are the big boys," Church continued. "Stryker APCs, reconnaissance vehicles, mobile gun systems, and fire support. None of them work, though."

"Any plans on repairing them?" James asked.

"Not that I've heard of. Just the Humvees for now. Oh, and these guys..." Church nodded at a pair of Abrams tanks on their left, sixty-plus short tons of menace, the hundred and twenty-millimeter cannons looming over them as they passed. "I guess those aren't too intimidating since you've been in one."

"Oh, they're still intimidating. They're amazing machines."

They pulled up to a large gray building with *Mechanics and Maintenance* written on a small brown sign. Six bay doors stood open, Humvees sitting inside with their hoods thrown up and Church drove around to the back, where several Humvees stood in a row, stripped down even more with pieces of armor and windows missing and tires removed.

"How do you get these pulled up if they don't run?"

"Sergeant Peterson puts out a call, and we grab some guys and gals who are on patrol to come help push pool. Once we get them parked, it's all up to Peterson and Diaz."

Church coasted to a stop and hit the horn. James got out and stepped around to the front as a man and woman walked out from the rows of Humvees, wearing sunglasses with their sleeves rolled up and grease spots on their arms and faces. Sergeant Peterson was tall and clean-cut with a thick, well-trimmed brown mustache while Diaz sported ink-black hair that was combed back and gathered in a tight bun on the back of her head.

Peterson was wiping grease off a wrench as they stepped over. "Who's this, Corporal?"

"This is James Burton. Hawkins wants him to help you rebuild some of these Humvees."

Peterson snorted and pushed his mirrored sunglasses higher on his nose. "Is that right?"

"That's right, Sergeant. It's a direct order from Hawkins."

Peterson paused and smiled, revealing a set of perfect white teeth. "He doesn't look like a mechanic, and we don't have time to train him."

"It's the other way around. The Colonel's putting him in charge of repairs for a day or three."

"Excuse me?" Diaz shook her head.

"I know my way around engines," James explained.

"But do you have any experience repairing these?" Peterson jerked his head toward the row of Humvees behind him.

"Fixed one up yesterday so I could bring Private Oswell here from La Porte. I've done plenty of wrenching back home, too."

"He's also the hero of Kansas City," Church broke in. "You know, the guy who fixed the tank during the attack?"

Peterson lowered his head and looked at James above his sunglasses. "That was you?"

"I wish people'd stop calling me that," James laughed. "The firing mechanism had a jam. It was no big deal."

Peterson nodded appreciatively, his tough exterior breaking just a bit. "Still. Okay, then. Maybe you won't be a pain in my backside, and we sure could use the help. Between you and me, Diaz and I are pretty fresh to motor pool... and we're struggling."

"We good here?" Church asked, and Peterson nodded.

"Go with Diaz. She's got a list of parts we need stripped. If you've got any tricks, don't be shy in sharing." Peterson flashed him a good-natured grin. "After all, the Colonel says you're the boss now."

"Mr. Burton, I'll be back in a few hours to show you where to get dinner." Church got back in the golf cart and took off.

"Come on," Diaz said with a wave as she turned away. "I'll show you around."

James followed Diaz through the rows. "How long have you been in the guard, Diaz?"

Diaz stopped in front of a Humvee with the hood open and a light strung up that shined down into the engine block. An empty cart stood nearby, and a small tool case rested on the engine.

"I signed up for eight years, and I was halfway done before all this happened. Looks like I'm in for life now." She grabbed a wrench, leaned in, and started loosening bolts.

"Sorry to hear that," James replied hesitantly. "So... what are we looking for? I assume alternators, pumps, hoses, and things like that?"

"Here's the list," she said gruffly and handed him a greasy piece of paper. "Start with that one over there. Retrieve the parts, load them onto the cart, go to the next vehicle and keep searching for more."

James looked over the items and nodded. "You don't want to work together?"

"I'll come check in on you. Contrary to Peterson's claim – and his own abilities – I'm not half bad at wrenching."

"Fair enough," he laughed. "Spare set of tools?"

"In the garage."

James went inside, found an old toolbox, and started collecting some ratchets and wrenches from the workbenches before heading back out to the cart. He hooked the battery-operated light up and moved the cord aside, diving in after his first part, starting with the hoses and fan belts to clear the crowded space between the motor and grill, then tackling the alternator and shifting to the front fuel lines, getting them out quickly and setting them on the engine block. Working in the back he got a few more wires, fuel pump and other odds and ends before he headed back to the cart and double-checked his list. Disconnecting the battery terminals, he hauled it out and arranged everything on the cart, placing the alternator last on the bottom shelf, separating the hoses, clamps, and extra nuts and bolts. Diaz backed out from the hood of her vehicle, face covered in a sheen of sweat and a smear of grease on her forehead.

Her eyes widened in surprise. "Not bad, James. Not bad at all."

The next few hours passed quickly as James fell into the work and put aside his pains and worries. He got lost in the nuts, bolts, and wires, getting sweaty and dirty again, reopening some of the cuts on his fingers and the backs of his hands. The headlamps came off, followed by the spark plugs and every clip and clamp he could find that he thought would be helpful in the final repairs.

As he worked, he noticed one and then two shadows periodically nearby as Diaz and Peterson first checked on him. The shadows came around with more frequency as the day went on, and the pair began to ask him questions, using his years of experience and general knowledgebase to guide their own work. Soon, the cart was full, the late-day sun was on its way down, and James was tiring as the ache in his side returned.

"Let's take this inside," Diaz said, and they grabbed the fully-laden cart and pushed it over to where Peterson was working on another repair.

"Yo, Peterson." Diaz called to him. "I think we're finished for the day."

The Sergeant turned, beaming at the pile of parts on the cart. "Damn fine work, the both of you! This is more than Diaz and I've pulled in, like, a week."

"Yeah, turns out the civvie's not too bad at wrenching." Diaz gave James a good-natured punch in the arm, and he laughed.

"I'm just glad to be of help to you all. Are we done for the day?"

"Yeah, you are." Peterson pointed at a clock mounted up on the wall. "Church'll be here in a few to collect you for dinner. Diaz and I will do a bit of inventory then hit the mess hall too."

As if on cue, Church pulled up in his golf cart and waved. "Ready for dinner, Mr. Burton?"

James smiled and jogged out to the golf cart, hopping in and resting back, cleaning off his hands with a rag. Church drove them to the barracks and up a side lane to a long building with picnic benches and about forty troops eating off trays. They parked by a set of golf carts and ATVs, heading inside, James smiling as aromas of beef and vegetables poured over him, his stomach starting to growl madly. After getting their trays, they found an empty spot at the end of the picnic bench and sat, James digging into the beef tips and noodles, green beans and bacon, finishing everything off with a brownie and a cold glass of milk.

"I feel like a king," he said.

"We're pretty lucky," Church agreed with a wave of his fork. "There are a lot of other outposts like La Porte who weren't so lucky. We've got a fair amount of supplies coming in... well, all except for the fuel. Once that starts rolling in, we'll be in good shape."

James looked up from his food and watched the sun descend toward the horizon, engrossed in the pinkish hues cast across the sky. "I'd like to think there'll be an end to this, but I don't know when or how."

"We haven't heard a thing from DC. We get our orders from Hawkins and do what needs to be done. Morale isn't great, but everyone works hard, and we're all grateful to be in here and not out there."

James dipped a piece of buttered bread into his beef gravy, cleaning off part of his tray before taking a large, satisfying bite. "You folks are doing a great job here. Any word on Oswell?"

"She's doing much better and getting some rest at the barracks. She'll return to patrol as soon as she's able."

"Good to know. She's been through a lot and deserves to be here with this outfit."

James finished his plate, stood, and rolled his shoulders, loosening any remaining tension and nodding to Church. "I'm ready to get back to work, Corporal. I want to get these vehicles repaired so I can get that horse and get out of here."

"You sure you don't want to get some sleep?"

"I'll sleep after I get that horse." James smiled.

"All right, Mr. Burton. Let's go."

They dropped off their trays, got in the golf cart, and headed back toward the shop, where Peterson and Diaz were already back and sorting through the parts and assigning them to the various trucks in the bay.

"Well, well, well," Peterson called. "Look who the hard worker is! You know, I bet Diaz she couldn't get one of these suckers fired up before you could."

Diaz wore a wry smile. "Are you ready to fix some Humvees, man?"

James laughed and got out. "Challenge accepted." At the last second, he turned back to Church. "Hey, can you do me a favor?"

"What is it?"

"Can you send a message to the refugee camps between Florida and Michigan? I'm looking for some people. I put my name in the refugee database at Kansas City, but my people hadn't made it to a camp yet."

"Consider it done. What are their names?"

"Alice, Jake, and Sarah Burton. My wife and kids."

CHAPTER TWENTY-FOUR

Ryan Cooper
Lansing, Michigan

Lightning cut the sky in jagged tears as dark clouds sped by, winds whipping the drizzle into stinging droplets, the scent of rain carried along with leaves and twigs that flew across the yard, Duchess and Diana barking and snapping at them as they gave chase.

"Settle down, you mutts!" Ryan bellowed, but only Diana paid him any mind and came trotting back as he and Helen tilted the last water tank upright at the corner of the house.

They'd cleaned out an additional two tanks, making that a total of five for drinking water, and an extra one at the corner of the house to catch rainwater off the roof via a downspout. They didn't have enough bricks to raise the additional tanks any higher, but repositioning them was a problem for the future. Ryan took a screwdriver from his pocket and started unscrewing the lower section of the downspout and pulling it off. He laid it along the side of the house and grabbed a flexible plastic spout, putting it over the metal one coming off the roof and screwing it in.

"I think we're in for a real doozy," he said. "If we can fill these extra tanks, we'll be in great shape. Should be able to increase the water pressure eventually, too."

Helen backed up and dusted her hands off. "The skies look absolutely terrible. It's going to come down hard."

"Good," Ryan chuckled and angled the flexible spout into the top of the tank. "The more the better."

The wind gusted hard, throwing more debris across the yard, whipping the drizzle into a blender. Out at the chicken coop, a couple of hens and the rooster stood outside, picking at the feed in spite of the wind being strong enough to ruffle their feathers and knock one hen sideways.

"Stupid birds," Ryan said, starting toward them. "You'd think they'd get inside and stay there with a storm about to hit."

"Sometimes they don't take the hint!" Helen called after him.

Ryan rushed out to the chicken coop, grabbing the door and sweeping the two hens in with his feet. He missed the rooster, who clucked and took off in the opposite direction. Cursing and slamming the door, Ryan turned to go after him, but Duchess sprinted up and planted her paws in front of the fleeing bird, her deep-chested chuff sending the bird right back at him. Ryan stepped aside and threw open the door before the rooster flew in, flapping and squawking.

"Good girl, Duchess!" He slammed the door and locked it. "Let's go!"

They rushed back to the house where Helen stood off to the side, pointing to the front gate as the wind blew her hair around. A woman was screaming and shouting above the storm, the howling wind carrying the sounds to them from a good distance away.

"What in the world is going on? Is that Sandy?"

"Looks like it," Helen said. "She's down at the gate, and it looks like she's in trouble."

"When is she not?" Ryan grumbled, coming around the corner to look down at the gate through his rifle scope. Sandy stood at the gate, hopping, waving, carrying on, and throwing glances over her shoulder. "She's all in a tizzy about something."

"We have to go help her. We can't just leave her down there."

Ryan clenched his fists and stared through the rain, finally sighing heavily. "Grab the dogs. I'll get your gun."

Ryan picked up Helen's rifle from the EV's hood while she got the dogs and put them on their leashes, and they once again began their trek down the long driveway. Once Sandy saw they were coming, she stopped screaming and waving but kept one eye on the road, her face drawn with strain and worry.

"What's wrong, Sandy?" Helen said when they got there. "Is there trouble?"

"Yes... no... sort of..."

"It's one or the other, woman." Ryan watched the road behind her. "Make up your damn mind."

"Someone's looking for me. They're looking for you, too."

"What in the world are you talking about?" Ryan asked, the hairs on the back of his neck starting to stand on end.

"Come on inside, Sandy." Helen unlocked the gate and opened it so she could squeeze in. Then she faced her and gave her shoulders a shake. "You're safe. No one's going to hurt you. Now, take a deep breath and tell us what's going on."

"Just tell us what you saw," Ryan said, softening his tone.

Sandy nodded, focusing, her voice shaky at first but growing steadier as she spoke. "Okay... so, I was coming back from looking for a well pump — and I got it, too!"

Ryan saw the cart and pump sitting on the other side of the fence. "Is that it there?"

"Yeah, I found it at a septic tank service place."

Ryan rubbed his jaw as he studied the shiny new pump. "It's different than the one I pulled out, but it'll work. Nice job."

"I was coming back with it when I saw a truck parked outside the Willoughby's camp. Not a pickup truck but a huge thing, like a dump truck. A... um... *salt truck.* You know the kind?"

"Yeah." Ryan walked over to the fence and gave the pump another look, glancing both ways down the road as well.

"There were a bunch of people in the truck bed with guns, and the three main guys were standing in the road and talking to Jack and Barb." Sandy's eyes rested on Helen. "I overheard them, and they were asking about you. At first, they said the *Coopers*, and I didn't put it together. Then I heard your first names, Ryan and Helen."

Helen squinted in confusion. "Why would they be asking about us?"

Ryan's voice turned deathly somber, his neck hairs feeling like they were trying to eject themselves from his skin. "What did they look like?"

Sandy turned. "The leader is kind of tall and skinny, and he's got one of those gray broom handle mustaches, and he was wearing a baseball hat."

"What about the others?"

Two of the guys he had with him were huge. Big and fat, dumpy with greasy hair. They were all wearing military coats and baseball hats if that helps."

Ryan walked the fence line, turned, and came back, racking his brain as to whom it could be. "Let's see. Skinny guy with a broom handle mustache and two big boys, all with military coats and... *wait a second.*" Ryan turned to Helen. "Could she be talking about Red Fletcher and his buddies? What were their names?"

"Reynolds and Hansen?" Helen asked. "Aren't they hunting buddies of yours?"

"I never hunted with Reynolds and Hansen. Met them once, but they're friends of Red's. I played golf and poker with Red a few times. Nice enough guy."

"They didn't seem nice. They shot Mike," Sandy said.

"They shot Mike Jones?" Ryan gaped. "Like, killed him?"

Sandy made a gunshot gesture to her temple. "In the back of the head. Boom."

"That doesn't sound right." Ryan shook his head. "Those were our neighbors from Grand Rapids."

"I remember them being sort of... intense the few times I saw Red." Helen said.

"They're veterans, but not *killers*." Ryan paused. "Well. As far as I know, anyway…"

"Apparently they are now." Helen swallowed hard. "Not that I'm all that surprised. You saw how the neighbors changed when this happened. Maybe Red and his friends changed too.

"Maybe."

"This isn't good, Ryan."

"Nope. No, it's not. Sandy, did they say why they wanted to find us?"

"No, they just kept demanding to know where you were and then shot Mike, then they started talking about *me* so I bolted here. It was the only thing I could think to do. I thought about grabbing Stephen, but I didn't know if I could get to the house without being seen. They think I was out scavenging, but if they find out the truth…"

"They'll punish you for it," Ryan said pointedly. "Or your boy."

Sandy went back to the gate and rested her hands on top. "Stephen is with my friend, but I don't know if she can keep him safe for very long. I'm so scared for him. Please, you've got to help me go get him."

"No way in hell." Ryan's response was immediate. "I'm sorry, Sandy, but I can't risk Helen and I's safety by leaving. *Especially* if Red Fletcher has lost his mind and is trying to find us."

"Please, Ryan." Sandy turned to him and took his arm. "He's my *son*!"

Ryan shrugged out of her grasp. "Look, I appreciate you getting the pump, but—."

"He was alone with Summer *because* I was trying to get this pump for you."

"For *you*, too," Ryan pointed out. "News flash – if you're going to be staying here, you'll need that pump as badly as we do."

"Ryan," Helen's words were sharp. "Don't talk that way. This isn't some random person or object we're talking about. It's her son."

He gestured angrily toward the road, frustration in his rising voice. "What do you want us to do, Helen? Take on the neighborhood *plus* a band of former military men?"

"You don't have to take them on," Sandy sputtered. "Just help me get Stephen out of there. We can do it quietly, under the cover of the storm."

Ryan shook his head. "I'm not a fighter. Not like this." He clenched his fists as turmoil burned in his chest, face twisting with a mixture of emotions.

"Ryan." Helen rested a hand on his chest and gazed up at him. "We have to help her. She's genuine."

"I don't—"

"Yes. You can. It's the right thing to do."

Ryan's eyes glassed over and he squeezed them shut, the raindrops mixing with his tears. Tilting his head back, he groaned and sighed deeply, then patted Helen's hand and turned to Sandy. "Okay. Let's go save your boy."

"Thank you!" Sandy wrapped her arms around him and Helen both, squeezing them tight. "Thank you so much!"

Ryan nodded and drew away. "Save your thanks for after we get him. You two stay here with the dogs. Let me run up to the house and grab a few things."

Ryan rushed up to the house as fast as he could limp, the wind battering him, his coat whipping around his waist, pant legs snapping. He threw open the door and went straight to the hall closet for the emergency supplies they'd stashed, taking James' rain-resistant jacket out, slipping it on, and grabbing a metal flashlight that could double as a weapon. Halfway to the front door, Ryan paused and went back. If Sandy was going with him, she might as well be armed. From the top shelf, he pulled a 9mm pistol and a couple of spare magazines, putting them in his pocket and zipping his coat up tight. He slammed the front door behind him and hurried back down to the gate where Helen and Sandy were holding the dogs' leashes, their hair swirling around their heads.

"Okay, I'm ready to go." Ryan took his rifle off the fence rail and slung it on his shoulder. "Where are we heading?"

"They were out front at the Willoughby's, but I don't know where they are now. I guess they could be in the camp in the Willoughby's back yard?"

Ryan nodded. "Okay. We'll head up the road and take a look."

"I love you, dear," Helen said, grabbing his jacket and pulling him close. "Stay safe."

"I love you too. Do me a favor? While we're going for Stephen, can you push that cart with the well pump to the house?"

"Of course."

"It's pretty heavy," Sandy said. "You may need to drag it over the gravel."

"I can manage."

"Keep the dogs inside the house with you and keep an eye out for us when we come back. We might need your help."

"I'll be watching the road." She gave him a pointed look. "You get Steven and come home safely, hear me?"

They walked into the road without looking back, and Ryan unslung his rifle and held it against his chest, bending into the wind. The darkness was complete, the storm blasting them and throwing them off balance, still more wind than rain, howling against the backdrop of the advancing lightning and thunder. Sandy strode beside him with her arms crossed, head bowed as she leaned into the wind, arms wrapped around herself.

Once they'd gotten a ways down the road, Ryan nodded to his left, speaking loudly a few inches from her ear. "What do you say we cut through these yards here, swing way around, and come at them from the east?"

"We'd have the cover of the woods."

"That's exactly what I was thinking. Get around behind them... what's their camp like?"

"They've got a bunch of RVs parked in a semicircle around a big bonfire. If we come at them from the east, we'll be coming up behind them."

"Perfect."

They cut between two houses, stepping over debris hidden in the tall grass, catching a whiff of charcoal drifting off the remains that mixed with the fresh rain. The Willoughby's campsite was a faint glow through the backyards, looking to be a quarter mile away or so.

"Yeah, I see them now."

The woods were straight ahead, and once they got within the tree line, they moved south through the brush, moving where there was the least resistance and cutting through gaps in the foliage.

"We'll check out the camp first," Ryan said, lips practically touching her ear, trying to keep anyone else who might be nearby from hearing them speak. "If Stephen isn't there, we'll circle to your house."

"Okay."

"It's likely we'll want to bring him back through the woods. The street will be too risky."

"Right."

They kept the campfire glow on their right at all times, smoke drifting by, voices reaching them above the rumbling thunder. Through the trees, Ryan saw the squarish shapes of RVs and tents highlighted in orange light, several makeshift sheds and carports set up as shelters. Shadows lingered near the bonfire, quietly talking beneath an awning, but Ryan couldn't tell whether they were members of Jack's crew or the new arrivals from Grand Rapids.

"We need to get a little closer."

They circled to the east behind the RVs, and Ryan moved to the edge of the woods just out of view. He parted the damp foliage and peered between the RVs where people milled around and talked quietly or laughed, patting each other on the backs, acting – as best as he could tell – like the best of friends. Two burly men stood out in the tangerine glow, framed in shadow but unmistakable as they tilted up bottles and drank.

"There's Hansen and Reynolds. Jack and Barb, too. Didn't you say they were arguing when you saw them last?"

"Yeah," Sandy said, puzzled as she leaned in beside him. "Seemed like the new people were going to kill them all."

"And now they're like best friends." Ryan narrowed his eyes. "That's a little *too* convenient. If they've teamed up... nevermind. We'll deal with that later."

Sandy started to move when Ryan stopped her. "Hold on a second. I got something for you." He reached into his jacket pocket, pulled out the pistol and magazines, and handed them over.

"What's this?"

"Just in case. If they're killing people, then you need a way to defend yourself."

Sandy put the magazines in her pocket. "Thanks, Ryan."

"You know how to shoot?"

"Yeah."

"Good. Don't use it unless I fire first or we're in a real tight spot. I'd prefer to do this quietly if possible."

"Okay."

"C'mon, let's move slowly and try to spot Stephen."

The bloated sky gave a burp of thunder that shook the woods, causing the people in camp to pause their revelries and look out from under their shelters, pointing at where a brilliant lightning strike had landed a mile or so away. Ryan felt the vibration in the sapling he was holding onto, wincing as a torrent of rain swiftly followed the lightning, the line of rain followed by a gale force wind that carried it sideways and well into the tree line to drench them.

Ryan grabbed Sandy and pulled her down. "This rain is going to be a problem."

She shook her head. "We're not going back. I'm not leaving without my son."

"Never said we were. C'mon."

Ryan threw up his hood and gestured for her to walk south along the tree line, surveilling the area, stopping to look between the RVs as the groups of people realized their lightweight shelters were doing nothing. A few ducked and ran with jackets over their heads, doors opened and slammed, and the people by the fire clustered beneath a carport for shelter as the firelight flickered and danced.

"I can't see anything in this," Ryan yelled into Sandy's ear, barely able to be heard as water dripped from his hood and ran off his chin.

"I see some people on the south side of the camp. Let's check it out!"

Ryan followed Sandy as she kept to the trees, their footsteps in the crackling brush drowned out by the rain. Soon, he saw what she was talking about, a small side camp constructed from pieces of plywood nailed to a cluster of trees, the low branches forming rafters with tarps hanging down, spiked to the ground as they whipped and fluttered.

"There!" Sandy stepped into the open and pointed to a group of kids who sat in the middle, protected from the wind and rain, a soft lantern glow lighting up their little space where they huddled over something on the ground. "Stephen's got to be with them!"

"Wait!" Ryan called and shook his head. The children were too far away from the adults, and while he could recall heading off on his own at a young age, none of it made any sense. The children by themselves in a storm, the adults partying like they were old friends; none of it added up. "I don't know, Sandy. Something doesn't seem right here. I just don't think—"

Sandy came back, grabbed his arm, and tugged it. "He's right *there*. I'll get him and meet you back here, okay?"

Before he could stop her, she took off toward the children and Ryan jumped out after her, rain thrown into his face, drenching his hair, and running down his neck. He got ten yards before he stopped and squatted. The bonfire was almost out, flames sputtering to stay alive but giving way to darkness, and the men and women who still remained under the carport continued to laugh and carouse. An RV door opened and a man ran outside with a flashlight, the pale beam jiggling and shaking with their movements, barely able to penetrate more than a few feet into the torrential downpour. Ryan crouched and froze, waiting for someone to shout and come after them, ready to cover Sandy and her son with gunfire if he had to, but the man with the flashlight headed back into the RV a few seconds later, seeking shelter from the storm.

Sandy's form was highlighted in the shelter's lantern light, making shadows on the interior walls as she grabbed Stephen's arm and backpack and hauled him into the rain. Ryan stood and backed up as they got closer, sweeping his rifle barrel across the camp and waiting for someone, *anyone*, to notice what was happening. A few seconds later Sandy and Stephen were past him, panting, half staggering on the slippery grass, holding their arms out for balance. Ryan turned and followed them back to the tree line where they disappeared into the woods and settled behind the bushes. Sandy grabbed Stephen in an embrace and shook him, planting a kiss on his forehead and hugging him yet again.

"Oh, my poor little man. I wasn't sure if you were okay."

"You said you'd be right home," Stephen cried, his eyes red and bloodshot. "I thought you left for good!"

"No way, kiddo." Sandy held his cheek. "I just couldn't come get you with those people around. Did any of them hurt you?"

Stephen shook his head.

"Good. Ryan, should we get some things from my house?"

"Absolutely not," Ryan said. He'd been watching the camp, waiting for someone to notice the three of them, but the kids stayed where they were and kept playing, and the men and women continued carrying on. "This is too weird. Too easy. Who leaves a bunch of kids out by themselves in a storm like this?"

"I don't know."

Ryan shook his head and growled. "Let's just get moving back to the house. I want to get home now."

They turned and pressed through the forest with the storm raging around them, the torrential downpour soaking the forest canopy with water dripping on their heads and leaving pools of filth on the ground. Soon everything was wet and soggy, the mud soft beneath their boots as they tried to move quickly in the darkness. Ryan couldn't have asked for better cover to use during an escape, but that didn't stop him from throwing glances over his shoulder as they hurried on.

CHAPTER TWENTY-FIVE

Alice Burton
Talladega National Forest, Alabama

A wave of dry heat rolled over them like a furnace, drying and superheating the air and singeing the hairs on her arms. Sarah cried out as she and Jake gripped their ears as the explosive sound boomed through the woods, the pressure threatening to crush their eardrums. Alice slammed her hands to her ears, too, pressing her cheek against the rumbling tree trunk that was getting struck by pieces of flaming debris. When the heat wave passed, they were left with fat chunks of wreckage hitting the forest floor and setting patches of woods on fire.

Alice removed her hands from her ears, the ringing intense, but she was still able to hear. "Let's go, follow me!"

Shaken, they crept quickly through the woods, circling to the northeast, the wind blowing cinders around and catching in their hair and on their clothing, forcing them to constantly pat at themselves and each other. The burning building cast shadows long across the forest floor until they reached the thickest part of the trees and were mostly out of sight.

"Okay, east toward the river."

"I can't believe you lured them in like that, mom."

"Yeah, well... I had to do something. Hopefully kids like Colton will take the hint and help the others escape."

"You did good mom," Jake squeezed her hand. "Real good."

People were shouting and running toward the burning building, but Alice kept her chin down and clung to Jake's arm, the three trying to make their way through the darkened forest without tripping and falling. Soon they were past the bunk houses and storage sheds and into the open fields where new constructions were going up with poorly-poured concrete foundations and shoddily constructed wooden floors, likely more sleeping quarters or, perhaps, another meth lab.

The smell of the river hit them far before they saw it, and they reached it a few moments later, descending a rocky bank covered in scree and scraggly bushes. Slipping along the shoreline, they watched the bunk houses and abandoned campfires where the food burned on the unattended grills. Lights had come on in the bunk houses and people were rushing toward the blaze where smoke curled into the sky, the fiery debris setting off smaller explosions and fires in the nearby buildings as propane and more stores of chemicals ignited. Screams echoed after the secondary explosions, though as far as Alice could tell they were from adults, not children.

The sloping shoreline rose slightly, hiding Alice and the kids from view if they stooped low enough, and she nudged them onward. "There's nobody at the campfires. Let's go."

They reached the south side of camp where a dead body still floated offshore, its feet caught in a tangle of branches, and Jake stopped and looked between it and Alice, but she only nodded and gestured for them to keep going. They climbed the bank and crept along the tree line past the spot where Alice had killed the three people, their bodies having been dragged out into the open and lined up in a neat row. The massive fire was plainly visible, but it was far off past the bunkhouses where the campground was littered with chunks of flaming debris on the roofs and in the yards, the fire spreading out of control. Shadows and shapes stood out against the glowing lights as people threw buckets of water, though their attempts were half-hearted as the fire outpaced them.

Alice knelt slowly next to the bodies and started feeling around in their pockets and belts.

"What are you doing?" Jake asked.

Sarah's jaw was slack for a second. "Did... you really kill these people?"

"Yep. None of this blood's mine."

"What are you doing?"

"Checking for weapons, tools – anything we can use." She glanced up nervously across the campsite. "It's not going to take them long to figure out we weren't in there."

"I'm on it," Jake said and joined her, rifling through the pockets of the deceased. "They don't have anything."

"Yeah. Crap. Stripped clean." Alice stood and gestured for Sarah to take the lead. "The horses are in a stable a few hundred yards away. If we can get to them, we can get out of here."

Right as she spoke, a man's voice rang out above the raging fire. "Riley's dead! They killed her! Find 'em! Now! I want their heads!"

Alice smiled coldly. "Looks like *I* wasn't the one who got to be burned alive. C'mon, move it."

She kept the kids moving, hastening her own pained gait, pushing through thick underbrush and past stiff stands of poplar saplings as they traversed down a hillside, a humid mist rising from the forest floor. Soon, the rough shape of the stables came into view with fog rolling up the walls and angry shouts pursuing them. As they stepped inside the stables through the crooked door, a huge smile spread on Sarah's face, and she ran to Stormy and threw her arms around the horse's neck. "I can't believe it," she said with a burst of cheer. "I never thought I'd see you guys again."

Buck and Rocky stamped their hooves and strained against their tethers as Alice pointed. "The saddles are over here, kids. Let's go... quickly now. We've only got a couple of minutes, max."

While the kids pulled the saddles from their hooks and started preparing their horses, Alice grabbed Buck's and immediately dropped it, clenching her side and wincing.

"I'll help you in a second, Mom," Jake said, and he mumbled himself through the steps of saddling Rocky. "Put the saddle on... leave three fingers between the front of the saddle and the neck... make sure the straps are firm but not pinching his skin..."

In less than five minutes, the kids had their horses saddled and came to help Alice while she stood and wondered how she'd mount up without some significant pain. When they were done, she walked right over and put her left foot in the stirrup, reaching for the saddle horn with no other choice but to do it. Jake and Sarah helped keep her stable as she climbed up, threw her leg over, and settled into an uncomfortable position with her legs spread and more weight on her lower back and chest. A fit of spasms hit her, and she leaned forward, breaths coming in shallow gasps, vision curling black around the edges until she caught her breath and relaxed with a short sigh.

"Are you okay?" Jake asked as he held Buck steady.

"Yeah," Alice gasped and clutched her side. "I'll live. Let's try to keep it that way."

Jake threw open a wider set of doors in the back of the stable, and they guided the horses out, finally outside and free in the cool night air. Every time Alice shifted for balance, her rib cage rebelled, her muscles tightening around her sides, squeezing, sending waves of pain through her torso. If she leaned to the right, the pain was slightly more tolerable, and she gave Buck a kick to send him into motion, galloping down the long lane leading out of the campground with the kids right behind her.

They rode westward a while, and Alice took the first northward trail they came to with the moonlight illuminating the bushes and tall swaying grasses bracketing the path. Alice slowed as they entered the trail, pushing beneath low-hanging branches and walking Buck up a slowly rising hill.

"You think we're safe now, mom?" Jake asked.

"Not till we're *very* far away from this forest."

"I wish we had Hercules." Sarah shoved vines out of her face. "Don't get me wrong – I'm glad we have these three, but...."

"I know. It's sad, but we can't go back for him. I'm sorry."

"Yeah...."

"Do you know where this trail leads?" Jake asked.

Alice chuckled. "As long as it takes us north away from the people trying to kill us, I don't care."

They rode in silence, navigating the treacherous slope with the trail littered with leaves and sticks, climbing hundreds of feet into the hills, finally reaching the top where the trees thinned and left a wide clearing spread out before them. Alice guided them around the right-hand edge which gave them a view of the camp through the gaps in the treetops. The silhouettes of buildings stuck out in the bright orange glow, the fires having spread from the meth lab to the outhouses, sheds, and trees, the conflagration raging out of control, the entire campground looking like a charcoal grill with a belly of open flames. Figures ran around, tossing buckets of water drawn up from the river while flashlight beams flashed through the woods.

"Looks like total chaos," Jake said with a raspy voice.

"That was the idea." Alice pointed at a series of lights that branched far off into the woods, heading north in the valley. "I wonder if those are some of the kids making a break for it?"

"I sure hope so." Sarah replied. "And for the record, I think you did a good job giving them a chance, mom. Thanks."

"Of course, hon." Alice patted Buck on the neck. "How're the horses feeling? Anyone limping or injured?"

"Rocky's good," Jake said, still in his jean shorts and old black T-shirt with the rock band design on it. "Tough as nails."

"Nothing's wrong with Stormy." Sarah's white T-shirt was smudged all over, her jean shorts torn in the front.

Sarah's button-up shirt hung from her shoulders, the plain blue camisole beneath it grungy and sweat-stained, just like she felt. They were all bruised, filthy and exhausted – but they were alive. "Can you see where the path starts up again?"

Sarah rose in her saddle and pointed. "I think I see it over there. Do we stay on it?"

"As long as it's heading north, yes."

"We are so screwed," Jake said with a dry laugh. "We lost everything. All the equipment we collected, the MREs, our weapons and ammunition..."

"We didn't lose everything, though." Alice walked Buck closer and grabbed his arm, smiling through the pain. "We have each other. After all this... nothing else matters as much as that."

"I'm glad you found us." Jake's eyes were glassy. "I still can't believe you survived that gunshot."

"Well, you better believe it." Alice turned her smile on Sarah. "This world will have to try harder if it wants to tear me away from you kids."

Sarah laughed through her tears and nodded. "I love you, Mom."

"What should we do now?" Jake asked. "I mean, I know *north* but what about after that?"

"Water, first. Then food and shelter." Alice gazed across the raging fires. "We'll survive, that's what. Just... survive."

A pink glow rose alongside the sun over the abandoned town, shot through with old fires and road wrecks, decayed bodies and bones picked clean and scattered across the highways, filling the bellies of turkey vultures and four-legged scavengers who'd fed well over the past weeks. Where there'd previously been bustling neighborhoods and a busy town center was nothing but a disturbing, unnatural peace and quiet. Creeper vines crawled unchecked up the high school walls, and the football field grass was almost a foot high. Birds were coming alive with song, their twittering and chirping filling the air, robins hopping through the weeds and tall grasses in search of a meal.

They were somewhere north of Talladega National Forest in a place marked by an old, crooked sign, *Munford*. Inside a small country grocery store, Alice used her pocketknife to break open a package of kitchen knives, handing one each to Sarah and Jake who promptly tucked them between their belt and jean shorts with the blades pointing backwards. On the checkout counter sat a bunch of canvas shopping bags half open to reveal a couple of gallons of water, several boxes of pasta, a small metal pot, and a few cans of concentrated soup.

Jake lifted the bags so the contents filled out the bottoms. "How far do you think this will get us?"

"Not far, but it's a treasure trove after we lost everything." Alice kept her movements steady and light, trying to avoid aggravating her injuries. "It'll sustain us for a few days. The best news is this water, though." She put her hand on the gallon jugs and closed her eyes, sighing with relief.

"You think Riley's people will come after us? It sounded like she didn't make it."

"Good." Alice's answer was very matter-of-fact. "I doubt very much that they'll follow us, but at least we have some minimal means of defense again."

"What I wouldn't give for our pools sticks," Jake grinned.

Alice laughed and ruffled his hair. "If you can manage to find some pool sticks, I'll be impressed."

They slipped the bag handles onto their arms and carried several each outside, crunching across the gravel lot where the horses were tied up behind a dumpster. They lashed the full bags and a few empty ones to the horses' saddles with pieces of twine and some bungee cables they'd found in the store's tiny automotive section, then untied the horses and mounted up, Alice grunting and gasping as she climbed up and settled, relaxing and waiting for the pain to pass. She nudged Buck into motion and guided them along a lane of brick buildings with old-style store signs hanging above the doors. The wide front windows were smudged and dirty, prices and sales covered in dust, a few windows shattered with glass gleaming on the sidewalks and reflecting sparkles of morning light. They passed a coffee shop and a deli, a vintage record store and a place that sold blinds and drapes.

"Hey, Mom." Jake pushed Rocky up beside her "There's a shoe store."

"I saw that. Let's check it out."

Hank's Shoes was − or had been − a small place with only a few aisles of boots and tennis shoes, slippers, and a big bargain bin full of socks. Some racks had signs that read *Buy one, get one free!* and there was a hallway in the back that led to some restrooms. Most of it had been picked over, but a fair amount was still left, survivors having been in more of a rush to get their hands on food and water instead of comfortable footwear.

"Oh, I'm all over these socks!" Sarah shouted, running to the bin and grabbing the biggest athletic socks she could find, slamming two pairs into her face and breathing deep. "Ugh," she pulled back with a grimace. "Smells like smoke."

"Are you *really* going to complain about fresh socks?" Alice raised an eyebrow and chuckled. "Set aside several packs for each of us on the counter up front, and add some ankle socks, too, if you can find them."

"Okay."

"Find some shoes that fit you, kids," Alice said. "Make it something we can travel in. I'm grabbing some boots, but you guys can get sneakers if you want."

"Hiking boots for me," Jake said with a firm nod, kicking off his ratty sneakers and checking the work boots against the wall for his size. "Waterproof."

"Good choice. Try for something durable and light, but I'd go with durable first. We'll hopefully be riding most of the way, but you never know."

While they searched through the store, Alice kept her eye on the horses who were tied up to the frame of a sedan askew out in the street. The town was deathly silent, even with all of their talking and noise-making, a welcome − though ominous − relief. Soon they had their shoe selections stacked by a row of chairs near the counter, swapping out their old dingy socks for new ones and then trying on shoes. Jake walked around in his rugged work boots and Alice found a similar pair in a woman's size, sitting back after lacing them up, wiggling her toes and thumping her heels and toes against each other to check the fit.

"These would have come in handy before."

"Hey, guys. Check it out." Sarah came walking down the middle row with a pair of big fuzzy slippers on her feet, her skinny, dirty legs in stark contrast to the fresh new footwear as she struck a pose. "What do you think?"

Jacob laughed and Alice smirked but pointed at the boot aisle. "Boots. *Now.*"

"Yes, Mom," Sarah said with a sideways grin.

They left the store in their new footwear, flexing and testing the fits before climbing into their saddles and walking the horses down the lane. They found some additional gallon-sized water jugs in another mini store at the end of the block along with a box of processed cupcakes, more canned soups, and assorted snacks. On the next corner stood a bank, and just past it was the wreckage of a gas station, its concrete pads in ruins after the main underground tanks had blown. The town proper ended after the gas station, giving way to old homes spaced far apart along the highway. Most of them were either destroyed or too fire damaged and unsafe to enter, though others stood empty and still on the roadside. They checked a two-story house on the right, something built in the forties or fifties, almost Victorian in its styling with its covered front porch and high peaks.

"I don't see any cars or trucks in the driveway. Think it's worth risking?" Alice asked Jake and Sarah. "We could use some flashlights or other basics, if we can find them."

"There's a garage out back," Sarah noted. "But I guess if it had cars, the place would've burned down already."

"Exactly. Hmm...." Alice stared at the house for a long moment. "Nobody's been at the windows and it seems deserted... I think we can take a chance. Just be ready to run like the wind if there's even a hint of someone there."

They followed the cracked blacktop driveway to the rear and tied the horses up to the posts of a large back porch that spanned the entire length of the house. Alice went up first, knife in one hand, the other pressed to the glass. Despite the older style of the place, the inside had reasonably modern furniture and a flat screen TV on the living room wall.

"I don't see anyone, but I guess we should still knock." Alice walked across the creaking floorboards and knocked on the back door, holding her knife low and staying a good three feet away from the big pane of glass where she could see the hardwood hallway and partially into the kitchen. When no noises came from inside the building, Alice shrugged. "I guess no one's home."

"Maybe they never made it back from wherever they were," Sarah said. "Kinda like us in Florida."

"You're probably right. Jake, can you find me a good-sized rock?"

"On it." Jake jumped into the yard and came back a moment later with a piece of brick from a flower bed. Alice tried to take it from him, but he gestured for her to move. "I've got this, Mom."

Alice stood aside and Jake drew the rock back and threw it through the glass with a crash. He reached in and unlocked the deadbolt, then pushed the door open and stepped inside, boots crunching over pieces of glass as he gave Alice and Sarah room. Alice followed him and immediately turned into the kitchen where the cabinets and pantry stood wide open with most of the food gone except for boxes of hard candies and chocolate, soft drinks and fruit juices.

"I guess I was wrong," Sarah whispered. "Yeah, these folks must've bugged out after the disaster. Maybe they had an electric car or something."

"Or someone came in here and looted the place before us. Can we take some stuff?"

"Whatever you can carry, sure. Looks like the owners – or whoever was in here – thought the same thing and took most stuff, though."

While Sarah gathered up some food, Jake and Alice walked through the house, having a careful look around for anything they could use, but finding no flashlights in any of the kitchen or living room drawers. The upstairs bedroom floors were covered with discarded clothes and suitcases as if the former occupants had made a hasty escape and in the master bedroom she found an assortment of women's clothing that was slightly bigger than her size, and she started sorting through them for a comfortable riding outfit.

Jake came in. "There are two girls' bedrooms back there and maybe some clothes for Sarah, but nothing for me."

"A man lived here..." Alice gestured to a different closet. "Try those jeans on. Even if they're a little too big, you can roll the pant legs up. There's a belt hanging from a hook there, and we can make our own belt holes and cut the end off if we have to. Sarah, honey!?"

Boots trounced up the stairs, and a moment later Sarah stood in the doorway. "Yeah, Mom?"

"Jake said there are a couple of girls' rooms at the end of the hallway. See if you can find some jeans and T-shirts. Maybe a jacket or windbreaker if you can find one."

"One of the girls likes foxes!" Jake called as he held up a pair of jeans to himself. "A... lot!"

"Foxes?" Alice asked.

"Yeah, she's got a *creepy* amount of fox posters all over her room."

The exclamation from the end of the hall told Alice and Jake both that Sarah must've been happy with her find, and a moment later, she came back with a pair of jeans that fit her perfectly, a dark brown belt which she'd tucked her knife into, a fresh white T-shirt, and a girl's red and yellow flannel shirt with a fox emblem over the left breast pocket.

"I love this stuff."

"Those fit you great, honey," Alice said as Sarah walked back and forth across the room. "Now find an extra change of clothes to take with us."

By that time, Jake had put on the man's underwear and pulled his jeans on, but they were way too big and barely stayed on his hips. Alice worked on the belt, making more holes and using her knife to saw off the excess leather. Pretty soon they had him dressed in oversized jeans, a black T-shirt with a motorcycle emblem on the front, and a medium-weight gray jacket that was way too big but would protect him from the elements. Alice found a couple pairs of jeans for herself, two nice-fitting camisoles, and a gray sweatshirt to go over them. The woman had some decent jackets, but none were made for traveling, so the sweatshirt would have to do.

"Okay, let's each find one set of extra clothing and get everything packed up."

With their items gathered on the kitchen counter, Sarah tried one of the spigots and found it working well enough to wet some paper towels and wash their faces, refreshing themselves as they scrubbed off the mud and dirt.

"How's your chest?" Sarah asked as she rubbed her arms clean and dried them with the towel.

Alice lifted her sweatshirt and her new black camisole to reveal the severe bruising that marked her left side and went all the way past her waistline. The kids both blanched as she showed them where the bullet had ricocheted and traveled down her side.

"Mom..." Jake shook his head and blinked back tears. "You... got really lucky. Sarah, we almost lost Mom."

"I know." Sarah replied, staring at Alice's injuries. "I thought she was a ghost when she walked into that meth lab. I thought I was going crazy for a second there."

The three hugged for a long moment in the kitchen before Alice wiped away her tears and extracted herself, favoring her sore side. "Reports of my death and all that. Let's continue this on the road, though, 'kay? After that campground, I don't really want to sit in one place for too long anymore."

They packed their things into the saddlebags and mounted up, walking the horses down the driveway and onto the highway where they turned north again.

"I feel so much better," Sarah said with an exaggerated sigh. "Those old clothes smelled horrible."

"Definitely," Jake laughed. "I don't think we changed for... who knows how long?"

"That is *not* a subject we're going to discuss," Alice snorted. "Let's just be thankful for what we have."

The morning wore on, growing into afternoon, and they found more patches of grass for the horses to walk on as they left the highway, always heading north. The landscape was riddled with destruction and death beneath clear blue skies and a bright, beautiful sun as they traversed through fields carpeted with long Bermuda grass and explosions of wildflowers. They saw fewer farmsteads and neighborhoods and entered a string of massive, round hills to the east, piled together under the sky and covered in rich forests. On one lonely highway, they came across a building burned to its foundation with the husks of cars flipped out front, and the remnants of a neon sign out front read *Whisker's Bar and Grill*. As they were passing it, Jake grinned and angled toward the building.

"Hey, what're you doing?" Alice asked.

"Check it out, Mom." He walked Rocky along the side of the establishment, hopping off for a moment before jumping back on the horse, holding a pair of pool cues.

"Well I'll be." Alice tilted back her head and laughed, genuinely, for the first time in days.

"Dude." Sarah accepted one of the cues as Jake tossed it to her. "We are seriously right back at square one again."

"No," Alice chuckled, nudging her horse to continue on, Jake and Sarah riding beside her. "Not square one. We're much closer to home, we've got reliable transportation, and a wealth of experience in our hands."

"And pool cues." Jake added, wiggling his eyebrows as he held one up.

"And pool cues," Alice grinned, laughing again as her family continued moving forward, ever north.

CHAPTER TWENTY-SIX

Ryan Cooper
Lansing, Michigan

Rain beat against the side of the house and the boarded-up windows, drumbeats of tiny hands trying to worm their way in through any crack and crevice possible. Ryan ignored the drips that emerged through the cracked glass and barricades, standing in the darkened dining room with his binoculars pressed to the glass, looking through gaps in the plywood. He was dripping wet, boots muddy on the hardwood flooring, clenching the binoculars and holding down the rising bile in his stomach. The tree line and road were clear, but the absence of movement did nothing to make him feel any better. The storm hadn't let up, rattling the rooftop, shaking the windows, and scaring the dogs who went from room to room every time thunder crashed above their heads.

The dogs were afraid of the storm but curious about Sandy and Stephen, who stood dripping on the floor by the dining room table. Helen was helping them, hanging Stephen's backpack on a chair and gathering their wet coats as Duke and Duchess sniffed at them with slowly wagging tails.

"If one candle isn't enough light." Helen nodded at the single candle burning on a table in the corner. "There are more in the kitchen."

"Thank you." Sandy nodded.

"No more light," Ryan growled. "One is enough."

Helen stared at him for a few seconds and frowned. "I'll just... put these wet coats in the laundry room and go up to get you all some dry clothes to get into. Just hang tight."

Sandy swept her wet hair back and walked a few steps back into the foyer, gazing up at the catwalk and vaulted ceiling. "This is a lovely home."

"Thanks." Ryan's reply was soft and distracted as he still stared through the window.

"I've only been inside once." Sandy coughed lightly. "A couple of years ago when Alice had a book club thing going."

"Mm-hmm."

"Anyway, I-I promise you, Stephen and I won't be a burden. We'll do our share of work and help out wherever we can." When Ryan didn't answer, Sandy half smiled and came to stand behind him. "It must be nice with just the two of you here. Plenty of room, with chickens and animals out back."

"More than enough for two people," Ryan muttered, "but when the rest of the family gets here, it'll be tight."

"You expect them home soon?"

"Any day now. We're just holding down the fort until then."

"I see." Sandy turned to Stephen, who was standing and shivering. "What do you have in your backpack, son? Any games?"

"Yeah, I have a chess game, and checkers, too."

"Oh, I'll bet Ryan loves those games. I'm sure he'll play with you."

Ryan ignored Sandy's comments, shifting to the other window, the one that had been completely boarded up after the intruders had crashed through it. Wind whistled through the gap and water slowly dripped through onto the floor, but the binoculars revealed nothing moving on the west side of the property.

"And I'll play if Ryan doesn't have... the time...." Sandy trailed off, wrapping her arms around herself and shifting back and forth awkwardly.

"I found some clothes," Helen announced, descending the stairs with a big stack of garments in her arms, putting three separate piles on the table. "I got some of Jake's clothes for you, Stephen. They might be a little big."

"Oh, don't worry about that," Sandy assured her. "We really appreciate this a *lot*."

Helen smiled. "You're a little taller than Alice, but she always wore her sweatpants and sweatshirts a size or two large, so I brought some of those for you. Dry socks for everyone, too."

"That's amazing," Sandy said. "Thank you. Where can we change?"

"Go down that hallway and take a right into the kitchen. The laundry room is just off that."

"Thanks again, Helen. I'd hug you, but..." Sandy gestured to her wet clothes.

"You can hug me when you get back," Helen laughed.

"Come on, Stephen," Sandy said, taking him down the hall with their clothes.

Helen folded her arms and walked up behind Ryan. "What's got you in a mood fouler than the weather, hon?"

Lightning flashed off to the left and scattered across the sky in a pattern of zigzagging flashes that lit the yard like a strobe light. The smaller, sturdier trees out in the middle of the yard thrashed wildly in the crushing winds while the row of maples bowed deeply, their heads whipping back and forth like fans at a rock concert.

"Watching and waiting."

"Why don't you sit down and rest?" When Ryan continued to stare through the binoculars, Helen sighed. "I'll make our guests some food. Do you want anything?"

"I'm good for now. Thanks."

Helen went down the hall to put something together while Sandy and Stephen came out and sat at the dining room table. Sandy wore Alice's black sweatpants and gray pullover with *Michigan State* written across the front, and Stephen had on a pair of Jake's blue jeans and a white T-shirt with a space design.

When Sandy came back into the kitchen she was carrying four plates, which she put down with a soft clank. "I tried to help Helen with the food, but she just handed me some plates and utensils and told me to come out here."

"Sit. Make yourself comfortable," Ryan said. "Best you don't wander right now."

A shadow passed over her face, but she nodded and guided Stephen back to the table where they waited in silence, listening to the constant thunder as the lightning tried to tear the sky asunder.

The smell of hot food preceded Helen carrying two big bowls into the dining room and setting them on the table. "These are leftovers, but still pretty good. We've got broccoli tuna casserole and spiced potatoes. I promise – the casserole isn't nearly as bad as it sounds."

"Are you kidding me?" Sandy asked, taking a big whiff of both bowls. "That smells *delicious*. We haven't had anything this good since...." She gave Stephen a sad glance. "Anyway, thank you. This looks incredible."

"No problem." Helen patted both Sandy and Stephen on the back. "It's good to see smiles on fresh faces."

Helen scooped potatoes and casserole on each plate, and Stephen and Sandy quickly began to eat. While they did, Helen went to the kitchen and returned with two glasses of milk, leaving the pair gaping in disbelief when they appeared in front of her.

"Milk?!" Sandy said around a mouthful of casserole. "This is heaven. Clearly we've died and gone to heaven."

"Ryan, are you sure you don't want anything?" Helen asked.

"Yes."

Helen brought a towel to Ryan and patted his head and neck. "You really should get dried off, dear. I put some spare clothes on the table for you."

"I said I'm fine, Helen," he said gruffly. "Just let me be."

"Why are you worried, dear? No one will show up in this storm. We're fine for now."

"No one's shown up *yet*."

"Would you look at it out there? Everyone will be hunkered down until this storm's over. We can wait until morning to start worrying."

"That's what they'll be expecting us to do." Shaking his head, he turned to Sandy and Stephen. "That was way too easy, Sandy. There *has* to be something going on."

"What do you mean?" Sandy swallowed her milk, wiping her mouth on a napkin.

Ryan put the binoculars down and leaned in and leveled a hard stare at Stephen. "What were you and your friends doing out in that shelter playing games?"

Stephen shrugged.

"Ryan...." Helen whispered, and he turned to Sandy again.

"Don't you think it's strange they put kids out there when it was about to storm? Why would they leave them there and not put them in a house or camper somewhere?"

"Well, it wasn't storming yet, dear." Helen moved in between Ryan and Sandy.

"They just put us there," Stephen said. "Some kids wanted to go out there, and I thought it would be fun. It was like camping out like my dad and I used to do."

Ryan closed his eyes and pushed aside a pang of guilt. "Well, who put you out there? Who actually *told* that you could sit outside and play?"

"Ms. Barb and Ms. Summer. They said we should play over there while the adults were talking."

"Barb and Summer." He glanced at Sandy, who was staring back at him.

"What are you thinking Ryan?" she asked, then her eyes widened in understanding. "Wait. Do you think we're working with them or something?!"

"You said they shot Mike."

"That's right."

"I didn't see the body. You could've made that up."

"*Ryan!*" Helen said. "Just what *are* you getting at? Why are you being such an..." she whispered the final word, "*ass*?"

"It was just..." He stepped back from the table, rubbing his hand across his face, glaring from Sandy to Stephen. "Come on... did they put you up to this? Did they help you find that well pump so they'd have someone on the inside here?"

Sandy dropped her fork on the table. "W-why would I do that?"

"One man kept asking me questions," Stephen said in a weak voice.

"What one man?" Ryan turned back to Stephen.

"One of the new people. He had a big bushy mustache."

"Did they call him Red? "

"I think so."

Ryan spun on Helen. "I knew it! They planted that boy out there to lure us in and see what we would do! Probably so they could watch me, see what weapons I brought to rescue him... figure out our status...."

"What could they have possibly learned that they wouldn't have found out from the neighbors?" Helen asked.

"It doesn't matter." Ryan walked back to the window with the binoculars and looked outside. "If those old coots killed Mike in cold blood, they're darker than I thought possible. I mean... if Sandy's telling the truth, they killed Mike in cold blood to get more information on us." He turned back to the table with his hands on his hips. "Hell, just knowing we're alive is more than worth the price of admission. But they'd need more, wouldn't they?" He spoke to himself, starting to pace, the hairs on his neck once again starting to rise. "Wait. If they planted your boy out there to lure us in... I wouldn't be surprised if... hold on a second."

Ryan raced over and snatched Stephen's backpack off the chair, throwing it on the table and rifling through it, opening the front flap, reaching in and pulling out a walkie-talkie with a piece of duct tape over the transmit button.

He brandished the radio at Sandy, shaking it in her face, teeth bared. "What the hell is this?!" He screamed and ripped the tape off the transmit button. "I was right, wasn't I?! You set us up!"

"No, Ryan. I swear." Sandy shook her head, tears streaming down her face. "I don't know how it got in there! I swear I just grabbed his backpack when I was trying to get him out of there. I didn't stop to look inside or anything!"

Ryan whirled on Stephen. "Then where did it come from? Did *you* put it in there, son?"

The dogs were feeding off Ryan's intensity, all of them standing around and watching him with their floppy ears raised, Duke growling low in the background.

Helen took Ryan's arm and tried to draw him back. "Ryan, stop!"

He shook off Helen's grip, banging his fist on the table. "Come on, Stephen! Tell me the truth!"

"I-I didn't put t-the radio in there!" Stephen's eyes were glassy, tears flowing freely down his cheeks as he bawled. "They g-gave it to me, s-said it had g-games in it!"

A low, coarse chuckle came through the radio speaker, like a rock being slowly dragged across sandpaper. "Well howdy there, Ryan Cooper. I'm guessin' all the silence on our end means you found our little toy. Good to talk to you again."

Ryan whirled away and strode over to the window, glaring at the gate through the binoculars but still seeing no one. He swallowed hard and kept his voice even. "Red Fletcher."

"You remember me. That's good, my friend."

"I'd hardly call us friends," Ryan growled.

"Oh, come on now. We were on a first-name basis. And bein' on a first-name basis is the first step to establishin' a long-lasting friendship, don't you think?"

"We played a few hands of poker and a bit of golf. We're acquaintances, not friends. What the hell do you want?"

The low chuckle came through again, and all three dogs growled at the sound. "Well, first of all, don't blame Sandy or her kid. It's not their fault. You're just too damn gullible. After all, remember the poker games? You never could see through a good bluff."

"What do you want?" Ryan repeated.

"We've come a long way to see you, of course. Look down at your gate, Cooper."

Ryan stood stiffly, a chill running up his spine as two people stepped off the road, walking up to their gate and resting their arms on the rail. He couldn't make out who they were, but they held rifles and appeared to be far too relaxed.

"You see them?"

"Easy targets for my thirty-aught-six."

"That's a long shot from your front door."

"Tell them to keep standing there for a couple of minutes, and they'll find out."

Red chuckled again, the sound grinding in Ryan's head, but he turned to Helen and gestured toward the back of the house. "Helen, check the windows, would you? Be ready."

Wordlessly, Helen grabbed a rifle off the table and marched down the hall with Diana and Duchess at her heels.

"We come in peace, Ryan. We just want a little bit of help. You're one of the only people with a working vehicle. Did you know that?"

"Is that what you want, my tractor?"

"You've got an electric car, too, I hear. At least that's what Jack told me."

"Jack's a liar."

"Now, Jack might be a lot of things," Red laughed, "but I don't think he'd lie to me."

"Why, because he's scared you'll do him the same as Mike?"

"Somethin' like that."

"What turned you into an animal, Red?"

"What turned you into a selfish *prick*, Ryan?" Red's voice changed, taking on a sinister note. "Jack and Barb filled me in on the situation, but I don't think I got the whole story quite yet. I know they were trying to steal from you, and you had every right to defend yourself. Still, you could've shown a bit of brotherly love to your neighbors. You could have brought them into the fold and had a few more bodies to defend the property, work the fields, stand guard."

"Stay off said property, or you'll regret it."

"Oh, come on now, Ryan." Red chuckled again. "Why not share willingly? We're not going away empty-handed."

"If you talked to Jack, then you know we held them off already. Killed some of them, too."

"Yeah. Five of 'em. Heard you have some hellhounds up there. But let me tell you something, Ryan. Jack isn't smart like me. He didn't bother surrounding your whole house while it was pouring rain so that you have no clue how many rifles are aimed at you and your pretty wife's heads right now. He didn't have a small army who's armed and trained and ready to do *anything* to get what they want. And he doesn't have the resources to bring something to knock that house down, with you inside of it if necessary. But I do, Cooper. I do."

Another cold chill ran down Ryan's spine. "What the hell are you talking about?"

An engine bellowed over the pounding rain, the chesty sound of a big diesel threatening to shout down the storm. Tires rumbled and chewed up the gravel and mud as a massive truck with a tall grill and side pipes billowing smoke appeared behind the tree line and roared toward the gate. Ryan's stomach dropped as the truck swerved straight at the gate, smashing through it, rails and fencing careening outward as another burst of lighting fired across the sky. As the lightning faded, the truck's headlamps kicked on and shined up the driveway, then more lights appeared in the trees and woods to the left and right, flashlights and laser beams alike.

"Helen!" Ryan bellowed, scanning the lights, trying to count them, unable to focus for the fear flowing through his body.

"I see them! They're around the back, too! Looks like a dozen at least!"

Ryan turned to grab his gun, his vision blurry and head dizzy as adrenaline flowed through his body. The vehicle didn't stop, though, merely trundled slowly between the maples and ponds, stopping in a spray of water just past where the driveway angled up, sitting there idling in the rain, its engine singing a low harmony to the rolling thunder.

Ryan stood shaking, jaw clenched tight, finally breaking his frozen stance, grabbing his rifle, and returning to the window. Calming himself with a deep breath, he raised the binoculars, tracking the figures moving through the trees on the east and west sides of the property. The dump truck's passenger door popped open, and Red stepped out to stand in the howling storm, waving up to him with a broad, smug grin before lifting the radio to his mouth.

"So, what'll it be, Ryan? Do you want to share your bounty with your friends? Or would you prefer to die instead?"

THE DEVOURING

CHAPTER ONE

Ryan Cooper
Lansing, Michigan

Ryan backed away from the window at the sight of the massive salt truck parked in their driveway, Red Fletcher still standing in the rain and lightning, the crackling skies illuminating his grim scowl as half a dozen people dispersed out of the back of the vehicle. Dread settled in Ryan's stomach, sweat crawling across his skin as he turned to Helen, his face pale.

"This isn't good."

"They wouldn't... really try to ram through the front of the house, would they?" Helen edged over to the window to peer between the cracks in the plywood.

"Yeah, I daresay they would. Even if they didn't, they've got enough people to take us down. Red's smart. He talked to Jack and his pack of idiots and learned from their mistakes. He knows we can't handle them."

"Isn't there... anywhere we can go?" Sandy asked, getting up from the table and putting her hands on her son's shoulders. "I have to protect Stephen. He's just a boy. He's not a part of this."

"We're all a part of this now, whether we like it or not." Ryan moved back to the window, squinting into the rainy night as a flash of lightning revealed Red with a poncho on, water dripping off his scruffy beard and down his front, still staring at the house.

"That's Reynolds driving and probably Hansen in the back. It's hard to tell, but those two giants are hard to mistake."

"How do you know?" Helen asked.

"Hansen and Reynolds sat in on the card games a few times. I hardly know anything about 'em."

"Well, they sure know us."

Ryan shook his head. "How did they find us, anyway? I never told Red about this place. Maybe I mentioned we were coming here to housesit, but that's it. I didn't give him an address or anything."

"Does that really matter right now?" Helen stepped away from the window. "What are we going to do?"

Ryan placed his rifle on the table and rubbed at his eyes with one hand, sighing deeply. "There's only one thing we can do, Helen." He gestured around. "All this, everything we have here – all we were protecting and trying to keep sacred and whole for Alice and James – we have to give it up."

Helen blanched. "Give up? You're joking!"

Ryan's jaw worked back and forth. "They've got us cornered. We can't take them all out, and if they don't shoot us, they'll just bring the house down around us."

"We can escape!" Helen pointed in the direction of the barn. "I didn't see any of them around the barn; we can just take off and go!"

"And slowly starve to death? No... no we have to try and stay alive here. Play for our lives, and figure out how to strike when the time's right."

"They said they'd trade. Maybe we can offer something, and they'll go away."

"Make no mistake, honey. They're here to take *everything*. Our lives are the best we can bargain for right now."

"I—"

The radio crackled, interrupting Helen. "My patience is a *very* limited resource these days, Cooper. I suggest you quit hand-wringing and hang the welcome sign."

"Take the dogs," Ryan looked at Sandy. "Get them to the barn, and lock them in, then get your butt back to the house with Helen."

"What are you plan—" Helen started.

"We don't have time for any more talk." Ryan moved toward the front door, slipping on his raincoat. "Just trust me. Keep the dogs alive, and pray that I manage to keep *us* alive, too."

Helen nodded. "I love you, Ryan. Stay safe."

Red's gruff voice piped through the speaker. "Last chance, Cooper. What'll it be?"

Ryan grimaced and swiped the radio off the table. "I'm coming out, Red. Give me a second."

"Good choice, Ryan." Red's saccharine tone sent a shiver down Ryan's spine. "Make sure you come out unarmed. We've all got itchy trigger fingers."

Looking at the rifle on the table, Ryan headed to the door, looking back to Helen. "Don't lose hope. We're not giving up. We're focusing on living to fight another day."

With a forceful tug, Ryan swung open the door, surrendering himself to the wrath of the tempestuous elements. Torrents of rain, not merely falling but charging horizontally across the landscape in sheets, bore the signature of the storm's relentless ferocity. The sky above was an arena of furious conflict, dense clouds churning and roiling in a ceaseless ballet of turmoil, punctuated by the spectral dance of lightning. The air vibrated with the grumbling bellows of thunder and the unknown of what was to come, the wild heartbeat of the storm vibrating in tune with Ryan's very soul.

Out in the driveway, Red stood near the truck, holding a radio in one hand and revolver in the other, water dripping from the barrel. "Come on over, Ryan!" He looked up into the sky, grinning madly. "It's a beautiful day, isn't it?"

Ryan stepped down the path to the driveway, turning and angling toward Red as armed men and women watched from beneath poncho hoods glistening with rainwater, lightning continually cracking and flashing in the sky.

Ryan stopped when he was ten yards away, nodding slowly. "Red. Can't say I'm happy to see you, but your group did well getting all the way here."

"And we're about to do much better," Red conceded, "now that we've got a new place to stay."

"I'm assuming things weren't good in Grand Rapids?"

"It was challenging," Red replied with a shrug.

"How'd you find us? I don't remember giving you directions to my daughter's property."

"We went to your condo. Sorry to report the place burned to the ground. There were a few things in the wreckage, though." Red turned and gestured to the passenger side of the truck where Martha was sitting up, peering over the dashboard, her wavy gray hair tumbling to her shoulders. "Martha found a letter from your daughter and son-in-law. Envelope was half-burned, but it gave us enough to go on."

"I figured it was something like that." Ryan stared at the pistol still clenched tight in Red's hand. "You plan on using that?"

"Depends on how you act. So, let's get down to business."

Ryan clenched his hands and nodded, taking on a businesslike tone. "We've got milk and eggs enough for your crew. We'd be happy to give you a supply of that right now as a peace offering. If you come back tomorrow, we can do some more trading."

Red chuckled low, glancing over his shoulder as Hansen and a shorter, rugged man came up to stand beside him, their feet spread, rifles pointed at the ground. "Well, that's pretty gracious of you, Ryan. What else you got?"

"We could discuss further trades after we established a bit of trust. There is a list of things we need if you'd be willing to—"

"Don't be making any demands of me, Cooper." Red's voice grew sharp in an instant, his eyes narrowing. "*I'm* in charge, and *I* set the rules."

Hansen stepped forward, poncho hood thrown back, rain pouring down his head and neck. "Why are we even talking to this guy?"

The smaller man nodded. "Just shoot him and let's take what we need."

"Now, Tyler," Red corrected him. "Ryan's a friend, *so far*. Until he gives me a reason to hurt him, we'll handle this in a civilized manner." He leveled an unsettling smile. "Come on, Ryan. What else do you have?"

Ryan wiped a hand across his face, glancing upward as another streak of lightning illuminated the sky. "If milk and eggs aren't enough for you, we could spare a couple of sheep. You could slaughter them and have meat for all your people and then some. Probably last you a month or more if you ration it out."

"Ration it out," Red smirked. "You hear that? Ryan wants us to ration things out."

Hansen laughed deep in his chest, a low resonant sound like a bull chuffing while Tyler only glared at Ryan with a bemused, ghoulish half grin. Behind the salt truck, Red's people were gathering, and more were creeping up through the fields and trees to join them, a dozen shadowy figures silhouetted in the washed-out moonlight with the sharp shapes of weapons in their hands.

"That's the best I can do for you." Ryan said. "Keeping a big crew full won't be easy, but I'm sure we can come to some sort of ongoing—"

"Shut up, Cooper," Red replied flatly. "You know something? I think the boys are right."

Red raised his revolver, water dripping off the burnished metal as he leveled it at Ryan's chest. "Maybe I should just go ahead and shoot you. It'd be a hell of a lot simpler than jabbering on and on."

Ryan ignored his racing heart and the pistol both, addressing Red as matter-of-factly as he could muster. "We run this farm and we know how to keep things going. If you just come in and take everything and sweep us aside, that would be foolish. You can't do that."

Red growled and stepped toward him, raising the pistol, holding it a foot away from Ryan's head. "You don't get to tell me what I can or can't take. What we want, we take. You hear me?"

The radio in Red's hand popped to life, Helen's shrill voice blasting through. "Red Fletcher, why are you pointing a gun at my husband? You promised not to hurt us if we cooperated!"

Another voice came from near Red as Martha squeezed between Hansen and Tyler, touching her husband's arm. "Red, honey. Listen to what Helen's saying. More killing isn't the answer."

Red started to snarl at Martha but quickly relaxed, though he didn't lower his weapon. "They're toying with us, Martha. They're trying to trick us and buy themselves time to hide things." He turned his glare on Ryan. "Well, I'll tell you what. It won't work." He thumbed the hammer back with a click.

"We're not hiding things," Ryan growled even as he squirmed. "How does that even make any sense?"

"Hang on now, Red." Martha's voice grew harder. "Maybe Ryan's right. Maybe we should let them keep running the place. Just with us in charge."

"We're all farmers. We'll handle it just fine."

"You know as well as I do that every farm has its quirks... its share of problem animals, the potential for disease. Do you want to take this place over only to have it fail by summer? Where will we be then?"

"You know she's right, Red. Farms are tricky. We've got this place operating nice and smooth."

Red's index finger played over the trigger for several agonizing seconds before he smiled, lowering the weapon and dropping the hammer. "My good wife is talking sense, as always. Tell you what. Let's go on up to the house and have a look around. I promise, and *Martha* promises, none of you will be hurt provided you don't raise a hand to us. That means putting down your weapons and keeping those dogs out of the way."

"The dogs are in the barn," Ryan silently prayed that Sandy had followed his instructions. "You won't get any trouble from them, or from us."

"You'll want to warn Helen to put down her guns, too. Unless you want to see her shot."

"No, Red. I don't want to see my wife of many years gunned down in front of me. I'll tell her soon as we get to the porch."

"Reynolds, come on out," Red called over his shoulder.

The driver's door opened with a squeal and slammed shut, and Reynolds came to stand by Red and Martha, with Tyler and Hansen on the other side.

"All right, then. Turn around and march, Ryan."

Ryan sighed and headed up to the house, boots squelching through the puddles, splashing in streams of water running down the driveway. He reached the walking path from the driveway to the front door, and his insides shriveled up as he stared across the brick house, the memories they'd made hanging on over the last few days and weeks, defending themselves with everything they had. The boot steps behind him, the invaders worming in like a virus, demanding their supplies, sustenance, and ruining everything – Ryan's fists curled at his sides.

"I'm telling you. If those dogs so much as snarl at us, we'll put them and you down."

When Ryan came to the front stoop, he shouted through the closed door, gesturing behind him. "Honey, we're going to let them have a look around. Martha's here, and she and Red promised we won't be hurt as long as we do what they say. Make sure you put your guns down when we come in, okay?"

Helen opened the door, peering over Ryan's shoulder at the shadowy figures trailing down the path, more coming up the driveway and through the yard and fields, all approaching the house. Exchanging a nod with Martha, Helen swung the door open and backed up, holding her rifle and pistol in each hand, then slowly placed them on the table. Ryan came in and stood to the side near Helen, clasping her hand as Red and his people filed in.

"Well, well, well!" Red grinned, making a complete turn as he looked around at the spacious home, craning his neck to see the kitchen and dining room. "Look what we have here! Tyler, this the Eden you were looking for?"

Tyler walked into the great room and looked around. "So far, so good. We'll see what they have out in the barns and chicken coop, though."

Red slapped Ryan on the shoulder, leaning in close. "Why don't you tell us where everything is? Save us a lot of trouble poking around." Red put his face inches away from Ryan's, his breath foul, teeth yellowed from too much coffee and not enough dental care. When Ryan didn't instantly respond, Red shrugged and grinned. "No problem. We'll make ourselves at home and have a look around."

Ryan raised an eyebrow at Helen. "Are the dogs still in the barn?"

"Yep, locked up tight."

"We'll keep them there till you're assured they aren't a threat to you, Red." Ryan watched Red making small circles in the entryway, looking around at the house and furniture.

"Don't worry, Cooper. I'll keep my word as long as you all behave." He gestured at the chairs around the dining room table. "Why don't ya'll just take a seat with Sandy and little Stephen. Someone'll keep an eye on you."

"I've got it," a bearded man replied as he entered the house.

Ryan took Helen by the arm and guided her to the other side of the table where they sat down under the watchful eyes of Red's group. "I'm sorry," Ryan whispered quietly, squeezing her hand.

"There's nothing to be sorry about," she replied, putting her other hand atop his. "You're still alive. That's all I care about."

"I should have done more... done something. I let you down. I let everyone down." He looked over at Sandy watching the intruders anxiously, holding Stephen's hand and keeping herself between him and the guard. "Even them."

"That's not true, Ryan."

Others filtered in, moving past Red and into the house and Ryan pointed down the hallway, raising his voice. "Watch out for those doorknobs out back. They've got razor blades on them."

Red gave Ryan a grin and grateful nod, then ordered Reynolds and Hansen upstairs to have a look around. Others walked out back, and Ryan shifted uneasily, squeezing Helen's hand harder, spreading the fingers of his other hand flat on the table to keep from making a fist. Pots and pans rattled in the kitchen as people got into things, someone shouting with joy when they opened the refrigerator to find gallons of milk stored inside. Red and Martha took seats at the table with Martha sitting across from Ryan and Helen, giving Helen a sympathetic look but staying quiet. Red sat at the head of the table, propped his feet up, and waved as Jack and Barb Willoughby stepped in.

"Look at the big bully." Jack grinned at Ryan. "Not so tough now, are you?"

"You got taken down a notch, didn't you?" Barb added with a smirk.

"Red," Martha glared at her husband. "We should handle this like adults."

"We are."

"Not with *them* acting this way."

"I told you we wouldn't kill him, Martha." Red dragged his feet off the table and leaned forward with the revolver in hand. "That's the only promise I made."

Martha stared openly at Jack and Barb. "You're forgetting, dear, that we met these people less than twenty-four hours ago. Do we really want to let them do what they want, especially to our *hosts?*"

Red ran his tongue over his teeth, leaning back in his chair as he considered Martha's words, then finally turned and gave the Willoughbys a heated stare. "Jack. Take your people out back and check things out.

"Don't go in the main barn just yet," Sandy interjected, "the dogs are out there."

"And stay out of the main barn." Red looked back at his wife. "That good enough for you, Martha?"

Martha relaxed with a quiet nod while Jack and Barb moved to the rear of the house, Jack rubbing his hands together greedily. A thin woman wearing full overalls and a ragged top tore off her poncho and tossed it haphazardly on the living room floor, brushing back her long, dark, wet hair.

"What do you want me to do, Red?" Nancy asked.

"Go check in the kitchen and bring us something good to drink."

She grinned, tucked her thumb into her overall bib, and moved into the kitchen with a swagger. A moment later she came back out with a milk mustache atop a wide grin, a stack of glasses in one hand and an unmarked gallon jug in the other, holding it up and sloshing the white liquid around inside.

"Howsabout this, Red? Good, fresh milk. I'll bet they've got a cow out back."

Red blinked in mock astonishment. "Is that true, Ryan? Do you have a heifer?"

"I told you we had milk, so obviously we have a cow." Ryan growled, clenching and unclenching his fist beneath the table. "Her name is Bessie."

"Very nice. Thank *you*, Ryan and Helen."

Nancy set out the glasses on the table, pouring a bit into each one, placing them in front of everyone at the table, then filling Red's to the top and handing it to him. "I haven't tasted milk this good before."

"Nothing beats fresh." Red raised the glass to his nose, inhaled deeply, then drained the glass dry before wiping his mouth with the back of his arm and giving a satisfied belch in Ryan's direction. "Whew, boy. That tastes good. Cold and refreshing. Hard to believe you've been keeping this all to yourself."

"Glad you enjoyed it." Ryan murmured, none of the others at the table bothering to drink theirs.

"There are at least seven more gallons in there." Nancy said. "And that's just the start of what they've got, too."

"Thanks, Nancy," Red gestured. "That'll be all. Get with Martha and start taking inventory. Martha?"

Martha stood and looked around, speaking softly. "Helen, do... do you have some notepads and pens?"

"In the bottom right kitchen drawer."

"Thank you."

Tyler came in the front door, slapping his knee and giving Red two thumbs up. "They've got a whole pen of chickens out there, Red. Plenty of sheep and a cow out back, too. That probably explains..."

"All the milk." Red gestured at the glasses. "Good work, Tyler. Get me an accurate headcount of all the animals."

"Yes, sir." Tyler gave him a brief, informal salute and walked off.

Reynolds and Hansen came tromping down the stairs and crossed the foyer to stand before Red. "We checked the upstairs," Reynolds said. "They've got a nice master bedroom, some kids' rooms, two bathrooms, and a small office. No other people."

"Any place for a man and his wife to lay their heads for a good night's rest?"

"I'd say the master bedroom. The bed's made."

"Ryan and Helen probably left the master bedroom alone, being it's their daughter's." He looked at Helen, who nodded, then he grinned. "But I'm not family, so Martha and I will take that room. Now, as for them..." Red took his boots off the table and leaned forward, but was cut off when Martha came back into the room.

"*Red.*"

"Oh good grief, woman. I'm not going to make them sleep out in the barn with the damn dogs. Reynolds, take these nice folks up to a spare bedroom and tuck them in nice and tight."

"Sure, Red." Reynolds gestured as Hansen chuckled next to him. "Come on, folks. You're way past your bedtime."

"Come on. Let's go," Ryan said to the others, standing and waiting for Helen, guiding her around the other side, away from Red. The four followed Reynolds upstairs, Ryan seething at the sounds of people rummaging through the house, his daughter's home being flipped upside down. At the guest bedroom, he pushed open the door and they all stepped inside.

"Don't try anything stupid," Reynolds said. "I'll be right outside the door. Do not lock it. And if I hear you messing with the windows, I'm coming in."

Reynolds pulled the door shut, and Ryan turned and squeezed past Helen and Sandy, gesturing to the twin-sized mattress. "I guess we should get comfortable. Sounds like we're going to be stuck up here for a while."

Helpless to do anything more, Ryan settled on the edge of the bed, turning his face away from the mirror that hung above the dresser. Outside, the storm raged on, pelting the house with heavy rainfall as lightning broke and raced across the sky.

CHAPTER TWO

Alice Burton
Somewhere in Tennessee...

The once idyllic Tennessee landscape lay bare beneath dark gray skies that looked down upon a road covered in glass, rubber, plastic and rusting metal. A faint fog drifted through the mid-morning air, a breeze carrying the faint scent of oil and antifreeze that sat in small puddles inside shredded pieces of metal and plastic.

Alice walked Buck along the side of the road with the gentle swish of his hooves in the tall grasses, her gaze drifting back and forth in search of anything that might injure him. Sarah came behind her on Stormy, slouching tiredly in the saddle and Jake was last, wearing the oversized clothes they'd modified for him, shirt and jeans hanging off his shoulders and hips, both requiring constant adjustments. It'd been a day since they'd found their new shoes, socks, and the remnants of food from the corner store, and already they were bone-weary from their ride, the promise of home still agonizingly distant.

They'd long since grown numb to the sight of corpses that lay in the wreckage, their limbs torn off and scattered, skin dehydrated and pulled taut over bleach-white skulls, lips peeled back, forming rictus grimaces. Alice didn't even bother to tell the children to look away; their experiences both before and after the camp had noticeably hardened them, and they both were quieter, more introspective, and spoke less than they had before encountering Mark and Christine. They'd had a few chances for quiet conversations during their ride, but true processing of what had taken place wouldn't be possible until they were safe back home.

Heading ever north, they navigated highways and back roads and small towns of the shattered land, scanning the horizon for signs of life or hope amid the devastation. The kids' faces were etched with weariness and defiance, their new clothes caked with grime and dust from just a day's ride. Buck, Stormy, and Rocky hung their heads as they navigated the Tennessee highway, passing through what remained of small towns with farmsteads and houses standing in fields of tall grass, overgrown with creepers stretching up the siding and brick. In the absence of humanity's control, nature was fierce in its reclamation of the world, grasses and weeds turning neat, rigid lines into blurred, organic ones as they wound their way through cracks and crevices.

Mailboxes lay crooked, the names ripped off or burned away, and in one yard an old car tire hung from an oak tree, swinging slowly in a soft breeze with no children to use it. Paper and plastic products tumbled everywhere, garbage cans rolled in the road and they passed beneath a tall pole with a tattered United States flag fluttering at the top, weather-worn with no one to care for it in weeks.

"How you doing, Mom?" Sarah asked, walking Stormy up beside her. "Your chest okay?"

Alice had been massaging her chest and winced as she pressed gingerly on it. "Not bad. It's still uncomfortable to ride, but it's getting better. This bruising, though...." She started to lift her camisole but drew her hand away. "It looks like a grape, but the edges are turning greenish."

"Greenish?" Jake made a disgusted sound. "Isn't that bad?"

"That means it's healing." Alice took a deep breath, the sharp pain stabbing her left side, forcing her to exhale with a wince. "See, not so bad."

"Are you kidding, Mom?" Sarah shook her head. "You need a doctor."

"Preaching to the choir, kiddo. I'd ride straight to the next hospital if we knew where that was."

"Yeah, I guess you're right."

Jake rode up beside her as they moved across a long stretch of rich green grass that came to the horses' knees with a brown wooden fence on the left and the highway on their right. "Where are we, anyway?"

"Somewhere in Tennessee." Alice shook her head. "At least, I think so. I saw signs for Hohenwald."

"How many miles to Hohenwald?" Jake asked.

"A lot. Let's keep riding." Almost as soon as she finished the sentence, Alice nodded ahead. "Hey, check it out. Is that a truck stop?"

"We can cut through that field to get around it," Sara replied.

"I'm thinking we might want to check it out."

"Are you sure? I thought you said we should stay away from people."

"We need supplies, though. We found enough for a couple days, but we're going to need a lot more than that."

"How should we approach this?" Jake eyed the store suspiciously.

"You guys stay back, spread out and keep an eye out for trouble. I'll ride up, check inside, and call you if the coast is clear. Any signs of trouble, shout your head off and we'll ride right on through. Got it?"

The kids nodded and started moving away from Alice while she nudged Buck in the flanks and trotted him toward the truck stop. It was a small, family-owned business with the remains of three semis in the lot along with a couple of vehicles out near what used to be the fuel stations. The store was small and squat with a big sign in the front window that read, "*Free Wi-Fi and showers with the purchase of a fill 'er up.*"

As Alice crossed the gravel parking lot, the kids stayed at the edge near the road, keeping a fair distance away from each other as they looked around for any signs of trouble. She walked Buck along the storefront and tried to see inside through the window's glare, but there were no signs of life or even any damage to the building. Alice swung her leg over the saddle, dismounted, and tied Buck to a concrete post. Hands pressed to the glass, she peered in, jaw dropping at the neatly spaced rows of goods and coolers that were untouched, looking as though someone had restocked them overnight before any customer had gotten a chance to come in.

Alice turned to the kids and waved them over.

"What's up?" Sarah arrived first, dismounting from Stormy and tying him beside Buck.

"This place looks pristine." Alice turned to look at the road, its view obscured by the destroyed fuel pumps and semis sitting out front. "If anyone's gone by, I bet they assumed the whole store went up and never bothered to check."

"No way," Jake said, coming over and mirroring her position at the window, surveying all the stocked shelves. "That's a first."

"Yeah." Alice grabbed the door handles and pulled, but they were locked tight. "I'll need a brick or something."

"I'll find something," Jake said.

"How did this place survive?" Sarah scratched her head as she walked along the window.

"You got me. It's a remote highway, so maybe it just got overlooked." Alice gestured toward the back. "The rigs out were probably parked too far away to cause any damage when they exploded."

"Lucky us."

Jake returned with a small, white pebble and grinned. "Stand back."

"Is that—" Alice turned, covering her and Sarah's eyes while Jake wound up and hurled the small piece of ceramic at the window, instantly turning the entire door into a spiderweb of cracks. One kick sent the shards flying, leaving a wide opening for them to pass through.

"Nice work. Wait out here a second; let me do a quick check and make sure we're alone."

Alice stepped inside, crunching on pieces of glass and listening for movement from the back of the store where it was too dark to see. She took out her flashlight, flipped it on, and walked down the main aisle, blinking at the array of food on the shelves. Beef jerky, salted cashews, and every type of gas station food anyone could want were in full supply. Toward the back was a fountain drink island and a rack of hot dogs, which strangely had accumulated no mold, but were merely shriveled and extra greasy looking.

Alice turned away with a shudder and moved to the counter where she leaned over and shined her light across a wall packed with cigarettes, a glass case of lottery scratch-offs, and the usual cash registers. In the back was a storeroom with an office, an old metal desk, and a computer with scattered papers on top. Alice turned a full circle, sighed, and left the room to head out front, waving for the kids to step in.

"Take all the water you can carry, and any nonperishable snacks. Peanuts, jerky, and anything in cans. Even the canned meat."

"This is dragon-lair level of treasure," Jake said, swinging his ratty backpack off his shoulder and moving straight to the canned food aisle while Sarah stepped in front of Alice with her fox backpack in hand.

"I'll have to ditch some of these clothes."

"That's fine. Food is more important right now. Just make sure you have at least one change of clothes." Alice shuffled to the door, favoring her left side where the aches and pains remained. "I'll grab my duffel bag off Buck, and you can fill that up, too."

She stepped out for the duffel bag and picked up some new plastic bags from behind the front counter, had another glance around, and returned to hand them all to Sarah except for two small plastic bags. Back at the front counter, Alice loaded up on batteries, double-bagging them and tying them shut before drifting to the other side of the store which served as a sandwich-making shop. She circled and checked the freezers and refrigerator, slamming the doors shut when the smell of rotten food wafted out.

Moving behind the counter, she stooped and searched the shelves, rifling through receipts and paperwork, locating a cardboard box labeled *Lost and Found* filled with old jackets, hats, and an empty wallet. She knocked over a pair of plastic cups and made a disgusted sound when her fingers slipped into an ashtray with old cigarette butts. Wiping her hands on a rag, she continued her search, grinning when her palm ran along a long, cylindrical metal object and she pulled out a pump-action shotgun, the barrel black and tarnished and the old wooden stock worn with a small crack running along the inside.

"Holy cow." She kept feeling around the shelf and came across an old shoebox with twelve shotgun shells. "Bingo!"

"What is it?" Sarah asked, coming over.

Alice stood, put her bags of batteries on the counter and held up the shotgun with two hands. She checked the magazine tube and pump-action slide, frowning when it seemed stuck at first until she jerked it and finally pushed it forward with the familiar *clack*.

"Whoa, great score, Mom. Think it'll work?"

"It's a little dirty and doesn't look like it's been maintained in forever, but it cycles okay. Should be fine. How are you guys making out?"

Sarah threw a thumb toward the front entrance. "We got tons of stuff."

"We'll be eating like kings!" Jake called from somewhere on the other side of the store.

"Take it outside and tie it to the saddles. Make it so it won't get in the way of our riding."

Alice checked around again, gathered up what she'd found, and walked outside, where Jake and Sarah were each holding a bottle of water and a stick of beef jerky. Sarah threw Alice a stick of jerky as well, which she stuck into her mouth before securing the bag of batteries alongside a duffel bag, anchored behind where her leg would be.

"I wish we still had Hercules." Sarah patted one of the bags tied to her saddle. "That big guy would have come in handy right about now."

Jake talked around his chewing. "Could've loaded the whole store on his back."

"Wilford'll be disappointed when we tell him what happened," Sarah added, tossing her jerky wrapper into a trashcan before dusting her hands off.

"I think, like me, he'll be happy we stayed alive through all that mess." Alice gestured to the horses. "Okay, let's mount up and ride."

Alice led them to the highway with the stuffed duffel and plastic bags bumping and clattering against the horses' sides, bulging with what they'd found, Alice riding with the shotgun loaded and resting across her knees. The day was clear as flocks of birds flew through the sky, banking in every direction while scores of turkey vultures circled as far as they could see, still feasting on the death – both old and recent.

Sarah suddenly pointed up ahead. "Train tracks, Mom."

Alice squinted. "Yep, and running parallel to the highway. Let's cross this bridge and move to the right-hand shoulder."

The train tracks merged with the road on the left-hand side, and Alice kept the horses over to the right, walking in a wide grassy field clear of debris and rubble, sections of marshy puddles covered in algae with insects dive-bombing them from every direction.

"Ugh, *horseflies*!" Sarah kicked Stormy ahead and splashed through the water, making frustrated sounds as she waved her hand around her head.

Jake and Alice shared a roll of their eyes and a laugh, then pushed forward to catch up. Soon, they were riding along the winding road with the train tracks stretching alongside them throughout the Tennessee hills. Alice found a pack of breath mints and ate one at a time, following it with a swig of water, sucking in air, and sighing. She'd only planned on eating a couple but had devoured most of the pack before stuffing it back in her pocket.

Jake nudged her in the side as he came up next to her. "Wow, Mom. That's a lot of breath mints you just ate."

"Hey, don't judge me. I haven't brushed my teeth in days. It's nice to have a minty fresh mouth again. Though I guess it would have been smart to look for toothbrushes there."

"I did." Jake ran his tongue over his teeth. "Feels like I've got an inch of slime on mine."

Sarah stared at Alice's pocket, reached out, and guided Stormy closer. "Can I have some, too?"

"Of course, dear." Alice handed her the rest of the pack. "Keep them. I've got more."

"Thanks," Sarah tossed back a mint and Alice handed one to Jake before he could ask, both of them nodding in thanks.

The deep, throaty vibrations of train wheels ground across the tracks sometime later that afternoon, and a half hour later the locomotive appeared, sleek and black with boxcars and flatbeds stretching as far as the trio could see behind them.

"Time to vamoose," Alice said. "Let's get off the road and out of sight."

"Why?" Jake asked. "It's not like anyone will jump off and chase us."

"You sure about that? I'm not, and we're not taking that chance." Alice started to guide Buck into the woods, intent on waiting until the train passed to resume their journey.

Sarah took her arm and pointed back. "Hold on a second, Mom. It looks like there are troops on the train."

Alice turned Buck, putting her hand to her forehead to shield her eyes from the bright daylight, squinting to make out a half-dozen figures with rifles and military fatigues standing on the boxcars, swaying gently back and forth in time with the motion of the train. Interspersed between the boxcars were flat trailers filled with supplies, crates, boxes and massive containers, all secured with rope and steel bindings. More troops rode on the flat cars, sitting on the cargo or loitering around the edges, leaning against support posts with their rifles shouldered, a few smoking cigarettes and talking as they rolled along.

"Do you think we should talk to them?" Sarah asked.

"I'm not sure...." Alice mused as the train approached, the big locomotive moving past and following with more boxcars and supply flatbeds. "C'mon, let's keep pace with them for a minute."

A couple military personnel on a boxcar roof stepped to the edge and waved, a woman calling out, "Afternoon, folks! You all okay?"

Alice turned back to the train with a half wave. "We're fine! Where are you coming from?"

"New Orleans. Before that, Houston."

"Where you headed?"

"Indiana."

"Gotcha." Alice walked Buck alongside the slow-moving train with Jake and Sarah trailing behind.

"We're on our way to Clarksville," the second guardsman added, "but we're stopping in Hohenwald. Need a ride?"

"Well, we hadn't planned on getting one, but it's mighty tempting."

The guardswoman pointed ahead, to the front of the train. "If you want a ride, meet us in town. We'll be around for the next day or so to exchange supplies. I'm Sergeant Smith. He's Private Dixon."

Alice smiled haltingly, the tension in her chest loosening. "We appreciate the offer, but we can't leave our horses behind."

"Don't worry, ma'am. We've got a few cars with horses and plenty of room left. We'll even load them for you."

Alice nodded as she thought about it. "Okay, that might work. I'm Alice, and these are my kids, Sarah and Jake."

"Nice to meet you folks. So, you think you'll be joining us? I can let the Captain know."

The road began to diverge from the railroad tracks, and the path next to the rails was too rough for the horses, so Alice shouted in response. "We'll catch up to you in town."

"Great!" Smith waved. "We'll watch for you."

"Thank you!" Alice called as the train rolled out of range and more cars trundled by, every guardsman on board nodding or smiling amicably as they passed.

"I've got a good feeling about them," Jake said.

"Me, too," Sarah added.

"Okay, kids," Alice nodded in hesitant agreement. "Looks like we may be getting home a little faster than we thought."

"Do you think they'll be able to get us all the way home?" Sarah asked.

"They said they were heading to Indiana," Alice replied, "and that's a lot closer than we are now. We'll see."

They ran the horses at a medium pace for a few minutes, banking off into the grass and trying to keep up with the train. Eventually, Alice drew Buck to a slow trot as the last car rolled out of sight around the next bend. Above the trees rose a scattering of tall buildings, name-brand hotels, restaurant signs, and cranes towering over the train yard.

"There's the town, Mom!" Sarah said, picking up the pace and trotting Stormy out ahead.

"I see. Come on!"

They galloped to the south edge of town where the train tracks swept off to the right, forcing them to take side roads and alleys that angled to the northeast. A warehouse district grew around them, wide supply buildings interspersed with vast parking lots scattered everywhere.

"We'll have to cut through this mess," Alice said as she nudged Buck into the thick of the warehouses, weaving between the wreckage of semis and trailers alike. "The train station is up ahead."

They caught the train as it was slowing, galloping past the last car as National Guard members jogged across the roofs toward the front and climbed down ladders on the sides. Alice waved the kids on faster with growing excitement only to hold up a hand and pull Buck to a sudden, panicked stop as the first firecracker pops of small arms fire reached them from just ahead.

CHAPTER THREE

James Burton
Shipshewana, Indiana

James tossed a wrench in the toolbox with a clatter and wiped the grease off his hands - doing more to spread it around than actually clean it off - then picked up a bundle of cables, an alternator and two hoses and carried them to a nearby cart where he placed them with the other stripped parts. The air was dry and dusty in the motor pool, a soft wind blowing through and tussling his longish hair, which was starting to droop into his eyes on account of not being cut in weeks. His fingers were sore from digging around in Humvee engines the past twenty-four hours, he was energized and encouraged by doing the work and keeping his mind occupied. Taking the cart by its handle, James pushed it over the cracked pavement and turned it into the rear bay where Diaz and Peterson were hammering away at a pair of Humvees they about had ready to roll out.

James parked the cart next to two others, grabbed an alternator from the bunch, and carried it over to Diaz. "Here you go, Diaz."

"You don't have to bring me the parts, man. I can get them myself."

James grinned and winked. "I'm trying to give you a chance to catch up with me. I'm on my third repair today. Where are you?"

Diaz made a disgusted face. "Just finishing my first, but none of the parts I tried worked."

"Ah, excuses," James said with a shrug. "Glad I don't need any."

Diaz shot him a sideways grin and threw a dirty rag at him, James ducking as it flew over his head.

"How you were ever accepted into the Guard with an aim like that, I'll never understand."

She chuckled and got back to work, leaning beneath the hood and finishing her repairs with a twist of a wrench. In the time James had been with them, they'd pushed out a dozen trucks, cleaned up the shop, and lined up another six vehicles to work on. The maintenance bay smelled of grease, fuel, antifreeze, and oil, with the stale odor of old trucks being put back in service. James moved quickly and efficiently, ensuring his repairs were clean and correct, falling into a steady rhythm and delivering engines that hummed. Every one he fixed started the first time, while Diaz and Peterson had their share of lingering hiccups and false starts, forcing them to either consult him for advice or recheck their work to find the faults.

"You're doing a great job, James." Sergeant Peterson stepped over, nodding in admiration. "I'd love to keep you around, and we could use the help. We've got years' worth of work ahead of us."

"That you do. I, on the other hand, cannot *wait* to get out of here. I'm hoping that'll be today." James glanced at the front of the shop where the bay doors stood wide open, letting in the sunlight and dust from outside. They had a stack of new tires at the entrance of bay one and a huge fuel tank that had been delivered earlier in the morning, fresh from a refinery at an undisclosed location. "Don't get me wrong. If I had my choice of a place to work during this disaster, it would be here. You run a great shop."

"Appreciate that." Peterson gave James a friendly slap on the back. "Think you can get a few more of these puppies out the door before Hawkins steals you away from us?"

"I think we can manage that."

The rest of the afternoon flew by, with James getting four more vehicles out the door, Diaz assisting him with changing the tires and fueling them up before parking them in the side lot. An hour before dinner, Corporal Church pulled up in the golf cart with Colonel Hawkins in the passenger seat, stopping outside bay door one.

"Be right back, Peterson," James said, jogging over and shaking each man's hand. "Hey, Church. Colonel Hawkins. Good to see you both again."

Hawkins turned a full circle, glancing into the side lot. "You folks do all that just today?"

"Yep," James nodded. "We've been busting them out."

Hawkins whistled low. "We're sure going to miss you."

"Peterson and Diaz can hold their own."

"I don't doubt that, but you've really bolstered production."

"Happy to do it. Now, uh... about what we had talked about...."

"James," Hawkins said with a wink. "I'm sorry to say that we've had a bit of an escape from the corral last night."

"You don't say?"

"It happens now and again. A primo horse ran away into the night."

James smirked. "That's just awful."

"Yeah, she had full tack and a saddle on her, too."

James winced. "Oh, that's got to sting. I hope someone finds her who can take care of her."

"Oh, I'm sure someone will. Funny thing, though... not only did that horse have tack and saddle, but it seems to have had a full stash of supplies."

"Horses stealing supplies? This world really *is* changing."

"Indeed. Oh, and there's one other thing."

James glanced back at the Humvees. "Dare I ask?"

"This is something you'll want to know about. We got a radio message a few hours back regarding one Alice Burton. I assume that's—"

The flesh on James' neck and arms crawled, hairs standing upright at the sound of his wife's name. "My wife. You heard about her?! How? *When?* Where is she?"

Hawkins took James by the arm, gestured to the stacks of tires. "Have a seat. You look like you're about ready to fall over."

Waves of dizziness passed over James, and he allowed himself to be guided over to the tires where he sat down. "I... thanks, Colonel. But what about my wife? What's wrong?"

"First thing's first," Hawkins said, glancing over at Church who stood near James, ready to catch him in case he passed out. "Alice is okay."

"What about Sarah and Jake? The—"

"Yes, they're okay, too. I don't have a lot of details, but they were picked up in Tennessee by the Oklahoma National Guard. The train they're on now will pass through Louisville and then hit Connersville, Indiana in about a day."

James' arms and neck prickled again. "That's... not far from here."

"Not at all. Hundred and fifty miles or so."

"That's only a few days of hard riding." James started to get up, but Church took his arm and gently pushed him back down. "Colonel, I'd like to leave as soon as possible."

"Just hang on a second, James." Hawkins lowered his voice and leaned in. "Under normal circumstances I wouldn't do any of this, but you've been such a huge asset, and you've put this outpost so far ahead of the curve on getting those old decommissions fixed up... well, I pulled a couple strings.

"There's a convoy arriving tonight that'll be pulling horse trailers. They'll pick up our horses from here at the outpost and head south, passing ten miles from the Connersville station where that train will be." Hawkins winked at James. "I hear that primo horse is a slippery girl, and she might just so happen to slip aboard one of the trailers and slip off again in Connersville with you."

The tension in James' shoulders melted away, replaced by warmth and relaxation that filled his very soul. "That's... you're... way too gracious. Thank you. I can't really believe any of this, to be honest."

"Believe it, James." Hawkins clapped him on the shoulder. "It's all arranged. I've got all the paperwork done... well, I guess you could say I *lost* some of it."

James chuckled, holding out a hand and clenching Hawkins' hand firmly. "I'm eternally grateful to you, sir. Thank you."

"I'm the grateful one. You've been an enormous asset and I'll be sad to see you go. Even if I gave you a handful of horses and supplies, it still wouldn't be enough to compensate for what you've done."

"When does all this get underway?"

"The convoy will arrive in a few hours, so you should get cleaned up, grab some chow, and pick up your supplies. Tell Corporal Church what you need – whatever you can carry, you can have."

"Thank you, I will."

"We'll radio to the train and tell them you'll meet them at Connersville before they hook east, and to make sure your wife and kids get off the train safely there."

Hawkins stood and James got to his feet, following him to the golf cart with a spring in his step, the Colonel swinging into the passenger seat with Church hopping in next to him.

"I'll send Church back for you in a while. Wrap up here, give the wrenches some motivation to keep going and then we'll get you ready to go."

"I'll be here. Thank you. See you soon, Church."

The golf cart turned and sped away in a high, electrical whine, Church flying down the road to the barracks. James stood and stared into the distance, basking in the warmth of the slowly receding sun, closing his eyes against a soft breeze that cooled the sweat of anticipation on his brow and neck. Butterflies tickled his stomach at the thought of actually seeing Alice and the kids again, though he dared not get his hopes too high, lest they be dashed by some unforeseen circumstance. *I'll see you soon*, he thought, heading back to the garage with a smile.

"I knew it," Diaz said with an exaggerated roll of her eyes. "He's leaving us, Sarge."

"That true, James?" Peterson asked, coming over with a grease-covered socket wrench in hand. "You leaving us already?"

"Yeah." James couldn't contain a grin. "Hawkins said I'm too good for you and he's shipping me out." The pair glanced at each other, confused, before James laughed. "No, I'm joking. You two have been great. Just keep things simple, y'know? Slow is smooth and smooth is fast."

Diaz smirked and leaned on a nearby hood. "Don't lie, James," she said in heavily accented English. "You're just afraid we're going to take all the credit for your work here."

"Hey, Hawkins gave me his personal number – you start pulling that, and I'm going to have a little chat with him." A dirty rag shot out of nowhere a few seconds later, forcing James to duck.

For the next forty-five minutes he helped tie up a few loose ends, putting an alternator and hoses into the next Humvee in line alongside Diaz and Peterson before Church pulled up in the golf cart with Oswell in the passenger seat.

"Well, guys. I guess this is it." James held his hand out to Peterson.

The tall, muscular mechanic gripped his hand, almost crushing it with his strength, pulling James' arm back and forth in an exaggerated shake. "Good luck, James. All the best to you and your family. We'll miss you."

"Yeah, good luck, man," Diaz said, coming over and embracing him ruefully with her grease-smudged arms, backing up with a reluctant grin. "If you ever need a job, head directly here. I'm sure we can find a place for you somewhere."

"I will. Good luck to you both. Stay safe, and good luck getting all these...." James turned and gestured out the rear bay door where an endless supply of partially decommissioned Humvees awaited upgrades.

"Thanks." Peterson clapped him on the back. "Safe travels, man."

James hustled over to where Church and Oswell waited for him, climbing in the rear seat, the added weight causing the electric motor to whine high as they pulled off.

"Thanks, Church. What are you doing here, Oswell?"

"Church swung by and picked me up." Oswell's eyes were glassy. "Hawkins figured I might want to say goodbye. Not that I do, of course."

"Oh yes, of course." James smiled, clinging to the seat as Church banked left and joined the main road back to the barracks, rocking them around as he whipped the wheel. "Yeah, it looks like I'm out of here."

Oswell nodded and faced forward. "Well, I'll miss the heck out of you."

"Yeah, me too."

"You know, for a civilian," Oswell gave a lighthearted chuckle, "you're not half bad. Thanks for having my back through all that BS. If the motor pool didn't want your butt all to themselves, I'd be asking you to sign up to help us grunts."

"I appreciate it, but..."

"Yeah, yeah. Something about your family." Oswell gave him a light punch in the shoulder. "I hope they realize how lucky they are."

"Not as lucky as I am." James smiled, looking off into the distance.

"Do you want to get cleaned up first?" Church asked. "Or grab some grub?"

"Shower first. It's going to be my last hot shower and good meal for a while, so I want to make it count. You eating dinner, Oswell?"

She glanced back, dark hair blowing across her cheeks, the weariness in her eyes having lessened after a good night of rest. "Darn right I am. It's our last meal together, and I don't want it to be beef jerky, cashews, and licorice sticks."

"Blugh. I'm good never eating that again," James said, pointing ahead. "Church, take me to the showers first if you would and I'll get cleaned up. Then we'll eat some real food."

"Yes, sir."

James scrubbed enthusiastically, trying to make his last hot shower last as long as possible. He'd borrowed a shaver after he was done and attacked his beard, cutting off big clumps and shaving it down to the skin, leaving his face clean, smooth, and a little itchy. Drying off in front of the mirror, pushing back his wet hair, James sighed and tried to dispel the haunted look that had stuck with him since Chicago. Only Alice and the kids could remedy his aching soul; to hear their voices and hold them tight was all he wanted. James leaned over the sink, splashed more cold water on his face, and dried it again, tossing the towel in a bin as he exited.

He met Oswell and Church outside and they drove up to the mess hall where they ate a few slices of pizza with an assortment of ingredients thrown on top of cheap dough. It wasn't much to look at but tasted divine and he ate his fill, fueling up for the final push. James and Oswell talked about their journey through the outskirts of Chicago, accompanied by a growing crowd of listeners, sharing theories on what had happened to the gangs and how messy it would be putting the world back together again.

"There's probably one gang in charge of the whole city by now," Oswell surmised.

"Bah, I don't know," James countered. "There are probably a lot of smaller factions establishing themselves, and none of them will go down without a fight." He shook his head in disgust. "Everyone's taking advantage of the catastrophe to carve out a piece of the aftermath for themselves."

"Not for long," Oswell said. "Leaders like Colonel Hawkins will knock things straight again."

"I sure hope so."

After eating, James, Church and Oswell found a table outside and had coffee by themselves, watching the sun go down, filling the horizon with pink and orange hues that saturated the treetops.

"It's so beautiful," Oswell leaned back against the table.

"Yeah, it is," James replied. "And it'll be even more beautiful when I watch it with Alice and the kids. No offense to you two."

"No offense taken," Church chuckled.

The trio sat in comfortable silence, sipping their coffee and watching the sunset, James constantly checking the road for the convoy that would take him to his loved ones.

CHAPTER FOUR

Alice Burton
Somewhere in Tennessee...

Alice drew Buck short and turned him in a full circle, scanning the area with a grim expression.

"Where are the shots coming from?" Sarah asked as she and Jake kept their horses next to Buck, staring across the warehouse park where huge liquid tanks sat up off to the left and adjacent warehouses filled the spaces in between.

"Up ahead. You kids stay here, and I'll ride forward to check it out." Alice hefted the shotgun in her right hand and guided Buck ahead with her left, giving him a nudge in the sides to get him moving.

"No way!" Jake rode after her. "We're not separating again."

"It's a bad idea to split up right now, Mom." Sarah pulled up on the other side of Alice, agreeing with Jake.

Alice slowed Buck. "Maybe we should skip the train altogether."

"Mom," Jake said, rising in his stirrups and trying to see farther ahead. "That's the National freaking Guard on the train. They can handle it. I mean, if we go off by ourselves, who knows what trouble we'll run into. Shouldn't we be staying with the good guys and try to help them?"

"Maybe..." Alice spoke slowly before finally nodding. "We can check it out, but you two stay behind me and keep your eyes open for trouble. Understand?"

Head down, leaning forward and ignoring her chest pain, Alice urged Buck on, trotting fast along the paved street, scanning ahead where the road angled toward the track's converging point where more tall cylinders stood connected by miles of catwalks and ductwork. The head of the train had nosed into a dark area with a series of loading platforms and stacked nearby were pallets of steel beams, piping, bricks, and other building materials. Thirty-thousand-gallon tanks sat poised atop concrete staging areas and cranes loomed tall on the north side of the loading yard, one holding a basket of equipment and supplies forty feet high, another sitting crooked with the winch hanging off the side.

Scattered among all of the industrial twists and turns were a dozen or more attackers clothed in jeans, dark jackets and balaclavas, all of them wielding rifles and pistols. They exchanged gunfire with the troops who'd fallen on their bellies on the boxcar roofs or dropped down inside the train cars. One guardsman tried to jump from one car to the next, landed, staggered, and was hit by a round and sent pitching over the side. More guard members rushed from the rear of the train, hopping off flatbeds to flank their attackers but the enemy was firing from a higher vantage point and had a great deal of cover, enabling them to slowly pick off troops, moving in teams of three and four as they edged closer to the locomotive.

Heart hammering in her chest, Alice crept around a large stack of logs atop Buck only to encounter four attackers squatting behind a pallet of bricks. As they turned toward her, their surprise evident on their faces, she raised her shotgun on pure instinct and fired at them. The buckshot had a devastating effect, shredding one of the men and injuring the other three, preventing them from immediately returning fire. Before the others even realized their comrade was dead, Alice charged her gun with a clack and fired again, the buckshot catching two more men square in the faces, throwing one against a skid and the other to the ground. The last one was holding the back of his neck, stung from stray shot, and he spun with a cry, firing wildly at Alice. She already had another shell loaded, though, and fired as she urged Buck to move, the weapon's stock punching her shoulder and knocking her backwards. She held on as the man dropped to the ground with a wet slap, pulled Buck up short, spun him in a circle, and charged the shotgun again.

With Alice's multiple shots coming from behind the main group of attackers, panic set in and they scattered, scrambling into the open and making themselves prime targets for the guardsmen. Rounds peppered the ground, striking arms and legs, cutting them down and spraying blood across the gravel. A few dropped their weapons and fled north, chased by bullets that nipped at their heels, screams and curses filling the air, though one tried to regroup them, holding his position and waving his people back. A few stopped, scrambled behind cover, and opened fire again. The leader shouted and pointed at Alice, swinging his rifle up to take a shot, but a guardsman put a round through his temple, face flashing with bewilderment as the bullet exited the other side of his head, taking pieces of skull and brains with it.

Sarah and Jake were closing in on the gunfire when Alice raced back, glancing over her shoulder to ensure she wasn't being chased, slowing only once they were all safely away from the fight.

"Geez, Mom," Sarah said. "What were you doing out there?"

"I didn't mean to." Alice spoke breathlessly, winded from the ride, adrenaline and her stinging shoulder. "I just came up on them so fast it was either them or me." She turned Buck back toward the train again, looking down at the shotgun in her hands before stowing it in one of the bags on the horse. "Jake, put the knife away."

Guardsmen were coming off the boxcars, filtering in from the rear cars and spreading out to capture surrendering attackers. After disarming them, they shoved them to the ground or sat them on skids, binding their hands behind their backs. Bodies were rolled over, pockets checked, and weapons confiscated, collected by a pair of guardsmen who ferried them back to one of the train cars.

A tall woman with brown hair spilling from her National Guard cap shouted orders as she moved around the industrial yard, and when she caught sight of Alice and the kids loitering on their horses nearby, she grabbed two guard members and marched over, her two companions keeping their rifles at the ready as they stared down Alice, Jake and Sarah.

The woman spoke roughly as she gave the trio a once-over. "I take it you're not with these jokers?"

"Not at all," Alice replied.

"So, you just stumbled into the fight?"

"Sort of... I spoke with Sergeant Smith and Private Dixon a short way back. They said to meet them here at the station if we wanted a ride, so we were just following up."

"So it was you who ambushed these assholes from behind, eh?"

"Accidentally. I was trying to see what was going on, surprised a few of them and did what I had to do."

"Great timing." She stepped closer, stroking Buck's head before giving Alice an affirmative nod. "I'm Captain Hechler, the one responsible for this train. I appreciate your help back there; pretty sure you're the reason why they broke down so fast."

"I'm Alice. Happy to help the good guys. Any idea who they were?"

Hechler shrugged. "Doesn't really matter. There's been plenty of idiots trying to raid the trains. These're just more of the same."

"Does the offer still stand for us to come aboard? We'd appreciate the lift, but only if it wouldn't be an imposition."

"Of course. Where are you heading?"

"North, as far as you can take us. We're trying to get home to Michigan, outside Lansing."

"Michigan? No, we're not going that far, but we can get you close."

"That's fantastic." Alice smiling at Jake and Sarah. "What'll it cost us?"

"Nothing at all," Hechler replied. "Follow me. I'll grab the Staff Sergeant and he'll get you folks situated."

Alice gestured for the kids to dismount and they walked the horses through the former field of battle toward the train. Blood soaked the loading area gravel and dripped from metal girders and piping, the guard members grabbing splayed bodies and piling them in a row while others marched prisoners toward one of the cars that was outfitted with barred windows. Two guardsmen walked alongside them, snatching off their balaclavas to reveal middle-aged men and women with a few young ones mixed in, wearing grizzled, shellshocked expressions as they stared at their fallen comrades.

Alice and the kids followed Hechler where she'd reached the train and Smith and Dixon were climbing off a boxcar, grins spreading when they saw the trio.

"We wondered who was shooting," Smith said. "Someone said they were on horseback, and I instantly thought of you."

"Yep, it was this little lady right here," Hechler replied. "She was on point with a shotgun. Took out five or six of them, I think."

"Just four," Alice corrected her with a slight smile. "And I got lucky."

"Ah, sorry. *Only* four. Anyway, Smith, these folks are yours. Get their horses loaded on car seven with the rest of the heavy supplies."

"Yes, ma'am," Smith said, gesturing for Alice and the kids to follow her.

Guardsmen came out of the train and resumed their normal activity, using the yard as a staging area to load and unload materials onto boxcars and stack them on flatbeds. A few of them nodded, smiled, and complimented her on her horses and shooting, and Alice replied in kind, the pain in her body subsiding momentarily as she focused on keeping Jake, Sarah and the horses within sight in the midst of all the hustle and bustle. At the seventh car back, Smith gestured to a pair of guards who'd affixed a ramp to the boxcar and stood aside to allow Alice to guide Buck into the car. Alice left Buck and walked up onto the deck, gaping at another twenty horses loaded into stalls on every wall, flanks pointed toward the middle and hay and manure scattered across the floor.

"Why are you transporting so many horses?"

"Federal orders," she replied with an almost imperceptible wince. "We're keeping any horses we find for the recovery effort."

"Wait a minute." Alice came down the ramp and took Buck's reins. "You want to take *our* horses?"

"Like I said... it's a federal order."

"Sorry, but you *can't* take our horses. They were given to us by a dear friend. We need them to get home to Michigan."

"I understand that ma'am, but—"

"I'm trying to get these kids back to their home and their father. I can't believe you'd keep me from doing that."

Smith waved to Dixon. "Dixon, can you go pull the list?"

"Yeah, I'm on it." Dixon turned and ran off. Replacing him were a pair of guardsmen who stepped over, eying Alice warily.

"Okay, where's Dixon going?" Alice turned her glare on Smith. "What's this list you're talking about?"

"Look, Alice. Everything's fine. And your horses will be returned once the recovery efforts wind down."

Alice turned Buck away, ready to head toward the road. "Which could take months or years."

"Possibly..." Smith agreed. "But I'd bet we'll get them back to you much sooner than that."

"Seriously, Mom?" Sarah's cheeks burned red, and she pulled Stormy a few steps away, mirroring Alice. "They're seriously going to take our horses?"

"They most certainly are not." Alice kept Buck behind her and pressed closer to the Sergeant, forcing her back a few paces. "Was that your plan all along? Did you trick me into bringing our horses here so you could steal them out from under us?"

"Ma'am, look... well... not exactly...."

"And after I saved your asses just now?" Alice snorted derisively. "You'd *still* take my horses?"

"Like I said, Alice. It's a federal order. We're not looking for trouble, but but—"

"You may not have been looking for trouble, but you've definitely found it." She swung under Buck's neck and started to grab her shotgun from her bag. "You'll take our horses over my dead body."

Dixon jogged up as the guards started to reach for their rifles, waving a notepad, shouting, and gesturing. "Hold up a second! Alice... you're Alice *Burton,* right?"

Confused, Alice dropped the shotgun back in the bag and stepped around to the other side. "How did you know my last name? I didn't give it to you."

"I was just checking the *list*, ma'am."

"What list?"

"The *refugee* list." Dixon explained, waving the notepad again and pointing at a single line. "Ma'am, do you know a James Burton?"

Alice's mouth opened and closed in shock for several seconds, trying to form the words but initially unable to do so. "James... that's my husband."

"Dad?" Sarah whispered from behind her.

"And then these two are Jake and Sarah?"

Alice nodded, dumbfounded.

"Thanks for confirming that. Hang tight a second," he said, turning away. "I need to confirm something."

Alice grabbed the Private's arm. "Do you know something about my husband?"

"That's what I'm trying to find out." Dixon glanced at her hand on his arm. "Please, ma'am."

Alice let go and fell against Buck's shoulder, knees weak and head overwhelmed by dizziness. Dixon took a radio off his belt and spoke into it as Sarah stepped over and took her arm.

"What's he talking about with Dad?"

"I don't know, but..." Alice swayed.

Jake gripped her arm. "Mom, are you okay?"

"Yeah, I'm just a little lightheaded."

Jake dropped Rocky's reins. "Come on, Mom. Let's sit you down." The kids walked her to a pallet of bricks and sat her down, the nearby guardsmen gathered around Dixon.

"Mom, what did he say?"

Alice shook her head. "I don't know, he just... I think they heard from your father."

Smith stepped over to her, holding out a bottle of water. "Don't be too surprised, Alice. We've been working doubly hard to reconnect families, so it's possible your name made it on a list somewhere. We're not bad people, I promise you."

Alice sipped the water, moistening her suddenly parched throat. "But we didn't put our names on any lists. How would... I don't understand."

"Well, maybe your husband did. We're trying to get the details, so just hang tight, okay?"

Alice nodded blankly and wrapped her arms around Jake and Sarah, clinging to them as the world spun around her, unable to make sense of the possibilities that were presenting themselves.

"And... Alice," Smith continued, lowering her voice. "I'll do everything I can to make sure your horses are returned to you as quickly as possible. I don't like this any more than you do, believe me."

Alice mumbled some half-hearted response, having momentarily forgotten about everything, her only thoughts focused solely on the fact that her husband, James, might still be alive. The pain they'd suffered through, the miles they'd traveled and the dangers they'd faced all paled in the face of it. To survive through Denver and whatever hells he had faced since then was unimaginable – but then again, so was what she and her own children had withstood.

Sarah stood and faced the guardswoman. "It's not fair. These horses are ours, and you can't take them."

"It's a *federal* order," Smith reiterated, "I'll do what I can, but...."

Alice gently took Sarah's arm and pulled her back, staring down Smith. "This conversation isn't over. You understand me?"

"Yes, ma'am." The guardswoman flinched ever so slightly. "You know where to find me."

"Can we at least get our supplies off them?"

"Yes, of course. Here, I'll help you."

Alice stood, pushing past the guardsmen gathered around. "No thanks. We'll do it ourselves."

While Smith and the other guard members around the car watched, Alice and the kids took their duffel bags, backpacks, and plastic sacks off the horses and set them off to the side. Alice gave Smith a cold look before stepping back to let two guard members lead the horses up into the car, the trio watching in simmering silence as Buck, Stormy, and Rocky climbed up the ramp and were placed on the right-hand side in three empty stalls.

"This is rotten," Jake said.

"I know. Just try to focus on your father being alive."

"If we can believe them." Jake made a disgusted sound, eyes moist as he watched Rocky go in last. "Maybe they're just trying to placate us."

"They'd have to know *something*. They couldn't have guessed our last name."

Sarah was on the verge of tears. "It's not right."

Alice stared at the guardsmen. "Nope. It's not."

Smith approached. "Okay, folks. I think we're ready for you to hop on. We can board you a few cars up. Refugee car."

Alice gave her a begrudging nod, and they picked up their things, slung them on their shoulders, and followed her as she led them to the next ramp where two dozen curious faces looked down at them from the boxcar's dark recesses.

"When are we leaving?" Alice asked.

"In a little while. Get comfortable and settle in." Smith gifted her with a half smile. "It'll be a bumpy ride, but won't take long once we get going." Smith started to head back when Alice called out.

"When will I know more about my husband?"

"Hard to say, ma'am." Smith replied, doing a half turn as she continued walking. "Dixon's still working on it, I'm sure. We'll let you know when we hear something."

Alice nodded and sighed, then gestured for the kids to go on up where they joined a half-filled boxcar full of listless faces, dirty and smudged from travel. Families had taken over parts of the car for their own, sectioned off by suitcases and duffel bags, backpacks, and bales of hay. One father stood outside a makeshift construction, staring at Alice, Sarah and Jake with a dark expression, shaking his head before disappearing behind a set of curtains. Single mothers and fathers, a mix of people still looking for loved ones, milled around the boxcar or sat in small groups. Alice spotted a clear section on the east side of the car and nodded for Sarah and Jake to go there and they put down their things, Sarah forming a barrier between them and the next family of four; a bright-faced little girl with a set of pigtails sticking out from the sides of her head watching them curiously.

As the three settled into their small space on the cramped, BO-laden train car, the established families eventually stopped staring at the newcomers and they were able to get a few minutes of peace to themselves. Placing Sarah's fox backpack beneath her head, Alice tried to lie down and get a few minutes of rest, but her spine ached from the day's ride, and her ribs glowed with a fiery pain that refused to subside. No matter which way she turned, she couldn't get comfortable on the hard floor, and eventually she stood and stepped close to the open door, joining Jake to watch the guardsmen load and offload equipment and supplies. Groups of them used rusted dollies and pushcarts to move crates of emergency supplies off of the boxcars while others brought on a few old, dilapidated Humvees and transport vehicles, strapping them down on flatbeds alongside scores of bales of hay, horse feed and other goods wrapped in plastic.

Jake whistled. "That's enough to supply a small army."

"Mmm" Alice crossed her arms. "How much of that's been taken from people, like the horses?"

"Not that I'm defending them – because I'm not – but is it *really* that different from us taking stuff from the gas station and that house?"

"Were any people there? Did we take more than was necessary, or just enough to get us by until we can get home?"

Jake grunted. "Yeah, I see your point."

"Like, I get them needing to requisition resources. But we did help them and they're taking our horses in return for it." Alice shook her head. "Whatever. At least we have a ride north with protection. That counts for something. Hopefully Smith's honest and will try to find a way to get them to us."

Jake put an arm on Alice's shoulder, giving her a hug. "If they really found Dad, who needs the horses, right?"

"If they reunite us with your father, *that* would be a fair trade. I'll admit that much."

A group of nearby guardsmen outside the train had found a pallet of bricks to sit on with their MREs spread out, frowning at the labels, trading off portions they didn't want and talking amongst themselves. Alice watched them closely, then patted Jake on the arm.

"Hey, I'll be right back." She turned back inside the car and walked to where Sarah was sitting on a bale of hay picking at bits of straw. "Hi, honey. You hanging in there?"

"I wish I had my e-reader." She wrapped her arms around her knees. "I loved that thing."

Alice kneeled by one of their duffel bags and began pulling out bags of chips and some candy bars they'd gotten from the truck stop. "The second we can find one for you, we will."

"Yeah, but it won't have all my favorite books. They were on my old one."

"I'm sorry, honey." Alice stroked her cheek. "Maybe we'll find one on the way home. Or, heck, if the world ever returns to normal again—"

"It'll never be normal again." Sarah's eyes turned glassy. "It'll never be the same."

Alice hugged her. "You're probably right about that, but people will always need entertainment, and there will always be people who want to tell their stories." She rubbed a dirt smudge off her cheek. "You know, I bet you could tell *our* story pretty well. We've been through some crazy stuff."

Sarah was quiet for a few seconds before nodding. "You know... that's not a bad idea." A small smile played at the edges of her mouth as her mood lifted a bit more. "I bet I could start a journal and turn it into a book later. Like, a memoir or something."

"You'd be awesome at it. Just like everything else you do."

"I don't suppose you found a notebook at that gas station, did you?"

"Notebooks weren't high on the priority list, but we'll find something." Alice winked at her. "I have a feeling that a notebook will be easier to come by than an e-reader."

Sarah nodded at the armful of snacks Alice had collected. "What are you doing with all that?"

"Honestly? I feel a little bad about giving Smith so much grief. She didn't give the order to have the horses seized, and neither did the captain. Who knows, maybe we can trade them for a notepad. Plus, we need to tell them about that camp. Want to come with me?"

Sarah stood and beamed. "Sure!"

They walked over to the door and down to mingle with the guardsmen, one man seeing them coming, tapping his buddies on the shoulder and pointing.

"Hey there." Alice held out the bags of chips and candy bars, motioning at their half-eaten MREs. "I've eaten enough of those in my life to know they suck after a while. Can I interest you in something to break up the monotony?"

The group looked around at one another, and the man who'd seen them coming raised an eyebrow. "Where'd you get all that?"

"We got lucky and found a gas station nobody had touched shortly before we ran into your train. We've got plenty; would you like some?"

"Absolutely." The man nodded enthusiastically. "What do you want for them?"

"It's on the house." Alice started placing the food on the table. "A token of thanks for giving us a ride north. And, well, there might be one thing we could use."

"What's that?" The guardsman asked as he tore open a bag of chips.

Alice nudged Sarah, who spoke. "I was looking for a notepad. Or two. If you have any?"

"Notepads?"

"Yeah, just something to write in. Maybe some pens or pencils if you have them. I wanted to start writing down some of the stuff we've been going through, since we've got some downtime on the train."

He nodded, speaking around a mouthful of sour cream and onion chips. "Kid, for this stuff, I'm sure we can track down some notepads, pens and pencils for you. I'll get you some before you leave."

"Thank you so much." Sarah smiled.

"One other thing, guys," Alice continued. "We... we ran into some trouble down south."

"What sort of trouble?"

"A meth lab with kids being basically kept as slaves."

A couple of the guardsmen paused mid-bite, staring blankly at her before one of them finally spoke. "Are... are you serious?"

"As a heart attack. I rescued my kids from a camp they'd set up, and when we got out it looked like some of the kids were escaping – we set half the place on fire – but I was hoping that you could tell someone higher up, and maybe the Guard could go in and try to rescue the kids?"

"Yeah, we definitely want to get that information. Hang on, let me grab one of those notebooks right now and get some information from you.

Fifteen minutes later, after explaining as much as she and Sarah could remember and securing a promise that someone would be alerted immediately about the situation, Alice and Sarah turned back to the train, greeted by Jake who was watching from the door.

"Nice work, mom. That's how you make friends."

"Food always goes a long way." Sarah replied. "I just hope they get to that camp soon."

"An army marches on its stomach." Alice put her arms around them as she and Sarah climbed back into the train car. "And it seemed like they were taking us pretty seriously. C'mon, let's get settled. I don't know when the train will leave, but—"

"Alice! Ms. Burton!" A voice – private Dixon's – interrupted Alice as they were heading back to their corner of the train car, and they turned to watch him dash between the busy troops, holding up a clipboard as he ran.

"What is it?" Alice asked, heart suddenly thudding hard in her chest, spine tickling with pinpricks of anticipation. "Is it about…"

"Yes, ma'am. It's your husband. I've got a message from him— well, not from James himself, but from Colonel Hawkins at a National Guard unit north of here in Shipshewana. He says they've got a James Burton there, and he'll meet you in Connersville, Indiana. In fact, he's being transported there now."

"He's… alive?" The words were a whisper, the world becoming a blur in Alice's vision as she staggered, grabbing for the side of the train car as she lowered herself down into a sitting position, the rest of the car's residents staring as Dixon cleared his throat and lowered his voice.

"Alive and well. He made it to the post a day or so ago."

"Dad?" Jake and Sarah spoke in unison, looking at each other, then Alice, who was staring unrelentingly at the private.

"Swear to me."

"Ma'am?"

Alice reached out, grabbing Dixon's wrist with an iron grip, her words spilling out in a low growl. "Swear to me that you're telling the truth. That this isn't some kind of lie or trick."

Dixon turned the clipboard around with his free hand, showing a handwritten message on an official-looking slip of paper with the National Guard letterhead. "Radio operator delivered it to me, and I'm delivering it to you. I swear, it's no trick."

"You said… Connersville?" Alice squeezed harder. "Where's that? How do I get there?"

Dixon glanced at Jake and Sarah. "Ms. Burton… it's right on our way. We'll be passing through it."

"Mom," Jake touched her hand lightly. "I think you're hurting him."

Her son's touch was electric, and Alice blinked several times, pulling her hand back. "Sorry. Passing through? I— I don't…"

"He's meeting us in Connersville. You'll be reunited." Dixon looked at Sarah. "Is she okay? Do I need to get the medic?"

"No. No, I'm…" Alice gasped, lightheaded from unknowingly holding her breath for a moment. "I'm fine. James is really going to be there? But… but how?"

"Hawkins is sending him as part of a convoy!" Dixon slapped his clipboard and grinned. "We'll meet some of Hawkins' people there, and they'll have James with them."

"Dad. We're… really going to see Dad." Sarah grinned, leaning on her mother.

"What about the horses?" Jake addressed Dixon, looking at Alice. "We'll still need them to get all the way home."

Dixon's grin faded slightly and he lowered his voice further. "I'll… try to talk to Captain Hechler directly and see if we can't let you keep at least one of your horses. You were a big help back there."

Alice straightened, taking a deep breath and patting both Jake and Sarah on the legs as she stood. "We appreciate whatever you can do for us."

Dixon nodded and turned, calling back as he headed through the throng of guardsmen preparing to get back on the train. "I'll let you know if there are any other updates on your husband!"

Alice, Jake and Sarah watched him go, then Sarah spoke quietly. "We're not going to let them keep our horses, are we?"

"No." Alice's response was frank and matter-of-fact, letting a slight smile play across her lips. "But don't worry about that right now. If they think *I'm* a pain to deal with, they haven't met your father. C'mon. Let's get back on board."

CHAPTER FIVE

Red Fletcher
East Lansing, Michigan

Red's crew had wasted no time spreading out across the homestead, spreading out in the house on the top and main floors and throwing up a few tents in the barnyard, camping out near the chicken coops with stoves blazing, eggs mixed with stir-fried vegetables stolen from the pantry. The Grand Rapids crew worked with Jack's group to walk the property at first light, getting an idea of what they had to work with, establishing patrols to guard the outskirts and performing repairs on the house as Red directed. Deep, fearsome barks from the barn had kept them from opening the door, though Red didn't bother to hide his frustration with the delay in exploring the space, stopped from killing the dogs only by Martha's insistence that they give Ryan and Helen a chance to acclimate the animals to the newcomers.

Martha had been the first in the shower in the morning, Red choosing to wait with his feet up on the kitchen table, staring out through the empty hole where a piece of plywood had been, surveying his new domain. A good night's sleep in a soft bed had left him wide awake, alert, enthusiastic – and with a full belly, to boot.

Red grinned as Martha came upstairs from the basement bathroom, rosy-faced and clean, her gray-streaked, wet hair pushed back, a towel around her neck. Nancy Likely had gone next while Jack and Barb sat with him at the table, a map of the local roads spread out in the center along with notepads filled with scribbles of inventory amounts, levels of propane left in the main tank and estimates for how much power they had available as well as the work each person would need to contribute to keep the water flowing.

Their limited power had become evident after Hansen had flipped several breakers on, distributing more power to the house than the batteries could handle, causing a blackout sometime around midnight. Red had responded by berating the man, ordering him to change everything back to how it had been and letting him know in no uncertain terms that they had to consult with Ryan before making such changes.

"We have a lot of work to do," Red arched his back and eased himself out of his chair as Nancy came up the stairs, "but this place is everything we needed and more."

Martha's smile was thin as she avoided Red's gaze. "Just remember we're guests here, Red."

"Oh, I will." Red grabbed a clean towel from a stack in the living room as he headed downstairs. "Just as long as they remember to be hospitable."

Upstairs, Helen finally gave up on trying to get any sleep, sitting upright to find Ryan sitting on the floor by the boarded-up window, peeking through the blinds and cracks in the wood as he kept tabs on the comings and goings of the 'occupiers' as he had begun to call them. Stephen lay in the middle of the bed with Sandy next to him, both of them sleeping, though each of them occasionally twitched or groaned quietly, their sleep anything but peaceful.

"Oh, Ryan." Helen stood next to him, rubbing his shoulder. "Did you get *any* sleep?"

"Not a wink." Ryan continued staring out the window. "I've been listening to them down there, going through everything, eating scads of food and probably drinking all the milk we've been saving up. The supplies won't last long at this rate and then they'll be starving all over again. *Dumbasses.*"

Helen huffed. "Well, I'm going down for coffee."

"Helen, don't—"

"No. It's still our house, and there's coffee enough for everyone." She got up, changed from her pajamas into jeans, a pink camisole, and slippers, and swung open the door to find Nancy sitting on a folding chair in the hall, a shotgun leaning up against the wall next to her.

"Get back inside." Nancy pointed at the room behind Helen.

"I'm getting us some coffee."

"Nope. Red said—"

"Last I checked, this is my daughter's house, we're the hosts and you're all *guests* here. Are you saying I'm a prisoner now?"

Nancy smirked. "No, I guess not. Go ahead."

Helen pushed past her and headed for the stairs and Ryan sat for a long moment with the door open, listening to Helen's footsteps on the steps as he watched people walking around on the edge of the property. Before Nancy could get up and shut the door, he got up and moved by her with a scowl, heading for the stairs and going down. At the bottom, he peeked into the living room where Reynolds was lounging on the couch, soft classic rock music coming from the speakers connected to the entertainment system.

Oh yes, just use more power, why don't you. Dumbasses. Ryan rolled his eyes as he came down the stairs, pausing on the landing as Helen's voice grew louder before she was cut off.

"I'll talk to Nancy," Red said. "But I want you all staying upstairs, out of my way."

"It's just coffee, Red." Martha gave him a soft smile and gripped his arm. "Let her get some, would you?"

Jack raised a finger. "If you're making coffee, bring me a cup, too."

Helen turned on Jack, tension rising in her voice, looking between him and Red. "No. I *won't* be a slave in my daughter's home, or a prisoner. This is still *our* place and I won't stand for you treating us like that."

Ryan eased down the stairs, catching a glimpse of Helen's clenched fists shaking ever so slightly at her sides, Red staring at her in amusement before chuckling and patting Martha on the back. "Well, I'll be damned. Helen, you've got some spunk. I like that." He turned and pointed at Jack. "Get your own coffee, and tell Nancy to back off with the tough guy routine. Helen, go ahead and get that coffee. Ryan, come sit with me?"

Helen walked past Red, giving Martha the faintest nod of thanks before heading into the kitchen.

"Come on, Ryan." Red gestured at the table. "I'd like you to sit here and be my advisor. Maybe we can work past all this nonsense, eh?"

Ryan ground his teeth and took a deep breath, resisting the urge to roll his eyes again before nodding and taking a seat across from the Willoughbys, who were finishing up breakfast.

"Thanks for letting us stay here," Barb spoke around mouthfuls of food. "It's charming, and the food's great, isn't it, Jack?"

"Damn good." Jack rested one arm on the table as he picked at his teeth with a toothpick. "Very hospitable of you to let us use the place, Ryan. I knew we could work things out if you had the right motivation. Glad Red came along to help you see the light."

Ryan said nothing, instead staring through the open window out into the yard, tracking the patrol from earlier who had reached the gate and was standing near it. Martha came from the kitchen with Helen behind her, fresh cups of coffee in each hand, both women sitting and sliding the mugs to their husbands. Martha took a seat between Jack and Red, closing her eyes and slouching wearily when Jack belched loudly.

Ryan flexed his jaw again, then stirred sugar and creamer into his coffee, taking a sip, trying to block out the noise of Red and his crew as they passed through the house, bringing mud and grass with them, asking for schedules and things to do. Red divvied up the general chores - who should be collecting the eggs, feeding the animals and preparing meals each day – before the subject shifted to the subject of Bessie when two men came in, asking when she should be slaughtered.

"Are you two really as stupid as you sound?" Helen glared at the men. "She's producing buckets of milk and you want to turn her into burgers?"

Red shook his head in disappointment at the two men who'd asked. "The lady of the house is right. The last thing we want to do is slaughter that cow if they've got her producing milk. Baking, cooking, coffee... that milk's worth its weight in gold. Now..." Red shifted forward. "The question is, which of you is going to milk her?"

The pair shared a confused look, and one replied, "Well, we don't know how to milk a cow, Red."

"Then why're you proposing we butcher her?" He held up a hand to stymie any response. "If you can't do farm work, you're on guard duty."

Both men nodded and continued on their way, quickly replaced by more, both from Red's original group and the locals, all of them coming to Red to give reports and receive instructions. Ryan listened intently as he stared out the window, still tracking the patrols, trying to find some pattern that could be exploited. When the talk shifted to the battery room and power, Ryan could barely suppress a grin. By his own calculations, they'd be out of juice before the day was through, leaving them struggling and complaining, maybe even starting to turn on each other.

"Now wouldn't that be something?"

A short time later, an older man squelched upstairs in a pair of Ryan's rubber shower shoes with a towel cinched around his waist, his gray hair dripping wet and half-covered in suds.

"Bob, why are you standing in the hallway dripping wet?" Red cocked his head to the side. "You got any sense in that brain of yours?"

"Yeah, sorry about that, Red," Bob replied sheepishly, one hand clutching the towel while he ran the other across his wet head. "The water pressure's basically gone. I barely got rinsed off before it turned into a squirt."

"You *didn't* get all the way rinsed off," Red replied, shifting over to Ryan. "What's the problem with the water?"

"The well pump burned out a few days ago. I built a manual one to draw water out of the well and we filled the tanks out back but it looks like you ran through them."

"So, what you're saying is that this house doesn't have good running water right now?"

"It does if you start pumping it by hand. I had Sandy fetch me a well pump right before you all moved in, but it's not hooked up."

"It's out back," Helen said. "You'll find it leaning against the house near the back door."

Red tilted his head back, pinching the bridge of his nose and rubbing his eyes. "And you were going to tell us this when?"

"You didn't ask."

Red started to speak, but paused for a few seconds as Martha laid her hand on his, then he relaxed and shrugged. "Fair enough," he said. "I'll volunteer one of my boys to fix that. That's what this is all about. Working together to come up with solutions."

"You're the boss."

Red stood and gestured at the broken dining room windows. "In fact, we'll go one step farther and fix all the damage Jack and his people did."

Ryan raised an eyebrow. "You storm in here and take what you want, nearly killing me in the process, then you run through our supplies like a bear in a bees' nest, and it's only been twenty-four hours. Now you're telling me you'll install the well pump and fix all the windows?"

"That's exactly what I'm saying."

"And why would you do that?"

Martha flinched ever so slightly as Red rested his hands on her shoulders. "Ever heard the saying, a happy wife makes for a happy life?"

"Once or twice."

"Reynolds!" Red called with a wink. "Hey, Reynolds. Man, are you in there?"

The music cut off, and Reynolds shuffled into the foyer. "Yeah, Boss?"

"Seems we've got a water pressure problem. Need a well pump installed. You grab someone to do that?"

"Yep, I'll get right on it." Reynolds started down the hall.

Red glanced at Martha. "We good?"

"Thank you, Red."

"Do me a favor, Reynolds!"

The big man stopped halfway to the kitchen. "Yeah, Boss?"

"Send Nancy in when you see her."

A few seconds later, Nancy stepped in wearing blue jeans and a baggy sweatshirt. "What do you need, Red?"

"I want you to take Hansen and a team and scout the area for new windows."

"Windows?"

"That's right. We owe it to our hosts, and *ourselves*, to repair what's broken around here. Nobody wants to live in a shot-up, boarded up place long term, now do we?"

Nancy nodded briskly. "Oh, yeah. Sure thing, Red. If we're going to live here, we might as well make it nice."

"Exactly what Martha and I were thinking. Get moving today, got it?"

"I'll grab Hansen right now, and we'll go around the neighborhood and see what's left."

"Good. Grab Bob and a couple of others and send them in here before you go."

"Right. Will do."

Ryan leaned back in his chair, staring at Red quizzically when the man turned to him.

"Something on your mind, Ryan?" Red asked. "I may be old but my ears still work well enough to pick up your snorts and snickers."

"Just wondering why you were about to kill me last night and now you're putting together people to repair my daughter's house."

"Ryan, you know good and well that we needed to secure the place. It wasn't ideal, but now that we've done it, we're all in this together." Red placed a hand on Martha's shoulder. "Isn't that right?"

"I'm glad things didn't turn violent." Martha ran her tongue across her lips, smiling thinly as she patted Red's hand.

"I don't blame you for being angry," Red continued, "but I'm sure you'll come to terms with things soon enough. On the way from Grand Rapids, all I could think about was finding a nice place to settle down until this disaster blows over. A place with plenty of food, water, friends, and a pillow to lay my head on. You can't blame us for wanting that."

"Not too happy you picked my daughter's house, but I'll live."

Ryan pushed his cup aside, placed his palms on the table, and got to his feet, shuffling toward the hall when Tyler grabbed his arm and swung him around.

"Just where do you think you're going, old man?"

Ryan looked Tyler over head to toe before jerking his arm free, turning back to Red. "To feed the animals and check on the dogs in the barn. They're past due for their feeding and probably thrown off and upset by all you people walking around out there. Best thing to do is leave the animals alone to avoid stirring them up and getting them rankled."

"Man's got a point," Martha said. "If we want our eggs coming regular and our chickens stress free, we need to keep them calm and happy. Best to let whoever's been taking care of them continue, so they don't start getting stressed out."

Red took Martha's hand, patting it and smiling. "That's my wife, always thinking."

"C'mon, Red, we can't—" Tyler grabbed for Ryan's arm again, prompting Ryan to push him back a few paces, and Tyler grabbed for the pistol on his hip.

"Watch it, old man. Shoving people around is a good way to get shot."

"This is *our* house." He turned to Red. "And you all are *guests* here. Which means *we* still have a say in what happens. Right? Or does that only apply when you want it to?"

"They know the farm and their animals better than we do." Martha spoke before Red could, staring down Tyler. "They should still be doing their normal routine, at least until we learn."

Red worked his jaw back and forth, mulling over Martha's and Ryan's words. "Makes sense to me. Tyler, go with him."

"I don't need a babysitter."

"Tyler's just going to make sure any lingering hard feelings aren't expressed in... negative ways." Red glanced at Tyler, who nodded in understanding.

"What can I do? You took our guns."

"Can't be too careful. I know good and well how resourceful us farmers can be."

"You haven't been a farmer in a long time, Red."

"Neither have you. Doesn't change a thing." Red raised a finger, cutting off Ryan before he could retort. "Listen, before you head out, there's something else I need."

"What's that?"

"I want the code to that safe in the basement."

"What safe?"

"Don't play stupid, Ryan. The gun safe in the half pantry, where the old bikes are stored."

"Oh, that safe. I don't have the code. Alice didn't give it to us."

"I find that hard to believe. You knocked off, what, half a dozen of Jack's people? Where'd you get the weapons and ammo to do that?"

"Do you really think Helen and I would travel anywhere unarmed?" Jack, who was standing in the next room over, ground his teeth together as Ryan replied matter-of-factly. "They're our weapons."

Martha put her hand on Red's again, and he leaned forward, sighing. "Mhm. Well, I'll let you get to work. If you manage to think of what that code might be, that'd be a great help to my patience."

Ryan didn't bother to reply, moving to the closet and grabbing a windbreaker, Tyler following close behind him. "I'm assuming the rain has stopped?"

"Yep." Tyler replied. "But it's muddy. Might want to put on your galoshes. Hate for you to hurt yourself, old man."

Ryan shrugged on his jacket and headed for the back door, grunting at the messy kitchen with plates of half-finished eggs, glasses with leftover milk, pots and pans dirty on the stove, and coffee grounds spilled across the counter. The pantry door stood open with several jars of canned vegetables gone along with a few boxes of pasta, and the oven was on, though whatever was cooking didn't exactly smell appetizing.

Ryan paused at the back door. Outside, a couple of the occupiers were tossing a football out past a run-down RV that someone had parked to the right of the chicken coop. Instead of wandering about quietly as they usually did, the chickens were agitated, flapping their wings and clucking loudly as Bob flicked twigs at them, chuckling whenever he managed to hit one. Ryan jerked the door open and stepped into the moist morning air with a cool breath of fall biting his cheeks, striding toward the chickens with a slight limp, focused on the man who was annoying them.

"Hey, idiot," Ryan growled, turning Bob around by the arm. "Leave the chickens alone."

A few years younger than Ryan with a chin of grey and white scruff, Bob chuckled, shaking off Ryan's arm with ease. "You ain't got no say here anymore." He flicked another twig, narrowly missing a hen. "Go milk a cow or somethin'."

Ryan jabbed a finger in Bob's face, coming a few millimeters from poking him in the nose. "You people say you want to survive the end of the world but then you harass the livestock." Ryan's hot scowl and gruff voice forced the man to back up. "Not a great survival strategy. Especially for a bunch of former farmers."

"Listen here you s—"

"All right now, boys." Tyler stepped between them. "Settle down. Bob, go find something else to do."

"What? You're taking *his* side?"

"Red's orders. Go take a hike. I've got this."

Bob shifted back and forth for a few seconds, then rolled his eyes and led with his shoulder as he walked away, knocking Ryan off balance.

Tyler cocked an eyebrow. "You want to dig your own grave, that's your business. But you're already walking on thin ice and the last thing you want to do is to start pushing people around. Red's not gonna—"

"Oh, shut the hell up." Ryan turned away, stalking past the coop and heading to the feed shed.

Tyler stood at the door, watching while Ryan got out the scratch and buckets, filling them up and carrying them to the coop. Chickens bolted toward him from every direction, clucking, crowing, and jostling to stay on his heels. Ryan scattered the feed, leading the chickens back and forth, scattering them out as evenly as possible so that they wouldn't be crowded. Out of the corner of his eye he spotted Red watching him from a back window, and he elected to ignore the occupier's leader's stare. It wasn't long before Red stepped outside with a small group of his crew, going around and pointing to all of the windows that had been broken or boarded up around the house.

"I want measurements taken of all these windows before you head out into the neighborhood to look for new panes. Make sure you pry these boards off first. Don't need any rot creeping in."

"Yes, sir. We're on it."

"Ryan, you got any tools around?" Red called.

"Basement. James has a workshop near the battery room. I'm sure you can show yourself in."

Red waved. "Good man, Ryan. I'll get my people right on it."

Ryan grumbled and returned to feeding the chickens, talking to them and leading them back and forth in front of the coop with the feed while Tyler stood by, watching with an eyebrow up.

"What *are* you doing, old man?"

"Moving them around a bit. Spreads the feed out and runs off any excess stress they might be feeling right now with all you people around harassing them."

"You're serious about that, aren't you? You care how these stupid birds feel."

"How many eggs we get depends on these chickens' happiness and overall health. I figured you would know that given you were a farmer."

"We never had chickens."

"That's no excuse for lacking common knowledge."

Ryan tossed the last handful of feed to the birds and returned to the shed to grab feed for the sheep and other barnyard animals. He dropped three buckets into a wheelbarrow, including one with dog food, turned it around inside the cramped shed, and pushed it outside toward the barn.

"Here," Tyler reached for the wheelbarrow. "Before you hurt yourself, old man."

"I never say no to free labor."

Tyler took the wheelbarrow handles and pushed it out to the barn, parking it in front of the door. As he followed, Ryan took in his surroundings, noting where Red's extended group of occupiers were settling in for the long haul. In addition to the RV, a small camp had sprung up between the shed and chicken coop with tents and tarps strung everywhere. Multiple pairs of guards were wandering the property on the patrol routes Ryan had first noticed springing up overnight, following the property line around in a steady, never-ending loop.

Red was with Reynolds, poking and prodding Ryan and Helen's electric vehicle, undoubtedly intending to use and abuse it like they were with everything else. Aside from the patrols, though, there weren't many people standing around, as they were either working inside, out searching for supplies or devouring the ones inside the house.

As he stepped through the wide-open barn gate after Tyler, Ryan spotted three pairs of guards in the barnyard; one pair was sitting out on the northwest corner and watching the woods while the others stood in scattered spots in the mud and grass, chatting among themselves, barely giving Tyler and Ryan a second glance.

When he and Tyler neared the barnyard shelter, the sheep, ducks, and fowl milled over, pressing toward the wheelbarrow in anticipation of their meal. Ryan tossed feed out, while Tyler watched, drawing the sheep and fowl off in opposite directions, scattering the feed wide in the grass to keep it from getting lost in the mud.

"That it?" Tyler asked.

"Mm. Good enough."

Ryan left the wheelbarrow and buckets at the front corner of the barn and went over to the door where Sandy had latched the door shut after getting the dogs inside the day before. Tyler stood a few feet behind him, hand on his pistol, staring through the cracks in the wood as the massive Great Pyrenees snuffled and snorted, growling as they sensed the men and the mixture of Ryan's scent with that of a stranger's.

"Hang on, guys. Settle down now!" Ryan shot Tyler a warning. "Stay outside. They're not exactly amenable to strangers. Ask Jack if you don't believe me."

"What do you need to do in there?"

"Just need to feed 'em and check on Bessie."

Tyler grunted. "Red wants the tractor in use pronto, and he wants someone milking that cow."

"That's the plan."

"Red also wants me to keep an eye on you. Can't do that while you're in there alone." Tyler flinched as one of the dogs flung themselves against the door, snarling at the strange voice.

Ryan shrugged. "Sure, if you want to go in, be my guest. Plenty of space out on the east side of the property for another grave."

"I'll just shoot the damn mutts." Tyler started to pull the pistol out of his holster when Ryan rolled his eyes.

"Oh yes, by all means, destroy a valuable resource. Red clearly didn't bring you along for your brains, did he?"

"The hell you talkin' about?"

"The dogs don't like strangers *now*. But with a few days of work, they could be acclimated to everyone here. Instead of thinking about killing them, why don't you try to imagine how much they'd help you when another group tries to take you out."

"Ain't nobody strong enough to do that."

"Yeah, that's what *we* thought, too. Look what happened to us. You really think Red would approve of you throwing away a resource like this, go ahead and shoot them before talking to him. That's on you, not me."

Tyler stewed on Ryan's words for a moment before lowering his pistol back into the holster and crossing his arms. "Fine. You've got ten minutes. You ain't back by then, I'm shooting the dogs *and* you."

"Fair enough."

Ryan grabbed the bucket of dog food and held his foot against the door. Lifting the crossbar with his free hand, he tossed it aside and slipped through, knee up as the dogs tried to push past him, barking and leaping as they spotted Tyler. Ryan seized the inside handle and swung his hips through, knocking Diana back and slamming the door with a clack of the latch, calling back to Tyler.

"Slide that crossbar back in place, quick now."

"All right. Hurry it up in there."

Ryan waited until the crossbar fell before turning and greeting the slavering dogs, grabbing Duke's forepaws and holding him upright where the animal licked his face and slobbered everywhere.

Ryan chuckled and walked him away from the door, speaking softly to the dogs. "All right, you big lumbering beasts. Settle down."

He pushed Duke off and let him drop, then got on his knee to hug Diana and Duchess who barked excitedly and circled him, swatting him with their tails, trying to crawl on his shoulders, and generally knocking him around. The dogs' combined weight was more than he could handle, and Ryan fell to the dirt floor, chuckling as they piled on.

"You guys better quit it, I've only got a few minutes!" Ryan rubbed the dogs' heads and flanks, satiating their desire for attention enough to be able to get up and dust himself off before taking a look around.

The barn was, miraculously, untouched, the tractor sitting next to the fuel tank, the hulking shapes dark and shadowy in the fractured light spilling in through cracks in the walls. Ryan walked over to a vertical beam where an electric lantern hung, turned it on, and doused the space in a soft yellow glow. Bessie lowed deeply and shifted in her stall in response to his intrusion, and he opened her gate, stepping in and running his hand along her side, stooping to feel her udders and giving her an affectionate pat on the side.

"Hey, old girl. You seem fit to burst, don't you? Don't worry... we won't let any of those idiots try to milk you if we can help it. I'll get Helen out here as soon as I can."

After pouring some dog food into a pile on the floor, Ryan took an old bucket off the wall and filled it from a water storage tank near the back of the barn, placing it near the food, then grabbed a second, larger bucket and filled up Bessie's trough in her stall. He repeated the process with her food trough, patting her side and speaking softly to her as she ate, the soft normalcy of the barn calming his heart rate and lowering his blood pressure all at once.

"How much longer, Ryan?" A banging came from the door, and Ryan's blood pressure skyrocketed again. He ground his teeth together, whispering a string of curses that only Bessie could hear before responding.

"Two minutes, Tyler. Just finishing up."

Moving swiftly out of Bessie's stall, Ryan patted the dogs as they hungrily devoured their food. He limped past the tractor, taking stock of the barn for general principles, just on the off-chance that there was something – anything – that could spark an idea. Aside from the farming equipment, there were a few tool chests, a pile of scrap wood, an old trailer and a stack of thick sheet metal resting against the wall. No weapons were readily visible, and nothing sprang to mind as a quick, get-out-of-jail-free card that he and Helen could use against their occupiers.

With one last glance at the piles of scrap wood and metal, Ryan headed for the door, banging on it loudly as he called to Tyler. "Lift up the crossbar. I'm coming out."

There was a squeak of wood on wood and the tension in the door relaxed, then Ryan unlatched the door and exited before the dogs noticed what he was doing.

"Well?" Tyler's arms were crossed as he stared Ryan down.

"All good. Bessie needs to be milked, though. She's fit to burst."

"Can't you do that?"

"Takes longer than ten minutes. I didn't feel like getting a few extra holes today."

"Mm. C'mon. Back to the house. We'll discuss this all with Red."

Tyler followed Ryan back to the house, dropping the wheelbarrow off at the shed on the way and heading in through the back door. Inside, the dining room was a whirlwind scene of construction, the wood boards having been pulled off the front of the windows, replaced by plastic tarps that were being stretched tight and stapled in place.

Red stood in the dining room, overseeing the workers both inside and out, and turned when Ryan and Tyler came up the stairs. In the time that Ryan had been outside, Sandy and Stephen had come down and were sitting next to Helen on the near side of the table while they ate a breakfast of scrambled eggs and bacon, none of them speaking as they watched the occupiers work.

"The plastic's just temporary," Red gestured to the front windows, "I've got Nancy and Hansen out looking for replacement windows for the whole front side. Looks like these are the main ones that need repair. Any others that you know of?"

"One upstairs that Jack and his degenerates shot up when they attacked the first time. We picked up the glass and boarded things up, but that needs to be replaced, too. And there're a lot of bullet holes in the front of the house. If those don't get plugged, rain'll keep coming in and this place will be infested with black mold inside a month."

"We'll get it done," Red nodded.

"Helen," Ryan turned to his wife, "Would you mind milking Bessie as soon as possible? She's full up and looking pretty uncomfortable. Besides, we need to keep the fridge stocked for our guests."

Helen stood and wiped off her hands on a napkin, addressing Ryan. "I'll take care of that right now."

"That sounds just great, Helen," Red said. "Let us know if we can help."

"I'll need someone to carry the containers back to the house when I'm done. I can't do that hill with those heavy things."

"You can grab Bob or Reynolds for that."

Helen nodded grimly and started to walk away when Red spoke again. "What about those dogs, Tyler? We gonna be able to use that barn soon?"

"Ask him," Tyler replied, hands on his hips as he nodded at Ryan. "Damn things nearly broke through the wall when they heard me out there. If you ask me, they need to be put down, but Mr. Expert here claims we can use them."

"Now, Ryan," Red drew out the words, affecting a bit of a southern drawl. "What use would I have for beasts that would sooner kill me as look at me?"

"Like I told him out there," Ryan replied. "You'd be an idiot if you threw away a resource."

"A resource." Red stared at him blankly. "Explain."

"Great Pyrenees are *big*, territorial and loyal to a fault. You give me a few days, maybe a week, and I'll have those dogs ready to treat your people like they do us. You can ask Jack and Barb, they'll tell you how useful the dogs can be if someone unwanted comes around."

Red tapped his fingers on his arm. "Seems... like a long shot to me, Ryan. Plus I assume you want to use the barn while you're doing it. That's a long time we won't have access to the tractor along with whatever else is out there."

"You don't just dispose of valuable weaponry," Ryan continued. "You figure out how to use it so that you *can* use it. Just give me some time. Sandy and Stephen can be the guinea pigs." Stephen started to open his mouth, but Sandy nudged him and pointed at his food. "That way your men won't be in any danger. As for the tractor, what do you need it for right now anyway? We already got all the crops in and did all the dirty work. Helen can milk Bessie, your people can cart the containers back and forth for her, and I'll get the dogs on better terms with you all."

Red glanced at Tyler, who shrugged, a hapless expression on his face. "Okay," Red finally replied. "Three days. You've got three days to get them under control. After that, if they show so much as a single tooth at me or my people, they get put down. Oh, and if I even *think* you're trying to pull a fast one over on me, your wife'll die first. Got it?"

Ryan nodded. "You'll be happy you gave me a chance."

"I'll be *happier* once I'm convinced you're telling me the truth. Nonetheless," He gestured around. "I like this new attitude everyone has. Working together, accomplishing goals, and most of all, keeping our bellies full. Let's keep it up, eh?"

CHAPTER SIX

James Burton
Shipshewana, Indiana

James strode across the grounds of the National Guard outpost, head held high, whistling in an off-key tune. Crossing into the lobby of the quartermaster's building, he passed several posters hanging on the walls, nodded to a few guardsmen standing off to one side and headed up to a young man sitting behind the main desk.

"Can I help you with something, mister...."

"James Burton. Yeah, hi..." James read the guardsman's name tag. "Corporal Denniston. Colonel Hawkins should have called about me?"

"Ohhh, yeah." Denniston checked his clipboard and nodded. "The Colonel must like you or something."

"Why's that?"

"He called over personally. You've got free run of the place. He said to give you any and everything you can carry."

"Well shoot," James chuckled and rubbed his clean-shaven jaw. "Don't I feel like the prize pig."

"Mm. Anyway, what do you want to start with?"

"I'm... not sure. What're my options?"

"Here, just write out your priorities. Weapons, food, other supplies." Denniston slid the clipboard over and placed a blank sheet of paper on top. "We'll flesh it out from there."

"Gotcha."

James took the pen he was offered and started writing: two duffel bags, a few weeks' worth of MREs for four people, water filters and purification tablets, and a flashlight and a blade for each member of his family.

Denniston had been watching him write. "Do you want four or seven-inch blades?"

"Do you have anything in the middle? Like, six? If not, we'll take four-inch. I'm looking for something with utility more than anything else."

"Understood. I'll see what we've got."

Next on the list he added a rifle, a pistol, and a reasonable amount of ammunition, then added an 'x2' so that Alice would have weapons as well. *Do Jake and Sarah need guns? Have they been using them already?* James' breath caught in his throat and he took a deep breath, glancing up apologetically as Denniston stared at him.

"Sorry. Just thinking about my kids."

"Don't apologize. The Colonel mentioned something about you reuniting. That's good. I hope more of us will experience that." Denniston gestured at the titanium staff James had leaned against the counter. "Want a new one of those, too?"

James touched the staff, smiling. It was dented, stained, and scratched, especially at the end where he'd used it as a weapon or to trek over rough terrain. But it was *his*. "No... I think I'll keep this one. We've been through a lot together. But if you have a few more, my wife and two kids could use them."

"Will do. Is that all?" Denniston held out his hand for the clipboard.

James nodded hesitantly and then with more certainty. "Yeah, that'll do it for me. Is that too much?"

The corporal looked over the list, then back up at James and shrugged. "You look like you can carry all of that. Orders are orders. Just have a seat and give us a bit."

Denniston gestured for a guardswoman standing off to the side to follow him into the back where supplies were stacked in tightly pressed rows, rising nearly to the ceiling. It took them a good thirty minutes to gather everything, Denniston coming out with one duffel bag and dropping it at James' feet, the guardswoman following close behind with a second and placing it with the first. A moment later, Denniston appeared with an ammunition vest, two pistols, and a pair of rifles, which he put on the counter.

"The vest'll get heavy, but it'll hold most of the rifle and pistol ammunition you requested. The rest is in the bag."

The first rifle was a newer carbine, military-grade without a mark on it while the second was a Springfield thirty-aught-six with a well-worn stock and a scope on top that gave it the look of a deranged sniper rifle.

"I would give you two carbines," Denniston gestured to the latter, "But we've only got one available. This Springfield's old and has seen hell, but it's used for instructional purposes, so it's well-maintained and should get you by just fine."

"It's a beauty. Thanks a lot, Corporal. I appreciate all your help." He nodded to the guardswoman. "You, too. Thanks."

James slung the rifles on his left shoulder along with a duffel bag, then he grabbed the second duffel bag and hoisted it on his right shoulder, the weight of it all causing him to slump ridiculously and laugh at his own discomfort.

"Yep, I can carry it all," James said. "Barely, but I'll manage. Thanks again, and take care of yourselves."

"You, too. Safe travels."

He shuffled out of the quartermaster's office and angled toward the end of the lot where Colonel Hawkins, Church, Oswell, and a group of guard members waited near a staging area.

As he came up, Hawkins raised an eyebrow. "Got enough supplies there?"

James would've shrugged if he could've. "Hey, you told them everything I can carry. You think I'm going to turn down an offer like that?"

Hawkins chuckled as James let the bags drop to the ground, readjusting the rifles from his shoulder to sling across his back. "That's very true. I'm glad you got what you needed. It should help you get home *and* repay you for your help."

"This is way more than enough. You have my sincere thanks."

Hawkins nodded and pointed to the northeast, where a trail of headlights approached around a bend in the road. "Looks like you made it out here just in time. Here comes that convoy." Hooves scratched on the pavement, followed by nickers and snorts, and Hawkins turned. "And here come the horses."

A dozen guard members brought up an equal number of horses, their coats freshly brushed and glistening in the glare of the overhead lights. As they were led around and lined up to wait for the convoy to show, a guardswoman brought a saddled ginger horse up to Hawkins.

"Here you are, sir." She held out the reins to Hawkins, giving James a side. "As you requested."

Hawkins took the reins and handed them to James, who patted the horse on the nose and stroked her side. "What's her name?"

The guardswoman shrugged. "We don't name them when they come in. Better to not get attached."

James nodded. "Makes sense." He stroked her long snout, a solid color to match the rest of her lack of markings. "She's beautiful. I think I'll call her Amber after the horse I lost back in the city."

"That's a fine name," Hawkins' reply was nearly drowned out by the chorus of thrumming diesel engines.

Three Humvees pulled off the road and swung into the lot, full of Marines and bristling with armaments and mounted machine guns. The ground shook, the vibrations felt in James' knees and teeth, and as they settled off to the side, four more Humvees pulling in long trailers and parked side-by-side in the parking lot in front of Hawkins. Guard members led the horses up and opened the gates, and the Colonel crossed to a lead Humvee and spoke with someone in charge of the convoy. After a brief conversation, he led the man over; a lean and thin guardsman with stiff shoulders and wire-rimmed glasses, every motion he made giving the impression of smooth efficiency.

"James, this is Captain Bragg out of Sturgis. He runs this convoy and will be taking you with them. Bragg, this is James Burton. In addition to his assistance at Kansas City, he's helped us get a dozen more Humvees battle-ready."

Bragg gave James a once over from head to foot as he extended a hand. "Very good to meet you, Mr. Burton. Colonel Hawkins filled me in on your exploits. It's great seeing a loyal, upstanding citizen like yourself stepping up for the cause. It's an honor to escort you to Connersville, sir."

James shook Bragg's hand, grip firm and steady. "Like I told the Colonel. I just did what anyone would do."

"What you did was more than *most* people would do on a good day."

"Thanks, Captain Bragg."

"Make sure you get him where he needs to go," Hawkins spoke to Bragg. "And see that his horse gets there, too."

"Yes, sir. We'll head straight from here to Connersville, and James will have a short, straight shot to the train station."

"Good."

"Want me to load Amber in one of these trailers?" James asked.

Bragg turned and waved to one of his guardsmen, and a man jogged over. "Put this one in trailer four. Make sure she's ready for a quick offload, understand?"

"Yes, sir." He took the reins from James and guided her away.

Bragg raised his voice. "We'll be ready to go in about fifteen minutes. We've got room for you and your things in the third Humvee with Garcia and Cortez."

"Thanks, Captain."

Guard members who'd driven in traded with a new group just coming on shift, the two sides exchanging information before the new drivers took over, and the old ones were directed to the nearby barracks for some rest. The entire exchange moved quickly and efficiently, with troops calling to each other, shaking hands, and loading gear onto the armored trucks.

"Colonel Hawkins." James held out his hand. "I appreciate everything you and your people have done for me. I haven't really had time to process that I'm going to see my wife and kids again soon and—well, thank you."

"We're only as good as the people we serve," Hawkins grasped James' hand firmly. "It's been a pleasure helping you out, and having you help us out, too. You take care of that family of yours, you hear?"

"I will."

A figure standing behind Hawkins hobbled closer as the Colonel stepped back to talk to his people, revealing herself to be Oswell walking with the aid of a cane and sporting fresh fatigues.

"Oswell?" James grinned. "Don't tell me you came out here to see me off?"

"You bet your bottom dollar I did," she grinned. "I couldn't let you go without a goodbye."

"Shouldn't you be working or something?"

"Oh I've got plenty of that ahead of me."

"Let's get you loaded up, James." Hawkins stepped back over to him. "They're almost done refueling."

Oswell hobbled forward to throw her free arm around James' neck, closing her fist and squeezing him tight for a long moment before finally letting go. "Thanks, James. For believing in me and forcing me to get on my feet back in that alley. If you hadn't done that, I wouldn't be here now."

"We saved each other," James corrected her, taking a final look around. "When this is over, I expect a phone call or a postcard or something, got it?"

"You're in the Government's database," Oswell grinned. "You bet your ass I'm going to check up on you and your family first chance I get."

With a smile and a final nod, James grabbed his duffel bags and slung them on his shoulders, bearing their weight across the parking lot to the third Humvee in the convoy. A guardsman opened the rear door and hatchback, gesturing for him to put his things in the back with the rest of the gear.

"It'll be a little cramped in the backseat," he said, "hope you don't mind."

James shrugged off his duffel bags and placed them inside, along with his guns and his ammunition vest. "Fine by me. You could duct-tape me to the top of one of the horse trailers and I'd be happy as a clam."

The guardsman slammed the hatchback with a chuckle and James climbed in the back, taking the left-hand seat, the right side filled with backpacks, rifles, and a couple of canisters of ammo for the mounted machine gun. As the other guardsmen got in, he nodded at the gun. "I don't know how to fire this thing if we get into trouble."

"Garcia will handle that," the driver replied with a chuckle.

A young man in the front passenger seat turned and grinned back at him. "Hello, James! I'm Private Garcia. And your driver for today's trip is Specialist Cortez. We do apologize for the lack of cushioning on the seats, but as the Captain says, your ass will grow callouses or die trying."

Cortez put his seatbelt on and started the Humvee with a low rumble, rolling his eyes. "Knock it off, Garcia. Don't start scaring the civvie."

"He'll have to do more than that, trust me." James secured his lap belt and leaned down, peering through the dirt-covered window.

As soon as the horses were loaded up and secured and the drivers switched out, Bragg strode to the passenger side of the first Humvee, put his hand up, and rolled his hand a few times. He got in the lead vehicle, and the convoy pulled out with the three Humvees in front, four horse trailers following behind, and two armored trucks bringing up the rearguard. There was the faint squelch of radio traffic that James couldn't make out as Garcia and Cortez received instructions in their earpieces, which they responded to with short, clipped replies.

They circled the lot and the quartermaster's office where Oswell, Hawkins, and Church watched them roll to the main highway and head south. The Humvees' headlamps cut through the dark, flat Indiana countryside, shaping twisted, contorted shadows as they passed by wilted cornfields, gently swaying trees, and small, ramshackle buildings.

James settled back, trying in vain for a few moments to find a comfortable spot on his seat, the slight scent of oil burning off the engine block permeating into the interior of the vehicle. The road spun beneath them as the military radio scratched and crackled with faint voices, Garcia and Cortez whispering as they wove along with the convoy, eating up the miles and the darkness. With only so much room available to him, James shifted sideways in the seat, curled up as best he could, and tried to get some sleep, though his thoughts soon turned to his family.

Alice, Sarah and Jake were alive – unless Hawkins had been lying to him for some reason – and he was going to see them again soon. Given the difficulties he had suffered in his journey, it was hard to fathom what they'd gone through, or that they truly could have come out the other side unscathed. Agony, elation, depression and joy surged through him in waves until he finally drifted off into a restless slumber, rolling in and out of consciousness along with the bumps and jostles of the road.

Two hours later, the trucks slowed, brakes squealing and the Humvee shuddered to a halt, startling James awake. The radio crackled to life, followed by the sounds of small arms fire and he flung his arms out, forgetting where he was, briefly imagining that he was back in the office in Chicago, listening to the gangs battle it out in the streets. As Garcia unbuckled himself, rose in the seat, and slipped up through the Humvee turret hatch, James came fully to his senses, his surroundings sharpening in focus as the attack intensified.

Rounds pinged off the convoy's armor, the incoming fire hitting from the left, striking his door and all along the side. Ducking and raising just high enough to see out the window, he watched red tracers light up the night in response, cutting into the woods, shearing branches off trees and slicing saplings to pieces. Figures sprinted through the darkness, bobbing and weaving, but the Humvee shook as the fifty continued to spew fire, hot casings raining down onto the roof of the vehicle, the chatter vibrating his skull.

Bragg's voice came through on a speaker in the front, and Cortez pressed a hand to his ear, listening intently before reaching back and grabbing Garcia's leg, pulling on it. "Garcia, hold your fire!"

Their Humvee joined the others in ceasing their attack, and the convoy sat silently for several minutes, eventually moving slowly south along the road, spotlights penetrating the gloom in search of more attackers. Gradually the convoy picked up speed again and sped on through the night, the diesel engines growling intensely, leaving James' body thrumming with adrenaline. Garcia dropped from the Humvee's hatch once they were a few miles down the road and slid back into his seat, a wide grin on his face as he punched Cortez in the arm and said something in Spanish.

Turning back to James, he shouted over the noise of the engine, "You okay back there, man?"

"Oh, yeah," James replied with a half salute. "All in a day's work out here, right gentlemen?"

The guardsmen nodded and chuckled. With the skirmish behind them, the convoy rolled on through the night beneath a blanket of moon-infused clouds, dark, billowing shadows highlighted in amber. Visibility on the ground was relatively good thanks to the glow, and James found himself checking the trees and woods, unable to sleep. His ears still echoed with the noise of the fifty, his nerves jittery, feet rolling in the brass that had tumbled through the hatch onto the floor.

"These kinds of attacks, have they been increasing?" James finally asked, and Garcia turned in his seat.

"Like you wouldn't believe. You'd think they'd get tired of getting their butts kicked."

"What are they after? It can't be food, right? Back at the outpost, I heard some talk about the feds dropping pallets of food all over the place."

"Nah, not food. Transportation. Transport's *everything* right now."

"These Humvees must be a prime target, then." James took a deep breath and tried to calm his still-jittery nerves.

"I mean, yes, sort of," Garcia shrugged, "but what they really want are the horses."

"You can't mount machine guns on horses."

"No, but think about it. Humvees need fuel to run, right, which means they need a way to refine that fuel. That's overhead. And they'll never get their hands on our refineries, so they'll never have the fuel to keep any vehicles they do manage to steal running for long." He jerked his thumb toward the rear where the horse trailers stuck close. "But horses... some water and grass and a good night's sleep and they'll take you anywhere you want to go."

James nodded and continued staring through the smudged, spiderweb-cracked bullet-resistant glass.

"But don't worry about anything," Cortez said confidently. "They've tried a hundred times, and we hold them off."

"Most of the time," Garcia added.

James snorted. "*Most* of the time? What does that mean?"

Cortez shrugged. "Of the convoys we've ridden in, nobody's ever taken us down. I heard that a few were overwhelmed, though. Half the vehicles were destroyed and all the supplies were left intact, but the horses were gone."

"Sounds about right," Garcia agreed.

"That's... not good."

"It's costing *them* a lot more than it's costing us," Cortez said. "They can't afford to keep trying. Most of the routes we've been traveling, they're settling down. That was probably just some farmers or something back there. Nothing organized."

"How long until we reach the rendezvous point near Connersville?"

Garcia referenced a map and checked for the next mile marker on the side of the road. Once past that, he turned and said, "About five more miles. Won't be long."

"It shouldn't take long for me to unload Amber and get out of your hair."

"Nah, we'll help you," Cortez smiled. "It's been a pleasure driving you. If Captain Bragg says you're worth it, then you are. He's a great—"

Their ear radios burst to life with static-filled shouts, a voice piping over the line, barely audible but with a rising note of panic coming through the professional tone.

"Hey," James pointed at the radio. "Can you turn that on?"

"Yeah, give me a second." Cortez fiddled with the knobs, tuning the radio that seemed recently installed with wires and cables hanging from beneath the dashboard.

A woman's voice suddenly came through clear. "... anyone within the vicinity of Connersville, Indiana. This is Captain Hechler of the Oklahoma National Guard. We're under heavy attack. Any friendly forces in the area? Over."

Without a moment's hesitation, Captain Bragg cut in on the line. "Captain Hechler, this is Captain Bragg from the forty-fourth, heading your way."

Hechler replied with audible relief. "Great news, Captain Bragg. How many can you bring?"

"I've got just over a dozen troops and some fifty-cals. Think that would help turn the tables?"

"Undoubtedly. Be advised the train was derailed when it entered town."

"The train?" James whispered, his stomach dropping precipitously.

"They've taken most of the rear cars, and we're holed up in the locomotive and a few passenger cars up front. We won't last long. What direction are you approaching from?"

There was a scrabble of paper and a whispered conversation before the captain answered. "We'll be coming in from the east side, it looks like."

"Sounds good, Captain Bragg. I'll let—dammit, get suppressing fire over there *now*!"

"Garcia. Tomlin." Bragg addressed the convoy. "Man the fifties. Assume anyone who *looks* hostile is. Look alive, people!"

Cortez shook his head and yawned dramatically, jerking his thumb at the turret. "Up you go, Garcia. Mr. Hero, can you grab a couple of canisters of ammo out of the back? We'll need you to keep Garcia supplied."

"Oh knock it off with the hero nonsense." James laughed as he unbuckled his seatbelt and twisted to grab an ammo can. "I've got him covered."

Even through the forced smile, James' heart and stomach grew heavy as his imagination ran wild, driven by abject fear of losing what he'd lost once already – and thought he was on the verge of regaining. Forcing a series of deep breaths, he checked that his pistols were loaded and moved one of the rifles from the rear of the vehicle to within arm's reach.

"Hold tight." The words slipped past clenched teeth. "We're coming."

CHAPTER SEVEN

Alice Burton
Louisville, Kentucky

Exhausted as she was, Alice struggled to catch a single iota of sleep as the train clacked its way north, thoughts of reuniting with James and being so much closer to home keeping her from resting. The train had set out in the late evening, the locomotive winding up and hauling the fully loaded cars behind it down the lengthy stretch of track toward Connersville. The air was cool and the cloud cover nearly complete with a broad yellow glow in the west where the sun was vanishing over the horizon, a near-full moon rising off to the east to take its brighter brethren's place in the sky. The low glows cast the landscape in eerie shadows, framing endless farmland and trees and an array of houses built right up to the tracks, leaving Alice to wonder how the homeowners could sleep or work or do *anything* with trains rolling by every day.

Sarah, at least, had fallen asleep shortly after the train had departed the station, snoring as she lay curled up on her spare set of clothing with her head on her fox backpack. Jake was awake, though, sitting in contemplative silence, leaning against the side of the train car, staring out the door as the sun finally vanished beneath the trees and the night began to take over. After sitting and lying for far too long, Alice had gotten up and walked to the wide-open train car door, sitting on the edge with a few other insomniacs, her feet kicking out as the train rolled onward, watching the forest go by, night creatures with yellow eyes glaring back from the gloom.

It wasn't until sometime after midnight she'd been tired enough to try and sleep again, reaching success in a tossing, turning half-doze with disturbing dreams centered around their journey and the joys and dangers they'd faced along the way. Wilford was there, upset when she told him the National Guard would be taking the horses despite doing everything in her power to stop them. And while she couldn't remember what Wilford said in the dream, his warm embrace lingered, and his voice echoed in her head.

James had been the next to show up, running through the woods as she found herself sitting back in the train car door, reaching out to take her hand but missing it at the last second. He stumbled and fell into the brush, vanishing as the train carried on. She had tried to jump to him, but froze, her muscles refusing to respond as the clack of the train's wheels grew louder, so much so that it hurt her ears and she grimaced, tossing and turning until her eyes flew open, the clacking still there, though with a sinister, alarming change.

"Mom!" Jake shook her by the shoulder and she sat up.

"Is that—"

"Gunfire. Yeah."

Distant pops came from the direction of the front of the train, then louder, bombastic carbines returned fire, bursts of hard rounds followed by shouts, screams, and someone yelling through a bullhorn. The train was slowing as well as the landscape changed from rural to urban, much like where they'd encountered it at its last stop. A few of the other people in the train car who were closer to the open door pulled it closed, locking it before huddling together in a small group.

Alice patted Sarah on the side, shaking her. "What's going on, Mom?" She finally woke, rubbing at her eyes.

"I don't know. Another attack, maybe." She looked at Jake, who had dropped down to kneel next to her and Sarah, whispering to the pair of them so as to not be heard by the rest of the train car's riders. "Be ready to move out if things go south, okay?"

Almost as soon as it started, the gunfire stopped, though everyone in the boxcar stayed well away from the door until the train had come to a complete halt. The sounds of guardsmen hopping down and moving around outside drew Alice to the door where she popped the latch and slid it open a few feet. A bright yellow glow filtered down from lights hanging from poles, illuminating a train yard filled with supplies, much like the previous stop had been. Ramps fell and guardsmen brought down loads of goods, helped by more of their compatriots who stepped out of the gloom.

"Hey, I'm going to hop off and see what's up." Alice patted Sarah and Jake on the shoulder. "Stay here and watch our stuff, 'k?"

"Okay," Sarah said, while Jake nodded next to her. "Be *careful*."

"I will."

Alice sat on the edge of the deck, eying the steep six-foot drop before hopping down, landing hard and wincing at the anticipated shock of pain up her left side. She leaned against the train momentarily until it receded and she could walk again, then she shuffled along the tracks and into the shipping yard, hanging out at the edge, staying out of the way as the guardsmen walked back and forth. There were no signs telling Alice where they'd stopped or how far they had left to reach Connersville, but she spotted an officer standing off to the side, directing troops to carry supplies toward a waiting line of Humvees equipped with a variety of enclosed and open trailers.

"Excuse me," Alice said, raising her hand in greeting as she came up.

The officer turned. "Yes?" He leaned forward and squinted. "You're not supposed to be out here. It's dangerous."

"Sorry, I know. I just needed to ask - I'm assuming this isn't Connersville?"

"No, ma'am. You've still got a ways to go."

"Where are we?"

"Near Louisville. We're doing an exchange of supplies and swapping out some manpower."

"How long will this take?"

"About forty-five minutes, then you should be pulling out again." The officer checked his watch, sighing wearily.

Alice gestured to the surrounding darkness. "Is everyone okay? We heard the gunshots."

"Couple of wounded, but nothing serious. Damned ungrateful pricks deciding that all the food they can eat isn't enough."

"Sounds like the people back where we got on the train in the last city."

"They're all along the train routes these days."

"Do you know who they are?"

The guardsman shrugged. "People who aren't happy." He pointed to the pallets of supplies. "We have more emergency aid than people could eat in a lifetime, but it's not good enough for them. They want to take everything we've got for themselves. Makes it hard to coordinate recovery operations."

Alice gestured to the stacks and skids of crates filled with food and water. "They seriously aren't happy with all of this?"

"They're going after our transportation. Cars, Humvees, motorcycles, bikes, and even the horses we're hauling."

"Don't say that." Alice shook her head. "We have horses on board."

"Don't worry. No one's getting our supplies, *or* your horses. They've tried many times and failed."

"I guess people are getting desperate." Alice shook her head. "I thought about trying to find bikes myself, but then we got the horses."

"Yeah, can't go wrong with those," the guardsman replied.

Another guardsman shouted from the front of the train, grabbing his attention. "Well, ma'am. I've got to finish up here. You'll be heading out soon. You should get back in your boxcar and get ready to move."

"Thanks," Alice replied with a smile, waving at him as he left.

She headed back to the kids, finding them standing near the edge of the boxcar, their bags near their feet, nervously looking around in anticipation of having to flee in a hurry.

"We're all good, guys. You can relax."

"So it was an attack?"

"Yeah, like the one we disrupted, it sounds like. I'm going to have a look around. You guys stay here, and don't get off the train, okay? We'll be moving out fairly soon."

"We'll be right here." Sarah replied, turning to speak with a young girl they'd briefly interacted with earlier on the ride while Jake sat on a bale of hay, talking with an older man wearing a gray jacket. Jake flashed her a smile and nodded that he'd heard her and Alice moved to the car's rear, pushed through the door, and strode across a short gangway to the next car. She stepped into a car full of feed and hay bales, maneuvering around workers and ducking beneath a pair of guardsmen who were tossing bales into the car and moving them around to make room for more.

The horsecar was next where she checked on Buck, Rocky, and Stormy. Their coats had been brushed by someone in a hurry, and all their gear was hanging on the wall, alongside other tack and saddles from more horses the guardsmen had taken aboard. After a few minutes of – hopefully not empty – promises that she wouldn't let them be taken anywhere, she headed into the next boxcar after hearing shouts and loud clatters.

When she opened the door, she stepped into chaos, with stacks of crates marked as *food*, *clothing*, and *clean water* being swung both in and out by a small crane worked by a pair of guardsmen outside the train. She slipped past the group as they were shouting and pointing at a stack of pallets out near the edge of the station, exploring the next few cars. Guardsmen activity had decreased the farther back she went, the supplies in the boxcars organized and strapped to rings on the walls and floor, ready for distribution at stops farther up the line.

As she stepped into another boxcar, a familiar voice called out, and she turned to see Dixon hurrying behind her, calling her name.

"Alice! What are you doing back here? These cars are off-limits to civilians."

"Oh, sorry. I didn't see any signs. Just stretching my legs and looking around."

"Uh huh. Yeah, I need you to get back to your boxcar." Dixon looked outside at the guardsmen going back and forth. "If someone realizes you're here, it'll be my ass."

"Sorry about that. Yeah I'll head back now." Alice began to head back through the boxcars, Dixon directly behind her as they wove through the piles of supplies.

"By the way, I talked to Captain Hechler."

"About the horses?"

"Yes. She's sounding amenable to you taking *one* horse so you can have some help getting home, but she's not budging on all three."

"That's a tough compromise," Alice said, looking out through an open boxcar door at the impenetrable darkness beyond the train station. "We can't all ride one horse."

"No, but one horse could carry your supplies, and the three of you could walk. With your husband along, it shouldn't be too difficult."

"Yeah, that's not fair."

"Alice, you know it's out of my ha—"

"No, not that. Well, that's unfair too. I mean bringing up James." She turned to him, a slight smile on her lips. "Trying to distract me with him isn't fair."

Dixon shrugged. "Whatever I have to do to keep the peace."

Alice was quiet for several long seconds as she stared out into the darkness, watching the shadows of trees as they swayed in the wind. "Well, if that's the best you can do, then that's the best you can do. I will hold you to getting them back when this is done, though."

"Of course. All of your information is being logged. I can assure you that neither the state nor the feds want to be dealing with horses long-term." Dixon's professionalism slipped ever so slightly as his shoulders sagged and he leaned in, speaking softly. "I mean, have you *smelled* them? And seen the mess they make?"

Alice laughed. "Fair point. I suppose you all are tired of cleaning up after them, huh?"

"You've got that right. Do you know which one you want?"

"It'll probably be the bay, Buck."

"I'll see to it. Thank you for understanding."

Alice shrugged. "Not like I have much choice in the matter. No sense in getting mad about something I can't control."

"Still. Not getting yelled at by yet another person is… refreshing."

Alice nodded. "So when are we leaving?"

"Shouldn't be too much longer. Just hang tight in your boxcar until then, okay?"

"Yeah, yeah. Back where I belong. I'm going."

He smiled. "Thanks, Alice. See you soon."

Alice watched Dixon jump off the boxcar and jog after a group of guardsmen before she navigated through the supply cars and ended up back in the boxcar with Sarah and Jake. Jake was still talking to the man on the bale of hay, while Sarah had fallen asleep between the stacks, using handfuls of hay stuffed in between their belongings as a pillow. The other passengers in the boxcar were similarly relaxed, eating and talking quietly amongst themselves, the worry from the initial attack having dissipated.

Jake glanced up at Alice and discreetly exited his conversation with the man, coming up to her as she crouched down to check on Sarah. "Hey, Mom."

"Hey. We're almost ready to roll out. Bad news, though. Dixon said we could take one horse, but the captain is refusing to give us all three."

"Seriously?! We can't let them do that!"

"Preaching to the choir, son," Alice said. "But what do you propose? Take on the National Guard with some pool cues and a shotgun?"

"I…" Jake groaned and sat down next to Sarah and Alice. "Yeah I guess not. Which one are we taking? Buck?"

"Yeah."

"Sarah won't be happy."

"I know." Alice stroked the side of Sarah's head. "What about you?"

"I'm pretty attached to Rocky, but there isn't much I can do about it."

"No, I'm afraid not. At least we'll get to see your father soon."

Jake grinned. "Now that, I can be happy about."

"You and me both, kiddo. C'mon, try to get some rest. We'll need it."

"Yeah, will do."

"Oh, and Jake?" Alice dropped her voice to the faintest whisper, leaning in to his ear. "If there's even the *slightest* opportunity to get all three, we're taking it. Understood?"

"You read my mind, mom."

"Good. The saddles and tack are hanging on a wall in the boxcar they're in. We may not get an opportunity, but…."

"Yup."

Alice ruffled his hair and squirmed her way down onto the floor of the boxcar to lay next to Sarah, Jake doing the same on Sarah's opposite side. A short time later, the locomotive came to life, throttling up with a high-pitched train whistle, the cars shaking and rumbling as they picked up speed. The sway of the car and its rhythmic squealing along the tracks became a lullaby to Alice, and soon her eyelids were drooping shut, her body's exhaustion enough to overcome her mind's racing thoughts about James.

A jolt threw Alice a foot off the deck, head slamming into the side of the boxcar, a flail of limbs in her face as the screech of metal pierced through her sleep. Sarah and Jake both were atop her, the boxcar lurching hard to the side, and as Alice groaned and twisted to get out from under them, the pressure on her chest violently reminded her that she was still dealing with a grievous bodily injury.

Gravity suddenly shifted in the opposite direction, and they were airborne as the boxcar left the rails, turning in a violent lurch, sending them rolling down the side of the rough wooden wall as it pitched unevenly. A chorus of screams rang out and hay bales went flying, detaching from their rope bindings and filling the air with dust and rough bits of straw. The boxcar lurched again, continuing its roll, and they were soon tumbling along the boxcar's roof, the passengers flailing and reaching for family members as they were shaken like a box of cracker jacks.

Alice grabbed for Sarah, clenching her tight, and grunted when her head slammed against something hard, and she flopped over, losing all sense of direction, her balance skewed in the violent whipping. The boxcar's front end flipped around and pointed downward, ramming into something unseen and sending everyone rolling toward the front, toppling over each other, limbs cartwheeling the boxcar finally, mercifully, came to a stop.

Alice breathed slowly in the darkness, shrouded in a din of silence with a thick haze lingering in the air. People grunted and groaned, sobbed quietly, shuffled, and called out for their loved ones. A child's muffled cries came from deep within the pile of bodies and hay, and she couldn't see for the darkness and swirl of straw and dust in the air.

"Jake? Sarah?"

Rolling onto her aching side, gasping, coughing, and choking on dust, Alice fished a small flashlight from her pocket, flipped it on, and waved it around. A thick golden haze filled the air, reflecting the light and deepening the shadows in every corner of the boxcar. People were moving, sitting with their heads in their hands, and starting to pick through tossed baggage and piles of straw in search of loved ones. Alice's beam finally hit Sarah, who'd tumbled toward the bottom with her feet resting on a pile of hay.

"Sarah, honey?" Alice coughed, her voice like sandpaper. "Sarah, where's your brother?"

Sarah blinked in disoriented confusion with her thick chestnut hair in a tangle, pieces of straw sticking out. "Mom? I-- I don't know."

Alice slid closer on her backside a few feet. "Over here, honey. Are you okay?"

"Yeah, I think so. What happened?"

"I think we derailed." She raised her voice. "Everyone, we've derailed! Find a way out! Take your friends and family and climb out through the door."

The boxcar had ended up partially upright in the end, and at least four people lay outside on a grassy slope, a couple of them crawling around and disoriented.

"Someone help me! People are buried under here!"

One of the passengers was kneeling, grabbing handfuls of hay and tossing them aside, virtually swimming through the pile to pull a teenage girl from the mess. The man in a gray jacket who Jake had been speaking with swept in behind him, took the girl by the hands, and dragged her clear, staggering with her toward the door. Alice shifted forward, rolled right, and got to her knees, taking Sarah by the wrist and pulling her close. "I'm going to help these people. Find your brother and get outside."

Sarah nodded. "Yeah, Mom. I'll find him. I just... I think I heard him a second ago."

"That's him over there." Alice pointed to where Jake was sliding sideways toward the door.

"Okay. Got him."

Alice slid to the edge of the hay where it had piled up with pieces of luggage, duffel bags, children's suitcases and other supplies that had been stacked inside the boxcar. She kicked some hay aside and started digging through the pile as a mother cried out next to her.

"My baby! She was right in my arms!"

"We'll find her," the man with the gray jacket replied. "Keep looking everyone! If you've got your family, please go outside so we know who's missing and who isn't."

Alice kept digging, scraping along the edge of the car, throwing handfuls of hay above her only to have them slide down again. "Someone form a line. Take all the hay and this luggage we toss up and throw it outside."

As people formed up behind her, she caught movement in the hay on her left and rolled in its direction with a sharp intake of air, the stretch of her chest sending stinging spikes through her whole body. Ignoring the pain, she dove forward, kicking and reaching, plunging her hand into the hay to wrap around someone's wrist. Leveraging on her left elbow, she pulled back, jerking, hauling a heavy weight with her. A young man about Jake's age emerged from the mess with a tuft of brown hair and straw sticking out. He spat and coughed, crawling out of the pile and Alice adjusted her grip, grabbing his shirt, leveraging herself backward as he got to his knees.

She patted him hard on the shoulder. "Are you okay, son?"

"I... I think so," he replied, spitting more hay and blinking. "What happened?"

"We derailed and flipped. Go outside. If you're not hurt, grab some of this luggage and take it with you. We need to clear this place out so we can search for more people. Hurry!"

Alice leaned forward and grabbed the suitcase handle, pulling it out in a burst of hay, handing it to him and pushing them both farther up the tilted car. It was at that moment, when she paused to take stock of where to search next, that she realized that gunshots had been echoing in the distance for the last few minutes.

Alice turned her flashlight around, illuminating Sarah and Jake as they crawled toward the door, then she shifted the beam back to the hay, skimming across it and looking for movement as more people joined them in the search. The line of passengers carried luggage and hay up and tossed it outside in piles and a moment later they found one person, then another. Alice spotted a lump moving just beneath the surface of the hay, and she dove toward it as a man wearing a skewed ball cap tried to crawl free, swimming with one arm up through the mess as Alice slid to meet him.

"Are you okay?" She averted her face as a new haze of dust rose from the pile.

"I think so," he replied, gasping, spitting, rolling upward, and dragging someone else with him. "I found this little one. She landed on me, and I just covered her up."

A bright, terrified face peered up from where she'd been tucked in the man's arm with her pigtails skewed on her head.

"Oh, honey. Your mom's looking for you."

The little girl gasped, blinked, then took a deep breath, letting it out in an ear-shattering wail that put a smile on Alice's face. She accepted the girl from the man, turning, crawling with her up the car's roof, searching for the mother, who came sliding down almost past her into the pile, but she was caught by two others nearby.

The mother snatched the girl from Alice. "Elise, oh my baby! I thought I lost you!"

"I think she's okay," Alice said, grinning through her own pain. "She's got quite a set of lungs on her."

The mother smiled, tears in her eyes. "Thank you so much!"

"Don't thank me." Alice nodded to the man with the hat who'd kept the young girl safe. "Thank him."

The woman waved to him and reached upward to helping hands, the joyous moment interrupted as more gunfire came from the front of the train. The search efforts continued for a few more moments in spite of it, and soon a dozen people were safe, being handed up to others, and helped out onto the gravel and grass next to the train car. Three more were found before Alice and the others finished and crawled out, and Sarah and Jake were standing off to the side, Sarah handing her a bottle of water as she came up.

"Oh, jeez," Alice croaked. She tilted up the bottle, swished her mouth out and spat. "You guys okay?"

"Yeah, Mom." Jake nodded and pointed up the tracks. "But that's getting closer."

In addition to their boxcar, several ahead of them had also derailed and toppled down a short slope, rolling and piling atop each other. Another dozen guardsmen were running along the tracks to join what appeared to be a fight up front, while a few helped more passengers get out of the boxcars, tending to those who had been seriously wounded while glancing uneasily in the direction of the gunfire.

"It has to be another attack," Alice said, moving past the toppled boxcar and climbing the slope to the train tracks, peering ahead where the bright lights of a fire illuminated what remained of the passenger cars.

Behind them, most of the supply cars were still on the tracks, including the cars carrying the horses and the flatbed hauling heavy equipment. More shouting and gunfire erupted from up ahead, lively flashes lighting up the woods and buildings.

"What now?" Jake asked, the gunfire reaching a fevered pitch as more guardsmen joined in, working to coordinate against the ambushers.

"We can't go that way, or we'll get caught in the crossfire, and I don't have my shotgun...." Alice shook her head, squinting, peering past the battle as the town rolled off ahead in the faint peach glow of buildings on fire. "Looks like the train station's still a mile or two down the tracks. We could try to make it there and circle around the fighting?"

"Whatever we decide, we should do it quick." Jake nodded ahead to where the National Guard was engaging the attackers. A brief burst of gunfire lit up the night like fireflies in the darkness. Guardsmen fell back, and shadowy figures leaped aboard the lead trains where more shooting ensued. Silhouetted in one of the rear windows, Alice watched as a handful of National Guard were overcome, pushed into the back of the train, and shot in a flash of gunfire.

"Okay, time to move." Alice whispered to the pair, the already-nervous group of passengers around them growing more so as the fighting intensified.

"We're heading for the horses?" Jake asked.

"Let's go try to find some of our things first. Quick, look around."

Alice and the kids scrambled back down the slope, Alice getting her flashlight out and shining it on the piles of luggage and duffel bags they'd emptied from the tipped car, pushing Jake and Sarah ahead to begin rifling through them.

Jake called out a few seconds later, "I've got the duffel bag, Mom!"

"I found the shotgun!"

Alice whipped the flashlight off to the left at the edge of the pile of belongings, where Sarah stood with the gun in hand.

"Okay, we're good then."

"What about the shells?"

"They're in the duffel bag." Alice waved to hurry them along. "All right. Let's get up to the tracks. Quickly now, hurry."

They climbed the slope, and she grabbed the shotgun from Sarah who was dragging her fox backpack behind her. As they reached the tracks, bellowed cries came from off to the side, and shadowy figures jogged toward them on the tracks from the front of the train. Alice shoved Jake and Sarah ahead of her and they sprinted for the big square shape of the horsecar, circling and climbing through the open door to the sound of the animals snorting and stomping in displeasure backsides bumping together as they backed up, unable to escape due to their tethers.

Jake scrambled up first, reaching for Sarah and then Alice who grabbed his hand, swung her leg up, and stood. "Jake, get them saddled. Sarah, help him. You two do it best."

"What about you?" Sarah asked breathlessly.

"Just hurry up!"

While the kids saddled the horses, Alice rested her shotgun against the wall and untethered a mare on the left-hand side of the car.

"Easy, girl," she said, backing her out of the stall, turning her, removing her bit and headgear, and pointing her toward the door.

She cracked the horse in the flank with a hard slap, and the mare launched forward with a high whinny, coming to the end of the car door and leaping out, landing on the side of the tracks and sprinting off through the grassy field. Alice continued down the line, backing the horses out, untethering them, and setting them free, watching as they ran off into the night with hooves flying. There were only a few left by the time Jake and Sarah were ready, and the sounds of feet flying up the tracks grew louder outside the car.

"Let's go, kids; move it!"

Jake and Sarah brought the three horses around to face the door, holding them there while Alice searched for a way to get them off the train without jumping several feet across and down. In the delay, two men ran up on them, panting hard, wearing dark coats and carrying rifles. One man with a ball cap on jerked his gun to his shoulder when he saw them.

"Whoa, there!" He swept his rifle across them. "Let those horses be. You ain't going nowhere."

Alice waved to get the kids to back up, smiling haltingly and stammering as she stood at the edge of the deck, shuffling toward the edge of the door. "Hey, wait, we're on your side. It sounds rough out there – what's happening?"

"It's more than rough," The man leered. "We're giving the guard a whipping."

"Th-that's great; we can join y—"

"Shut up and stay right there. Don't *move*. Cover her, will you, Sam?" The man in the baseball cap glanced into the field, watching as the last of the horses ran off into the woods. "You... you assholes let the horses go. Which one of you did it?!" He pointed at Sarah and Jake standing between the horses.

"I did it." Alice held her hands where they could see them, gesturing at their horses, taking another small step toward the edge of the door. "These three were ours before the National Guard took them, and I didn't want the others to get trapped on the train in case a fire broke out. There are more horses, though, and—"

"Shut up!"

The other man shifted his weapon toward Alice, shaking his head, spitting. "The whole point of this was those damn horses! Now we've got to round them up!"

"I—I didn't know, I'm sorry! I can help you!"

One of the men fired into the air out of frustration, and Buck pulled out of Jake's grip and circled in the boxcar, tossing his head and hopping, hooves clopping on the wooden deck. Jake let Rocky go and lunged to get Buck back under control, grabbing his reins as the man called Sam shouted at him.

"Quit screwing with the horses and get out here!"

"Quit shooting!" Sarah screamed back. "You're scaring them!"

"Maybe you didn't hear me, little girl," Sam warned. "Climb down out of that boxcar. All three of you. Right now!"

The brief distraction was all Alice was waiting for, and she lunged the last foot toward the edge of the boxcar door, scooped up the shotgun, jerked it to her shoulder with a cry, and squeezed the trigger. The gun – not full seated against her shoulder – kicked hard, her tendons and bones screaming in pain, the shock rattling through her whole body. She fought past it, racking another shell, swinging the gun toward the two men as they flailed with their weapons, firing again, sending blood and sinew spraying across the ground. His compatriot was snarling and cursing from the blood-splattered gravel, crawling for the rifle he'd dropped a few feet away. Alice took careful aim, racked another shotgun shell, and fired, peppering his upper torso and quieting his swearing mouth.

Alice racked another shell, aiming between the two bodies for a few seconds, her mind taking extra long to catch up with reality thanks to the adrenaline flooding through her.

"Mom!" Sarah pulled her by the arm. "More are coming!"

Alice glanced up the tracks, more footfalls accompanied by shadows, lights and yelling. "Time to go! Mount up, kids. Let's go!"

Alice swung under Buck's neck and got on his left side, jamming her foot into the stirrup.

"We have to get them out of the car first," Sarah said. "We can't ride them off the deck!"

"Mount up!" Alice growled, rasping. "*Now*, Sarah, before those men get here and finish what the other two started!"

The horses stomped around in the wooden boxcar as the kids tried to calm them enough to climb up on their backs. Stormy and Rocky finally settled enough for Sarah and Jake to swing into their saddles, the horses bumping their flanks and shoulders, Sarah almost falling off as she tried to situate her backpack.

"Come on, kids. Go *now*!" Alice gripped the reins, staring into the night, the darkness like a cliff dropping into nothingness. While her gut churned, and her brain screamed *No!,* Alice kicked Buck's flanks and whipped the reins, shouting, "Go, Buck! Go, boy!"

Buck launched himself through the door, his massive weight carrying Alice into the open air. They hung suspended in the empty darkness for a fraction of a second before plummeting, Alice lifting from her saddle, almost flying free until Buck's front hooves hit the ground with a sudden jolt. She plunged forward, face pressed against his neck, his bulk shifting and flexing beneath her. Gripping the reins and saddle horn with everything she had, knees clenched tight, Alice stayed on as Buck raced down the tracks, banking into the vast green field toward the woods.

The kids cried out a second later, catching up to her in an instant, the hooves of the three beasts pounding through the sweeping grasses as the wind howled past their heads. Gunshots went off behind them, forcing Alice to lay flatter and stay down to avoid the zipping rounds. It was only when she'd reached the edge of the woods that she glanced back, checking to make sure Jake and Sarah were behind her.

"Go, Mom! Go!"

With her heart hammering like a piston, every breath beyond painful, Alice whipped the reins to the left, turning and launching them full-on into the woods.

CHAPTER EIGHT

Ryan Cooper
Lansing, Michigan

Ryan and Helen sat in chairs in front of the window in their small room, looking out into the cold, bleak night. Reynolds had removed the boards Ryan had nailed up with a warning not to try anything stupid, followed by a laugh and mumbled comment about breaking both legs from the fall. A single candle burned on the dresser, providing just enough light to not stub their toes without preventing them from seeing out into the dark. The driveway cut between the maples rocking in the breeze, losing more leaves by the day as the season's change became inevitable. The clouds lay across the sky in broken shapes, soft swaths miles long, painted by golden moonlight around the edges, the thin rays touching the swaying grass.

Sandy and Stephen were lying on the twin bed while Ryan and Helen kept watch, Sandy with her knees drawn up, wearing a pair of Alice's sweatpants, T-shirt and thick socks. "You sure you want first watch?"

"We're just happy to have someone to share it with," Ryan replied. "For a long time, it was just the two of us. We'll take first watch, you can have second."

"Do you think they would actually try anything with us after all this?" Sandy asked. "Like... would they hurt us *now*?"

"They're acting nice enough, but it's only because we know a lot about the farm. They can't run it without us, but after they get the lay of the place, I have a bad feeling they'll have less and less use for us."

"Martha's helped too," Helen said. "She doesn't seem like the rest of them. Especially not like Red."

"Mm. I don't think she'll matter once Red gets a bug up his butt. My biggest fear is that those dummies will run out of food and start kicking people out, starting with us."

Helen nodded slowly. "I'm surprised it hasn't happened already with the way they're wasting nearly as much as they eat."

Ryan leaned forward, rubbing his hands together slowly as he watched a two-man patrol stop near the gate. "Keeping Red happy is our priority right now."

"It's not easy" Helen looked at Sandy, who nodded quickly in agreement. "He seems ready to blow his top all the time. And you agitating his men isn't helping things."

"I know, I know. I've about bit my tongue off a hundred times so far and it's not getting any easier. I just... I just need some time. I think I might have the start of a plan."

"What kind of plan?" Helen asked.

601

"It revolves around the tractor, but that's all I'll say right now. I need a few days in the barn, alone, to put things together."

Helen's eyes crinkled from her sly smile. "You cheeky devil. That's why you used the dogs like that."

"Guilty as charged. But until I can formulate this plan some more..." He glanced at Sandy and Stephen. "We need to lay low and do what these people want. Get along with everyone and try to look small and insignificant. That means all of us."

Sandy swung her legs over the edge of the bed and sat up. "I've heard a few of them talking about us."

"Like?" Ryan asked.

"They say we're dead weight and aren't worth much. Especially because..." She blinked at them in apology.

"You can tell us, dear," Helen said. "You won't offend anyone here."

"Well, they said we were dead weight because you two are... well, *old*."

"Let them think that," Ryan nodded. "To them, dead weight means useless which means harmless which means under-estimating us."

"The one big guy, Reynolds, I think? He said we couldn't contribute much, either. Said he didn't trust us after what Jack said about Stephen and I."

"Okay, that could be a real problem. If that's what they really think, then we need to act on it." Ryan flexed his fist. "We'll have to *do* more and be *extra* nice to them. Prove our worth to them so they won't think about kicking us out of here in the next few days."

"I could make it a point to start cooking for everyone," Helen said decidedly, "finish some canning, and even tidy up around the place. Sandy can help."

"Good. Anything to make ourselves feel indispensable."

"And you know something?" Helen looked at Sandy. "I bet we could get Martha alone. Try to talk to her. See if there's anything there we can use to our advantage."

"She seems sad and nervous and doesn't say much." Ryan snorted in realization. "Hang on – do you think her and Red could be on the rocks?"

"It would explain a lot. Maybe we could use that to our advantage. She's been sympathetic to us so far."

"We have to be careful," Sandy said pointedly. "We're all vulnerable here, and I won't do anything to risk my son's life. If we're trying to stall for time, we should *really* go along with them and put our hearts into it. For all their faults, some of them can see through a charade pretty well."

Ryan turned in his chair. "Yup. I'd say we need to become a troupe of actors and immerse ourselves in our roles. Like the man once said, it ain't a lie if you believe it."

"So, are we agreed on what to do?" Helen asked. "How about you, Stephen? You on board with us and your mom?"

Stephen nodded slowly, shyly. "Yeah, just do what they say and be friendly. Even if they're mean?"

"That's right." Ryan gave him a half grin. "You've got the easy job, really. Just stay close to your mother, and follow her lead."

"I can do that."

"While you all are playing along, I'll work around the barn and get things ready. I think Red bought my argument, but you never know, so I'll have to work fast."

"If you need any help, let us know," Helen said. "Until then, we'll lay low and be... helpful."

Sandy shrugged. "Nothing else to do, right? Shouldn't be too hard."

Ryan shifted and faced the window again, kicking his feet against the floor and setting the rocking chair in motion. "All right, then. It's settled. Let the show begin."

Helen was up before the break of dawn, dressing herself in a clean pair of jeans, a gray camisole, and a blue, long-sleeve, button-up shirt.

"Looks like you're ready for work," Ryan sat up from the bed and threw off the light blanket he'd tossed over himself when Sandy had taken over the watch, still fully dressed from the day before.

"I'll take that as a compliment." She raised an eyebrow at him. "You'd better at least put some clean underwear on."

"Oh, come on now, I'm fine." Ryan sniffed at his underarm and twisted his mouth. "Ugh. I'd go shower but I don't really want to be at my most vulnerable in this nest of vipers."

Standing with a groan of discomfort, Ryan joined her at the mirror, putting his arm around her waist. "I don't know how you keep yourself looking so beautiful."

She leaned into him affectionately. "Oh, thank you, dear."

"We don't have to do this if you don't want to. We can just... walk out of here. I'm sure they'd let us go."

"And then what?"

"Well... yeah."

"What is your end goal anyway, Ryan?" Sandy spoke from the other side of the room, where she'd been keeping watch out the opposite window.

Ryan glanced at the closed door, gesturing for Sandy to come closer, and he lowered his voice until he was barely audible. "Live to fight another day. If my plan works, we'll hopefully be able to make off with some valuables, enough to keep ourselves safe for a while and plan how we're going to take this place back. Of course, that relies on my having a few days to work on this – and a cup or three of good luck, too."

"We'll play our part." Helen rested her hand on Ryan's arm, looking at Sandy who nodded in agreement. "I'll just be my normal self and treat them like old friends we've lost touch with. I reckon it'll be easier for us two than it will be for you."

"If I keep grinding my teeth like this, I'm going to need a dentist."

"It's just how we'll have to do things for a while."

Sandy went into the connected bathroom to wash her face and came out in a fresh shirt taken from Alice's stash, tying her hair up into a ponytail with a deep sigh. "Okay. Let's do this."

"You sure you're good?" Helen asked.

"It'll be hard, considering what Jack and Barb did to me." Sandy touched her cheek. "I'll be okay, though."

"You won't be alone." Ryan put his arms around Helen and Sandy. "If we stick together, we'll get through this. And... if at any time either of you feel threatened, just pull one of us aside and talk to us."

"Three days." Sandy nodded. "I can do three days."

"Right. Okay. You ladies go down first." Ryan finished tying his boots, straightening with a groan. "I'll be down a few minutes later to check things out and try to get to the barn again for as much of the day as possible."

Sandy and Helen opened the door with a glance at each other, emerging to find an older woman from Red's group sitting in the hall on a folding chair, pistol on her hip and book in her hands. She started to get up, reaching for her pistol, and Helen held up her hands.

"I know, I know. We're not supposed to be out unless Red says so," Helen was saying. "But we just wanted to make breakfast and do a little cleaning around the house."

"I don't know..." The guard glanced across the hall where the master bedroom door was shut tight. "I don't want to wake Red up right now. He mentioned wanting to sleep in today."

"No need to wake him up. We're just going down to help. Red would *want* that, don't you think? He's been encouraging cooperation and all. I'm sure he'd appreciate a nice plate full of steaming hot eggs when he wakes up."

The woman stared at the master bedroom door for several long seconds before relenting. "Well, I guess as long as you don't try to leave..."

"Where else would we go? Come on. We'll make sure you get the first plate, and we'll throw in some extra bacon, too" Helen leaned in and lowered her voice. "Consider it a thank you for letting us out to get some work done."

"Since you put it that way," she replied with a grin, "I guess that would be okay."

Helen smiled warmly. "Thank you. What's your name?"

"Elisabeth Mott."

"Okay, Elisabeth," Helen said. "One plate of eggs and bacon coming up. Give us a bit, okay?"

Helen gently closed the door, leaving Ryan and Stephen in the room, leading Sandy downstairs and suppressing a frown at the sight of a group of people sleeping in the great room who'd dragged out coverlets, blankets, and spare pillows from the closet. Reynolds stepped in from the kitchen and paused when he caught the women standing at the threshold. He'd removed his military coat but wore a heavy flannel shirt over a white T-shirt, camouflage pants, and dirty socks as he padded across the carpet.

"What are you two doing down here?" he growled.

Helen met him with a beaming smile and a cheerful tone. "Heya, Reynolds. We're starting breakfast. Want some?"

"Red didn't authorize it. You two need to get back upstairs and wait until he gets up."

"We could do that... or, we know a lot of you've been on shift all night, guarding the place and working hard, and we thought we'd whip up some breakfast to help out. What do you say?"

Reynolds frowned from the depths of his bearded, round face, and Sandy smiled as well, gushing at him. "I make *award-winning* scrambled eggs. That's what everyone's always said, anyway. I'll let you be the judge, though."

"I... I don't know. Red didn't say—"

"Oh, Red'll be fine with it." Helen slipped down the hallway. "By the way, did you boys manage to fix the water?"

"Yeah, new pump's in and it works fine." He scratched his beard, casting a glance up at Red's room.

"Good, we can get this place cleaned up and get things hopping. C'mon, Sandy."

Reynolds turned the corner and followed them a few steps as they headed into a kitchen overflowing with piles of unwashed dishes and garbage everywhere. A stack of plates stood tall in the sink with water dripping from the tap, grease and splatters of raw and cooked food covering nearly every horizontal surface. Helen and Sandy began gathering the dirty dishes and bringing them to the counter, though rather than run the dishwasher, they did them by hand, Helen scrubbing them and Sandy rinsing them next to her in a sink full of hot water before setting them in a rack off to the side. After half an hour of intense scrubbing, they managed to cut through most of the mess, finishing off with some sanitizing of the countertops.

"Well, this is looking better," Helen said with the sweep of a rag.

"Much," Sandy replied. "Now, let's get that cooking island cleaned up so we can start the food."

"You start on that, and I'll get the coffee going."

Tyler came up from the basement and stopped in the kitchen. "What's going on in here?"

"Morning, Tyler," Helen chirped, hefting a bag of coffee grounds. "Want some coffee?"

Tyler narrowed his eyes but nodded. "Yeah, a cup of coffee sounds pretty good."

"Cream and sugar with that? Sorry, but we only have powdered creamer unless you want milk."

"Milk's fine," he said, leaning against the counter, watching the pair work until Helen got his coffee ready, brought it over, and set it in front of him with a smile.

"There you go. What's on the agenda for today?"

Tyler sipped his coffee with an appreciative nod. "Thanks. Um... patrolling the grounds. There's a lot to watch out for around here."

"Make sure you go out past the north fence. The woods go almost all the way to the highway." Helen rested her hands on the cooking island, trying to keep a smile plastered on her face in spite of the scratches, stains and scorch marks that had been left on the wood. She took a sponge from under the sink and started scrubbing, glancing sidelong at Tyler. "We saw some military convoys on the highway back there a few days ago."

"Military?" Tyler tensed and tilted his head. "You mean Army? Marines? Guard?"

"Not sure the branch." Helen scrubbed some butter on the cooking countertop. "It was a big convoy of armored trucks of all sizes and shapes."

"Did you talk to them?"

"Oh, goodness no, we didn't talk to them, but we waved," she lied, "and they waved back. Seemed very friendly."

"Did they stop at all?"

"Nope. They seemed in a hurry to get wherever they were going."

Tyler glanced back up at Red's room again, digesting the information. "Well, uh, thanks for the coffee. I best get to it."

"Want me to put that coffee into something to keep it hot for you?"

Tyler held out the cup hesitantly. "Sure? Uhh... thanks."

Helen got an insulated cup from the cabinet and made the exchange. "Please bring it back so we can wash it. Don't be leaving things sitting around. Makes it a lot harder to clean and keep everything orderly."

"I can do that." Tyler raised the cup and walked to the stairs, stopping on the first step before shaking his head and going out the back door.

Over the kitchen counter, Helen could just make out that the razor blades had been removed from the doorknob, leaving pieces of epoxy resin in their place.

"They seem pretty skeptical," Sandy whispered as she scrubbed the island next to Helen.

"Give it a little time," Helen replied, waving to a pair walking by the front windows. "Just smile and wave and be absolutely saccharine."

"You got it."

Just when they were about to finish the last of the cleanup, Martha came downstairs to the kitchen, giving it an appreciative once-over. "Look at you two ladies going at it. What's the occasion?" She put her hands on the cooking island and leaned in.

"No occasion." Helen turned with an overly sober expression. "There's been enough violence in the world over for a lifetime. It's time someone stirred in a little love and good intentions."

Martha nodded, looking up in the direction of the master bedroom. "I can't disagree with that." She released a long sigh. "Sometimes Red gets so wound up with things."

"I noticed. But Ryan's the same way. When all this started, he was on edge all the time."

"How about now? I'm sure he's not too happy about us being here."

Helen moved a short stack of dishes closer to the sink for Sandy to take. "Well, it's not ideal. I'm just glad we resolved things without violence."

"How about a cup of coffee to start things off?" Sandy raised a mug and shook it back and forth before putting it on a drying rack. "It's hot and fresh!"

"That sounds great. I can get it myself."

Helen made a flourishing gesture toward the coffee maker. "Have at it. Fair warning. We're low on sugar, so go easy."

"I only take mine with a little milk." Martha circled the cooking island, grabbed a clean white mug from the cupboard, and poured herself a cup.

"We've got two dozen eggs in the fridge," Helen said, peeking in. "That'll barely get us through today what with all of these hungry mouths. After breakfast, we'll gather some eggs."

"How about if I go gather the eggs?" Martha asked, her smile faltering. "We're... guests here, after all."

Helen turned and rested her fists on her hips. "Sandy, can you get some potatoes chopped up and frying and throw on a couple of pieces of bacon? There's more down in the cellar. It's in the refrigerator over by the HVAC. I'll take Martha out to show her around the chicken coop."

"Sure thing, Helen," Sandy replied.

Helen put down her coffee cup. "Ready to go out now? We can make this a fantastic breakfast if we get another dozen right now."

"I'm ready." Martha said. "I'll grab Nancy, too. She'll want to know the ins and outs of the place, and she's got farming experience."

"Meet you back here in a couple of minutes?"

"Yeah, be right back."

While Martha fetched Nancy, Helen spoke softly to Sandy. "Here we go."

"Time to work your magic."

"Heh, we'll see. She's clearly not happy with this arrangement, but how far that goes is anyone's guess."

"Good luck."

Helen found her jacket in the hall closet, shrugging it on and zipping it up tight. While it was comfortable in the house thanks to all of the people inhabiting it, the cold grip of winter was rapidly descending on them, faster – it seemed – than normal. A moment later, she met Martha and Nancy in the kitchen, Nancy in ragged jeans, a dirt-stained long-sleeved shirt, and a blue vest that had seen better days.

"Heya, Nancy." Helen walked right up and rubbed the tattered coat sleeves between her fingers. "We need to find you a better vest. My daughter, Alice, has some she stored in a bin downstairs. Since you two are about the same size, you can borrow one of hers. How does that sound?"

A thin woman with sunken cheeks and pale blue eyes, Nancy gave Helen a side-eyed look before succumbing to Helen's smile, replying with a shrug. "Yeah. Sure. I'm not turning down new clothes."

Helen patted her arm. "We'll run yours through the spinner as soon as Red gives us permission to switch the power to them."

At that moment, Sandy dropped a block of butter on a hot griddle, the instant sizzle and smell coming off it causing Helen's stomach to grumble. "That smells good already, Sandy. We'll be back soon to check on things."

"Happy egg hunting!" Sandy raised a knife, already most of the way through the cutting of the potatoes.

"After you," Martha gestured to the back door.

Helen stepped out into the cold morning air, her breath coming in warm gusts, the brisk breeze sweeping it away and slapping her awake.

Martha hugged herself. "It's a little nippy out this morning."

"The winter's likely to be bad," Helen said darkly, "right when we don't need it."

"You're probably right." Martha glanced at the EV parked off to their left. "Does that car actually run?"

"For now it does." Helen nodded as they started moving toward the chicken coop. "But the roads aren't in good shape. I guess you know all about that though. Ryan and I tried to drive on the highway at the start of all this, but it didn't go so well. The wreckage got too thick, and we were forced to turn back."

"Same thing happened to us. Good thing Red... he got us the dump truck." Martha cleared her throat, looking off to the side, avoiding Helen's gaze. "We ran into a lot of that on the way from Grand Rapids, but we plowed right through it."

"Smash and crash," Nancy added with a growl.

They reached the feed shed, and Helen showed them where to get the chicken scratch and a bucket to refill the chickens' water. "Nancy, why don't you run down to the spigot and see if you can get some water out of it? Reynolds said they replaced the well pump, so the pressure should be good now."

"Alright," Nancy grabbed the bucket and headed for the spigot.

"So, are we just feeding them or just gathering eggs?" Martha asked.

"We'll do it all in one shebang."

"How much do you feed them? We got rid of ours years ago. Without the kids at home it was just too much work."

"Oh yeah, they're a lot. Handy, now though. Six scoops should do it, spread out nice and even on the ground. Keeps 'em busy and distracted." Helen retrieved the chicken feed out of the nearby plastic-lined garbage can and heading outside with Martha in tow.

The chickens saw them coming and made a beeline in their direction, heads bobbing, with the rooster out front and clucking up a storm.

"This rooster is a real pecker," Helen said, grabbing a small handful of feed and tossing it off to the left where the birds banked in a flock of squawks and feathers. "He's another reason to keep things spread out. Alice's told me a few times she's about to cook him up, and I can't say I blame her." She kept walking, taking another handful and throwing it off to the right, drawing more of the chickens that way, then grabbing a third handful and tossing it toward the house where the remaining chickens bobbed and waddled off. "See what I mean?"

"You have a nice place here for them."

"Well, it's all James and Alice's setup. We're just watching over it for them. Oh, over to the right are some baskets and some moving blanket scraps. I usually line the baskets with cloth since they're on an angle, to roll the eggs out after they lay them. Though we might switch to grass or something soon." Helen picked up the corner of a scrap and wrinkled her nose. "We already have enough extra laundry."

"Do you have an incubator setup somewhere?"

"No, they never got around to that, unfortunately. I think we'll need to do that sooner than later, though, what with all the extra people in the group."

"I can help with that. Did my fair share back in the day."

"Didn't we all." Helen smiled. "I remember when our chicks helped cover for quite a few bills back in the day."

"Oh yes, us too. Red... well." Martha stiffened. "We didn't do it for long."

Helen held up the basket after a few seconds of awkward silence, changing the subject. "Not bad for one day. The hens are laying about the same as normal, so far."

"That's good news."

"One of your people was out here harassing the chickens yesterday, though. Ryan said he was flicking sticks at them or something."

Martha sighed. "I know... I heard about that, and we're sorry. Red had a conversation with him."

"Thank you. These animals need to be our top priority right now, what with winter fast approaching. We'll need them more than ever."

Martha nodded quietly and the pair finished up and headed back to the house.

Ryan came downstairs a few minutes after Helen went outside, giving the women enough space to get started while leaving Stephen to read a book in the bedroom, where Sandy had indicated she'd prefer him to remain. Stepping into the foyer, wearing jeans and his usual old jacket, Ryan walked to the dining room table, forcing a smile when he saw Jack and Barb seated on the other side.

"Everybody hard at work already?" Ryan leaned on a dining room chair, looking over at the people still snoring on the floor of the living room.

"Mm. We're just reviewing the inventory until Red gets up." Jack put the clipboard down on the table, gesturing at it. "You've got a lot more than you were letting on."

"We didn't think it was wise to shoot our mouths off," Ryan replied, "but now that you're here... it's all yours, I guess."

"Don't play the victim with us." Jack rolled his eyes. "We had to bring in another group to get you to cooperate. What does that say about you?"

Ryan forced a half smile. "I hate to admit it, but you're right. From what I've seen over the past few days, we'll be better off with more people. More people equal better defensive capabilities. I know we've had our differences, Jack, but I hope we can get along from here on out."

Ryan leaned across the table, holding his hand out. Jack stared at it momentarily, then clasped it. "The old man comes around, huh? This doesn't make up for what you did to us."

"Nor you to us. Truce?"

"For now, old man. For now."

Ryan released Jack's hand and looked around. "Helen go outside?"

"She went out to get more eggs. Sandy's on breakfast. Oh, there she is now."

Sandy came out of the kitchen with several plates, placing them down at the table in preparation for Red's crew to start coming in to eat. "Ryan! Fancy some breakfast?"

"Eggs and coffee would be great. I'll get it."

"No, no, have a seat, and I'll bring you a plate."

"Appreciate that, Sandy. Thank you."

Ryan sat across from Barbara and Jack as the occupiers finally began to stir from the smell of the eggs and bacon. Figures passed through the kitchen, grabbing cups of coffee and plates of eggs before wandering outside, the guard shifts changing out. Red tromped down the stairs with his boots unlaced, standing in the foyer, stretching, yawning, his gray hair combed straight back and his beard trimmed shorter and neater than the previous evening.

"Hey, boys and girls." He took a seat at the head of the table. "How's everyone this fine morning? Jack, what do you have for me?"

"We've got a list of the provisions here, Red. When do you want to go over them?"

"Later. Are we okay for the next few days?"

Jack nodded and gestured at the notepad in front of him. "Yeah, we should be fine for a few days, but we've got a long list of things to go over to prep for the long term."

"All right. I see we've got breakfast served," Red said. "Why don't we talk about things while we eat some of this fantastic-looking grub?"

"Helen and Sandy did a great job getting the kitchen clean and getting things started this morning," Ryan offered. "Trying to be helpful and all."

"Well, I'll be damned." Red stared at Ryan for a moment, his grin broadening as he relaxed and threw his arm over the back of his chair. "I knew this would work out somehow, but I didn't know just how much. Looks like everyone's pulling together. Reynolds! Hey, Reynolds! You in here?"

Lumbering footsteps sounded in the hallway, and Reynolds appeared, cleaner than he had been earlier when Ryan had spotted him, but still wearing the same dirt-covered clothes.

"You get yourself a shower this morning?"

"Yeah, Boss."

"Couldn't find any clothes?"

"Nothing that would fit, but I've got a few spare sets in the laundry room I'm saving. Martha said we should gather everyone's stuff and do some wash later today."

"With this many people we'll need to run that washer all day, every day," Red looked over at Ryan. "What kind of strain will that put on the solar panels?"

Ryan sipped his coffee. "I haven't checked on our current load since you all arrived, but I suspect we're pushing the absolute limits of what the solar can do unless we cut back in places. Don't forget, though – those hot water heaters are propane, and that's going to run out at some point."

"Good point. Reynolds, how's the water pump working?"

Reynolds leaned back. "We installed it yesterday and it's... okay. Pressure seems like it could be better."

"Can you help the boys with the water pump, Ryan? I'll give you Reynolds and Tyler."

Ryan nodded. "Probably something with how it's seated." He turned and addressed Reynolds. "What did you do to install it?"

"Uhhh, we just followed the directions on the box," Reynolds scratched his head. "Pulled the old one out along with the fifty or sixty feet of PVC, removed the old pump and got the new one put on and lowered it back in."

"Did you clean off the pipe as you lowered it back in?"

"Well, yeah. Didn't want any grass and dirt getting in there."

"Good." Ryan nodded. "What about shocking the well?"

"Of course. We added a few cups of bleach and ran the pump for a while to get it all out before finishing the hookups in the well head."

"It's probably a clog or kink or loose fitting between the well head and the house. We'll check everything out, make sure it's good and figure it out." Ryan looked over at Red. "Shouldn't be too much trouble. Maybe an hour or so of no water while we sort it out."

"Splendid," Red tapped on the table. "This is great."

"I was going to suggest something else..." Ryan said.

"Go on."

"It's about the water heaters. I think we need to source electric water heaters sooner rather than later, so we can stretch the propane out as much as possible. Hygiene's incredibly important right now. We don't want disease spreading around because people aren't washing properly. Plus, hot showers will go a long way to maintaining morale."

"I like the way you think, Ryan. I could put a group together and have them look for a couple of water heaters. I assume some homes still in the area could have them."

"Yep. I'd check the plumbers around here too. They probably have some stock if they have a warehouse."

Red gestured to Jack. "You getting all this down?"

Jack had been listening intently to the conversation but not writing anything down, and Red's pointed question made him sit up and grab his clipboard. "Oh, yeah. I'll add it to the to do list. Reseat the water pump and get it up and running. Source a couple of electric water heaters. Got it, Red."

"Good. Remember we need windows still, too." Red jerked his thumb behind him at the flapping plastic tarps. "All this cold air coming in has me nervous about winter."

"There's another thing Helen and I had been meaning to get to," Ryan said, pointing to Jack to write the next bit down. "The field needs to be cleaned up, the old plant matter mulched up and spread. The earth tilled and all. It might be a good idea to create a second field, what with all the extra people, so it's ready for springtime."

"Now you're thinking, Ryan," Red agreed with a quick finger jab. "And that's exactly why I want to get to that tractor sooner rather than later. You getting all that, Jack?"

"Yeah, Boss." Jack held up the notepad. "I've got Reynolds on the pump, Nancy and Hansen on scavenging, Martha and Helen on cooking and cleaning duties, and Tyler in control of the guard shifts."

"Good," Red said, leaning forward and clasping his hands together. "Looks like we have everything shored up pretty well for now, and our scavenging teams can start making progress around the place."

"Where can we put children?" Barb asked. "We've still got some people up at the trailers at our place. Some grandkids, nephews, and a few others."

Red shook his head. "They can stay right where they are for now."

"You said everyone was welcome here, Red." Barb's expression darkened. "Our kids are the most important of us."

"This'll be our base of operations. That doesn't mean we can't have smaller camps along the main road here."

"Or," Ryan leaned in to add to the discussion. "We could use that salt truck you've got out there to pull one or two of the trailers up here in the yard and put them on the edge of the property. You could house guards in them. Move a couple more onto the east side of the property and put your defenseless folks there. Kids, older folks. Heck, you could even make an infirmary out of one of the trailers."

Red stared at Ryan a long time before laughing admirably. "Well, dang, Ryan. You've really thought this thing through."

"I'm just throwing ideas out there to see what sticks. A few trailers could be hooked up to propane generators or more solar panels if we can source them. That's farther out in the future, though."

Jack continued to furiously jot down notes on his clipboard, trying to keep up with Red and Ryan's conversation. Plates of eggs and bacon, glasses of milk and fresh cups of coffee soon arrived as Helen and Martha came back into the house, and soon the conversations fell to soft-spoken discussions as everyone ate with utensils clinking on plates and quiet sips.

"Well, this is just great," Red finally said, dropping his fork onto his plate and pushing it away. "This is all coming together quite well. I'm just worried we can't sustain this."

"As you should be," Jack added.

Helen stood behind Ryan, interrupting before Jack could continue. "It's a strain on our resources. The hens are doing well, and the egg production is stable. Milk, too. We probably have enough vegetables to last this group most of the winter, but we'll be out of sugar, flour and other staples before we know it."

"We're way ahead of you on that, Helen. Ryan has offered some good advice for shoring things up, including what we need to do to get those fields in shape for the spring. Jack will maintain the list of tasks and supplies we need, and we have the rest of the fall and winter to prepare. I'll have teams going out today to assemble the bigger pieces of what needs to happen."

Smiling, Helen squeezed Ryan's shoulders. "I do have one request... the ladies and I will make a pass through the house and clean things up today, but we'll need your support in making some rules for everyone, or we'll be living in a dump. Stuff like throwing garbage away, cleaning up after yourselves, even things as basic as carrying dishes to the sink instead of leaving them on the table."

"Yeah, that's something to consider, too."

"I think there should be a strikes system," Martha added, nodding in agreement with Helen. "Three strikes and you're no longer welcome in the house."

"Anyone who can't live like a human being inside this house will be camping out with the animals." Red affirmed.

"Sounds like a plan." Ryan planted his hands on the table, scooting his chair back and standing. "If you don't mind, Red, I want to take Sandy's boy, Stephen, out with me to feed the animals and train the dogs. He can also help me transport milk back to the house."

"We already fed the chickens and picked up the eggs," Helen said.

Ryan nodded. "I figured as much. I can spend more time with the dogs." He turned to Red. "Once we get them in line, you'll see how right I am about them. They're loyal, and they'll patrol the perimeter without question. A good dog with good ears and keen senses is better than three or four men."

"You don't need Reynolds or Tyler to help out there?"

"Not today, but I'll let you know. I don't want to risk anyone by having them around the dogs for now. I might grab some clothes from different people, so they can get used to their scents."

Red clapped. "Good enough. I appreciate everyone getting along. In fact, I think it would be a great idea to meet here at this table every morning and go over things like this. Jack, I'll expect an update on what the scavenging teams bring back, and Ryan can let us know how he's coming along with the dogs. Reynolds, after the morning meeting, you, me, Hansen, and Tyler will sit here and talk about moving trailers in and going over our defenses. How's that sound?"

"Sounds good to me, Boss."

Red clapped again. "Okay, everyone. Let's get to it."

Ryan picked up his empty plate and coffee cup and started to take it back when Helen took both and nodded toward the stairs. "Go on up and get Stephen. I'll clear this up."

Ryan gave her a kiss on the cheek before heading upstairs to fetch Stephen, favoring his still-sore calf while leaning carefully on the prosthetic. Steps were always difficult to manage, especially in the mornings when he wasn't quite fully awake and had a lot on his mind. In the room, Stephen had discarded his book and was getting his clothes changed into some of Jake's clothes that were a few sizes too big for him.

"Here, son," Ryan said, pointing to his pant legs. "You'll want to roll those up. Do you have a belt?"

Stephen nodded and held one up, starting to weave it through his jean loops. "Yeah, I've got this."

Ryan watched him finish getting ready, picking up a coat of Jake's that Sandy had left on the bed. "Make sure you dress warm. It'll be chilly out there."

When they were done, Ryan opened the door to see Elizabeth Mott lingering in the loft, over by the rail and looking downstairs. "You probably won't need to guard the door anymore." Ryan spoke loudly enough to be heard downstairs. "I don't want to put words in Red's mouth, but you could probably go down and see if anyone else needs help with something."

Elizabeth peered down into the foyer, looking at Red who glanced back, giving her a thumbs up. "All right... I'll do that."

Ryan headed downstairs with Stephen in tow, slipping past where Red was gathering his people, dividing them into different groups and handing out their assignments. They stood around the table, ten rough-looking men and women like Reynolds and Hansen, all armed with rifles, shotguns, and pistols. Red had spread out a map and was pointing things out to them as Ryan turned Stephen into the kitchen. It was bustling with people coming and going, bringing back plates after breakfast and setting them on the counter where Martha directed them.

"Want a refresher on that coffee?" Helen called from the sink.

"Sounds good." Ryan swung by to let her fill his cup. "The boy hasn't eaten yet."

Sandy appeared with a small plate of eggs, bacon and fried potatoes and a tall glass of milk. "Sit, Stephen. You can eat real quick before you head out."

Ryan stood to the side, watching the groups come and go while Stephen sat on a stool on the opposite side of the counter eating. "You ladies have got a good rhythm going."

"Thanks, dear," Helen replied. "We're going to expand the operation to the rest of the house."

"We're getting some cleaning supplies together now," Martha added, drying her fingers on the towel hanging over her shoulder. "This house needs a serious once over. Sorry, Helen."

"Oh, you know. It happens. I just hope we can keep it from happening again."

Stephen brought his plate and cup to the sink, giving Sandy a hug before joining Ryan near the back door.

"Ready, Stephen?"

"Yeah, Mr. Cooper."

"That's my dad," Ryan chuckled. "Just call me Ryan."

"Oh. Okay... Ryan."

Stephen was wiry with dark eyebrows and hair like his mother, swimming in Jake's coat and throwing nervous glances around as the bigger men moved through the house.

"All right, son." He ruffled the boy's hair. "Let's put you to work. You remember our dogs?"

"Yeah."

"Well, we'll be training them today after we feed the barnyard animals."

"Can I pet the animals?"

"Nope. We're all business today. No time for messing around."

"Okay."

Ryan opened the door and gestured for him to go first. Outside, the late morning sun was bathing the yard in warm light, burning off the frost that coated the grass, tents, and the EVs' windows. Touching Stephen's shoulder and pointing toward the barn, the pair walked past the guards as the late sleepers began to stir. More guards stood on the property's east and west sides with a handful of people at the north fence where they'd pulled up a burn barrel and made a fire. Ryan guided Stephen around the chicken coops and campers, swinging into the feed shed and gathering buckets for the animals.

"See that bag over there, son?" he asked, pointing to the plastic-lined dog food trashcan at the end of the shelves.

"Yeah. Is that for the dogs?"

"Yup. Get that big coffee can full of dog food and put it in the wheelbarrow. I'll gather the rest of the feed."

As Ryan swung the wheelbarrow around and pushed it outside, a guard strolled up, keeping his distance with his shotgun resting in his arms. Ryan nodded to him in greeting and angled the wheelbarrow toward the barn, driving up to the shelter where the animals came to greet them, sheep and goats bleating while the fowl and ducks loitered around the group.

"We'll try to lead the ducks and peafowl back with the chickens at some point." Ryan wheeled up to the barn door and set the wheelbarrow down. "Or maybe they'll work their way back down on their own, we'll see."

Stephen grinned at the animals, holding his hands out as the sheep crowded around with their heads up, the bleating noise reaching a crescendo, threatening to topple him over.

Ryan chuckled, stepping closer before he could be overwhelmed. "Stephen, the first thing you want to learn is that these ferocious beasts will want something to nibble on right off, so grab a handful of feed and toss some out that way."

Stephen did as instructed, turning and tossing it over the sheep's heads, half of the animals breaking off while the rest licked at his hands and pushed against the wheelbarrow.

"That's it. Now do the same again the other way."

While Stephen fed the larger animals, Ryan got the attention of their peafowl and guided them off to the side, dropping a liberal amount of feed for them. When he and Stephen were done, he gestured to the barn door and removed the wooden bar, grabbing the latch and pulling it open, allowing it to swing wide a few inches.

"Come on inside, quickly. Don't let the dogs out."

They pushed their way inside, Ryan using his knee to keep Duke, Dutchess, and Diana from coming through the door, securing it from the inside with the latch and a piece of scrap wire hanging nearby on the wall.

"Doggone mutts – you three need to settle down!" Ryan laughed as he rubbed their heads, the trio jumping around and atop each other, bumping and pushing against Ryan and Stephen both.

"Uhhh, Mr. Cooper?"

"Ryan."

"Ryan..." Stephen's voice was strained, and Ryan spoke sharply to the dogs.

"Hey! Settle down!" The three's antics lessened, and Ryan patted Stephen on the shoulder. "You're fine. They won't hurt you – well, unless they knock you over by accident. They're used to you. They're just a little excited right now."

"Hey!" Ryan shouted as Diana started pawing at the door. "Heel, Diana. *Heel!*"

Diana loped back, circled, and sat at his side. A moment later, a shadow appeared at the door, and the sound of someone pounding on it was accompanied by a shout.

"What's going on in there?"

"We're all good!" Ryan called, motioning at the dogs with his palm to stay still as he walked back to the door, Stephen taking over and giving the dogs the attention they craved.

Opening the door a crack, Ryan nodded at the man standing outside, hand on the rifle on his shoulder. "Hey, sorry about that. It's going to be noisy in here as we get the dogs used to everyone."

The guard craned his head to see past Ryan, though the barn's interior was too dark for him to make anything out. "It sounded like someone was trying to break down the door."

"Yeah, these are *big* dogs." Ryan quickly changed the subject. "Hey, listen, do me a favor and spread the word – anyone that's able, have them come hang out by this door sometimes, okay? Part of what I'm doing with the dogs is letting them get used to everyone's scent."

"What's the other part?"

"Oh, that's what the kid's for." Ryan chuckled darkly. "The dogs don't really like him much, and Red didn't want to risk any of his people on getting them acclimated to strangers, so... yeah."

"Holy *cow*." The guard whistled. "I know Red's cold, but that is *cold* cold."

"Yeah, I think the little dude's gonna be okay though. Listen, I need to get back to it, but anytime you can walk by the door, just give it a quick knock so I can bring the dogs over and let them sniff, okay? I'll keep them from breaking it down, don't worry."

"Yeah, yeah. Sure." The guard slammed the door shut and his shadow moved hastily away.

Ryan let out a long breath and went back over to Stephen, who was watching him closely with a raised eyebrow. "That didn't sound entirely truthful, Ryan."

"All's fair in love and war, kid. And make no mistake – we are at *war*."

"What do you want me to do?" Stephen asked.

"Stand here by the door and keep an eye on the guard through the crack here."

"So we're *not* training them?"

Ryan grinned, rubbing Duke's head and stroking his neck. "If anyone asks, then yes, that's what we're doing. But do you really want these killing machines to be friends with these people? No, what we're actually going to be doing is something else."

"Your plan?"

"You got it."

"What is your plan, anyway?"

Ryan stood straight, hands on his hips, staring across the barn at the tractor and piles of scrap next to it. "We're going to build something."

CHAPTER NINE

James Burton
Connersville, Indiana

The Humvees raced down the highway through the whipping storm, splatters of rain, drizzle, and high winds hitting them in sporadic bursts. They took the curves as fast as they dared, tires swerving on the pavement, rubber slewing on the wet road, the frames of the old vehicles rattling as they tried not to spin out of control. The vehicles pulling the horse trailers were doing a fair job of keeping up, their drivers using every straightaway to their advantage to stay tight behind the rest of the convoy.

"Take it easy, Cortez," Garcia hissed as he held his weapon tightly and gripped the door.

"I'm just trying to keep up with Bragg. He's driving like a bat out of hell."

James clung to his rifle, moving with the dips and turns of the armored truck as they wove west toward the train station in Connersville. His stomach rolled, his shoulders tense watching the road, willing them forward, jaw locked tight, ready to pass up ammunition or launch himself out the door depending on what came next.

James nodded past the Humvees' taillights where an orange glow illuminated the horizon. "Oh crap. Another explosion."

"Yeah this doesn't look good," Cortez said.

"All right, people," Bragg's voice came through the CB's speaker and the two men's earpieces. "I want Cortez and Garcia to swing up front and lay down suppressing fire with the fifty-cal. The rest of you prepare to dismount and follow me in on foot. Got it?"

The fire team leaders responded in the affirmative, and the convoy slowed as the glow from the fires intensified, casting flickering light across the matte-black locomotive.

"Sons of bitches are going to regret this," Garcia said, resting his carbine next to his seat and twisting upward to push through the roof hatch.

Wind and rain burst in, spraying James in the face, Garcia's boots kicking as he climbed up and sat in the gunner's turret, James adjusting to see around his legs.

"James, toss up another canister."

"Yeah." James reached into the cargo area, grabbed a heavy canister with two hands, and handed it up, Garcia snatching it up and dropping it on the roof with a thud.

The next few minutes were a race against time as more explosions ripped through the approaching train station. James could make out a platform in the staging area dead ahead at the end of a long road, fire rolling up from warehouses and liquid container tanks in the background. The massive locomotive had three passenger cars still attached, all quiet with no lights shining in the conductor's cabin or cars. The first two trucks spread into the terminating gravel lot with Cortez slamming the accelerator and shooting between them.

"On the right," Bragg piped through the speaker. "Garcia, are you seeing this?"

Garcia stooped and spotted figures across the tracks. "Got them!"

Their Humvee charged past other military vehicles, most of them still ablaze from the attack that was taking place. Before James knew what was happening, tracers split the darkness, flashing brighter than the flames that lit up the background as Garcia opened up the fifty. The rounds zipped through the air, chewing up gravel and blistering the warehouse walls as he cut running figures to pieces. Hot brass rained down to sting James' cheeks, forcing him to cover his face as he kept an eye out the window for his family.

Cortez swept the Humvee around to the right, coming in sideways and lurching to a tire-shuddering halt, the fifty still howling as Garcia rotated right and left, responding to shouts in his earpiece of enemy locations. A few of Bragg's people moved in a swath of woods past the locomotive, calling out their position and status over the radio, and even more had moved up into the warehouse yard where they exchanged fire with the ambushers. Gunfire flared to life along the train tracks where several cars had derailed and a flash of bright lightning lit up the open, grassy areas between the tracks and the warehouses, revealing torn fencing and strips of brush and trees dividing the two sides.

The radio crackled again, and Bragg came through. "Let's go, people! We have our window! Move, move, move!"

"That means you too, James. Hustle!" Cortez shouted at him and the pair clambered out of the vehicle.

The area fell into a dead silence as they closed their doors and crouched down, waiting on the main force to move up to meet them. In the dim orange light, James fell in behind Cortez and hand signals were exchanged between the guardsmen as more from a second Humvee split off to the right to head toward the station while Bragg's team, Cortez, and James broke left toward the locomotive. With no military training, he could only mirror their movements, cross-stepping, keeping his barrel pointed downward and the rifle stock tucked against his shoulder. They broke into a run and hit the locomotive, backs thrown against an overturned train car, listening for any signs of the enemy.

"With me!" Bragg gestured for the guardsmen to follow him up into the car sitting on its side next to the tracks.

James remained where he was until Cortez, standing at the top of the stairs, motioned him up. After assembling the group inside the passenger car, Bragg guided them inside and down the center aisle of a passenger boxcar bathed in blood. The air stank of death, and a cold hand of fear gripped James around the neck. A dozen people lay dead in their seats – most of them guardsmen – and the windows and walls were filled with bullet holes with the fire's glow shining through them. The second and third cars were the same, with several corpses sprawled in the seats on the right-hand side, at least fifteen slaughtered by bullets and blunt force trauma. James held his breath as he rolled them over, sighing with relief when they turned out to be strangers, trying to brush away the guilt over his relief.

Soon he'd fallen behind, and Cortez waved for him to catch up. James kicked over plates and trays, sending dishes and utensils clattering and rattling. Smoke drifted in through the broken windows as they stepped to the rear door and down a set of stairs to the tracks again. Facing the fires, they watched the crumbling buildings as they crashed and fell to pieces, devoured by the flames.

"What now, sir?" Cortez asked.

"I can't raise anyone from the Oklahoma Guard on the radio," Bragg replied. "There's a chance no one survived."

James crept over, staying low in the flickering light. "What about down the tracks there? I see a bunch of derailed train cars about two hundred yards down. There might be more wounded in that direction."

"All right," Bragg replied. "Be careful, and try to confirm your targets before you fire. Last thing we need are friendly casualties."

As they stalked the tracks a pair of bodies appeared, sprawled across the rails, and Cortez and another guardsman rushed over to check them out, coming back to say they were members of the Oklahoma unit.

Cortez scowled. "Blood's still coming from the wounds. They weren't killed that long ago."

"Be ready, people."

The group continued along the tracks, James searching the firelight around the far buildings for moving shadows. The drifting embers and swirling cinders swept through the trees on a cool breeze, sizzling and hissing as they mixed with drizzle. Their boots crunched on the gravel, their breathing low and heavy as they approached the next set of boxcars.

"I can't see a thing," Cortez said.

"Stay low," Bragg replied. "Keep trying them on the radio."

While the troops focused to the west, James kept glancing at the spilled boxcars off to his left in a ditch, catching voices on the rising breeze.

"Captain? I see people by that derailed car," he said. "Some are standing on the hill behind them, where the rest are still on the track. Civilians, maybe?"

Bragg rose briefly and flicked on a flashlight in the indicated direction, catching the tail end of the derailed boxcar sticking up and a few people gathered on the hill.

"Definitely civilians," Bragg agreed, snapping off his light. "Spread out. We'll see if they're hostile or not."

Between their location and the derailed cars, fifty yards away in an area filled with spilled crates, gunfire erupted, aimed into the trees at an approaching force in the woods.

"Those are our weapons!" Garcia called out.

"Identify yourselves!" Bragg yelled over the radio. "Or we will open fire!"

"Captain Bragg? I'm with Captain Hechler's unit! We're at the midpoint of the train, firing on ambushers in the forest!"

"Looks like we found the Oklahoma Guard," Bragg called. "Let's hit those bastards coming through the trees. Come on, people. Light 'em up!"

The guardsmen took knees, weapons shouldered, spraying a hail of gunfire at the tree line. Guns turned their way, muzzles flashed, and bullets zipped by, striking the rails and gravel mounds. James aimed his weapon and gave the trees several bursts before Cortez shuffled over and grabbed him by the shoulder.

"Bragg wants you to go find your family! Now! The boys up ahead know you're coming, just stay behind them!"

Nodding, firing one more tight burst into the woods, James turned and sprinted along the tracks, keeping low, wincing at the zips and ricochets flying past him. His long strides carried him behind the Oklahoma Guard members taking cover behind spilled crates they'd formed into a nest. He didn't spare them a glance but ran on by another fifty yards, angling to the left and sliding feet-first down the hillside on the wet grass, hitting rocks and debris on the way. Grunting, rolling, and tumbling into a depression, James came to a hard stop at the bottom, landing in a six-inch trough of drainage. Soaking wet, he pushed himself into a sitting position and stared at the shadows of people approaching. A flashlight flipped on, blinding him with light.

"Hold it right there, buddy!" a man said. "Are you one of *them?*"

James threw his hand up to shield his eyes. "My name is James. I'm here with the National Guard from Shipshewana."

The flashlight beam dipped, and a man wearing a gray jacket stepped up, holding a broken piece of wood like he was ready to swing it at James' head. "You're a civilian?"

"Yeah."

"You're not with any of those other assholes?"

"No! Like I said, I came with the guardsmen. They're up on the tracks fighting now."

Sporadic gunfire continued to rip off, singing harmonies with the lightning cracks that filled the sky, casting the billowing clouds in mint-green light.

"All right. Come on, man. Get out of the water." He took James' hand and helped him stand on the slope.

"I'm here looking for my wife and kids," James said breathlessly. "Their names are Alice, Jake, and Sarah. Has anyone seen them?"

"There were so many families on the train," the man replied. "I... I'm not great with names."

James raised his voice and motioned at the people sitting on the hillside amongst spilled suitcases and bales of hay. "Has anyone here seen Alice Burton? She'd be about this tall, with dark brown hair, and two kids with her, Jake and Sarah. Teens, both of them."

"Yeah, I know who you're talking about." A tall man pointed back up at the tracks. "She and her kids helped us get people off the train, then they took off up the hill. I think they went for the horsecar. The lady had a shotgun."

With a sudden, restless anxiety building in his gut, James thanked him and waved to the person on the hill before trudging back up to the tracks. He took an immediate left, staying low, glancing between the flashing gunfire and the horsecar. When he reached the car he side-stepped over a pair of bodies, then grabbed the edge and climbed up, standing on the leaning deck amidst the aroma of manure and hay, aged from hundreds of miles of travel. Aside from a few gentle snorts from the rear corner of the car, it was empty, though.

"Alice! Jake! Sarah!"

James leaped down and called out again, jogging down the tracks where more train cars had derailed, some resting on their sides, others tipped over, still more tilted with their contents spilled across the rails. No one moved, no fires burned, leaving everything shrouded in darkness. An open field spread out ahead of him with shadowy woods in the distance, the moonlight illuminating the treetops, punctuated by flashes of lightning. He drew out his flashlight, angling toward the flipped boxcars but stopped and grimaced into the darkness.

Where are you guys?

With a frustrated sigh, he crept to the opposite side of the tracks and headed back north, keeping well away from where the fighting was happening as he swung his light back and forth. A few cars forward revealed a slew of bodies scattered about, most wearing National Guard uniforms, and all showing signs of having been engaged in both distanced and close-range combat.

He searched through the bodies, rolling them over, shining his flashlight on their faces, checking for survivors along with any signs of his family. A groan came from nearby, and he turned and crawled up the red-slick slope to a woman lying amidst the troops with a body on top of her. He grabbed the dead guardsman and shoved him off, aiming his flashlight into the face of a guardswoman with blood spatters on her cheeks and neck, her expression drawn in pain.

"Here, c'mon, sit up." James reached for the woman, and she gasped and flailed around, looking for her gun.

James laid down his carbine and grabbed hers before she could turn it on him. "Whoa, easy there! I'm with Captain Bragg. He's fighting on the other side of the tracks right now."

She nodded and groaned, every syllable requiring an intense effort. "Oh... good. He made... it. I'm... Captain Hechler."

"Okay, Captain. Let me help you up."

James wrapped his left arm around her shoulder and gripped her bloodied jacket in his right hand. On the count of three, he lifted her into a seated position where she slumped forward and held her stomach. James placed his flashlight down with the beam shining at the pavement, giving him enough light to see Hechler's face.

"What happened here?"

Hechler grabbed James' coat with a gasp, holding the tension in her shoulders until the pain passed. "They... did something to the tracks. Derailed us. Threw everything into... confusion. We got our asses kicked..."

James turned a nearby backpack over, flipping it open and rifling through the contents before tossing it aside. "Do you have a first aid kit? Maybe someone in your group was a medic?"

"I don't..." Hechler was breathless with pain, searching his face in confusion. "Don't know."

"Bragg! We have someone wounded over here!" James shouted, trying to be heard over the gunfire before he spoke to Hechler again. "I'm sorry we didn't get here faster. As soon as Bragg can, I'm sure he'll send someone over here."

Hechler's mouth moved, a faint word spilling out. "Who... who are you?"

"I'm James... James Burton. Colonel Hawkins up in Shipshewana sent me this way. He said he'd talked to your people about my family... Alice, Jake, and Sarah."

Hechler nodded and wheezed. "I... know them."

"You *do?*"

"We got word you were... coming." She coughed and gasped weakly. "Glad you m-made it. Wish... I could've given you a better reunion. Your wife t-told us all about you. Dixon... and some others..." The Captain grimaced in pain, her desperate gaze resting on the scattered, bullet-ridden bodies around her. "Where's Dixon?"

"I don't know a Dixon." James leaned closer, locking eyes with her. "Captain, can you tell me where my wife and kids might've gone? Any direction at all? Or even if... if they're still....""

"Alice... took off on horses... horses they brought with them. Saw... saw them. Before we were gunned down."

"So, they got away?" James leaned even closer, his voice a hard whisper.

"Yes and... no. Got away... th-three men were chasing them... horseback."

"Where?"

With intense effort, she raised her shaking arm, fingers smeared with blood as she pointed behind her. "Through the woods... other side. I hope you... f-find..."

"Thank you, Captain." James rose and looked back to where Bragg and his guard members were filtering west toward some broken fencing and firing into the warehouse area. "Bragg!" James shouted again, his voice growing hoarse, but no reply came. "Son of a... Captain, do you have a radio here? I can call Bragg, get him to send a medic over to our side and—"

James looked back down as Hechler went limp in his arms, her head dropping to the side, staring blankly off into space, a single tear breaking from the corner of her eye to roll down her cheek. James rested her back and lowered her hat to cover her face, whispering a prayer for her before creeping north and then back over the tracks. Bragg and his troops were hunkered in a shallow ditch at the fence line, firing through the trees to the warehouse district where shadows moved. James put his head down and sprinted over, hitting the ground and rolling into the ditch next to Cortez.

Cortez grabbed him by the jacket and hauled him upright. "Are you crazy, man? You should have been long gone."

"I just found Hechler and her people. They're all dead, on the other side of the train. I won't leave you guys here to get torn apart."

"Hechler's dead?" Bragg asked. "Dammit!"

Cortez ducked as the gunfire picked up, a barrage pinging off the metal fence posts and chain mesh, dirt kicking into their faces as branches from the surrounding brush were cut to pieces and fell.

"We'll be fine, man." Cortez shoved him toward Bragg. "Tell him, Captain."

Bragg rose and fired two quick bursts across the lot before ducking. "He's right, James." Bragg was almost nonchalant as he skillfully picked more targets out of the darkness. "The rest of the convoy is on the way, and we have another unit dropping in from the north. We'll make sure Hechler and her people are avenged. Go find your wife and kids."

"Are you sure, Captain? I can stay here and fight."

"This fight isn't yours." Bragg stopped firing, turned, and slammed his hand on James's shoulder, squeezing it tight. "Go before I kick your ass out of here myself."

"Thanks, Captain. Good luck."

Bragg shouted down the line. "Come on, people! Suppressing fire!"

The guardsmen raised from the ditch and unleashed a barrage of automatic gunfire that lit the night brighter than the fires burning around them, driving the surviving ambushers back into the cover of darkness. James wasted no time climbing out of the ditch, ducking and running, hitting the tracks and circling to the opposite side of the train, then sprinting south past Captain Hechler and her dead troops, all the way to the horsecar where Alice and the kids had surely been.

He tossed his gun onto the deck, grabbing the edge and hauling himself up, slipping to the back corner where he'd heard the snorts earlier. In a makeshift stall tucked in behind the others, he spotted a dappled gray flank sticking out that belonged to a gelding who stomped on the wooden deck and shook his head nervously.

"Well, at least I've got a ride," James murmured, looking out over the edge of the boxcar. "But did you guys seriously take the horses out of here onto that slope?"

It was a four-foot drop from the deck to the top of the slope, the boxcar's lean making it higher and more awkward. The horse gave a chesty chuff, and James shouldered his rifle and went to draw him from his stall.

"Hey there, buddy. Hey, boy. Did they leave you behind? Did all your friends take off?"

The horse nickered and whinnied softly as James approached and ran his hand along the horse's flank. He was nosed into the corner, barely able to turn to see him, one eye rolled up in his head as he tugged on his tether.

"It's okay, boy. Settle down. I'll get you out of here." James rested his hand on the horse's flank, stroking his back, the soft, gray-mottled coat practically glowing in the darkness. "Okay, truth be told... I'm going to need a ride. Think you can work with me on that?"

James shimmied between the horse and the stall, patting the animal's neck, stretching to untie his tether. He swung around to face the horse and gently pushed and encouraged him to back out of the stall, the dappled gray chuffing and snorting in response, pawing at the floor, hooves striking hard.

"There you go, my boy. Good boy. Back on out."

By the time he'd gotten the fidgety horse out, sweat was trickling down his temples and neck. Once free of the confines of the stall, the horse calmed and nudged James shyly.

"That's it, boy," James said, stroking his nose. "Are you a riding horse? Let's see." He reluctantly let go of the tether and stepped into the stall, grabbing the harness and tack hanging from the wall. "Okay, you don't have a saddle... great. Just great."

Gear in hand, James placed the bit into the horse's mouth and looped the reins over his head to rest them on his neck. He guided the horse to the edge of the train car deck then paused to reload his rifle from his ammunition vest, then slung the carbine securely across his back so it couldn't come loose.

"Can you jump down, buddy?" James tugged the bridle in hopes the horse would simply leap off, but when the dappled gray only tossed his head with an annoyed snort, James swallowed down a lump and rested his cheek against the horse's side. "Okay. I guess we'll have to do this the hard way. Heaven help me... bareback on a jump like that. If I survive this, I'm going to give that riding instructor a piece of my mind."

With a nervous twitch in his stomach, James buried his fingers into the horse's mane, gripped it firmly, and laid his other hand on the horse's back. He gathered himself to make the jump and lunged, swinging his leg up and across the smooth coat, relying on his momentum to carry him, wiggling and squirming, into a seated position. The dappled gray grunted and shifted the entire time, moving sideways away from him and only stopping when James was in place. Ducking and reaching up, James found he had about two feet of clearance for his head. Taking a moment to adjust to the horse's swaggering gait, and with time running out, James kicked the horse's flanks with a "Hee-yah!"

The horse rose on its rear hooves, twelve-hundred pounds of muscle tensing beneath him and leaping with a sudden lurch. James leaned forward to keep as much of his chest and belly resting along the curved spine as he could, avoiding the top of the boxcar at all costs. An instant later they were airborne, James with nothing to cling to except the mane, clenching his knees tight and preparing for an off-balance landing. They hit hard, James pitching to the side, almost toppling off but using his leverage to stay mounted, squeezing tight to the horse's chest with his legs. As the dappled gray flew toward the grassy field, he started to slide off to the right but quickly adjusted, shifting his hips, clinging with his knees, and staying low. James let him run about thirty yards before sitting up and gently pulling the reins in his shaking hands.

"Whoa, boy! Whoa... slow down!"

Leaning back and tugging the reins, he got the dappled gray to pull up and stop, the anxious horse doing a quick circle, breath puffing in the brightening moonlight. The field stretched before him, the train station and warehouse area off to his right still burning brightly, and the woods and deep shadows formed on his left.

Focusing on the woods, he tried to imagine where Alice and the kids would ride if they had pursuers on their heels. Looking back at the train, then through the woods, he saw a narrow path had been cut through the branches, with pieces of them broken off, and he turned the gray, giving him a sharp kick to take off. Flying through the tall grasses between the trees, wind blowing past him, they pounded across the moist earth beneath the velvet cloud cover with golden moonlight painting the sky a shade of purple-green. The woods didn't last long; only forty yards of trees and brush before they reached a dirt road, James pulling the gray to a sharp stop. He started to turn left but swung the horse the other way where the path led back to the city.

"Where would you have gone, sweetie? Back toward the tracks or try to get north around the city?"

Heading back to where she'd escaped seemed unlikely, so he turned to the north road and squeezed the horse's flanks, urging him onward. Wind blew through his hair as hooves pounded the dirt, sending gravel, dust, and mud flying off behind them, every muscle and bone in James' body jolting with the rough locomotion, trying to keep him steady. He leaned forward and tried to bounce along with the horse's motion, peering around his neck to get a good view of the road.

James had expected the road to bend back toward the city, but it instead swung to the northwest and the landscape changed from warehouses and loading yards to wide-open fields, swaths of trees, and gentle hills rising off to the west. The flames and gunfire from the train station battle faded with the distance, leaving only moonlight to see by, an eerie luminance that lay across the shadows, giving very little sense of depth or shape to his surroundings. After a quarter mile of fast riding, James raised himself up and slowed the gray to a trot. The horse tossed his head and snorted, James calming him with a pat on the neck.

"You're okay, boy," he said absently, "I'm just hurting from all this bouncing."

The landscape had completely changed from urban to rural, with wide-open fields cut through by the curving country road. He crossed a bridge over a small creek, old crumbling barns with rusted farm equipment squatting nearby, and after a moment of rest for his sore backside, James pushed his horse into a trot, rounding a bend where more square plots of fields hugged the road. A dilapidated fence ran parallel to the road on the left-hand side, fifteen feet from the shoulder and two horses stood at the rail, restless and shifting from one leg to the other.

As James rode closer, he spotted the dark shape of a person lying in the grass at their feet and he slid off the gray's back, hitting the ground on shaky legs and sweeping under the horse's neck to fall to his knees beside the body. He turned it over to find it was a man in dark clothing, moonlight revealing a bearded face with pale eyes staring at the clouds. Blood soaked the front of his coat, and when James spread it open, he saw the spray of buckshot embedded in his chest and neck.

"Alice?" James looked up, looking around for his family, finding nothing as the moon vanished behind a cloud, darkening the world around him. "Did you guys do this?"

James looked at the horses before placing his hands on the rail, half climbing it and getting a view over the long grass surrounding a flat field that had been cleared in preparation for planting in the spring. He started to call out but clamped his mouth shut, biting off the words before he could warn a potential assailant that he was there. Leaving the dappled gray horse standing by the fence by the others and dropping into the tall grass, he swung his rifle off his shoulder and stepped straight through the muddy field. Boots squelching in cold puddles and pulling out with suctioning sounds and globs of mud, he pressed forward, barely able to make out a series of trails through the grass ahead.

At the far edge of the field, a moist dirt trail led off through the mud and grass, and he stooped and got his flashlight out, shining it down to reveal a scattering of hoof prints and what might have been the boots of a large man imprinted deeply along the edges. He wasn't a tracker, and the assortment of prints left him confused as to their composition; he only knew they were heading deeper into the grass and toward another field. Snapping off the light, James jogged ahead and broke through a copse of trees, slowing and crouching as he entered the field.

On a gently rising slope, he caught a hint of movement, and he fell into a crouch and crept closer, faster, breath coming in ragged gasps as an overwhelming sense of panic overtook him. Several figures took shape near the top; two were smaller than the rest, standing poised behind a woman with her hair in a ponytail and holding a long gun in her hands, silhouette standing out against the glowing mist. Two other figures stood off to the right, both of them larger than the woman, though he couldn't see if they were armed or not.

"...teach this bitch a lesson!" The voice seemed to come from one of the two figures on the right, a man.

"Did you idiots not learn from your friends?" The woman snarled, the sound of her voice turning James's blood cold as recognition crept over him. "Leave us the hell alone or you'll end up just like them!"

"Is that..." James whispered, creeping through the grass, trying to angle himself to approach the figures on the right without being seen.

"Not if we spread out." The men split apart, revealing they were both armed, rifles aimed at the trio they were menacing.

The woman whipped her rifle between the two men, finally settling on one when a voice rang out from somewhere behind the group, loud and clear, and once again James had the distinct impression that he recognized the voice from somewhere.

"Put down your weapons!"

The voice was enough to create a pause between the combatants, and they started arguing with each other and the unseen third party, snarling and growling in voices he couldn't hear. James was a long way off, but he moved faster up the sweeping slope, raising his rifle, fully intending to fire upon the two men, but waiting until he could be sure the others were who he thought they were. Halfway there, their words become clearer, though his vision was obscured as he entered a wide, deep ditch with a small stream trickling through.

"...you won't shoot us!" One man said.

"They need to pay for what they've done!" Another one spoke. "You give us them, and we'll leave peacefully!"

"The answer is no. I will not warn you a third time. Lower your weapons and leave with your lives, or you will become fertilizer for our fields." The last voice was the same one who'd shouted at the group to get them to lower their weapons to begin with.

"Just leave us alone!" A young girl's voice cried out loud and clear, and James's heart dropped into his stomach, chills running up and down his back and arms.

"Sarah?" He whispered, clambering faster up the slope of the ditch on the other side, rising above the grass, barely catching sight of the shadowed figures as someone else shouted.

Multiple muzzles flashed in response, bathing the area in a dark, agonizing orange glow and three of the five figures who'd been standing in the open dropped to the ground. A black tunnel closed around James's vision and he stood up, abandoning all pretense of stealth, charging forward with a blood-curdling scream.

619

CHAPTER TEN

Oliver and Claire
Christchurch, New Zealand

Oliver stood on the dirt track leading up into the hills from the corrals, watching Emily and Maggie drive a hundred sheep to the northwest field, the women walking strategically behind the flock, sometimes jogging or running, always gesturing with open arms and capturing any strays that tried to wander off.

Oliver wore knee-high boots covered in mud and dung, his coveralls sweaty from a day of working the farm, grooming sheep in one of their broad, flat barns amidst the grain and feed silos and shelters. Their main homestead sat nestled into the woods on the east side of the property, anchoring it all together in a beautiful layout of buildings, gravel paths, and dozens of corrals filled with murmuring, bleating sheep.

Hands on his hips, Oliver gave a stiff sigh and turned as Claire came up. "Are they ready to go, dear?"

"We've got all thirty separated out, all like they requested."

"Good. These thirty will match the government quota."

Claire studied his face. "You don't seem too happy."

"Oh, no. I'm fine with it." Oliver removed his wide-brimmed hat and wiped the sweat off his brow. "I'm happy to contribute to the cause, but it's a little more than what we normally would have slaughtered this year. I'm just concerned we won't be able to make up for it, not at the numbers the Ministry of Civil Defense wants us to reach."

"We'll adjust," Claire said, resting a hand on his shoulder and looking at the thirty sheep in the corral. "We've done it before, and we'll do it again."

"Of course we will. I'm still concerned about how this will affect our feed supply. It's not like the regular boats are coming into Christchurch anymore."

"Things have changed," Claire agreed. "But I'm grateful we have enough to give back when it really matters."

Oliver nodded slowly and walked over to the gate. "All right, then. Let's get these sheep up to the trading lot."

The gate came open and the sheep remained clustered, watching Oliver with their flat stares until Claire slid around the right side and began pushing, cajoling and guiding them through. Slowly walking them in a shallow arc, Oliver pointed them north toward the northeast run.

"Thirty sheep is easy enough work," he thought, calling to one stray and trotting out to ensure he got back in line with the others.

The late morning sun was warm, the skies vivid blue, so sharp it almost hurt to look up, a scene that seemed unnatural given the state of the world. The pasture was covered in long, green grass with the livestock run cutting up through it toward the northeast, the sheep with their finely trimmed coats gleaming against the hillside, each marked with blue tags on their ears. The chorus of bleating grunts filled the air in a wall of sound as they bumped up the path with Oliver and Claire to guide them. It was the part of his life that Oliver loved the most, sharing the day with the woman he'd spent the past forty years with, honing their skills together, wordlessly herding the animals to where they needed them to go, all punctuated with an occasional smile across the white bobbing heads.

Once the flock realized where their owners wanted them to go, they fell in line and Oliver and Claire swept in behind them, strolling together up the long trek to the top of the hill that provided a majestic view of their property. Twisting shelter belts ran throughout the landscape, swaths of oaks, poplars, willows, and local woods adding a tropical flavor. They'd planted many of the trees years ago to form protective barriers against the wind, elements, and sea gales that battered farms along the shoreline during the harsh stormy months, and the growth had done its job admirably.

"I'll never get used to this view." Oliver gazed south across the property. "It's as beautiful as the day we bought this place."

Claire stepped closer and held his hand. "And I love you as much as the day we moved in with a flock of... how many sheep did we have?"

"A hundred to begin with after borrowing and begging for the money to buy the place." They turned and jogged to keep up with the sheep, moving steadily along the high ridge with slight depressions, the land opening around them with an excellent view of the other farms in the area. A wind blew up from the valley below, sweeping through the trees and hitting them square on, drying the sweat on Oliver's face.

"I just hope they're putting the animals to good use."

"You know they will be, darling. You don't look thrilled."

"I wish we had more of a say in things is all."

"The mobilization of resources is necessary for the benefit of everyone. Those hit hardest by what happened in the cities need our help."

Oliver stepped off to the left, jogging to catch a couple of strays and guide them back in with the rest. "I know, dear," he replied with a bright smile. "We may take a hit profit-wise, but it could be an opportunity to grow in other ways."

"They promised more than enough feed to expand the operation." Claire gave him a hopeful smile. "It'll set us back a couple of years, nothing more. And think about what it will do for the country. Think of the good *we* can do. We always talk about paying it forward..."

"You're right, of course. The way folks pull together around here, we'll be fine."

"After all," Claire said, "it's not like the sheep can be shipped anywhere anyway – there are hardly any boats left, and you know what the port looks like."

"How could I forget?" Recollections of those first few news reports flashed through his mind: Christchurch burning, the port destroyed, ships sunk out in the harbor, the water on fire, the screams of the dying carried to them in the night air. "I still regret getting out the field glasses for a better look."

Claire rested her hand on his shoulder, weathered features etched with concern.

"I still..." Oliver swallowed a hard lump as those disturbing emotions resurfaced, forcing him to put his arm around Claire's waist to keep his hand from shaking. "I still regret not being able to help."

"There was nothing we could do then, dear," Claire whispered. "And that's why we're helping *now*. What we've built here on our beautiful farm will do so much for everyone. And think of how much better off we are than many other countries."

"We should be thankful that we're fairly isolated for once," Oliver agreed. "And we don't have to worry about borders. We'll recover faster than most, at least in some respects."

"Let's just hope the Yanks get back on their feet sooner than later. Soon we'll see a flotilla of their ships on the horizon." Claire glanced east where the noonday light highlighted the gray horizon. "We'll be back to regular trading again soon enough."

Oliver slowly nodded, looking across at where an assortment of vegetables grew in the west-side fields: greens, potatoes, peppers, carrots, onions, and sweetcorn. "For now, we do what the Prime Minister said and focus on our people here at home."

"We'll be fine, dear," Claire said. "We've got the necessities."

The pair caught up with the sheep as they wove their way up the hill another quarter mile, joined by other local farmers who were driving their own flocks toward the trading lots. Large lines of sheep made their way up the rise from different directions, some so large that farmers needed helpers on horseback to herd them.

"There's George Lancaster." Claire pointed. "Looks like he has a hundred sheep. Wheaton's pushing out even more. Makes our thirty not look so bad."

"Nope, not at all."

Oliver watched the procession as George's and Honey's people kept their large flocks in line and moving up the designated paths to the wide dirt lot in the distance. Honey's sheep were marked with yellow tags, and George's were red, colors they'd all agreed on many years ago as they sometimes needed to rotate the flock to different fields, ensuring they kept all the animals well-fed and happy. At the top of the hill, the sheep were driven into the lot and stood bleating and mingling with the brightly colored tags gleaming in the sunlight.

George dismounted and strode up, using a walking stick for support. "Hello there," he called, waving the stick. "Heckuva morning, wouldn't you say?"

"Absolutely beautiful." Oliver removed his hat and wiped the sweat off his forehead.

"Great day," Claire replied with a smile. "How are you, George?"

"Oh, fine... just fine."

"Hey, guys and gals!" Honey Wheaton climbed from her dappled gray horse, her wild, blonde hair jutting from her sun hat and a pink scarf tied around her neck. "How is everyone today?"

"Good, Honey," Oliver nodded and shook her hand.

"Could be better, I suppose," George added with a brief wave. "You faring well, Honey?"

"Yeah, all things considered." She stood with her hands on her hips, her baggy blouse gusting in the wind as she watched the flocks and herders. "You hear about them wanting us to increase production?"

"Yep," Oliver replied. "Claire's sure they'll give us enough feed. I s'pose she's probably right."

"They've been pretty good to us so far," George said, crossing his arms and wearing a comfortable smile. "If they say we'll have the feed, we'll have it."

"Sure hope so. Say, we need to get together and discuss the new field rotation soon."

George clapped Oliver's back. "Anytime, my friend. Just come on over, or we can stop by."

"Hey, Honey," Oliver said, "we'll have a crop harvest soon. Let's talk about trading some of what we have for a pair of horses, male and female."

"We can talk about it," Honey replied, winking at him and Claire. "Breeding horses are extremely valuable, though. Might take you a few years to pay them off."

"Whatever it takes, Honey." Oliver grinned. "Oh, here comes the government."

A long line of vehicles approached up a winding hill from the highway, each hauling a trailer that left a trail of dust behind it as they rolled into the lot, swinging off to the right, slowing as they neared the wandering sheep and parking in a rigid line with the backs of the trailers facing the farmers. A contingent of workers stepped out of the trucks wearing blue coveralls with government seals on their shoulders, two conferring briefly before making their way over to the ranchers. The head official picked his way through the flocks, a tall, stiff man with his shirt buttoned up to his chin, a tussle of brown hair on top, and a clean-shaven face.

He waved his clipboard. "Hello there. I think you all know my name, but if not, I'm Reginald Ross." He stopped, checked something on his clipboard, and pointed at George. "You're... George Lancaster." He moved down the line. "Oliver and Claire Melton, and... Honey Wheaton? I first want to thank you all for being here and bringing such marvelous flocks." He gestured at the surrounding sheep. "It's quite a beautiful sight, and it'll go a long way to helping stabilize things."

"Happy to help," George replied. "So, how is this all going to work?"

"Should be very fairly easy," Ross said. "I'll have you sign a few papers, we'll check the quotas, and our people will load up the livestock in those trailers. In return, you'll each receive feed in a designated silo." He turned and gestured to the brand-new, freshly painted silos off to their left, with fences and locked gates, the manual augers locked tight. "Make sense?"

The ranchers exchanged looks and nodded.

"All right then. Please take your paperwork from my staffers and check it over."

Two staffers stepped up with stacks of clipboards, calling names and giving them to the ranchers when they raised their hands.

"Right here!" Oliver said when his name was called, and a young woman gave him a clipboard with his papers.

He and Claire stood shoulder to shoulder, each holding a corner of the clipboard as they reviewed the specifications of the trade deal. Oliver scratched his head, frowning. "Um, ma'am?"

The staffer leaned in. "You have a question, Mr. Melton?"

"That's right. This shows our feed allotment for the sheep we're providing." Oliver pointed to the two lines in question.

"That's right."

"This is... not enough. By my estimates, it'd be about half of what we could afford from selling to our normal buyer in Christchurch."

The staffer was already nodding. "Exchange rates... well, to be frank, they don't exist right now. I assure you, though, we're working on bumping the numbers up as soon as we can bring in more supplies from Australia."

Oliver nodded. "I see. What happens if someone doesn't sign the papers and refuses the trade?"

The staffer shrugged. "We'd send it up the chain. Some folks are understandably reluctant to jump in, but we're certain they'll be right on board when they see the results of what we're doing and the lives we're saving."

"Fair enough." Oliver smiled, took the pen from her, and signed the paperwork.

George and Honey followed suit along with several other farmers who'd brought their flocks up to add to the growing numbers. The staffers handed out the keys to the silos and moved on as the government herders filtered in to load the sheep into the trailers, George's and Honey's people joining in to help handle the animals, receiving thanks and smiles in return. Ross guided the proceedings for a short time until things ran smoothly, at which point he stood back and watched.

Oliver stood next to him with his arms crossed. "So, Ross. As long as we continue to bring our quotas, those silos will stay full?"

"That's right, Mr. Melton. And we'll be giving bonuses for any wool you can provide."

"Well, we've got plenty of that," Claire stated, standing on Oliver's left. "Is it true they want us to expand?"

"Yes, ma'am. We're hoping to subsidize doubling or even tripling your production. We're working on getting more feed from Australia, so these trades will become even more valuable to you than before all this happened."

Oliver exchanged a pleased nod with Claire. "How long do you think this will last?"

"It could be months... probably years. Plan on staying in it for the long haul, my friend, and you'll come out of this on top."

"That's good to hear," Oliver replied. "I hate to say we're benefiting off something like this when we're just happy to contribute, but regardless, we'll do what we can."

"That's the kind of attitude we're hoping for."

Oliver wrapped his arm around Claire's waist, standing by as the workers gained more confidence, driving the sheep into the trailers by the dozens, packing them in comfortably but tightly, finally slamming the gates shut and preparing to go. The armed guards climbed back into their vehicles with Ross and his staffers giving a hearty wave and a call of farewell.

"God Defend New Zealand!"

The ranchers raised their fists in reply, clasping forearms, and shouting enthusiastically. Honey galloped up with two of her people as George climbed into his saddle.

"How does two days from now sound?" George asked. "For our meeting, I mean."

"Perfect," Honey replied, looking at Oliver and Claire, who nodded in affirmation. "We'll figure out how to solve this looming field rotation problem. See you then!"

Oliver and Claire waved as the ranchers galloped down the livestock run before branching off toward their separate farms, leaving dust in their wakes. Oliver squeezed Claire to him and watched the two departing groups, the government people driving the flocks to the city while the ranchers were left to their peaceful farms.

"I guess I shouldn't be too upset about our legacy," Oliver said.

"What do you mean?"

"We wanted to give the farm to the kids when we retired, but I guess there's a greater cause now."

"A greater cause indeed, dear. We'll be feeding hundreds and maybe even thousands of people." She smiled and gave a little shiver of pleasure. "It kind of thrills me, to be honest. And there's nothing that says we can't leave it to them one day anyway."

"Aye. We'll make it work." Oliver held up the silo key. "Let's go down and grab the cart, and Ellie and Maggie, and start hauling down some of this feed. It's time to start expanding."

Arm in arm, they walked the winding livestock run beneath the brilliant blue sky and promises of a glowing future.

CHAPTER ELEVEN

Alice Burton
Connersville, Indiana

Buck's fluid gait carried her into a short patch of woods, Jake and Sarah hot on her heels, their pursuers calling out after them. They ducked and dodged, weaving through the saplings, hitting dips and climbing quickly with the horses' sides heaving, their chests billowing like wind machines, three freight trains of muscles between their knees as they thundered over the soft, loamy ground. They pounded onto a dirt road stretching north and south, giving them more options than she wanted. If she went left, it would lead them straight back to the train tracks, but heading right appeared as though it would take them closer to the city where James might find them after he discovered what happened to the train.

Sarah and Jake rode onto the road behind her with Jake turning Rocky in a circle. "Where now, Mom?" he asked, breathless with vertigo.

"I'm not sure," Alice replied, grimacing with indecision. "I think we're far enough away from them now that we can take a momen—"

Men shouted and cursed, flashlights bobbed in the distance, and horses plodded after them through the woods.

"Forget I said that. They're coming. Let's go!"

She turned Buck north on the dirt road, kicking him into motion, holding on as he galloped, throwing up clumps of mud and rocks. Gunshots went off sporadically in the distance, bullets whizzing by and striking trees, buildings and the road.

"Stay low and go!" Alice pressed herself to Buck's back, urging the surging steed on, hitting the next bend with a vengeance to put the curve of trees between them and their pursuers. The gunfire stopped momentarily as Jake and Sarah caught up, and Alice continued to push them forward, seizing the opportunity afforded by the break in the gunfire. As the cloud cover drifted out from in front of the moon, she caught sight of a small creek behind them, and a city in the distance even farther back.

"This road isn't going where I thought it would!"

"What do we do?" Sarah gasped breathlessly. "They're not far away!"

"Think they'll make that jump?" Alice nodded to a fence line coming up on the left.

"I don't know, Mom. Can we?!"

Jake squinted into the night. "That's at least four feet high, mom!"

"We can make it... we *have* to! Come on!"

A flurry of gunfire came from behind, one of the rounds nicking Alice's shoulder, and she clenched her teeth in pain. "Go! Faster!"

She charged Buck along the right-hand side of the lane, taking a wide angle for the fence, standing slightly in her saddle and sizing up the height of the jump.

"Come on, Buck. You can do this, boy..." Alice turned him in a sharp arc toward the dusty rails. "Up, Buck! Come on, boy. Up!" Alice dug her heels into his flanks and tensed, eyes closed.

Buck gathered himself and leaped, and they were airborne once again, weightless, the click of his hoof against the wooden rail sounding a split second before they plunged toward the ground, landing and continuing onward. She slowed for a few seconds, looking back to see if Jake and Sarah had made it, only to see them fly past her on both sides.

"Keep going!" Alice shouted, swinging Buck around and readying her shotgun.

Their pursuers were angling toward the rail, weapons lowered as they prepared to jump, but Alice aimed at the leading assailant, firing a burst of buckshot that ripped the man from his saddle, sending him toppling to the ground with a crunch. Buck raised on his back legs with a cry, nearly kicking her off, and she pulled on the reins, steadying him before she could fall off.

One of the pursuer's horses swung away from the fence and raced on down the lane, taking its hapless rider with it while the man on the middle horse made the jump, flying over the rail at an angle and hitting a patch of mud on the other side, his horse slipping and sliding, flailing as it tried to right itself. Alice kicked Buck into motion, racing hard after the kids as they pounded through a muddy field.

"Mom, there's a path!" Jake called from the edge of the field, pointing at a trail bending off into the grass.

The horse and rider who hadn't made it over the fence came back around to the rail, the rider sliding off and over the fence, hitting the mud with a splatter, falling to his knees before getting up and waving to the man who'd made the jump, both taking aim at Alice and the kids.

"Go!" Alice snapped. "Ride!"

Jake angled them around the edge of the field, mirroring the tree line and using the thick brush as cover, Sarah next to him, and Alice in hot pursuit. When Alice caught up to the pair, she pointed toward an open field on their left and they raced through the darkness, unable to see if the two men had found their trail and were following on the single horse or if they'd gotten lost. After a quarter mile they reached the top of a shallow rise with moonlight highlighting the swaying grasses and Alice pulled Buck to a halt.

"Whoa, easy boy!"

Jake and Sarah drew up beside her, their horses gasping in billowing breaths, foam dripping from their lips as they snorted and chuffed.

"What is it, Mom?" Sarah said. "Why did we stop?"

Alice pointed north. "I think we're on someone's property now."

In the velvet glow of the moonlight, sheds and barns stood out against the shadows, square blocks with peaked roofs, farmsteads facing each other across a long dirt lane that led off into the distance with chimneys trickling smoke into the sky, and soft glows in a few of the windows. Fences stood everywhere with pens and cattle runs between them, and a few old horse-drawn plows were parked on the sides.

"Farmers?" Jake asked.

"Yeah. Looks that way."

"Well, let's go." Jake trotted Rocky ahead a few yards before looking back.

Alice glanced behind them where the moonlight gave no hint of movement nor signs of pursuit.

"Let's go on down and try to find a place to hide out for a while. But take it slow. I don't want to run into *more* people with guns."

"Yeah, let's not get shot," Sarah agreed, catching her breath and urging Stormy ahead.

The three trotted in a tight formation toward the farmsteads when the swift and sudden gallop of hooves thundered toward them. Whipping the reins to the left, Alice spun Buck with a warning cry. A horse and rider charged out of the shadows, plowing between the kids' horses, sending them rearing and staggering away, both Jake and Sarah toppling over. A massive revolver raised and fired point-blank at Alice, then there was a sting in her shoulder, raw-hot pain that forced her to recoil. The attacker swerved at the last second but not before ramming into Buck with the broad side of his horse, sending Alice and Buck both lurching sideways as lightning rod agony raced down Alice's arm. Buck whipped the other way, and she flew from her saddle, airborne for a breathless moment before slamming in the mud on her right arm, a sharp cry of pain ripping from her throat.

Alice clenched her teeth on a scream, crawling a couple of feet to grab her shotgun and struggling up to see Sarah and Jake were lying in the grass a few feet away. "You guys okay?"

"I think so," Jake said, getting up and helping Sarah who blinked in confusion.

"Put down your gun, lady!" The man on foot charged in from the right with a rifle in his hand, and the rider slid from his saddle, revolver raised, joining his partner as they closed in.

Alice shoved the kids behind her. "You drop *yours!*" She growled through the pain with the shotgun stock resting against her hip, unable to lift it to her shoulder due to the numbness gripping her arm.

"Won't tell you again, woman!" The one with the rifle jerked the weapon to his shoulder and stopped ten yards away, his barrel flashing between Alice and the kids.

"You killed Chester back there," the other man bellowed, pulling back the hammer on his revolver and settling it on the kids.

Glaring fiercely, Alice screamed at them, keeping the shotgun level with the pair. "Stay the hell *back!*"

"Oh no, woman." He snarled in response. "You and your little brats are going to pay!"

The revolver swiveled to point at Jake and Sarah. "We'll take her and shoot the kids. That'll teach this bitch a lesson!"

"Did you idiots not learn from your friends?" Alice snarled. "Leave us the hell alone or you'll end up just like them!"

"Not if we spread out." The one holding the rifle took five quick steps to his right, and both men closed in at different angles as Alice swung the shotgun back and forth between them.

With a gasp of pain Alice managed to jerk the shotgun to her shoulder, fingers squeezing on the trigger, freezing at a man's deep-throated, imposing shout from behind.

"Put down your weapons!"

The declaration froze Alice and her attackers, and all eyes turned north where buildings lay spread out across the moon-bathed fields. A pair of men strode briskly toward them, coats billowing, wide-brimmed hats perched on their heads, each of them bearing a rifle aimed at the group. One was older and taller than the other, gray-haired and stiff-jawed, while the youngest had a bright red bushel of hair sticking from beneath his hat.

"What in God's green earth is going on here?" The older man glanced over Alice, Jake and Sarah and turned his shotgun aside, aiming at one of her accosters.

Alice took a few steps toward the newcomers but threw hot glances at their attackers. "These two men are chasing us and have been trying to kill us!"

"This woman stole our horses," the man carrying the rifle spat. "And killed our buddy!"

"We did not steal *your* horses!" Alice snapped back. "These are ours! You and your people attacked and crashed the train we were on! You tried to kill everyone, and now you're trying to kill *us!*"

"I—the hell, no!" The other one stuttered, flustered as the two men advanced on the group. "Train? What train? It was you and these troublemakers you got with you... these damn kids! You came in and stole our horses!"

The pair of newcomers gave each other a look and continued to advance, their weapons still up and continuing to aim more at the pair of men than at Alice and the kids. "Everyone back away from each other, and drop their weapons."

Alice shook her head. "I'm sorry, I can't do that. I'm not letting them hurt my children."

"Come on, mister. Do we look like the kind of people who'd try to derail a train?"

The older man raised an eyebrow. "Derail? Who said anything about derailing a train?"

"Father," the younger man said, stepping closer and narrowing his eyes at the man with the revolver. "I know him. He's one of the men who tried to steal from us when we first arrived here."

The older man nodded knowingly. "I thought I recognized him. That's right... you're one of those thieves."

Alice, Jake and Sarah shifted backwards as the father and son sidestepped to put themselves between Alice and the men.

"Listen, boys. I'm done being peaceable. You tried to steal from us, and you got to live. Testing my patience twice is not a good idea. Best vacate this area *now.*"

One of the attackers sneered, gesturing at the shotguns that the father and son bore. "What do you think you're going to do with *them?* Nothing, that's what. I know your kind of people." When the father and son still didn't back down, the man rose on his toes and jeered. "You won't shoot us."

"They need to pay for what they've done! You give us them, and we'll leave peacefully."

"The answer is no. I will not warn you a third time. Lower your weapons and leave with your lives, or you will become fertilizer for our fields."

The man with the revolver switched his aim slightly, a twitch of his shoulder, and Alice threw herself onto Jake and Sarah as an explosion echoed from in front of them, filling the air with flame and smoke. Both of the attackers fell before they could get a shot off, collapsing to the ground as the father and son fired their shotguns simultaneously.

A desperate scream cut through the ensuing silence, echoing louder than the shotguns, and both men leveled their shotguns at another man charging through the grass, carrying a carbine and hollering at the top of his lungs.

"Alice! *Alice!*"

As the father and son exchanged a look of confusion, Alice pushed herself up from the ground, heart racing, scarcely willing to believe her own ears.

"James?" She whispered, then called out louder, eyes wide, hope surging from the depths of her soul. "*James!*"

CHAPTER TWELVE

Helen Cooper
East Lansing, Michigan

Dishes rattled and water poured hot from the spigot, topping off the rinse water in the right-hand sink. The kitchen smelled of lemon-fresh dish soap as Helen and Martha worked together to clean up the mess after a loud and hectic lunch, Helen scrubbing the bowls and Martha rinsing, wiping and stacking them. The crew had been in and out all afternoon in between chores, with the women serving vegetable soup from a big pot, Helen wearing a smile the entire time despite watching their valuable supplies shrink in real time before her eyes. Just one week at the pace they were going would drain them significantly, and two weeks would wipe them out.

"When will the scavenging teams get started?" Helen asked as she scrubbed another dish and handed it over.

"Red's already on it. Got them out there looking for water heaters and other things."

"Oh, that's good."

Martha shot her a sidelong glance. "Something wrong, Helen?"

"Not at all."

"It's okay. You can tell me."

"I guess having so many people in the house all of a sudden is a little... I don't know. It's a *lot*."

"I can't blame you for feeling... put out," Martha replied, voice growing softer. "I'd feel the same. I told Red as much already so many times, but there's no talking to him, especially when he gets his mind fixed on something."

Helen grabbed a couple of dirty glasses with milk crusted around the rims and on the bottoms. She pushed the scrubber all the way, twirling it to get everything before handing them to Martha.

"Red's certainly a forward thinker," Helen suppressed a roll of her eyes. "That's why he and Ryan get along so well. I hope they both want what's best for everyone here."

Martha smiled falteringly. "I know it's been said a hundred times, but we're in this together, and we'll make it work." She dried the last two glasses and put them in the dish rack, turning to Helen and leaning on the counter. "I can't imagine how hard this must be for you. You've been through so much already before we showed up." She cast a dark look into the great room. "Jack and Barb Willoughby. They're not the most gracious of people, are they?"

Helen sighed. "No, they're not. Good thing for us Jack isn't a good shot, or we'd be dead."

Martha clicked her tongue and shook her head. "I'm so sorry to hear about the spat you got into with them before we came."

Helen forced herself to wave it off. "It's nothing. I won't focus on that negativity now, not when everything is going so well."

"Good to hear that, Helen. It really is."

With a clatter of buckets, a mop, and cleaning supplies, Sandy and Nancy came in from the foyer and dropped their things at their feet, Nancy giving an audible groan as she stretched her right arm over her head and yawned. The women had their sleeves rolled up, wet spots on their knees, and scrubbing powder speckling their shirts.

"That's the last of the bathrooms," Sandy said, covered in beads of sweat.

"There's still one in the basement," Helen announced with a sly grin.

Sandy and Nancy shared a tired look and started to pick up their things.

"On to that one, then," Sandy said. "What about after that?"

Helen pointed to the small hallway leading to the laundry room. "That could use a good scrubbing down, and after that we can probably get Ryan to turn some breakers on so we can run the washer and dryer for a few hours."

Nancy rolled her eyes. "I'll be last in line."

"We'll toss yours in first and get you in the shower. You'll be smelling like a rose before the night's out."

"I've never smelled like a rose," Nancy said flatly.

"Well, get ready for it," Helen forced a smile.

Martha rested her hand on Helen's shoulder and addressed the cleaning crew. "Go on, ladies. We'll save you some soup."

Sandy and Nancy headed down the hallway with their buckets of supplies and Helen strode to the back door and pushed the curtain aside to peer into the yard where Red, Reynolds, and a few whose names she didn't know were trying to reseat the well pump. They had the entire contraption lifted out of the pipe with the long PVC tubing stretched across the length of the side yard, Reynolds doing most of the work with the others standing around watching and talking amongst themselves.

"I can't wait to get regular pressure again."

"I'm just impressed you had a backup system." Martha turned the water on briefly and watched it trickle from the spigot before shutting it off again. "That's some smart thinking."

"Ryan's clever like that. I'm glad Red decided to listen to reason."

"You and me both," Martha smiled wanly.

Helen walked over to the cooking island and leaned against it, looking at the refrigerator and counter where several stacks of supplies had been brought up and left. "We've got such a big crew here now that we need to start thinking about making food in larger, simpler batches. We can give them a buffet line for breakfast with eggs, pancakes, and possibly some dried or caned fruit and berries for breakfast. We won't have any fresh crops from the fruit trees until next year though."

"We could do oatmeal and dried fruit, too... granola?"

"We've got big bags of that in the downstairs pantry," Helen replied. "It'll go with almost anything. Oatmeal or just plain with milk."

"There you go," Martha nodded. "What do you think for dinner tonight?"

"We've got some hamburger meat down in the freezer. It's been down there for a while, way at the bottom. We can use several pounds of that, mix in some beans and a few spices and make some chili. It'll match the weather nicely, too."

Martha leaned out and touched Helen's hand. "That sounds amazing. I can't believe how we went from barely scraping by to eating like kings. Thank you."

Helen gestured to the messy cooking island with grease, crumbs, and egg splatters on the surface and caked on the burners. "Should we make the girls clean this up?"

"We're done with the dishes. Let's give them a hand."

The pair grabbed their scrubbers and a pan of warm, soapy water and began wiping down the appliances and cabinets. Through the window, Helen noticed Tyler and some others in the barnyard standing around piles of wood and supplies.

"What's Tyler working on?" Helen asked.

"I overheard they wanted to put up some new fencing for the animals they're hoping to bring back from nearby farms."

"Do you think there are a lot?"

"When all the farms went up around us, a lot of animals escaped. I'd wager there are flocks of sheep, chickens, and goats roaming everywhere around here, but the problem back in Grand Rapids was that one group corralled them all…" A shadow passed over her face.

"It's okay, Martha. You can tell me anything. What happened back in Grand Rapids? I mean, aside from our condominium burning to the ground."

"I'm sorry we had to bring you that news. We salvaged some whiskey from the basement. You're more than welcome to some."

"Ryan will be glad to hear that," Helen said. "He had a few expensive bottles." She waited for Martha to go on, picking up a pair of burner grates and placing them aside with a soft clank, scrubbing the baked-on food.

"A group of some former military yahoos took over the town," Martha said. "They took over the strip malls and a big department store downtown."

"No!"

"Oh, yes."

"I thought a couple of your group are former military. Isn't Red?"

"Some are, but it's like they say… it's not what you know, it's *who* you know. And I guess we weren't friends with the right people." Martha worked on the opposite end of the cooking island, talking as she scrubbed at the grease spots. "They had fifty, maybe seventy-five people. Huge group. They scavenged all the supplies… I mean all of them. Just took it all for themselves. We had one cow left on Nancy Likely's farm and Jed slaughtered it for us, but the group pushed in on us and took it."

"They came in and stole it from you?" Helen kept her eyes down, not daring to look up for fear of her voice growing thick with sarcasm. "That's awful."

"Yes, well…" Martha hesitated a moment, and Helen could very nearly hear the woman's shoulders sag in defeat. "It's dark out there, Martha. There are things… terrible things going on."

"I know. Believe me, I do."

Martha started to say more, but Sandy came in, frowning when she saw them cleaning the cooking island. "Hey, I was going to do that."

"Well, there's the kitchen table, too."

"On it." Sandy set her bucket down, taking out a rag and wiping the table surface. "It's like a lunchroom cafeteria at the school I used to work in. Except three times a day instead of two."

"I don't know if Red mentioned to the crew yet the part from before about everyone picking up after themselves," Martha shrugged in apology. "Sorry. I'll mention it to him."

"It's fine," Helen said. "I'm just glad people are getting solid food."

"Some of us hadn't eaten properly for weeks. I just hope we can keep everything up here and keep adding new things. Like the water heaters Ryan was talking about."

The women fell quiet, working as country music played in the living room courtesy of one of the crew members getting into Alice and James's CD collection. After a few minutes Sandy and Helen exchanged a look, Helen cutting her eyes toward Martha with a slight rock of her head, and Sandy cleared her throat. "So, Martha. You know Helen from before?"

"Not directly. Just through our husbands. We lived in the same general area in Grand Rapids, but I don't think we talked much at all before."

"What made you all come this way? Red mentioned you'd gone to Helen and Ryan's condo?"

"Yes." Martha's voice went quiet again, and she took a long breath, forcing a slight smile. "I was just telling Helen about the situation back in Grand Rapids. Things weren't good, and a violent group threatened us. Red decided it was time to get out and he… thought here might be good. The road wasn't kind to us, though."

"What do you mean?"

"We got down here in the salt truck, but we didn't start that way." Martha wiped down a burner grate and set it aside. "Once we decided to leave, we walked from our place at the remains of one of the farms to your condo, Helen. There were… there were a lot of people who weren't exactly friendly along the way. Very territorial."

"Guarding whatever they had left," Helen avoided Martha's gaze again. "Can't say I blame them."

There was another pause before she resumed. "Anyway, there we were hoofing it across town, everything we owned in grocery store baskets and carts, rattling along like some homeless convoy which, to be fair, I guess we were." Martha's laugh was devoid of levity. "Red had everyone pretty worked up after a pack of dogs came at us, ready to shoot anyone who threatened us. We went through some houses and ran into a little... trouble."

"What kind of trouble?"

"I, uh. I was outside. But they got jumped by some homeowners, and Red and the boys were forced to shoot. There were screams, too."

"Screams?" Helen looked at Martha, then at Sandy, who had paused her cleaning to listen to Martha's story.

"Red... well, Red told me a husband and wife jumped Hansen and Reynolds, and the boys shot them. Or maybe it was Tyler. I didn't get the whole story and it seemed..." She shook her head. "Anyway, those were the first people who they killed."

Helen and Sandy shared a quick, dark look, Sandy mouthing something Helen couldn't make out. "It's tough to live with." Helen replied to Martha. "I mean, killing people is hard."

"We ran into more trouble near your condo." Martha walked to the sink, turned on the spigot to a trickle of warm water, and rinsed off her sponge. She started to go back to the cooking island but leaned over the counter, staring out through the window. "A family came at us out of the shadows."

"A family?"

"I—they might've just been scavengers going through the ruins. But—I... I'll never forget that girl's eyes."

"What happened?" Helen paused at the corner of the cooking island and blinked at Martha. "Did Red...."

The words spilled out. "Red told the father to stop multiple times, but he kept coming. The family was standing back in the shadows. Hansen shot first, and then the mother and children they came running out and... you... you can imagine what happened next." Martha's chest heaved from the expulsion of the heavy words, eyes glassy and arms trembling.

"Oh, Martha. You..." Helen chose her words carefully, trying to balance her end goal with the raw, true emotional impact she was feeling. "Red really did that?"

Martha nodded sadly. "After that, we made our way east, swinging through a few towns, running from people mostly. We ended up in a podunk town with a maintenance building and what we hoped would be supplies. Ended up getting that truck from a couple of guardsmen who were in the process of confiscating it."

"Did Red...."

"Yeah," Martha replied breathlessly, wiping tears out of her eyes and turning back to dry the soapy burners. "I told him not to, told him how bad it was, what he was doing, but he didn't listen. I... that man won't listen to anyone when he's fixated on something." Martha's jaw worked back and forth as she stared out the window at the group working on the well pump.

"Ladies," Helen spoke softly. "I can finish up here. Why don't you take some hot tea out to the workers? While you're at it, ask them how long it'll be till we get proper water pressure again."

"That sounds great," Sandy said as she circled the cooking island and began rooting through the cupboards for a thermal coffee urn. "Martha, there are teabags in the pantry. Can you grab five or ten out?"

"Oh. Yeah... yeah, sure," Martha said, drying her cheeks and giving Sandy a slight smile. "Thank you both for listening."

As they worked on the batch of tea, Nancy came in carrying her supplies and set them down by the wall. "All done in the laundry room. Want me to start gathering clothes to wash?"

"Why don't you help me take tea out?" Sandy asked, gesturing to the assemblage of mugs and hot tea they were throwing together.

"Yeah, sure."

Helen continued cleaning while they steeped the teabags in hot water, filling the room with a rich but bitter aroma. Sandy and Nancy each carried a tray of mugs and two urns outside while Helen held the door for them, waving and shutting it behind them to lock out the chill. She stood beside Martha with her back to the counter, arms folded as she watched them balance their trays and carry them out to the waiting group. "That'll warm them up nicely."

"They'll appreciate it," Martha replied. A dark look crossed her face followed by a sharp intake of breath. "I just... want you to know that I'm *so* sorry for this. I wish I could have made Red *not* come. The way he looked at Ryan, and nearly—I'm sorry."

Helen patted Martha's arm. "That's nice of you, Martha, but you don't—"

"No, there's no need to act happy about it. If a group of... violent people came to our farm and took it over, I don't know what I'd do."

Helen pursed her lips and leaned back, once again choosing her words with extreme care. "Could Red be... convinced to leave?"

"No, no he wouldn't up and leave," Martha whispered, crossing her arms to mirror Helen's posture. "And despite his promises to do better, all I see is that he's changed for the worse since all this started. He's cruel and callous, not the gentle man he was before."

"I'm so sorry, Martha. Ryan and I will have a hard time putting up with this long-term," Helen admitted. "There are just too many people here, and once James and Alice make it back, they're not going to be happy with a couple dozen or more visitors."

"I'd be a complete fool to think you and Ryan would be happy with this. I can tell Ryan barely holds his anger in, especially when he looks at Jack."

Helen shrugged. "Well, Jack did shoot Ryan in the leg."

Martha snorted before she could stop herself. "Sorry. That's not funny at all. Ryan's got some kind of restraint to not strangle Jack in his sleep."

"Oh, I'm sure he's thinking about it nonstop."

They laughed together, Helen holding her stomach and allowing some pent-up tension to escape. Their laughter faded, and she took a deep breath and sighed. "I appreciate the talk, Martha. It's nice to know that not everyone here is out to get us. I just hope we can all keep getting along..."

Martha's visage sank again, and she forced a slight smile, nodding in agreement with Helen before staring back out the window, lost in thought.

Sandy almost dropped her tray descending the steps, tripping on a pair of screwdrivers someone had left in the way. The mugs and urn of tea tilted precariously before she paused to grab it with both hands, chuckling nervously in triumph.

"Nice catch," Nancy said.

"I was a waitress a long time ago, so I got a lot of practice."

"I did a stint at a diner." Nancy balanced her tray in one hand, six mugs around the urn. "Who would have thought it would come in handy at the end of the world?"

"It brings out those all-important skills we thought we'd forgotten." Sandy stepped over some hoses, lengths of pipe and tubes of sealant. Red and Reynolds were both soaked with water, both of them holding on to the well pump and tightening a clamp on the bottom of the device.

"This should fix the leak," Red said. "Let's lower it back into the well pipe."

"You all want some tea before you do that? It's nice and hot!" Sandy swung around to a small plastic table someone had brought out, covered in various tools. Setting the tray down, she accidentally knocked a drill off. "My bad. I'll get that."

Nancy angled in the other direction toward the EV and placed her tray on the hood. "I've got some over here, too. Plenty to go around."

The group looked at Red as he removed his hat and wiped his arm across his sweaty brow. "Yeah, it's time for a break. Go on, grab yourself some hot tea."

Nancy and Sandy poured everyone a mug, and soon they were standing around sipping and peering up into the late afternoon sun, still warm as it cast the treetops in golden light and fell across their shoulders. Pairs of guards walked the yard perimeter, and a second burn barrel blazed up in the north part of the barnyard with an even bigger crowd gathered around it. The animals milled beneath their shelter, with a few stray sheep and ducks wandering along the fence line, nudging the rails and nibbling at the weeds.

Red finished draining his cup and nodded appreciatively. "I'm not usually one for tea, but that hit the spot. Much obliged, ladies. Reynolds... you ready to put this pump in?"

"Yeah, Boss."

While the others finished their drinks, Reynolds and Red lifted the pipe and gingerly maneuvered to lower the pump in first, then began dropping it down the well shaft, using hand towels from one of the bathrooms to wipe the dirt and grass from the pipe as it went down.

Red leaned in as they neared the end of the pipe. "Okay, hold it. You've got to seat it in the harness and work it so that it fits into the pipe running into the house."

"I've got it, Boss. Hey, can you move a bit?"

Red backed away as Reynolds lowered the pump three more feet, shoulders and arms bulging as he twisted the PVC around and settled it in place. "Almost got it." The pump dropped a little more before he jerked the tool free. "I think that did it, Red."

"Excellent work, Reynolds. Now, we need to test it. Somebody get Ryan and tell him to make it so we can switch this thing back on from the panel."

"I'll get him," Sandy said, grabbing two mugs and an urn. "I'm sure they could use some tea, too. Won't take but a few minutes."

"Thanks, Sandy. Everyone take ten – we're almost done here."

Sandy headed through the yard past the chicken coops, weaving her way around where a small group sat on buckets between tents, cleaning weapons and talking. She passed through the barnyard gate where Tyler and the others were gathered by the fencing supplies and Sandy smiled and nodded at them, angling toward the barn doors where she stopped at the sight of a sign that read "*Do not enter. Dogs in training.*"

With her hands full, she kicked the door three times.

"Who is it?" Ryan's gruff voice called from inside.

"It's Sandy. I brought some tea for you and a request from Red."

"Come on in."

"I've got my hands full. Could use some help."

The door popped wide a few inches, and Stephen's smile greeted her. "Come on in, Mom," he said, holding the door open with one arm and backing up enough for her to slide through. As soon as she was inside, he quickly shut the door and latched it.

"Is it going well in here?" Sandy asked, stepping in and looking for a place to put the tray, setting it on a workbench Ryan had built from two sawhorses and a piece of plywood. "My, my... You've been busy."

"Come on over, Sandy. Keep your voice low."

Ryan had a welding torch in hand, a tank next to him, and several pieces of metal positioned around the tractor. He turned off the torch and lifted the long gray mask, revealing a sweat-stained face.

"We've got to be extremely careful," he spoke quietly, putting the torch down and removing his welding gloves as he gestured toward the door. "They all think we're training the dogs."

Duke, Duchess, and Diana lounged by the stalls in the barn, watching Ryan curiously as he worked. Three shaggy heads turned to Sandy as she leaned down to pet them, their tails wagging in furious excitement.

"I assume this is your plan, huh? Mind telling me what it is?"

Ryan winked. "I'm working with this metal, and that's all you need to know right now."

"Well, Red wants you down by the house. They've got the well pump reinstalled and want to test it out. Guess they want you to do something with the breaker panel."

"I guess it's good to be needed. Here, give me a hand with this real quick."

Together, they picked up the heavy pieces of steel and moved them aside, stacking them randomly against vertical beams and walls, presenting a messy appearance that wouldn't give away his work should unwanted eyes peer into the barn.

"Here, have a quick drink before we go up." Sandy poured two mugs and stirred in a little sugar as steam rose in twisting tendrils.

"Thank you. How are things going back at the house?" Ryan asked with another wink. "You ladies getting along well?"

"Better than I thought. Helen and Martha are like sisters, and Nancy and I have been cleaning the house all morning. Boy, what a mess those people leave."

"What do you expect?" Ryan snorted. "They came in here acting like they own the place. Makes you wonder what their houses looked like."

"I think Helen's got them thinking about rationing more. They're supposed to put together some bigger, simpler meals for the crew, trying to cut back on everyone grabbing whatever they want."

"That's my Helen. A smart lady." Ryan put his empty mug down. "Okay, let's head up and see the damage."

Ryan took one more look over the work area, ensuring the tank and welder were tucked away before they exited the barn and shut the doors behind them, throwing the wooden bar in place.

"That sign's pretty smart," Sandy said, nodding toward the sign as they moved outside and walked together back up to the house.

Ryan chuckled. "I figured it would help remind those numbskulls to steer clear of the barn and let me work in peace."

Red greeted them at the well with a wave. "There's the big man himself. We've got everything installed and think we have the leaks patched up. Just need you to get the electricity on for us so we don't mess anything up."

"All right. Let me check the well out first."

Reynolds and Red stood aside as Ryan leaned closer to the well head, holding his hand out for a flashlight. Shining the beam inside, he inspected the bleach-streaked grime, ensuring the pump was seated in the horseshoe-shaped cradle, sealed tight against the opening leading into the house.

He stood and nodded. "Yeah, that looks pretty good. Nice work."

"Good." Red clapped him on the shoulder. "Go throw the magic switch for us, then!."

Those gathered around gave an enthusiastic cheer as Ryan waved them off, more embarrassed than anything. "You can thank me when it works."

"How's things in the barn?" Red asked, walking toward the back door along with Ryan, Reynolds trailing behind them.

"Just doing my job, training the dogs."

"It's going well? I haven't seen you bring anyone in."

"Well yeah, I don't want someone getting mauled." Ryan smiled disarmingly. "Stephen's in there getting them used to having a stranger around, and I've asked your people to walk around the door anytime they're around so the dogs can get used to their scents. Another day or two and I'll have your people meeting them face-to-face, and then they can start taking them on guard patrols."

Red grunted amiably. "Sounds almost too good to be true."

"It'll be a huge help around here. And other than that, I'm doing some maintenance on the tractor to get it ready for a lot of use. I assume you'll be wanting to put it to work?"

"You assumed right." Red eyed him carefully as Ryan opened the back door. "Let's get this pump back on so you can get back to work, eh?"

"Yup, let's go. I'll show you what to do."

"All right. Reynolds, with us."

The three men headed inside, Ryan exchanging glances with Helen as she and Martha were preparing things on the counter for dinner.

"We're having chili tonight, dear," Helen called out, waving and smiling at the three men.

"Sounds delicious." Ryan led Red and Reynolds down the basement stairs, where a few low white light bulbs cast the room in a dim glow.

Ryan showed them where the tanks were connected to the internal filter and he unscrewed the hose, rolled it up, and hung it from a hook by the half-open window. Heading back to the filtration system, he grabbed the external well line where it hung from a nail and reconnected it, tightening it with a wrench.

"This is where you connect the water, whether you're using the tanks or the pump."

Red nodded. "Good. Time to turn on the power?"

"Yep. Hopefully nobody's touching a live wire," he chuckled. "The pressure gauge should start rising a few seconds after I turn the power on."

"Do you need to shut anything off?"

"Yeah, I'll cut off some lights and things. The well pump has a pretty strong draw, especially when it first starts up."

Ryan walked over to the breaker box, opened the door, and gestured to the two sides, one for the incoming city power and the other for the battery room, currently feeding them a steady supply of electricity.

"All right, Ryan," Red said. "Let 'er rip."

Ryan flipped several switches off and turned on the well pump, setting off a slight vibration as water began pouring through the pipe into the house. "There it is. Do you hear it?"

"Yep, I hear it," Red said with a nod.

Ryan stepped between Reynolds and Red, circling to the water filter where the well hose was connected. He tapped on the gauge and watched the pressure rise past forty-five pounds per square inch and settle around the fifty-five mark. "Would you look at that. We've got pressure now."

"Ha!" Red slapped Reynolds on the back. "No more relying on those damned tanks."

"Just make sure we keep an eye on it for a few days. Let whoever comes down here know to take note if the pressure drops off or acts funny and let us know. Other than that, we should be good."

"Well, that's great, Ryan." Red clapped him on the back. "Isn't that great, Reynolds?"

"It sure is, Boss."

"Now, if your boys can come up with those water heaters, we'll be in even better shape."

"They'll get them." Red looked pointedly at Reynolds, who nodded in assurance. "Where do we put them?"

Ryan motioned to the general area. "Right here will be fine. We'll set them up on bricks and daisy chain them to the propane ones until the propane runs out. After that, we can disconnect them or just keep them in line. There're enough people that even two tanks might not be enough to keep up with demand, so overflow of hot water during slow times would be a boon."

"Smart thinking. We'll need your help on that one."

"I figured as much. I'm no plumber, but I can do a fair amount."

"Hey, Boss," Reynolds said. "I'll head up and tell everyone who hasn't cleaned up that they can go ahead with the water now."

"You do that," Red replied.

As Reynold's boots trod up the stairwell, Ryan shoved his hands into his pockets. "Nice work on getting that installed, Red. I'll get back to work."

As he started to walk away, Red grabbed his arm and leaned in. "You better not be up to anything out there."

Ryan recoiled. "What are you talking about? We've been cooperating, haven't we?"

"A little too much, I'd say." Red's eyes narrowed, his voice dropping with a hint of malice. "I just can't imagine a man like you would give up this place so easily."

"We're not giving up my daughter's home. We're *sharing* it." Ryan gently pulled out of Red's grip, forcing a neutral expression to remain on his face. "Like I said before, I'm not happy you're here, and I wish Helen and I had the place to ourselves still, but that's not how things turned out, is it?"

"That doesn't explain how easy you've made things for us. All the cooking, cleaning, working outside, being friendly – the whole nine yards."

Ryan took a deep breath, shoved his hands deeper into his pockets, and gave a long, forced sigh, shrugging exaggeratedly. "I've come to terms with reality, Red. You're here, whether we like it or not, and if we want to survive, we have to get along with your crew. Even Jack – and believe me, Red, dealing with that bastard is the hardest thing of all. But I've made my peace with how things turned out. You'll get no trouble from me."

Red stared at him for a long moment, searching his face for a lie before nodding and patting Ryan on the shoulder. "Fair enough, Ryan. I don't expect you to like us being here, but your support is what matters. Keep it up and you won't get trouble from us."

"You got it, Red."

"C'mon, let's head up."

"Sure thing."

Ryan waited for Red to get ahead and peeked into a ten-foot square supply room that was missing its door. A safe stood against the wall, bolted to the floor, illuminated by an electric lantern. Its edges were chipped and dented by the tools scattered around; screwdrivers, metal files, a saw, and a sledgehammer stood in testimony to the failed attempts to pry open the door and get at what was inside.

CHAPTER THIRTEEN

James Burton
Connersville, Indiana

"James?" Both the father and son spoke in tandem, lowering their weapons before the father stepped forward and repeated the question. "James *Burton*?"

"You... what?" James looked between the pair of men before turning to the three other figures as they got to their feet in front of him. He had to be dreaming – there was no other explanation for what was going on. Death had finally overtaken him – or he'd fallen and hit his head *exceptionally* hard.

"Alice? Jake? Sarah?" The words felt uncomfortable on his lips.

His family was haggard, Alice much thinner than he remembered, swimming in a button-up shirt and camisole. Jake was dressed in oversized jeans and a T-shirt, his dark brown hair wild and windblown and Sarah's cheeks were smudged with dirt, but her eyes were bright, full of life, confirming that he was still very much alive, and his dreams – not his nightmares – had finally come to life.

"Dad!"

James dropped his gun and sprinted forward, reaching for family, sweeping them together in a crushing embrace. He breathed them in, their physical contact sending a rush of adrenaline through his body, more than when he'd run from the gangs in Chicago or rushed to save Oswell from certain death or leapt from the boxcar on the back of his horse. Gasping, holding his breath behind clenched teeth, James squeezed them with all his strength, daring the world to try and take them away again.

"Dad?!" Jake hugged back, blinking tears of disbelief. "You found us?!"

Sarah buried her head in the crush of bodies. "Oh, Dad. It's you. It's *really* you!"

Alice pressed her face against his, his cheeks wet with her tears before she grabbed his jaw and kissed him squarely on the lips. Backing up to lock eyes with him, she whispered, "You finally found us."

He nodded, words escaping him until he managed to croak out a whisper. "I love you."

"You have no idea. I love you too." They drew apart, and Alice touched his face again and ran her hand through his hair, her eyes betraying love, sadness, and... pain.

James took an extra step back, holding her by the shoulders and looking her up and down. "Alice, honey. Are you okay?"

"I had a little... accident a few days ago." Her smile faltered, but she shook her head and threw herself against him, arms wrapping tight while Jake and Sarah hugged them both from either side, all four of them sobbing in relief and elation.

Eli and Abram stood nearby, pale faces glowing in the darkness like apparitions until Eli smiled wide and stepped forward, handing his shotgun to Abram.

"Well, I'll be," he said. "God's miracles never cease. It *is* you, James."

James stepped back from Alice, Sarah and Jake, giving Eli and Abram a look of disbelief, overcome with dizziness that threatened to topple him to the ground. Eli reached out as James swayed, steadying him, taking his hand firmly.

"Eli?" James looked at the red-haired man. "Abram?"

"Aye. It is a joy to see you again." Eli's smile grew, and James released the man's hand, embracing the older man in a fierce hug, laughter mixing with his tears of joy, his vision growing blurry and his nose congested.

"It's good to see you, too," James replied in a rush, releasing Eli and taking Abram's proffered hand before giving him a hug as well, then turning back to his family, jaw dropping open, words failing him. "I... I can't believe it."

"If this is who I think it is," Eli gestured at Alice, Jake and Sarah, "Then I imagine you must feel as though this is a dream."

"You have *no* idea. Eli, Abram... this is... well, it's my family. Alice, Jake and Sarah. Guys, these..." He struggled for words again until they tumbled out.

"Well, Eli and Abram are friends I met on the road. That's kind of underselling it though..."

"I am truly blessed to be witnessing such a grand reunion." Eli's grin stretched from ear to ear as he looked at Abram, who merely stood smiling and slowly shaking his head. "We have thought of you often, and prayed for you just as much."

"I... I mean... wha... HOW?!" James finally shouted, throwing his hands in the air in exasperated joy. "How did *any* of you get here?"

"Connersville was always our destination," Eli said. "As it was for you and your family, it would seem. We never got a chance to tell you the city we were heading toward, but we had faith that we would cross paths again someday. I never imagined it would be so soon."

Alice looked back and forth between the Amish men and James. "Wait... you know these men?"

"Yeah, Dad," Jake said. "Are they with you?"

"I mean, kind of?" James laughed, still stammering as his mind reeled with disbelief. "I met Eli and his family a week or two ago? Longer than that maybe? It's... there's been a lot going on." James tried to reform the events of the past few weeks into a coherent timeline in his mind. "We met around Fayette, Missouri and split up around Hannibal."

"Your husband, Mrs. Burton, saved my family's lives," Eli said.

"They saved *mine* too, just to be clear." James' bright expression faltered. "Oh Abram. I... I'm sorry, but Amber... she fell in Chicago. I was ambushed and...."

"James." Eli smiled. "*You* are alive. If Amber served you well, then we give thanks for her sacrifice, and that it was not in vain."

James swallowed a lump. "Better than well."

"Good." Eli shifted to Alice. "Mrs. Burton, I apologize for this lackluster greeting. I was not expecting to see my friend again so soon, nor his beautiful family. You have caught me off-guard, and I apologize."

"Apologize?" Alice broke from Jake, Sarah and James and embraced Eli, surprising the man who went stiff, smiling uncomfortably at James over Alice's shoulder. "Eli, you just saved our lives. Thank you. Sincerely." She let him go and he coughed lightly, adjusting his coat.

"I am glad we could be of service to a friend in need."

James ran his hands through his hair as he looked at Alice, Sarah and Jake, giving them another hug as tears ran freely. "Eli. Abram. I owe you more than I can ever repay. Thank you for protecting my wife and children."

Eli nodded, smiling warmly. "Again, I must apologize for this lackluster greeting, but... welcome to our home. I can scarcely believe you found us, but you did."

"I can't believe it either. Did everyone make it here in one piece?"

"Aye, we did." Eli nodded, taking one of the shotguns back from Abram. "Albeit through the darkest valleys filled with shadow, and after a test that changed us fundamentally, but that's a conversation for later. For now, I'd like to get to know your family properly."

"Right. This is my wife, Alice, my son Jake, and my daughter, Sarah." James gestured to each one in turn.

All three of them shook Eli and Abram's outstretched hands before Alice spoke. "Thank you both, again. I have no idea who you both are, but if my husband says you're friends, then you're our friends, too."

"Indeed, we are." Eli smiled at all of them. "God has truly blessed us on this night."

"Eli! Are my eyes deceiving me?" A woman rushed out of the darkness in a swish of skirts, mouth open in shock and surprise. "Oh, God bless us - it really *is* you, James! I heard your voice and had to come see if it was true." She circled Eli, rose on her toes, and threw her arms around James' neck, knocking him back a few paces before he steadied himself and returned her embrace.

"Clara! It's great to see you again!" James laughed, eyes filling with tears again. "I want you to meet my wife and kids. Alice, this is—"

Clara stepped back, smiling broadly. "One moment, James. If we're doing introductions, we might as well do them all at once." Clara turned and bustled past Eli and Abram, stopping to wave and gesture to a group of people standing on the nearest farmstead porch some fifty yards away, silhouetted by warm light shining from the door. At Clara's signal, they rushed off the porch and flowed toward them in a wave of dresses and suspenders, followed by a man in dark pants holding an oil lamp.

"Can you believe God's blessing on us?" Eli gestured grandly. "It's James! And he found his family!"

"James!" The cry went up from the whole family as they crowded around Eli, Clara and Abram.

"Alice, Jake, Sarah, This is Clara, Eli's wife. That's Betty, Abram's wife. Betty, where are..." James and then Alice gave Betty a hug as two smaller forms squeezed in. "There you are, Sadie and John!"

The man with the lantern stepped near with a woman by his side, waiting patiently until James recognized her blue dress and his stark black beard.

"Ha! There you are!" James beamed. "This is Esther and her husband, Jacob. The best riverboat rider this side of the Mississippi!"

"It's wonderful to see you again, James." Jacob grinned, shaking his hand and nodding to Alice, Sarah and Jake as a boy poked his head between Esther and Jacob and smiled.

"And your boy, Levi! I couldn't forget you." James grinned and stood back, gesturing wide to his family. "Everyone, these are the ones I told you about: Alice, Jake, and Sarah."

A rousing chorus went up as the Amish crowded around the smaller family, giving hugs and handshakes as they talked over each other. Clara's tears broke free as she locked arms with Eli and as the Amish overwhelmed them, Alice laughed, trying to both greet everyone and remember their names, eventually finding James again and throwing her arms around his waist and kissing him again.

"You smell awful," she said with a laugh. "But I don't mind a bit."

James hugged her tight, grinning broadly. "You smell like death warmed over, but I don't care either. I just can't believe it's really you."

Clara raised her hand and snapped her fingers repeatedly, shouting over the din. "Everyone! Enough crowding around and overwhelming these poor souls. Let's get them back to the house and make them comfortable."

James started to give an excuse that they couldn't impose on them, but Clara took his arm and turned him toward the house with a scowl. "Not. One. Word. I will *not* hear of it."

Eli walked on the far side. "You must stay at least the night."

"At *least* that," Clara agreed enthusiastically. "Much more if I have my way."

"Okay, okay," James responded, holding his hands up in surrender. "But any longer than that..."

Eli raised his shotgun and grinned. "Don't make me threaten you, James Burton!"

James laughed. "Yeah, you and I are going to have a *long* conversation about that!"

"So, there I was with Private Oswell, limping through a junkyard as all these people were trying to hunt us down and find us." James stabbed a pile of green beans with his fork. "We took shelter in a sewer, of all places. It was the only safe place to rest up and figure out what to do next."

He took a bite, looking down the table where Alice and the kids sat to his right, with the Amish family spread along the left-hand side with Eli seated opposite him at the head of the table. Jake, Sarah and the older Amish children listened intently as James told his story while the younger ones ate quietly at the opposite end of the table. Abram occupied the chairs to Eli's right while Betty, Jacob, and Esther bustled around the table, delivering food and drinks from Clara who was preparing everything from the kitchen a few feet away.

"That sounds absolutely horrifying, James," Clara called. "How in the world did you both escape the city?"

James swallowed the warm green beans soaked in butter, salt, and pepper. "We just went any direction we could, running away from the shooting and fighting. Oswell was in bad shape, so it was slow going."

Jake nodded knowingly. "Sounds like when we were running through the forest after escaping the camp, right, Mom?"

"Pretty close," Alice agreed and talked around a mouthful of potatoes. "That was after I was shot and we blew the meth lab up."

James blinked, fork suspended in midair halfway to his mouth. "You... blew up a meth lab? In a forest?"

"In a summer camp in a forest," Jake said. "It was *crazy*."

"It's a long story," Alice admitted.

James scooped another bite. "Well, we've got time. I want to know *everything*. How did you even get out of Florida?"

Alice started with the trouble at the restaurant, the people they'd fought off with pool sticks back at the beach house, and their trek up the beach, crowded with refugees. She retold their experience that night at Andrea's motel and how Alice had begun piecing together what had happened with the fuel supply after hearing Andrea tell her how their generators were still working while others in the business district had inexplicably exploded. The short trip in the EV came next. "I wish we could have driven it farther, but we ran out of luck somewhere around the Florida-Georgia line."

"Someone shot the car," Jake said. "A lot of someones, actually."

"Son of a..." James glanced at Eli. "Sorry."

Eli's lips upturned mischievously. "These are fascinating tales. Please, continue."

Sarah continued. "Yeah, Mom was going around a roadblock, but they were shooting at us the whole time. They hit the batteries."

"It caught fire," Alice finished flatly. "Quite vigorously. We salvaged a few things but pretty much lost everything else."

Esther swept in and refilled a cup of tea for Alice. "So, you were back to walking then?"

"Yep. We hiked a little more and came upon Monticello Horse Farm."

"That's where we met Wilford." Sarah continued the story, telling them about Wilford's kindness, meeting the horses they'd ridden for so many miles, and being attacked one night at the stables.

"That's just incredible. I can't believe you went through that and..." James' voice faltered, and he shook his head sadly. "I just wish I could've been there to protect you."

"Well, we had Wilford," Sarah said, "I hope you get to meet him one day. He's so cool, and he knows everything about horses."

James raised his eyebrows. "Sounds to me like you kids know quite a bit about horses, too."

"It took some practice," Jake said, "but we got it down pretty quick. I dunno what we would have done without those lessons, though. We rode from there to... what happened next, Mom?"

Alice grinned warmly. "We met little Ethan soon after that."

"Oh, yeah!" Sarah's eyes widened and she smiled broadly. "How could we forget Ethan?"

Alice told how they'd met Nate and his wife Elaine and delivered their baby with no help or hospital equipment. Clara in particular listened with rapt attention, giving Alice a hug when she got to the part where the baby came out healthy and screaming.

Eli shook his head through it all, sipping on his tea after finishing his meal. "How about you, James? What happened after you and Private Oswell escaped Chicago?"

James continued his story about finding the bikes and driving them eastward for miles, avoiding people when they could and barely escaping desperate groups trying to take their bikes and supplies. He ended his part with them reaching the abandoned National Guard facility in La Porte, saving Oswell's life again, fixing a Humvee, and driving it north to Colonel Hawkins' outpost in Shipshewana.

"I had quite a few bumps and bruises I hadn't noticed, and Doctor Agarwal thought I might have cracked a rib or two." James touched his left side.

"I might have one or three to match." Alice winked.

"You have broken ribs?"

Sarah leaned in breathlessly. "She got *shot*, Dad. Remember?"

"Holy—sorry, Eli. I nearly forgot!" James's fork dropped to his plate, clattering noisily. "What happened?!"

The table sat enraptured as Alice, Jake and Sarah took turns finishing their tale: the trip on horseback through the Georgia hills, meeting Christine and Mark, Alice being shot and the kids captured and taken to an old summer camp where the leaders were cooking drugs.

"That's where blowing up the meth lab came from?" James asked, finishing the last bites of his meal.

"Yep." Alice frowned darkly. "That was after I rescued the kids and..." Her face darkened, her whole body sagging. "Did some things."

James nodded slowly. "We can wait to tell the rest later. Eli, why don't you tell me what happened after we were forced to split up."

"I'm afraid our story isn't quite as exciting as yours or your wife's."

"Uh huh," James smirked looking across the room at the pair of shotguns hanging above the mantle, "Eli, the last time we spoke, you were an ardent pacifist. *Something* must have happened."

"That's true." Eli's expression betrayed neither shame nor pride. "I suppose it was a rousing journey in more ways than one."

"I hope me taking Amber didn't make it any harder. I'm just... so sorry about her, Eli." James looked at Abram. "And to you, too, Abram. She saved my life multiple times."

"James, you *must* stop apologizing for Amber," Abram said.

Clara stepped in to collect the dirty plates. "Amber was a gift from God, and her service to you eases our hearts."

"Plus, we have many new horses now," Eli added, "and even more thanks to Alice setting them free from the horsecar. We've got men out rounding them up now. No, James. With God's blessing, Amber kept you alive and guided you past many dangers – saving us in the process – and that is all we could ever ask for."

Eli paused for a moment while drinks were refilled, then continued. "Back in Hannibal, as James distracted our potential attackers, we sped away in our wagons."

"I saw you tearing down the road."

"Aye, we did. And they did not see us, praise be. We rode hard for two days without rest or incident. On the third day, as we neared Connersville, however, we were set upon by the same sort of ambushers you saw when you first met us." Eli shook his head. "Rough men, desperate and – dare I say - evil."

"While we do not wish to call any of God's creations such," Clara put her hand on Eli's shoulder, and he rested his hand on hers. "It is clear to us that they were twisted and vile."

"Indeed. They came upon us while we were breaking for supper. We'd found a secluded place near some woods, a park with swings and slides nearby. I remember thinking how the place must have rung with children's laughter before the world caught fire. We unfolded our table and broke bread when they surrounded us, and we quickly moved the children inside the wagons and faced them. I offered them food and even invited them to sup with us, but they wanted to take everything. We begged them to leave us alone, but they refused to listen—and they tried to put their hands on Clara and Betty."

"Is that when you..."

Eli nodded grimly. "Yes. If they had merely wanted our possessions, we would have surrendered them and gone on our way. But it was clear they wanted more than that. Abram and Jacob and I had discussed your words ever since we parted ways. It was with a simple nod to them that we turned our plowshares into swords." He glanced at Abram sitting next to him. "The shotguns were hidden on the wagons. We gathered them up quickly, our pretense being that we were unloading our supplies for the men. I had intended for Abram and Jacob and I to be the ones with blood on our hands, but Clara—" Eli choked up for a moment, and Clara continued, speaking matter-of-factly.

"I retrieved the shotgun from beneath the seat and laid the leader low, shooting true and spilling his insides. We struck them all down, our firearms roaring like thunder, laying low our enemies before they could harm our family."

"I still wish—" Clara interrupted Eli before he could continue.

"The Lord guided my hand, husband, and I did what needed to be done for the sake of my loved ones."

"You and I have more in common in that regard than you realize," Alice replied.

"The long and short of it," Eli said, "was that we arrived here safe and sound. But every evening since then, when the sun goes down, I'm plagued with much doubt and guilt over my actions."

"If you hadn't," James spoke softly, "then you and your family wouldn't be here today."

"Even still. To go against one of our most sacred beliefs has been... challenging."

"I can't even imagine. I still think you did the right thing, though. You didn't kill out of malice or ill will – you did it in defense of those you love."

"I agree. Yet it wasn't the only time. There were more times when we defended ourselves, learning in our nascent way how to do so. And, truly, it was your words that saved us – and your wife and children, in fact. When we heard the shouts and gunfire we came armed, prepared to defend ourselves, but found we had to defend others, instead. More growth for us, and more pondering and reflection too, in time, I'm sure."

"Eli," James reached his hand out. "I can't thank you enough for saving them. I'm sorry you had to compromise your values, but without your willingness to change, our families would be gone."

"Oh, we didn't compromise our values, James. Please, don't mistake my wallowing in guilt and questions for that. We simply gained a new perspective on our values. And though we had to shed blood, we buried the dead properly and will do so again, on the morrow. They are still people, after all, as misguided and twisted as they've become."

"You're a wise man, Eli. Very wise indeed."

The sound of crickets was nearly overwhelming as a soft, cool breeze blew across the old porch, its wooden slats, decorative railings and beams holding up a creaking awning, all of it bathed in a pale light from a pair of oil lamps hanging from hooks. James rocked slowly in his chair next to Alice, holding her hand and a cup of coffee as they looked out across the fields, dirt lanes and homes of the Amish community.

"Jake and Sarah are so good with the kids." Alice smiled, hearing them inside as they entertained the younger Amish children.

"They're so different now than when I last saw them. They've changed."

"It was the whole thing that did it, but most of all I think it was that national park. I wish we'd never gone that way."

"What happened? Besides what you told me about what you had to do."

"Sarah was the first to notice that Hunter and Mia weren't actually Mark and Christine's kids. Not being able to help them really tore Sarah up on the inside. Jake, too, to some degree." Alice glanced over her shoulder through the front door where the children laughed. "And I guess being in that camp with all those kids - seeing how they were beaten and forced to work in terrible conditions - changed them."

"I hope for the better."

"Better? I don't know if that would change anyone for the better. For the wiser, though? Yeah." Alice sighed. "Then again, I'm changed as well – most definitely not for the better. There are moments when I... I feel like a different person."

"The world changed you. It changed *all* of us. But you're here now. That's what matters."

Alice squeezed his hand. "We're not splitting up again, understand me? No more business trips and meeting us for vacations."

"No, never again," James said. "Next vacation or business trip, we're all going together or not at all. Well... I guess that's *if* there are more trips and vacations."

They sat quietly for a few minutes staring out into the darkness, listening to the restless night and singing bugs.

"Do you think Mom and Dad are okay?" Alice's voice was nearly inaudible.

"There's no reason to think otherwise. They're both competent people and know how to run a farm."

"But they're older, and they haven't had a farm in years."

"Doesn't matter. Ryan is a tough old man who can hold his own. And your mother's no slouch, either."

"Do you think the barn went up with the fuel tank? If *that* exploded, it might have taken out some of the animals."

James shrugged. "We purchased that fuel way before any of this happened. I don't remember exactly when we got it; it had to have been at least six months before the explosions. That... should be far enough back before the fuel was tainted?"

"I can't help but worry."

"Worrying is sometimes part of love," James smiled at her. "And things aren't all bad in this new world. We found each other, didn't we?"

"Against every odd in the universe," Alice squeezed his hand tight.

"But we did it, so there's no reason to think we won't walk up the driveway and find your Mom and Dad waiting for us. They would've harvested the field and got the solar panels setup and – heck, they're probably living better than ninety-nine percent of anyone out here."

"Maybe not the Amish." Alice raised her cup. "Good grief, this is some great coffee."

"Grew the beans themselves, according to Eli."

"Ugh. Heaven in a cup. I'm going to miss this when we leave."

Heavy boots trod on the wooden floor, boards squeaking as Eli stepped onto the porch, cup in hand, thumb hooked into his suspenders. "Good evening to both of you. I hope I'm not interrupting. I promised Clara I'd give you some time to catch up."

"You're not interrupting at all, Eli," Alice replied. "We were just enjoying the evening and your amazing coffee."

"It's a vice, but a slight one." He winked at them.

"Growing your bean plants right on the property?" James whistled low. "You truly are self-sufficient. If you start trading, you could get top-dollar for these."

"Before the world went up in flames, we traded much, both with the Amish and the English. I'm sure we'll do so again. There are many here – as there are everywhere – who need aid. We'll do what we can to assist."

"Don't take this the wrong way, Eli," James said, "but I hope you're not going to overextend yourselves. Your family has to come first."

Eli smiled. "Our family is God's family, which includes all of His children. We're expanding the fields, and the bounty will help feed the needy. We've already welcomed some to live near us, and they understand they'll need to work hard to earn what they receive."

"We won't be a burden on you," Alice said. "We'll be out of your hair in a day."

"While you have the means to go at any time – those are some beautiful horses you obtained – you could never be a burden. Your husband is the reason my family still lives. There will always be a warm bed and a hot meal here for you, no matter what."

Alice smiled. "Thank you, Eli. You're far too kind. We will need to get going soon, though. My parents are at our house and we need to get back to them, to see how they are and get back to our own farm."

"That's why you want to leave us so soon?"

"Oh, I mean, yes," Alice gushed. "but it's certainly not for any lack of hospitality. This place is incredible... and your family is kinder than anyone I've met before."

"Clara and I understand the burning need to reunite with your family," Eli said, looking back toward the interior of the house. "In fact... hmm. I believe we may be able to help you get home in a more timely manner. Come with me."

James shared a curious glance with Alice, and the two stood and followed Eli inside where Clara and Betty had cleared off the table, replacing dishes and cups with a large map.

"What is this?" James asked.

"We took the liberty of trying to map you a way home, after some of our talk at the dinner table. I hope you don't mind."

"Are you serious?" Alice blinked. "I... thank you! Of course we don't mind."

"We've pieced together several maps of Indiana here," Eli traced the area with a finger, "and Michigan here. Now, these maps are old, but the highways won't have changed much over the years." Eli followed a line of marks heading north. "I took some time to sketch a path for you from here up to Shipshewana and onward. Here's where you can cross the border and get home."

"Looks like about three hundred miles," James replied. "How long do you think that'll take us on horseback?"

Alice leaned over the maps, tracing the path herself. "If we push them to the max, we can get there in eight days, give or take."

"Your wife is correct. That will be hard on the animals, but it is doable."

"Not bad... maybe give ourselves an extra few days, though. Who knows what we'll run into. Thank you; this map is extremely helpful, Eli."

"Oh, no," Eli smiled as Jacob and Abram stepped into the room. "This map is not what I was speaking of."

Abram held out a sack he was carrying, and Eli reached inside and retrieved a black box about a foot long and seven inches in width with an assortment of knobs, dials, and a keypad on the bottom.

"What's this?" James asked, taking the device from Eli. "Is this a radio?"

"It is a military shortwave radio. We received it from the local National Guard units. They made contact with us the day after we arrived, and after a pleasant exchange – something we've had too few and far between these days – we entered into an accord with them."

"The National Guard has been great to me this whole time," James agreed. "What was the deal?"

"As you may have surmised, we take great pride in caring for our horses and have generations of experience caring for them and training them. Myself and Abram are experienced farriers, and most Amish grow up learning basic care from a young age. We agreed to help shelter and care for any horses they obtain, and in return they are providing us with goods we can't grow or make ourselves yet. They have also assured us that since we will be in possession of, in their words 'Government Property,' that we can call on them if we ever need assistance."

James turned the radio over. "Judging by the fact that you had this in a sack, I'm guessing you haven't called them, huh?"

"We have not required their assistance, and our use of their radio would be something we would have to..." he looked at Clara sitting in a chair near the fireplace, "discuss. In any case, the National Guard is due to pick up the first shipment of horses we've been nursing and perhaps – based on your story – you may know the name of someone who can assist you with traveling north."

"Eli," James held the radio up, grinning broadly. "I think I know *just* the person to call. Have you turned it on yet?"

"No."

"Well, let's give it a try."

James sat at the dining room table with the radio in front of him, checking the battery compartment and plugging in wires for the microphone and an antenna which Eli had one of the children hold. Meanwhile, Jacob and Abram pushed aside the maps to give them room and sat opposite James, with Alice sitting directly to his right. Clara and Betty appeared regular as clockwork again, bearing fresh coffee, bread, butter and jam, placing it all on the table before gathering around.

"I'm not complaining." Alice reached for some bread. "But I'm pretty sure I've gained back all the weight I've lost just since we arrived here."

Clara laughed. "The road is long, and you need plenty of nourishment along the way!"

A piece of paper with frequencies written on it was taped to the back of the radio, and James turned the radio to the first frequency after switching it on, raising the volume. He took the handset off the cradle and pressed the transmit button.

"Hello? My name is James Burton." James paused and held the handset out as he waited for a response. "This is James Burton – I'm calling for any National Guard units who might be in the area. Can anyone read me? Please respond." A good twenty seconds passed before James glanced at Eli. "Did they mention which channel would get a response?"

"I'm afraid not. They just gave us the radio and told us to try the channels written on the back."

"Hrm." James pushed the button again. "Hello, this is James Burton, calling from Connersville, Indiana, calling for—"

"This is the Fort Wayne National Guard," a woman's distorted voice burst through the tiny speaker. "State your name and business."

"James Burton," he replied loudly. "I'm calling from Connersville, Indiana. I'm using a radio given to us by National Guard troops from your facility. I'm with an Amish community taking care of your horses down here."

A long pause preceded her response. "I don't have a James Burton on my list of contacts from the community."

"Yeah, that's a long story... listen, I have a request. Who am I speaking with?"

"Private Drury."

"Well, Private Drury. I know Colonel Hawkins from the Shipshewana outpost. I'm hoping you can get me in touch with him."

"Shipshewana?"

"Yeah. Is there any way we can do a three-way call or something? I need to speak with Colonel Hawkins as soon as possible. He sent me south with a convoy to reach a supply train here in Connersville. I was traveling with Captain Bragg, but the train was derailed and attacked. I'm sure Colonel Hawkins would want to know what happened."

"I see." Drury's voice tightened. "Give me a minute."

"Thank you."

While they waited, James shared an expectant look with Alice and Eli. Squelches and static hit the line, and he reached for the volume knob, dialing it down until a voice burst through, tinnier than Drury's had been.

"This is Colonel Hawkins from the National Guard facility in Shipshewana. Who am I speaking to?"

"This is James Burton. Good to hear your voice again, Colonel!"

"James Burton! Holy hell, we thought we might have lost you at the train station. Captain Bragg radioed and said they'd driven off the attackers but lost track of you when he sent you off for your family. He hoped you'd made it out safe."

James briefly recounted the story of what had happened after he left Captain Bragg back at the train station. "It's a miracle, Colonel. I traveled with Eli and his family weeks ago, and our paths crossed once again, right here. The Guard unit out of Fort Wayne gave them a radio, so I thought I'd take a chance and call you. It's good to know Captain Bragg and his troops are safe."

"I'm glad you made it and found your family, James! Why are you calling me, though, and not Captain Bragg? He's still in the area, last I heard."

"Oh, yeah, I'm sure he is. But uhhh... look. I hate to ask you for another favor, but with the train derailment and everything, I kind of lost all my supplies, and..."

"Let me guess," Hawkins' wry grin came through the radio clear as day. "You need another favor?"

James chuckled. "You might say that, Colonel. You might say that."

CHAPTER FOURTEEN

Marco
Venice, Italy

Thunderclouds rolled overhead, blotting out the sun above Venice, throwing the afternoon into a darkness that threatened to swallow everything, matching Marco's mood. He stood in the back of a gondola with Lucia up front, both of them poling their way through the narrow waterways as pieces of motorboats, charred wood, and the occasional bodies floated by.

They would've dragged any corpses out of the water and taken them to a burn site, but he and Lucia weren't on corpse duty that day, and they had to keep moving, so they both whispered a prayer for each of the dead they encountered and continued pushing. Both were dressed in black clothing; jeans, leather boots, and undershirts beneath heavy, dark military coats they'd gotten out of supply. Lucia stood splay-legged upfront, shifting her pole from one side to the other, her inky silken hair drawn back in a ponytail, wearing no jewelry or accouterments of any kind, nothing that might reflect light and give them away.

Passing beneath bridges, they cruised smoothly and quietly over the gently lapping waters, making fast progress up the Rio de la Guerra toward the northwest side of the city, weaving between homes built right up to the water, with open archways one could drive a gondola through. The older, rustic architecture was an assortment of Baroque and Byzantine, ancient Gothic arches and pointed structures, oddly shaped roofs with clusters of windows centered between solid edges to give the buildings a sturdier appearance.

Arms straining, sweat beading on his face and arms despite the cool breezes, Marco glanced at the duffel bag in the middle of the gondola, loaded with rifles and pistols and hundreds of rounds of ammunition as Lucia spoke. "Big piece ahead," she called as a heap of floating debris approached, her voice high and clear, a singsong tone she'd used to charm crowds at the local opera in a day gone by.

"I see it."

The back half of a boat floated, overturned, its wooden hull jutting above the surface, scorch marks making intricate patterns along the wood, pieces of tarps and other garbage clinging to it in the gently bobbing waves. On up the Rio Della Misericordia, the channel widened, revealing cafés, hotels, and lounges being used as trading posts for goods coming into and out of the city where neighborhoods came to barter and trade. Half-sunken motorboats and water taxis floated in pools of oil and fuel that hadn't ignited and the walls were marked with hellish, black-ash designs that crawled up the brick. Other structures had caught fire but had been doused by residents before they could spread and destroy the surrounding blocks. Cleanup crews and corpse collectors were out in canoes and flat-bottomed boats, doing their best to clean things up, nodding to Marco and Lucia as they drifted by.

The channel widened by another twenty feet, reaching a small, bustling dock area where boats lined up and people divided into teams. Bumping between the other vessels, offering apologies, Marco shoved them up next to a large flatbed motorboat with a pieced-together engine, grease-stained and leaking smoke, the driver looking just as rough. Leaving their boat moored there, Marco and Lucia grabbed their duffel bags and leaped onto the flatbed, joining another dozen people who were tethering smaller boats to the larger one with chains and hooks.

"Filippo," he said to the driver.

Filippo nodded back. "Marco. Lucia."

Once the team of sixteen was assembled, Filippo shoved off from the dock and revved the motor, driving them away from the crowd and into the open waters of the lagoon on the north side of Venice. The waves kicked up, the boat dipping and rocking harder, forcing Marco and Lucia to sit near the back where the smaller flatbeds bobbed and bumped behind them.

"We're hoping for a good haul today," Filippo said in Italian.

Marco stared out over the wide channel, the train tracks stretching across the Bridge of Liberty to the mainland. No trains ran anymore, and the tracks were covered with barricades and guards. Distant gunshots, shouts, explosions and thumps created a constant din. Along the framework shoreline, flaming bottles arced through the air and struck buildings, sending tiny fires springing up before being quickly doused by fire brigades.

"We *always* hope for a good haul," Marco replied.

"Things are getting desperate," Filippo said. "The attacks on our shores are growing in number."

A burst of gunshots rattled off to the northeast, and heads turned to see two Venetian patrol boats filled with city defenders with white dots on their sleeves surround a smaller boat inbound from the mainland. Two people lay dead over the rail of the intruding boat, bleeding into the water while others in back held their hands up in surrender.

"You'd think they'd pick a better time to come," Lucia said as she checked her weapons. "If they want to succeed."

"Our patrols can handle anything." Marco tried to sound confident, his words held together by a fierce grimace that faltered. "Day or night. They will never succeed."

"The problem, my friends," Filippo replied. "Is that the raiders are disguising themselves as city workers. There have been too many close calls already."

Marco looked at the painted markings on his sleeve. "Good thing the Captain changes our designations every day. They could kill us, take our coats, and still not make it into the city."

Filippo shrugged. "Yes, but they'll figure something else out. One day, perhaps, they will simply come in great enough numbers to overwhelm us."

Marco's cheeks flushed. "What do we have here that they don't on the mainland? They have the supplies, not us."

Filippo stood and gestured as they passed beneath the Bridge of Liberty, firelights on the tracks glowing as daylight faded. "Our city still stands as it was before the world went up in flames. There is shelter here, protection."

"But homes can be rebuilt," Marco argued. "We are the ones who have to come out to get food. They can grow crops and raise livestock over there."

"So, why don't you move there then?" Filippo stated flatly, sitting with his arms folded across his chest, letting the boat steer itself for a moment.

Off to the left stood Santa Croce and Cannaregio, the major shipyards, the grand complexes, taverns, and restaurants of Venice where they'd turned the parking lots into refugee space where stuck tourists could live until help could arrive.

Lucia regarded him with dark eyes. "We could never leave Venice... *never*. One day, the Playhouse will open again. Some say it will be *very* soon."

Filippo gestured broadly with one arm as he steered. "Entertainment lives on! That is why we will weather these great and terrible times, my friends. We still have angels like Lucia with beautiful voices to sing songs of the time that once was. Please, Lucia, sing a song now."

Lucia smiled politely but shook her head, returning to her weapons checks. The glowing flames of the mainland still burned, though the ones in Venice never lasted long thanks to the city's fire teams. Her dreams felt miles – centuries – away, a stark contrast from her former life. Instead of singing, she was destined to continue volunteering to steal goods on the mainland, part of the scavenging teams... the *Squadra di Recupero*, the *Recs*.

Filippo drove them slowly through Port Tronchetto, an L-shaped port of entry to Venice where cargo containers stood in wide shipyards, left untouched next to crooked, useless cranes and long warehouses that had burned to the ground. With the engine idling low, they crept past sunken trade ships and lingered at the port exit until darkness fell and a half moon gleamed off the silent, bouncing waves.

The raiders were quiet, checking the ropes and keeping an eye on the small flat boats they were hauling behind them. Finally, Filippo gave a silent gesture and revved the engine to life, pulling them across the lagoon toward the mainland. They passed dead boats on both sides; fishing trawlers, cargo vessels, and sunken raiders with their hulls and sails jutting up or rolled onto their sides. An occasional body floated by, exposed shoulders, arms and skull always picked clean by the birds, clothing hanging in soggy tatters, the corpse infecting the water with rot.

Halfway across the lagoon, Lucia handed him his rifle and he pressed a magazine into the magazine well, then chambered a round with a swift clack of the lever action. He accepted the pistol from Lucia which she'd already loaded and charged, and holstered it on his hip. The remaining boat crew did the same with their weapons, hunkering down as they angled southeast along the mainland shoreline, Filippo searching for an inlet to try. He mumbled to himself, stood, and balanced with eerie precision as the waves rocked the boat back and forth. Occasionally, he lifted a pair of binoculars to scout the area before sitting again and adjusting course.

"I see a way in."

Angling sharply to the right, kicking the engine up a little higher to fight the sluggish current, he steered them into a wide canal with long, angular docks and large flatbottomed boats sunk at the bottom of the lagoon with their tops sticking out, smokestacks and exhaust pipes jutting from the dark waves. Filippo motored past those, staying in the center of the narrow channel as they headed two miles inward past inlets and side branches, islands with skeletons of warehouses and storage sheds, shipping containers, huge coal piles, stacks of wooden timbers and other building materials used to maintain Venice in the lagoon. Filippo angled them up an industrial canal, even more of a concrete jungle with heavy equipment crushed and decrepit, useless ships scuttled at the piers.

"So much gone to waste," Marco said with an emotionless stare.

Filippo gestured toward the front. "If you want to see a waste, feast upon the sight of the Ocean Princess."

The Recs all rose and turned to look north at the massive cruise liner sitting at its pier, the sharp bow of the ship angled up slightly, tipped to the stern side with lightless cabin windows pointed toward the water. Flame-devoured corpses lay sprawled on the decking, radio antennas and communication arrays hung by cables, lifeboats dangling over the side. The boat had pulled loose from its boarding ramps and had char marks up its sides, the rear section containing a massive hole, the size and scope of the wreckage a testament to the horrors of what had occurred.

The Recs cursed, prayed and made the sign of the cross before the gargantuan ship passed out of sight behind another row of warehouses and maintenance bays. The area around them devolved into administration buildings, stores, and a few apartment complexes with collapsing fronts. The canal narrowed even further with small piers slipping by on either side, most with motorboat wreckage built up in the channel and causing Filippo to weave between it, stopping once to have the Rec team push debris out of the way with poles. Eventually, they came to a quiet dock, Filippo cutting the engine and leaping out to tie them up tight and catch the flatbed boats as they drifted up.

"I need two to guard the boat," Filippo said, drawing his pistol and checking the chamber. "I give the rest four hours to get what you need, then we leave."

Marco and Lucia led their team up the set of winding, concrete steps, long since fallen to decay, the entire landing skewed slightly to the left, its imminent demise hurried by the explosions that had occurred along the docks and thrown the area into ruin. The mainland streets were filled with dirt lots and piles of materials for mixing concrete and pitch, but eventually they reached their first residential area, a long block of tightly packed apartments built in an old Renaissance style. The roof angles and walls were symmetrical and perfectly proportional, some with columns and pediments along the fence lines. Where the warehouse district was mostly burned to the ground, there had been efforts to save the civilian structures. A few buildings dripped with leaking pipes and dribbling sprinkler systems and hoses were still connected to water spigots, but the water had been of no use against the flames.

Shouts and echoes swelled in the concrete streets, voices drifting around them, shapes shifting in the alleyways. They slipped through the streets, keeping to one side or the other, weapons sweeping in every direction, barrels pointing into the shadows, looking for signs of ambushers. Marco avoided the open streets, steering clear of conflict, angling the Recs ahead toward a large block of shopping centers and restaurants.

The city dripped with menace, a forlorn chaos permeating from every pore, alleyway, and scorched stoop. Many of the denizens who were left behaved more like insects than people, scattering before the fast-moving, well-armed scavengers who swept by in their dark clothing and matte-black weapons. Marco caught flashes of bright garb in the gloom, poor souls with matted hair, more mongrel than human. Some showed signs of organization, survivors picking through the wreckage but staying far out of the Recs' way.

Marco led them down a long set of stone stairs marking the start of a plaza. Within it stretched a wide, debris-strewn square, bracketed by rows of stores, a tourist's paradise with a touch of traditional Italian architecture. A stone man on horseback stood in the center of a fountain, the horse rearing up and pawing at the sky, a two-foot wall encircling the statue and fountain. Beyond it stood a row of abandoned vendor's carts beneath the shadow of a mountainous stone church that stretched a hundred feet tall with a pointed steeple that stabbed the darkened sky. He gestured for the team to break into groups of four, each group headed into a separate store along the extensive row that hadn't been fire damaged.

Lucia, Valentin and Antonio followed Marco into a candy store, stopping to listen for sounds. Amidst the strewn chairs and candy-striped decor, the glass counter was shattered with shards scattered across the floor.

"Why are we here?" Lucia asked.

Marco placed his finger over his lips and shushed her, then he grinned and led them deeper into the shop, past over-turned tables and chairs, slipping along a wall-shelf full of books and entering a supply area at the rear of the store. Racks of boxed confectioneries, chocolates, and Italian hard candies sat on shelves, but most of them had been taken, the shelves stripped, broken boxes on the floor covered in boot prints, smashed and inedible.

"Marco, this is a waste of time," Antonio said. "We need to be looking for real food, not junk food like this."

Valentin agreed. "Let's move on before the others take all the good stuff."

"The good stuff?" Marco asked with a cocked eyebrow, finding a side door and slipping into a small manufacturing area with a large oven and candy-making appliances. "The sign out front said homemade candy."

"Yeah?" Antonio replied. "Who cares?"

Stepping around a large table, Marco pointed above a workstation where flour had spilled everywhere and boxes, tins, and other baking goods were stacked. "This is chocolate, sugar, flour..." He ran his fingers through the spillage on the table and held it up, his fingertips glowing in Lucia's flashlight beam. "You don't think the cooks back in the city will trade high for these items?"

Their faces brightened all at once, their expressions suddenly eager as they looked greedily across the shelves of goods.

"We can't even carry all this," Valentin said, gaping in awe.

Marco grinned broadly. "Now you see why this is a gold mine."

"Yes, yes, Marco," Antonio replied, grabbing two sacks of confectioner's sugar. "You're a genius. Is that what you want me to say?"

"Yes, actually." Marco nodded and gestured toward the ovens and closets around. "Put whatever you can carry in your duffel bags. The rest we will hide in the ovens and any other place you can find. We'll come back for it later." He took Lucia by the shoulder. "This will bring us good trades, my dear."

"Yes, Marco." Her smile stretched from ear to ear. "It was a great call."

"Okay, people. Let's get to work."

After hiding everything they could and packing their duffel bags full to bursting, Marco and his team left the candy store. On the way out, Marco grabbed two books, *La Divina Commedi* and *Le Città Invisibili* and stepped outside. Along the treasure chest of storefronts, the teams had tossed piles of goods on the sidewalk - useless things like pots and glassware, furniture, paintings, and chairs. Someone opened a door and threw a pan outside where it hit the pile and rattled across the cobblestones.

Marco clicked his tongue and gestured angrily. "Keep it down or you'll draw the *rats*."

"Um, Marco?"

Lucia was shining her flashlight across the lane, wearing a concerned but curious expression. Marco followed her gaze to a little girl sitting on a cornerstone next to a café. She wore a bright blue dress, torn around the knees, her dirty shoes kicking back against the cornerstone, her hair a mess of pigtails and braids. She held a shiny red apple in her hand and, watching them intently, the girl sank her teeth into the apple and chewed, the juice dripping down her chin and onto her dress.

"Come on, Marco." Lucia snagged his arm and drew him across the plaza.

He called over his shoulder. "Antonio. Valentin. Stay here. Make sure the others get out quickly and quietly."

Valentin ran off while Antonio occupied the store corner, looking north across the cobblestone square with its statues and imposing church steeple on the other side.

"Hey," Lucia said when they reached the child. "Are you lost? Do you need help?"

The girl blinked at them, face betraying no sign of emotion, her shoes making soft scuffling noises as they bounced against the cornerstone.

"Do you have family here? A mom or dad?" Marco asked.

When the girl didn't respond, Lucia pressed. "Brother or sister?" She glanced at Marco. "Is she mute or something?"

All Marco saw in the girl's face was an echo of the grim world they lived in, the raw reality of what they'd also become if they didn't strive for something more; civility, art, literature... life. He felt the weight of the books inside his coat, glad he'd grabbed them and promising himself to get more on the next trip.

The girl's cold blue eyes shifted to Marco, chilling him with an emotionless stare that sent tiny fingers of dread dancing up his spine. "There might've been a little girl in there once," he murmured, "but she's gone now."

"Don't say that Marco," Lucia whispered harshly. "You don't know what she's been through."

"I've got a good idea. Anyway, there's nothing we can do for her. Let's leave her alone."

"Hey, Marco," Antonio hissed. "Come here."

Antonio was standing at the corner, nodding northward and holding his weapon against his chest. Marco trotted over and stared into the stirring shadows menacing the square.

"What is it, man? What do you see?"

"Movement over by the church. A lot of it."

Nodding, he called for Lucia, but she was holding the girl's feet, trying to talk to her, pleading with her to come down off the cornerstone.

"Lucia! Come on. We've got company."

"Let's hide you, little girl," Lucia was saying. "I... I'll take you with me when we leave, okay?"

Lucia got beneath her arms and lifted her off the stone perch, putting her down behind it and forcing her to squat. The girl clung to her apple, her expression never changing while Lucia maneuvered her into position.

"That's it," Lucia walked backward, smiling and nodding, holding up her palms and making a pushing gesture. "Stay right here. I'll be back, okay?"

"Come on, Lucia," Marco hissed. "We need to check this out..."

"Okay, I'm coming!"

Shoulder to shoulder, they ran toward the fountain and the stone horse pawing at the sky. Antonio and Valentin fell in behind them, pounding over the cobblestones with echoing footfalls. Marco and Lucia reached the fountain first, squatting with their weapons resting across the wall, peering north where the church and its connecting buildings sat in eerie silence. Shadows slithered along a wrought iron fence to the left, and more moved on the right-hand corner block with its tall, arcing lamp post. Marco turned and pointed at Antonio and three others, gesturing off to the right, sending them slipping off into the darkness. Rounding up Valentin and two others, he shoved them toward the café where overturned tables and chairs lay scattered across the cobblestones and shattered glass.

"Go there," he told them. "Use the tables for cover and watch for anyone coming in through the building."

Marco and Lucia stayed in cover, peering around the statue, crouched with their rifles pointed in the general direction of the church. The shadows played tricks with Marco's vision, dark shapes moving in the thickening night, accentuated by a glow of mist rising from sewer grates. He blinked and shook his head to clear his vision, focusing again, picking up new shapes that seemed to have a physical presence beyond mere tricks of the light.

"There," he said, grabbing Lucia and pulling her to his side of the statue, pointing to the cluster of vendor carts. "Do you see them?"

"No, what do you see?"

Marco rested his rifle on the stone wall and took aim. "Legs."

With a squeeze of the trigger, the gun cracked in a bright flash of light, followed by a hollow scream. A shape fell between the wheels of the cart, someone clenching their knee and rolling back and forth on the ground. Marco fired again and the shape jerked and quieted. He blinked through a waft of gun smoke as three figures raised up and fired in retaliation, their muzzle flashes giving away their location. Marco grabbed Lucia and dragged her down as rounds peppered the brick wall, one pinging off the statue in a cloud of stone dust.

Rifle fire erupted from the left and right, but Marco left Antonio and Valentin to handle it because the people behind the cart charged toward the statue across the market square, heads down and running, shooting as they came. Marco and Lucia opened fire, working their charging levers like pistons and loading new shells into the firing chambers one after the other. One figure was trying to circle to the left, and Marco tracked and shot him in the side to send him twisting into the mist. A round from Lucia's gun struck the one running up the middle, a stomach shot that doubled him over and put him down with a heavy grunt. Their third attacker turned and bolted, and Marco started to fire but paused, electing to save his ammunition.

"Good shooting," he said.

"You, too." She rested her hand on his shoulder, searching the steamy night for more attackers.

Antonio ran up with his folks from the street. "We drove them back, but they are regrouping... bringing more."

"Okay, let's leave."

Marco turned and jogged back to the stores with the group right behind him, meeting Valentin's people from the café and drawing them along toward the piles of looted goods.

"You were right," Valentin said, panting as he ran. "They tried to flank us through the café, but we sent them running."

"Good work, my friend," Marco replied in a breathless rush as the heat of the moment thrummed through his body. "Let's get our things and go before more come."

Duffel bags were slung on shoulders, and anything extra stuffed into pockets or inside jackets. They were about to race to the stone stairs when Antonio took Marco by the shoulder and turned him. Lucia was by the cornerstone, squatting and calling out, trying to find the girl who seemed to have disappeared like a ghost.

"Lucia!" Marco hissed, snapping his fingers to get her attention.

She stood and moved to her left, peering into the deep shadows and alleys, stooping with her hands on her knees. "Where are you?"

"Lucia, come *on*!" Marco snapped. "*Lu-cia*!" The child had likely been a part of an ambush strategy, but Lucia's heart was big, and leaving the child a challenge.

Lucia turned and staggered over to them, grabbing her duffel bag and slinging it on her shoulder. "Let's go!" Marco bellowed, slapping them on their backs, waving them, shoving them along.

The Recs jogged past the long avenue of shops and restaurants, up stone stairs that twisted up to bridges and dead, whispering spaces, scuffling shoes following, chasing them. With supplies rattling in the duffel bags they ducked, slipped, and wove through the ruble of Mestre, taking as roundabout of a path as possible to throw off any possible pursuers. After thirty minutes of running, they reached the dock where Filippo waited.

"Put your stuff there." Filippo pointed at the deck. "Good haul?"

Marco nodded as they jumped on board, the flatbed swaying as they lined up their duffel bags in a haphazard row. Marco dropped his, straightened it out, and climbed up to stand at Filippo's side.

"What'd you get?"

"Baking materials," Marco said. "Chocolate, sugar, and flour."

Filippo whistled. "That'll make Reggie and the bakers *extremely* happy."

The next hour was a waiting game for the remaining Recs, Marco and the others spreading out around the area, watching for "rats," paranoid that someone had followed them back to the boat. But no attacks came, no gunshots in the night, only Raul's team returning late, barely making the four-hour deadline, piling cases of bottled water, canned goods, and clothing in the boats. Marco went to Raul as he tossed a soccer ball from one hand to the other and watched his team finish loading.

"Plan on doing some playing?"

Raul smiled crookedly. "I'm not a soccer player, but my kid brother is. I'll give it to him."

"What did *you* get?"

Marco shrugged. "Nothing."

"Oh, come on. We all bring back trinkets for our loved ones."

"It's not a trinket, but..." He opened his coat and showed Raul the books he'd gotten from the candy shop.

"Very nice. We need stuff like that. No more TV."

"Exactly," Marco nodded.

"All right, everyone," Filippo called. "We're leaving."

With everything loaded onto the flatbeds and morning fast approaching, Filippo started the motorboat with a cough and a sputter, slowly turning them around, leading the tethered flatbeds and making sure they didn't tangle or tip. Then he was driving them down the canal, puttering into the open waters, bouncing, rolling back and forth, swaying with waves rippling from side channels and shipping lanes. The massive cruise ship passed by on their left, silent and dead, the corpse of the vessel a monument to their new world. Marco didn't spare it a glance, focusing ahead until they reached the open lagoon and angled toward the L-shaped Tronchetto district and home.

In the distance, the Bridge of Freedom was lit up in a fiery glow as raiders from the mainland made a bold, headlong approach, running into Venetian resistance by way of tracer rounds lighting the sky, arcing bottles of fuel that burst and sprayed flames across flesh and stone. The screams of their enemies, once compatriots, filled the night sky, bodies toppling off the highway arches to plunge into the lagoon.

Marco put his arm around Lucia, drawing her close as cinders drifted into the sky and were carried across the wind-swept waters. "Are you okay?"

She nodded and tucked her chin, wet cheeks lit by the fiery glow.

"What's wrong? It was a successful run, no? No one was hurt."

"Yes, I know. I am grateful for that."

"Are you upset that you had to shoot someone?"

Lucia shook her head, tears falling to her chin, hanging at her jawline until she wiped them away. She grabbed her coat and pulled it tight. "I have killed before... too many times to count." With a gasp and a sob, she buried her face in her coat and shook her head. "It's nothing."

Marco swung to knees and faced her. "Then what is it, Lucia?" He leaned in, craning his neck to get her to look at him. "Tell me what I can do to make it better. Is it something I said?"

She let go of her coat and held his face. "No, Marco. I love you. It's just... the *girl*." She gazed toward the mainland. "I promised her we would bring her home, and we didn't."

"How could we, Lucia? She ran away. She wasn't there anymore."

"I should have kept her close. I... I should have held her *hand*."

"And drag her along while we ran? It wasn't your fault she ran off. I'm telling you – they were using her."

"She was just scared," Lucia said, sobbing and throwing her arms around him.

Marco comforted and held her, keeping his thoughts to himself as he kept his arms around her and let her cry it out, swaying with the boat's movements as they raced back to Venice with their treasures.

CHAPTER FIFTEEN

Ryan Cooper
East Lansing, Michigan

"You say you got three of them heaters?"

It was early the following day as Hansen and Tyler led Red into the kitchen toward the front door. Ryan was already looking out the window, leaning to the side to see the salt truck with the tailgate down, the crew having lined up two electric water heaters on the driveway while they wrestled the third one out.

"Yep. Right there, Boss." Hansen nodded, pulling the door open for Red. "We found them right where you said they'd be, down at that appliance shop. Two are brand spanking new, too."

"Well, I'll be damned." Red shot Ryan a glance. "I guess that appliance place came through for us."

"Well, they only had the two left at the supply store," Hansen said. "The third one we got from the neighbor's house down the road. You can see it's a little older than the other two."

Ryan gave a studious grunt. "It's about ten years old, I'd say, just based on the design. Should be fine, though."

"You know a lot about water heaters?" Red asked. "Never figured you for an expert in them."

"Not an expert, but I've had to replace my fair share."

"Think you and Tyler could sort out getting them installed?"

"We could give it a try. I don't see the point in putting them all to use right away. Three's overkill."

"Two's what we need right now," Red countered. "Rip out the two old ones down there and keep the third in the barn as a spare."

Ryan folded his arms and rubbed his chin, staring at the water heaters. "Like I was saying yesterday, better to keep them in sequence as holding tanks with the current ones. The third can sit in a corner somewhere in case we need it in a pinch."

"You don't think that's going to be too crowded?"

Ryan shrugged. "Not much more than it already is. You throw one in the barn and it's liable to have the cow kick it or someone run the tractor into it and puncture it."

"Well shoot. That's a fair point." Red looked over at Martha, smiling. "It's a good thing we kept this son of a gun around – he's a smart cookie."

Martha nodded at him without saying anything, returning to her work with Helen. The pair were in the kitchen, pouring over inventory numbers and working on planning future meals, trying to calculate the calories they'd need to keep everyone healthy while not draining the pantry.

"Besides, you want to have all of your equipment where you can hook it up quickly in case something goes wrong." Ryan pressed the point. "A water heater isn't life or death, but it would be good to have them in one spot where all we need to do is throw a few switches and swap out some pipes. Would make it easier to perform maintenance on them, too."

"Yeah, I get the gist." Red rolled his eyes. "You can stop now."

"You asked for my advice," Ryan shrugged. "I'm just trying to give it. Put all three new ones downstairs, and Tyler and I will get them hooked up."

Red stiffened, his jaw tense as he stared Ryan down, a crimson hue rising from his neck onto his face. "Reynolds? Hansen?"

"Yeah, Boss," Reynolds replied.

"I'm here," Hansen said.

"First thing I want you to do is tear out those pieces of crap water heaters down there and let me know when it's done." Red stared at Ryan the entire time while giving the instructions, speaking through clenched teeth.

Hansen was already heading toward the basement door. "On it, Red."

Reynolds was right behind him, taking a three-pound hammer off his tool belt when Ryan stepped past Red and grabbed Reynold's arm before he got to the door. "Don't tear out a thing. Leave it alone, both of you."

Red grabbed Ryan by the arm and jerked him back, pushing his face close into Ryan's, the veins on his neck beginning to throb. "You don't *touch* my people, you got that? You don't give the orders, and you don't put a hand on them!"

Ryan didn't back down, his voice rising to meet Red's. "And you don't get the final say in whatever the hell you want about this house! We had an agreement th—"

"Ain't no *agreement*!" Red screamed at him, spittle flecking outward, his face a mask of pure rage.

"It was understood Helen and I would have run of this house," Ryan growled. "We'd have the final say regarding major changes."

Red raised a finger and jabbed it into Ryan's chest. "Listen to me, Ryan Cooper. If you don't step back..."

"Wait! Hold on just a second." Helen rushed in and tried to get between the two bristling men, arms on both of their chests. "This is *not* that big of a deal – we don't need to have a shouting match."

"*He* turned it into a shouting match," Ryan scowled.

Red's glare dripped venom. "It doesn't matter if it's a big deal or a small deal - your husband doesn't understand that I do *not* care what he thinks."

"Now, Red," Helen pleaded. "This is our family's home, and despite everything that's happened, we should have a say over any permanent changes. We've been helpful and cooperative, and Ryan knows a *lot* about this place that you all still don't. I know you're in charge, but I think some respect for our wishes is owed to us."

"She's right, honey," Martha joined Helen, circling to the other side and taking Red's arm. "We're here as their guests, remember? We should be respectful of that. It's the right thing to do."

Red's crew was filtering in from all parts of the house and outside, a few looking through the bay window and others standing in the hallway, all curious as to the source of the uproar. Ryan was acutely aware of Hansen and Reynolds towering over him, flexing their fists, ready to pounce at Red's command. Still, others nudged each other, whispering, and Red looked around at the assembled group.

"Maybe we should put it to a vote," someone murmured from the living room, just barely loud enough to hear.

Red spun on them, searching the crowd. "Who said that? Who the *hell* said that?"

When no one responded, Red drew his revolver from its holster, eyes narrowing, nostrils flaring as he glared from one person to the next. "Coward." He spun back, hand flexing on the revolver's handle. "Martha, Helen... stay out of this. It doesn't concern either of you." Red's attention swung back to Ryan. "Now, listen Ryan-"

"It certainly *does* concern me." Helen's voice rose, shaking slightly, determination compelling her to continue even as Ryan shook his head at her.

"Honey." Ryan looked at Red. "Step back, please. Red, there's no reason we need to do this over some water heaters."

"Like your husband said," Red growled. "Back *up*." He shoved Helen aside, then pushed Martha after her, the pair falling backward onto the kitchen island, barely catching themselves to keep from topping over.

Ryan tried to retaliate, but Red shoved him into the kitchen table, knocking cups and mugs over and forcing Ryan to grab the chairs to stay upright. Crying out, Martha seized Red's arm and jerked hard, trying to pull him off. Ryan fended off Red's next push with a sweep of his arm, and Martha used her leverage to haul Red backward a few steps, off balance and staggering. Red spun on her, nostrils flaring, eyes bulging in fury as he left Ryan alone for the moment and backed Martha into the living room, frothing at the mouth as he screamed at her.

"*I'm* the one in charge. *Me!* No one tells me what to do around here, you got that?" He held up a finger, pointing at her, then at the rest of the crew who were still staring at him. "This ain't a damned democracy! I'm in charge, you got that?" Red whirled on Helen, stalking toward her. "How about *you?* You got that?!"

Ryan pushed off the kitchen furniture, knocking chairs to the floor as he launched himself at Red, nearly grabbing him before being stopped by Hansen.

"You touch her, you're a dead man, Red!" Ryan pushed back against Hansen as Red loomed over Helen, razor-edged vitriol overflowing in a sharp bellow. "And don't talk to me about respect or how this is still *your* family home because it isn't. It's mine now. *Mine,* dammit!"

Ryan shoved against Hansen's immovable bulk, twisting and squirming in his heavy-handed grip, reaching to grab Red's shirt but unable to break Hansen's hold.

"I'm telling you, Red," Ryan growled. "If you touch her..."

"You'll do *what,* Ryan?" Red, chest heaving, his voice dangerously, menacingly soft, spoke over his shoulder without taking his eyes off Helen. "You'll do *what?*"

Ryan forced himself to remain calm and stop struggling against Hansen. "Red. It's water heaters. There's no need to talk to our wives like this. Come on, man, have some respect."

"Respect? *Respect?* That's what this whole thing's about, Cooper! It ain't about no damned water heaters, it's about the lack of respect!"

"We respect you, Red," Ryan said. "We do. We've shown that every step of the way. All we're asking is—"

Red raised the pistol, flicking his shoulder back, pointing the gun straight at Ryan's head.

"Whoa!" Hansen said, releasing Ryan and recoiling, hands in the air. "Don't get any blood on me, Boss. I just got cleaned up!"

Ignoring Hansen, Red shook the weapon at Ryan and then shifted it around the entire group, aiming at everyone from Nancy to Reynolds to Martha, swinging in a full circle before coming to rest on Ryan again.

Red's arm stiffened and his index finger twitched on the guard, brushing against the edge of the trigger. "I'm sick and tired of being fed *bullshit.*" He drew the hammer back with his thumb. "You know what I do with bullshit? I hose it down the drain."

Ryan's heart was pounding as he stood his ground, staring Red down, trying to keep his gaze off the barrel and the full cylinder pointed at his face. "All right, Red. We can do it your way. Two heaters downstairs, one in the barn."

Red's stare lingered, then he chuckled darkly. "No... no, after this load of BS, you need to be made an example of."

"Red Fletcher, you listen to me right now!" Martha was suddenly back in the kitchen, putting herself between Ryan and the gun barrel as she pressed forward toward her husband. "You will *not* do this. Not *this* kind of violence. Not again!"

In spite of the fact that the revolver's silver barrel was pointed at his wife's head, Red's aim was steady, and for a fraction of a second Ryan thought Red might just squeeze the trigger.

"Why the *hell* are you siding with *them?*" Red lowered the gun, finally taking his eyes off of Ryan. "Why are you defending *them?*"

"I'm not defending them," Martha replied, softer. "I'm just trying to get through this day without seeing someone's brains spread all over the ground. Please, Red."

Ryan sidestepped Red, taking Helen by the hand and pulling her through the crowd, voice shaking. "I'm going out to check on the solar panels. Do whatever you want, Red! Burn the place down if that's what you want to do!"

Outside, cool air blew across his face, drying his sweaty skin and washing away the stifling heat of the kitchen. Ryan led Helen out to the solar panels, scowling at the back door, half expecting Red to come charging outside, revolver in hand once again.

"That was way too close," Helen whispered, squeezing Ryan's hand, her knuckles turning white.

"What the hell was his problem? It's *water heaters* for heaven's sake."

"He's lost his mind."

With nowhere for his adrenaline-fueled energy to go, Ryan squatted and peered beneath the layer of panels, reaching under and fiddling with the frame, loosening the ball joint and angling two panels west a few degrees. None of it was necessary, but it occupied his hands and mind, preventing him from doing something he'd regret.

"I mean, there's something *seriously* wrong with him," Helen continued, keeping an eye on the door.

"I didn't think that would set him off... well, maybe I was poking him a little. Still not enough to warrant *that* response. Did you see him pointing that thing at Martha? Plus all of the rest of his people?"

"That man is borderline *insane*."

"We need to change our plans."

"Meaning?"

"This whole resisting them from the inside isn't going to keep working for much longer."

"Well, I've already been working on Martha. Of course, if she were to tell Red what Sandy and I were talking to her about...."

"We'd probably all end up with extra holes in our heads."

Helen nodded. "Yeah. You're right; we need to go."

Hansen appeared in the bay window, watching Ryan and Helen, and Ryan turned to kneel and duck beneath a panel. "Yeah, and we need to do it tonight."

Helen pretended to be helping him. "Tonight? Are we even ready?"

"Maybe? We don't have much of a choice, honestly."

"Okay. Tell me how I can help."

"After things settle down, gather up anything you can. Food, clothing, weapons – just grab kitchen knives if that's all we've got. We'll be taking the trailer with us."

"Are we going to take the EV?"

"No. The tractor. We'll meet at the barn later when there's a change of guards."

Helen nodded. "Okay... I'll wait for a chance to go back inside."

The chance came thirty minutes later when Martha stepped outside and came over with her hands clasped in front of her, smiling nervously as she glanced back toward the house.

"Helen, Ryan... I'm so sorry about what happened. Red... he's having a bad day. Not that it's an excuse for what he did and said."

Ryan backed out from beneath the panels, standing, dusting off his pants and forcing a thin smile. "Thanks, Martha. I guess he feels under pressure, huh?"

"Everyone's under pressure, but no one else is acting like that." She wrapped her arms around herself and turned to look at the house again. "That was... way out of line, obviously."

"Yeah that's not exactly the phrase I'd use to describe my husband pointing a loaded gun at my head, but sure."

"What's he doing now?" Helen asked, jabbing Ryan in the side with her elbow before Martha turned back around.

"He's in the dining room with Jack and Tyler, reaming them for something."

"Good," Ryan chuckled dryly. "Better them than us. Maybe he could use a swig from one of those bourbon bottles Helen said you had."

"Oh, *no*." Martha shook her head a few seconds too long. "No, no, no, no. That would be bad. He's... he can't drink. No. No, everything's fine. He'll take it out on folks for a minute then be right as rain."

"I hope so." Helen took Martha's hands. "Is there anything we can do?"

"Come inside and help us plan dinner."

"Oh, I don't know. If it's still tense in there..."

"It's not, I swear. Sandy and Nancy are asking for you and—we *really* need you in there, Helen. Actually, if everyone could just see you, it might help settle things down even more. You too, Ryan."

"Oh, no, Martha." Ryan shrugged. "I think I'll just stay out here and work for a while double-checking the panels and then head in to take care of the dogs some more. I don't think Red needs to see me. If Helen wants to go in, that's fine. Just make sure she's safe, okay?"

"She'll be fine, Ryan," Helen said. "I promise."

"Good luck inside," Ryan squeezed Helen's hand.

"I'll meet up with you later. Good luck with your work."

"Thanks, good luck with dinner."

Ryan watched them go in, letting out a breath and flexing his fists a few times, trying to release the tension. The afternoon wore on, as Ryan busied himself with feigning work on the solar panels, going over what his remaining tasks were in his plan, trying to decide what things he could afford to let go and what would be required.

"No sense delaying any further, Cooper," he said. "Time to get on with this."

After rechecking a last bit of wiring on the solar panels, Ryan stood, dusted off his hands, and started toward the barn. Halfway there, the back door of the house flew open and Red came jogging out after him. "Hey, Cooper! Hold up!"

Ryan took a deep breath and let the air slip slowly out, turning, offering Red a smile. Red jogged out to him with a travel mug of coffee in his hand and his baseball cap flipped backward, covering the last few yards with a swaggering gait.

"Yeah, Red. What is it?"

"I just wanted to say sorry for that little argument back there."

"It's all right, Red. It happens." Ryan let his smile linger and turned to go, but Red took him by the shoulder.

"No, really. Listen up."

Ryan paused and reversed back. "Seriously, Red. No apology necessary. Like you said, it's your house now."

"What? Oh, no no. I'm not apologizing for that. I'm apologizing for almost *burying* you and Helen out there." Red's smile spread as he gestured with his mug out toward the edge of the field.

"I... excuse me?"

"Now, don't thank me." Red continued, sipping from his coffee as he looked at the distant piles of dirt. "Thank Martha. She kept me from making a decision today that would have gone poorly for you."

"I see." Ryan's jaw clenched tight. "Well, thank you. And I'll make sure to tell Martha as much the next time I see her."

Red clapped him hard on the shoulder. "That's exactly why you're still with us. You've got an even temper and a lot of patience. We're going to get along great."

"Live and learn, Red." Ryan stuck out his hand, and Red took it, gripping it tight.

"That's right. We live and learn." Red stared at him for a long moment before releasing his hand. "All right then. I'll let you get back to whatever you're doing."

"Thanks, Red." Ryan watched him saunter back up to the house, waving at a few of his crew along the way.

Ryan grumbled under his breath and headed down to the barn, waving to the guards at the north side of the property, bumping against the door bar that was leaning against the wall.

"Hello?" Ryan knocked on the door. "Who's in there?"

After some shuffling the door opened a crack, revealing Helen peering over his shoulder. "Get in here. Hurry up."

"I didn't see you get away," he replied, slipping in to the sounds of the dogs snuffling in the background.

"I just got here a minute ago. Martha has dinner under control, so I pointed out we were already running low on milk."

"So you're milking the cow and I guess Red figures I'm working with the dogs again or something." Ryan shook his head. "Just pray we don't get caught."

"I think the worst of it's behind us – I brought out the supplies already. There was a window when no one was out here when you were with the solar panels so I took a chance." Helen led him to a crate over by the wall and opened it to show a stack of canned goods, jars full of vegetables, and a few canisters of water, milk and eggs.

Ryan grinned. "How on earth did you get all of that collected up?"

"I started squirreling some things away yesterday." She smiled thinly. "I didn't know what would happen, but I figured it could come to this. Took me two trips to get it out here. I think it'll last us a week or two, if we ration it."

Ryan turned and wrapped his arms around Helen, squeezing her tight. "This is better than I'd dreamed it could be. Go ahead and put everything into the small trailer for me. Spread them out so they're covered and protected against bumps – there's going to be quite a few of those. When we're ready to leave, we'll put the dogs in the trailer with them."

Helen nodded at a few metal sheets resting against the tractor. "So this is your plan, I take it?"

"Yep. It's not much to look at, but it'll work, I think."

Ryan walked around the small tractor, pointing at the pieces of steel as he went. "I got everything cut and measured, and started on some of the welding, too. The back of the cab will be covered from top to bottom, as will the fuel tank and the rear hydraulic lines."

"What about the tires?"

"They're foam-filled. Doesn't matter if they take a shot or not."

"We're really just going to drive out of here?"

"Yep. We'll lay down some kind of distraction and go straight out of the barn, down the driveway and through the gate. We'll rob them of a vital piece of equipment they'll need to work the fields in the process."

"That cab looks pretty tight... are you sure two people can fit in there?"

Ryan snickered. "Oh, come on, I figured you'd like some tight quarters. It's romantic."

"Uh huh." Helen rolled her eyes, smiling at him. "What about the dogs? If they're in the trailer...."

"I'll put some steel over the trailer gate. Don't want to add too much or we'll risk getting bogged down if I have to go off-roading."

"This seems like—"

"A half-baked, cockamamie plan?"

"Well. I don't know if I would put it *quite* like that. But yes."

Ryan shrugged. "You work with what you've got. What we've got right now with this whole stay-here-and-try-not-to-get-killed strategy isn't working, so we're going to work with something else and hope it goes better."

How much more work do you have to do on the... *tank*?"

"A few more hours. Go ahead and milk Bessie while I work. Both of us can't be gone for too long or else they'll get suspicious."

Ryan pulled his welding tools out from behind a stack of bins and quickly got to work again. For the next half hour he finished reinforcing the tractor cab, welding pieces around the frame on the back and rear sides, letting them cool, and testing their strength.

"It doesn't have to be perfect," he said after finishing up with a piece of steel across the rear of the trailer. "Just enough to shield us on the way out the door."

Helen loaded the trailer with supplies, stacking them inside and placing blankets and handfuls of hay between them so they wouldn't break on the ride out.

"I'm going back up to the house and make myself known."

"Good idea. Be careful."

"I'll be back before too long. Are you sure we need to leave so soon?" Ryan stared at her for several long seconds until she said what he was thinking. "No, you're right. Red might..."

"Exactly."

After Helen left, Ryan redoubled his efforts, stacking pieces of wood and bricks to hold up sheets of steel level across the lower section of the cab, igniting the torch and running it along the seam. Sweat trickled down his face as he fused metal to metal, bright sparks of light and purple flames dancing as his hands moved, his long-gone experience with the craft slowly returning to him the more he worked. After reinforcing the cab's rear he worked on the right-hand side, waves of heat rolling off the metal sheets as Ryan rushed the last few joints, nearly enclosing the entire cabin. By the time he was done, Ryan's shirt was soaked, and two more hours had passed.

"Not the best seams I've ever made, but they'll hold." Ryan removed his mask and set it down, exchanging it for a rag to wipe himself dry. "I think we're just about ready to go." He looked over at the dogs, who had fallen asleep in a corner of the barn. "How about you three? You ready to ride in a trailer while under heavy fire? Yeah, me neither."

Knocks hammered the barn door, and before Ryan could hide any of his equipment, the door flew open, Helen and Sandy slipping in. Sandy slammed the door and turned to them as Helen carried a handful of boxed food over to the trailer. "How's it going out here?"

"We've nearly got it ready to go." Ryan gestured at the tractor. "What are you doing out here? Where's Stephen?"

"He's safe, up in the bedroom. Red and his crew are down in the basement trying to tear out those propane heaters, so Helen pulled me out here with her."

Sandy took two steps farther into the barn, eyes widening as they adjusted to the dim lighting and she saw the tractor and trailer lined up. "Wow. This looks like a killdozer."

"Come again?" Ryan raised an eyebrow.

"Nevermind. Is it done?"

"For the most part."

"Why didn't you tell me about this?" Sandy looked at Helen, then back at Ryan. "Don't... you want me and Stephen to come?"

Helen and Ryan exchanged a glance, and Helen responded. "We hadn't really talked about it, honestly."

"You should probably stay, Sandy," Ryan replied. "Helen and I are the targets of Red and his crew. You and Stephen can stay in the background and stay safe here."

"Safe? *Safe?* Do you really think it's safe here?"

"It's better than dodging gunfire as you drive away in a tractor with barely any food or other supplies."

"I seriously doubt that."

"Sandy," Helen touched the younger woman's arm, looking at Ryan, who nodded at her. "We're not leaving for good."

"Wait, what? But I thought—"

"Look, we won't be gone long," Ryan said. "Just long enough to regroup and figure out how to run these assholes off of my daughter's property."

"But I can *help*," Sandy replied. "Stephen and I can both help you. You can't leave us here with them!"

"That's part of why I want you to stay here." Ryan said.

"I agree." Helen squeezed Sandy's hand. "Stay here, play along, keep yourselves safe - and be ready for when we return. Keep working on Martha, too. From what she's said, there's real potential there to turn her into an ally."

"Are you *sure?*" Sandy wrung her hands. "I... I don't know if I should stay here. Maybe we should just leave when you both do, even if we don't go with you."

"I don't think so, Sandy." Helen replied. "Ryan's right. The best place for you is here. There's food, a roof over your head, other people. And remember – they hate *us*, not you. You'll be okay."

Emotions washed across Sandy's face, sadness and anxiety changing into a fierce look of determination. "Fine, I'll stay and keep Stephen safe here, but promise me you'll come back."

"We promise," Ryan replied. "Just stay safe here, and don't provoke them."

"I won't. I'll see what I can do about Martha."

"Good." Ryan nodded. "Soften them up for us. We'll find a way to communicate with you once we're out and decide what we're doing next."

"How will I know how to—"

Footsteps crunched through the dirt outside a second before a heavy fist struck the barn door, knocking, hammering on the old wood, freezing them where they stood.

CHAPTER SIXTEEN

James Burton
Connersville, Indiana

Morning broke across the fields and hills, golden sunlight cascading through the treetops to reveal beautifully crafted barns, sheds, and greenhouses nestled in the lush green landscape. Flocks of birds soared overhead, cutting between the trees before sailing upward across the vibrant sky. Several farmsteads crowded a short lane leading to the paved main road running north to south that divided the small, rustic homes from the larger fields.

James stretched and yawned, taking in the vibrant scenery illuminated by the new day as groups of locals walked gravel paths between yards and gardens butting up to wide front porches. A few farmsteads sat close together with families meeting in the backyards beneath awnings and canopies, sharing in the sunshine and the bustle of morning chores. Two wide, diagonal fields sat nestled between two large farmhouses, and women with white bonnets and men with wide-brimmed hats had been busy tilling them since the early morning, finishing up preparations for next season.

"This is beautiful," James said to Alice, who stood beside him with her arm locked in his. "I could live in a place like this."

"Hon," Alice gently batted his shoulder, "we *do* live in a place like this."

"I know... but you know what I mean."

"It seems like a beautiful existence." Alice nodded. "Lots of people working together, living peacefully."

"Do you think the kids would like it?"

"Jake probably would," she replied, "but Sarah would be dead set on finding books to rebuild her collection from home. I can almost picture her in the ruins of society, scrounging inside of libraries. I doubt they'd like what she was reading... all that fantasy stuff."

"What you're saying is... our daughter would be a rebel."

"A bit, yeah."

Eli stepped onto the porch with coffee, wearing a bright white suspender shirt. He'd forgone his wide-brimmed hat, and his dark gray hair was cut short on top and nearly shaved on the sides, apart from his sideburns that swept down to join his beard. Moving to the rail, he gazed into the bright, vivid day.

"Oh, what a beautiful morning the Lord has blessed us with." He tapped on the wooden railing. "The only thing that would make it more glorious is if you'd stay with us this day and enjoy another supper and a good night's rest."

"That sounds great, but we really do have to get going." James stood next to Eli's right. "We'd love to stay, but we need to get home, back to the farm and Alice's parents."

"Yes, you have your own family and farm to attend to. I understand. It's just sad you must go so soon. You've been wonderful company. Your children in particular have been such a blessing with the children."

The sounds of girls laughing exploded from inside the house, giggles and snickers that lingered from the previous night.

"Honestly, seeing my kids again has been wonderful, but to hear their laughter..." James choked up for a moment. "It makes my heart do somersaults."

"It's truly been a joyous reunion," Eli agreed. "And how are you, Alice?"

"This is something I doubted I might ever see," Alice said, moving to Eli's other side and resting her hands on the rail. "I never gave up hope on James, but... sometimes it was so bad out there that I couldn't imagine a moment like this. A *morning* like this."

"I'm sure you felt the same way when you finally got here," James said to Eli. "Obviously, you were received with open arms."

Eli nodded to the Amish walking through the community and working in the fields. "Aye, they opened their hearts and homes to us. But never forget, you are always welcome here as well."

"We'll be back to visit at some point," James said. "And again, thank you for your generosity and help."

"The best time to make a friend is before you need one." Eli gave James an affectionate smile. "Of course, we needed you more than we could have ever imagined, before we became friends, even."

"Turns out we needed each other," James replied. "Okay, honey. You ready?"

"I think so. Let me get the kids rounded up."

"While she's doing that, let's go meet my sons." Eli gestured toward the lane where Abram and Jacob were leading four horses fully saddled and laden with supplies.

"Hey, there they are!" James called. "The bay horse is Buck?"

"Yup." Alice waved. "And there's Stormy and Rocky."

"They're gorgeous." James squinted at the fourth horse, a ginger mare with a glistening coat. "Well, I'll be. Looks like Captain Bragg dropped off Amber with the rest of the supplies Hawkins gave me."

Eli smiled. "I had hoped that would be more of a surprise, but Bragg's people brought her over early this morning so we could check her out and make sure she was ready to travel. We've even put shoes on them all."

"What can I say? Thank you!"

"Amber?" Alice asked. "Isn't that...."

"Yeah, I named her after..." He glanced at Eli. "After the wonderful horse Eli gave to me."

"Bless her equine heart," Eli said wistfully, clapping James on the back. "Amber is a beautiful horse, James, and an apt tribute to the old girl."

Alice squeezed James' hand. "I'll go in and get the kids ready."

They left their coffee cups on the rail, and Eli gestured for James to follow him down the steps. The two men walked out into the yard and down to the dirt and gravel lane where Jacob and Abram brought the horses up.

James petted Amber's snout. "She's a beauty, isn't she?"

"That she is." Abram affirmed.

"Someday, I'll make it up to you."

"I assure you, James, no more apologies are necessary," Abram replied somberly. "You don't need to make *anything* up. Your survival and your family's survival are what matter the most."

The men brought the horses into the yard and up near the porch, and James whistled low at the sheer number of supplies loaded onto them. "Colonel Hawkins is a good man, and so is Captain Bragg and his troops. They fought well last night."

"As did you and your family," Eli said with a rising tone. "God has truly blessed us this day and punished those who would bring evil to us." He looked to his right, into the field where they'd shot the two men the previous evening. "May He protect you on the rest of your journey home."

"Thanks, Eli. He will."

Eli placed his hand on a set of radios hanging from Amber's saddle. "It looks like Captain Bragg wants your family to stay together, too. He gave you these radios to stay in touch with each other should you ever get separated again."

James walked over, grinning. "And you have the frequencies we'll be using? Just in case we need to get a hold of you for something."

Eli chuckled and winked. "We may use the radio from time to time, though I sincerely doubt it. At the very least, we can have someone who is not in our community to monitor them... after all, we'll be working with many outside our community in the near future."

Alice and the kids stepped onto the porch wearing the same clothes as before, freshly laundered after Clara and Betty had put them through the washer and hung them out to dry overnight. Alice came off the porch with the kids, laughing and smiling, and James embraced her and took a deep breath of her freshly washed hair, trimmed and put up in a ponytail out of her face.

Jake stepped over to look over the horses, talking to James and Abram and reviewing their equipment and supplies. Sarah came out last, rosy-cheeked from laughing with the Amish children, her hair held in a blue ribbon behind her head, falling in a tangle of waves down the middle of her back. The Amish gathered around them, Clara, Betty, and Esther with their arms around each other, the kids pressing in close and taking Alice's and James' hands while Eli held his arms up as if embracing the entire group.

"It is with a heavy heart that we come together this fine morning to say farewell to our friends," Eli said. "James, Alice, Jake, and Sarah."

There were smiles all around, and a few tears, and Eli continued. "You seldom meet such good friends in this world, especially with it crumbling around us. Where evil attacks us at every turn, we look toward love and friendship to see us through, and none have been there for us like James and our brothers and sisters here in Connersville. The stories we told last night, and the food we shared, are a testament to our lasting friendship and good fortune under the Lord's watchful eye. We have lost much in this world, sharing heartbreak, death, and enduring enough evil for a lifetime."

Clara wiped a tear from her eye, and Betty and Esther were nodding. Alice's eyes glimmered wetly, and James put his arm around her shoulders and squeezed her gently.

Eli finished with a flourish. "But we look forward to meeting again, God willing, to break bread and fellowship together."

A chorus of amens went around the group, then vehicles approaching up the main road from north to south caught everyone's attention, and they watched as a cloud of dust trailed from behind a long row of vehicles. Jacob, Abram, and Eli grabbed shotguns off the porch, stepping down the lane between the squat farmhouses to challenge the trucks, then Eli stopped and waved.

"It's the convoy we've been expecting!"

The Amish lowered their weapons and strode to the end of the lane to wait for the trucks to roll up while the families swept in behind them.

James leaned over to Alice, whispering. "I'll never get used to seeing them with firearms."

Three Humvees led the pack, all dented, rusted vehicles that had seen better days, followed by nearly a dozen horse trailers and assorted supply trucks, old vans, SUVs, ATVs, and a flatbed with an APC resting on it. Bringing up the rear were more Humvees, light assault vehicles, and troop transports. The growling diesel engines and rattling frames made such a noise as to draw the Amish from their homes to stand on their porches and point or whisper at the mechanized line as it pulled to a halt with the third Humvee stopping at the intersection.

Eli, Abram, and Jacob waved to the guardsmen who stood in their turrets, receiving casual waves back as the gunners relaxed their stance upon entering the Amish's territory. James and Alice caught up to the group a moment later with the rest of their group staying with the horses several yards behind them.

Captain Bragg stepped out of the third Humvee and waved to James. "James Burton. Glad to see you all in one piece. And with your wife, I presume?"

James stepped in to shake the Captain's hand. "Captain Bragg. Good to see you too. How did you and your people fare?"

The Captain's hard edge softened. "Two dead and a handful wounded. We put at least thirty of those bastards in the ground, though." He looked over at Eli. "Oh, sorry about that. Beg your pardon."

Eli smiled warmly. "We shall pray for your people, and the ones they killed. A life lost is never something to celebrate – even though it is sometimes necessary."

Captain Bragg nodded. "I appreciate that. Couldn't agree more."

The lead vehicle's passenger door popped open and a wide-chested officer stepped out wearing a pair of dark sunglasses, his square jaw locked tight as he looked around, spotting James and marching up to him.

"Colonel Hawkins?" James grinned as the Shipshewana commander approached, flanked by two guardsmen. "What on earth are you doing out here?"

"Well, well, well. The hero of Kansas City himself! Fancy running into you again."

They shook hands, patting each other on the shoulder as Alice watched on with a bemused expression. "Hero of Kansas City?"

James shrugged, cheeks turning red, directing his attention back to Hawkins. "Alice, this is Colonel Hawkins – Colonel, this is my wife, Alice."

"Glad you were able to link up, James. Pleasure to meet you, ma'am."

"Likewise."

"What brings you so far from Shipshewana, Colonel?" James asked.

"I thought I'd swing by and oversee this transport myself. This is a big one, as you can tell." Hawkins motioned to the line of horse trailers stretching around the bend. "And it's our first time working with our Amish friends here, so I thought I'd come down and introduce myself."

James stepped aside and gestured to Eli. "This is who you'll want to speak with, then. This is Eli and his sons, Abram and Jacob. I actually know them from a few weeks back. Fantastic people – you can't go wrong working with them."

"It is a pleasure to speak with you in person, Colonel Hawkins," Eli shook the Colonel's hand, "We'll take good care of your horses, of that I can promise you."

"Excellent. Glad to hear it." Hawkins nodded and looked off to the side where Jake and Sarah were watching from near their horses.

"I see you didn't just find your wife, Burton."

"I got them all back, thanks to your help, Colonel. That's my son, Jake and my daughter, Sarah."

"We appreciate you returning James to us," Alice spoke up again. "It's almost been a day so far and we're still having trouble believing it."

"I'm glad to hear it. Your husband's a good man – and a valuable asset. I didn't want to give him up... he's lucky he's not part of the service." Hawkins winked. "In his short time at the Shipshewana outpost, he helped our wrench monkeys get their production skyrocketing. I'm happy to do what I can for him... I'm even happier to see you folks reunited."

"Well, I'm not sure how to repay you for this next favor," James chuckled nervously. "It's a pretty big one after that first ride you gave me."

Hawkins folded his arms across his chest. "You kidding me? Even after all this, I still owe you a favor or three. Between your help with those Humvee repairs and what you showed Diaz and Peterson, we got another dozen trucks up and running already. Whatever pep you put in their step, it's helping. A *lot*."

"Well, thanks. They're good mechanics. I appreciate you rescheduling your run on such short notice."

"I'm happy to oblige," Hawkins shifted to Eli. "I was told your people would be mostly unarmed and might need some protection from time to time." He looked down at the shotgun Eli held in his left hand, raising an eyebrow. "Looks to me like that might not be entirely accurate?"

Eli put a hand on James' shoulder. "While we have had a bit of a change of perspective ourselves thanks to our mutual friend here, we are still very much in favor of pacifism over violence, so any and all assistance would be appreciated."

"We'll make it happen for you." Hawkins glanced at his watch. "It's time we get loaded up and head north. Ten minutes and we're gone."

He spun his finger in the air, bringing forth a group of guard members who partnered up with the Amish to get all the horses and supplies exchanged. Clara, Betty, and the rest of Eli's family joined in and began sorting and placing things on carts while James, Alice, and the kids stood back and watched as Eli and Colonel Hawkins directed the trades and oversaw the work. When they were done, Hawkins shook hands with Eli one last time and circled his arm in the air. "Two minutes, people!"

James met Eli at the intersection and clasped his arm. "We'll see you real soon, Eli. I know you called me an angel, but in that field last night, *you* were the angel. Thank you for saving my family."

"Mutual angels, then, perhaps, my friend?" Eli smiled slightly as James nodded, then Eli turned to Alice. "It was a pleasure meeting you and your lovely children. Please make haste to rejoin us as soon as possible. Our door is always open to your family."

"Thank you Eli. Thank you, Clara – your whole family. Thank you. For everything."

"Take care of this one," Eli shook James's hand one last time. "He is a good man."

Alice locked arms with James. "Don't you worry about that. We're not letting him out of our sight ever again."

Eli's family descended on them, dusty and sweaty from their work, smiling as they hugged Sarah and Jake in turn, then Alice and James. When they were done with their goodbyes, Hawkins led them to the lead Humvee, where James, Alice, and the kids got into the back and the Colonel patted the vehicle's roof and slipped in the front passenger seat. They pulled out in a slow, wide turn that took them away from the clean wooden homes and gardens and the smiling faces as they waved and pointed at the winding line of steel cutting through the fields and farms and out to the main highway and heading north.

The road hummed beneath their wheels, the convoy stretching into the early morning under steel blue skies and enough sunlight to paint the landscape in a vivid, golden hue. The grass stood out green and vibrant, the flat, wooded landscape swept by gentle winds that brought the scents of honeysuckle and moist earth. James couldn't help but glance at Alice every minute or so, their shoulders resting together, hips touching in the crowded confines of the vehicle.

"What?" Alice whispered when she noticed him staring at her.

James gave her a smile and shook his head. "Nothing... just glad to be back next to you, that's all." He turned to Hawkins who was poring over a map he'd spread out in his lap, glancing up at the occasional road sign and giving orders through the radio handset.

"Colonel Hawkins," James said. "I don't mean to interrupt, but how long will it take us to get there?"

"No more than a few hours. We'll drop you and the family off with your horses a few miles south of Lansing proper where we have a small outpost at Angola. They can outfit you with anything else you need to take north."

"I'm not sure what else we'll need," James replied. "You've already given us so much."

"From there, it should just be a few hours ride to East Lansing – and then another hour home?" Alice asked.

Hawkins raised the map so everyone could see, tracing a line from the Angola outpost to East Lansing. "That sounds about right based on what I know about horses, ma'am. We're talking just a few hours from there."

"Thanks, Colonel Hawkins."

Hawkins grinned from beneath his dark, shiny sunglasses. "Just relax and enjoy the ride. We'll have you there in a jiffy."

James settled back and closed his eyes, holding Alice's hand. When she leaned against him and smiled, he kissed her on the forehead. "I love you."

"I love you too. I can't believe we're almost home."

By midday, they'd reached Fort Wayne, Indiana, their journey made all the faster thanks to scouts riding ahead on light reconnaissance vehicles, motorcycles, and ATVs to clear the way and check for ambushes and any potential detours that might need to be taken. Flat fields in perfect squares stretched to either side of Highway 1, divided by old country roads and swaths of deciduous forest, packed with numerous varieties of oak and cedars that filled the air with a fresh, evergreen musk.

The fields gave way to parks and recreation areas along Highway 1, and they passed Ossian, Yoder, and finally entered the outskirts of Fort Wayne. The convoy took I-469 east around the city, the way already cleared of most debris, car husks shoved to the shoulders or piled in semi-neat rows in the grassy fields like apocalyptic junkyards. On the eastern side of town, near New Haven, a small tent city had been erected, and military trucks and guards patrolled the area. Groups of refugees lined the roads to watch the convoy pass, some children waving and eliciting honks from the drivers.

Once north of the city, they jumped back on I-69 and drove several miles to a National Guard recruiting station in Angola, pulling off into a grassy field near a small set of warehouses used for commercial storage. Bright new chain-link fencing surrounded the facility, and temporary structures dotted the area, the buildings marked with military designations and large spray-painted arrows. Guards patrolled the perimeter, and plywood and sandbag installations with heavy gunners were stationed at all four corners.

James, Alice, and the kids waited by the trailers as Hawkins spoke with the outpost leader, a tall woman with sandy brown hair tucked into a camouflage hat, before heading over and telling his people to start unloading the horses. The crew got out, secured their weapons, and popped the trailer doors open, slowly backing the animals out, leading them by tethers. Hawkins led James, Alice, and the kids to one trailer as their horses were guided out, saddled and loaded up with supplies for their journey.

"Here you go, Burtons. All ready to go and delivered as promised." Hawkins stood by the horses, looking them over as James and his family approached.

"Colonel Hawkins... I don't know what to say. You've helped us more than I can believe or have the ability to thank you for. But thank you all the same."

Alice approached the Colonel, hugging him tight, wiping tears from her eyes. "I can practically smell home from here. Thank you."

"Glad we could help," Hawkins replied, a slight smile spreading across his face. "I wish you all the luck in the world." He shook their hands one by one before turning to point off in the distance.

"Follow that little dirt road there through the north gates. The guards will let you through, and you can continue along the backroads with the maps we gave you, which should take you all the way to East Lansing. I'd stay off I-69 if I were you. The horses can handle it, but the last thing you need is to run into a gung-ho guard outfit who wants to take your things from you."

"Yeah, we'd prefer to avoid that, too."

"You folks have your weapons?"

James tapped his shoulder to show his rifle slung there, and Alice did the same. Jake hoisted his shotgun, and Sarah had the pistol James had given her in a holster on her right hip.

"I think we're set here, Colonel. We've got the radios as well. I don't know if they'll have the range to reach you, but I hope we get the chance to say hi again once this all calms down."

"As do I, James. As do I." They shook hands one last time, and James waved to Captain Bragg, who was working with Cortez and Garcia on hauling some items out of a nearby van.

James turned to Alice, Jake and Sarah. "Alright, guys. Let's get this show on the road."

Climbing into their saddles, they got the horses moving toward the gate, Jake and Sarah galloping out ahead a little before slowing their horses to a trot. He raised an eyebrow at Alice, and she only shrugged and smiled. "I told you things've changed."

"No kidding. They look like naturals."

The gate guards waved them past, and they moved between shady patches of trees with dappled sunlight breaking through the gaps to touch the earth. Creeper vines hung in twisted streamers from up high, and bugs buzzed past their heads as leaves drifted into the road in a scatter of gold and red. Birds chirped, and the distant knock of a woodpecker echoed off the verdant canopy as James took a deep breath of the woods' fragrance, the hint of fall in the air.

"You okay?" Alice asked.

"Very. It smells like home."

"I know *exactly* what you mean." She watched as Sarah and Jake rode up a way ahead. "No offense to the beach and the south, but I can do without the heat and humidity for the rest of my lifetime, thank you very much."

"No kidding. If I see another city again, it'll be way, way too soon."

"Same." Alice paused. "We did good, all of us, to get this far."

"How about you? Are you okay?"

"I couldn't be happier."

"No, I mean on the *inside*. After... you know."

Alice grew quiet as she and James rode next to each other along the road, staring at Jake and Sarah ahead of them. When she finally spoke, it was so soft that James could barely hear her. "No. No I'm not."

"What can I do to help?"

Alice smiled sadly at him. "I don't think anyone can help with this. But it's okay." She nodded ahead, at their children. "I'd do it again, for them."

"You shouldn't have to carry that around."

"Don't tell me it's not fair, James. Life isn't fair. And you did plenty of things that'll be with you for the rest of yours, too."

"Yeah..." It was James's turn to stare off into space for a moment. "I'd do it again, too." He reached out and took Alice's hand, squeezing it tightly. "We might not be okay, but we'll *be* okay."

Alice nodded, and they rode silently for another minute before she spoke. "I'm getting butterflies in my stomach about Mom and Dad. I really hope they're okay."

"We'll find out soon enough. What do you say we pick up the pace a little?" He squeezed Amber's sides and settled back as she broke into a trot.

"Hey, wait up!" Alice called.

Soon all four were riding briskly along the broad path that stretched off into the distance, watching the scenery and constant, fluttering movement of birds in the upper boughs. They reached the main highway and turned north, the horses' hooves clattering on the broken pavement as they wove between old wrecks and burned-out vehicles, skeletons on the road touched only by the slow, inexorable passage of time. Old farmsteads passed by in the distance on both sides of the road, most in disrepair with vines creeping up their sides, grass growing wild around the foundations, nature coming to claim what had always been hers.

"You know, it's not going to be a picnic when we get home," Alice said. "There's going to be a lot of work to do."

James nodded. "With everything we've seen on the road, it's bound to be ten times harder than we can ever imagine. I'm sure your parents have gotten a good jump on things, though."

"Undoubtedly. I'm sure they're far better off there than they would have been in Grand Rapids, too."

They rode for another two hours, the sun setting, the light fading by the minute until orange and pink hues spread through the treetops and left them riding in cool shadows.

"We should probably find someplace to stop soon."

"Take your pick of luxurious accommodations," Alice replied, gesturing to a pair of homes, each half-burned to the ground. "That is if we can find one that's not going to collapse on us in the night."

"Yeah, no thanks. And the intact ones, judging by the drawn blinds, could be occupied. The last thing I want to do is get into a gunfight with someone right now."

"What do you suggest?"

"Let's just keep our eyes open."

At the end of a bend where maple and ash trees stretched bare branches to the sky, they passed a tall sign with "*Coldwater Fairgrounds*" written in flourishing script. A winding gravel road led into the fields where long buildings and squares of dirt and concrete were laid out for vendor booths. Between the plots stood park areas with overgrown gardens, bushes, and tangles of brush with promises of seclusion and safety.

"This looks *perfect*," James said.

A Ferris wheel rose above the treetops, rusted cars bolted into the steel frame, and as they cut through an open field and approached the fairgrounds, more evidence of rides could be seen spread across several square miles of weaving paths, both paved and covered in gravel, dirt tracks barely wide enough for bicycles or motorcycles leading into the forest. The land was mostly flat with a few long, halfhearted rises forming ridge lines for hikers to follow. On the south side stood the fairgrounds proper, with rusted swings hanging from contraptions with axles that spun in the wind, crooked signs for things like *Tilt-O-Whirl* and *Screaming Eagle* rattling ominously.

"Yeah, no thanks," Sarah said, nodding at the carousel where it stood like a rotten tooth. "Have you guys ever *watched* a horror movie?"

Jake pointed. "That's where you have to sleep tonight, sis. All by yourself in the creepy carousel with the weird horses."

"Come on you two, let's go." Alice rolled her eyes as they moved on, walking the horses through the fairgrounds and into the campgrounds where signs for camping and hiking stood at the base of a hill.

"I'm thinking we can head up one of those trails." James pointed at the signs. "Find a nice little secluded spot to rest and set up camp."

"We'll make a Dakota fire to cut down on the smoke and light," Jake said. "Just in case anyone's nearby."

"You remember how to do that?" James cocked an eyebrow.

"We've practiced a time or two on the trail."

They walked through the campground on the well-worn gravel and dirt paths running between each site and down a short hill fed by a creek off to the north.

"That looks like a good place," Alice walked her horse around in circles at a secluded site at the back of the campgrounds where they were surrounded by trees, isolated from any potential prying eyes. "Sarah and I will set up camp while you two walk the perimeter and check things out."

James gave her a tip of an imaginary hat. "Yes, ma'am. We'll be back in a jiffy."

Alice and Sarah dismounted while Jake and James took their horses back down the path. Beneath the gently waving branches, the shade was cool, their way dark enough for James to take out a flashlight and shine it up ahead. The slow clopping of their horses' hooves on the soft dirt gave him an intense sense of peace and solitude he hadn't felt in weeks.

"So, I imagine your mother set watch shifts for you guys while you were traveling north?"

"Oh, yeah. Mom was pretty on top of things, but Sarah and I got the hang of it pretty fast. By the time we reached Connersville, we were practically doing everything ourselves."

James side-eyed Jake. "Did you grow an inch or something? You seem a *lot* older than you did a month ago."

"No, Dad," Jake laughed.

They stopped at an overlook where long green fields swept out below, bathed in the fading daylight, the sky a mix of orange and gray as the birds nestled in for the evening, and the bats claimed their place in the night sky.

"It's beautiful up here," Jake whispered.

"It sure is. I never thought we'd get to see all this again."

"You sure we don't want to press on and get home tonight?"

James shook his head. "No, better we get some sleep and rest up. One night won't make a difference, and if we're alert and ready, it'll be worth it. C'mon, let's take one more ride around this place and get back to camp to help the girls."

"Yeah, that sounds good. Hup, Rocky. Let's go, boy."

They got the horses moving along the dirt track that wove in and between the stretch of hills surrounding the fairgrounds. The trees were a tangle of bare branches and vines, deadfall shed from high above to deteriorate and dry rot. They followed the creek for a short way north, cutting back across a wooden bridge with the horses' hooves clapping across the old wood, then they headed up the side of a hill where oaks gripped the banks and leaves spilled down over the rocks to scatter at their feet.

They rode a couple of miles around the fairgrounds, James with his rifle ready, watching the woods for any signs of people, either camped out or stalking through the wilderness in search of prey. They reached the highway and circled south to the fairgrounds again with its Ferris wheel, carousel, and dilapidated ice cream parlor. Cutting sharply back east, they took the same gravel track up to the campsite.

Alice and Sarah were almost done when they arrived, the fire blazing deep in a hole in the ground surrounded by a stone circle. Alice and Sarah were both chopping up logs and breaking sticks they'd dragged up next to the campfire, and after securing their horses, James and Jake began to assist with the work.

"This looks cozy," James said, picking up a piece of deadfall and tossing the bits into a pile at the edge of camp.

"Sarah's laying the tents out over there." Alice nodded to where Sarah was straightening the nylon pieces and organizing the rods, poles, and spikes.

"Jake, why don't you help your sister?"

Jake nodded to James and joined his sister in working with the tents. Thirty minutes later, they had a pile of wood stacked up by the fire, the smoke almost nonexistent thanks to the design of the fire pit, the light dim as the orange glow swelled over the sides to bake the earth around it. The kids had the tents set up a short time later, spiked down with the tent flaps thrown open and blankets and sleeping bags tossed inside. James and Alice pulled over some logs to sit on near the fire, but paused as Alice winced, holding her side.

"You good?" James put a hand on her shoulder as she stood bent over, taking long, shallow breaths.

"Yeah. It's been a lot better but sometimes it just... hurts."

"Here, sit down. I'll finish setting up."

It took some doing, but an hour and a half after they'd arrived, they were all seated around the campfire, Jake and Sarah on one side, James and Alice on the other, and between them on a steel grate, aluminum foil-wrapped bundles sizzled and steamed.

"These sausages and vegetables are going to be great," James said. "Eli said they just made them that morning."

"They treated us so well back there." Alice locked arms with James and rested her head against his shoulder. "I haven't slept on a bed that comfortable in a long time."

"Yeah, they're good people." James used a stick to flip the foil bundles, some of the juices leaking through the seals and landing on the flames below.

Ten minutes later they each cradled a packet of food atop thin aluminum plates. They picked at the steaming cocoons, opening them and emptying the contents onto their plates before using sporks and knives to cut into the meat and vegetables, the aromas washing across the campsite, mixing with the smell of the fire. After a few bites, Sarah brought a bottle of water around and filled their tin cups, Alice raising hers as she looked around at her husband and children.

"Here's to family and togetherness."

"And to being home, finally, tomorrow." James added.

CHAPTER SEVENTEEN

Ryan Cooper
East Lansing, Michigan

Helen clutched Ryan's arm, whispering. "Who's that?"

"I don't know," Ryan grabbed a large ratchet off the nearby crate, looking around at the scattering of tools around the barn. "Whoever it is, we don't have time to get all this cleaned up. We might have to make a break for it."

"Stay back," Sandy said, rushing over to the door. "I'll try to get rid of them."

Ryan stood off to the side with his weapon at the ready, Helen behind them, clinging to a tire iron she'd picked up off the floor. The knock came again, and Sandy opened the door a few inches only for Stephen to push past his mother and enter, looking around until he spotted Ryan and Helen.

"Red's looking for you."

"Who's he asking for?" Ryan lowered his weapon.

"You or Mrs. Cooper," Stephen replied.

"Tell him one of them will be up in a minute." Sandy pushed him toward the door.

"Wait a second, son." Ryan pointed the ratchet at a two-gallon bucket of milk sitting on a nearby bench. "It might look suspicious if he comes back empty-handed. Honey?"

Helen headed over and picked the container up, bringing it back and handing it to Stephen, who leaned backward under its weight.

Ryan leaned in. "You sure you've got that?"

"Yeah, I can do it." Stephen used his knee to hoist it higher on his chest.

"If anyone asks," Ryan said, "tell them you saw us working with the dogs at the barn, and someone will be up in a minute. Now, go. Be careful."

Stephen waddled outside, and Sandy shut the door behind him with the clack of the latch. She leaned against the door, sighing heavily, sweat glistening on her forehead. "One of you needs to head back right now. I don't want Stephen there by himself. If they start to ask questions, he could—"

"I know, he's just a boy," Ryan nodded. "We can't have him spilling the beans without meaning to."

"I'll go head off Red." Helen started to grab the door handle, but Ryan intercepted her and turned her away, stepping between her and the exit.

"I can't let you do that, Helen. You've seen how Red is. Even with Martha on our side, there's no telling what he might do to you if he thinks you're hiding something."

"Don't be silly, Ryan." Helen removed his hand and pushed him gently away. "You have to stay here and finish getting things ready. Sandy and I will go back. I'll put on a brave face and see if I can't smuggle anything else out of the house while I'm there."

Ryan fixed her with a worried, skeptical look. "Be *very* careful, Helen. Red's lost his damn mind, and there's no telling what he might do."

"I'll play it extra safe. You know good and well it's better for me to go than you."

Ryan drew her close and kissed her on the forehead. "You're probably right. If I go up there, I'll end up punching him in the throat. Then Hansen and Reynolds will blow me away, and that'll be the end of it. Just be careful."

Helen squeezed his hands one final time. "Come on, Sandy. Let's go."

Sandy followed closely behind Helen as she grabbed the latch and opened the door a little, shooting Ryan a glance. "Get everything done here while I'm gone, okay? Be ready to leave at a moment's notice if necessary."

Ryan nodded, heart sinking as the door latched shut and the women's shadows moved away and disappeared, watching the door another few seconds before returning to finish the remaining preparations.

Helen and Sandy walked arm in arm past the tents and the chicken coop under the scrutinizing gaze of the guards and crew members lingering around the EV. Tyler was leaning into the EV's rear hatch and shifting supplies around, pointing at a backpack for someone to hand it to him.

"Where are they going?" Sandy asked.

"Who knows? Honestly, I don't care anymore."

Inside, a few people sat at the kitchen table as Martha and Nancy prepared a late-night meal for those coming off duty. Martha and Helen exchanged a smile and a nod before Helen guided Sandy toward the basement door, calling out to Martha.

"We're going to head downstairs to—"

A callused hand grabbed Helen's wrist before she could reach the doorknob. The firm grip turned her arm backward, bending her wrist almost painfully as Red stepped in from the hall wearing a thin, cold grin with a flicker of fire in his eyes.

"And just what might you ladies be up to?"

Helen turned, backing into Sandy, pulling her hand free before he could get a better hold. "We're heading downstairs to do some inventory and bring some things up for tomorrow's meals."

"I see. What were you doing out in the barn?"

"Helping Ryan with the dogs and Bessie." She gestured to the two-gallon milk container sitting inside the door. "I had Stephen bring that up to pasteurize later."

Red stared at her for a moment. "Tell me about this inventory you're talking about. I've already had Jack and Barb go over everything."

"There's another storage closet in the back by the safe. Last I saw, Jack and Barb missed it – probably because of all the commotion over the safe. Given how fast everyone's going through food, I thought we'd go down and take stock of what we have there and see if James and Alice had anything that's expiring soon that we can eat, or need to get rid of. Want me to bring the numbers up to Jack and Barb when I'm done?"

Red sighed, seemingly satisfied by her explanation. "Of course those two dimwits missed supplies. Yeah, I guess that would be good. Good to know there's a little extra. That'll give the scavenging teams time to find more supplies. Oh, and Helen... if you happen to remember the combination to that safe, let me know."

"I can't remember something I never knew," Helen said in a matter-of-fact tone, pulling open the door and stepping inside with Sandy coming behind her until Red grabbed her arm in turn.

"Stay up here. I need you to work on something."

Sandy flashed Helen a look before turning away with a nod. "Yeah, sure thing, Red. What do you need?"

The door shut behind her, leaving Helen alone on the stairs with the soft basement lights below, the smells of dust and oil, grease, and the burning scent of solder and flux as the men downstairs worked on the water heaters. She went down, passing by the pair of propane heaters pushed off to the side, cobwebs hanging from the cut piping and nozzles. Helen slid by toward the room with the safe, catching an odd look from Reynolds and his helpers before she stepped in and turned left where a short wall of shelves was stocked full of canned goods, powdered beverages and boxed meals. Helen picked up a notepad and pen on the center shelf and dug into the inventory, writing things down and adding to the list, partially making a list for Jack and Barb but mostly feigning being busy until she was certain she wasn't going to be snuck up on. Out in the other room, Reynolds cursed at the men as they tried to figure out how to assemble and install the new water heaters, clanking pipes around, sawing, and using a handheld torch.

Ryan would have all that in less than an hour. Helen smiled smugly to herself. *Keep being idiots, idiots.*

After a while, Helen reached into a plastic bin and pulled out a small sack. Spreading it open, she grabbed two glass jars each of pickles, potatoes, tomatoes, and canned meat and placed them inside. With a glance over her shoulder, Helen got on her knees and reached beneath the last shelf where the back was completely open. James and Alice had built the secret compartment soon after constructing the house, Alice divulging its existence to Helen during one of their mother-daughter canning sessions one evening. Apparently, James had wanted to keep spare weapons hidden there for a "just-in-case" situation.

"This is just in case, James... so what do you have for me?" she murmured, finally drawing out two nine-millimeter pistols and several boxes of ammunition. She wrapped them in cloth and placed them in the sack with a few more jars lying on top.

Cinching the sack tight, Helen grabbed the inventory list and left the room, moving past Reynolds and his men. She was just about to turn up the stairs when Reynolds' shadow appeared to cut her off.

"Hey, uh, Helen...?"

Helen went up one step, stopping and sighing. "Yes, Reynolds?"

"I was just wondering..." Reynolds grinned.

"Wondering *what*?"

"Well, me and some of the guys have a bet going on how long you and Ryan are going to make it here."

"Is that right?"

"Yeah... see, most of the guys think you'll be dead and in the ground in under a week – if Red doesn't just leave you out in a field for the coyotes - but I think you'll make it a lot longer."

Helen raised her chin. "Oh, yeah? How long?"

"I think three weeks."

"And what are you all betting?"

"Three bottles of whiskey."

Ignoring the grins and whispered words from Reynolds' helpers, she gave him a brisk nod, jaw tight as she spoke. "We'll try to hang around as long as we can for you."

"Great, Helen. Thanks."

Helen headed back up the stairs, heading for the back door when a voice called out behind her.

"Hey, what are you doing?"

Helen took two more steps before the stern voice came again.

"Helen, stop!"

She turned with a smile to face Hansen standing at the entrance to the great room. The kitchen was empty except for one guard at the table, sipping sullenly at a cup of coffee.

"Yeah?"

"Where are you going?"

"I'm heading back to the barn... did you need something?"

"What's in the bag?"

"Some spoiled food I'm taking out to the animals."

"Spoiled food?"

Helen placed the sack on the kitchen table, loosened the drawstrings, and reached for the canned meat, pulling it out to show Hansen the marbled pieces floating in yellow liquid and spices.

"Yeah, like this meat here."

Hansen made a disgusted face as he craned his neck to look at the jar from different angles. "*That's* meat?"

Helen chuckled. "Yes... well, it used to be. Alice and I tried to can some last year. Clearly, it's no good."

"You can *can* meat?"

"Oh sure. Some of it down there is still good. This stuff, though...."

How'd it get that way?"

"Sometimes the seals can break when you're canning stuff." Helen held the jar up and tapped on the top with her index finger. "If the seal breaks even a little bit and lets in the least bit of air, it'll spoil everything. You don't want to feed this stuff to anyone. Unless they want botulism, that is." She made a show of putting the can back in the sack and wiping her hands on her pants, and Hansen drew away from her, mouth twisted.

"That's nasty. But the animals can eat it?"

"Oh yeah. Those dogs have stomachs like iron. It won't hurt them a bit. Saves us from using some dog food for a meal or two."

Hansen's heavy brow narrowed. "I guess so, yeah."

"Oh, can you give this list to Jack and Barbara? Red wanted them to have it when I was done." Helen handed him the notepad with the inventory she'd written on it.

"Oh, sure. Yeah. I'll take it to Red right now. Thanks, Helen."

"No problem. Glad to help. Talk to you at dinner." Helen brightened. "I hope you've got a big appetite."

A smile finally broke out on Hansen's face at the mention of food. "All the time."

"We'll take care of you, don't worry." She reached out and patted his stomach with a wink. "See you soon."

Helen stepped outside, pulling the door shut behind her, pausing to let out a shuddering sigh before she headed down to the barn and knocked softly on the door, waiting for Ryan to answer.

"Who is it?"

"It's me, dear."

The door popped open, and Helen slipped inside and placed the sack down. "I brought a few more things."

Ryan pushed the edges of the sack over the pile of jars. "Good work on this food. I had no idea—" He spotted the weapons and boxes of ammunition, glancing at Helen as she folded her arms and smiled.

"Did I do okay?"

"Helen, this is incredible." Ryan lifted a pistol and ejected the magazine, racking the slide to check the chamber. "Where did you get these?"

"You know how we hid food and a few extra weapons around the house just in case?"

"Yeah. Is this from one of our caches?"

"Nope. One of Alice and James's. Alice and I were canning food a couple of years ago; she told me they had a little space at the bottom shelf to keep a few things hidden, just in case." Helen grinned and picked up the other pistol, turning it over. "I hadn't thought much about it until we started talking about leaving. Imagine my surprise when I found the guns there."

"Brilliant!" Ryan held the back of her head and planted a kiss on her lips. "A couple of guns makes this whole thing a *lot* more feasible." He nodded toward the armored tractor. "We've got offense now, plus defense and enough food for a week or two. That'd be enough time for us to scavenge and figure out what we're going to do."

"I was afraid before, but I'm not anymore."

Ryan stopped and looked at her. "What do you mean?"

"As soon as I stepped in the house, Red grilled me, and when I was leaving, Hansen gave me the business."

"Oh, yeah? How'd you get past them?"

"I told Red the truth, and I told Hansen I was bringing this food out to feed the dogs and that the meat was bad."

Ryan chuckled. "He's never had canned meat, has he?"

"Apparently not. Is there any way we can leave right *now*? I don't want to be here longer than we have to."

"We need to wait a little while, at least until the sun goes all the way down. I don't want to make it any easier for them to shoot us than humanly possible."

Helen nodded and stepped away, folding her arms in thought.

"What's on your mind, honey?"

"I was just thinking... we should try another kind of distraction, before we leave."

"What do you mean?" Ryan asked, following curiously behind her.

"When I was talking to Hansen in there, I insinuated he'd better be ready for a big dinner. I say we give them one."

Ryan squinted in confusion. "What? Why?"

"We could do up a big dinner for everyone tonight – some really filling, buttery, fat-filled food. I'll bring in Nancy, Sandy, and Martha to help. We'll tell Red it's an apology for everything earlier, the arguments and all that."

"Why would we do all that?"

Helen smiled. "You know how you are when you've had a huge meal. If everyone's half-asleep with their bellies full, it might make it a bit easier for us to get out of dodge."

"With everyone fat and happy, we could slip out of the house and no one would be the wiser." Ryan nodded and grinned. "You're a smart woman, Helen. Do it. I'll sneak the pistols inside, too, just in case we need them."

"I'll grab Sandy and tell her the plan, and we'll get started on dinner."

CHAPTER EIGHTEEN

President Birk
Camp David, New Hampshire

The armored convoy rolled through the lush, forested Catoctin Mountain Park grounds with a thrum of diesel engines and plumes of exhaust. Tall aspens and wide oaks crowded the roadsides in walls of brown and green, the branches stretching over them quivering from the passing of heavy machinery. LAV-25 armored vehicles led the charge, racing toward the compound in single-file formation with gunners sitting in the turrets, swiveling their machine guns back and forth as they watched for unknown dangers. Humvees rumbled behind them, loaded for bear while green and black camouflaged ATVs rode through the surrounding woods, scouting for signs of trouble and potential ambushes.

President Birk rode with Harris in the fifth Humvee back, an up-armored vehicle with no turret designed to make a fast getaway if the column came under fire. The rest of the Humvees bore thick steel plates, reinforced, bullet-resistant windows, and two missile launchers for expanded ground operations, though none of the vehicles were in good condition, all of them having been salvaged, repaired and retrofitted from old, mothballed stock.

Birk leaned forward between the seats, craning his neck to see the first signs of Camp David, and as they swept up the entry road toward the main structures, the site's destruction was clear.

"I wanted to believe it was still there," Birk growled softly, shoulders slumping. "Dammit, General. What happened?"

"I don't know, sir. We lost contact with Camp David weeks ago."

The Camp David main house had been a multi-leveled, saddle-shaped structure with a peaked roof on either side that framed a flat middle. Glass doors and windows built into the upper terrace reflected sunlight and clear blue skies on a usual day, and pear and maple trees had dotted the yard, crowding the front stoop and entrance lane, the wide branches providing shade across the lush, grassy slope.

The main complex had been turned to ash, all the foliage burned to the ground, leaving only sprigs and jutting branches sticking up. The compound's rustic beauty had been turned into a smoky nest of charred beams poking from the coals, the west end of the house buckled, windows smashed, and the old brick and gray siding spilled into the yard. The convoy came to a rolling stop in front of the building with brakes squealing and engines throttling down, leaving them idling silently.

Birk blinked in astonishment. "What happened here, General?"

"We're going to wait here and find out, Mr. President. We should have some information soon."

The General spoke into a handset, and Marines exited their armored vehicles and filtered through the grounds, disappearing around the back where the pool, guest rooms, and driving range would be. The minutes ticked by, and Birk could only stare at the sheer complete destruction as emotions of anger, resentment, and concern battled within him. A voice piped low from Pulaski's radio, and he listened in rapt attention before his face clouded over with worry.

"Are you sure? You've checked everywhere? All right. Yes. I'll let him know. Sir..." Pulaski turned to address Birk. "Sir, the Marine fire teams have scouted the area. The guest house, adjoining buildings, and main house are gone. No signs of survivors. There's no evidence of a fight or intruders, and they think the fires could have been started in the generator rooms or vehicles parked in the garage."

"Were the usual staff here at the time?"

"I would presume so, but that's unknown."

Birk swallowed. "What about bodies?"

"None as of yet. We can start sifting through the wreckage soon. Do you want to check out the rest of the place?"

Birk nodded. "Yes, I want to see it."

"Very well. Harris?"

Agent Harris popped his door and got out, scanning the woods and surrounding area before joining Birk as he strode through the yard past the LAVs, up to the main house. The front porch and brick facing had collapsed inward, leaving about two feet of rubble crushing the flowerbeds and bushes that had once decorated the place. Harris followed Birk east around the winding stone pathways, the President walking stiffly.

"I just... I can't *believe* this," Birk said, stopping at the rear corner on a terrace of decorative stone. "I was just here... what, a month and a half ago?"

"The weekend retreat after the G20 summit," Harris nodded.

Birk reached out to touch a wooden beam still standing. "We had the Canadians come in with their families for a round of talks."

The President stepped off the rocky terrace and took another rubble-strewn path through a rear garden, debris crunching beneath their shoes, coming to stand by the pool where lawn furniture and debris floated in black water. Colonel Crow and General Pulaski stood close, Marines patrolling in and around the grounds all the while. "Sue and I finally got an hour to relax after everyone went to bed."

"Yes, sir. I believe that was at around 2 a.m., and you wanted to get in the jacuzzi on a whim."

Something stirred in Birk's heart as he pondered memories of his wife. "I think that was the last time that she and I had any time to ourselves."

"I'm sorry, sir."

Birk inhaled deeply, shaking off the thoughts, clapping his hands together. "All right, folks. I've seen enough. Let's go."

He led the way, moving briskly away from the destruction, back along the stone paths and across the overgrown grass to their Humvee. Harris got the door for him, and Birk climbed inside, settling between the agent and another Marine.

"Let's head on to Site R, General."

"Yes, sir," Pulaski got in, rocking the Humvee with his bulk.

"Shangri-La is no more," Birk said. "So much history just... *gone*. This has been a place of peace and negotiation for decades. Who would've thought it would end up burned to the ground?"

"I don't think anyone, sir."

"I think I was supposed to be hosting the UK Prime Minister here sometime this month," Birk said. "But now...."

The Marines jogged back to their Humvees and the LAVs rolled out, churning up the ground and leaving deep tire marks in the grass as they tore out ahead of the convoy. Above the mass of vehicles, drones buzzed above the trees, disturbing flocks of birds as they scanned the ground and skies across the spectrum, searching for threats that could not be spotted from the ground.

"I didn't know we had drones still functioning." Birk commented.

"Just a few of them. Like this old heap," Pulaski hit his fist against the Humvee's roof a couple of times, "it's whatever we could get running that was mothballed."

Putting Camp David behind them, they continued through the Maryland woodlands, approaching Site R at the head of a mountain pass with sweeping valleys and twisting roads, switchbacks and tunnels swollen with spreading crowns of white oaks, tall beeches with flat, gray bark and jagged leaves. Stands of hemlocks and poplars swept away from them as they rose higher along the hillside perch with the view of the vales below.

"What a view," Birk said. "Sue would've loved it up here. Almost makes you forget that anything happened."

"Almost, sir." Harris said, looking out the opposite window where a rocky bank of trees rose up, a forest wall rising to the upper plateau nestled in a layer of fine mist.

"I never would've seen this place if things weren't so bad." He chuckled darkly. "It's not like Site R receives presidential visitors."

"I wouldn't imagine so, sir," Harris replied.

"Here we are now." Pulaski indicated they'd reached the top of the mountain, straightening in his seat.

The narrow roadway opened into a larger staging area perched on the slope. Two gun placements stood on the western edge with Marines stationed nearby, standing guard and watching the road and valley where streams cut through and created bright green lines of foliage. A set of blast doors were built into the wall with a thick steel frame and hinges as tall as the Humvee was long. They stood open, guarded by Marines outfitted in full body armor, camouflaged in woodland colors with their faces painted green, black, and brown. More Marines moved in groups of twelve or in teams of four, patrolling the road and going back and forth into and out of the mountain.

The convoy didn't slow as it rolled into the yawning cavern, the scenery transforming from green and natural to one filled with the sound of industrial machinery, marching boots and shouted orders. Bright light glowed from the ceiling, illuminating rough-hewn gray walls and shiny floors coated in oil paint. Squeals of tires echoed through the chamber as the vehicles rolled up to a series of passages cutting into the hill and parked. Nearby, in a large parking lot, mechanics swarmed a line of Humvees, armored vehicles, and a half-dozen tanks, readying them to move.

Harris disembarked and Birk went after him, looking around and whistling. "Not bad, General. Not bad... looks like this place is in pretty good shape, all things considered."

Pulaski slammed his door, pointing to where the rows of armor were being worked on. "All these have been brought in from the outside and are fully functional already. It's a bit slower in other places, but all in all the refits of old stock have been going well. At this point, fuel appears to be our main bottleneck."

"Somehow that doesn't surprise me."

A half-dozen staffers poured from a side entrance, heading straight to the President's entourage. Sandy Strode and Colonel Crow moved to intercept the group, asking and answering questions, getting updates, and finding out where they needed to go. After a moment, Crow gestured for General Pulaski to bring them along.

"Right this way, sir," Pulaski said, following behind Birk as he flipped through a clipboard full of paper. As they entered the passage, Pulaski continued with various updates. "We're still working on getting communication links rerouted for full C&C capability. It'll take a few more hours. Losing so many satellite comms centers revealed some unexpected weaknesses."

"Understandable."

"Between the East and West coasts, we've strengthened our air capabilities a bit, if you can call it that: an additional thirty-six F-16s, two F-22s, one AWAC, and four B-22s are up and running. That's in addition to what we had operating before, including the C-130s that have been making supply drops."

"I assume jet fuel's the bottleneck there still?"

Birk followed Crow and Strode along the rough-hewn passage with military markings and heavy steel doors every few feet, each group they passed pausing and moving aside to give them room.

"Correct, though it's not entirely bad news. We've got an Arizona refinement facility partially online and are producing jet fuel in limited amounts. We're not going to have birds in the sky twenty-four seven for a while, but production should continue to increase and give us the flexibility we so desperately need."

"What about this place?" Birk gestured to the walls and ceiling. "Are we going to experience another Mount Weather?"

"Absolutely not. Thanks to a training exercise that was going on, we have nearly five hundred combined Army, Marine, and Navy personnel on site. More importantly, unlike the Mount Weather facility, Site R is a nuclear bunker. Conventional explosives won't scratch the paint on those blast doors."

"Good."

Strode guided Birk into a corridor on the left-hand side. "Right this way, Mr. President."

Another long passageway stretched forever, their boots echoing and squeaking on the tiled floors. At the end of the hall, they stepped through another large steel door, entering a conference room with staffers standing near the seats and coffee urns, ready to serve the road-weary officers and staff. Birk immediately took his position at the far end of the table, bracketed by the United States flag and the Presidential Standard behind him. Pulaski, Crow, Spencer, and others took seats on the right while the civilian staffers, scientists, and tech teams sat on the left.

"Good to see you all." Birk accepted a tablet and a cup of coffee from a staffer, looking through the device while he drank. After a moment, he continued. "General Pulaski, go ahead and start us off with a general status update."

"Yes sir," Pulaski replied stiffly, shuffling some papers around on the table. "We're getting more regular updates from NORTHCOM and our command and control abilities are estimated to be greatly enhanced – if not fully online – within four hours. National Guard units across the country are shoring up key supply routes along major highways and providing crucial logistics support, particularly when it comes to getting older vehicles up and running. Right now, they're the backbone of this whole operation. It'll be a while more before we can try to re-enter the cities and establish some order there, but we're working on plans to make that a reality as soon as possible.

"The Army Corps of Engineers and Marines are working to secure the White House grounds and begin rebuilding the area to restore some normalcy to governmental operations. It'll take months, but it's an important step just for the sake of optics."

"What about international relations?"

"We've established communication with many of our allies and assured them the US government is still very much here and capable. While South America is mostly unresponsive, we're hearing from New Zealand, Australia, and our European friends across the pond. Most seem to be in boats similar to ours – plenty of resources, but a lack of transportation. The Mexican military forces are crippled, and Canada's CAF is spread pretty thin, but we're trying to hammer out ways to help each other as much as possible."

Birk tapped the table with his pen. "Who's faring the best in all of this? Because I'm sure it's not us."

"South Africa, Japan, Australia, and New Zealand all appear to be on top of the crisis."

"On *top*?" Birk groaned. "How on earth are *they* on top of it?"

"In the case of New Zealand..." Pulaski shuffled through his papers, "Their natural isolation's proven to be their strength – that and their low population numbers. Their livestock industry weathered the storm quite well, and they're in the growing season. They're hurting for imports, but have pivoted quickly to producing what they need internally. And, frankly, they just had less people die."

"Those are the sort of people we need to get boats to, so we can start trading with them as soon as possible."

"We're still working on bolstering our naval capabilities. They're not quite as bad as our air capabilities, but it's no walk in the park. The San Francisco Naval shipyard was finally secured last week – National Guard to thank again for that, too – and they're dragging in anything that still floats and repairing it. Pearl Harbor's also getting some work done. They've got four cargo ships ready to sail, and three destroyers – old, but functional – to escort them to the New Zealand shipyards once they're able to approach." Pulaski smirked. "One of the destroyers was a museum piece and in less than two weeks they were able to get engines and cannons in her. Our people do good work."

"Damn straight. How do we fare compared to the rest?"

"As far as we can tell, China and Russia are still trying to weld together rust and don't have anything more than a few fishing vessels ready to go. We've spotted debris from their submarines as well so we're confident that our basic capabilities will be enough to keep us on top – for the time being."

"Good. Anything else of importance right now?"

"We're starting to see some improvements in rural areas. Kansas City, Indianapolis, Pittsburgh... all starting to shore up. Guard units are working with the locals, employing them and helping oversee basic trade and production as we're getting ready for fall and winter to set in. The big cities are a mess, but we'll get there. Did you want to talk casualty numbers now?"

Birk waved his hand. "No, I'll go over those later."

"Yes, sir." General Pulaski sat, sweeping his papers into a single pile.

"I'll be frank with you all." Birk took a drink from his bottle of water and addressed the table. "You've all done a hell of a job. It may not seem like it a lot of the time, but things *are* improving. To use a metaphor that my late wife, Sue, loved – we're knitting a quilt. Prior to all of this, we had a pretty big quilt and were just adding to it. Now, though? We're starting with scraps. Pieces of thread and bits of cloth, all in a jumble, disorganized and torn apart. In these early days we're just trying to start sewing a few pieces together. It doesn't look like much or feel like much, but we'll continue to add to the quilt – to the tapestry of this great country."

The room was quiet as Birk continued, all eyes on him.

"We are resilient, unwavering, and determined to stand where so many others would fail. What happens next, and how we conduct ourselves, will determine whether our Republic spirals into despair or soars to greatness. This rests squarely upon our shoulders, and we will meet this challenge head-on, bruised but not beaten, bloodied but unbowed."

CHAPTER NINETEEN

Ryan Cooper
East Lansing, Michigan

"Are you sure we're not using too much food?"

Red stood near two pots bubbling furiously on the stove, one with leftover chili and the other packed with potatoes, ham, green beans and a variety of other ingredients pulled out of freezers.

"Not according to our estimates," Martha replied as she stirred the stew, periodically adding small amounts of pepper and salt, tasting the broth between stirs. "We've measured everything out. Relax, honey. Everything's fine."

Helen leaned against the counter, forcing the most natural smile she could muster. "We're providing the best caloric value *and* saving on supplies by making larger batches. It's the best way to feed so many people all at once."

"Well, all right," Red nodded. "I trust you ladies know what you're doing."

The crew was in high spirits, Hansen and Reynolds the loudest at the table as they spooned in mouthfuls of chili, dripping it on themselves and the table without so much as a second glance. Martha had given Sandy and Nancy the night off once both pots were filled, and the two women had joined the rest of the crew at the table and in the living room. Sandy occasionally swung through the kitchen to refill drinks and bowls, glancing at Helen each time who always responded with a raised eyebrow and a slight shake of her head.

Helen ran a tight kitchen, throwing herself into the meal, keeping the food moving, the plates washed and the counters clean, and toward the end of the night, Martha came up, wiping her hands clean with a towel after cleaning up the kitchen table.

"Can you believe this? We did a fantastic job here."

"I hope everyone enjoyed themselves." Helen smiled, focusing on the stack of cups she was washing.

"Oh, they did. I don't think anyone's been this full in weeks. I'm a little worried we can't keep up this level of... well, perfection, though."

Helen nodded, looking toward the people sitting at the kitchen table and in the great room, one woman seated in James' recliner, others squatting on the stone hearth as they ate and talked quietly. "It's a lot to put together, but keep one thing in mind, Martha... this is our job now, and we have to do the best we can. As long as they keep up with the farming and scavenging, we'll make sure hot meals keep rolling out each and every day."

"That's a comforting thought," Martha replied.

"I just hope everyone else can keep up." Helen offered a smile. "Again, not our problem. That's up to Tyler and his scavenging teams."

"I'm sure Red will keep them working hard if it means meals this good. This ham is..." Martha reached into a bowl and pulled out a piece, tossing it in her mouth. "Maybe the juiciest ham I've ever eaten. What's your secret?"

Helen shrugged. "I just keep it simple. Basic seasonings, and don't overcook it." She waved as Ryan stepped in from outside, half-smiling at her as he carried tools to the basement door and went downstairs.

"What's Ryan up to?"

"He volunteered to help Reynolds with the water heaters after I told him it wasn't going so well."

"Do you think Ryan can help?"

"He'll try," Helen said. "It seemed like a mess when I was down there earlier."

Martha leaned in. "That's why I'm *so* glad to have you two on our side. You two really know how to get things—"

"I'll have one more helping." Red appeared at the center island, holding his bowl out. "I've got to say, this is probably some of the best stew I've had in a while."

"I was just saying the same thing," Martha said.

"Glad you like it." Helen brought his bowl over to the pot and filled it. "It's pretty simple - ham, potatoes, green beans, other odds and ends. Dinner of champions."

Red accepted his bowl, eating a mouthful as he stood in front of them. When he was done chewing and swallowing, he gestured with the utensil. "The crew thanks you both for this."

"It was Helen's idea to throw it all together," Martha said.

"With all the arguing and carrying on today, I wanted to make it as an apology... you know, to make amends with you, Red."

Red nodded and dipped his spoon into the bowl for another bite. "Maybe we should argue more often if it inspires dinner like this."

Martha and Helen shared a nervous look, and Martha smiled at Red, giving him a slight smile. "I'm glad to see you in a good mood again, honey. Everything falls in line when you're happy."

Red pointed his spoon at her, talking around his food. "Make sure you two get yourselves some, too."

Without waiting for a response, he turned and walked back to the dining room. As the evening wore on, crew members began to get up to go to sleep or take care of their guard shifts, rubbing their distended bellies, laughing sluggishly, grabbing their weapons, and heading out the door. A few came in for third and fourth helpings, which Helen enthusiastically doled out, all while watching the basement door for Ryan. With midnight approaching, more crew members retired to the second-floor loft or their camping spots outside, and Sandy lit a few candles.

"Two cups of coffee, please." Jack stepped in and Helen nodded and turned to pour them when thuds rose from the basement stairs. The door flew open, and Ryan shuffled into the kitchen with smears of dirt on his cheeks and cuts on his hands.

"Water heaters are installed. We should have hot water within the hour."

Jack took the coffee from Helen and stood by the hall entrance. "Good work, Ryan. I'll let Red know."

"I'll tell him myself." Ryan started to push past Jack. "I want to ask him about grabbing some showers."

Jack quickly stepped in his way. "Don't worry about it, man. Red said the guards coming off second shift get first dibs."

"I've been working on those water heaters for three hours." Ryan held up his dirty, bleeding hands. "Can't I just get a quick one?"

"Nope, Red already gave the order." Jack grinned. "*His* people go to the head of the line. If you want to argue with Red about it, be my guest."

Ryan bristled before quickly deflating. "Fine. As soon as Helen's done in the kitchen, we'll head to bed."

"Get some rest, Ryan." Jack started down the hall. "Lots more to get done for us tomorrow."

"Come here, dear." Helen gestured to a chair at the kitchen table. "Sit down."

Ryan sat heavily and held his hands out in front of him, exposing the thin cuts from work he'd been doing, both in the basement and out in the barn. Helen sat next to him, wiping a warm cloth gently across his sore palms.

Ryan sighed. "Thanks, hon."

"Is it time?" Helen whispered.

"Close." Ryan raised his voice. "Hey, Martha, I'll help Helen straighten up and put this food away. Why don't you relax for a while."

"Are you sure?"

"I'm positive."

Martha peeked into the forty-quart pot of stew. "They wiped out the *entire* pot, and the chili took a good hit, too."

"You ladies sure do know how to throw a dinner."

"I'm proud of us." Martha wiped her hands with a towel and tossed it on the counter. "Are you sure, Ryan? You've been working all day and night."

"It's all part of our daily routine," Ryan replied assuredly. "I work all day and into the night, then meet my wife back here in the kitchen where we get things cleaned up. Usually, we have a cup of coffee at the kitchen table, but I think we'll take ours upstairs and sit by the window tonight."

"Well, if you say so."

"It really is the little things." Helen took Ryan's arm as Martha poured herself a cup of coffee and went to join Red outside. Resting her forehead on Ryan's chest, she whispered to him. "My heart is pounding."

"You okay?"

"Absolutely. I can't stand this, Ryan. Watching these people in our daughter's home, tearing it up, holding guns to our heads... it makes me sick to my stomach. I'd rather die than see any more of this."

"We're not dying. In fact, what we're going to do is give these bastards something to remember us by." He kissed her head. "Let's clean this kitchen and head upstairs."

Helen sat on the edge of the bed, her hands resting in her lap, heel bouncing nervously against the floor. In the darkness, Ryan paced by the window, watching the guard shifts out front change as midnight came and went. Sandy and Stephen had fallen asleep an hour and a half prior after a brief discussion about the pair leaving and more reassurances that Helen and Ryan would indeed be returning.

"I hope Red doesn't take this out on them," Helen whispered.

Ryan looked over at the sleeping pair. "Me too, but it's a risk we'll have to take. You and I are on the chopping block, and we can't be sticking around any longer."

Taking a break from watching out the window, Ryan splashed cold water in his face to cool the impatience growing inside him. He'd occasionally pace over to the door, putting his ear to it whenever he heard footsteps on the stairs or someone speaking in the loft, but he always returned to the window, monitoring the guards and ensuring they weren't breaking from their usual routine. It was almost 2 a.m. before things settled down enough for them to consider leaving, when the voices downstairs had faded followed by Red and Martha coming upstairs and heading down the hall to the master bedroom.

"We'll give them a little time to fall asleep." Ryan whispered to Helen, easing himself into a chair to take the weight off of his prosthetic and aching calf.

The bullet wound wasn't close to being healed, but he'd adjusted to it, the trick being not to let it get too stiff, and as the slow creep of night wore on, he stood and gestured toward the door.

"Helen. It's time to go."

Donning their coats and removing their pistols from a spare pair of rubber boots Ryan had secreted them in, they moved to the door and Helen grabbed two extra sacks of supplies she'd managed to purloin from the pantry. Ryan gripped the doorknob, turned it, and gave it a tug, revealing the loft where a dozen of the crew were camped out in sleeping bags or blow up mattresses. Ryan and Helen stepped carefully past them and at the head of the stairs, Ryan leaned back and peered over the rail into the living room where several people were huddled beneath blankets. When no one moved, he led Helen downstairs, slowing to a crawl toward the bottom. Waiting for a moment, he listened to the hollow sound of his breathing, Helen's jacket rustling, the distant hum of the refrigerator, and someone snoring nearby.

Stepping into the foyer, wincing as the hardwood creaked, Ryan peeked into the dining room to find it empty except. A small electric lantern sat in the middle of a series of maps Red had marked up with ink and pushpins buried straight into the table. With a roll of his eyes, Ryan continued down the hallway toward the back door, wincing every time a board creaked, the squeal like shattering glass in the darkness. Helen stopped him at the back door, tapping Ryan on the shoulder and heading over to snuff out a candle with a soft hiss when a large shadow shifted across the kitchen floor.

"Where the hell are you going?"

Ryan froze, dropping his hand off the doorknob as he turned. Jack Willoughby stood in the hallway in overalls and socks, wearing a holster strapped beneath his left arm.

"Just heading out to finish some work," Ryan replied, swallowing a lump in his throat and resting his arm against the pistol inside his waistband beneath his shirt.

Helen nodded and reached for the door handle, pulling it open with a soft suck of air as she held the bags aloft. "Red wanted us to take a few things out to the guards. I hate having to go out there at this hour, but..." She shrugged. "Gotta do what we gotta do."

Jack shook his head slowly, looking between the pair. "A few things, huh?" He drew his revolver in a surprisingly quick motion. "No. No... I don't think so. Both of you, get back upstairs right now."

"What the hell, Jack? You trying to piss off Red or something?" Ryan looked up toward the master bedroom. "Put that thing away and let us do what he told us to do."

"No, somethin's not right here." Jack waved the revolver toward the great room where a few of the people sleeping had started to stir. "Get back over there by the TV while I go get Red."

"So you're going to go wake up Red," Ryan hissed. "Thereby pissing him off at you and resulting in him telling you what I've already told you? Do you really think that's a smart idea?"

"Shut up, Ryan. Red told me to keep an eye on you two. He said that—*unf!*"

Jack's body crumpled over as Helen swung one of the sacks – primarily containing canned goods – directly at Jack's head, striking him in the side across the temple.

"Go!" Ryan shouted as he drew his pistol, firing at Jack and again at the guards who had started to reach for their own weapons, forcing them to dive back toward the floor.

He and Helen turned, shuffling out the door, slamming it shut behind them before they took off through the yard past the outside crewmembers who were starting to stir thanks to the gunshots. A group of guards jogged from the west side of the property, shouting and pointing toward the house where the lights were slowly coming on.

"Damn! This is *not* going according to plan." Ryan picked up the pace, limping heavily, holding his pistol close to his body as he took one of the bags from Helen to lighten her load.

"Just go, and try not to attract their attention." Helen whispered to him as she held onto his arm.

A woman stumbled out of a nearby tent and sprinted toward the house without a glance at them and two men jogged in from the east side of the property, joining the rising confusion as the back door flew open and shouts erupted.

"Stop them!"

"What happened!?"

"The Cooopers! They shot Jack! Where the hell are they?"

"Find them!"

"Where'd they go?"

"I don't know. Get some lights on out here!"

The shouts continued as Ryan and Helen made it to the barn, slipping inside as shots finally rang out in their direction, rounds clipping the wall and showering them with dust and splinters.

"There they are! Get 'em!"

Ryan threw the door shut, grabbed a nearby t-post and jammed it across the door so that it couldn't be opened from the outside, then shuffled over to the trailer to toss his bag inside. Helen was behind him, dropping hers in as well, bending in to shift things around.

"The whole camp is waking up," Helen said, wincing as more rounds struck the barn and the shouts drew closer.

"Doesn't matter," he huffed. "I'll get the welding tools and throw them in the trailer. You grab the dogs. We've got maybe two minutes before they'll have this place surrounded."

"On it."

"Duke, Duchess!" Helen slapped her hands on her thighs. "Heel! *Heel!*"

The dogs turned in her direction but didn't obey until Ryan slammed his hand on the side of the tractor. "*Hey!* Heel!"

Heads low, they rushed over, wrapping themselves around Ryan's and Helen's legs, whining and sniffing. Shadows approached the doors, and the dogs' demeanor changed, lowering their heads and growling, their protective nature overriding their fear of the noises outside.

"Stay," Ryan ordered them, grabbing his welding tools, swinging the propane tank inside the trailer along with a toolbox and a couple of extra spare sheets of steel.

"The dogs aren't going to fit on the trailer." Helen had just finished putting their leashes on. "Where do we put them?"

"Oh, geez…" Ryan said, stepping back and checking the arrangement of supplies stacked on the small trailer, trying to move things around as more voices joined the others outside the barn. "We don't have time to move anything around. Let's put them in the bucket. Here, I'll get this thing fired up."

Ryan climbed into the cabin, jerked the lever on his left into the neutral position, stomped on the brake pedal and turned the key. The tractor started with a loud rumble and a belch of exhaust, and he grabbed a lever and raised the bucket to about knee level, then stepped down and circled to help Helen get the dogs inside of it.

"Come on, Duke." Ryan coughed in the fumes, wrapping his arms around the massive dog as he hauled him up, dropping him awkwardly into the bucket, ripping his pants on the bucket's steel teeth when Duke tried to wiggle out of his grasp. "Dang it! Stay, boy. *Stay*."

Duke whined and wagged his tail as Ryan reached for Duchess. Together, they got her in with Duke and put Diana in last, the massive dogs trying to turn in the confined space, bumping into each other, sniffling and growling.

"How are we going to keep them inside?" Helen asked. "They'll jump right out."

"Tie their leashes tight to the framework and hope they're smart enough to stay put." Ryan reached behind the bucket, wrapped Duke's leash around the stabilizing bars several times, and made a loose knot. Helen finished with the other two as the sounds of clucking came from somewhere in the barn. Ryan spun, spotting two chickens as they shot by. As one pulled to a stop, he scooped it off the ground and took it to the trailer, stuffing it inside a duffel bag.

"Helen, can you-"

Helen had already scooped the other bird up and was bringing it over with both arms wrapped around it, stuffing it in with the other one. By then, the dogs were whining loudly, barking at the growing shadows outside, shapes shifting in flashlight beams, several voices rising from the roiling darkness in shouts and warnings.

"Open the doors!"

"You're just digging yourselves a bigger hole!"

A woman hammered her fist on the wood and shouted. "Break the doors down!"

Ryan shuffled to the bucket and hugged all three dogs. "Stay here, guys. Sit. That's it. *Stay*!" As he spoke, he fixed each with the sternest look he could muster, all three drawing quiet and watching him intently. "Okay, Helen. Let's go."

They circled to the side of the tractor, and Ryan helped Helen up the steps, pulling the heavy door open and clearing the way for her to slip inside.

"Sit on the ledge behind be. Just put your legs around to the side. Watch the controls—there you go." He climbed in after her and fell into the seat, slamming the door and working the foot pedals, hand on the gearshift.

Fists hammered on the front doors, heavy blows caused dents to appear. Off to the side, the man door began to splinter, straining inward against the t-post. "Open up!" a man bellowed. "Open up right now!"

Ryan took a deep breath and edged back in his seat. "Ready?"

Helen nodded quietly, reaching over his shoulder to grab his arm, hugging him awkwardly in the cramped, single-seat interior. "No. Let's go."

"We'll be back, and we'll make them pay."

More gunshots sounded, holes showing through the man door around the latch, one pinging off the bucket, startling the dogs. Ryan raised the bucket just high enough to keep the dogs above eye level, tilting it back, causing the dogs to fall back and settle in the deepest part.

"Hang on, Helen!"

Ryan threw the tractor into low gear, checked that four-wheel drive was engaged, pushed the throttle as high as it would go and tromped down on the accelerator. The diesel engine roared, smoke billowing from the exhaust as they trundled forward with the trailer in tow, rocking back and forth on the way to obliterate the barn doors and whoever stood behind them. They hit the doors with a crash of wood and flying timbers, metal hinges torn out of the walls, dogs yelping in surprise as the tractor frame shuddered, though the vehicle didn't slow at all.

Ryan briefly spotted a few faces jerking upward in dumbfounded confusion as the armored tractor ran right over them, hitting two men square on and burying them beneath the chassis, the left front tire slamming into one as he attempted to dive away, snapping his leg with a crack punctuated by a bloodcurdling scream. The tractor frame bumped and rocked as the wheels hit a divot, the dogs, supplies in the trailer and Ryan and Helen all lurching back and forth.

Ryan took a sharp left, hitting a man with the edge of the bucket and spinning him to the ground, then he flipped on the headlamps, illuminating another man's terrified face as the bucket knocked him down and the left tires rolled directly over his chest.

It wasn't until they reached the barnyard gate that Red's crew recovered, lurching to their feet, finding their weapons in the dark and the mud, unleashing a barrage on the armored tractor. Bullets pinged off the metal plates around the enclosed trailer, ricocheting off in sparks of light, from single *clanks* to flat sprays of buckshot sounding like hail against their sides, but none penetrated through to the cab's interior.

"Hold on! I'm turning for the driveway!"

As they trundled through the spread of tents and campers, a woman rushed in, grabbing the door, climbing up, waving a pistol, and trying to get it over the steel plate. Holding onto the wheel with one hand, Ryan opened the window and held his pistol up and over the plate, firing three quick shots downward and she fell off with a cry of pain that was silenced as the trailer rolled over her.

They rolled past the squawking, flapping chickens in the coop and angled left as Red, Reynolds, and Hansen rushed from the back door, shouting as they raised their weapons. The tractor took multiple shots, Ryan clinging to the wheel with one hand, biding his time until they could turn, then he quickly raised up the pistol and took several shots at the porch, sending the trio diving for cover.

Ryan growled to himself, focusing on maneuvering the tractor away from the house while keeping the non-armored front of it from being exposed to potential fire. "That's what you get for screwing with me. Out of my way!" He fired two more shots before whipping the tractor toward the garage, heading straight for the dump truck parked off to the side.

Turning the tractor away at the last second, he raised his pistol above the side plate again, emptying the last of the magazine into the dump truck's fuel tank mounted on the side. The first round struck gravel, but the rest hit true, releasing sprays of diesel that streamed down into the gravel.

The last trigger pull ended in a click, and Ryan straightened the tractor, handed the pistol to Helen and angled down the driveway, switching to high gear with the accelerator pressed to the floor. Helen swapped magazines in his pistol as several crew members jogged behind, firing on the run. Rifle rounds struck the backplate, dented it, and bounced off, and Helen twisted her arm to fire out the window over the steel plate as Ryan had, hitting a woman square in the face, her body collapsing in a heap, the others with her scattering for cover.

"Are they coming after us in the EV?"

"I don't think so," Helen said breathlessly as she swayed back and forth, clinging to Ryan's shoulder with one hand and pushing against the roof of the cap with the other to keep her balance.

"Damn fine work there."

"You too. I'd say we recovered nicely after Jack almost ruined everything for us."

"Darn right, we did." Ryan chuckled darkly. "Red might have been expecting us to try to get away, but I don't think he expected *this*."

They quickly drove between the red oaks, past the ducks and ponds, until they reached the road, Ryan glancing back as rounds continued to be fired at them, though fewer were finding their marks the farther away they got.

"Gate!" Helen called.

"I know... just hold on." Ryan and Helen braced themselves as they drove through the freshly-repaired gate which Red's crew had fixed a day prior, sending the silver metal piece flying across the road as the dogs whined loudly from the front bucket.

"Sorry!" Ryan called to them.

"Which way now?"

"South, past town. First we put some distance between us and them, then we'll find a quiet place to hide out."

Ryan swung the tractor left on the road, the trailer rattling behind them, the dogs continuing to whine. After a few hundred feet the dirt road changed to a paved one, and their speed increased even more. Taking his pistol back from Helen, he stuffed it into his pants pocket and killed the lights on the tractor, squinting into the darkness. The road swung around to the right, intersecting with another, and Ryan took a left, taking them past the supply stores for three miles until they reached a stoplight. Ryan stopped at the side of the road, sat back, and eased back on the throttle, watching the rearview window for signs of pursuit.

"How soon do you think they'll come after us?" Helen asked. "Or will they bother?"

"Red will want to, but he'll find that pretty difficult when most of his fuel is gone from that salt truck of his." Ryan stared at the road, trying to calculate what it would take to fix it. "All they'll have is the EV and a couple miles in the salt truck."

"What about the ATV?"

"I don't think Red will commit the EV and ATV to looking for us. Plus that ATV is *loud*. As crazy as he is, he's not stupid. No, if they try to look for us, they'll use the EV. Good luck to them, though – they'll never get enough juice from the solar panels to recharge it and keep the whole house running."

"Let's go." Helen looked through the back window. "Just in case."

Ryan put the tractor in gear and throttled back up, lurching forward on the gloomy, moonlit road.

The old, half-burned-down barn with its leaky roof and charred rafters sat nestled in a copse of birches and maples in a field of knee-high grass, one of a hundred similar places they'd seen while taking the old Michigan back roads, narrow lanes with the woods growing right up to the pavement, a mosaic of gnarled branches hanging over them.

The tractor was parked behind the barn, covered in trees and branches to hide any jutting pieces of metal that might capture a flashlight beam or other light source. Inside, the smell of charred wood still lingered from the weeks-ago fires, the right side of the barn completely collapsed, though the left was still mostly intact. They'd stacked up some old crates and hay bales to form a bit of a barrier between them and the blackened section of fallen beams and a campfire burned on a soft patch of dirt, the smoke drifting up through cracks in the roof, the light partially hidden by old farm equipment and wooden pallets stacked in rows.

Ryan stood next to the fire, turned a full circle and nodded. "Well. This sucks. But it should be good enough to hide us."

Helen sat on a box near the fire, her hair lit in a tangerine glow as she leaned down and patted Duke's side where he lay near the fire next to Duchess and Diana.

"Come on, dear. Sit by the fire and get warm. We need to rest."

Ryan made one more round around the barn before stepping over Duke and sitting next to her. A pan sat on a grate above the fire, and Ryan stirred the contents, clacking the spoon on the side and setting it on a nearby stone.

"Stewed tomatoes. Hrm."

"I can add some of the canned meat," Helen sighed, "but I was going to save it for tomorrow."

"Save it. Tomatoes are fine for tonight. I'm thankful for what we've got, as little as it is. We're alive and we have food and water."

"And a couple of chickens."

"And a couple of chickens. What else can we really ask for right now?"

"The house back?"

Ryan glanced at the supplies they'd brought into the barn, including a few cans stacked on a crate, light reflecting off the glass and illuminating dark chunks suspended in an oily liquid. "What kind of meat is it?"

"Lamb, I think."

"Sounds nice."

"How long do you think we'll be out here?" Helen leaned against him, exhaustion creeping into her voice.

"No clue, but we can't go too far. We have to be here when Alice and the kids show up." Ryan put his arm over her shoulders. "We don't want them walking into that."

"That's the *last* thing we want." Helen sniffed and leaned against him, locking arms tightly. "But...."

"What?"

"What if they don't show up anytime soon? What will *we* do?"

"Find the right time to hit them hard and take back the house. We killed at least four, maybe five people on our way out. That had to sting."

"We'll have to do it soon. As much as I love the dogs, they eat more than a person and we don't have the supplies to keep them fed for very long." She patted Duke's head again. "How are we going to hit them hard, anyway? Just drive back up in the tractor?"

Ryan fixated on the flames as they wove intricate patterns around the triangular shaped stack of wood, tendrils flickering in the cool air. "Sandy said something in the barn that got me thinking."

"What was that?"

"She mentioned a 'killdozer'."

"Oh, yes. I remember that... what on earth was she talking about?"

"I had no idea at the time, but as we smashed through the barn doors, it came to me. It was this guy who – well, never-mind the details. It's complicated. Suffice it to say that he got really, really mad and took a bulldozer, welded plate steel all over it, made some gun ports and demolished a small town before the police were able to stop him."

Helen sat back up, pulling back and staring at him with a raised eyebrow. "You're going to turn the tractor into a tank?"

"Yeah, why do you think I brought all this scrap metal? It's already mostly there. It just needs steel over the front and top – oh, and the engine bay – and then it'll be set."

"What're you going to do with it? Just roll up the driveway like he did in his salt truck to us?"

Ryan put his arm around Helen and stared into the fire, nodding slowly. "You're damn right I am."

"As much as I love this idea, there are a *few* pro—"

Duke's head popped up, a low growl building in his throat, staring past the fire at something beyond it in the burned-out section of the barn.

"What is it, Duke?" Ryan whispered, watching the shadows, reaching for his pistol. "Get it, boy. Go on – go get it."

All three dogs scrambled to their feet, walking slowly around the fire, creeping toward the stacked crates and hay bales sniffing and snorting and whining at each other. Ryan pointed for Helen to move off to the side as he circled the box they were sitting on, focusing on a particular patch of darkness, raising his pistol and speaking loudly.

"Who the hell is out there? You want to lose a limb to one of our dogs, keep slinking around!"

A voice came from the darkness. "Oh, come on. Duke's just a big baby, aren't you boy? And anyway – I like that kill-dozer idea. Want a hand with it?"

CHAPTER TWENTY

James Burton
East Lansing, Michigan

"I see a way between the houses there."

Jake pointed west at a pair of bi-level homes, one untouched by the fires, the other having survived with only a few black streaks across the siding, though its windows were smashed, and the front door was lying on its porch, evidence of scavengers roaming through the area.

The neighborhood they'd passed through had been brimming with chaos, two groups of survivors fighting in front of a house that had been set aflame. The focus of one of the groups seemed to be the defense of several homes with lights in the windows, field fence and barbed wire stretched between the structures keeping a motley collection of animals contained. They'd barely managed to avoid being spotted by the groups by skirting the edge of the neighborhood and crossing through the shallow edge of a lake, the sounds of fighting fading off into the distance as they'd moved forward, the evening sun at their backs.

"Good idea," James agreed, turning Amber in the direction of the houses, heading between two other front yards and into a long, open backyard. "Keep moving. Just a couple more hours..."

Alice came up beside him. "We'll ride through the night if we have to."

"Absolutely. We're sleeping in our beds – no more camping for this family."

James pulled out a map he had tucked into his jacket, spreading it open as Alice guided her horse closer, their legs pressed between the horses' sides as she leaned in. He pointed his flashlight at the crumpled paper finger resting on a spot off to the east of East Lansing.

"We're about here. We'll take this road up, cut through here, then we'll be home."

"Home," Sarah smiled. "The streets and neighborhoods are starting to look familiar."

"Um, Dad?" Jake was staring toward the woods behind them. "I think someone's following us."

James rested his hand on his rifle and turned Amber around, watching as a pair of flashlights bobbed beneath corkscrew willow branches that drooped to the ground near the lake.

"Someone must have seen us come back here. Okay, let's get going before they take a potshot at us. C'mon, Amber!"

The four took off, putting distance between them and the bobbing flashlights, running across open fields of swaying overgrown grass and weeds, occasionally following or cutting across trails left by deer and other wildlife. The wind cooled their sweat as they rode across a wide, grassy field dotted with abandoned farm equipment, rusted marks on an otherwise unblemished landscape. Racing along the edge of the woods, James kept his focus forward, searching for the highway to take them home. He pulled Amber to a stop when they reached the fence line of an old farmstead, the main house fifty yards off, gutted by fire.

"The barn's still standing," Jake said, pointing to the back field behind the house.

"Don't tempt me," James laughed, "we're not stopping for anything till we get home."

A break in the fence line allowed them through, and they rode into the yard and along the gravel driveway that twisted between crouching trees, terminating in a two-lane highway where a pair of sedans had been crushed together in a head-on collision.

"Here we go," James said, drawing Amber up and turning her back to face the others. "If we go east along this road, it should get us in the general vicinity of home."

"Yeah, Rick lives around here," Jake said, looking up and down the highway. "A couple miles that way, I think. Home's this way."

"All right, then," James nodded. "Lead on, son."

Jake took off ahead with Alice and Sarah behind them, James bringing up the rear, soon reaching the shoulder of a long bend where a stone retaining wall held a hillside in check. Deep-rooted oak trees stretched out over the road and broke through the wall in spots, pushing mortar out in crumbles. A few minutes later the road straightened, and the woods gave way to open fields and a slope that they rode toward, finally reaching the top of the rise where they stopped.

"Is that our house?" Jake asked, pointing north toward a faint orange glow in the distance.

"I think it is," Sarah said, rising from her stirrups and grinning.

"Yep, that's it." Alice gave James a crooked smile. "It looks... intact. That's good news."

"C'mon. Less dawdling, more riding." James reached for Alice's hand, grinning broadly. "I'd say another twenty minutes, and we'll be home, guys."

Jake took Rocky to the edge of the road and pumped his fist in the air. "We're almost home! We're almost-"

"Hold on, Jake!" James rode up next to him, staring off into the distance.

"Oh, sorry. Noise. Right."

"No, it's not that." James squinted. "Something doesn't look right. It's... Someone hand me the binoculars."

"Right here," Sarah said, digging them out and stretching to give them over.

James raised the binoculars and scanned the area around their property, his view obscured by the rows of trees along the property line. "The lights are on... Your dad's EV is parked in the back it looks like, but there's another truck there, too. Is that a... dump truck?"

"A dump truck?" Alice replied, her expression darkening. "What would Mom and Dad be doing with a dump truck?"

"I don't know, but I think I see people standing around it. Five or six, it looks like. I see flashlights around the barn and the yard and.... what in the world?"

Alice stood in her stirrups. "What is it?"

"Are those... tents? I think those are tents and an RV parked next to the house."

"Tents?" Alice snapped angrily. "What are people doing on our property... with tents and an RV?! Where are my mother and father?"

"That's what I'd like to know," James said, lowering the binoculars. "I think someone's taken over the farm."

"Who would want to take our house?" Jake asked, Sarah starting to speak over him until James climbed off his horse and shushed them both.

"Calm down – we don't know that something's wrong or that it's been taken over. It could be someone they teamed up with the neighbors or something." James stared through the binoculars for another moment before handing them to Alice, checking that he was carrying ammunition for his rifle and grabbing his staff from a bag on Amber's back.

"Where are you going?" Alice asked.

James shifted the rifle on his shoulder, searching for his walking stick on Amber's back. "I'm going down there on foot to check it out."

"You're not going alone." Alice reached across Amber and grabbed the walking stick. "No way, James. We talked about splitting up."

"Someone needs to check it out, and it'll be easier for me on foot."

"The only way down there is by taking the road or crossing through the fields out in the open." Alice shook her head and gestured. "No. No, someone could see you."

"There's that drainage tunnel that runs beneath the road and the ditch along the property line. I'll use that and the trees for cover. They'll never spot me."

"I still don't like it," Alice was looking through the binoculars. "That's a *lot* of people."

James grabbed a flashlight and took the binoculars back, hanging them around his neck. "I'll be back soon."

"James, don't," Alice said. "Let's go down together."

James ducked beneath Amber's neck and handed the reins up to Alice. "One person moves faster and quieter than two. Stay here. I'll be back shortly."

"Dad, we *just* got you back." Sarah started to get off of her horse. "Don't go."

"Guys." James pointed down at the house. "I'm going across the field, not the country. Trust me – I'll be fine. Just stay here."

Before they could say anything else, James was off, jogging over the open field at an angle toward the nearby road. He followed it for a few hundred feet, staying on the opposite side to take advantage of the cover provided by the woods, then used the drainage tunnel to cross over, staying low in the deep ditch that ran along their property line. James moved carefully through the ditch, splashing through a shallow trickle of water and staying below the large bushes that grew on either side.

Once he was halfway up their property, he pushed up the bank through the loose tangle of brush and crunched over dead leaves and brittle deadfall. Overhead, the sun had completely vanished over the horizon and the moon was high overhead, its glow lending just enough light to see by. The woods on the property line quickly turned into the rich patch of evergreens and pines, angry shouts penetrating the wall of green, the sounds of a large group of people coming from near the house. James craned his neck, sidestepping over forest debris, picking his way slowly forward, finally catching sight of the house and lights in the windows.

Slipping his rifle off of his shoulder, James pressed forward, angling east and steering away from a burn barrel sitting by the fence rail. One man stood near it, looking back toward the house, his whole focus on the fracas taking place. James paused and squinted, but couldn't make out who it was, so he continued east around the fence line closest to the barn where the evergreens thinned out.

The animals stirred beneath their shelter, grunting and bleating nervously, huddled close together in fear as the shouts from up near the house continued. Fingers tracing the steel field fence he'd installed a few years prior, James moved to his left, watching the people in the yard as they slowly came into view. One group was up by the barnyard gate where wood had been piled, appearing to be organized into teams. A rustle nearby froze him on the spot, two black eyes with moonlight glinting in them staring at him from a foot away. He started to recoil but relaxed when the sheep bleated softly, ignoring him after deeming him not to be a threat, going back to picking through the deadfall for green sprigs.

"You scared the crap out of me," he whispered. "Stupid sheep...."

Swallowing a lump in his throat, James continued left along the fence line, getting a better view of the people who were clustered around the barn and spotting several bodies lying motionless in a row by the barnyard gate along with a stack of wood.

A woman groaned loudly from nearby, out of sight, and someone else cursed loudly, in pain or anger, or both.

"If you want this shard of wood out of your gut, Gil," a man shouted, "you gotta hold still!"

"What's going on here?" James murmured. "Why do I smell diesel?"

Down by the porch, the EV started up, lights coming on, someone driving it in a circle until it faced down the driveway. People were at the chicken coop, bringing out baskets of eggs, one quickly shutting the door to keep the birds from getting out. The forms of others stood silhouetted in the house windows, moving in the kitchen or standing on the porch, some wearing military-style jackets, blending with the darkness. Almost all were armed with shotguns and rifles, bulges of pistols beneath their coats.

"Somehow I don't think Ryan and Helen teamed up with you people..." James continued moving down the fence line, more of the property drawing into view.

An older woman with combed-back gray hair stepped outside with a shorter woman, both heading over to the dump truck parked outside the front of the house. The property was littered with flimsy tents, burn barrels, and campfires in between the barn and the house, in addition to the RV they'd spotted. Motion back at the barn drew his attention, and he shifted a few yards back the way he'd walked, hunkering down where the fence met the forest as the voices grew loud enough to hear.

"I can't believe you idiots," a man said, his voice rough and strained. "I warned you that Ryan and Helen were up to something, but you took your eyes off the ball and look what happened! You *screwed up!*"

Curious, James slipped a little more to his right, focusing on some people standing in front of the barn, facing the barn door.

"I left you in charge, and *you* let *me* down! You let *all* of us down! Look inside that barn. Did anyone see what they were doing? Did anyone notice the *welding torch!?*"

"But Boss, the old man was supposed to be working with the dogs," a baritone replied, "and Helen was in the house most of the time. How could we know they'd beef up the tractor and break out?"

"Shut the hell up, Hansen!" the first voice snapped.

"But, Red," another man started.

"Shut up with your excuses, Tyler." The man named Red yelled again. "You were supposed to be watching the old man and the dogs!"

"I got put on a different shift and figured *someone* was watching them."

"Well, you figured wrong!" Red's voice had risen to the verge of hysteria, and the people off to the side of the barn that James could see flinched and backed up.

"You're all a bunch of screw-ups! I should have known better than to put you on point."

"Come on, Red," Tyler said. "We did everything you asked."

"Not everything." Red paused a moment before starting up again. "And you! You knew what was going on, too, didn't you, Sandy?"

A woman with a boy in her arms recoiled. "I swear, we didn't know anything, Red."

"You were with one of them the whole time."

"What? No we weren't! Stephen was helping him with the dogs!" The young boy said something that was too quiet for James to make out, then the woman continued. "I tried to talk to Helen, but she acted like nothing was wrong. After you used Stephen to trick them, they didn't trust us anymore. Ryan was ready to kill me himself - they wouldn't have told me *anything.*"

"Shut up. I'm tired of hearing you talk."

James gripped the fencing hard, squeezing the field fence, bending it out of place. His home was, indeed, occupied. Helen and Ryan appeared to have escaped - not long ago, by the sound of things - though where they were was anyone's guess.

"There's going to be hell to pay for this." Red continued his tirade. "And don't be surprised if some of you get kicked out of here! I'm going to be watching all of you *very* closely. You idiots cost us good workers, the barn's torn to hell and the damn *tractor* - the thing we needed more than anything - is *gone!* Not to mention the damn truck's out of commission until we repair the fuel tank!"

"We still have that ATV they've got in that other barn," a voice whined. "It's not a total loss."

"An ATV. Fantastic. We'll just till and plow with an ATV. Marvelous idea. I've got a better idea - shut the hell up and get back to work. Guards back on duty, and no screwing around or I'll turn you into fertilizer for the gardens like those others lined up by the gate!" Red sucked in a lungful of air and let it out in a deranged, screeching shout. "And I want Ryan and Helen, and that tractor they took found!"

The group of people began jogging away from the barn in different directions, and James heard Red's voice again.

"Hansen. Grab these dead bodies and stack them up with the others. Then put together a work detail to get them buried. Strip them down, first."

"Okay, Boss."

Two guards appeared at the corner of the barn, walking almost directly at James, glancing back as they mumbled.

"Red's always on our backs," one said.

"Yeah, we're the ones who got shot at," replied the other. "My friend *died*, man."

James eased back into the shadows of the trees, turned, and crept south along the fence line, dipping low back into the ditch to mask his movement. After reversing his course through the ditch and along the road, he sprinted across the wide-open field and climbed the short hill where Alice and the kids sat on the ground next to the horses, greeting him with a wave.

Alice stood and embraced him briefly. "We thought you'd gotten stuck down there," she said in a shaky voice. "What's going on?"

"It's not good. I mean, the house is standing and so is the barn and the animals are all there, but there are people crawling all over the property. I got a good look at the place and heard a little speech by the guy who seemed to be running things. They were calling him Red."

"Doesn't sound familiar."

"Yeah, never heard of him myself." James sat on the ground, catching his breath. "But it's worse than we feared. These people, whoever they are, have taken over everything. They've got run of the property and are digging in."

"How many are there?"

"I guess about fifteen or twenty, give or take. But I didn't see everyone. Could be a lot more inside for all I know."

"What about Mom and Dad?"

"That's the kicker – it sounds like they escaped. *Tonight*, no less. Red was screaming at a bunch of people about Ryan and Helen escaping and taking the tractor. He's *pissed* about it."

Alice gasped. "Mom and Dad are alive?!"

"I think so. And this Red guy is pretty pissed off about it." James grinned. "I'm guessing your dad might be the cause for that."

"No doubt." Alice stood, looking at the house. "We need to find them."

James nodded, standing and reaching for Amber. "Agreed. After we find them, we'll decide what to do about the property." Shadows moved down at the house, the warm glow from the windows shifting as people walked through the rooms.

"Decide?" Alice snorted. "What decision is there?"

"There are a *lot* of people there, and—"

Her expression darkened, voice lowering to a snarl. "And I've *dealt* with a *lot* of people before, James. I dealt with them once and I'll deal with them again."

James held his hands up. "Easy. I'm on your side – and I agree. I just mean our strategy. We're not abandoning our home."

"Good. First step is finding Mom and Dad."

"Agreed." James climbed into his saddle, the others following suit.

Jake spoke. "Maybe we should head down near the end of the driveway, see if we can find any tracks?"

"Worth a shot." James looked at Alice, both of them nodding in agreement.

They took the horses across the field to the nearby road and headed down until they reached a turn, taking a right and moving from pavement to a mixture of dirt and gravel. With the driveway up ahead, they moved slowly, weapons at the ready, spread out across the width of the road in case of an ambush.

"Okay, that's close enough," James said when they came to the edge of the woods at the end of their driveway, able to see all the way up the gravel track that cut between their ponds and red oaks.

"There's the front gate," Sarah said, pointing to a drainage ditch on the side of the road opposite their property.

"Five bucks says Ryan and Helen did that with the tractor. Come on, let's go before they see us." James led them back south, slowing down once they got a few hundred yards away.

Alice named each family as they passed their neighbors. "Well, there's the Willoughbys. I see some lights way back on their property. Maybe they've got a camp."

"I don't think they'd have stopped so close to the house."

"Agreed. And there's the Crenshaws next door. Looks like no one's home. I hope Sandy made it out okay."

"Sandy?" James asked. "Sandy Crenshaw?"

"Yeah."

"I think Sandy was up at the barn. Red was giving her all kinds of grief for not ratting on your parents or something."

"You think more of our neighbors are up there?"

"I don't know, but maybe? The way he was throwing orders around, he's set up more or less as a king there."

"Not for long." Alice shook her head, frowning. "At least we know Sandy is alive."

"There was a kid with her, too. I think his name was Stephen?"

"Oh yeah, that's her. Good to know they're okay."

"Maybe... the way that guy was talking, though, they might not be for long." Ryan urged Amber ahead and they circled around to where they'd first come in on the dirt road. At the intersection, Ryan turned Amber in a circle, squinting into the darkness in frustration.

"Any thoughts about which way they would have gone? Did Ryan or Helen know anyone in town? Friends they might have sought out? Anyone we'd know?"

"Not that I know of," Alice replied. "Dad probably would have taken them south to get as far away from here as possible, especially if they thought those people were chasing them."

"Yeah, but there'd be more resources closer to town. Your father's resourceful - they might have gone that way looking for supplies and to find a place to hide the tractor."

"What about the park down in town?" Sarah suggested.

"The park's a solid idea. Lots of space, plenty of trees... it's big, too." Alice looked over at James. "I say we try down there."

"The dirt's all cut up with tire tracks here," James pointed his flashlight at the ground, flicking it on briefly, "so they went at least this far. Yeah... let's try down there, see what we can find. Worst case we'll bed down for the night somewhere down there by ourselves."

They continued south, past the supply stores, following the long path toward the small town in the darkness, their flashlights off, navigating by the light of the moon and their memories of the area. Sweat trickled down James' sides and face, his shirt sticking to his skin, back aching from the long ride.

"Are you okay?" Alice galloped beside him with her ponytail bouncing against her back.

"I'm just... we came all this way for nothing."

"Not nothing. Everything's still there." Alice smiled. "We just have some varmints to get rid of."

"True. And we know how to get rid of those."

"Yes. Yes we do...."

James held up his hand as they approached town, forcing them to slow to a trot as they reached the intersection with the main thoroughfare. The single streetlamp hung silent and dead and the corner gas station no longer existed, its fuel tanks having set the nearby buildings on fire, debris scattered across the road and nearby fields.

"The park's this way," James said, angling off to the left, walking Amber down the street. "No shouting for them, okay? We don't want to draw any unwanted attention."

The other three nodded, and they continued for another two blocks. A laundromat, Chinese restaurant and pizza shop sat on the right, their facades the only things remaining after the fires. A couple of old Victorian-style houses that had been built when the town was first established filled the next block, the remnants of one of their peaked roofs pointing upward into the sky. A small stone church followed, its exterior scarred with smoke, a large oak tree that had once stood out front having toppled over as it burned, lying twisted against the steeple.

"Here we are." They approached the park corner. "I don't see any signs of them. No light. No voices..."

"And no sign of the tractor." Alice flicked on her flashlight and pointing it at the ground, finding no signs of marks in the grass. "Absolutely nothing."

"Don't," James said, turning to Sarah. "Honey, why did you suggest coming to the park?"

"Grandpa and Grandma *loved* bringing us here back when we were little." She pointed at the swings. "Grandpa loved to spin us on the old roundabout before they took it out. Someone on the city council said it was too dangerous, but Grandpa only laughed and called them wimps. He said kids his days got their badges of honor on that ride, and a few skinned knees, too."

"There's a baseball field behind these trees," Jake said, "and some barns and ponds off to the left. I used to love coming here with Grandpa, too. We'd walk around and look at ponds and throw frozen peas to the ducks sometimes."

"It is the perfect place to hide..." Alice walked Buck a few steps into the park, stopping where the sidewalk ended and the grass started. "Maybe we should check it out a bit."

"Camp might be good for now," James replied. "Then we can start fresh in—"

Alice stood suddenly in her stirrups and pointed. "Look."

"Huh?" James rose to see what she was looking at, squinting, straining his eyes in the darkness. Finally, as the moon appeared from behind the clouds, he spotted a thin tendril of gray smoke rising above the tree line and drifting up into the empty sky. "Smoke?"

"Yep." Alice dismounted and handed the reins to James. "You stay here with the kids."

"But–"

"No buts." Her face began to grow dark again. "You went off by yourself last time. It's my turn this time. Just stay here with the kids, and I'll be back in a jiffy. I'll fire three shots if I get in trouble."

"But—"

"If you hear shots, come running."

Alice jogged across the grass, ignoring James as he tried to protest again, slowing as pain pulled on her side, reminding her of her ribs, the bruising, and the shot she'd taken to the chest. Clutching her shirt, Alice stepped onto a gravel path cutting through the park, looking down to find it disturbed in a similar pattern to how it had been back on the dirt road.

"It *has* to be you." She whispered.

She passed the playground and bathrooms and slipped into the woods, passing gleaming fences bordering the baseball field. Up ahead stood a long, squarish shape; a barn with smoke drifting between cracks in the roof. The rear section was demolished, but the front half was still intact, and a whisper of light leaked from split boards, the orange glow of a fire illuminating the blackened timbers on the fallen side. Alice worked her way closer, stepping through the knee-high grass, circling to her right to get behind the building. Nestled in the trees, covered with branches and leaves, stood a machine, a familiar-looking tractor and trailer, though they were covered with sheet metal on multiple sides. Alice took a path that wove through crusted, scorched wood and collapsed roofing, creeping closer to the light, crouching, tilting her head as soft voices filtered through.

"...going to hit them hard, anyway? Just drive back up in the tractor?"

"Sandy said some-thing in the barn that got me thinking."

"What was that?"

"She mentioned a 'killdozer'."

"Oh, yes. I remember that... what on earth was she talking about?"

"I had no idea at the time, but as we smashed through the barn doors, it came to me. It was this guy who – well, never mind the details. It's complicated. Suffice it to say that he got really, really mad and took a bulldozer, welded plate steel all over it, made some gun ports and demolished a small town before the police were able to stop him."

Alice stood with tears streaming down her cheeks, choking back a sob, swimming forward through the tangle of fallen wood as the voices continued.

"What're you doing to do with it? Just roll up the driveway like he did in his salt truck to us?"

Ryan put his arm around Helen and stared into the fire, nodding slowly. "You're damn right I am."

"As much as I love this idea, there are a few pro—"

The voices stopped, and a growl came from the direction of the firelight, followed by the distinct whines of a pair of other animals.

"What is it, Duke?" Her father's voice came again. "Get it, boy. Go on – go get it. Who the hell is out there? You want to lose a limb to one of our dogs, keep slinking around!"

Alice finally cleared her throat, laughing as she spoke, tears still streaming down her cheeks. "Oh, come on. Duke's just a big baby, aren't you boy? And anyway – I like that killdozer idea. Want a hand with it?"

She stepped from behind a pile of fallen timbers into the light to find her parents standing between her and the fire. Their pistols wavered in their hand as she smiled at them, dropping to their sides as recognition set in, her mother's falling to the dirt with a soft clatter as Helen reached out, eyes welling with tears, her tired, ragged voice whispering a single word.

"Alice?"

THE REDEMPTION

CHAPTER ONE

The Burton/Cooper Family
Somewhere outside East Lansing, Michigan

Ryan and Helen stood stock-still, looked at each other, then back at the figure standing before them. Time slowed, the sounds of the crickets and crackling fire drawing out into infinity, their heartbeats thumping loud in their ears, dizziness overtaking both of them as the sheer improbability crashed down like a wave. After several seconds – or hours, the difference was impossible to distinguish – time resumed its steady pace as both pistols slipped from motionless hands and dropped to the dirt with soft thumps. Ryan and Helen rushed forward, wrapping their arms around their daughter in a fierce, unhesitant, unrelenting embrace.

"Alice?" Helen choked out the word again, running a hand across her daughter's head and back. The figure looked real, felt real, but reality was often a cruel mistress, and she couldn't trust that she wasn't somehow hallucinating what she saw, felt and heard. "Is that really you, baby?"

"It's me, Mom." Alice wept freely, tears pouring down her cheeks in rivers, squeezing tight to her parents. "I can't believe we found you guys."

"You made it, girl." Ryan's eyes were tightly shut, face buried in his daughter's hair, arms tight around her. "Took you long enough."

Alice laughed, pulling back just enough to wipe an arm across her face, clearing the tears and snot as she looked at her parents. They were the same as she recalled – same faces, same wrinkles, same ferocity behind the eyes – but they'd grown thinner, more haggard and had a look of desperation around them she couldn't quite pin down.

"Are you guys okay? Are you hurt?"

Ryan squeezed her again and she winced. "We could ask the same of you, girl." He held her by the shoulders, ignoring the three dogs as they bounced around the trio, nearly landing in the fire on more than one occasion. "What's wrong?"

"I got... it's a long story, Dad. I'm fine though. I promise." Alice looked to her mother, giving her another hug before holding both of their hands. "I knew you two would be okay. Somehow I just knew it."

"We're too stubborn to die." Ryan snorted, looking past Alice, his expression darkening. "Wait... are you alone? Where's—"

"Oh, *crap*." Alice turned, cupping her hands to her mouth, her voice cracking as she bellowed out into the darkness. "James! Jake! Sarah!! Get over here!"

"You... *all* made it?" A hesitant smile formed on Helen's lips, broadening when three more figures stepped forward into the firelight, tears streaming down her cheeks again as Jake and Sarah ran forward, nearly knocking her over as they grabbed her from both sides.

"Grandma!" They shouted in unison, laughing, Duke, Duchess and Diana growing more excited as they wove between the figures, barking and pushing for attention.

Setting his rifle down on a nearby crate, James watched the reunion, catching Ryan's eye with a brief nod and a wry smile. Ryan's eyes welled up again and he wiped them, nodding at James as he clung to Alice, hugging her tight before letting her go and stalking over to his son-in-law.

"James."

"Ryan." James looked at the older man bemusedly for a few seconds before they, too, embraced, laughing, Ryan slamming his hands against James's back, his tears dampening the back of James's shirt.

"You brought her back," Ryan whispered into James's ear, clinging tighter, choking the breath out of James as he struggled to match Ryan's ferocity in his hug. "You brought our baby back to us. Thank you."

"I'm—"

"Ryan..." James put a hand on his father-in-law's shoulder. "If you apologize one more time, I'm going to have to kick your butt up one side and down the other. It's okay. Seriously."

"Listen to him, Dad. Do you really want to get beaten up in front of your grandkids?"

The group of six sat on crates around the fire, Jake and Sarah between their grandparents, with James and Alice close by on one side. Duke, Duchess and Diana lay on the ground in front of them, long having exhausted themselves, content to receive a never-ending stream of scratches and belly rubs from their returned masters. Ryan stared at his daughter for a long moment, then nudged Jake, leaning in and whispering conspiratorially.

"You got my back in this?"

"Yeah, I'll go for the legs, and you finish him off."

"Now hold on just a second," James laughed, holding his hands up in mock surrender. "You'd really beat up on your dad so soon after getting him back?"

Jake's expression was flat as he looked at James, then at Ryan, then James again before he shrugged. "Eh, we've had you back for a few days. Grandpa's fresh and new."

"Wow..." James chortled as Alice jabbed him in the side. "Betrayed by my own flesh and blood!"

All six laughed together, weeks of tensions slipping away in the face of the renewed bonds of familial company. After a moment, Ryan cleared his throat and continued, arm wrapped around Jake, squeezing him tight.

"I know I've said this a million times already, but we're really glad to have you all back. And we truly are sorry for losing the house." Ryan's eyes glistened, his voice catching in his throat. "We did all we could, but in the end it came down to our lives or letting those *bastards* in, so...."

"Dad. It's okay." Alice patted her father's leg as he wiped his sleeve across his eyes. "You're safe. That's all that matters."

"Stop apologizing, please. It wouldn't matter if the place had been burned to the ground. You two are what matter. Though I'm kind of wondering *why* you didn't burn the place to the ground, rather than letting them take over. Who are they? I got close enough to the house to see there were people there and could tell they were really pissed off at you guys, but..."

"They're our – well, *your* neighbors. And ours."

"Come again?" Alice blinked a few times. "*Our* neighbors?"

"Yeaaaah." Ryan shifted on his crate, looking at Helen. "You want to tell them the whole story?"

"You go ahead. I'll jump in if you forget something."

Outside the barn, one of the horses whinnied in annoyance and Sarah stood up. "I'll go get them fed. Be back in a minute."

Ryan nodded. "Holler if you need help." Turning back to the others, he began. "Well, it started with everything going up in smoke. Your neighbors at the end of the driveway had their garage go up in flames. We helped them fight it and saw that things weren't looking too pretty around the rest of the area, so we figured we should probably go back to Grand Rapids and just check stuff out. I'm sure you can imagine how well that went."

"Did you even get out on the highway?" Alice asked.

"Oh yes. We spent... what, an hour or two moving stuff out of the way to get down the road, didn't we?" Ryan looked at Helen, who nodded in affirmation. "I kept thinking things might clear up after a while, but once we figured out this was so big, we turned around and went back to your place. After that we hunkered down for a while and things were okay."

"Until Jack and Barb and a bunch of others tried to break into the house."

"I'm sorry, *what*?!" James tilted his head at Helen. "Jack and Barb *Willoughby*?"

"Those are the ones." Helen nodded slowly. "Their little raiding party shot Ryan, but we drove them off and killed a couple of them," she leaned down and patted Duke, stroking his back and side, "thanks to your pups."

"Duke took center stage in that defense. Leapt straight off the catwalk and plowed into one of them. Tore his throat out – or was it one of the women?" Ryan asked Helen, who shrugged.

"It's all a blur at this point."

"Hold on, Mom." Alice stammered. "Are-are you seriously telling me that you guys killed people?"

"In self-defense." Ryan's gaze was piercing. "Though something tells me you four have seen your fair share of death as well."

"More than you know." James answered. "But finish your story first. You drove them off, I take it?"

"Tails between their legs," Helen patted Duke again, chuckling darkly. "No offense, boy."

"Mm. Things were fine for a day or three after that. Just trying to take care of things around the place. That's when Sandy entered the picture, needing help for her boy. Infection or somesuch. Her husband was one of the ones that died in the attack, and she seemed not to mind too much so we gave her some of your antibiotics from the cupboard."

"I know Sandy," Alice interjected. "She's good people."

Sarah came back in and sat down, warming her hands near the fire.

"Ryan had his doubts at first." Helen added. "But she turned out to be all right in the end. I get the distinct impression that her husband was physically abusing her. Maybe Stephen, too."

"That's..." Alice hesitated. "Not surprising, when I think about it. Sad, but not really surprising."

Ryan took a drink from a jar of water before continuing. "We talked with her for a while, then the neighbors tried to use her to get to us – that failed, obviously. Then everything just kind of fell apart from there. We went from trying to get Sandy to get a replacement well pump – you've got a new well pump, by the way, James."

"It finally kicked the bucket, eh?"

"Yep. New one works well, though."

"Solar's enough to run it and everything else?"

"It is after I put in some new panels." Ryan winked. "It's a damn good setup you've got there, son. Too good, really. It's the whole reason why Red and his posse of idiots wanted the place so much."

"Okay, who is this *Red*?" Alice looked at Ryan, then James. "Is that the guy who was shouting at everyone and giving orders when you spied on the house?"

"I think so. Real mean-looking guy, baseball cap, acted like God died and left him in charge."

"That's him," Ryan nodded. "And he's a piece of work."

"How do you know him, Dad?"

Ryan stared at the jar of water in his hand for a long moment, silently watching the flames crackling through the liquid as he swirled it around, mouth opening and closing a few times in silence before he took a long breath, wiping away a tear forming at the edge of one eye. "My biggest regret is that I opened my big mouth, hon. I'm so sorry."

"It's not your fault." Helen leaned over, wrapping an arm around Ryan and addressing Alice and James. "Red's an acquaintance of your father's from home. They played golf sometimes, and a bit of poker. They were farmers in the area – most of the people he brought with him were, at one point, way back in the day. Apparently one of them remembered Ryan mentioning your place here offhand once and they decided to make the trip out here."

"The traveled from Grand Rapids out to here? For *our* place?" James was incredulous. "Did you tell them we had stockpiles of gold bullion or something?"

"James..." Alice shook her head.

"Sorry... Ryan, I didn't mean—"

"No. No, you *should* mean it." Ryan arched his back, sitting straight and looking at his daughter and son-in-law. "My big mouth got your house taken. I never thought bragging about my kids would lead to something like this, but it's my fault, through and through."

"Dad. No. It's not your fault."

"Listen to your daughter, you old man." Helen squeezed Ryan's hand. "You can't keep beating yourself up for the actions of a..." Helen glanced at Jake and Sarah. "Of a... *despicable, vile* person."

"Like I said," James said, smiling, "it's not your fault. Don't you remember what I said I'd do if you apologized again?"

A slight smile spread across Ryan's face. "Just you try it."

"All right, before we make space for a fistfight, finish telling us about this Red fellow." Alice said, looking to her father. "What's he like, what're his people like, all that stuff."

"He looked like a dictator to me." James said. "And he was *really* torqued off about you two escaping."

"As he should be, given we took what's probably the only working tractor for fifty miles around." Ryan smiled, looking over at the partially obscured vehicle. "And yes, he's a dictator, to put it mildly. I think he's got some sort of military background, but I'm not sure. A couple of his people do – I'm pretty sure one's Marines, and don't know what the other is or was."

"Is he working with the neighbors, then? Like Jack and Barb and the rest?" Alice asked.

"I don't know if 'working with' is as accurate as 'lording over.' He and the group he brought from Grand Rapids are the ones in charge, without a doubt. From what Sandy told us, they rolled into town in the salt truck parked in front of the house and straight-up shot one of the neighbors to get their attention, then they all decided to pledge their fealty to him. After that, they drove straight through the gate and up to the house."

"Nearly killing Ryan in the process." Helen's lips were thin, her jaw working back and forth as she spoke. "I think he would have, if it hadn't been for Martha."

"And she is?" James asked.

"Red's wife." Ryan nodded, looking at Helen. "There's some kind of weird dynamic going on with those two. Abusive, it seems to me."

"Undoubtedly. The man pointed a gun at her and threatened to kill her, and she barely batted an eye."

"I still think she might end up being an ally, in the end." Ryan replied.

"Okay," James stood, stretching his back and twisting gingerly back and forth. "Before we start delving into the nuances of each person's personality, let me make sure I've got this straight. There's a group of your neighbors and our neighbors who have taken over our home, numbering in the couple dozen plus range, if my headcount was remotely accurate. The one leading them is borderline psychopathic and I'm sure would have zero issues in killing us if we marched up there and asked nicely for the keys back."

"They're moderately well-armed, too." Helen's smile was slight, casting a glance at Alice, who shared a similar wry grin as James continued speaking.

"Moderately well-armed, too, yes, thank you. Perfect. Wonderful." James looked around. "And we have four adults, two children, a tractor, some horses and a modest amount of supplies. Does that sound about right?"

Ryan nodded. "More or less. Though it sounds too fatalistic when you put it like that."

"It's been a long ride and I'm cranky. Sorry."

"Do you have a point with this," Alice asked, crossing her arms and looking up at him. "Or are you just trying to depress all of us?"

"Oh, yeah. I guess I'm wondering what the plan is."

Ryan raised an eyebrow, smiling. "I thought you'd never ask."

Gnats, smoke particulates and dust swirled in the face of the narrow flashlight beam. Above, the moon passed behind another cloud, magnifying the light's effect, and James turned it slightly toward the ground, shaking his head in mock sadness. "Ryan... what on earth did you do to my tractor?"

"Saved our lives, that's what I did." Ryan pulled at the branches he and Helen had placed across the vehicle's frame, revealing the misshapen angles and rushed welding work that had gone into it.

James walked around the tractor and trailer, examining a few places where bullets had snuck in between the steel plates, leaving small holes in their wake. "Looks like a good job, considering everything you had going on. I don't see any damage to any vital systems. A few holes in the tires, which don't matter. Nice work. Very nice work."

"I appreciate that — she's not done yet, though."

"You and mom were talking about a 'Killdozer' before, Dad." Alice stood near her father, holding Helen's hand. "That sounds familiar. I'm not sure why."

"I don't remember the names or the place, but there was a mechanic a long while back who felt wronged by his town — I think they cut off access to his building or something? Anyway, he covered a bulldozer with steel plating. Turned it into a full-fledged tank, with portholes for shooting out of it and everything, and made it so that it couldn't be broken into. He then proceeded to demolish half the town before the thing finally took enough small arms fire that it broke down."

"Holy..." Jake whispered, a smile slowly spreading across his face. "That's *awesome*. We're gonna build something like that?"

"I don't think we have enough steel to make a full-on tank — not to mention this little tractor probably doesn't have the horsepower to hold it — but that's the general idea, yes."

"You want to demolish our house?" James knelt down, examining a bundle of hydraulic cables that peeked out from one of the steel plates, checking for damage. Nearby, hobbled by their leads, the horses ignored the conversation, chewing on tender grass near the trees.

"Absolutely not. But their little tent city out there? Yes. Plus, an impenetrable place to fire from will be an invaluable distraction."

"Pass me that blanket?" James pointed at a lightweight blanket that had been stuffed into the trailer, and Alice picked it up and handed it to James, who spread it out on the ground under the tractor before crawling underneath. "It's a good idea, Ryan. I'm all for it."

"It was already a little sluggish on the drive over here. I know some of that was the trailer, but I'm not sure how much more weight we can put on it before the engine stresses too much."

"Oh, don't worry about that." James smiled, checking more hydraulic lines before crawling back out and dusting his hands off. "Here, check this out."

Popping the hood of the tractor, James squatted on the right-hand side, pointing at a small section next to the engine block. "I can get us another ten, maybe fifteen horsepower out of this sucker easy. Won't take fifteen minutes — well, no, that's not true. If we had an angle grinder it'd take fifteen minutes." He tapped a small, cylinder, spinning a cover with his thumb and forefinger.

"How do you expect to do that?"

"This model's got twenty-five horses; one of the reason I bought it was so that I wouldn't have to mess with all the stupid computer controls that are required for anything over twenty-five. But the engine itself is the exact same one that they use in the thirty-five horse models."

Ryan's brow was furrowed, then his eyes widened and he grinned as realization set in. "That's the fuel screw, isn't it?"

"Exactly." James stood up, patting Ryan on the shoulder. "Just need to remove that cover and then we can get another ten easy out of her, maybe more if we're careful."

"That's genius!" Ryan laughed. "How on earth did you come up with that?"

James shrugged. "It's a pretty common modification for this model. I was going to wait till she was out of warranty to do it, but somehow I don't think the warranty much matters anymore."

"If you can get another ten or fifteen horses out of this, then we can put some *serious* armor on it." Ryan walked around the tractor himself, looking over his work, taking note of each bad weld, gap in the plating and area that could use more steel.

"Yeah, I mean we can add gun ports, cover the whole thing halfway down the wheels and possibly even build some kind of extension off of the cab for someone to sit in and fire out of."

"That sounds like a *dreadful* amount of work," Helen said, glancing at Alice and the kids. "Do you really think we can manage all that?"

James shone his light across the supplies in the back of the trailer, then looked back at the tractor. "Looks like we have enough steel."

"I meant more along the lines of food..." Helen's tone took on an embarrassed air. "We were barely able to get what we got, and I'm not sure it'll be enough for six people for more than a day or two at most. And we can't exactly eat horse feed."

"We'll scavenge and stretch things out, hon." Ryan put an arm around her, smiling at James, Alice, Jake and Sarah. "We've got them back – that's all that matters."

"You've got more than us back," Alice said, she and James grinning as they looked across at the horses, still saddled and fully-loaded as they grazed in the darkness nearby. "We didn't come empty-handed."

CHAPTER TWO

Red Fletcher
Somewhere outside East Lansing

Dawn's early light peeked over the eastern horizon, casting rays through the thick line of trees bordering the edge of the Burtons' property. Shovels plunged into the earth and sweat dripped to the ground as long graves were dug next to existing ones, the manual labor made all the more agonizing by who the graves were for. Long shadows grew more distinct as the sun slowly rose, the animals milling about as they waited for their food, growing increasingly agitated as their anticipated feeding time came and went with no signs of their usual masters. A smattering of guards walked along the edge of the property, whispering to themselves as they cast wary glances toward the large house sitting atop a slight hill near the center of the forty acres. From the direction of the house, on a flat part of the driveway out in front of it, the muffled sounds of cursing, metal striking metal and shouts of annoyance echoed through the morning's mist, carrying with them a sense of dread and malaise that had settled over the place.

"This crap ain't bonding!" Reynolds was on his back, laying atop a comically-undersized creeper, half of his body underneath the front of the large salt truck's lefthand fuel tank. "There's still diesel dripping out and I can't get it to stay! Dammit – it almost went in my eye!"

Hansen's wide stomach, chest, then shoulders appeared as he squeezed out from underneath the truck, sitting up and wiping at his cheek with his shirt sleeve. A gray, metallic-looking substance smeared across his cheek and he winced, standing up and pointing toward the small group of people near him. "Get me some water! Now! Jeez, it's burning!"

Reynolds handed over a cup of water he had been drinking from and a handkerchief from his back pocket, and Hansen doused the cloth with the water before swabbing his cheek, finally removing the substance to reveal a bright red streak. "Told you you shoulda worn goggles." Reynolds chuckled, taking back the cup from Hansen.

"Shut up, or get under there yourself."

"What's the problem anyway?"

"I told you, it won't bond!"

"Did you sand it down first?"

"Did I—of course I sanded it down, you idiot!" Reynolds touched at the red streak on his cheek, wincing. "There's still diesel dripping out and I guess that's keeping the stuff from bonding and curing." He gestured to a few five-gallon buckets at the edge of the driveway, speaking to the group of people watching him. "Why didn't you get it all out, huh?"

"You boys doing okay?" A soft voice came from behind, and both men turned to see Martha approaching with several cups of coffee on a small tray. "It looked like you all were having trouble so I thought some coffee might help."

"Thanks, Martha." Reynolds took one of the cups, sipping at it. "It's this stupid tank we're trying to fix. The holes on the top are fine, but the ones near the bottom are giving me a fit."

"I hate to bear bad news, but Red's going to be coming out in a minute." Martha whispered as she finished handing out the coffee to the others. "He's in a frightful state. I don't think he slept a wink last night."

"Great," Reynolds moaned. "And I'm the one who's going to get his butt chewed out."

"Calm down," Hansen put a hand on Reynolds' shoulder. "Take a breath."

"Don't tell me to calm down," Reynolds slapped Hansen's hand away, rubbing at the red mark on his cheek. "How about you give him the bad news, huh?"

"Bad news? Gentlemen – bad news is *not* a phrase I want to hear." Hansen's shoulders tensed as a new voice came from behind him, and before he could turn to greet them, Red Fletcher was already at his side, arms crossed, looking him over top to bottom. "What the hell happened to you, Hansen?"

"It's the liquid metal, Red. It won't bond to the tank."

"And why not?" Red's voice was eerily calm.

"Because *some people* didn't do their job draining the tank all the way. I've got diesel all over me and it keeps seeping out of the holes and keeping the stuff from sticking to the tank and hardening. The epoxy isn't working either. It's the diesel, Red."

Red closed his eyes, rubbing them with his thumb and forefinger, chewing on his upper lip before speaking. "Hansen. Your one job was to fix the tank. Are you telling me that you can't do that?"

"Red, *nobody* can. It's not—"

"I am so *damned* tired," Red's voice rose with each word, "of people telling me it's not. Their. Fault!" The last word exploded out of his mouth, and Red pushed Hansen backwards, arms windmilling as his bulk crashed up against the side of the salt truck. The others around him moved back, including Martha, who stood near the rear of the truck. "It's *your* job so it's *your* responsibility which means it's *your* fault! Get it?!"

Hansen nodded meekly as Red gave him another shove on the chest with his arm before turning to the rest of the assembled group, all of whom had gained a strong interest in gazing at their feet.

"As for the rest of you – do we really need *five* people standing around with their thumbs up their butts?" He stalked over to the buckets of diesel and peered into them, shaking his head. "Why the hell did you save this stuff? We've got a whole *tank* of it in the barn!"

"You told us t—" Reynolds started.

"Shut up!" Red turned on him. "And aren't you supposed to be out on guard duty?"

"N-no, that's later today, after—"

"Get out there *now*, Reynolds, unless you want my boot where the sun don't shine!"

As Reynolds hurried off, Red turned to the rest of the group, gesticulating at them as he continued shouting. "Get moving, all of you! Find something productive to do! We're down *six* people and a bunch of meds thanks to taking care of Jack before he kicked the bucket! If you don't have a place to be, I want you to get inside so I can give you new assignments. Move it!"

The crowd dispersed as quickly as humanly possible, and Red turned to Martha, his stern visage softening for a few seconds before he noticed three people at the top of the driveway, outside the garage. "Come here!" He pointed at the figures, shouting at them, and they began walking down toward the truck.

"You need me, Red? Nancy Lively asked, standing behind Sandy and Stephen.

"No. Go find something to do." Nancy turned and jogged off without another word, leaving Sandy and Stephen standing alone, Martha far off to the side, with Red facing them. "You know, I had a lot of time to think last night. And I spent a *lot* of that time thinking about you, Sandy."

"W-why?" Sandy's mouth grew dry, and she licked her lips, trying to force a smile. "Do you need me to do something? I was going to get breakfast going."

"Breakfast can wait." Red's voice lowered again, eyes narrowing. "I want to talk to you about Ryan and Helen."

"What a-about them?" Sandy still tried to force a smile.

"I was thinking... you and Helen were *awfully* close, it seemed to me. Nancy told me herself, that you and Helen were like that." Red twisted his forefinger and middle finger around each other. "If that were the case, I just think that you'd have known that they were going to try and escape. And if you *did* know, and didn't tell us, then it would be entirely *your* responsibility that we lost six people plus a tractor and a pile of supplies to boot."

"Red, I swear—"

"Swearing's not right, Sandy." Red stepped forward, "Especially when you know it's a lie." He looked down at Stephen, a cruel smile on his face. "Isn't that right, son? Isn't lying wrong?"

"Red…" Martha came in from the side, laying her hand on his arm. "I don't think Stephen would lie to you. Would you, Stephen?"

"N-no s-sir, I mean, uhm, m-ma'm."

"My son isn't a part of anything, Red." Sandy put her arms around Stephen's chest. "And neither am I. Helen and Ryan were kind to me, for a while, but after what you did with Stephen to get in here, plus what the rest did with me to try and get to them before you arrived… well, they didn't trust me at all. I had *no* idea they were going to do what they did. I would have told you had I known – this affects my son and I just as much as the rest of you."

Red was silent, staring into Sandy's eyes as she fought to meet his gaze without blinking, until finally he shook his head and sighed. "Get out of my sight and get started on the food. We'll continue this conversation later."

Sandy nodded, taking Stephen with her as she turned, hurrying back toward the house. Martha headed after them, giving Red a slight smile which he acknowledged with a frown and shake of his head before turning back on Hansen, who was still standing next to the salt truck, watching the proceedings with wide eyes.

"Hansen," Red tilted his head and neck back and forth until a slight crack finally sounded. "How long until this truck is ready." It was a statement, not a question, and Hansen swallowed hard, racking his brain for some sort of answer that wouldn't lead to a further tongue-lashing.

"Honestly, Red? It's going to take a while. Two days, maybe?"

"Two—" The word exploded out, then Red clamped his mouth shut and closed his eyes, jaw clenching and unclenching fiercely for a moment before he spoke again, calmer, but tone tinged with frustration and a dark anger. "Two days? Why two, Hansen? Why not two *hours?*"

"I'm almost out of the liquid metal, Red. And this epoxy's dissolving on contact with the diesel." Hansen half-turned, pointing at the fuel tank. "We need to drill another hole in the very bottom of the tank, or find a pump or something, so that every last drop can be cleaned out. We'll probably have to weld patches on the holes, so any fuel fumes in there will be a very very bad thing. I'm going to need help, too. They weren't just standing around, Red, they were helping and I need them if I'm going to get this done. Someone's got to go find some welding gear, and someone else needs to drain the tank, and—"

"All right, I get it." Red held up a hand, then shouted. "Reynolds! Get over here!"

"What's up, Red?"

"I—what do you mean, 'what's up'? Are you twelve?" Red rolled his eyes. "I need a team put together. Go out searching for what Hansen needs to repair this piece of crap. I want it back by the end of the day. Welding gear, steel to make a new fuel tank, whatever he needs. Understand?"

"Yeah, no problem, Red. I'll get it done."

"Good." Red started to turn back to Hansen.

"Uhh… Red?"

Red sighed deeply at the sound of Reynold's voice. "I swear, this'd better be a *really* good question."

"I was just wondering something."

"Spit it out!"

"Well, I mean, why do we need this truck back up and running so fast? Don't we have everything we need here?"

"Reynolds…" Hansen's eyes were wide, his head shaking slightly behind Red as he made a cutting motion across his neck, which Reynolds ignored as he plowed on with his questions.

"I mean, we've got the ATV and that EV of theirs and power and food and everything, right? Why do—*urk!*" Reynolds' barrage of questions were cut off as Red circled around the man before shoving him sideways, slamming him against the side of the salt truck, arm pinned across Reynolds' neck. He choked and gasped, struggling meekly against Red, who ignored the man's flailing arms, slapping him on the side of the face and head, punctuating every other word with a blow.

"Ryan Cooper is out there! He's alive, and he's going to want revenge! We lost people and we need *all* resources at top strength, including this truck!"

"B—but, Red," Reynolds gasped for air, clinging to Red's arm, trying to pull it away from his windpipe, "we've got all we need here. We have more people, supplies… everything. What c-can he do to us?"

Red let up on Reynolds' neck for a second before slamming the man harder against the side of the salt truck. Reynolds' vision went blurry and spotted with a variety of colors for a few seconds, Red's voice a bellow that cut through the visual static, his spittle flying into Reynolds' face. "And *he* has a tractor! And supplies! And, apparently," Red gestured to the fuel tank, letting off of Reynolds long enough for the man to take a few quick breaths, "he has *guns*, too! We've got one lousy ATV, an electric car that's locked to Ryan and Helen's fingerprints, and a truck that can't do *jack*!"

"We… w-we still outnumber h-him, Red." Reynolds sputtered out a reply.

"You don't get it, do you?" Red snorted disdainfully. "Of course you don't, *idiot*." Red glanced around to see that a crowd had formed, both near the salt truck and farther away, everyone stopped in their tracks and duties to listen and watch as Red berated Reynolds. He looked back to Reynolds and slapping him once more upside the head before releasing him, Reynolds sinking slowly to the ground as Red turned to the assembled crowd, voice raising. "None of you get it! This man is *dangerous*! He *will* be back, and we *need* to get ready! But none of you are going to be ready, are you? No, of course you won't, because you let him get away in the first place! If you were any good at your jobs you would have stopped him!"

Red paused from his gesticulation-laden berating of his crew, crimson-faced and panting. A woman – one of the local neighbors – approached him slowly, flanked by two other people whose eyes were downcast as they shuffled behind her. "Red?" She spoke quietly.

"What *is* it?!" Red bellowed at her. "Just tell me what it is!"

"We… we're back from the first search. The tire tracks stopped at the paved road. We kept going for a while, looking for any signs of where they went, but there was nothing."

"This is exactly what I mean." Red put both hands to the sides of his face, squeezing as he pulled down on his cheeks, groaning loudly. "None of you know how to do *anything* properly! Just get back out there and *find him!!*"

With a final hoarse, cracked, spit-filled scream, Red stomped up the driveway, Martha meeting him halfway, whispering something to him that no one else could hear. He shook off the hand she tried to put on his shoulder, but she persisted, speaking to him and patting his back and arm as she walked next to him all the way back up to the house, following him inside and closing the door behind them.

Reynolds and Hansen looked at each other, then at the woman and her search party, before everyone shrugged and shook their heads. They spoke quietly to each other as they resumed their tasks, the trio heading to get some food and water before going back out on another search, and Reynolds and Hansen resuming their work on the salt truck.

An hour after the screaming and berating had stopped, there was a soft tick of a door being opened, then another of it being softly shut. Martha appeared at the top of the stairs a second later, descending them slowly, giving Sandy and Stephen a slight smile as she caught sight of them sitting at the dining room table, Stephen reading while Sandy sat with a notebook and pen, writing down meal ideas for the next few days. Martha looked back at the top of the stairs and sighed, shoulders slumping as she sat down next to Sandy.

"He asleep?" Sandy whispered.

"Yes. Thank goodness." Martha took off her glasses, closed her eyes and slowly massaged them. "I'm sorry, Sandy." Martha put her glasses back on and took Sandy's hand, squeezing it. "He shouldn't have threatened you again. He shouldn't be speaking to anyone like he is."

"Was he always like this?" Sandy asked.

The answer took a moment. Martha clung to Sandy's hand, gazing out the front window at the men working on the salt truck, the guards patrolling at the edges of the property, and the trees and broad, grey sky beyond. "Sometimes" she finally said, softly, not a whisper, but quietly enough that she couldn't be heard beyond the table. "It was never this bad, though. And he'd been mellowing out the last few years. Quite a lot, actually. But this… it's driven him mad."

Sandy rubbed at a series of yellowish marks on her arm, bruises that had almost healed, but still showed signs of their existence. "It's not okay for him to treat you like this, either."

"It's okay, Sandy."

"It's *not*, Martha." Sandy took Martha's hands, looking her in the eye. "He pointed a gun at you. Not by accident. He was considering *killing* you."

"I..." Martha's mouth opened momentarily before shutting again, her eyes turning glassy. She wiped at them, taking a deep breath and summoning a smile before patting Sandy's hand. "Don't worry about me, dear. You need to think about yourself, and your son. Red's got his eye on you. That's not a good thing."

"I wish we had escaped with Ryan and Helen – that I had known about it, and could have gone with them." Sandy's voice was barely audible. She searched Martha's face for signs of surprise, but the older woman merely nodded slowly, patting Sandy's hand again.

"Try to stay out of Red's way, dear. I'll help you as best as I can."

"We'll help each *other*, Martha. I'm not alone right now, and neither are you."

Martha's forced smile turned genuine at Sandy's words and she nodded slowly, a silent thanks as they sat hand in hand, Stephen next to them, all three staring out the window as they contemplated what was to come.

CHAPTER THREE

Agent Harris
Site R, Pennsylvania

"Seven percent?"

"Seven percent."

Birk rubbed his eyes wearily, tossing the paper he was looking at back onto the table with a sigh. "It's a sad day when *seven* percent of the electrical grid being operational is going to seem like a miracle."

"It's the state of the world, sir."

"Yep." Birk arched his back, stretching and cracking it before returning to the stack of papers. "So three weeks for that, then oil processing is...."

"Two percent at this moment." Pulaski leaned in, pointing to a chart on the page. "Old, out of commission refineries are producing all we have at the moment. We're currently pulling nothing out of the ground. We expect it to take three months to return domestic production and processing to ten to fifteen percent of pre-collapse capacity."

"Fifteen percent? Good heavens."

"I know that sounds low, but—"

"No, that sounds *incredibly* ambitious."

"Ambitious, but doable. Despite their proximity to many of the initial fires, we were able to pull out a sizeable number of employees and contractors from the top five drilling and refinery companies. It's a matter of infrastructure at this point. The Corps of Engineers has it as their top priority, still."

"I assume most of the production is centered around diesel production?"

"Diesel and jet fuel. Gasoline is taking a back seat right now for obvious reasons."

"Good." Birk nodded. "Good to hear. Sounds like some desperately-needed progress. What else do you have for me?"

The background drone of Site R's air conditioning and filtration systems mixed with the buzz of the overhead lights, filling the silence left as Pulaski shuffled through more paperwork, still adjusting to his new, multipurpose role. Normally strictly in charge of military affairs, he'd taken on the role of coordinator, briefer and all-around advisor as others in Birk's orbit had been forced to take on additional roles themselves, spreading through the Site R complex to collect information and deliver it to Pulaski and Birk.

"Sorry, sir. One moment."

"Relax, Pulaski. Take your time." Birk looked over and gave Harris a sly smile, the younger agent returning it before Birk spoke to him. "How's your mattress treating you, Harris?"

"It smells like a cross between mildew and urine. Other than that, it's fine."

"Mine too." Birk chuckled. "I don't think they really expected to have to host anyone here in the overflow barracks."

"Here we are," Pulaski said, pulling a stapled-together collection of papers out of one of his stacks and thumbing through it. "Updates on transportation acquisitions, civilian morale and general, uh, 'feelings' of the country." He looked at Birk. "Sir, I'm really not the one to try and update you on this. Could we get Ms. Strode in to—"

"Nope. This is you and me, General. Nancy's got her own set of tasks to take care of."

"As you wish." Pulaski squared his shoulders. "Methods of transportation are being acquired – organic and mechanical alike. National Guard posts – the ones that are still intact, that is – are taking point on this. Old vehicles are being turned around and repaired and refitted, and they're using any intact civilian vehicles including electric ones as well."

"What do you mean by organic methods of transportation? Horses?"

"Yes, sir. Horses are the main source of transportation right now in areas that aren't near the three main train routes that are operating. It looks like we're taking down information whenever possible so that the owners can be compensated or what's taken can be returned at a later date. Most of the time these resources are abandoned, but when they aren't, civilians aren't generally happy to be forced to give up their property."

"Understandable." Birk nodded. "You'd think that the resource drops and aid camps and such would be helping them understand we're legitimately on *their* side."

"Not according to these report summaries." Pulaski replied. "They're still suspicious of the camps and aid drops, and attacks on National Guard posts and train convoys have been increasing dramatically. If you'll forgive the frankness...."

"General, just say what's on your mind; stop asking for permission."

"People have lost their damn minds."

Birk and Harris both laughed at the General's words, glancing at each other before their chuckles grew louder. "I'll give it to you, Pulaski... that *was* frank. Any thoughts from either of you on what we can do? County, city and state-level connections and relationships will only go so far if the people feel like they're on their own and don't have any sort of connection to their leaders."

"Have we released any PR campaigns, sir?" Harris spoke first, the other two men turning to him.

"PR campaigns?" Birk shook his head. "Not to my knowledge. We've been focused on getting aid where it needs to be. Do you think that's what we're missing?"

"Might be, sir."

"Explain, Mr. Harris." Pulaski's words were a statement, not a question, and he gestured to a seat next to him at the small table.

Harris rose from his seat near the door and circled around to sit at the table. "I guess I'm thinking of it from their perspective and, well... I can understand some of their reactions. A major disaster has happened, a large percentage of the American public is *dead* and their government is just throwing food and water and aid camps at the problem."

"We're doing *far* more than that," Pulaski bristled, holding up reams of paper. "Have you been listening to what we've been discussing?"

"General, you know we're doing a lot, and I know we're doing a lot, but does Joe Public know? Are they aware that we're going to be at ten percent refining capability in three months? Do they know that power will be back on soon for sections of the country? Have they been informed, en masse, about what we're doing with their horses that we take, and how we're ensuring they'll get them back?"

"Of course they are. We tell anyone we see what we're doing."

Harris looked at Birk. "Sir, you're a politician. Do you see what I'm saying?"

Birk's slow, steady nod during Harris's questions grew stronger as the agent addressed him directly. "I do. I see exactly what you're saying. And you're right. Dead on. We need a PR campaign, Pulaski."

"Sir?" Pulaski, already out of his depths as an informal advisor and secretary to the President, appeared even more lost.

Birk pushed back from the table, standing and starting to pace around the room as he talked. "We're reaching individuals, but we're not reaching *America* as a whole. That's a huge problem in situations like this, because if we don't reach the American people as a whole, the individual conversations are meaningless. We need to shift focus here. I need a dedicated team – the press secretary's gone, so find me someone who's got even a modicum of press or PR experience and get them ready for a meeting. We need videos, radio statements, daily updates for the public." Birk stopped at the pile of papers in front of Pulaski, jabbing a finger at it. "*This* is what the public needs to know. The good, the bad and the ugly."

"Sir, our adversaries—"

"Do not matter one whit. We've already established that anyone with any capabilities were crippled just like we were. So let's be an example – to our people and theirs – of how you respond to a beatdown like this." Birk clenched the back of his chair, knuckles turning white, laughing derisively at himself. "Son of a... I'm a damned politician. How did *I* not realize what we were missing? How did – no offense, Harris – a *bodyguard* figure this out?"

Harris smiled. "None taken, sir. And it's pretty simple – you've been busy leading, not politicking."

"It's long past time to do both again. Pulaski – find me all the people you can who have backgrounds in PR and media. I'll also need to know how far we can push video and voice messages. Videos can be sent to aid camps and played on screens there at a minimum, but we can push voice messages out farther than that, surely."

Pulaski nodded in understanding. "Give me an hour, sir. I'll have an update for you then."

"Excellent. Thank you." Birk gestured at Harris. "Come on. I'm going for a walk."

Water cascaded down a manmade waterfall into a massive reservoir a thousand feet long and wide, the echo deafening in the enclosed space in the back portion of the Site R facility. The fresh water – sourced from underground rivers and pumped from aquifers a thousand feet or more underground – served to nourish both the humans living inside the facility as well as the twin nuclear reactors that provided the power necessary to maintain all of the site's infrastructure.

As a well-known and publicly referenced location in popular media and general culture, Raven Rock's long-term strategic value had diminished over the years, leading to a declination in appearance and upkeep. The complex – once top-secret and protected from all prying eyes – had, over the years, turned into a facility similar in nature to Mount Weather and even Cheyenne Mountain. While certain operations were still located at such facilities – and their internal workings secret to all but the privileged few – they were nonetheless deprioritized in favor of other complexes that received modern upgrades and amenities.

"Smells like mildew back here, too." President Birk wrinkled his nose as he and Harris walked across the catwalk that extended across the reservoir, the swirling waters beneath their feet lit by dozens of bright yellow bulbs that hung from the rock ceiling.

"It reminds me of this little grocery store I went to all the time when I was a kid." Harris replied. "You'd walk in and just get hit by this wave of mildew. I couldn't stand the place, but my mother liked going there over any of the bigger places."

Birk stopped and gripped the handrail, peering over the edge into the dark, roiling waters just a few feet below. "It reminds me of the basement bunker of the White House. They put new paint and carpets in there to try and cover it up, but it never helps." Glancing back down the way they came at the group of Marines following at a distance, Birk raised a mischievous eyebrow. "C'mon. Let's go see the reactors."

"Sir? I don't think we—"

"Who's in charge, Harris?"

Harris sighed. "I think they're past the reservoir, up a level."

"That's the spirit." Birk winked and continued onward, Harris rushing to catch up with him.

The pair exited from the reservoir space through a large pair of metal doors, leaving the rush of water behind. Following signs marked with radiation warnings, they headed up a flight of stairs, the President saluted by various members of the military as he took the lead, nodding and returning each one he received. When he and Harris reached the doors marked with signs for the nuclear reactors, a man in a white lab coat rose from a desk and ran for the doors, blocking their way.

"I—who are you? You can't be down... wait... are you...."

"I am." Birk towered over the smaller man. "And I'm taking a little self-guided tour of the facility. I'd like to see the reactors."

"This... this isn't done. It's just not done!"

"Doctor... Kepler." Birk put an arm on the man's shoulder, giving him a soft smile. "The gentleman standing behind me is my personal Secret Service agent. His job is to make sure no threats get through to me, and he takes his job *very* seriously. You don't want him to think you're a threat, do you?"

The man's eyes widened, a series of sputtering, stuttering words coming from his lips, though no actual words were formed in the process. Birk gave him a wink and gently pushed him aside, opening the doors with both hands. "We'll just be a minute, Doctor! Thank you for your cooperation!"

The room containing the twin reactors was fifty feet wide by two hundred feet long, with circular guardrails at either end surrounding twin chambers full of water. A blue glow emanated from both chambers, and Birk and Harris approached the nearest one, staring down into the water. The water was still compared to the rush of the reservoir they had walked over previously, but it nonetheless bubbled, the glow growing and receding in strength in a steady rhythm.

"So much power," Birk muttered, leaning over the rail, staring down into the water. "Limitless power for destruction or for good, all contained in the palms of our hands. Makes you think, doesn't it, Harris?"

The agent moved cautiously to the handrail, peeking gingerly over the side. "Is it... safe to be here?"

Birk chuckled. "Perfectly. You'd need to go lick the reactor rods to get a dose that would hurt you."

"I didn't realize you knew anything about nuclear reactors, sir."

"I wanted to be a nuclear physicist," Birk looked around the room, elbow on the edge of the guardrail as he leaned against it. "But I couldn't handle the math. E&M kicked my butt out of the room and then I went with my backup. A JD wasn't my first choice, but it landed me here, so... not all bad." Birk's gaze returned to the water. "That blue glow is Cherenkov radiation. It's caused when particles travel faster through a medium than light can pass through the same medium. Like a sonic boom, but for your eyes."

"Is there... something on your mind?" Harris asked. "I don't want to pry, but this isn't like you, sir."

Birk's smile was more strained. "I need your opinion, Harris."

"On?"

Birk gestured with both hands in large, sweeping motions. "All of *this*. The new updates, what we're doing, our future plans... all of it. Don't give me bullshit – I want your candid opinion."

"I... wonder how things are really going out there, on the streets. I question the reliability of some of the reports you're getting. Mostly I'm wondering how things will get resolved. I've seen the sort of rebuilding that goes on during and after wars. That seems like a walk in the park compared to what we have to do here and now."

Birk pointed a finger at Harris, narrowing one eye. "And that's why I keep you around, Harris. You know, Pulaski and Crow both tried to get you replaced a few times since this mess all started. Said they wanted to assign someone more experienced. I told them that if they tried they'd be out in the streets." Harris opened his mouth to speak, but Birk waved him off. "Oh, save it. Good intentions, but those two are hammers and anvils. Weapons to be pointed in the right directions. I need thinking – like what you did back there in that conference room. We've all been so worried about *doing* the right things that we haven't paid a lick of attention to *telling* people what we're doing. The message is just as important – hell, it's usually *more* important – than the actions. So, in answer to your question: that's what's on my mind. Getting creative. Figuring out our blind spots. What have we missed? What are we overlooking? What are we screwing up? You keep helping me with those things and we're going to do just fine."

"Thank you, sir. I appreciate the vote of confidence."

"Damn straight." Birk looked back down in the water. "You know you can swim in that, right?"

"Swim? In a reactor chamber?"

"Yep. It's perfectly safe."

"Sir, I—"

"Relax, Harris. I'm not going to put you through watching me jump in." Birk laughed, turned from the rail and slapped the agent on the back. "Come on. Let's do some more sightseeing then get back. We've got a country to save."

"Yes, sir."

CHAPTER FOUR

The Burton/Cooper Family
Somewhere outside East Lansing

Dawn's first light crept up over the eastern tree line behind the park, and for the first time in weeks, it was not accompanied by sadness, grief, exhaustion or worry, but with joy, laughter, hope – and the smell of bacon and eggs. Four horses grazed lazily in the grass outside the dilapidated barn where the smells and sounds emanated from, their burdens having been relieved from them the night before, saddles hung from the barn's walls and coats given a hasty brushing. Their leads were long, giving them the freedom to escape from some of the merriment that went on from inside the structure, but it was not far enough, and they snorted and chuffed when the voices grew in pitch, annoyed by events beyond their understanding.

"Hot! Jeez, give me a cloth or something, quick! Bacon's gonna burn!" Ryan blew on his fingers as he pulled them from the piece of sheet metal set atop the fire. Helen jumped from her seat and took a dishrag from one of their duffel bags, throwing it at him, and he used it to move the metal from the fire to the top of a nearby crate. After sliding the bacon off onto another, smaller piece of sheet metal, he put the larger one back over the fire and waved at Alice and Helen. "Okay, your turn. If I have to touch that stupid thing again I think I'd rather go hungry."

Ryan's daughter giggled as she pulled out eggs from one of her parents' bags, cracking a dozen of them into the bacon grease as her mother used a spatula to stir and scramble them. "Hang on," James said, rooting through one of their bags before he pulled out two small wooden cylinders. "Yep, I thought they gave us salt and pepper. Here, Helen."

"They gave you salt and pepper, too?" Helen twisted the tops off of the cylinders, revealing coarsely ground pepper and thick flakes of sea salt. "You four really got the royal treatment, didn't you?"

"Yeah, well, when you save a whole family from certain death, they tend to be thankful." James grinned as Jake poked him in the side.

"Sheesh, Dad, finally taking some credit for what you did?"

James shrugged. "Just a little bit. Hey, you know we have some mix for bread and biscuits too, right? Clara made them up for us."

"Amish bread?" Sarah groaned, looking up from the trailer just outside the barn where she was busy organizing the supplies that Ryan and Helen had brought with them. "Tell me they gave us butter and some jam, too. *Please*."

"Yep. A few meals' worth, even if we stuff ourselves."

"More like one meal worth if *Sarah* stuffs herself." Jake called out, grinning as his comment had the desired effect.

"Shut *up*!"

"Cool it, you two," Alice warned. "We spent weeks without you two getting at each other's throats. The least you can do is wait until we're back in our house before you start up again."

"Speaking of," James raised an eyebrow at Jake, who nodded, "after we eat, we need to get started on that plan. We've got supplies here for at least two weeks, if we ration and stretch everything as thin as we can, but I don't want to wait that long. I didn't go through hell and high water just to give up at my own doorstep."

"I agree," Ryan replied, accepting a stack of thin aluminum army trays from James. "We probably have enough gear here to do most of the work, but depending on what you want to do, we might have to scavenge for more."

"You're the one who did all of that to the tractor," James nodded over his shoulder in the direction of the heavily-modified vehicle. "I figured you had some ideas."

"I'm not the engineer here, or the – what was it Alice said they called you?"

"Hero of Kansas City I think, wasn't it?" Helen shared a smile with Alice as James groaned.

"Oh knock it off. I unjammed a firing pin."

"The smallest action can have the greatest consequences." Ryan finished divvying up the bacon and eggs onto the plates and began to pass them around. "And I'm not wrong – you *are* the engineer. One look at those welds'll tell you I don't have the foggiest notion about what I'm doing."

A slight smile played at the corners of James' mouth as he took his plate. "Thanks for cooking this up, Ryan." James looked upward, closing his eyes. "And thank *you* for carrying us this far. Bless this food – and our hands, and deliver our enemies into them." A chorus of amens went around the group, followed by sporks scraping against the metal trays. Once everyone had a few bites, James continued. "No, you did a good job with the tractor given the pressure you were under. I'll redo some of the welds, but that's mostly because I have some ideas for additions to it."

"I'm all ears."

Half an hour later, mugs of steaming coffee in hand, Ryan, Helen, James and Alice stood around the tractor while Jake and Sarah continued organizing their supplies and tended to the dogs and horses inside the barn, keeping them from getting underfoot and in the way outside. James knelt down and looked beneath the rear of the tractor, using a piece of charred wood to draw black lines on both the steel plating and the tractor body itself, mumbling to himself under his breath as he went. Handing his cup to Alice, he leaned down underneath the front of the vehicle, then stood back up and lifted the hood.

"Is he okay?" Helen whispered to Alice.

"He's thinking," Alice smiled, her husband's hand motions and murmurs at once so familiar yet so strange for lack of togetherness over the past weeks. "Just give him a minute."

Closing the hood of the tractor, James stepped back and looked at it from the front, eying the steel plates Ryan had installed that covered the windows, his hands rotating back and forth at forty-five and ninety degree angles to the steel plates and curves of the tractor's chassis. Alice silently held out his coffee cup, which he accepted before circling the tractor once again before heading to the trailer. Squatting down next to the pile of steel plates Ryan had loaded into the trailer, he looked between them and the tractor several times before standing and draining the rest of the coffee in the thin metal mug.

"Yep." James looked at Ryan. "We're going to need to scavenge. Not a lot, but we'll need another tank for the welder and at least three more pieces of steel plate, plus some poles for structural support. And do any of you have any string?"

"Slow down there, tiger," Alice laughed. "Care to explain to us what you have up your sleeve?"

"Well, we're going to do what Ryan was talking about, what with making a Killdozer, but we're going to take it a step farther." James walked to the side of the tractor and opened the door. "Instead of just plate steel over the windows, we'll build compartments off of the sides of the tractor. We're also going to fully enclose everything stem to stern and add gun ports in the main cab and in the side compartments."

"Side compartments?" Helen was the first to ask the question on everyone's minds. "Are people going to sit in them?"

"I thought about it, but no. Too risky." James tapped on the tractor's door window. "But they won't know that. See – my thought is that the tractor's going to be the distraction while the rest bring the fight to them from behind, but in order to do that we have to make them think that we're committing ourselves fully to the tractor in the assault." Grabbing one of the rifles from one of the bags given to him by the National Guard, he hefted it. "We've got enough rifles and hand-guns that I can rig up some stands for them, and with the help of some pulleys and string, we can make it *look* like there are three or more people inside this thing, firing through multiple gun ports."

"Holy Toledo." Ryan whistled, long and low. "That... that could work. Red would freak if he thought there were a few of us in there; he'd divert everyone to attack the tractor."

"That was my assumption based on what I saw and what you were telling us about him." Ryan swung the cab door closed again. "We can use plywood for the underside, to save on steel, but we need solid steel for the sides of it, so rounds have less of a chance of penetrating through into the cab from the sides."

"So where do we source the materials?" Alice asked.

"There's that strip of businesses back down the road a ways. The well place and that electrical contractor, y'know? We can start there – they're bound to have welding gear."

"That's where Sandy got the well pump, isn't it?" Helen looked at Ryan.

"I think so, yeah." Ryan scratched his chin. "That'll take us dangerously close to the house... are you sure you don't want to search farther out? Red's bound to send people out looking for us. He's not stupid enough to think we tucked tail and ran for good."

James snorted. "Let them search for us. By the time they find us, we'll be geared up and ready to go. No – we're not moving farther away. We're going to have this ready in a couple days, maybe three at the most, and we're taking the fight to them."

"Someone should do recon on the house." Sarah's voice came from behind the group, and they all turned to her. "Grandma and Grandpa killed several people on their way out, so maybe they changed how they're doing things there."

"She's not wrong," Alice looked at James. "I can do that one night – and don't you argue with me, James."

James held up both hands, taking a step back from Alice. "Easy now, I'm on your side. I think that's a good idea – but I'll need all hands on deck for getting the tractor ready. Once it's done, let's run recon on the place if at all possible."

"Well, what do you need, James?" Ryan rubbed his hands together. "Anyone got any paper or a pen so we can make a list?"

"Right here!" Jake called before Sarah could answer, holding up one of the pads of paper they'd received on the train from the National Guard. James took the pad, along with a pencil, nodding in thanks.

"Excellent. Here's what we need."

The sun's higher position in the sky did little to alleviate the chill in the air, particularly as another strong breeze swept across the park, finding each and every crack in the old barn's walls, worming its way through to the inhabitants within. The fire – temporarily abandoned after breakfast – had been refueled in light of the cooler weather, and was soon roaring again, though its hunger meant there was yet another task that had to be added to the list of "must-dos." Said list was already uncomfortably long, even with six people available to tackle it, though needs, as the saying went, must.

"I want you two to keep your eyes open."

"Yes, sir."

"I'm serious – these people are *dangerous*."

"Dad...."

"No, listen to me. If something happens to us... well, nothing's going to happen. But if it did, you'd probably be best making your way back south, to Eli's."

"Honey." A gentle hand rested on James' shoulder where he sat with Jake and Sarah. Alice squatted next to him, patting him on the back. "Jake and Sarah can handle themselves."

"I just want—"

"I know you mean well, but...." Alice's smile was warm, and James' shoulders slumped as understanding flowed through him.'

"Sorry, kids. I'm still having trouble dealing with some of these changes. I keep forgetting what you two have gone through with your mom."

"It's gonna be okay, dad." Sarah looked at Jake. "Trust us – after everything that's happened, we're just as prepared as you are."

"Uh huh."

"They're not wrong," Alice couldn't keep a grin down. "The pair of them could probably kick your butt."

"Yeah, well, still. They're going to be here by themselves. That makes me nervous."

"We won't be alone, Dad." Sarah wrapped an arm around Duke's wide, floofy neck and squeezed. "We've got these three here. Grandma says they're bonafide killers and protectors. Plus we can always use the horses to get away in a hurry if we have to. We'll be fine!"

"I think they get the point, hon." Alice stood up, holding out a hand and helping to pull James to his feet. He dusted off his pants and sighed, rolling his head backward and stretching his shoulders.

"Yeah, I get it. 'Lay off' – message received. Just be careful, okay?"

"We will."

"Keep the dogs and horses hidden inside, and don't go out of sight of the barn." Alice looked down at the pair. "If you even *think* you hear someone, get back to the barn. And don't hesitate to shoot."

"Mom, jeez, we're just going to be gathering firewood." Sarah rolled her eyes. "We're going to be *fine*."

"Jake, you locked and loaded?"

"Yep."

"Good." Alice exhaled deeply before looking at James. "You ready?"

"Nope. Doesn't matter."

Alice and James headed out of the barn to the trailer where Ryan had laid a long piece of plywood across the back half of the trailer. The duffel bags that James and Alice had brought with them were loosely piled in the trailer proper, having been emptied of supplies. The fresh food, MREs and water filtration equipment were stacked in the front of the trailer, while the rifles, handguns and shotgun that Alice had managed to hold on to were laid out across the plywood. Ryan and Helen stood side-by-side on the right side of the trailer, loading rounds from thin cardboard boxes into polymer magazines, filling every single one of the dozens that the military had provided them with.

"Ryan." James nodded to his father-in-law, coming up with Alice to stand on the opposite side of the small trailer. "Helen. Things going okay?"

"Excellent," Ryan nodded. "You got a *ton* of equipment from those folks. They must have really liked you."

"They owed me a favor or two," James grinned, "and I made sure to phone them in."

"Good man. I wish we had a couple more rifles, but four pistols – minus one for the kids – two rifles and a shotgun aren't bad."

"Kind of puts a damper on my idea to have multiple guns firing inside the tractor, though." James mused.

"I bet we can find a few during our runs today and tomorrow," Alice said, hefting the shotgun, losing herself briefly in the memory of shooting the pair of men at the train before shaking it off and continuing. "There's bound to be a few cars or homes with pistols or rifles in them."

"Hey that's a good idea. Just look for the ones with the manufacturer stickers on the back windows," James chuckled. "Helen, you're a natural with that loading."

"Oh, don't you worry about me, dear." Helen's grey-stained fingers moved swiftly from the box of 5.56 to the magazine in hand, scooping several rounds up and clacking them into place, her left thumb red from constantly pushing down on the top round. "I prefer mixing up something in the kitchen, but I can handle myself with one of these." After loading the last magazine, she picked up one of the rifles, slammed the magazine in, charged the handle and ticked the safety on. "In case you can't tell, I'm just a wee bit pissed off."

Alice and James exchanged a glance, both of them chuckling before Alice answered. "Yeah, I can see that, Mom. Spring-loaded, I'd say. Dad, I think we're good here, yes?"

"What about the horses?" Ryan asked, casting an eye toward the barn. "Are they going to be part of our plan?"

Alice and James both answered at the same time. "No."

"Okay... care to fill me in on why we wouldn't want to?" Ryan raised an eyebrow and James nodded at Alice to go first.

"Three of those are Wilford's horses – if they were injured, I'd never forgive myself."

"And," James continued, "I'm not risking Amber, either. We're never going to win on firepower and bravado. We're going to have to sneak in. Horses are going to be the opposite of that. Way too obvious – they'll slow us down and make it impossible for us to do what we need to do."

"Even while we're patrolling or going around looking for supplies, horses are going to be too big and obvious. If we can use them to haul something, maybe, but I'd still rather use the tractor." Alice finished.

Ryan nodded as he stacked up several pistol and rifle magazines, dividing them into four equal piles before pushing a box of shotgun shells across the plywood toward his daughter. "Makes sense to me. You know, this reminds me of that time, back on the old farm."

"With the dogs?" Alice's question received a nod from her father, and a raised eyebrow from her mother. "That's the second time in the last week I've thought about that night."

"The camp?" Her mother asked.

"Yeah." Alice paused, hand half-full of shells she was transferring to one of her pockets, her voice a faint whisper. "That was something else."

"I'm so sorry, sweetie." Ryan reached out and took her hand, squeezing it. "When you're ready to talk more about it, we're all here for you. I know it had to have been *so* hard."

"That's what scares me, Dad." Alice looked at James, who nodded slightly. "It wasn't hard at all. I did what had to be done."

"And saved our children – and hopefully many more in the process." James put an arm around Alice, pulling her toward him.

"Why wasn't it hard, though? It should have been so much more difficult for me to do that. Killing... so many people." Alice's expression twisted, eyes filling with tears. "Am I a monster?"

"I said it the first time you asked me that, and I'll keep saying it: no. You're a hero."

Alice dropped the shells from her hand into her pocket, then held both hands out, turning them over. "I don't feel like a hero."

James turned, twisting Alice around with him to face the barn where Jake and Sarah were talking as they pushed each other while petting the dogs, giggling and laughing quietly. "Those two are alive solely because of you. *You* made that miracle happen."

Another magazine slammed home into the second rifle, and Ryan charged it, ticked the safety on, and shouldered it. "We're going to make another miracle happen."

"Remember our time limit – three hours, no more. No going more than a couple miles away from camp here, and no heading in the direction of the house." James picked up the pair of radios and handed one to Helen. "Keep the volume low and keep in constant contact – every fifteen minutes, even if you have nothing to report. If we hear three shots, we drop everything and come running back here. Do *not* overload yourselves – I'm talking to you in particular, Ryan. We're going to figure out where everything is first, then we'll take the tractor and trailer around and do a fast pickup later."

"Take care of yourselves." Ryan looked at Helen as she picked up one of the pistols from the trailer. "Ready?"

"Ready."

"Kids," James called, "we're heading out. Get the rest of these guns tucked away in the barn and cover up the trailer and tractor. Remember – three shots. Got it?"

"Got it, dad!" Jake called. "Stay safe!"

After a brief round of hugs, Ryan and Helen headed off through the trees while James and Alice went back through the park and open areas, sticking to the edge of the trees whenever possible, angling for the main road. While Ryan and Helen searched primarily for firearms and some of the materials needed for the tractor outfitting in a nearby neighborhood, James and Alice's job was to find the plate steel, filler rods and another tank of Argon gas.

Once out to the main road, James and Alice paused, looking back and forth down the abandoned stretch of pavement. The road was still as cracked and pothole-laden as it had been for years, the small town's finances unable to keep up with the maintenance required to fight against Michigan's harsh winters. A few cars were in ditches on the sides of the road, but it was clear for the most part, and the pair headed in the direction of the town's outskirts where the small strip of maintenance businesses sat.

Under normal conditions, heading into town meant that the rush of traffic from Interstate 69 would be audible, as would the sound of trucks and passenger vehicles from around the town proper. The silence was intense, at least in the artificial spectrum, and though birdsong, insects and the rush of breezes filled in many of the gaps, the lack of sound had a nauseating quality to it. Things were more natural and – arguably – more at peace, but that peace had come at a terrible, unshakable price that was impossible to completely push out of one's mind.

"It's way too quiet." Alice finally said, speaking just to fill the void.

"You realize that by saying that, you've condemned us to some sort of horrible fate, right?" James elbowed her in the arm, grinning.

"Oh no. Something horrible. However will we survive that." Alice rolled her eyes.

"I missed your sarcasm," James grinned. "And I missed this place, too. Can't say I much like walking down this road, though. It's nearly as bad as driving it."

"Mmm. So much for getting any more road repairs, ever."

"Not unless folks do it themselves."

"At least the feds are clearing the highways. Dad said there were two convoys they saw. Think we could get any help from them with our house situation? Call in that favor again?"

James chuckled. "I think *two* rides and four horses completely expended our favors with the Guard. My fixing up some vehicles only goes so far."

"Yeah... you're right. Plus, if we need them again in the future we want to be on their good side."

"And I don't want any blowback on Eli's family."

"Oh, that too... I didn't think about that." Alice sighed. "Oh well. Hey – there's Peterson's place. Think he'll have what you need for the welding stuff?"

"Yeah, he should. Might not have the right type of filler rods but anything'll work in a pinch. Hm. Tubing or t-posts would be good, too, for structural support. Not as great as solid steel made for the job, but I can't complain too much."

The pair entered the parking lot for *Peterson Plumbing Services LLC*, continuing to turn in full circles as they went, checking for signs of anyone that might be lurking around. The building itself was intact, though the parking area out front had two vans, three pickup trucks and a sedan that had all burned down to their core. The windows on the front of the plumbing store had been broken from the outside, and James entered first, stepping high to avoid a jagged row of glass at shin-level.

"Careful." He whispered, rifle at the ready. "Go left."

Alice nodded, shotgun to her shoulder as she headed to the left of the store, glancing down each darkened aisle as James did the same to the right. Several seconds later a loud whisper came from his direction as he called out an all-clear, and she did the same in return before meeting him back near the entrance.

"Keep an eye while I search?" James asked.

"On it. This place doesn't look like they took much, does it?"

James shrugged. "What's the average person going to get from a plumbing store that'd be useful right now, besides, like... water filters. I bet those are gone. Most of the rest is probably still intact."

"All right, well get to searching. Don't load up with too much."

"Only what we can carry." James slipped an empty duffel bag off his left shoulder and slung the rifle across his back.

Heading down the nearest aisle, James clicked on one of the small flashlights he'd received from the Guard, scanning the items before switching to another aisle, then another. On the fourth he finally found what he was looking for – welding filler rods, thin rods of metal used in the welding process to help bond together what the person was welding, as well as fill in any gaps that might need it. Ideally, the type of filler rod would match the material being welded – copper rods for copper, steel rods for steel, aluminum rods for aluminum – but try as he might, James could only find copper rods.

"I mean," he looked over the package, hemming and hawing as he mumbled to himself, "it's better than nothing. It'll bond reasonably well, but... just not ideal. Whatever." James stuffed three packs of the rods into his bag, then continued down the aisle, searching for tall black cylinders filled with Argon gas.

Nodding to Alice who was standing near the front of the store, watching out the broken window, James scoured the rest of the aisles before heading behind the broad counter. There was still no sign of the cylinders, so he continued through the double doors behind the counter that led to a small storage area with tall steel shelving units covered in thick pieces of wood. It didn't take long to cover the storage area, and soon James found what he was looking for – a dozen cylinders with varying labels on them, including two marked as Argon gas. At fifty or so pounds each, the steel cylinders weren't very heavy, but their length made them awkward to carry, and James had to throw the duffel on his back and carry the cylinders with both hands sideways through the double doors back into the shop.

"Get back!" Alice was at his side as he pushed through the doors, and he nearly dropped the cylinders as he stumbled backward, barely hanging on to them.

"What are—" James started to shout, but Alice clamped a hand over his mouth and shook her head vigorously, eyes wide in panic. He raised both eyebrows in question, looking over toward the doors and she nodded. "Three of them." Alice whispered. "We need to hide."

Still carrying the cylinders, James rushed back to where he'd found them and placed them among the others, then unslung his rifle and whispered to Alice. "Where are they?"

"Right out front by now. They snuck up on me – I barely heard them in time to sneak behind the counter, then you were coming through." She peeked out from behind a shelf to look at the double doors leading into the shop, trying to get a view through the rectangular windows set into each door. "Damn. They're out there."

A loud voice drifted from the front of the store, confirming what Alice said, and she spun to James. "I think we can take them."

"And what happens when they don't return? They'll send more people out to where these ones were sent." James shook his head. "Come on, farther back into the shelves. There's some boxes we can hide inside." The pair moved forward, Alice following after James into the far corner of the room where large boxes, crates and pallets were haphazardly stacked atop each other near a locked and chained rear door. Slipping behind the pile, they quickly pulled some of the cardboard atop themselves and stayed crouched low, still able to see through cracks in the pile.

"—see why we have to search *this* place. It's for friggin' plumbers." A male voice grew suddenly louder as the double doors swung open, loudly crashing against the walls as the three figures threw them open, looking into the darkened storage area beyond. "Why would they come *here*?"

"Red's gone crazy." A woman spoke next. "You want to try to lie to him and tell him we searched everywhere when we didn't, that's on your head. I'm not getting killed for you."

A dissatisfied grunt was the only reply as the three sets of footsteps clomped down between the rows of shelving units, each accompanied by a flashlight beam that swung around in fast, wide arcs indicative of a half-hearted search effort. James slowly reached for the radio clipped to his waist and turned the volume knob all the way down as the figures reached the back of the storage area, their backs to the pile of refuse as they gathered together again.

"Satisfied?" The original voice spoke again. "Or should we take a picture to show Red that we did our job?"

"Both of you shut up, or Red's going to hear from me that neither of you did your jobs." A third voice, another man, spoke, cutting off the woman as she started to reply.

"Like he'll believe you over the both of us?" the woman spoke harshly.

"He will because I'm with him and you two were just picked up along the way." The third voice spoke disdainfully. "And you'd better stop insulting him or I *will* tell him what you're saying."

The original two voices groaned and grumbled but said nothing more, and the three pairs of footsteps retreated as the third person spoke again. "Two more places to check then we're moving down a street. Get moving."

The voices grew indistinct once again and faded altogether, though Alice and James remained where they were for a few moments afterward. Moving slowly through the cardboard and wood pile, James emerged after holding up an index finger to Alice, rifle at the ready as he tip-toed across the back of the storage area, ensuring they were truly alone before finally relaxing.

"We're good. Man, that sucked."

"I guess we know who they were with, huh?" Alice came out, still standing behind the end of a row of shelves, peeking out at the double doors at the front of the room.

"No kidding." James headed up to the doors and watched through the windows for a moment before pulling the radio from his belt. He turned the volume knob back up and thumbed the transmit button. "Two, this is one. Come back." James repeated his message two more times before there was a click and a voice.

"We hear you. Anything wrong?" Ryan's voice was barely recognizable through the static and compression used by the radios, and though none of them thought that Red's group had any radios in their possession capable of picking up on their transmissions, not using names or specific locations was deemed to be the safest course of action regardless.

"We encountered three a while ago. No contact, but they're actively searching. Any signs at your end?"

"Completely dead. Do you need help?"

"Nope. We've found some of what we need, but we're going to keep searching and stay well clear of them."

"We'll keep our eyes open. Thanks for the heads up."

"Stay safe." James clipped the radio back on his belt and turned the volume knob down to the halfway mark. "Okay," he turned to Alice, "they're safe, thankfully."

"Good. Let's finish up here and get back to the kids... I don't like being out here if there are people actively searching for mom and dad. You had those gas tanks in your arms; do we need to take those with us?"

"No, they're too bulky; let's get them out and put them in the back of one of those cars in the parking lot so we can quickly pick them up with the tractor tomorrow when we do the final run. Here, get the doors for me and I'll grab 'em."

James retrieved the pair of cylinders again, carrying them across both arms through the double doors and the broken front windows of the store with Alice close by his side, watching in both directions. Heading to the sedan in the parking lot, James put the cylinders down near the rear and pushed open the blackened trunk, pieces of it falling off and coating his hands in rust and ash. He pushed both cylinders into the trunk and let the lid fall down, the spring tension that once held it open completely gone, then stepped back and nodded.

"Okay, we're good here."

"Where to next?"

James pointed down the road, toward the other businesses. "They said they were moving to a different street after they check a couple other places, so I'm guessing they went that way. We should go after them, but slowly, and see if we can find the plate steel."

"Let's go."

They skipped the next building – a combination dental office and accounting firm – and headed directly for a squat, wide brick structure, that housed a boat repair, servicing and storage business. The parking lot of the boat repair company was similar to that of the plumbing supply company, with all of the vehicles having been turned to scrap. Pausing behind a blackened, rusty shell of a van near the front of the store, James watched the storefront for a moment to ensure it was empty while Alice was next to him, looking at the van's paneling up and down.

"Why couldn't we use this?" She asked, and James turned to her.

"What?"

"Why couldn't we use the sides of some cars, like this van?"

"Ah." James turned back to look at the building. "Too much work, and too thin. We'd have to cut everything which would take a while, and the fire and rust will have compromised the already thin metal. It might stop a .22, but anything larger would punch through."

"Oh."

"I have a good feeling about Burt's here, though. C'mon – let's hurry."

James and Alice jogged toward the front of the store and passed through the broken windows that were once again broken from the outside. The inside of the store was largely intact, like the plumbing supply store had been, the people who'd broken in having not known what to do with the contents of the place, much like a dog catching a car.

"What about this?" Alice pointed to a nearby wall that was covered top to bottom and side to side with samples of materials used in building and repairing boats, from interiors to exteriors. Two foot by two foot sections of cloth, aluminum, plastic, vinyl and other materials were all labelled, and James skimmed them over, shaking his head at each one.

"No... nothing here'll work. Come on, let's check in back."

Once again, they walked through a double set of doors and entered a warehouse-like environment, though it was one that was far more open and larger than at the previous location. A few sets of tall shelves containing supplies sat off to one side, but most of the space was taken up by boats and boat trailers in various states of repair. A few were suspended by chains, some were up on lifts and a handful were on trailers, awaiting their turns for repair that would never come. The space was empty, most importantly, and if the men who'd come into the plumbing store had entered the boat shop, they'd already left, leaving no trace of their presence.

James passed by the rows of boats, glancing over them, running a hand along their sides as he whispered to himself, moving quickly to where a trailer was half-disassembled by the far wall. A grinder, welding torch and pieces of scrap metal were on the floor next to the trailer and he picked up one of the pieces of metal and examined it, turning it over in his hands.

"You find something?" Alice appeared and crouched down next to him.

"This is steel." James hefted the piece of metal, looking at the trailer. "Someone had a *steel* trailer? Why would they have that? Aluminum's what most of them are made out of."

"Maybe it's old?"

"Doesn't look like it."

"Are we... arguing about you finding something that we need?" Alice smirked and James snorted at himself, shaking his head.

"Yeah, sorry about that. I got lost in my own thoughts a bit there." James put the piece of scrap back down and stood up. "This means they've got steel here somewhere, though. Hopefully some big pieces. C'mon, let's check their storage shelves."

The pair passed through the rows of shelves until James found what he was looking for on the bottom of one of them – two large, bulky, impractically heavy pieces of three-quarter inch steel plating. James stood over the pieces, grinning from ear to ear as he kicked at the pieces with his foot. "Shoot... this is exactly what we need. I just don't know how we're going to get it out of here, though."

"Can't we just bring the tractor in?" Alice asked.

"Maybe?" James walked to the end of the aisle, looking at the large rows of rollup doors where the boats and trailers would be pulled into and out of the repair bays. "Good grief, though. We're going to make so much noise doing this."

"How long will it take to finish the tractor up once we have all the supplies?"

"A full day's worth of work. Maybe a day and a half." James kicked at the plating again. "I'll have to cut these to size before I can weld them, and then there's the whole getting them installed... hrm." James left the steel plate behind, walking toward the repair bays with Alice trailing behind him.

"What are you thinking now?"

"Well, for one thing, I'm glad they were smart enough to drain the tanks on the boats so they didn't go up in flames. But it's these hoists, the ones they have these boats on... they'd make the work on the tractor go a lot easier."

"You want to bring one of those back to camp, too?" Alice raised an eyebrow. "I don't think they'll fit on our little trailer. Not to mention how much they weigh."

"No, I'm thinking we bring everything *here*." James motioned to the room at large. "Look at all this stuff – they've got welding equipment, the hoists, the steel, and plenty of tools. It's perfect."

"It's also on the beaten path, where that Red fellow has people searching for mom and dad."

"True. Maybe we should go find them and kill them."

"*What?*" Alice was incredulous, and James turned to look at her.

"What do you mean, *what?*"

"My husband just casually suggested that we go kill people. That's *what*."

James shrugged. "Nothing casual about it. They took our home and want to kill *us*."

"I..." Alice let out a long, exasperated sigh. "I guess that's true. Still sounds very weird coming from your mouth."

"Believe me, there are a lot of things I've said and done the last few weeks that are weirder than that." James shook the chains of a hoist standing empty off to the side and nodded. "I still think this might be better than the camp for putting everything together. But we should talk to Ryan and Helen about it, see what they think."

"You ready to go back?"

James looked around, patting his duffel bag. "I've got the only thing we can really carry for now that we need, so yeah. Let's head back and see what they found." Thumbing the radio's volume knob up, James depressed the transmit button. "Two, this is one. All is good here. Found what we need and we're heading back. We'll talk once we're there."

CHAPTER FIVE

Red Fletcher
Somewhere outside East Lansing

"It's a... *safe*! How... can it be!?"

From upstairs, sitting in the dining room looking through the newly-repaired windows out at the long driveway, Martha flinched at every screamed, unintelligible word that filtered through the floorboards and up the staircase in the other room. Her fingers tightened around her mug as more shouting followed, her lips pressed tightly together, eyes closed as she breathed deeply in and out.

"Hey." A soft voice came from next to Martha and a hand patted her arm. "You okay?"

"Mm." Martha didn't open her eyes. "You should make yourself scarce. He's in a bad mood again."

"It seems like that's more common than not." Sandy sat down next to Martha, taking the older woman's free hand in her own, squeezing back as Martha gripped her hand fiercely. "You sure you're okay?"

"It wasn't supposed to be like this." A tear slipped from between Martha's left eyelid, running down her cheek. "First it was that couple, then the family, then those soldiers and now...." Martha inhaled deeply, opening her wet eyes to look at Sandy. "Go on. He'll be up any minute. Go be busy. Hurry."

Sandy stayed seated for a few seconds until another shout was followed by heavy clomping on the stairs. She squeezed Martha's hand once more, Martha nodded in response, then Sandy got up and hurried through the kitchen into the laundry room. The clomps on the stairs grew louder until the door to the basement was finally thrown open by the human maelstrom that had emerged from beneath the earth.

Dressed in dirt-covered jeans and a long-sleeved flannel shirt stolen from Ryan's belongings, Red Fletcher stormed through the living room and into the kitchen, turning on the tap and grabbing a plastic cup from a pile near the sink. He filled it with water and swallowed noisily, spitting some back out, rinsing his mouth, then swallowing more. Throwing the cup back down onto the counter, Red took a hand towel from the counter next to the sink and stalked through the kitchen into the dining room, circling around Martha to stand directly in front of her, blocking her view as he looked through the window.

"Things aren't going well, I take it?" Martha spoke quietly, closing her eyes and gripping her mug tight again.

"Damn straight it's not going well." Red turned, throwing his arms in the air, the built-up tension and desire to rant finally letting loose. "Those idiots can't get a freaking *safe* open even with power tools and days to work on it. 'Oh it's too hard, oh it's just not working, oh we can't' – no, *I* just can't with *them*. They're useless, Martha. Absolutely useless!"

"I'm sorry."

Red flopped into the chair next to her, grabbing her hand, nearly spilling her coffee in the process. "This was supposed to be easier than it's been, you know? Then those two assholes had to go and *ruin* everything. How're we supposed to get food in the ground in the Spring without the tractor? The barn's all torn to hell so the animals can get out whenever they want, too."

"And people died." Martha's voice was still quiet.

"Yeah, we lost some good labor. Maybe we shoulda just stayed where we were. Less trouble that way." Red sighed and picked up Martha's coffee, sniffing it. "Then again, we wouldn't have this if we'd stayed put."

"Nope." A slight, forced smile appeared as Martha turned to look at her husband, then back out the window.

"Well, you keep up your good work. I'm going back down there to kick their butts some more." Red stomped on the floor, yelling at it. "Here that? I'm on the way back down!"

Red took a drink from Martha's coffee cup, put it down and stood, tromping his way through the dining room and living room back to the basement door before throwing it back open and heading down the stairs. At the table, Martha looked at the coffee cup for a long moment before closing her eyes and sighing yet again, fist clenched so tight her knuckles and fingers were white.

The normally semi-dark basement was aglow with half a dozen flashlights and lanterns, and the smell of body odor was deep, permeating into the concrete walls of the small room where three men were crowded around together, grumbling and shoving as they worked. Two stood shoulder-to-shoulder near the entrance to the room, one holding a lantern while the other held a flashlight, both of them pressing a hand to one ear, tilting their other ear against their shoulder. The third man, on his knees in front of the two, had a set of shooting ear guards on, and he wielded a cutoff tool that smoked as he pressed it against the safe, a dozen broken cutting wheels scattered on the ground in front of him.

Sweat flowed from the third man's face as he pushed in with the cutting tool, the alloy wheel glowing shades of red and orange as it progressed down a long, slender trough in the metal, extending the cut millimeter by agonizing millimeter. A shower of sparks flew across the plastic shield covering his face and the thick leather jacket he had on backwards to cover his chest, and every once in a while one of the men behind him would grab a spray bottle filled with water and use it to douse a spark that landed on cloth, hair, or a nearby wooden shelf.

Even with the high-pitched wailing of metal upon metal blocking almost all sound, Red Fletcher's reappearance was unmissable, his form darkening the glow of lanterns that were set up in the adjoining room, the smell of rank coffee breath coming in long, shallow wheezes behind the three men. He stood silent for a few long moments, hands over his ears as he watched the man work at the safe with the grinding wheel until it, too, finally shattered.

"Son of a—" the man exclaimed, turning in frustration and catching sight of Red's boots through the legs of the other two men. "Red? Look, man, I'm sorry, okay? I get about two inches from each of these damned things before they break."

"Get out of the way." Red growled. The two men shuffled past Red, avoiding his gaze. "You too, Tyler."

As Tyler pushed himself up off the floor, he spotted a long steel tube in Red's hand, seven feet tall and covered in paint and stains. "You got a plan, Red?"

"I *always* have a plan." Red glared at Tyler. "Get out of my way and pass me that prybar off the workbench."

Handing Red the long red prybar, Tyler stood out of the way with the other two men, none of them daring to leave the basement without an explicit dismissal from Red. As they watched, Red looked the waist-high safe over, pushing back and forth on it, though it was rock-steady, not moving so much as a hairsbreadth.

"This isn't right." Red grunted, pushing on the safe again with all his weight, but it still didn't budge. "Hm."

Frowning, Red ran his finger along the L-shaped cut that had been made in the safe's door at the upper left corner, approximately one foot long on each side. He and the others had tried to get a look at the safe's contents through the crack, but nothing was visible, and it was unknown whether or not the cuts were deep enough to even pierce all the way through the door or not. Taking the prybar in hand, he jammed it into the upper corner of the cut at an angle, getting it a couple of inches deep before the increasing thickness of the bar's end prevented it from penetrating any farther. Once the prybar was secured, Red moved the steel pipe into place over the end of the prybar, sliding it down until the pipe itself was touching the body of the safe, effectively extending the handle of the tool by an additional seven feet.

"Get over here and help me push," Red called over his shoulder as he began pushing up on the pipe, flexing the prybar against the steel of the safe. Tyler came to his aid and they pushed together, maneuvering the pipe around the ceiling joists and cabling that ran between them. Working from the far end of the pipe, they were easily able to begin prying the cut corner of the door outward, first by an inch, then by two, then three. Before long, the pipe was hitting the ceiling subflooring atop the joists, and they were out of room to continue leveraging the prybar against the safe door, so Red called for a halt and let off of the pipe, the prybar sliding out of it and clattering to the ground.

"Holy cow, Red." Tyler whistled. "It's open!"

"Not hardly. Give me a flashlight." Red held out his hand until one of the other men slapped a light into it, then he handed the pipe to Tyler and leaned in over the newly-created hole in the safe, peering inward. "Just what I thought. Look."

Tyler stood next to Red, examining the couple-inch gap to find a space inside the door and another piece of steel on the backside of the space. "Double-walled?"

"Looks like it." Red nodded. "C'mon, let's pry this open more so we can get at the mechanism in the middle easier."

"What for?"

"You'll see." Red looked over his shoulder at the two men standing in the next room. "You, go get a roll of aluminum foil. Grate it through a cheese grater, then run it through a food processor in the kitchen. I want aluminum powder. Needs to be no coarser than coffee grounds – understand me?" The first man nodded and Red turned his attention to the second man. "Get a putty knife or something and a jar or jug. Go around and collect up rust."

"R-rust?" The man stammered.

"Rust."

"Where do I find Rust, Red?"

Red's eyes widened as the volume of his voice raised. "We live in *Michigan* you idiot! There's rust *everywhere* around here! Get it off of cars, buildings, your ass – I don't care, just get me a couple soda cans worth of it, understand me?"

"I... yeah, Red." The second man looked at the first, and they both nodded in unison. "Yeah we got it."

"You two have half an hour. Make it snappy."

"Red?" Tyler asked after the two men fell over each other to escape their leader's wrath.

"What."

"You making thermite?"

"Crude thermite, but yes." Red grinned as he directed his attention back at the safe. "Now c'mon. Let's get this thing pried open some more."

Just under thirty minutes later, after an intense amount of effort on the part of Red and Tyler, the safe's front door panel had been peeled outward on the upper lefthand side like a soup can top, revealing a steel box near the center of the door that penetrated through both layers, containing the locking mechanism. The two men leaned against the walls of the room, sweating and panting as they looked over their work, waiting for the other pair to come back with the ingredients Red had demanded.

"Why... why don't we just burn it open from the top?" Tyler panted, the prybar in his hands bent in multiple places, most of its red paint gone.

"I'm gonna let you think about that one for a hot second and let you tell *me* why that's a bad idea."

Tyler narrowed his eyes at the safe for several long seconds before widening them in realization. "Oh. It might burn through and damage what's inside."

Red bopped Tyler in the head a few times with a fist. "Exactly. Speaking of burning – where are those two idiots? Those stairs are playing hell with my knees and I do *not* want to head back up there."

The sound of multiple feet stomping through the house was followed by the throwing open of the basement door, and the owners of the footsteps rapid descent down the basement stairs. The pair who'd been there with Tyler before emerged, each holding out a mason jar, one filled with an orange powder and the other filled with a silver powder.

"Here you go, Red." The one holding the iron oxide panted. "I got most of it from piles of junk around the back woods, and the rest from some cars at the neighbors house down at the end of the driveway."

Red took the jars and shook them, nodding in approval. "Good work. The aluminum could be finer."

"Red, I've had the food processors – both of 'em – going nonstop. The blades are dull and they don't have any spares. I swear this is the best we can do."

"It'll have to be enough." Red nodded. "Get out of here, both of you. Find some fans and start getting some air circulating down here. We're about to make a *lot* of smoke."

Placing both jars down on top of the safe, Red grabbed a spoon sitting on a nearby shelf, glancing over the jars of food with a raised brow before turning to Tyler. "Find me some matchbooks. I need a couple dozen matches."

"Matches. Right. On it, Red." Tyler hurried out into the basement proper, heading up the stairs to ask around for matches.

Using the spoon, Red measured out a small amount of aluminum and approximately three times as much iron oxide, mixing it together in one of the jar lids until the powders were thoroughly blended together. By the time he finished, Tyler had returned with a large box of matches which Red took and retrieved a small handful from, breaking most of them off at the head. He first spread thermite on the box inside the door, placing several match heads atop the pile, with one intact match sticking out of the top of the pile, then made a larger pile on the far right front corner of the safe, above where the bolts would hold the door in place to the frame of the safe.

"Red? Why're you putting it on the edge?"

"Belt and suspenders, Tyler. I think we'll be just fine burning through to the mechanism so we can turn those bolts and open this sucker up, but just in case that doesn't work like I think, we'll just burn this entire corner off so that the door'll swing freely."

"Ain't that gonna burn through to the inside of the safe?"

"It might. Which is why we're gonna do that *after* we see if burning through the mechanism works first. You ready?"

Tyler nodded, taking a step back and nearly bumping into a fan that had been set up on the floor outside the room. "Yeah. Give it a rip. I'll get the fans turned on."

Red grunted in affirmation, then took a single match from the box, striking it on the side and holding it to the one sticking out of the pile of thermite sitting inside the door, atop the mechanism's sheath. "One opened safe, coming up."

The match atop the pile flared to life then died down, the flame making its way across a couple of centimeters of wood with no sign of fanfare. When it reached the match heads sitting atop the pile, though, they whooshed to life, and their ignition started a chain reaction in the aluminum and iron oxide that seemed brighter than the sun itself. The entire pile glowed a brilliant white, sending off waves of heat, sparks and smoke that drove Red back, waving his hand in front of his face as he coughed violently.

Backing out of the room, Red turned the fan around so that it began pulling air out of the enclosed space, and Tyler went ahead of him, doing the same to the rest of them until a chain of fans was pulling smoke into the basement at large, and through the open windows and doors near the walkout section. The hiss of the burning thermite was loud even through the three walls separating the men from the chemical reaction, and Tyler shouted to Red to be heard. "How long's it gonna take?"

"Couple of minutes at most. Go find a fire extinguisher, just in case the shelves catch fire."

"Okay!" Tyler ran upstairs to find an extinguisher while Red lingered near a window, leaning in to glance down the hallway every few seconds to check and ensure that nothing else in the room was aflame.

By the time Tyler returned with an extinguisher from under the kitchen cabinet, the thermite reaction had all but burned out, though Red refrained from entering the small room until the fans had run for several more minutes. Smoke still hanging heavy in the air, he and Tyler ventured in, covering their mouths and noses with the tops of their shirts.

"Nothing's burning," Tyler looked around the small room. "That's good."

Red ignored the man, kneeling down in front of the safe with a flashlight to look inside the peeled-open door. The boxy covering over the center mechanism had been turned to slag where the thermite had been the thickest, much of the metal dripping down to the base of the inside of the door, though some of it still hung suspended where it had re-solidified, resembling silvery droplets of water suspended in midair.

Most importantly, the internals of the protective casing appeared to have been thoroughly destroyed, and Red held a hand up, wiggling his fingers at Tyler. "Water."

Tyler ran out of the room, retuning a moment later with a cup of water which Red took and poured over the damaged mechanism inside the safe's door, the water hissing slightly as it made contact with the heated metal. After cooling it down, Red reached in and felt the rod that extended from the back of the safe's door, gingerly gripping the jagged end and turning it. It resisted movement for a moment, then gave way with a soft *clunk*. Red smiled and stood up, handing the cup back to Tyler before gesturing to the safe with a flourish.

"I present to you," he said, pulling on the door, "one opened safe."

Creaking as the damaged corner rubbed against the side of the safe's body, the door opened without hesitation, revealing a deep, tall space inside that brightened as an internal light clicked on, revealing the contents therein.

"What the hell kind of safe is *that?*" Tyler asked from behind Red, both men cocking their heads at an angle in simultaneous confusion.

While most safes were symmetric in design, designed to be bolted to studs, joists or concrete flooring, the safe in the Burton household was neither symmetric nor bolted to the concrete floor. From the outside, it appeared as though it was a small, four-foot high steel box, when in actuality the safe's interior extended another four feet below the floor, the lower half surrounded by concrete which kept it safe and virtually impossible to remove without demolition equipment. The door to the safe was located on the top half of the structure, which helped give the impression that it was smaller than it actually was.

"I have no idea," Red said, looking the safe over from the left and right before shrugging. "Clever design though. You couldn't get that out of there without a jackhammer or dynamite."

"Good thing the door lock sucked, huh?" Tyler chuckled, giving Red a light punch on the arm before the man's stern glare cut Tyler's laugh off in his throat.

Kneeling down in front of the safe, Red looked inside, his trademark insidious smile growing. He reached down into the safe, grabbing boxes of ammunition and handed them to Tyler, who shuffled out of the room and placed them on a workbench before coming back for more. Once the ammunition was out of the safe, Red retrieved an antique-looking revolver and a double-barrel shotgun, both of which Tyler took to the workbench as well.

"That it, Red?" Tyler said, hands on his hips as he watched Red continue to fish around inside the safe.

"I dunno. Seems like an awfully small arsenal to keep in here."

"Maybe they have another one hidden in the house?"

"Probably. But I can't help but think this one—ha!" Feeling around on the velvety interior of the steel box, Red finally located a small string and pulled it. One of the soft walls of the safe collapsed in response, revealing a small, hidden interior compartment separate from the main one. Grabbing at the pocket, Red pulled out a long tan barrel weighing around twenty-five pounds, then a receiver and stock assembly in the same color, weighing another fifteen pounds.

"Jeez, these are heavy." Tyler complained as he hauled the pieces to the workbench, followed by Red. "That it?"

"Yep. Safe's empty."

"Not much in there besides ammo, huh?"

"Mm." Red pushed the shotgun and revolver aside. "Take these upstairs, figure out who needs a gun, and distribute them."

"What about that?" Tyler pointed at the two pieces of tan metal lying side-by-side on the workbench.

Red grinned. "This one's mine."

Sandy hummed quietly to herself as she stood in front of a sink filled with soapy water, allowing the rhythmic back and forth of the scrubbing to take over her mind and distract her from the worries that threatened to consume her. Each plate received twelve scrubs with the sponge in the left sink – five back and forth in one direction, then five more perpendicular, then one swirl on the top, and a swirl across the bottom – before it was dunked into the right sink for a quick rinse, then handed off to Martha who dried and stacked things up.

As Sandy was passing a plate to Martha to dry, the windows of the house all rattled as a small explosion went off out front, and Martha fumbled the plate, dropping it to the hardwood floor where it shattered, making both women jump a second time. Another explosion followed the first, and Sandy nearly slipped on a large piece of broken ceramic as she whirled, heart thumping.

"What's going on?!" Martha shouted, grabbing Sandy's hand, both women looking at each other, then out through the front windows.

"I—" Another explosion rang out, followed by a faint shout from someone – not of pain, but exhilaration and joy. "I don't know!" Sandy finished her sentence.

Both she and Martha ran to the front windows in the dining room, stepping over the largest shards of plate on the floor, both still thankfully wearing their shoes instead of just being in socks or bare feet. A fourth explosion rattled the glass again, both women covering their ears as they looked through the windows to find the source, spotting Red lying in the front yard with a large rifle on his shoulder, aiming at the pond several hundred feet away. He fired for a fifth time, fire erupting from the tan barrel of the Barrett M107A1, the shock wave rippling through the air, visibly moving the hair and clothing of those around him, and causing the windows in the house to all rattle again.

Out at the edge of the pond, a pile of feathers and splotch of red indicated that one of Red's initial shots had landed, turning one of the ducks into nothing more than a fine mist. The rest of them had scattered, though, taking to the sky to circle the house while they quacked frantically. The barnyard animals were responding more violently to the disturbance, though, with a sixth shot at one of the colorful Koi swimming in the pond sending the sheep bumping against each other and the fence, bending one of the fenceposts over a few inches before they panicked in a new direction. The chickens circled amongst the sheep, a few of them getting stepped on by the larger animals as they clucked and flapped, and from inside the barn Bessie's lowing was long and loud.

"Red Fletcher!" Martha pushed down the window and shouted, her voice cutting through the coarse laughter of the men assembled out front. "What the *hell* do you think you're doing?!"

Red pushed himself up off the ground, lifting the rifle and grinning as he walked toward the front of the house. "Just testing my new toy out! What do you think? The scope is *good* – only took me two shots to hit a duck, and a few more to hit one of those fish! I'm gonna turn Ryan and Helen into some fine pink mist with this sucker, just you watch!"

"Are you out of your mind?" Martha's normally quiet, acquiescent manner was temporarily gone, fire burning in her eyes and voice as she pointed at the barnyard. "You're killing things we might need to eat one day, and scaring other parts of our food supply half to death!"

Red looked over at the cluster of animals and shrugged, dropping the butt end of the rifle to rest on his foot, pushing the hot barrel back and forth between his hands. "They'll live. Who pissed in your cereal this morning?"

"*You* did. Knock it off with that thing; go shoot it in the back field if you want to waste your time and valuable ammunition playing around. Stop jeopardizing what we need to survive!" Martha shook her head and slammed the window back down, rubbing her eyes with the palms of both hands.

"You okay?" Sandy asked, putting an arm around Martha to lead her through the dining room and back into the kitchen. "You want something to drink? Coffee?"

Martha sighed and nodded. "Sure. Thanks, Sandy. I shouldn't yell at him like that – especially not when he's so irritable – but...."

"We might need those animals to survive. Even the ducks."

"I don't think there's a 'might' about it." A new voice came from the direction of the basement stairs where Nancy Likely emerged, holding a notebook in her hand.

"Oh no." Martha groaned. "Don't tell me there's *more* bad news. I don't think Red can handle more of that right now."

"Bad news? No, this is *awful* news." Nancy circled to the far side of the tall counter opposite Martha and Sandy, eying the younger woman suspiciously before slapping her notebook down with a sharp crack.

"You have a problem with me, Nancy?" Sandy stirred some milk into a cup of coffee before handing the cup to Martha.

"I think it's Red who's going to have the problem." Nancy pushed the notebook across the counter. "Our stores of food are *not* matching what you and Helen wrote down before. We have *maybe* a couple weeks' worth of food left."

Sandy picked up the notebook, looking at the two columns on it. The first appeared to be the numbers that she and Helen had made note of previously, though many of them were scratched out and replaced with different numbers in Nancy's handwriting. All of the replacements were smaller than the original numbers, and a few were circled several times and had exclamation points off to the side.

"I don't know what you're getting at, Nancy." Sandy put the notebook back down, meeting Nancy's stern gaze head-on, ignoring the rapid increase in her heart rate. "Helen did the writing; I just counted things and reported them to her."

"Uh huh. We'll see what Red has to say about that." Nancy glanced at Martha. "Where is he, anyway?"

"Out front, playing the fool." Martha sipped from her coffee. "If you want to accuse people here of doing something wrong, just come out with it. Otherwise, go away and let us get our work done."

Taking the notebook back, Nancy marched off toward the front door while Martha and Sandy exchanged a look. "Red's not going to be happy," Martha spoke first.

"I—I really didn't—"

Martha held up a hand. "Despite appearances to the contrary, I'm no fool. Please don't treat me like one. What you did or didn't do is of no concern to me. The only thing I care about is making sure Red doesn't threaten – or God forbid harm – anyone else here again. This mess has gotten far too out of control for me to care about anything else."

"Thanks, Martha."

"Don't thank me yet." Martha patted Sandy's hand. "Come on. Let's get some food started before he comes storming in here."

'Storming' was the appropriate descriptor, for a veritable hurricane blew through the door ten minutes after Nancy Likely had gone outside. Red Fletcher slammed into the door as he twisted the handle, releasing it to send it flying back and bounce off the drywall with a crunch, leaving a half-inch dent in the wall and a slight crack in the wood of the door itself. Nancy followed after him, along with a couple of stragglers who had been with Red out front as he fired the Barrett, one of them taking the gun as he half-handed, half-threw it at them.

"Where is she?!" Red bellowed as he stomped through the dining room, pointing a finger at Sandy and Martha as they stood at the counter, large mixing bowls in front of them. "There you are, you *snake*!"

"Red..." Martha started, patting his arm with a flour-coated hand. "I don't know what's going on, but please calm down? Some of the kids are sleeping upstairs. We don't need to be yelling, no matter what it is."

Red glared at Martha for a few seconds, then spoke slightly quieter, teeth clenched, words spat through them in a hiss. "Nancy just told me about our food situation, about how we have *far* less than we thought!" He pointed at Sandy and thrust the notebook forward. "It's *your* fault! You were with Helen, tallying up the supplies, weren't you? You wrote in this book, didn't you?"

"I—I wrote the numbers down, yes. But I didn't count most of the stuff, I swear. Helen did that and told me numbers to write down." She pointed at a few lines that hadn't been crossed out by Nancy. "I counted these, Red. That's why they're correct. I swear I didn't count the others, though; she must have told me the wrong numbers on purpose. I'm sorry, Red."

"Ignorance? Really? That's the excuse you're going with?" Red turned from Sandy, shifting his ire to his wife. "And what's your excuse, huh? Why didn't you catch this?"

"Red, I—"

"These are *huge* discrepancies, Martha!" Red's face began to flush as he started to shout again. "Look at this – two hundred cans of soup. We have *twelve*. Twelve! Sixty five-gallon jars of glassed eggs turns out to be twenty!" Martha took the notebook, casting a wary glance at Red as he whirled, continuing his rant as he paced between the kitchen and dining room. "We don't have anywhere *near* the amount of food we all thought we did. Those lying sacks of...." Red put his hands to his face and groaned.

"How much do we have?" Sandy asked.

"Bout two weeks or so, give or take." Nancy answered from the other side of the counter from where she'd been watching the goings-on. "That's if we just eat two meals a day, a couple thousand calories per person."

"Under normal conditions that would be fine," Martha flipped through the pages of the notebook, "but given we're all expending a lot more energy than we otherwise would...."

"Exactly." Red rolled his neck back and forth until a sharp crack finally came from it. "Now you see the predicament we're all in, thanks to the damned Coopers." Red looked over at Sandy, then Martha. "Don't think you're off the hook. Both of you should have caught this."

"This is bad," Martha agreed, closing the notebook and putting it on the counter. "But I think it's time we focused on solutions rather than pointing fingers at people who aren't here anymore."

"And what sort of solutions do you have in mind?" Nancy snorted, continuing as Red nodded in agreement. "The bit of scavenging we've done around here hasn't turned up much so far."

"We can expand outward?" Sandy suggested. "Once the truck is fixed, a group can head out and about – maybe even to the city? There's that tank of diesel in the barn, right?"

"We'd be lucky to get anything from the city," Nancy answered before Red could, again receiving a nod of agreement from him. "We need to focus on the long-term. That's why you came here, right, Red?"

"Yes it is." He growled. "Stored food will only take us so far. We need to get crops planted and more animals rounded up. But that takes time, which we don't have, since we need stored food to get us through the winter and into spring. And if there's none around, then we're up a creek without a paddle." Red sighed and strode to the front window, looking down at the barnyard. "We may need to think about slaughtering some of those animals sooner rather than later."

"Slaughtering the animals?" Martha came up beside him. "You want to *kill* our food sources?"

"What do we get out of the sheep?"

"Milk, used to make cheese. The chickens give us eggs and the cow gives us milk. How is our long-term outlook going to be improved if we start killing our meager supply of food providers right now? Maybe in a year or two, once we have a lot more chickens and sheep, we can start culling a few here and there for meat. But look at them," Martha pointed out at the flocks. "Not all of them will survive the winter or predators as it is. And you want to kill them, too?"

Contrary to his usual reaction, Red was quiet for a few minutes as he watched the people and animals milling about outside. "Okay," he finally replied, calm and collected in contrast to his previous outbursts. "You might have a point. *Might*. But we still have a major problem of too many mouths to feed and *way* too little food to go around."

"I'm sure we can figure a way through it," Martha took his arm, smiling thinly. "Wider scavenging runs, perhaps? Trying to find some more animals in the surrounding area to bolster the flocks? Maybe we can find some cattle and butcher and freeze them."

"All well and dandy, but we gotta think short term, too." Red pointed out at the small tent and RV collection in the side yard, off to the side of the house and barn. "All those people are eating off of what we've got here. We need to figure out who's critical and who can be cut loose."

"If you do that," Sandy spoke up from in the kitchen, nervously glancing at Nancy, "people are going to be pretty mad. Don't you think they might fight you on that?"

Red walked over to the front entry where the man had placed the rifle, hefting the forty-pound gun as he moved back into the dining room. His arms strained as he examined the weapon, turning it over a few times before he looked up at Sandy, mouth twisted into a maniacal grin. "Let them try. Let. Them. Try."

CHAPTER SIX

The Burton/Cooper Family
Somewhere outside East Lansing

James and Alice stayed off the roads the entire way back to the campsite, preferring the depths of the trees and thick brush and tall, browning stalks of cornfields to anything that was paved with asphalt, dirt or gravel. They neither heard nor saw any signs of more search parties from the people who occupied their home, and after a short time finally arrived back at the old ramshackle barn. Sarah, Jake, Helen and Ryan were nowhere to be seen until they were practically inside the barn, at which point the dogs leapt up and greeted their masters, followed by the people who'd been lurking in the shadows, guns at the ready to deliver a measure of harm upon any who would seek to do the same to them.

"Were you followed?" Ryan asked, looking past his daughter and son-in-law.

"No, we took the woods and fields." Alice looked at James. "Neither of us wanted to risk being spotted walking in this direction."

"Any idea who it was who was there with you?"

"None." James shook his head. "They didn't say any names other than Red's. And I'm guessing there's only one Red around here worth talking about. How about you two – any signs of people?"

"We heard voices a couple miles from here, around the neighborhood, but no idea if it was Red's people or not. After that, and what you said on the radio, we stuck to the trees as well."

"Good." James and Alice both visibly relaxed, and James took the duffle bags off his back, throwing them to the ground.

"I thought you said you got all you needed," Ryan raised an eyebrow, looking at the bags. "Is that all you need?"

"No, the rest was too heavy to carry. All I've got in there are the welding sticks. The gas and steel plates are at the plumbing shop and the boat repair place. That's actually what I wanted to talk to you all about."

"Here," Helen circled around the fire, two mugs clutched in her left hand by the handles which she held out to James and Alice. "Before you all start talking again, take these. Coffee with some hot chocolate powder mixed in. Poor man's mocha – drink up, both of you."

"Thanks, mom." Alice smiled and James nodded in appreciation as they both took their steaming mugs and took a few sips.

"Alright, out with it, boy," Ryan put his mug down on a cinderblock near the edge of the fire to keep the drink warm. "What's this you wanted to talk about?"

"I think we should move camp." James looked at Alice, who shrugged, and Helen and Ryan both gave each other a look before Ryan responded.

"Move camp? To... where, exactly?"

"The boat repair shop."

"Why?" Jake asked. "Isn't this safe here where we are?"

"That's... yes, yes this is safer." James conceded. "But hear me out. We need to get a move-on with our plans. A day or two max to finish up armoring up the tractor and then taking the fight to Red before he can recruit more people or hunt us down. We can spend a few hours trundling along in that thing to pick up the supplies, lug them back here and start working and hope we don't need to do what you *always* have to do for a home improvement project – go back to the store fifteen times - or we can just take everything to the hardware store and save all that hassle."

"And it's not safer because?" Alice gave James a pointed look.

"Because the boat repair shop's on the main thoroughfare. Thanks much. That was shockingly good." James smiled at Helen as he finished his mug of coffee and put it down. "And the main thoroughfare's where the plumbing supply store is, which is where that group was when they nearly tripped over us."

"Much higher chance to be found by Red... I don't like it." Ryan's jowls jiggled slightly as he shook his head. "No, no I don't like that at all."

"To be fair, we don't know that this place is really all *that* safe," Alice shrugged, "but I kind of have to agree with Dad on this. Sorry, hon."

"Don't be." James dismissed her with a wave of his hand. "If you guys think it's safer to stay here and work, then we'll do that and figure it out as we go along. Speaking of work, though – did you two find what you were looking for?"

"Ah!" Ryan stood up from the crate he was seated on and smiled, pointing to a duffle on a makeshift table in the corner. "Yes indeed, yes indeedy we did. Come look."

Unlike James's duffle bag, Ryan's was misshapen and overflowing to nearly bursting, with hard protrusions in multiple places on its sides and the zipper only halfway closed. Opening it, Ryan began to hand its contents to James, who laid them out on the large piece of plywood that served as a table. Three handguns, two rifles, several boxes of ammunition and a dozen magazines for the weapons came out first, followed by some shelf mounting brackets, balls of twine, screws, a cordless screwdriver and a small toolbox with screwdrivers and a few common sizes of sockets along with a large and small ratchet.

"What you said about putting extra guns in the tractor got me thinking that you'd need something to mount them *with*, so I figured you could weld these steel shelf brackets to the inside of the compartments for a makeshift set of mounts."

"Nice thinking, Ryan." James picked through the pile of supplies. "This is perfect. Looks like there's plenty of ammo for the rifles, so we'll use those. It'll be more intimidating to have the rifle barrels poking through the metal anyway."

"Do you think that'll really matter to these people?" Helen asked. "I don't think they'll be easily frightened."

"It's not about scaring them," Ryan answered before James could. "Psychology's half of warfare. Anything we can do to make them think they're at a disadvantage bumps up our chances of success."

"Make no mistake, mom – this *is* war." Alice picked up one of the pistols, hefting it and ejecting an empty magazine before clearing the chamber and looking inside for signs of wear and tear.

"Oh I know it, sweetie. And it's one we're going to win." Helen's thin smile chilled James to the core.

"You're a frightening woman sometimes, Helen. C'mon, let's get the trailer uncovered and get the tractor ready to go out on that salvage run. Oh, Ryan, did you find any kind of steel bars for supports?"

"Yep, couldn't fit them into the bag, though."

"How far away are they?"

Ryan wagged his head back and forth. "Ehh... three miles, maybe, give or take."

"We'll leave those for the time being, then. The boat repair place has some that I think will work, and they're closer. I don't want to be out and about with an engine running for longer than we—"

"Dad!" Jake ran into the barn from where he and Sarah had been standing outside with the dogs keeping watch. "Someone's coming!"

The four adults glanced at each other before dropping the items they'd been poring over and grabbing their weapons that they'd put down earlier. Alice gestured for Jake and Sarah to hurry inside, and they were followed by the three dogs who kept looking behind and growling out at the open field of the park beyond the barn.

"Where are they?" James took to one knee and shouldered his rifle as he stared out in the direction his children had pointed when they came in. Jake stood behind him, gesturing to the outline of park equipment in the far distance.

"We saw someone moving out there by the swingsets and stuff. We waited a minute because we didn't know for sure if we really saw someone, but then we saw two more of them."

"Crap." James glanced at Alice. "What're the chances it's *not* those yahoos from the store?"

"Slim to none I'd say. What do you want to do?"

"I don't exactly want to get in a shootout, but if they come over here and find us then we're going to have a shootout on our hands." James leaned out, looking over at the tractor and trailer, the former of which was parked in a thick stand of bushes and the latter of which was covered in a tarp, branches and piles of dead leaves. "I don't think that concealment's going to work if they get up close."

"We can spread out," Ryan stood on the other side of the doorframe, also watching for the people Jake and Sarah had seen. "In the trees and in the barn. When they get close we take them all down at once. Easy as pie."

"We're close enough to the house that they might hear the gunshots. If they come investigating…"

"Did you recognize them?" James asked Alice.

"Who?"

"The three from the store – did you recognize them? Because I didn't."

"No, but—"

"Okay. I know what to do. Kids stay in the barn with the dogs – do *not* let them out unless a fight breaks out. Alice, you and your parents spread out. Stay well-hidden. I'm going to meet these people and see if I can talk my way out of them coming closer." James nodded out toward the open area of the park. "There they are, by the trees. I need to go."

"You're going *out?*" Helen hissed at him. "Are you crazy?!"

"No way. You're not going out there." Alice grabbed at his shoulder.

James leaned his rifle against the door and unbuckled the holster from his belt, taking his pistol and tucking it into his pocket before scooping some dirt and mud from the ground and rubbing it on his face and clothes, smearing it on his shirt and pants on both the front and back. "They don't *know* me, guys. Will you just trust me? If anything goes south, I'll drop flat on the ground and you'll have a clear target to taking them out."

Slipping out of Alice's grasp, James adopted a slight limp as he ran out of the barn, hands up in the air, shouting at the trio of men. Behind him, the others looked at each other before scrambling to spread out in the barn and behind the tractor off to the side of it, forming a wide firing arc, all while Alice silently prayed that her husband hadn't just run head-long to his own demise.

"I still don't see why we need to search out here." A man in a long, dark coat gestured to the park as he and two others walked past the playground equipment. "There's no tire tracks – not that you could see 'em even if there was – and why would two old farts pick a park to hide in?"

"They're probably long gone," one of the others agreed, "but if we don't search…."

"Yeah, yeah."

"Will you two shut up and just keep your eyes open?" The third man, older than the pair and one of Red Fletcher's original group from Grand Rapids, admonished them. "Do you want to let them know we're looking for them?"

"Oh, come on, that old man can't hear worth anything. And his wife's the same way."

"I said, shut *up.*" The older one clutched his rifle to his shoulder and pointed ahead. "I hear someone coming."

The sounds of something crashing through the undergrowth in the woods nearby drew the trio's attention, and a shape soon emerged. A man staggered out, covered in dirt and grime, hands held up as he caught sight of the three men, eyes wide in fright. "Oh sh—please, please don't kill me!" The man dropped to his knees, hands still up, voice cracking as he sobbed. "No, please! I'm just trying to find some food! Please don't kill me!"

"Who the hell's that?" The older man asked the other two, who both shrugged.

"Never seen him before."

"Same. Dunno, he could be anyone."

"Who are you?" The leader of the group kept his rifle at the ready, though it wasn't pointed at the filthy man in front of them.

"Carver! Jimmy Carver! I—I'm just tryin' t' find some food, man, that's all."

"Where'd you come from?"

"Back there," James pointed in the direction of the dilapidated barn, hand shaking in an exaggerated fashion as he kept his gaze low, avoiding the men's eyes in a deferential pose. "Found a barn I've been squatting in. Man I'm so hungry though. You guys have anything you can spare? Haven't had anything to eat since I found couple garter snakes a couple days ago."

"You seen an old man and lady?" One of the two locals stepped to the side a few paces, craning to see the barn in the distance. "Would have been driving a tractor with a trailer and three dogs, too."

"Dogs?" James's eyes widened and he slowly stood to his feet, gaze occasionally flicking to the older of the three men, watching for signs that he might grow aggressive. "I wish I'd seen some dogs. That would be some good eating. Please, though – you gotta help me. Don't you have any food? You boys look really well-fed."

"We don't have any food, so stop asking." The other local growled, and the older of the group nodded in agreement. "Just answer the question, did you see an older couple in the last day or so? Or hear an engine going?"

"Maybe we should check the barn over," the one who'd stepped off to the side suggested. "Just to make sure."

"No, man," James addressed the original question. "I haven't heard a damn thing. But that's probably on account of all the diarrhea and throwing up... I had a couple frogs from a pond but I think they had something wrong with them." Each of the trio took a step back, lips twisting in revulsion as they all looked James up and down before exchanging worried glances, and James pressed his advantage, taking a step forward, hands clasped. "Anything you've got would help... an energy bar or piece of fruit or *anything*."

"Get the hell back," the leader shouted, raising his rifle. "Stay away from us!"

"Sorry!" James put his hands up, stepping rapidly backward and making a show of nearly tripping over his own feet. "I'm sorry!"

"We gonna go check his barn out?" The one wearing the long coat whispered to the taller man. "Because if you want to do that, I volunteer *you* to go step in whatever messes he made."

"Ugh." The man rolled his eyes, then spoke to the one who'd side-stepped to look at the barn from a distance. "You see anything over there? Tractor or people or anything?"

"Nuh-uh," the man shook his head. "It's half-collapsed and looks like the other half'll fall down any day. Hopefully it'll take him with it."

"Let's go, then." The leader pointed across the park. "We'll cut through to the neighborhood and search there before we head back."

As the group began to walk away, James took a few steps toward them, hands outstretched. "Please don't leave me! I can help you, honest! I'll help you find whoever you need. I just need some food! Please!"

"Back. Off." The older man raised his rifle and once again James moved back a few paces. "One more move toward us and you won't have to worry about being hungry again!"

James backpedaled, nearly tripping and falling as he protested with hoarse cries of "sorry" and "please" though he made no further moves toward the men as they cut perpendicular across the open space, each of them giving a final glance in the direction of the barn before they moved into the woods, toward a neighborhood on the opposite side where Ryan and Helen had been searching earlier in the day.

Once the three were out of sight and earshot, James straightened and brushed some of the dirt off his shirt and pants, smirking in the direction the men had traveled. "Idiots."

"That," a voice from behind him whispered, "was *way* too close."

"You think so?" James turned and smiled at Alice, who was walking through the woods toward him, shaking her head in disapproval. "I thought it went pretty well."

"You're insane. You know that, right?"

James laughed, heading back in the direction of the barn with Alice by his side. "Those guys certainly thought so."

"What did you even say to them? It looked like they were eying the barn, then they started backing off."

"I told them I ate some frogs and crapped myself. They became *very* uninterested in checking the barn out after that."

"Ew..." Alice punched him in the arm and laughed. "You're insane *and* gross."

"Hey, whatever works, right?" James grinned, though it quickly faded. "But we've got serious problems even with them gone. They said they were going to check out the neighborhood on the other side of the park before they headed back to our house."

"That's good, right?"

"No, not really. It means we can't do any work until tonight without risking them hearing us. And who knows if they'll have more people searching out nearby tomorrow, too."

"You want to move to the boat shop, don't you?"

"It's enclosed, so less chance of being seen or heard and more protection in case they do find us. We can barricade the doors, keep someone on lookout duty, keep the horses in the outbuilding behind it so they're out of sight and sound... it's way better all around."

"I'm starting to agree with you on that." Alice sighed. "It's going to be a pain to move everything there."

"Nah, a few hours to load everything up while those idiots are out searching, then we make our move tonight and work through the night and all day tomorrow."

"James," Ryan stepped out of the barn, looking around, rifle clutched to his chest. "You good?"

"Yep, all good. But we need to talk about what to do next." After a brief explanation of what the trio had said while encountering James, Ryan slowly began nodding in agreement.

"I don't like moving, but I like it less out here knowing that they're actively searching for us."

"You're a fool for what you did, James Burton – but you did good." Helen admonished him with a smile. "And I agree. This place is too open and exposed."

"So we're agreed we should move tonight?" James looked around, all of them nodding. "Good. Then we should discuss our actual plan of assault on the house."

"I don't like that word. *Assault*." Helen wrapped her arms around her, shuddering. "We're not an Army."

"We're going to have to become one." James looked at them all in turn, including Jake and Sarah. "All of us are going to have to play a role in this, like it or not."

"I think the first thing we should do is call your military friends and ask them for help." Alice held up a hand before James could protest. "I know we already talked about it, but hear me out. I don't think there'll be any blowback for Eli. And what's the worst they can do or say? Sorry, we can't help you? We say thank you if that's the case and continue on ourselves."

"I just really don't think that's the best idea, hon."

"Will you just listen to me on this? They were *really* nice. They couldn't stop talking about you and what you did for them. I think you've got more deviant credit than you realize."

James sighed, rubbing his eyes with his thumb and forefinger before groaning and holding out his other hand. "Get me one of the radios."

"Thank you." Alice gave him a kiss before hurrying to the table in the corner of the barn, grabbing one of the radios they'd been gifted, and bringing it back to him.

"You realize that these might not reach them, right?" James hefted it, switching it on and unfurling the long, flexible antenna from a snap on the side of the device. "Jake, take this and hold it up as high as you can."

"Yep. I think it's worth trying, though." Alice said as Jake grabbed the antenna and stretched it out.

After punching in one of the frequencies from a note taped to the back of the radio, James stared at it, thumb over the transmit button. "Do I use my real name?"

"Why not?"

"If someone else is listening...."

"Red's a lot of things, but a possessor of a military radio is *not* one of them." Ryan answered.

"All right. Here goes nothing." James took a deep breath and pressed the button. "This is James Burton calling for Colonel Hawkins. Please respond." Digital static was the only answer and he tried again. "This is James Burton. I'm trying to reach Colonel Hawkins about an urgent matter. If anyone in the National Guard can hear me, please respond."

More static came, and James was about to transmit again when a booming voice burst through, instantly recognizable. "Burton? How the hell are you doing, son?"

"Colonel Hawkins? Is that you?"

"In the flesh, James. Didn't expect to hear from you so soon. We just departed the guard post an hour ago – you'd have missed me if you'd called any later. What's going on?"

"I didn't want to call you, Colonel – and I fully expect you to say no to this – but we're having... some trouble."

"What sort of trouble? Speak fast; we're going to be out of range in a few minutes."

"We found my wife's parents, but our home's been taken over by a pretty big group. They tried to kill my wife's parents, and killed other people along the way. Alice thought that you all might be able to help, but I don't want to bother you after all you've done for us."

"James – if you need anything, I don't want you to hesitate to call me, understand?" Alice raised an eyebrow as she crossed her arms, giving James an 'I told you so' look.

"Sorry about that, Colonel. I know we've been an imposition already, though, and—"

"I would love to help you, but we've been tasked with moving equipment back down south. We wouldn't be free until... Captain! When will we be up in this area again?" There was some garbled mumbling and shouting in the background, then the Colonel came back again. "Won't be for another two weeks. Can you hold out that long? I might be able to get some armor up there to give you a hand at that point."

"I'm not sure, Colonel... I'll have to talk to my family and see what they think. Our supplies might stretch that far, but we're being actively hunted – these people are *really* pissed off that my wife's parents escaped them."

"Understood, James. Listen – I'll give you the frequency of the post we dropped you off at. If you get in a real bind, you give us a call, okay? You probably won't get a response, but someone's always listening, and they'll relay the message to me. My hands are tied right now, but if I can pull any strings for you, I will."

"Thank you, Colonel, we appreciate that greatly."

"Here, the Captain'll give you the frequency. Good speaking with you James – stay in touch."

After receiving the frequency, James switched the radio back off and folded the antenna back up as Alice spoke. "That went well, huh? What'd I tell you?"

"Yeah I wasn't really expecting that sort of a response."

"It's not much use, though, is it?" Ryan growled. "We can't just cool our jets for two weeks. Feeding six people off of our supplies and keeping below Red's radar isn't going to work."

"He's right," James said, looking at Alice. "As good as it was of him to offer to help, I don't think we can wait two weeks. We need to start getting ready *now*."

"I agree." Alice nodded. "We tried them, and they can't help us, so now we know we have to do it on our own."

"What we really need," Ryan intoned darkly, "is a plan. Seeing as we're going to be waiting here till it gets dark to really do anything, we should be discussing that."

"Agreed," James affirmed. "I have thoughts on that very subject."

"Somehow I figured you might." Ryan grinned at him. "Should we make some more coffee first?"

"Yeah, and I want us all to stay clustered in the barn with the kids keeping watch from the windows on either side. If those guys change their minds and head back in this direction, we need to be ready for them."

"We're on it, dad." Sarah and Jake looked at each other. "Can we have a scope or some binoculars or something?"

"Yep, check the duffle bags. Stay out of sight and get us if you see *anything*, understand?"

"We will." Sarah nudged her brother. "C'mon, let's go."

James watched the pair head off to get the equipment they needed before they split up into opposite sides of the barn, settling down in front of broken-out windows to begin their watch. Having his children in harm's way – even if it was something as simple as keeping watch – was enough to make his stomach churn.

"They're going to be okay." Helen squeezed his hand, smiling at him and Alice both. "I promise."

"I sure hope so." James looked at Alice. "I'm starting to wish we could have known about this. Maybe we could have left them down at Eli's, or—"

"Nuh-uh." Alice shook her head. "Nope. You don't get to pull that kind of nonsense. We didn't know, and even if we had, there's no way *I* would have left them anywhere except right by my side."

"I'm just worried about them."

"Surprisingly, I'm not." Alice snorted as she spoke the words. "That feels weird to say. Like I'm a bad mom or something. I watched those kids survive that hell at the camp they were at, and the train, and all the stuff before it and they are just as capable as you and I. Probably more so, to tell the truth. So stop worrying about them. We're not putting them on the driveway with guns and marching them in. At least I hope that's not your plan."

James chuckled. "No, I haven't gone *quite* that crazy. But it's still a bit of a crazy plan."

"Well, stop keeping us in suspense," Ryan handed out mugs of fresh coffee that he'd poured. "Tell us what we're going to do."

"Based on what you've told me about Red, he's an angry man. Paranoid, too."

"Yep."

"So we're going to lean into that." Ryan nodded in the direction of the tractor and trailer. "The tractor's the lynchpin – without it, I don't think we have a snowball's chance of doing this. There are going to be empty steel-plated compartments on both doors with gun ports on the front of each one. Someone's going to drive it straight up the driveway when the time comes, and you'll be firing from the guns with strings tied to the triggers. The goal of the tractor isn't to actually do much to anyone, but more to provide the biggest, noisiest, most intimidating distraction that we can muster. And, by all means, you should be in high gear at the start and run over anyone you can." During his talking, James had shifted from speaking to the group at large to addressing Helen directly.

"James... why are you looking at me?" Helen asked, eyes narrowing at him in suspicion.

"Don't take this the wrong way, Helen, but as far as I know, you've got the least firearm experience of the four of us, right?"

"Yes, but I don't know how to drive a tractor!" Helen protested, raising her voice as she looked between James and Ryan. "I mean, I—I did back in the day, but not anymore!"

"They haven't changed, hon," Ryan patted her hand. "They're easier to drive than most cars, honestly."

"Don't tell me you agree with him!"

"I..." Ryan shrugged sheepishly. "I kind of do?"

"I never..." Helen sighed heavily, then rolled her eyes. "You think you're done raising kids and then they expect you to go and drive a tractor into battle for them."

"Dad and James are right, Mom." Alice put an arm around Helen. "If James or Dad were in the tractor, we'd lose a good gun in the fight."

"Exactly." James nodded. "So... you okay with that, Helen? You'll be safe, I promise. Unless they've got an RPG or... something else which I can't imagine they have." James' smile faltered for a split second, then he continued. "You'll just need to drive around and into things, tearing stuff up and keeping them occupied."

"That, I can do." Helen sighed. "What I'd *like* to do is take Red Fletcher by the—"

"Aaaanyway..." James grinned. "Okay, so the tractor will go up first. The rest of us adults will split up and come in from the sides of the property. Our first goals will be to take out guard patrols from behind as they approach the tractor, as well as any other stragglers that might be lurking around the outer edges of the property. We want to be as quiet as possible. If you can get the drop on someone and use a knife, do it. Otherwise, fire sparingly unless your life is on the line."

"What about the kids? And the dogs? I assume you're keeping them together?"

"Yeah, that was my plan. Give them plenty of protection." James rubbed at the back of his neck. "Beyond that, I'm not sure what to have them do. I don't want to leave them here, necessarily, but having them out there, even at a safe distance, sounds risky."

Alice lowered her voice so that Jake and Sarah couldn't hear her. "I don't know either. Here feels safer in some ways, but up there feels better in others."

"Well, it wouldn't be *here* here. They'd be at the boat shop which would provide them with some protection." James scratched absently at the stubble growing in on his chin. "I guess we could leave them with one of the radios. That would impact us, though, and how we can communicate."

"Will it?" Ryan asked. "If we're in four separate groups and only have two radios, are they going to be all that effective?"

"Yeah, good point." James sighed. "Maybe we should leave one with the kids and I'll hold on to the other, or Alice can."

"So we're going to leave them at the shop?" Alice asked. "If we do that, we could just leave Duke with them, and take Duchess and Diana with us."

"Oh, yeah, smart. I like that." James nodded emphatically. "I like that a lot. Okay, so we'll leave them at the shop, and one of us will keep the other radio. If something happens they can call Hawkins. I'm pretty sure he'd move heaven and earth to take care of them and get them to Eli's family."

"They won't like that at all."

"Too bad." James glanced over at Jake and Sarah, both of whom showed no signs that they had heard the conversation.

"So we approach the house, subdue anyone along the way... then what?" Ryan took a sip from his mug. "We won't have the kind of leverage they had when they approached. We'll be outnumbered and outgunned still."

"Someone needs to get inside the house. Ideally you or I, Ryan, and then we need to take out Red. Though I guess that's a question I should have asked – if we kill him, will they give up?"

Helen shuddered next to Ryan, pulling her coat tighter around herself. "This talk of just *killing* people like we're going to the grocery store, all casual-like... it's disturbing."

"It's necessary." Alice's voice was cold.

"I suppose...." Helen sighed.

"In answer to your question," Ryan continued, "yes, I think they will. Jack – if he's alive – will put up a fight, as will Barb. Maybe a couple others. The rest are following Red and kowtowing to him. If he's gone, they won't know what to do."

"Hopefully we can keep the bloodshed to a minimum, then." James stood, putting his half-filled mug near the edge of the fire as he walked to the barn entrance, staring out over the wide-open space beyond. "If they don't, then we use our position inside the house to kill anyone else who tries to visit harm upon us. We give them one chance for mercy." James turned back to the group. "Just one. After that, it's fair game. Agreed?"

Alice, Helen and Ryan all nodded in agreement and James arched his shoulders back, stretching his neck to crack it and his back. "All right. Let's get started gathering everything up to get to the shop later this evening."

Ryan and Helen nodded and moved off together toward the trailer to start working on it. James and Alice lingered near the door to the barn for a few moments, Alice waiting until they had left before she spoke to James, voice barely above a whisper.

"The kids are going to hate being left behind."

"Yeah. They'll probably try to come after us or something." James sighed, looking over his shoulder at his son and daughter. "Not that I'd blame them if they did. I'll see if I can have a talk with them about it."

"Won't do much good."

"Mm."

"Hey," Alice stepped closer to him, crossing her arms. "What was that hesitation about?"

"What hesitation?"

"When we were talking about who would ride in the tractor, you didn't seem very comfortable with it for a second."

"Oh." James leaned around the doorway, watching Helen and Ryan as they pulled branches off of the trailer and began to organize the gear in the back. "It's nothing."

"Just tell me."

"I just... if this guy is as messed up as they say he is, I wonder if he'll manage to get through the safe in the basement."

"The safe? It's hidden behind a false wall."

"No, not that one. The one in the little storage room."

"Oh, right. What's... oh. *Oh.*" Realization dawned and Alice nodded slowly. "The Barrett?"

"Yeah. If they got that out...." A chill ran up James' spine at the thought. "That would really complicate things."

"No point in worrying about that right now." Alice patted his arm before starting off to the trailer herself, calling out behind her as she went. "We'll deal with whatever happens when it comes along."

"Yeah." James murmured.

He stayed at the entrance to the barn for a few more long minutes, watching his wife and her parents working together, memories of the time they'd all spent together flowing through his mind. Shaking off the reverie, he looked around the barn at the duffle bags and other equipment, then at his two children, steeling himself for the unpleasant conversation that was yet to come.

"Guess I'd better get this over with." With a sigh, James headed back into the barn toward Jake and Sarah.

CHAPTER SEVEN

Red Fletcher
Somewhere outside East Lansing

"I don't want to go up there."

"Well, you have to."

"Why me?"

"Because," Nancy Likely's eyes narrowed, "I told you to."

"He never put you in charge." The woman Nancy was speaking to – one of the neighbors that had glommed onto the group the day after they'd taken it from Ryan and Helen – shook her head vehemently at Nancy, walking away from the base of the stairs. "You go up there and talk to him if you're so important. I'm going get some eggs or help milk the cow or something."

Nancy Likely reached out after the woman, but she slipped out of Nancy's grasp, quickly hurrying through the back door. Looking around, no one else in the living room or kitchen – including Sandy and Martha – would meet her eyes. She groaned as she looked up the stairs, each step stretching out before her into a warped, infinite pattern. It wasn't that the journey was particularly long or that she cared that much about how much her knees hurt. It was more about the fact that Red Fletcher had grown more erratic and paranoid by the hour, and checking on him seemed to yield worse and worse results.

"Fine," she grumbled, planting a boot on the first step and hand on the rail, pulling herself by the slick wood as much as she pushed off of the horizontal surface beneath her foot. "I'll do it myself."

At the top of the sixteen stairs – she had been up and down enough in the light and dark that memorizing how many there were was a necessity – she took a right, heading for the far bedroom, a large, open space above the garage. Ryan had fired at her friends from the space when they'd initially stormed the house days, weeks, months – however long ago it had been. Time was growing more indistinct, the days blurring into each other since they lacked rigid structure and definition. Regular sleep schedules, going to work, picking kids up from school, paying bills and grocery shopping had been replaced with catching a few hours of sleep at irregular hours, scavenging for scraps of food while facing down a dwindling supply, waiting in line with a dozen others for a few minutes' worth of a hot shower and chasing chickens around to find any eggs they'd laid outside of their nests.

Her old problems couldn't compare. No one's could, even when measured against the relative safety and security she had found with Red Fletcher's group. But that safety was dwindling, slipping out of her hands like droplets of water, splashing to the group and evaporating in the sun. His obsessions had grown reckless, and his focus was on the wrong things, at least in her mind. Steeling herself at the half-closed door to the bedroom, she took a deep breath before giving a slight rap on the door as she pushed it open.

Red sat in a folding chair at the window overlooking the front driveway, the same spot he'd taken up residence in shortly after the accusations he'd leveled at his wife and Sandy about the food supplies. The window was cracked and the imposing .50's folding bipod rested on the window frame, barrel sticking out the window with the stock of the gun resting on a card table. Red's right hand sat on the back half of the gun, thumb and forefinger stroking the metal while his left hand held a monocular that he swept to and fro over the front of the property. He muttered to himself as she approached, the name 'Ryan' distinct amidst the unintelligible mumblings.

"Red?" Nancy coughed slightly, but he still didn't stir. "Red?" She asked again, reaching out to touch him on the shoulder.

"Who?!" Red jerked to the side as her fingers brushed his shirt, jumping out of his chair, hand reaching for a pistol strapped to his hip.

Nancy backed up a few feet, raising her hands as she spoke louder, trying to calm him down. "It's me! It's just Nancy, Red! I'm sorry!"

Red stood stock still for several seconds, hand on the pistol half-pulled from its holster, his eyes wide as he looked her over until recognition registered. His body relaxed, shoulders sagging as he released the gun and shook his head angrily at her. "Damn you, Nancy! Knock when you're coming in the door!"

"I... I did knock. And I said your name, too. You were talking to yourself. I don't think you heard me."

"Course I didn't hear you. Woulda said something if I did." Dropping back into his chair, he spat at the open crack of the window, the saliva hitting the glass instead, bubbly as it slid toward the lift. "What do you want, anyway?"

"I heard the yelling earlier when the boys came up to talk to you. Just wanted to make sure things were okay."

"Okay?" He spat again, missing the gap a second time. "How do you think things are, *Nancy*?" Her name came out between clenched teeth, hissed instead of spoken. "We lost good people, our food's running out and Ryan and Helen are *still* out there."

"I wanted to ask you about that, Red. About them."

"What about them?" Red put the monocular back to his left eye, twisting the focusing knob with his index finger.

"Should we really be putting so much effort into finding them?"

"Yes."

"But... why?"

Red held up his right hand, extending his fingers in rapid-fire fashion as he spoke. "They have a tractor that we need. They took supplies we need. We need to kill them before they can try to carry out some revenge. They killed our people. They lied to us and stole from us."

"I mean..." Nancy shifted back and forth on her feet. "We have enough people still we can get the fields ready by hand. And they wouldn't dare try anything here on their own. It's bad we lost what we did, but we can make up for it if we put the manpower into more scavenging instead of searching for them."

Red lowered his monocular and inhaled slowly, and while his back was to her, Nancy had the distinct impression that his eyes were screwed shut. "I've given my answer already." His voice was low and quiet, barely audible. "I don't want to hear any more arguments. Understand?"

"O—okay. Sure thing." Nancy's head bobbed up and down fiercely. "What can I do to help you? Can I get you anything?"

Red stood suddenly, monocular at his eye as he peered down at the end of the driveway. He put it down and sat back in the chair, shouldering the large rifle and swiveling it to aim in the same direction he'd just been looking. After a few seconds of looking through the scope, he put the rifle down and turned to her, smiling. "Yes. Run down and tell that patrol I want to see them in the kitchen *now* for a report."

Martha and Sandy paused from their cooking to watch Nancy take the stairs two at a time on her way down, clutching the banister as she swung around and headed for the front door, throwing it open and closed again without as much as a word or look in their direction. Stepping into the kitchen, Sandy looked at the window as Nancy jogged toward a group of three men who were heading up the driveway, then she headed back into the kitchen with Martha.

"Looks like another patrol's back."

"Red probably sent Nancy to bring them inside." Martha sighed. "I don't know if I want to be around for the conversation they're going to have."

"Is it a conversation if it's one side doing all the yelling?" Sandy glanced at Martha, trying to gauge how the comment landed when Martha snorted and smiled.

"No... no it's not."

"Martha... don't you think we should do something about this?"

The older woman lifted the spoon she'd been using to stir the vat of chicken noodle soup, tasting a bit of the broth before shaking in more salt and resuming her stirring. "What part?"

"I don't want to overstep, but he's been up there all day yelling at people while he sits next to that gun. Every time someone comes down they're whispering about how... unhinged he sounds." Sandy winced slightly as she finished her sentence. "I'm sorry. I shouldn't talk about him like that – he's your husband."

Martha was quiet as she stirred, staring into the pot at the carrots, noodles, celery, chunks of chicken swirling around, steam rising up around her face. When she spoke it was barely a whisper, and Sandy had to move closer to hear. "I don't think he's been that in a long time."

"I—I'm sorry, Martha. I shouldn't have—"

Martha turned, eyes glassy as she patted Sandy on the arm. "No, sweetie, it's not your fault." Looking upward, in the direction of the room Red had sequestered himself in, Martha sighed yet again. "Ever since we lost the farm, he's been like this."

"I didn't know you lost your farm. Was it recent?"

"Oh no, no, no. It's been fifteen, sixteen years at this point." Martha took another sip of the soup, putting the ladle down across the edge of the pot as she twisted the pepper mill above the liquid. "The state was putting in a bypass and used imminent domain to take a swath of farms out our way. We got triple what the place was worth, but the money didn't matter to Red. I told him we could start over, somewhere else, without worrying about being financially strained but he had no desire to do it. So we settled down in the country on a few acres and I think he just gave up on life at that point." A half-hearted smile tugged at one corner of her mouth. "You never really notice things as they happen, do you? Then one day you realize that they've happened to you and you wonder where it all went wrong. You wonder how you got to the point where..." Martha's jaw flexed, and Sandy finished her sentence.

"Where your husband points a loaded gun at your head?"

"And kills an innocent family. And steals a home from a former friend." Martha's shoulders straightened with a sharp inhale. "And, yes, threatens to kill his wife."

"What can we do? I... I worry about Stephen more than anyone else in all this."

"I don't think... well." Martha stopped, considering her words. "No, I don't think I can say that he wouldn't hurt a child. I don't know what to do, though."

"If... if there was a chance for Stephen and I to escape, would you help me?" The question was a whisper, asked hesitantly as Sandy studied Martha's face for any signs of betrayal.

"Yes." The answer came instantly. "I don't—"

Before Martha could continue, the front door burst open, slamming against the wall, rattling the glass so hard it sounded as though it could shatter at any second. Nancy led the group of three men inside, all of them heading into the dining room next to the kitchen where they took off their jackets and laid their weapons at the table, rubbing their hands together to warm them.

"C'mon," Sandy nudged Martha with a smile. "We'll talk more later." She nodded at the men, raising her voice and smiling at them. "Welcome back! Coffee for all of you gentlemen? We've got a big batch of soup for dinner tonight and it is smelling *good*."

The oldest of the group nodded, his voice gruff as he leaned against one of the dining room chairs. "Coffee, please. That smells amazing. I could eat half a dozen bowls right now."

"I don't think we have that much. Red's been pretty adamant about us rationing the supplies." Nancy laughed and winked at him. "But seeing as you've been working so hard out there, I'll make sure your bowl's extra full."

"Much obliged, thank you."

"Anything for you boys — you're doing the hard work out there while we ladies cook and clean all day. Speaking of hard work, did you have any luck in your search?"

One of the other men, younger than the leader of the trio, rolled his eyes and answered first. "If you count finding a fat lot of *nothing* as luck, then yeah, we had all the luck in the world."

"'Nothing' is not what I like to hear, Jimmy." The voice came from the catwalk above the living room and main entryway, and the three men looked up toward it to see Red Fletcher leaning against the rail, arms folded together. "That doesn't make me very happy."

"Red." The eldest of the trio nodded in deference. "You want the full rundown on where we went?"

"Please." Red descended the stairs, pausing at the first landing to look out the windows at the fields beyond before continuing. He sat at the head of the table, looking expectantly at Martha and Sandy, the latter of whom gave him one of the cups of coffee she'd made for the returning group before hurrying back to prepare another cup. "Tell me," he said, sipping at the steaming mug, "where you went and how you managed to come up with nothing after spending the entire day wandering around."

"I had these two," the older man motioned at the pair sitting next to him, "tell me where any stores and populated areas are in the area. We started in the town and checked every building inside and out. I don't mean a cursory glance, either. We went into every shop and checked every single room. Plenty of looting, but nothing that looked recent and no signs of people. No tracks, either — not that there would be, on pavement."

The door opened and Red turned, nodding to a woman who came in carrying a basket of eggs in one hand and a pail of milk in the other, heading for the kitchen with them. "Well then," he turned back to face the men, "where did you go after the stores?"

"We cut through a park campground type place and went through a neighborhood on the other side."

"So there were no people there, either, huh?"

"Some of the houses were burned down, some were intact. We checked the intact ones, but whoever was there left a while ago, I'd wager."

"They probably left for greener pastures, or they're dead. Wasn't anyone around — or if there was, they stayed pretty well hidden. Well, except that one homeless guy who crapped himself." One of the other two, a local, interjected, and Red's eyes narrowed.

"A homeless guy? Explain."

"It wasn't Ryan," Jimmy answered. "He was living out of a half-collapsed barn. Came out and begged us for food, said he hadn't had anything to eat but... what was it?" Jimmy looked at the man who'd spoken up.

"Frogs."

"Frogs. That's what it was. Started going on about how he was spewing from both ends from them. We didn't stick around long after that."

"What did he look like? Maybe it was Ryan in a disguise." Red continued to press the issue.

"Nah, I promise you it wasn't Ryan. Much younger, mid or late 30's. Dark brown hair, kinda tallish, taller than Ryan by half a foot at least."

"Did he have green eyes?" The question came not from Red, but from the woman in the kitchen who was handing the eggs and milk to Martha and Sandy. Red turned to her, an eyebrow raised, then he looked back at the trio.

"Well? Answer the lady."

"As a matter of fact," the older man nodded slowly, "he did. Yeah, he definitely did."

"Sharp chin and jawline?" The woman asked.

"Hard to tell under the stubble and dirt and crap all over him. Maybe?" Jimmy looked at the other two who'd seen the man, and both of them shrugged helplessly.

"What are you getting at... who are you, exactly?" Red asked the woman who'd spoken up.

"Terry. I live—lived, I guess—the next road over. We were with the Willoughby's when you and your people showed up."

"Terry." Red snapped his fingers, nodding. "That's right, I remember you there, hiding in the back with the rest." He waved absently at her, motioning toward Jimmy. "How do you know what this homeless frog-eater looks like?"

"Well," Terry hesitated, "I think he might be James Burton."

"James Burton." Red repeated the name, running his tongue across his teeth, tasting the syllables as they spilled out. "*Burton.* Why does that sound familiar?"

"He's the guy who owns this place. Him and his wife, Alice. Ryan and Helen are Alice's parents."

Red's eyes widened as he stared down Terry, then he abruptly leapt to his feet, crossing the distance between himself and Terry in two steps, looming over her, his voice harsh and quiet at the same time. "Are you certain." It was a statement, not a question. "Are you absolutely, without a doubt, positively certain."

"I—I—I don't—I can't be—" Terry stammered, trying to back up, but she was pressed against the counter with Martha and Sandy on either side of her and no easy way to escape.

Red whirled back to the trio still sitting at the table, all three of them more alert than they'd been since they walked in. "Where is this park."

"Few miles down the road, near the town." Jimmy motioned with his head in the general direction of the place.

"But you only saw this one person." Red spoke to himself more than anyone else, turning from Terry to go back into the dining room and stare out the windows down the long driveway. "You're sure you didn't see anyone else? There was no one else in the barn?"

"Not that we saw." Jimmy shook his head. "We didn't go into the thing, though."

Red froze midway through a turn back to the table, closing his eyes. "You didn't check the barn?"

"No. It was falling down, halfway collapsed. There was nobody else in it."

"But you didn't check it." Another statement instead of a question. "You didn't bother to go *check* the building." Red's arm quivered as he pinched his brow, the skin on his fingers and around his nose turning white from the pressure. His rage finally released as he slammed his fist down on the table, rattling the coffee mugs and sloshing coffee out of two of them as he screamed, spittle flying from his mouth. "Why the *hell* would you not *check* the building?!"

"Red, it was just the one guy, how do we even know he's—"

"Tyler!" Red bellowed, and a moment later the man appeared, huffing and puffing from running through the basement and up the stairs.

"What's going on, Red?"

"These *idiots* might have inadvertently stumbled across Ryan's deadbeat family, and quite possibly missed out on finding Ryan and Helen entirely." Red gestured to the three men sitting at the table, eyes aflame with rage. "I want you, Jimmy and a couple of the local yokels to take the ATV and head back out to find this frog-eating barn-dweller. Find him and kill him, then search the area for any signs of Ryan and Helen."

"Kill him?" Jimmy blanched. "What if he's not related to Ryan at all?"

"Did I ask for your input?!" Red turned on Jimmy, inches from the man's face, flecks of white foam flying from his mouth. "Do you want me to go with you? No? Then get your asses moving! Now!"

Tyler, Jimmy and the two men at the table hurried out the front door, jogging down around the house, past the barn, RV and tents, beelining for the small outbuilding where the ATV sat. Red watched them go until they disappeared around the side of the house, then headed back upstairs, muttering under his breath and stomping hard on each creaky step. In the kitchen, Terry, Martha and Sandy looked at each other quietly, Terry's face pale as she put a hand to her mouth.

"I... I hope I didn't... I don't want anyone else to get *hurt*."

Sandy and Martha exchanged a glance, and Sandy shook her head, returning to the dough on the counter that she was kneading for biscuits. "You should have thought about that before you told Red anything. Now an innocent man might die because of it."

"I...." Terry grew paler, then exited the kitchen, heading out the back door.

"Personally," another voice came from the opposite side of the counter where Nancy Likely was seated in a cushioned chair, watching out over the back fields. "I hope it *is* James and the whole family's there with him. It'd be good to see this get over and done with once and for all so we can focus on what's important."

"You don't see anything wrong with killing people, do you, Nancy?" Sandy asked.

"Nope. Not one bit."

CHAPTER EIGHT

Somewhere in Northern California

In a time in the not-so-distant past – which had been forever lost to the rapidly accumulating annals of history – the Benton Farmer's Market in Northern California would draw tens of thousands of visitors every day on the weekends. Its existence had been existentially threatened thanks to the events of the prior several weeks, but for the first time since death and destruction had begun to spread it was open, and a faint glimmer of hope had appeared with its reopening.

Spread across an eighty-acre swath of land, the thirty acres that had once been solely devoted to parking were instead taken up by the same makeshift tents that covered much of the other fifty acres. Green, blue, gray and tan tarps stretched over tent poles and two-by-fours, shielding vendors and visitors alike from the sun as it crept higher in the sky. Despite the ramshackle look of the place, it still possessed the same heart as the old Farmer's Market, much of that due to the presence of the same vendors that had made up its lifeblood in the past. Their survival had been down to luck as much as it had been to their isolation, and though they were not strangers to sacrifice and tribulation, they had persevered and come through to the other side stronger – and looking to sell or trade their goods with each other and with other, more urban survivors.

Crowds of civilians dressed in all manner of clothing from intact to ragged wandered amidst the maze of tents, carrying sacks of goods they had brought to trade or had purchased, and more than a few pulled wagons behind them as well, children riding among the piles of greenery, freshly butchered meat and small white orbs delicately placed in rows of crumpled up newspaper and piles of straw. The attendance of the purchasers and traders was normal even if their appearance had changed, but the heavy presence of armed men and women that passed through the crowds was a distinct difference compared to how the market had looked in the past.

"You boys want something to drink?" A voice called out, drawing the attention of two guardsmen who were walking side by side down the main thoroughfare of the market. Don Crowl and Jeff Hodgson turned simultaneously, smiling and nodding at an older woman who stood behind a rickety table filled with crates of lemons, her husband working a hand crank juicer at a smaller table behind her. "It's on the house – for you and your friends."

"Beautiful looking fruit, ma'am." Don nodded at her as he and Jeff stepped closer. "Thank you, but no. We appreciate it, though."

"You boys just come back here if you get thirsty, understand?" She winked at them. "We've got plenty to spare for the folks who're helping keep us safe and protected here."

"We'll keep that in mind, ma'am." Don smiled, touching the edge of his helmet. "Have a nice one; I hope you sell out."

"God bless you, son!" The woman called out as the pair continued on, both of them waving at her.

"*I'm* thirsty," Jeff said once they'd gotten out of earshot. "And that looked like some *damned* good lemonade."

"Uh huh. Keep walking, soldier." Don grinned. "If we accept every offer these people have been making, we'd both be about twenty pounds heavier right about now."

"They're just trying to show their appreciation." Jeff smiled and nodded at another vendor who waved at the pair as they passed.

"Like I said, keep walking."

The pair reached one of the main intersections in the farmer's market, pausing to watch as a few customers argued with a vendor on the corner. A pair of Sheriff's deputies appeared a moment later at the opposite side of the intersection, and the guardsmen exchanged a nod of recognition with the deputies before they met in the middle.

"Think we should do something about this?" Jeff asked one of the officers, a woman with short-cropped blonde hair and a name tag reading *Correll*.

"Nah," she dismissed him with a wave. "That's just Frank being Frank. He's one of the original vendors. Always in a bad mood, never willing to give out bulk discounts. They've been going like that since we last came by, about twenty minutes ago."

"Fair enough." Don nodded. "We'll leave 'em to you, then. Any particular place you'd like us to attend to?"

"It's been pretty quiet today, but if you want to be helpful, there's a white tent down the way." Correll turned and pointed back the way she and her partner had come. "They brought some goats to sell, but their fencing is *awful* and I'm pretty sure they're going to break out soon."

"Well," Don grinned, patting the large rucksack on Jeff's back, "it's a good thing we've come prepared. C'mon, let's go see to some goats."

Leaving behind a pair of chuckling officers behind them, the guardsmen turned and headed down the gravel path that Correll had indicated, Jeff grumbling immediately once they were out of earshot.

"Join the Guard, they said. See the world, they said."

"I thought one of the best parts of the Guard was that you *don't* get shipped all over the world," Don countered.

"Yeah, well, some excitement might be nice right about now. It'd beat patrolling a farmer's market and fixing goat pens."

"Hey," Don's voice grew serious. "What we're doing is important. If you'd been in one of the groups sent into the cities you'd realize that. Places like this are going to make the difference for the recovery of the country. It's up to *us* to protect them, keep the peace, and do whatever we can to help people rebuild."

"Sorry." Jeff mumbled.

"No, I mean it – have you even seen pictures of what the cities look like?" Don pressed in. "Because I know you weren't sent in to try and rescue anyone. And I'm pretty sure you weren't on any trains, either."

"I mean..." Jeff shifted uncomfortably under his backpack, face flushing under the questioning. "I've seen videos, yeah."

"Yeah. That ain't *nothing*. Videos don't have smells. They don't get into your brain and clamp down and refuse to let you sleep at night."

"Okay, okay, I get it."

"Nah, you don't." Don clapped Jeff on the shoulder. "But that's okay. Just remember why we're here, okay?"

"Yeah, I got it."

"Good man." Jeff stopped and gestured to a white tent on their right. "I think we found the place, if the bleating's a clue."

"Ya think?" Jeff grinned, nodding at the woman who looked over at them from behind a makeshift fence build out of pallets. "How you doing, ma'am?"

"Oh, you know – hey! Knock it off!" She shouted and swung a pool noodle at a goat who had started to headbutt one of the pallets, shaking the whole line of them. "I'm okay, I guess."

"Can we offer some assistance?" Don asked, looking down at her with a bemused grin. "We've got some supplies and can help you shore up this fence."

"You... could you?" The woman's face lit up at the offer, and she nodded vigorously. "That would be incredible. I sold several of them, but it's the feisty ones left, and without their buddies they're getting kind of grouchy."

"No problem at all, ma'am." Jeff swung his backpack off and dropped it to the ground with a dull metallic thud. Unzipping the main pocket, he pulled out a small box of nails and a hammer, then looked up at Don. "See if you can find some scrap wood anywhere?"

"Oh, I've got some in the back of my wagon, behind the tent." The woman let go of one of the goats to point at a horse drawn wagon, then lunged for the animal as it tried to headbutt the nearest pallet again. "No, you get back here!"

"I've got it, just hang on." Don jogged around the tent and reached into the back of the wagon, pulling out several short pieces of scrap wood, bringing them back to Jeff who was already hammering more nails into the pallets that were loose and falling apart from the repeated impacts.

"Okay, hold it up on the top first. Yeah, like that. Perfect." As Don held up a two-foot piece of wood across two pallets, Jeff drove nails into either side, joining the pair of pallets first at the top, then at the bottom with another piece of wood.

Repeating the process along the four sides of the pallet fence, the pair rapidly turned the wire-joined loose pallets into a proper, sturdy fence, before driving a few more nails in at the corners to keep the whole structure stable. When they'd finished, they helped the woman drive a few stakes into the ground, then each man held onto a couple of goats while the woman tied leads to their necks and then to the stakes, separating them from each other and keeping them from repeatedly attacking the fence.

When all was said and done, the three stood at the front of the woman's tent, breathing heavily as they exchanged handshakes. "You two are amazing. Just amazing."

"Our pleasure, ma'am." Don nodded.

"Please, call me Angie. If you need anything – you just ask, you hear me? I've got cold water, some wine, hardboiled eggs, fresh goat milk, smoked sausages and bacon, and plenty of greens to go with them. Anything you boys want, you just ask."

"That's real kind of you, Ms. Angie," Jeff answered, Don watching silently with a raised eyebrow, "but we've got to be moving on. Lots of other folks to help out."

"I'm here all weekend, so don't be strangers, okay?" Angie reached into her apron, pulling out a pair of small packages wrapped in wax paper, pressing them into the guardsmen's hands.

"Just a couple of hardboiled eggs each."

"Oh, no, we can't—"

"You hush up, young fella." She shushed Jeff's protestations. "They'll keep your energy up. Keep doing good work out there, and don't be strangers."

"We won't; have a good one, ma'am!" Don smiled, holding up his package in thanks.

"Angie!"

"Have a good one, Angie! Thank you kindly. Hope you sell all of those fine animals you mean to!"

"Thank *you!*" Angie waved at them as they headed off down the row of vendors, back toward the main intersection.

Stopping once again to look around at the crowd of people as he opened his package to find a pair of salted and peppered eggs inside, Don chuckled, prompting a question from his fellow guardsman. "What? You laughing at me?"

"No, you did great back there. And that was the perfect answer to her." Don pointed at the opposite side of the intersection, where the vendor that Correll had pointed out was still shouting and waving his arms, though it was at an entirely new group of customers. "Looks like she was right about that guy."

"Frank being Frank." Jeff snorted. "Think we should have a word with him?"

"Nah." Don unwrapped his eggs as well, taking a bite out of one. "If Correll isn't worried, I'm not worried." Don tilted his head to the side, chewing as he spoke. "C'mon, let's make another round. Maybe we can find another goat herder to help."

"See, I knew you'd come around on the food front."

"Uh huh." Don rolled his eyes. "Just keep walking."

The pair of guardsmen continued down the main thoroughfare, passing by vendors, customers, fellow guardsmen and police, the sea of humanity thick and full of hope, shoulders pressing together as they carried out their business. Some groused, a few complained, but most laughed and smiled, happy not because of their situation but in spite of it, choosing to respond to their surroundings with positivity and happiness instead of hopelessness and fear. While the population had been decimated by the disaster, it had not been completely wiped out, and as the survivors crawled from the ashes into the dawn of a new world, they found their hopes bolstered by their fellow man. Hopes for continued survival, rebuilding, fellowship and a world made slightly – even if imperceptibly so – better each and every day.

CHAPTER NINE

The Burton/Cooper Family
Somewhere outside East Lansing

The afternoon had quickly turned into the evening, and the evening had transformed into a rich, thick blackness that had settled over the region, the onset of Fall evident in the rapidity of the sun's departure beneath the horizon. Across the park and campgrounds, the area was quiet and dark, the only source of light and sound coming from out of and next to the half-collapsed barn where the family worked to finish up their loading of the trailer and tractor, preparing for a move to what would hopefully be a safer locale.

With the help of four additional people, the trailer had been reorganized from the ground up, and it contained virtually all of their supplies along with space for four people to ride, albeit not exactly in comfort. While keeping the dogs in the bucket of the tractor had initially been a last-minute desperation move, it was the best place for them, and they had already been loaded up and clipped in with shortened leashes, instructed by James and Alice both to stay still, a command they obeyed with no small amount of angst.

"We good here?" James stood inside the barn next to the fire, hands alternating between outstretched and rubbing together as he looked around the interior of the structure.

"I think so," Ryan affirmed, tipping over the piece of wood they'd used as a table inside the building and pushing it up against a wall to reduce the evidence that anyone had been staying in the place. "Other than the fire."

"Yeah, that can't really be helped." James accepted a rusty bucket filled with dirt from Jake and poured it out over the flames, extinguishing them in a few seconds and keeping the billowing smoke to a minimum. "Go ahead and get another bucketful and pour it on over the edges," he spoke to his son, who took the bucket and ran off.

"Hon?" Alice stepped inside the barn. "We're all ready out here. I've got Stormy, Amber and Buck's leads tied off to Rocky and I'm ready to follow you all."

"Cool, we're just finishing up inside; we'll be out in a minute. Go ahead and get everyone loaded in the trailer." James and Ryan waited until Jake returned with another bucket of dirt and dumped it out over the remaining coals of the fire, then threw the bucket into the back of the barn.

"I guess that does it." Ryan took a final look around. "Not that I'm glad to be on the move again, but I will *not* miss this place."

"It served its purpose. Home's calling, though, and we're going to answer." James started heading out of the barn. "C'mon, get loaded up in the trailer while I get the tractor fired up."

Ryan and Jake joined Helen and Sarah in the trailer while James pulled open the door to the tractor and climbed inside, closing the side with a whooshing *thunk* that brought back memories of brush hogging, tilling and moving piles of mulch for days and weeks at a time. "Well, hello there, Wiley." James patted the steering wheel, rubbing the dirt and oil-stained emblem of a howling coyote in the center of the steering column. "Been a while, hasn't it?"

The tractor wasn't particularly large or unique or even special – except to James. It had been his first true farm-related purchase after they'd moved to their property, and the tractor had a special place in his heart in spite of its relatively diminutive stature compared to other machines on nearby plots. Sitting in the cab, closed off from the outside world with a deep, throaty diesel engine rumbling from his feet all the way through his chest was a feeling that made him smile each and every time he turned the key, and that night was no different.

After depressing the brake and checking to ensure he was in neutral, James gave the key a turn backwards, the dashboard lighting up and the engine heating unit kicking on. He waited the requisite ten or fifteen seconds until the heater notification turned off, then turned the key the opposite direction. The engine growled to life in an instant, deep and rumbling, sending a wave of vibrations through the cab. A slight squeal came from under the hood as he pushed up on the throttle lever and he snorted.

"Whoops. Guess I should've tightened that up before my trip, huh? Sorry about that, girl. Don't worry – we're going to do some work to you. Turn you into a tank. You'll like it, I promise."

Throttling up to half power, James turned in his seat and waved to the group in the trailer and Alice on her horse, receiving thumbs-ups in response. He depressed the back pedal and turned the wheel to the left, maneuvering the trailer and tractor backwards next to the barn, swinging the vehicle out of the trees and bushes where it had been hidden, then pushed forward through the grass, the trailer swinging around and straightening out with a jolt. Raising the bucket a foot and tilting it back slightly he checked to make sure Duke, Duchess and Diana were secure then pushed the throttle all the way up.

The small convoy passed through the campground and park in rapid succession, James maneuvering through the shortest grass onto rougher surfaces as quickly as he could, reducing the tracks they left to a minimum, though with the trailer loaded for bear it was impossible not to leave a pair of wheel marks as they passed over the greenery. Keeping the lights off to avoid drawing even more attention than the engine would draw on its own, James had to operate partially by memory of the area and partially by moonlight as it peeked out from behind cloud cover. Once on the main road, James turned toward the road near town where he and Alice had explored the stores, and twenty minutes later the boat shop's sign appeared through the inky black of the night, its white background glowing under the light of the moon.

"Here we go..." James murmured, heart suddenly racing. Thoughts came unbidden into his mind, wondering if the shop had somehow been found by other survivors, or by the group occupying his home, and they had deduced his plan for the tractor and laid a trap for his family. "You're being paranoid again..."

Shaking off the worry, James pulled the trailer around to the side of the building where the row of roll-up doors stood, then throttled down the tractor, lowered the bucket to the ground and shut off the engine. Alice hopped off of Rocky and tied his lead to the back of the trailer as he finished getting the tractor turned off, then he climbed out, drew his pistol from a holster on his waistband and moved to the trailer, speaking in a low voice to the rest of the family.

"I'm going to go make sure the place is how we left it. Ryan, you want to unhook Duke and bring him in, too?"

"Yup." The older man grunted as he stepped out of the trailer, accepting a rifle from Alice.

He threw the weapon's strap across his chest and headed for the tractor bucket, unlatching Duke's lead and giving the dog a few sharp, quiet commands. The animal clung to Ryan's side, giving repeated looks at James, picking up on the tension in the atmosphere as it obeyed and stayed close and quiet.

"Door around this way was unlocked when we left." James pointed ahead. "Follow me."

"Right behind you."

The three headed up to the building and James pushed open the door, leading his way into the building with the pistol, a flashlight clutched in his other hand, ready to thumb it on at the first sign of trouble. The interior was quiet and dark, though, the skylights the only source of illumination in the place, and after a few seconds of waiting and listening to naught but the sound of Duke's panting, James clicked the flashlight on to get a look around the place.

It was exactly as they had left it – all the doors were still closed, tools were in the same places they had been, boats still sitting or hanging in various states of repair. There was no sign anyone had been in the place to even check it out after he and Alice had left it earlier in the day, though he still took a quick walk through the place just to be on the safe side. Once he was certain that it was empty and they were alone, he holstered his pistol and headed back to Ryan and Duke who were waiting at the entrance.

"We good?" Ryan asked.

"I think so," James nodded. "Place looks exactly like it did when we were here before."

"You weren't kidding about what they've got here." Ryan whistled as James turned around, passing the beam of his flashlight across the interior of the room again. "This place is a gold mine."

"Yeah, it's got everything we need to get that Killdozer plan of yours working."

"*Our* plan, you mean. Mine was just going to involve a few more plates of steel on the tractor and calling it good. You're the one who came up with the idea to make them think we're all piled in there so they're distracted by it."

"It's a team effort." James smiled, heading out the door when Ryan caught him by the arm. "What's up?"

"Has Alice talked to you about how she and the kids are doing?" Ryan looked back toward the door, voice dropping. "Helen and I are worried about them."

James' shoulders sagged. "I am, too. She's talked about it some. I've gotten enough details to piece everything together, but she... I think she's scared of herself. I think the kids made out better than she did, and they were the ones who were kidnapped and abused at that camp."

"That's what I noticed, too. Is there anything we can do about it? To help her, I mean?"

"I don't think we can do anything for any of them right now except what we're doing. And even if we *could*, I'm not sure that would be healthy."

"How do you mean?"

"Alice – and Sarah and Jake to some degree – they're going to need a *lot* of processing time. We can't afford to do that right now. And if we give them a break, if we give them some quiet time to collect their thoughts and start processing what happened to them, I'm afraid they might just break down." James hesitated. "And... I don't think we can afford that right now. Sorry; I know that sounds callous."

"No, you're right." Ryan nodded, tears forming in his eyes. "I just... it's killing me to see my baby like this. And then my grandkids, too. I don't mean to leave you out; I know you've gone through hell, too, but I just—"

"Ryan," James smiled, opening his arms and giving the older man a fierce, back-slapping hug. "That means the world. To all of us. We're gonna help them once this is over. Help them, help me, help you and Helen. We're gonna get through this and once we're on the other side, we'll be okay. It'll take a long, long time... but we'll make it. Okay?"

Ryan swiped at his eyes with his shirt sleeves, nodding gruffly. "Yeah. We will. Sorry about...."

"Don't apologize." James smiled, patting Ryan on the shoulder. "Our family's love for each other is just about the only thing holding us together. Don't hold that inside; let it out. Now, c'mon, let's get that outbuilding checked over and get the horses stashed in there with some feed, then get these doors open and get everyone inside so we can get to work."

Two in the morning came and went by the time they got fully situated into the boat shop. The trailer and hookup were pulled off the 3-point hitch and set to the side, and a few worktables were cleared off near the tractor. Getting hoists into position for holding up the steel plates came next, then James got to work on the welding job while Ryan and Jake scrounged up pulleys for use with the guns on the inside of the compartments James was busy creating. Alice, Helen and Sarah took turns patrolling around the outside of the structure, and those who weren't patrolling worked on stripping down the new firearms that Ryan and Helen had found so that they could be cleaned, lubricated and reassembled. The spare magazines were filled and organized, and after finding needles, thread and fabric used for repairing boat seats and sails, they set to work fashioning magazine carriers that could be looped around their chests and waists.

Twisted upside down beneath a section of steel plates suspended by a hoist as he welded, James was too distracted to notice the sudden appearance of Sarah in the building, followed quickly by everyone getting up and rushing toward her. It was only when Ryan ran over and slapped his leg that he stopped welding and looked over at the group as they were mid-conversation.

"What's going on?" Putting the welding torch down, he took off his gloves and helmet, placing them on the workbench.

"She saw someone." Alice's eyes were wide, and James nearly tripped over a coil of rope on the floor as he hurried over.

"How many and where?"

"I... I don't know. They were on the ATV – *our* ATV!"

"Are you sure it was our ATV?" James asked.

"*Yes*! They had two guys on the ATV and it was pulling the little wagon mom uses to haul the hay bales around in, and there was one, no, I think it was two in the wagon."

"Did you see any guns?"

"It was dark, dad, I—I don't know. Maybe?"

"Okay, just calm down. Breathe, honey." James gave her the warmest smile he could muster, putting his hands on her arms and rubbing up and down on them. "We're okay. We're going to stay okay. Just talk me through what you saw."

Sarah took several long, deep breaths and closed her eyes, reciting from memory what had happened. "Duke and I were out in front of the building circling around, and I decided to go across the street because Mom and Grandma have been doing that too, just to widen the patrol a bit."

"Okay, not a bad idea." James nodded.

"Well, we were over there and I heard an engine. I thought it was my imagination but I definitely heard it, and it was coming up *fast*. I was going to try to get back across the road but there wasn't any time, so I grabbed Duke and we got into the ditch along the road. That's when that ATV went just screaming past – I mean *screaming*, dad. They were driving it like you always tell us not to, overloaded and throttle in the red."

"Small favor might be that they burn out the engine before they can get much more use out of it." Ryan spoke quietly from behind Sarah, receiving a murmur of agreement from Alice.

"They were gone real fast, but the guys on the ATV had flashlights so I could make them out, and the glow made me think there were people in the trailer too, but I'm not sure... maybe it was just the two guys on the ATV."

"You came back here after they drove by?"

"Yeah, ran back as soon as they turned down the road to the right around the bend."

"That way?" James pointed in the general direction of the park.

"No, they were coming *away* from the park."

James looked at Alice, then Ryan, the three exchanging worried looks. "I guess that trickery didn't work all too well if they went back to check out the park again."

"Maybe they described you to someone at the house, or one of the guys there *did* recognize you and they were just playing dumb to go back and get reinforcements." Ryan scratched his chin, starting to pace back and forth.

"Regardless, it's got to be at least three people, otherwise they wouldn't have the trailer." James patted Sarah on the shoulder. "Good work, hon. You did great. Get a drink, and you and your brother get into the office back there. Take a pistol with you."

"But—"

"No 'buts'," James interrupted his son. "Both of you and the dogs in the office *now*. When we need you, we'll call for you. Until then, I want you in the safest room of this place."

"What do you want to do?" Ryan moved closer to James, arms crossed, leaning in as the four adults clustered together.

"We need to keep eyes and ears on the road. We should have heard them but between the welding torch and the hammering and talking, we completely missed them."

"How soon till they come back, do you think? Alice asked.

"This is pure guesswork based on a few days spent with that lunatic," Ryan ran a hand through his hair, staring off into the distance as he verbalized his thoughts. "But my guess is that Red told them to find us come hell or high water. If they came from the direction of the park, they *probably* already visited the barn and figured out we left. They know we left because of the tire tracks, but they won't be able to track us on the road, so they'll have to start searching places again."

"I bet they're doing a quick overview first," James glanced in the direction of the road. "Then they'll come back through on foot and go through the shops again."

"Can we pack up and go somewhere else, before they get here?" Helen was wringing her hands, voice trembling slightly with worry. "This was supposed to be a safe place for us to get ready, but if they're out searching for us...."

"Is anywhere really safe?" James snorted, then twisted around to look at Ryan's wristwatch. "Look, I need another... two hours, maybe three to finish up the compartments. Then figure another hour or two to get the gun holes cut and get the guns mounted, so we're looking at dawn by the time the tractor's ready to go."

"Will we have that much time before they search near here and find us?" Alice asked.

"I dunno. But every minute I spend talking here is another minute I'm wasting not getting that sucker ready." James started walking back over to the tractor, grabbing his helmet and gloves. "You three put together some kind of patrol or lookout plan while I'm working, and throw me a gun if worst comes to worst." The sounds of the welding torch came a moment later, and Ryan, Helen and Alice all moved to the opposite side of the large space, near the office where the kids were sitting on chairs inside, watching them while petting the dogs.

"So, thoughts on a plan?" Ryan looked expectantly at Alice.

"You're the guy who lived with those people for a few days and got yourself and Mom out safely. I want to hear what you think we should do first."

"Hmmm." Ryan pulled out a rolling stool from underneath a nearby table and sat down, massaging each thigh in turn as he talked. "Red's going to have sent out at least one of his own men, maybe two. I think we should assume there are four of them in total, so there are probably a couple of locals mixed in there as well to give directions to his people and help them find their way around."

"Four people should be easy to spot, regardless of whether they're on foot or not." Alice turned and looked at the dogs in the office, smiling at Jake and Sarah as they sat watching her. "We could keep one person inside and then two people outside, each with one of the dogs. At the first sign of trouble we hightail it back inside and get ready for them to try and come through one of the doors."

"I really don't like our defenses in this building," Ryan said, gesturing to the walls. "No windows, multiple doors for them to enter through and divide our attention."

"We gotta do the best we can with what we've got. And what we've got is this."

"I'll go outside with Alice," Helen declared, putting a hand on Ryan's shoulder as he tried to stand up, pushing him back down into the stool. "And I'm not taking any arguments from you."

"Helen—"

"I said no arguments! You've been going nonstop since we left – we've barely sat down in, what, a week? I'm surprised you can still walk. Are you popping painkillers every hour or more often?"

Ryan started to argue, then his shoulders sagged and he lowered his head. "We ran out of the ibuprofen this morning. It wasn't doing much, but it was keeping the edge off."

"For the love of... *Dad*!" Alice admonished him. "Why wouldn't you say anything?!"

Ryan shrugged. "There are more important things going on. I'm not having my wife out there. Not when I'm able to get out there myself."

"Oh, really? So you're okay with your daughter going out there, just not Mom?"

"I—" Ryan held up a finger then dropped it, brow creasing as he shook his head at her. "You really are your mother's child. You know that, right?"

"Stubborn to the last." Helen patted Ryan on the back. "Rest your legs, you're going to need them later."

"And check the duffle bags we brought with us," Alice added. "They gave us a lot of stuff. Might be some painkillers in there you can pop before we leave later in the morning."

"Don't go wandering far out there, you hear me?" Ryan watched both women as they went to the bags containing their weapons and supplies, Alice taking her shotgun and Helen taking one of the pistols she'd grabbed from the supply room before they made their escape. "We'll hear a gunshot in here no matter what's going on, so don't even *think* about hesitating to fire."

"We'll be fine, Dad." Alice glanced through the office windows. "Take care of them, okay? And keep an eye on James so that he doesn't hurt himself."

"Will do." Ryan rolled his stool over to the table to grab a rifle and spare magazine for himself while Alice and Helen took Duke and Duchess from the office, saying a few words to Jake and Sarah before they left. Ryan rolled over to the office door and propped it open, sitting in the doorway with his back against the doorframe, alternating between massaging his left and right legs as he talked with the kids.

"How're you two holding up?"

"Not bad." Sarah shrugged.

"Tired of sitting around not *doing* anything." Jake groaned.

"Are you kidding me? You two are the best danged lookouts I've ever met. You spotted the guys back at the barn and Sarah warned us about the ATV. We'd be in hot water if not for that work."

"Yeah, but it's not *real* work."

"There'll be plenty of that once we get back into your house, don't you worry about that. Lots of cleanup to do, lots of planting to take care of in the Spring, plus the animals to take care of. We'll be keeping *very* busy, don't you worry about that."

As Ryan, Jake and Sarah continued to talk, Diana lay on the floor between them, occasionally raising her head when James would grunt or drop something, but otherwise staying calm in spite of the new environment. Outside, Duke and Duchess were another matter as Alice and Helen exited the building, opting to stick together as they circled around the building in slow, roving patrols. Their pair of dogs pulled at their leads repeatedly, occasionally growling into the darkness before stopping and acting as if nothing was wrong. The night air had gone from chilly to cold, and all four of their exhalations were visible in the pale moonlight in large puffs of mist that drifted upward, dissipating slowly into the dark.

"*Heel*." Alice hissed at Duke, pulling sharply at his lead. "They really backslid on their training since we were here last. He never used to be like this."

"Oh, that's probably our fault," Helen said. "We never really did much with them – it was so doggone busy since it all... you know."

"Not your fault at all. I just don't know what's gotten into them." Alice stopped and knelt down next to Duke, roughly rubbing his shaggy head, sending his ears flopping back and forth. "You see someone out there, boy? You smell something?" Duke merely whined in response, and Alice stood up again and shrugged. "I'm half-tempted to turn him loose, but he might just smell a deer or turkey or something out there."

"Duchess seems fine," Helen patted the dog's head as they began moving around the building again. "You can tell when they sense a person versus an animal. Duke's probably just being Duke."

Alice chuckled. "Right? I'm sorry you had to deal with them for so long."

"Oh, they were great. Saved our lives, actually." Helen's smile faded, her voice growing hard. "That night the neighbors broke in... if not for the dogs, we wouldn't have made it."

"He really leapt over the catwalk, huh?"

"It was a movie scene come to life."

"Kind of wish I could have seen that."

"We wish you could have been here, too. But you're here now, and that's all... all that..." Helen trailed off as Duchess stopped, forcing Helen to turn and tug on the lead. "Come on, girl. C'mon."

"Mom." Alice's tone made Helen whirl to see Alice pointing off into the distance down the road where a bright light had appeared and was rapidly growing larger. "Quick, mom, back around the building!"

Pulling on Duke and Duchess's leads, Alice and Helen ran around to the front of the building to where the burned-out vehicles were. The approaching light was moving quickly, and was accompanied a few seconds later by the scream of an engine being pushed to its limits. Just as the four got behind the husk of a large work van, an ATV tore past, a trailer hooked to it bumping and twisting behind it, fishtailing hard. The ATV was gone as soon as it had appeared, its taillights vanishing along with the sound of the engine as it went around a curve in the road back in the direction of the park, the opposite way it had come the first time Sarah saw it.

"There was only one person on it." Alice looked at Helen. "Right?"

Helen nodded slowly. "I only saw one, too."

"That's... that's really not good."

"We need to go warn the others."

Both women pushed off of the vehicle they'd been leaning against and began heading for the front door of the boat shop when Alice pulled on her mother's arm, stopping her in her tracks before jerking her back behind the vehicle.

"Down there!" Alice hissed, looping Duke's lead around her arm to pull him tight to her, other hand clutching her shotgun tight.

"What is it?" Helen asked, pulling Duchess close to her in a mimicry of Alice's action.

"Two lights. They're close. Really close."

"How close?" Helen leaned out to peek, then ducked back, eyes wide as she looked over at Alice, whispering frantically. "They're *right there*! How did they sneak up on us?"

"I don't know. We need to get back inside and warn the others."

A shout went up from one of the figures who was approaching on the front side of the building, his voice carrying through the still night. "Try the back doors, I'll check around front!"

"Got it!" Another, more distance voice came in response.

"We have to do something," Helen said.

"I'm about to." Alice tugged on Duke, pulling him back to her. His ears were back and a low growl was emanating from his and Duchess's throats, the scent of the men caught in their noses. Kneeling down, she put her shotgun on the ground and unlatched Duke's lead from his collar, whispering to him as she held him back with two fingers. "You smell him, boy? Yeah, you want to get him?" He strained against her, his growls growing deeper as the man's footsteps became audible around the other side of the burned-out van.

———

Walking toward the front door of the boat repair shop, the figure stopped in his tracks as a low, organic-sounded rumbling came from somewhere nearby. Looking around, he frowned, passing his light across the wrecks in the parking lot, the street nearby, and the front of the building.

"The hell is that noi—"

The words froze on his lips as the scrable of claws on pavement replaced the rumbling, and a large, white shape emerged from behind the nearest wreck of a vehicle, bounding toward the ten or so feet that separated them. Recognition flashed behind his eyes as his light passed over the shape and he tried to raise his pistol, but his reaction time was nothing in comparison to Duke's ravenous, uninhibited ferocity. The hundred-and-fifty pound creature launched himself at the man, front paws landing on his chest, knocking both his light and his gun out of his arms, jaws clamping first around the man's face, then his neck, turning his abrupt scream of agony into a muffled gurgle.

"Stay here."

Turning around the van, shotgun to her shoulder, Alice took in the scene in a second, leaving the dog to do his work while she sprinted for the front of the building, stealth abandoned as a shout went up from the man on the other side of the building, asking if his partner was okay or not. Slamming into the front door shoulder-first, Alice ran through the receptionist area through into the main work area, sliding to a stop on the slick floors, all eyes in the room turning toward her.

"They're here!" When no one moved, she pointed at the rolling doors at the back of the building. "They're right outside the doors! Get up *now*!"

A gunshot from behind the building went up, followed by a shout of "They're here!" from a pair of voices out back and the interior of the building exploded in motion. James dropped his welding equipment to the floor and grabbed a rifle off a nearby table, then sprinted for a corner on the far wall, kneeling down behind a steel tool chest, rifle sweeping across the three rolling doors in preparation for who might come through.

Alice ran back out front, helping her mother get inside, then called for Duke, yelling at him several times before he finally released the figure's neck, his skull dropping to the ground with a sickening crunch of bone and flesh. His muzzle was covered with blood, dripping across the pavement and floor of the building as he bounded inside. Helen and Duchess followed as Alice beckoned to them, and as they were crossing the threshold, a series of gunshots echoed from down at the end of the building, bullets ricocheting off of the ground behind Helen and Duchess.

Twisting the lock to the front door of the building, Alice dashed back inside, yelling to her mother over her shoulder. "Let Duchess off her lead, then get in the office with the kids!"

"Gladly!" Helen shouted back, struggling with the large animal before finally getting the latch undone, releasing Duchess to run into the main room where she beelined for Duke, the pair snarling and growling at the rolling doors and the front door in an alternating fashion.

"How many?" Ryan shouted, kneeling still on his rolling stool, though he was sheltered behind a large steel tool chest much like James was, though Ryan's rifle was pointed at the door his wife and daughter had just entered through.

"No clue!" Alice ran to the office to check on the kids, motioning for them to drop down to the floor. "Duke took one down, but there could be two or three more. Someone drove by on an ATV a minute before they showed up, though, so he could be back any minute."

"I *saw* you Helen Cooper!" The shout came from outside the front door, causing Helen to freeze in place and exchange a wide-eyed stare with Ryan. "We can still do this peacefully, you know! Red just wants to talk!"

James gave a quiet *hsst* to get everyone's attention and put his finger to his lips, shaking his head. Responding would only harm them, not help. They all nodded, and then James pantomimed grabbing the dogs' collars and holding them, which Alice, Helen and Ryan each did with Duke, Duchess and Diana in turn.

"Come on, Helen! Come on, Ryan! We can make this work! Hell, if you just give us the tractor then we'll tell Red we couldn't find you both. I'm sure he'd be happy with just the tractor back!"

There was a soft *click* from James' direction as he ticked his safety off and pointed at both the front entrance and the far rolling door in the back where some scratching and shuffling was coming from. "Get ready." He whispered, barely loud enough to hear.

Without the benefit of seeing each other, the man out front and the one out back had to rely on shouting at each other to coordinate their attempted incursion into the boat repair shop, which had the unfortunate side effect of revealing the entirety of their ill-fated moves to their enemies. A loud "Now!" came from the front, accompanied by breaking glass, and a second later the rolling back door began to lift. While Ryan covered the entryway into the front reception area, James shuffled out of cover from behind the tool chest and dropped to the ground, gaining a clear sight on the rolling door from beneath a suspended boat.

The dim lights from the interior of the building were a spotlight in comparison to the inky blackness outside, and the groping hands of the man pulling up the rolling door were clear as day, followed by the sight of his feet and shins. James fired as the door rolled up past the man's knees, his three shots striking the edge of the door, just slightly higher than he had intended thanks to the unusual firing position he'd adopted. The reaction from the man outside was instantaneous, though, as he dropped the door while falling backwards, preventing his entry into the building but also keeping James from firing upon him.

"I've got the back doors on lock," James called out, no longer concerned with the pretense of stealth. "Watch the front!"

Ryan grunted in acknowledgement, but did not move, keeping his rifle wedged against his shoulder, cheek welded to it as he sat behind the tool chest, right hand holding the rifle and left hand holding onto Diana. Alice was also watching the front door, from the opposite side as her father as she held onto Duke, though she had switched from her shotgun to a pistol so as to better control the straining animal. The next few minutes stretched on in agony, every sound magnified and every movement excruciating. Aside from the breaking glass at the front of the building, there had been no further signs of incursion from that direction, and the three rolling doors had been left alone as well.

When the two men finally came into the building proper, their entrance was foreshadowed by some soft grunts, the sound of crackling glass underfoot, and the gentle thud of bodies slamming up against the wall of the reception area on the other side of the door. James glanced in the direction of the entrance but kept his focus on the back doors, leaving the defense of the main entrance in the hands of Ryan and Alice.

When the two men came through the door, they did so in tandem, back to back with a pair of pistols held in their leading hands, firing indiscriminately into the room. While the rounds were too high to hit anyone, they did have the desired effect of forcing Alice and Ryan to duck down low, allowing the men to squeeze in and dash in opposite directions, one finding cover behind a boat while another hid behind a tool chest.

"They're inside!" Helen screamed, pulling both Jake and Sarah low to the ground, releasing Diana in the process, though try as she might by throwing herself against the glass of the windows and doors of the small office, she couldn't escape.

In the main shop floor, Duke and duchess were straining against Alice and Ryan, snarling and barking, and finally Alice yelled out to her father. "Let 'em go!"

Both dogs frenzied at her call, pulling away and scrabbling to find purchase on the slick concrete floor. When they finally did, their bulky bodies slammed against tools and workbenches as they careened along toward where the two men were hiding. Both men heard the dogs coming and one stood up, trying to get a bead on the animals before they could reach him, receiving several shots to the shoulder and chest at close range courtesy of Alice. His screams attracted both dogs, which pivoted in his direction, and a second later the yelling turned to muffled shrieking that was quickly silenced.

"Dammit!" The other man yelled, scrambling on all fours for the door, but Ryan rose out of his stool and tracked the man as he tried to retreat, hitting him several times in the back, the final round going through the man's head, causing his body to go limp and drop to the floor.

The reverberation and echo of the gunshots slowly faded from the room, and James slowly stood from his position near the rear doors, calling out to the ones near the front. "Was that all of them? Are we good?"

"I-I don't know." Alice kept her pistol trained on the door to the reception area in the front of the shop, moving forward with her dad on the opposite side, both of them stepping over the bodies of the men they'd killed to lean forward and look through the doorway. "Maybe?"

"What about the one on the ATV?" Ryan asked, looking back at James, who shrugged.

"I don't think there's anyone else back here. Maybe he was one of them, and we just didn't realize?"

"I don't think so." Alice took a step out into the reception area, looking around, when another gunshot rang out, accompanied by Alice's scream.

"Alice!" James bolted for the door, shoving past Ryan who was nearly there himself when another shot rang out, striking the doorframe near James' head.

"No!"

A shout came from the parking lot and James crouched down next to where his wife lay groaning on the floor, firing in the direction of the voice. A series of curses went up along with a howl of pain, then came running footsteps and the thrum of the ATV's engine. The vehicle tore through the darkness with just its red running lights on, fleeing the scene in a haphazard, meandering path with the vague shape of one man on the back of it. James started to get up to go out and pursue the vehicle but stopped, looking back down at Alice. Before he could reach for her, Ryan was in the doorway, pushing James away.

"I've got her. Go after him. He *cannot* get back to Red!"

James nodded and dashed across the broken glass and out the door, firing rounds at the ATV's red lights in the distance, one after the other, the sound echoing through the night. Stopping at the edge of the parking lot, James squeezed off a final shot and then paused, watching as the running lights of the ATV swerved and vanished around a bend in the road. He dropped the rifle and cursed under his breath, slamming a fist against the nearby wreck in frustration. The sight of Alice on the ground in the reception area flashed through his mind and he turned back to the building, running inside and skidding to a stop. Alice was sitting up against the wall, Ryan at her side, holding her hand and talking to her. James dropped to one knee to check on her, glancing at Ryan with both eyebrows raised.

"Is she…"

"She's fine."

"I am, James. I promise." Alice pointed to a gash in her left shoulder, wincing as her father pulled some gauze off of it, doubled it over and then pressed it back again. "I got snagged on a big piece of glass when I slipped and fell."

"You fell?" James looked at the wound as Ryan answered for her.

"She just fell – I told you, she's fine."

"Thank heavens for small favors." James let out a breath of relief as he stood and went back to the entrance to the store, looking out at the direction the ATV had gone. "I don't know if I hit him or not, but he drove off pretty far."

"That's not good." Ryan growled. "Red will come in full force."

"Then we need to be ready to meet him if he does." James looked down at Alice again. "Are you *sure* you're okay?"

"I promise I'm fine."

"Okay. Ryan – can you all handle the bodies?"

"We've got it. You get back to welding."

"Yep, exactly what I was thinking." James handed the older man his rifle and headed back onto the shop floor, nodding at Helen, Jake and Sarah as they stood in the office, arms around each other. "You all okay?"

A chorus of nods and yeses came in response and James waved at them, then gathered up his welding gear. His heart was still throbbing as the adrenaline surge started to fade, but he did his best to ignore the wave of dizziness and shock that washed over him. There were more pressing matters at hand, ones that required his full attention, and self-care would have to wait. Ticking the welding torch back on, James allowed himself one long, deep, shuddering breath before lowering the visor on his helmet and getting back to work, the tool crackling loud in the enclosed space.

CHAPTER TEN

Rockport, MA

Waves broke against rocks in a steady, unrelenting rhythm, their rush carried on the cool ocean breeze as a gentle whisper that reached far inland, no longer hindered by the roar of traffic and engines and bells and whistles. Creaking wood, dipping oars and a shout of encouragement or request for assistance occasionally came with the water's murmurs, and the steady scream of gulls overhead punctuated the calm serenity, adding a reminder that not all life had been disrupted so many weeks ago.

Two fishing boats rose and sank on the swells as they slowly made their way to the main docks in the Rockport Harbor. The engines that had once tamed the seas and driven them forward no matter the wind or current had long since been ripped out to reduce weight in the vessel, as there was no more fuel to be found for them and they were more effective as anchors than as propulsion devices. Instead, they were driven forward by manpower alone – six men sat on makeshift benches nailed to the deck of the boat on either side, twelve in total, each grasping a long oar and pulling in time to a song that they all hummed under their breaths. One man stood on the bow of each vessel to call out directions and any obstacles while another stood in the cabin at the wheel, each ship being guided to opposite sides of the same dock that protruded out into the bay.

When the boats came up alongside the dock, several of the deckhands who had been loitering at the back of each craft threw thick ropes to the people waiting on the docks. Oars were retracted at the same time, and the boats were pulled up alongside the dock and lashed firmly, everyone aboard and on the docks waving and grinning as another successful harvest had been concluded. Those on board the ships exited without any additional work, taking lunch pails and thermoses with them while they greeted and talked with the crew that was coming aboard to unload the catch and prepare to take the vessels out again within an hour.

The steady cadence of fishing with both boats had been maintained day and night for two weeks straight, and though it was hard work that required all in the small town to pull their weight and pitch in, the results spoke for themselves. Smokers had been set up across the town in every front and backyard where there was room, and barrels of salt had been passed out and were constantly restocked and refreshed by a small team on horseback. Once the fish were smoked and salted, a small portion were reserved by the families who performed the work and the rest were sent to city hall to be stored away and carefully monitored for spoilage.

It was simple work, truth be told, but with many moving parts, each of which required constant care and maintenance. Boats had to be checked for leaks, lines and nets for frays, people for injuries they might not have noticed, and supplies monitored so that none ran out. For some of those in the town, the work had been their way of life for generations and came as naturally as breathing, but for most it was a constant learning experience as they adapted from their lives in the before to their lives in the after.

"Jason!" A young woman in overalls and a bright red long-sleeved shirt waved from the shore as the men filed in off the boats.

One of the men, shoulders slumped and face downcast in weariness perked up at the sound of his name, returning the wave, picking up his speed to greet the young woman with a hug and a smile. "Sandy! What're you doing here?"

"Figured I'd come meet you today." She beamed, holding out a small, insulated mug. "Kids are watching the smoker for me."

"You didn't have to do that."

"I know, but…" she shrugged. "C'mon, get back to the house so I can start on dinner. We got some eggs today, finally."

"Eggs? Are you serious?"

"Yep. Them two are finally starting to pull their weight."

"I'm not sure that a few eggs in six months is really pulling their weight, but it's a start I guess."

Sandy took Jason's lunch pail and thermos while he drank deep from his mug, the pair moving away from the docks with the rest of the men that had been on the boats as their replacement shifts finished the unloading and prepared for the next shift that would take place overnight. The unusual arrangement had been established by the people of Rockport weeks prior, shortly after the fires that had consumed many of their homes, cars and boats. Isolated as they were, the sea promised a way to survive and thrive amid the harshness of the coming winter, but only if they worked ceaselessly to make it happen.

After repairing two boats, the townsfolk had decided to engage in a series of three shifts that would rotate each day, enabling the vessels to be on the water day and night while also giving the crews enough time to rest and recuperate between each shift. It was hard work, brutal even, but the results spoke for themselves. With no one else on the water, the boats were able to fill their cargo holds with fish and crustaceans each time they went out, adapting their methods and locations to the time of day and weather. In a few short weeks, the surviving members of the town had stockpiled enough food to last them all halfway through the winter, and with a few more weeks' worth of work, they'd be set to survive through its entirety without having to go out on the water again.

Fingers interlaced, Sandy and Jason headed inland from the docks, waving and shouting greetings to their neighbors as they passed, finally arriving at their small home just a couple of blocks from the seashore. Perched near the top of a small rocky bluff overlooking the shoreline, they had a few hundred square feet of yard in the front and double the same in the back. Surrounded on all sides by a quintessential small-town white picket fence, the home was two-stories tall with steeply-angled roof lines and red paint that showed years of wear and tear. Smoke drifted from the small chimney on one side of the house and from another source in the backyard, and the smell of smoked meat grew stronger as the pair crossed through the waist-high gate out front and walked around the house to the backyard.

"Hey, dudes!" Jason smiled at the sight of his eleven and eight year-old sons, both of whom were sitting near a trio of fifty-gallon drums that had smoke pouring out of their cracks.

"Dad!" The youngest turned first, jumped up and ran to give his father a hug, pulling back after a moment and twisting his nose. "You still stink."

"He always stinks." Their eldest grinned playfully. "But it's okay to stink these days."

"Not for little boys it's not," Jason smiled, grabbing both of them, pulling them in and squeezing them tight. "How have you been for your mom? Helpful? Not helpful?"

"Helpful," they both said in unison.

"Uh huh. I know what that means."

"They've been surprisingly great today, actually." Sandy walked around the makeshift smokers, checking that they all had enough wood chips. "Cutting wood, chipping it up, helping with the house, everything. They even got some water heated up for our baths already."

"No way." Jason beamed. "You guys got the bath water ready?"

"All three tubs should be ready. We sold six more of the circulators while you were on your shift, too – we're all out."

"No kidding? What'd we get for them?"

Sandy looked upward with a squint, touching her fingers in turn as she tried to remember the list of items. "Four thermal blankets, the promise of thirty pounds of fish, a set of pots and pans, a box of books, some schoolbooks and another box of old magazines. Outdoors stuff, mostly."

"You traded some circulators for old magazines?" Jason raised an eyebrow.

"Hon, when winter hits and you aren't out there every other day tearing your body to bits fishing, you're going to be *very* glad we have some entertainment. I'm already worried enough about your boys – I don't need you climbing the walls, too. I'm really hoping to get us some board games, but I think people are starting to realize how handy those will be. Nobody wants to part with them."

"Fair enough." Jason finished draining his mug and handed it to his youngest son, who ran inside with it. "I'll get started on making some more later tonight, after I get that bath." He stretched and groaned, touching his back where a sharp twinge had made itself known. "Maybe... tomorrow?"

"Tomorrow. There's a meeting tonight anyway that we need to attend."

"Ugh. What about now?"

"Just general status and updates for everyone, as far as I know." Sandy smiled and squeezed his hand again. "C'mon, get yourself cleaned up so we can get something to eat before we have to leave."

A few hours later, all four family members had gone through their new thrice-weekly cleaning regimen and were sparkling, clean and smelling fresh. While waiting for their sons to get dressed, Jason picked up a bottle of liquid soap that they'd all used as a body wash and shampoo and tilted the container back and forth. "We're running low."

"Yeah," Sandy nodded. "I tried to trade one of the circulators for more, but Agatha had already traded it all away. She said we're next on the list though."

"That's something, I guess. We've still got those bars in the closet, right?"

"All ten of them, for all the good they'll do."

"Maybe someone wants them?"

"Someone who likes having their skin dried out, cracked and bleeding?"

Jason snorted. "Good point." Looking up at the stairwell, he raised his voice. "Boys! C'mon already. We're gonna be late!"

A series of thuds came from the floor above as the two boys pounded out of their room and down the hall, then flew down the stairs, taking them two and three at a time before landing in front of their parents. "We're ready!"

"Just had to do my hair! Let's go, what're you waiting for?"

Jefferson, their oldest, raced out the door, throwing the question behind him as he went. Ted, their youngest, followed his older brother and the pair were at the gate by the time Jason and Sandy were out the door. Jason locked it behind him and tucked his keys into his pocket, taking his wife's arm.

"You don't have to do that, you know."

"What? Hold your arm?"

"No, lock the front door."

"Heh." Jason chuckled dryly. "Old habits die hard."

"We know *literally* everyone in town at this point."

"Still. Never know when someone new might show up. Or someone old might get a bad idea."

"Mhmm." Sandy patted his arm as they followed their boys back down the road toward the shoreline. "You worry too much."

"Sometimes I wonder if we're not worrying enough." Jason gestured to the people walking to and fro, much of the small seaside town looking exactly as lively and carefree as it always had. "Insulation isn't always a good thing."

"And neither is worrying. Come on now, cheer up. You've got the next day and a few hours off, so stop fretting and enjoy our company, hm?" Sandy gave him a kiss on the cheek and he blushed, smiling and nodding.

"Fine... I'll do my best. You make it pretty easy, though."

Their conversation became lost amid the wash of outside voices as they all filed into the city hall building, squeezing past people talking loudly in the entryway, then milling about while they found four seats side-by-side in the middle of the left side of the main room. The place was packed with at least two hundred souls, a hundred in chairs and another hundred standing and leaning off to the sides, and even with such a larger number of people in one place, the mood was nothing short of joyous – one might even call it festive.

"Thank you all for coming!" An artificially loud voice came from the front of the room, warped by electrical circuitry, and the first several rows of people winced and covered their ears. "Sorry... sorry." The voice became quieter as the short, rotund man standing at the podium twisted a dial on the side of the megaphone he was holding. "My son was playing with this earlier today; turned the volume all the way up." He coughed, clearing his throat to re-center himself, and started over again with a broad smile.

"As I was saying, thank you all for coming! I am beside myself with joy over how our little community's pulled together and keeps working so well with each other, and the mood in here tonight reflects that. In spite of everything we've managed to all keep our bellies full, our beds warm and our lives largely intact. Different, to be sure, but intact nonetheless." He pointed out across the room. "Everyone is contributing and we're all reaping the rewards. You should all be *very* pleased with yourselves."

A round of applause broke out, and he waited a moment before waving his hands to quiet it down. "I won't keep you long – I know you all have lots to get to, and we've gone over the numbers at other meetings. I just want to reiterate – we're *making it*. Winter's fast approaching, but we've already secured over sixty percent of what we need – as a community – to feed everyone for the entire season." Another round of applause and cheers broke out. "I'm also pleased to tell you, for the first time, that a *third* boat is very nearly repaired. It's one of the largest ones, and we're planning to take it out deeper in the water for a more varied catch, as well as some potential exploratory trips."

The mayor-by-default – for he wasn't the elected mayor, but rather a bean counter in the mayor's office who had risen to the challenge in the days shortly after the disaster – continued on for a few more moments, detailing new bits of information that hadn't yet been shared with the town. After ten or fifteen minutes he looked at his wristwatch and began to wrap up.

"I said I didn't want to keep you all for long, and I won't. Thank you all for coming – and as you're leaving, we do have one last surprise for you all. Please make sure to pick up a bottle of Gertie's homemade apple cider at the door. There's more than enough for everyone to take one, children included, and I don't think I'm exaggerating when I say that it's her *best* yet."

Applause rang out once again and the crowd grew raucous again as everyone began to stand and shuffle toward the entrance of the building. Jason's family moved with them, but were stopped abruptly by a tap on Jason's shoulder. He turned to find the mayor-by-default standing behind him, grinning from ear to ear and holding a small cardboard box that had been taped shut.

"Jason! Glad to see you here!"

"Wouldn't miss it, Simon." Jason nodded cordially at the man who stood a full foot and a half shorter than him.

"I was wondering..." Simon lowered his voice and looked around conspiratorially. "You wouldn't happen to have one of your little devices available, would you?"

"Devices?" Jason asked. "Oh, you mean a circulator?"

"Indeedy do." Simon's smile only broadened as he rocked back and forth on his shining leather shoes. "I've heard great things, simply *marvelous* things about them and my wife is just *dying* for one. Heating our water in buckets is getting very tiresome."

Jason smiled, glancing at Sandy bemusedly. "That's exactly why I started building them. I don't have any right now, but I'm going to spend my day off tomorrow building a few more. I can add you to the list if you'd like though it might be a while."

"Mmmm." Simon looked over at a cluster of the town's leadership who were talking in the corner, receiving a nod of affirmation from them. "I've actually been talking to a few people about this. The Council, the boat captains, and some of the crew. Taking the temperature of the people, so to speak." Simon pushed his rounded glasses further up on his face. "With winter coming, we're going to need warmth more than ever, and your circulators are *just* what everyone in town needs. How would you like to switch occupations?"

"Switch?" Jason's brow creased. "I'm not following."

"The general consensus is that we need you building your devices more than we need you pulling in nets on a boat. With a third boat getting in the water in a couple of days, we'll have even more men out on the water, which means more food."

"Are you asking my husband to build his circulators full-time?"

"I suppose I should have said that outright." Simon chuckled. "That is, indeed, what we're asking. If you'd be willing to do so?"

"How would that work, exactly?" Jason asked. "Right now the work I do on the boats helps ensure we've got food to eat, and the circulators I build on the side are for trading for things we need. We'd be getting less in the end than if I just kept doing it part time on my days off."

"Nope! You'd still be trading, and as someone performing an *essential* town service, you and your family would have your food allocated the same as if you were on a boat. We wouldn't dream of asking you to do this at a detriment to yourself."

"That's... that's a big ask, Simon." Jason smiled. "But I really appreciate it."

"Is that a yes?"

"That's a 'let me think about it overnight' – if that's okay?"

"Take whatever time you need," Simon smiled, handing the cardboard box to Sandy. "And, in the meantime, take this. Hopefully it gives you some encouragement, hmm?"

After thanking Simon, the pair headed once again toward the entrance to the hall, catching up to their sons who were waiting outside, each holding two bottles of cider which they raised above their heads to show their parents. "We picked 'em up for you!"

"Yeah, they were starting to run out and had to go get more boxes, but we got some for us!"

"Nicely done, boys," Sandy smiled, tucking the cardboard box under one arm and taking a bottle of cider with her free hand. "Twenty ounce bottles? Gertie must've been working overtime."

"Here, let's see what ol' Simon's trying to bribe me with." Jason took the box from under Sandy's arm, peeled back the tape and lifted the flaps. "Son of a..." Jason groaned.

"What? What'd he give us?"

"A box of cigars, two bottles of shampoo and... a card game? *Mille Bornes*, it says." Jason repeated the French phrase a few times.

"So it *is* a bribe. Something for you, something for me, and a game for the whole family. I guess he really wants you to work on those circulators. Are you going to say yes?"

"How can I say no? The boats are dangerous, and this would give me more time at home to help out around the house." Jason ran a hand through his hair. "Although it would be a *lot* more work... and we'd have to do some scrapping in the burned-out houses to find enough copper. And the heating blocks take time to mill...." He trailed off.

"Sounds like you'll be busy, then." Sandy took his arm again, patting it as the four turned onto the lane leading up toward their house.

"*Really* busy."

"Jason!" A voice called out, and Jason turned to the house at the corner of the intersection.

"Jeffrey, hey, how's it going? Missed you at the meeting!"

"Oh," an older, liver-spotted man shrugged and waved in a dismissive gesture. "I went to the one this morning. You get some cider?"

"A bottle each." Sandy lifted her bottle and smiled.

"Great, great..." The older man scratched the back of his neck, looking around self-consciously. "Listen... uhh..."

"You need one too, huh?" A smile crept into the corners of Jason's mouth, one eyebrow raising.

"It's the arthritis," Jeffrey rubbed at his hands, "makes it hard to work the smoker. I've been sharing Deb's, but she's getting tired of it, so...."

Jason chuckled and nodded as he and Sandy started walking again. "Swing by tomorrow and I'll add you to the list."

"You're a life-saver, Jason!" The older man beamed. "I'll come by after lunch!"

"Bring me some copper tubing if you have it," Jason called back. "I'm running low!"

"Will do!"

Jason continued to chuckle as they walked the steep road back up to the house, their sons already inside the gate and heading for the front door. "That old coot's playing up his arthritis."

"I don't blame him," Sandy said. "You've only been making them for a week and you've got half the town wanting one and the mayor asking you to change jobs."

"Strange how such a tiny thing as hot water can mean so much right now." Jason paused at the gate and looked back down at the buildings along the shoreline, the docks, and the faint outlines of the boats out in the water beyond. "Makes you wonder how all the rest of the world's doing."

"Not sure I'd like to find out." Sandy rubbed her arm, shivering involuntarily. "I think we got lucky."

"I just hope the luck holds out." Jason sighed. "C'mon, let's get inside. I need your help with some inventory-taking while we've still got the light."

"Oh, so now I'm your assistant, is that it?" Sandy took a playful swipe at him as Jason pushed through the gate, narrowly missing her hand.

"Best assistant in the world!" He called, jogging toward the front door as she laughed and followed up behind him, leaving Rockport behind for the moment to continue quietly working away, a small beacon of light in the darkness of the world.

CHAPTER ELEVEN

Red Fletcher
Somewhere outside East Lansing

On the Burton's forty-acre farm, their ATV was most often used to pull a cart back and forth across the length of the property, transporting animals, firewood, supplies and occasionally their children. James kept it well-maintained even though it was by far the least used vehicle on the property, and had replaced its battery, fuel filter and one of the tires only two months prior to the world going up in flames. While having a new fuel filter and tire had proven useful to the group from Grand Rapids that had taken the house, it was the new battery that ultimately proved to be most valuable, as it allowed the flashing taillights of the vehicle to stay lit for several hours overnight and into the next morning. The tire tracks and the trail of leaking fuel didn't draw attention to the ATV's location shortly after dawn, but the flashing red tail-light did, blinking steadily on and off in a thick pile of brush, catching the eye of one of the search party who shouted at the others on the opposite side of the road.

It took several minutes more for the group to get through the thick branches, briars and vines that the ATV had become embedded in, and another ten to find the former driver of the vehicle, who had been thrown a dozen feet away when the ATV had collided with a particularly thick oak tree. The front of the vehicle had crumpled, a wheel had become dislodged and one of the handlebars was a full two inches inside the tree itself, causing the only real damage to the oak that was visible. The ATV was a total loss, failing to start as one of the men sat upon it and repeatedly turned the key while the other two searched the area for signs of the rider.

When he was finally located nearly twenty minutes after the ATV had first been spotted, it was feared that he was dead, or close enough to it that there would be no point in trying to carry him back to shelter. The first man who happened upon him slapped him in the face a few times before noticing that his right leg was twisted backwards at the knee, his face blanching at the sight of the white bone sticking out from the wound. He turned to vomit, accidentally spewing some of it on the feet of the second man who'd come to check on the status of the driver, setting off an argument that lasted until the one on the ATV finally came over and shouted at them both to, as he put it, "focus up, you knuck-leheads."

A pulse was finally found on the rider's neck, and enough leaves and dirt were cleared from his face to identify him as Tyler, one of the few who Red personally relied upon to carry out his whims from day to day. Nervous glances were exchanged between the three men as they kneeled around the body, each man contemplating what Red's reaction would be to the news, and how it would – not 'could' but 'would' - blow back on them. None of the three belonged to Red's group from Grand Rapids, and they had seen firsthand how he treated those from the local area differently than those from his 'squad' as some referred to it.

"We... could just leave him here." One of the three finally voiced what they were all thinking.

"It's obvious someone was here, though." Another pointed back the way they'd come. "We left footprints and cleared crap off of him. We can't."

"What if we take the body somewhere and dump it?"

"He's *alive*, Curtis." The third man spoke up. "I'm *not* going to murder someone. Not in cold blood like this."

"You didn't have a problem when it was that old couple." The one who'd made the original suggestion snarled.

"No. We're bringing him back to Red." The third man stood, looking around. "We're not that far from the property. I'll take his torso, you two grab a leg each." Grumbling, the other two took a leg each and began to lift him, only to be shouted at by the third man. "No, watch his leg! It's gonna snap off—no, the other way. Yes!"

It took twice as long to get out of the wooded area and back onto the road as it had to locate Tyler in the first place, and all three men were sweating and puffing as they trudged down the road, shifting Tyler's body every few paces to try and maintain a grip on it. Their only saving grace was that he had crashed a quarter mile from the house, though it did take close to another hour to haul Tyler's considerable bulk that distance. When they reached the gate, they laid him on the ground and Curtis ran to get help, recruiting a pair of guards who were patrolling near the pond. They, in turn, brought a wheelbarrow down to the end of the driveway, and Tyler was carefully loaded into it and taken up to the house where a flurry of commotion erupted as their procession was finally spotted by those inside.

Red was the first one through the door, erupting from the house in a manner similar to an enraged hornet whose nest had been struck with a baseball or long stick. He was trailed by a few other people including Martha and Sandy who stopped on the porch to watch as Tyler was brought up to the steps. Red met the wheelbarrow at the bottom of the steps and looked at Tyler's broken, bloody and barely-bleeding body for a few seconds before directing his ire at the three who'd brought him back.

"What. Happened." As was his habit, it was a statement, not a question.

"No idea." Curtis spoke first, blurting out what they'd found. "The ATV was up against a tree like he'd wrecked it and he was like this in the woods. Took us forever to drag him out on account of the bones and everything."

"The ATV's wrecked?" Red looked out at the expanse of the driveway stretching down to the road. "Can it be repaired?"

"Not unless you've got a brand-new one to donate all its parts to the old one." The one who'd refused to leave Tyler in the woods spoke. "About the only thing that works is the battery, and that's been drained all night."

"You a mechanic, Jerry?"

"Sixteen years small engine repair."

Red fixed the man with a snarl. "Then why the *hell* aren't you helping with getting the truck fixed up? Or figuring out how to bypass the damned lock on that stupid electric piece of crap out back?"

Jerry's face was a mask of confusion, looking around at the others as he struggled to understand Red's anger. "I... small engine repair. I don't know anything about EVs. And how am I supposed to repair a fuel tank when you've got people on it already?"

Red's hand twitched near the holster on his hip, the large revolver still ever-present, as much a menacing presence as he himself was. "Then what use are you around here, huh?"

"I'll... I'll get to helping with the truck."

"Good boy." Red watched the man walk off for a moment before turning his attention to Tyler, questioning Curtis in the process. "So he's alive still?"

"Barely. His leg's all messed up and he's lost a lot of blood."

"Martha!" Red called.

Martha exchanged a look with Sandy before heading down the stairs to stand next to Red. "I'm here."

"Oh, good. Didn't know you were outside." Red gestured vaguely at Tyler's dirty, bloody, broken body. "You know something about first aid. What can you do here?"

"I know how to put bandages on and maybe put a suture or two in, hon. He needs a doctor, *bad*."

"Unless someone here's a doctor," Red raised his voice, looking at the group of people who were assembled around the front of the house, "you'll have to figure it out. You two, bring him inside." Red pointed at the two men who, along with Jerry, had found Tyler. "Someone get a tarp laid out on the floor. Don't want blood all over my floors." Turning,

Red spotted Sandy. "You help my wife. If Tyler dies before I get answers to my questions, it's on your head, understand me?"

"Red…" Martha touched his arm, but Red recoiled, snapping at her. "*Something* happened to him and I want to know *what* it was. If it was Ryan and Helen then I want to know exactly where they were and what happened to the rest of the people with him. Get me answers – after that, let him die." With his final proclamation made, Red headed back up the stairs and reentered the house, going to the top floor to resume his watch through the rifle, wholly ignoring the flurry of activity below that took place in his absence.

"You two!" Martha's commanding voice cut through the murmur of the crowd. "Push the wheelbarrow inside. Sandy, find a tarp down in the basement and get it spread out on that carpet in the side room opposite the kitchen."

"Got it." Sandy headed off as Martha stood in front of the pair of men who were pushing the wheelbarrow up the steps, wincing with every bounce of the wheel.

"Caref—*careful!* For goodness's sake, the man's got a *bone* sticking through his leg. Can we *not* do more damage, please?"

Once the wheelbarrow was inside, Martha pointed to Nancy Likely, who'd been standing at the front window watching the goings-on. "Nancy, help these two get Tyler out onto the tarp. The rest of you clear out! I just want these two in here helping me!"

"Hell no." Nancy snorted derisively as the rest of the onlookers quickly exited the house. "I'm not getting—"

"Should I get Red and see what he says? He put me in charge of trying to save Tyler's life, and I intend to do just that. I'd hate to tell him you were working against him." Martha's eyes flashed with unconcealed rage, and Nancy slowly nodded.

"Fine."

"Good. Sandy, hold the corners of the tarp. Gentle with him, tip up the wheelbarrow some. Not too far… good, no, watch his leg! Are you *trying* to hurt him more? Yes, like that. Yes, okay now flat. Just lay his legs down there, yes. Good. Okay, get the wheelbarrow out of here, and bring me a couple pairs of scissors, some of those disposable gloves from the drawer near the sink, and some wipes. I need to see what we're dealing with."

Despite her complete lack of medical training, Martha had jumped into the work like she was born for it. Using the scissors, she cut through Tyler's jeans first, slicing each pant leg up to the waist to expose his legs. Once the first pair dulled she switched to the second pair, then cut his shirt off as well, peeling the filthy fabric back and pressing it down against the tarp. Glancing briefly at his leg, she focused on his torso first, listening at his mouth for his shallow breathing and taking his pulse while she observed his shallow chest movements.

"That leg looks *bad*," Sandy whispered from next to her.

"I have no idea how to set a bone, let alone one that's broken so badly it's poking out through the skin." Martha whispered back. "The blood loss is the bigger issue, though. He's *very* pale. I wonder if the artery in his leg was nicked when his leg broke." Martha gingerly prodded Tyler's leg from top to bottom, then felt around on his upper torso and arms, then examined his head. "Nasty egg on his head there. Probably has a concussion, maybe a TBI?"

"What's a TBI?" Nancy asked from across the tarp.

"Traumatic brain injury. That plus shock are probably why he's out." Martha looked up at Nancy. "I'm just guessing here based on what I've read and picked up."

"Well start 'guessing' on how to fix him up."

"I…." Martha put the backs of her wrists against her forehead. "I'm not sure where to start. I could try to push the bone back in, make it meet up and maybe make a cast. But I'm pretty sure they usually put pins in the bone to keep it joined, right?"

"I have no idea." Nancy's mouth was twisted into a nauseous knot.

"That's what they did for my brother when he broke his leg." Sandy nodded slowly. "That was… ten years ago, I think. It probably hasn't changed much since then."

Martha took a deep breath in a vain effort to calm her nerves, then reached for the piece of bone that was sticking out of the skin, taking his leg in her other hand. She pushed against the broken piece, moving his leg, trying to get the bone to go back where it belonged, but each push and shove only made more blood ooze from the wound.

"I don't think I can do this. Plus, it's filthy inside there and it'll get massively infected." Martha leaned back, squatting with her elbows resting on her knees, arms outstretched.

"Then what are you going to do?" Sandy asked.

"Cut it off." The words came from above, and all three women looked up to see Red staring down at them from the catwalk, arms crossed and resting on the rail. "Just make sure he lives, or it's on *all* your heads."

Red stalked back to his overwatch vigil, and Nancy glared at Martha across the tarp, hissing at her. "Thanks a *lot*."

"In for a penny," Sandy shot back, receiving an even colder glare than the one delivered to Martha.

"Quiet, both of you." Martha manipulated the bone again, trying to push it in. She managed to get it a few centimeters closer to the gash in the skin, but gave up after another trickle of blood emerged. "I think he's right."

"You're going to cut off Tyler's leg?" Sandy's face grew pale.

"What else can I do? He won't survive with the bone sticking out and I can't just hack and slash at him to try and mend it without killing him."

"He's going to die from this. You know that, right?" Nancy gestured toward the gruesome injury.

"And what's your brilliant suggestion?" Martha snapped at the younger woman.

Nancy's mouth opened and closed several times as she looked over Tyler's body, trying to come up with some other suggestion that would avoid the inevitable. "I'll get some gloves." She finally responded, her jaw clicking as she clenched and unclenched it repeatedly.

"Good. Find me something sharp, too. It needs teeth – serrations – like a bread knife or something." Martha looked at Sandy, lowering her voice to a whisper as Nancy rummaged through the drawers in the kitchen. "If something goes wrong here, you and Stephen need to run."

"Do you really think he'll hurt me if Tyler dies?"

Martha's eyes were moist, her voice quivering even as she forced her jaw to remain firm in the face of the unknown. "I have no clue."

"How about an electric carving knife?" Nancy called from the kitchen.

"That'll work. We need to sanitize it. Is there a lighter or butane torch or something?"

"Uhhh... not that I know of?"

"What about the stove?" Sandy suggested.

"Perfect." Martha nodded. "Run the blades over the flames several times, Nancy."

"Wait, we're doing this *now?*"

"He's still losing blood; we either do this now and have a slim chance of saving his life, or we just let him die."

A muttered curse came from the kitchen, followed by the clicking of a stovetop burner being ignited. While Nancy busied herself with preparing the surgical instrument, Martha gave Sandy more instructions. "Get gloved up, and find some rubbing alcohol, fishing line, needles and get some water from the storage room downstairs. A couple of their glass jars should be enough. And plenty of towels. And all the gauze and bandages and medical tape you can find from any first aid kits. I need to clean this site off and sanitize everything as best as I can, then we'll get to cutting."

Several minutes later, Sandy arrived back at the living room with everything Martha had requested, taking the needles to Nancy to sterilize before putting on a pair of gloves and opening the jars of water, handing them to Martha. "I should've opened those before I put on the gloves... sorry. Should I get a new pair?"

"No," Martha shook her head. "It's going to be impossible to keep everything sanitized perfectly. We'll do our best and hopefully that'll be good enough."

Placing one of the jars of water down next to Tyler, Martha poured one over his leg, rubbing at the dirt, sweat and blood as she did so, cleaning the skin and irrigating the wound at the same time. The next jar of water went on after, finishing the job, and she used a towel to mop up the mess of water from around his legs.

"Alcohol." Martha held out her hand, accepting a large, 1-liter plastic jug of 70% rubbing alcohol that Sandy had found on a basement shelf. "Open a window or two, please. This stuff smells awful."

After the windows were opened, Martha poured the alcohol on her dirty glove first, washing away some of the blood and dirt, then poured it directly onto where the bone was sticking out, flushing out the wound with the potent liquid and cleaning the skin around it as well. "Okay, here," she said, handing the bottle back to Sandy, who put it off to the side of the tarp. "Nancy? You have that carving knife ready?"

"Yeah I ran it over the flames this whole time. It's hot as hell but I got the blades back in the knife handle."

"Is there a plug that we can reach from over here?"

"It's battery-powered. Says it's eighty-five percent charged."

"Lord have mercy. A battery-powered turkey carver." Martha muttered. "And I'm about to take off a man's leg with it." Taking a deep breath, Martha continued. "Bring me the carver. Sandy, your job is going to be *very* critical with this. I'm guessing the artery wasn't cut, otherwise he'd have been dead in the first five minutes he was out there in the woods. We're going to *have* to cut it, though, but I'm going to try to expose it first, so that you can tie it off with the fishing line before I cut through it."

"Okay." Sandy's gulp was audible.

"This is going to be nasty. Try not to vomit directly into the wound if you can help it, okay?"

Sandy nodded. "I'll do my best."

"Losers do their best," Martha intoned in a bad Scottish accent.

"Huh?" Nancy said, giving Martha a quizzical look as she held out the carving knife.

"Nothing. Just a line from a movie. Okay, we ready to start? Too bad."

Without waiting for a response from either Sandy or Nancy, Martha pressed the button on the side of the carving knife and the blades clattered to life, sliding back and forth inside the knife handle in opposite directions a mere two millimeters from each other. The wound on Tyler's leg was longer than it was wide, though it was widest at the top near his knee, which is where Martha pressed the top of the carving knife. The blades cut through the flesh like it wasn't even there, and she jerked them back momentarily, stunned by the rapidity at which they had penetrated.

Adjusting the angle at which she was cutting, she went in again, rocking the carver up and down to try and cut through the flesh evenly, aiming to get as much of the internals exposed as possible so that they could tie off his femoral artery. The blades ground noisily as she touched the remaining bone that the broken portion had splintered off from, and she went around them, expanding the wound bit by bit, the blood flow virtually nonexistent thanks to much of the flesh already having started to die off from the hours he'd spent lying in the woods.

On the far side of the wound, after just a few small incisions, Martha stopped, pulling the knife out and motioning to Sandy. "Get to the other side. I think that's it, right there." She pointed to what looked like a thick piece of twine, though it was red and pulsating slightly in tune with Tyler's faint heartbeat. "Get the fishing line underneath, right up there near the top. Yep. Okay, tie it good and tight. There you go."

To her credit, Sandy worked without complaint or regurgitation of her stomach contents, focusing on the details of what she was doing to drown out the details around it. The fishing line went around the artery twice, then she cut it short and tied a knot, pulling it tighter gently, watching as the portion of the artery below the knot began to deflate, its pulsations growing weaker until they ceased all together. "I think I got it."

"Nancy, heat up a butter knife or something. Red hot, if you can. After I cut this, I want you to cauterize it."

"*Me?!*"

"In for a penny. Hurry up."

Grumbling again, Nancy stood and ran into the kitchen, clicking the stovetop back on and using a pair of tongs again to heat the butterknife as she had done to the carving blades. While she did so, Martha resumed work with the carver, severing the last remaining bits of flesh that attached the leg to the rest of Tyler's body. When Nancy came back with the knife, the handle was wrapped with a pot-holder and she knelt down opposite Martha again.

"Okay. I'm going to cut the artery first. As soon as I do, Sandy will hold it up and Nancy will cauterize it. Then I'm going to cut through the bone, and then we're going to wrap this leg up *very* tightly with all the gauze and bandages and tape we have. Understand?"

Their initial squeamishness had all but vanished in the face of the monumental task they were working on, and both Nancy and Sandy nodded seriously, readying themselves to do as Martha had instructed.

"On three, then. One. Two. Three."

The artery jerked and jiggled briefly as the carver's blades struggled to find purchase, then it snapped into two pieces, sending more blood oozing out from Tyler's leg. Martha ignored Sandy and Nancy as they cauterized the end of the artery, turning the carving knife's blades onto the remaining piece of bone that held Tyler's leg to the rest of his body. The blades, having been used infrequently, were still razor-sharp, and it took less than a minute for her to finish cutting through the bone, getting as close to the flesh inside his remaining stump as possible.

Dropping the carving knife on the tarp next to her, Martha picked up the remainder of the isopropyl alcohol and dumped it out on the exposed flesh of Tyler's leg, soaking every nook and cranny. "I hope this doesn't give him blood poisoning or something. Too much of this absorbed into the skin is bad news."

"Are you ready for bandages?" Sandy asked, tearing off her old pair of gloves and putting on a new pair.

"Yes. I'll get the initial layers on and then you come in with the rest." After waiting a moment for as much of the alcohol to evaporate as possible, Martha began to pack gauze into Tyler's leg, filling out the spaces and gaps as much as she could before she signaled to Sandy. "Wrap it. Nice and tight."

Sitting back, Martha took several slow, deep breaths as she watched Sandy work, Nancy occasionally reaching in to help as well. A few moments later, Tyler's leg stump was fully encased in gauze and bandages, and Sandy placed it gently back down on the floor to rest atop a clean towel when Red's voice came from above again.

"Well done, you three. You look like professional surgeons."

Martha clenched her teeth and slowly stood, angling to look up at Red. "He's still alive – barely. But I can't make any promises on how he'll do from here."

"Let's hope he makes it."

There's a giant mess down here to clean up, Red."

"I suggest you three get—a"

"*No.*" Martha cut him off, her voice rising with anger. "I was just wrist-deep in someone's *insides*, and so were they. We are *not* cleaning this up. Bully someone else into doing it, or get down here and do it yourself." Turning to Sandy and Nancy, Martha nodded at them both. "Thank you for your help. If you'll excuse me, I need to clean myself up and vomit." She touched her stomach. "Maybe not in that order."

Martha hurried out of the room, heading for the nearest bathroom while Red watched her go from the catwalk above, eyebrow raised, bemused smile on his face. When she'd vanished, he looked down at Nancy and Sandy for a long moment, finally rolling his eyes and pushing himself up off the railing.

"You two get out of my sight. I'll get someone else to clean up the mess and move him somewhere to recover."

The two women had vanished into other bathrooms in the house by the time Red came to the bottom of the stairs. He crouched near the tarp, lip curled in disgust at Tyler's condition and at his detached leg that was lying in a pool of blood and viscera. "You'd better wake up soon, you stupid asshole, and tell me where they are." Red snorted. "Otherwise I'll take off your other leg and beat you to death with both of 'em."

By some strange miracle, Tyler managed to stay alive for the next two hours, though he hadn't woken up from his unconscious state even after being roughly moved from the floor, wiped down with wet rags and placed on the sofa with a blanket across his chest. Red had gradually moved his vigil from the top floor of the house to the main floor, standing in the dining room for much of the time and periodically walking back to "check" on Tyler. Unlike Martha, who would occasionally check Tyler's temperature and pulse, Red's idea of "checking" consisted of slapping the sides of the man's face hard enough to turn his cheeks bright pink and yelling in his ear. Martha had asked him once to stop, but Red's only response was to insist that he needed information as quickly as possible.

"You're not going to wake him up by beating him." Martha stepped in between Red and the sofa, forcing him to back up a couple of steps. "He's either going to wake up on his own, or maybe never at all. He might be fine when he wakes up or he might be so brain-damaged he can't speak."

"I told you to fix him!"

"How on *earth* am I supposed to *fix* brain damage? Do you hear yourself?" Martha argued back. "Whatever you want to get out of him is going to have to wait until he actually wakes up. Now quit doing more damage to him!"

For the few seconds that Red stood stock-still in front of his wife, glaring into her eyes, she tried to keep her breathing steady and not think about how he had pointed a loaded revolver at her head a couple of days prior. "Fine," he said. "I'll take care of this myself."

"And just what are you going to do?"

"Something happened to him." Red jabbed a finger at Tyler. "I'm going to get everyone together and we're going to go find out exactly what it was."

Red turned to leave, but Martha took his arm, softening her tone. "Honey, can you talk to me about this, just for a minute? Like we used to?"

A flicker of recognition passed through Red's eyes and he halted, half-turning toward her. "What do you want?"

"To talk. Please?" Martha pulled at his arm, directing him into the dining room where they sat down at the table. They both watched a few groups working outside through the front window before she continued. "Far be it from me to tell you how to do your things. You got us here, got us a house, plenty of supplies—"

"Not nearly enough," he grumbled.

"Well, see, that's what I'm getting at." She smiled faintly. "Taking everyone and marching them off to try and find out what happened to Tyler and the men he was with would mean less people getting ready for winter. It would also mean putting the house at risk." Martha shifted in her chair, gesturing to the salt truck out front. "You came in and took this place very easily because we had a large, united group. What if there's another group out there who's as big as we are? Maybe bigger?"

Red's brow furrowed, his thick eyebrows nearly touching at the center. "You think this wasn't Ryan and Helen?"

"How could two people do that to Tyler? Plus whatever happened to the others with him."

"So what're you saying? *Don't* go out there and find out what happened?"

Martha put a hand atop his, squeezing gently. "I'm saying we should use caution and... restraint. Send out a smaller group to see what's going on? Have them come back frequently and check in?"

"I suppose that could work." Red nodded slowly, looking back and forth between the groups of people working outside. "Maybe I'll get Reynolds to lead this one. Stupid as he is, he's smarter... smarter than... than... what the...."

Red rose from his chair mid-sentence, walking over to the window as Martha got up and stood next to him. "What's going on?"

"You see that... that smoke?"

A slight puff of smoke alternated between white and dark grey, traveling along behind the trees near the end of the driveway. The source of it drew into view right before it turned sharply, its overall form obscured as it plowed directly through the gate that had just been put back up, knocking it to the side with a metallic clang that could be heard all the way up at the house.

"What *is* that?" Martha asked, eyes wide.

"It's... it's a frigging *tank*!"

CHAPTER TWELVE

The Burton/Cooper Family
Somewhere outside East Lansing

"You really need to tell him you didn't cut your shoulder on glass." Helen whispered to her daughter as she continued cleaning Alice's wound, which still hadn't fully clotted.

"He's got enough stress as it is, Mom. Besides, I've been shot... twice more so far, and I'm fine?" Alice winced as Helen pushed down with a thick piece of gauze and wrapped a piece of tape around her arm two times. "Is duct tape *seriously* the only thing you could find?"

"Sorry." Helen shrugged. "There were about six inches of medical tape in the first aid kit and that's not going to hold the gauze on."

"Uh huh." A slight smile appeared. "Something tells me you might be enjoying this just a *little* bit."

"What's wrong with me enjoying a bit of painful poking and prodding of my daughter while we're in the midst of a life and death situation?" Helen squeezed and moved Alice's arm in multiple directions, finally nodding and grunting. "You're as good as I can fix you up."

"Cool." Alice stood from the swivel chair in the office and moved her arm back and forth. "I'll send you the bill for the rash this tape is going to give me."

"And I'll send you *my* bill for my medical expertise." Helen winked at her. "Come on, I need to go out there and help your father keep watch."

"I'll come too." The two women exited the office and Alice motioned at Jake and Sarah, who were sitting around a table, occasionally helping James by fetching tools and supplies that he requested. "We're going outside to keep watch. You good in here?"

Jake nodded, and Sarah jumped up, coming over to Alice. "Are you sure you're okay?"

"Yep. Grandma fixed me right up. I'm heading out with her to check on your grandfather. Keep an ear out for us and help your dad, okay?"

"Okay." Sarah went back to the table, and Alice and Helen both picked up a shotgun and rifle respectively as they headed out the door.

Outside, the darkness was just as thick as it had been before, and it took their eyes a few minutes to adjust to the darkness. The lights James had hooked up to the several spare batteries he'd found on a shelf were still going strong, enabling him to work without stopping, but they did have the disadvantage of ruining their night vision for several minutes after going out. Alice, Helen and Ryan had all offered to help James multiple times, but he continued to tell them that their best use was being outside, keeping an eye out for more potential intruders.

"Over here." Ryan called to the pair softly from across the parking lot, where he was sitting on the ground near the burned-out van in a position to watch for signs of people coming from the front of the building.

"Anything?" Helen asked, standing next to him.

"Not a peep. I'm half-tempted to go figure out where that ATV went."

"I'd considered that myself," Alice stood on the other side of her father. "But splitting up like that never quite works out well in the movies."

"We're not in a movie, kiddo. This is life and death." Ryan pushed himself up, waving off Alice's proffered arm of assistance. "How you doing? That 'glass' cut on your arm okay?"

"Yeah. Sorry... I just can't have him worrying about me right now."

"I understand. I'm not helping you once he finds out, though. He'll wring my neck first, then come after your mother." Ryan chuckled.

Alice laughed, and they all lapsed into silence as they stared out into the night, Alice and Helen's eyesight gradually growing better, the moon's pale glow revealing more details the longer they stared out into the shadows. Finally, she patted Helen on the back and gestured off to the side with a turn of her head. "I'm going to start walking around the building a few times. You want to come?"

"Sure. You staying here?" Helen asked Ryan, who nodded.

"Yep. Both legs have been aching pretty bad, so I'm going to plant myself here where I can watch the road real close."

"Give a shout or a shot if you see anyone."

"You do the same. Stay safe, you two."

While Helen, Alice and Ryan kept watch outside in the darkness, James continued his work inside, his focus entirely on turning his tractor into something that would resemble a tank as much as humanly possible. Steel plating had already been added to the back and undersides of the vehicle, and he had rerouted multiple hydraulic lines to ensure that they couldn't be cut either by someone getting too close or getting off a lucky shot.

The side 'boxes' of the vehicle were nearly finished as well, and while his original plan called for some wood to be used, he had found enough steel to make them entirely out of metal, increasing both their weight and protectiveness. A square, ruler, sharpie and few minutes on each box had given him the places he would need to cut into the plates, a task he was saving until he'd completed all of the welding.

The front of the tractor was proving to be the trickiest job of all. He'd enclosed most of the engine bay, leaving the top and front partially exposed with strategic gaps for air intake and heat dissipation, but finding a way to give the driver enough of a view while also ensuring that it would be difficult to shoot inward was stymying him. Lying beneath the vehicle, rerouting more hoses and cables, the possible solution came to him, and he rolled out from under the tractor and began rummaging through the drawers and shelves in the shop.

"C'mon... you *have* to have one. Even a simple—ha!" One of the drawers had what James was looking for, and he pulled out a borescope camera, used for inspecting hard-to-reach places. The label on the back of the smudged and stained box containing the video screen indicated that it delivered a "HI-RES" feed, though based on his personal experience with consumer units, that meant very little as to the actual quality. He powered up the borescope and waited for the screen to finish going through its startup sequence, then an image flickered to life of the floor of the shop. Grabbing the end of the ten-foot-long cable, he waved the small camera around, watching the video on the small screen and nodding in surprise.

"Huh. Not bad." Swinging it around to point at a darkened corner of the building, he watched as the quality went down somewhat, though it was still more than adequate and – most importantly – there was almost no latency in the feed. "Yep," James muttered to himself, hefting the borescope in both hands. "This'll work."

He set the device to the side on a work table and went back to his welding with a renewed vigor, finishing up the engine bay a half hour later. Instead of making the right side of it completely covered by a solid, immovable plate of steel, he attached hinges to the piece on the right, which allowed him to raise and lower it so that he could get at the fuel screw when he was ready to increase the horsepower. Next came the basic structure for the front of the tractor's cab, though he didn't put the piece in front of the front windows up immediately. Instead, he used a torch to cut a wide slit in the front piece of steel that was around three inches high, saving the piece he'd cut out off to the side before he finished putting the front piece on.

With the large piece of plate steel attached to the front window of the tractor completed, the welding work was all but done, so he turned his attention to the slit he had cut. Like the piece on the right side of the engine bay, he welded hinges to the piece he'd cut out, re-attaching it to the main piece of metal in such a way that it could be rotated back and forth into a closed and open position with the help of a piece of twine that he ran through an air vent at the bottom of the window where it met the body of the tractor.

When the metal piece was pulled upward, it fully blocked the front hatch hole, providing the driver with added protection, but no visibility. This problem was solved by drilling a small hole in the front plate next to the hatch and threading the borescope cable through the same air vent, and then securing the camera in place in the drilled hole and the video screen on the interior of the tractor. Thusly, when the front hatch had to be closed for safety reasons, the driver would still have a view of the outside world, albeit one that was limited.

"Good enough for government work." James sat in the tractor and used the twine to open and close the hatch several times, checking to see if it could get stuck. "Time to work on the engine."

His motivation, determination and adrenaline were all starting to flag by the time he'd adjusted the fuel screw and tested the new configuration of the engine, and he took a few minute break to relieve himself in a small bathroom inside the shop. When he came out, Jake and Sarah handed him the warmed-up contents of an MRE and a steaming cup full of instant coffee, both of which he accepted without hesitation.

"Thanks, guys." James sat down at a table and spooned the chili mac into his mouth.

"You kept waving us off when we tried to help, so we figured food was the least we could do." Sarah patted her father's arm.

"You can't keep going at this all night by yourself, Dad." Jake agreed.

"It's just easier when I know what I'm doing to do it myself, rather than explain along the way. Faster, too."

"Uh huh. You're going to keel over if you keep going like this." Sarah shook her head. "Do you want me to get Mom?"

"Oh, come on now. That's not very fair." James chuckled, draining half his coffee cup in between bites of a graham cracker. "But fine. You two can help me with figuring out how to mount the guns inside the firing boxes."

"Is that what you're calling those wing things on the sides of the tractor?"

"Huh." James swiveled on his seat, looking over at the shining monstrosity. "I guess if wings were boxy, short and useless for flying, then yeah."

"We actually had an idea for that," Sarah said, taking a folded piece of paper out of her pocket. "Jake came up with it and I sketched it out."

"Hrm." James took the paper and unfolded it, flattening it out onto the work table. "Let's take a look and see."

On the paper, drawn in ballpoint pen, were several three-dimensional representations of cubes, at an angle to the viewer, with the back walls shaded with hatch marks. On one of the near sides of one cube, a small square hole in the cube was demarcated by dashed lines, and a simple sketch of a pistol was drawn near it, with the barrel of the pistol resting level with the hole, and the bottom of the grip touching the base of the cube. Another cube depicted the same scene, except zoomed in, showing that the grip was resting not directly on the surface of the bottom of the cube, but inside of a 'well' of metal, square in shape, that rose to just under the trigger guard of the weapon.

"If you have one gun per box or wing or whatever, then you can keep the guns in place by building a little hole for them to stand in. They could even be taller on the back, to help with recoil." Jake pointed at the drawing.

"And then my idea was to have a small pulley on the back – but I think it would work without it too – so that whoever's driving can sort of pull back and at an angle with the string, and it'll go around the opposite side of the pistol to put the right amount of force on the trigger." Sarah added.

"They could bounce out of the holder hole things," Jake continued, "but you could help offset that by securing the trigger guard to the bottom of the box, or to the holders. Even some strong tape would probably do it."

James was quiet for a moment as he chewed on the last few bits of his chili mac, spoon in one hand and drawing in the other, the torn-open MRE package sitting on the table. Finally he put the paper down and looked at Jake and Sarah both in turn, his neutral expression growing into a broad grin.

"You two came up with this on your own?"

"Yep." Sarah nodded. "We were supposed to be helping you but you wouldn't let us, so what else were we going to do?"

"Be the absolutely brilliant children who I am reminded, again, that I am *overjoyed* to see." James put the piece of paper down on the work table and tapped on it enthusiastically. "It's fantastic. Won't take me but half an hour to build holders for the pistols. You two can help by finding some scraps and doing some measuring of the guns and marking up the scraps."

James spent a few more minutes guiding the pair through what would be most helpful, then sent them off to hunt through the shop, the pair chattering away as they consulted the notes they'd taken and the drawings they'd done. For the briefest of moments, their present circumstances slipped out of his mind entirely, focused as he was on his two children. In the moment there was only a sense of pride, love and peace that welled up from the inside, suffusing through his whole body and driving out the stress, worry and fear that had plagued him for weeks.

He took a long breath, and with that the feeling was gone. He picked up his welding helmet and found his cutting torch, focusing once again on his task at hand. There would be time enough for feelings later. His family might have been reunited and safe for the time being, but their home was still very far away, and there was a great deal of work left to do before they could reclaim it and call themselves truly safe.

"Aren't you going to test-fire it?"

The tractor's right-hand door was open, Helen sitting in the driver's seat while Alice and Ryan examined James' work. Ryan reached into the boxy wing and rattled the pistol in its holster, tugging back and forth on it sharply. "Seems pretty stable to me."

"I don't know," Alice looked at James. "It makes me nervous. Mom in here all by herself, pulling strings to fire guns that are just kind of... sitting in there."

"Test-firing would waste ammo and draw unnecessary attention." James patted Alice's back. "It's okay, really."

"Seems simple enough to me." Helen tugged on the twine attached to the front window port, raising and lowering the shield before turning off the monitor attached to the borescope. "I'm going to be fine, hon. It's you three who I'm most worried about." Helen eased herself out of the seat and descended the two steps to the ground, Ryan holding her hand the whole way. "I'll be behind armor while you all are on your own two feet."

"It's not fair!" Jake yelled from across the room where he and Sarah were watching out the front entrance to the shop. "We can handle ourselves just fine!"

"You hush and keep your eyes open." James pointed at Jake, speaking a no-nonsense tone. "We're not having this discussion again."

"But—" Sarah tried to protest, but quieted when Alice gave her a look.

After Alice, Helen and Ryan had come in from outside to check on James' progress, the topic of their eventual assault on the house had naturally come up, as had the adults' decision to have Jake and Sarah remain at the boat shop with Duke as protection. Both of them were less than pleased with the decision – to put things mildly – but no argument would be brooked, and no amount of whining and wheedling could convince James and Alice to change their minds.

"It's *not* fair, though!" Sarah said, taking a few steps toward her parents.

"Enough!" James very nearly roared back at her, causing her to retreat back to her seat with wide eyes. "I am *not* having my children out there on the front lines of this! It's bad enough your mother, grandmother and grandfather will be out there risking their lives. But my children? No!" He closed his eyes for a few seconds, gritting his teeth and taking a few long breaths through his nose before addressing them again, his tone calm in a forced way. "I appreciate that you want to help. But you're staying here with Duke and a radio. If things go wrong, we'll tell you, and then you're going to head south for Eli and the National Guard to take care of you."

"But—" It was Jake's turn to start to speak, and he too fell quiet as James put up a hand.

"End. Of. Discussion."

Turning back to the group, James rubbed his eyes and groaned softly, receiving a pat on the back and nod of approval from Alice. "They'll be fine here."

"Yeah." Shaking off his emotions, James continued. "Anyway, so do you feel comfortable with operating the tractor, Helen?"

"I think so. Give me five minutes of practice driving around the building before we leave and I'll feel a lot better. It's like riding a bike, though, I'm sure." She winked at Ryan.

"You'll remember soon enough, hon." Ryan grunted as he pushed the door of the tractor closed. "How much more is there to do before we head out?"

"Not much." James looked down at the table they were standing around, half of it covered with the guns and ammunition they were taking with them, and the other half covered in a crude permanent marker drawing of the house and surrounding land.

Stick figures and looping lines marked where Ryan knew patrols had been set up before he and Helen had left, and a series of small triangles marked the small tent city out between the house and main barn. Fencelines and ditches had been drawn in, along with thick stands of trees and any rises or falls in the property itself or the neighboring ones, if they were enough to potentially provide cover or concealment. The four had gone over their approach several times in the last hour, refining what they wanted to do based on their supplies and capabilities as well as Red's temperament and greater fighting force. Their plan was sound and risk-averse, designed to protect themselves first and foremost while being open to change based on the fluidity of Red's response to their attack. Much would be decided in the first few moments of their arrival, though when it came down to it, all of the planning and contingencies they had discussed boiled down to one thing: cutting off the head of the snake.

"We've talked through everything and have a plan. Best thing we can do now is get a bit of rest and get ready. We've got..." James pushed up his sleeve to check his watch. "Three hours till we should move out. I'll head outside and keep watch while you all rest up."

"Nope." Alice took the rifle that James was starting to pick up. "You've been working your butt off all night long. You're going to lay down over there in the corner and get some shuteye. Two hours, minimum. Then you can get up and check everything over one last time like I know you're going to want to do."

Too tired to protest, James plodded over to the small bed that they'd put together out of boat cushions and a thin blanket from one of their bags. He was snoring in less than a minute, and Alice turned to her parents. "Three hours till we leave. How do you want to divvy up this lookout stuff?"

"We're heading out," Ryan said, looking over to where Jake and Sarah were sitting at their table, faces sullen. "I think you have some mother-children time you need to spend."

"Thanks, Dad." Alice smiled at her father. "Give a shout if you need anything."

"We will." Helen picked up one of the pistols off the table, accompanying Ryan to the front door, stopping at Jake and Sarah's table to give them each a hug and whisper something to them before heading outside.

Alice waited until her parents had exited the building before heading over to Jake and Sarah herself, easing herself into a seat across from them. They kept their focus on the tabletop, neither speaking to her or looking at her until she cleared her throat. "Well. C'mon, then. Out with it."

Sarah and Jake both exploded at the same time, speaking over each other in a flurry of "it's not fair" and "we can handle ourselves" and "don't you remember the camp?!"

Alice held both hands up and grimaced, gesturing to where James was snoring in the far corner of the room. "Easy, easy... one at a time. Don't wake your dad up, okay? He needs some rest."

"Mom," Sarah started up again before Jake had a chance. "We were *good* at the campground! We were really good!"

"And with Wilford? Do you seriously think we can't handle ourselves after *that*, too?!" Jake added.

"Kids." Alice's smile was sad, reflecting the harsh reality of the situations they'd found themselves in. "Nobody ever said you couldn't handle it. I bet you'd handle it better than the rest of us."

"Then why can't we go? We've been in danger this whole time, mom!" Sarah looked at her brother, who nodded vigorously.

"All of those times, we had no choice but for you to be in danger. We were trying to get home and I couldn't exactly leave you behind and come back for you later, even if I had wanted to." Alice's chest grew tight, her voice hitching in her throat. "All I've ever wanted is to keep you safe. I haven't felt safe much at all for weeks, but with home right around the corner I kind of do now? But it's also unsafe – *very* unsafe. And with all the people we know turning against us, apparently, there's no one here I trust to keep you safe, so that's why you're going to stay here, with Duke, until we get the house back and if we don't, then you'll have the radio and you know what to do." The words came out in an emotional flood.

Both Jake and Sarah sat quietly for a moment, looking down at the table, until Jake finally nudged his sister and answered, letting out a deep sigh of capitulation. "Okay. We'll stay here. But please keep you and Dad safe."

"And Grandpa and Grandma." Sarah added.

"And Duchess and Diana." Jake smiled, eliciting a chuckle from Alice.

"We'll be fine. And by this time tomorrow," Alice took each of their hands, looking them in the eyes in turn. "I promise you that we'll be sleeping in our own beds again."

"All right, people. We ready to do this?" James addressed his wife and parents-in-laws as they stood around the armored tractor, backpacks and duffel bags on their shoulders, pistols on their hips and long guns in their hands.

"Absolutely not," Ryan replied with a thin smile. "So let's get on with it."

While Ryan opened the door of the tractor and helped Helen up into the driver's seat, Alice crouched down at the rolling door behind the tractor and motioned for James to start lifting it up. He did so a few inches and sunshine poured in through the crack, eliciting a grunt of surprise from Alice. "Guess I forgot how bright it is out there. Last time I went out was before sunrise."

"Been a long night for everyone." James nodded toward the door. "All clear?"

Alice pressed her head against the floor, peering out at the gravel lot behind the building, the trees behind the lot and the shapes of buildings beyond. "Looks like it." She grabbed the door with him and together they hefted it upward, then James grabbed the chain off to one side and pulled, raising the door the rest of the way up into the ceiling of the building. James ventured out a few steps, rifle at the ready, but after a moment of listening to leaves and branches rustling and birds chirping from the upper boughs, he turned back to Ryan, Helen and Alice.

"I think we're good." Raising his arm, he looked at his watch. "I've got it as... ten twenty-seven and thirty, thirty-one, thirty-two. You all have the same still?"

"Yep." Alice nodded.

"I'm one second slow." Ryan frowned at his watch.

"I'm good." Helen called from the interior of the tractor.

"Guess I should recalibrate mine." Ryan began to take off his watch when James shook his head.

"One second off is fine. Just remember the times, and consult your notes if you're unsure of something." James took the radio off his hip and looked deeper into the building, where Jake and Sarah stood, Jake holding onto Duke's leash. "I'm going to keep this cranked up to where I can hear it. Don't call me unless it's an emergency, unless I call first, okay?"

"Sure wish we had a few more of those." Ryan grumbled.

"We do what we can with what we've got, Dad." Alice gave him a wry smile, which broadened as he rolled his eyes. "Hey, don't give me that. You're the one who used to tell me that all the time."

"Oh believe me, I know. Nobody lets me forget, that's for sure."

"Okay, Helen, get it started up." Helen nodded, checking that the tractor was in neutral, then depressed the brake and turned the key. The entire thing sputtered and coughed, then roared to life, belching smoke inside the shop, though the fresh breeze from outside immediately dissipated it as James raised his voice and continued. "Alice, get the dogs in the trailer. Ryan, you and Alice and Duchess are first out at the eastern ditch. Stay spread out, and don't forget to keep their muzzles on until you're ready. Helen, I'm getting in the bucket with Diana – remember to slow down where I told you, okay?"

"I won't run you two over, don't worry." Helen grinned.

"Okay." James took a deep breath. "Last thing – we're going to see faces we recognize. Ryan and Helen, from when they were at the house with those people, and Alice and I from years' worth of living around them. Ignore the familiarity. Unless it's Sandy or Stephen, we shoot to kill. Am I clear?"

All three nodded, and Ryan growled as he began to step into the trailer, following Alice and Duchess. "Believe me, I won't have any problems with that."

"Good." James whistled for Diana as Helen lowered the bucket, gesturing for her to jump in, and following after her. He slapped the metal plating on the front of the cab's window and gave one final shouted command.

"Let's get going, Helen. Take us home!"

CHAPTER THIRTEEN

Somewhere outside East Lansing

The engine sounded mostly the same, aside from a slightly throatier roar – and the plume of dark smoke that emerged from the exhaust when the throttled was pegged to full – but even riding in the bucket, James could *feel* the difference adjusting the fuel screw had made. The engine was, on paper, limited to twenty-five horsepower, but to save money the manufacturer had put the same engine in their twenty-five horsepower models as was in the thirty-fives. The thirty-fives had the computers and gizmos that would meet mandated pollution controls whereas the twenty-fives weren't required to have such things, but the twenty-fives still had, in effect, a thirty-five horsepower engine, except that it was artificially limited from reaching its true capacity.

Adjusting the fuel screw to gain another ten horses wasn't *technically* against the law for an end user to perform, though it did void the warranty, risk damage to the block if the modification wasn't done properly and really should have involved proper tuning of other parts of the machine. That would be for later, though. For the time being, the extra power did exactly what it was supposed to do: it put some pep in the small tractor's overloaded step.

The added weight of carrying four people, two dogs, supplies and several hundred pounds of plate steel welded to the sides had virtually no effect on the machine's ability to get up and go. It responded to Helen's feathered touch of the pedal like it wasn't loaded down at all, tearing down the road as fast as it was capable of traveling, taking each turn and change in direction in stride without showing any strain on the engine whatsoever.

"Bet it's putting strain on the axles, though." James muttered to himself, glancing back over the bucket at the front wheels of the tractor as they spun across the pavement. Patting Diana's head as she whined, he spoke to her. "It's okay girl. I know you don't like the tape. We'll have you free and ready to howl and bite before you know it."

As much as it had pained James to do, he had wrapped Diana and Duchess' muzzles with some blue painting tape they'd found in a drawer in the shop so that the animals would remain quiet during the family's approach to the farm. The tape was just sticky enough to remain on while not being enough so as to pull on their fur and cause them any pain when removed, though as they were unused to any sort of confinement beyond a leash, both of them were scratching and snorting at the brief confinement.

"Easy, girl. I know." James glanced at his watch. "Twenty minutes and you'll be out of it, I promise. Better this than us getting shot right off the bat. You guys are supposed to bark at anything you don't like. You just don't know how, do you? Yeah, it's okay. Twenty minutes and you can bark all you want." Placated by James' scratches but still not in agreement with him, Diana ceased her whining as she shook her head around and snorted, voicing her displeasure in the only way she knew how.

"We're going, right?"

"Duh." Sarah rolled her eyes at her brother as she looked at the front door of the boat shop, watching down both sides of the road as she'd been instructed by both of her parents.

"When, exactly?" Jake spread his arms and shook his head at her. "They're getting *way* ahead of us, you know."

"When we're *sure* that they won't be coming back because they forgot something." Sarah turned and glared at him. "Do you want to deal with that from them? I don't."

Jake grinned and tapped his temple with his forefinger. "Smart thinking. Very smart."

"I try."

The pair stood at the doorway for a few more minutes, listening for the sound of the tractor and watching for any signs of movement. When both were satisfied that their parents and grandparents had actually left. Sarah turned to her brother. "We should go."

"Yep. Which way? Just... down the road?"

"Why not?"

Jake shrugged. "I dunno. It seems dangerous around here, that's all."

"We know the people around here, though. They're fine people." Sarah's forced smile faltered. "Mostly."

"Yeah, sure. That's why they took our home from Grandpa and Grandma. Because they're 'fine people.' Do you even hear yourself?"

"What's your bright idea then?"

Jake stepped out through the door and into the parking lot, trailed by Sarah and Duke. The sun was rising higher in the sky behind him as he pointed off toward the north-northwest. "Our farm's over there, right?"

"Yeah, I think so."

"So why don't we cut straight through the woods and stuff between us and home? It'll save us time and we'll avoid anyone who might be watching the road. We should come out at the HVAC place across from the house."

"Taking the horses would be faster, even if we both rode on one." Jake looked back at the outbuilding where Rocky, Stormy, Amber and Buck were still being housed.

"And get spotted in an instant? No way. Besides, I bet we'll be faster without them since we can cut through the trees."

"Yeah, but that's where all the neighbor's houses are the thickest, too. I don't really want to be *there*."

"They'll all be at *our* house, dummy." Jake rolled his eyes.

"Ohhhh. Right. And they'll be distracted by...."

"Exactly. Speaking of which... what exactly are we going to do?" Though the initial topic of going along had come up between them as soon as they had been forbidden from doing so, their precise goal had never actually been discussed.

"Help them? Rescue them if they need help?" Sarah leaned over and rubbed Duke's head, flopping his ears back and forth. "Siccing Duke on the bad guys so he can tear their throats out?"

"Or get caught or shot because we're kids and this is crazy for us to be doing."

"Okay, who took my brother and replaced him with a wimpy pod person?" Sarah nudged Jake in the ribs, her expression playful until she noticed his somber face. "Hey. You okay?"

Jake's eyes were glassy and a tremble had taken over his voice. "Mom died."

"What? No, she—"

"We thought she was dead, Sarah." He looked at her, tears running down both cheeks. "He shot her and we thought she was dead and gone and we had no one left. And now we've got her back, and dad and grandma and grandpa but they've all gone off to die. And we're going to be left alone *again*."

"Whoa, whoa, whoa." Sarah wrapped her arms around her brother, pulling his head in to her chest as a pained sob broke free. "Where's this coming from? They're not dead and they're not going to die. What's gotten into you?"

"I'm so tired." Jake clutched tight to Sarah's jacket, his knuckles whitening, words interspersed with more sobbing and crying. "I'm so, so tired. I just want to be home. Home and in bed and get up and eat breakfast and do schoolwork and get in trouble for forgetting to take the trash out and... and all of it."

Sarah's stoutness finally broke, and she too began to cry, pulling Jake tighter to her until her hands and arms ached almost as much as her heart. A whine came from next to them as Duke pushed against their legs, covering their pant legs in drool as he pushed his snout in, staring up at them, scratching gently at their jeans. Jake finally let go, then Sarah did, both of them laughing as they wiped tears and snot from their faces and knelt down next to Duke, hugging him and petting his shaggy white fur.

"I'm sorry." Jake cleared his throat, his voice cracking. "I don't know what... what I was thinking."

"You're tired, dude. So am I." Sarah smiled and reached out to pat his arm.

Jake nodded, silent for a moment as he stared at Duke. "What was the place we were going to eat at when it all started?" He finally spoke. "Do you remember the name?"

"Uhhhh... oh, wait, you mean the seafood place in Florida?"

"Yeah, that one. 'Seafood' something, wasn't it?"

Sarah chortled. "Seafood Jack's!"

"Yes! Gosh what a dumb name for a restaurant."

"Hey, maybe Jack wasn't very creative."

"I wish we could have eaten there."

"Ew." Sarah wrinkled her nose. "Why would you want your last proper meal to be from a place called Seafood Jack's?"

"Fair point." Jake inhaled deeply and let it all out in a rush as he stood up, looking off to the northwest. "We're going to get through this, right?"

"I promise." Sarah stood and took Jake's hand, squeezing it tight.

When riding inside the tractor, James' rear end started feeling sore after thirty or so minutes of bumping around – less if he was driving over old furrows out in the parts of the field that they had yet to till down to level ground. Riding in the bucket, though, was even worse, and virtually every part of him was hurting within the first few minutes. Slouched over to the side with the bucket tilted up, James kept a low profile, clinging to Diana's collar with one hand and using his other to alternate between keeping his gun on his shoulder and adjusting his position so that he wouldn't fall out.

"Almost there..." James whispered, clenching his jaw against the inevitable bumps and jolts that were soon to come.

They were a hundred feet from the turn-off of the paved road onto the dirt one that they lived off of, and then another hundred from the spot where Alice, Ryan and Duchess would be let off. James and Diana would be dropped off a short distance later, and Helen would wait with the tractor for a few minutes before tearing onto the driveway and raising hell.

The tractor and trailer shook violently as Helen took the transition from paved road to dirt road at speed, and James and Diana both lifted a few inches into the air before slamming back down into the bucket. Looking back through the open porthole, James caught a glimpse of Helen, who gave a wave of apology and a shrug of her shoulders. She let off the accelerator a few seconds later, coasting to stop, and there was a thump and rattle from the back as Ryan, Alice and Duchess climbed off the trailer. Alice took Duchess into the ditch without looking back while Ryan detached the lightweight trailer from the back of the tractor and pushed it off the side of the road. He then followed his daughter into the ditch, giving a wave at Helen and Ryan before vanishing down the slope into the thick brush.

Helen accelerated again, bringing them ever-closer to the end of their driveway, throttling down the engine to reduce the amount of noise they made as they had previously discussed. When she stopped at the previously agreed-upon location, she lowered the bucket and leveled it out. Diana leapt out of it, stumbling as she hit the ground while James half rolled, half stepped out, taking a few staggering steps to get his balance. Finally finding it, he grabbed Diana's leash and they headed off onto the side of the road opposite the house, sticking to the trees and keeping a close eye on the burned-down homes and barns that belonged to their neighbors.

"We're behind by a minute," James said to Diana, checking his watch. "C'mon girl. Let's hustle. Nobody's going to be down here; they're all up at our place."

James and Diana took off at a run, only slowing briefly when he looked across the dirt road at the gate at the end of his driveway. Emotions briefly swirled at the sight of their house sitting atop a hill a third of a way back on the property, but he pushed back on them and refocused on his objective, continuing through the fallen leaves, winding around the trees as they passed by the driveway, heading to the western side of the property.

Once he was roughly across from the property line separating his farm from the small creek that marked the border, he and Diana crossed over, looking both ways but seeing no one in either direction except for the idling tractor waiting near the entrance to the property. Water splashed up on his legs, waist and face as he and Diana pushed through the creek at a fast jog. She breathed hard next to him and he considered removing her muzzle, but instead slowed a bit and patted her on the back.

"Almost there, girl. I promise."

She whined in return, and he was about to talk to her further when a flash of movement through the trees and fence line caught his eye and he halted in the creek, crouching down to one knee, pulling Diana close to him. She saw the movement as well and growled, straining against her muzzle, and James spoke softly into her ear.

"Easy, girl. Calm down." James checked his watch. "Just a few more minutes."

He and Diana tracked the man as he walked slowly down the perimeter of the fenceline, speaking to someone who was out of sight, his voice muffled at first then growing audible when he was in line with the pair.

"...obsessed. Absolutely obsessed. Sheri wants to get out of here and it's starting to sound better and better to me."

"Did you hear about the food?"

"You mean the lack thereof? I know, man. Sheri squirreled away three cans of beans and I think I might be able to get a couple more, but, like, what are we going to do with five cans of beans? Winter's gonna be here soon."

"Not to mention the whole...." Their voices faded away as they passed James and Diana, their footsteps still loud as they shuffled and crunched through dead weeds and leaves scattered along the fence line.

James checked his watch again. "One more minute." He looked down at Diana. "I'm gonna take it off now, okay? You need to be quiet, though."

Her large, brown eyes tracked his movements as he quickly unwrapped the few layers of blue tape from around her muzzle, and she snuffed loudly, opening and closing her mouth a few times, acting as though she'd been muzzled for years instead of less than half an hour.

James checked his watch one last time and smiled thinly. "Okay. Time to go over the fence."

"I'm pretty sure this is the first time I've seen the house from this side of the fence."

"You guys didn't visit the neighbors often?"

"More like we just stuck to our side of the line and let them stick to theirs."

"They could use to trim back some of the burrs and briars."

"I'm sure they'll get right on that, dad."

Alice stifled a snicker as she and her father crept along the edge of the fence, whispering to each other more to calm their nerves than anything else. Thick pine trees growing along the fence line blocked their view to the house, and Ryan had assured her that he only ever saw people patrolling on the inner side of the trees. They traveled together for the first few hundred feet, then when they reached the first incursion point, Alice gave her father a brief hug and wished him luck before continuing on, leaving Duchess with him. Like Diana, Duchess was similarly muzzled, and Alice glanced back to see Ryan stroking her head and whispering quietly in her ear to keep her calm and quiet.

Fifty feet later, her father was out of view thanks to the thick brush and tree cover on the neighbor's side of the fence, and Alice once again found herself wandering along through hostile territory. *Just breathe*, she repeated to herself over and over again, the words coming in time with her footsteps. *Just breathe. They're safe. Jake's safe. Sarah's safe. Just breathe.*

Each word was accompanied by another step, leaves and deadfall crunching beneath her shoes. She looked down at them, the sneakers worn and tattered from traveling for weeks across the country, stained by grass, dirt, horse manure, and the dark brownish red of dried blood. In a private moment at Eli's house when she'd been in the bathroom, she had tried to scrub the blood out, but it had merely faded, the splash refusing to leave the white and grey fabric. At a glance, it could be mistaken for another dirt stain, but the truth remained with her, marring her mind and soul as much as the fabric.

A voice, faintly carried on the wind, made Alice stop, and she dropped to the ground, scooting up next to the base of an oak as she scanned the trees on the other side of the fence. Her right hand went not for her pistol, but for the knife she carried in a sheath attached to one of the straps of her backpack, hanging upside down for easy access. A second voice accompanied the first, both of them growing louder, and she relaxed, returning the knife fully into its sheath, though her hand remained on the handle, gripping it tight.

Must be one of the patrols. Alice checked her watch. *11:03. Two more minutes.*

Minute-accurate synchronization had been agreed upon by the group, as it was the only way to ensure that they could sow the most chaos with their limited numbers and supplies. 11:05 AM was the agreed-upon time to begin their planned activities, the oddity of the time purposeful on the off-chance that the guards changed routines precisely on the hour, and catching them a few minutes after could offer some advantages. The chances were slim, but five minutes wasn't that long to wait unless it involved sitting in an idling tractor with virtually no way to see what was going on outside.

"One more minute." Helen's right leg jiggled up and down in a rapid-fire motion as she sat inside the tractor, staring at her watch. Closing her eyes hadn't helped with the intense feelings of claustrophobia, and watching through the smart porthole at the front only intensified them. "One more minute...."

When her watch read thirty seconds left, she took a deep breath and checked that her seatbelt was still latched, then put her right hand on the throttle. "Okay. Showtime."

Dark smoke belched from the tractor's exhaust as she pushed the throttle all the way to the max and stepped down on the accelerator, sending her lurching backward in her seat. Without the encumbrance of the trailer, two dogs and three adults weighing it down, the machine almost felt nimble in spite of its plate steel armor. Helen crossed the couple hundred feet and reached the driveway entrance just as her watch beeped to indicate that it was 11:05. She turned wide before swinging directly in toward the driveway, cringing as the mass of trees whipped past and turned into a view of the dented gate that had been re-mounted to the posts.

"Sorry!" Helen whispered the word through clenched teeth to no one in particular as she tore through the gate at full speed, sending it bouncing along for several feet before the corner of the bucket caught it and sent it flying off to the side with an ear-piercing metallic clang.

The tractor bounced hard on a pothole and she would have hit her head on the ceiling of the cab if she hadn't been buckled in. The house appeared in a flash through the narrow porthole but was gone just as quickly as the tractor tilted back downward, continuing its acceleration forward down the driveway. If people were near her and shouting, she couldn't hear it through the armor and roar of the engine, though she was just barely able to pick up on the impact of something – bullets, she assumed – hitting the metal.

"Crap!" Nearly forgetting one of the most important parts of her plan, Helen closed the porthole and turned the tractor sharply to the right, looking for the source of the bullet impacts.

A flash of movement appeared on the camera screen, and she saw two guards backpedaling as they fired at the vehicle, fear turning into desperation as the tractor picked up speed, barreling through the grass toward them. Tugging on the strings attached to the pistols in the wings, Helen yelped at the loud reports in the enclosed space, deafening through her makeshift earplugs. The discharge of the weapons had the desired effect, though, as the two men turned tail and ran, one of them tripping over the strap on his rifle, rolling along the ground for several feet before abandoning the weapon and scurrying into the trees along with his comrade. Emboldened by the abject fear on display, Helen turned the tractor back toward the driveway and began trundling forward, pulling on each of the strings once more while she laid on the button for the tractor's horn, announcing her arrival with all the fanfare she could muster.

"It's a *tank!*" Red repeated himself, his voice shrill and cracking. "Where did they get a *tank?!*"

"Who?" Martha pressed her hands to the glass, watching as a large, silvery vehicle chased a pair of guards, smoke and puffs of flame erupting from its front before turning back around to continue up the driveway.

"It's *them!*"

"Ryan and Helen?" Martha shook her head. "How would they have gotten a tank?"

"Red! Red!" The back door flew open, and a man ran into the living room, looking around until he spotted Red, then bounded into the dining room. "Something's going on, man! We've got problems!"

"What was your first clue?!" Red snarled. "I can see the problem right there!"

"Wha—what?" The man looked through the window, blinking several times. "No, th—that's not what I'm talking about. There were gunshots, both sides of the property. Somebody's out there, and nobody sees the patrols that are supposed to be on the sides." The man stepped closer to the window, squinting at the silvery vehicle rumbling slowly up the drive. "Is that... a tank?"

"Get your ass back outside! Find out what happened to those patrols, and get anyone who's around the house inside *now*!" Red whirled to Martha. "I *told* you it was them!"

"Red, how could it be Ryan and Helen?" Martha stiffened, closing her eyes under Red's verbal assault. "If there's gunshots on both sides of the property, it has to be a larger group."

"Ryan Cooper is involved. Of that, I am certain." Red stared at the Tractor as it began to ascend the slight sloping portion of the driveway leading to the house, then smoke and fire erupted from the sides of the vehicle, one of the dining room windows shattered and Red spun to the side, hiding behind the window frame as Helen did the same. "Is that thing *armed*?!"

"What are we supposed to do?" Martha was breathless, pressed against the wall, waiting for another shot.

Sandy ran up the stairs as Martha was speaking, Stephen in tow, eyes wide. "What's happening? I heard shouting and glass breaking!"

"What did you know about this?" Red roared, stomping toward her, hands outstretched as she froze.

"Know about w-what?" Sandy stammered, looking between Red and Martha, who was still in the dining room.

"Leave her alone, Red! You need to get on that big gun of yours and protect us!"

Red paused, considering Martha's words, then nodded. "You're right. As for you," he pointed at Sandy and Stephen, "I'll deal with you *later*."

Grabbing the end of the railing, he ascended the steps, quickly crossing over the catwalk. Martha took a peek out the window to see that the armored vehicle had veered off of the driveway and was heading around the barn, gunfire still erupting from two boxy portions sticking out from either side. She ran across the dining room and threw her arms out, motioning for Sandy and Stephen to head into the room behind them, where she spoke in a low voice.

"I don't know what's going on, but you should take Stephen and try to leave."

"What *is* going on? We were downstairs taking inventory and trying to think up some recipes to make."

Marth glanced over her shoulder as scattered gunfire erupted both from the front porch, and farther out across the property. "I don't know. Someone's attacking, though. Go on, back down into the basement. If things get bad, you should take off. Grab some food and just go. Understand?"

Sandy nodded, holding tight to Stephen's hand. "We will. Thank you, Martha. Will you... be okay? With him? I mean, if we're gone...."

"I've survived this long." Martha took a deep breath, raising her chin defiantly. "I'll survive a little longer."

CHAPTER FOURTEEN

Somewhere outside East Lansing

"I don't hear *anything*." Jake cupped his hands around both ears. "They should have started by now and I don't hear gunshots or anything."

"It's just now eleven o'five." Sarah shrugged. "Maybe they got delayed by a minute or two."

"Or something bad happened." Jake grumbled.

Faint staccato gunshots echoed across the treetops, a series of pops that wouldn't have stood out in ordinary life pre-collapse in the rural setting. Both kids stopped in their tracks and looked at each other, then another volley came and their eyes widened.

"That's not a hunter." Jake gulped. "They started."

"Sounds like it." Sarah nudged him. "Hurry up. We can be there in just a few more minutes if we run."

With a nod, Jake put his head down and took off at a run, Sarah close behind. They wound through the thick forest, the lack of leaves and general foliage enabling them to carry on at a faster pace than if it had been spring or summer. Still, they had to dodge low-hanging branches every few feet, navigate across boggy areas still wet from recent rainfall without getting their shoes stuck and somehow stay on course through what looked like an impenetrable wall of bark. Sarah's estimate held true, though, and they emerged from the trees onto the edge of a paved road four minutes later, covered in burrs and scratches, but all the more closer to their goal.

"Hurry up!" Sarah called as she bounded across the road, down a short slope and across an overgrown grassy field next to a large metal structure that had half-collapsed in on itself. "The road's just up here!"

"I'm lugging *this* thing with me!" Jake muttered to himself, adjusting the rifle on his shoulder yet again as it slipped and bumped against his back and side as he caught up to Sarah.

Several more gunshots rang out – much louder than before, and they were followed by another explosive report, though it sounded more like an actual explosion than gunfire. "That sounds like..." Jake whispered.

"I know. Hurry up."

When James had opened fire on the two guards, dispatching them first with shots to their backs and then their heads, he assumed that the echoing reports were just that – echoes. More came afterward, though, three more in a rapid-fire row, from the far side of the property, then all went silent. James knelt next to the bodies, keeping his head just above the tall weeds that grew nearly up to the edge of the fence line, his view of the house blocked by both the weeds and a series of large spruces that had been planted halfway between the fence and the house. He heard nothing except the distant roar of the tractor, though, and saw nothing except the top of the house, still standing in all of its glory.

"I hope they're okay." He finally spoke, whispering to Diana as he turned the men over, checking their pockets for magazines, ejecting the ones in their weapons and checking them for compatibility with either his pistol or rifle.

"Two more for the AR." James nodded. "Good stuff. And they only had one each. Either this Red fellow hasn't been preparing his people for a protracted gunfight or he just doesn't have the ability to." With one final check of the men, James looked at Diana. "You ready to go, girl?"

Diana's tail wagged eagerly as she sniffed around the bodies, then she looked up at him, whining softly. "Yeah, yeah, I know. You'll get your chance soon enough, killer."

Patting his leg and ordering Diana to follow him, James walked into the weed field, quickly losing almost all sense of direction amidst the six, seven, and eight-foot-tall plant matter. When he and Alice had purchased the property years prior, they had made grand plans for the entirety of their forty acres, but between work, school and day to day life, their progress had been slowed on many occasions. Instead of using the entirety of the acreage all at once, they had been forced to do things in chunks each year. The first year was spent clearing several acres and planting fruit trees, the next was spent planting and cleaning around the house, barn and other outbuildings, the next spent preparing and planting their acres of gardens, and on and on. Progress had been slow and steady, though there was still much to do – like clearing more of the fields for a paddock for horses and several additional cows to raise for additional milk and for beef.

"Wonder where we'll get the cows now, huh, girl?" James patted Diana's head, stopping at the edge of the tall weeds, one hand on her collar. "All right, let's see what's going on out there...."

The roar of the tractor's engine grew louder, and several more gunshots came, along with a concussive blast several times louder than any of the other gunshots. James froze in place at the sound, recognizing it, but in denial over what it actually was.

"They broke into the safe." He whispered. "Come on, Diana! Helen's in trouble!"

While James had taken Diana's mauling opportunity from her with his well-placed gunshots, Duchess took full advantage of hers. After being lifted over the fence by Alice and Ryan and having her muzzle removed, Duchess had tackled one of the men from behind, wrapped her jaws around his neck and shaken him hard, snapping his spinal cord in a matter of seconds. The other man barely had time to stumble backwards and fumble with his rifle before Ryan and Alice both fired on him, her slugs and his pistol fire combining to end his life in a few short seconds.

It took a moment to get Duchess off the first man. His blood was mixed with her foamy saliva, a frothy mix of bubbles and dripping, stickiness. Alice tugged at her, then Ryan tried, then Alice finally told her *Leave it!* in a sharp tone and she finally listened. Panting heavily, she looked back at the man several times, whining as the three moved along the tree line, getting away from where they'd used their weapons in case anyone came looking to see what happened.

"Is that... what they did the first time?"

"Worse." Ryan pulled a ratty handkerchief from his pocket and wiped a trail of bloody saliva from his hand.

"Think anyone heard us?"

"Undoubtedly. But with your mom stirring up trouble, I don't think we're going to be the main priority."

"How many people do they have left, do you think?"

"I've been trying to figure that out and I'm not sure. If they had a few groups out on patrol then the numbers at the actual house have to be pretty small though. Maybe a dozen or so left?" Ryan shrugged, shaking his head. "We'll know when we know."

"Helpful."

"Just giving you my honest opinion."

"Come on, we need to move in. I think we're close to the shed now. Hold this real quick. I'll go down low, check things out before we push through."

Alice handed her shotgun to Ryan and got on her stomach. The space underneath the evergreens' thick foliage was only a couple of feet tall, and she slithered forward, ignoring the sap, bird droppings and thick weeds and grass as she went. The small outbuilding that had housed the ATV along with a variety of supplies that they didn't need to access very often was sitting just off to her left, and the house was farther down and to the left, several hundred feet away.

"Dad!" Alice hissed for him. "We're clear!"

Alice continued crawling forward until she was out from underneath the evergreen, then stood to her feet. There was a rustle and shake of the branches of a few trees behind her as Ryan and Duchess both emerged, and Ryan handed Alice her shotgun. "Good. Nobody running this way is excellent."

"Did they have people positioned on the back side of the house before?" Alice pointed.

"No, just around the edges."

"I'm thinking we should go in nice and quiet, and see if we can't get inside directly from here. Cut the head off that snake right quick."

"I like the sound of that. Let's move."

The trio moved around the side of the outbuilding for cover, pausing to check again for signs of people before they began jogging toward the house. They'd only made it a third of the way there when gunfire erupted from the front side, and the tractor's roar echoed out across the fields. A few more gunshots sounded, then a thunderous roar, far louder than that of the other gunshots, echoed out. Alice paused in her tracks, grabbing Ryan's arm, face turning white.

"What is it?" Ryan looked back at her, stopping as well.

"Did you hear that?"

"Sounds like some kind of explosion. Fuel tank? Propane tank maybe? Those idiots in their little tent city had propane tanks by the dozens...."

"Dad." Alice shook her head, swallowing hard. "That wasn't a propane tank."

Helen Cooper had never been a particularly in-your-face sort of person, even when she was younger, and her warmth and kindness had only grown since she became a grandmother. Anytime there was an argument or situation with conflict or the potential thereof, Helen was the rational voice in the room who talked everyone down and helped find a mutually beneficial resolution if there was one to be found. Even when Red Fletcher and his band of misfits had violated her home and traveled to her daughter's house and taken it over, nearly killing her husband in the process, Helen's responses had been muted – to say the least.

There was something about the tractor that undid it all. Whether it was the armor providing a feeling of invincibility or the reclamation of what belonged to her family that fanned the flames, Helen Cooper was a changed woman. Bouncing up and down in her seat, eyes glued to the camera screen, she turned the wheel sharply as she chased after a group of people firing ineffectively upon her, laughing as she pulled the strings for both pistols simultaneously twice in a row, one of the rounds striking an attacker in the leg, causing her to fall to the ground. She pushed hard on the accelerator as the woman tried to crawl away, then roll to the side, but Helen turned at the last second as well, her laugh fading to a cold, thin smile as the tractor's right wheels rolled over the woman's chest and midsection.

"Thought you could get away with it, did you?" Helen mumbled to herself as she swung the tractor back around, firing one of the pistols again in the direction of a group at the front of the house, sending them scattering in all directions. "You... *bastards* thought you could get away with it, huh?"

More gunfire rattled off from the group she'd scattered, and she picked one of them – an older man, one of Red's minions she half-recognized – to chase after. Pushing the accelerator back down to the floor, the tractor trundled along across the hill of the front yard, gunfire ricocheting helplessly off the thick steel armor – then there was a hot flash, a massive explosion, and a concussive blast inside the cab of the tractor.

A flurry of sparks accompanied the noise and blast of energy, a flurry of orange that soared in from the right wing of armor, ricocheting around inside the cab a few times before sputtering out into nothingness. A sharp pain on Helen's right arm came a fraction of a second later and she swatted at her arm, feeling a sharp sting as her fingertips and palm brushed against several small metal fragments that had been embedded in her skin. Overwhelmed by the sound and confused about its origin, she briefly lost control of the vehicle, heading down the hill at the front of the house and rounding to the side.

"What the *hell* was that?!" Helen screamed, picking at the metal fragments in her arm, pulling them out one by one and dropping them on the floor.

Her fingers were sticky with blood by the time she got the last one out, and she wiped her left hand on her pants before grabbing the wheel and turning it sharply, heading around to the back of the house. Once she reached the back, more gunfire erupted from an upper floor, and she winced, expecting another explosion of light and sound, but the rounds plinked off of the armor as they had at first. Breathing hard, Helen tried to focus, to remember what her job was and what she was supposed to be doing.

"Oh, no." Helen looked at her watch. "I'm late... I'm late, I'm late, I'm late." Pushing the tractor to its max again, she roared past the back of the house, avoiding both the solar panels and their EV, making a beeline for the RV and tent city. "Come on, come on... follow me...."

With no way to check behind her to see if she was being followed, Helen focused on the task at hand. Gripping the steering wheel tight and wincing slightly, she rolled through a trio of tents and campfires that had been set up in the large grassy area between the house and barn. The tractor didn't slow and the engine didn't strain as it scattered pots, pans, clothing and personal effects, nor did the presence of a couple of wooden dressers in one tent provide any sort of an obstacle. Veering slightly to the right, she hooked the corner of the bucket in the side of a fifth wheel, the aluminum siding screeching as the side of the small mobile home was torn open like a soup can. Insulation, accordioned metal and glass scattered under the wheels of the tractor. Unlike the tents, the destruction of the 5th wheel prompted a response, and there were a series of loud yells she could barely make out, followed by gunfire.

Once again Helen cringed at the gunfire, waiting for another explosion through the interior of the tractor, but they all ricocheted off harmlessly. "What *was* th—"

The beginnings of the assumption of safety vanished as a corner of the left wing of armor vanished, its disappearance accompanied by a flood of sunlight, an ear-splitting roar and another spray of orange-hot metal fragments that bounced around a few times before their glow dissipated. Helen screamed and twisted the tractor to the left, and another explosion rang out, though there was no accompanying damage to the tractor unlike the first two times.

Turning around at the tail end of the small campground setup, she caught sight of movement off in the trees as two figures emerged from the pines, running toward a different cluster of pines situated off on the back of the house. A slight smile passed across her lips before she continued back through a few more tents, pulling on the strings attached to the pistols and turning the wheel back and forth, chasing down a few of the braver souls who had ventured down from the house to try and attack her at close range.

"Yeah... pay attention to the tank. There you go..." More gunfire chattered out, and there was a fourth explosion, but whatever had caused it also missed the tractor, though she still winced and cried out in expectation of it hitting her again. "They hit me out front and out here, but not out back..." Helen mumbled to herself, knuckles white on the steering wheel as the tractor bounced back and forth over a refrigerator someone had hauled out in the grass next to their tent.

A thought occurred to Helen, and she turned the tractor in the direction of the house again, beginning an ascent up the hill that the structure rested upon. As the angle of the camera pitched up with the vehicle, she caught sight of movement in an upper window. A person was at the window, and a long tan piece of metal jutted out, smoke curling from the end of it. *A gun*, she thought. *A really, really big gun.* The barrel of the weapon was aimed in her direction, but the person wielding it had yet to fire a fifth time, so she twisted the wheel sharply and headed back down the hill, swooping behind the 5th wheel she had damaged before heading in a zig-zag fashion toward the barn. With no idea how someone was penetrating the armor of the tractor, all she could hope for was to try and continue distracting Red's people long enough for James, Helen or Ryan to get to the house and finish things once and for all.

A fifth explosion finally sounded out, and there was a loud bang from the top of the tractor as something heavy and forceful bounced off the armor on the top of the cab, and Helen screamed as she kept swerving back and forth on her way to the barn.

"Preferably without dying in the process!"

"There ain't no three people in that thing! I saw through the crack, it's just one person driving it!"

One of the neighbors – Martha had never learned his name, as he was one of the many that mostly kept to the tents and RVs outside – ran in through the front door, huffing and puffing, shouting up at Red.

"What??" Red's voice bellowed down. "Can't hear a damn thing! Stupid earplugs don't do *nothing*!"

"I said—" The man started to shout again, but Martha touched his arm and pointed at the ceiling.

"Go up to him. He's not going to be able to hear you from down here."

The man nodded and ran up the stairs, taking them two and three at a time, leaving a trail of wet grass and dirt in his wake. Martha spun to the window, pressing the side of her face against the glass as she watched the armored vehicle swerve back and forth on its way to the barn.

"Maybe... maybe it *is* them." Her words were a whisper, but a voice near her ear replied regardless.

"Ryan and Helen?"

Martha flinched, glancing to the side, then held a hand to her heart. "Do you *want* to give me a heart attack? Keep your voice down. That Nancy woman likes to lurk just out of sight."

"She's outside, with the others." Sandy pointed at a group trailing behind the armored vehicle, following it to where it had vanished around the opposite side of the barn.

"I'm no expert, but would you say that looks like the driver is trying to draw people after it?"

"They did a number on the tents and RVs. Tore up a bunch of tents, ripped up the side of one of the fifth wheels too. Whoever they are, they want to get some kind of attention." Sandy looked behind her to check on Stephen, who was sitting on a chair in the corner of the kitchen, clutching a few books as he stared at her. "We're ready to go, like you said. Bags are downstairs near the basement door."

"Good." Martha's nostrils flared, her jaw working back and forth. "I have to figure out what to do here."

"Do?"

"If that's Ryan and Helen...."

A long moment of silence passed between the two women, sporadic gunfire and the loud voices of Red and the man who'd gone upstairs the only sounds to punctuate it.

"You're going to help them, aren't you?"

"I would never." The response was pure instinct. She caught herself at the end, mouth opening and closing a few times before she nodded firmly to finish convincing herself of her own words. "I would never work against my husband."

"Honey," Sandy glanced back at the kitchen, and up at the catwalk. "A man who points a gun at your head is *not* your husband, no matter what vows you took or piece of paper you put your name on."

Martha watched out the window as the armored vehicle took a wide circle in front of the barn before disappearing back behind it, a scream and more gunfire following. "We should get some first aid kits ready... if anyone's left alive we need to help them."

Martha left the dining room, heading for the laundry room before Sandy could say another word, leaving the younger woman to watch out the window.

"If it is you," Sandy spoke softly, "I wish you all the luck in the world."

"Dad's going to be *pissed* about the fence!"

"Dad has worse things to worry about than the fence, and *we* have worse things to worry about, too. Hurry your butt up, Jake!"

Still trailing behind his sister and Duke, Jake cast a worried glance back at the field fence that was sagging heavily. A few of the fence ties had broken off when he and his sister had climbed up and over the fence in a middle section between t-posts, something that their father had warned them time and again not to do. Sarah was right, though – there were worse things to worry about, like the overly-loud gunshots that kept echoing across the fields.

"That's dad's gun." Jake caught up to his sister, wrapping the strap for his rifle around his arm a couple of times as he adjusted his grip.

"I know."

"That thing will destroy the tractor."

"I know."

"How are we—"

"I don't know, Jake." Sarah glanced at him, eyes flashing with worry-laden frustration. "Just shut up and hurry up."

"No!" Jake grabbed Sarah's arm as she turned, pulling her back around. "What are we going to even do here?"

"We're going to help Mom and Dad and Grandma and Grandpa. That's why we're here!"

"Yeah but, like, *what* are we going to do? Storm the castle? Sneak around and take out the guards?"

Sarah hesitated for a moment as she processed Jake's question. "I... I don't know. Help them? We can figure it out as we go."

"I don't like that."

"I know you don't. It's going to be okay…" Looking past Jake in the direction where Duke was tugging at his lead and whining, Sarah's face paled and she pointed further down the fence line, swallowing hard. "I think we're following in Mom or Dad's footsteps."

"What? Wh—oh, *jeez*." Jake grimaced, averting his eyes from the corpses lying in the grass. "Gross. Let's just get going."

"I thought you didn't like not knowing what we're going to do."

"I don't. So let's try to figure it out before we get to the house."

Stopping at the edge of the weed field, Jake and Sarah gave each other a look as a smattering of gunfire was overpowered by another immense explosion. Without a word, the trio plunged into the weeds, winding their way toward their home.

It didn't take more than a few minutes for the pair to reach the edge of the weed field. They crouched low, watching the portions of the house that weren't masked by trees, and watching the commotion at the barn beyond it. The sound of the tractor came from around the barn, and there were groups of people shouting, firing guns and running around the structure as thick white and black smoke rose in the air from the tractor's exhaust.

Farther down the field, where it widened and came up next to the driveway for a few hundred feet, they spotted a lone figure and a white shape running across the driveway before vanishing in the tall grasses and reeds that bordered the marshy areas around their pond.

"There's dad!" Jake pointed, inadvertently shouting before clamping his mouth shut as Sarah shushed him.

Duke had spotted, smelled or both his master, and was pulling at his lead, forcing Sarah to wrap the leash around her hand and arm a few times. "Should we follow?"

"No way. He'll *kill* us. We should try to help grandma, or make a distraction for whoever's in the house shooting dad's Barrett."

"You want to distract the person who's shooting dad's fifty-cal?" Sarah turned and gave her brother a skeptical look, one eyebrow shooting up. "You really have gone crazy, haven't you?"

"Do you have any better ideas?" Jake threw his hands in the air, wagging his head back and forth. When Sarah didn't immediately respond, he nodded. "Yeah, that's what I thought. Come on, I bet there's nobody out back behind the house. We might be able to sneak in."

Without waiting for an answer, Jake retreated a few steps into the field of weeds and began jogging toward the back of the property. Sarah and Duke followed a moment later, hurrying to catch up with him. After a short distance they came to a stand of pines and moved out from the weeds, pushing aside the thick layers of branches. At the edge of the trees they could make out the backside of the tall, three-story house, with the rows of solar panels off to the left and their grandparents' electric car still parked near the back door. No one else was in sight, and all of the shouts and gunfire were still coming from out beyond the house, toward the barn.

"Hurry!" Jake took off for the back door at a sprint, leaving Sarah to hiss after him, grabbing for his jacket and missing entirely.

"Wait! What about Duke?!" Looking down at the dog, she wrapped the leash around her arm even further, her tone turning to a desperate plea. "Stay close to me, boy. Don't try to go running off, okay?"

Pushing forward, Sarah tugged on Duke's lead and he followed, sticking close to her side, eyes glued to Jake as he reached the back door to the house. Sarah was slower than Jake, but close on his tail, and she'd just about drawn even with the solar panels when there was a familiar, distant shout off to her left.

"Sarah! Watch out!!"

CHAPTER FIFTEEN

Somewhere outside East Lansing

Martha, Sandy and Stephen were back in the dining room when Red came storming down the stairs, his normally fast gait slowed by the enormous rifle he had stretched across both arms along with two green ammunition canisters, one in each hand. He pushed them aside as he approached the dining room table, tossing the cans onto it before sliding the rifle forward on his arms, wincing as it dug into his forearm and scraped off several layers of skin.

"You want to give me a hand here?" Red snarled at the women, finally getting the rifle into his hands and waving off Martha, who had turned toward him. "No, no, I'll just deal with it myself. You keep being helpful watching out the window. Real great." His gaze flicked over to Stephen, who was sitting on a chair in a corner, knees drawn up to his chest. "You're old enough to get out there and help. Why aren't you out there?"

"Leave him alone, Red. He's a child. And why do you have that thing down here? Are you trying to blow our eardrums out with it or something?"

"The last casing got jammed. I gotta get it out then I'm going outside. Whoever's in that stupid 'tank' or whatever it is got wise and they're staying behind the barn. Pretty sure I put a hurtin' on 'em, though. This sucker put some nice fat holes in their armor."

Red patted the rifle, then turned it on its side, ejecting the empty magazine from the well. He pulled back on the bolt with one hand and stuck a finger up inside the well, trying to push on a large .50 caliber shell casing that had gotten stuck at an angle in the ejector slot. Try as he might, though, he couldn't push the shell back into the chamber from the outside, and his hands were too large to reach up inside the magwell and try to free it from the inside.

"You want a spoon or a butter knife or screwdriver or something?" Martha asked, stepping away from the window as she spoke to him.

Red grunted as he tried to push a finger up inside the magwell again, and shook his head. "No. You, kid. Get over here and make yourself useful."

"No!" Sandy answered before Martha could, moving quickly to stand near Stephen's side. "You are *not* involving my son in this!"

Red growled as he reached for the revolver on his hip, thumb rubbing across the wooden grain of the handle. "He helps or he dies. It's that simple. Everyone has to pull their weight, and his time has come."

"M-Mom... it's okay." Stephen stepped around Sandy, body trembling. "I can do it."

"No. Not happening." Sandy pulled hard on his shoulders, maneuvering back around in front of him once again. "Just give it to me. I've got small fingers."

"Nope. The kid does it." Red's fingers wrapped around the handle, his thumb moving to the steel hammer, running along its grooves. "You've already pulled your weight with cooking and cleaning. He's been nothing but a consumer, hiding away and reading nonstop."

"Red...." Martha eased a hand onto his gun arm. "He's just a boy. You have bigger things to worry about."

Red looked out the window, listening to the sound of gunfire and shouting for a few seconds. "Nah, sounds like they've got everything under control for the moment. I won't tell you again, Sandy. The boy helps out, or he dies."

Sandy watched Red closely, weighing her options. She glanced at Martha who stood slightly behind Red, nodding her head ever so slightly. "Fine. I'm helping him, though."

"Whatever you say, buttercup." Red grinned as Stephen stepped out again. "C'mere kid, lend me the use of those nimble little fingers you've got."

Red let go of his revolver and hefted the rifle in both hands, flipping it over and dropping it hard onto the table. The gun rocked over to the side as the scope on top shuddered under the impact, and Red grabbed it to keep it from sliding any farther. After sitting down in a chair in front of the rifle, Red rolled it back over so that the magwell was facing him, then he motioned for Stephen to step closer.

"In here," Red pointed. "See the jam?"

Stephen leaned down close to the gun, Sandy next to him, and looked in where Red indicated. His whole hand fit inside the magwell, and his fingers slid around the jammed shell with ease. Try as he might to pull it out, though, it refused to move.

"I... I can't get it." Stephen grunted, looking up at his mother.

"You heard him. He tried, but he's not strong enough." Sandy put an arm around Stephen, but Red shook his head.

"Nope. Try again, kid. Get a solid grip on it and pull the front part right there down while I haul back on the bolt carrier." Red grabbed the bolt with his left hand as Stephen nodded in understanding. "Ready? One, two, three!"

Stephen wrapped his hand around the casing as Red began to count, then started tugging once he reached "two," putting all of his strength into the task as Red shouted "three." Red simultaneously jerked back hard on the bolt carrier, sending a shudder down the length of the rifle as its multiple disparate parts flexed against the pins that held them together. The motion – plus Stephen's effort – was enough to make a difference, and the young boy nearly fell over backwards as his hand exited the magwell, shell casing still held in his fist. Red let go of the bolt with a whoop and it slammed back home, sending another shudder down the length of the weapon.

"Hot damn, son! You did it!" Red clapped Stephen on the back as he stood up, then moved around the table, pushing Sandy, Stephen and Martha out of the way as he went. "I gotta grab more ammo, then I'm taking a little walk outside to put an end to whoever's driving that stupid tank."

Red headed through the entryway and had one hand on the end of the banister and was about to turn and head up the stairs when he looked across the living room and out through the window. Stopping in his tracks, he squinted and slowly began walking across the living room as he called out in a loud voice.

"Hey, whose kids are those?"

Martha headed through the kitchen and met him at the window next to the back door, looking out at a young boy and girl who were running across the back yard. The girl was nearly to the basement door and the boy and a large dog had just exited a stand of pine trees and were following in her tracks.

"Holy— that's one of their dogs!" Red shouted, fumbling with the back doorknob with his left hand while fishing his revolver out of its holster with his right.

"That's Duke, mom." Stephen and Sandy were standing next to Martha, and Stephen spoke in a voice that was barely louder than a whisper. His mother held a finger to her lips and shook her head before she exchanged a look with Martha, who shrugged.

Before either of the women could say anything, Red had stepped out the back door onto the deck and was raising his revolver, aiming for the boy and the dog that were crossing the yard, seemingly unaware of his presence.

"Sarah!" A voice cut through across the grass, causing Red to turn and grab for his holster` as he searched for its origin. "Watch out!"

"When did he buy *that*?" Ryan asked, grunting as he tugged on Duchess's lead to keep the dog focused and with him.

"I don't know, a year or two ago? Someone was selling it for dirt cheap and he got a wild hair." Alice pushed back tree branches, holding them for her father as they crept forward amidst the stand of pines, getting closer to the house.

"Was it in a basement safe?"

"Yeah. Did they crack it open?"

"They were trying to, before we got out of there. It didn't look big enough to hold a fifty, though."

"It's sunken into the floor so that most of it's underground."

"Oh." Ryan paused. "That thing can punch holes through the tractor's armor."

"I know... anytime he takes it out back and shoots it, he likes to drag an old appliance out there. Has a lot of fun filling them with holes. Shot clean through an engine one of his buddies brought over once, too."

"I'd hate to see what that can do to a person."

"Yeah you really don't want to. It's the sort of thing that, if you get hit pretty much anywhere, you'd better hope there's a hospital within arm's reach."

"This isn't helping my anxiety...." Ryan swallowed hard, muttering under his breath.

They continued in silence for a couple more minutes until Alice held up a hand and they stopped, dropping to their knees and then their stomachs to peer under the lowest branches of the pines and spruces. "I think this is as good as we can get," she whispered. "From here it's a pretty straight shot to the ba—wait. The *hell?!*"

The blood drained from Alice's face as she looked over to their right and caught sight of movement in the tall weeds out where the lawn changed to a field. Her gut instinct was to assume that the movement was from people who were associated with the group occupying her home. That changed an instant later when she saw how small they were, and that there was a large white shape lurking next to them.

"What? What's going on?" Ryan asked, unable to see what she was staring at from his perspective.

"*It's the kids!*" Alice hissed through clenched teeth. "What are they *doing* here?" Her urge to call out at them was overwhelming, tempered only by the knowledge that there could be – and likely were - adversaries nearby who would hear her.

The forms started moving out from the tangle of weeds, revealing themselves to indeed be Jake and Sarah, with Jake taking the lead, sprinting across the grass, heading directly for the basement door. Alice scrambled forward, reaching out with an arm, still unable to bring herself to shout at them. Movement flashed from behind the windows on the second floor of the house, and a figure moved toward the door leading out onto the deck. It was a tall, bearded figure, wearing a worn hunting jacket and sporting a ballcap with something large in his hand. Off to the right, movement flashed again as Sarah and Duke charged out of the weeds, following Jake in toward the house. The door leading out to the deck opened and the figure started to step out, and Alice could hold her tongue no longer.

"Sarah! Watch out!"

The figure out on the deck reacted faster to her shout than did her two children, whirling in place, hand going for a bulge on his hip.

Sarah and Jake turned simultaneously, recognizing their mother's voice, their forward movement and momentum halting as they both realized how much trouble they were in. Before they could respond, there was a rustle from the porch above and Jake turned to see a figure step to the edge, raise a large revolver in the direction of his sister and squeeze the trigger. The weapon bucked against the wrinkled, dirty fingers wrapped around its handle, the long barrel providing much-needed stability against the recoil forced upon it by the .357. A scream came from behind Jake, along with a yelp, and then a clatter of boots on wooden stairs before a strong arm wrapped around his neck and began dragging him upward.

"Get your hands off my son!"

Jake heard his mother's voice again though he was unable to see her, so focused was he on the arm around his neck. Blood thudded in his temples as he struggled against his captor, though his blows and scratches were meaningless. A flash of heat exploded across his neck and he went limp, recognizing what had been pressed against his chin, gruff words accompanying the hot, still-smoking steel.

"Quit your thrashing or your brains'll be all over the deck!" Red's voice grew louder as he addressed Alice. "And you – drop your guns and come out with your hands up!"

"Let my son go!" Alice's hoarse shout was backdropped by the sounds of Duke's heavy whining and yelping. "Let him go you son of a—"

"Tut tut!" Red used his heel to kick open the door to the house, stepping up and inside, still dragging Jake in front of him. "Language, little miss, language! Just drop the guns and your precious little brat can go."

"Not happening, Red." Another voice echoed across the yard, from the same general direction as Alice's. "You don't want to hurt any kids. I know you d—"

"You don't know *jack*!" Red's scream was earsplitting, causing Jake to wince and try to pull away, though Red only tightened his hold. "I *knew* you were behind this, Ryan! And who's this, then? This your little grandson? Sending him in to do your dirty work, huh?"

There was a long pause before Ryan continued speaking. "He's not supposed to be here, Red. Just let him go and I'll come out. I'll drop my gun and come out, I swear."

"Prove it!" Red stopped just inside the open back door to the house, revolver still pressed up against Jake's neck, finger massaging the side of the trigger guard and trigger in a steady, circular motion.

"You can't go out there, Dad!" Alice looked at her father's weapon which he had just finished handing to her. "He's going to kill you!"

"And if I don't, he's going to kill Jake and then Sarah, too."

Alice turned back toward the house, peering through the thick pine boughs. "Where even... oh my word. *Sarah*!" Alice hissed beneath her breath.

"What?"

"She just went inside the basement door! She's going inside, the damn fool girl!"

"Then I have to get going right now." Ryan straightened and raised his voice into a shout, addressing Red. "He's not supposed to be here, Red. Just let him go and I'll come out. I'll drop my gun and come out, I swear."

"Prove it!" The shout echoed across the yard, and Ryan looked back at Alice.

"I love you, sweetheart."

"Dad, no!" Alice blinked, hot tears stinging her cold, wind-chapped cheeks. "You can't!"

"Crap." Ryan pushed through the branches. "Red must've hit Duke. There's blood all over the grass, but...."

"But what?"

"Duke's gone, too."

"Did he follow Sarah?"

"I have no clue, hon. Look, just try to—"

"Time's up, Ryan! I guess you want your grandson to have no more head, huh?"

"I'm coming out! Dammit, Red! Hold your fire!" Leaving Duchess behind with Alice who quickly tied her lead to the trunk of one of the pines, Ryan finished pushing through the branches, raising his arms high above his head as he exited the pine trees.

"And there he is, the man of the hour!" Red crowed, throwing his head back even as he kept the revolver barrel pressed tight against Jake's neck. "Now who was that other voice there? Your annoying wife? It didn't sound like her!"

"Look at yourself for one dang minute, Red!" Ryan advanced slowly through the yard, arms raised, a sudden gust of wind whipping leaves up around him in a swirl. "You're holding a gun to the head of a child! A *child*! Is that really who you are?"

"Whatever I have to do to survive, Cooper."

"What the *hell* is the meaning of this?!" A new voice came from behind Red and he rolled his eyes before twisting his head around, forcing a smile.

"Honey! You're just in time to see who I—"

"Is that a *child*?!" Martha's horrified screech brought a thin smile to Ryan's lips. "Red Fletcher! It's not bad enough you point a gun at your own *wife* but you have to threaten to kill children, too?!"

"Martha...." Red grimaced, keeping Jake between himself and Ryan as he tried to reason with his wife. "This is Ryan Cooper's grandson."

"I don't care whose grandson it is! Take your gun off the boy's neck right now!"

"Martha...." Red's voice dropped low as he growled at her. "Get back inside."

"Hi Martha!" Ryan called out, waving one of his raised hands, taking another step toward the porch. "Good to see you again!"

"Shut up, Cooper!" Red took another step inside the house, still keeping Jake in front of him. "Where's the other one, his mother? I want her out here right now!"

Ever since Red had grabbed him and dragged him up the stairs, Jake had gone mostly limp, providing his body with just enough support to reduce the pressure of Red's arm and gun on his neck. As a result, Red's attention on his captor had reduced as he continued shouting at Ryan and talking to his wife, and his grip on Jake's neck had reduced. Seizing the moment, Jake threw his hands up into the underside of Red's arm, digging in with his fingernails. Red shouted, his gun arm waving about for a few seconds as he struggled to get Jake under control, finally slamming the butt of the revolver against the side of Jake's head. A tidal wave of pain radiated through Jake's skull, and his vision went blurry as bursts of stars exploded outward in all directions.

"You little—" Red jammed the revolver barrel back into Jake's neck, eliciting a cry from the stand of pines.

"No!" Alice stumbled out through the branches, throwing her and Ryan's guns to the ground and raising her hands above her head. "Please, no! Don't hurt him!"

"Well, well, well! I assume this is your daughter?" Red glanced at Ryan, then squeezed tighter on Jake's neck before turning the revolver on Alice.

"Red..." Ryan cautioned. "Don't do anything stupid."

"Stupid? Stupid, he says!" Red looked back at Martha. "He comes here and tries to start something with me and calls *me* stupid!" A rattle of gunfire from the other side of the house and beyond the barn drew Red's attention for a moment and he looked upward, closing his eyes. "That's your doing too, isn't it? That tank or whatever it is that's been running people down? Mm, doesn't matter – frankly, I don't care. Too many mouths to feed already."

"Red, let's talk about this. You hate *me* and want to hurt *me*, not my grandson or my daughter."

"Daughter?" Red's eyebrows scrunched together. "What daughter?"

"Is this guy losing it or what?" Alice whispered to Ryan as she stood next to him, both of their arms raised.

"Oh!" Red shouted, before Ryan could answer her. "Right! Daughter! What's your name, princess?" Red pressed the gun barrel back into Jake's neck. "What's your mommy's name?"

"A-Alice." Jake choked out the words. "Please, just—"

"Zip it, kid." Red tightened his arm again, causing Jake to fall silent. "Alice! Ryan! I decided what we're going to do. I'm going into the house, nice and easy. You two will come up onto this deck nice and easy, then come inside and sit down. We're going to have ourselves a nice... a nice little... chit... what the *hell* is that noise?"

While Red had been talking, the sound of the tractor's engine had grown steadily louder until the armored beast finally roared around the side of the house, leaning hard to the right as Helen turned the wheel sharply. Between the four-wheel-drive and the large, knobby tires, the wheels dug deep into the soft soil, leaving a twin pair of ruts in its wake. The tractor's horn blared several times as Helen circled around the solar panels, all eyes on the vehicle as it turned toward the house, engine revving to its max. Red stumbled backward as the tractor accelerated toward the back deck, his arm loosening from Jake's neck just enough for him to wriggle free, and he darted across the deck and flew down the stairs four at a time, running perpendicular to the oncoming tractor.

"What are you *doing*?!" Red screamed, turning and reaching for the Barrett. Weighing over thirty pounds, the rifle was not meant to be shouldered, but Red tried anyway, screaming as he lifted the weapon in the general direction of the tractor and pulled the trigger.

The effects were instantaneous, devastating and widespread. Red's whole body twisted as the rifle slammed into his right shoulder, snapping bone as it jumped up and backwards, flying out of his hands to slam down on the sofa behind him. Every pane of glass in the back door shattered from the concussive blast of the rifle, and while Red's ear protection saved him from shattering his eardrums, Martha was not so lucky. She clutched her head and shrieked in harmony with his own bellow of pain, his right arm dangling uselessly, the bulge under his shirt at his shoulder speaking to the destruction that had been caused.

The round that Red had fired had gone wild, sailing high over the heads of all of his intended targets, but the rifle's sound had its intended effect of making Helen turn the tractor before she reached the porch. Amidst the distraction provided by the tractor and Red's shouts of pain, Jake, Alice and Ryan retreated breathlessly back into the trees.

"Are you okay?" Both Alice and Ryan reached for non-existent weapons, momentarily startled by the voice until they realized who it was.

"Dad! You're safe!" Jake whispered, grabbing for Duchess' lead as Diana pulled on her lead, eager to be reunited with the other members of her family.

"Jake, what are you—"

"They came, both of them." Alice interrupted, daggers leaping from her eyes as she stared at Jake. "Sarah's nowhere to be found. Duke got hit but she must have dragged him off somewhere."

"Yeah, I know. Through the basement door."

"*What?!*" Alice grabbed James by the arm, squeezing tight. "She's *inside* the house?"

"Her and Duke both. The a-hole on the porch – great guy, by the way, holding a gun at my son's head – hit Duke in the thigh. Sarah pulled him inside when he was distracted threatening to kill Jake."

"This whole plan is falling apart and *fast*." Ryan groaned, peeking through the tree limbs. "Helen seems to be doing well, though."

"Aside from the holes in the steel plates, yeah." Alice swallowed hard. "I could see clear inside through one of them."

"Somehow I doubt that'll be a problem anymore." James gestured in the direction of the house. "Pretty sure that dude broke his whole arm when he tried to shoulder-fire the fifty."

"What are we going to do about Sarah?" Alice turned their attention back to the crisis at hand.

"I'm going in after her." James' fingers and knuckles turned white as he twisted them around his rifle. "You two get your guns and cover me. I'll head in through the basement door, hopefully without being seen."

"And then?"

James shrugged at his wife. "Stick to the plan as best we can. Cut the head off the snake."

Shouts and arguing came from the direction of the house before James could exit the stand of pines, and the three adults stood, staring at each other for a moment as they tried to glean what information they could from the exchange. Jake finally tried to speak, but they all shushed him, glaring at him in silent admonition. The tractor's engine noise began to ramp up again a moment later, drowning out the shouting, but gunfire followed closely behind it.

"She's coming around again. I think they're fir—get down!" Branches snapped as several rounds shot through the trees and Ryan dragged Alice downward while James practically leapt atop Jake to force him to the ground.

"They're not firing at *her*!" Alice hissed. "They're trying to flush *us* out!"

"Crawl, spread out! I've got Diana! Hurry, go!"

James grabbed Diana's lead and shuffled forward, deeper into the field of weeds. Alice grabbed Jake's hand as they moved off to the left while Ryan took Duchess and moved off to the right. The tractor's engine was a loud roar as it passed between the field and the house, but the hail of fire into the trees didn't abate, Helen's distraction no longer enticing enough to keep Red's attention.

CHAPTER SIXTEEN

Somewhere outside East Lansing

The front door opened and slammed repeatedly as the surviving members of Red's group poured into the house, tracking mud, grass and animal droppings across the tile, hardwood and carpets. A pair of them took up positions near the front windows while the rest headed to the back side of the house, torn between staring at their leader writhing on the floor and watching the tank drive back and forth outside. With each turn that it made, gunfire belched from three separate locations on it, hitting the siding and windows of the house, and they all returned fire, shattering glass and amplifying the ringing in the few eardrums that still remained.

"Ignore the damn tank!" The words were forced between clenched teeth, coming from the floor of the living room where Red lay, twisting in agony as his wife cut his shirt from his chest. "Shoot *them*! The trees! They're in the trees!"

"Quiet!" Martha shouted at Red, wincing as the gunfire increased. "And hold still so I can see how badly you hurt yourself!"

"*Me*?! *They* did this to me! I knew it was them! I knew they'd be back!"

"Sandy!" Martha shouted above the noise. "I need help here!" Appearing on the catwalk above the living room with Stephen in her arms, Sandy shook her head, but Martha persisted, pleading. "I need you *now*! Leave Stephen in your room and get down here!"

Sandy hesitated for a few seconds, then she leaned down and whispered to Stephen before pushing him in the direction of the bedroom. With a final look down at Martha, Sandy hurried down the stairs and crossed the living room, her eyes half-closed, wincing at the report of every gunshot.

"What do you need?" Sandy knelt down on the other side of Red, shouting to be heard over the noise.

"Hold his other arm, keep him from thrashing. I don't care if you have to sit on him – I need to take a look what the damn fool did to his shoulder."

Sandy nodded and held Red's left arm down. She put a knee on it, keeping it pinned to the ground before pressing down on his upper torso with her arms, leaning out across him. Martha nodded at her and leaned down, turning Red's right arm to examine the back of his shoulder. He yelped in pain and tried to wriggle free, but Sandy pressed down harder, putting her full body weight on him.

"Massive bruising, looks like broken bones... good heavens." Martha's muttering was nearly inaudible over the gunfire. "I don't know how I'm going to fix this. He needs a doctor – no, a surgeon."

Sandy turned her head and leaned further to see what Martha was pointing at. "You can practically see the bruise spreading in real time. And this bit here," she gently prodded at a hard lump sticking out on the back of his shoulder, which was twisted and misshapen. "This isn't supposed to be here."

"Did he dislocate it?"

"I think he *shattered* it."

"That's not good."

"No. I don't think there's anything we can do for him."

"I'm *still here*!" Red shouted, twisting hard against Sandy until he loosened his arm.

Pushing hard, Red shoved Sandy off to the side, then did the same for Martha, yelping as his right shoulder hit the floor in the process. Leveraging his bulk with his left arm, he turned and got on his knees, then finally forced himself to his feet, his right arm still dangling at his side.

"Get me something to keep this thing from flopping around." Red shouted at Martha, nodding downward at his loose arm. "And some painkillers! Oxy if they've got it!"

Sandy put a hand on Martha's arm. "I'll go check. I'll grab a pillowcase or something. You can bind his arm with that."

Martha nodded, then turned to address Red, hands on her ears, still wincing at every gunshot. "Red, *please* tell them to stop shooting! My ears are already gone from that big gun you fired! This is just making it worse!"

"Nobody's stopping anything 'til they're all dead!"

"They're gone, Red! Look!" Martha nodded out toward the back. "Nobody's there!"

Red took a few tentative steps forward, left arm curled around his right, pulling it tight to his side. He watched out the back window for a long moment before raising his voice, shouting to the half dozen or so of his people who were still alive. "Hold up! Stop firing!"

A few more stray rounds went out into the trees and weed field beyond before they all listened to his orders and stopped shooting. In the absence of the gunfire, the silence became deafening, everyone's ears – or at least the ones still intact – filling with a slight ringing. Even Red, who'd been wearing hearing protection, shook his head to try and clear the tinnitus to no effect.

"Anyone see them?" Nancy Likely coughed amid the cloud of gunsmoke that had formed a haze in the house, swirling in the breeze coming through the door's broken glass.

"I never saw 'em to start!" One of the last remaining members of Red's group shouted back.

Red looked back and forth among the faces standing up against the windows, counting their numbers, struggling against the throbbing in his head. "Where *is* everyone?"

"What do you mean?" Nancy asked.

"Everyone else. Where are they? Hiding from that tank?" The roar of the tractor grew from the front of the house, along with a couple of gunshots.

"I think she means this is all we have, Red." Martha looked at Nancy, who nodded in affirmation.

"You mean they ran away?" Red's upper lip curled. "Figures. Bunch of cowards."

"They're *dead*." Nancy wiped her arm across her forehead, scowling at the streak of blood from a gash she'd sustained outside. "The ones patrolling haven't radioed and one of your guys said he saw one of them dead, and then that stupid tank or whatever it is ran over or shot a bunch of them. A few might've run away, but most of 'em are still out there, bleedin' out into the grass."

Martha's face blanched. "Did... did it go that poorly out at the barn?"

Nancy nodded. "I got there late, after most of whatever happened already finished. Good thing too, otherwise I'd have joined them. A couple got pinned between the barn and that thing, then a couple more got mowed down by whoever's in there shooting."

"*Helen*. It *has* to be."

Nancy ignored Red's interjection, continuing to talk to Martha, glancing over at Sandy as she came down the stairs, a small tote in her hands. "That stupid thing's faster than it looks. Three of your people couldn't outrun it out in the open. Whoever's driving it did a number on us."

"Doesn't matter." Red grunted as Sandy put the tote on the back of the sofa and began to open packages of athletic tape. "We have more than enough people left to take care of this problem. We just gotta be smart about it."

"Anybody hit?"

A hundred feet out in the tall weeds, James crouched low as he looked at Ryan, Alice and Jake. All three of them shook their heads before looking down and checking Duchess and Diana.

"Good." James pinched the bridge of his nose. "That was a cluster and a half."

"I think we put a hurting on them," Alice forced a smile. "They looked scared to death of the tractor."

"They were more interested in *us* than it by the end. And we've got a bigger problem." James stared down Jake. "How could you two be so foolish as to come out here?"

"I..." Jake shrugged. "We just wanted to try and help."

"Your 'help' got your sister trapped inside the house with those lunatics." James responded harshly.

"And nearly got you killed!" Alice pushed on Jake before pulling him in, wrapping him tight, tears streaming down both cheeks. "What were you *thinking*?!"

"There'll be time enough for blame and consequences and all that later." Ryan put a hand on Alice's shoulder, then on James'. "Right now we need to finish what we started. We've got to get Sarah out of that house."

"Do you still have your radio?" Jake looked at Ryan, then his father as Alice let him go. "She was carrying ours... you could just radio her."

James, Alice and Ryan looked at each other, eyes widening before James began to fumble at his waistband beneath his jacket.

"Hush, boy. Shhh." Sarah stroked Duke's ear as he whined softly.

One hand rubbed his head and muzzle while she kept her other pressed to his leg, a dirty cloth she'd come across on the utility room floor while scrabbling to hide after getting the massive animal through the basement door. When Duke had gone down, she only had a few seconds to think, and defaulted to saving her pet and guardian in spite of the potential repercussions from her decision.

The basement had been blessedly empty of any intruders, though, and she'd managed to help Duke get through it and into a small utility room in a far corner of the basement. Tucked away in the darkness, pressed up between and behind a large tank and a stack of crates and boxes she sat cross-legged with Duke's bulk resting on her legs. Flexing her muscles every few seconds to keep her legs and feet from going to sleep from a lack of circulation, she tried to calm her breathing as best as she could while the incoherent shouting went on above her. Gunshots followed, along with more screams and shouts and the sound of the tractor roaring by, and Sarah tucked herself deeper into the corner, pulling Duke close to her chest.

Tears came at the height of the gunshots as images sprang into her mind of her family being torn apart by the rounds. She tried more times than she could keep track of to get up and head upstairs, but fear kept her rooted to the spot. After a few moments the gunfire eased up and then stopped altogether. She turned her head, craning around to try and listen to the voices upstairs, but couldn't make out what they were saying.

"Those don't sound like happy voices." Sarah whispered to Duke. "Maybe Mom and Dad are okay?" Duke whined again, licking her chin as he kicked his injured leg, trying to throw her arm off of it. "Still, boy. Be still."

The utility room was nearly pitch black, the only source of light a thin strip of daylight emanating from beneath the door. Unable to check on the status of his wound visually, she tried to do it by hand, feeling around both sides of his leg. The hole was sticky and wet, but there was no flow of blood, only matted fur.

"You're still with me, so I guess it was... what, through and through? Is that right?" Sarah took a deep breath. "We have to do something, boy. Who knows what happened to Mom and Dad and... oh jeez. Jake is probably getting chewed out right now. And grandpa, and grandma..." She groaned, resting her head back against the rough cinderblocks that made up the interior wall of the utility room. "I don't even have my gun on me. What am I supp—"

Sarah's quiet whispering was interrupted by a squelch of static and a beep that came from her jacket pocket, and she nearly threw Duke off of her as she scrabbled for the radio she'd forgotten was there, turning the volume down before putting it up to her ear.

"Sarah? Sarah Burton?" Her mother's voice filtered through, followed by her father.

"What the—what other Sarahs would be out here?!"

"I don't know!" Sarah could practically hear her mother's eyes rolling into the back of her head.

"I'm here!" Sarah depressed the transmit button, holding the radio close to her mouth, whispering as she stared upward into the darkness. "I'm here, guys."

"Sarah! Are you safe?"

"I'm in the corner utility room, with all the crates. I've got Duke here with me. He's hurt but he's okay."

"Oh thank goodness." Alice let out a breath that sounded like it had been held for weeks. "We're going to get you out of there, okay?"

"How are we going to do that?" Ryan's voice was tinny and distant. "Tell her to stay put. We'll come up with something and radio her back."

"Hon, we're—"

"I heard him, mom. Can you put dad on?"

There was a short pause before James' voice came through. "What's up, sweetie?"

"I think I dropped my gun somewhere. Is there one down here anywhere?"

"Crap. Uhhh... hang on, let me think." Sarah clutched the radio tight, counting down to ten for each inhale and exhale until her father came back on. "Okay, are you alone down in the basement?"

"Yeah. They were all shooting and shouting upstairs, but I just hear talking now."

"Okay, good. You remember where we put all the Christmas decorations last year, under the stairs to the basement?"

"Yeah."

"You remember how you can get to that space through the hole in the wall from the room you're in now?"

"I think so... I can't see anything in here, though. It's totally dark."

"It's okay, you can go by feel. What you want to do is go through into that little space under the stairs. If you go all the way to the other side of it, up against the wall, all the way at the top is where I hung a couple of our old hunting shotguns. There're some shells there, too."

"They searched the house top to bottom, James." Ryan's voice came again, hard to make out over the static. "They probably found those and have been using them."

"They're *really* stuck up in there and well-hidden. I'm betting they didn't find them. It's worth a shot, at least. She needs *something* to defend herself with." James' voice grew louder as he spoke directly into the radio again. "You hear that, hon? There's a chance they aren't there, but I'm betting they are. If you find them both, take the one with the shorter barrel. The shells will fit both, though."

"Just be *careful*. You hear me?" Sarah's mother chimed back in. "After you get it, you get back into that room and stay hidden in a corner with Duke. He'll protect you."

"I know... I'll be okay, mom. I'm really sorry about this... it's my fault he's hurt."

"We'll talk about it later, hon. Just stay safe. We'll call you back when we have a plan ready to go."

"K. I love you."

"We love you two, sweetie." Alice's voice hitched and then the radio went dead, the small green light dying out as the transmission stopped.

Sarah took a deep breath and clipped the radio to her belt. She leaned down, wrapping both arms around Duke's neck, whispering into his ear. "Time for us to get a plan of ours going, huh, buddy?"

It took Sarah several tries to get Duke to stay still on the floor instead of following her. Every time she started to crawl away from him he began to whine and shuffle along after her, but he finally relented, though his soft whines persisted as she crossed the room. Her eyesight had adjusted as best as it could after spending twenty or so minutes in the utility room, and she was able to make out vague shapes thanks to the glow underneath the door. Using her hands to guide her, she eventually found her way to the other side of the room and found the hole that led to the space beneath the stairs.

She squeezed her eyes shut out of habit as she tried to recall the layout of the space, drawing on her memories of putting away the decorations. Seven opaque plastic totes were along one wall of the space, with the tree suspended on hangers underneath the stairs to keep it up off the floor. There were two thick plastic bags hanging on the back wall, and she had been sent to put away a few small boxes around a corner, her small stature enabling her to easily squeeze into the area.

It was into that same corner that she traveled again, hands sliding across the stacks of plastic totes on one side and the plastic bags on the other, head brushing against the needles of the Christmas tree overhead. The corner her father had told her about was another foot ahead and to the side, and she groped around, tapping against the studs and dusty back of the drywall that formed the wall on the opposite side of the space.

Standing up slowly to avoid hitting her head, Sarah's fingers finally transitioned from rough wood and drywall to cold steel and slick, polished wood. Running her hands along the weapon, she tried to imagine its total length before reaching higher to search for the second weapon. It was sitting a few inches above the first, and was several inches shorter than the one on the bottom, and felt more like plastic and metal than wood and metal.

"Okay, now for the shells...." Sarah lifted the top shotgun off of its hooks and leaned it on the wall in front of her, then reached back up, arms spread wide as she felt for the box of shells her father had told her about. "Come on... where are they... ha!"

The fingers of her left hand brushed against a small cardboard box and she reached for it, inadvertently knocking it over. The clatter of the shells on the concrete floor sounded impossibly loud in the small space and she froze, eyes screwed shut, shoulders hunched as she waited for the voices upstairs to grow louder as they would undoubtedly come to see what had made the racket. The talking and shouting continued unabated, though, and after a moment she stooped down and began collecting the spilled shells, stuffing them into her pockets.

Once she'd found all of the shells she could, Sarah took the shotgun and began her crawl back out of the small space back through the hole in the wall between the studs, re-entering the utility room once again. Duke's whines and the faintest outlines of the objects in the space guided her back to the corner where she sat upright and laid the shotgun out on her lap. Duke's head quickly invaded her space and she rubbed his ears and under his chin before scooting away from him and telling him to stay still, then she got to work on trying to load the shotgun in the dark.

The weapon wasn't entirely unfamiliar to her. It was a polymer pump-action with a pistol grip and a barrel that was as short as possible without crossing into SBR territory, perfect for home defense. She'd seen her father use it a few times and watched him and Jake load and unload it for practice, but had never done so herself. The memories were quick to come back, though, and she soon had the first shell inserted, then followed up with several more. After finding the disconnector release button on the left side she racked the slide, chambering a round before she realized she had no idea how to tell if the safety was engaged or not – or where it even was.

"Crap." Sarah whispered to Duke. "Uhhh... let's set this over here, ok?" Sarah leaned the shotgun up against the wall next to her, staying far away from the pistol grip and trigger area, then unclipped the radio from her belt and turned the volume back up. "Dad? Are you there?"

The response was nearly instantaneous. "We're here. Did you find it?"

"Yeah. It was right where you told me. Uhh..."

"What's wrong?" Her mother's voice cut in.

"Nothing's wrong... I just can't see very well in here, and I have no idea where the safety is on this thing. It's not near the trigger."

James chuckled, the genuine humor in his voice a balm to Sarah's nervousness. "It's on the top, right behind the rear sight. Slide the switch back for safe, forward for fire."

"Okay, hang on." Sarah put the radio down on the floor next to her and took the shotgun back in her hands, groping for the top of it until she felt a large, textured switch that slid back and forth when she pressed and pulled on it. "Got it. Thanks, Dad."

"You got it, honey. You got it all loaded?"

"Yeah."

"Good. Those are buckshot. They have a bit of spread to them so just keep that in mind if you have to use it."

Sarah's jaw clenched as she thought over the plan she'd been devising while retrieving the gun, trying desperately to work up the courage to vocalize it. "Hey, did you guys figure out what you're going to do yet?"

"Not yet. Those yahoos are still at the back windows and your grandma hasn't come back around yet. I don't think she's drawing them out anymore – probably hurt or killed too many of them for them to want to mess with her."

"Okay, so... I know you're going to yell at me and tell me not to do this, so I want you to know up front that I'm turning the radio off after I finish." Alice tried to speak, but Sarah closed her eyes and kept talking over her. "I think Duke can walk, so we're going to provide a distraction. Once you hear or see gunfire inside the upstairs, start shooting at them from the outside. They'll be fish in a barrel through the windows. Duke and I will get to a safe spot. We'll be fine, I promise. Just watch for the first shots."

James and Alice both tried to interject, but Sarah – as promised – turned her radio volume knob all the way down until it clicked off. Duke whined at her and Sarah rubbed his ears again, a nervous chuckle escaping her throat. "If we get out of this alive, I'm pretty sure they're going to take turns killing me."

"I'll kill her."

"Hon."

"Strangle. Just... I'll strangle her!"

"I know... I know. Just... try to stay calm, okay."

Alice's eyes burned with anger and frustration. "Stay *calm*?! My *daughter* is about to use a shotgun and a dog for some sort of... I don't even know what! An assault?!"

"Sweetie." Ryan put his hand on Alice's shoulder. "I agree wholeheartedly that she shouldn't be doing whatever she's going to do. But she's going to. So we need to focus on that. And then – once this is all over – I'll be first in line to hold her down so you can strangle her. Okay?"

Alice's scowl began to break around the edges, and she laughed for a few seconds before it turned to tears and then sobs. She leaned into James' chest as he wrapped his arms around her, holding her tight for a moment, his own tears dampening the top of her head.

"It really will be okay. I promise."

"My baby girl shouldn't be in there... none of this should be happening. None of it."

"Mom?" Jake put a hand on Alice's shoulder. "Remember the camp? She was strong then. She's going to be strong here, too."

Alice let go of James and smiled at Jake, pulling him for a hug as well. "Expecting you two to stay put was a pretty dumb idea, wasn't it?"

"Uh, yeah. Duh." Jake grinned at her.

"Mhm. You're getting strangled along with your sister, I hope you know."

"I figured."

Alice arched her back, closing her eyes and turning her face upward, the eight and nine foot tall weeds scratching at her from all sides. She exhaled slowly and nodded slowly, looking between her father, husband and son. "Okay. Let's finish this."

"Okay, boy. We can do this." Sarah stood in front of the door to the utility room, shotgun in her right hand and Duke's lead in her left, whispering to herself. "C'mon. Just open the door. Open it, you coward. Come on... just do it. Hurry up."

All of the psyching up in the world did nothing to calm the raging storm in her chest, her heart beating so fast and loud that dizziness passed through her in waves, threatening to knock her to the floor. Duke whined at her, pressing his head into her thigh and waist as he sensed her nervousness and fear.

"I'm glad *you're* feeling up to doing this, Duke." Sarah forced a smile, patting the oversized beast on the head and back. "I guess it takes more than a gunshot to get you to slow down, huh?"

Duke shifted back and forth as he continued to whine at her, trying in vain to ease the pressure on his wounded leg. When Sarah had started moving for the door he had hopped up immediately to join her, his injury forgotten as he sought to help his ward. Nudging against the door, Duke's whines turned into a low growl and there was the distinct creak of someone moving around at the top of the stairs.

"Shhh!"

Sarah shushed Duke and quickly opened the utility room door, pulling up on the door handle to keep the hinges from squeaking. A woman's voice that Sarah didn't recognize came from the top of the stairs, shouting incoherently. Footsteps followed, along with some grumbling and grouching, the person clearly not happy about having to do whatever it is she was about to do.

"What was that lady's name..." Sarah tried to remember the woman her grandparents had talked about. "She's got a son... Stephen... Sandy!" The name came to Sarah just as the person finished tromping down the stairs, still out of sight around a short hallway.

"...think he is anyway. Comes in actin' all high and mighty and can't even shoot a damn gun without crackin' all his bones. Then *I* have to go searching for painkillers? These goody-two-shoe idiots aren't going to have morphine or oxy or anything like that in their frickin' basement..."

The voice faded as the woman went the other direction in the expansive basement. Sarah looked down at Duke as he pulled against his lead, his growl low and his hackles up.

"I'm guessing that's not Sandy, huh?" Sarah took a deep breath and choked up on Duke's lead, putting her fingers around the release lever attached to his collar. "You want to get her?" Duke's growls increased and he strained harder against Sarah, dragging her forward a few inches across the floor. "Okay. Go get 'er."

The moment the latch came off Duke's collar, the dog bounded forward, nails digging into the concrete and then scrabbling across the hardwood and tile at the far end of the hallway. Sarah followed him, and turned the corner just in time to see a woman at the opposite end of the basement throw her hands in the air and let out a muffled scream before it was cut off as Duke leapt onto her chest. Burying his jaws into the soft of her neck he squeezed and shook, cutting off Nancy Likely's ability to call for help and draining the life from her in a matter of seconds.

Sarah ran to Duke's side as he released Nancy, the woman's head falling to the hard floor with a wet crunch. A wave of nausea passed through Sarah's gut but she ignored it, taking Duke by the collar and leading him away from the woman's body before putting his lead back on. "Jeez, buddy. I sure *hope* that wasn't the nice lady...." She looked upward as footsteps tromped back and forth above her head. "I wonder how long till they notice she's missing. Should we make our move now?"

Blood dripped from Duke's muzzle as he looked up at Sarah then at the ceiling, alternating between a soft whine and low growl as the voices grew louder. "I guess that answers my question, huh?"

With one final glance back at the mangled corpse lying in a steadily expanding pool of blood, Sarah pulled at Duke's lead and began heading back toward the stairs, sweaty fingers squeezing tight around the shotgun's pistol grip.

"*Advil?* That's it?"

Red held the cerulean-colored bottle aloft in his good hand, his mouth twisted in a scowl as he lobbed it at Sandy. Missing her by a good two feet, it bounced off the hardwood floor and the top flew off, spilling the softgels. Sandy retreated with the small plastic bin of medical supplies, looking apologetically at Martha.

"Red." Martha's lips thinned, her jawline working back and forth as she clenched. "You need to stop this and think rationally."

"Just what's that supposed to mean, woman?" Red turned to her, instinctively trying to raise his right hand only to groan in pain before raising his left.

"What it means, *husband*, is that you should know when to admit defeat and be able to handle that like a man."

"So you want to give up, huh?" Red gestured to the room at large. "You want to give up on all this? Then what?" His voice grew louder. "Crawl back to Grand Rapids? Try to eke out a living somehow? Beg the *government* for handouts? That's even *if* we could get past Ryan and Helen and that stupid... tank or whatever the hell it is!"

"Are you done?"

"I don't know! Maybe!"

"Tell me when you're done yelling at me so I can respond."

Red rolled his eyes, turning to the few remaining members of his group standing near the windows. "Oh I haven't even *begun* to yell! I'm just getting started! What about these idiots, huh? Can't hit the broad side of a barn! What are we supposed to do, Martha?" Red turned back to her. "Why don't you tell me? Go on! I'm done now – tell me!"

Martha's voice was calm and steady, but a razor's edge, unlike anything Sandy had heard slip past the older woman's lips. "We left our home to find something better, Red. And somewhere along the way you changed. Maybe it was that couple you killed. Or that family. Or those workers. Or maybe you didn't change at all, and I've just been a willfully ignorant fool to not see it for all these years." Martha's words grew louder, cutting off any attempts Red made to speak over her.

"You've gotten a couple *dozen* people killed doing this Red, plus all the ones you had a hand in killing directly. And for

MIKE KRAUS

what? A big house? Some land? Things that we didn't find, but *stole* from good, hardworking neighbors. No, not neighbors. *Friends*. People we *knew*. You are an *evil* man, Red Fletcher. I was a fool to think you were anything but."

Red took a step closer, his good hand clenched into a fist, but Martha continued unabated, her voice a shout, echoing through the whole room. "What I *want* you to do is go out there, hands to the sky, and beg for mercy. Throw yourself at their feet and pray that they let us leave with our lives. It's the only decent thing left for you to do! What do I *expect* you to do, though?" Martha's gusto faltered, her shoulders slumping, voice dropping to a near-whisper. "To keep doing the wrong thing."

Red stared at his wife for a long moment, good fist clenching and unclenching repeatedly. Martha slumped down in a nearby chair, head in her hands, not meeting his gaze. Finally, he spoke.

"Someone go find me painkillers. Ones that'll actually work."

"I checked the bathrooms upstairs," Sandy volunteered with an audible gulp. "They didn't have anything except what I brought. I'll go back up and keep looking, though. We'll find you something, I promise."

"You," Red turned to look at Nancy. "Look downstairs and hurry up with it. I'm pretty sure that I'm hallucinating from the pain. Find me something strong. They've got to have something lying around."

Nancy Likely nodded at Red before heading toward the stairs, talking under her breath the whole way. Ignoring the looks from the others standing at the back windows, Red stood and stared at the fields for a few moments before sweeping his left arm over them.

"We're going to need to deal with that tank somehow. You two, get the fifty and get upstairs. Fill that sucker with holes. Don't shoulder fire it, though." The two men Red had pointed at looked at each other, then back at Red.

"You already shot it a few times, though, and it didn't do jack."

"The rounds penetrated through it, though, didn't they? So you keep penetrating it until the driver's turned to a pink mist. Got it?"

A simultaneous "oh" came from the pair and Red rolled his eyes, pacing back and forth across the floor, left hand massaging his upper right arm. "The rest of us will need to head out back and flush Ryan and his daughter and grandson out of hiding."

"You're really going to keep doing this, aren't you?" Martha asked from her seat on the couch.

"Yes I am, *wife*."

Sarah ascended the basement steps gingerly, keeping Duke tight to her leg, tugging on his lead every time he tried to whine or growl. Smiling as she hit the fourth step, she silently apologized to her parents for all the complaining she'd done when she'd been roped into helping them replace the boards a few months prior. The squeaking from the stairs had gotten unbearable, and while the work had been annoying, it was paying off in ways she'd never imagined.

"Yes I am, *wife*."

A man's voice was audible as he started to shout, and she kept moving, stopping two steps from the door which was mostly closed. Peeking through the cracks, she saw a man in a red baseball hat standing near the windows as he talked to a woman sitting on the sofa. The others in the room were all watching him, and Sarah whispered to Duke.

"That a bad guy, boy?" Duke pulled against the lead again, and Sarah had to cinch up on her grip to keep him still.

"And I don't appreciate your attempts to undermine me, either." The man in the red cap continued. "I might be 'evil' in your eyes, but I'm still doing my damned best to take care of us and keep us alive! And if that means I have to kill people to keep us alive, then so be it!"

"Even if they're your friends?" The woman sitting on the sofa spoke again.

"Ryan Cooper is not and never was my friend!"

"You played golf and poker with him. That makes him more than the strangers you gunned down!"

"Okay, so that's *definitely* the guy grandma and grandpa talked about." Sarah murmured. "His wife doesn't sound so bad, though."

"Oh please!" The man threw up his left arm, turning so that Sarah could see that his right arm was bound tight to his chest, his shirt torn at the right shoulder to expose an unnatural lump and bright purple and red bruises. "I'd kill whoever I need to!" The man whirled to a pair of other men who were standing near the staircase going to the upper floor, one of

798

which was holding a large gun that Sarah immediately recognized. "And you two – get your butts upstairs and take out that tank!"

"Okay, boy. It's now or never."

Sarah's stomach whirled and her breaths came fast and short as she surged up the last two stairs, letting out just enough of Duke's lead to bring her left hand up to the shotgun and hold it to her shoulder. She pushed open the door with the barrel and turned the shotgun toward the two men nearest her, targeting the one holding her father's gun. Her shoulder burned the instant she pulled the trigger, the shotgun kicking her like a mule.

"Drop it!"

Sarah's scream echoed after the shotgun blast, though the words were unnecessary as the man holding the fifty-caliber rifle took the brunt of the shotgun blast in his chest, turning his sweat-stained t-shirt a deep crimson as he collapsed on the floor, howling in agony. Duke began snarling and barking, pulling against Sarah, but she braced her hip on the basement stair doorway, tucking her right shoulder into it as well so that she could whip the shotgun back and forth across the people standing in the room.

Red's right hand tried to instinctually go for his hip, and though the bandages kept it tight in place, the muscle movement lit a fire that coursed through his entire limb. The large rifle fell awkwardly to the ground, the long barrel striking the second man who'd been tasked to go to the top floor in the back of his knees. He fell to the floor, drawing Sarah's attention for a second before she swiveled back to keep the man in the red cap in view.

"Nobody move!" The hardness in Sarah's words surprised even herself, and she took a step forward, Duke glued to her leg and hip as she walked, his fangs bared and a low growl in his throat.

"You're gonna want to put that gun down there, little missy." Red nodded down at his injured arm. "Otherwise you'll end up like me."

Behind Red, one of his followers started moving laterally toward the kitchen but Sarah picked up on the motion, swinging the shotgun toward him and firing again. Unlike her first shot, which had landed squarely thanks to how close she was to her target, her second shot went wide, only catching the man in one arm with a few of the pellets. The auditory force of the blast was lessened from the first shot – no doubt thanks to the hearing damage she'd suffered – but the physical force was more potent, and the shotgun nearly left her hands. As she fumbled with it, the man who'd collapsed on the floor near to her lunged forward, clawing and scrabbling along.

Duke snarled and pulled on his lead but Sarah held him firm, not seeing the man who was only a couple of feet away. He reached out, pushing up off the floor and grabbed the shotgun's barrel, pushing hard to knock her off-balance, then tugging to jerk it out of her grip. Sarah staggered back, nearly falling, only stopping because of the wall behind her, Duke's lead still clutched tight. The massive beast was in a frenzy, a mixture of foam and blood flying from his jaws as he barked and snapped, standing in between Sarah and the others in the room to protect her as best as he could.

"Put that mutt—wait, no!" Red strode forward, gesturing for one of the men behind him to come forward. "Put *her* down, then secure the mutt. We can always train it and use it."

"Red! No!" Martha shouted, started to rise from her seat, but he kicked at her, knocking her to the ground.

"With pleasure." The man grinned wickedly.

The man started to move to the left to get a clear shot at Sarah, raising his rifle once he was clear of Red when his whole body slumped like a puppet whose strings had been cut. Red and white colored gore mixed with his blonde hair as it exploded from the side of his head and he crumpled to the floor like a flattening accordion. The gunshot's report echoed from the back field an instant later, and the room erupted into chaos.

"You sure we shouldn't spread out?"

"We don't have radios," James whispered back to his wife, silently counting the seconds between each inhale and exhale, trying to keep his heart rate under control. "We should stick together for now."

"What're they doing?" Ryan asked from the other side of James, holding on to the leads for both Duchess and Diana.

Peering unblinking through the scope, James provided a running commentary. "The big one's talking to a couple of women... one of them's going upstairs, the other's heading for the basement."

"Sarah." Alice wrung her hands. "Can't we do *something*?"

"I'm tracking her through the windows. If I can do something to help Sarah, I will. Wait. Okay, the lady's going in the opposite direction of where Sarah's hiding." James angled the rifle back to the right, careful to keep his movements restrained to avoid being seen amid the tall weeds and pine branches. "There's movement at the other end... I think it's— wait, that's got to be Duke and Sarah. They're following the lady and—" James pulled back from the scope, eyes wide.

"Did they just do what I think they did?" Jake asked, no small amount of pride in his voice.

"Pretty sure, yeah."

"Duke is one helluva dog." Ryan smiled grimly.

"Yeah, holy cow. He's *covered* in red." James managed a nervous chuckle. "Okay, uhhh, looks like they're moving back the other way, toward the stairs. Yep, she's gone." James lowered the rifle, rubbing his eye before returning it to the scope. "Everyone upstairs is still there, near the back windows. I'd take out Fletcher but he's half behind a wall. Son of a gun... hold on, there's movement. Two heading for the stairs going up, and one of them's got—oh crap! *Sarah*!"

"They've got her?!"

"No, no, but she's there, at the top of the stairs and—oh, *jeez*." The shotgun blast was somewhat muffled but still audible, and James tracked the two men who fell down in its wake. "She shot a couple of them, it looks like. Good girl... okay, time to help her out."

James ticked the safety off on the rifle and adjusted in his crouch, leaning up against Ryan to help steady his aim. The seconds ticked by, stretching out as he watched the figures moving around, only able to see their top halves due to the angle he was viewing them at. Sarah moved further into the room, then there was a hand reaching for her shotgun, ripping it from her grasp, then there was a flash of white as Duke jumped upward and retreated to guard her. Swiveling to the left, James spotted more movement as one of the men standing behind Red moved into view, lifting a rifle, pointing it at his daughter.

"No."

James exhaled the word in a breath that came as he squeezed the trigger. The rifle bucked in his grip, a hole appeared in one of the house's back windows, the man who'd been threatening his daughter collapsed to the floor and utter chaos broke out in the living room of the Burton family home.

CHAPTER SEVENTEEN

Somewhere outside East Lansing

"Run! Take the back porch! I'm circling around to the front!"

Ryan was the first up, his legs throbbing as they went from resting to pumping in an instant. He angled toward the side of the house, crashing through the tall weeds and pine trees, exiting out into the yard, heading for the slope of the hill on the side of the house where the water tanks and well pump were located. While going up the hill would have been painful and exhausting in any other situation, having Duchess practically pulling him the entire way made it far easier. While his main goal was to flank and provide crossfire from the front of the house, his worries about Helen's state weighed heavily on him. The tractor hadn't appeared out back since he, Alice and James had retreated into the field, and his fears grew a hundredfold when he spotted the vehicle tipped over onto its side out near the barn, a pair of deep ruts behind it.

"Son of a…" Ryan paused just long enough to glance at the house, then over at the tractor before snapping back into motion, running for the vehicle as he panted and muttered under his breath, trying to keep Duchess under control while simultaneously looking for any potential threats. "I'm coming, hon… I'm coming… please be okay."

"Ryan!" A voice caught his attention and he raised his pistol by force of habit, turning to where it'd come from.

"Helen?!" Ryan angled back up toward the house, lowering his gun as he spotted his wife leaning on one of the closed garage doors, her face and shirt stained with blotches of red, a rifle gripped tight in her hands. "What happened? Are you okay?"

"I'm fine. Hit my head something fierce when I turned over the tractor. Took a turn way too sharp." Helen smiled tenaciously as Duchess licked at her arms and hands. "What are *you* doing up here?"

"Everything went to hell." Ryan nodded at her rifle. "You good to shoot?"

"You'd better believe it."

"Can you handle Duchess?"

"Yep."

"Good, come on. Sarah's inside and she's in trouble. Alice and James are out back and we need to go in through the front."

"Sarah's *inside*?!"

"Come on!"

Ryan ignored her question and rounded the front flowerbeds, Helen and Duchess close behind as they headed for the front door. Instead of waiting and listening, Ryan opted for the less subtle approach of bursting in through the door with as much noise as possible, stopping just inside the entryway, pistol raised as he glanced around, trying to take in what was going on.

Two men were lying dead on the floor of the living room and two more were standing near the back door out to the porch, facing off against James, Alice, Jake and Diana who stood just inside the back door. Martha Fletcher was trying to pull herself up off the living room floor, and behind her the last remaining member of Red's people stood with his back against the door leading down to the basement where Duke snarled, barked and banged against it, all in an effort to get to Sarah, his barks exciting both Duchess and Diana who joined in the din, pulling at their respective leads.

"Sarah!" Ryan shouted. "Are you okay?"

"She's *fine*, Ryan, and she'll *stay* fine so long as all of you back off!"

Red Fletcher stood with his back to the fireplace, a few feet from his own wife, his good arm wrapped around Sarah's neck, pulling her up to her tiptoes. The bandages holding his right arm to his body had been pulled loose and Red was holding a knife to Sarah's neck, the pain from doing so evident as he continued to lick his lips and grit his teeth, sweat pouring down his face.

"Let her go!" James shouted.

"Drop your guns!" Alice screamed at the pair of neighbors still loyal to Red, their recognition of the Burtons obvious as they faltered, their rifles quivering and shaking.

"You do *not* drop your guns!" Red's face turned crimson as he shouted back. "We've finally got them *exactly* where we want them!"

"You've got a knife, your two idiots are outgunned and outnumbered and if any of you take a single shot, you'll have two dogs at your throats faster than you can blink. Three once Duke gets through that door." Ryan snarled. "You're up a creek, Red, but if you let my granddaughter go, we'll let you walk out of here alive. You have my word."

"Listen to him, Red, please!" Martha was on her knees, staring up at him from just a few feet away, one hand on the sofa, still trying to push herself up. "We can walk away!"

"So we walk off and *die*? No! Hell no!" Red's broken arm shook, the knife dropping half an inch as he tried to steady it and fight off the pain.

"She's a *child*, Red!" Martha managed to get her right foot underneath of her as she pleaded with her husband. "You're threatening to kill a *child*! Can't you hear yourself?"

"She's an obstacle." Red growled, gripping Sarah tighter with his left arm. "And she's leverage. For me – for *us*! For us to actually *live*!"

"Us?" Martha spat, voice rising as she slowly rose. "*Us?!* You held a gun to my head! You threatened to kill three separate children, not to mention the whole families you already killed!"

Martha stood tall, her right arm swinging up to reveal she was holding Red's large stainless steel revolver which she pointed at the side of his head, her grip firm and her aim steadier than stone. Tears fell from her eyes and her voice dropped, barely a whisper.

"No... there is no 'us' anymore, Red Fletcher."

Red's grip loosened on Sarah, dropping her as Martha began to squeeze the trigger. He turned toward his wife, swinging the knife at her, mouth open in a silent scream that never got a chance to come to fruition. The six-inch barrel of the revolver belched fire as the knife impacted with Martha, the round passing into, through and out of Red's skull as his blade completed its swing, cutting deep into the side of Martha's neck. Both husband and wife fell to the floor, one dead before he finished moving, the other crying out in anguish as her essence exited her body in dark red gushes, the pain of her mortal wound nothing compared to that of being forced to take the life of the one she had once loved.

"If I see you anywhere, anytime, for *any* reason, you're *dead*!"

Alice's shout chased the three surviving members of Red Fletcher's followers – her own neighbors – as they fled down the driveway, stumbling and falling to the gravel more than once before they managed to make it to the end and disappear around the corner. Satisfied that they were gone, Alice called Jake over.

"Stand guard, would you? I don't think they'll be back, but better safe than sorry."

"Will do." Jake looked over at the living room where Ryan, Helen and Sandy had knelt in a circle. "Is she..."

"She will be soon, yes. Could you take Sandy's son, Stephen out on the porch with you? Sarah, too. And keep the dogs outside. We could use some space in here."

"We've got it."

While Jake went into the dining room to get Stephen and Sarah and round up the three dogs, Alice hurried back into the living room and knelt down next to the others. Sandy had a bandage pressed firmly against Martha's neck, but it was soaked through with blood that stained her fingers and soaked into the carpet. She looked up at Helen, eyes glassy, shaking her head ever so slightly.

"It's too deep. I can't... even if she had an ambulance, I don't think she'd make it."

"Don't.... want to... make it." Martha's hand came up and Helen took it, gripping it tight.

"We can't thank you enough for what you did, honey." Helen's smile was laced with sadness, tears running down her cheeks. "I'm so sorry you had to."

"Don't be." Martha's words were a whisper, her breathing labored and heavy. "He... he was going to hurt her. Is she..."

"She's fine, thanks to you." James said, brushing a few hairs out of Martha's eyes. "She's my daughter, and I'm indebted to you for saving her."

"Daughter." Martha's eyes flitted to Alice. "You... mother?"

"I am. Alice. Alice Burton."

"I'm sorry. Sorry... for what we did... did to... home..."

"Shh, don't talk, you're just making it worse." Alice took Martha's other hand, looking over at her mother. "We can't do anything?"

Helen shook her head and held tight to Martha's hand, she and the others lapsing into silence as they listened to Martha's final, slow breaths that eventually stopped, her hands going limp and slipping from Helen and Alice's fingers. The four stayed with Martha for a time, unmoving, their eyes closed as they gave silent thanks for an imperfect person who, when it truly mattered, sacrificed everything she had for the good of another.

EPILOGUE

Six months later

"Are you *sure* you're going to be alright?" Alice held her mother's hands, squeezing tight. "We can call it off right now. I don't mind!"

"Will you shut up and get out of here already?" Ryan came up from behind Helen, rolling his eyes as he playfully pushed on his daughter's shoulder. "It's *you* we should be worried about, going on a two-week trip back down south."

"Don't you try to turn this around on me, Dad. We've got the US military babysitting us the whole way. Who do you guys have, huh?"

"Sandy, her son, three bonafide killer dogs... oh, and the *US military*. Seriously, we don't need our own babysitters!"

"Don't look at me. Talk to James if you don't like it! But then you'll probably have to talk to that Hawkins fellow, and between you and me I think he's pretty annoyed that he missed out on helping us take back the house, so he's overcompensating."

"That's my daughter, making the oddest friends." Helen gave Alice a final hug, then Ryan did the same. "You four stay safe, you hear me?"

"You too. We'll radio daily if the phones stop working."

"We'll pick up – if we're not too busy." Ryan winked at Alice as Stephen came running up, followed closely by Sandy. "With Jake and Sarah gone I'm going to put this guy to work on repairing the barn."

"You haven't left yet?" Sandy asked, checking her watch before giving Alice a quick hug as well.

"Yeah, yeah, I know. We're outta here." Alice nodded. "We'll be back."

"You'd better!" Ryan called, waving as Alice jogged down the front steps, around the curving walkway and down the driveway to where the convoy was waiting. She hopped a few times to catch a glimpse through the slats of a trailer behind one of the Humvees as she went, finally patting it with satisfaction before continuing on.

"Sheesh, Mom, we were gonna leave without you!" Jake yelled out through the back hatch of an armored personnel carrier, eliciting an eyeroll from his mother. Alice climbed into the vehicle, sitting in the seat next to James, smiling as he and a woman sitting across from them finished their laughing conversation.

"You did *not*!" the woman threw her head back, slapping one leg.

"Hand to heart, when I woke up I thought – just for a few seconds mind you – that I was in some kind of zombie horror movie."

"Well it's no wonder you were smashing through the door like you were going to kill something!" the woman wiped a tear from her eye and grinned. "Also, your wife is *just* as lovely as you described."

Alice grinned as she caught sight of the woman's name tag, standing up to give her a quick embrace before they both sat back down. "Private Oswell – so good to finally meet you in person. From what James told me, you two had a pretty rough go of it."

"You can say that again." Oswell's cheerful demeanor vanished. "If it wasn't for him helping me out, I'd be a rotting corpse in some no-name alley in Chicago."

"As I've told you a hundred times, we saved each other." James grinned. "It was awesome of Colonel Hawkins to send you along."

"Oh, please, I would have chewed his arm off if he hadn't. Escorting your family during a supply run down south and back up? Highlight of my year."

"When do we see the Colonel anyway?"

"He's on the first stop!" Oswell pulled a notebook from one of her vest pockets and flipped it open. "He'll be waiting for us with your Amish friends."

"Have there been any changes with the other stops we're making?" Alice leaned up, trying to catch sight of the paper.

"Nope!" Oswell smiled, turning the notebook around. "Everything's on track!"

"And Eli and his family are okay with what we requested? And you all are, too?"

Oswell's eyes grew big. "Uhhh... the less said about that the better. But yes, we're meeting that request."

Alice leaned back in her seat, exhaling in relief. "Good."

"You all ready to rock and roll?" A uniformed figure peeked into the vehicle, stiffening when he spotted James. "Mr. Burton! Good to see you! We appreciate the refuel. Wasn't necessary, but it's much appreciated."

"It's our way of contributing to this venture." James smiled. "You're letting us tag along, so we should pay for our way in some form."

"Roger that. Well, buckle in. This old girl gets bumpy at high speeds."

James and Alice buckled their belts while Oswell double-checked Jake and Sarah's, then James took Alice's hand, squeezing it tight. "You sure you want to do this?"

Alice smiled, her heart jumping as she imagined the stops they were about to make. "Wild horses couldn't stop me."

"James Burton." The barrel-chested Colonel couldn't disguise his grin as he greeted the Burton family exiting the APC. "You sure do seem to turn up quite a lot."

"Colonel." James shook the man's hand, exchanging a pat on the shoulder before Alice, Jake and Sarah shook his hand in turn. "Thank you a—"

"What the..." Hawkins lowered his voice conspiratorially for the next word. "*Hell* did I tell you about thanking me?"

"Eli's got you on a short leash, huh?"

Hawkins rolled his eyes, groaning good-naturedly. "They've got ears everywhere. One of us so much as tries to make a sound they don't like and they're all over us with chastisements. Surprised they didn't beat me to meeting y—ah, speak of the... nevermind. Here they come."

Hawkins stepped back as a group of smiling and laughing adults and children hurried down a dirt path from their homes. "James!" The man at the head of the group called out. "You arrived!"

"Eli!" James strode forward to greet the man, the pair foregoing a handshake for a bear hug, instead.

Eli took a step back, gripping James' shoulders, grinning. "You've gotten healthier since we last saw you!"

James threw his head back, laughing. "Did you just call me fat, Eli?"

"Nonsense! I would never say such a thing." Eli's smile persisted as he, Clara and the rest of his family greeted James, Alice, Jake and Sarah.

"Come now!" Clara declared, nodding at her husband. "I've been told in no uncertain terms by *Colonel* Hawkins that you all are leaving tomorrow morning, so we need to get you all up to the houses, show you to your rooms and get your bellies filled with something better than that awful mush they call 'food.' Come on now!"

"Ma'am," Hawkins raised a hand. "I also said that they'll be staying longer when they come back up this way."

Ignoring the Colonel, Clara and her family led the Burtons up to the houses, James falling behind to lean in and whisper in Hawkins' ear. "That is the *shortest* leash I've ever seen."

"They're lucky we need them," Hawkins snorted, "Otherwise..."

"James!" Eli called. "You'd best hurry, or I'll catch an earful from my Clara!"

"Now who's on a short leash, huh?" Hawkins once again couldn't suppress a smile as James hurried off, turning and jogging backwards for a moment to give a retort.

"Uh huh, keep talking Colonel! You going to join us?"

"For dinner!" Hawkins called out. "I've got a job to do first!"

James laughed, waving off the Colonel's remark before turning back around and running after his family and friends.

"Whyyyyyy do we have to get up *so* early?"

The early Spring sun hadn't even begun to think about peeking over the horizon as Jake stumbled into his seat in the APC, nearly tripping over his own feet in the process.

"It's a long trip down to Florida, even for the United States military." James wrapped an arm around his son, pulling him tight. "They finished getting everything secured yet?"

Jake yawned. "Almost. Mom's all paranoid about whether they got them loaded up right or not and Sarah's trying to reassure her."

Alice's voice drifted along, growing louder as she approached the APC, with Sarah periodically reassuring her.

"...just saying!"

"Mom, it's okay."

"No, what if they get hungry, huh? Thirsty?"

"Mom, they know what they're doing. They transport them every day."

"That doesn't mean they know what they're doing! I loaded them up yesterday, and then they went and did it on their own without me this morning!"

"Private Oswell was just trying to help, mom. She knows what she's doing – besides, Abram insisted on helping. They know how much the horses mean to us, okay? Dad – help me out here?" Sarah threw her arms up in exasperation as she and Alice came into view of the back of the APC and began climbing in.

"Oh no, no, no. I'm staying out of this." James shook his head emphatically. "Not a chance."

"That is probably wise, my friend." Eli appeared around the back of the APC, leaning in with a smile, Clara, Jacob and Abram close behind her, all of them carrying large wicker baskets.

"Eli! We already said goodbye. What're you all doing here?"

"I know we will see you again in a week, but Clara insisted—"

"Eli..." Clara nudged him, and Eli relented.

"*We* are insisting that you take these with you. For you, and those you're traveling to see."

"I know better than to try to tell you no, Eli, so thank you – all of you. We're all very much looking forward to getting back here to see you, and helping you out, too."

"Don't worry, my friend." Eli winked. "We'll have plenty of field work for you to help us with."

After a final round of goodbyes, Eli's family left and were quickly replaced by Private Oswell climbing back into the APC and sealing the hatch. "Alrighty, folks. Everything's accounted for, except for one of our four-legged friends. No idea where it went – must have broken free." Oswell grinned at Alice, who nodded appreciatively.

"Thank you. I know it's a lot to ask."

"Nah, not anymore it's not. They're returning them to a lot of people these days anyway. We just sped things along a bit." Oswell flipped through her notebook. "Oh, about that other matter...."

Alice sat forward in her seat, as did Jake and Sarah. "The kids?"

"Mhm. We did some digging, and I can confirm for you that twenty-eight children were picked up by a patrol about three weeks after you and your kids were on the train and told them about it."

Alice sagged back, head against the bulkhead. "Thank goodness. And they're all okay?"

"I don't have any details, but I promise you they were well looked-after."

"That's a load off her shoulders," Sarah rested her head on Alice's shoulder. "Thank you for finding that out."

"No problem at all." Oswell clapped her notebook shut and put it back in her vest. "Best get buckled in – we leave in two, and it's going to be a long few days' trip."

———

Four days later, Alice, Jake and Sarah were the first to emerge from the back of the APC into the heat, humidity and brightness of their new surroundings. After taking a moment to stretch and get their things in order, James gave Alice a hug and a smile.

"You three have fun. Shout when you want us to come in, okay?"

"Thanks, hon. Give us fifteen or twenty minutes max."

"Just make sure he doesn't shoot you, okay?"

Alice grinned, and she, Jake and Sarah headed over to the horse trailer where the leads for Buck, Stormy, Rocky and Cleveland – a horse gifted to them courtesy of Colonel Hawkins – were being held by Oswell and three other members of the convoy. The trio took the horses – Alice taking Stormy and Cleveland while Jake and Sarah handled the other two, and together they began walking down the long lane, past the sign out front which read "Monticello Manor Horse Farm."

Halfway down the driveway, there was a loud shout, and a figure stepped out from behind one of the trees lining the driveway. "Hold up! Hands where I can... mercy me!" Wilford's thick Irish accent was nearly palpable as he moved onto the lane, lowering the shotgun in his hands, his mouth and eyes wide in disbelief. "'Tis... you! Alice Burton?!"

"Wilford!" Jake and Sarah both shouted out in unison, dropping the leads as they ran toward him, grabbing him on either side in a hug that threatened to topple him over.

"Oof! Easy there lad, easy lass! My ribs've only been healed a fortnight and you'll crack 'em again if you aren't careful!"

Taking the dropped leads, Alice maneuvered the four horses down the lane to Wilford, stopping a few feet away, her smile wide as she watched him look from animal to animal, then finally back to her. "Y'made it home, then, Alice?"

Alice dropped the leads and accepted Wilford's embrace, the old man squeezing her tight, patting her on the back as tears sprang into both of their eyes. "We did, Wilford. Thanks in no small part to you, we made it." Alice pulled back, wiping her eyes and cheeks, her smile faltering. "I have to apologize, though. Some bad things happened and... we lost Hercules. We were fortunate enough to come across this boy, though, and we brought him along."

"Oh, Alice." Wilford stroked Cleveland's nose. "I don't give a flying fig about that. He kept you safe and that's all that matters t'me. This looks like a fine boy, but I have to ask – why in hell's bells are y'three even back down here?"

"We came to visit you!" Sarah's grin was contagious.

"And return your horses!" Jake added.

"And to see how we can help you," Alice smiled. "We made some good friends on the way home and want to help you any way we can."

"Under any other circumstances I'd say no, but I won't lie – it's been rough going." Wilford's smile faltered a bit, and Alice noticed for the first time that he appeared to have lost several pounds, and smelled like he hadn't showered a single time.

"You look like you've had a rough go of it. I was worried you might not have made it at all."

"Oh, it's been touch and go a few times. But I'm too stubborn to die." Wilford winked at her. "Now what's this you say about help?"

Alice grabbed the radio off her belt and pressed the transmit button. "Colonel Hawkins, we're ready for you."

"Copy. On our way."

———

"You are a *miracle*, Alice Burton." Wilford's voice was muffled as he dried his hair with a towel, shaking his head back and forth to clear the water from his ears. "No, a miracle's miracle."

Alice laughed as Wilford tossed the towel on a nearby folding chair and ran his fingers through his hair, straightening the thin white locks. "You like the portable shower, huh? The water pressure's not great, but it's hot."

"Are y'kidding me? It's heavenly! And the food – where did you get homemade apple butter and bread and smoked beef?"

"That'd be courtesy of our friends up north."

"The ones I'll be working with?!"

"The same."

"Oh mercy me. I'm going to get t'be too fat to walk. They'll have to roll me around from horse to horse."

Alice laughed. "What *have* you been eating, anyway?"

"Oh, you know. Rabbits, quail, an alligator, plenty of fish. Bit of horse."

"Oh, Wilford. You didn't eat one of the *horses*, did you?"

"Just the one who broke her leg – poor girl stumbled in a hole when some ruffians came onto the farm last month."

"I'm sorry we couldn't get anyone down here to help you sooner."

"Oh, stuff your sorries in a sack, missy." Wilford picked up a thick ream of paper from a folding table and held it aloft. "This right here is going to keep me busier than a one-legged arse-kicker."

"You're happy with the terms?"

"Happy? It's my dream! Paid by the United States government to work with wonderful people doing what I know and love?" Wilford made a show of pinching his arm exaggeratedly, wincing, then gestured to the bustle of activity going on around them. "Nope, not dreaming! It's *better* than a dream!"

"I'm glad to hear it." Alice smiled as Wilford sat down next to her, the pair of them watching Jake, Sarah and Oswell as they led horses from one of the stables down to a horse trailer.

"Alice?" Wilford put a hand on Alice's arm, his voice quiet. "Don't lie to an old man – why did y'come back and do this for me?"

Alice took Wilford's hand and squeezed it tight, leaning back in her chair to stare upward at the sunlight filtering through the leaves of a two-hundred year old oak tree. The skies had cleared considerably since their trip up through the state, and though the day was humid and hotter than she preferred, the Spring weather was tolerable – if only just. Two of the large trailers carried by the convoy had been deployed, offering the passengers a fully-stocked kitchen, bathroom and shower facilities which all used to refresh themselves after the trip.

"When I think back on all the people who were kind to us, who helped us and kept us safe, you were at the top of the list. You helped us, gave us shelter, protected us, and even gave us a way to get home faster than we otherwise could have. How can I look myself in the mirror if I didn't try to do my best to help you and anyone else I can?"

Wilford nodded, then patted her on the arm before standing up. "It means the world t'me, Alice. Now if you'll excuse me, I need to help them wrangle that stud. Hey – hey, hold on just a minute!" Wilford hurried off, his thick Irish accent cutting across the field.

Alice sat quietly for a few moments, eyes closed, listening to the hustle and bustle before she heard footsteps nearby. "Hey," James sat down next to her. "How's he doing? I saw you two talking."

"I think he's going to be out of his gourd with happiness. Thanks for convincing Hawkins to do yet another favor."

"Favor? The man was thanking *me*. They're still dependent on horses in a lot of areas, and Wilford's experience is going to help them out a lot. I'm pretty sure you just got us restocked on favors that Hawkins owes us."

"Are they still going all the way down south after this?"

"Yep. And they still have that last stop on the way. They'll check in on Andrea and make sure she gets anything she needs."

"I guess them being overloaded on supplies is a good thing for everyone still alive, huh? Pity it means that there are so *few* left."

"Yeah... that's way beyond our pay grade, though." James put an arm around Alice and leaned in, the two of them watching Jake and Sarah work with Wilford on a huge, seventeen-hand Belgian. "Oh, Hawkins said to tell you that we'll have another two days here, then we're heading back up north. They'll start taking the horses up in groups later today."

"Two days is good." Alice smiled. "We could use the break."

"Want to take a walk? Get away from the noise? This place looks big enough to have some quiet spots."

Alice chuckled, standing and taking James' hand in hers. "Oh it is. Come on."

Alice and James wove through the throngs of people, vehicles and animals, making their way down one of the side lanes on the property hand-in-hand, letting the silence slowly envelope them until the only noise was that of the wind in the trees, the chitter of insects and birdsong. Alice closed her eyes once more as they emerged from under the shade of the trees into the sun, its warmth joining with that which she felt on the inside. At long last she was at peace, reunited with her friends and loved ones, and in that she had finally found her way home.

WANT MORE AWESOME BOOKS?

Find more fantastic tales at books.to/readmorepa.

If you're new to reading Mike Kraus, consider visiting his website (www.mikekrausbooks.com) and signing up for his free newsletter. You'll receive several free books and a sample of his audiobooks, too, just for signing up, you can unsubscribe at any time and you will receive absolutely *no* spam.

Special Thanks

Special thanks to my awesome beta team, without whom this book wouldn't be nearly as great.

Thank you!

WANT MORE AWESOME BOOKS?

Find more fantastic tales right here at books.to/readmorepa.

***

If you're new to reading Mike Kraus, consider visiting his website at www.mikekrausbooks.com and signing up for his free newsletter. You'll receive several free books and a sample of his audiobooks, too, just for signing up, you can unsubscribe at any time and you will receive absolutely *no* spam.

www.ingramcontent.com/pod-product-compliance
Ingram Content Group UK Ltd.
Pitfield, Milton Keynes, MK11 3LW, UK
UKHW051447040725

6733UKWH00032B/751